The Editor

A native of Germany, EDGAR ROSENBERG received his Ph.D. at Stanford University and since 1965 has been Professor of English and Comparative Literature at Cornell University. He is the author of *From Shylock to Svengali* and some fifty pieces of short fiction, translations, and articles in journals ranging from *Esquire* and *Commentary* to *The Dickensian*. He has taught at San Jose State College and Harvard University, has been Visiting Professor at Stanford and the University of Haifa, and has received Guggenheim, Fulbright, Bread Loaf, and Stanford Fiction Fellowships as well as the Clark Distinguished Teaching Award at Cornell.

W. W. NORTON & COMPANY, INC.
Also Publishes

THE NORTON ANTHOLOGY OF AFRICAN AMERICAN LITERATURE
edited by Henry Louis Gates Jr. and Nellie Y. McKay et al.

THE NORTON ANTHOLOGY OF AMERICAN LITERATURE
edited by Nina Baym et al.

THE NORTON ANTHOLOGY OF CONTEMPORARY FICTION
edited by R. V. Cassill and Joyce Carol Oates

THE NORTON ANTHOLOGY OF ENGLISH LITERATURE
edited by M. H. Abrams and Stephen Greenblatt et al.

THE NORTON ANTHOLOGY OF LITERATURE BY WOMEN
edited by Sandra M. Gilbert and Susan Gubar

THE NORTON ANTHOLOGY OF MODERN POETRY
edited by Richard Ellmann and Robert O'Clair

THE NORTON ANTHOLOGY OF POETRY
edited by Margaret Ferguson, Mary Jo Salter, and Jon Stallworthy

THE NORTON ANTHOLOGY OF SHORT FICTION
edited by R. V. Cassill and Richard Bausch

THE NORTON ANTHOLOGY OF THEORY AND CRITICISM
edited by Vincent B. Leitch et al.

THE NORTON ANTHOLOGY OF WORLD LITERATURE
edited by Sarah Lawall et al.

THE NORTON FACSIMILE OF THE FIRST FOLIO OF SHAKESPEARE
prepared by Charlton Hinman

THE NORTON INTRODUCTION TO LITERATURE
edited by Jerome Beaty, Alison Booth, J. Paul Hunter, and Kelly J. Mays

THE NORTON INTRODUCTION TO THE SHORT NOVEL
edited by Jerome Beaty

THE NORTON READER
edited by Linda H. Peterson, John C. Brereton, and Joan E. Hartman

THE NORTON SAMPLER
edited by Thomas Cooley

THE NORTON SHAKESPEARE, BASED ON THE OXFORD EDITION
edited by Stephen Greenblatt et al.

For a complete list of Norton Critical Editions, visit
www.wwnorton.com/college/english/nce.welcome.htm

GREAT EXPECTATIONS

AUTHORITATIVE TEXT
BACKGROUNDS
CONTEXTS
CRITICISM

A NORTON CRITICAL EDITION

Charles Dickens

GREAT EXPECTATIONS

AUTHORITATIVE TEXT

BACKGROUNDS

CONTEXTS

CRITICISM

Edited by

EDGAR ROSENBERG

CORNELL UNIVERSITY

W • W • NORTON & COMPANY • *New York* • *London*

Copyright © 1999 by W. W. Norton & Company, Inc.

The text of this book is composed in Electra with the display set in Bernhard Modern.
Composition by PennSet, Inc. Manufacturing by Courier Companies, Inc.

Library of Congress Cataloging-in-Publication Data

Dickens, Charles, 1812–1870.
    Great expectations : authoritative text, backgrounds, contexts,
criticism / Charles Dickens ; edited by Edgar Rosenberg.
        p.   cm. — (A Norton critical edition)
    Includes bibliographical references (p.   ).

            ISBN 0-393-96069-2 (pbk.)

    1. Dickens, Charles, 1812–1870. Great expectations.
I. Rosenberg, Edgar.
PR4560.A1   1999.
823'.8—DC20   91-43432
                                                        CIP
                                                        Rev.

W. W. Norton & Company, Inc., 500 Fifth Avenue, New York, N.Y. 10110
www.wwnorton.com
W. W. Norton & Company Ltd., Castle House, 75/76 Wells Street,
London W1T 3QT

6 7 8 9 0

Contents

Illustrations

Preface

T. S. Eliot somewhere envisioned a work of literature that would cut across all stratifications of taste. I suppose that on the available evidence *Great Expectations* lives up to Eliot's ideal as nearly as any novel in English now being read; and in the past sixty years, certainly, since Bernard Shaw's judgment of it as Dickens's "most compactly perfect book," it has retained not only its place in the pantheon of English fiction but also its overarching appeal. Its idolators range from the adolescent in Roger Martin du Gard's *Les Thibault* who "wept ecstatically for having guessed from the outset that Pip would give poor Biddy up for the exotic charms of cruel Miss Estella" to the frostbitten explorers in James Michener's *Journey* who try to keep warm in their hut in the Klondike by reading *Great Expectations* not once but twice (" 'This,' said Trevor Blythe, 'is a damned fine novel' ")—though even two readings aren't enough to keep them from being hexed by a woman named Favisham. Closer to home, a recent nationwide poll among college teachers ranked it first among the novels that, given the choice of any one novel, they should most like to teach; and some twenty-five years earlier George Ford, tabulating Dickens's most widely read novels in England and in America by looking at sales figures and indulging in some intelligent guesswork, found *Great Expectations* coming in second in both stables—since *David Copperfield* ranked first in England with *A Tale of Two Cities* coming in seventh, and *A Tale of Two Cities* ranked first in the States with *David Copperfield* coming in sixth, *Great Expectations* easily totes up the highest combined point value. Crossing the Atlantic and the Channel, we find that some fifteen years before Ford's survey, in a competition sponsored by *Figaro Littéraire* to pick the dozen greatest nineteenth-century "foreign" novels (the jury including François Mauriac and André Maurois), *Great Expectations* took first honors handily. The French seem anyhow to enjoy a special rapport with the book. The best two full-length studies we have are the productions of French critics: Anny Sadrin's cogent discussion and René Belletto's big poststructuralist exercise; one of the finest editions remains Sylvère Monod's *Les grandes espérances*, which he prepared for Garnier in 1960, and if the author of the third (forthcoming) scholarly text happens to be an American specialist in the field—Jerome Meckier—at least his name *sounds* French. And though every Dickensian knows that Dickens called *David Copperfield* "his favourite child," it's nice to discover that the father of fifteen placed *Great Expectations* next in line—in this assessment, by the way, light-years ahead of his contemporaries.

To be sure, *Great Expectations* has never quite enjoyed the legendary fame thrust on *Oliver Twist* or *A Christmas Carol*—books that almost dissociate themselves from their author and attain to the near-anonymity that is one of the trademarks of mythopoeic literature. In still purer form, this kind of literature would include books like *Robinson Crusoe* or, for that matter, the

Sherlock Holmes stories: if you asked, say, fifty college seniors how many had heard of *Robinson Crusoe*, chances are that they would look insulted, but if you asked them who wrote it three would be likely to raise their hands. *Great Expectations* contains no characters who have turned into household words on the order of Scrooge, a name that can be found in any dictionary—a recent student of mine who happened not to know the meaning of "miser," once I explained the meaning to him, said, "Oh, you mean a scrooge!" (In much of Continental Europe, Latin America, and the Middle East, books like *Oliver* are taught—like *Robinson Crusoe* and *Uncle Tom's Cabin*—as juvenile classics, first cousins to *Ivanhoe* and *Treasure Island*.) *Webster's* may record a "Scrooge" and a "Pecksniff," but it has yet to register a "Pip" or a "Pumblechook." And in a recent radio interview, the director of the new *Lolita* movie quoted a friend of his telling him, "I'll bet you called her Lolita because she is one!"

A book like *Great Expectations*, then, is apt to appeal both to readers of these nearly anonymous fictions and to the more learned specimens who, though they may not know whether Goncharov wrote *Oblomov* or Oblomov wrote *Goncharov*, know that Dickens alone could have written *Great Expectations*. On the level of narrative, *Great Expectations* maintains a degree of suspense that few books of its caliber can match. But this suspense itself is rooted in deeply troubling questions, questions that touch on the problematic sources of wealth (how can money have both such literally criminal and affectively altruistic origins and uses?); on the sham claims of emotional and petty financial parasites; on the rights and wrongs (mostly the wrongs) of the legal machinery and the judiciary; on the "process" by which venal men turn spoiled young women into spoiled and embittered hags; on the ways in which the past mines the present; and on all the evil committed under the sun by "that friendly foe, Great Expectations." These are the salient motifs of many of Dickens's novels, from *Oliver* to *Our Mutual Friend*. But in *Great Expectations* they are given a special urgency; and it's hardly a coincidence that the opening of the novel is one of the most celebrated in fiction. *Great Expectations* begins almost as a Christmas requiem: in a graveyard on Christmas Eve; the chimes that ring in the festive rites are the great guns from the prison ships a few miles off, warning that convicts are on the loose, of whom one "has a secret way pecooliar to himself, of getting at a boy, and at his heart, and at his liver"; the Christmas dinner itself culminates in a hideously spun-out fantasy in which the child-hero is butchered and turned into roast pig—as novels go, surely Pip's Christmas meal is equaled by the one young Stephen Dedalus recollects.

Remembrance is of the essence of *Great Expectations*, and of Dickens's three first-person novels this is surely the most poignantly satisfying. Not that Pip teases us as an "unreliable narrator": given his small leads and great illusions, Pip is remarkably frank—more candid than his favored older brother, David, and more of a piece than Esther, the much admired, much maligned heroine of *Bleak House*, who half the time forgets who she is and talks pure Dickens. The striking thing about Pip's recital lies not least in his beautifully nuanced and pliant range of emotive language—and in that still rarer quality that Graham Greene defines when he detects in the novel "the tone of Dickens's secret prose, that sense of a mind speaking to itself with no one there to listen." Greene goes on to quote the passage from chapter 35 in which Pip returns to his childhood home to confront a death in the family and reflects how "the very breath of the beans and clover whispered to my heart that the day must come when it would be well for my memory that others walking in the sunshine should be softened as they thought of me." The long passage two pages later that describes his sister's burial happens also to be one of the funniest in the book, without Dickens's generating the least discomfort at such indecorous mirth in funerals. How he manages to lull us into these genial mood swings remains, I suppose, his trade secret.

II

The text of the present edition of *Great Expectations* (like the texts of the Norton Critical Editions of *Hard Times* and *Bleak House*) has been established by a thorough comparative study of all surviving versions of Dickens's novel. These consist of the "Wisbech" manuscript—the only major Dickens MS that is not shelved in either of the two chief repositories, the Forster Collection of the Victoria and Albert Museum in London or the Pierpont Morgan Library in New York, but is hidden away in the Fens of Cambridgeshire. We have next two earlier fragmentary sets of corrected proof at the V & A, of which the first is almost certainly first proof; a nearly complete set of what is ostensibly very late proof at the Morgan Library; the American serial run in *Harper's Weekly*, a version the more revealing to students of Dickens's texts for having been set up from uncorrected proof sheets; the serial version in Dickens's own weekly *All the Year Round*; and the book editions that appeared in Dickens's lifetime. The only significant early texts are the first three-volume edition of 1861 and, less pressingly, the "Charles Dickens Edition" of 1868; this, in turn, is based largely on the earlier "Library Edition" of 1862 and not only perpetuated most of its errors but added a few of its own. In selecting my copy-text, I have not only departed from the practice of using the fallible '68 edition, which has been adopted (without serious damage to the integrity of the book) by a lot of modern trade publishers, but (more gamely) departed from using the first book edition of '61, which has served the editors of the variorum Clarendon Dickens and most Norton Critical Editions of Dickens as copy-text.

In setting aside the principles followed by editors like John Butt, Kathleen Tillotson, and Sylvère Monod, I have been guided by a number of principles, if you can call them that. For one thing, compared with the changes Dickens introduced in proof in his other novels, the changes he introduced in *Great Expectations* are very slight—possibly because of the unpremeditated mode of publication he found himself forced to adopt a mere eight or nine weeks before the book began to appear in *All the Year Round*. As K. J. Fielding pointed out long ago, nearly all changes in proof are virtually exhausted by changes in accidentals, chiefly in punctuation. Thus, by the time *Great Expectations* came out in book form, the text had to all intents been established, apart from a number of substantive changes—by no means all for the better— that he prepared for the '61 edition. Second, as my parenthesis suggests, on the few occasions on which *All the Year Round* and first edition go separate ways without my being satisfied that the road not taken by earlier editors was the road Dickens himself chose not to take, I selected what struck me as both the more plausible and more plausive reading, a procedure that, in nine cases out of ten, led me back to *All the Year Round*. Third, if the proximity of serial to manuscript bears any relevance and the proof on which *All the Year Round* is based shows no changes in wording or accidentals, the text closest to the MS seemed to be the more dependable—though I realize that this is not always a textually watertight argument. (*Harper's*, of course, is textually insignificant, except as a literary curiosity.) Fourth, it seemed to me reasonable to assume that both as editor of *All the Year Round* and contributor to it, Dickens, who spent hours in correcting the sentences of his journalistic hirelings, would be more than ordinarily vigilant in going over the weekly portions about to be sent to as many as one hundred thousand readers, and though not downright cavalier in introducing later changes, he appears to have been comparatively "relaxed." On the other hand, where the '61 reading suggests an intentional change, I have (reluctantly) adopted the '61 reading; and with a much better conscience I have restored manuscript readings where both the MS reading is clearly superior and the printed reading rests almost certainly on a typesetter's error. How much Dickens's printers had to put up with and how astoundingly few mistakes they committed is something I discuss in the essay on Dickens's compositional habits. If I had to allege yet a fifth reason for choosing one text over another, I should have to express my assurance that out of, say, fifty thousand readers of *Great Expectations*, perhaps as many as thirty would notice the difference; and they are all friends of mine.

III

"All works which describe manners," Dr. Johnson observes with his customary air of having settled *that* hash, "require footnotes, in sixty years or less." He doesn't specify the number of footnotes, though, nor legislate their length. Annotators have their choice. Thomas Mann, perhaps to justify the length of a thousand-page book, writes that "only the truly exhaustive is truly amusing," and one of Macaulay's dinner companions complained to his host that "the gentleman gives more information than society needs." Assuming Dr. Johnson's figure to be reasonably realistic, I note that the moratorium on easily accessible information expired at least as far back as 1921 if we use the publication date of *Great Expectations* as our yardstick, and some forty years earlier if we go by the date of action. To check my own tendency toward opulence, I tossed the whole problem of footnotes to four bright seniors and two graduate students, handed each a copy of *Great Expectations* (I forget the edition I gave them) and asked them to underline whatever they thought needed explanation. They underlined everything, underlined so unsparingly that I had to deprive them of a few notes. Naturally, there is only so much you can say about a "jack-towel" or a "whitlow" or the distinctive features of Brentford, once you have gotten beyond its dirt. On the other hand, we have gone to extensive and sometimes peculiar lengths to explain features that strike us as important features of Regency England but are apt to be lost on the present-day reader, especially the American reader: things like early-nineteenth-century penology, elementary education, and amusements, from fictitious dirigibles to debased *Hamlets*. In their introductory note to *Bleak House*, the Norton editors point out that of the novel's fourteen opening words only seven are intelligible to the nonspecialist (including two prepositions, a connective, the definite article, and the place-name London), but what are lay readers to make of "Michaelmas Term," "Lord High Chancellor," and "Lincoln's Inn Hall"? *Great Expectations* is a less densely topical book than *Bleak House*, and so ours is a correspondingly less taxing job. Even so, nobody is born with a knowledge of "Hulks" (even Pip pretends not to know what they are), nor the difference between a hackney-coach and a hackney-cab, nor, for that matter, between an Inn and an inn. Then also (to descend to the perishable vocabulary on which comedy thrives) people no longer call each other "Bounceables" or talk about "dabs" and "lags." Nor are they intercepted at birth by a specimen known as an "accoucheur-policeman." They no longer wear "mourning rings" left to them by condemned convicts, nor ride down Main Street on caparisoned coursers, or plain coursers. In coping with dated and substandard vocabulary, I have occasionally relied on earlier lexicographers of slang and cant on the order of Grose and Hotten—Hotten published the second edition of his glossary the same year Dickens began to write *Great Expectations* and is thus doubly useful. Once in a while I have even briefly explained a word that readers could look up easily enough in even a medium-good dictionary—on the presumption that they won't. As someone who still speaks Remedial English himself, I am naturally sympathetic to anybody who wants to know what a plenipotentiary does for a living, and a potman.

In dealing with the entertaining subject of entertainment and with Dickens's zany literary allusions, I have followed the practice of earlier annotators who, instead of merely citing chapter and verse ("from a glee for three voices by Thomas Moore"), convey a much better sense of Dickens's tomfooleries by quoting a few lines from his sources. The procedure provides its own rewards in demonstrating in epitome the range—and limits—of Dickens's culture: in nearly all his allusions beyond references to biblical commonplaces, he zeroes in on Shakespeare, on eighteenth-century drama and verse, and on mythology, and in talking about them he can barely keep a straight face. Often in annotating a prominent fixture of Pip's England, I have found the most helpful sources in Dickens's own descriptions elsewhere in these crowded books, not least in his early *Sketches by Boz*, which are especially useful as near-contemporaries of Pip, and in the later polemical pieces, in which he expresses his views in the transparent language more suited to the writer of editorials than of romance. Similarly, where I have unearthed a striking verbal or pictorial or narrative echo or analogue in his other novels, I have cf.'d the pertinent note as a way of calling attention to some of Dickens's abiding tics and fixations. In a very few instances I have gone even further afield. Words and social customs that call attention to themselves in *Great Expectations* have a way of popping up in very different, unneighborly writers—Austen, James, Conrad, Aldous Huxley—and where I thought these pick-ups informative, as hitchhikers often are, I hauled them on board. But "vether it's worth while goin through so much, to learn so little, as the charity boy said ven he got to the end of the alphabet," is a matter of taste.

For that matter, where I have found the procedure helpful, I have even foisted footnotes on the backpage essays, over and above the page references the writers themselves have provided. More often than not their allusions are as remote to students as anything to be found in *Great Expectations*. What on Earth is an Apprentice's Vade Mecum? It sounds like patent medicine, or a requiem. If somebody owns an antimacassar, does it follow that he owns a macassar? Probably not. Thanks to *Les Mis* everybody knows all about Jean Valjean. But Marcel? Odette? And what newborn male infant has ever been heard to betray his good manners by thrice crowing "*A boire! A boire! A boire!*" I pause for a reply.[1] I have unstintingly raided earlier annotators of *Great Expectations*; where I felt that my creditor held a monopoly on the note I stole, I have indicated the source of my piracy. To Edward Guiliano, Philip Collins, and Sylvère Monod I owe a special debt for filching as many notes as I did; their names appear at the foot of the page with embarrassing regularity. If David Paroissien were not about to publish whatever there is to be annotated in *Great Expectations* in the series of substance notes issued by Helm Information, I might lay to my soul the flattering unction that the next editor of *Great Expectations* would borrow from me as I have borrowed from those who preceded me. For that, to paraphrase Miss Prism's definition of fiction—that is what scholarship means.

IV

The rationale for the selection of the pieces filed away under the brief rubric "Contexts" is very simply my own sense of fitness or "relevance," which may be no rationale at all. Even so, certain extracts ought to stand the test of suitability. *Great Expectations* starts out with a scene in a churchyard; our selection starts out with an "irreligious cross" between a parody and a replay of the scene in the same churchyard. Given Pip's early experiences, it would seem perverse not to say something about the conditions of childhood in Regency and early Victorian England and the obtrusive link to the world of criminals, from Dickens's impressions of fairy-tale Captain Murderers to Pip's experiences of real murderers about to be shipped off in real prison ships. The Nurse's spine-chilling stories at the young Dickens's bedside are separated by a very few years from their social correlatives: the sadistic or else appallingly inept kinds of "education" to which wealthy fathers and pauperized gammers submitted their young: either by treating them to an edifying outing to view a hanging man or by placing an illiterate crone in charge of indigent schoolchildren and cramming the lot into a classroom (or cellarage) that is generically "close, crowded, and dirty." Even before he succumbs to the narcotic effects of the village school, and many years before his London tutor defines the nature of true gentility, Pip gets his first taste of a "gentleman"—who is also a suave and cowardly convict about to be remanded to Botany Bay, where gentlemen of his ilk thrive like mushrooms. And since there can be no great expectations where there is no Botany Bay, I devote some pages to the subject (a recurrent topos in the Victorian novel) of penal servitude down under. If criminal spectacles like hangings formed one of the

---

1. In annotating, I have drawn the line in one respect: I can't bear the idea of annotating my own sesquipedalia, Latin commonplaces, and allusions to Marx, *Midsummer Night's Dream*, and the Apocrypha. It's perfectly fine to annotate Peter Brooks where he hasn't footnoted Gide, or Ian Watt where he hasn't footnoted Erik Erikson, but to footnote myself for some reason strikes me as asinine. You will therefore not find a clue to Roger Martin du Gard, the cruel Estella, and *de haut en bas*, though had anybody else used any of them, I should certainly have explained them.

Londoner's grand entertainments, he found more sanitary escapes to other killing fields: pantomime, melodrama, and all the pop theatricals Dickens and Pip delighted in—not only the Dickens of Pip's young manhood but the middle-aged magician of whom a friend remarked that the great man thrilled to the sight of elephants dancing onstage. To valorize this part of Pip's experience, I have turned back the clock to the eighteenth century and paired those spectacular rivals, Samuel Richardson and Henry Fielding. The *Hamlet* scene in *Great Expectations* surely warrants a free ticket to Garrick's Hamlet in Fielding's *Tom Jones* ("Compare Eighteenth- and Nineteenth-Century Versions of Parody and Critique"); and if Richardson's manual dwells on the temptations lying in ambush for young London rakes rather than rustics like Pip, the play he recommends as a universal prophylactic happens also to be the most important drama Dickens exploits in *Great Expectations*. My aim has been to straddle reminiscences, juvenile fiction, reports of governmental commissions, some brief letters, personal and polemical essays by and about Dickens, twentieth-century commentaries, and Literature.

The inclusion of the pieces by Humphry House and especially Robin Gilmour displays the futility of drawing the line between criticism and the sort of miscellany I have heaped together under the earlier rubric. Still, most of us recognize criticism when we see it, even in hybrid form. The contemporary reviews make for a mixed bag of goods—which is the way I chose them—but even where we ourselves might cry foul their very intemperance is refreshing. So are their irreconcilable differences. Take Wemmick (whom you haven't met yet any more than you have met Biddy, the cruel Estella, and the bewitching Miss Favisham). Wemmick is a middle-aged clerk in an attorney's office who lives in an imitation castle with his deaf father and courts a middle-aged lady. One reviewer calls Wemmick "a specimen of oddity run mad." Another calls him "a conception worthy of Dickens's happiest days." Another describes him as "the great creation of the book, and his marriage as the funniest incident," and he goes on to ask the kind of rhetorical question a reviewer ought never to ask: "How often will future jokers observe, 'Halloa, here's a church; let's have a wedding.'" Beginning with Gissing and Shaw[2] and continuing with the later commentators I have bagged, things get slightly trickier and more ponderous. I should say "we" have bagged since I picked the critical essays the way I picked the footnotes: I ran some hundred essays by my students and told them to grade the whole stack and to pick anywhere from a dozen to twenty pieces they wanted Norton to print. Some of the critics, like Wemmick, naturally gave rise to sordid arguments. A number of the essays collect themselves: Shaw's, Van Ghent's, Moynahan's, Brooks's. Others—Gervais, Raphael—we felt ought to be better known than they are. Our choices finally came down to our plain admiration for the critical commentary, the range and variety of interpretation, and their usefulness in providing a kind of running argument. Shaw argues with Dickens's (unprinted) enemies. House argues with Shaw. Moynahan argues with Van Ghent. Fielding argues with House and Moynahan. The E. M. Forster whose paragraph

---

2. Shaw is everywhere. In calling him "the Nestor of our age" in his obituary notice in 1950, Mann no doubt had in mind not only Shaw's longevity but his fabled memory and invincible loquaciousness. Thus he appears not only in his own right in his essay but also in his comments on Dickens's letters, the double ending and the sins of Bulwer-Lytton, Dickens's thefts from Charles Lever, and much else.

ushers in the "Essays" is at odds with the E. M. Forster who strikes the fashionably *de haut en bas* Bloomsbury note in his most famous critical work a year later. *Great Expectations* (to get the mandatory truism down and out) has been immensely written about: George Worth had collected more than eleven hundred entries by the time he completed his great bibliography— fifteen years ago. Confronted with so much plenty, an editor is bound to display a certain waffliness.[3] I have supplied linking bridges in the few instances where the complexity of the essay or the length of the omitted matter seemed to me to call for these aids, but not elsewhere.

At Norton's prodding, I have no sooner let the hero and heroine loose in chapter 59 than I have stalked them with long textual commentaries. A good deal of this material has already appeared in one packaging or another. The essay on the endings has been cited often enough (and even provoked a rebuttal twice as long as my own longueurs) to justify its inclusion, I think—I have of course taken into account the literature that has appeared since I published the piece and performed a couple of critical somersaults in the hope of provoking a few more long articles. A few other random passages have been lifted from a still more megalosaurian article. The essays on the preliminaries to the novel and on the Wisbech manuscript, apart from one sustained section, are mostly new. Some of these materials necessarily overlap (a few may even contradict each other), but I have preferred to risk a sense of déjà *lu* to the omission of what seemed to me substantive issues where the context called for a second take. What I have tried to do in most of these pieces is to go beyond the immediate (and ostensible) subject to convey some ideas about Dickens's editorial practices, the sort of journal in which *Great Expectations* got its start, Dickens's (often astonishing) working habits, both the sloppy and the fastidious fellow novelists who as it were fed into and out of *Great Expectations*. Along the way, I have tried to say something about the demands of serial writing, the nature of Dickensian coincidence, the advice he dished out to aspiring writers.

The monthly installments are indicated by Roman numerals in brackets on left-hand pages, while the weekly installments are indicated by Roman numerals on the right-hand pages as well as by a printer's mark at the end of each weekly; this information, together with the serial dates of publication and the corresponding monthly divisions as Dickens conceived (and paginated) them, appears more fully in Tables 1 and 2 on pages 400–02. The numbered cue lines are intended to expedite the location of words and phrases to which the textual matter refers. And to convey the richness and novelty of Dickens's vocabulary in *Great Expectations* as this is reflected in

3. I keenly regret the omission of five essays in particular: Elliot L. Gilbert's "In Primal Sympathy: *Great Expectations* and the Secret Life"; Robert Newsom's "The Hero's Shame"; Murray Baumgarten's "Calligraphy and Code: Writing in *Great Expectations*"; Jeremy Tambling's "Prison-Bound: Dickens and Foucault"; and Jay Clayton's "Is Pip Postmodern? Or, Dickens at the End of the Twentieth Century." I couldn't have reprinted any of them in their entirety, and to edit them would have been a rather daunting job as well as a disservice to the writers. Providentially, the first three have been assembled in one volume (*Dickens Studies Annual* 11 [1983]); at least Gilbert's and Tambling's pieces have been anthologized elsewhere, and Clayton's is one of a handful of essays in Janice Carlisle's edition of *Great Expectations*, which appeared so recently that it would have been idle even to ask for a poaching license. Next time.

the many citations from the novel that have found their way into the *Oxford English Dictionary*, I have signaled their inclusion by placing the bracketed abbreviation [OED] at the end of the pertinent footnote. In other words, these are illustrative examples taken from *Great Expectations* to pinpoint the meaning of a given word at a particular date by reference to the novel. The parenthetical notation (OED) merely gives the dictionary as a source of the note.

Acknowledgments

"To Miss Ramona Slupski, Miss Heidi Lim Choo Tan, Miss Piper Vathek, and Miss Joylene Aguilar Garcia Rosario, all of the Graduate Section of British Studies, Yourgrau College, my thanks for collating material and answering swiftly my transatlantic letters and demands; to Miss Gudrun Naismith, for immaculately typing many drafts of this work and deciphering my nearly illegible and at times tormented handwriting, my deepest thanks. And to all my former colleagues at Yourgrau (Wyola Campus), who, by urging me forward in my work, reversed my fortunes, my grateful thanks for assisting me in this undertaking."[1]

An edition that has been twice as long in the making as the Jarndyce suit in *Bleak House* and the construction of the Great Wall of China faces minimally four handicaps. For one thing, nobody in the editor's position can expect to fulfill expectations he has aroused for decades and well-meaning colleagues have, all embarrassingly, aired in print for decades. For another, the people who might have retained the faith in and even a certain curiosity about this project have long fallen asleep with boredom and turned their attention to greener pastures. For a third, since the mill of Dickensians grinds at an alarming pace, the discoveries I should have been the first to bring to light, as if they were so many lost plays of Aeschylus—the location of the novel's first ending in proof, the single sustained change Dickens undertook between manuscript and first printed version, the autobiographical touches he removed as too close to home, the marketing of the first editions—have long since been found out by my colleagues, even if I anticipated them in unloading all this booty on learned journals.[2] I am, of course, most grateful to the editors who published chunks of the articles I reprint below, especially the editors of *The Dickensian, Dickens Studies Annual,* and *Dickens Quarterly,* and to Professor Joel Brattin for inviting me to take the manuscript essay for a brief airing.

By far the saddest penalty I have to pay for my truancies is that so many of my creditors are beyond the reach of my acknowledgments. I would particularly like to record my thanks to the late Mrs. Madeline House for allowing me to inspect her file of the Dickens letters; to the Wisbech and Fenland

---

1. From *World's End and Other Stories* (Boston, 1980). Reprinted by permission of Houghton Mifflin Company. I have had to place this paragraph in quotation marks and provide it with a superscript because I didn't write it, obviously, and because the writer, Paul Theroux, has done for acknowledgments what Cervantes has done for prefaces and dedications—crippled any attempt to express a sensible "valentine" without cracking up.
2. Dr. Margaret Cardwell will forgive me, I hope, for mentioning (for the record merely) that a lot of the more exciting features of her scrupulous edition of *Great Expectations* in the Clarendon Dickens—including the items I just docketed—were first excavated and printed by me. I should not bother to raise this issue if the reviewers of her edition hadn't singled out just these excavations for their special tribute to Dr. Cardwell's text. This in the friendliest and most collegial spirit and without the least imputation, I trust, of my sounding like somebody out of *Pale Fire* or "Pierre Menard." Though I had done my textual homework by the time her edition appeared, I greatly profited by her apparatus in verifying my textual annotation.

Museum for (unlimited) access to the manuscript; to the Victoria and Albert Museum for permission to mine the corrected proof shelved in the Forster Collection; to the Pierpont Morgan Library, especially to Ms. Anna Lou Ashby, Assistant Curator of Printed Books, and to the former Curator of Manuscripts and Modern Books, Mr. Douglas C. Ewing, for expediting my detective work in uncovering the unhappy ending (literally, by the application of steam), as well as permission to reproduce it (Pierpont Morgan Library, New York, *PML 6640*); to the Dickens House for giving me access, year in year out, to their marvellous research facilities and accommodating me in their study; to the Berg Collection of The New York Public Library for permission to use Pailthorpe's watercolor for our cover illustration; to the Kent County Council and the Rochester upon Medway Studies Centre, particularly Ms. K. I. Woollacott, Centre Manager of the Civic Centre, Strood, Rochester, and to my friends Laurie and Inge Hack of Hollingbourne, Kent, for providing me with guides to Pip's native grounds; to Dr. Ronald Grim and Ms. Charlotte Hunts of the Library of Congress for selecting half a dozen maps of Regency London for me; to the London Transport Museum for fortifying my meager knowledge of hackney-coaches and scullers and for donating from their collection a priceless map of the Pool of London; to the London Science Museum; and not least to the staff of the Cornell University Library for their tireless help.

To Mr. William Bennett of the Temple and Mr. Colin Arnold of West Walton, Wisbech, I owe thanks for guiding me through the technicalities of English law; to Professor Jane Rabb for sharing her unique knowledge of Dickens's illustrators;[3] and, for providing every kind of information, to the late Mr. Leslie Staples, the late Professor Noel Peyrouton, Professors Murray Baumgarten, Janice Carlisle, Philip Collins, Edward Guiliano, Fred Kaplan, Dan H. Laurence, Philip Marcus, Sylvère Monod, Ada Nisbet, Robert Patten, Martin Quinn, Michael Slater, Harry Stone, and Kathleen Tillotson. It is a pleasure to pay special tribute to three colleagues: Professor Kenneth Fielding, for making available his typed transcript of the Morgan proof at a time when he himself thought of preparing a "rival" edition; to Professor Anny Sadrin, for donating her chapter on the chronology of the novel; and to Professor Jerome Meckier, who, while sharing the editorship with me, provided more information than I can acknowledge in a note. If I register an occasional quibble with him, no doubt I do as much for my other benefactors. If I were to add the names of my colleagues in the Departments of Classics, Comparative Literature, English, and History at Cornell, this roster would bring Rabelais to his knees.

This leaves me with two great unrepayable debts: to the late Miss Marjorie Pillers, former Curator of the Dickens House, for her personal and professional hospitality, which spanned decades; and to the late Mr. Wilfred L. Hanchant, Librarian of the Wisbech and Fenland Museum, who not only allowed me to pore over the leaves of the *Great Expectations* manuscript long past closing hours but provided me with an invaluable microfilm of the manuscript. To my many hosts in Wisbech, in particular Dr. and Mrs. Peter Cave

---

3. I owe apologies to my colleague and friend Dr. Jane Rabb for not including a concisely excellent essay on the early illustrations that she wrote at my request (and meticulously revised a number of times) at the time I began this project. The truth is that after years in the desert I didn't have the heart (or guts) to ask her once more to update her piece and pay the price of my own delinquencies. All my shaming regrets.

and the late Dr. Kenneth Elliott and Mrs. Elliott, I am much indebted for making me feel as if I were an honorary citizen of the Fens. Opulent as this list already is, it would be churlish not to thank the students who have had a hand in the research and the cartography: Annie Ballantyne, Carolynn Bruce, Claire Colton, Laurie Fields, Susan Forster, Laura Garrity, Jacaranda Henkel, Kat Hickey, Ioannis Kantzaris, Lynn Kovach, Jean Kwon, Kathleen Morkes, Elise Shin, John Skurchak, Jacqueline Sobota, Kwan-Sen Naguib Wen, and my most persistent junta: Max Junker, Rehana Kaderali, Julie Orringer, Kelly Quimby, and Ann Tappert. And I am deeply indebted to my first editor, the late John Benedict, and (presumably) my last editor, Carol Stiles Bemis, whose desk for the past ten years has been staggering under the heavy weight of my brittle letters. That these people should have shown so much forbearance, good humor, and solicitude speaks well for all of us.

My single greatest debt is to my colleague Dr. Jean Callahan. Apart from writing the essay on the reading version, she has been complicit in compiling the bibliography, composing large chunks of the textual history, and verifying the text. Her collaboration, more than anyone else's, has vastly benefited our sponsor—Dickens or Norton, whoever comes first. At that (having done my donnish duty by Paul Theroux) I may leave it.

Abbreviations

Cardwell: *Great Expectations*, ed. Margaret Cardwell (Oxford: Clarendon Press, 1993)

Collins: *Dickens: Interviews and Recollections*, ed. Philip Collins (2 vols. Totowa, N.J.: Barnes & Noble Books, 1981)

Dickensian: Dickensian, ed. Malcolm Andrews (London: The Dickens Fellowship, 1905–)

DQ: Dickens Quarterly, ed. David Paroissien (Amherst, Mass.: The Dickens Society, 1984–)

DSA: Dickens Studies Annual: Essays on Victorian Fiction, vols. 1–7 ed. Robert Partlow (Carbondale: Southern Illinois Press, 1971–78); vols. 8 to date ed. Michael Timko, Fred Kaplan, and Edward Guiliano (New York: AMS Press, 1980–)

DSN: Dickens Studies Newsletter, ed. Duane DeVries (Louisville, Ky.: The Dickens Society, 1971–84)

Falconer: William Falconer, *A New and Universal Dictionary of the Marine* . . . [1769], ed. William Burney (London: T. Cadell, 1830)

Forster: John Forster, *The Life of Charles Dickens* (Boston: Estes & Lauriat, 1872–74), ed. A. J. Hoppé (2 vols. London: Dent, 1969)

Guiliano/Collins: *Great Expectations* in *The Annotated Dickens*, ed. Edward Guiliano and Philip Collins (2 vols. New York: Crown Publishers, 1986), vol. 2, 822–1115

Grose: Francis Grose, *Classical Dictionary of the Vulgar Tongue* [1785] (Facsimile rept. Menston, Yorkshire: The Scolar Press, 1968)

Hill: T. W. Hill, "Notes on *Great Expectations*," *Dickensian* 53–56 (1957–60)

Hotten: John Camden Hotten, *A Dictionary of Modern Slang, Cant, and Vulgar Words* (2nd ed. London: John Camden Hotten, 1860)

McMaster: R. D. McMaster, *Great Expectations* (Toronto: Macmillan Co. of Canada, 1965)

Monod: *Les grandes espérances*, ed. Sylvère Monod (Paris: Editions Garnier Frères, 1959)

NL: *The Letters of Charles Dickens*, ed. Arthur Waugh (3 vols. Bloomsbury [London]: The Nonesuch Press, 1938)

OED: *New Oxford English Dictionary*

PL: *The Letters of Charles Dickens*, ed. Madeline House, Graham Storey, Kathleen Tillotson, K. J. Fielding, et al. (The Pilgrim Edition. Oxford: Clarendon Press, 1965–)

Sadrin: Anny Sadrin, *Great Expectations* (Unwin Critical Library. London: Unwin Hyman, 1988)

Speeches: *The Speeches of Charles Dickens*, ed. K. J. Fielding (Oxford: Clarendon Press, 1960)

The Text of
GREAT EXPECTATIONS

GREAT EXPECTATIONS

BY

CHARLES DICKENS.

IN THREE VOLUMES.

VOL. I.

LONDON:

CHAPMAN AND HALL, 193, PICCADILLY.

MDCCCLXI.

Dickens and the Rev. Chauncy Hare Townshend (1798–1868), the dedicatee of *Great Expectations*, first met in 1840 as fellow devotees of mesmerism—Townshend as practitioner, Dickens as avid student. The two were brought together by the Dickenses' family doctor, John Elliotson (1791–1868), whose own pioneering advocacy of mesmerism cost him his professorship at London University in 1838. Townshend's life was marked by physical delicacy, which kept him from pursuing his ministry and which he cultivated (between his first volume of verse and his second he paused for thirty years); the novelist Bulwer-Lytton, himself an enthusiastic believer, described Townshend's career as the perfect "beau ideal of happiness—elegant rest, travel, lots of money—and he is always ill and melancholy." Despite their friendship, Townshend emerges from Dickens's letters as somebody perpetually engaged in guarding against catarrhs. But Townshend was totally dedicated to his scientific pursuits: his *Facts in Mesmerism*, a pleasingly written defense and exposition of the subject, which Edgar Allan Poe praised as "a work to be valued properly in a day to come," appeared in 1840; *Mesmerism Proved True* in 1859. Under his tutelage, Dickens became an accomplished hypnotist, whose single most widely publicized experiment—begun during his sojourn in Genoa in 1844—on the English-born wife of a Swiss banker, provoked perhaps unfounded anxieties in Mrs. Dickens. Townshend, commuting between his mansion in London and his villa in Lausanne in pursuit of his health—kept alive en route by "every description of physic, old brandy, East India Sherry, sandwiches, oranges, cordial waters, newspapers, pocket handkerchiefs, shawls, flannels, telescopes, compasses, repeaters, and finger-rings of great value"—idolized Dickens and immortalized him in verse twice: in the volume *Sermons in Sonnets*, 1850 ("Man of the genial mind! To thee a debt / No usurer records I largely owe!") and *The Three Gates*, 1859, in a dedicatory dime-store poem ("It is not for thy worldly fame / That thou art dear to me; / It is not for thy lofty name / That I so cherish thee," etc.). Townshend died during Dickens's visit to America; on his return, Dickens found himself charged, as Townshend's literary executor, with the job of editing a chaotic mass of manuscripts: "notes and reflections" on theological matters, "distributed in the strangest fragments through the strangest note-books, pocket-books, slips of paper and what not, [producing] a most incoherent and tautological result." These appeared as *The Religious Opinions of the Late Rev. Chauncy Hare Townshend* (conversationally Dickens referred to them as Townshend's Religious Hiccoughs) in December 1869. Townshend chiefly aimed at divesting religion of its metaphysical trappings, which he thought detrimental to rational discourse on questions of faith.

Dickens's interest in mesmerism is most clearly reflected in his last (unfinished) novel, *The Mystery of Edwin Drood*, in which he deals with the subject head-on; but as the authority on the subject (Fred Kaplan, *Dickens and Mesmerism*) has pointed out, his fascination with mesmeric and hypnagogic states can be found in almost every one of his novels—the reader of *Great Expectations* may look for instances in the episodes in which the attorney "tames" his domestic by a virtually hypnotic imposition of his will (chapter 26); in the hero's inability to identify the means by which the heroine has tamed *him* when they first meet (chapter 8); his trancelike response to the return of an unwelcome visitor (chapter 40); the (again trancelike) heightened consciousness produced in moments of extreme physical tension (chapter 53). Dickens presented Townshend with the manuscript of *Great Expectations* at the time of its publication in book form; Townshend bequeathed the MS to the Wisbech and Fenland Museum in Wisbech, a small market town some thirty miles north of Cambridge, on the border of Norfolk and Cambridgeshire, close to his birthplace.

Frederick Lehmann

To Chauncey Hare Townshend

25. 1861.

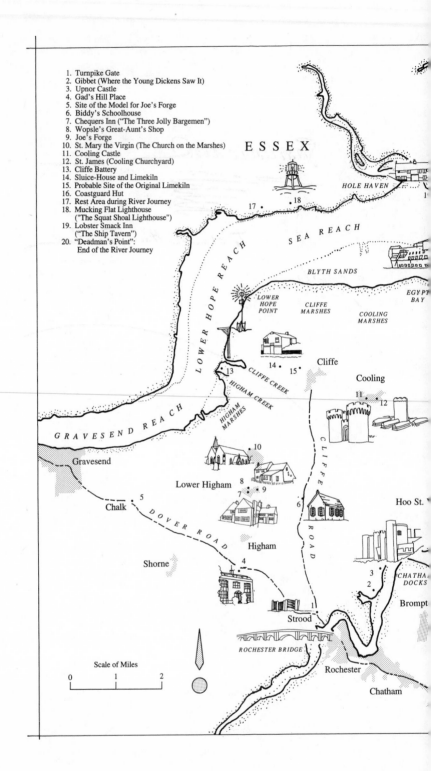

1. Turnpike Gate
2. Gibbet (Where the Young Dickens Saw It)
3. Upnor Castle
4. Gad's Hill Place
5. Site of the Model for Joe's Forge
6. Biddy's Schoolhouse
7. Chequers Inn ("The Three Jolly Bargemen")
8. Wopsle's Great-Aunt's Shop
9. Joe's Forge
10. St. Mary the Virgin (The Church on the Marshes)
11. Cooling Castle
12. St. James (Cooling Churchyard)
13. Cliffe Battery
14. Sluice-House and Limekiln
15. Probable Site of the Original Limekiln
16. Coastguard Hut
17. Rest Area during River Journey
18. Mucking Flat Lighthouse
     ("The Squat Shoal Lighthouse")
19. Lobster Smack Inn
     ("The Ship Tavern")
20. "Deadman's Point":
     End of the River Journey

ESSEX

HOLE HAVEN

SEA REACH

BLYTH SANDS

EGYPT
BAY

LOWER
HOPE
POINT

CLIFFE
MARSHES

COOLING
MARSHES

Cliffe

Cooling

CLIFFE CREEK

HIGHAM CREEK

HIGHAM
MARSHES

Gravesend

Lower Higham

Hoo St.

Chalk

DOVER ROAD

Higham

CLIFFE ROAD

CHATHAM
DOCKS

Shorne

Brompt

Strood

ROCHESTER BRIDGE

Rochester

Chatham

Scale of Miles

0   1   2

6

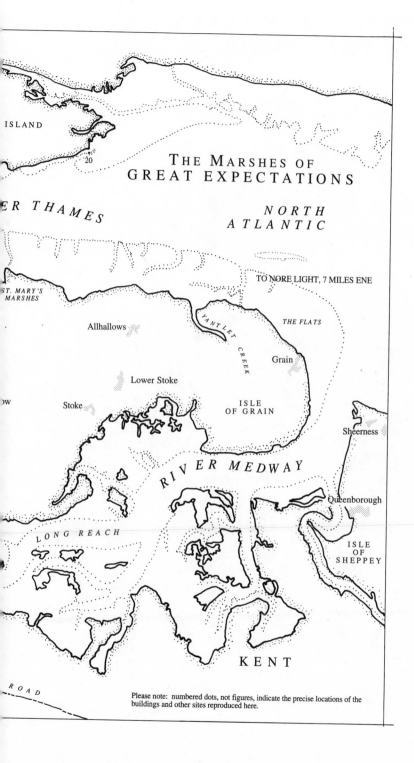

ISLAND

20

THE MARSHES OF
GREAT EXPECTATIONS

ER THAMES

*NORTH
ATLANTIC*

TO NORE LIGHT, 7 MILES ENE

*ST. MARY'S
MARSHES*

Allhallows

THE FLATS

YANTLET CREEK

Grain

Lower Stoke

DW

Stoke

*ISLE
OF GRAIN*

Sheerness

RIVER MEDWAY

Queenborough

LONG REACH

*ISLE
OF
SHEPPEY*

KENT

ROAD

Please note: numbered dots, not figures, indicate the precise locations of the
buildings and other sites reproduced here.

Chapter I.

My father's family name being Pirrip, and my christian name Philip, my infant tongue could make of both names nothing longer or more explicit than Pip. So, I called myself Pip, and came to be called Pip.

I give Pirrip as my father's family name, on the authority of his tombstone and my sister—Mrs. Joe Gargery, who married the blacksmith. As I never saw my father or my mother, and never saw any likeness of either of them (for their days were long before the days of photographs),[1] my first fancies regarding what they were like, were unreasonably derived from their tombstones. The shape of the letters on my father's, gave me an odd idea that he was a square, stout, dark man with curly black hair. From the character and turn of the inscription, "*Also Georgiana Wife of the Above*," I drew a childish conclusion that my mother was freckled and sickly. To five little stone lozenges,[2] each about a foot and a half long, which were arranged in a neat row beside their grave, and were sacred to the memory of five little brothers of mine—who gave up trying to get a living, exceedingly early in that universal struggle[3]—I am indebted for a belief I religiously entertained that they had all been born on their backs with their hands in their trousers-pockets, and had never taken them out in this state of existence.[4]

Ours was the marsh country, down by the river, within, as the river wound, twenty miles of the sea.[5] My first most vivid and broad impression of the identity of things, seems to me to have been gained on a memorable raw afternoon towards evening. At such a time I found out for certain, that this bleak place overgrown with nettles was the churchyard; and that Philip Pirrip, late of this parish, and also Georgiana wife of the above, were dead and buried; and that Alexander, Bartholomew, Abraham, Tobias, and Roger, infant children of the aforesaid, were also dead and buried; and that the dark flat wilderness beyond the churchyard, intersected with dykes and mounds and gates, with scattered cattle feeding on it, was the marshes; and that the low leaden line beyond, was the river; and that the distant savage lair from which the wind was rushing, was the sea; and that the

---

1. Some thirty years earlier. Louis-Jacques-Mandé Daguerre (1789–1851) to all intents invented photography, using silvered copper plates, in 1839, the same year in which W. H. Fox Talbot (1800–1877) announced the first photographic print on light-sensitive paper to the Royal Society. By 1860 photography had become all the rage.
2. In the original sense of slabs, or tombstones. The meaning is more clearly suggested in French, in which the word *lozenge* translates as "rhomboid."
3. The phrase echoes chapter 3 ("Struggle for Existence") of Darwin's *Origin of Species*, which had appeared in November 1859, less than a year before Dickens started to write *Great Expectations*.
4. The concluding image recalls the scene in *Oliver Twist*, chapter 5, in which the coffin lids in Sowerberry's funeral parlor appear "in the dim light, like high-shouldered ghosts with their hands in their breeches-pockets." See also *Edwin Drood*, chapter 6, in which the Reverend Crisparkle bears the Christian name "Septimus, because six little brother Crisparkles before him went out . . . as they were born, like six weak little rushlights before they were lighted."
5. The marshes (or meshes) of the Hoo Peninsula, the sparsely populated tongue of land stretching east between the Thames and the Medway estuaries in northern Kent. The Kentish fenland, from one mile to three miles wide, is everywhere intersected with muddy ditches and covered with rushes and rank vegetation. As Guiliano/Collins point out, Dickens, in evoking Pip's childhood home, gives virtually no identifiable place-names—whereas in his description of London every building, street, and back alley is accounted for.

small bundle of shivers growing afraid of it all and beginning to cry, was Pip.[6]

"Hold your noise!" cried a terrible voice, as a man started up from among the graves at the side of the church porch. "Keep still, you little devil, or I'll cut your throat!"

A fearful man, all in coarse grey, with a great iron on his leg. A man with no hat, and with broken shoes, and with an old rag tied round his head. A man who had been soaked in water, and smothered in mud, and lamed by stones, and cut by flints, and stung by nettles, and torn by briars; who limped, and shivered, and glared and growled; and whose teeth chattered in his head as he seized me by the chin.

"O! Don't cut my throat, sir," I pleaded in terror. "Pray don't do it, sir."

"Tell us your name!" said the man. "Quick!"

"Pip, sir."

"Once more," said the man, staring at me. "Give it mouth!"[7]

"Pip. Pip, sir."

"Show us where you live," said the man. "Pint out the place!"

I pointed to where our village lay, on the flat in-shore among the alder-trees and pollards,[8] a mile or more from the church.[9]

The man, after looking at me for a moment, turned me upside-down, and emptied my pockets. There was nothing in them but a piece of bread. When the church came to itself—for he was so sudden and strong that he made it go head over heels before me, and I saw the steeple under my legs—when the church came to itself, I say, I was seated on a high tombstone, trembling, while he ate the bread ravenously.

"You young dog," said the man, licking his lips at me, "what fat cheeks you ha' got."

I believe they were fat, though I was at that time undersized for my years, and not strong.

"Darn Me if I couldn't eat 'em," said the man, with a threatening shake of his head, "and if I han't half a mind to't!"

I earnestly expressed my hope that he wouldn't, and held tighter to the tombstone on which he had put me; partly, to keep myself upon it; partly, to keep myself from crying.

"Now then, lookee here!" said the man. "Where's your mother?"

"There, sir!" said I.

He started, made a short run, and stopped and looked over his shoulder.

"There, sir!" I timidly explained. "Also Georgiana. That's my mother."

"Oh!" said he, coming back. "And is that your father alonger your mother?"

"Yes, sir," said I; "him too; late of this parish."

"Ha!" he muttered then, considering. "Who d'ye live with—supposin' you're kindly let to live, which I han't made up my mind about?"

6. See Carlyle's *Sartor Resartus* (1836) 2.7: "Wherefore, like a coward, dost thou forever pip and whimper and go cowering and trembling?" Elsewhere Pip's name has been pressed into service as a palindrome, a seed, Sir Philip Sidney, a figure out of *The Maid and the Magpie*, and a refrain in a nursery rhyme.
7. Theatrical slang. "A rude request to an actor or orator [to] speak up" (Hotten).
8. Trees cut back to the trunk to promote the growth of young branches and dense heads of foliage.
9. The church, with its twenty-foot steeple, is located at Lower Higham, four miles north of Rochester. But Dickens relied on his composite skills in drawing Pip's village: the lozenge-shaped tombstones are imported from the churchyard at Cooling, another three miles northeast, Dickens reducing the actual number of gravestones from thirteen to five; and Joe's forge in chapter 2, Pip's home, is borrowed from the village of Chalk (the site of Dickens's honeymoon), between Gravesend and Rochester.

"My sister, sir—Mrs. Joe Gargery—wife of Joe Gargery, the blacksmith, sir."

"Blacksmith, eh?" said he. And looked down at his leg.

After darkly looking at his leg and at me several times, he came closer to my tombstone, took me by both arms, and tilted me back as far as he could hold me; so that his eyes looked most powerfully down into mine, and mine looked most helplessly up into his.

"Now lookee here," he said, "the question being whether you're to be let to live. You know what a file is."

"Yes, sir."

"And you know what wittles[1] is."

"Yes, sir."

After each question he tilted me over a little more, so as to give me a greater sense of helplessness and danger.

"You get me a file." He tilted me again. "And you get me wittles." He tilted me again. "You bring 'em both to me." He tilted me again. "Or I'll have your heart and liver out." He tilted me again.

I was dreadfully frightened, and so giddy that I clung to him with both hands, and said, "If you would kindly please to let me keep upright, sir, perhaps I shouldn't be sick, and perhaps I could attend more."

He gave me a most tremendous dip and roll, so that the church jumped over its own weather-cock. Then, he held me by the arms, in an upright position on the top of the stone, and went on in these fearful terms:

"You bring me, to-morrow morning early, that file and them wittles. You bring the lot to me, at that old Battery over yonder.[2] You do it, and you never dare to say a word or dare to make a sign concerning your having seen such a person as me, or any person sumever, and you shall be let to live. You fail, or you go from my words in any partickler, no matter how small it is, and your heart and your liver shall be tore out, roasted, and ate. Now, I ain't alone, as you may think I am. There's a young man hid with me, in comparison with which young man I am a Angel. That young man hears the words I speak. That young man has a secret way pecooliar to himself, of getting at a boy, and at his heart, and at his liver. It is in wain for a boy to attempt to hide himself from that young man. A boy may lock his door, may be warm in bed, may tuck himself up, may draw the clothes over his head, may think himself comfortable and safe, but that young man will softly creep and creep his way to him and tear him open. I am a keeping that young man from harming of you at the present moment, with great difficulty. I find it wery hard to hold that young man off of your inside. Now, what do you say?"

I said that I would get him the file, and I would get him what broken bits of food I could, and I would come to him at the Battery, early in the morning.

"Say Lord strike you dead if you don't!" said the man.

I said so, and he took me down.

"Now," he pursued, "you remember what you've undertook, and you remember that young man, and you get home!"

"Goo-good night, sir," I faltered.

1. Victuals.
2. Cliffe Creek Battery, about a mile west of Pip's village, was one of the earliest fortifications (1539) built to defend the Thames and so guard the approach to London from the sea. By Pip's time no more than a mound of dirt.

"Much of that!" said he, glancing about him over the cold wet flat. "I wish I was a frog. Or a eel!"

At the same time, he hugged his shuddering body in both his arms—clasping himself, as if to hold himself together—and limped towards the low church wall. As I saw him go, picking his way among the nettles, and among the brambles that bound the green mounds, he looked in my young eyes as if he were eluding the hands of the dead people, stretching up cautiously out of their graves, to get a twist upon his ankle and pull him in.

When he came to the low church wall, he got over it, like a man whose legs were numbed and stiff, and then turned round to look for me. When I   10 saw him turning, I set my face towards home, and made the best use of my legs. But presently I looked over my shoulder, and saw him going on again towards the river, still hugging himself in both arms, and picking his way with his sore feet among the great stones dropped into the marshes here and there, for stepping-places when the rains were heavy, or the tide was in.

The marshes were just a long black horizontal line then, as I stopped to look after him; and the river was just another horizontal line, not nearly so broad nor yet so black; and the sky was just a row of long angry red lines and dense black lines intermixed. On the edge of the river, I could faintly make out the only two black things in all the prospect that seemed to be standing   20 upright; one of these was the beacon by which the sailors steered—like an unhooped cask upon a pole—an ugly thing when you were near it; the other, a gibbet[3] with some chains hanging to it which had once held a pirate. The man was limping on towards this latter, as if he were the pirate come to life, and come down, and going back to hook himself up again. It gave me a terrible turn when I thought so; and as I saw the cattle lifting their heads to gaze after him, I wondered whether they thought so too. I looked all round for the horrible young man, and could see no signs of him. But, now I was frightened again, and ran home without stopping.

Chapter II.

My sister, Mrs. Joe Gargery, was more than twenty years older than I, and   30 had established a great reputation with herself and the neighbours because she had brought me up "by hand."[1] Having at that time to find out for myself what the expression meant, and knowing her to have a hard and heavy hand, and to be much in the habit of laying it upon her husband as well as upon me, I supposed that Joe Gargery and I were both brought up by hand.

She was not a good-looking woman, my sister; and I had a general impression that she must have made Joe Gargery marry her by hand. Joe was a fair man, with curls of flaxen hair on each side of his smooth face, and with eyes of such a very undecided blue that they seemed to have somehow got mixed with their own whites. He was a mild, good-natured, sweet-tempered,   40

3. Gallows: an upright post with a projecting arm from which criminals were hanged. The habit of displaying corpses by leaving them hanging in chains along the river and main approaches to London persisted well into Pip's day. In his *Child's History of England*, chapter 19, Dickens traces the custom back to the thwarted rebellion of the Kentish leader Wat Tyler against Richard II. "Unhooped cask": the beacon at Cliffe Creek was an elevated cage in which a fire could be lit as a signal.

1. The phrase (Pip deliberately misconstrues it) means "bottle-fed," a more expensive method than breast-feeding. Hence Mrs. Joe's bragging below and Joe's approving comments in chapter 7. Presumably Pip's mother died in childbirth or soon after, before she could breast-feed him.

easy-going, foolish, dear fellow—a sort of Hercules in strength, and also in weakness.[2]

My sister, Mrs. Joe, with black hair and eyes, had such a prevailing redness of skin that I sometimes used to wonder whether it was possible she washed herself with a nutmeg-grater instead of soap.[3] She was tall and bony, and almost always wore a coarse apron, fastened over her figure behind with two loops, and having a square impregnable bib in front that was stuck full of pins and needles. She made it a powerful merit in herself, and a strong reproach against Joe, that she wore this apron so much. Though I really see no reason why she should have worn it at all: or why, if she did wear it at all, she should not have taken it off, every day of her life.

Joe's forge adjoined our house, which was a wooden house, as many of the dwellings in our country were—most of them, at that time. When I ran home from the churchyard, the forge was shut up, and Joe was sitting alone in the kitchen. Joe and I being fellow-sufferers, and having confidences as such, Joe imparted a confidence to me, the moment I raised the latch of the door and peeped in at him opposite to it, sitting in the chimney-corner.

"Mrs. Joe has been out a dozen times, looking for you, Pip. And she's out now, making it a baker's dozen."[4]

"Is she?"

"Yes, Pip," said Joe; "and what's worse, she's got Tickler with her."

At this dismal intelligence, I twisted the only button on my waistcoat round and round, and looked in great depression at the fire. Tickler was a wax-ended piece of cane, worn smooth by collision with my tickled frame.[5]

"She sot down," said Joe, "and she got up, and she made a grab at Tickler, and she Ram-paged out. That's what she did," said Joe, slowly clearing the fire between the lower bars with the poker, and looking at it: "she Ram-paged out, Pip."

"Has she been gone long, Joe?" I always treated him as a larger species of child, and as no more than my equal.

"Well," said Joe, glancing up at the Dutch clock,[6] "she's been on the Rampage, this last spell, about five minutes, Pip. She's a coming! Get behind the door, old chap, and have the jack-towel[7] betwixt you."

I took the advice. My sister, Mrs. Joe, throwing the door wide open, and finding an obstruction behind it, immediately divined the cause, and applied

2. In strength physically; in weakness in being henpecked. Hercules's physical feats, crowned by the Twelve Labors he performed for Eurystheus (slaying the Hydra, cleansing the Augean stables, etc.) are proverbial; sold into slavery to Omphale, queen of Lydia, he disgraced himself by spinning wool and swapping his lion's skin for women's wear.

3. The image recalls David Copperfield's recollections (chapter 2) of "the touch of Peggotty's forefinger . . . roughened by needlework, like a pocket nutmeg-grater" (Monod).

4. Thirteen. The custom dates back to the thirteenth century. In one of the earliest statutes (51 Henry III), bakers received a stiff penalty if they short-changed their customers. To guard against this, they added an extra piece: hence "baker's dozen." Against this, Grose: "fourteen, that number of rolls being allowed to the purchasers of a dozen."

5. Schoolmasters placed wax on the end of the cane to keep it from splitting. "Tickler": perhaps from "tickle tail," slang for rod [OED]. "Tickler" had already appeared as the sword-stick carried by the fire-eating American Major Hannibal Chollop ("a splendid sample of our na-tive raw material") in Martin Chuzzlewit, chapter 23—along with his great knife "Ripper."

6. Deutsch, really: the clocks, almost entirely of wood, cheap, and hence popular with the poor, originated in the Black Forest, home of the cuckoo clock.

7. Coarse roller towel: Jaggers is described as using one in chapter 26. In the States, often a fixture in public lavatories. The auxiliary "Jack" is frequently extended to ordinary appliances that may have replaced the services of a live Jack—a servant or general handyman. See "bootjack" below and the variety of Jacks in chapters 8 and 54.

Tickler to its further investigation. She concluded by throwing me—I often served her.as a connubial missile—at Joe, who, glad to get hold of me on any terms, passed me on into the chimney and quietly fenced me up there with his great leg.[8]

"Where have you been, you young monkey?" said Mrs. Joe, stamping her foot. "Tell me directly what you've been doing to wear me away with fret and fright and worrit, or I'd have you out of that corner if you was fifty Pips and he was five hundred Gargerys."

"I have only been to the churchyard," said I, from my stool, crying and rubbing myself.   10

"Churchyard!" repeated my sister. "If it warn't for me you'd have been to the churchyard long ago, and stayed there. Who brought you up by hand?"

"You did," said I.

"And why did I do it, I should like to know!" exclaimed my sister.

I whimpered, "I don't know."

"I don't!" said my sister. "I'd never do it again! I know that. I may truly say I've never had this apron of mine off, since born you were. It's bad enough to be a blacksmith's wife (and him a Gargery), without being your mother."

My thoughts strayed from that question as I looked disconsolately at the fire. For, the fugitive out on the marshes with the ironed leg, the mysterious 20 young man, the file, the food, and the dreadful pledge I was under to commit a larceny on those sheltering premises, rose before me in the avenging coals.[9]

"Hah!" said Mrs. Joe, restoring Tickler to his station. "Churchyard, indeed! You may well say churchyard, you two." One of us, by-the-by, had not said it at all. "You'll drive me to the churchyard betwixt you, one of these days, and oh, a pr-r-recious pair you'd be without me!"

As she applied herself to set the tea-things, Joe peeped down at me over his leg, as if he were mentally casting me and himself up, and calculating what kind of pair we practically should make, under the grievous circumstances foreshadowed. After that, he sat feeling his right-side flaxen curls and 30 whisker, and following Mrs. Joe about with his blue eyes, as his manner always was at squally times.

My sister had a trenchant way of cutting our bread-and-butter for us, that never varied. First, with her left hand she jammed the loaf hard and fast against her bib—where it sometimes got a pin into it, and sometimes a needle, which we afterwards got into our mouths. Then, she took some butter (not too much) on a knife and spread it on the loaf, in an apothecary kind of way as if she were making a plaister[1]—using both sides of the knife with a slapping dexterity, and trimming and moulding the butter off round the crust. Then, she gave the knife a final smart wipe on the edge of the plaister, and then 40 sawed a very thick round off the loaf: which she finally, before separating from the loaf, hewed into two halves: of which Joe got one, and I the other.

8. Old-fashioned fireplaces, found especially in the country, built into the hollow of one wall, were large enough to accommodate two or more people who sat on a stool or low chairs close to the fire.
9. The phrase may hark back to the association of coals and vengeance in Romans 12.19–21: "Vengeance is mine; I will repay, saith the Lord. Therefore if thine enemy hunger, feed him; if he thirst, give him to drink: for in doing so thou shalt heap coals of fire on his head." Between Paul and Pip (but closer to Pip) we have young Clifford's war-whoop during the Lancastrian rout in Shakespeare's 2 *Henry VI* 5.3.33–36: "Oh war, thou son of hell, / Whom angry heavens do make their minister, / Throw in the frozen bosoms of our part / Hot coals of vengeance!" But see also the "coals of fire" Joe heaps on Pip's head in chapter 27.
1. Poultice.

On the present occasion, though I was hungry, I dared not eat my slice. I felt that I must have something in reserve for my dreadful acquaintance, and his ally the still more dreadful young man. I knew Mrs. Joe's housekeeping to be of the strictest kind, and that my larcenous researches might find nothing available in the safe. Therefore I resolved to put my hunk[2] of bread-and-butter down the leg of my trousers.

The effort of resolution necessary to the achievement of this purpose, I found to be quite awful. It was as if I had to make up my mind to leap from the top of a high house, or plunge into a great depth of water. And it was made the more difficult by the unconscious Joe. In our already-mentioned freemasonry[3] as fellow-sufferers, and in his good-natured companionship with me, it was our evening habit to compare the way we bit through our slices, by silently holding them up to each other's admiration now and then—which stimulated us to new exertions. To-night, Joe several times invited me, by the display of his fast-diminishing slice, to enter upon our usual friendly competition; but he found me, each time, with my yellow mug of tea on one knee, and my untouched bread-and-butter on the other. At last, I desperately considered that the thing I contemplated must be done, and that it had best be done in the least improbable manner consistent with the circumstances. I took advantage of a moment when Joe had just looked at me, and got my bread-and-butter down my leg.

Joe was evidently made uncomfortable by what he supposed to be my loss of appetite, and took a thoughtful bite out of his slice, which he didn't seem to enjoy. He turned it about in his mouth much longer than usual, pondering over it a good deal, and after all gulped it down like a pill. He was about to take another bite, and had just got his head on one side for a good purchase on it, when his eye fell on me, and he saw that my bread-and-butter was gone.

The wonder and consternation with which Joe stopped on the threshold of his bite and stared at me, were too evident to escape my sister's observation.

"What's the matter now?" said she, smartly, as she put down her cup.

"I say, you know!" muttered Joe, shaking his head at me in very serious remonstrance. "Pip, old chap! You'll do yourself a mischief. It'll stick somewhere. You can't have chawed it, Pip."

"What's the matter now?" repeated my sister, more sharply than before.

"If you can cough any trifle on it up, Pip, I'd recommend you to do it," said Joe, all aghast. "Manners is manners, but still your elth's your elth."

By this time, my sister was quite desperate, so she pounced on Joe, and, taking him by the two whiskers, knocked his head for a little while against the wall behind him: while I sat in the corner, looking guiltily on.

"Now, perhaps you'll mention what's the matter," said my sister, out of breath, "you staring great stuck pig."[4]

Joe looked at her in a helpless way; then took a helpless bite, and looked at me again.

"You know, Pip," said Joe, solemnly, with his last bite in his cheek, and speaking in a confidential voice, as if we two were quite alone, "you and me

---

2. A thick slice. Also "hunch": thus early in chapter 8 Pip notices that Pumblechook's "shopman took his mug of tea and hunch of bread-and-butter on a sack of peas."
3. Secret fraternal order that evolved from the medieval guilds. Freemasons were known to use secret signs to communicate with each other in the presence of noninitiates.
4. A pig with its throat cut.

is always friends, and I'd be the last to tell upon you, any time. But such a"
—he moved his chair and looked about the floor between us, and then again
at me—"such a most oncommon Bolt as that!"[5]

"Been bolting his food, has he?" cried my sister.

"You know, old chap," said Joe, looking at me, and not at Mrs. Joe, with
his bite still in his cheek, "I Bolted, myself, when I was your age—frequent
—and as a boy I've been among a many Bolters; but I never see your Bolting
equal yet, Pip, and it's a mercy you ain't Bolted dead."

My sister made a dive at me, and fished me up by the hair: saying nothing
more than the awful words, "You come along and be dosed."   10

Some medical beast had revived Tar-water in those days as a fine medicine,
and Mrs. Joe always kept a supply of it in the cupboard; having a belief in
its virtues correspondent to its nastiness.[6] At the best of times, so much of this
elixir was administered to me as a choice restorative, that I was conscious of
going about, smelling like a new fence. On this particular evening the urgency of my case demanded a pint of this mixture, which was poured down
my throat, for my greater comfort, while Mrs. Joe held my head under her
arm, as a boot would be held in a boot-jack.[7] Joe got off with half a pint; but
was made to swallow that (much to his disturbance, as he sat slowly munching
and meditating before the fire), "because he had had a turn." Judging from   20
myself, I should say he certainly had a turn afterwards, if he had had none
before.

Conscience is a dreadful thing when it accuses man or boy; but when, in
the case of a boy, that secret burden co-operates with another secret burden
down the leg of his trousers, it is (as I can testify) a great punishment. The
guilty knowledge that I was going to rob Mrs. Joe—I never thought I was
going to rob Joe, for I never thought of any of the housekeeping property as
his—united to the necessity of always keeping one hand on my bread and
butter as I sat, or when I was ordered about the kitchen on any small errand,
almost drove me out of my mind. Then, as the marsh winds made the fire   30
glow and flare, I thought I heard the voice outside, of the man with the iron
on his leg who had sworn me to secrecy, declaring that he couldn't and
wouldn't starve until to-morrow, but must be fed now. At other times, I
thought, What if the young man who was with so much difficulty restrained
from imbruing his hands in me, should yield to a constitutional impatience,
or should mistake the time, and should think himself accredited to my heart
and liver to-night, instead of to-morrow! If ever anybody's hair stood on end
with terror, mine must have done so then. But, perhaps, nobody's ever did?

It was Christmas Eve, and I had to stir the pudding for next day, with a
copper-stick,[8] from seven to eight by the Dutch clock. I tried it with the load   40
upon my leg (and that made me think afresh of the man with the load on

5. "To Bolt: . . . to swallow meat without chewing" (Grose). Grose singles out Kent as notorious for its
Bolters.
6. Tar-water, a concoction of pine extract and fir extract, the most widely touted panacea of the eighteenth
century, thanks to Bishop Berkeley (1685–1753), who, in his essay *Siris: A Chain of Philosophical
Inquiries Concerning the Virtues of Tar Water* (1774), prescribed it as a cure for everything from
"foulness of blood" and "ulceration of the bowels" to pleurisy, erysipelas, dropsy, and "hysteric cases."
As Berkeley urges a smaller dosage for "children and squeamish persons," Pip's horror at being force-
fed a pint makes sense.
7. Short board equipped with a hook, which held the heel of the boot in place to help in pulling it off.
8. Ordinarily used to stir laundry boiling in the "copper[-kettle]" on washing days, but itself so deterged
by the procedure that Pip could put it to work as a food blender.

his leg), and found the tendency of exercise to bring the bread-and-butter out at my ankle, quite unmanageable. Happily, I slipped away, and deposited that part of my conscience in my garret bedroom.

"Hark!" said I, when I had done my stirring, and was taking a final warm in the chimney corner before being sent up to bed; "was that great guns, Joe?"

"Ah!" said Joe. "There's another conwict off."

"What does that mean, Joe?" said I.

Mrs. Joe, who always took explanations upon herself, said, snappishly, "Escaped. Escaped." Administering the definition like Tar-water.   10

While Mrs. Joe sat with her head bending over her needlework, I put my mouth into the forms of saying to Joe, "What's a convict?" Joe put *his* mouth into the forms of returning such a highly elaborate answer, that I could make out nothing of it but the single word "Pip."

"There was a conwict off last night," said Joe, aloud, "after sunset-gun.[9] And they fired warning of him. And now, it appears they're firing warning of another."

"*Who's* firing?" said I.

"Drat that boy," interposed my sister, frowning at me over her work, "what a questioner he is. Ask no questions, and you'll be told no lies."[1]   20

It was not very polite to herself, I thought, to imply that I should be told lies by her, even if I did ask questions. But she never was polite, unless there was company.

At this point, Joe greatly augmented my curiosity by taking the utmost pains to open his mouth very wide, and to put it into the form of a word that looked to me like "Sulks." Therefore, I naturally pointed to Mrs. Joe, and put my mouth into the form of saying, "her?" But Joe wouldn't hear of that, at all, and again opened his mouth very wide, and shook the form of a most emphatic word out of it. But I could make nothing of the word.

"Mrs. Joe," said I, as a last resource, "I should like to know—if you wouldn't   30 much mind—where the firing comes from?"

"Lord bless the boy!" exclaimed my sister, as if she didn't quite mean that, but rather the contrary. "From the Hulks!"[2]

"Oh-h!" said I, looking at Joe. "Hulks!"

Joe gave a reproachful cough, as much as to say, "Well, I told you so."

"And please what's Hulks?" said I.[3]

"That's the way with this boy!" exclaimed my sister, pointing me out with

9. Not a special type of weaponry; a cannon fired at sunset, generally near military installations. Toward the end of chapter 15 Pip refers to it as a "signal cannon": a signal, that is, to mark the escape of convicts from the hulks.

1. Oliver Goldsmith, *She Stoops to Conquer, or The Mistakes of a Night* (1771, performed 1773), act 3: "Ask me no questions and I'll tell you no fibs." Goldsmith's *Vicar of Wakefield* was one of the most widely read novels in Dickens's household.

2. The revolt of the American colonies in 1775 brought on a critical breakdown in the transportation of convicts to the New World, since the sixteenth century the harshest penalty short of the death sentence. In '75 the government recommended the use of dismantled ships, moored off the mudbanks of the Thames estuary, as temporary prison depots, all convicts to be sentenced to hard labor. Though the hulks were set up as a stopgap measure to relieve the pressure on the overflowing jails at a time when the country recognized two hundred capital crimes, many of them commutable to transportation, the enormous influx of prisoners of war during the Napoleonic Wars persuaded the government not only to perpetuate the hulks but to increase their number. The physical conditions in the hulks were among the most appalling in British penal history; between 1776 and 1795, of some fifty-eight hundred prisoners aboard, nearly two thousand died of infection and malnutrition. The Penal Servitude Acts of 1853 and 1857 replaced transportation with equivalent terms of imprisonment in England.

3. On the embattled question about Pip's question, see p. 442.

her needle and thread, and shaking her head at me. "Answer him one question, and he'll ask you a dozen directly. Hulks are prison-ships, right 'cross th' meshes." We always used that name for marshes, in our country. "I wonder who's put into prison-ships, and why they're put there?" said I, in a general way, and with quiet desperation. It was too much for Mrs. Joe, who immediately rose. "I tell you what, young fellow," said she, "I didn't bring you up by hand to badger people's lives out. It would be blame to me, and not praise, if I had. People are put in the Hulks because they murder, and because they rob, and forge, and do all sorts of bad; and they always begin by asking questions. Now, you get 10 along to bed!"

I was never allowed a candle to light me to bed, and, as I went up-stairs in the dark, with my head tingling—from Mrs. Joe's thimble having played the tambourine upon it, to accompany her last words—I felt fearfully sensible of the great convenience that the Hulks were handy for me. I was clearly on my way there. I had begun by asking questions, and I was going to rob Mrs. Joe.

Since that time, which is far enough away now, I have often thought that few people know what secrecy there is in the young, under terror. No matter how unreasonable the terror, so that it be terror. I was in mortal terror of the 20 young man who wanted my heart and liver; I was in mortal terror of my interlocutor with the ironed leg; I was in mortal terror of myself, from whom an awful promise had been extracted; I had no hope of deliverance through my all-powerful sister, who repulsed me at every turn; I am afraid to think even now of what I might have done, upon requirement, in the secrecy of my terror.

If I slept at all that night, it was only to imagine myself drifting down the river on a strong spring tide, to the Hulks; a ghostly pirate calling out to me through a speaking-trumpet, as I passed the gibbet-station, that I had better come ashore and be hanged there at once, and not put it off. I was afraid to sleep, even if I had been inclined, for I knew that at the first faint dawn of 30 morning I must rob the pantry. There was no doing it in the night, for there was no getting a light by easy friction then; to have got one, I must have struck it out of flint and steel, and have made a noise like the very pirate himself rattling his chains.[4]

As soon as the great black velvet pall outside my little window was shot with grey, I got up and went down stairs; every board upon the way, and every crack in every board, calling after me, "Stop thief!" and "Get up, Mrs. Joe!" In the pantry, which was far more abundantly supplied than usual, owing to the season, I was very much alarmed, by a hare hanging up by the heels, whom I rather thought I caught, when my back was half turned, wink- 40 ing. I had no time for verification, no time for selection, no time for anything, for I had no time to spare. I stole some bread, some rind of cheese, about half a jar of mincemeat[5] (which I tied up in my pocket-handkerchief with my last night's slice), some brandy from a stone bottle (which I decanted into a glass bottle I had secretly used for making that intoxicating fluid, Spanish-

4. Friction matches were unknown in England before 1827; phosphorus-tipped matches were first marketed commercially in the thirties; and safety matches as we know them came later still. In Pip's day, getting a light involved the process Pip describes in chapter 53: of igniting tinder with the sparks struck off by the percussion of flint and steel.
5. A mixture of finely chopped (or minced) currants, raisins, sugar, suet, apples, etc., sometimes including bits of meat. Mincemeat pies are traditionally served at Christmas.

liquorice-water, up in my room: diluting the stone bottle[6] from a jug in the kitchen cupboard), a meat bone with very little on it, and a beautiful round compact pork pie. I was nearly going away without the pie, but I was tempted to mount upon a shelf, to look what it was that was put away so carefully in a covered earthenware dish in a corner, and I found it was the pie, and I took it, in the hope that it was not intended for early use, and would not be missed for some time.

There was a door in the kitchen, communicating with the forge; I unlocked and unbolted that door, and got a file from among Joe's tools. Then, I put the fastenings as I had found them, opened the door at which I had entered 10 when I ran home last night, shut it, and ran for the misty marshes.

Chapter III.

It was a rimy morning, and very damp. I had seen the damp lying on the outside of my little window, as if some goblin had been crying there all night, and using the window for a pocket-handkerchief. Now, I saw the damp lying on the bare hedges and spare grass, like a coarser sort of spiders' webs; hanging itself from twig to twig and blade to blade. On every rail and gate, wet lay clammy; and the marsh-mist was so thick, that the wooden finger on the post directing people to our village—a direction which they never accepted, for they never came there—was invisible to me until I was quite close under it. Then, as I looked up at it, while it dripped, it seemed to my oppressed 20 conscience like a phantom devoting me to the Hulks.

The mist was heavier yet when I got out upon the marshes, so that instead of my running at everything, everything seemed to run at me. This was very disagreeable to a guilty mind. The gates and dykes and banks came bursting at me through the mist, as if they cried as plainly as could be, "A boy with Somebody-else's pork pie! Stop him!" The cattle came upon me with like suddenness, staring out of their eyes, and steaming out of their nostrils, "Halloa, young thief!" One black ox, with a white cravat on—who even had to my awakened conscience something of a clerical air[1]—fixed me so obstinately with his eyes, and moved his blunt head round in such an accusatory manner 30 as I moved round, that I blubbered out to him, "I couldn't help it, sir! It wasn't for myself I took it!" Upon which he put down his head, blew a cloud of smoke out of his nose, and vanished with a kick-up of his hind-legs and a flourish of his tail.

All this time, I was getting on towards the river; but however fast I went, I couldn't warm my feet, to which the damp cold seemed riveted, as the iron was riveted to the leg of the man I was running to meet. I knew my way to the Battery, pretty straight, for I had been down there on a Sunday with Joe, and Joe, sitting on an old gun, had told me that when I was 'prentice to him regularly bound, we would have such Larks there! However, in the confusion 40

6. Heavily glazed piece of pottery. "Spanish-liquorice-water": Pip is being funny: liquorice water is no more intoxicating than prune juice.
1. Since clergymen wore white collars, the black ox "with a white cravat on" perhaps scares Pip all the more for the religious authority Pip imputes to him.

of the mist, I found myself at last too far to the right, and consequently had
to try back along the river-side, on the bank of loose stones above the mud
and the stakes that staked the tide out. Making my way along here with all
despatch, I had just crossed a ditch which I knew to be very near the Battery,
and had just scrambled up the mound beyond the ditch, when I saw the man
sitting before me. His back was towards me, and he had his arms folded, and
was nodding forward, heavy with sleep.

I thought he would be more glad if I came upon him with his breakfast,
in that unexpected manner, so I went forward softly and touched him on the
shoulder. He instantly jumped up, and it was not the same man, but another   10
man!

And yet this man was dressed in coarse grey, too, and had a great iron on
his leg, and was lame, and hoarse, and cold, and was everything that the other
man was; except that he had not the same face, and had a flat broad-brimmed
low-crowned felt hat on. All this, I saw in a moment, for I had only a moment
to see it in; he swore an oath at me, made a hit at me—it was a round weak
blow that missed me and almost knocked himself down, for it made him
stumble—and then he ran into the mist, stumbling twice as he went, and I
lost him.

"It's the young man!" I thought, feeling my heart shoot as I identified him.   20
I dare say I should have felt a pain in my liver, too, if I had known where it
was.

I was soon at the Battery, after that, and there was the right man—hugging
himself and limping to and fro, as if he had never all night left off hugging
and limping—waiting for me. He was awfully cold, to be sure. I half expected
to see him drop down before my face and die of deadly cold. His eyes looked
so awfully hungry, too, that when I handed him the file, and he laid it down
on the grass, it occurred to me he would have tried to eat it, if he had not
seen my bundle. He did not turn me upside down, this time, to get at what
I had, but left me right side upwards while I opened the bundle and emptied   30
my pockets.

"What's in the bottle, boy?" said he.

"Brandy," said I.

He was already handing mincemeat down his throat in the most curious
manner—more like a man who was putting it away somewhere in a violent
hurry, than a man who was eating it—but he left off to take some of the
liquor. He shivered all the while, so violently, that it was quite as much as
he could do to keep the neck of the bottle between his teeth, without biting
it off.

"I think you have got the ague,"[2] said I.   40

"I'm much of your opinion, boy," said he.

"It's bad about here," I told him. "You've been lying out on the meshes,
and they're dreadful aguish. Rheumatic, too."

"I'll eat my breakfast afore they're the death of me," said he. "I'd do that,
if I was going to be strung up to that there gallows as there is over there,
directly arterwards. I'll beat the shivers so far, I'll bet you."

He was gobbling mincemeat, meat-bone, bread, cheese, and pork pie, all
at once: staring distrustfully while he did so at the mist all round us, and

---

2. Fever and chills.

often stopping—even stopping his jaws—to listen. Some real or fancied sound, some clink upon the river or breathing of beast upon the marsh, now gave him a start, and he said, suddenly:

"You're not a deceiving imp? You brought no one with you?"

"No, sir! No!"

"Nor giv' no one the office to follow you?"[3]

"No!"

"Well," said he, "I believe you. You'd be but a fierce young hound indeed, if at your time of life you could help to hunt a wretched warmint, hunted as near death and dunghill as this poor wretched warmint[4] is!"   10

Something clicked in his throat, as if he had works in him like a clock, and was going to strike. And he smeared his ragged rough sleeve over his eyes.

Pitying his desolation, and watching him as he gradually settled down upon the pie, I made bold to say, "I am glad you enjoy it."

"Did you speak?"

"I said I was glad you enjoyed it."

"Thankee, my boy. I do."

I had often watched a large dog of ours eating his food; and I now noticed a decided similarity between the dog's way of eating, and the man's. The man 20 took strong sharp sudden bites, just like the dog. He swallowed, or rather snapped up, every mouthful, too soon and too fast; and he looked sideways here and there while he ate, as if he thought there was danger in every direction, of somebody's coming to take the pie away. He was altogether too unsettled in his mind over it, to appreciate it comfortably, I thought, or to have anybody to dine with him, without making a chop with his jaws at the visitor. In all of which particulars he was very like the dog.[5]

"I am afraid you won't leave any of it for him," said I, timidly; after a silence during which I had hesitated as to the politeness of making the remark. "There's no more to be got where that came from." It was the certainty 30 of this fact that impelled me to offer the hint.

"Leave any for him? Who's him?" said my friend, stopping in his crunching of pie-crust.

"The young man. That you spoke of. That was hid with you."

"Oh ah!" he returned, with something like a gruff laugh. "Him? Yes, yes! *He* don't want no wittles."

"I thought he looked as if he did," said I.

The man stopped eating, and regarded me with the keenest scrutiny and the greatest surprise.

"Looked? When?"   40

"Just now."

"Where?"

"Yonder," said I, pointing; "over there, where I found him nodding asleep, and thought it was you."

He held me by the collar and stared at me so, that I began to think his first idea about cutting my throat had revived.

3. "Nor tipped off the police?"
4. Vermin. But the term could be used colloquially to describe any type of rascal.
5. Except for Joe's allusion to the dog in his conversation with Jaggers in chapter 18, this is the last we hear of it.

"Dressed like you, you know, only with a hat," I explained, trembling; "and—and"—I was very anxious to put this delicately—"and with—the same reason for wanting to borrow a file. Didn't you hear the cannon last night?"

"Then, there *was* firing!" he said to himself.

"I wonder you shouldn't have been sure of that," I returned, "for we heard it up at home, and that's further away, and we were shut in besides."

"Why, see now!" said he. "When a man's alone on these flats, with a light head and a light stomach, perishing of cold and want, he hears nothin' all night, but guns firing, and voices calling. Hears? He sees the soldiers, with their red coats lighted up by the torches carried afore, closing in round him. Hears his number called,[6] hears himself challenged, hears the rattle of the muskets, hears the orders 'Make ready! Present! Cover him steady, men!' and is laid hands on—and there's nothin'! Why, if I see one pursuing party last night—coming up in order, Damn 'em, with their tramp, tramp—I see a hundred. And as to firing! Why, I see the mist shake with the cannon, arter it was broad day.—But this man;" he had said all the rest, as if he had forgotten my being there; "did you notice anything in him?"

"He had a badly bruised face," said I, recalling what I hardly knew I knew.

"Not here?" exclaimed the man, striking his left cheek mercilessly with the flat of his hand.

"Yes! There!"

"Where is he?" He crammed what little food was left, into the breast of his grey jacket. "Show me the way he went. I'll pull him down, like a bloodhound. Curse this iron on my sore leg! Give us hold of the file, boy."

I indicated in what direction the mist had shrouded the other man, and he looked up at it for an instant. But he was down on the rank wet grass, filing at his iron like a madman, and not minding me or minding his own leg, which had an old chafe upon it and was bloody, but which he handled as roughly as if it had no more feeling in it than the file. I was very much afraid of him again, now that he had worked himself into this fierce hurry, and I was likewise very much afraid of keeping away from home any longer. I told him I must go, but he took no notice, so I thought the best thing I could do was to slip off. The last I saw of him, his head was bent over his knee and he was working hard at his fetter, muttering impatient imprecations at it and at his leg. The last I heard of him, I stopped in the mist to listen, and the file was still going.

Chapter IV.

I fully expected to find a Constable[1] in the kitchen, waiting to take me up. But not only was there no Constable there, but no discovery had yet been made of the robbery. Mrs. Joe was prodigiously busy in getting the house ready for the festivities of the day, and Joe had been put upon the kitchen door-step to keep him out of the dustpan—an article into which his destiny

6. Convicts were given numbers instead of names, to stigmatize them as nonpersons and to keep them from being identified. On the other hand, carriages and hotel rooms (like ships) were entitled to names instead of digits.
1. Local officer in charge of keeping the peace who handled minor criminal and other judicial affairs.

II   CHAPTER IV   23

always led him sooner or later, when my sister was vigorously reaping the floors of her establishment.

"And where the deuce ha' *you* been?" was Mrs. Joe's Christmas salutation, when I and my conscience showed ourselves.

I said I had been down to hear the Carols. "Ah! well!" observed Mrs. Joe. "You might ha' done worse." Not a doubt of that, I thought.

"Perhaps if I warn't a blacksmith's wife, and (what's the same thing) a slave with her apron never off, *I* should have been to hear the Carols," said Mrs. Joe. "I'm rather partial to Carols, myself, and that's the best of reasons for my never hearing any." 10

Joe, who had ventured into the kitchen after me as the dustpan had retired before us, drew the back of his hand across his nose with a conciliatory air when Mrs. Joe darted a look at him, and, when her eyes were withdrawn, secretly crossed his two forefingers, and exhibited them to me, as our token that Mrs. Joe was in a cross temper. This was so much her normal state, that Joe and I would often, for weeks together, be, as to our fingers, like monumental Crusaders as to their legs.[2]

We were to have a superb dinner, consisting of a leg of pickled pork and greens, and a pair of roast stuffed fowls. A handsome mince-pie had been made yesterday morning (which accounted for the mincemeat not being 20 missed), and the pudding was already on the boil. These extensive arrangements occasioned us to be cut off unceremoniously in respect of breakfast; "for I an't," said Mrs. Joe, "I an't a going to have no formal cramming and busting and washing up now, with what I've got before me, I promise you!"

So, we had our slices served out, as if we were two thousand troops on a forced march instead of a man and boy at home; and we took gulps of milk and water, with apologetic countenances, from a jug on the dresser. In the mean time, Mrs. Joe put clean white curtains up, and tacked a new flowered-flounce across the wide chimney to replace the old one, and uncovered the little state parlour across the passage, which was never uncovered at any other 30 time, but passed the rest of the year in a cool haze of silver paper, which even extended to the four little white crockery poodles on the mantel-shelf, each with a black nose and a basket of flowers in his mouth, and each the counterpart of the other. Mrs. Joe was a very clean housekeeper, but had an exquisite art of making her cleanliness more uncomfortable and unacceptable than dirt itself. Cleanliness is next to Godliness, and some people do the same by their religion.[3]

My sister having so much to do, was going to church vicariously; that is to say, Joe and I were going. In his working clothes, Joe was a well-knit characteristic-looking blacksmith; in his holiday clothes, he was more like a 40 scarecrow in good circumstances, than anything else. Nothing that he wore

2. In the thirteenth century, as part of a short-lived vogue in the construction of church monuments, the recumbent effigies of knights began to perk up a little by crossing their legs, bending their knees, grasping their swords, etc. This gave rise to the popular delusion (to which Dickens himself seems to have subscribed) that any knight memorialized by crossed legs had taken part in the Crusades and that the higher up he crossed them the more numerous his campaigns: legs crossed at the feet, one campaign; at the knees, two campaigns; at the thighs, three.
3. See John Wesley's sermon *On Dress* (1791): "Slovenliness is no part of religion. . . . Cleanliness is next to godliness"; and Francis Bacon's *Advancement of Learning* (1605): "Cleanliness of the body was ever deemed to proceed from a due reverence to God" (Hill). But really a commonplace of all major religions. As Guiliano/Collins point out, the English noted with satisfaction that this axiom was entirely unknown in France.

then, fitted him or seemed to belong to him; and everything that he wore then, grazed him. On the present festive occasion he emerged from his room, when the blithe bells were going, the picture of misery, in a full suit of Sunday penitentials.[4] As to me, I think my sister must have had some general idea that I was a young offender whom an Accoucheur-Policeman had taken up (on my birthday) and delivered over to her, to be dealt with according to the outraged majesty of the law.[5] I was always treated as if I had insisted on being born, in opposition to the dictates of reason, religion, and morality, and against the dissuading arguments of my best friends. Even when I was taken to have a new suit of clothes, the tailor had orders to construct them like a kind of Reformatory, and on no account to let me have the free use of my limbs.

Joe and I going to church, therefore, must have been a moving spectacle for compassionate minds. Yet, what I suffered outside, was nothing to what I underwent within. The terrors that had assailed me whenever Mrs. Joe had gone near the pantry, or out of the room, were only to be equalled by the remorse with which my mind dwelt on what my hands had done. Under the weight of my wicked secret, I pondered whether the Church would be powerful enough to shield me from the vengeance of the terrible young man, if I divulged to that establishment. I conceived the idea that the time when the banns were read and when the clergyman said, "Ye are now to declare it!" would be the time for me to rise and propose a private conference in the vestry. I am far from being sure that I might not have astonished our small congregation by resorting to this extreme measure, but for its being Christmas Day and no Sunday.[6]

Mr. Wopsle, the clerk at church, was to dine with us; and Mr. Hubble the wheelwright and Mrs. Hubble; and Uncle Pumblechook (Joe's uncle, but Mrs. Joe appropriated him), who was a well-to-do corn-chandler in the nearest town, and drove his own chaise-cart.[7] The dinner hour was half-past one. When Joe and I got home, we found the table laid, and Mrs. Joe dressed, and the dinner dressing, and the front door unlocked (it never was, at any other time) for the company to enter by, and everything most splendid. And still, not a word of the robbery.

The time came, without bringing with it any relief to my feelings, and the company came. Mr. Wopsle, united to a Roman nose and a large shining bald forehead, had a deep voice which he was uncommonly proud of; indeed it was understood among his acquaintance that if you could only give him his head, he would read the clergyman into fits; he himself confessed that if the Church was "thrown open," meaning to competition, he would not despair of making his mark in it. The Church not being "thrown open," he

4. Black clothes, perhaps used here ironically to suggest mourning garments [OED].
5. "Accoucheur": male midwife. Here a policeman who serves as midwife in emergencies. As Pip uses the term, the accoucheur punishes babies for being born by taking them into custody at birth.
6. From the "Solemnization of Matrimony" in *The Book of Common Prayer*, official text of the Anglican church since 1549: "I require and charge you both . . . that if either of you know any impediment, why ye may not be lawfully joined together in matrimony, ye do now confess it." The formula followed by the curate in calling the banns on "three several Sundays or holidays" preceding the wedding. As Pip notes, the banns are not called on Christmas.
7. Light horse-drawn carriage strengthened to serve as a tradesman's vehicle. Joe's and Pumblechook's references to it as a "shay cart" in chapters 7 and 8 reflect the assumption, common to their stations, that *chaise* is plural: there may be two shays but only one shay. "Corn-chandler": a retail grain merchant.

was, as I have said, our clerk.[8] But he punished the Amens tremendously;[9] and when he gave out the psalm—always giving the whole verse—he looked all round the congregation first, as much as to say, "You have heard our friend overhead;[1] oblige me with your opinion of this style!"

I opened the door to the company—making believe that it was a habit of ours to open that door—and I opened it first to Mr. Wopsle, next to Mr. and Mrs. Hubble, and last of all to Uncle Pumblechook. N.B.[2] I was not allowed to call him uncle, under the severest penalties.

"Mrs. Joe," said Uncle Pumblechook: a large hard-breathing middle-aged slow man, with a mouth like a fish, dull staring eyes, and sandy hair standing 10 upright on his head, so that he looked as if he had just been all but choked, and had that very moment come to; "I have brought you, as the compliments of the season—I have brought you, Mum, a bottle of sherry wine—and I have brought you, Mum, a bottle of port wine."

Every Christmas Day he presented himself, as a profound novelty, with exactly the same words, and carrying the two bottles like dumbbells. Every Christmas Day, Mrs. Joe replied, as she now replied, "Oh, Un—cle Pum—ble—chook! This IS kind!" Every Christmas Day, he retorted, as he now retorted, "It's no more than your merits. And now are you all bobbish, and how's Sixpennorth of halfpence?"[3] meaning me. 20

We dined on these occasions in the kitchen, and adjourned, for the nuts and oranges and apples, to the parlour; which was a change very like Joe's change from his working clothes to his Sunday dress. My sister was uncommonly lively on the present occasion, and indeed was generally more gracious in the society of Mrs. Hubble than in any other company. I remember Mrs. Hubble as a little curly sharp-edged person in sky-blue, who held a conventionally juvenile position, because she had married Mr. Hubble—I don't know at what remote period—when she was much younger than he. I remember Mr. Hubble as a tough high-shouldered stooping old man, of a sawdusty fragrance, with his legs extraordinarily wide apart: so that in my short days I 30 always saw some miles of open country between them when I met him coming up the lane.

Among this good company, I should have felt myself, even if I hadn't robbed the pantry, in a false position. Not because I was squeezed in at an acute angle of the table-cloth, with the table in my chest, and the Pumble-chookian elbow in my eye, nor because I was not allowed to speak (I didn't

8. Wopsle's job as parish clerk is that of a lay reader who leads the congregation in the responses, reads out notices in the church, helps the priest in performing the sacraments, collects money for the parish poor and, more generally, keeps order during the service—whipping stray dogs from the church and poking sleepy parishioners to attention.
9. "Gave the Amens all he had"; "hit them hard." One of the clerk's stock duties: Grose cites "Amen Curler" as slang for parish clerk. Cf. Shakespeare's *Richard II* 4.1.163–64 (Richard scolding the rebel nobility): "God save the King! Will no man say 'Amen'? / Am I both priest and clerk? Well then, Amen."
1. Allusion to the three-decker pulpit, a fixture of the post-Reformation church, which incorporated the reading pew. As clerk, Wopsle occupies the lowest stall; "our friend overhead," the parson, reads the prayers and litany from the box above his and climbs to the top deck to deliver the sermon. Standing at the east end of the nave the pulpit blocked the view of the altar and invited somnolence among clergy and congregation alike. In William Cowper's *The Task* (1785), book 1, lines 94–96, "Sweet sleep enjoys the curate in his desk / The tedious rector drawling o'er his head / And sweet the clerk below."
2. *Nota bene*: Latin for "mark well."
3. A lot of small change, hence a little squirt. "Bobbish": in high spirits [*OED*].

want to speak), nor because I was regaled with the scaly tips of the drumsticks of the fowls, and with those obscure corners of pork of which the pig, when living, had had the least reason to be vain. No; I should not have minded that, if they would only have left me alone. But they wouldn't leave me alone. They seemed to think the opportunity lost, if they failed to point the conversation at me, every now and then, and stick the point into me. I might have been an unfortunate little bull in a Spanish arena, I got so smartingly touched up by these moral goads.

It began the moment we sat down to dinner. Mr. Wopsle said grace with theatrical declamation—as it now appears to me, something like a religious cross of the Ghost in Hamlet with Richard the Third—and ended with the very proper aspiration that we might be truly grateful. Upon which my sister fixed me with her eye, and said, in a low reproachful voice, "Do you hear that? Be grateful."

"Especially," said Mr. Pumblechook, "be grateful, boy, to them which brought you up by hand."

Mrs. Hubble shook her head, and contemplating me with a mournful presentiment that I should come to no good, asked, "Why is it that the young are never grateful?" This moral mystery seemed too much for the company until Mr. Hubble tersely solved it by saying, "Naterally wicious." Everybody then murmured "True!" and looked at me in a particularly unpleasant and personal manner.

Joe's station and influence were something feebler (if possible) when there was company, than when there was none. But he always aided and comforted me when he could, in some way of his own, and he always did so at dinnertime by giving me gravy, if there were any. There being plenty of gravy today, Joe spooned into my plate, at this point, about half a pint.

A little later on in the dinner, Mr. Wopsle reviewed the sermon with some severity, and intimated—in the usual hypothetical case of the Church being "thrown open"—what kind of sermon *he* would have given them. After favouring them with some heads of that discourse, he remarked that he considered the subject of the day's homily, ill chosen; which was the less excusable, he added, when there were so many subjects "going about."

"True again," said Uncle Pumblechook. "You've hit it, sir! Plenty of subjects going about, for them that know how to put salt upon their tails. That's what's wanted. A man needn't go far to find a subject, if he's ready with his salt-box. Why," added Mr. Pumblechook, after a short interval of reflection, "Look at Pork alone. There's a subject! If you want a subject, look at Pork!"

"True, sir. Many a moral for the young," returned Mr. Wopsle; and I knew he was going to lug me in, before he said it; "might be deduced from that text."

("You listen to this," said my sister to me, in a severe parenthesis.)

Joe gave me some more gravy.

"Swine," pursued Mr. Wopsle, in his deepest voice, and pointing his fork at my blushes, as if he were mentioning my christian name; "Swine were the companions of the prodigal.[4] The gluttony of Swine is put before us, as an example to the young." (I thought this pretty well in him who had been

---

4. Luke 15.15: "And he went and joined himself to a citizen of that country and he sent him into the fields to feed the swine." The story of the prodigal son is given in verses 11–32.

praising up the pork for being so plump and juicy.) "What is detestable in a pig, is more detestable in a boy."

"Or girl," suggested Mr. Hubble.

"Of course, or girl, Mr. Hubble," assented Mr. Wopsle, rather irritably, "but there is no girl present."

"Besides," said Mr. Pumblechook, turning sharp on me, "think what you've got to be grateful for. If you'd been born a Squeaker——"[5]

"He *was*, if ever a child was," said my sister, most emphatically. Joe gave me some more gravy.

"Well, but I mean a four-footed Squeaker," said Mr. Pumblechook. "If you had been born such, would you have been here now? Not you——"

"Unless in that form," said Mr. Wopsle, nodding towards the dish.

"But I don't mean in that form, sir," returned Mr. Pumblechook, who had an objection to being interrupted; "I mean, enjoying himself with his elders and betters, and improving himself with their conversation, and rolling in the lap of luxury. Would he have been doing that? No, he wouldn't. And what would have been your destination?" turning on me again. "You would have been disposed of for so many shillings according to the market price of the article, and Dunstable the butcher would have come up to you as you lay in your straw, and he would have whipped you under his left arm, and with his right he would have tucked up his frock to get a penknife from out of his waistcoat-pocket, and he would have shed your blood and had your life. No bringing up by hand then. Not a bit of it!"

Joe offered me more gravy, which I was afraid to take.

"He was a world of trouble to you, ma'am," said Mrs. Hubble, commiserating my sister.

"Trouble?" echoed my sister; "trouble?" And then entered on a fearful catalogue of all the illnesses I had been guilty of, and all the acts of sleeplessness I had committed, and all the high places I had tumbled from, and all the low places I had tumbled into, and all the injuries I had done myself, and all the times she had wished me in my grave and I had contumaciously refused to go there.

I think the Romans must have aggravated one another very much, with their noses. Perhaps, they became the restless people they were, in consequence.[6] Anyhow, Mr. Wopsle's Roman nose so aggravated me, during the recital of my misdemeanours, that I should have liked to pull it until he howled. But, all I had endured up to this time, was nothing in comparison with the awful feelings that took possession of me when the pause was broken which ensued upon my sister's recital, and in which pause everybody had looked at me (as I felt painfully conscious) with indignation and abhorrence.

"Yet," said Mr. Pumblechook, leading the company gently back to the theme from which they had strayed, "Pork—regarded as biled—is rich, too; ain't it?"

"Have a little brandy, uncle," said my sister.

---

5. In one of its meanings, slang for bastard. "To stifle the squeaker: to murder a bastard" (Grose).
6. Pip refers to the awesome Roman conquests: over the course of more than six hundred years, from the fourth century B.C. to the third century A.D., the Romans invaded territories as far-flung as present-day Turkey, Libya, Germany, France, the Crimea, Egypt, Mauritania, and, of course, Britain. Dickens apparently liked this conceit: in *Hard Times*, Mrs. Sparsit, a genteelly impoverished widow, is afflicted with a "Coriolanian nose."

O Heavens, it had come at last! He would find it was weak, he would say it was weak, and I was lost! I held tight to the leg of the table under the cloth, with both hands, and awaited my fate.

My sister went for the stone bottle, came back with the stone bottle, and poured his brandy out: no one else taking any. The wretched man trifled with his glass—took it up, looked at it through the light, put it down—prolonged my misery. All this time, Mrs. Joe and Joe were briskly clearing the table for the pie and pudding.

I couldn't keep my eyes off him. Always holding tight by the leg of the table with my hands and feet, I saw the miserable creature finger his glass 10 playfully, take it up, smile, throw his head back, and drink the brandy off. Instantly afterwards, the company were seized with unspeakable consternation, owing to his springing to his feet, turning round several times in an appalling spasmodic whooping-cough dance, and rushing out at the door; he then became visible through the window, violently plunging and expectorating, making the most hideous faces, and apparently out of his mind.

I held on tight, while Mrs. Joe and Joe ran to him. I didn't know how I had done it, but I had no doubt I had murdered him somehow. In my dreadful situation, it was a relief when he was brought back, and, surveying the company all round as if *they* had disagreed with him, sank down into his 20 chair with the one significant gasp, "Tar!"

I had filled up the bottle from the tar-water jug. I knew he would be worse by-and-by. I moved the table, like a Medium of the present day, by the vigour of my unseen hold upon it.[7]

"Tar!" cried my sister, in amazement. "Why, how ever could Tar come there?"

But, Uncle Pumblechook, who was omnipotent in that kitchen, wouldn't hear the word, wouldn't hear of the subject, imperiously waved it all away with his hand, and asked for hot gin-and-water. My sister, who had begun to be alarmingly meditative, had to employ herself actively in getting the gin, 30 the hot water, the sugar, and the lemon-peel, and mixing them. For the time at least, I was saved. I still held on to the leg of the table, but clutched it now with the fervour of gratitude.

By degrees, I became calm enough to release my grasp and partake of pudding. Mr. Pumblechook partook of pudding. All partook of pudding. The course terminated, and Mr. Pumblechook had begun to beam under the genial influence of gin-and-water. I began to think I should get over the day, when my sister said to Joe, "Clean plates—cold."

I clutched the leg of the table again immediately, and pressed it to my bosom as if it had been the companion of my youth and friend of my soul. 40 I foresaw what was coming, and I felt that this time I really was gone.

"You must taste," said my sister, addressing the guests with her best grace,

---

7. A topical gibe (rare in *Great Expectations*) at the spiritualists, who created a stir in the 1850s and '60s. Dickens's distaste for clairvoyants and table-rappers is reflected in a dozen pieces he contributed to or accepted for *Household Words* and *All the Year Round*: see his "Stores for the First of April," "Well-Authenticated Rappings," "Rather a Strong Dose," and "The Martyr Medium" (*HW*, March 7, 1857, and February 20, 1858; *AYR*, March 21 and April 4, 1863). An unconscious party to the vice he condemned, Dickens appeared as a figure from the spirit world to one of the century's foremost mediumists, Arthur Conan Doyle, expressly to clear up the mystery of *Edwin Drood* for him; or so Doyle claimed.

"you must taste, to finish with, such a delightful and delicious present of Uncle Pumblechook's!"

Must they! Let them not hope to taste it!

"You must know," said my sister, rising, "it's a pie; a savoury pork pie."

The company murmured their compliments. Uncle Pumblechook, sensible of having deserved well of his fellow-creatures, said—quite vivaciously, all things considered—"Well, Mrs. Joe, we'll do our best endeavours; let us have a cut at this same pie."

My sister went out to get it. I heard her steps proceed to the pantry. I saw Mr. Pumblechook balance his knife. I saw reawakening appetite in the Roman nostrils of Mr. Wopsle. I heard Mr. Hubble remark that "a bit of savoury pork pie would lay atop of anything you could mention, and do no harm," and I heard Joe say, "You shall have some, Pip." I have never been absolutely certain whether I uttered a shrill yell of terror, merely in spirit, or in the bodily hearing of the company. I felt that I could bear no more, and that I must run away. I released the leg of the table, and ran for my life.

But, I ran no further than the house door, for there I ran head foremost into a party of soldiers with their muskets: one of whom held out a pair of handcuffs to me, saying, "Here you are, look sharp, come on!"

Chapter V.

THE apparition of a file of soldiers ringing down the butt-ends of their loaded muskets on our door-step, caused the dinner-party to rise from table[1] in confusion, and caused Mrs. Joe, re-entering the kitchen empty-handed, to stop short and stare, in her wondering lament of "Gracious goodness gracious me, what's gone—with the—pie!"

The sergeant and I were in the kitchen when Mrs. Joe stood staring; at which crisis I partially recovered the use of my senses. It was the sergeant who had spoken to me, and he was now looking round at the company, with his handcuffs invitingly extended towards them in his right hand, and his left on my shoulder.

"Excuse me, ladies and gentlemen," said the sergeant, "but as I have mentioned at the door to this smart young shaver"[2] (which he hadn't), "I am on a chase in the name of the King,[3] and I want the blacksmith."

"And pray what might you want with *him?*" retorted my sister, quick to resent his being wanted at all.

"Missis," returned the gallant sergeant, "speaking for myself, I should reply, the honour and pleasure of his fine wife's acquaintance; speaking for the King, I answer, a little job done."

1. Victorian usage. Similarly, below, "out of window," "put on table," "anything on table," etc.
2. "A subtle fellow, one who trims close" (Grose). By Dickens's time, the term could be used to describe any precocious youngster.
3. George III (1738–1820), crowned 1760. The "old, mad, blind, despised, and dying king" of Shelley's sonnet. The sergeant's toast notwithstanding, the King, intermittently insane since 1788, when "the flying gout flew from his legs to his head and stayed there," broke down completely in 1811.

This was received as rather neat in the sergeant; insomuch that Mr. Pumblechook cried audibly, "Good again!"

"You see, blacksmith," said the sergeant, who had by this time picked out Joe with his eye, "we have had an accident with these, and I find the lock of one of 'em goes wrong, and the coupling don't act pretty. As they are wanted for immediate service, will you throw your eye over them?"

Joe threw his eye over them, and pronounced that the job would necessitate the lighting of his forge fire, and would take nearer two hours than one. "Will it? Then will you set about it at once, blacksmith," said the off-hand sergeant, "as it's on His Majesty's service. And if my men can bear a hand anywhere,   10 they'll make themselves useful." With that, he called to his men, who came trooping into the kitchen one after another, and piled their arms in a corner. And then they stood about, as soldiers do; now, with their hands loosely clasped before them; now, resting a knee or a shoulder; now, easing a belt or a pouch; now, opening the door to spit stiffly over their high stocks,[4] out into the yard.

All these things I saw without then knowing that I saw them, for I was in an agony of apprehension. But, beginning to perceive that the handcuffs were not for me, and that the military had so far got the better of the pie as to put it in the background, I collected a little more of my scattered wits.   20

"Would you give me the Time?" said the sergeant, addressing himself to Mr. Pumblechook, as to a man whose appreciative powers justified the inference that he was equal to the time.

"It's just gone half-past two."

"That's not so bad," said the sergeant, reflecting; "even if I was forced to halt here nigh two hours, that'll do. How far might you call yourselves from the marshes, hereabouts? Not above a mile, I reckon?"

"Just a mile," said Mrs. Joe.

"That'll do. We begin to close in upon 'em about dusk. A little before dusk, my orders are. That'll do."   30

"Convicts, sergeant?" asked Mr. Wopsle, in a matter-of-course way.

"Ay!" returned the sergeant, "two. They're pretty well known to be out on the marshes still, and they won't try to get clear of 'em before dusk. Anybody here seen anything of any such game?"

Everybody, myself excepted, said no, with confidence. Nobody thought of me.

"Well!" said the sergeant, "they'll find themselves trapped in a circle, I expect, sooner than they count on. Now, blacksmith! If you're ready, His Majesty the King is."

Joe had got his coat and waistcoat and cravat off, and his leather apron on,   40 and passed into the forge. One of the soldiers opened its wooden windows, another lighted the fire, another turned to at the bellows, the rest stood round the blaze, which was soon roaring. Then Joe began to hammer and clink, hammer and clink, and we all looked on.

The interest of the impending pursuit not only absorbed the general attention, but even made my sister liberal. She drew a pitcher of beer from the cask, for the soldiers, and invited the sergeant to take a glass of brandy.[5] But

---

4. Stiff collars worn by the military.
5. Mrs. Joe dispenses the drinks according to rank, reserving the most expensive—the brandy—for the suave sergeant (Guiliano/Collins).

Mr. Pumblechook said, sharply, "Give him wine, Mum. I'll engage there's no Tar in that:" so, the sergeant thanked him and said that as he preferred his drink without tar, he would take wine, if it was equally convenient. When it was given him, he drank His Majesty's health and Compliments of the Season, and took it all at a mouthful and smacked his lips.

"Good stuff, eh, sergeant?" said Mr. Pumblechook.

"I'll tell you something," returned the sergeant; "I suspect that stuff's of *your* providing."

Mr. Pumblechook, with a fat sort of laugh, said, "Ay, ay? Why?"

"Because," returned the sergeant, clapping him on the shoulder, "you're a 10 man that knows what's what."

"D'ye think so?" said Mr. Pumblechook, with his former laugh. "Have another glass."

"With you. Hob and nob,"[6] returned the sergeant. "The top of mine to the foot of yours—the foot of yours to the top of mine—Ring once, ring twice— the best tune on the Musical Glasses! Your health. May you live a thousand years, and never be a worse judge of the right sort than you are at the present moment of your life!"

The sergeant tossed off his glass again and seemed quite ready for another glass. I noticed that Mr. Pumblechook in his hospitality appeared to forget 20 that he had made a present of the wine, but took the bottle from Mrs. Joe and had all the credit of handing it about in a gush of joviality. Even I got some. And he was so very free of the wine that he even called for the other bottle and handed that about with the same liberality, when the first was gone.

As I watched them while they all stood clustered about the forge enjoying themselves so much, I thought what terrible good sauce for a dinner my fugitive friend on the marshes was. They had not enjoyed themselves a quarter so much, before the entertainment was brightened with the excitement he furnished. And, now, when they were all in lively anticipation of "the two 30 villains" being taken, and when the bellows seemed to roar for the fugitives, the fire to flare for them, the smoke to hurry away in pursuit of them, Joe to hammer and clink for them, and all the murky shadows on the wall to shake at them in menace as the blaze rose and sank and the red-hot sparks dropped and died, the pale afternoon outside, almost seemed in my pitying young fancy to have turned pale on their account, poor wretches.

At last, Joe's job was done, and the ringing and roaring stopped. As Joe got on his coat, he mustered courage to propose that some of us should go down with the soldiers and see what came of the hunt. Mr. Pumblechook and Mr. Hubble declined, on the plea of a pipe and ladies' society; but Mr. Wopsle 40 said he would go, if Joe would. Joe said he was agreeable, and he would take me, if Mrs. Joe approved. We never should have got leave to go, I am sure, but for Mrs. Joe's curiosity to know all about it and how it ended. As it was, she merely stipulated, "If you bring the boy back with his head blown to bits by a musket, don't look to me to put it together again."

The sergeant took a polite leave of the ladies, and parted from Mr. Pumblechook as from a comrade; though I doubt if he were quite as fully sensible

6. "Give and take"; literally, "have and have not." Toast or invitation to drink. In the ritual that follows, the sergeant suits the action to the words: the phrase "Ring once, ring twice" is attended by the touching of glasses; hence the reference to "Musical Glasses" [OED].

of that gentleman's merits under arid conditions, as when something moist
was going. His men resumed their muskets and fell in. Mr. Wopsle, Joe, and
I, received strict charge to keep in the rear, and to speak no word after we
reached the marshes. When we were all out in the raw air and were steadily
moving towards our business, I treasonably whispered to Joe, "I hope, Joe,
we shan't find them." And Joe whispered to me, "I'd give a shilling if they
had cut and run, Pip."

We were joined by no stragglers from the village, for the weather was cold
and threatening, the way dreary, the footing bad, darkness coming on, and
the people had good fires in-doors and were keeping the day. A few faces   10
hurried to glowing windows and looked after us, but none came out. We
passed the finger-post,[7] and held straight on to the churchyard. There, we
were stopped a few minutes by a signal from the sergeant's hand, while two
or three of his men dispersed themselves among the graves, and also examined
the porch. They came in again without finding anything, and then we struck
out on the open marshes, through the gate at the side of the churchyard. A
bitter sleet came rattling against us here on the east wind, and Joe took me
on his back.

Now that we were out upon the dismal wilderness where they little thought
I had been within eight or nine hours and had seen both men hiding, I   20
considered for the first time, with great dread, if we should come upon them,
would my particular convict suppose that it was I who had brought the soldiers
there? He had asked me if I was a deceiving imp, and he had said I should
be a fierce young hound if I joined the hunt against him. Would he believe
that I was both imp and hound in treacherous earnest, and had betrayed him?

It was of no use asking myself this question now. There I was, on Joe's
back, and there was Joe beneath me, charging at the ditches like a hunter,
and stimulating Mr. Wopsle not to tumble on his Roman nose, and to keep
up with us. The soldiers were in front of us, extended into a pretty wide line
with an interval between man and man. We were taking the course I had   30
begun with, and from which I had diverged in the mist. Either the mist was
not out again yet, or the wind had dispelled it. Under the low red glare of
sunset, the beacon, and the gibbet, and the mound of the Battery, and the
opposite shore of the river, were plain, though all of a watery lead colour.

With my heart thumping like a blacksmith at Joe's broad shoulder, I looked
all about for any sign of the convicts. I could see none, I could hear none.
Mr. Wopsle had greatly alarmed me more than once, by his blowing and
hard breathing; but I knew the sounds by this time, and could dissociate them
from the object of pursuit. I got a dreadful start, when I thought I heard the
file still going; but it was only a sheep bell. The sheep stopped in their eating   40
and looked timidly at us; and the cattle, their heads turned from the wind
and sleet, stared angrily as if they held us responsible for both annoyances;
but, except these things, and the shudder of the dying day in every blade of
grass, there was no break in the bleak stillness of the marshes.

The soldiers were moving on in the direction of the old Battery, and we
were moving on a little way behind them, when, all of a sudden, we all
stopped. For, there had reached us on the wings of the wind and rain, a long

---

7. Signpost, its crossbeams terminating in the shape of a finger; the "wooden finger . . . directing people
to our village" mentioned in chapter 3 and pictured in Pailthorpe's drawing reproduced on the cover
of this Norton Critical Edition.

shout. It was repeated. It was at a distance towards the east, but it was long and loud. Nay, there seemed to be two or more shouts raised together—if one might judge from a confusion in the sound.

To this effect the sergeant and the nearest men were speaking under their breath, when Joe and I came up. After another moment's listening, Joe (who was a good judge) agreed, and Mr. Wopsle (who was a bad judge) agreed. The sergeant, a decisive man, ordered that the sound should not be answered, but that the course should be changed, and that his men should make towards it "at the double." So we slanted to the right (where the East was), and Joe pounded away so wonderfully, that I had to hold on tight to keep my seat.   10

It was a run indeed now, and what Joe called, in the only two words he spoke all the time, "a Winder."[8] Down banks and up banks, and over gates, and splashing into dykes, and breaking among coarse rushes: no man cared where he went. As we came nearer to the shouting, it became more and more apparent that it was made by more than one voice. Sometimes, it seemed to stop altogether, and then the soldiers stopped. When it broke out again, the soldiers made for it at a greater rate than ever, and we after them. After a while, we had so run it down, that we could hear one voice calling "Murder!" and another voice, "Convicts! Runaways! Guard! This way for the runaway convicts!" Then both voices would seem to be stifled in a struggle, and then   20 would break out again. And when it had come to this, the soldiers ran like deer, and Joe too.

The sergeant ran in first, when we had run the noise quite down, and two of his men ran in close upon him. Their pieces were cocked and levelled when we all ran in.

"Here are both men!" panted the sergeant, struggling at the bottom of a ditch. "Surrender, you two! and confound you for two wild beasts! Come asunder!"

Water was splashing, and mud was flying, and oaths were being sworn, and blows were being struck, when half a dozen more men went down into the   30 ditch to help the sergeant, and dragged out, separately, my convict and the other one. Both were bleeding and panting and execrating and struggling; but of course I knew them both directly.

"Mind!" said my convict, wiping blood from his face with his ragged sleeves, and shaking torn hair from his fingers; "I took him! I give him up to you! Mind that!"

"It's not much to be particular about," said the sergeant; "it'll do you small good, my man, being in the same plight yourself. Handcuffs there!"

"I don't expect it to do me any good. I don't want it to do me more good than it does now," said my convict, with a greedy laugh. "I took him. He   40 knows it. That's enough for me."

The other convict was livid to look at, and, in addition to the old bruised left side of his face, seemed to be bruised and torn all over. He could not so much as get his breath to speak, until they were both separately handcuffed, but leaned upon a soldier to keep himself from falling.

"Take notice, guard—he tried to murder me," were his first words.

"Tried to murder him?" said my convict, disdainfully. "Try, and not do it? I took him, and giv' him up; that's what I done. I not only prevented him

8. That is, Joe's exertions take the wind out of him [OED].

getting off the marshes, but I dragged him here—dragged him this far on his way back. He's a gentleman, if you please, this villain. Now, the Hulks has got its gentleman again, through me. Murder him? Worth my while, too, to murder him, when I could do worse and drag him back!"

The other one still gasped, "He tried—he tried—to—murder me. Bear—bear witness."

"Lookee here!" said my convict to the sergeant. "Single-handed I got clear of the prison-ship; I made a dash and I done it. I could ha' got clear of these death-cold flats likewise—look at my leg: you won't find much iron on it—if I hadn't made discovery that *he* was here. Let *him* go free? Let *him* profit by the means as I found out? Let *him* make a tool of me afresh and again? Once more? No, no, no. If I had died at the bottom there;" and he made an emphatic swing at the ditch with his manacled hands; "I'd have held to him with that grip, that you should have been safe to find him in my hold."

The other fugitive, who was evidently in extreme horror of his companion, repeated, "He tried to murder me. I should have been a dead man if you had not come up."

"He lies!" said my convict, with fierce energy. "He's a liar born, and he'll die a liar. Look at his face; ain't it written there? Let him turn those eyes of his on me. I defy him to do it."

The other, with an effort at a scornful smile—which could not, however, collect the nervous working of his mouth into any set expression—looked at the soldiers, and looked about at the marshes and at the sky, but certainly did not look at the speaker.

"Do you see him?" pursued my convict. "Do you see what a villain he is? Do you see those grovelling and wandering eyes? That's how he looked when we were tried together. He never looked at me."

The other, always working and working his dry lips and turning his eyes restlessly about him far and near, did at last turn them for a moment on the speaker, with the words, "You are not much to look at," and with a half-taunting glance at the bound hands. At that point, my convict became so frantically exasperated, that he would have rushed upon him but for the interposition of the soldiers. "Didn't I tell you," said the other convict then, "that he would murder me, if he could?" And any one could see that he shook with fear, and that there broke out upon his lips, curious white flakes, like thin snow.

"Enough of this parley," said the sergeant. "Light those torches."

As one of the soldiers, who carried a basket in lieu of a gun, went down on his knee to open it, my convict looked round him for the first time, and saw me. I had alighted from Joe's back on the brink of the ditch when we came up, and had not moved since. I looked at him eagerly when he looked at me, and slightly moved my hands and shook my head. I had been waiting for him to see me, that I might try to assure him of my innocence. It was not at all expressed to me that he even comprehended my intention, for he gave me a look that I did not understand, and it all passed in a moment. But if he had looked at me for an hour or for a day, I could not have remembered his face ever afterwards, as having been more attentive.

The soldier with the basket soon got a light, and lighted three or four torches, and took one himself and distributed the others. It had been almost dark before, but now it seemed quite dark, and soon afterwards very dark.

Before we departed from that spot, four soldiers standing in a ring, fired twice into the air. Presently we saw other torches kindled at some distance behind us, and others on the marshes on the opposite bank of the river. "All right," said the sergeant. "March."

We had not gone far when three cannon were fired ahead of us with a sound that seemed to burst something inside my ear. "You are expected on board," said the sergeant to my convict; "they know you are coming. Don't straggle, my man. Close up here."

The two were kept apart, and each walked surrounded by a separate guard. I had hold of Joe's hand now, and Joe carried one of the torches. Mr. Wopsle 10 had been for going back, but Joe was resolved to see it out, so we went on with the party. There was a reasonably good path now, mostly on the edge of the river, with a divergence here and there where a dyke came, with a miniature windmill[9] on it and a muddy sluice-gate. When I looked round, I could see the other lights coming in after us. The torches we carried, dropped great blotches of fire upon the track, and I could see those, too, lying smoking and flaring. I could see nothing else but black darkness. Our lights warmed the air about us with their pitchy blaze, and the two prisoners seemed rather to like that, as they limped along in the midst of the muskets. We could not go fast, because of their lameness, and they were so spent, that two or three 20 times we had to halt while they rested.

After an hour or so of this travelling, we came to a rough wooden hut and a landing-place. There was a guard in the hut, and they challenged, and the sergeant answered. Then, we went into the hut where there was a smell of tobacco and whitewash, and a bright fire, and a lamp, and a stand of muskets, and a drum, and a low wooden bedstead, like an overgrown mangle[1] without the machinery, capable of holding about a dozen soldiers all at once. Three or four soldiers who lay upon it in their great-coats, were not much interested in us, but just lifted their heads and took a sleepy stare, and then lay down again. The sergeant made some kind of report, and some entry in a book, 30 and then the convict whom I call the other convict was drafted off with his guard, to go on board first.

My convict never looked at me, except that once. While we stood in the hut, he stood before the fire looking thoughtfully at it, or putting up his feet by turns upon the hob,[2] and looking thoughtfully at them as if he pitied them for their recent adventures. Suddenly, he turned to the sergeant, and remarked:

"I wish to say something respecting this escape. It may prevent some persons laying under suspicion alonger me."

"You can say what you like," returned the sergeant, standing coolly looking 40 at him with his arms folded, "but you have no call to say it here. You'll have opportunity enough to say about it, and hear about it, before it's done with, you know."

"I know, but this is another pint, a separate pint. A man can't starve; at least *I* can't. I took some wittles, up at the willage over yonder—where the church stands a'most out on the marshes."

9. Small mechanism equipped with blades, used to control the flow of tidal waters into the ditches and dykes that drain the marshes.
1. Household device that uses hand-cranked rollers to press laundry. A monstrous piece of machinery in Pip's day—some six feet long by three feet wide (Hill).
2. A projection or ledge built into a fireplace, where food can be kept warm.

"You mean stole," said the sergeant.

"And I'll tell you where from. From the blacksmith's."

"Halloa!" said the sergeant, staring at Joe.

"Halloa, Pip!" said Joe, staring at me.

"It was some broken wittles[3]—that's what it was—and a dram of liquor,[4] and a pie."

"Have you happened to miss such an article as a pie, blacksmith?" asked the sergeant, confidentially.

"My wife did, at the very moment when you came in. Don't you know, Pip?"   10

"So," said my convict, turning his eyes on Joe in a moody manner, and without the least glance at me; "so you're the blacksmith, are you? Then I'm sorry to say, I've eat your pie."

"God knows you're welcome to it—so far as it was ever mine," returned Joe, with a saving remembrance of Mrs. Joe. "We don't know what you have done, but we wouldn't have you starved to death for it, poor miserable fellow-creatur.—Would us, Pip?"

The something that I had noticed before, clicked in the man's throat again, and he turned his back. The boat had returned, and his guard were ready, so we followed him to the landing-place made of rough stakes and stones,   20 and saw him put into the boat, which was rowed by a crew of convicts like himself. No one seemed surprised to see him, or interested in seeing him, or glad to see him, or sorry to see him, or spoke a word, except that somebody in the boat growled as if to dogs, "Give way, you!" which was the signal for the dip of the oars. By the light of the torches, we saw the black Hulk lying out a little way from the mud of the shore, like a wicked Noah's ark.[5] Cribbed and barred and moored by massive rusty chains, the prison-ship seemed in my young eyes to be ironed like the prisoners. We saw the boat go alongside, and we saw him taken up the side and disappear. Then, the ends of the torches were flung hissing into the water, and went out, as if it were all over   30 with him.

★

Chapter VI.

MY state of mind regarding the pilfering from which I had been so unexpectedly exonerated, did not impel me to frank disclosure; but I hope it had some dregs of good at the bottom of it.

I do not recall that I felt any tenderness of conscience in reference to Mrs. Joe, when the fear of being found out was lifted off me. But I loved Joe—perhaps for no better reason in those early days than because the dear fellow let me love him—and, as to him, my inner self was not so easily composed. It was much upon my mind (particularly when I first saw him looking about

3. Here used to mean leftovers.
4. One-eighth of a fluid ounce. Here it refers to the amount of liquor Magwitch can down in one gulp.
5. Cf. David Copperfield's nocturnal impressions as he "toils into Chatham" on his flight to Dover in chapter 13: "A mere dream of chalk, and drawbridges, and mastless ships in a muddy river, roofed like Noah's arks."

for his file) that I ought to tell Joe the whole truth. Yet I did not, and for the reason that I mistrusted that if I did, he would think me worse than I was. The fear of losing Joe's confidence, and of thenceforth sitting in the chimney corner at night staring drearily at my for ever lost companion and friend, tied up my tongue. I morbidly represented to myself that if Joe knew it, I never afterwards could see him at the fireside feeling his fair whisker, without thinking that he was meditating on it. That, if Joe knew it, I never afterwards could see him glance, however casually, at yesterday's meat or pudding when it came on to-day's table, without thinking that he was debating whether I had been in the pantry. That, if Joe knew it, and at any subsequent period of our 10 joint domestic life remarked that his beer was flat or thick, the conviction that he suspected Tar in it, would bring a rush of blood to my face. In a word, I was too cowardly to do what I knew to be right, as I had been too cowardly to avoid doing what I knew to be wrong. I had had no intercourse with the world at that time, and I imitated none of its many inhabitants who act in this manner. Quite an untaught genius, I made the discovery of the line of action for myself.

As I was sleepy before we were far away from the prison-ship, Joe took me on his back again and carried me home. He must have had a tiresome journey of it, for Mr. Wopsle, being knocked up,[1] was in such a very bad temper that 20 if the Church had been thrown open, he would probably have excommunicated the whole expedition, beginning with Joe and myself. In his lay capacity, he persisted in sitting down in the damp to such an insane extent, that when his coat was taken off to be dried at the kitchen fire, the circumstantial evidence on his trousers would have hanged him if it had been a capital offence.

By that time, I was staggering on the kitchen floor like a little drunkard, through having been newly set upon my feet, and through having been fast asleep, and through waking in the heat and lights and noise of tongues. As I came to myself (with the aid of a heavy thump between the shoulders, and the restorative exclamation "Yah! Was there ever such a boy as this!" from 30 my sister) I found Joe telling them about the convict's confession, and all the visitors suggesting different ways by which he had got into the pantry. Mr. Pumblechook made out, after carefully surveying the premises, that he had first got upon the roof of the forge, and had then got upon the roof of the house, and had then let himself down the kitchen chimney by a rope made of his bedding cut into strips; and as Mr. Pumblechook was very positive and drove his own chaise-cart—over everybody—it was agreed that it must be so. Mr. Wopsle, indeed, wildly cried out "No!" with the feeble malice of a tired man; but, as he had no theory, and no coat on, he was unanimously set at naught—not to mention his smoking hard behind, as he stood with his back 40 to the kitchen fire to draw the damp out: which was not calculated to inspire confidence.

This was all I heard that night before my sister clutched me, as a slumberous offence to the company's eyesight, and assisted me up to bed with such a strong hand that I seemed to have fifty boots on, and to be dangling them all against the edges of the stairs. My state of mind, as I have described it, began before I was up in the morning, and lasted long after the subject

---

1. "Tired, jaded, used up, done for" (Hotten). In another sense "to put together," "to construct": thus the items Pip thinks of "knocking up" as gifts for Miss Havisham in chapter 15.

had died out, and had ceased to be mentioned saving on exceptional occasions.

Chapter VII.[1]

AT the time when I stood in the churchyard, reading the family tombstones, I had just enough learning to be able to spell them out. My construction even of their simple meaning was not very correct, for I read "wife of the Above" as a complimentary reference to my father's exaltation to a better world; and if any one of my deceased relations had been referred to as "Below," I have no doubt I should have formed the worst opinions of that member of the family. Neither, were my notions of the theological positions to which my Catechism bound me, at all accurate; for, I have a lively remembrance that I supposed my declaration that I was to "walk in the same all the days of my life," laid me under an obligation always to go through the village from our house in one particular direction, and never to vary it by turning down by the wheelwright's or up by the mill.[2]

When I was old enough, I was to be apprenticed to Joe,[3] and until I could assume that dignity I was not to be what Mrs. Joe called "Pompeyed," or (as I render it) pampered. Therefore, I was not only odd-boy about the forge, but if any neighbour happened to want an extra boy to frighten birds, or pick up stones, or do any such job, I was favoured with the employment. In order, however, that our superior position might not be compromised thereby, a money-box was kept on the kitchen mantel-shelf, into which it was publicly made known that all my earnings were dropped. I have an impression that they were to be contributed eventually towards the liquidation of the National Debt, but I know I had no hope of any personal participation in the treasure.[4]

Mr. Wopsle's great-aunt kept an evening school in the village; that is to say, she was a ridiculous old woman of limited means and unlimited infirmity, who used to go to sleep from six to seven every evening, in the society of youth who paid twopence per week each, for the improving opportunity of seeing her do it.. She rented a small cottage, and Mr. Wopsle had the room up-stairs, where we students used to overhear him reading aloud in a most dignified and terrific manner, and occasionally bumping on the ceiling. There was a fiction that Mr. Wopsle "examined" the scholars, once a quarter. What he did on those occasions, was to turn up his cuffs, stick up his hair, and give us Mark Antony's oration over the body of Cæsar. This was always followed by Collins's Ode on the Passions, wherein I particularly venerated

1. Chapters 6 and 7 are run as one chapter in manuscript.
2. Pip's gloss on the "Baptismal Service" in *The Book of Common Prayer*, at which his godparents promised that he would "renounce the devil and all his works," "believe all the articles of the Christian faith," "and thirdly, that [he] should keep God's holy will and commandments and walk in the same all the days of [his] life." Autobiographical touch: according to Mary Weller, the slavey from the Chatham Workhouse whom the Dickenses hired as servant, Dickens labored under the same delusion as Pip (Guiliano/Collins citing *Lippincott's Magazine* [June 1874]: 773).
3. For the regulations governing Pip's apprenticeship, see p. 79, n. 5.
4. The sharp rise of the national debt during and after the Napoleonic Wars between 1805 and 1815 had stirred up much public anxiety: Pip's fantasy may be rooted in the actualities of the day (Monod). Typically, the pennies in his money-box would be deposited in one of the savings banks established in the eighteenth century.

Mr. Wopsle as Revenge, throwing his blood-stain'd sword in thunder down, and taking the War denouncing trumpet with a withering look.[5] It was not with me then, as it was in later life: when I fell into the society of the Passions, and compared them with Collins and Wopsle, rather to the disadvantage of both gentlemen.

Mr. Wopsle's great-aunt, besides keeping this Educational Institution, kept—in the same room—a little general shop. She had no idea what stock she had, or what the price of anything in it was; but there was a little greasy memorandum-book kept in a drawer, which served as a Catalogue of Prices, and by this oracle, Biddy arranged all the shop transactions. Biddy was Mr. Wopsle's great-aunt's granddaughter; I confess myself quite unequal to the working-out of the problem, what relation she was to Mr. Wopsle. She was an orphan like myself; like me, too, had been brought up by hand. She was most noticeable, I thought, in respect of her extremities; for, her hair always wanted brushing, her hands always wanted washing, and her shoes always wanted mending and pulling up at heel. This description must be received, however, with a week-day limitation. On Sundays, she went to church elaborated.

Much of my unassisted self, and more by the help of Biddy than of Mr. Wopsle's great-aunt, I struggled through the alphabet as if it had been a bramble-bush; getting considerably worried and scratched by every letter. After that, I fell among those thieves,[6] the nine figures, who seemed every evening to do something new to disguise themselves and baffle recognition. But, at last I began, in a purblind[7] groping way, to read, write, and cipher, on the very smallest scale.

One night, I was sitting in the chimney corner with my slate, expending great efforts on the production of a letter to Joe. I think it must have been a full year after our hunt upon the marshes, for it was a long time after, and it was winter and a hard frost. With an alphabet on the hearth at my feet for reference, I contrived in an hour or two to print and smear this epistle:

"MI DEEr JO i OPE U R krWitE wEll i OPE i sHAl soN B HaBelL 4 2 teeDge U JO aN theN wE sHOrl B sO gLOdd aN wEn i M preNgtD 2 u JO woT larX aN bLEvE ME inF xn PiP."

There was no indispensable necessity for my communicating with Joe by letter, inasmuch as he sat beside me and we were alone. But, I delivered this written communication (slate and all) with my own hand, and Joe received it as a miracle of erudition.

"I say, Pip, old chap!" cried Joe, opening his blue eyes wide, "what a scholar you are! An't you?"

"I should like to be," said I, glancing at the slate as he held it: with a misgiving that the writing was rather hilly.

---

5. "The Passions: An Ode for Music" (1746), the last of the *Odes on Several Descriptive and Allegorical Subjects* by William Collins (1721–1759), a favorite among vocal exhibitionists. A dozen personified Passions—Fear, Hope, Joy, etc.—grouped around the figure of Music take turns at snatching her instruments from her: in stanza 6, "with a Frown, / Revenge impatient rose, / He threw his blood-stain'd Sword in Thunder down, / And with a with'ring Look, / the War-denouncing Trumpet took," etc. "Mark Antony's oration," of course, is the one he delivers in *Julius Caesar* 3.2.70 ff.
6. See the parable of the good Samaritan: "And Jesus answering said, 'A certain man went down from Jerusalem to Jericho and fell among thieves, which stripped him of his raiment, and wounded him, and departed, leaving him half dead'" (Luke 10.30).
7. Partly blind, dim-sighted, or slow to perceive. Originally, totally blind—"pure blind."

"Why, here's a J," said Joe, "and a O equal to anythink! Here's a J and a O, Pip, and a J-O, Joe."[8]

I had never heard Joe read aloud to any greater extent than this monosyllable, and I had observed at church last Sunday when I accidentally held our Prayer-Book upside down, that it seemed to suit his convenience quite as well as if it had been all right. Wishing to embrace the present occasion of finding out whether in teaching Joe I should have to begin quite at the beginning, I said, "Ah! But read the rest, Joe."

"The rest, eh, Pip?" said Joe, looking at it with a slowly searching eye, "One, two, three. Why, here's three Js, and three Os, and three J-O, Joes in 10 it, Pip!"

I leaned over Joe, and, with the aid of my forefinger, read him the whole letter.

"Astonishing!" said Joe, when I had finished. "You ARE a scholar."

"How do you spell Gargery, Joe?" I asked him, with a modest patronage.

"I don't spell it at all," said Joe.

"But supposing you did?"

"It *can't* be supposed," said Joe. "Tho' I'm oncommon fond of reading, too."

"Are you, Joe?"   20

"On-common. Give me," said Joe, "a good book, or a good newspaper, and sit me down afore a good fire, and I ask no better. Lord!" he continued, after rubbing his knees a little, "when you *do* come to a J and a O, and says you, 'Here, at last, is a J-O, Joe,' how interesting reading is!"

I derived from this, that Joe's education, like Steam, was yet in its infancy.[9] Pursuing the subject, I inquired:

"Didn't you ever go to school, Joe, when you were as little as me?"

"No, Pip."

"Why didn't you ever go to school, Joe, when you were as little as me?"

"Well, Pip," said Joe, taking up the poker and settling himself to his usual 30 occupation when he was thoughtful, of slowly raking the fire between the lower bars: "I'll tell you. My father, Pip, he were given to drink, and when he were overtook with drink, he hammered away at my mother, most onmerciful. It were a'most the only hammering he did, indeed, 'xcepting at myself. And he hammered at me with a wigour only to be equalled by the wigour with which he didn't hammer at his anvil.—You're a listening and understanding, Pip?"

"Yes, Joe."

" 'Consequence, my mother and me we ran away from my father, several times; and then my mother she'd go out to work, and she'd say, 'Joe,' she'd 40

---

8. In Joe's analphabetic orgy Dickens retrieves some of his own impressions in learning his letters: "the jolly letter O, the crooked S, with its full benevolent turns, the curious G, and the Q, with its comical tail that first awoke in me a sense of the humorous" (To the Printers' Pension Society, April 6, 1864; *Speeches*, p. 364).
9. "Steam . . . in its infancy" was one of the clichés of the day. Though James Watt (1736–1819) patented his engine as early as 1769, to all intents the infancy of steam coincided with Pip's. The first steamboat was launched in 1801; Robert Fulton ran his steamer up the Hudson five years later, opening up steam navigation commercially; and the use of steam pumps in collieries followed in 1814. Steam had been the in topic for decades, conversationally and in poetry; thus Erasmus Darwin in his *Botanic Gardens* (1791), canto 16: "The Giant-Power from earth's remotest caves / Lifts with strong arm her dark reluctant waves * * * / Soon shall thy arm, UNCONQUERED STEAM! afar / Drag the slow barge, or drive the rapid car; / Or on wide-waving winds expanded bear / The flying chariot through the fields of air."

say, 'now, please God, you shall have some schooling, child,' and she'd put me to school. But my father were that good in his hart that he couldn't abear to be without us. So, he'd come with a most tremenjous crowd and make such a row at the doors of the houses where we was, that they used to be obleeged to have no more to do with us and to give us up to him. And then he took us home and hammered us. Which, you see, Pip," said Joe, pausing in his meditative raking of the fire, and looking at me, "were a drawback on my learning."

"Certainly, poor Joe!"

"Though mind you, Pip," said Joe, with a judicial touch or two of the 10 poker on the top bar, "rendering unto all their doo, and maintaining equal justice betwixt man and man,[1] my father were that good in his hart, don't you see?"

I didn't see; but I didn't say so.

"Well!" Joe pursued, "somebody must keep the pot a biling, Pip, or the pot won't bile, don't you know?"

I saw that, and said so.

" 'Consequence, my father didn't make objections to my going to work; so I went to work at my present calling, which were his too, if he would have followed it, and I worked tolerable hard, I assure *you*, Pip. In time I were 20 able to keep him, and I kep him till he went off in a purple leptic fit.[2] And it were my intentions to have had put upon his tombstone that Whatsume'er the failings on his part, Remember reader he were that good in his hart."

Joe recited this couplet with such manifest pride and careful perspicuity, that I asked him if he had made it himself?

"I made it," said Joe, "my own self. I made it in a moment. It was like striking out a horseshoe complete, in a single blow. I never was so much surprised in all my life—couldn't credit my own ed—to tell you the truth, hardly believed it *were* my own ed. As I was saying, Pip, it were my intentions to have had it cut over him; but poetry costs money, cut it how you will, 30 small or large, and it were not done. Not to mention bearers,[3] all the money that could be spared were wanted for my mother. She were in poor elth, and quite broke. She weren't long of following, poor soul, and her share of peace come round at last."

Joe's blue eyes turned a little watery; he rubbed, first one of them, and then the other, in a most uncongenial and uncomfortable manner, with the round knob on the top of the poker.

"It were but lonesome then," said Joe, "living here alone, and I got acquainted with your sister. Now, Pip;" Joe looked firmly at me, as if he knew I was not going to agree with him; "your sister is a fine figure of a woman." 40

I could not help looking at the fire, in an obvious state of doubt.

"Whatever family opinions, or whatever the world's opinions, on that subject may be, Pip, your sister is," Joe tapped the top bar with the poker after every word following, "a—fine—figure—of—a—woman!"

I could think of nothing better to say than "I am glad you think so, Joe."

"So am I," returned Joe, catching me up. "*I* am glad I think so, Pip. A

---

1. Garbled version of Romans 13.7: "Render therefore all their dues: tribute to whom tribute is due; custom to whom custom," etc.
2. Gargerism for apoplectic fit.
3. Pallbearers.

little redness, or a little matter of Bone, here or there, what does it signify to Me?"

I sagaciously observed, if it didn't signify to him, to whom did it signify? "Certainly!" assented Joe. "That's it. You're right, old chap! When I got acquainted with your sister, it were the talk how she was bringing you up by hand. Very kind of her too, all the folks said, and I said, along with all the folks. As to you," Joe pursued, with a countenance expressive of seeing something very nasty indeed: "if you could have been aware how small and flabby and mean you was, dear me, you'd have formed the most contemptible opinions of yourself!"   10

Not exactly relishing this, I said, "Never mind me, Joe."

"But I did mind you, Pip," he returned, with tender simplicity. "When I offered to your sister to keep company, and to be asked in church at such times as she was willing and ready to come to the forge, I said to her, 'And bring the poor little child. God bless the poor little child,' I said to your sister, 'there's room for *him* at the forge!' "

I broke out crying and begging pardon, and hugged Joe round the neck: who dropped the poker to hug me, and to say, "Ever the best of friends; an't us, Pip? Don't cry, old chap!"

When this little interruption was over, Joe resumed: 20

"Well, you see, Pip, and here we are! That's about where it lights; here we are! Now, when you take me in hand in my learning, Pip (and I tell you beforehand I am awful dull, most awful dull), Mrs. Joe mustn't see too much of what we're up to. It must be done, as I may say, on the sly. And why on the sly? I'll tell you why, Pip."

He had taken up the poker again; without which, I doubt if he could have proceeded in his demonstration.

"Your sister is given to government."

"Given to government, Joe?" I was startled, for I had some shadowy idea (and I am afraid I must add, hope) that Joe had divorced her in favour of the   30 Lords of the Admiralty, or Treasury.[4]

"Given to government," said Joe. "Which I meantersay the government of you and myself."

"Oh!"

"And she an't over partial to having scholars on the premises," Joe continued, "and in partikler would not be over partial to my being a scholar, for fear as I might rise. Like a sort of rebel, don't you see?"

I was going to retort with an inquiry, and had got as far as "Why——" when Joe stopped me.

"Stay a bit. I know what you're a going to say, Pip; stay a bit! I don't deny   40 that your sister comes the Mo-gul over us, now and again.[5] I don't deny that

---

4. Until the passage of the Matrimonial Causes Act in 1857, divorce could be granted only by parliamentary dispensation, a privilege beyond the reach of the poor. Pip's shadowy idea of divorce as an everyday occurrence really suggests a response more appropriate to 1860 than 1813 (Monod). The MS wording slightly palliates this anachronism: the sentence "I had some idea . . . that Joe had obtained a divorce and settled [his wife] on the Lords of the Admiralty" begins to suggest the effort and maneuvering involved in divorce proceedings that the printed text ignores.

5. The Moguls became a byword for despotism in two centuries of political rule. The last Mogul emperor, Bahadur Shah II, was overthrown by the British in 1857 for his passive complicity in the Indian Mutiny, an event within very recent memory that played into Dickens's Christmas story for 1857, *The Perils of Certain English Prisoners*. In nicknaming his friend John Forster "the Mogul," Dickens kids Forster's self-importance and often compulsive rudeness.

she do throw us back-falls,[6] and that she do drop down upon us heavy. At such times as when your sister is on the Ram-page, Pip," Joe sank his voice to a whisper and glanced at the door, "candour compels fur to admit that she is a Buster."[7]

Joe pronounced this word, as if it began with at least twelve capital Bs.

"Why don't I rise? That were your observation when I broke it off, Pip?"

"Yes, Joe."

"Well," said Joe, passing the poker into his left hand, that he might feel his whisker; and I had no hope of him whenever he took to that placid occupation; "your sister's a master-mind. A master-mind."   10

"What's that?" I asked, in some hope of bringing him to a stand. But, Joe was readier with his definition than I had expected, and completely stopped me by arguing circularly, and answering with a fixed look, "Her."

"And I an't a master-mind," Joe resumed, when he had unfixed his look, and got back to his whisker. "And last of all, Pip—and this I want to say very serous to you, old chap—I see so much in my poor mother, of a woman drudging and slaving and breaking her honest hart and never getting no peace in her mortal days, that I'm dead afeerd of going wrong in the way of not doing what's right by a woman, and I'd fur rather of the two go wrong the t'other way, and be a little ill-conwenienced myself. I wish it was only me   20 that got put out, Pip; I wish there warn't no Tickler for you, old chap; I wish I could take it all on myself; but this is the up-and-down-and-straight on it, Pip, and I hope you'll overlook short-comings."

Young as I was, I believe that I dated a new admiration of Joe from that night. We were equals afterwards, as we had been before; but, afterwards at quiet times when I sat looking at Joe and thinking about him, I had a new sensation of feeling conscious that I was looking up to Joe in my heart.

"However," said Joe, rising to replenish the fire; "here's the Dutch-clock a working himself up to being equal to striking Eight of 'em, and she's not come home yet! I hope Uncle Pumblechook's mare mayn't have set a fore-   30 foot on a piece o' ice, and gone down."

Mrs. Joe made occasional trips with Uncle Pumblechook on market days, to assist him in buying such household stuffs and goods as required a woman's judgment; Uncle Pumblechook being a bachelor and reposing no confidences in his domestic servant. This was market day, and Mrs. Joe was out on one of these expeditions.

Joe made the fire and swept the hearth, and then we went to the door to listen for the chaise-cart. It was a dry cold night, and the wind blew keenly, and the frost was white and hard. A man would die to-night of lying out on the marshes, I thought. And then I looked at the stars, and considered how   40 awful it would be for a man to turn his face up to them as he froze to death, and see no help or pity in all the glittering multitude.

"Here comes the mare," said Joe, "ringing like a peal of bells!"

The sound of her iron shoes upon the hard road was quite musical, as she came along at a much brisker trot than usual. We got a chair out ready for Mrs. Joe's alighting, and stirred up the fire that they might see a bright window, and took a final survey of the kitchen that nothing might be out of its place. When we had completed these preparations, they drove up, wrapped

6. Wrestling jargon.
7. "[Lung]-buster": Her Ram-paging leaves Mrs. Joe gasping for air [OED].

to the eyes. Mrs. Joe was soon landed, and Uncle Pumblechook was soon
down too, covering the mare with a cloth, and we were soon all in the kitchen,
carrying so much cold air in with us that it seemed to drive all the heat out
of the fire.

"Now," said Mrs. Joe, unwrapping herself with haste and excitement, and
throwing her bonnet back on her shoulders where it hung by the strings: "if
this boy an't grateful this night, he never will be!"

I looked as grateful as any boy possibly could, who was wholly uninformed
why he ought to assume that expression.

"It's only to be hoped," said my sister, "that he won't be Pompeyed. But I　10
have my fears."

"She an't in that line, Mum," said Mr. Pumblechook. "She knows better."

She? I looked at Joe, making the motion with my lips and eyebrows, "She?"
Joe looked at me, making the motion with *his* lips and eyebrows, "She?" My
sister catching him in the act, he drew the back of his hand across his nose
with his usual conciliatory air on such occasions, and looked at her.

"Well?" said my sister, in her snappish way. "What are you staring at? Is
the house a-fire?"

—"Which some indiwidual," Joe politely hinted, "mentioned—she."

"And she is a she, I suppose?" said my sister. "Unless you call Miss Ha-　20
visham a he. And I doubt if even you'll go so far as that."

"Miss Havisham, up town?" said Joe.

"Is there any Miss Havisham down town?" returned my sister. "She wants
this boy to go and play there. And of course he's going. And he had better
play there," said my sister, shaking her head at me as an encouragement to
be extremely light and sportive, "or I'll work him."

I had heard of Miss Havisham up town—everybody for miles round, had
heard of Miss Havisham up town—as an immensely rich and grim lady who
lived in a large and dismal house barricaded against robbers, and who led a
life of seclusion.　30

"Well to be sure!" said Joe, astounded. "I wonder how she come to know
Pip!"

"Noodle!" cried my sister. "Who said she knew him?"

—"Which some indiwidual," Joe again politely hinted, "mentioned that
she wanted him to go and play there."

"And couldn't she ask Uncle Pumblechook if he knew of a boy to go and
play there? Isn't it just barely possible that Uncle Pumblechook may be a
tenant of hers, and that he may sometimes—we won't say quarterly or half
yearly, for that would be requiring too much of you—but sometimes—go there
to pay his rent? And couldn't she then ask Uncle Pumblechook if he knew　40
of a boy to go and play there? And couldn't Uncle Pumblechook, being always
considerate and thoughtful for us—though you may not think it, Joseph," in
a tone of the deepest reproach, as if he were the most callous of nephews,
"then mention this boy, standing Prancing here"—which I solemnly declare
I was not doing—"that I have for ever been a willing slave to?"

"Good again!" cried Uncle Pumblechook. "Well put! Prettily pointed!
Good indeed! Now Joseph, you know the case."

"No, Joseph," said my sister, still in a reproachful manner, while Joe apologetically drew the back of his hand across and across his nose, "you do not
yet—though you may not think it—know the case. You may consider that you　50

do, but you do *not*, Joseph. For you do not know that Uncle Pumblechook, being sensible that for anything we can tell, this boy's fortune may be made by his going to Miss Havisham's, has offered to take him into town to-night in his own chaise-cart, and to keep him to-night, and to take him with his own hands to Miss Havisham's to-morrow morning. And Lor-a-mussy me!"[8] cried my sister, casting off her bonnet in sudden desperation, "here I stand talking to mere Mooncalfs,[9] with Uncle Pumblechook waiting, and the mare catching cold at the door, and the boy grimed with crock[1] and dirt from the hair of his head to the sole of his foot!"

With that, she pounced upon me, like an eagle on a lamb, and my face 10 was squeezed into wooden bowls in sinks, and my head was put under taps of water-butts, and I was soaped, and kneaded, and towelled, and thumped, and harrowed, and rasped,[2] until I really was quite beside myself. (I may here remark that I suppose myself to be better acquainted than any living authority, with the ridgy effect of a wedding-ring, passing unsympathetically over the human countenance.)[3]

When my ablutions were completed, I was put into clean linen of the stiffest character, like a young penitent into sackcloth, and was trussed up in my tightest and fearfullest suit. I was then delivered over to Mr. Pumblechook, who formally received me as if he were the Sheriff, and who let off upon me 20 the speech that I knew he had been dying to make all along: "Boy, be for ever grateful to all friends, but especially unto them which brought you up by hand!"

"Good-bye, Joe!"

"God bless you, Pip, old chap!"

I had never parted from him before, and what with my feelings and what with soap-suds, I could at first see no stars from the chaise-cart. But they twinkled out one by one, without throwing any light on the questions why on earth I was going to play at Miss Havisham's, and what on earth I was expected to play at. 30

★

8. "Lord have mercy upon me!"
9. Congenital idiots. Behind the insult lies the ancient belief in the malign power of the moon to produce monstrous births. In Shakespeare's *Tempest* 2.2.128–31, the monster Caliban, "the man-i-the-moon that was," is saluted as "mooncalf" by his fellow triumvir Stephano.
1. Smut and soot, perhaps from contact with crockery [OED]. In this sense Dr. Johnson: "The black or soot of a pot or kettle."
2. Worked on with a coarse file.
3. The detail may be an unconscious borrowing. In *Mr. Gilfil's Love Story* (1858), in a scene dealing with the rearing of a waif, George Eliot remarks that "cleanliness is sometimes a painful good, as any one can vouch who has had his face washed the wrong way, by a pitiless hand with a gold ring on the third finger." In a letter to Eliot of January 18, 1858, Dickens singles out "the sad love story of Mr. Gilfil" for special praise (see *Dickensian* 20 [1924]: 98–99).

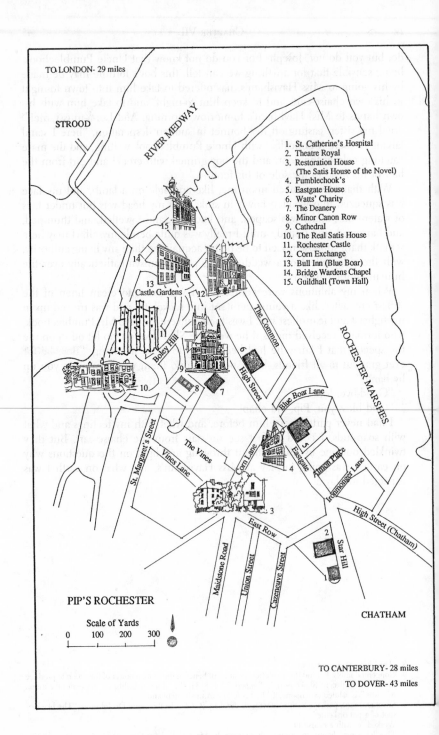

TO LONDON- 29 miles

STROOD

RIVER MEDWAY

1. St. Catherine's Hospital
2. Theatre Royal
3. Restoration House
   (The Satis House of the Novel)
4. Pumblechook's
5. Eastgate House
6. Watts' Charity
7. The Deanery
8. Minor Canon Row
9. Cathedral
10. The Real Satis House
11. Rochester Castle
12. Corn Exchange
13. Bull Inn (Blue Boar)
14. Bridge Wardens Chapel
15. Guildhall (Town Hall)

ROCHESTER MARSHES

Castle Gardens

Boley Hill

The Common

High Street

Blue Boar Lane

The Vines

Vines Lane

St. Margaret's Street

Corn Lane

Eastgate

Union Place

Ironmonger Lane

High Street (Chatham)

East Row

Maidstone Road

Union Street

Cazeneuve Street

Star Hill

CHATHAM

PIP'S ROCHESTER

Scale of Yards

0   100   200   300

TO CANTERBURY- 28 miles

TO DOVER- 43 miles

Chapter VIII.

MR. PUMBLECHOOK'S premises in the High-street[1] of the market town,[2] were of a peppercorny and farinaceous character, as the premises of a corn-chandler and seedsman should be. It appeared to me that he must be a very happy man indeed, to have so many little drawers in his shop; and I wondered when I peeped into one or two on the lower tiers, and saw the tied-up brown paper packets inside, whether the flower-seeds and bulbs ever wanted of a fine day to break out of those jails, and bloom.

It was in the early morning after my arrival that I entertained this specu-lation. On the previous night, I had been sent straight to bed in an attic with a sloping roof, which was so low in the corner where the bedstead was, that   10 I calculated the tiles as being within a foot of my eyebrows. In the same early morning, I discovered a singular affinity between seeds and corduroys. Mr. Pumblechook wore corduroys, and so did his shopman; and somehow, there was a general air and flavour about the corduroys, so much in the nature of seeds, and a general air and flavour about the seeds, so much in the nature of corduroys, that I hardly knew which was which. The same opportunity served me for noticing that Mr. Pumblechook appeared to conduct his busi-ness by looking across the street at the saddler, who appeared to transact *his* business by keeping his eye on the coachmaker, who appeared to get on in life by putting his hands in his pockets and contemplating the baker, who in   20 his turn folded his arms and stared at the grocer, who stood at his door and yawned at the chemist. The watchmaker, always poring over a little desk with a magnifying glass at his eye, and always inspected by a group in smock-frocks[3] poring over him through the glass of his shop-window, seemed to be about the only person in the High-street whose trade engaged his attention.

Mr. Pumblechook and I breakfasted at eight o'clock in the parlour behind the shop, while the shopman took his mug of tea and hunch of bread-and-butter on a sack of peas in the front premises. I considered Mr. Pumblechook wretched company. Besides being possessed by my sister's idea that a morti-fying and penitential character ought to be imparted to my diet—besides   30 giving me as much crumb as possible in combination with as little butter, and putting such a quantity of warm water into my milk that it would have been more candid to have left the milk out altogether—his conversation con-sisted of nothing but arithmetic. On my politely bidding him Good morning, he said, pompously, "Seven times nine, boy!" And how should *I* be able to answer, dodged in that way, in a strange place, on an empty stomach! I was

1. Main Street.
2. The market town, though never specifically named, is Rochester, Kent, some thirty miles east of London on the Dover Road, the locale associated with Dickens's childhood and his final years of prosperity at Gad's Hill Place. In Pip's day, Rochester numbered some sixty-five hundred souls; the much more commercialized Chatham next door, with its large naval yards—the town in which Dick-ens lived from age five to age ten—was twice as large. Now as then, Rochester's chief attractions include its Norman Cathedral and Castle, its Guildhall, and the buildings described below. Elsewhere in Dickens's work the town appears as Winglebury (*Sketches by Boz*); Mudfog (*The Mudfog Papers*); Dullborough (*The Uncommercial Traveller*); Cloisterham (*Edwin Drood*); and, as Rochester, in *Pick-wick Papers*, the Christmas story *The Seven Poor Travellers*, and a number of papers in *Household Words*.
3. Loose-fitting knee-length garments of coarse linen, usually worn by farm laborers over or instead of a coat; elsewhere the loose garment worn by artists over their clothes.

hungry, but before I had swallowed a morsel, he began a running sum that lasted all through the breakfast. "Seven?" "And four?" "And eight?" "And six?" "And two?" "And ten?" And so on.[4] And after each figure was disposed of, it was as much as I could do to get a bite or a sup, before the next came; while he sat at his ease guessing nothing, and eating bacon and hot roll, in (if I may be allowed the expression) a gorging and gormandising manner.

For such reasons, I was very glad when ten o'clock came and we started for Miss Havisham's; though I was not at all at my ease regarding the manner in which I should acquit myself under that lady's roof. Within a quarter of an hour we came to Miss Havisham's house, which was of old brick, and 10 dismal, and had a great many iron bars to it. Some of the windows had been walled up; of those that remained, all the lower were rustily barred. There was a court-yard in front, and that was barred; so, we had to wait, after ringing the bell, until some one should come to open it. While we waited at the gate, I peeped in (even then Mr. Pumblechook said, "And fourteen?" but I pretended not to hear him), and saw that at the side of the house there was a large brewery; no brewing was going on in it, however, and none seemed to have gone on for a long long time.

A window was raised, and a clear voice demanded, "What name?" To which my conductor replied, "Pumblechook." The voice returned, "Quite 20 right," and the window was shut again, and a young lady came across the court-yard, with keys in her hand.

"This," said Mr. Pumblechook, "is Pip."

"This is Pip, is it?" returned the young lady, who was very pretty and seemed very proud; "come in, Pip."

Mr. Pumblechook was coming in also, when she stopped him with the gate.

"Oh!" she said. "Did you wish to see Miss Havisham?"

"If Miss Havisham wished to see me," returned Mr. Pumblechook, discomfited. 30

"Ah!" said the girl; "but you see she don't."

She said it so finally, and in such an undiscussible way, that Mr. Pumblechook, though in a condition of ruffled dignity, could not protest. But he eyed me severely—as if I had done anything to him!—and departed with the words reproachfully delivered: "Boy! Let your behaviour here be a credit unto them which brought you up by hand!" I was not free from apprehension that he would come back to propound through the gate, "And sixteen?" But he didn't.

My young conductress locked the gate, and we went across the court-yard. It was paved and clean, but grass was growing in every crevice. The brewery 40 buildings had a little lane of communication with it, and the wooden gates of that lane stood open, and all the brewery beyond stood open, away to the high enclosing wall, and all was empty and disused. The cold wind seemed to blow colder there, than outside the gate; and it made a shrill noise in howling in and out at the open sides of the brewery, like the noise of wind in the rigging of a ship at sea.

She saw me looking at it, and she said, "You could drink without hurt all the strong beer that's brewed there now, boy."

4. Pumblechook's arithmetical torture is redolent of the punishment inflicted on David Copperfield by his stepfather in chapter 4.

"I should think I could, miss," said I, in a shy way.

"Better not try to brew beer there now, or it would turn out sour, boy; don't you think so?"

"It looks like it, miss."

"Not that anybody means to try," she added, "for that's all done with, and the place will stand as idle as it is, till it falls. As to strong beer, there's enough of that in the cellars already, to drown the Manor House."

"Is that the name of this house, miss?"

"One of its names, boy."

"It has more than one, then, miss?"

"One more. Its other name was Satis; which is Greek, or Latin, or Hebrew,[5] or all three—or all one to me—for enough."

"Enough House," said I; "that's a curious name, miss."

"Yes," she replied; "but it meant more than it said. It meant, when it was given, that whoever had this house, could want nothing else.[6] They must have been easily satisfied in those days, I should think. But don't loiter, boy."

Though she called me "boy" so often, and with a carelessness that was far from complimentary, she was of about my own age—or very little older. She seemed much older than I, of course, being a girl, and beautiful and self-possessed; and she was as scornful of me as if she had been one-and-twenty, and a queen.

We went into the house by a side door—the great front entrance had two chains across it outside—and the first thing I noticed was, that the passages were all dark, and that she had left a candle burning there. She took it up, and we went through more passages and up a staircase, and still it was all dark, and only the candle lighted us.

At last we came to the door of a room, and she said, "Go in."

I answered, more in shyness than politeness, "After you, miss."

To this, she returned: "Don't be ridiculous, boy; I am not going in." And scornfully walked away, and—what was worse—took the candle with her.

This was very uncomfortable, and I was half afraid. However, the only thing to be done being to knock at the door, I knocked, and was told from within to enter. I entered, therefore, and found myself in a pretty large room, well lighted with wax candles. No glimpse of daylight was to be seen in it. It was a dressing-room, as I supposed from the furniture, though much of it was of forms and uses then quite unknown to me. But prominent in it was a draped table with a gilded looking-glass, and that I made out at first sight to be a fine lady's dressing-table.

Whether I should have made out this object so soon, if there had been no fine lady sitting at it, I cannot say. In an arm-chair, with an elbow resting on the table and her head leaning on that hand, sat the strangest lady I have ever seen, or shall ever see.

She was dressed in rich materials—satins, and lace, and silks—all of white.

---

5. Latin.

6. Another instance of Dickens's composite art. In describing Havisham's residence Dickens grafted the name of one Rochester building onto the architectural details of another. According to local tradition, Satis House, a whitestone mansion in back of the Castle Gardens, owes its name to Elizabeth I, who, on a visit in 1573, after listening to her host's apologies for the modesty of the accommodations, assured him, "Satis"—"good enough." But the essential features of the fictional Satis House are borrowed not from the historical one but from a handsome redbrick late-Tudor mansion downtown, "Restoration House," named for another royal visitor, Charles II, who (almost certainly) overnighted there on the eve of his return to London in May 1660, before the throne was restored to him.

Her shoes were white. And she had a long white veil dependent from her hair, and she had bridal flowers in her hair, but her hair was white. Some bright jewels sparkled on her neck and on her hands, and some other jewels lay sparkling on the table. Dresses, less splendid than the dress she wore, and half-packed trunks, were scattered about. She had not quite finished dressing, for she had but one shoe on—the other was on the table near her hand—her veil was but half arranged, her watch and chain were not put on, and some lace for her bosom lay with those trinkets, and with her handkerchief, and gloves, and some flowers, and a prayer-book, all confusedly heaped about the looking-glass.

It was not in the first moments that I saw all these things, though I saw more of them in the first moments than might be supposed. But, I saw that everything within my view which ought to be white, had been white long ago, and had lost its lustre, and was faded and yellow. I saw that the bride within the bridal dress had withered like the dress, and like the flowers, and had no brightness left but the brightness of her sunken eyes. I saw that the dress had been put upon the rounded figure of a young woman, and that the figure upon which it now hung loose, had shrunk to skin and bone. Once, I had been taken to see some ghastly wax-work at the Fair, representing I know not what impossible personage lying in state. Once, I had been taken to one of our old marsh churches to see a skeleton in the ashes of a rich dress, that had been dug out of a vault under the church pavement. Now, wax-work and skeleton seemed to have dark eyes that moved and looked at me. I should have cried out, if I could.

"Who is it?" said the lady at the table.

"Pip, ma'am."

"Pip?"

"Mr. Pumblechook's boy, ma'am. Come—to play."

"Come nearer; let me look at you. Come close."

It was when I stood before her, avoiding her eyes, that I took note of the surrounding objects in detail, and saw that her watch had stopped at twenty minutes to nine, and that a clock in the room had stopped at twenty minutes to nine.

"Look at me," said Miss Havisham. "You are not afraid of a woman who has never seen the sun since you were born?"

I regret to state that I was not afraid of telling the enormous lie comprehended in the answer "No."

"Do you know what I touch here?" she said, laying her hands, one upon the other, on her left side.

"Yes, ma'am." (It made me think of the young man.)

"What do I touch?"

"Your heart."

"Broken!"

She uttered the word with an eager look, and with strong emphasis, and with a weird smile that had a kind of boast in it. Afterwards, she kept her hands there for a little while, and slowly took them away as if they were heavy.

"I am tired," said Miss Havisham. "I want diversion, and I have done with men and women. Play."

I think it will be conceded by my most disputatious reader, that she could hardly have directed an unfortunate boy to do anything in the wide world more difficult to be done under the circumstances.

"I sometimes have sick fancies," she went on, "and I have a sick fancy that I want to see some play. There, there!" with an impatient movement of the fingers of her right hand; "play, play, play!"

For a moment, with the fear of my sister's working me before my eyes, I had a desperate idea of starting round the room in the assumed character of Mr. Pumblechook's chaise-cart. But, I felt myself so unequal to the performance that I gave it up, and stood looking at Miss Havisham in what I suppose she took for a dogged manner, inasmuch as she said, when we had taken a 10 good look at each other:

"Are you sullen and obstinate?"

"No, ma'am, I am very sorry for you, and very sorry I can't play just now. If you complain of me I shall get into trouble with my sister, so I would do it if I could; but it's so new here, and so strange, and so fine—and melancholy——" I stopped, fearing I might say too much, or had already said it, and we took another look at each other.

Before she spoke again, she turned her eyes from me, and looked at the dress she wore, and at the dressing-table, and finally at herself in the looking-glass. 20

"So new to him," she muttered, "so old to me; so strange to him, so familiar to me; so melancholy to both of us! Call Estella."[7]

As she was still looking at the reflexion of herself, I thought she was still talking to herself, and kept quiet.

"Call Estella," she repeated, flashing a look at me. "You can do that. Call Estella. At the door."

To stand in the dark in a mysterious passage of an unknown house, bawling Estella to a scornful young lady neither visible nor responsive, and feeling it a dreadful liberty so to roar out her name, was almost as bad as playing to order. But, she answered at last, and her light came along the long dark 30 passage like a star.

Miss Havisham beckoned her to come close, and took up a jewel from the table, and tried its effect upon her fair young bosom and against her pretty brown hair. "Your own, one day, my dear, and you will use it well. Let me see you play cards with this boy."

"With this boy! Why, he is a common labouring-boy!"

I thought I overheard Miss Havisham answer—only it seemed so unlikely —"Well? You can break his heart."

"What do you play, boy?" asked Estella of myself, with the greatest disdain.

"Nothing but beggar my neighbour, miss." 40

"Beggar him," said Miss Havisham to Estella. So we sat down to cards.[8]

It was then I began to understand that everything in the room had stopped,

---

7. From Latin *stella*, "star." The name Estella was to all intents popularized by *Great Expectations*: in England the name hardly appears (if at all) before 1861.
8. Beggar My Neighbour, or Beat Your Neighbour Out of Doors, is a simple turn-up card game for two. Pip shuffles; Estella cuts. Pip and Estella each hold half the pack face down and take turns playing his or her top card face up. So long as each plays cards of ten or lower, the cards are placed on the common pile. By and by Pip plays an ace or face card and Estella has to pay a penalty: four cards if Pip plays an ace, three for a king, two for a queen, one for a jack (or knave). But if Estella's pay-off cards themselves contain an ace or face card, she turns the tables on Pip and adds the cards to her own. Excitement mounts as high card follows high card—till Estella wins all the cards with her last trump and thoroughly beggars Pip.

like the watch and the clock, a long time ago. I noticed that Miss Havisham put down the jewel exactly on the spot from which she had taken it up. As Estella dealt the cards, I glanced at the dressing-table again, and saw that the shoe upon it, once white, now yellow, had never been worn. I glanced down at the foot from which the shoe was absent, and saw that the silk stocking on it, once white, now yellow, had been trodden ragged. Without this arrest of everything, this standing still of all the pale decayed objects, not even the withered bridal dress on the collapsed form could have looked so like grave-clothes, or the long veil so like a shroud.

So she sat, corpse-like, as we played at cards; the frillings and trimmings   10
on her bridal dress looking like earthy paper. I knew nothing then, of the discoveries that are occasionally made of bodies buried in ancient times, which fall to powder in the moment of being distinctly seen; but, I have often thought since, that she must have looked as if the admission of the natural light of day would have struck her to dust.

"He calls the knaves, Jacks, this boy!" said Estella with disdain, before our first game was out.[9] "And what coarse hands he has. And what thick boots!"

I had never thought of being ashamed of my hands before; but I began to consider them a very indifferent pair. Her contempt for me was so strong, that it became infectious, and I caught it.   20

She won the game, and I dealt. I misdealt, as was only natural, when I knew she was lying in wait for me to do wrong; and she denounced me for a stupid, clumsy labouring-boy.

"You say nothing of her," remarked Miss Havisham to me, as she looked on. "She says many hard things of you, but you say nothing of her. What do you think of her?"

"I don't like to say," I stammered.

"Tell me in my ear," said Miss Havisham, bending down.

"I think she is very proud," I replied, in a whisper.

"Anything else?"   30

"I think she is very pretty."

"Anything else?"

"I think she is very insulting." (She was looking at me then, with a look of supreme aversion.)

"Anything else?"

"I think I should like to go home."

"And never see her again, though she is so pretty?"

"I am not sure that I shouldn't like to see her again, but I should like to go home now."

"You shall go soon," said Miss Havisham, aloud. "Play the game out."   40

Saving for the one weird smile at first, I should have felt almost sure that Miss Havisham's face could not smile. It had dropped into a watchful and brooding expression—most likely when all the things about her had become transfixed—and it looked as if nothing could ever lift it up again. Her chest had dropped, so that she stooped; and her voice had dropped, so that she spoke low, and with a dead lull upon her; altogether, she had the appearance

9. The knave card carries the initial J to obviate the confusion occasioned by the initials of king and knave. The class prejudice that the distinction implied persisted for more than a century: see the discrimination between "U" (Upper) and "Non-U" first formulated by the linguist Alan Strode Campbell Ross in 1954 and popularized by Nancy Mitford in her collection of essays *Noblesse Oblige* two years later, in which "Knaves" and "Jacks" retain their social definitions.

of having dropped, body and soul, within and without, under the weight of a crushing blow.

I played the game to an end with Estella, and she beggared me. She threw the cards down on the table when she had won them all, as if she despised them for having been won of me.

"When shall I have you here again?" said Miss Havisham. "Let me think."

I was beginning to remind her that to-day was Wednesday, when she checked me with her former impatient movement of the fingers of her right hand. 10

"There, there! I know nothing of days of the week; I know nothing of weeks of the year. Come again after six days. You hear?"

"Yes, ma'am."

"Estella, take him down. Let him have something to eat, and let him roam and look about him while he eats. Go, Pip."

I followed the candle down, as I had followed the candle up, and she stood it in the place where we had found it. Until she opened the side entrance, I had fancied, without thinking about it, that it must necessarily be night-time. The rush of the daylight quite confounded me, and made me feel as if I had been in the candle-light of the strange room many hours. 20

"You are to wait here, you boy," said Estella; and disappeared and closed the door.

I took the opportunity of being alone in the court-yard, to look at my coarse hands and my common boots. My opinion of those accessories was not favourable. They had never troubled me before, but they troubled me now, as vulgar appendages. I determined to ask Joe why he had ever taught me to call those picture-cards, Jacks, which ought to be called knaves. I wished Joe had been rather more genteelly brought up, and then I should have been so too.

She came back, with some bread and meat and a little mug of beer.[1] She 30 put the mug down on the stones of the yard, and gave me the bread and meat without looking at me, as insolently as if I were a dog in disgrace. I was so humiliated, hurt, spurned, offended, angry, sorry—I cannot hit upon the right name for the smart—God knows what its name was—that tears started to my eyes. The moment they sprang there, the girl looked at me with a quick delight in having been the cause of them. This gave me power to keep them back and to look at her: so, she gave a contemptuous toss—but with a sense, I thought, of having made too sure that I was so wounded—and left me.

But, when she was gone, I looked about me for a place to hide my face in, and got behind one of the gates in the brewery-lane, and leaned my sleeve 40 against the wall there, and leaned my forehead on it and cried. As I cried, I kicked the wall, and took a hard twist at my hair; so bitter were my feelings, and so sharp was the smart without a name, that needed counteraction.

My sister's bringing up had made me sensitive. In the little world in which children have their existence whosoever brings them up, there is nothing so finely perceived and so finely felt as injustice. It may be only small injustice

1. In Dickens's time and earlier beer was drunk with nearly all meals—very often upper-class households brewed their own. Water, which had to be drawn from the well, was nothing so refreshing as it is today; tea and coffee were too expensive for most families. The beer Pip was served would be the thin brew given to children. The social status of brewers is mordantly described by Herbert Pocket in chapter 22.

that the child can be exposed to; but the child is small, and its world is small, and its rocking-horse stands as many hands high, according to scale, as a big-boned Irish hunter.[2] Within myself, I had sustained, from my babyhood, a perpetual conflict with injustice. I had known, from the time when I could speak, that my sister, in her capricious and violent coercion, was unjust to me. I had cherished a profound conviction that her bringing me up by hand, gave her no right to bring me up by jerks. Through all my punishments, disgraces, fasts and vigils, and other penitential performances, I had nursed this assurance; and to my communing so much with it, in a solitary and unprotected way, I in great part refer the fact that I was morally timid and very sensitive.

I got rid of my injured feelings for the time, by kicking them into the brewery wall, and twisting them out of my hair, and then I smoothed my face with my sleeve, and came from behind the gate. The bread and meat were acceptable, and the beer was warming and tingling, and I was soon in spirits to look about me.

To be sure, it was a deserted place, down to the pigeon-house in the brewery-yard, which had been blown crooked on its pole by some high wind, and would have made the pigeons think themselves at sea, if there had been any pigeons there to be rocked by it. But, there were no pigeons in the dovecot, no horses in the stable, no pigs in the sty, no malt in the storehouse, no smells of grains and beer in the copper or the vat. All the uses and scents of the brewery might have evaporated with its last reek of smoke. In a by-yard, there was a wilderness of empty casks, which had a certain sour remembrance of better days lingering about them; but it was too sour to be accepted as a sample of the beer that was gone—and in this respect I remember those recluses as being like most others.[3]

Behind the furthest end of the brewery, was a rank garden with an old wall: not so high but that I could struggle up and hold on long enough to look over it, and see that the rank garden was the garden of the house, and that it was overgrown with tangled weeds, but that there was a track upon the green and yellow paths, as if some one sometimes walked there, and that Estella was walking away from me even then. But she seemed to be everywhere. For, when I yielded to the temptation presented by the casks, and began to walk on them, I saw *her* walking on them at the end of the yard of casks. She had her back to me, and held her pretty brown hair spread out in her two hands, and never looked round, and passed out of my view directly. So, in the brewery itself—by which I mean the large paved lofty place in which they used to make the beer, and where the brewing utensils still were. When I first went into it, and, rather oppressed by its gloom, stood near the door looking about me, I saw her pass among the extinguished fires, and ascend some light iron stairs, and go out by a gallery high overhead, as if she were going out into the sky.

It was in this place, and at this moment, that a strange thing happened to my fancy. I thought it a strange thing then, and I thought it a stranger thing

2. Large agile horse, bred by crossing an English Thoroughbred and an Irish Draft, used for cross-country hunting.
3. The unflattering comparison of hermits to stale beer vats reflects not only Dickens's uncomplicated antimedievalism and anti-Romanism—like Milton, he would have placed "eremites and friars" on a par with "embryos and idiots"—but his bigotry against people whose marginal lifestyle repelled and perhaps even frightened him.

long afterwards.[4] I turned my eyes—a little dimmed by looking up at the frosty light—towards a great wooden beam in a low nook of the building near me on my right hand, and I saw a figure hanging there by the neck. A figure all in yellow white, with but one shoe to the feet; and it hung so, that I could see that the faded trimmings of the dress were like earthy paper, and that the face was Miss Havisham's, with a movement going over the whole countenance as if she were trying to call to me. In the terror of seeing the figure, and in the terror of being certain that it had not been there a moment before, I at first ran from it, and then ran towards it. And my terror was greatest of all, when I found no figure there.[5]

Nothing less than the frosty light of the cheerful sky, the sight of people passing beyond the bars of the court-yard gate, and the reviving influence of the rest of the bread and meat and beer, would have brought me round. Even with those aids, I might not have come to myself as soon as I did, but that I saw Estella approaching with the keys, to let me out. She would have some fair reason for looking down upon me, I thought, if she saw me frightened; and she should have no fair reason.

She gave me a triumphant glance in passing me, as if she rejoiced that my hands were so coarse and my boots were so thick, and she opened the gate and stood holding it. I was passing out without looking at her, when she touched me with a taunting hand.

"Why don't you cry?"

"Because I don't want to."

"You do," said she. "You have been crying till you are half blind, and you are near crying again now."

She laughed contemptuously, pushed me out, and locked the gate upon me. I went straight to Mr. Pumblechook's, and was immensely relieved to find him not at home. So, leaving word with the shopman on what day I was wanted at Miss Havisham's again, I set off on the four-mile walk to our forge; pondering, as I went along, on all I had seen, and deeply revolving that I was a common labouring-boy; that my hands were coarse; that my boots were thick; that I had fallen into a despicable habit of calling knaves Jacks; that I was much more ignorant than I had considered myself last night, and generally that I was in a low-lived bad way.

★

---

4. Sentence not in MS, modified in proof. Dickens may have added it to alert the reader to the recurrence of the fantasy (see next note) and to stress the retrospective quality of Pip's narrative. Similar reminders ("as it now appears to me" and locutions like it), clearly interpolated as second thoughts, are scattered throughout the MS.
5. In 1849 George Manning and his Belgian-born wife Maria (the alleged model for the feral French maid Hortense in *Bleak House*), killed their lodger—Maria's lover—Patrick O'Connor in their home in southeast London for petty gain and threw his body into a pit of quicklime Manning had dug beneath the kitchen floor. The Mannings were hanged on top of Horsemonger Lane Gaol in Southwark (the first husband-and-wife execution since 1700) on November 13 before a crowd of thirty thousand. In his sketch "Lying Awake" (*Household Words*, October 30, 1852) Dickens is haunted by the memory of the two bodies, the woman's form "dangling on the top of the entrance gateway . . . quite unchanged in its trim appearance as it slowly swung from side to side," and Dickens retrieves this phantom here and again in chapter 49.

Chapter IX.

WHEN I reached home, my sister was very curious to know all about Miss Havisham's, and asked a number of questions. And I soon found myself getting heavily bumped from behind in the nape of the neck and the small of the back, and having my face ignominiously shoved against the kitchen wall, because I did not answer those questions at sufficient length.

If a dread of not being understood be hidden in the breasts of other young people to anything like the extent to which it used to be hidden in mine—which I consider probable, as I have no particular reason to suspect myself of having been a monstrosity—it is the key to many reservations. I felt convinced that if I described Miss Havisham's as my eyes had seen it, I should not be understood. Not only that, but I felt convinced that Miss Havisham too would not be understood; and although she was perfectly incomprehensible to me, I entertained an impression that there would be something coarse and treacherous in my dragging her as she really was (to say nothing of Miss Estella) before the contemplation of Mrs. Joe. Consequently, I said as little as I could, and had my face shoved against the kitchen wall.

The worst of it was that that bullying old Pumblechook, preyed upon by a devouring curiosity to be informed of all I had seen and heard, came gaping over in his chaise-cart at tea time, to have the details divulged to him. And the mere sight of the torment, with his fishy eyes and mouth open, his sandy hair inquisitively on end, and his waistcoat heaving with windy arithmetic, made me vicious[1] in my reticence.

"Well, boy," Uncle Pumblechook began, as soon as he was seated in the chair of honour by the fire. "How did you get on up town?"

I answered, "Pretty well, sir," and my sister shook her fist at me.

"Pretty well?" Mr. Pumblechook repeated. "Pretty well is no answer. Tell us what you mean by pretty well, boy?"

Whitewash on the forehead hardens the brain into a state of obstinacy perhaps. Anyhow, with whitewash from the wall on my forehead, my obstinacy was adamantine. I reflected for some time, and then answered as if I had discovered a new idea, "I mean pretty well."

My sister with an exclamation of impatience was going to fly at me—I had no shadow of defence, for Joe was busy in the forge—when Mr. Pumblechook interposed with "No! Don't lose your temper. Leave this lad to me, ma'am; leave this lad to me." Mr. Pumblechook then turned me towards him, as if he were going to cut my hair, and said:

"First (to get our thoughts in order): Forty-three pence?"

I calculated the consequences of replying "Four Hundred Pound," and, finding them against me, went as near the answer as I could—which was somewhere about eightpence off. Mr. Pumblechook then put me through my pence-table[2] from "twelve pence make one shilling," up to "forty pence make three and fourpence," and then triumphantly demanded, as if he had done for me, "Now! How much is forty-three pence?" To which I replied, after a long interval of reflection, "I don't know." And I was so aggravated that I almost doubt if I did know.

1. In this sense not morally depraved but resolutely bad-tempered and stubborn.
2. Multiplication table for shillings and pence. A shilling is one-twentieth of a pound.

Mr. Pumblechook worked his head like a screw to screw it out of me, and said, "Is forty-three pence seven and sixpence three fardens,[3] for instance?" "Yes!" said I. And although my sister instantly boxed my ears, it was highly gratifying to me to see that the answer spoilt his joke, and brought him to a dead stop.

"Boy! What like is Miss Havisham?" Mr. Pumblechook began again when he had recovered; folding his arms tight on his chest and applying the screw. "Very tall and dark," I told him.

"Is she, uncle?" asked my sister.

Mr. Pumblechook winked assent; from which I at once inferred that he   10 had never seen Miss Havisham, for she was nothing of the kind.

"Good!" said Mr. Pumblechook, conceitedly. ("This is the way to have him! We are beginning to hold our own, I think, Mum?")

"I am sure, uncle," returned Mrs. Joe, "I wish you had him always: you know so well how to deal with him."

"Now, boy! What was she a doing of, when you went in to-day?" asked Mr. Pumblechook.

"She was sitting," I answered, "in a black velvet coach."

Mr. Pumblechook and Mrs. Joe stared at one another—as they well might—and both repeated, "In a black velvet coach?"   20

"Yes," said I. "And Miss Estella—that's her niece, I think—handed her in cake and wine at the coach-window, on a gold plate. And we all had cake and wine on gold plates. And I got up behind the coach to eat mine, because she told me to."

"Was anybody else there?" asked Mr. Pumblechook.

"Four dogs," said I.

"Large or small?"

"Immense," said I. "And they fought for veal cutlets out of a silver basket."

Mr. Pumblechook and Mrs. Joe stared at one another again, in utter amaze-   30 ment. I was perfectly frantic—a reckless witness under the torture—and would have told them anything.

"Where *was* this coach, in the name of gracious?" asked my sister.

"In Miss Havisham's room." They stared again. "But there weren't any horses to it." I added this saving clause, in the moment of rejecting four richly caparisoned coursers[4] which I had had wild thoughts of harnessing.

"Can this be possible, uncle?" asked Mrs. Joe. "What can the boy mean?"

"I'll tell you, Mum," said Mr. Pumblechook. "My opinion is, it's a sedan-chair. She's flighty, you know—very flighty—quite flighty enough to pass her days in a sedan-chair."[5]   40

"Did you ever see her in it, uncle?" asked Mrs. Joe.

"How could I?" he returned, forced to the admission, "when I never see her in my life? Never clapped eyes upon her!"

"Goodness, uncle! And yet you have spoken to her?"

"Why, don't you know," said Mr. Pumblechook, testily, "that when I have

---

3. Farthings (fourthlings): quarter pennies. Discontinued as legal tender in 1960.
4. "Caparison" is to deck out or harness. Since the seventeenth century, a courser usually designates a swift horse or racer. By now the expression is used only poetically or rhetorically.
5. One-passenger vehicle: enclosed portable chair carried by "chairmen" by means of long wooden poles in front and back. In fashionable use from the seventeenth to the early nineteenth century. "Flighty": crazy.

been there, I have been took up to the outside of her door, and the door has stood ajar, and she has spoke to me that way. Don't say you don't know *that*, Mum. Howsever, the boy went there to play. What did you play at, boy?" "We played with flags," I said. (I beg to observe that I think of myself with amazement, when I recall the lies I told on this occasion.) "Flags!" echoed my sister.

"Yes," said I. "Estella waved a blue flag, and I waved a red one, and Miss Havisham waved one sprinkled all over with little gold stars, out at the coach-window. And then we all waved our swords and hurrahed."

"Swords!" repeated my sister. "Where did you get swords from?"   10
"Out of a cupboard," said I. "And I saw pistols in it—and jam—and pills. And there was no daylight in the room, but it was all lighted up with candles."

"That's true, Mum," said Mr. Pumblechook, with a grave nod. "That's the state of the case, for that much I've seen myself." And then they both stared at me, and I with an obtrusive show of artlessness on my countenance, stared at them, and plaited the right leg of my trousers with my right hand.

If they had asked me any more questions I should undoubtedly have be-trayed myself, for I was even then on the point of mentioning that there was a balloon in the yard,[6] and should have hazarded the statement but for my invention being divided between that phenomenon and a bear in the brewery.   20 They were so much occupied, however, in discussing the marvels I had al-ready presented for their consideration, that I escaped. The subject still held them when Joe came in from his work to have a cup of tea. To whom my sister, more for the relief of her own mind than for the gratification of his, related my pretended experiences.

Now, when I saw Joe open his blue eyes and roll them all round the kitchen in helpless amazement, I was overtaken by penitence; but only as regarded him—not in the least as regarded the other two. Towards Joe, and Joe only, I considered myself a young monster, while they sat debating what results would ensue to me from Miss Havisham's acquaintance and favour.   30 They had no doubt that Miss Havisham would "do something" for me; their doubts related to the form that something would take. My sister stood out for "property." Mr. Pumblechook was in favour of a handsome premium for binding me apprentice to some genteel trade—say, the corn and seed trade for instance. Joe fell into the deepest disgrace with both, for offering the bright suggestion that I might only be presented with one of the dogs who had fought for the veal cutlets. "If a fool's head can't express better opinions than that," said my sister, "and you have got any work to do, you had better go and do it." So he went.

After Mr. Pumblechook had driven off, and when my sister was washing   40 up, I stole into the forge to Joe, and remained by him until he had done for the night. Then I said, "Before the fire goes out, Joe, I should like to tell you something."

6. Pip is talking about the hydrogen airship invented by the Montgolfiers and the Brothers Charles in 1783. Its presence in the Satis House yard—had Pip stuck to his story—would have introduced an element of the futuristic: though the first airship went up in 1784 (taking off, as skeptics liked to point out, from a spot close to Bedlam, with a cat as passenger), ballooning did not come into its own in England before the 1820s. From the mid-thirties on, serious balloon ascents began to enjoy a fantastic vogue as the star attractions in Vauxhall Gardens and Cremorne—the amusement parks of early-Victorian England—thanks largely to the aeronaut Charles Green, who went up more than five hundred times between 1821 and 1852, taking with him such fetching clients as "a lady and her pet leopard," an acrobat gyrating on a trapeze, and a French actress ("Europa") astride a bull.

"Should you, Pip?" said Joe, drawing his shoeing-stool near the forge. "Then tell us. What is it, Pip?"

"Joe," said I, taking hold of his rolled-up shirt sleeve, and twisting it between my finger and thumb, "you remember all that about Miss Havisham's?"

"Remember?" said Joe. "I believe you![7] Wonderful!"

"It's a terrible thing, Joe; it ain't true."

"What are you telling of, Pip?" cried Joe, falling back in the greatest amazement. "You don't mean to say it's——"

"Yes I do; it's lies, Joe."

"But not all of it? Why sure you don't mean to say, Pip, that there was no   10 black welwet co——ch?" For, I stood shaking my head. "But at least there was dogs, Pip. Come, Pip," said Joe, persuasively, "if there warn't no weal cutlets, at least there was dogs?"

"No, Joe."

"A dog?" said Joe. "A puppy? Come?"

"No, Joe, there was nothing at all of the kind."

As I fixed my eyes hopelessly on Joe, Joe contemplated me in dismay. "Pip, old chap! this won't do, old fellow! I say! Where do you expect to go to?"

"It's terrible, Joe; an't it?"

"Terrible?" cried Joe. "Awful! What possessed you?"   20

"I don't know what possessed me, Joe," I replied, letting his shirt sleeve go, and sitting down in the ashes at his feet, hanging my head; "but I wish you hadn't taught me to call Knaves at cards, Jacks; and I wish my boots weren't so thick nor my hands so coarse."

And then I told Joe that I felt very miserable, and that I hadn't been able to explain myself to Mrs. Joe and Pumblechook, who were so rude to me, and that there had been a beautiful young lady at Miss Havisham's who was dreadfully proud, and that she had said I was common, and that I knew I was common, and that I wished I was not common, and that the lies had come of it somehow, though I didn't know how.   30

This was a case of metaphysics, at least as difficult for Joe to deal with, as for me. But Joe took the case altogether out of the region of metaphysics, and by that means vanquished it.

"There's one thing you may be sure of, Pip," said Joe, after some rumination, "namely, that lies is lies. Howsever they come, they didn't ought to come, and they come from the father of lies,[8] and work round to the same. Don't you tell no more of 'em, Pip. *That* ain't the way to get out of being common, old chap. And as to being common, I don't make it out at all clear. You are oncommon in some things. You're oncommon small. Likewise, you're a oncommon scholar."   40

"No, I am ignorant and backward, Joe."

"Why, see what a letter you wrote last night! Wrote in print even! I've seen letters—Ah! and from gentlefolks!—that I'll swear weren't wrote in print," said Joe.

---

7. "You said it!" or "You can say that again!" The expression allegedly gained currency from the stock phrase of one of the characters in *The Green Bushes, or A Hundred Years Ago*, a domestic drama by the prolific actor-playwright John Buckstone (1802–1879). As Buckstone's play appeared in 1845, the expression was either already current much earlier or Joe is guilty of an anachronism. In chapter 25, in reply to Pip's query about Jaggers, " 'Dread him,' said Wemmick. 'I believe you they dread him.' "

8. The devil. So used in John 8.44.

"I have learnt next to nothing, Joe. You think much of me. It's only that."

"Well, Pip," said Joe, "be it so or be it son't, you must be a common scholar afore you can be a oncommon one, I should hope! The king upon his throne, with his crown upon his ed, can't sit and write his acts of Parliament in print, without having begun, when he were a unpromoted Prince, with the alphabet—Ah!" added Joe, with a shake of the head that was full of meaning, "and begun at A too, and worked his way to Z. And I know what that is to do, though I can't say I've exactly done it."

There was some hope in this piece of wisdom, and it rather encouraged me.   10

"Whether common ones as to callings and earnings," pursued Joe, reflectively, "mightn't be the better of continuing fur to keep company with common ones, instead of going out to play with oncommon ones—which reminds me to hope that there were a flag perhaps?"

"No, Joe."

"(I'm sorry there weren't a flag, Pip.) Whether that might be or mightn't be, is a thing as can't be looked into now, without putting your sister on the Rampage; and that's a thing not to be thought of as being done intentional. Lookee here, Pip, at what is said to you by a true friend. Which this to you the true friend say. If you can't get to be oncommon through going straight,   20 you'll never get to do it through going crooked. So don't tell no more on 'em, Pip, and live well and die happy."

"You are not angry with me, Joe?"

"No, old chap. But bearing in mind that them were which I meantersay of a stunning and outdacious sort—alluding to them which bordered on weal cutlets and dog-fighting—a sincere well-wisher would adwise, Pip, their being dropped into your meditations when you go up-stairs to bed. That's all, old chap, and don't never do it no more."

When I got up to my little room and said my prayers, I did not forget Joe's recommendation, and yet my young mind was in that disturbed and unthank-   30 ful state, that I thought long after I laid me down, how common Estella would consider Joe, a mere blacksmith: how thick his boots, and how coarse his hands. I thought how Joe and my sister were then sitting in the kitchen, and how I had come up to bed from the kitchen, and how Miss Havisham and Estella never sat in a kitchen, but were far above the level of such common doings. I fell asleep recalling what I "used to do" when I was at Miss Havisham's; as though I had been there weeks or months, instead of hours, and as though it were quite an old subject of remembrance, instead of one that had arisen only that day.

That was a memorable day to me, for it made great changes in me. But,   40 it is the same with any life. Imagine one selected day struck out of it, and think how different its course would have been. Pause you who read this, and think for a moment of the long chain of iron or gold, of thorns or flowers, that would never have bound you, but for the formation of the first link on one memorable day.

Chapter X.

THE felicitous idea occurred to me a morning or two later when I woke, that the best step I could take towards making myself uncommon was to get out of Biddy everything she knew. In pursuance of this luminous conception I mentioned to Biddy when I went to Mr. Wopsle's great-aunt's at night, that I had a particular reason for wishing to get on in life, and that I should feel very much obliged to her if she would impart all her learning to me. Biddy, who was the most obliging of girls, immediately said she would, and indeed began to carry out her promise within five minutes.

The Educational scheme or Course established by Mr. Wopsle's great-aunt may be resolved into the following synopsis.[1] The pupils ate apples and put straws down one another's backs, until Mr. Wopsle's great-aunt collected her energies, and made an indiscriminate totter at them with a birch-rod. After receiving the charge with every mark of derision, the pupils formed in line and buzzingly passed a ragged book from hand to hand. The book had an alphabet in it, some figures and tables, and a little spelling—that is to say, it had had once. As soon as this volume began to circulate, Mr. Wopsle's great-aunt fell into a state of coma; arising either from sleep or a rheumatic paroxysm. The pupils then entered among themselves upon a competitive examination on the subject of Boots, with the view of ascertaining who could tread the hardest upon whose toes. This mental exercise lasted until Biddy made a rush at them and distributed three defaced Bibles (shaped as if they had been unskilfully cut off the chump-end of something), more illegibly printed at the best than any curiosities of literature[2] I have since met with, speckled all over with ironmould, and having various specimens of the insect world smashed between their leaves. This part of the Course was usually lightened by several single combats between Biddy and refractory students. When the fights were over, Biddy gave out the number of a page, and then we all read aloud what we could—or what we couldn't—in a frightful chorus; Biddy leading with a high shrill monotonous voice, and none of us having the least notion of, or reverence for, what we were reading about. When this horrible din had lasted a certain time, it mechanically awoke Mr. Wopsle's great-aunt, who staggered at a boy fortuitously and pulled his ears. This was understood to terminate the Course for the evening, and we emerged into the air with shrieks of intellectual victory. It is fair to remark that there was no prohibition against any pupil's entertaining himself with a slate or even with the ink (when there was any), but that it was not easy to pursue that branch of study in the winter season, on account of the little general shop in which the classes were holden—and which was also Mr. Wopsle's great-aunt's sitting-room and bed-chamber—being but faintly

1. Wopsle's great-aunt manages a so-called Dame School, a ludicrously inept form of private schooling for the working classes, especially for younger children, practiced in large parts of England before the introduction of free national schooling later in the century. The Dame Schools swarmed with teachers destitute of all training. Classes met in the evening to leave teachers and students free to work during the day. Dickens, who briefly attended a Dame School in Chatham at age six, recalled some of its dismal features in the piece "Our School" (*Household Words*, October 11, 1851). On the conditions of the Dame Schools, see the Report of the Newcastle Commission, pp. 588–92.
2. This phrase is no doubt a dig at the opus of the same title by Isaac D'Israeli (1766–1848), the Prime Minister's father, a six-volume collection of pithy historical, literary, and miscellaneous anecdotes ranging from "Dethroned Monarchs" and "Literary Dutchmen" to "Infectious Diseases." *Chump-end*: blunt end [OED].

illuminated through the agency of one low-spirited dip-candle and no snuffers.[3]

It appeared to me that it would take time, to become uncommon under these circumstances: nevertheless, I resolved to try it, and that very evening Biddy entered on our special agreement, by imparting some information from her little catalogue of Prices, under the head of moist sugar,[4] and lending me, to copy at home, a large old English D which she had imitated from the heading of some newspaper, and which I supposed, until she told me what it was, to be a design for a buckle.

Of course there was a public-house in the village, and of course Joe liked   10 sometimes to smoke his pipe there. I had received strict orders from my sister to call for him at the Three Jolly Bargemen, that evening, on my way from school, and bring him home at my peril.[5] To the Three Jolly Bargemen, therefore, I directed my steps.

There was a bar at the Jolly Bargemen, with some alarmingly long chalk scores in it on the wall at the side of the door, which seemed to me to be never paid off. They had been there ever since I could remember, and had grown more than I had. But there was a quantity of chalk about our country, and perhaps the people neglected no opportunity of turning it to account.[6]

It being Saturday night, I found the landlord looking rather grimly at these   20 records, but as my business was with Joe and not with him, I merely wished him good evening, and passed into the common room at the end of the passage, where there was a bright large kitchen fire, and where Joe was smoking his pipe in company with Mr. Wopsle and a stranger. Joe greeted me as usual with "Halloa, Pip, old chap!" and the moment he said that, the stranger turned his head and looked at me.

He was a secret-looking man whom I had never seen before. His head was all on one side, and one of his eyes was half shut up, as if he were taking aim at something with an invisible gun. He had a pipe in his mouth, and he took it out, and, after slowly blowing all his smoke away and looking hard at   30 me all the time, nodded. So, I nodded, and then he nodded again, and made room on the settle[7] beside him that I might sit down there.

But, as I was used to sit beside Joe whenever I entered that place of resort, I said "No, thank you, sir," and fell into the space Joe made for me on the opposite settle. The strange man, after glancing at Joe, and seeing that his attention was otherwise engaged, nodded to me again when I had taken my seat, and then rubbed his leg—in a very odd way, as it struck me.

"You was saying," said the strange man, turning to Joe, "that you was a blacksmith."

"Yes. I said it, you know," said Joe.   40

---

3. Ordinarily, candle-extinguishers; here their opposite: scissorlike contraptions used to trim off the wick (or snuff) and keep the candle tidy without putting out the flame. "Dip-candle": unlike the expensive wax candles used in Satis House, dirt-cheap type (known also as "farthing dip"), made by dipping the wick into melted tallow; popular among the needy.
4. Inferior unrefined or partly refined sugar.
5. Mrs. Joe would hardly have allowed Joe to smoke indoors; the use of tobacco in the presence of ladies was taboo. In wealthier, more commodious households, men might retire to a special male enclave, such as a billiard room, to smoke, frequently wearing a smoking jacket and cap to keep their other clothes and their hair from reeking of tobacco. The "Three Jolly Bargemen" has been identified as the Chequers Inn in Lower Higham, a mile south of the cemetery in chapter 1.
6. The "quantity of chalk" is reflected in the place name Chalk: see p. 10, n. 9.
7. Long high-backed wooden seat or bench, usually with armrests.

"What'll you drink, Mr.——? You didn't mention your name, by-the-by."

Joe mentioned it now, and the strange man called him by it.

"What'll you drink, Mr. Gargery? At my expense? To top up with?"

"Well," said Joe, "to tell you the truth, I ain't much in the habit of drinking at anybody's expense but my own."

"Habit? No," returned the stranger, "but once and away, and on a Saturday night too. Come! Put a name to it, Mr. Gargery."

"I wouldn't wish to be stiff company," said Joe. "Rum."

"Rum," repeated the stranger. "And will the other gentleman originate a sentiment?"

"Rum," said Mr. Wopsle.

"Three Rums!" cried the stranger, calling to the landlord. "Glasses round!"

"This other gentleman," observed Joe, by way of introducing Mr. Wopsle, "is a gentleman that you would like to hear give it out.[8] Our clerk at church."

"Aha!" said the stranger, quickly, and cocking his eye at me. "The lonely church, right out on the marshes, with the graves round it!"

"That's it," said Joe.

The stranger, with a comfortable kind of grunt over his pipe, put his legs up on the settle that he had all to himself. He wore a flapping broad-brimmed traveller's hat, and under it a handkerchief tied over his head in the manner of a cap: so that he showed no hair.[9] As he looked at the fire, I thought I saw a cunning expression, followed by a half laugh, come into his face.

"I am not acquainted with this country, gentlemen, but it seems a solitary country towards the river."

"Most meshes is solitary," said Joe.

"No doubt, no doubt. Do you find any gipsies, now, or tramps, or vagrants of any sort out there?"

"No," said Joe; "none but a runaway convict now and then. And we don't find *them*, easy. Eh, Mr. Wopsle?"

Mr. Wopsle, with a majestic remembrance of old discomfiture, assented; but not warmly.

"Seems you have been out after such?" asked the stranger.

"Once," returned Joe. "Not that we wanted to take them, you understand; we went out as lookers-on; me, and Mr. Wopsle, and Pip. Didn't us, Pip?"

"Yes, Joe."

The stranger looked at me again—still cocking his eye, as if he were expressly taking aim at me with his invisible gun—and said, "He's a likely young parcel of bones that. What is it you call him?"

"Pip," said Joe.

"Christened Pip?"

"No, not christened Pip."

"Surname Pip?"

"No," said Joe; "it's a kind of a family name what he gave himself when a infant, and is called by."

"Son of yours?"

"Well," said Joe, meditatively—not, of course, that it could be in anywise

---

8. In leading the congregation in the responses.
9. Since convicts had their hair shaven, the stranger may be covering his head to conceal that he has recently been discharged from jail.

necessary to consider about it, but because it was the way at the Jolly Bargemen to seem to consider deeply about everything that was discussed over
pipes; "well—no. No, he ain't."

"Nevvy?" said the strange man.

"Well," said Joe, with the same appearance of profound cogitation, "he is
not—no, not to deceive you he is *not*—my nevvy."

"What the Blue Blazes is he?" asked the stranger. Which appeared to me
to be an inquiry of unnecessary strength.

Mr. Wopsle struck in upon that; as one who knew all about relationships,
having professional occasion to bear in mind what female relations a man   10
might not marry; and expounded the ties between me and Joe.[1] Having his
hand in, Mr. Wopsle finished off with a most terrifically snarling passage from
Richard the Third, and seemed to think he had done quite enough to account
for it when he added, "—as the poet says."[2]

And here I may remark that when Mr. Wopsle referred to me, he considered it a necessary part of such reference to rumple my hair and poke it into
my eyes. I cannot conceive why everybody of his standing who visited at our
house should always have put me through the same inflammatory process
under similar circumstances. Yet I do not call to mind that I was ever in my
earlier youth the subject of remark in our social family circle, but some large-   20
handed person took some such ophthalmic steps to patronise me.[3]

All this while the strange man looked at nobody but me, and looked at me
as if he were determined to have a shot at me at last, and bring me down.
But he said nothing after offering his Blue Blazes observation, until the glasses
of rum-and-water were brought; and then he made his shot, and a most
extraordinary shot it was.

It was not a verbal remark, but a proceeding in dumb-show, and was pointedly addressed to me. He stirred his rum-and-water pointedly at me, and he
tasted his rum-and-water pointedly at me. And he stirred it and he tasted it:
not with a spoon that was brought to him, but *with a file*.[4]   30

He did this so that nobody but I saw the file; and when he had done it he
wiped the file and put it in a breast-pocket. I knew it to be Joe's file, and I
knew that he knew my convict the moment I saw the instrument. I sat gazing
at him, spell-bound. But he now reclined on his settle, taking very little notice
of me, and talking principally about turnips.

1. See p. 24, n. 6. In the Anglican marriage service the couple must confess to "any impediment"
   to their being "lawfully joined together." Under canon law, "consanguinity" (blood ties) and "affinity"
   (relation by marriage) constitute two such impediments. As parish clerk, Wopsle can be expected to
   know by heart Archbishop Parker's "Table of Kindred and Affinity" (1563), which dockets every degree
   of relationship in which marriage is disallowed as unlawful.
2. *Richard III*, because a play in which the hero marries the niece whose father he killed, murders his
   brother and nephews, and is himself killed by the nephews' presumptive brother-in-law (who succeeds
   him as king), lends itself to the demonstration of tangled domestic alliances. Though the play teems
   with snarling passages, a good place to start looking is 4.2.62 ff. ("I must be married to my brother's
   daughter," * * * Murder her brothers, and then marry her?") but 1.2.215–250 or Queen Margaret's
   malediction in 1.3.185–230 ("What? Were you snarling all before I came, / Ready to catch each other
   by the throat * * * Thou elvish-marked, abortive, rooting hog, * * * Thou loathèd issue of thy father's
   loins," etc.) also fit the bill.
3. Opthalmia is an inflammation of the eyes. Pip suggests that Wopsle's antics bring on the disease
   instead of curing it. In the same vein, *Oliver Twist*, chapter 26: "Why, the sight of you, Mr. Fagin,
   would cure the hoptalmy!" (i.e., "Aren't *you* a sight for sore eyes!")
4. Dickens is being awfully high-handed in allowing the file to travel so freely among criminals. Very
   likely it would have been taken from the convict at the time of his capture in chapter 5. Dickens's
   textual disinfectant is discussed on p. 449.

There was a delicious sense of cleaning-up and making a quiet pause before going on in life afresh, in our village on Saturday nights, which stimulated Joe to dare to stay out half an hour longer on Saturdays than at other times. The half-hour and the rum-and-water running out together, Joe got up to go, and took me by the hand.

"Stop half a moment, Mr. Gargery," said the strange man. "I think I've got a bright new shilling somewhere in my pocket, and if I have, the boy shall have it."

He looked it out from a handful of small change, folded it in some crumpled paper, and gave it to me. "Yours!" said he. "Mind! Your own."   10

I thanked him, staring at him far beyond the bounds of good manners, and holding tight to Joe. He gave Joe good-night, and he gave Mr. Wopsle good-night (who went out with us), and he gave me only a look with his aiming eye—no, not a look, for he shut it up, but wonders may be done with an eye by hiding it.

On the way home, if I had been in a humour for talking, the talk must have been all on my side, for Mr. Wopsle parted from us at the door of the Jolly Bargemen, and Joe went all the way home with his mouth wide open, to rinse the rum out with as much air as possible. But I was in a manner stupefied by this turning up of my old misdeed and old acquaintance, and   20 could think of nothing else.

My sister was not in a very bad temper when we presented ourselves in the kitchen, and Joe was encouraged by that unusual circumstance to tell her about the bright shilling. "A bad un, I'll be bound," said Mrs. Joe, triumphantly, "or he wouldn't have given it to the boy! Let's look at it."

I took it out of the paper, and it proved to be a good one. "But what's this?" said Mrs. Joe, throwing down the shilling and catching up the paper. "Two One-Pound notes?"[5]

Nothing less than two fat sweltering one-pound notes that seemed to have been on terms of the warmest intimacy with all the cattle markets in the   30 county. Joe caught up his hat again, and ran with them to the Jolly Bargemen to restore them to their owner. While he was gone, I sat down on my usual stool and looked vacantly at my sister: feeling pretty sure that the man would not be there.

Presently, Joe came back, saying that the man was gone, but that he, Joe, had left word at the Three Jolly Bargemen concerning the notes. Then my sister sealed them up in a piece of paper, and put them under some dried rose-leaves in an ornamental teapot on the top of a press[6] in the state parlour. There, they remained, a nightmare to me, many and many a night and day.

I had sadly broken sleep when I got to bed, through thinking of the strange   40 man taking aim at me with his invisible gun, and of the guiltily coarse and common thing it was, to be on secret terms of conspiracy with convicts—a feature in my low career that I had previously forgotten. I was haunted by the file too. A dread possessed me that when I least expected it, the file would reappear. I coaxed myself to sleep by thinking of Miss Havisham's, next

5. On the discontinuance of one-pound notes from 1821 (elsewhere the date is given as 1826) until 1914, see pp. 542–43. From 1971, when Britain adopted the decimal standard, the denominations given here to explain the sums used in *Great Expectations* became officially obsolete.
6. Movable closet or case for clothes, linen, etc.

Wednesday; and in my sleep I saw the file coming at me out of a door without seeing who held it, and I screamed myself awake.[7]

Chapter XI.

AT the appointed time I returned to Miss Havisham's, and my hesitating ring at the gate brought out Estella. She locked it after admitting me, as she had done before, and again preceded me into the dark passage where her candle stood. She took no notice of me until she had the candle in her hand, when she looked over her shoulder, superciliously saying, "You are to come this way to-day," and took me to quite another part of the house.

The passage was a long one and seemed to pervade the whole square basement of the Manor House. We traversed but one side of the square, 10 however, and at the end of it she stopped, and put her candle down and opened a door. Here, the daylight reappeared, and I found myself in a small paved court-yard, the opposite side of which was formed by a detached dwelling-house, that looked as if it had once belonged to the manager or head clerk of the extinct brewery. There was a clock in the outer wall of this house. Like the clock in Miss Havisham's room and like Miss Havisham's watch, it had stopped at twenty minutes to nine.

We went in at the door, which stood open, and into a gloomy room with a low ceiling, on the ground floor at the back. There was some company in the room, and Estella said to me as she joined it, "You are to go and stand 20 there, boy, till you are wanted." "There," being the window, I crossed to it, and stood "there," in a very uncomfortable state of mind, looking out.

It opened to the ground, and looked into a most miserable corner of the neglected garden, upon a rank ruin of cabbage-stalks, and one box-tree that had been clipped round long ago, like a pudding, and had a new growth at the top of it, out of shape and of a different colour, as if that part of the pudding had stuck to the saucepan and got burnt. This was my homely thought, as I contemplated the box-tree.[1] There had been some light snow over-night, and it lay nowhere else to my knowledge; but, it had not quite melted from the cold shadow of this bit of garden, and the wind caught it 30 up in little eddies and threw it at the window, as if it pelted me for coming there.

I divined that my coming had stopped conversation in the room, and that its other occupants were looking at me. I could see nothing of the room except the shining of the fire in the window-glass, but I stiffened in all my joints with the consciousness that I was under close inspection.

There were three ladies in the room and one gentleman. Before I had been standing at the window five minutes, they somehow conveyed to me that they were all toadies and humbugs, but that each of them pretended not to know that the others were toadies and humbugs: because the admission that he or 40 she did know it, would have made him or her out to be a toady and humbug.

7. Probably Pip echoes the opening line in Macbeth's soliloquy before he murders King Duncan (2.1.33): "Is this a dagger which I see before me." *Macbeth* was one of Dickens's favorite plays.
1. Shrub with deep-green leaves of a thick leathery texture, often used in ornamental gardening.

They all had a listless and dreary air of waiting somebody's pleasure, and the most talkative of the ladies had to speak quite rigidly to suppress a yawn. This lady, whose name was Camilla, very much reminded me of my sister, with the difference that she was older and (as I found when I caught sight of her) of a blunter cast of features. Indeed, when I knew her better I began to think it was a Mercy she had any features at all, so very blank and high was the dead wall of her face.

"Poor dear soul!" said this lady, with an abruptness of manner quite my sister's. "Nobody's enemy but his own!"[2]

"It would be much more commendable to be somebody else's enemy," said the gentleman; "far more natural." 10

"Cousin Raymond,"[3] observed another lady, "we are to love our neighbour."

"Sarah Pocket," returned Cousin Raymond, "if a man is not his own neighbour, who is?"[4]

Miss Pocket laughed, and Camilla laughed and said (checking a yawn), "The idea!" But I thought they seemed to think it rather a good idea too. The other lady, who had not spoken yet, said gravely and emphatically, "*Very* true!"

"Poor soul!" Camilla presently went on (I knew they had all been looking 20 at me in the mean time), "he is so very strange! Would any one believe that when Tom's wife died, he actually could not be induced to see the importance of the children's having the deepest of trimmings to their mourning? 'Good Lord!' said he, 'Camilla, what can it signify so long as the poor bereaved little things are in black?' So like Matthew! The idea!"

"Good points in him; good points in him," said Cousin Raymond; "Heaven forbid I should deny good points in him; but he never had, and he never will have, any sense of the proprieties."

"You know I was obliged," said Camilla, "I was obliged to be firm. I said, 'It WILL NOT DO for the credit of the family.' I told him that, without deep 30 trimmings, the family was disgraced. I cried about it from breakfast till dinner. I injured my digestion. And at last he flung out in his violent way, and said with a D, 'Then do as you like.' Thank Goodness it will always be a consolation to me to know that I instantly went out in a pouring rain and bought the things."

"*He* paid for them, did he not?" asked Estella.

"It's not the question, my dear child, who paid for them," returned Camilla, "*I* bought them. And I shall often think of that with peace, when I wake up in the night."

The ringing of a distant bell, combined with the echoing of some cry or 40 call along the passage by which I had come, interrupted the conversation and caused Estella to say to me, "Now, boy!" On my turning round, they all looked at me with the utmost contempt, and, as I went out, I heard Sarah

---

2. Cicero referring to Caesar in his *Letters to Atticus* (68–44 B.C.) 10.8: "He is his own worst enemy." But Dickens may have picked up the expression from Henry Fielding's *Tom Jones* (1749) 4.5: "Tom, though an idle, thoughtless, rattling rascal, was nobody's enemy but his own."
3. From MS through *All the Year Round* Raymond appears, in this scene only, as "Cousin John"; a few pages later he turns into "Raymond." Almost certainly Dickens's error—unless he planned to introduce two different characters and then decided that he had enough Pockets to make his point.
4. Perhaps an oblique allusion to the lawyer's question in Luke 10.29, "And who is my neighbour?" which launches the parable of the good Samaritan.

Pocket say, "Well I am sure! What next!" and Camilla add, with indignation, "Was there ever such a fancy! The i-de-a!"

As we were going with our candle along the dark passage, Estella stopped all of a sudden, and facing round said in her taunting manner with her face quite close to mine:

"Well?"

"Well, miss?" I answered, almost falling over her and checking myself. She stood looking at me, and, of course, I stood looking at her.

"Am I pretty?"

"Yes; I think you are very pretty."   10

"Am I insulting?"

"Not so much so as you were last time," said I.

"Not so much so?"

"No."

She fired when she asked the last question, and she slapped my face with such force as she had, when I answered it.

"Now?" said she. "You little coarse monster, what do you think of me now?"

"I shall not tell you."

"Because you are going to tell, up-stairs. Is that it?"   20

"No," said I, "that's not it."

"Why don't you cry again, you little wretch?"

"Because I'll never cry for you again," said I. Which was, I suppose, as false a declaration as ever was made; for I was inwardly crying for her then, and I know what I know of the pain she cost me afterwards.

We went on our way up-stairs after this episode; and, as we were going up, we met a gentleman groping his way down.

"Who have we here?" asked the gentleman, stopping and looking at me.

"A boy," said Estella.

He was a burly man of an exceedingly dark complexion, with an exceed- 30
ingly large head and a correspondingly large hand. He took my chin in his large hand and turned up my face to have a look at me by the light of the candle. He was prematurely bald on the top of his head, and had bushy black eyebrows that wouldn't lie down but stood up bristling. His eyes were set very deep in his head, and were disagreeably sharp and suspicious. He had a large watch-chain, and strong black dots where his beard and whiskers would have been if he had let them. He was nothing to me, and I could have had no foresight then, that he ever would be anything to me, but it happened that I had this opportunity of observing him well.

"Boy of the neighbourhood? Hey?" said he.   40

"Yes, sir," said I.

"And how do *you* come here?"

"Miss Havisham sent for me, sir," I explained.

"Well! Behave yourself. I have a pretty large experience of boys, and you're a bad set of fellows. Now mind!" said he, biting the side of his great forefinger as he frowned at me, "you behave yourself!"

With those words, he released me—which I was glad of, for his hand smelt of scented soap—and went his way down stairs. I wondered whether he could be a doctor; but no, I thought; he couldn't be a doctor, or he would have a quieter and more persuasive manner. There was not much time to consider 50 the subject, for we were soon in Miss Havisham's room, where she and everything else were just as I had left them. Estella left me standing near the door, and I stood there until Miss Havisham cast her eyes upon me from her dressing-table.

"So!" she said, without being startled or surprised; "the days have worn away, have they?"

"Yes, ma'am. To-day is——"

"There, there, there!" with the impatient movement of her fingers. "I don't want to know. Are you ready to play?"

I was obliged to answer in some confusion, "I don't think I am, ma'am." 10

"Not at cards again?" she demanded, with a searching look.

"Yes, ma'am; I could do that, if I was wanted."

"Since this house strikes you old and grave, boy," said Miss Havisham, impatiently, "and you are unwilling to play, are you willing to work?"

I could answer this inquiry with a better heart than I had been able to find for the other question, and I said I was quite willing.

"Then go into that opposite room," said she, pointing at the door behind me with her withered hand, "and wait there till I come."

I crossed the staircase landing, and entered the room she indicated. From that room too, the daylight was completely excluded, and it had an airless 20 smell that was oppressive. A fire had been lately kindled in the damp old-fashioned grate, and it was more disposed to go out than to burn up, and the reluctant smoke which hung in the room seemed colder than the clearer air—like our own marsh mist. Certain wintry branches of candles on the high chimney-piece faintly lighted the chamber: or it would be more expressive to say, faintly troubled its darkness. It was spacious, and I dare say had once been handsome, but every discernible thing in it was covered with dust and mould, and dropping to pieces. The most prominent object was a long table with a tablecloth spread on it, as if a feast had been in preparation when the house and the clocks all stopped together. An épergne[5] or centre-piece of 30 some kind was in the middle of this cloth; it was so heavily overhung with cobwebs that its form was quite undistinguishable, and, as I looked along the yellow expanse out of which I remember its seeming to grow like a black fungus, I saw speckled-legged spiders with blotchy bodies running home to it, and running out from it, as if some circumstance of the greatest public importance had just transpired in the spider community.

I heard the mice too, rattling behind the panels, as if the same occurrence were important to their interests. But, the black-beetles took no notice of the agitation, and groped about the hearth in a ponderous elderly way, as if they were short-sighted and hard of hearing, and not on terms with one 40 another.

These crawling things had fascinated my attention and I was watching them from a distance, when Miss Havisham laid a hand upon my shoulder. In her other hand she had a crutch-headed stick[6] on which she leaned, and she looked like the Witch of the place.

5. Elaborate ornamental stand for the dinner table, consisting of grouped dishes for fruit, dessert, etc. [OED].
6. Walking stick with a transverse handle, like the head of a crutch. Its association with magic survived Miss Havisham (and Dickens) by decades: the idea is captured as late as 1902 in Henry James's novel *The Wings of the Dove* (4.1), in which one of the major/minor characters is described by the heroine as a "fairy godmother" and whimsically imagined as "brandishing [her] magic crutch."

"This," said she, pointing to the long table with her stick, "is where I will be laid when I am dead. They shall come and look at me here."

With some vague misgiving that she might get upon the table then and there and die at once, the complete realisation of the ghastly waxwork at the Fair, I shrank under her touch.

"What do you think that is?" she asked me, again pointing with her stick; "that, where those cobwebs are?"

"I can't guess what it is, ma'am."

"It's a great cake. A bride-cake. Mine!"

She looked all round the room in a glaring manner, and then said, leaning 10 on me while her hand twitched my shoulder, "Come, come, come! Walk me, walk me!"

I made out from this, that the work I had to do, was to walk Miss Havisham round and round the room. Accordingly, I started at once, and she leaned upon my shoulder, and we went away at a pace that might have been an imitation (founded on my first impulse under that roof) of Mr. Pumblechook's chaise-cart.

She was not physically strong, and after a little time she said "Slower!" Still, we went at an impatient fitful speed, and as we went, she twitched the hand upon my shoulder, and worked her mouth, and led me to believe that 20 we were going fast because her thoughts went fast. After a while she said, "Call Estella!" so I went out on the landing and roared that name as I had done on the previous occasion. When her light appeared, I returned to Miss Havisham, and we started away again round and round the room.

If only Estella had come to be a spectator of our proceedings, I should have felt sufficiently disconcerted; but, as she brought with her the three ladies and the gentleman whom I had seen below, I didn't know what to do. In my politeness, I would have stopped; but, Miss Havisham twitched my shoulder, and we posted on—with a shamefaced consciousness on my part that they would think it was all my doing.   30

"Dear Miss Havisham," said Miss Sarah Pocket. "How well you look!"

"I do not," returned Miss Havisham. "I am yellow skin and bone."

Camilla brightened when Miss Pocket met with this rebuff; and she murmured, as she plaintively contemplated Miss Havisham, "Poor dear soul! Certainly not to be expected to look well, poor thing. The idea!"

"And how are *you*?" said Miss Havisham to Camilla. As we were close to Camilla then, I would have stopped as a matter of course, only Miss Havisham wouldn't stop. We swept on, and I felt that I was highly obnoxious to Camilla.

"Thank you, Miss Havisham," she returned, "I am as well as can be 40 expected."

"Why, what's the matter with you?" asked Miss Havisham, with exceeding sharpness.

"Nothing worth mentioning," replied Camilla. "I don't wish to make a display of my feelings, but I have habitually thought of you more in the night than I am quite equal to."

"Then don't think of me," retorted Miss Havisham.

"Very easily said!" remarked Camilla, amiably repressing a sob, while a hitch came into her upper lip, and her tears overflowed. "Raymond is a witness what ginger and sal volatile[7] I am obliged to take in the night. Raymond is a witness what nervous jerkings I have in my legs. Chokings and nervous jerkings, however, are nothing new to me when I think with anxiety of those I love. If I could be less affectionate and sensitive, I should have a better digestion and an iron set of nerves. I am sure I wish it could be so. But as to not thinking of you in the night—The idea!" Here, a burst of tears.

The Raymond referred to, I understood to be the gentleman present, and him I understood to be Mr. Camilla. He came to the rescue at this point, and said in a consolatory and complimentary voice, "Camilla, my dear, it is well known that your family feelings are gradually undermining you to the extent of making one of your legs shorter than the other."

"I am not aware," observed the grave lady whose voice I had heard but once, "that to think of any person is to make a great claim upon that person, my dear."

Miss Sarah Pocket, whom I now saw to be a little dry brown corrugated old woman, with a small face that might have been made of walnut-shells, and a large mouth like a cat's without the whiskers, supported this position by saying, "No, indeed, my dear. Hem!"

"Thinking is easy enough," said the grave lady.

"What is easier, you know?" assented Miss Sarah Pocket.

"Oh yes, yes!" cried Camilla, whose fermenting feelings appeared to rise from her legs to her bosom. "It's all very true! It's a weakness to be so affectionate, but I can't help it. No doubt my health would be much better if it was otherwise. Still I wouldn't change my disposition if I could. It's the cause of much suffering, but it's a consolation to know I possess it, when I wake up in the night." Here another burst of feeling.

Miss Havisham and I had never stopped all this time, but kept going round and round the room: now, brushing against the skirts of the visitors, and now giving them the whole length of the dismal chamber.

"There's Matthew!" said Camilla. "Never mixing with any natural ties, never coming here to see how Miss Havisham is! I have taken to the sofa with my staylace cut,[8] and have lain there hours, insensible, with my head over the side, and my hair all down, and my feet I don't know where——"

("Much higher than your head, my love," said Mr. Camilla.)

"I have gone off into that state, hours and hours, on account of Matthew's strange and inexplicable conduct, and nobody has thanked me."

"Really I must say I should think not!" interposed the grave lady.

"You see, my dear," added Miss Sarah Pocket (a blandly vicious personage), "the question to put to yourself is, who did you expect to thank you, my love?"

"Without expecting any thanks, or anything of the sort," resumed Camilla, "I have remained in that state, hours and hours, and Raymond is a witness of the extent to which I have choked, and what the total inefficacy of ginger has been, and I have been heard at the pianoforte-tuner's across the street, where the poor mistaken children have even supposed it to be pigeons cooing at a distance—and now to be told——" Here Camilla put her hand to her throat, and began to be quite chemical as to the formation of new combinations there.

7. Aromatic mixture used in smelling salts. Ginger cures indigestion; sal volatile, migraines.
8. Dr. Johnson: a "kind of stiff waistcoat made of whalebone, worn by ladies."

When this same Matthew was mentioned, Miss Havisham stopped me and
herself, and stood looking at the speaker. This change had a great influence
in bringing Camilla's chemistry to a sudden end.

"Matthew will come and see me at last," said Miss Havisham, sternly,
"when I am laid on that table. That will be his place—there," striking the
table with her stick, "at my head! And yours will be there! And your husband's
there! And Sarah Pocket's there! And Georgiana's there![9] Now you all know
where to take your stations when you come to feast upon me. And now go!"

At the mention of each name, she had struck the table with her stick in a
new place. She now said, "Walk me, walk me!" and we went on again.   10

"I suppose there's nothing to be done," exclaimed Camilla, "but comply
and depart. It's something to have seen the object of one's love and duty, for
even so short a time. I shall think of it with a melancholy satisfaction when
I wake up in the night. I wish Matthew could have that comfort, but he sets
it at defiance. I am determined not to make a display of my feelings, but it's
very hard to be told one wants to feast on one's relations—as if one was a
Giant[1]—and to be told to go. The bare idea!"

Mr. Camilla interposing, as Mrs. Camilla laid her hand upon her heaving
bosom, that lady assumed an unnatural fortitude of manner which I supposed
to be expressive of an intention to drop and choke when out of view, and kiss-   20
ing her hand to Miss Havisham, was escorted forth. Sarah Pocket and Georgiana contended who should remain last; but, Sarah was too knowing to be
outdone, and ambled round Georgiana with that artful slipperiness, that the
latter was obliged to take precedence. Sarah Pocket then made her separate effect of departing with "Bless you, Miss Havisham dear!" and with a smile of
forgiving pity on her walnut-shell countenance for the weaknesses of the rest.

While Estella was away lighting them down, Miss Havisham still walked
with her hand on my shoulder, but more and more slowly. At last she stopped
before the fire, and said, after muttering and looking at it some seconds:

"This is my birthday, Pip."   30

I was going to wish her many happy returns, when she lifted her stick.

"I don't suffer it to be spoken of. I don't suffer those who were here just
now, or any one, to speak of it. They come here on the day, but they dare
not refer to it."

Of course I made no further effort to refer to it.

"On this day of the year, long before you were born, this heap of decay,"
stabbing with her crutched stick at the pile of cobwebs on the table but not
touching it, "was brought here. It and I have worn away together. The mice

9. How are these people related anyway? In chapter 22, Herbert identifies his father as Miss Havisham's
cousin; in chapter 23, Camilla is identified as his sister and Georgina as his cousin. Presumably Sara is another
sister of his: in MS chapter 29, Pip, in speaking to her about Matthew, tells her: "Your brother and
family are very well." (But this sounds too chummy; so Pip corrects himself: "Mr. Pocket and family
are very well.") Very likely all three women are cousins of Havisham's; but as a writer in *The Dickensian* (20 [1924]: 217–18) notes, the word "cousin" could be extended to embrace more distant
relatives and was often used as a term of familiarity.

1. In the Olympian creation myth, after castrating his father, Uranus, Kronos—to keep one of his own
sons from taking charge in turn—annually swallowed the children he fathered on his sister Rhea. But
at the birth of Zeus, Rhea tricked him into eating not Zeus but a diapered stone. As cupbearer at
Kronos's court, Zeus plied his father with a concoction of salt and honey that induced him to vomit
up the other children, and with the aid of his disgorged brothers Hades and Poseidon he killed Kronos
with a thunderbolt. But the reference may be, less ornately, to the story of Jack the Giant Killer.
Nothing about the parenthetical Giant in the MS.

have gnawed at it, and sharper teeth than teeth of mice have gnawed at me."

She held the head of her stick against her heart as she stood looking at the table; she in her once white dress, all yellow and withered; the once white cloth all yellow and withered; everything around, in a state to crumble under a touch.

"When the ruin is complete," said she, with a ghastly look, "and when they lay me dead in my bride's dress on the bride's table—which shall be done, and which will be the finished curse upon him—so much the better if it is done on this day!"

She stood looking at the table as if she stood looking at her own figure 10 lying there. I remained quiet. Estella returned, and she too remained quiet. It seemed to me that we continued thus for a long time. In the heavy air of the room, and the heavy darkness that brooded in its remoter corners, I even had an alarming fancy that Estella and I would presently begin to decay.

At length, not coming out of her distraught state by degrees, but in an instant, Miss Havisham said, "Let me see you two play at cards; why have you not begun?" With that, we returned to her room, and sat down as before; I was beggared, as before; and again, as before, Miss Havisham watched us all the time, directed my attention to Estella's beauty, and made me notice it the more by trying her jewels on Estella's breast and hair.   20

Estella, for her part, likewise treated me as before; except that she did not condescend to speak. When we had played some half-dozen games, a day was appointed for my return, and I was taken down into the yard to be fed in the former dog-like manner. There, too, I was again left to wander about as I liked.

It is not much to the purpose whether a gate in that garden wall which I had scrambled up to peep over on the last occasion was, on that last occasion, open or shut. Enough that I saw no gate then, and that I saw one now. As it stood open, and as I knew that Estella had let the visitors out—for, she had returned with the keys in her hand—I strolled into the garden and strolled all over it. It was quite a wilderness, and there were old melon-frames and 30 cucumber-frames[2] in it, which seemed in their decline to have produced a spontaneous growth of weak attempts at pieces of old hats and boots, with now and then a weedy offshoot into the likeness of a battered saucepan.

When I had exhausted the garden, and a greenhouse with nothing in it but a fallen-down grape-vine and some bottles, I found myself in the dismal corner upon which I had looked out of window. Never questioning for a moment that the house was now empty, I looked in at another window, and found myself, to my great surprise, exchanging a broad stare with a pale young gentleman with red eyelids and light hair.

This pale young gentleman quickly disappeared, and reappeared beside 40 me. He had been at his books when I had found myself staring at him, and I now saw that he was inky.

"Halloa!" said he, "young fellow!"

Halloa being a general observation which I have usually observed to be best answered by itself, I said "Halloa!" politely omitting young fellow.

"Who let *you* in?" said he.

"Miss Estella."

---

2. Low glass-covered boxes for the planting of seedlings.

"Who gave you leave to prowl about?"

"Miss Estella."

"Come and fight," said the pale young gentleman.

What could I do but follow him? I have often asked myself the question since: but, what else could I do? His manner was so final, and I was so astonished, that I followed where he led, as if I had been under a spell.

"Stop a minute, though," he said, wheeling round before we had gone many paces. "I ought to give you a reason for fighting, too. There it is!" In a most irritating manner he instantly slapped his hands against one another, daintily flung one of his legs up behind him, pulled my hair, slapped his 10 hands again, dipped his head, and butted it into my stomach.

The bull-like proceeding last mentioned, besides that it was unquestionably to be regarded in the light of a liberty, was particularly disagreeable just after bread and meat. I therefore hit out at him and was going to hit out again, when he said, "Aha! Would you?" and began dancing backwards and forwards in a manner quite unparalleled within my limited experience.

"Laws of the game!" said he. Here, he skipped from his left leg on to his right. "Regular rules!"[3] Here, he skipped from his right leg on to his left. "Come to the ground, and go through the preliminaries!" Here, he dodged backwards and forwards, and did all sorts of things while I looked helplessly 20 at him.

I was secretly afraid of him when I saw him so dexterous; but, I felt morally and physically convinced that his light head of hair could have had no business in the pit of my stomach, and that I had a right to consider it irrelevant when so obtruded on my attention. Therefore, I followed him without a word, to a retired nook of the garden formed by the junction of two walls and screened by some rubbish. On his asking me if I was satisfied with the ground, and on my replying Yes, he begged my leave to absent himself for a moment, and quickly returned with a bottle of water and a sponge dipped in vinegar. "Available for both," he said, placing these against the wall. And then fell to 30 pulling off, not only his jacket and waistcoat, but his shirt too, in a manner at once light-hearted, business-like, and bloodthirsty.

Although he did not look very healthy—having pimples on his face, and a breaking out on his mouth—these dreadful preparations quite appalled me. I judged him to be about my own age, but he was much taller, and he had a way of spinning himself about that was full of appearance.[4] For the rest, he was a young gentleman in a grey suit (when not denuded for battle), with his elbows, knees, wrists, and heels, considerably in advance of the rest of him as to development.

My heart failed me when I saw him squaring at me with every demonstra- 40 tion of mechanical nicety and eyeing my anatomy as if he were minutely choosing his bone. I never have been so surprised in my life, as I was when

---

3. Since we are told that Herbert "second[s] himself according to form," the "regular rules" by which he abides very likely preceded the London Prize Ring rules of 1838, which specified that "each man shall be attended to the ring by two seconds and a bottle-holder." The seconds were obliged to sponge "their principal"; they were not to "interfere, advise, or direct the adversary of their principal" and were bound to "refrain from all offensive and irritating expressions." If, on the other hand, Pip implies that Herbert had to "second himself" in the absence of seconds mandated by the London rules, the match would have to take place after 1838, a date that is difficult to square with the chronology of the book. Either way, Pip and Herbert of course fought bareknuckled; the Marquess of Queensberry rules date from 1867.

4. Shifty; pretending to be stronger than he is.

I let out the first blow, and saw him lying on his back looking up at me with a bloody nose and his face exceedingly fore-shortened.

But, he was on his feet directly, and after sponging himself with a great show of dexterity began squaring again. The second greatest surprise I have ever had in my life was seeing him on his back again, looking up at me out of a black eye.

His spirit inspired me with great respect. He seemed to have no strength, and he never once hit me hard, and he was always knocked down; but, he would be up again in a moment, sponging himself or drinking out of the water-bottle, with the greatest satisfaction in seconding himself according to form, and then came at me with an air and a show that made me believe he really was going to do for me at last. He got heavily bruised, for I am sorry to record that the more I hit him, the harder I hit him; but, he came up again and again and again, until at last he got a bad fall with the back of his head against the wall. Even after that crisis in our affairs, he got up and turned round and round confusedly a few times, not knowing where I was; but finally went on his knees to his sponge and threw it up: at the same time panting out, "That means you have won."

He seemed so brave and innocent, that although I had not proposed the contest I felt but a gloomy satisfaction in my victory. Indeed, I go so far as to hope that I regarded myself while dressing as a species of savage young wolf, or other wild beast. However, I got dressed, darkly wiping my sanguinary face at intervals, and I said, "Can I help you?" and he said "No thankee," and I said "Good afternoon," and *he* said "Same to you."

When I got into the court-yard, I found Estella waiting with the keys. But, she neither asked me where I had been, nor why I had kept her waiting; and there was a bright flush upon her face, as though something had happened to delight her. Instead of going straight to the gate, too, she stepped back into the passage, and beckoned me.

"Come here! You may kiss me, if you like."

I kissed her cheek as she turned it to me. I think I would have gone through a great deal to kiss her cheek. But, I felt that the kiss was given to the coarse common boy as a piece of money might have been, and that it was worth nothing.

What with the birthday visitors, and what with the cards, and what with the fight, my stay had lasted so long, that when I neared home the light on the spit of sand off the point on the marshes was gleaming against a black night-sky, and Joe's furnace was flinging a path of fire across the road.

Chapter XII.

MY mind grew very uneasy on the subject of the pale young gentleman. The more I thought of the fight, and recalled the pale young gentleman on his back in various stages of puffy and incrimsoned countenance, the more certain it appeared that something would be done to me. I felt that the pale young gentleman's blood was on my head, and that the Law would avenge it. Without having any definite idea of the penalties I had incurred, it was clear to me that village boys could not go stalking about the country, ravaging the houses of gentlefolks and pitching into the studious youth of England, without laying themselves open to severe punishment. For some days, I even kept close at home, and looked out at the kitchen door with the greatest caution and trepidation before going on an errand, lest the officers of the County Jail should pounce upon me. The pale young gentleman's nose had stained my trousers, and I tried to wash out that evidence of my guilt in the dead of night. I had cut my knuckles against the pale young gentleman's teeth, and I twisted my imagination into a thousand tangles, as I devised incredible ways of accounting for that damnatory circumstance when I should   10 be haled before the Judges.

When the day came round for my return to the scene of the deed of violence, my terrors reached their height. Whether myrmidons[1] of Justice, specially sent down from London, would be lying in ambush behind the gate? Whether Miss Havisham, preferring to take personal vengeance for an outrage done to her house, might rise in those grave-clothes of hers, draw a pistol, and shoot me dead? Whether suborned[2] boys—a numerous band of mercenaries—might be engaged to fall upon me in the brewery, and knock me about until I was no more? It was high testimony to my confidence in the spirit of the pale young gentleman, that I never imagined *him* accessory to   20 these retaliations; they always came into my mind as the acts of injudicious relatives of his, goaded on by the state of his visage and an indignant sympathy with the family features.

However, go to Miss Havisham's I must, and go I did. And behold! nothing came of the late struggle. It was not alluded to in any way, and no pale young gentleman was to be discovered on the premises. I found the same gate open, and I explored the garden, and even looked in at the windows of the detached house; but, my view was suddenly stopped by the closed shutters within, and all was lifeless. Only in the corner where the combat had taken place, could I detect any evidence of the young gentleman's existence. There were traces   30 of his gore in that spot, and I covered them with garden-mould from the eye of man.

On the broad landing between Miss Havisham's own room and that other room in which the long table was laid out, I saw a garden-chair—a light chair on wheels, that you pushed from behind. It had been placed there since my last visit, and I entered, that same day, on a regular occupation of pushing Miss Havisham in this chair (when she was tired of walking with her hand upon my shoulder) round her own room, and across the landing, and round the other room. Over and over and over again, we would make these journeys, and sometimes they would last as long as three hours at a stretch. I insensibly   40 fall into a general mention of these journeys as numerous, because it was at once settled that I should return every alternate day at noon for these purposes, and because I am now going to sum up a period of at least eight or ten months.

1. Literally, ant people (*myrmex*, Gr. ant), from the myth in which Aeacus begs his father, Zeus, to populate his plague-stricken island by transforming its ants into men. In the *Iliad*, the loyal island-subjects who sail with Aeacus's grandson Achilles to Troy; by extension, any loyal (or servile) follower or brutal henchman. By Pip's time almost always a put-down of the police; thus Byron's reference to the "Bow-street Myrmidons" in his *English Bards and Scotch Reviewers* (1819), 1.467.
2. Incited or bribed to commit a crime.

As we began to be more used to one another, Miss Havisham talked more to me, and asked me such questions as what had I learnt and what was I going to be? I told her I was going to be apprenticed to Joe, I believed; and I enlarged upon my knowing nothing and wanting to know everything, in the hope that she might offer some help towards that desirable end. But, she did not; on the contrary, she seemed to prefer my being ignorant. Neither did she ever give me any money—or anything but my daily dinner—nor ever stipulate that I should be paid for my services.

Estella was always about, and always let me in and out, but never told me I might kiss her again. Sometimes, she would coldly tolerate me; sometimes, she would condescend to me; sometimes, she would be quite familiar with me; sometimes, she would tell me energetically that she hated me. Miss Havisham would often ask me in a whisper, or when we were alone, "Does she grow prettier and prettier, Pip?" And when I said yes (for indeed she did), would seem to enjoy it greedily. Also, when we played at cards Miss Havisham would look on, with a miserly relish of Estella's moods, whatever they were. And sometimes, when her moods were so many and so contradictory of one another that I was puzzled what to say or do, Miss Havisham would embrace her with lavish fondness, murmuring something in her ear that sounded like "Break their hearts, my pride and hope, break their hearts and have no mercy!"

There was a song Joe used to hum fragments of at the forge, of which the burden was Old Clem.[3] This was not a very ceremonious way of rendering homage to a patron saint; but, I believe Old Clem stood in that relation towards smiths. It was a song that imitated the measure of beating upon iron, and was a mere lyrical excuse for the introduction of Old Clem's respected name. Thus, you were to hammer boys round—Old Clem! With a thump and a sound—Old Clem! Beat it out, beat it out—Old Clem! With a clink for the stout—Old Clem! Blow the fire, blow the fire—Old Clem! Roaring dryer, soaring higher—Old Clem! One day soon after the appearance of the chair, Miss Havisham suddenly saying to me, with the impatient movement of her fingers, "There, there, there! Sing!" I was surprised into crooning this ditty as I pushed her over the floor. It happened so to catch her fancy, that she took it up in a low brooding voice as if she were singing in her sleep. After that, it became customary with us to have it as we moved about, and Estella would often join in; though the whole strain was so subdued, even when there were three of us, that it made less noise in the grim old house than the lightest breath of wind.

What could I become with these surroundings? How could my character fail to be influenced by them? Is it to be wondered at if my thoughts were dazed, as my eyes were, when I came out into the natural light from the misty yellow rooms?

Perhaps, I might have told Joe about the pale young gentleman, if I had not previously been betrayed into those enormous inventions to which I have confessed. Under the circumstances, I felt that Joe could hardly fail to discern in the pale young gentleman, an appropriate passenger to be put into the

3. To honor their patron saint, Pope Clement I (pontificate 88?–102?, third in succession to Peter), the blacksmiths of Chatham Dockyard staged an annual parade on St. Clement's Day (November 23); there Dickens presumably picked up the tune as a boy.

black velvet coach; therefore, I said nothing of him. Besides: that shrinking from having Miss Havisham and Estella discussed, which had come upon me in the beginning, grew much more potent as time went on. I reposed complete confidence in no one but Biddy; but, I told poor Biddy everything. Why it came natural to me to do so, and why Biddy had a deep concern in everything I told her, I did not know then, though I think I know now.

Meanwhile, councils went on in the kitchen at home, fraught with almost insupportable aggravation to my exasperated spirit. That ass, Pumblechook, used often to come over of a night for the purpose of discussing my prospects with my sister; and I really do believe (to this hour with less penitence than I ought to feel), that if these hands could have taken a linchpin out of his chaise-cart, they would have done it. The miserable man was a man of that confined stolidity of mind, that he could not discuss my prospects without having me before him—as it were, to operate upon—and he would drag me up from my stool (usually by the collar) where I was quiet in a corner, and, putting me before the fire as if I were going to be cooked, would begin by saying, "Now, Mum, here is this boy! Here is this boy which you brought up by hand. Hold up your head, boy, and be for ever grateful unto them which so did do. Now, Mum, with respections to this boy!" And then he would rumple my hair the wrong way—which from my earliest remembrance, as already hinted, I have in my soul denied the right of any fellow-creature to do—and would hold me before him by the sleeve: a spectacle of imbecility only to be equalled by himself.

Then, he and my sister would pair off in such nonsensical speculations about Miss Havisham, and about what she would do with me and for me, that I used to want—quite painfully—to burst into spiteful tears, fly at Pumblechook, and pummel him all over. In these dialogues, my sister spoke of me as if she were morally wrenching one of my teeth out at every reference; while Pumblechook himself, self-constituted my patron, would sit supervising me with a depreciatory eye, like the architect of my fortunes who thought himself engaged in a very unremunerative job.

In these discussions, Joe bore no part. But, he was often talked at, while they were in progress, by reason of Mrs. Joe's perceiving that he was not favourable to my being taken from the forge. I was fully old enough now, to be apprenticed to Joe;[4] and when Joe sat with the poker on his knees thoughtfully raking out the ashes between the lower bars, my sister would so distinctly construe that innocent action into opposition on his part, that she would dive at him, take the poker out of his hands, shake him, and put it away. There was a most irritating end to every one of these debates. All in a moment, with nothing to lead up to it, my sister would stop herself in a yawn, and catching sight of me as it were incidentally, would swoop upon me, with "Come!

---

4. Fourteen. Pip's statement earlier in the chapter that "a period of at least eight or ten months" is being summed up needn't perhaps be taken literally; beyond marking Pip's age at three or four given points, Dickens is pleasantly vague in his signals, and his very imprecision suggests the equally plausible inference that years, not months, have passed since Pip's first summons to Satis House. Against this, it has been argued that Dickens simply didn't bother with such technicalities as the legal age of apprentices and meant Pip to be considerably younger than fourteen at this point. At worst, this raises the objection that Pip's moody confidences to Biddy in chapter 16, which occur one year later, sound oddly precocious in the mouth of a ten-year-old; fifteen or sixteen would sound more likely.

There's enough of *you*! *You* get along to bed; *you've* given trouble enough
for one night, I hope!" As if I had besought them as a favour to bother my
life out.

We went on in this way for a long time, and it seemed likely that we should
continue to go on in this way for a long time, when, one day Miss Havisham
stopped short as she and I were walking, she leaning on my shoulder; and
said with some displeasure:

"You are growing tall, Pip!"

I thought it best to hint, through the medium of a meditative look, that
this might be occasioned by circumstances over which I had no control.   10

She said no more at the time; but, she presently stopped and looked at me
again; and presently again; and after that, looked frowning and moody. On
the next day of my attendance when our usual exercise was over, and I had
landed her at her dressing-table, she stayed me with a movement of her
impatient fingers:

"Tell me the name again of that blacksmith of yours."

"Joe Gargery, ma'am."

"Meaning the master you were to be apprenticed to?"

"Yes, Miss Havisham."

"You had better be apprenticed at once. Would Gargery come here with   20
you, and bring your indentures, do you think?"[5]

I signified that I had no doubt he would take it as an honour to be asked.

"Then let him come."

"At any particular time, Miss Havisham?"

"There, there! I know nothing about times. Let him come soon, and come
alone with you."

When I got home at night, and delivered this message for Joe, my sister
"went on the Rampage," in a more alarming degree than at any previous
period. She asked me and Joe whether we supposed she was door-mats under
our feet, and how we dared to use her so, and what company we graciously   30
thought she *was* fit for? When she had exhausted a torrent of such inquiries,
she threw a candlestick at Joe, burst into a loud sobbing, got out the
dustpan—which was always a very bad sign—put on her coarse apron, and
began cleaning up to a terrible extent. Not satisfied with a dry cleaning, she
took to a pail and scrubbing-brush, and cleaned us out of house and home,
so that we stood shivering in the back yard. It was ten o'clock at night before
we ventured to creep in again, and then she asked Joe why he hadn't married
a Negress Slave at once? Joe offered no answer, poor fellow, but stood feeling
his whisker and looking dejectedly at me, as if he thought it really might have
been a better speculation.[6]   40

---

5. The terms governing apprenticeships were laid down by the Statute of Artificers in 1563: an apprenticeship period to last seven years, normally from ages fourteen to twenty-one; the drawing up of formal
indentures—a written contract binding the apprentice to the master, so called because its edges were
indented to prevent forgery—and the payment of a premium from the apprentice's parents or guardians
to the master to defray the expenses of training and maintenance. (Pip would be especially sensitive
to a passage in the *Apprentice's Guide*, a popular manual of the day, in which the aspirant is "reminded
of the fate of George Barnwell, should he have unsuitable female acquaintances"—on this see chapter
15.) Though the apprenticeship clause of 1563 was repealed in 1814, a lot of the earlier customs
lingered throughout the early years of the nineteenth century. Pumblechook's roster of prohibitions
appears in chapter 13.
6. Bargain.

Chapter XIII.

IT was a trial to my feelings, on the next day but one, to see Joe arraying himself in his Sunday clothes to accompany me to Miss Havisham's. However, as he thought his court-suit[1] necessary to the occasion, it was not for me to tell him that he looked far better in his working dress; the rather, because I knew he made himself so dreadfully uncomfortable, entirely on my account, and that it was for me he pulled up his shirt-collar so very high behind, that it made the hair on the crown of his head stand up like a tuft of feathers.

At breakfast-time my sister declared her intention of going to town with us, and being left at Uncle Pumblechook's, and called for "when we had done 10 with our fine ladies"—a way of putting the case, from which Joe appeared inclined to augur the worst. The forge was shut up for the day, and Joe inscribed in chalk upon the door (as it was his custom to do on the very rare occasions when he was not at work) the monosyllable HOUT, accompanied by a sketch of an arrow supposed to be flying in the direction he had taken.

We walked to town, my sister leading the way in a very large beaver bonnet, and carrying a basket like the Great Seal of England in plaited straw, a pair of pattens,[2] a spare shawl, and an umbrella, though it was a fine bright day. I am not quite clear whether these articles were carried penitentially or ostentatiously; but, I rather think they were displayed as articles of property— 20 much as Cleopatra or any other sovereign lady on the Rampage might exhibit her wealth in a pageant or procession.[3]

When we came to Pumblechook's, my sister bounced in and left us. As it was almost noon, Joe and I held straight on to Miss Havisham's house. Estella opened the gate as usual, and, the moment she appeared, Joe took his hat off and stood weighing it by the brim in both his hands: as if he had some urgent reason in his mind for being particular to half a quarter of an ounce.

Estella took no notice of either of us, but led us the way that I knew so well. I followed next to her, and Joe came last. When I looked back at Joe in the long passage, he was still weighing his hat with the greatest care, and 30 was coming after us in long strides on the tips of his toes.

Estella told me we were both to go in, so I took Joe by the coat-cuff and conducted him into Miss Havisham's presence. She was seated at her dressing-table, and looked round at us immediately.

"Oh!" said she to Joe. "You are the husband of the sister of this boy?"

I could hardly have imagined dear old Joe looking so unlike himself or so like some extraordinary bird; standing, as he did, speechless, with his tuft of feathers ruffled, and his mouth open, as if he wanted a worm.

"You are the husband," repeated Miss Havisham, "of the sister of this boy?"

It was very aggravating; but, throughout the interview Joe persisted in ad- 40 dressing Me instead of Miss Havisham.

---

1. Clothes worn on a visit to royalty: Joe's Sunday's best.
2. Elevator boots: overshoes or clogs with thick wooden soles raised a few inches above ground by means of a metal support to keep the feet from mud or wet. "Great Seal of England": The Lord Chancellor's seal, required on all legal documents—the Lord Chancellor is the highest judicial functionary in Britain and chairman of the House of Lords. Pip's analogy is to the pouch in which the seal is carried.
3. The Nubian Queen (69–30 B.C.), as Shakespeare describes her, is remarkable equally for her sovereign rages and her gorgeous regalia.

I present Joe to Miss Havisham.

Frederic W. Pailthorpe, "I Present Joe to Miss Havisham"

"Which I meantersay, Pip," Joe now observed in a manner that was at once expressive of forcible argumentation, strict confidence, and great politeness, "as I hup and married your sister, and I were at the time what you might call (if you was anyways inclined) a single man."

"Well!" said Miss Havisham. "And you have reared the boy, with the intention of taking him for your apprentice; is that so, Mr. Gargery?"

"You know, Pip," replied Joe, "as you and me were ever friends, and it were look'd for'ard to betwixt us, as being calc'lated to lead to larks. Not but what, Pip, if you had ever made objections to the business—such as its being open to black and sut,[4] or such-like—not but what they would have been attended to, don't you see?"

"Has the boy," said Miss Havisham, "ever made any objection? Does he like the trade?"

"Which it is well beknown to yourself, Pip," returned Joe, strengthening his former mixture of argumentation, confidence, and politeness, "that it were the wish of your own hart." (I saw the idea suddenly break upon him that he would adapt his epitaph to the occasion, before he went on to say) "And there weren't no objection on your part, and Pip it were the great wish of your hart!"

It was quite in vain for me to endeavour to make him sensible that he ought to speak to Miss Havisham. The more I made faces and gestures to him to do it, the more confidential, argumentative, and polite, he persisted in being to Me.

"Have you brought his indentures with you?" asked Miss Havisham.

"Well, Pip, you know," replied Joe, as if that were a little unreasonable, "you yourself see me put 'em in my 'at, and therefore you know as they are here." With which he took them out, and gave them, not to Miss Havisham, but to me. I am afraid I was ashamed of the dear good fellow—I *know* I was ashamed of him—when I saw that Estella stood at the back of Miss Havisham's chair, and that her eyes laughed mischievously. I took the indentures out of his hand and gave them to Miss Havisham.

"You expected," said Miss Havisham, as she looked them over, "no premium with the boy?"

"Joe!" I remonstrated; for he made no reply at all. "Why don't you answer——"

"Pip," returned Joe, cutting me short as if he were hurt, "which I meantersay that were not a question requiring a answer betwixt yourself and me, and which you know the answer to be full well No. You know it to be No, Pip, and wherefore should I say it?"

Miss Havisham glanced at him as if she understood what he really was, better than I had thought possible, seeing what he was there; and took up a little bag from the table beside her.

"Pip has earned a premium here," she said, "and here it is. There are five-and-twenty guineas in this bag.[5] Give it to your master, Pip."

As if he were absolutely out of his mind with the wonder awakened in him

---

4. Dirt and soot.
5. In the ensuing conversation guineas and pounds are used interchangeably. Either way, the riches Joe takes it for: roughly the equivalent of his half-yearly earnings. (Patrick Colquhoun's *Treatise on Indigence*, published about ten years before this—in 1806—estimates the average annual income for blacksmiths at £55.) The guinea, a coin worth one pound and one shilling, ceased to be minted in 1813 and has been out of general circulation since 1817. See Sadrin's discussion below, pp. 540–42.

by her strange figure and the strange room, Joe, even at this pass, persisted in addressing me.

"This is wery liberal on your part, Pip," said Joe, "and it is as such received and grateful welcome, though never looked for, far nor near nor nowheres. And now, old chap," said Joe, conveying to me a sensation, first of burning and then of freezing, for I felt as if that familiar expression were applied to Miss Havisham; "and now, old chap, may we do our duty! May you and me do our duty, both on us by one and another, and by them which your liberal present—have—conweyed—to be—for the satisfaction of mind—of—them as never—" here Joe showed that he felt he had fallen into frightful difficulties, until he triumphantly rescued himself with the words, "and from myself far be it!" These words had such a round and convincing sound for him that he said them twice.

"Good-by, Pip!" said Miss Havisham. "Let them out, Estella."

"Am I to come again, Miss Havisham?" I asked.

"No. Gargery is your master now. Gargery! One word!"

Thus calling him back as I went out of the door, I heard her say to Joe, in a distinct emphatic voice, "The boy has been a good boy here, and that is his reward. Of course, as an honest man, you will expect no other and no more."

How Joe got out of the room, I have never been able to determine; but, I know that when he did get out he was steadily proceeding up-stairs instead of coming down, and was deaf to all remonstrances until I went after him and laid hold of him. In another minute we were outside the gate, and it was locked, and Estella was gone.

When we stood in the daylight alone again, Joe backed up against a wall, and said to me, "Astonishing!" And there he remained so long, saying "Astonishing!" at intervals, so often, that I began to think his senses were never coming back. At length he prolonged his remark into "Pip, I do assure you that this is as-TON-ishing!" and so, by degrees, became conversational and able to walk away.

I have reason to think that Joe's intellects were brightened by the encounter they had passed through, and that on our way to Pumblechook's he invented a subtle and deep design. My reason is to be found in what took place in Mr. Pumblechook's parlour: where, on our presenting ourselves, my sister sat in conference with that detested seedsman.

"Well?" cried my sister, addressing us both at once. "And what's happened to you? I wonder you condescend to come back to such poor society as this, I am sure I do!"

"Miss Havisham," said Joe, with a fixed look at me, like an effort of remembrance, "made it wery partick'ler that we should give her—were it compliments or respects, Pip?"

"Compliments," I said.

"Which that were my own belief," assented Joe—"her compliments to Mrs. J. Gargery——"

"Much good they'll do me!" observed my sister; but rather gratified too.

"And wishing," pursued Joe, with another fixed look at me, like another effort of remembrance, "that the state of Miss Havisham's elth were sitch as would have—allowed, were it, Pip?"

"Of her having the pleasure," I added.

"Of ladies' company," said Joe. And drew a long breath.

"Well!" cried my sister, with a mollified glance at Mr. Pumblechook. "She might have had the politeness to send that message at first, but it's better late than never. And what did she give young Rantipole[6] here?"

"She giv' him," said Joe, "nothing."

Mrs. Joe was going to break out, but Joe went on.

"What she giv'," said Joe, "she giv' to his friends. 'And by his friends,' were her explanation, 'I mean into the hands of his sister Mrs. J. Gargery.' Them were her words; 'Mrs. J. Gargery.' She mayn't have know'd," added Joe, with an appearance of reflection, "whether it were Joe, or Jorge."   10

My sister looked at Pumblechook: who smoothed the elbows of his wooden arm-chair, and nodded at her and at the fire, as if he had known all about it beforehand.

"And how much have you got?" asked my sister, laughing. Positively, laughing!

"What would present company say to ten pound?" demanded Joe.

"They'd say," returned my sister, curtly, "pretty well. Not too much, but pretty well."

"It's more than that, then," said Joe.

That fearful Impostor, Pumblechook, immediately nodded, and said, as he   20 rubbed the arms of his chair: "It's more than that, Mum."

"Why, you don't mean to say——" began my sister.

"Yes I do, Mum," said Pumblechook; "but wait a bit. Go on, Joseph. Good in you! Go on!"

"What would present company say," proceeded Joe, "to twenty pound?"

"Handsome would be the word," returned my sister.

"Well, then," said Joe, "It's more than twenty pound."

That abject Hypocrite, Pumblechook, nodded again, and said, with a patronising laugh, "It's more than that, Mum. Good again! Follow her up, Joseph!"   30

"Then to make an end of it," said Joe, delightedly handing the bag to my sister; "it's five-and-twenty pound."

"It's five-and-twenty pound, Mum," echoed that basest of swindlers, Pumblechook, rising to shake hands with her; "and it's no more than your merits (as I said when my opinion was asked), and I wish you joy of the money!"

If the Villain had stopped here, his case would have been sufficiently awful, but he blackened his guilt by proceeding to take me into custody, with a right of patronage that left all his former criminality far behind.

"Now you see, Joseph and wife," said Pumblechook, as he took me by the   40 arm above the elbow, "I am one of them that always go right through what they've begun. This boy must be bound, out of hand.[7] That's *my* way. Bound out of hand."

---

6. Blusterer; literally, raving head. Dickens's readers would have recognized this as a nickname for Napoleon III, who was much in the news in 1860: waging war on Austria in support of Italian independence (and then concluding a secret treaty with her), while maintaining a garrison at Rome to defend Pius IX from the Italians. Queen Victoria thought him "the *universal disturber* of the *world*" (italics hers). But Rantipole is also the family name of two wicked children in Mary Butt Sherwood's scary juvenile classic, *The History of the Fairchild Family* (1818). (The term appears in a later edition than the one from which the excerpt below, pp. 585–88, is taken.)

7. Without delay.

"Goodness knows, Uncle Pumblechook," said my sister (grasping the money), "we're deeply beholden to you."

"Never mind me, Mum," returned that diabolical corn-chandler. "A pleasure's a pleasure, all the world over. But this boy, you know; we must have him bound. I said I'd see to it—to tell you the truth."

The Justices were sitting in the Town Hall near at hand,[8] and we at once went over to have me bound apprentice to Joe in the Magisterial presence. I say, we went over, but I was pushed over by Pumblechook, exactly as if I had that moment picked a pocket or fired a rick;[9] indeed, it was the general impression in Court that I had been taken red-handed, for, as Pumblechook shoved me before him through the crowd, I heard some people say, "What's he done?" and others, "He's a young 'un too, but looks bad, don't he?" One person of mild and benevolent aspect even gave me a tract ornamented with a woodcut of a malevolent young man fitted up with a perfect sausage-shop of fetters, and entitled To BE READ IN MY CELL.

The Hall was a queer place, I thought, with higher pews in it than a church—and with people hanging over the pews looking on—and with mighty Justices (one with a powdered head) leaning back in chairs, with folded arms, or taking snuff, or going to sleep, or writing, or reading the newspapers—and with some shining black portraits on the walls, which my unartistic eye regarded as a composition of hardbake and sticking-plaister.[1] Here, in a corner, my indentures were duly signed and attested, and I was "bound;" Mr. Pumblechook holding me all the while as if we had looked in on our way to the scaffold, to have those little preliminaries disposed of.

When we had come out again, and had got rid of the boys who had been put into great spirits by the expectation of seeing me publicly tortured, and who were much disappointed to find that my friends were merely rallying round me, we went back to Pumblechook's. And there my sister became so excited by the twenty-five guineas, that nothing would serve her but we must have a dinner out of that windfall, at the Blue Boar,[2] and that Pumblechook must go over in his chaise-cart, and bring the Hubbles and Mr. Wopsle.

It was agreed to be done; and a most melancholy day I passed. For, it inscrutably appeared to stand to reason, in the minds of the whole company, that I was an excrescence on the entertainment. And to make it worse, they all asked me from time to time—in short, whenever they had nothing else to do—why I didn't enjoy myself. And what could I possibly do then, but say I *was* enjoying myself—when I wasn't?

---

8. The Rochester Guildhall, built in 1687, meeting place of the city council. "Justices": Justices of the Peace, local magistrates, usually unsalaried, who perform routine municipal functions. Dating from 1327, Justices were appointed by the king's special commission to keep the peace; their jurisdiction allowed them to commit offenders to trial and, in cases of minor infractions, to convict and punish. In rural districts, Justices were usually picked from among unsalaried country gentry and acted as judges; in the larger cities, their duties included those of police magistrates.
9. Set fire to a haystack. To appreciate Pip's fantasies in the lines following, one has to remember that during the eighteenth century children under age ten were hanged (on one occasion ten were strung up together as a warning to men and a spectacle to delight the angels); that as late as 1808 a brother and sister aged seven and eleven suffered the same barbarity; and that later still, in 1831, a boy of nine was publicly hanged for arson. The threats to juvenile offenders are spelled out by Jaggers in chapter 51 and in Hawkins's essay, esp. p. 594.
1. Gummed adhesive strips of thin cloth used to cover minor sores. "Hardbake": almond toffee.
2. Modeled on The Royal Victoria and Bull Hotel across the street from the Guildhall. In Pip's day simply The Bull, Princess Victoria having yet to overnight there in 1836, when the flooding of the Medway obstructed her passage across Rochester Bridge. Dickens took the name from The Blue Boar down the street from The Bull.

However, they were grown up and had their own way, and they made the most of it. That swindling Pumblechook, exalted into the beneficent contriver of the whole occasion, actually took the top of the table; and, when he addressed them on the subject of my being bound, and fiendishly congratulated them on my being liable to imprisonment if I played at cards, drank strong liquors, kept late hours or bad company, or indulged in other vagaries which the form of my indentures appeared to contemplate as next to inevitable, he placed me standing on a chair beside him, to illustrate his remarks.

My only other remembrances of the great festival are, That they wouldn't let me go to sleep, but whenever they saw me dropping off, woke me up and 10 told me to enjoy myself. That, rather late in the evening Mr. Wopsle gave us Collins's ode, and threw his blood-stain'd sword in thunder down, with such effect, that a waiter came in and said, "The Commercials underneath sent up their compliments, and it wasn't the Tumbler's Arms."[3] That, they were all in excellent spirits on the road home, and sang O Lady Fair! Mr. Wopsle taking the bass, and asserting with a tremendously strong voice (in reply to the inquisitive bore who leads that piece of music in a most impertinent manner, by wanting to know all about everybody's private affairs) that *he* was the man with his white locks flowing, and that he was upon the whole the weakest pilgrim going.[4]   20

Finally, I remember that when I got into my little bedroom I was truly wretched, and had a strong conviction on me that I should never like Joe's trade. I had liked it once, but once was not now.

★

Chapter XIV.

It is a most miserable thing to feel ashamed of home. There may be black ingratitude in the thing, and the punishment may be retributive and well deserved; but that it is a miserable thing, I can testify.

Home had never been a very pleasant place to me, because of my sister's temper. But, Joe had sanctified it, and I had believed in it. I had believed in the best parlour as a most elegant saloon; I had believed in the front door, as a mysterious portal of the Temple of State whose solemn opening was 30 attended with a sacrifice of roast fowls; I had believed in the kitchen as a chaste though not magnificent apartment; I had believed in the forge as the glowing road to manhood and independence. Within a single year, all this was changed. Now, it was all coarse and common, and I would not have had Miss Havisham and Estella see it on any account.

How much of my ungracious condition of mind may have been my own fault, how much Miss Havisham's, how much my sister's, is now of no mo-

---

3. Hangout for circus performers, or a spot featuring acrobats and circus folks as entertainers. "Commercials": traveling salesmen.
4. Take-off on a popular glee for three voices (Lady Fair, Ancient Pilgrim, Hostess) written and set to music in 1802 by the Irish poet Thomas Moore (1779–1852). "Hostess: 'Oh Lady Fair where art thou roaming / The sun has sunk, the night is coming. . . . And who is the man with his white locks flowing, / Oh Lady Fair where is he going?' " etc. Moore's melodies easily outnumber those of any other tunesmith in Dickens's novels.

ment to me or to any one. The change was made in me; the thing was done. Well or ill done, excusably or inexcusably, it was done.

Once, it had seemed to me that when I should at last roll up my shirt-sleeves and go into the forge, Joe's 'prentice, I should be distinguished and happy. Now the reality was in my hold, I only felt that I was dusty with the dust of small-coal, and that I had a weight upon my daily remembrance to which the anvil was a feather. There have been occasions in my later life (I suppose as in most lives) when I have felt for a time as if a thick curtain had fallen on all its interest and romance, to shut me out from anything save dull endurance any more. Never has that curtain dropped so heavy and blank, as when my way in life lay stretched out straight before me through the newly-entered road of apprenticeship to Joe.[1]

I remember that at a later period of my "time" I used to stand about the churchyard on Sunday evenings when night was falling, comparing my own perspective with the windy marsh view, and making out some likeness between them by thinking how flat and low both were, and how on both there came an unknown way and a dark mist and then the sea. I was quite as dejected on the first working-day of my apprenticeship as in that after-time; but I am glad to know that I never breathed a murmur to Joe while my indentures lasted. It is about the only thing I *am* glad to know of myself in that connexion.

For, though it includes what I proceed to add, all the merit of what I proceed to add was Joe's. It was not because I was faithful, but because Joe was faithful, that I never ran away and went for a soldier or a sailor. It was not because I had a strong sense of the virtue of industry, but because Joe had a strong sense of the virtue of industry, that I worked with tolerable zeal against the grain. It is not possible to know how far the influence of any amiable honest-hearted duty-doing man flies out into the world; but it is very possible to know how it has touched one's self in going by, and I know right well that any good that intermixed itself with my apprenticeship came of plain contented Joe, and not of restlessly aspiring discontented me.

What I wanted, who can say? How can *I* say, when I never knew? What I dreaded was, that in some unlucky hour I, being at my grimiest and commonest, should lift up my eyes and see Estella looking in at one of the wooden windows of the forge. I was haunted by the fear that she would, sooner or later, find me out, with a black face and hands, doing the coarsest part of my work, and would exult over me and despise me. Often after dark, when I was pulling the bellows for Joe and we were singing Old Clem, and when the thought how we used to sing it at Miss Havisham's would seem to show me Estella's face in the fire with her pretty hair fluttering in the wind and her eyes scorning me,—often at such a time I would look towards those panels of black night in the wall which the wooden windows then were, and would fancy that I saw her just drawing her face away, and would believe that she had come at last.

After that, when we went in to supper, the place and the meal would have

1. The foregoing passage recalls the famous passage in *David Copperfield*, chapter 11, in which David, enslaved at the warehouse of Murdstone & Grinby, feels permanently severed from his childhood. Dickens's autobiographical fragment, the source for all later comment on the Warren's Blacking episode on which the Murdstone chapters are based, is given in Forster's biography, 1.2.

a more homely look than ever, and I would feel more ashamed of home than ever in my own ungracious breast.

Chapter XV.

As I was getting too big for Mr. Wopsle's great-aunt's room, my education under that preposterous female terminated. Not, however, until Biddy had imparted to me everything she knew, from the little catalogue of prices, to a comic song she had once bought for a halfpenny. Although the only coherent part of the latter piece of literature were the opening lines,

When I went to Lunnon town sirs,
  Too rul loo rul
  Too rul loo rul
Wasn't I done very brown sirs,
  Too rul loo rul
  Too rul loo rul

—still, in my desire to be wiser, I got this composition by heart with the utmost gravity; nor do I recollect that I questioned its merit, except that I thought (as I still do) the amount of Too rul somewhat in excess of the poetry.[1] In my hunger for information, I made proposals to Mr. Wopsle to bestow some intellectual crumbs upon me: with which he kindly complied. As it turned out, however, that he only wanted me for a dramatic lay-figure,[2] to be contradicted and embraced and wept over and bullied and clutched and stabbed and knocked about in a variety of ways, I soon declined that course of instruction; though not until Mr. Wopsle in his poetic fury had severely mauled me.

Whatever I acquired, I tried to impart to Joe. This statement sounds so well, that I cannot in my conscience let it pass unexplained. I wanted to make Joe less ignorant and common, that he might be worthier of my society and less open to Estella's reproach.

The old Battery out on the marshes was our place of study, and a broken slate and a short piece of slate pencil were our educational implements: to which Joe always added a pipe of tobacco. I never knew Joe to remember anything from one Sunday to another, or to acquire, under my tuition, any piece of information whatever. Yet he would smoke his pipe at the Battery with a far more sagacious air than anywhere else—even with a learned air— as if he considered himself to be advancing immensely. Dear fellow, I hope he did.

It was pleasant and quiet out there with the sails on the river passing beyond the earthwork, and sometimes, when the tide was low, looking as if they belonged to sunken ships that were still sailing on at the bottom of the water. Whenever I watched the vessels standing out[3] to sea with their white sails

1. No single source for this has been found. Probably Dickens's own version of a popular song, "The Astonished Countryman" ("When first I came to London Town") or a music hall duet, "The Time of Day" ("I came up to town scarce six months ago . . . Too ral loo ral loo") or a fantasia on several such pieces. Joe makes the most of the refrain in chapter 27.
2. Wooden model of the human body with movable joints, which artists manipulate to copy its positions in motion. Here Pip obviously serves as Wopsle's dummy.
3. Starting out.

spread, I somehow thought of Miss Havisham and Estella; and whenever the light struck aslant afar off, upon a cloud or sail or green hill-side or water-line, it was just the same.—Miss Havisham and Estella and the strange house and the strange life appeared to have something to do with everything that was picturesque.

One Sunday when Joe, greatly enjoying his pipe, had so plumed himself on being "most awful dull," that I had given him up for the day, I lay on the earthwork for some time with my chin on my hand descrying traces of Miss Havisham and Estella all over the prospect, in the sky and in the water, until at last I resolved to mention a thought concerning them that had been much 10 in my head.

"Joe," said I; "don't you think I ought to make Miss Havisham a visit?"

"Well, Pip," returned Joe, slowly considering. "What for?"

"What for, Joe? What is any visit made for?"

"There is some wisits p'r'aps," said Joe, "as for ever remains open to the question, Pip. But in regard of wisiting Miss Havisham. She might think you wanted something—expected something of her."

"Don't you think I might say that I did not, Joe?"

"You might, old chap," said Joe. "And she might credit it. Similarly she mightn't." 20

Joe felt, as I did, that he had made a point there, and he pulled hard at his pipe to keep himself from weakening it by repetition.

"You see, Pip," Joe pursued, as soon as he was past that danger, "Miss Havisham done the handsome thing by you. When Miss Havisham done the handsome thing by you, she called me back to say to me as that were all."

"Yes, Joe. I heard her."

"ALL," Joe repeated, very emphatically.

"Yes, Joe. I tell you, I heard her."

"Which I meantersay, Pip, it might be that her meaning were—Make a end on it!—As you was!—Me to the North and you to the South!—Keep in 30 sunders!"

I had thought of that too, and it was very far from comforting to me to find that he had thought of it; for, it seemed to render it more probable.

"But, Joe."

"Yes, old chap."

"Here am I, getting on in the first year of my time, and since the day of my being bound I have never thanked Miss Havisham, or asked after her, or shown that I remember her."

"That's true, Pip; and unless you was to turn her out a set of shoes all four round—and which I meantersay as even a set of shoes all four round might 40 not act acceptable as a present, in a total wacancy of hoofs——"

"I don't mean that sort of remembrance, Joe; I don't mean a present."

But Joe had got the idea of a present in his head and must harp upon it. "Or even," said he, "if you was helped to knocking her up a new chain for the front door—or say a gross or two of shark-headed screws[4] for general use —or some light fancy article, such as a toasting-fork when she took her muffins—or a gridiron when she took a sprat or such like——"

---

4. Roundheaded (or pointed) screws as opposed to flatheaded ones. Roundheads did not come into use until the nineteenth century; so Joe refers to a fairly recent commodity [OED]. Joe goes on to name a few other simple items Pip could "knock up" on the anvil. "Gridiron": grill.

"I don't mean any present at all, Joe," I interposed.

"Well," said Joe, still harping on it as though I had particularly pressed it, "if I was yourself, Pip, I wouldn't. No, I would *not*. For what's a door-chain when she's got one always up? And shark-headers is open to misrepresentations. And if it was a toasting-fork, you'd go into brass and do yourself no credit. And the oncommonest workman can't show himself oncommon in a gridiron—for a gridiron IS a gridiron," said Joe, steadfastly impressing it upon me, as if he were endeavouring to rouse me from a fixed delusion, "and you may haim at what you like, but a gridiron it will come out, either by your leave or again your leave, and you can't help yourself——"   10

"My dear Joe," I cried, in desperation, taking hold of his coat, "don't go on in that way. I never thought of making Miss Havisham any present."

"No, Pip," Joe assented, as if he had been contending for that, all along; "and what I say to you, is, you are right, Pip."

"Yes, Joe; but what I wanted to say, was, that as we are rather slack just now, if you could give me a half-holiday[5] to-morrow, I think I would go up-town and make a call on Miss Est—Havisham."

"Which her name," said Joe, gravely, "ain't Estavisham, Pip, unless she have been rechris'ened."

"I know, Joe, I know. It was a slip of mine. What do you think of it, Joe?"   20

In brief, Joe thought that if I thought well of it, he thought well of it. But, he was particular in stipulating that if I were not received with cordiality, or if I were not encouraged to repeat my visit as a visit which had no ulterior object but was simply one of gratitude for a favour received, then this experimental trip should have no successor. By these conditions I promised to abide.

Now, Joe kept a journeyman at weekly wages whose name was Orlick.[6] He pretended that his christian name was Dolge—a clear impossibility—but he was a fellow of that obstinate disposition that I believe him to have been the prey of no delusion in this particular, but wilfully to have imposed that name 30 upon the village as an affront to its understanding.[7] He was a broad-shouldered loose-limbed swarthy fellow of great strength, never in a hurry, and always slouching. He never even seemed to come to his work on purpose, but would slouch in as if by mere accident; and when he went to the Jolly Bargemen to eat his dinner, or went away at night, he would slouch out, like Cain or the Wandering Jew,[8] as if he had no idea where he was going and no intention of ever coming back. He lodged at a sluice-keeper's[9] out on the marshes, and on working days would come slouching from his hermitage, with his hands in his pockets and his dinner loosely tied in a bundle round his neck and dangling on his back. On Sundays he mostly lay all day on sluice gates, or 40

---

5. A half day off, usually taken on Saturday.
6. As a journeyman Orlick has completed his apprenticeship and thus qualified himself to work for daily or (as here) weekly wages.
7. On Orlick's name, see p. 462. Orlick's third-person self-references to "Old Orlick" may carry suggestions of the devil, traditionally "Old Nick," "the Old One," etc.
8. Murderers and pariahs. In Genesis 4.12, following the fratricide, Cain is condemned to be "a fugitive and a vagabond in the earth"; in the legend of the Wandering (or Eternal) Jew, as Jesus toiled up to Calvary, Caiaphus (elsewhere Ahasuerus) drove him from his door with the taunt, "Go faster!", incurring the curse of immortality in Jesus's ironic reply, "I shall go, but *you* shall stay." Though the story lacks scriptural sanction, it may derive from Matthew 16.28 and Mark 9.1.
9. The sluice-keeper's job was to control the flow of water through the marshes by means of sluices, or floodgates.

stood against ricks and barns. He always slouched, locomotively, with his eyes on the ground; and, when accosted or otherwise required to raise them, he looked up in a half resentful, half puzzled way, as though the only thought he ever had, was, that it was rather an odd and injurious fact that he should never be thinking.

This morose journeyman had no liking for me. When I was very small and timid, he gave me to understand that the Devil lived in a black corner of the forge, and that he knew the fiend very well: also that it was necessary to make up the fire once in every seven years, with a live boy, and that I might consider myself fuel.[1] When I became Joe's 'prentice, he was perhaps confirmed in 10 some suspicion that I should displace him; howbeit, he liked me still less. Not that he ever said anything, or did anything, openly importing hostility; I only noticed that he always beat his sparks in my direction, and that whenever I sang Old Clem, he came in out of time.

Dolge Orlick was at work and present, next day, when I reminded Joe of my half-holiday. He said nothing at the moment, for he and Joe had just got a piece of hot iron between them and I was at the bellows; but by-and-by he said, leaning on his hammer:

"Now, master! Sure you're not a going to favour only one of us. If Young Pip has a half-holiday, do as much for Old Orlick." I suppose he was about 20 five-and-twenty, but he usually spoke of himself as an ancient person.

"Why, what'll you do with a half-holiday, if you get it?" said Joe.

"What'll I do with it! What'll he do with it? I'll do as much with it as him," said Orlick.

"As to Pip, he's going up-town," said Joe.

"Well then as to Old Orlick, he's a going up-town," retorted that worthy. "Two can go up-town. Tan't only one wot can go up-town."

"Don't lose your temper," said Joe.

"Shall if I like," growled Orlick. "Some and their up-towning! Now, master! Come. No favouring in this shop. Be a man!"   30

The master refusing to entertain the subject until the journeyman was in a better temper, Orlick plunged at the furnace, drew out a red-hot bar, made at me with it as if he were going to run it through my body, whisked it round my head, laid it on the anvil, hammered it out—as if it were I, I thought, and the sparks were my spirting blood—and finally said, when he had hammered himself hot and the iron cold, and he again leaned on his hammer:

"Now, master!"

"Are you all right now?" demanded Joe.

"Ah! I am all right," said gruff Old Orlick.

"Then, as in general you stick to your work as well as most men," said Joe, 40 "let it be a half-holiday for all."

My sister had been standing silent in the yard, within hearing—she was a most unscrupulous spy and listener—and she instantly looked in at one of the windows.

"Like you, you fool!" said she to Joe, "giving holidays to great idle hulkers

---

1. Buried in Orlick's story may be bits and pieces of the St. Dunstan legend, which Dickens ridiculed in *A Child's History of England*, chapter 4. A blacksmith and great liar, Dunstan claims to have been tempted in his forge by Satan, "whereupon, having his pincers in the fire, red hot, he seized the devil by the nose, and put him to such pain that his bellowings were heard for miles and miles."

like that. You are a rich man, upon my life, to waste wages in that way. I
wish *I* was his master!"

"You'd be everybody's master, if you durst," retorted Orlick, with an ill-
favoured grin.

("Let her alone," said Joe.)

"I'd be a match for all noodles and all rogues," returned my sister, beginning to work herself into a mighty rage. "And I couldn't be a match for the
noodles without being a match for your master, who's the dunder-headed[2]
king of the noodles. And I couldn't be a match for the rogues, without being
a match for you, who are the blackest-looking and the worst rogue between   10
this and France. Now!"

"You're a foul shrew, Mother Gargery," growled the journeyman. "If that
makes a judge of rogues, you ought to be a good 'un."

("Let her alone, will you?" said Joe.)

"What did you say?" cried my sister, beginning to scream. "What did you
say? What did that fellow Orlick say to me, Pip? What did he call me, with
my husband standing by? O! O! O!" Each of these exclamations was a shriek;
and I must remark of my sister, what is equally true of all the violent women
I have ever seen, that passion was no excuse for her, because it is undeniable
that instead of lapsing into passion, she consciously and deliberately took   20
extraordinary pains to force herself into it, and became blindly furious by
regular stages; "what was the name he gave me before the base man who
swore to defend me? O! Hold me! O!"

"Ah-h-h!" growled the journeyman, between his teeth, "*I'd* hold you, if you
was my wife. I'd hold you under the pump, and choke it out of you."

("I tell you, let her alone," said Joe.)

"O! To hear him!" cried my sister, with a clap of her hands and a scream
together—which was her next stage. "To hear the names he's giving me! That
Orlick! In my own house! Me, a married woman! With my husband standing
by! O! O!" Here my sister, after a fit of clappings and screamings, beat her   30
hands upon her bosom and upon her knees, and threw her cap off, and pulled
her hair down—which were the last stages on her road to frenzy. Being by
this time a perfect Fury[3] and a complete success, she made a dash at the
door, which I had fortunately locked.

What could the wretched Joe do now, after his disregarded parenthetical
interruptions, but stand up to his journeyman, and ask him what he meant
by interfering betwixt himself and Mrs. Joe; and further whether he was man
enough to come on? Old Orlick felt that the situation admitted of nothing
less than coming on, and was on his defence straightway; so, without so much
as pulling off their singed and burnt aprons, they went at one another like   40
two giants. But, if any man in that neighbourhood could stand up long against
Joe, I never saw the man. Orlick, as if he had been of no more account than
the pale young gentleman, was very soon among the coal-dust and in no
hurry to come out of it. Then, Joe unlocked the door and picked up my sister,
who had dropped insensible at the window (but who had seen the fight first,

2. Blockheaded. The *OED* suggests as possible origin the Scottish *donner*, "to stun with a blow or loud
   noise," heavy enough to stupefy one for life.
3. The Furies, or Erinyes, are the avenging goddesses of Greek mythology. They specialize in avenging
   family crimes.

I think), and who was carried into the house and laid down, and who was recommended to revive, and would do nothing but struggle and clench her hands in Joe's hair. Then, came that singular calm and silence which succeed all uproars; and then, with the vague sensation which I have always connected with such a lull—namely, that it was Sunday, and somebody was dead—I went up-stairs to dress myself.

When I came down again, I found Joe and Orlick sweeping up, without any other traces of discomposure than a slit in one of Orlick's nostrils, which was neither expressive nor ornamental. A pot of beer had appeared from the Jolly Bargemen, and they were sharing it by turns in a peaceable manner. The lull had a sedative and philosophic influence on Joe, who followed me out into the road to say, as a parting observation that might do me good, "On the Rampage, Pip, and off the Rampage, Pip—such is Life!"

With what absurd emotions (for we think the feelings that are very serious in a man quite comical in a boy), I found myself again going to Miss Havisham's, matters little here. Nor how I passed and repassed the gate many times before I could make up my mind to ring. Nor, how I debated whether I should go away without ringing; nor, how I should undoubtedly have gone, if my time had been my own, to come back.

Miss Sarah Pocket came to the gate. No Estella.

"How, then? You here again?" said Miss Pocket. "What do you want?"

When I said that I only came to see how Miss Havisham was, Sarah evidently deliberated whether or no she should send me about my business. But, unwilling to hazard the responsibility, she let me in, and presently brought the sharp message that I was to "come up."

Everything was unchanged, and Miss Havisham was alone. "Well?" said she, fixing her eyes upon me. "I hope you want nothing? You'll get nothing."

"No indeed, Miss Havisham. I only wanted you to know that I am doing very well in my apprenticeship, and am always much obliged to you."

"There, there!" with the old restless fingers. "Come now and then; come on your birthday.—Ay!" she cried suddenly, turning herself and her chair towards me, "you are looking round for Estella? Hey?"

I had been looking round—in fact, for Estella—and I stammered that I hoped she was well.

"Abroad," said Miss Havisham; "educating for a lady; far out of reach; prettier than ever; admired by all who see her. Do you feel that you have lost her?"

There was such a malignant enjoyment in her utterance of the last words, and she broke into such a disagreeable laugh, that I was at a loss what to say. She spared me the trouble of considering, by dismissing me. When the gate was closed upon me by Sarah of the walnut-shell countenance, I felt more than ever dissatisfied with my home and with my trade and with everything; and that was all I took by *that* motion.

As I was loitering along the High-street, looking in disconsolately at the shop-windows, and thinking what I should buy if I were a gentleman, who should come out of the bookshop but Mr. Wopsle. Mr. Wopsle had in his hand the affecting tragedy of George Barnwell, in which he had that moment invested sixpence, with the view of heaping every word of it on the head of

Pumblechook, with whom he was going to drink tea.[4] No sooner did he see me, than he appeared to consider that a special Providence had put a 'prentice in his way to be read at; and he laid hold of me, and insisted on my accompanying him to the Pumblechookian parlour. As I knew it would be miserable at home, and as the nights were dark and the way was dreary, and almost any companionship on the road was better than none, I made no great resistance; consequently, we turned into Pumblechooks's just as the street and the shops were lighting up.

As I never assisted at any other representation of George Barnwell, I don't know how long it may usually take; but I know very well that it took until half-past nine o'clock that night, and that when Mr. Wopsle got into Newgate,[5] I thought he never would go to the scaffold, he became so much slower than at any former period of his disgraceful career. I thought it a little too much that he should complain of being cut short in his flower after all, as if he had not been running to seed, leaf after leaf, ever since his course began.[6] This, however, was a mere question of length and wearisomeness. What stung me, was the identification of the whole affair with my unoffending self. When Barnwell began to go wrong, I declare that I felt positively apologetic, Pumblechook's indignant stare so taxed me with it. Wopsle, too, took pains to present me in the worst light. At once ferocious and maudlin, I was made to murder my uncle with no extenuating circumstances whatever; Millwood put me down in argument, on every occasion; it became sheer monomania in my master's daughter to care a button for me; and all I can say for my gasping and procrastinating conduct on the fatal morning, is, that it was worthy of the general feebleness of my character. Even after I was happily hanged in my public character and Wopsle had closed the book, Pumblechook sat staring at me, and shaking his head, and saying, "Take warning, boy, take warning!" as if it were a well-known fact that in my private capacity, I contemplated murdering a near relation, provided I could only induce one to have the weakness to become my benefactor.

It was a very dark night when it was all over, and when I set out with Mr. Wopsle on the walk home. Beyond town we found a heavy mist out, and it

4. George Barnwell, the hero of *The London Merchant* (1731) by the English playwright George Lillo (1693?–1740), is an eighteen-year-old city apprentice, diligent, loyal, beloved by his master's daughter. A wily and venal whore, Millwood, a "scandal to her sex and a curse of ours," takes advantage of his adolescent infatuation to talk him into embezzling from his employer, then, on pain of deserting him, into killing his nearest kinsman, a rich rural uncle. To avert suspicion of complicity in the murder, she betrays George to the police, the more readily on discovering that in the panic of killing his uncle, George forgot to rob him. In the event, both malefactors are hanged. Barnwell's "history" had turned into a piece of popular culture, circulating in ballad form, long before Lillo picked it up. The play owes its spectacular vogue to Lillo's success in preaching the value of honest shopkeeping to a nation of shopkeepers, while showering blessings on English commercial prosperity; and it was ritually performed for the benefit of apprentices during the Christmas and Easter holidays and on Lord Mayor's Day. As an early specimen of "bourgeois tragedy," it enjoyed vast prestige on the Continent; Goethe allowed that he "yawned through most of it and cried at the end"; and the aged Duke of Hesse-Darmstadt, who refrained from watching tragedies on principle as injurious to his health but couldn't be kept away from Lillo's play, had the satisfaction of finding his principles vindicated by dying of a heart attack in the middle of the performance, after sundry approving moral commentaries and with a "Bravo!" lodged in his throat.
5. Dickens's detail. Lillo's stage directions read simply "a dungeon," "a room in a prison," "the place of execution." The New Gate, one of the entries to London, stood in the western wall of the city, Newgate Street passing through it. The jail bore its name from the thirteenth century; by the end of the sixteenth century it had become a byword for prisons. Newgate was rebuilt a number of times before it replaced Tyburn as the place of execution at the end of the eighteenth century; it was demolished in 1902.
6. Loose paraphrase of Barnwell's exit lines, 5.10.3–30. But Dickens is being unfair: though prosy, George "groan[s] but murmur[s] not."

fell wet and thick. The turnpike lamp[7] was a blur, quite out of the lamp's usual place apparently, and its rays looked solid substance on the fog. We were noticing this, and saying how that the mist rose with a change of wind from a certain quarter of our marshes, when we came upon a man slouching under the lee of the turnpike house.

"Halloa!" we said, stopping. "Orlick there?"

"Ah!" he answered, slouching out. "I was standing by a minute, on the chance of company."

"You are late," I remarked.

Orlick not unnaturally answered, "Well? And *you're* late." 10

"We have been," said Mr. Wopsle, exalted with his late performance, "we have been indulging, Mr. Orlick, in an intellectual evening."

Old Orlick growled, as if he had nothing to say about that, and we all went on together. I asked him presently whether he had been spending his half-holiday up and down town?

"Yes," said he, "all of it. I come in behind yourself. I didn't see you, but I must have been pretty close behind you. By-the-bye, the guns is going again."

"At the Hulks?" said I.

"Ay! There's some of the birds flown from the cages. The guns have been 20 going since dark, about. You'll hear one presently."

In effect, we had not walked many yards further, when the well-remembered boom came towards us, deadened by the mist, and heavily rolled away along the low grounds by the river, as if it were pursuing and threatening the fugitives.

"A good night for cutting off in," said Orlick. "We'd be puzzled how to bring down a jail-bird on the wing, to-night."

The subject was a suggestive one to me, and I thought about it in silence. Mr. Wopsle, as the ill-requited uncle of the evening's tragedy, fell to meditating aloud in his garden at Camberwell.[8] Orlick, with his hands in his 30 pockets, slouched heavily at my side. It was very dark, very wet, very muddy, and so we splashed along. Now and then the sound of the signal cannon broke upon us again, and again rolled sulkily along the course of the river. I kept myself to myself and my thoughts. Mr. Wopsle died amiably at Camberwell, and exceedingly game on Bosworth Field, and in the greatest agonies at Glastonbury.[9] Orlick sometimes growled, "Beat it out, beat it out—old

---

7. Turnpike, literally a revolving crossbar armed with spikes, used as a tollgate designed to enforce the collection of small levies for road repairs. At night the turnpike barriers were marked by a lamp to keep pedestrians from slipping past the tollkeeper.
8. In act 2.5–7, just before the murder, Barnwell's uncle entertains presentiments of death and speculates à la Hamlet on the reality of the hereafter. Dickens found this soliloquy singularly imbecile. "Camberwell": a borough in Southwark, some two and a half miles south of the Thames.
9. Wopsle is cheering himself up with lively death scenes. "Camberwell": see preceding note. "Bosworth Field": battle in which Richard III is killed: 5.8 in Shakespeare's play. But Shakespeare's Richard dies—exceedingly game—in a stage direction ("Enter Richard and Richmond. They fight. Richard is slain. Retreat and flourish"). Wopsle may be doing the kingdom-and-horse-trading passage immediately preceding or writhing to death in pantomime. "Glastonbury": a puzzle. Dickens may have confused it with Swinstead Abbey, the setting, in Shakespeare's *King John*, of John's death by poison. ("There is so hot a summer in my bosom / I crumble up to dust / * * * Within me is a hell, and there the poison / Is, as a fiend, confined * * * "). One of Shakespeare's least performed plays today, it enjoyed a good deal of popularity in the nineteenth century; it played on English anti-Catholic sentiments and became a favorite vehicle of England's leading tragedian, Dickens's friend Charles Macready ("My dying scene was my best"). No mention of Glastonbury in the manuscript.

Clem! With a clink for the stout—old Clem!" I thought he had been drinking, but he was not drunk.

Thus we came to the village. The way by which we approached it, took us past the Three Jolly Bargemen, which we were surprised to find—it being eleven o'clock—in a state of commotion, with the door wide open, and unwonted lights that had been hastily caught up and put down, scattered about. Mr. Wopsle dropped in to ask what was the matter (surmising that a convict had been taken), but came running out in a great hurry.

"There's something wrong," said he, without stopping, "up at your place, Pip. Run all!"   10

"What is it?" I asked, keeping up with him. So did Orlick, at my side.

"I can't quite understand. The house seems to have been violently entered when Joe Gargery was out. Supposed by convicts. Somebody has been attacked and hurt."

We were running too fast to admit of more being said, and we made no stop until we got into our kitchen. It was full of people; the whole village was there, or in the yard; and there was a surgeon, and there was Joe, and there were a group of women, all on the floor in the midst of the kitchen. The unemployed bystanders drew back when they saw me, and so I became aware of my sister—lying without sense or movement on the bare boards where she   20 had been knocked down by a tremendous blow on the back of the head, dealt by some unknown hand when her face was turned towards the fire— destined never to be on the Rampage again while she was wife of Joe.

★

Chapter XVI.

WITH my head full of George Barnwell, I was at first disposed to believe that I must have had some hand in the attack upon my sister, or at all events that as her near relation, popularly known to be under obligations to her, I was a more legitimate object of suspicion than any one else. But when, in the clearer light of next morning, I began to reconsider the matter and to hear it discussed around me on all sides, I took another view of the case, which was more reasonable.   30

Joe had been at the Three Jolly Bargemen, smoking his pipe, from a quarter after eight o'clock to a quarter before ten. While he was there, my sister had been seen standing at the kitchen door, and had exchanged Good Night with a farm-labourer going home. The man could not be more particular as to the time at which he saw her (he got into dense confusion when he tried to be), than that it must have been before nine. When Joe went home at five minutes before ten, he found her struck down on the floor, and promptly called in assistance. The fire had not then burnt unusually low, nor was the snuff of the candle very long; the candle, however, had been blown out.

Nothing had been taken away from any part of the house. Neither, beyond   40 the blowing out of the candle—which stood on a table between the door and my sister, and was behind her when she stood facing the fire and was struck— was there any disarrangement of the kitchen, excepting such as she herself had made in falling and bleeding. But, there was one remarkable piece of evidence on the spot. She had been struck with something blunt and heavy on the head and spine; after the blows were dealt, something heavy had been thrown down at her with considerable violence as she lay on her face. And on the ground beside her, when Joe picked her up, was a convict's leg-iron which had been filed asunder.

Now, Joe, examining this iron with a smith's eye, declared it to have been filed asunder some time ago. The hue and cry going off to the Hulks, and people coming thence to examine the iron, Joe's opinion was corroborated. They did not undertake to say when it had left the prison-ships to which it undoubtedly had once belonged; but they claimed to know for certain that that particular manacle had not been worn by either of two convicts who had escaped last night. Further, one of those two was already retaken, and had not freed himself of his iron.

Knowing what I knew, I set up an inference of my own here. I believed the iron to be my convict's iron—the iron I had seen and heard him filing at, on the marshes—but my mind did not accuse him of having put it to its latest use. For, I believed one of two other persons to have become possessed of it, and to have turned it to this cruel account. Either Orlick, or the strange man who had shown me the file.

Now, as to Orlick; he had gone to town exactly as he told us when we picked him up at the turnpike, he had been seen about town all the evening, he had been in divers companies in several public-houses, and he had come back with myself and Mr. Wopsle. There was nothing against him, save the quarrel; and my sister had quarrelled with him, and with everybody else about her, ten thousand times. As to the strange man; if he had come back for his two bank notes there could have been no dispute about them, because my sister was fully prepared to restore them. Besides, there had been no alter-cation; the assailant had come in so silently and suddenly that she had been felled before she could look round.

It was horrible to think that I had provided the weapon, however unde-signedly, but I could hardly think otherwise. I suffered unspeakable trouble while I considered and reconsidered whether I should at last dissolve that spell of my childhood, and tell Joe all the story. For months afterwards, I every day settled the question finally in the negative, and reopened and reargued it next morning. The contention came, after all, to this;—the secret was such an old one now, had so grown into me and become a part of myself, that I could not tear it away. In addition to the dread that, having led up to so much mischief, it would be now more likely than ever to alienate Joe from me if he believed it, I had the further restraining dread that he would not believe it, but would assort it with the fabulous dogs and veal cutlets as a monstrous invention. However, I temporised with myself, of course—for, was I not wavering between right and wrong, when the thing is always done!—and resolved to make a full disclosure if I should see any such new occasion as a new chance of helping in the discovery of the assailant.

The Constables, and the Bow-street men from London—for, this happened in the days of the extinct red waistcoated police[1]—were about the house for a week or two, and did pretty much what I have heard and read of like

---

1. Actually the Runners (see next note) were plainclothesmen, but they were sometimes popularly known as "redbreasts" from the uniform of their colleagues on the Bow Street Foot [Night] Patrol—whom the young Pip has had no chance to see.

authorities doing in other such cases. They took up several obviously wrong people, and they ran their heads very hard against wrong ideas, and persisted in trying to fit the circumstances to the ideas, instead of trying to extract ideas from the circumstances. Also, they stood about the door of the Jolly Barge-men, with knowing and reserved looks that filled the whole neighbourhood with admiration; and they had a mysterious manner of taking their drink, that was almost as good as taking the culprit. But not quite, for they never did it.[2]

Long after these constitutional powers had dispersed, my sister lay very ill in bed. Her sight was disturbed, so that she saw objects multiplied, and grasped at visionary teacups and wine-glasses instead of the realities; her hear- 10 ing was greatly impaired; her memory also; and her speech was unintelligible. When, at last, she came round so far as to be helped down stairs, it was still necessary to keep my slate always by her, that she might indicate in writing what she could not indicate in speech. As she was (very bad handwriting apart) a more than indifferent speller, and as Joe was a more than indifferent reader, extraordinary complications arose between them, which I was always called in to solve. The administration of mutton instead of medicine, the substitution of Tea for Joe, and the baker for bacon, were among the mildest of my own mistakes.[3]

However, her temper was greatly improved, and she was patient. A trem- 20 ulous uncertainty of the action of all her limbs soon became a part of her regular state, and afterwards, at intervals of two or three months, she would often put her hands to her head and would then remain for about a week at a time in some gloomy aberration of mind. We were at a loss to find a suitable attendant for her, until a circumstance happened conveniently to relieve us. Mr. Wopsle's great-aunt conquered a confirmed habit of living into which she had fallen,[4] and Biddy became a part of our establishment.

It may have been about a month after my sister's reappearance in the kitchen, when Biddy came to us with a small speckled box containing the whole of her worldly effects, and became a blessing to the household. Above 30 all, she was a blessing to Joe, for the dear old fellow was sadly cut up by the constant contemplation of the wreck of his wife, and had been accustomed, while attending on her of an evening, to turn to me every now and then and say, with his blue eyes moistened, "Such a fine figure of a woman as she once were, Pip!" Biddy instantly taking the cleverest charge of her as though she had studied her from infancy, Joe became able in some sort to appreciate the greater quiet of his life, and to get down to the Jolly Bargemen now and then for a change that did him good. It was characteristic of the police people that they had all more or less suspected poor Joe (though he never knew it),

2. The Bow Street Runners, England's first police detectives, date from 1749, the invention of Henry Fielding, who doubled as magistrate and novelist. Though they mostly operated locally out of their Bow Street headquarters in London, the Runners were occasionally called in to assist in cases outside the city. Sir Robert Peel's introduction of the Metropolitan London Police (the "Peelers," or "Bob-bies") in 1829 superseded the Bow Street constabulary. Dickens's contempt for the Runners, already evident in his portrayal of Blathers and Duff, the bungling investigators in *Oliver Twist*, chapter 31, contrasts sharply with his idolatry of the New Police.

3. Mrs. Joe's case has drawn professional notices in the medical journals. In the language of the eminent neurosurgeon Lord Brain, Mrs. Joe suffers from "a severe contusion of the left temporoparietal region causing jargon aphasia and word deafness and some traumatic dementia, with injury to the third and sixth cranial nerve leading to diplopia." Brain compares Dickens's diagnoses of neurological states, in their accuracy and minuteness, with those of "clinicians of genius," doubly remarkable considering the meagerness of neurological data in Dickens's day.

4. An echo of Sir Thomas Browne's *Urn Burial*, 5 (1658): "The long habit of living indisposeth us for dying" (Hill).

and that they had to a man concurred in regarding him as one of the deepest spirits they had ever encountered.

Biddy's first triumph in her new office, was to solve a difficulty that had completely vanquished me. I had tried hard at it, but had made nothing of it. Thus it was:

Again and again and again, my sister had traced upon the slate a character that looked like a curious T, and then with the utmost eagerness had called our attention to it as something she particularly wanted. I had in vain tried everything producible that began with a T, from tar to toast and tub. At length it had come into my head that the sign looked like a hammer, and on my 10 lustily calling that word in my sister's ear, she had begun to hammer on the table and had expressed a qualified assent. Thereupon, I had brought in all our hammers, one after another, but without avail. Then I bethought me of a crutch, the shape being much the same, and I borrowed one in the village, and displayed it to my sister with considerable confidence. But she shook her head to that extent when she was shown it, that we were terrified lest in her weak and shattered state she should dislocate her neck.

When my sister found that Biddy was very quick to understand her, this mysterious sign reappeared on the slate. Biddy looked thoughtfully at it, heard my explanation, looked thoughtfully at my sister, looked thoughtfully at Joe 20 (who was always represented on the slate by his initial letter), and ran into the forge, followed by Joe and me.

"Why, of course!" cried Biddy, with an exultant face. "Don't you see? It's him!"

Orlick, without a doubt! She had lost his name, and could only signify him by his hammer. We told him why we wanted him to come into the kitchen, and he slowly laid down his hammer, wiped his brow with his arm, took another wipe at it with his apron, and came slouching out, with a curious loose vagabond bend in the knees that strongly distinguished him.

I confess that I expected to see my sister denounce him, and that I was 30 disappointed by the different result. She manifested the greatest anxiety to be on good terms with him, was evidently much pleased by his being at length produced, and motioned that she would have him given something to drink. She watched his countenance as if she were particularly wishful to be assured that he took kindly to his reception, she showed every possible desire to conciliate him, and there was an air of humble propitiation in all she did, such as I have seen pervade the bearing of a child towards a hard master. After that day, a day rarely passed without her drawing the hammer on her slate, and without Orlick's slouching in and standing doggedly before her, as if he knew no more than I did what to make of it. 40

Chapter XVII.

I NOW fell into a regular routine of apprenticeship-life, which was varied, beyond the limits of the village and the marshes, by no more remarkable circumstance than the arrival of my birthday and my paying another visit to Miss Havisham. I found Miss Sarah Pocket still on duty at the gate, I found Miss Havisham just as I had left her, and she spoke of Estella in the very same way, if not in the very same words. The interview lasted but a few minutes, and she gave me a guinea when I was going, and told me to come again on my next birthday. I may mention at once that this became an annual custom. I tried to decline taking the guinea on the first occasion, but with no better effect than causing her to ask me very angrily, if I expected more? Then, and after that, I took it.

So unchanging was the dull old house, the yellow light in the darkened room, the faded spectre in the chair by the dressing-table glass, that I felt as if the stopping of the clocks had stopped Time in that mysterious place, and, while I and everything else outside it grew older, it stood still. Daylight never entered the house as to my thoughts and remembrances of it, any more than   10
as to the actual fact. It bewildered me, and under its influence I continued at heart to hate my trade and to be ashamed of home.

Imperceptibly I became conscious of a change in Biddy, however. Her shoes came up at the heel, her hair grew bright and neat, her hands were always clean. She was not beautiful—she was common, and could not be like Estella—but she was pleasant and wholesome and sweet-tempered. She had not been with us more than a year (I remember her being newly out of mourning at the time it struck me), when I observed to myself one evening that she had curiously thoughtful and attentive eyes; eyes that were very pretty and very good.   20

It came of my lifting up my own eyes from a task I was poring at—writing some passages from a book, to improve myself in two ways at once by a sort of stratagem—and seeing Biddy observant of what I was about. I laid down my pen, and Biddy stopped in her needlework without laying it down.

"Biddy," said I, "how do you manage it? Either I am very stupid, or you are very clever."

"What is it that I manage? I don't know," returned Biddy, smiling.

She managed our whole domestic life, and wonderfully too; but I did not mean that, though that made what I did mean more surprising.

"How do you manage, Biddy," said I, "to learn everything that I learn, and   30
always to keep up with me?" I was beginning to be rather vain of my knowledge, for I spent my birthday guineas on it, and set aside the greater part of my pocket-money for similar investment; though I have no doubt, now, that the little I knew was extremely dear at the price.

"I might as well ask you," said Biddy, "how you manage?"

"No; because when I come in from the forge of a night, any one can see me turning to at it. But you never turn to at it, Biddy."

"I suppose I must catch it—like a cough," said Biddy, quietly; and went on with her sewing.

Pursuing my idea as I leaned back in my wooden chair and looked at   40
Biddy sewing away with her head on one side, I began to think her rather an extraordinary girl. For, I called to mind now, that she was equally accomplished in the terms of our trade and the names of our different sorts of work, and our various tools. In short, whatever I knew, Biddy knew. Theoretically, she was already as good a blacksmith as I, or better.

"You are one of those, Biddy," said I, "who make the most of every chance. You never had a chance before you came here, and see how improved you are!"

Biddy looked at me for an instant, and went on with her sewing. "I was your first teacher though; wasn't I?" said she, as she sewed.   50

"Biddy!" I exclaimed, in amazement. "Why, you are crying!"

"No, I am not," said Biddy, looking up and laughing. "What put that in your head?"

What could have put it in my head, but the glistening of a tear as it dropped on her work? I sat silent, recalling what a drudge she had been until Mr. Wopsle's great-aunt successfully overcame that bad habit of living, so highly desirable to be got rid of by some people. I recalled the hopeless circumstances by which she had been surrounded in the miserable little shop and the miserable little noisy evening school, with that miserable old bundle of incompetence always to be dragged and shouldered. I reflected that even in those untoward times there must have been latent in Biddy what was now developing, for, in my first uneasiness and discontent I had turned to her for help, as a matter of course. Biddy sat quietly sewing, shedding no more tears, and while I looked at her and thought about it all, it occurred to me that perhaps I had not been sufficiently grateful to Biddy. I might have been too reserved, and should have patronised her more (though I did not use that precise word in my meditations), with my confidence.

"Yes, Biddy," I observed, when I had done turning it over, "you were my first teacher, and that at a time when we little thought of ever being together like this, in this kitchen."

"Ah, poor thing!" replied Biddy. It was like her self-forgetfulness, to transfer the remark to my sister, and to get up and be busy about her, making her more comfortable; "that's sadly true!"

"Well!" said I, "we must talk together a little more, as we used to do. And I must consult you a little more, as I used to do. Let us have a quiet walk on the marshes next Sunday, Biddy, and a long chat."

My sister was never left alone now; but Joe more than readily undertook the care of her on that Sunday afternoon, and Biddy and I went out together. It was summer time and lovely weather. When we had passed the village and the church and the churchyard, and were out on the marshes and began to see the sails of the ships as they sailed on, I began to combine Miss Havisham and Estella with the prospect, in my usual way. When we came to the riverside and sat down on the bank, with the water rippling at our feet, making it all more quiet than it would have been without that sound, I resolved that it was a good time and place for the admission of Biddy into my inner confidence.

"Biddy," said I, after binding her to secrecy, "I want to be a gentleman."

"Oh, I wouldn't, if I was you!" she returned. "I don't think it would answer."

"Biddy," said I, with some severity, "I have particular reasons for wanting to be a gentleman."

"You know best, Pip; but don't you think you are happier as you are?"

"Biddy," I exclaimed, impatiently, "I am not at all happy as I am. I am disgusted with my calling and with my life. I have never taken to either, since I was bound. Don't be absurd."

"Was I absurd?" said Biddy, quietly raising her eyebrows; "I am sorry for that; I didn't mean to be. I only want you to do well, and to be comfortable."

"Well then, understand once for all that I never shall or can be comfortable—or anything but miserable—there, Biddy!—unless I can lead a very different sort of life from the life I lead now."

"That's a pity!" said Biddy, shaking her head with a sorrowful air.

Now, I too had so often thought it a pity, that, in the singular kind of quarrel with myself which I was always carrying on, I was half inclined to shed tears of vexation and distress when Biddy gave utterance to her sentiment and my own. I told her she was right, and I knew it was much to be regretted, but still it was not to be helped.

"If I could have settled down," I said to Biddy, plucking up the short grass within reach, much as I had once upon a time pulled my feelings out of my hair and kicked them into the brewery wall: "if I could have settled down and been but half as fond of the forge as I was when I was little, I know it 10 would have been much better for me. You and I and Joe would have wanted nothing then, and Joe and I would perhaps have gone partners when I was out of my time, and I might even have grown up to keep company with you, and we might have sat on this very bank on a fine Sunday, quite different people. I should have been good enough for *you*; shouldn't I, Biddy?"

Biddy sighed as she looked at the ships sailing on, and returned for answer, "Yes; I am not over particular." It scarcely sounded flattering, but I knew she meant well.

"Instead of that," said I, plucking up more grass and chewing a blade or two, "see how I am going on. Dissatisfied, and uncomfortable, and—what 20 would it signify to me, being coarse and common, if nobody had told me so!"

Biddy turned her face suddenly towards mine, and looked far more attentively at me than she had looked at the sailing ships.

"It was neither a very true nor a very polite thing to say," she remarked, directing her eyes to the ships again. "Who said it?"

I was disconcerted, for I had broken away without quite seeing where I was going. It was not to be shuffled off now, however, and I answered, "The beautiful young lady at Miss Havisham's, and she's more beautiful than anybody ever was, and I admire her dreadfully, and I want to be a gentleman on 30 her account." Having made this lunatic confession, I began to throw my torn-up grass into the river, as if I had some thoughts of following it.

"Do you want to be a gentleman, to spite her or to gain her over?" Biddy quietly asked me, after a pause.

"I don't know," I moodily answered.

"Because, if it is to spite her," Biddy pursued, "I should think—but you know best—that might be better and more independently done by caring nothing for her words. And if it is to gain her over, I should think—but you know best—she was not worth gaining over."

Exactly what I myself had thought, many times. Exactly what was perfectly 40 manifest to me at the moment. But how could I, a poor dazed village lad, avoid that wonderful inconsistency into which the best and wisest of men fall every day?

"It may be all quite true," said I to Biddy, "but I admire her dreadfully."

In short, I turned over on my face when I came to that, and got a good grasp on the hair on each side of my head, and wrenched it well. All the while knowing the madness of my heart to be so very mad and misplaced, that I was quite conscious it would have served my face right, if I had lifted it up by my hair, and knocked it against the pebbles as a punishment for belonging to such an idiot.   50

Biddy was the wisest of girls, and she tried to reason no more with me. She put her hand, which was a comfortable hand though roughened by work, upon my hands, one after another, and gently took them out of my hair. Then she softly patted my shoulder in a soothing way, while with my face upon my sleeve I cried a little—exactly as I had done in the brewery yard— and felt vaguely convinced that I was very much ill used by somebody, or by everybody; I can't say which.

"I am glad of one thing," said Biddy, "and that is, that you have felt you could give me your confidence, Pip. And I am glad of another thing, and that is, that of course you know you may depend upon my keeping it and 10 always so far deserving it. If your first teacher (dear! such a poor one, and so much in need of being taught herself!) had been your teacher at the present time, she thinks she knows what lesson she would set. But it would be a hard one to learn, and you have got beyond her, and it's of no use now." So, with a quiet sigh for me, Biddy rose from the bank, and said, with a fresh and pleasant change of voice, "Shall we walk a little further, or go home?"

"Biddy," I cried, getting up, putting my arm round her neck, and giving her a kiss, "I shall always tell you everything."

"Till you're a gentleman," said Biddy.

"You know I never shall be, so that's always. Not that I have any occasion 20 to tell you anything, for you know everything I know—as I told you at home the other night."

"Ah!" said Biddy, quite in a whisper, as she looked away at the ships. And then repeated, with her former pleasant change; "shall we walk a little further, or go home?"

I said to Biddy we would walk a little further, and we did so, and the summer afternoon toned down into the summer evening, and it was very beautiful. I began to consider whether I was not more naturally and whole-somely situated, after all, in these circumstances, than playing beggar my neighbour by candlelight in the room with the stopped clocks, and being 30 despised by Estella. I thought it would be very good for me if I could get her out of my head, with all the rest of those remembrances and fancies, and could go to work determined to relish what I had to do, and stick to it, and make the best of it. I asked myself the question whether I did not surely know that if Estella were beside me at that moment instead of Biddy, she would make me miserable? I was obliged to admit that I did know it for a certainty, and I said to myself, "Pip, what a fool you are!"

We talked a good deal as we walked, and all that Biddy said seemed right. Biddy was never insulting, or capricious, or Biddy to-day and somebody else to-morrow; she would have derived only pain, and no pleasure, from giving 40 me pain; she would far rather have wounded her own breast than mine. How could it be then, that I did not like her much the better of the two?

"Biddy," said I, when we were walking homeward, "I wish you could put me right."

"I wish I could!" said Biddy.

"If I could only get myself to fall in love with you—you don't mind my speaking so openly to such an old acquaintance?"

"Oh dear, not at all!" said Biddy. "Don't mind me."

"If I could only get myself to do it, *that* would be the thing for me."

"But you never will, you see," said Biddy.   50

It did not appear quite so unlikely to me that evening, as it would have done if we had discussed it a few hours before. I therefore observed I was not quite sure of that. But Biddy said she *was*, and she said it decisively. In my heart I believed her to be right; and yet I took it rather ill, too, that she should be so positive on the point.

When we came near the churchyard, we had to cross an embankment, and get over a stile[1] near a sluice-gate. There started up, from the gate, or from the rushes, or from the ooze (which was quite in his stagnant way), old Orlick.

"Halloa!" he growled, "where are you two going?"   10

Where should we be going, but home? "Well then," said he, "I'm jiggered if[2] I don't see you home!"

This penalty of being jiggered was a favourite supposititious case of his. He attached no definite meaning to the word that I am aware of, but used it, like his own pretended christian name, to affront mankind, and convey an idea of something savagely damaging. When I was younger, I had had a general belief that if he had jiggered me personally, he would have done it with a sharp and twisted hook.

Biddy was much against his going with us, and said to me in a whisper, "Don't let him come; I don't like him." As I did not like him either, I took 20 the liberty of saying that we thanked him but we didn't want seeing home. He received that piece of information with a yell of laughter, and dropped back, but came slouching after us at a little distance.

Curious to know whether Biddy suspected him of having had a hand in that murderous attack of which my sister had never been able to give any account, I asked her why she did not like him?

"Oh!" she replied, glancing over her shoulder as he slouched after us, "because I—I am afraid he likes me."

"Did he ever tell you he liked you?" I asked, indignantly.

"No," said Biddy, glancing over her shoulder again, "he never told me so; 30 but he dances at me, whenever he can catch my eye."

However novel and peculiar this testimony of attachment, I did not doubt the accuracy of the interpretation. I was very hot indeed upon old Orlick's daring to admire her; as hot as if it were an outrage on myself.

"But it makes no difference to you, you know," said Biddy, calmly.

"No, Biddy, it makes no difference to me; only I don't like it; I don't approve of it."

"Nor I neither," said Biddy. "Though *that* makes no difference to you."

"Exactly," said I; "but I must tell you I should have no opinion of you, Biddy, if he danced at you with your own consent."   40

I kept an eye on Orlick after that night, and, whenever circumstances were favourable to his dancing at Biddy, got before him, to obscure that demonstration. He had struck root in Joe's establishment, by reason of my sister's sudden fancy for him, or I should have tried to get him dismissed. He quite

---

1. Step or steps constructed to get over a fence, wall, or ditch, designed to keep the cattle in and let pedestrians out.
2. "I'll be damned if," "curse me if" [OED]. "A common form of mild swearing" (Hotten). In one of its meanings—a jigger is one who dances a jig—the phrase may relate to Orlick's conduct toward Biddy below. In this sense the "jig of anxiety" performed by the "second Jew" in chapter 20. In his *After Many a Summer Dies the Swan* (1939), chapter 2, Aldous Huxley defines it specifically to mean "I'm damned," and, like Dickens, draws attention to the oddity of the locution (Monod).

understood and reciprocated my good intentions, as I had reason to know thereafter.

And now, because my mind was not confused enough before, I complicated its confusion fifty thousand-fold, by having states and seasons when I was clear that Biddy was immeasurably better than Estella, and that the plain honest working life to which I was born, had nothing in it to be ashamed of, but offered me sufficient means of self-respect and happiness. At those times, I would decide conclusively that my disaffection to dear old Joe and the forge was gone, and that I was growing up in a fair way to be partners with Joe and to keep company with Biddy—when all in a moment some confounding 10 remembrance of the Havisham days would fall upon me, like a destructive missile, and scatter my wits again. Scattered wits take a long time picking up; and often, before I had got them well together, they would be dispersed in all directions by one stray thought, that perhaps after all Miss Havisham was going to make my fortune when my time was out.[3]

If my time had run out, it would have left me still at the height of my perplexities, I dare say. It never did run out, however, but was brought to a premature end, as I proceed to relate.

Chapter XVIII.

It was in the fourth year of my apprenticeship to Joe, and it was a Saturday night. There was a group assembled round the fire at the Three Jolly Barge- 20 men, attentive to Mr. Wopsle as he read the newspaper aloud. Of that group, I was one.

A highly popular murder[1] had been committed, and Mr. Wopsle was imbrued in blood to the eyebrows. He gloated over every abhorrent adjective in the description, and identified himself with every witness at the Inquest. He faintly moaned, "I am done for," as the victim, and he barbarously bellowed, "I'll serve you out," as the murderer. He gave the medical testimony, in pointed imitation of our local practitioner; and he piped and shook, as the aged turnpike-keeper who had heard blows, to an extent so very paralytic as to suggest a doubt regarding the mental competency of that witness. The 30 coroner, in Mr. Wopsle's hands, became Timon of Athens; the beadle, Coriolanus.[2] He enjoyed himself thoroughly, and we all enjoyed ourselves, and were delightfully comfortable. In this cosy state of mind we came to the verdict Wilful Murder.[3]

Then, and not sooner, I became aware of a strange gentleman leaning over

3. "When I had completed my apprenticeship."

1. In the sense of a widely publicized one.

2. The coroner, like Shakespeare's Timon, has turned cynic and misanthrope; the beadle emulates Coriolanus in his scorn for the rabble. "Beadle": minor official who kept order in the parish, punished petty offenders, and acted as general factotum. Thanks to Oliver's nemesis Bumble (the leading exemplar of beadledom in fiction), a byword for officiousness and bullying.

3. In cases of unnatural deaths, the coroner was required to inspect the body in the presence of at least twelve jurors whose verdict (accidental death, homicide, suicide) guided subsequent court proceedings. The beadle rounded up the jurors and kept the crowd in line. The scene here recapitulates in miniature the account of the coroner's inquest in *Bleak House*, chapter 11, which terminates, as this one does, in some postmortem horseplay in a public house.

the back of the settle opposite me, looking on. There was an expression of contempt on his face, and he bit the side of a great forefinger as he watched the group of faces. "Well!" said the stranger to Mr. Wopsle, when the reading was done, "you have settled it all to your own satisfaction, I have no doubt?"

Everybody started and looked up, as if it were the murderer. He looked at everybody coldly and sarcastically.

"Guilty, of course?" said he. "Out with it. Come!"

"Sir," returned Mr. Wopsle, "without having the honour of your acquaintance, I do say Guilty." Upon this, we all took courage to unite in a confirm- 10 atory murmur.

"I know you do," said the stranger; "I knew you would. I told you so. But now I'll ask you a question. Do you know, or do you not know, that the law of England supposes every man to be innocent, until he is proved—proved —to be guilty?"

"Sir," Mr. Wopsle began to reply, "as an Englishman myself, I——"

"Come!" said the stranger, biting his forefinger at him. "Don't evade the question. Either you know it, or you don't know it. Which is it to be?"

He stood with his head on one side and himself on one side in a bullying interrogative manner, and he threw his forefinger at Mr. Wopsle—as it were 20 to mark him out—before biting it again.[4]

"Now!" said he. "Do you know it, or don't you know it?"

"Certainly I know it," replied Mr. Wopsle.

"Certainly you know it. Then why didn't you say so at first? Now, I'll ask you another question;" taking possession of Mr. Wopsle, as if he had a right to him. "Do you know that none of these witnesses have yet been cross-examined?"

Mr. Wopsle was beginning, "I can only say——" when the stranger stopped him.

"What? You won't answer the question, yes or no? Now, I'll try you again." 30 Throwing his finger at him again. "Attend to me. Are you aware, or are you not aware, that none of these witnesses have yet been cross-examined? Come, I only want one word from you. Yes, or no?"

Mr. Wopsle hesitated, and we all began to conceive rather a poor opinion of him.

"Come!" said the stranger, "I'll help you. You don't deserve help, but I'll help you. Look at that paper you hold in your hand. What is it?"

"What is it?" repeated Mr. Wopsle, eyeing it, much at a loss.

"Is it," pursued the stranger in his most sarcastic and suspicious manner, "the printed paper you have just been reading from?" 40

"Undoubtedly."

"Undoubtedly. Now, turn to that paper, and tell me whether it distinctly states that the prisoner expressly said that his legal advisers instructed him altogether to reserve his defence?"

"I read that just now," Mr. Wopsle pleaded.

"Never mind what you read just now, sir; I don't ask you what you read just now. You may read the Lord's Prayer backwards, if you like—and, per-

---

4. The bullying forefinger recalls Inspector Bucket's still more obtrusive "fat forefinger [which rises] to the dignity of a familiar demon" in *Bleak House*, chapter 53.

haps, have done it before to-day.[5] Turn to the paper. No, no, no, my friend; not to the top of the column; you know better than that; to the bottom, to the bottom." (We all began to think Mr. Wopsle full of subterfuge.) "Well? Have you found it?"

"Here it is," said Mr. Wopsle.

"Now, follow that passage with your eye, and tell me whether it distinctly states that the prisoner expressly said that he was instructed by his legal advisers wholly to reserve his defence? Come! Do you make that of it?"

Mr. Wopsle answered, "Those are not the exact words."

"Not the exact words!" repeated the gentleman, bitterly. "Is that the exact substance?"

"Yes," said Mr. Wopsle.

"Yes!" repeated the stranger, looking round at the rest of the company with his right hand extended towards the witness, Wopsle. "And now I ask you what you say to the conscience of that man who, with that passage before his eyes, can lay his head upon his pillow after having pronounced a fellow-creature guilty, unheard?"

We all began to suspect that Mr. Wopsle was not the man we had thought him, and that he was beginning to be found out.

"And that same man, remember," pursued the gentleman, throwing his finger at Mr. Wopsle heavily; "that same man might be summoned as a juryman upon this very trial, and, having thus deeply committed himself, might return to the bosom of his family and lay his head upon his pillow, after deliberately swearing that he would well and truly try the issue joined between Our Sovereign Lord the King and the prisoner at the bar, and would a true verdict give according to the evidence, so help him God!"[6]

We were all deeply persuaded that the unfortunate Wopsle had gone too far, and had better stop in his reckless career while there was yet time.

The strange gentleman, with an air of authority not to be disputed, and with a manner expressive of knowing something secret about every one of us that would effectually do for each individual if he chose to disclose it, left the back of the settle, and came into the space between the two settles, in front of the fire, where he remained standing: his left hand in his pocket, and he biting the forefinger of his right.

"From information I have received," said he, looking round at us as we all quailed before him, "I have reason to believe there is a blacksmith among you, by name Joseph—or Joe—Gargery. Which is the man?"

"Here is the man," said Joe.

The strange gentleman beckoned him out of his place, and Joe went.

"You have an apprentice," pursued the stranger, "commonly known as Pip? Is he here?"

"I am here!" I cried.

The stranger did not recognise me, but I recognised him as the gentleman I had met on the stairs, on the occasion of my second visit to Miss Havisham. His appearance was too remarkable for me to have forgotten. I had known

---

5. Improbable, unless Wopsle consorts with witches and satanists: "the strange gentleman" is talking about a spell to conjure up the devil, a feature of the Black Mass. In Marlowe's *Dr. Faustus* 1.3.8–9, Jehovah's name is "forward and backward anagrammatized."

6. Wopsle's interrogator soars into professional mimicry of the oath the court clerk administers to jurors. The oath is cited in Hawkins's piece, p. 595.

him the moment I saw him looking over the settle, and now that I stood confronting him with his hand upon my shoulder, I checked off again in detail, his large head, his dark complexion, his deep-set eyes, his bushy black eyebrows, his large watch-chain, his strong black dots of beard and whisker, and even the smell of scented soap on his great hand.

"I wish to have a private conference with you two," said he, when he had surveyed me at his leisure. "It will take a little time. Perhaps we had better go to your place of residence. I prefer not to anticipate my communication, here; you will impart as much or as little of it as you please to your friends afterwards; I have nothing to do with that."   10

Amidst a wondering silence, we three walked out of the Jolly Bargemen, and in a wondering silence walked home. While going along, the strange gentleman occasionally looked at me, and occasionally bit the side of his finger. As we neared home, Joe vaguely acknowledging the occasion as an impressive and ceremonious one, went on ahead to open the front door. Our conference was held in the state-parlour, which was feebly lighted by one candle.

It began with the strange gentleman's sitting down at the table, drawing the candle to him, and looking over some entries in his pocket-book. He then put up the pocket-book and set the candle a little aside: after peering round   20 it into the darkness at Joe and me, to ascertain which was which.

"My name," he said, "is Jaggers, and I am a lawyer in London. I am pretty well known. I have unusual business to transact with you, and I commence by explaining that it is not of my originating. If my advice had been asked, I should not have been here. It was not asked, and you see me here. What I have to do, as the confidential agent of another, I do. No less, no more."

Finding that he could not see us very well from where he sat, he got up, and threw one leg over the back of a chair and leaned upon it; thus having one foot on the seat of the chair, and one foot on the ground.

"Now, Joseph Gargery, I am the bearer of an offer to relieve you of this   30 young fellow, your apprentice. You would not object to cancel his indentures, at his request and for his good? You would not want anything for so doing?"

"Lord forbid that I should want anything for not standing in Pip's way!" said Joe, staring.

"Lord forbidding is pious, but not to the purpose," returned Mr. Jaggers. "The question is, Would you want anything? Do you want anything?"

"The answer is," returned Joe, sternly, "No."

I thought Mr. Jaggers glanced at Joe, as if he considered him a fool for his disinterestedness. But I was too much bewildered between breathless curiosity and surprise, to be sure of it.   40

"Very well," said Mr. Jaggers. "Recollect the admission you have made, and don't try to go from it presently."

"Who's a going to try?" retorted Joe.

"I don't say anybody is. Do you keep a dog?"

"Yes, I do keep a dog."

"Bear in mind then, that Brag is a good dog, but Holdfast is a better.[7] Bear that in mind, will you?" repeated Mr. Jaggers, shutting his eyes and nodding

---

7. "Better to keep your word than shoot your mouth off" [Holdfast = keep a promise]. Cf. Pistol's parting shot to Mistress Quickly in Shakespeare's *Henry V* 2.3.42–43: "Trust none, for oaths are straws, men's faiths are wafer-cakes, / And Holdfast is the only dog, my duck."

his head at Joe, as if he were forgiving him something. "Now, I return to this young fellow. And the communication I have got to make is, that he has great expectations."[8]

Joe and I gasped, and looked at one another.

"I am instructed to communicate to him," said Mr. Jaggers, throwing his finger at me, sideways, "that he will come into a handsome property. Further, that it is the desire of the present possessor of that property, that he be immediately removed from his present sphere of life and from this place, and be brought up as a gentleman—in a word, as a young fellow of great expectations."

My dream was out; my wild fancy was surpassed by sober reality; Miss Havisham was going to make my fortune on a grand scale.

"Now, Mr. Pip," pursued the lawyer, "I address the rest of what I have to say, to you. You are to understand first, that it is the request of the person from whom I take my instructions, that you always bear the name of Pip.[9] You will have no objection, I dare say, to your great expectations being encumbered with that easy condition. But if you have any objection, this is the time to mention it."

My heart was beating so fast, and there was such a singing in my ears, that I could scarcely stammer I had no objection.

"I should think not! Now you are to understand secondly, Mr. Pip, that the name of the person who is your liberal benefactor remains a profound secret, until the person chooses to reveal it. I am empowered to mention that it is the intention of the person to reveal it at first hand by word of mouth to yourself. When or where that intention may be carried out, I cannot say; no one can say. It may be years hence. Now, you are distinctly to understand that you are most positively prohibited from making any inquiry on this head, or any allusion or reference, however distant, to any individual whomsoever as *the* individual in all the communications you may have with me. If you have a suspicion in your own breast, keep that suspicion in your own breast. It is not the least to the purpose what the reasons of this prohibition are; they may be the strongest and gravest reasons, or they may be mere whim. That is not for you to inquire into. The condition is laid down. Your acceptance of it, and your observance of it as binding, is the only remaining condition that I am charged with, by the person from whom I take my instructions, and for whom I am not otherwise responsible. That person is the person from whom you derive your expectations, and the secret is solely held by that person and by me. Again, not a very difficult condition with which to encumber such a rise in fortune; but if you have any objection to it, this is the time to mention it. Speak out."

Once more, I stammered with difficulty that I had no objection.

"I should think not! Now, Mr. Pip, I have done with stipulations." Though he called me Mr. Pip, and began rather to make up to me, he still could not

---

8. The most frequently cited source for the phrase appears in sonnet 21 of Sir Philip Sidney's sonnet sequence *Astrophil and Stella* (about 1582), lines 6–8: "that to my birth I owe / Nobler desires, lest else that friendly foe, / Great expectations, wear a train of shame." But the expression was fairly common: Dickens himself had used it at least once before, in *Martin Chuzzlewit*, chapter 6. On its timely appearance in Charles Lever's *A Day's Ride*, see p. 422.

9. This, as a condition of his great expectations, is now Pip's legal name. In chapter 30, he refers to himself as Mr. Pip in his snotty communiqué to Trabb, and in chapter 44 Wemmick addresses a note to "Mr. Philip Pip, Esquire"; as a lawyer's clerk, Wemmick is not likely to err on this score.

get rid of a certain air of bullying suspicion; and even now he occasionally shut his eyes and threw his finger at me while he spoke, as much as to express that he knew all kinds of things to my disparagement, if he only chose to mention them. "We come next, to mere details of arrangement. You must know that, although I have used the term 'expectations' more than once, you are not endowed with expectations only. There is already lodged in my hands, a sum of money amply sufficient for your suitable education and mainte- nance. You will please consider me your guardian. Oh!" for I was going to thank him, "I tell you at once, I am paid for my services, or I shouldn't render them. It is considered that you must be better educated in accordance with your altered position, and that you will be alive to the importance and ne- cessity of at once entering on that advantage."

I said I had always longed for it.

"Never mind what you have always longed for, Mr. Pip," he retorted; "keep to the record. If you long for it now, that's enough. Am I answered that you are ready to be placed at once, under some proper tutor? Is that it?"

I stammered, yes, that was it.

"Good. Now, your inclinations are to be consulted. I don't think that wise, mind, but it's my trust. Have you ever heard of any tutor whom you would prefer to another?"

I had never heard of any tutor but Biddy and Mr. Wopsle's great-aunt; so, I replied in the negative.

"There is a certain tutor, of whom I have some knowledge, who I think might suit the purpose," said Mr. Jaggers. "I don't recommend him, observe; because I never recommend anybody. The gentleman I speak of, is one Mr. Matthew Pocket."

Ah! I caught at the name directly. Miss Havisham's relation. The Matthew whom Mr. and Mrs. Camilla had spoken of. The Matthew whose place was to be at Miss Havisham's head, when she lay dead, in her bride's dress on the bride's table.

"You know the name?" said Mr. Jaggers, looking shrewdly at me, and then shutting up his eyes while he waited for my answer.

My answer was, that I had heard of the name.

"Oh!" said he. "You have heard of the name. But the question is, what do you say of it?"

I said, or tried to say, that I was much obliged to him for his recommen- dation——

"No, my young friend!" he interrupted, shaking his great head very slowly. "Recollect yourself!"

Not recollecting myself, I began again that I was much obliged to him for his recommendation——

"No, my young friend," he interrupted, shaking his head and frowning and smiling both at once; "no, no, no; it's very well done but it won't do; you are too young to fix me with it. Recommendation is not the word, Mr. Pip. Try another."

Correcting myself, I said that I was much obliged to him for his mention of Mr. Matthew Pocket——

"*That's* more like it!" cried Mr. Jaggers.

—And (I added), I would gladly try that gentleman.

"Good. You had better try him in his own house. The way shall be prepared for you, and you can see his son first, who is in London. When will you come to London?"

I said (glancing at Joe, who stood looking on motionless), that I supposed I could come directly.

"First," said Mr. Jaggers, "you should have some new clothes to come in, and they should not be working clothes. Say this day week. You'll want some money. Shall I leave you twenty guineas?"

He produced a long purse,[1] with the greatest coolness, and counted them out on the table and pushed them over to me. This was the first time he had taken his leg from the chair. He sat astride of the chair when he had pushed the money over, and sat swinging his purse and eyeing Joe.

"Well, Joseph Gargery? You look dumbfoundered?"

"I *am*!" said Joe, in a very decided manner.

"It was understood that you wanted nothing for yourself, remember?"

"It were understood," said Joe. "And it are understood. And it ever will be similar according."

"But what," said Mr. Jaggers, swinging his purse, "what if it was in my instructions to make you a present, as compensation?"

"As compensation what for?" Joe demanded.

"For the loss of his services."

Joe laid his hand upon my shoulder with the touch of a woman. I have often thought him since, like the steam-hammer, that can crush a man or tap an egg-shell, in his combination of strength with gentleness. "Pip is that hearty welcome," said Joe, "to go free with his services to honour and fortun', as no words can tell him. But if you think as Money can make compensation to me for the loss of the little child—what come to the forge—and ever the best of friends!——"

O dear good Joe, whom I was so ready to leave and so unthankful to, I see you again, with your muscular blacksmith's arm before your eyes, and your broad chest heaving, and your voice dying away. O dear good faithful tender Joe, I feel the loving tremble of your hand upon my arm, as solemnly this day as if it had been the rustle of an angel's wing!

But I encouraged Joe at the time. I was lost in the mazes of my future fortunes, and could not retrace the by-paths we had trodden together. I begged Joe to be comforted, for (as he said) we had ever been the best of friends, and (as I said) we ever would be so. Joe scooped his eyes with his disengaged wrist, as if he were bent on gouging himself, but said not another word.

Mr. Jaggers had looked on at this, as one who recognised in Joe the village idiot and in me his keeper. When it was over, he said, weighing in his hand the purse he had ceased to swing:

"Now, Joseph Gargery, I warn you this is your last chance. No half measures with me. If you mean to take a present that I have it in charge to make you, speak out, and you shall have it. If on the contrary you mean to say——" Here, to his great amazement he was stopped by Joe's suddenly working round him with every demonstration of a fell[2] pugilistic purpose.

"Which I meantersay," cried Joe, "that if you come into my place bull-

---

1. A bag, usually of leather, that could be folded to fit into one's pocket.
2. Deadly.

baiting³ and badgering me, come out! Which I meantersay as such if you're a man, come on! Which I meantersay that what I say, I meantersay and stand or fall by!"

I drew Joe away, and he immediately became placable; merely stating to me, in an obliging manner and as a polite expostulatory notice to any one whom it might happen to concern, that he were not a going to be bull-baited and badgered in his own place. Mr. Jaggers had risen when Joe demonstrated, and had backed to near the door. Without evincing any inclination to come in again, he there delivered his valedictory remarks. They were these.

"Well, Mr. Pip, I think the sooner you leave here—as you are to be a 10 gentleman—the better. Let it stand for this day week, and you shall receive my printed address in the mean time. You can take a hackney-coach at the stage-coach⁴ office in London, and come straight to me. Understand that I express no opinion, one way or other, on the trust I undertake. I am paid for undertaking it, and I do so. Now, understand that, finally. Understand that!"

He was throwing his finger at both of us, and I think would have gone on, but for his seeming to think Joe dangerous, and going off.

Something came into my head which induced me to run after him, as he was going down to the Jolly Bargemen where he had left a hired carriage.

"I beg your pardon, Mr. Jaggers."   20

"Halloa!" said he, facing round, "what's the matter?"

"I wish to be quite right, Mr. Jaggers, and to keep to your directions; so I thought I had better ask. Would there be any objection to my taking leave of any one I know, about here, before I go away?"

"No," said he, looking as if he hardly understood me.

"I don't mean in the village only, but up town?"

"No," said he. "No objection."

I thanked him and ran home again, and there I found that Joe had already locked the front door, and vacated the state-parlour, and was seated by the kitchen fire with a hand on each knee, gazing intently at the burning coals. 30 I too sat down before the fire and gazed at the coals, and nothing was said for a long time.

My sister was in her cushioned chair in her corner, and Biddy sat at her needlework before the fire, and Joe sat next Biddy, and I sat next Joe in the corner opposite my sister. The more I looked into the glowing coals, the more incapable I became of looking at Joe; the longer the silence lasted, the more unable I felt to speak.

At length I got out, "Joe, have you told Biddy?"

"No, Pip," returned Joe, still looking at the fire, and holding his knees tight, as if he had private information that they intended to make off some- 40 where, "which I left it to yourself, Pip."

---

3. Like bear-baiting and boar-baiting, an English pastime that dates at least from the twelfth century, in which dogs were let loose on a tied-up and sometimes blinded animal. Ambassadors to Queen Elizabeth's court might be entertained not only with an opulent banquet but also by the baiting of bears and bulls with sturdy "English dogs," such as the native mastiff. Bull-baiting had virtually played itself out by the nineteenth century.

4. A hackney-coach (p. 129, n. 3), functionally a forerunner of the taxi, could be hired off the street, while a stage-coach, functionally a forerunner of the bus, traveled between fixed places at fixed hours. The typical stage-coach engaged four horses and seated about eight passengers, had some such name as "Tally-Ho," "Defiance," or "Rapid," traveled at between five and ten miles an hour, and bore the proprietor's name on the door, as well as the names of the principal towns it touched on or connected with.

"I would rather you told, Joe."

"Pip's a gentleman of fortun' then," said Joe, "and God bless him in it!"
Biddy dropped her work and looked at me. Joe held his knees and looked
at me. I looked at both of them. After a pause, they both heartily congratulated
me; but there was a certain touch of sadness in their congratulations that I
rather resented.

I took it upon myself to impress Biddy (and through Biddy, Joe) with the
grave obligation I considered my friends under, to know nothing and say
nothing about the maker of my fortune. It would all come out in good time,
I observed, and in the mean while nothing was to be said save that I had
come into great expectations from a mysterious patron. Biddy nodded her
head thoughtfully at the fire as she took up her work again, and said she
would be very particular; and Joe, still detaining his knees, said, "Ay, ay, I'll
be ekervally partickler, Pip;" and then they congratulated me again, and went
on to express so much wonder at the notion of my being a gentleman, that
I didn't half like it.

Infinite pains were then taken by Biddy to convey to my sister some idea
of what had happened. To the best of my belief, those efforts entirely failed.
She laughed and nodded her head a great many times, and even repeated
after Biddy the words "Pip" and "Property." But I doubt if they had more
meaning in them than an election cry, and I cannot suggest a darker picture
of her state of mind.[5]

I never could have believed it without experience, but as Joe and Biddy
became more at their cheerful ease again, I became quite gloomy. Dissatisfied
with my fortune, of course I could not be; but it is possible that I may have
been, without quite knowing it, dissatisfied with myself.

Anyhow, I sat with my elbow on my knee and my face upon my
hand, looking into the fire, as those two talked about my going away, and
about what they should do without me, and all that. And whenever I
caught one of them looking at me, though never so pleasantly (and they often
looked at me—particularly Biddy), I felt in a manner offended: as if they were
expressing some mistrust of me. Though Heaven knows they never did by
word or sign.

At those times I would get up and look out at the door; for our kitchen
door opened at once upon the night, and stood open on summer evenings
to air the room. The very stars to which I then raised my eyes, I am afraid I
took to be but poor and humble stars for glittering on the rustic objects among
which I had passed my life.

"Saturday night," said I, when we sat at our supper of bread-and-cheese
and beer. "Five more days, and then the day before *the* day! They'll soon
go."

"Yes, Pip," observed Joe, whose voice sounded hollow in his beer mug.
"They'll soon go."

"Soon, soon go," said Biddy.

"I have been thinking, Joe, that when I go down town on Monday, and
order my new clothes, I shall tell the tailor that I'll come and put them on

5. Dickens's dim view of parliamentary hokum and electioneering cant, perhaps conditioned by his
boring spell as a parliamentary reporter in the early thirties, is a staple of his fiction, from "The Election
for Beadle" in *Sketches by Boz* (1836), "Our Parish," 4 to the description of Veneering's candidacy
in *Our Mutual Friend* (1866) 2.3.

there, or that I'll have them sent to Mr. Pumblechook's. It would be very disagreeable to be stared at by all the people here."

"Mr. and Mrs. Hubble might like to see you in your new gen-teel figure too, Pip," said Joe, industriously cutting his bread, with his cheese on it, in the palm of his left hand, and glancing at my untasted supper as if he thought of the time when we used to compare slices. "So might Wopsle. And the Jolly Bargemen might take it as a compliment."

"That's just what I don't want, Joe. They would make such a business of it—such a coarse and common business—that I couldn't bear myself."

"Ah, that indeed, Pip!" said Joe. "If you couldn't abear yourself——" 10

Biddy asked me here, as she sat holding my sister's plate, "Have you thought about when you'll show yourself to Mr. Gargery, and your sister, and me? You will show yourself to us; won't you?"

"Biddy," I returned with some resentment, "you are so exceedingly quick that it's difficult to keep up with you."

("She always were quick," observed Joe.)

"If you had waited another moment, Biddy, you would have heard me say that I shall bring my clothes here in a bundle one evening—most likely on the evening before I go away."

Biddy said no more. Handsomely forgiving her, I soon exchanged an af- 20 fectionate good night with her and Joe, and went up to bed. When I got into my little room, I sat down and took a long look at it, as a mean little room that I should soon be parted from and raised above, for ever. It was furnished with fresh young remembrances too, and even at the same moment I fell into much the same confused division of mind between it and the better rooms to which I was going, as I had been in so often between the forge and Miss Havisham's, and Biddy and Estella.

The sun had been shining brightly all day on the roof of my attic, and the room was warm. As I put the window open and stood looking out, I saw Joe come slowly forth at the dark door below, and take a turn or two in the air; 30 and then I saw Biddy come and bring him a pipe and light it for him. He never smoked so late, and it seemed to hint to me that he wanted comforting, for some reason or other.

He presently stood at the door immediately beneath me, smoking his pipe, and Biddy stood there too, quietly talking to him, and I knew that they talked of me, for I heard my name mentioned in an endearing tone by both of them more than once. I would not have listened for more, if I could have heard more: so, I drew away from the window, and sat down in my one chair by the bedside, feeling it very sorrowful and strange that this first night of my bright fortunes should be the loneliest I had ever known. 40

Looking towards the open window, I saw light wreaths from Joe's pipe floating there, and I fancied it was like a blessing from Joe—not obtruded on me or paraded before me, but pervading the air we shared together. I put my light out, and crept into bed; and it was an uneasy bed now, and I never slept the old sound sleep in it any more.

★

Chapter XIX.

MORNING made a considerable difference in my general prospect of Life, and brightened it so much that it scarcely seemed the same. What lay heaviest on my mind was the consideration that six days intervened between me and the day of departure; for, I could not divest myself of a misgiving that something might happen to London in the mean while, and that, when I got there, it would be either greatly deteriorated or clean gone.

Joe and Biddy were very sympathetic and pleasant when I spoke of our approaching separation; but they only referred to it when I did. After breakfast, Joe brought out my indentures from the press in the best parlour, and we put them in the fire, and I felt that I was free. With all the novelty of my eman- 10 cipation on me, I went to church with Joe, and thought, perhaps the clergyman wouldn't have read that about the rich man and the kingdom of Heaven, if he had known all.[1]

After our early dinner I strolled out alone, purposing to finish off the marshes at once, and get them done with. As I passed the church, I felt (as I had felt during service in the morning) a sublime compassion for the poor creatures who were destined to go there, Sunday after Sunday, all their lives through, and to lie obscurely at last among the low green mounds. I promised myself that I would do something for them one of these days, and formed a plan in outline for bestowing a dinner of roast beef and plum-pudding, a pint 20 of ale, and a gallon of condescension, upon everybody in the village.

If I had often thought before, with something allied to shame, of my companionship with the fugitive whom I had once seen limping among those graves, what were my thoughts on this Sunday, when the place recalled the wretch, ragged and shivering, with his felon iron and badge! My comfort was, that it happened a long time ago, and that he had doubtless been transported a long way off, and that he was dead to me, and might be veritably dead into the bargain.

No more low wet grounds, no more dykes and sluices, no more of these grazing cattle—though they seemed, in their dull manner, to wear a more 30 respectful air now, and to face round, in order that they might stare as long as possible at the possessor of such great expectations—farewell, monotonous acquaintances of my childhood, henceforth I was for London and greatness: not for smith's work in general and for you! I made my exultant way to the

---

1. "It is easier for a camel to go through the eye of a needle than for a rich man to enter into the kingdom of God." The text for this prescribed Sunday morning sermon appears in Matthew 19.25, Mark 10.25, and Luke 18.25; it would be nice to latch on to this information to date the action once and for all. Before its revision in 1867, the lectionary printed at the beginning of the prayer book used to appoint three days in the year (not two, as now) on which each of the New Testament lessons were to be read—nine days for us to choose from. Since Pip's departure takes place in late spring or summer (it's warm enough for him to fall asleep outdoors, and he refers to "summer evenings" a few pages earlier), the dates prescribed in the lectionary can be narrowed to three: May 21 (Matthew), June 9 (Mark), July 6 (Luke) [Hill]. Assuming the main action of *Great Expectations* to take place sometime between 1800 and 1830, this leaves out Mark—no Sunday, June 9, between 1805 and 1833. Matthew is possible but unlikely: it would fix the year as 1815, which is improbably early. Luke is much our best bet: July 6 falls on a Sunday in 1823. From this we can infer some other dates. Pip, "in the fourth year of his apprenticeship," is presumably seventeen. His birthday—as he informs us in chapter 36—comes in November; and he has just turned seven when the novel opens. Accordingly, Pip leaves his village on Saturday, July 12, 1823; the novel begins on Thursday, December 24, 1812; and Pip was born in November 1805. Against this, Sadrin's sensible objection (p. 537, n. 2), and that masterplotter Wilkie Collins's, that "readers [do not] test an emotional book by the base rules of arithmetic."

old Battery, and, lying down there to consider the question whether Miss Havisham intended me for Estella, fell asleep.

When I awoke, I was much surprised to find Joe sitting beside me, smoking his pipe. He greeted me with a cheerful smile on my opening my eyes, and said:

"As being the last time, Pip, I thought I'd foller."

"And Joe, I am very glad you did so."

"Thankee, Pip."

"You may be sure, dear Joe," I went on, after we had shaken hands, "that I shall never forget you."   10

"No no, Pip!" said Joe, in a comfortable tone, "I'm sure of that. Ay, ay, old chap! Bless you, it were only necessary to get it well round in a man's mind, to be certain on it. But it took a bit of time to get it well round, the change come so oncommon plump; didn't it?"

Somehow I was not best pleased with Joe's being so mightily secure of me. I should have liked him to have betrayed emotion, or to have said, "It does you credit, Pip," or something of that sort. Therefore, I made no remark on Joe's first head: merely saying as to his second that the tidings had indeed come suddenly, but that I had always wanted to be a gentleman, and had often and often speculated on what I would do if I were one.   20

"Have you though?" said Joe. "Astonishing!"

"It's a pity now, Joe," said I, "that you did not get on a little more, when we had our lessons here; isn't it?"

"Well, I don't know," returned Joe. "I'm so awful dull. I'm only master of my own trade. It were always a pity as I was so awful dull; but it's no more of a pity now, than it was—this day twelvemonth—don't you see?"

What I had meant was, that when I came into my property and was able to do something for Joe, it would have been much more agreeable if he had been better qualified for a rise in station. He was so perfectly innocent of my meaning, however, that I thought I would mention it to Biddy in preference.   30

So, when we had walked home and had had tea, I took Biddy into our little garden by the side of the lane, and, after throwing out in a general way for the elevation of her spirits, that I should never forget her, said I had a favour to ask of her.

"And it is, Biddy," said I, "that you will not omit any opportunity of helping Joe on, a little."

"How helping him on?" asked Biddy, with a steady sort of glance.

"Well! Joe is a dear good fellow—in fact, I think he is the dearest fellow that ever lived—but he is rather backward in some things. For instance, Biddy, in his learning and his manners."   40

Although I was looking at Biddy as I spoke, and although she opened her eyes very wide when I had spoken, she did not look at me.

"Oh, his manners! Won't his manners do then?" asked Biddy, plucking a black currant leaf.

"My dear Biddy, they do very well here——"

"Oh! they *do* very well here?" interposed Biddy, looking closely at the leaf in her hand.

"Hear me out—but if I were to remove Joe into a higher sphere, as I shall hope to remove him when I fully come into my property, they would hardly do him justice."   50

"And don't you think he knows that?" asked Biddy.

It was such a very provoking question (for it had never in the most distant manner occurred to me), that I said, snappishly, "Biddy, what do you mean?"

Biddy having rubbed the leaf to pieces between her hands—and the smell of a black currant bush has ever since recalled to me that evening in the little garden by the side of the lane—said, "Have you never considered that he may be proud?"

"Proud!" I repeated, with disdainful emphasis.

"Oh! there are many kinds of pride," said Biddy, looking full at me and shaking her head; "pride is not all of one kind——"   10

"Well? What are you stopping for?" said I.

"Not all of one kind," resumed Biddy. "He may be too proud to let any one take him out of a place that he is competent to fill and fills well and with respect. To tell you the truth, I think he is: though it sounds bold in me to say so, for you must know him far better than I do."

"Now, Biddy," said I, "I am very sorry to see this in you. I did not expect to see this in you. You are envious, Biddy, and grudging. You are dissatisfied on account of my rise in fortune, and you can't help showing it."

"If you have the heart to think so," returned Biddy, "say so. Say so over and over again, if you have the heart to think so."   20

"If you have the heart to be so, you mean, Biddy," said I, in a virtuous and superior tone; "don't put it off upon me. I am very sorry to see it, and it's a —it's a bad side of human nature. I did intend to ask you to use any little opportunities you might have after I was gone, of improving dear Joe. But after this, I ask you nothing. I am extremely sorry to see this in you, Biddy," I repeated. "It's a—it's a bad side of human nature."

"Whether you scold me or approve of me," returned poor Biddy, "you may equally depend upon my trying to do all that lies in my power, here, at all times. And whatever opinion you take away of me, shall make no difference in my remembrance of you. Yet a gentleman should not be unjust neither,"   30
said Biddy, turning away her head.

I again warmly repeated that it was a bad side of human nature (in which sentiment, waiving its application, I have since seen reason to think I was right), and I walked down the little path away from Biddy, and Biddy went into the house, and I went out at the garden gate and took a dejected stroll until supper-time; again feeling it very sorrowful and strange that this, the second night of my bright fortunes, should be as lonely and unsatisfactory as the first.

But morning once more brightened my view, and I extended my clemency to Biddy, and we dropped the subject. Putting on the best clothes I had, I   40
went into town as early as I could hope to find the shops open, and presented myself before Mr. Trabb, the tailor: who was having his breakfast in the parlour behind his shop, and who did not think it worth his while to come out to me, but called me in to him.

"Well!" said Mr. Trabb, in a hail-fellow-well-met kind of way. "How are you, and what can I do for you?"

Mr. Trabb had sliced his hot roll into three feather beds,[2] and was slipping butter in between the blankets, and covering it up. He was a prosperous old

---

2. A feather bed is a thick quilt stuffed with feathers; Dickens uses the image to suggest the fat buttered mouth-filling rolls with which Trabb is gorging himself.

bachelor, and his open window looked into a prosperous little garden and orchard, and there was a prosperous iron safe let into the wall at the side of his fireplace, and I did not doubt that heaps of his prosperity were put away in it in bags.

"Mr. Trabb," said I, "it's an unpleasant thing to have to mention, because it looks like boasting; but I have come into a handsome property."

A change passed over Mr. Trabb. He forgot the butter in bed, got up from the bedside, and wiped his fingers on the tablecloth, exclaiming, "Lord bless my soul!"

"I am going up to my guardian in London," said I, casually drawing some 10 guineas out of my pocket and looking at them; "and I want a fashionable suit of clothes to go in. I wish to pay for them," I added—otherwise I thought he might only pretend to make them—"with ready money."

"My dear sir," said Mr. Trabb, as he respectfully bent his body, opened his arms, and took the liberty of touching me on the outside of each elbow, "don't hurt me by mentioning that. May I venture to congratulate you? Would you do me the favour of stepping into the shop?"

Now, Mr. Trabb's boy was the most audacious boy in all that country-side. When I had entered he was sweeping the shop, and he had sweetened his labours by sweeping over me. He was still sweeping when I came out into 20 the shop with Mr. Trabb, and he knocked the broom against all possible corners and obstacles, to express (as I understood it) equality with any blacksmith, alive or dead.[3]

"Hold that noise," said Mr. Trabb, with the greatest sternness, "or I'll knock your head off! Do me the favour to be seated, sir. Now this," said Mr. Trabb, taking down a roll of cloth, and tiding it out in a flowing manner over the counter, preparatory to getting his hand under it to show the gloss, "is a very sweet article. I can recommend it for your purpose, sir, because it really is extra super. But you shall see some others. Give me Number Four, you!" (To the boy, and with a dreadfully severe stare: foreseeing the danger of that 30 miscreant's brushing me with it, or making some other sign of familiarity.)

Mr. Trabb never removed his stern eye from the boy until he had deposited number four on the counter and was at a safe distance again. Then, he commanded him to bring number five and number eight. "And let me have none of your tricks here," said Mr. Trabb, "or you shall repent it, you young scoundrel, the longest day you have to live."

Mr. Trabb then bent over number four, and in a sort of deferential confidence recommended it to me as a light article for summer wear, an article much in vogue among the nobility and gentry, an article that it would ever be an honour to him to reflect upon a distinguished fellow-townsman's (if he 40 might claim me for a fellow-townsman) having worn. "Are you bringing numbers five and eight, you vagabond," said Mr. Trabb to the boy after that, "or shall I kick you out of the shop and bring them myself?"

I selected the materials for a suit, with the assistance of Mr. Trabb's judgment, and re-entered the parlour to be measured. For, although Mr. Trabb

---

3. Like a lot of Dickens's comic figures, Trabb's boy remains unidentified except in relation to somebody else—who happens to be less amusing than his dependent. Elsewhere in *Great Expectations* we have characters—the Avenger, the Aged P., old Gruffandgrim—who seem to remain anonymous even when their names appear in the text. Who ever remembers that the Avenger's name is Pepper?

had my measure already, and had previously been quite contented with it, he said apologetically that it "wouldn't do under existing circumstances, sir —wouldn't do at all." So, Mr. Trabb measured and calculated me, in the parlour, as if I were an estate and he the finest species of surveyor, and gave himself such a world of trouble that I felt that no suit of clothes could possibly remunerate him for his pains. When he had at last done and had appointed to send the articles to Mr. Pumblechook's on the Thursday evening, he said, with his hand upon the parlour lock, "I know, sir, that London gentlemen cannot be expected to patronise local work, as a rule: but if you would give me a turn now and then in the quality of a townsman, I should greatly esteem 10 it. Good morning, sir; much obliged.—Door!"

The last word was flung at the boy, who had not the least notion what it meant. But I saw him collapse as his master rubbed me out with his hands, and my first decided experience of the stupendous power of money, was, that it had morally laid upon his back, Trabb's boy.

After this memorable event, I went to the hatter's, and the bootmaker's, and the hosier's, and felt rather like Mother Hubbard's dog whose outfit required the services of so many trades.[4] I also went to the coach-office and took my place for seven o'clock on Saturday morning. It was not necessary to explain everywhere that I had come into a handsome property; but when- 20 ever I said anything to that effect, it followed that the officiating tradesman ceased to have his attention diverted through the window by the High-street, and concentrated his mind upon me. When I had ordered everything I wanted, I directed my steps towards Pumblechook's, and, as I approached that gentleman's place of business, I saw him standing at his door.

He was waiting for me with great impatience. He had been out early with the chaise-cart, and had called at the forge and heard the news. He had prepared a collation[5] for me in the Barnwell parlour, and he too ordered his shopman to "come out of the gangway" as my sacred person passed.

"My dear friend," said Mr. Pumblechook, taking me by both hands, when 30 he and I and the collation were alone, "I give you joy of your good fortune. Well deserved, well deserved!"

This was coming to the point, and I thought it a sensible way of expressing himself.

"To think," said Mr. Pumblechook, after snorting admiration at me for some moments, "that I should have been the humble instrument of leading up to this, is a proud reward."

I begged Mr. Pumblechook to remember that nothing was to be ever said or hinted, on that point.

"My dear young friend," said Mr. Pumblechook, "if you will allow me to 40 call you so——"

I murmured "Certainly," and Mr. Pumblechook took me by both hands again, and communicated a movement to his waistcoat that had an emotional appearance, though it was rather low down, "My dear young friend, rely upon my doing my little all in your absence, by keeping the fact before the mind

4. In Sarah Catherine Martin's nursery rhyme "The Comic Adventures of Mother Hubbard and Her Dog" (1805), Mother Hubbard, to fit out her dog, requisitions the services of a tailor, hatter, barber, cobbler, seamstress, and hosier.
5. A light meal. The term originates in the frugal supper taken by monks after the readings from the *Collationes*, or "Lives of the Fathers."

of Joseph.—Joseph!" said Mr. Pumblechook, in the way of a compassionate adjuration. "Joseph!! Joseph!!!" Thereupon he shook his head and tapped it, expressing his sense of deficiency in Joseph.

"But my dear young friend," said Mr. Pumblechook, "you must be hungry, you must be exhausted. Be seated. Here is a chicken had round from the Boar, here is a tongue had round from the Boar, here's one or two little things had round from the Boar, that I hope you may not despise. But do I," said Mr. Pumblechook, getting up again the moment after he had sat down, "see afore me, him as I ever sported with in his times of happy infancy? And may I—may I——?"   10

This May I meant, might he shake hands? I consented, and he was fervent, and then sat down again.

"Here is wine," said Mr. Pumblechook. "Let us drink, Thanks to Fortune, and may she ever pick out her favourites with equal judgment! And yet I cannot," said Mr. Pumblechook, getting up again, "see afore me One—and likeways drink to One—without again expressing—May I—may I——?"

I said he might, and he shook hands with me again, and emptied his glass and turned it upside down. I did the same; and if I had turned myself upside down before drinking, the wine could not have gone more direct to my head.

Mr. Pumblechook helped me to the liver wing, and to the best slice of   20
tongue (none of those out-of-the-way No Thoroughfares of Pork now),[6] and took, comparatively speaking, no care of himself at all. "Ah! poultry, poultry! You little thought," said Mr. Pumblechook, apostrophising the fowl in the dish, "when you was a young fledgling, what was in store for you. You little thought you was to be refreshment beneath this humble roof for one as— Call it a weakness, if you will," said Mr. Pumblechook, getting up again, "but may I? may I——?"

It began to be unnecessary to repeat the form of saying he might, so he did it at once. How he ever did it so often without wounding himself with my knife, I don't know.   30

"And your sister," he resumed, after a little steady eating, "which had the honour of bringing you up by hand! It's a sad picter, to reflect that she's no longer equal to fully understanding the honour. May——"

I saw he was about to come at me again, and I stopped him.

"We'll drink her health," said I.

"Ah!" cried Mr. Pumblechook, leaning back in his chair, quite flaccid with admiration, "that's the way you know 'em, sir!" (I don't know who Sir was, but he certainly was not I, and there was no third person present); "that's the way you know the noble minded, sir! Ever forgiving and ever affable. It might," said the servile Pumblechook, putting down his untasted glass in a   40
hurry and getting up again, "to a common person, have the appearance of repeating—but may I——?"

When he had done it, he resumed his seat and drank to my sister. "Let us never be blind," said Mr. Pumblechook, "to her faults of temper, but it is to be hoped she meant well."

At about this time I began to observe that he was getting flushed in the face; as to myself, I felt all face, steeped in wine and smarting.

6. The inedible parts—"those obscure corners of pork"—forced down Pip's throat at the Christmas dinner in chapter 4. "Liver wing": the right wing of the chicken, served as a special delicacy with the liver tucked under it—again, in contrast to the "scaly tips of the drumsticks" doled out to Pip earlier.

I mentioned to Mr. Pumblechook that I wished to have my new clothes sent to his house, and he was ecstatic on my so distinguishing him. I mentioned my reason for desiring to avoid observation in the village, and he lauded it to the skies. There was nobody but himself, he intimated, worthy of my confidence, and—in short, might he? Then he asked me tenderly if I remembered our boyish games at sums, and how we had gone together to have me bound apprentice, and, in effect, how he had ever been my favourite fancy and my chosen friend? If I had taken ten times as many glasses of wine as I had, I should have known that he never had stood in that relation towards me, and should in my heart of hearts have repudiated the idea. Yet for all 10 that, I remember feeling convinced that I had been much mistaken in him, and that he was a sensible practical good-hearted prime fellow.

By degrees he fell to reposing such great confidence in me, as to ask my advice in reference to his own affairs. He mentioned that there was an opportunity for a great amalgamation and monopoly of the corn and seed trade on those premises, if enlarged, such as had never occurred before in that, or any other neighbourhood. What alone was wanting to the realisation of a vast fortune, he considered to be More Capital. Those were the two little words, more capital. Now it appeared to him (Pumblechook) that if that capital were got into the business, through a sleeping partner,[7] sir: which sleeping partner 20 would have nothing to do but walk in, by self or deputy, whenever he pleased, and examine the books—and walk in twice a year and take his profits away in his pocket, to the tune of fifty per cent—it appeared to him that that might be an opening for a young gentleman of spirit combined with property, which would be worthy of his attention. But what did I think? He had great confidence in my opinion, and what did I think? I gave it as my opinion, "Wait a bit!" The united vastness and distinctness of this view so struck him, that he no longer asked if he might shake hands with me, but said he really must— and did.

We drank all the wine, and Mr. Pumblechook pledged himself over and 30 over again to keep Joseph up to the mark (I don't know what mark), and to render me efficient and constant service (I don't know what service). He also made known to me for the first time in my life, and certainly after having kept his secret wonderfully well, that he had always said of me, "That boy is no common boy, and mark me, his fortun' will be no common fortun'." He said with a tearful smile that it was a singular thing to think of now, and I said so too. Finally, I went out into the air with a dim perception that there was something unwonted in the conduct of the sunshine, and found that I had slumberously got to the turnpike without having taken any account of the road. 40

There, I was roused by Mr. Pumblechook's hailing me. He was a long way down the sunny street, and was making expressive gestures for me to stop. I stopped, and he came up breathless.

"No, my dear friend," said he, when he had recovered wind for speech. "Not if I can help it. This occasion shall not entirely pass without that affability on your part.—May I, as an old friend and well-wisher? May I?"

We shook hands for the hundredth time at least, and he ordered a young

---

7. A partner who shares in financing a business without participating in its management. In the U.S., "silent partner." Here and elsewhere Dickens capitalizes on the deviousness of active partners in blaming the sleeping ones for every disagreeable transaction. More specifically, see p. 200 and n. 5.

carter out of my way with the greatest indignation. Then, he blessed me and stood waving his hand to me until I had passed the crook in the road; and then I turned into a field and had a long nap under a hedge before I pursued my way home.

I had scant luggage to take with me to London, for little of the little I possessed was adapted to my new station. But I began packing that same afternoon, and wildly packed up things that I knew I should want next morning, in the maintenance of a fiction that there was not a moment to be lost.

So, Tuesday, Wednesday, and Thursday, passed; and on Friday morning I went to Mr. Pumblechook's, to put on my new clothes and pay my visit to 10 Miss Havisham. Mr. Pumblechook's own room was given up to me to dress in, and was decorated with clean towels expressly for the event. My clothes were rather a disappointment, of course. Probably every new and eagerly expected garment ever put on since clothes came in, fell a trifle short of the wearer's expectation. But after I had had my new suit on, some half an hour, and had gone through an immensity of posturing with Mr. Pumblechook's very limited dressing-glass in the futile endeavour to see my legs, it seemed to fit me better. It being market morning at a neighbouring town some ten miles off, Mr. Pumblechook was not at home. I had not told him exactly when I meant to leave, and was not likely to shake hands with him again 20 before departing. This was all as it should be, and I went out in my new array: fearfully ashamed of having to pass the shopman, and suspicious after all that I was at a personal disadvantage, something like Joe's in his Sunday suit.

I went circuitously to Miss Havisham's by all the back ways, and rang at the bell constrainedly, on account of the stiff long fingers of my gloves. Sarah Pocket came to the gate, and positively reeled back when she saw me so changed; her walnut-shell countenance likewise, turned from brown to green and yellow.

"You?" said she. "You? Good gracious! What do you want?"   30

"I am going to London, Miss Pocket," said I, "and want to say good-by to Miss Havisham."

I was not expected, for she left me locked in the yard, while she went to ask if I were to be admitted. After a very short delay, she returned and took me up, staring at me all the way.

Miss Havisham was taking exercise in the room with the long spread table, leaning on her crutched stick. The room was lighted as of yore, and at the sound of our entrance, she stopped and turned. She was then just abreast of the rotted bride-cake.

"Don't go, Sarah," she said. "Well, Pip?"   40

"I start for London, Miss Havisham, to-morrow," I explained, exceedingly careful what I said, "and I thought you would kindly not mind my taking leave of you."

"This is a gay figure, Pip," said she, making her crutched stick play round me, as if she, the fairy godmother who had changed me, were bestowing the finishing gift.

"I have come into such good fortune since I saw you last, Miss Havisham," I murmured. "And I am so grateful for it, Miss Havisham!"

"Ay, ay!" said she, looking at the discomfited and envious Sarah with delight. "I have seen Mr. Jaggers. *I* have heard about it, Pip. So you go to-morrow?"

"Yes, Miss Havisham."

"And you are adopted by a rich person?"

"Yes, Miss Havisham."

"Not named, eh?"

"No, Miss Havisham."

"And Mr. Jaggers is made your guardian?"

"Yes, Miss Havisham."

She quite gloated on these questions and answers, so keen was her enjoy- 10 ment of Sarah Pocket's jealous dismay. "Well!" she went on; "you have a promising career before you. Be good—deserve it—and abide by Mr. Jaggers's instructions." She looked at me, and looked at Sarah, and Sarah's counte-nance wrung out of her watchful face a cruel smile. "Good-by, Pip!—you will always keep the name of Pip, you know."

"Yes, Miss Havisham."

"Good-by, Pip!"

She stretched out her hand, and I went down on my knee and put it to my lips. I had not considered how I should take leave of her; it came naturally to me at the moment, to do this. She looked at Sarah Pocket with triumph 20 in her weird eyes, and so I left my fairy godmother, with both her hands on her crutched stick, standing in the midst of the dimly lighted room beside the rotten bride-cake that was hidden in cobwebs.

Sarah Pocket conducted me down as if I were a Ghost who must be seen out. She could not get over my appearance, and was in the last degree con-founded. I said "Good-by, Miss Pocket;" but she merely stared, and did not seem collected enough to know that I had spoken. Clear of the house, I made the best of my way back to Pumblechook's, took off my new clothes, made them into a bundle, and went back home in my older dress, carrying it—to speak the truth, much more at my ease too, though I had the bundle 30 to carry.

And now those six days which were to have run out so slowly, had run out fast and were gone, and to-morrow looked me in the face more steadily than I could look at it. As the six evenings had dwindled away to five, to four, to three, to two, I had become more and more appreciative of the society of Joe and Biddy. On this last evening, I dressed myself out in my new clothes for their delight, and sat in my splendour until bedtime. We had a hot supper on the occasion, graced by the inevitable roast fowl, and we had some flip[8] to finish with. We were all very low, and none the higher for pretending to be in spirits.

I was to leave our village at five in the morning, carrying my little hand- 40 portmanteau,[9] and I had told Joe that I wished to walk away all alone. I am afraid—sore afraid—that this purpose originated in my sense of the contrast there would be between me and Joe, if we went to the coach together. I had pretended with myself that there was nothing of this taint in the arrangement; but when I went up to my little room on this last night I felt compelled to

---

8. Mixture of beer, liquor, sugar, heated with a red-hot poker, popular at Christmas.
9. Originally a case or bag for use on a trip; in its more frequent current sense, a stiff leather suitcase, hinged and made to open into two compartments.

admit that it might be so, and had an impulse upon me to go down again and entreat Joe to walk with me in the morning. I did not.

All night there were coaches in my broken sleep, going to wrong places instead of to London, and having in the traces, now dogs, now cats, now pigs, now men—never horses. Fantastic failures of journeys occupied me until the day dawned and the birds were singing. Then, I got up and partly dressed, and sat at the window to take a last look out, and in taking it fell asleep.

Biddy was astir so early to get my breakfast, that, although I did not sleep at the window an hour, I smelt the smoke of the kitchen fire when I started 10 up with a terrible idea that it must be late in the afternoon. But long after that, and long after I had heard the clinking of the teacups and was quite ready, I wanted the resolution to go down stairs. After all, I remained up there, repeatedly unlocking and unstrapping my small portmanteau and locking and strapping it up again, until Biddy called to me that I was late.

It was a hurried breakfast with no taste in it. I got up from the meal, saying with a sort of briskness, as if it had only just occurred to me, "Well! I suppose I must be off!" and then I kissed my sister who was laughing and nodding and shaking in her usual chair, and kissed Biddy, and threw my arms around Joe's neck. Then I took up my little portmanteau and walked out. The last I saw of 20 them was when I presently heard a scuffle behind me, and looking back, saw Joe throwing an old shoe after me and Biddy throwing another old shoe.[1] I stopped then, to wave my hat, and dear old Joe waved his strong right arm above his head, crying huskily "Hooroar!" and Biddy put her apron to her face.

I walked away at a good pace, thinking it was easier to go than I had supposed it would be, and reflecting that it would never have done to have had an old shoe thrown after the coach, in sight of all the High-street. I whistled and made nothing of going. But the village was very peaceful and quiet, and the light mists were solemnly rising as if to show me the world, and I had been so innocent and little there, and all beyond was so unknown 30 and great, that in a moment with a strong heave and sob I broke into tears. It was by the finger-post at the end of the village, and I laid my hand upon it, and said, "Good-by, O my dear, dear friend!"

Heaven knows we need never be ashamed of our tears, for they are rain upon the blinding dust of earth, overlying our hard hearts. I was better after I had cried, than before—more sorry, more aware of my own ingratitude, more gentle. If I had cried before, I should have had Joe with me then.

So subdued I was by those tears, and by their breaking out again in the course of the quiet walk, that when I was on the coach, and it was clear of the town, I deliberated with an aching heart whether I would not get down 40 when we changed horses, and walk back, and have another evening at home, and a better parting. We changed, and I had not made up my mind, and still reflected for my comfort that it would be quite practicable to get down and walk back, when we changed again. And while I was occupied with these deliberations, I would fancy an exact resemblance to Joe in some man coming

1. This farewell-and-good-luck ritual, nowadays chiefly inflicted on newlyweds, can be traced back to ancient Hebrew practice. Monod cites Ruth 4.7: "Now this was the manner in former times in Israel concerning redeeming and concerning changing, for to confirm all things: a man plucked off his shoe, and gave it to his neighbour: and this was a testimony in Israel."

along the road towards us, and my heart would beat high. As if he could possibly be there!

We changed again, and yet again, and it was now too late and too far to go back, and I went on. And the mists had all solemnly risen now, and the world lay spread before me.

THIS IS THE END OF THE FIRST STAGE OF PIP'S EXPECTATIONS.

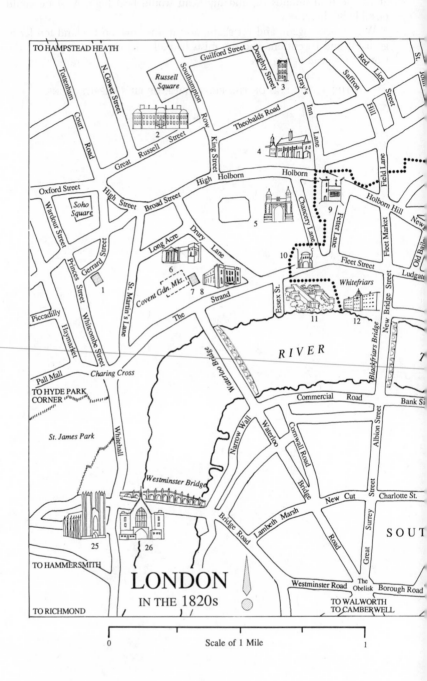

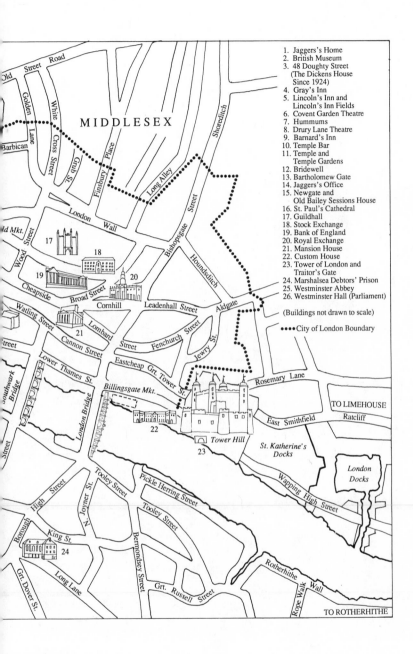

MIDDLESEX

1. Jaggers's Home
2. British Museum
3. 48 Doughty Street
   (The Dickens House
   Since 1924)
4. Gray's Inn
5. Lincoln's Inn and
   Lincoln's Inn Fields
6. Covent Garden Theatre
7. Hummums
8. Drury Lane Theatre
9. Barnard's Inn
10. Temple Bar
11. Temple and
    Temple Gardens
12. Bridewell
13. Bartholomew Gate
14. Jaggers's Office
15. Newgate and
    Old Bailey Sessions House
16. St. Paul's Cathedral
17. Guildhall
18. Stock Exchange
19. Bank of England
20. Royal Exchange
21. Mansion House
22. Custom House
23. Tower of London and
    Traitor's Gate
24. Marshalsea Debtors' Prison
25. Westminster Abbey
26. Westminster Hall (Parliament)

(Buildings not drawn to scale)

●●●●City of London Boundary

Chapter XX.

THE journey from our town to the metropolis was a journey of about five hours. It was a little past mid-day when the four-horse stage-coach by which I was a passenger, got into the ravel of traffic frayed out about the Cross-Keys, Wood-street, Cheapside, London.[1]

We Britons had at that time particularly settled that it was treasonable to doubt our having and our being the best of everything: otherwise, while I was scared by the immensity of London, I think I might have had some faint doubts whether it was not rather ugly, crooked, narrow, and dirty.

Mr. Jaggers had duly sent me his address; it was Little Britain,[2] and he had written after it on his card, "just out of Smithfield, and close by the coach-office." Nevertheless, a hackney-coachman,[3] who seemed to have as many capes to his greasy great-coat as he was years old, packed me up in his coach and hemmed me in with a folding and jingling barrier of steps, as if he were going to take me fifty miles. His getting on his box, which I remember to have been decorated with an old weather-stained pea-green hammercloth,[4] motheaten into rags, was quite a work of time. It was a wonderful equipage, with six great coronets outside,[5] and ragged things behind for I don't know how many footmen to hold on by, and a harrow[6] below them, to prevent amateur footmen from yielding to the temptation.

I had scarcely had time to enjoy the coach and to think how like a straw-yard it was, and yet how like a rag-shop,[7] and to wonder why the horses' nose-bags were kept inside, when I observed the coachman beginning to get down, as if we were going to stop presently. And stop we presently did, in a gloomy street, at certain offices with an open door, whereon was painted MR. JAGGERS.

"How much?" I asked the coachman.

The coachman glanced at Mr. Jaggers's name and answered, "A shilling—unless you wished to make it more."

I naturally said I had no wish to make it more.

"Then it must be a shilling," observed the coachman. "I don't want to get into trouble. I know him!" He darkly closed an eye at Mr. Jaggers's name, and shook his head.

1. Terminus for the Rochester coach route. "Cross-Keys": the coaching inn at which Dickens alighted when he came up to London, "packed like game," in the winter of 1822–23. The yards and stables attached to these taverns made them ideal traffic stops.
2. Street north of St. Paul's, named for the Dukes of Briton (Brittany), whose town mansions were located in the area. Jaggers's is one of a great many legal offices in the area, which is close to the criminal courts.
3. "A machine called a hackney-coach, licensed to carry six people, redolent of damp straw, driven by a still damper coachman, was the principal mode of locomotion [from the seventeenth to the early nineteenth century]" (Serjeant William Ballentine, quoted by Hill in *Dickensian* 39 [1943]: 26). A hackney was hired, or "borrowed"; hence the term "hackneyed" to mean unoriginal. Dickens describes it as "a great lumbering square concern of a dirty yellow colour (like a bilious brunette), with very small glasses, but very large frames; the panels are ornamented with a faded coat of arms, in shape something like a dissected bat" ("Hackney Coach Stands," *Sketches by Boz*, "Scenes," 7).
4. Cloth or blanket covering the driver's seat; literally a box containing a hammer and other tools kept on hand for emergency road repairs.
5. The armorial devices on the door panels indicate that the coach had once been the property of the nobility.
6. Spiked metal bars designed to keep freeloaders from riding on the back.
7. The floor of the coach might be covered with straw to keep the passengers' feet warm. Rag-shop suggests that it was littered with junk.

When he had got his shilling, and had in course of time completed the ascent to his box, and had got away (which appeared to relieve his mind), I went into the front office with my little portmanteau in my hand, and asked, Was Mr. Jaggers at home?

"He is not," returned the clerk. "He is in Court at present. Am I addressing Mr. Pip?"

I signified that he was addressing Mr. Pip.

"Mr. Jaggers left word would you wait in his room. He couldn't say how long he might be, having a case on. But it stands to reason, his time being valuable, that he won't be longer than he can help."   10

With those words, the clerk opened a door, and ushered me into an inner chamber at the back. Here we found a gentleman with one eye, in a velveteen suit and knee-breeches, who wiped his nose with his sleeve on being interrupted in the perusal of the newspaper.

"Go and wait outside, Mike," said the clerk.

I began to say that I hoped I was not interrupting——when the clerk shoved this gentleman out with as little ceremony as I ever saw used, and tossing his fur cap out after him, left me alone.

Mr. Jaggers's room was lighted by a skylight only, and was a most dismal place; the skylight eccentrically patched, like a broken head, and the distorted   20 adjoining houses looking as if they had twisted themselves to peep down at me through it. There were not so many papers about, as I should have expected to see; and there were some odd objects about, that I should not have expected to see—such as an old rusty pistol, a sword in a scabbard, several strange-looking boxes and packages, and two dreadful casts on a shelf of faces peculiarly swollen, and twitchy about the nose.[8] Mr. Jaggers's own high-backed chair was of deadly black horsehair, with rows of brass nails round it like a coffin; and I fancied I could see how he leaned back in it, and bit his forefinger at the clients. The room was but small, and the clients seemed to have had a habit of backing up against the wall: for the wall, especially op-   30 posite to Mr. Jaggers's chair, was greasy with shoulders. I recalled, too, that the one-eyed gentleman had shuffled forth against the wall when I was the innocent cause of his being turned out.

I sat down in the cliental chair placed over against Mr. Jaggers's chair, and became fascinated by the dismal atmosphere of the place. I called to mind that the clerk had the same air of knowing something to everybody else's disadvantage, as his master had. I wondered how many other clerks there were up-stairs, and whether they all claimed to have the same disparaging mastery of their fellow-creatures. I wondered what was the history of all the odd litter about the room, and how it came there. I wondered whether the   40 two swollen faces were of Mr. Jaggers's family, and, if he were so unfortunate as to have had a pair of such ill-looking relations, why he stuck them on that dusty perch for the blacks[9] and flies to settle on, instead of giving them a place at home. Of course I had no experience of a London summer day, and my spirits may have been oppressed by the hot exhausted air, and by the dust and grit that lay thick on everything. But I sat wondering and waiting in Mr.

8. Authentic detail. On a two-hour tour of Newgate on November 5, 1835, Dickens was shown just such casts, "the faces of . . . two notorious murderers," the body snatchers Bishop and Williams, who furnished hospitals with the cadavers of their victims and were hanged at Newgate in 1831.
9. Soot.

Jaggers's close room, until I really could not bear the two casts on the shelf above Mr. Jaggers's chair, and got up and went out.

When I told the clerk that I would take a turn in the air while I waited, he advised me to go round the corner and I should come into Smithfield.[1] So I came into Smithfield, and the shameful place, being all asmear with filth and fat and blood and foam, seemed to stick to me. So I rubbed it off with all possible speed by turning into a street where I saw the great black dome of Saint Paul's bulging at me from behind a grim stone building which a bystander said was Newgate Prison. Following the wall of the jail, I found the roadway covered with straw to deaden the noise of passing vehicles;[2] and from this, and from the quantity of people standing about, smelling strongly of spirits and beer, I inferred that the trials were on.

While I looked about me here, an exceedingly dirty and partially drunk minister of justice[3] asked me if I would like to step in and hear a trial or so: informing me that he could give me a front place for half-a-crown, whence I should command a full view of the Lord Chief Justice[4] in his wig and robes—mentioning that awful personage like waxwork, and presently offering him at the reduced price of eighteenpence. As I declined the proposal on the plea of an appointment, he was so good as to take me into a yard and show me where the gallows was kept, and also where people were publicly whipped, and then he showed me the Debtors' Door,[5] out of which culprits came to be hanged: heightening the interest of that dreadful portal by giving me to understand that "four on 'em" would come out at that door the day after tomorrow at eight in the morning, to be killed in a row.[6] This was horrible, and gave me a sickening idea of London: the more so as the Lord Chief Justice's proprietor wore (from his hat down to his boots and up again to his pocket-handkerchief inclusive) mildewed clothes, which had evidently not belonged to him originally, and which, I took it into my head, he had bought cheap of the executioner.[7] Under these circumstances I thought myself well rid of him for a shilling.

I dropped into the office to ask if Mr. Jaggers had come in yet, and I found he had not, and I strolled out again. This time I made the tour of Little Britain, and turned into Bartholomew Close;[8] and now I became aware that other people were waiting about for Mr. Jaggers, as well as I. There were two men of secret appearance lounging in Bartholomew Close, and thoughtfully

1. London's principal cattle market from 1150 to 1855, north of St. Paul's. Dickens crusaded against the brutal treatment of livestock and the appalling conditions of the market generally in the paper "The Heart of London," *Household Words*, May 4, 1850; an earlier view of Smithfield appears in the famous description in *Oliver Twist*, chapter 21.
2. The traffic at the time Pip arrived in London made as much of a racket as it makes today. To deaden the noise of horses' hooves and metal-rimmed wheels, streets were covered with straw, especially outside hospitals and law-courts (Guiliano/Collins).
3. Sarcastic reference to the gatekeeper at Newgate.
4. Principal judge of the High Court, next in rank to the Lord Chancellor.
5. So named for the heavy debt the prisoners were about to pay on the gallows.
6. In 1783 public executions were transferred from the gallows or "hanging tree" at Tyburn (now Marble Arch) to Newgate, providing Londoners with an enormously popular spectator sport—at one of these entertainments, the execution of the murderers Haggerty and Holloway on February 22, 1807, twenty-eight fans were trampled to death. A lifelong opponent of public executions, Dickens argued vehemently against them in letters to the *Daily News* and the *Times* in 1846 and 1848. "Eight in the morning": the hour at which criminals were traditionally executed. Thus in *Oliver Twist*, chapter 52: "At eight, [Fagin] would be the only mourner in his funeral train." Public executions were abolished in 1868.
7. Who himself generally appropriated the clothes of his victims.
8. "Close": originally, cathedral precincts; here a narrow street near Bartholomew Church in the Smithfield area.

fitting their feet into the cracks of the pavement as they talked together, one of whom said to the other when they first passed me, that "Jaggers would do it if it was to be done." There was a knot of three men and two women standing at a corner, and one of the women was crying on her dirty shawl, and the other comforted her by saying, as she pulled her own shawl over her shoulders, "Jaggers is for him, 'Melia, and what more *could* you have?" There was a red-eyed little Jew who came into the Close while I was loitering there, in company with a second little Jew whom he sent upon an errand; and while the messenger was gone, I remarked this Jew, who was of a highly excitable temperament, performing a jig of anxiety under a lamp-post, and accompa-   10
nying himself, in a kind of frenzy, with the words, "Oh Jaggerth, Jaggerth, Jaggerth! all otherth ith Cag-Maggerth,[9] give me Jaggerth!" These testimonies to the popularity of my guardian made a deep impression on me, and I admired and wondered more than ever.

At length, as I was looking out at the iron gate of Bartholomew Close into Little Britain, I saw Mr. Jaggers coming across the road towards me. All the others who were waiting saw him at the same time, and there was quite a rush at him. Mr. Jaggers, putting a hand on my shoulder and walking me on at his side without saying anything to me, addressed himself to his followers.

First, he took the two secret men.   20

"Now, I have nothing to say to *you*," said Mr. Jaggers, throwing his finger at them. "I want to know no more than I know. As to the result, it's a toss-up. I told you from the first it was a toss-up. Have you paid Wemmick?"

"We made the money up this morning, sir," said one of the men, submis-sively, while the other perused Mr. Jaggers's face.

"I don't ask you when you made it up, or where, or whether you made it up at all. Has Wemmick got it?"

"Yes, sir," said both the men together.

"Very well; then you may go. Now, I won't have it!" said Mr. Jaggers, waving his hand at them to put them behind him. "If you say a word to me,   30
I'll throw up the case."

"We thought, Mr. Jaggers——" one of the men began, pulling off his hat.

"That's what I told you not to do," said Mr. Jaggers. "*You* thought! I think for you; that's enough for you. If I want you, I know where to find you; I don't want you to find me. Now I won't have it. I won't hear a word."

The two men looked at one another as Mr. Jaggers waved them behind again, and humbly fell back and were heard no more.

"And now *you*!" said Mr. Jaggers, suddenly stopping, and turning on the two women with the shawls, from whom the three men had meekly sep-arated.—"Oh! Amelia, is it?"   40

"Yes, Mr. Jaggers."

"And do you remember," retorted Mr. Jaggers, "that but for me you wouldn't be here and couldn't be here?"

"Oh yes, sir!" exclaimed both women together. "Lord bless you, sir, well we knows that!"

"Then why," said Mr. Jaggers, "do you come here?"

"My Bill, sir!" the crying woman pleaded.

---

9. Dealers in "cag-mag," or scraps of refuse, mainly in rotten meat. On the popular stage, Jews were habitually afflicted by lisps. In his *Sanity of Art* (1908), Bernard Shaw famously cites Jaggerth's Jew as a classic case of "echolalia"—the pathological repetition of meaningless rhyming words.

"Now, I tell you what!" said Mr. Jaggers. "Once for all. If you don't know that your Bill's in good hands, I know it. And if you come here, bothering about your Bill, I'll make an example of both your Bill and you, and let him slip through my fingers. Have you paid Wemmick?"

"Oh yes, sir! Every farden."

"Very well. Then you have done all you have got to do. Say another word— one single word—and Wemmick shall give you your money back."

This terrible threat caused the two women to fall off immediately. No one remained now but the excitable Jew, who had already raised the skirts of Mr. Jaggers's coat to his lips several times.   10

"I don't know this man!" said Mr. Jaggers, in the same devastating strain. "What does this fellow want?"

"Ma thear Mithter Jaggerth. Hown brother to Habraham Latharuth!"

"Who's he?" said Mr. Jaggers. "Let go of my coat."

The suitor, kissing the hem of the garment again before relinquishing it, replied, "Habraham Latharuth, on thuthpithion of plate."[1]

"You're too late," said Mr. Jaggers. "I am over the way."[2]

"Holy father, Mithter Jaggerth!" cried my excitable acquaintance, turning white, "don't thay you're again Habraham Latharuth!"

"I am," said Mr. Jaggers, "and there's an end of it. Get out of the way."   20

"Mithter Jaggerth! Half a moment! My hown cuthen'th gone to Mithter Wemmick at thith prethent minute, to hoffer him hany termth. Mithter Jaggerth! Half a quarter of a moment! If you'd have the condethenthun to be bought off from the t'other thide—at hany thuperior prithe!—money no object!—Mithter Jaggerth—Mithter——!"

My guardian threw his supplicant off with supreme indifference, and left him dancing on the pavement as if it were red-hot. Without further interruption, we reached the front office, where we found the clerk and the man in velveteen with the fur cap.

"Here's Mike," said the clerk, getting down from his stool, and approaching   30
Mr. Jaggers confidentially.

"Oh!" said Mr. Jaggers, turning to the man, who was pulling a lock of hair in the middle of his forehead, like the Bull in Cock Robin pulling at the bell-rope;[3] "your man comes on this afternoon. Well?"

"Well, Mas'r Jaggers," returned Mike, in the voice of a sufferer from a constitutional cold; "arter a deal o' trouble, I've found one, sir, as might do."

"What is he prepared to swear?"

"Well, Mas'r Jaggers," said Mike, wiping his nose on his fur cap this time; "in a general way, anythink."

---

1. Detained on the charge of having stolen or received stolen silver plate.
2. Engaged by the other party; prosecuting the case for the crown. As distinct from a barrister (a lawyer who has been called to the bar after graduating from one of the Inns of Court—in effect, a university man—and who is qualified to plead directly before the high courts), Jaggers, as a solicitor who has been trained, like Wemmick, in a lawyer's office, ordinarily acts as a legal advisor. Where this entails litigation, he prepares his client's case and submits the documentation to the barrister whom he engages to plead in court. But Jaggers in effect crosses the lines: in chapter 56, it is clearly not he but the unnamed barrister who is "saying what could be said" for the defendant; on the other hand, in a case like the one discussed here, *Lazarus v. the Crown*, he may himself prosecute. It has been suggested that this relaxation of the rules was mandated by the vast number of capital crimes, which so taxed the courts that solicitors were needed to pitch in as de facto barristers to prosecute minor offenses. By Dickens's time, the terms "solicitor" and "attorney" had become virtually interchangeable.
3. In stanza 13 of the old nursery rhyme (first published in 1744), the bull[finch] volunteers to toll the bell at Cock Robin's funeral. Pulling one's forelock: a sign of deference, generally from a country yokel to a member of the gentry.

Mr. Jaggers suddenly became most irate. "Now, I warned you before," said he, throwing his forefinger at the terrified client, "that if you ever presumed to talk in that way here, I'd make an example of you. You infernal scoundrel, how dare you tell ME that?"

The client looked scared, but bewildered too, as if he were unconscious what he had done.

"Spooney!" said the clerk, in a low voice, giving him a stir with his elbow. "Soft Head! Need you say it face to face?"

"Now, I ask you, you blundering booby," said my guardian, very sternly, "once more and for the last time, what the man you have brought here is   10 prepared to swear?"

Mike looked hard at my guardian, as if he were trying to learn a lesson from his face, and slowly replied, "Ayther to character, or to having been in his company and never left him all the night in question."

"Now, be careful. In what station of life is this man?"

Mike looked at his cap, and looked at the floor, and looked at the ceiling, and looked at the clerk, and even looked at me, before beginning to reply in a nervous manner, "We've dressed him up like——" when my guardian blustered out:

"What? You WILL, will you?"   20

("Spooney!" added the clerk again, with another stir.)

After some helpless casting about, Mike brightened and began again: "He is dressed like a 'spectable pieman. A sort of a pastrycook."

"Is he here?" asked my guardian.

"I left him," said Mike, "a settin on some door-steps round the corner."

"Take him past that window, and let me see him."

The window indicated was the office window. We all three went to it, behind the wire blind,[4] and presently saw the client go by in an accidental manner, with a murderous-looking tall individual, in a short suit of white linen and a paper cap. This guileless confectioner was not by any means   30 sober, and had a black eye in the green stage of recovery, which was painted over.

"Tell him to take his witness away directly," said my guardian to the clerk, in extreme disgust, "and ask him what he means by bringing such a fellow as that."

My guardian then took me into his own room, and while he lunched, standing, from a sandwich-box and a pocket flask of sherry (he seemed to bully his very sandwich as he ate it), informed me what arrangements he had made for me. I was to go to "Barnard's Inn,"[5] to young Mr. Pocket's rooms, where a bed had been sent in for my accommodation; I was to remain with   40 young Mr. Pocket until Monday; on Monday I was to go with him to his

---

4. Strong wire netting designed to keep burglars (and the light and heat) out.
5. One of the legal fraternities and dorms for students who planned to be called to the bar. As an "Inn of Chancery," Barnard's stood in a sort of "satellite relationship" to one of the four Inns of Court (Lincoln's Inn, Gray's Inn, Middle Temple, Inner Temple), the societies that alone had the right to certify students as barristers. A prospective student would thus serve his apprenticeship at an Inn of Chancery before being admitted to the Inn of Court that controlled it—Barnard's was affiliated with Gray's Inn. As neither Pip nor his roommate planned to be lawyers, clearly occupancy in these Inns was no longer restricted to future barristers; Dickens himself had rented chambers at Furnival's Inn as a young man. The legal fraternities were all conveniently clustered within easy distance of one another south of Holborn. The Inns of Chancery became increasingly obsolete after the Law Society established itself as a training ground for attorneys; only two survived the nineteenth century.

father's house on a visit, that I might try how I liked it. Also I was told what my allowance was to be—it was a very liberal one—and had handed to me from one of my guardian's drawers, the cards of certain tradesmen with whom I was to deal for all kinds of clothes, and such other things as I could in reason want. "You will find your credit good, Mr. Pip," said my guardian, whose flask of sherry smelt like a whole cask-full, as he hastily refreshed himself, "but I shall by this means be able to check your bills, and to pull you up if I find you outrunning the constable.[6] Of course you'll go wrong somehow, but that's no fault of mine."

After I had pondered a little over this encouraging sentiment, I asked Mr. Jaggers if I could send for a coach? He said it was not worth while, I was so near my destination; Wemmick should walk round with me, if I pleased.

I then found that Wemmick was the clerk in the next room. Another clerk was rung down from up-stairs to take his place while he was out,[7] and I accompanied him into the street, after shaking hands with my guardian. We found a new set of people lingering outside, but Wemmick made a way among them by saying coolly yet decisively, "I tell you it's no use; he won't have a word to say to one of you;" and we soon got clear of them, and went on side by side.

Chapter XXI.

CASTING my eyes on Mr. Wemmick as we went along, to see what he was like in the light of day, I found him to be a dry man, rather short in stature, with a square wooden face, whose expression seemed to have been imperfectly chipped out with a dull-edged chisel. There were some marks in it that might have been dimples, if the material had been softer and the instrument finer, but which, as it was, were only dints. The chisel had made three or four of these attempts at embellishment over his nose, but had given them up without an effort to smooth them off. I judged him to be a bachelor from the frayed condition of his linen, and he appeared to have sustained a good many bereavements; for, he wore at least four mourning rings,[1] besides a brooch representing a lady and a weeping willow at a tomb with an urn on it. I noticed, too, that several rings and seals hung at his watch-chain, as if he were quite laden with remembrances of departed friends. He had glittering eyes—small, keen, and black—and thin wide mottled lips. He had had them, to the best of my belief, from forty to fifty years.

"So you were never in London before?" said Mr. Wemmick to me.

"No," said I.

---

6. Originally, fleeing from arrest for debt; generalized to mean overspending or living beyond one's income.

7. Lawyers' clerks are of three sorts. In chapter 31 of *Pickwick Papers* Dickens gives an amusing account of their social gradations and lifestyles. All three work in the offices of qualified attorneys. Highest on the ladder is the articled clerk, in effect an attorney-in-training, whose parents or patrons remunerated the firm by paying a premium. Next, the salaried clerk, a long-term employee without prospects of advancement to solicitor: Wemmick falls into this category. At the bottom, a copying clerk, who, as his name suggests, copies legal documents by hand. Probably the best-known copying clerk in Dickens is Snagsby in *Bleak House;* the best-known in all of Anglophone literature, Melville's Bartleby the Scrivener (1856). Copying clerks often doubled as office boys.

1. Rings worn as remembrances of the deceased. Mourning brooches (usually of jet) are more properly worn by women. Dickens reverts to these gifts in chapter 24.

"*I* was new here once," said Mr. Wemmick. "Rum[2] to think of now!"

"You are well acquainted with it now?"

"Why, yes," said Mr. Wemmick. "I know the moves of it."

"Is it a very wicked place?" I asked, more for the sake of saying something than for information.

"You may get cheated, robbed, and murdered, in London. But there are plenty of people anywhere who'll do that for you."

"If there is bad blood between you and them," said I, to soften it off a little.

"Oh! I don't know about bad blood," returned Mr. Wemmick; "there's not much bad blood about. They'll do it, if there's anything to be got by it." 10

"That makes it worse."

"You think so?" returned Mr. Wemmick. "Much about the same, I should say."

He wore his hat on the back of his head, and looked straight before him: walking in a self-contained way as if there were nothing in the streets to claim his attention. His mouth was such a post-office of a mouth that he had a mechanical appearance of smiling. We had got to the top of Holborn Hill[3] before I knew that it was merely a mechanical appearance, and that he was not smiling at all. 20

"Do you know where Mr. Matthew Pocket lives?" I asked Mr. Wemmick.

"Yes," said he, nodding in the direction. "At Hammersmith,[4] west of London."

"Is that far?"

"Well! Say five miles."

"Do you know him?"

"Why, you're a regular cross-examiner!" said Mr. Wemmick, looking at me with an approving air. "Yes, I know him. *I* know him!"

There was an air of toleration or depreciation about his utterance of these words, that rather depressed me; and I was still looking sideways at his block 30 of a face in search of any encouraging note to the text when he said here we were at Barnard's Inn. My depression was not alleviated by the announcement, for I had supposed that establishment to be an hotel kept by one Barnard, to which the Blue Boar in our town was a mere public-house. Whereas I now found Barnard to be a disembodied spirit, or a fiction, and his inn the dingiest collection of shabby buildings ever squeezed together in a rank corner as a club for Tom-cats.

We entered this haven through a wicket-gate, and were disgorged by an introductory passage into a melancholy little square that looked to me like a flat burying-ground. I thought it had the most dismal trees in it, and the most 40 dismal sparrows, and the most dismal cats, and the most dismal houses (in number half a dozen or so), that I had ever seen. I thought the windows of the sets of chambers into which these houses were divided, were in every

---

2. Slang for "odd," "curious."
3. Stretch of road leading from the western boundaries of the City (see p. 144, n. 5) toward Newgate: for a brook (Olde Bourne) that ran down the Fleet River before the road was bridged over. Dubbed "Heavy Hill" by prisoners forced to trudge up the street from Newgate en route to being hanged at Tyburn.
4. Before being swallowed up by metropolitan London, a semirural suburb southwest of town. MS has "Hornsey, north of London." Hammersmith serves convenient narrative ends in its location fairly close to the Thames.

stage of dilapidated blind and curtain, crippled flower-pot, cracked glass, dusty decay and miserable makeshift; while To Let To Let To Let, glared at me from empty rooms, as if no new wretches ever came there, and the vengeance of the soul of Barnard were being slowly appeased by the gradual suicide of the present occupants and their unholy interment under the gravel. A frouzy[5] mourning of soot and smoke attired this forlorn creation of Barnard, and it had strewn ashes on its head, and was undergoing penance and humiliation as a mere dust-hole. Thus far my sense of sight; while dry rot and wet rot and all the silent rots that rot in neglected roof and cellar—rot of rat and mouse and bug and coaching-stables near at hand besides—addressed themselves 10 faintly to my sense of smell, and moaned, "Try Barnard's Mixture."[6]

So imperfect was this realisation of the first of my great expectations, that I looked in dismay at Mr. Wemmick. "Ah!" said he, mistaking me; "the retirement reminds you of the country. So it does me."

He led me into a corner and conducted me up a flight of stairs—which appeared to me to be slowly collapsing into sawdust, so that one of these days the upper lodgers would look out at their doors and find themselves without the means of coming down—to a set of chambers on the top floor. Mr. Pocket, Jun., was painted on the door, and there was a label on the letter-box, "Return shortly."
20
"He hardly thought you'd come so soon," Mr. Wemmick explained. "You don't want me any more?"

"No, thank you," said I.

"As I keep the cash," Mr. Wemmick observed, "we shall most likely meet pretty often. Good day."

"Good day."

I put out my hand, and Mr. Wemmick at first looked at it as if he thought I wanted something. Then he looked at me, and said, correcting himself,

"To be sure! Yes. You're in the habit of shaking hands?"

I was rather confused, thinking it must be out of the London fashion, but 30 said yes.

"I have got so out of it!" said Mr. Wemmick—"except at last.[7] Very glad, I'm sure, to make your acquaintance. Good day!"

When we had shaken hands and he was gone, I opened the staircase window and had nearly beheaded myself, for the lines had rotted away, and it came down like the guillotine.[8] Happily it was so quick that I had not put my head out. After this escape, I was content to take a foggy view of the Inn through the window's encrusting dirt, and to stand dolefully looking out, saying to myself that London was decidedly overrated.

Mr. Pocket, Junior's, idea of Shortly was not mine, for I had nearly mad- 40 dened myself with looking out for half an hour, and had written my name with my finger several times in the dirt of every pane in the window, before I heard footsteps on the stairs. Gradually there arose before me the hat, head, neckcloth, waistcoat, trousers, boots, of a member of society of about my own

5. Dirty.
6. Almost certainly a spoof on the slogan "Try . . . 's Mixture," with which tobacco merchants or patent-medicine sellers promoted their cheap blends.
7. Except at hangings. Wemmick appears to be bemused by Pip's handshake, a gesture he associates with the farewell handshake to a criminal just before he is hanged.
8. Sash window: literally "guillotine windows" in French (Monod).

standing. He had a paper-bag under each arm and a pottle[9] of strawberries in one hand, and was out of breath.

"Mr. Pip?" said he.

"Mr. Pocket?" said I.

"Dear me!" he exclaimed. "I am extremely sorry; but I knew there was a coach from your part of the country at mid-day, and I thought you would come by that one. The fact is, I have been out on your account—not that that is any excuse—for I thought, coming from the country, you might like a little fruit after dinner, and I went to Covent Garden Market[1] to get it good."

For a reason that I had, I felt as if my eyes would start out of my head. I acknowledged his attention incoherently, and began to think this was a dream.

"Dear me!" said Mr. Pocket, Junior. "This door sticks so!"

As he was fast making jam of his fruit by wrestling with the door while the paper-bags were under his arms, I begged him to allow me to hold them. He relinquished them with an agreeable smile, and combated with the door as if it were a wild beast. It yielded so suddenly at last, that he staggered back upon me, and I staggered back upon the opposite door, and we both laughed. But still I felt as if my eyes must start out of my head, and as if this must be a dream.

"Pray come in," said Mr. Pocket, Junior. "Allow me to lead the way. I am rather bare here, but I hope you'll be able to make out tolerably well till Monday. My father thought you would get on more agreeably through to-morrow with me than with him, and might like to take a walk about London. I am sure I shall be very happy to show London to you. As to our table, you won't find that bad, I hope, for it will be supplied from our coffee-house here, and (it is only right I should add) at your expense, such being Mr. Jaggers's directions. As to our lodging, it's not by any means splendid, because I have my own bread to earn, and my father hasn't anything to give me, and I shouldn't be willing to take it, if he had. This is our sitting-room—just such chairs and tables and carpet and so forth, you see, as they could spare from home. You mustn't give me credit for the tablecloth and spoons and castors,[2] because they come for you from the coffee-house. This is my little bedroom; rather musty, but Barnard's *is* musty. This is your bedroom; the furniture's hired for the occasion, but I trust it will answer the purpose; if you should want anything, I'll go and fetch it. The chambers are retired, and we shall be alone together, but we shan't fight, I dare say. But, dear me, I beg your pardon, you're holding the fruit all this time. Pray let me take these bags from you. I am quite ashamed."

As I stood opposite to Mr. Pocket, Junior, delivering him the bags, One, Two, I saw the starting appearance come into his own eyes that I knew to be in mine, and he said, falling back:

"Lord bless me, you're the prowling boy!"

"And you," said I, "are the pale young gentleman!"

9. Small wicker basket.
1. Originally "Convent Gardens," the site of the abbots of Westminster. London's principal fruit, vegetable, and flower market, in the theater district from the eighteenth century to 1973, when it was moved to Battersea.
2. Salt and pepper shakers, from which these and other condiments are cast, or sprinkled.

Chapter XXII.

THE pale young gentleman and I stood contemplating one another in Barnard's Inn, until we both burst out laughing. "The idea of its being you!" said he. "The idea of its being *you!*" said I. And then we contemplated one another afresh, and laughed again. "Well!" said the pale young gentleman, reaching out his hand good humouredly, "it's all over now, I hope, and it will be magnanimous in you if you'll forgive me for having knocked you about so."

I derived from this speech that Mr. Herbert Pocket (for Herbert was the pale young gentleman's name) still rather confounded his intention with his execution. But I made a modest reply, and we shook hands warmly.   10

"You hadn't come into your good fortune at that time?" said Herbert Pocket.

"No," said I.

"No," he acquiesced: "I heard it had happened very lately. *I* was rather on the look-out for good fortune then."

"Indeed?"

"Yes. Miss Havisham had sent for me, to see if she could take a fancy to me. But she couldn't—at all events, she didn't."

I thought it polite to remark that I was surprised to hear that.

"Bad taste," said Herbert, laughing, "but a fact. Yes, she had sent for me   20
on a trial visit, and if I had come out of it successfully, I suppose I should have been provided for; perhaps I should have been what-you-may-called it to Estella."

"What's that?" I asked, with sudden gravity.

He was arranging his fruit in plates while we talked, which divided his attention, and was the cause of his having made this lapse of a word. "Affianced," he explained, still busy with the fruit. "Betrothed. Engaged. What's-his-named. Any word of that sort."

"How did you bear your disappointment?" I asked.

"Pooh!" said he, "I didn't care much for it. *She's* a Tartar."   30

"Miss Havisham?" I suggested.

"I don't say no to that, but I meant Estella. That girl's hard and haughty and capricious to the last degree, and has been brought up by Miss Havisham to wreak revenge on all the male sex."

"What relation is she to Miss Havisham?"

"None," said he. "Only adopted."

"Why should she wreak revenge on all the male sex? What revenge?"

"Lord, Mr. Pip!" said he. "Don't you know?"

"No," said I.

"Dear me! It's quite a story, and shall be saved till dinner-time. And now   40
let me take the liberty of asking you a question. How did you come there that day?"

I told him, and he was attentive until I had finished, and then burst out laughing again, and asked me if I was sore afterwards? I didn't ask him if *he* was, for my conviction on that point was perfectly established.

"Mr. Jaggers is your guardian, I understand?" he went on.

"Yes."

"You know he is Miss Havisham's man of business and solicitor, and has her confidence when nobody else has?"

This was bringing me (I felt) towards dangerous ground. I answered with a constraint I made no attempt to disguise, that I had seen Mr. Jaggers in Miss Havisham's house on the very day of our combat, but never at any other time, and that I believed he had no recollection of having ever seen me there.

"He was so obliging as to suggest my father for your tutor, and he called on my father to propose it. Of course he knew about my father from his connexion with Miss Havisham. My father is Miss Havisham's cousin; not that that implies familiar intercourse between them, for he is a bad courtier 10 and will not propitiate her."

Herbert Pocket had a frank and easy way with him that was very taking. I had never seen any one then, and I have never seen any one since, who more strongly expressed to me, in every look and tone, a natural incapacity to do anything secret or mean. There was something wonderfully hopeful about his general air, and something that at the same time whispered to me he would never be very successful or rich. I don't know how this was. I became imbued with the notion on that first occasion before we sat down to dinner, but I cannot define by what means.

He was still a pale young gentleman, and had a certain conquered languor 20 about him in the midst of his spirits and briskness, that did not seem indicative of natural strength. He had not a handsome face, but it was better than handsome: being extremely amiable and cheerful. His figure was a little ungainly, as in the days when my knuckles had taken such liberties with it, but it looked as if it would always be light and young. Whether Mr. Trabb's local work would have sat more gracefully on him than on me, may be a question; but I am conscious that he carried off his rather old clothes much better than I carried off my new suit.

As he was so communicative, I felt that reserve on my part would be a bad return unsuited to our years. I therefore told him my small story, and laid 30 stress on my being forbidden to inquire who my benefactor was. I further mentioned that as I had been brought up a blacksmith in a country place, and knew very little of the ways of politeness, I would take it as a great kindness in him if he would give me a hint whenever he saw me at a loss or going wrong.

"With pleasure," said he, "though I venture to prophesy that you'll want very few hints. I dare say we shall be often together, and I should like to banish any needless restraint between us. Will you do me the favour to begin at once to call me by my christian name, Herbert?"

I thanked him, and said I would. I informed him in exchange that my 40 christian name was Philip.

"I don't take to Philip," said he, smiling, "for it sounds like a moral boy out of the spelling-book,[1] who was so lazy that he fell into a pond, or so fat that he couldn't see out of his eyes, or so avaricious that he locked up his

---

1. Herbert refers to *The English Spelling Book Accompanied by a Progressive Series of Easy and Familiar Lessons* (1801) by the Reverend William Fordyce Mavor (1758–1837), a prolific author of tourist guides, creator of a "Universal Stenography," and compiler of educational manuals. Mavor's textbook, which combined improving stories for the young with spelling exercises of graduated length, had allegedly reached its thirty-second edition within twenty-five years—at about the time Herbert raised his objection. Mavor's cautionary tales end less catastrophically than Herbert's borrowed (but nearly identical) instances; nor have I come across any Philips among Mavor's juvenile delinquents.

cake till the mice ate it, or so determined to go birds'-nesting that he got himself eaten by bears who lived handy in the neighbourhood. I tell you what I should like. We are so harmonious, and you have been a blacksmith— would you mind it?"

"I shouldn't mind anything that you propose," I answered, "but I don't understand you."

"Would you mind Handel for a familiar name? There's a charming piece of music by Handel, called the Harmonious Blacksmith."[2]

"I should like it very much."

"Then, my dear Handel," said he, turning round as the door opened, "here is the dinner, and I must beg of you to take the top of the table, because the dinner is of your providing."

This of course I would not hear of, so he took the top, and I faced him. It was a nice little dinner—seemed to me then, a very Lord Mayor's Feast[3]— and it acquired additional relish from being eaten under those independent circumstances, with no old people by, and with London all around us. This again was heightened by a certain gipsy character that set the banquet off: for while the table was, as Mr. Pumblechook might have said, the lap of luxury —being entirely furnished forth from the coffee-house—the circumjacent region of sitting-room was of a comparatively pastureless and shifty character: imposing on the waiter the wandering habits of putting the covers on the floor (where he fell over them), the melted butter in the arm-chair, the bread on the book-shelves, the cheese in the coal-scuttle, and the boiled fowl into my bed in the next room—where I found much of its parsley and butter in a state of congelation when I retired for the night. All this made the feast delightful, and when the waiter was not there to watch me, my pleasure was without alloy.

We had made some progress in the dinner, when I reminded Herbert of his promise to tell me about Miss Havisham.

"True," he replied. "I'll redeem it at once. Let me introduce the topic, Handel, by mentioning that in London it is not the custom to put the knife in the mouth—for fear of accidents—and that while the fork is reserved for that use, it is not put further in than is necessary. It is scarcely worth mentioning, only it's as well to do as other people do. Also, the spoon is not generally used over-hand, but under. This has two advantages. You get at your mouth better (which after all is the object), and you save a good deal of the attitude of opening oysters, on the part of the right elbow."

He offered these friendly suggestions in such a lively way, that we both laughed and I scarcely blushed.

"Now," he pursued, "concerning Miss Havisham. Miss Havisham, you must know, was a spoilt child. Her mother died when she was a baby, and her father denied her nothing. Her father was a country gentleman down in your part of the world, and was a brewer. I don't know why it should be a

---

2. Nickname attached in the nineteenth century to the "Air and Variations" of Handel's *Harpsichord Suite No. 5 in E Major* (1720), which vaguely resemble the sound of hammer strokes (or the patter of raindrops). Though popular lore long traced the origin of this to a blacksmith in whose forge Handel hid during a downpour, the nickname first appears in 1819. Dickens is nowhere more typically English than in his partiality for Handel's music.
3. The lavish banquet in Guildhall (or City Hall, the center of civic government) given annually to Cabinet members and other prominents on the second Saturday in November by the newly elected Lord Mayor of London.

crack thing to be a brewer; but it is indisputable that while you cannot possibly be genteel and bake, you may be as genteel as never was and brew. You see it every day."[4]

"Yet a gentleman may not keep a public-house; may he?" said I.

"Not on any account," returned Herbert; "but a public-house may keep a gentleman. Well! Mr. Havisham was very rich and very proud. So was his daughter."

"Miss Havisham was an only child?" I hazarded.

"Stop a moment, I am coming to that. No, she was not an only child; she had a half-brother. Her father privately married again—his cook, I rather 10 think."

"I thought he was proud," said I.

"My good Handel, so he was. He married his second wife privately, because he was proud, and in course of time *she* died. When she was dead, I apprehend he first told his daughter what he had done, and then the son became a part of the family, residing in the house you are acquainted with. As the son grew a young man, he turned out riotous, extravagant, undutiful—altogether bad. At last his father disinherited him; but he softened when he was dying and left him well off, though not nearly so well off as Miss Havisham. Take another glass of wine, and excuse my mentioning that society as a body 20 does not expect one to be so strictly conscientious in emptying one's glass, as to turn it bottom upwards with the rim on one's nose."

I had been doing this, in an excess of attention to his recital. I thanked him and apologised. He said, "Not at all," and resumed.

"Miss Havisham was now an heiress, and you may suppose was looked after as a great match. Her half-brother had now ample means again, but what with debts and what with new madness wasted them most fearfully again. There were stronger differences between him and her than there had been between him and his father, and it is suspected that he cherished a deep and mortal grudge against her, as having influenced the father's anger. Now, I 30 come to the cruel part of the story—merely breaking off, my dear Handel, to remark that a dinner-napkin will not go into a tumbler."

Why I was trying to pack mine into my tumbler, I am wholly unable to say. I only know that I found myself, with a perseverance worthy of a much better cause, making the most strenuous exertions to compress it within those limits. Again I thanked him and apologised, and again he said in the cheerfullest manner, "Not at all, I am sure!" and resumed.

"There appeared upon the scene—say at the races, or the public balls, or anywhere else you like—a certain man, who made love to Miss Havisham. I never saw him, for this happened five-and-twenty years ago (before you and 40 I were, Handel), but I have heard my father mention that he was a showyman, and the kind of man for the purpose. But that he was not to be, without ignorance or prejudice, mistaken for a gentleman, my father most strongly asseverates; because it is a principle of his that no man who was not a true gentleman at heart, ever was, since the world began, a true gentleman in manner. He says, no varnish can hide the grain of the wood; and the more

4. Miss Havisham's father evidently owes his prosperity to his brewery business; and, as Herbert makes a point of explaining to Pip, brewers enjoyed an astonishingly high social status—you could probably find as many rich brewers among the peerage as wealthy attorneys, lord chancellors, and military heroes. Thus, the barren vestiges of the brewery yard behind Satis House suggest a more considerable and poignant fall from high estate than we would suspect.

varnish you put on, the more the grain will express itself. Well! This man pursued Miss Havisham closely, and professed to be devoted to her. I believe she had not shown much susceptibility up to that time; but all the susceptibility she possessed, certainly came out then, and she passionately loved him. There is no doubt that she perfectly idolised him. He practised on her affection in that systematic way, that he got great sums of money from her, and he induced her to buy her brother out of a share in the brewery (which had been weakly left him by his father) at an immense price, on the plea that when he was her husband he must hold and manage it all. Your guardian was not at that time in Miss Havisham's councils, and she was too haughty   10 and too much in love, to be advised by any one. Her relations were poor and scheming, with the exception of my father; he was poor enough, but not time-serving or jealous. The only independent one among them, he warned her that she was doing too much for this man, and was placing herself too unreservedly in his power. She took the first opportunity of angrily ordering my father out of the house, in his presence, and my father has never seen her since."

I thought of her having said, "Matthew will come and see me at last when I am laid dead upon that table;" and I asked Herbert whether his father was so inveterate against her?   20

"It's not that," said he, "but she charged him in the presence of her intended husband with being disappointed in the hope of fawning upon her for his own advancement, and, if he were to go to her now, it would look true—even to him—and even to her. To return to the man and make an end of him. The marriage day was fixed, the wedding dresses were bought, the wedding tour was planned out, the wedding guests were invited. The day came, but not the bridegroom. He wrote her a letter——"

"Which she received," I struck in, "when she was dressing for her marriage? At twenty minutes to nine?"

"At the hour and minute," said Herbert, nodding, "at which she afterwards   30 stopped all the clocks. What was in it, further than that it most heartlessly broke the marriage off, I can't tell you, because I don't know. When she recovered from a bad illness that she had, she laid the whole place waste, as you have seen it, and she has never since looked upon the light of day."

"Is that all the story?" I asked, after considering it.

"All I know of it; and indeed I only know so much, through piecing it out for myself; for my father always avoids it, and, even when Miss Havisham invited me to go there, told me no more of it than it was absolutely requisite I should understand. But I have forgotten one thing. It has been supposed that the man to whom she gave her misplaced confidence, acted throughout   40 in concert with her half-brother; that it was a conspiracy between them; and that they shared the profits."

"I wonder he didn't marry her and get all the property," said I.

"He may have been married already, and her cruel mortification may have been a part of her half-brother's scheme," said Herbert. "Mind! I don't know that."

"What became of the two men?" I asked, after again considering the subject.

"They fell into deeper shame and degradation—if there can be deeper— and ruin."   50

"Are they alive now?"

"I don't know."

"You said just now, that Estella was not related to Miss Havisham, but adopted. When adopted?"

Herbert shrugged his shoulders. "There has always been an Estella, since I have heard of a Miss Havisham. I know no more. And now, Handel," said he, finally throwing off the story as it were, "there is a perfectly open understanding between us. All that I know about Miss Havisham, you know."

"And all that I know," I retorted, "you know."   10

"I fully believe it. So there can be no competition or perplexity between you and me. And as to the condition on which you hold your advancement in life—namely, that you are not to inquire or discuss to whom you owe it— you may be very sure that it will never be encroached upon, or even approached, by me, or by any one belonging to me."

In truth, he said this with so much delicacy, that I felt the subject done with, even though I should be under his father's roof for years and years to come. Yet he said it with so much meaning, too, that I felt he as perfectly understood Miss Havisham to be my benefactress, as I understood the fact myself.   20

It had not occurred to me before, that he had led up to the theme for the purpose of clearing it out of our way; but we were so much the lighter and easier for having broached it, that I now perceived this to be the case. We were very gay and sociable, and I asked him, in the course of conversation, what he was? He replied, "A capitalist—an Insurer of Ships." I suppose he saw me glancing about the room in search of some tokens of Shipping, or capital, for he added, "In the City."[5]

I had grand ideas of the wealth and importance of Insurers of Ships in the City, and I began to think with awe of having laid a young Insurer on his back, blackened his enterprising eye, and cut his responsible head open. But,   30 again, there came upon me, for my relief, that odd impression that Herbert Pocket would never be very successful or rich.

"I shall not rest satisfied with merely employing my capital in insuring ships. I shall buy up some good Life Assurance shares, and cut into the Direction.[6] I shall also do a little in the mining way. None of these things will interfere with my chartering a few thousand tons on my own account. I think I shall trade," said he, leaning back in his chair, "to the East Indies, for silks, shawls, spices, dyes, drugs, and precious woods. It's an interesting trade."

"And the profits are large?" said I.   40

"Tremendous!" said he.

5. The commercial center of England, the independent area ruled by the Lord Mayor and the Corporation of London. Hardly larger than a square mile, the City conforms to London's ancient boundaries, extending from Holborn to Aldgate and Smithfield to Southwark. The smallest local government area in the country, it maintains its own police force and fire brigade. Before the migration to the suburbs began in the early 1960s, some 125,000 residents still dwelled in a sector now almost exclusively occupied by offices and by more than a million daily commuters and workers. In *Villette* (1853) 1.6, Charlotte Brontë draws the distinction between the City and fashionable London: "I have seen the West-end, the parks, the fine squares; but I love the city far better. The city seems so much more in earnest: its business, its rush, its roar, are such serious things, sights, and sounds. The city is getting its living—the West-end but enjoying its pleasure."

6. "Buy my way into the directorship." On the changes Dickens introduced between MS and print in the conversation between Pip and Herbert that follows, see pp. 570–71.

I wavered again, and began to think here were greater expectations than my own.

"I think I shall trade, also," said he, putting his thumbs in his waistcoat pockets, "to the West Indies, for sugar, tobacco, and rum. Also to Ceylon, specially for elephants' tusks."

"You will want a good many ships," said I.

"A perfect fleet," said he.

Quite overpowered by the magnificence of these transactions, I asked him where the ships he insured mostly traded to at present?

"I haven't begun insuring yet," he replied. "I am looking about me."   10

Somehow, that pursuit seemed more in keeping with Barnard's Inn. I said (in a tone of conviction) "Ah-h!"

"Yes. I am in a counting-house, and looking about me."

"Is a counting-house profitable?" I asked.

"To——do you mean to the young fellow who's in it?" he asked, in reply.

"Yes; to you."

"Why, n-no: not to me." He said this with the air of one carefully reckoning up and striking a balance. "Not directly profitable. That is, it doesn't pay me anything, and I have to——keep myself."

This certainly had not a profitable appearance, and I shook my head as if   20 I would imply that it would be difficult to lay by much accumulative capital from such a source of income.

"But the thing is," said Herbert Pocket, "that you look about you. *That's* the grand thing. You are in a counting-house, you know, and you look about you."

It struck me as a singular implication that you couldn't be out of a counting-house, you know, and look about you; but I silently deferred to his experience.

"Then the time comes," said Herbert, "when you see your opening. And you go in and you swoop upon it and you make your capital, and then there you are! When you have once made your capital, you have nothing to do   30 but employ it."

This was very like his way of conducting that encounter in the garden; very like. His manner of bearing his poverty, too, exactly corresponded to his manner of bearing that defeat. It seemed to me that he took all blows and buffets now, with just the same air as he had taken mine then. It was evident that he had nothing around him but the simplest necessaries, for everything that I remarked upon, turned out to have been sent in on my account from the coffee-house or somewhere else.

Yet, having already made his fortune in his own mind, he was so unassuming with it that I felt quite grateful to him for not being puffed up. It was a   40 pleasant addition to his naturally pleasant ways, and we got on famously. In the evening we went out for a walk in the streets, and went half-price to the Theatre;[7] and next day we went to church at Westminster Abbey, and in the afternoon we walked in the Parks;[8] and I wondered who shod all the horses there, and wished Joe did.

On a moderate computation, it was many months, that Sunday, since I

---

7. A function of the opulent theatrical fare in Victorian London. Beginning as early as 6 P.M., a typical evening's program featured a melodrama, a farce, and short in-betweenities, akin to the double features the movies used to offer. Patrons who entered the theater about 8:30 got in at half price.
8. The large public parks north of Kensington Road, Knightsbridge, and Piccadilly—Kensington Gardens, Hyde Park, Green Park, and St. James's Park—are landmarks of the fashionable West End.

had left Joe and Biddy. The space interposed between myself and them, partook of that expansion, and our marshes were any distance off. That I could have been at our old church in my old church-going clothes, on the very last Sunday that ever was, seemed a combination of impossibilities, geographical and social, solar and lunar. Yet in the London streets so crowded with people and so brilliantly lighted in the dusk of evening, there were depressing hints of reproaches for that I had put the poor old kitchen at home so far away; and in the dead of night, the footsteps of some incapable impostor of a porter mooning about Barnard's Inn, under pretence of watching it, fell hollow on my heart.   10

On the Monday morning at a quarter before nine, Herbert went to the counting-house to report himself—to look about him, too, I suppose—and I bore him company. He was to come away in an hour or two to attend me to Hammersmith, and I was to wait about for him. It appeared to me that the eggs from which young Insurers were hatched, were incubated in dust and heat, like the eggs of ostriches, judging from the places to which those incipient giants repaired on a Monday morning. Nor did the counting-house where Herbert assisted, show in my eyes as at all a good Observatory; being a back second floor up a yard, of a grimy presence in all particulars, and with a look into another back second floor rather than a look out.   20

I waited about until it was noon, and I went upon 'Change,[9] and I saw fluey[1] men sitting there under the bills about shipping, whom I took to be great merchants, though I couldn't understand why they should all be out of spirits. When Herbert came, we went and had lunch at a celebrated house which I then quite venerated, but now believe to have been the most abject superstition in Europe, and where I could not help noticing, even then, that there was much more gravy on the tablecloths and knives and waiters' clothes, than in the steaks. This collation disposed of at a moderate price (considering the grease, which was not charged for), we went back to Barnard's Inn and got my little portmanteau, and then took coach for Hammersmith. We arrived 30 there at two or three o'clock in the afternoon, and had very little way to walk to Mr. Pocket's house. Lifting the latch of a gate, we passed direct into a little garden overlooking the river, where Mr. Pocket's children were playing about. And unless I deceive myself on a point where my interests or prepossessions are certainly not concerned, I saw that Mr. and Mrs. Pocket's children were not growing up or being brought up, but were tumbling up.

Mrs. Pocket was sitting on a garden chair under a tree, reading, with her legs upon another garden chair; and Mrs. Pocket's two nursemaids were looking about them while the children played. "Mamma," said Herbert, "this is young Mr. Pip." Upon which Mrs. Pocket received me with an appearance 40 of amiable dignity.[2]

"Master Alick and Miss Jane," cried one of the nurses to two of the children, "if you go a bouncing up against them bushes you'll fall over into the river and be drownded, and what'll your pa say then!"

9. The Royal Exchange, or London Stock Market, on Cornhill in the heart of the City, built in 1566–67. Here Lloyd's, the insurers, conducted their business, with brief intermittences, from 1774 to 1928.
1. Covered with dirt, hair, and dust [OED]. No reason for merchants to be covered in "flue"; possibly Dickens uses the term in the sense of its Latin origin to mean "shaggy"—which more nearly conforms with his description of them as looking "out of spirits."
2. On the change in the conception of Mrs. Pocket, see pp. 455–61.

At the same time this nurse picked up Mrs. Pocket's handkerchief, and said, "If that don't make six times you've dropped it, Mum!" Upon which Mrs. Pocket laughed and said, "Thank you, Flopson," and settling herself in one chair only, resumed her book. Her countenance immediately assumed a knitted and intent expression as if she had been reading for a week, but before she could have read half a dozen lines, she fixed her eyes upon me, and said, "I hope your mamma is quite well?" This unexpected inquiry put me into such a difficulty that I began saying in the absurdest way that if there had been any such person I had no doubt she would have been quite well and would have been very much obliged and would have sent her compliments, 10 when the nurse came to my rescue.

"Well!" she cried, picking up the pocket-handkerchief, "if that don't make seven times! What ARE you a doing of this afternoon, Mum!" Mrs. Pocket received her property at first with a look of unutterable surprise as if she had never seen it before, and then with a laugh of recognition, and said, "Thank you, Flopson," and forgot me, and went on reading.

I found, now I had leisure to count them, that there were no fewer than six little Pockets present, in various stages of tumbling up. I had scarcely arrived at the total when a seventh was heard, as in the region of air, wailing dolefully. 20

"If there ain't Baby!" said Flopson, appearing to think it most surprising. "Make haste up, Millers."

Millers, who was the other nurse, retired into the house, and by degrees the child's wailing was hushed and stopped, as if it were a young ventriloquist with something in its mouth. Mrs. Pocket read all the time, and I was curious to know what the book could be.

We were waiting, I supposed, for Mr. Pocket to come out to us; at any rate we waited there, and so I had an opportunity of observing the remarkable family phenomenon that whenever any of the children strayed near Mrs. Pocket in their play, they always tripped themselves up and tumbled over 30 her—always very much to her momentary astonishment, and their own more enduring lamentation. I was at a loss to account for this surprising circumstance, and could not help giving my mind to speculations about it, until by-and-by Millers came down with the baby, which baby was handed to Flopson, which Flopson was handing it to Mrs. Pocket, when she too went fairly head-foremost over Mrs. Pocket, baby and all, and was caught by Herbert and myself.

"Gracious me, Flopson!" said Mrs. Pocket, looking off her book for a moment, "everybody's tumbling!"

"Gracious you, indeed, Mum!" returned Flopson, very red in the face; 40 "what have you got there?"

"I got here, Flopson?" asked Mrs. Pocket.

"Why, if it ain't your footstool!" cried Flopson. "And if you keep it under your skirts like that, who's to help tumbling! Here! Take the baby, Mum, and give me your book."

Mrs. Pocket acted on the advice, and inexpertly danced the infant a little in her lap, while the other children played about it. This had lasted but a very short time, when Mrs. Pocket issued summary orders that they were all to be taken into the house for a nap. Thus I made the second discovery on that first occasion, that the nurture of the little Pockets consisted of alternately tumbling up and lying down.

Under these circumstances, when Flopson and Millers had got the children into the house like a little flock of sheep, and Mr. Pocket came out of it to make my acquaintance, I was not much surprised to find that Mr. Pocket was a gentleman with a rather perplexed expression of face, and with his very grey hair disordered on his head as if he didn't quite see his way to putting anything straight.

Chapter XXIII.

MR. POCKET said he was glad to see me, and he hoped I was not sorry to see him. "For I really am not," he added, with his son's smile, "an alarming 10 personage." He was a young-looking man, in spite of his perplexities and his very grey hair, and his manner seemed quite natural. I use the word natural, in the sense of its being unaffected; there was something comic in his distraught way, as though it would have been downright ludicrous but for his own perception that it was very near being so. When he had talked with me a little, he said to Mrs. Pocket, with a rather anxious contraction of his eyebrows, which were black and handsome, "Belinda, I hope you have welcomed Mr. Pip?" And she looked up from her book, and said, "Yes." She then smiled upon me in an absent state of mind, and asked me if I liked the taste of orange-flower water?[1] As the question had no bearing, near or remote, on any 20 foregone or subsequent transaction, I considered it to have been thrown out, like her previous approaches, in general conversational condescension.

I found out within a few hours, and may mention at once, that Mrs. Pocket was the only daughter of a certain quite accidental deceased Knight,[2] who had invented for himself a conviction that his deceased father would have been made a Baronet[3] but for somebody's determined opposition arising out of entirely personal motives—I forget whose, if I ever knew—the Sovereign's, the Prime Minister's, the Lord Chancellor's, the Archbishop of Canterbury's, anybody's—and had tacked himself on to the nobles of the earth in right of this quite supposititious fact. I believe he had been knighted himself for storm- 30 ing the English grammar at the point of the pen in a desperate address engrossed on vellum, on the occasion of the laying of the first stone of some building or other, and for handing some Royal Personage either the trowel or the mortar. Be that as it may, he had directed Mrs. Pocket to be brought up from her cradle as one who in the nature of things must marry a title, and who was to be guarded from the acquisition of plebeian domestic knowledge. So successful a watch and ward had been established over the young lady by this judicious parent, that she had grown up highly ornamental, but perfectly helpless and useless. With her character thus happily formed, in the

1. Mild tonic water, spiked with the distillation of bitter oranges.
2. Accidentally knighted, not accidentally deceased. That is, Mrs. Pocket's father owes his knighthood to political maneuvering or to carelessness, like Sir Thomas Tippins in *Our Mutual Friend* 1.10, who was "knighted in mistake for somebody else by His Majesty King George the Third."
3. The baronetcy, a title created in 1611 and one notch above knighthood, is hereditary, as knighthood is not; hence Mrs. Pocket's chumminess with Drummle, the future baronet.

first bloom of her youth she had encountered Mr. Pocket: who was also in
the first bloom of youth, and not quite decided whether to mount to the
Woolsack, or to roof himself in with a Mitre.[4] As his doing the one or the
other was a mere question of time, he and Mrs. Pocket had taken Time by
the forelock (when, to judge from its length, it would seem to have wanted
cutting), and had married without the knowledge of the judicious parent. The
judicious parent, having nothing to bestow or withhold but his blessing, had
handsomely settled that dower upon them after a short struggle, and had
informed Mr. Pocket that his wife was "a treasure for a Prince." Mr. Pocket
had invested the Prince's treasure in the ways of the world ever since, and it   10
was supposed to have brought in but indifferent interest. Still Mrs. Pocket
was in general the object of a queer sort of respectful pity, because she had
not married a title; while Mr. Pocket was the object of a queer sort of forgiving
reproach because he had never got one.

Mr. Pocket took me into the house and showed me my room: which was
a pleasant one, and so furnished as that I could use it with comfort for my
own private sitting-room. He then knocked at the doors of two other similar
rooms, and introduced me to their occupants, by name Drummle and Startop. Drummle, an old-looking young man of a heavy order of architecture,
was whistling. Startop, younger in years and appearance, was reading and   20
holding his head with both hands, as if he thought himself in danger of
exploding it with too strong a charge of knowledge.

Both Mr. and Mrs. Pocket had such a noticeable air of being in somebody
else's hands, that I wondered who really was in possession of the house and
let them live there, until I found this unknown power to be the servants. It
was a smooth way of going on, perhaps, in respect of saving trouble; but it
had the appearance of being expensive, for the servants felt it a duty they
owed to themselves to be nice in their eating and drinking, and to keep a
deal of company down stairs. They allowed a very liberal table to Mr. and
Mrs. Pocket, yet it always appeared to me that by far the best part of the   30
house to have boarded in, would have been the kitchen—always supposing
the boarder capable of self-defence, for, before I had been there a week, a
neighbouring lady with whom the family were personally unacquainted, wrote
in to say that she had seen Millers slapping the baby. This greatly distressed
Mrs. Pocket, who burst into tears on receiving the note, and said it was an
extraordinary thing that the neighbours couldn't mind their own business.

By degrees I learnt, and chiefly from Herbert, that Mr. Pocket had been
educated at Harrow[5] and at Cambridge, where he had distinguished himself;
but that when he had had the happiness of marrying Mrs. Pocket very early
in life, he had impaired his prospects and taken up the calling of a Grinder.   40
After grinding a number of dull blades[6]—of whom it was remarkable that
their fathers, when influential, were always going to help him to preferment,

---

4. Whether to aspire to the top secular or clerical office. "Woolsack": as highest judicial functionary in
   Britain and Chairman of the House of Lords, the Lord Chancellor is seated on a cushion stuffed with
   wool, a custom dating from Tudor England and a reminder of her prosperity in the wool trade.
   "Mitre": the tall, peaked headdress worn by the Pope, archbishops, and bishops; by extension, the title
   of bishop.
5. One of England's oldest (1571) public schools—in America "private schools." Our nearest equivalents
   to Harrow would be schools like Andover or Exeter.
6. That is, "after tutoring a number of lowbrows." A grinder is a private tutor who usually preps students
   for their exams. "Blades": easygoing gadabouts; else, sharp and cunning ones—in this latter sense of
   "sharpster" or "rogue" Wemmick refers to the forger of wills in chapter 24.

but always forgot to do it when the blades had left the Grindstone—he had wearied of that poor work and had come to London. Here, after gradually failing in loftier hopes, he had "read"[7] with divers who had lacked opportunities or neglected them, and had refurbished divers others for special occasions, and had turned his acquirements to the account of literary compilation and correction, and on such means, added to some very moderate private resources, still maintained the house I saw.

Mr. and Mrs. Pocket had a toady[8] neighbour; a widow lady of that highly sympathetic nature that she agreed with everybody, blessed everybody, and shed smiles and tears on everybody according to circumstances. This lady's name was Mrs. Coiler, and I had the honour of taking her down to dinner on the day of my installation. She gave me to understand on the stairs, that it was a blow to dear Mrs. Pocket that dear Mr. Pocket should be under the necessity of receiving gentlemen to read with him. That did not extend to Me, she told me, in a gush of love and confidence (at that time, I had known her something less than five minutes); if they were all like Me, it would be quite another thing.

"But dear Mrs. Pocket," said Mrs. Coiler, "after her early disappointment (not that dear Mr. Pocket was to blame in that), requires so much luxury and elegance——"

"Yes, ma'am," said I, to stop her, for I was afraid she was going to cry.

"And she is of so aristocratic a disposition——"

"Yes, ma'am," I said again, with the same object as before.

"—that it *is* hard," said Mrs. Coiler, "to have dear Mr. Pocket's time and attention diverted from dear Mrs. Pocket."

I could not help thinking that it might be harder if the butcher's time and attention were diverted from dear Mrs. Pocket; but I said nothing, and indeed had enough to do in keeping a bashful watch upon my company-manners.

It came to my knowledge, through what passed between Mrs. Pocket and Drummle while I was attentive to my knife and fork, spoon, glasses, and other instruments of self-destruction, that Drummle, whose christian name was Bentley,[9] was actually the next heir but one to a baronetcy. It further appeared that the book I had seen Mrs. Pocket reading in the garden was all about titles,[1] and that she knew the exact date at which her grandpapa would have come into the book, if he ever had come at all. Drummle didn't say much, but in his limited way (he struck me as a sulky kind of fellow) he spoke as one of the elect, and recognised Mrs. Pocket as a woman and a sister. No one but themselves and Mrs. Coiler the toady neighbour showed any interest in this part of the conversation, and it appeared to me that it was painful to Herbert; but it promised to last a long time, when the page came in with the announcement of a domestic affliction. It was, in effect, that the cook had mislaid the beef. To my unutterable amazement, I now, for the first time, saw Mr. Pocket relieve his mind by going through a performance that struck

7. Tutored.
8. Obsequious, fawning.
9. Presumably an in-joke. Drummle's first name and Dickens's way of calling attention to it suggest a snide reference to Dickens's old enemy, the publisher Richard Bentley (1794–1871), owner of *Bentley's Miscellany*, who hired Dickens in 1837 to launch his weekly as its first editor and with whom Dickens broke two years later after endless squabbles about editorial policy, publishing contracts, and money.
1. Debrett's *Peerage*, the "Who's Who" of the British nobility, first published in 1802 as *The New Peerage, or Ancient and Present State of the Nobility of England, Scotland and Ireland*, by John Field Debrett (d. 1822), and still going strong as an essential reference work.

me as very extraordinary, but which made no impression on anybody else, and with which I soon became as familiar as the rest. He laid down the carving-knife and fork—being engaged in carving at the moment—put his two hands into his disturbed hair, and appeared to make an extraordinary effort to lift himself up by it. When he had done this, and had not lifted himself up at all, he quietly went on with what he was about.

Mrs. Coiler then changed the subject, and began to flatter me. I liked it for a few moments, but she flattered me so very grossly that the pleasure was soon over. She had a serpentine way of coming close at me when she pretended to be vitally interested in the friends and localities I had left, which 10 was altogether snakey and fork-tongued; and when she made an occasional bounce upon Startop (who said very little to her), or upon Drummle (who said less), I rather envied them for being on the opposite side of the table.

After dinner the children were introduced, and Mrs. Coiler made admiring comments on their eyes, noses, and legs—a sagacious way of improving their minds. There were four little girls, and two little boys, besides the baby who might have been either, and the baby's next successor who was as yet neither. They were brought in by Flopson and Millers, much as though those two non-commissioned officers had been recruiting somewhere for children and had enlisted these: while Mrs. Pocket looked at the young Nobles that ought 20 to have been, as if she rather thought she had had the pleasure of inspecting them before, but didn't quite know what to make of them.

"Here! Give me your fork, mum, and take the baby," said Flopson. "Don't take it that way, or you'll get its head under the table."

Thus advised, Mrs. Pocket took it the other way, and got its head upon the table; which was announced to all present by a prodigious concussion.

"Dear, dear! Give it me back, mum," said Flopson; "and Miss Jane, come and dance to baby, do!"

One of the little girls: a mere mite who seemed to have prematurely taken upon herself some charge of the others: stepped out of her place by me, and 30 danced to and from the baby until it left off crying, and laughed. Then all the children laughed, and Mr. Pocket (who in the mean time had twice endeavoured to lift himself up by the hair) laughed, and we all laughed and were glad.

Flopson, by dint of doubling the baby at the joints like a Dutch doll,[2] then got it safely into Mrs. Pocket's lap, and gave it the nutcrackers to play with: at the same time recommending Mrs. Pocket to take notice that the handles of that instrument were not likely to agree with its eyes, and sharply charging Miss Jane to look after the same. Then, the two nurses left the room, and had a lively scuffle on the staircase with a dissipated page who had waited at 40 dinner, and who had clearly lost half his buttons at the gaming-table.[3]

I was made very uneasy in my mind by Mrs. Pocket's falling into a discussion with Drummle respecting two baronetcies while she ate a sliced orange steeped in sugar and wine, and forgetting all about the baby on her lap: who did most appalling things with the nutcrackers. At length, little Jane perceiving its young brains to be imperilled, softly left her place, and with many small artifices coaxed the dangerous weapon away. Mrs. Pocket finishing her orange at about the same time and not approving of this, said to Jane:

2. Wooden doll, with jointed legs.
3. In a pinch, silver or gold-plated buttons could be substituted for coins on gambling tables.

"You naughty child, how dare you? Go and sit down this instant!"

"Mamma dear," lisped the little girl, "baby ood have put hith eyeth out."

"How dare you tell me so!" retorted Mrs. Pocket. "Go and sit down in your chair this moment!"

Mrs. Pocket's dignity was so crushing, that I felt quite abashed: as if I myself had done something to rouse it.

"Belinda," remonstrated Mr. Pocket, from the other end of the table, "how can you be so unreasonable? Jane only interfered for the protection of baby."

"I will not allow anybody to interfere," said Mrs. Pocket. "I am surprised, Matthew, that you should expose me to the affront of interference."   10

"Good God!" cried Mr. Pocket, in an outbreak of desolate desperation. "Are infants to be nutcrackered into their tombs, and is nobody to save them!"

"I will not be interfered with by Jane," said Mrs. Pocket, with a majestic glance at that innocent little offender. "I hope I know my poor grandpapa's position. Jane, indeed!"

Mr. Pocket got his hands in his hair again, and this time really did lift himself some inches out of his chair. "Hear this!" he helplessly exclaimed to the elements. "Babies are to be nutcrackered dead, for people's poor grandpapa's positions!" Then he let himself down again, and became silent.

We all looked awkwardly at the tablecloth while this was going on. A pause   20 succeeded, during which the honest and irrepressible baby made a series of leaps and crows at little Jane, who appeared to me to be the only member of the family (irrespective of the servants) with whom it had any decided acquaintance.

"Mr. Drummle," said Mrs. Pocket, "will you ring for Flopson? Jane, you undutiful little thing, go and lie down. Now, baby darling, come with ma!"

The baby was the soul of honour; and protested with all its might. It doubled itself up the wrong way over Mrs. Pocket's arm, exhibited a pair of knitted shoes and dimpled ankles to the company in lieu of its soft face, and was carried out in the highest state of mutiny. And it gained its point after all, for   30 I saw it through the window within a few minutes, being nursed by little Jane.

It happened that the other five children were left behind at the dinner-table, through Flopson's having some private engagement and their not being anybody else's business. I thus became aware of the mutual relations between them and Mr. Pocket, which were exemplified in the following manner. Mr. Pocket, with the normal perplexity of his face heightened and his hair rumpled, looked at them for some minutes as if he couldn't make out how they came to be boarding and lodging in that establishment, and why they hadn't been billeted by Nature on somebody else. Then, in a distant Missionary way he asked them certain questions—as why little Joe had that hole in his frill:[4]   40 who said, Pa, Flopson was going to mend it when she had time—and how little Fanny came by that whitlow:[5] who said, Pa, Millers was going to poultice it when she didn't forget. Then, he melted into parental tenderness, and gave them a shilling apiece and told them to go and play; and then as they went out, with one very strong effort to lift himself up by the hair he dismissed the hopeless subject.

In the evening there was rowing on the river. As Drummle and Startop had each a boat, I resolved to set up mine, and to cut them both out. I was

4. Ornamental flared or ruffled edge worn by children around the collar.
5. Inflammation under or near the fingernail.

pretty good at most exercises in which country-boys are adepts, but as I was conscious of wanting elegance of style for the Thames—not to say for other waters—I at once engaged to place myself under the tuition of the winner of a prize-wherry[6] who plied at our stairs, and to whom I was introduced by my new allies. This practical authority confused me very much, by saying I had the arm of a blacksmith. If he could have known how nearly the compliment lost him his pupil, I doubt if he would have paid it.

There was a supper-tray after we got home at night, and I think we should all have enjoyed ourselves, but for a rather disagreeable domestic occurrence. Mr. Pocket was in good spirits, when a housemaid came in, and said, "If you please, sir, I should wish to speak to you."

"Speak to your master?" said Mrs. Pocket, whose dignity was roused again. "How can you think of such a thing? Go and speak to Flopson. Or speak to me—at some other time."

"Begging your pardon, ma'am?" returned the housemaid, "I should wish to speak at once, and to speak to master."

Hereupon, Mr. Pocket went out of the room, and we made the best of ourselves until he came back.

"This is a pretty thing, Belinda!" said Mr. Pocket, returning with a countenance expressive of grief and despair. "Here's the cook lying insensibly drunk on the kitchen floor, with a large bundle of fresh butter made up in the cupboard ready to sell for grease!"

Mrs. Pocket instantly showed much amiable emotion, and said, "This is that odious Sophia's doing!"

"What do you mean, Belinda?" demanded Mr. Pocket.

"Sophia has told you," said Mrs. Pocket. "Did I not see her with my own eyes and hear her with my own ears, come into the room just now and ask to speak to you?"

"But has she not taken me down stairs, Belinda," returned Mr. Pocket, "and shown me the woman, and the bundle too?"

"And do you defend her, Matthew," said Mrs. Pocket, "for making mischief?"

Mr. Pocket uttered a dismal groan.

"Am I, grandpapa's granddaughter, to be nothing in the house?" said Mrs. Pocket. "Besides, the cook has always been a very nice respectful woman, and said in the most natural manner when she came to look after the situation, that she felt I was born to be a Duchess."

There was a sofa where Mr. Pocket stood, and he dropped upon it in the attitude of the Dying Gladiator.[7] Still in that attitude he said, with a hollow voice, "Good night, Mr. Pip," when I deemed it advisable to go to bed and leave him.

---

6. Light rowboat that could be hired, rather like a water taxi, along with its owner—this one evidently a champion in wherrymen's races. The stairs leading from the bank of the Thames down to the water indicated the pick-up stops.
7. "The Dying Gaul," the Roman copy of a third century B.C. Greek statue—possibly part of a sculptured group—in the Capitoline Museum in Rome, was given a new lease on life in Byron's *Childe Harold's Pilgrimage*, canto 4 (1818), stanza 140: "He leans upon his hand—his manly brow / Consents to death but conquers agony / And his drooped head sinks gradually low," etc.

Chapter XXIV.

After two or three days, when I had established myself in my room and had gone backwards and forwards to London several times, and had ordered all I wanted of my tradesmen, Mr. Pocket and I had a long talk together. He knew more of my intended career than I knew myself, for he referred to his having been told by Mr. Jaggers that I was not designed for any profession, and that I should be well enough educated for my destiny if I could "hold my own" with the average of young men in prosperous circumstances. I acquiesced, of course, knowing nothing to the contrary.

He advised my attending certain places in London, for the acquisition of such mere rudiments as I wanted, and my investing him with the functions 10 of explainer and director of all my studies. He hoped that with intelligent assistance I should meet with little to discourage me, and should soon be able to dispense with any aid but his. Through his way of saying this, and much more to similar purpose, he placed himself on confidential terms with me in an admirable manner; and I may state at once that he was always so zealous and honourable in fulfilling his compact with me, that he made me zealous and honourable in fulfilling mine with him. If he had shown indifference as a master, I have no doubt I should have returned the compliment as a pupil; he gave me no such excuse, and each of us did the other justice. Nor did I ever regard him as having anything ludicrous about him—or any- 20 thing but what was serious, honest, and good—in his tutor communication with me.

When these points were settled, and so far carried out as that I had begun to work in earnest, it occurred to me that if I could retain my bedroom in Barnard's Inn, my life would be agreeably varied, while my manners would be none the worse for Herbert's society. Mr. Pocket did not object to this arrangement, but urged that before any step could possibly be taken in it, it must be submitted to my guardian. I felt that his delicacy arose out of the consideration that the plan would save Herbert some expense, so I went off to Little Britain and imparted my wish to Mr. Jaggers. 30

"If I could buy the furniture now hired for me," said I, "and one or two other little things, I should be quite at home there."

"Go it!" said Mr. Jaggers, with a short laugh. "I told you you'd get on. Well! How much do you want?"

I said I didn't know how much.

"Come!" retorted Mr. Jaggers. "How much? Fifty pounds?"

"Oh, not nearly so much."

"Five pounds?" said Mr. Jaggers.

This was such a great fall that I said in discomfiture, "Oh! more than that." 40

"More than that, eh?" retorted Mr. Jaggers, lying in wait for me, with his hands in his pockets, his head on one side, and his eyes on the wall behind me; "how much more?"

"It is so difficult to fix a sum," said I, hesitating.

"Come!" said Mr. Jaggers. "Let's get at it. Twice five; will that do? Three times five; will that do? Four times five; will that do?"

I said I thought that would do handsomely.

"Four times five will do handsomely, will it?" said Mr. Jaggers, knitting his brows. "Now, what do you make of four times five?"

"What do I make of it?"

"Ah!" said Mr. Jaggers; "how much?"

"I suppose you make it twenty pounds," said I, smiling.

"Never mind what *I* make it, my friend," observed Mr. Jaggers, with a knowing and contradictory toss of his head. "I want to know what *you* make it."

"Twenty pounds, of course."

"Wemmick!" said Mr. Jaggers, opening his office door. "Take Mr. Pip's written order, and pay him twenty pounds." 10

This strongly marked way of doing business made a strongly marked impression on me, and that not of an agreeable kind. Mr. Jaggers never laughed;[1] but he wore great bright creaking boots, and in poising himself on these boots, with his large head bent down and his eyebrows joined together, awaiting an answer, he sometimes caused the boots to creak, as if *they* laughed in a dry and suspicious way. As he happened to go out now, and as Wemmick was brisk and talkative, I said to Wemmick that I hardly knew what to make of Mr. Jaggers's manner.

"Tell him that, and he'll take it as a compliment," answered Wemmick; 20 "he don't mean that you *should* know what to make of it.—Oh!" for I looked surprised, "it's not personal; it's professional: only professional."

Wemmick was at his desk, lunching—and crunching—on a dry hard biscuit; pieces of which he threw from time to time into his slit of a mouth, as if he were posting them.

"Always seems to me," said Wemmick, "as if he had set a man-trap and was watching it. Suddenly—click—you're caught!"

Without remarking that man-traps were not among the amenities of life, I said I supposed he was very skilful?

"Deep," said Wemmick, "as Australia." Pointing with his pen at the office 30 floor, to express that Australia was understood for the purposes of the figure, to be symmetrically on the opposite spot of the globe. "If there was anything deeper," added Wemmick, bringing his pen to paper, "he'd be it."

Then, I said I supposed he had a fine business, and Wemmick said, "Capi-tal!" Then, I asked if there were many clerks? to which he replied:

"We don't run much into clerks, because there's only one Jaggers, and people won't have him at second hand. There are only four of us. Would you like to see 'em? You are one of us, as I may say."

I accepted the offer. When Mr. Wemmick had put all his biscuit into the post, and had paid me my money from a cash-box in a safe, the key of which 40 safe he kept somewhere down his back and produced from his coat-collar like an iron pigtail,[2] we went up-stairs. The house was dark and shabby, and the greasy shoulders that had left their mark in Mr. Jaggers's room, seemed to have been shuffling up and down the staircase for years. In the front first floor, a clerk who looked something between a publican and a rat-catcher— a large pale puffed swollen man—was attentively engaged with three or four people of shabby appearance, whom he treated as unceremoniously as everybody seemed to be treated who contributed to Mr. Jaggers's coffers. "Getting

---

1. He laughed (briefly) thirty lines earlier.
2. Pigtails were much in vogue among sailors.

evidence together," said Mr. Wemmick, as we came out, "for the Bailey."[3]
In the room over that, a little flabby terrier of a clerk with dangling hair (his
cropping seemed to have been forgotten when he was a puppy) was similarly
engaged with a man with weak eyes, whom Mr. Wemmick presented to me
as a smelter who kept his pot always boiling, and who would melt me anything
I pleased—and who was in an excessive white-perspiration, as if he had been
trying his art on himself.[4] In a back room, a high-shouldered man with a
face-ache tied up in dirty flannel, who was dressed in old black clothes that
bore the appearance of having been waxed, was stooping over his work of
making fair copies of the notes of the other two gentlemen, for Mr. Jaggers's 10
own use.

This was all the establishment. When we went down stairs again, Wemmick
led me into my guardian's room, and said, "This you've seen already."

"Pray," said I, as the two odious casts with the twitchy leer upon them
caught my sight again, "whose likenesses are those?"

"These?" said Wemmick, getting upon a chair, and blowing the dust off
the horrible heads before bringing them down. "These are two celebrated
ones. Famous clients of ours that got us a world of credit. This chap (why
you must have come down in the night and been peeping into the inkstand,
to get this blot upon your eyebrow, you old rascal!) murdered his master, 20
and, considering that he wasn't brought up to evidence,[5] didn't plan it badly."

"Is it like him?" I asked, recoiling from the brute, as Wemmick spat upon
his eyebrow and gave it a rub with his sleeve.

"Like him? It's himself, you know. The cast was made in Newgate, directly
after he was taken down.[6] You took a particular fancy for me, didn't you, Old
Artful?" said Wemmick. He then explained this affectionate apostrophe, by
touching his brooch representing the lady and the weeping willow at the tomb
with the urn upon it, and saying "Had it made for me, express!"

"Is the lady anybody?" said I.

"No," returned Wemmick. "Only his game. (You liked your bit of game, 30
didn't you?) No; deuce a bit of a lady in the case,[7] Mr. Pip, except one—and
she wasn't of this slender lady-like sort, and you wouldn't have caught *her*
looking after this urn—unless there was something to drink in it." Wemmick's
attention being thus directed to his brooch, he put down the cast, and polished the brooch with his pocket-handkerchief.

"Did that other creature come to the same end?" I asked. "He has the
same look."

"You're right," said Wemmick, "it's the genuine look. Much as if one
nostril was caught up with a horsehair and a little fish-hook. Yes, he came to
the same end; quite the natural end here, I assure you. He forged wills, this 40

---

3. The Old Bailey, the Central Criminal Court of London (Londoners still affectionately refer to it by
   its old name)—so called for the Roman wall, or "bailey," encircling the city. The inmates of Newgate,
   the prison attached to the court, were tried at the Old Bailey and, if sentenced to death, remanded
   to Newgate before being hanged outside the door of the Old Bailey. A graphic view of the Old Bailey
   in session appears in chapter 54.
4. Wemmick is showing off a receiver of stolen goods who "in the esoteric language peculiar to [Dick-
   ens's] criminals" (Monod) converts the thieves' haul of silver or gold cups, spoons, and the like into
   liquid assets. Perhaps more generally, Wemmick's way of saying that the metaphorical smelter, like
   Mike, could be trusted to follow the lawyer's instructions in manipulating his "evidence."
5. That is, was too untaught in the ways of the law to know what could be used in evidence.
6. From the gallows.
7. "Certainly no lady involved!" In Victorian usage, "deuce" often introduces a violent negative. "Game":
   colloquial, here to indicate the opposite of a dangerous liaison; an easy-come-easy-go affair.

blade did, if he didn't also put the supposed testators to sleep too.[8] You were a gentlemanly Cove,[9] though" (Mr. Wemmick was again apostrophising), "and you said you could write Greek. Yah, Bounceable![1] What a liar you were! I never met such a liar as you!" Before putting his late friend on his shelf again, Wemmick touched the largest of his mourning rings, and said, "Sent out to buy it for me, only the day before."

While he was putting up the other cast and coming down from the chair, the thought crossed my mind that all his personal jewellery was derived from like sources. As he had shown no diffidence on the subject, I ventured on the liberty of asking him the question, when he stood before me, dusting his hands.

"Oh yes," he returned, "these are all gifts of that kind. One brings another, you see; that's the way of it. I always take 'em. They're curiosities. And they're property. They may not be worth much, but, after all, they're property and portable. It don't signify to you with your brilliant look-out, but as to myself, my guiding-star always is, "Get hold of portable property.""

When I had rendered homage to this light, he went on to say, in a friendly manner:

"If at any odd time when you have nothing better to do, you wouldn't mind coming over to see me at Walworth,[2] I could offer you a bed, and I should consider it an honour. I have not much to show you; but such two or three curiosities as I have got, you might like to look over; and I am fond of a bit of garden and a summer-house."

I said I should be delighted to accept his hospitality.

"Thank'ee," said he, "then we'll consider that it's to come off, when convenient to you. Have you dined with Mr. Jaggers yet?"

"Not yet."

"Well," said Wemmick, "he'll give you wine, and good wine. I'll give you punch, and not bad punch. And now I'll tell you something. When you go to dine with Mr. Jaggers, look at his housekeeper."

"Shall I see something very uncommon?"

"Well," said Wemmick, "you'll see a wild beast tamed. Not so very uncommon, you'll tell me. I reply, that depends on the original wildness of the beast, and the amount of taming. It won't lower your opinion of Mr. Jaggers's powers. Keep your eye on it."

I told him I would do so with all the interest and curiosity that his preparation awakened. As I was taking my departure, he asked me if I would like to devote five minutes to seeing Mr. Jaggers "at it?"

For several reasons, and not least because I didn't clearly know what Mr. Jaggers would be found to be "at," I replied in the affirmative. We dived into the City, and came up in a crowded police-court, where a blood-relation (in the murderous sense) of the deceased with the fanciful taste in brooches, was standing at the bar, uncomfortably chewing something; while my guardian had a woman under examination or cross-examination—I don't know which

8. Murdered those who had presumably made their wills; or, plausibly, those whose wills he had forged.
9. "A sham, a fellow, a rogue" (Grose). Frequently used in a chummy or an amiably dismissive sense.
1. Windbag; sometimes chiseler. "Bounce: a showy swindler" (Hotten).
2. District two miles south of the Thames. In Pip's day virtually a separate village consisting of market gardens and scattered houses and cottages; now part of the borough of Southwark. For an extended description of this windswept "accursed locality," see the "Uncommercial" paper in *All the Year Round*, March 24, 1860.

—and was striking her, and the bench, and everybody present, with awe. If anybody, of whatsoever degree, said a word that he didn't approve of, he instantly required to have it "taken down." If anybody wouldn't make an admission, he said, "I'll have it out of you!" and if anybody made an admission, he said, "Now I have got you!" The magistrates shivered under a single bite of his finger. Thieves and thief-takers hung in dread rapture on his words, and shrank when a hair of his eyebrows turned in their direction. Which side he was on, I couldn't make out, for he seemed to me to be grinding the whole place in a mill; I only know that when I stole out on tiptoe, he was not on the side of the bench, for he was making the legs of the old gentleman 10 who presided, quite convulsive under the table, by his denunciations of his conduct as the representative of British law and justice in that chair that day.

★

Chapter XXV.

BENTLEY DRUMMLE, who was so sulky a fellow that he even took up a book as if its writer had done him an injury, did not take up an acquaintance in a more agreeable spirit. Heavy in figure, movement, and comprehension—in the sluggish complexion of his face, and in the large awkward tongue that seemed to loll about in his mouth as he himself lolled about in a room—he was idle, proud, niggardly, reserved, and suspicious. He came of rich people down in Somersetshire,[1] who had nursed this combination of qualities until they made the discovery that it was just of age and a blockhead. Thus Bentley 20 Drummle had come to Mr. Pocket when he was a head taller than that gentleman, and half a dozen heads thicker than most gentlemen.

Startop had been spoilt by a weak mother and kept at home when he ought to have been at school, but he was devotedly attached to her, and admired her beyond measure. He had a woman's delicacy of feature, and was—"as you may see, though you never saw her," said Herbert to me—"exactly like his mother." It was but natural that I should take to him much more kindly than to Drummle, and that even in the earliest evenings of our boating, he and I should pull homeward abreast of one another, conversing from boat to boat, while Bentley Drummle came up in our wake alone, under the over- 30 hanging banks and among the rushes. He would always creep in-shore like some uncomfortable amphibious creature, even when the tide would have sent him fast upon his way; and I always think of him as coming after us in the dark or by the back-water, when our own two boats were breaking the sunset or the moonlight in mid-stream.

Herbert was my intimate companion and friend. I presented him with a half-share in my boat, which was the occasion of his often coming down to Hammersmith; and my possession of a half-share in his chambers often took me up to London. We used to walk between the two places at all hours. I have an affection for the road yet (though it is not so pleasant a road as 40 it was then), formed in the impressibility of untried youth and hope.

1. County in southwestern England. In chapter 43 his home is said to be Shropshire, which is nowhere near, nor anything like, Somersetshire. Shropshire, which borders on Wales, is largely hilly country; Somersetshire (now Somerset), south of the Bristol Channel, is comparatively flat, its eastern regions marked by large tracts of moor.

When I had been in Mr. Pocket's family a month or two, Mr. and Mrs. Camilla turned up. Camilla was Mr. Pocket's sister. Georgiana, whom I had seen at Miss Havisham's on the same occasion, also turned up. She was a cousin—an indigestive single woman, who called her rigidity religion, and her liver love. These people hated me with the hatred of cupidity and disappointment. As a matter of course, they fawned upon me in my prosperity with the basest meanness. Towards Mr. Pocket, as a grown-up infant with no notion of his own interests, they showed the complacent forbearance I had heard them express. Mrs. Pocket they held in contempt; but they allowed the poor soul to have been heavily disappointed in life, because that shed a feeble 10 reflected light upon themselves.

These were the surroundings among which I settled down, and applied myself to my education. I soon contracted expensive habits, and began to spend an amount of money that within a few short months I should have thought almost fabulous, but through good and evil I stuck to my books. There was no other merit in this, than my having sense enough to feel my deficiencies. Between Mr. Pocket and Herbert I got on fast; and, with one or the other always at my elbow to give me the start I wanted, and clear obstructions out of my road, I must have been as great a dolt as Drummle if I had done less. 20

I had not seen Mr. Wemmick for some weeks, when I thought I would write him a note and propose to go home with him on a certain evening. He replied that it would give him much pleasure, and that he would expect me at the office at six o'clock. Thither I went, and there I found him, putting the key of his safe down his back as the clock struck.

"Did you think of walking down to Walworth?" said he.

"Certainly," said I, "if you approve."

"Very much," was Wemmick's reply, "for I have had my legs under the desk all day, and shall be glad to stretch them. Now, I'll tell you what I have got for supper, Mr. Pip. I have got a stewed steak—which is of home 30 preparation—and a cold roast fowl—which is from the cook's-shop. I think it's tender, because the master of the shop was a Juryman in some cases of ours the other day, and we let him down easy. I reminded him of it when I bought the fowl, and I said, 'Pick us out a good one, old Briton, because if we had chosen to keep you in the box another day or two, we could easily have done it.'[2] He said to that, 'Let me make you a present of the best fowl in the shop.' I let him, of course. As far as it goes, it's property and portable. You don't object to an aged parent, I hope?"

I really thought he was still speaking of the fowl, until he added, "Because I have got an aged parent at my place." I then said what politeness 40 required.

"So, you haven't dined with Mr. Jaggers yet?" he pursued, as we walked along.

"Not yet."

"He told me so this afternoon when he heard you were coming. I expect you'll have an invitation to-morrow. He's going to ask your pals, too. Three of 'em; ain't there?"

---

2. That is, Wemmick, for the price of a fowl, keeps the case from being dragged out. Protracted trials were as much of a nuisance as they are today, since jurors—like sequestered jurors today—were unable to pursue their businesses as long as the trial lasted.

Although I was not in the habit of counting Drummle as one of my intimate associates I answered, "Yes."

"Well, he's going to ask the whole gang;" I hardly felt complimented by the word; "and whatever he gives you, he'll give you good. Don't look forward to variety, but you'll have excellence. And there's another rum thing in his house," proceeded Wemmick, after a moment's pause, as if the remark followed on the housekeeper was understood; "he never lets a door or window be fastened at night."

"Is he never robbed?"

"That's it!" returned Wemmick. "He says and gives it out publicly, 'I want to see the man who'll rob me.' Lord bless you, I have heard him, a hundred times if I have heard him once, say to regular cracksmen[3] in our front office, 'You know where I live; now, no bolt is ever drawn there; why don't you do a stroke of business with me? Come; can't I tempt you?' Not a man of them, sir, would be bold enough to try it on, for love or money."

"They dread him so much?" said I.

"Dread him," said Wemmick. "I believe you they dread him. Not but what he's artful, even in his defiance of 'em. No silver, sir. Britannia metal,[4] every spoon."

"So they wouldn't have much," I observed, "even if they——"

"Ah! But he would have much," said Wemmick, cutting me short, "and they know it. He'd have their lives, and the lives of scores of 'em. He'd have all he could get. And it's impossible to say what he couldn't get, if he gave his mind to it."

I was falling into meditation on my guardian's greatness, when Wemmick remarked:

"As to the absence of plate, that's only his natural depth, you know. A river's its natural depth, and he's his natural depth. Look at his watch-chain. That's real enough."

"It's very massive," said I.

"Massive?" repeated Wemmick. "I think so. And his watch is a gold repeater,[5] and worth a hundred pound if it's worth a penny. Mr. Pip, there are about seven hundred thieves in this town who know all about that watch; there's not a man, a woman, or a child among them, who wouldn't identify the smallest link in that chain, and drop it as if it was red-hot, if inveigled into touching it."

At first with such discourse, and afterwards with conversation of a more general nature, did Mr. Wemmick and I beguile the time and the road, until he gave me to understand that we had arrived in the district of Walworth.

It appeared to be a collection of back lanes, ditches, and little gardens, and to present the aspect of a rather dull retirement. Wemmick's house was a little wooden cottage in the midst of plots of garden, and the top of it was cut out and painted like a battery mounted with guns.

"My own doing," said Wemmick. "Looks pretty; don't it?"

I highly commended it. I think it was the smallest house I ever saw; with

3. Burglars.
4. Alloy of tin, copper, and antimony, introduced by pewterers about 1800. Polished to look like silver, it might fool prospective burglars.
5. A watch that strikes the hour, or fraction of the hour, when a lever or spring is pressed. Useful especially in the dark, repeaters went out of style once the invention of matches obviated their usefulness.

the queerest gothic windows (by far the greater part of them sham), and a gothic door, almost too small to get in at.

"That's a real flagstaff, you see," said Wemmick, "and on Sundays I run up a real flag. Then look here. After I have crossed this bridge, I hoist it up —so—and cut off the communication."

The bridge was a plank, and it crossed a chasm about four feet wide and two deep. But it was very pleasant to see the pride with which he hoisted it up and made it fast; smiling as he did so, with a relish and not merely mechanically.[6]

"At nine o'clock every night, Greenwich time," said Wemmick, "the gun fires. There he is, you see! And when you hear him go, I think you'll say he's a Stinger."

The piece of ordnance referred to, was mounted in a separate fortress, constructed of lattice-work. It was protected from the weather by an ingenious little tarpaulin contrivance in the nature of an umbrella.

"Then, at the back," said Wemmick, "out of sight, so as not to impede the idea of fortifications—for it's a principle with me, if you have an idea, carry it out and keep it up; I don't know whether that's your opinion——"

I said, decidedly.

"At the back, there's a pig, and there are fowls and rabbits; then I knock together my own little frame, you see, and grow cucumbers; and you'll judge at supper what sort of a salad I can raise. So, sir," said Wemmick, smiling again, but seriously too as he shook his head, "if you can suppose the little place besieged, it would hold out a devil of a time in point of provisions."

Then he conducted me to a bower about a dozen yards off, but which was approached by such ingenious twists of path that it took quite a long time to get at; and in this retreat our glasses were already set forth. Our punch was cooling in an ornamental lake, on whose margin the bower was raised. This piece of water (with an island in the middle which might have been the salad for supper) was of a circular form, and he had constructed a fountain in it, which, when you set a little mill going and took a cork out of a pipe, played to that powerful extent that it made the back of your hand quite wet.

"I am my own engineer, and my own carpenter, and my own plumber, and my own gardener, and my own Jack of all Trades," said Wemmick, in acknowledging my compliments. "Well; it's a good thing, you know. It brushes the Newgate cobwebs away, and pleases the Aged. You wouldn't mind being at once introduced to the Aged, would you? It wouldn't put you out?"

I expressed the readiness I felt, and we went into the Castle. There we found, sitting by a fire, a very old man in a flannel coat: clean, cheerful, comfortable, and well cared for, but intensely deaf.

"Well, aged parent," said Wemmick, shaking hands with him in a cordial and jocose way, "how am you?"

"All right, John; all right!" replied the old man.

"Here's Mr. Pip, aged parent," said Wemmick, "and I wish you could hear

6. In describing Wemmick's castle, Dickens spoofs the mania for the revival of Gothic interiors early in the century, of which features like window casements were characteristic. But Dickens may also have borrowed features from Commodore Trunnion's quirky quarters in Tobias Smollett's *Peregrine Pickle* (1751), always a favorite with Dickens; see especially chapters 11 and 14. Dickens seems to have shared Wemmick's penchant for raising his flag: one of the maid's duties at Gad's Hill was to hoist the Union Jack whenever Dickens returned from his trips.

his name. Nod away at him, Mr. Pip; that's what he likes. Nod away at him, if you please, like winking!"

"This is a fine place of my son's, sir," cried the old man, while I nodded as hard as I possibly could. "This is a pretty pleasure-ground, sir. This spot and these beautiful works upon it ought to be kept together by the Nation, after my son's time, for the people's enjoyment."

"You're as proud of it as Punch; ain't you, Aged?" said Wemmick, contemplating the old man with his hard face really softened; "there's a nod for you;" giving him a tremendous one; "there's another for you;" giving him a still more tremendous one; "you like that, don't you? If you're not tired, Mr. 10 Pip—though I know it's tiring to strangers—will you tip him one more? You can't think how it pleases him."

I tipped him several more, and he was in great spirits. We left him bestirring himself to feed the fowls, and we sat down to our punch in the arbour; where Wemmick told me as he smoked a pipe that it had taken him a good many years to bring the property up to its present pitch of perfection.

"Is it your own, Mr. Wemmick?"

"Oh yes," said Wemmick, "I have got hold of it, a bit at a time. It's a freehold,[7] by George!"

"Is it, indeed? I hope Mr. Jaggers admires it?"

"Never seen it," said Wemmick. "Never heard of it. Never seen the Aged. 20 Never heard of him. No; the office is one thing, and private life is another. When I go into the office, I leave the Castle behind me, and when I come into the Castle, I leave the office behind me. If it's not in any way disagreeable to you, you'll oblige me by doing the same. I don't wish it professionally spoken about."

Of course I felt my good faith involved in the observance of his request. The punch being very nice, we sat there drinking it and talking, until it was almost nine o'clock. "Getting near gun-fire," said Wemmick then, as he laid down his pipe; "it's the Aged's treat."

Proceeding into the Castle again, we found the Aged heating the poker, 30 with expectant eyes, as a preliminary to the performance of this great nightly ceremony. Wemmick stood with his watch in his hand, until the moment was come for him to take the red-hot poker from the Aged, and repair to the battery. He took it, and went out, and presently the Stinger went off with a Bang that shook the crazy little box of a cottage as if it must fall to pieces, and made every glass and teacup in it ring. Upon this, the Aged—who I believe would have been blown out of his arm-chair but for holding on by the elbows—cried out exultingly, "He's fired! I heerd him!" and I nodded at the old gentleman until it is no figure of speech to declare that I absolutely could not see him. 40

The interval between that time and supper Wemmick devoted to showing me his collection of curiosities. They were mostly of a felonious character; comprising the pen with which a celebrated forgery had been committed, a distinguished razor or two, some locks of hair, and several manuscript confessions written under condemnation—upon which Mr. Wemmick set particular value as being, to use his own words, "every one of 'em Lies, sir." These were agreeably dispersed among small specimens of china and glass, various

7. Legal term to indicate that Wemmick holds a title to the property instead of paying rent as a tenant.

neat trifles made by the proprietor of the museum, and some tobacco-stoppers[8] carved by the Aged. They were all displayed in that chamber of the Castle into which I had been first inducted, and which served, not only as the general sitting-room, but as the kitchen too, if I might judge from a saucepan on the hob, and a brazen bijou over the fireplace designed for the suspension of a roasting-jack.[9]

There was a neat little girl in attendance, who looked after the Aged in the day. When she had laid the supper-cloth, the bridge was lowered to give her means of egress, and she withdrew for the night. The supper was excellent; and though the Castle was rather subject to dry-rot insomuch that it tasted 10 like a bad nut, and though the pig might have been farther off, I was heartily pleased with my whole entertainment. Nor was there any drawback on my little turret bedroom, beyond there being such a very thin ceiling between me and the flagstaff that when I lay down on my back in bed, it seemed as if I had to balance that pole on my forehead all night.

Wemmick was up early in the morning, and I am afraid I heard him cleaning my boots. After that, he fell to gardening, and I saw him from my gothic window pretending to employ the Aged, and nodding at him in a most devoted manner. Our breakfast was as good as the supper, and at half-past eight precisely we started for Little Britain. By degrees, Wemmick got dryer 20 and harder as we went along, and his mouth tightened into a post-office again. At last, when we got to his place of business and he pulled out his key from his coat-collar, he looked as unconscious of his Walworth property as if the Castle and the drawbridge and the arbour and the lake and the fountain and the Aged, had all been blown into space together by the last discharge of the Stinger.

Chapter XXVI.

IT fell out, as Wemmick had told me it would, that I had an early opportunity of comparing my guardian's establishment with that of his cashier and clerk. My guardian was in his room, washing his hands with his scented soap, when I went into the office from Walworth; and he called me to him, and 30 gave me the invitation for myself and friends which Wemmick had prepared me to receive. "No ceremony," he stipulated, "and no dinner dress, and say to-morrow." I asked him where we should come to (for I had no idea where he lived), and I believe it was in his general objection to make anything like an admission, that he replied, "Come here, and I'll take you home with me." I embrace this opportunity of remarking that he washed his clients off, as if he were a surgeon or a dentist. He had a closet in his room, fitted up for the purpose, which smelt of the scented soap like a perfumer's shop. It had an unusually large jack-towel on a roller inside the door, and he would wash his hands, and wipe them and dry them all over this towel, whenever he 40 came in from a police-court or dismissed a client from his room. When I and my friends repaired to him at six o'clock next day, he seemed to have

---

8. Contrivance used to press down the tobacco in the bowl of a pipe.
9. Ornamental brass bracket or crane over the fireplace. *Bijou* (French for "jewel"), with its suggestion of exquisite workmanship, is perhaps used euphemistically.

been engaged on a case of a darker complexion than usual, for we found him
with his head butted into this closet, not only washing his hands, but laving
his face and gargling his throat. And even when he had done all that, and
had gone all round the jack-towel, he took out his penknife and scraped the
case out of his nails before he put his coat on.

There were some people slinking about as usual when we passed out into
the street, who were evidently anxious to speak with him; but there was something so conclusive in the halo of scented soap which encircled his presence,
that they gave it up for that day. As we walked along westward, he was recognised ever and again by some face in the crowd of the streets, and when- 10
ever that happened he talked louder to me; but he never otherwise recognised
anybody, or took notice that anybody recognised him.

He conducted us to Gerrard-street, Soho,[1] to a house on the south side of
that street. Rather a stately house of its kind, but dolefully in want of painting,
and with dirty windows. He took out his key and opened the door, and we
all went into a stone hall, bare, gloomy, and little used. So, up a dark brown
staircase into a series of three dark brown rooms on the first floor. There were
carved garlands on the panelled walls, and as he stood among them giving
us welcome, I know what kind of loops I thought they looked like.

Dinner was laid in the best of these rooms; the second was his dressing- 20
room; the third his bedroom. He told us that he held the whole house, but
rarely used more of it than we saw. The table was comfortably laid—no silver
in the service, of course—and at the side of his chair was a capacious dumb-
waiter,[2] with a variety of bottles and decanters on it, and four dishes of fruit
for dessert. I noticed throughout, that he kept everything under his own hand,
and distributed everything himself.

There was a bookcase in the room; I saw, from the backs of the books, that
they were about evidence, criminal law, criminal biography, trials, acts of
parliament, and such things. The furniture was all very solid and good, like
his watch-chain. It had an official look, however, and there was nothing 30
merely ornamental to be seen. In a corner, was a little table of papers with a
shaded lamp: so that he seemed to bring the office home with him in that
respect too, and to wheel it out of an evening and fall to work.

As he had scarcely seen my three companions until now—for he and I had
walked together—he stood on the hearth-rug, after ringing the bell, and took
a searching look at them. To my surprise, he seemed at once to be principally
if not solely interested in Drummle.

"Pip," said he, putting his large hand on my shoulder and moving me to
the window, "I don't know one from the other. Who's the Spider?"

"The Spider?" said I.   40

"The blotchy, sprawly, sulky fellow."

"That's Bentley Drummle," I replied; "the one with the delicate face is
Startop."

1. Soho, a residential area between Oxford Street and Leicester Square, used to be a quiet sanctuary
   peopled by artists and foreigners, chiefly French Huguenots; best known in Dickens as the home of
   the emigré Manette family in A Tale of Two Cities. The area retains its foreign character in its cluster
   of foreign restaurants and porn shops. Gerrard Street, just north of Leicester Square, is memorable
   for its eighteenth-century artistic echoes: John Dryden and Edmund Burke owned houses on Gerrard
   Street; Dr. Johnson and Sir Joshua Reynolds founded their literary club at the Turk's Head Tavern
   there.
2. Or mute waiter. Device for serving food: typically, a movable upright pole with two or more revolving
   trays for dishes, condiments, etc.

Not making the least account of "the one with the delicate face," he returned. "Bentley Drummle is his name, is it? I like the look of that fellow."

He immediately began to talk to Drummle: not at all deterred by his replying in his heavy reticent way, but apparently led on by it to screw discourse out of him. I was looking at the two, when there came between me and them, the housekeeper, with the first dish for the table.

She was a woman of about forty, I supposed—but I may have thought her younger than she was. Rather tall, of a lithe nimble figure, extremely pale, with large faded-blue eyes, and a quantity of streaming hair. I cannot say whether any diseased affection of the heart caused her lips to be parted as if 10 she were panting, and her face to bear a curious expression of suddenness and flutter; but I know that I had been to see Macbeth at the theatre, a night or two before,[3] and that her face looked to me as if it were all disturbed by fiery air, like the faces I had seen rise out of the Witches' caldron.[4]

She set the dish on, touched my guardian quietly on the arm with a finger to notify that dinner was ready, and vanished. We took our seats at the round table, and my guardian kept Drummle on one side of him, while Startop sat on the other. It was a noble dish of fish that the housekeeper had put on table, and we had a joint of equally choice mutton afterwards, and then an equally choice bird. Sauces, wines, all the accessories we wanted, and all of 20 the best, were given out by our host from his dumb-waiter; and when they had made the circuit of the table, he always put them back again. Similarly, he dealt us clean plates and knives and forks, for each course, and dropped those just disused into two baskets on the ground by his chair. No other attendant than the housekeeper appeared. She set on every dish; and I always saw in her face, a face rising out of the caldron. Years afterwards, I made a dreadful likeness of that woman, by causing a face that had no other natural resemblance to it than it derived from flowing hair, to pass behind a bowl of flaming spirits in a dark room.

Induced to take particular notice of the housekeeper, both by her own 30 striking appearance and by Wemmick's preparation, I observed that whenever she was in the room, she kept her eyes attentively on my guardian, and that she would remove her hands from any dish she put before him, hesitatingly, as if she dreaded his calling her back, and wanted him to speak when she was nigh, if he had anything to say. I fancied that I could detect in his manner a consciousness of this, and a purpose of always holding her in suspense.

Dinner went off gaily, and, although my guardian seemed to follow rather than originate subjects, I knew that he wrenched the weakest part of our dispositions out of us. For myself, I found that I was expressing my tendency to lavish expenditure, and to patronise Herbert, and to boast of my great 40 prospects, before I quite knew that I had opened my lips. It was so with all of us, but with no one more than Drummle: the development of whose inclination to gird in a grudging and suspicious way at the rest, was screwed out of him before the fish was taken off.

It was not then, but when we had got to the cheese, that our conversation turned upon our rowing feats, and that Drummle was rallied for coming up behind of a night in that slow amphibious way of his. Drummle upon this, informed our host that he much preferred our room to our company, and

3. One. Pip spent the night before last at the Castle.
4. Macbeth 4.1.

that as to skill he was more than our master, and that as to strength he could scatter us like chaff. By some invisible agency, my guardian wound him up to a pitch little short of ferocity about this trifle; and he fell to baring and spanning his arm to show how muscular it was, and we all fell to baring and spanning our arms in a ridiculous manner.

Now, the housekeeper was at that time clearing the table; my guardian, taking no heed of her, but with the side of his face turned from her, was leaning back in his chair biting the side of his forefinger and showing an interest in Drummle, that, to me, was quite inexplicable. Suddenly, he clapped his large hand on the housekeeper's, like a trap, as she stretched it 10 across the table. So suddenly and smartly did he do this, that we all stopped in our foolish contention.

"If you talk of strength," said Mr. Jaggers, "I'll show you a wrist. Molly, let them see your wrist."

Her entrapped hand was on the table, but she had already put her other hand behind her waist. "Master," she said, in a low voice, with her eyes attentively and entreatingly fixed upon him. "Don't."

"I'll show you a wrist," repeated Mr. Jaggers, with an immovable determination to show it. "Molly, let them see your wrist."

"Master," she again murmured. "Please!"   20

"Molly," said Mr. Jaggers, not looking at her, but obstinately looking at the opposite side of the room, "let them see *both* your wrists. Show them. Come!"

He took his hand from hers, and turned that wrist up on the table. She brought her other hand from behind her, and held the two out side by side. The last wrist was much disfigured—deeply seamed and scarred across and across. When she held her hands out, she took her eyes from Mr. Jaggers, and turned them watchfully on every one of the rest of us in succession.

"There's power here," said Mr. Jaggers, coolly tracing out the sinews with his forefinger. "Very few men have the power of wrist that this woman has. It's remarkable what mere force of grip there is in these hands. I have had 30 occasion to notice many hands; but I never saw stronger in that respect, man's or woman's, than these."

While he said these words in a leisurely critical way, she continued to look at every one of us in regular succession as we sat. The moment he ceased, she looked at him again. "That'll do, Molly," said Mr. Jaggers, giving her a slight nod; "you have been admired, and can go." She withdrew her hands and went out of the room, and Mr. Jaggers, putting the decanters on from his dumb-waiter, filled his glass and passed round the wine.

"At half-past nine, gentlemen," said he, "we must break up. Pray make the best use of your time. I am glad to see you all. Mr. Drummle, I drink to 40 you."

If his object in singling out Drummle were to bring him out still more, it perfectly succeeded. In a sulky triumph, Drummle showed his morose depreciation of the rest of us, in a more and more offensive degree until he became downright intolerable. Through all his stages, Mr. Jaggers followed him with the same strange interest. He actually seemed to serve as a zest to Mr. Jaggers's wine.

In our boyish want of discretion I dare say we took too much to drink, and I know we talked too much. We became particularly hot upon some boorish sneer of Drummle's, to the effect that we were too free with our money. It 50 led to my remarking, with more zeal than discretion, that it came with a bad grace from him, to whom Startop had lent money in my presence, but a week or so before.

"Well," retorted Drummle: "he'll be paid."

"I don't mean to imply that he won't," said I, "but it might make you hold your tongue about us and our money, I should think."

"*You* should think!" retorted Drummle. "Oh Lord!"

"I dare say," I went on, meaning to be very severe, "that you wouldn't lend money to any of us, if we wanted it."

"You are right," said Drummle. "I wouldn't lend one of you a sixpence. I wouldn't lend anybody a sixpence." 10

"Rather mean to borrow under those circumstances, I should say."

"*You* should say," repeated Drummle. "Oh Lord!"

This was so very aggravating—the more especially, as I found myself making no way against his surly obtuseness—that I said, disregarding Herbert's efforts to check me:

"Come, Mr. Drummle, since we are on the subject, I'll tell you what passed between Herbert here and me, when you borrowed that money."

"*I* don't want to know what passed between Herbert there and you," growled Drummle. And I think he added in a lower growl, that we might 20 both go to the devil and shake ourselves.

"I'll tell you, however," said I, "whether you want to know or not. We said that as you put it into your pocket very glad to get it, you seemed to be immensely amused at his being so weak as to lend it."

Drummle laughed outright, and sat laughing in our faces, with his hands in his pockets and his round shoulders raised: plainly signifying that it was quite true, and that he despised us as asses all.

Hereupon, Startop took him in hand, though with a much better grace than I had shown, and exhorted him to be a little more agreeable. Startop, being a lively bright young fellow, and Drummle being the exact opposite, 30 the latter was always disposed to resent him as a direct personal affront. He now retorted in a coarse lumpish way, and Startop tried to turn the discussion aside with some small pleasantry that made us all laugh. Resenting this little success more than anything, Drummle without any threat or warning pulled his hands out of his pockets, dropped his round shoulders, swore, took up a large glass, and would have flung it at his adversary's head, but for our entertainer's dexterously seizing it at the instant when it was raised for that purpose.

"Gentlemen," said Mr. Jaggers, deliberately putting down the glass, and hauling out his gold repeater by its massive chain, "I am exceedingly sorry to 40 announce that it's half-past nine."

On this hint we all rose to depart. Before we got to the street door, Startop was cheerily calling Drummle "old boy," as if nothing had happened. But the old boy was so far from responding, that he would not even walk to Hammersmith on the same side of the way; so, Herbert and I, who remained in town, saw them going down the street on opposite sides; Startop leading, and Drummle lagging behind in the shadow of the houses, much as he was wont to follow in his boat.

As the door was not yet shut, I thought I would leave Herbert there for a moment, and run up-stairs again to say a word of apology to my guardian. I 50 found him in his dressing-room surrounded by his stock of boots, already hard at it, washing his hands of us.

I told him that I had come up again, to say how sorry I was that anything disagreeable should have occurred, and that I hoped he would not blame me much.

"Pooh!" said he, sluicing[5] his face, and speaking through the water-drops; "it's nothing, Pip. I like that Spider though."

He had turned towards me now, and was shaking his head, and blowing, and towelling himself.

"I am glad you like him, sir," said I—"but I don't."   10

"No, no," my guardian assented, "don't have too much to do with him. Keep as clear of him as you can. But I like the fellow, Pip; he is one of the true sort. Why, if I was a fortune-teller——"

Looking out of the towel, he caught my eye.

"But I am not a fortune-teller," he said, letting his head drop into a festoon of towel, and towelling away at his two ears. "You know what I am, don't you? Good night, Pip."

"Good night, sir."

In about a month after that, the Spider's time with Mr. Pocket was up for good, and, to the great relief of all the house but Mrs. Pocket, he went home   20 to the family hole.

Chapter XXVII.

"MY DEAR MR. PIP,

"I write this by request of Mr. Gargery, for to let you know that he is going to London in company of Mr. Wopsle and would be glad if agreeable to be allowed to see you. He would call at Barnard's Hotel Tuesday morning 9 o'clock, when if not agreeable please leave word. Your poor sister is much the same as when you left. We talk of you in the kitchen every night, and wonder what you are saying and doing. If now considered in the light of a liberty, excuse it for the love of poor old days. No more, dear Mr. Pip, from

"Your ever obliged, and affectionate   30
"Servant,
"BIDDY.

"P.S. He wishes me most particular to write *what larks*. He says you will understand. I hope and do not doubt it will be agreeable to see him even though a gentleman, for you had ever a good heart and he is a worthy worthy man. I have read him all, excepting only the last little sentence, and he wishes me most particular to write again *what larks*."

I received this letter by the post on Monday morning, and therefore its appointment was for next day. Let me confess exactly, with what feelings I looked forward to Joe's coming.   40

Not with pleasure, though I was bound to him by so many ties; no; with considerable disturbance, some mortification, and a keen sense of incongru-

---

5. Pouring water over.

ity. If I could have kept him away by paying money, I certainly would have paid money. My greatest reassurance was, that he was coming to Barnard's Inn, not to Hammersmith, and consequently would not fall in Bentley Drummle's way. I had little objection to his being seen by Herbert or his father, for both of whom I had a respect; but I had the sharpest sensitiveness as to his being seen by Drummle, whom I held in contempt. So, throughout life, our worst weaknesses and meannesses are usually committed for the sake of the people whom we most despise.

I had begun to be always decorating the chambers in some quite unnecessary and inappropriate way or other, and very expensive those wrestles with Barnard proved to be. By this time, the rooms were vastly different from what I had found them, and I enjoyed the honour of occupying a few prominent pages in the books of a neighbouring upholsterer. I had got on so fast of late, that I had even started a boy in boots[1]—top boots—in bondage and slavery to whom I might have been said to pass my days. For, after I had made this monster (out of the refuse of my washerwoman's family) and had clothed him with a blue coat, canary waistcoat, white cravat, creamy breeches, and the boots already mentioned, I had to find him a little to do and a great deal to eat; and with both of those horrible requirements he haunted my existence.[2]

This avenging phantom was ordered to be on duty at eight on Tuesday morning in the hall (it was two feet square, as charged for floorcloth), and Herbert suggested certain things for breakfast that he thought Joe would like. While I felt sincerely obliged to him for being so interested and considerate, I had an odd half-provoked sense of suspicion upon me, that if Joe had been coming to see *him*, he wouldn't have been quite so brisk about it.

However, I came into town on the Monday night to be ready for Joe, and I got up early in the morning, and caused the sitting-room and breakfast-table to assume their most splendid appearance. Unfortunately the morning was drizzly, and an angel could not have concealed the fact that Barnard was shedding sooty tears outside the window, like some weak giant of a Sweep.

As the time approached I should have liked to run away, but the Avenger pursuant to orders was in the hall, and presently I heard Joe on the staircase. I knew it was Joe by his clumsy manner of coming up-stairs—his state boots being always too big for him—and by the time it took him to read the names on the other floors in the course of his ascent. When at last he stopped outside our door, I could hear his finger tracing over the painted letters of my name, and I afterwards distinctly heard him breathing in at the keyhole. Finally he gave a faint single rap, and Pepper—such was the compromising name of the avenging boy—announced "Mr. Gargery!" I thought he never would have done wiping his feet, and that I must have gone out to lift him off the mat, but at last he came in.

"Joe, how are you, Joe?"

"Pip, how ARE you, Pip?"

With his good honest face all glowing and shining, and his hat put down

---

1. Literally a hotel servant who cleans boots à la Sam Weller in *Pickwick Papers*; generalized to mean any young male factotum. *Top boots:* knee-high boots, the cuff usually of a different color or make from the rest of the boot. Until mid-century, more likely to be worn by gentry and clergy than by Pip's errand boy.
2. Presumably an allusion to *Frankenstein, or The New Prometheus* (1818) by Mary Shelley (1797–1851), in which the legendary monster is assembled by Dr. Frankenstein from bits and pieces of human flesh. See Pip's reference to "the imaginary student" in chapter 40.

on the floor between us, he caught both my hands and worked them straight up and down, as if I had been the last-patented Pump.

"I am glad to see you, Joe. Give me your hat."

But Joe, taking it up carefully with both hands, like a bird's-nest with eggs in it, wouldn't hear of parting with that piece of property, and persisted in standing talking over it in a most uncomfortable way.

"Which you have that growed," said Joe, "and that swelled, and that gentlefolked;" Joe considered a little before he discovered this word; "as to be sure you are a honour to your king and country."

"And you, Joe, look wonderfully well."   10

"Thank God," said Joe, "I'm ekerval to most. And your sister, she's no worse than she were. And Biddy, she's ever right and ready. And all friends is no backerder, if not no forarder.[3] 'Ceptin' Wopsle; he's had a drop."

All this time (still with both hands taking great care of the bird's-nest), Joe was rolling his eyes round and round the room, and round and round the flowered pattern of my dressing-gown.

"Had a drop, Joe?"

"Why yes," said Joe, lowering his voice, "he's left the Church, and went into the playacting. Which the playacting have likeways brought him to London along with me. And his wish were," said Joe, getting the bird's-nest under   20
his left arm for the moment and groping in it for an egg with his right; "if no offence, as I would 'and you that."

I took what Joe gave me, and found it to be the crumpled playbill of a small metropolitan theatre,[4] announcing the first appearance in that very week of "the celebrated Provincial Amateur of Roscian renown,[5] whose unique performance in the highest tragic walk of our National Bard[6] has lately occasioned so great a sensation in local dramatic circles."

"Were you at his performance, Joe?" I inquired.

"I were," said Joe, with emphasis and solemnity.

"Was there a great sensation?"   30

"Why," said Joe, "yes, there certainly were a peck of orange-peel. Partickler, when he see the ghost. Though I put it to yourself, sir, whether it were calc'lated to keep a man up to his work with a good hart, to be continiwally cutting in betwixt him and the Ghost with 'Amen!' A man may have had a misfortun' and been in the Church," said Joe, lowering his voice to an argumentative and feeling tone, "but that is no reason why you should put him out at such a time.[7] Which I meantersay, if the ghost of a man's own father cannot be allowed to claim his attention, what can, Sir? Still more, when his

---

3. About the same; no worse but no better either. "Ekerval": equal.
4. In the early-nineteenth-century theater, leading roles could be bought by actors like Wopsle—"donkeys who are prevailed upon to pay for permission to exhibit their lamentable ignorance and boobyism on the stage of a private theatre," the price calibrated "in proportion to the scope afforded by the character for the display of their imbecility." Thus Richard III "is well worth two pounds, because he has it all to himself," and besides "the soliloquies alone are well worth fifteen shillings," to say nothing of "the stabbing of King Henry—decidedly cheap at three-and-sixpence"; so it all adds up. See "Private Theatres," *Sketches by Boz*, "Scenes," 13.
5. From Quintus Roscius Gallus (d. 62? B.C.), the greatest Roman comic actor of his time and, with yearly earnings equaling half a million pounds, the richest. During the 1804–05 season—at about the time of Pip's birth—a twelve-year-old Irish prodigy, Master William Betty (1791–1874), nicknamed "Young Roscius," took London by storm as lead in Shakespeare's great tragic roles.
6. *Hamlet.*
7. Joe evidently takes the chorus of "Amens" with which the audience boos Wopsle as a gibe at his "drop" in the Church. With Joe's reaction to the Ghost (*Hamlet* 1.4 and 1.5) compare that of Partridge, the superstitious backwoods schoolmaster in Fielding's *Tom Jones*, in the excerpt on pp. 611–14.

mourning 'at is unfortunately made so small as that the weight of the black feathers brings it off, try to keep it on how you may."

A ghost-seeing effect in Joe's own countenance informed me that Herbert had entered the room. So I presented Joe to Herbert, who held out his hand; but Joe backed from it, and held on by the bird's-nest.

"Your servant, Sir," said Joe, "which I hope as you and Pip"—here his eye fell on the Avenger, who was putting some toast on table, and so plainly denoted an intention to make that young gentleman one of the family, that I frowned it down and confused him more—"I meantersay, you two gentlemen—which I hope as you gets your elths in this close spot? For the present may be a wery good inn, according to London opinions," said Joe, confidentially, "and I believe its character do stand i; but I wouldn't keep a pig in it myself—not in the case that I wished him to fatten wholesome and to eat with a meller flavour on him."

Having borne this flattering testimony to the merits of our dwelling-place, and having incidentally shown this tendency to call me "sir," Joe, being invited to sit down to table, looked all round the room for a suitable spot on which to deposit his hat—as if it were only on some very few rare substances in nature that it could find a resting-place—and ultimately stood it on an extreme corner of the chimney-piece, from which it ever afterwards fell off at intervals.

"Do you take tea, or coffee, Mr. Gargery?" asked Herbert, who always presided of a morning.

"Thankee, Sir," said Joe, stiff from head to foot, "I'll take whichever is most agreeable to yourself."

"What do you say to coffee?"

"Thankee, Sir," returned Joe, evidently dispirited by the proposal, "since you *are* so kind as make chice of coffee, I will not run contrairy to your own opinions. But don't you never find it a little 'eating?"

"Say tea then," said Herbert, pouring it out.

Here Joe's hat tumbled off the mantelpiece, and he started out of his chair and picked it up, and fitted it to the same exact spot. As if it were an absolute point of good breeding that it should tumble off again soon.

"When did you come to town, Mr. Gargery?"

"Were it yesterday afternoon?" said Joe, after coughing behind his hand, as if he had had time to catch the whooping-cough since he came. "No it were not. Yes it were. Yes. It were yesterday afternoon" (with an appearance of mingled wisdom, relief, and strict impartiality).

"Have you seen anything of London, yet?"

"Why, yes, Sir," said Joe, "me and Wopsle went off straight to look at the Blacking Ware'us.[8] But we didn't find that it come up to its likeness in the red bills at the shop doors; which I meantersay," added Joe, in an explanatory manner, "as it is there drawd too architectooralooral."[9]

---

8. Manufacturer of black shoe polish at 97 High Holborn. Clearly the building doesn't live up to its pretentious ads. Dickens obsessively introduced into his novels—and into party word games—the name of Warren's Blacking, where he had slaved for roughly four months as a lad of twelve while his family was lodged in the Marshalsea Debtors' Prison.
9. Probably because the syllables "tooral-ooral-ooral" are a common way of substituting nonsemantic crooning for words. Clearly an echo of the "comic song" Biddy imparts to Pip in chapter 15 (p. 88). The syllables "tooral-ooral-ooral" are, of course, a common way of substituting nonsemantic crooning for words.

I really believe Joe would have prolonged this word (mightily expressive to my mind of some architecture that I know) into a perfect Chorus, but for his attention being providentially attracted by his hat, which was toppling. Indeed, it demanded from him a constant attention, and a quickness of eye and hand, very like that exacted by wicket-keeping.[1] He made the most extraordinary play with it, and showed the greatest skill; now, rushing at it and catching it neatly as it dropped; now merely stopping it midway, beating it up, and humouring it in various parts of the room and against a good deal of the pattern of the paper on the wall, before he felt it safe to close with it; finally splashing it into the slop-basin, where I took the liberty of laying hands upon it.   10

As to his shirt-collar, and his coat-collar, they were perplexing to reflect upon—insoluble mysteries both. Why should a man scrape himself to that extent, before he could consider himself full dressed? Why should he suppose it necessary to be purified by suffering for his holiday clothes? Then he fell into such unaccountable fits of meditation, with his fork midway between his plate and his mouth; had his eyes attracted in such strange directions; was afflicted with such remarkable coughs; sat so far from the table, and dropped so much more than he ate, and pretended that he hadn't dropped it; that I was heartily glad when Herbert left us for the City.

I had neither the good sense nor the good feeling to know that this was all   20 my fault, and that if I had been easier with Joe, Joe would have been easier with me. I felt impatient of him and out of temper with him; in which condition he heaped coals of fire on my head.[2]

"Us two being now alone, Sir"—began Joe.

"Joe," I interrupted, pettishly, "how can you call me Sir?"

Joe looked at me for a single instant with something faintly like reproach. Utterly preposterous as his cravat was, and as his collars were, I was conscious of a sort of dignity in the look too.

"Us two being now alone," resumed Joe, "and me having the intentions and abilities to stay not many minutes more, I will now conclude—leastways   30 begin—to mention what have led to my having had the present honour. For was it not," said Joe, with his old air of lucid exposition, "that my only wish were to be useful to you, I should not have had the honour of breaking wittles in the company and abode of gentlemen."

I was so unwilling to see the look again, that I made no remonstrance against this tone.

"Well, Sir," pursued Joe, "this is how it were. I were at the Bargemen t'other night, Pip;" whenever he subsided into affection, he called me Pip, and whenever he relapsed into politeness he called me Sir; "when there come up in his shay-cart, Pumblechook. Which that same identical," said Joe, going   40 down a new track, "do comb my 'air the wrong way sometimes, awful, by giving out up and down town as it were him which ever had your infant companionation and were looked upon as a playfeller by yourself."

"Nonsense. It was you, Joe."

"Which I fully believed it were, Pip," said Joe, slightly tossing his head, "though it signify little now, Sir. Well, Pip; this same identical, which his

---

1. Wickets are the two "goals" in cricket, sets of three vertical stumps at opposite ends of the playing area; and a wicketkeeper, a distant relation to the catcher in baseball, positions himself behind the batsman of the opposing team to catch or intercept the ball or take advantage of any foul the batsman commits.
2. Proverbs 25.22 and Romans 12.20. To overcome evil with good. See Pip's "avenging coals" and p. 14, n. 9.

manners is given to blusterous, come to me at the Bargemen (wot a pipe and a pint of beer do give refreshment to the working man, Sir, and do not over stimilate), and his word were, 'Joseph, Miss Havisham she wish to speak to you.' "

"Miss Havisham, Joe?"

" 'She wish,' were Pumblechook's word, 'to speak to you.' " Joe sat and rolled his eyes at the ceiling.

"Yes, Joe? Go on, please."

"Next day, Sir," said Joe, looking at me as if I were a long way off, "having cleaned myself, I go and I see Miss A."   10

"Miss A., Joe? Miss Havisham?"

"Which I say, Sir," replied Joe, with an air of legal formality, as if he were making his will, "Miss A., or otherways Havisham. Her expression air then as follering: 'Mr. Gargery. You air in correspondence with Mr. Pip?' Having had a letter from you, I were able to say 'I am.' (When I married your sister, Sir, I said 'I will;' and when I answered your friend, Pip, I said 'I am.') 'Would you tell him, then,' said she, 'that which Estella has come home and would be glad to see him.' "

I felt my face fire up as I looked at Joe. I hope one remote cause of its firing, may have been my consciousness that if I had known his errand, I   20 should have given him more encouragement.

"Biddy," pursued Joe, "when I got home and asked her fur to write the message to you, a little hung back. Biddy says, 'I know he will be very glad to have it by word of mouth, it is holiday-time, you want to see him, go!' I have now concluded, Sir," said Joe, rising from his chair, "and, Pip, I wish you ever well and ever prospering to a greater and a greater heighth."

"But you are not going now, Joe?"

"Yes I am," said Joe.

"But you are coming back to dinner, Joe?"

"No I am not," said Joe.   30

Our eyes met, and all the "Sir" melted out of that manly heart as he gave me his hand.

"Pip, dear old chap, life is made of ever so many partings welded together, as I may say, and one man's a blacksmith, and one's a whitesmith,[3] and one's a goldsmith, and one's a coppersmith. Diwisions among such must come, and must be met as they come. If there's been any fault at all to-day, it's mine. You and me is not two figures to be together in London; nor yet anywheres else but what is private, and beknown, and understood among friends. It ain't that I am proud, but that I want to be right, as you shall never see me no more in these clothes. I'm wrong in these clothes. I'm wrong out   40 of the forge, the kitchen, or off th' meshes. You won't find half so much fault in me if you think of me in my forge dress, with my hammer in my hand, or even my pipe. You won't find half so much fault in me if, supposing as you should ever wish to see me, you come and put your head in at the forge window and see Joe the blacksmith, there, at the old anvil, in the old burnt apron, sticking to the old work. I'm awful dull, but I hope I've beat out something nigh the rights of this at last. And so GOD bless you, dear old Pip, old chap, GOD bless you!"

---

3. Tinsmith; worker in metal.

I had not been mistaken in my fancy that there was a simple dignity in him. The fashion of his dress could no more come in its way when he spoke these words, than it could come in its way in Heaven. He touched me gently on the forehead, and went out. As soon as I could recover myself sufficiently, I hurried out after him and looked for him in the neighbouring streets; but he was gone.

Chapter XXVIII.

IT was clear that I must repair to our town next day, and in the first flow of my repentance it was equally clear that I must stay at Joe's. But when I had secured my box-place[1] by to-morrow's coach and had been down to Mr. Pocket's and back, I was not by any means convinced on the last point, and 10 began to invent reasons and make excuses for putting up at the Blue Boar. I should be an inconvenience at Joe's; I was not expected, and my bed would not be ready; I should be too far from Miss Havisham's, and she was exacting and mightn't like it. All other swindlers upon earth are nothing to the self-swindlers, and with such pretences did I cheat myself. Surely a curious thing. That I should innocently take a bad half-crown of somebody else's manufacture, is reasonable enough; but that I should knowingly reckon the spurious coin of my own make, as good money! An obliging stranger, under pretence of compactly folding up my bank notes for security's sake, abstracts the notes and gives me nutshells; but what is his sleight of hand to mine, when I fold 20 up my own nutshells and pass them on myself as notes!

Having settled that I must go to the Blue Boar, my mind was much disturbed by indecision whether or no to take the Avenger. It was tempting to think of that expensive Mercenary publicly airing his boots in the archway of the Blue Boar's posting-yard;[2] it was almost solemn to imagine him casually produced in the tailor's shop and confounding the disrespectful senses of Trabb's boy. On the other hand, Trabb's boy might worm himself into his intimacy and tell him things; or, reckless and desperate wretch as I knew he could be, might hoot him in the High-street. My patroness, too, might hear of him, and not approve. On the whole, I resolved to leave the Avenger 30 behind.

It was the afternoon coach by which I had taken my place, and, as winter had now come round, I should not arrive at my destination until two or three hours after dark. Our time of starting from the Cross Keys was two o'clock. I arrived on the ground with a quarter of an hour to spare, attended by the Avenger—if I may connect that expression with one who never attended on me if he could possibly help it.

At that time it was customary to carry Convicts down to the dockyards by stage-coach. As I had often heard of them in the capacity of outside-passengers,[3] and had more than once seen them on the high road dangling 40 their ironed legs over the coach roof, I had no cause to be surprised when Herbert, meeting me in the yard, came up and told me there were two

1. Seat beside the driver's.
2. Yard in back of the inn, where exhausted horses are exchanged for fresh ones.
3. For "inside seats" read "first class"; for "outside," read "tourist class."

convicts going down with me. But I had a reason that was an old reason now, for constitutionally faltering whenever I heard the word convict.

"You don't mind them, Handel?" said Herbert.

"Oh no!"

"I thought you seemed as if you didn't like them?"

"I can't pretend that I do like them, and I suppose you don't particularly. But I don't mind them."

"See! There they are," said Herbert, "coming out of the Tap.[4] What a degraded and vile sight it is!"

They had been treating their guard, I suppose, for they had a gaoler with them, and all three came out wiping their mouths on their hands. The two convicts were handcuffed together, and had irons on their legs—irons of a pattern that I knew well. They wore the dress that I likewise knew well. Their keeper had a brace of pistols, and carried a thick-knobbed bludgeon under his arm; but he was on terms of good understanding with them, and stood, with them beside him, looking on at the putting-to of the horses, rather with an air as if they were an interesting Exhibition not formally open at the moment, and he the Curator. One was a taller and stouter man than the other, and appeared as a matter of course, according to the mysterious ways of the world both convict and free, to have had allotted to him the smaller suit of clothes.[5] His arms and legs were like great pincushions of those shapes, and his attire disguised him absurdly; but I knew his half-closed eye at one glance. There stood the man whom I had seen on the settle at the Three Jolly Bargemen on a Saturday night, and who had brought me down with his invisible gun!

It was easy to make sure that as yet he knew me no more than if he had never seen me in his life. He looked across at me, and his eye appraised my watch-chain, and then he incidentally spat and said something to the other convict, and they laughed and slued themselves round[6] with a clink of their coupling manacle, and looked at something else. The great numbers on their backs, as if they were street doors; their coarse mangy ungainly outer surface, as if they were lower animals; their ironed legs, apologetically garlanded with pocket-handkerchiefs;[7] and the way in which all present looked at them and kept from them; made them (as Herbert had said) a most disagreeable and degraded spectacle.

But this was not the worst of it. It came out that the whole of the back of the coach had been taken by a family removing from London, and that there were no places for the two prisoners but on the seat in front behind the coachman. Hereupon, a choleric gentleman, who had taken the fourth place on that seat, flew into a most violent passion, and said that it was a breach of contract to mix him up with such villainous company, and that it was poisonous and pernicious and infamous and shameful and I don't know what

---

4. Pub.

5. Twenty-five years earlier, in *Pickwick Papers*, chapter 2, the impostor Jingle talked about the "mysterious dispensations of Providence—all the short men get long coats—all the long men short ones"; so the remark may be said to frame the Dickens canon (Monod).

6. Spun round.

7. Convicts were allowed to brighten their leg irons with handkerchiefs, almost certainly modeled on those popularized by James (Jem) Belcher (1781–1811), the Bristol pugilist, whose tastes in kerchiefs (white dots on dark blue) were adopted alike by prisoners and virtuous men.

else.[8] At this time the coach was ready and the coachman impatient, and we were all preparing to get up, and the prisoners had come over with their keeper—bringing with them that curious flavour of bread-poultice, baize, rope-yarn, and hearthstone,[9] which attends the convict presence.

"Don't take it so much amiss, sir," pleaded the keeper to the angry passenger; "I'll sit next you myself. I'll put 'em on the outside of the row. They won't interfere with you, sir. You needn't know they're there."

"And don't blame *me*," growled the convict I had recognised. "*I* don't want to go. I am quite ready to stay behind. As fur as I am concerned any one's welcome to *my* place."   10

"Or mine," said the other, gruffly. "*I* wouldn't have incommoded none of you, if I'd a had *my* way." Then they both laughed, and began cracking nuts, and spitting the shells about.—As I really think I should have liked to do myself, if I had been in their place and so despised.

At length it was voted that there was no help for the angry gentleman, and that he must either go in his chance company or remain behind. So he got into his place, still making complaints, and the keeper got into the place next him, and the convicts hauled themselves up as well as they could, and the convict I had recognised sat behind me with his breath on the hair of my head.   20

"Good-by, Handel!" Herbert called out as we started. I thought what a blessed fortune it was that he had found another name for me than Pip.

It is impossible to express with what acuteness I felt the convict's breathing, not only on the back of my head, but all along my spine. The sensation was like being touched in the marrow with some pungent and searching acid, and it set my very teeth on edge. He seemed to have more breathing business to do than another man, and to make more noise in doing it; and I was conscious of growing high-shouldered on one side, in my shrinking endeavours to fend him off.

The weather was miserably raw, and the two cursed the cold. It made us   30 all lethargic before we had gone far, and when we had left the Half-way House behind,[1] we habitually dozed and shivered and were silent. I dozed off, myself, in considering the question whether I ought to restore a couple of pounds sterling to this creature before losing sight of him, and how it could best be done. In the act of dipping forward as if I were going to bathe among the horses, I woke in a fright and took the question up again.

But I must have lost it longer than I had thought, since, although I could recognise nothing in the darkness and the fitful lights and shadows of our lamps, I traced marsh country in the cold damp wind that blew at us. Cowering forward for warmth and to make me a screen against the wind, the   40 convicts were closer to me than before. The very first words I heard them

---

8. Evidently a very large coach, seating fourteen: four passengers inside; the driver and a passenger up front; four passengers behind them on a bench; four passengers benched in back of the carriage.
9. May designate either a stone used to build a hearth or, more probably here, a soft kind of stone mixed with clay and used to whiten hearths or doorsteps. "Bread-poultice": a soft mass of some substance (such as bread), usually made with boiling water, spread on muslin or other material and applied to the skin to supply moisture or warmth. "Baize": a coarse woolen cloth. "Rope-yarn": most often used as a nautical term for a single yarn that forms part of a strand or rope. Convicts were frequently set to labor untwining ropes.
1. Generally any inn located between two major points. Here presumably The Guy, Earl of Warwick, an inn at Welling, roughly midway between London and Gravesend, and in fact dubbed The Halfway House.

interchange as I became conscious, were the words of my own thought, "Two One Pound notes."

"How did he get 'em?" said the convict I had never seen.

"How should I know?" returned the other. "He had 'em stowed away somehows. Giv him by friends, I expect."

"I wish," said the other, with a bitter curse upon the cold, "that I had 'em here."

"Two one pound notes, or friends?"

"Two one pound notes. I'd sell all the friends I ever had, for one, and think it a blessed good bargain. Well? So he says——?"

"So he says," resumed the convict I had recognised—"it was all said and done in half a minute, behind a pile of timber in the Dockyard—'you're a going to be discharged?' Yes, I was. Would I find out that boy that had fed him and kep his secret, and give him them two one pound notes? Yes, I would. And I did."

"More fool you," growled the other. "I'd have spent 'em on a Man, in wittles and drink. He must have been a green one. Mean to say he knowed nothing of you?"

"Not a ha'porth.[2] Different gangs and different ships. He was tried again for prison-breaking, and got made a Lifer."

"And was that—Honour!—the only time you worked out, in this part of the country?"

"The only time."

"What might have been your opinion of the place?"

"A most beastly place. Mudbank, mist, swamp, and work; work, swamp, mist, and mudbank."

They both execrated the place in very strong language, and gradually growled themselves out, and had nothing left to say.

After overhearing this dialogue, I should assuredly have got down and been left in the solitude and darkness of the highway, but for feeling certain that the man had no suspicion of my identity. Indeed, I was not only so changed in the course of nature, but so differently dressed and so differently circumstanced, that it was not at all likely he could have known me without accidental help. Still, the coincidence of our being together on the coach, was sufficiently strange to fill me with a dread that some other coincidence might at any moment connect me, in his hearing, with my name. For this reason, I resolved to alight as soon as we touched the town, and put myself out of his hearing. This device I executed successfully. My little portmanteau was in the boot[3] under my feet; I had but to turn a hinge to get it out; I threw it down before me, got down after it, and was left at the first lamp on the first stones of the town pavement. As to the convicts, they went their way with the coach, and I knew at what point they would be spirited off to the river. In my fancy, I saw the boat with its convict crew waiting for them at the slime-washed stairs,—again heard the gruff "Give way, you!" like an order to dogs —again saw the wicked Noah's Ark lying out in the black water.

I could not have said what I was afraid of, for my fear was altogether undefined and vague, but there was great fear upon me. As I walked on to the hotel, I felt that a dread, much exceeding the mere apprehension of a

2. Not half a penny's worth; that is, nothing.
3. Luggage compartment beneath the driver's seat.

painful or disagreeable recognition, made me tremble. I am confident that it took no distinctness of shape, and that it was the revival for a few minutes of the terror of childhood.

The coffee-room at the Blue Boar was empty, and I had not only ordered my dinner there, but had sat down to it, before the waiter knew me. As soon as ever he had apologised for the remissness of his memory, he asked me if he should send Boots for Mr. Pumblechook?

"No," said I, "certainly not."

The waiter (it was he who had brought up the Great Remonstrance from the Commercials[4] on the day when I was bound) appeared surprised, and took the earliest opportunity of putting a dirty old copy of a local newspaper so directly in my way, that I took it up and read this paragraph:

"Our readers will learn, not altogether without interest, in reference to the recent romantic rise in fortune of a young artificer in iron of this neighbour-hood (what a theme, by the way, for the magic pen of our as yet not universally acknowledged townsman TOOBY, the poet of our columns!), that the youth's earliest patron, companion, and friend, was a highly-respected individual not entirely unconnected with the corn and seed trade, and whose eminently convenient and commodious business premises are situate within a hundred miles of the High-street. It is not wholly irrespective of our personal feelings that we record HIM as the Mentor of our young Telemachus,[5] for it is good to know that our town produced the founder of the latter's fortunes. Does the thought-contracted brow of the local Sage or the lustrous eye of local Beauty inquire whose fortunes? We believe that Quentin Matsys was the BLACKSMITH of Antwerp. VERB. SAP.[6]"

I entertain a conviction, based upon large experience, that if in the days of my prosperity I had gone to the North Pole, I should have met somebody there, wandering Esquimaux or civilised man, who would have told me that Pumblechook was my earliest patron and the founder of my fortunes.

Chapter XXIX.

BETIMES in the morning I was up and out. It was too early yet to go to Miss Havisham's, so I loitered into the country on Miss Havisham's side of

---

4. Kidding reference to the objections that the commercial travelers voiced at the apprenticeship hoopla in chapter 13. "Great Remonstrance": the petition, passed by the Puritan parliament in November 1641, lodging a series of grievances against Charles I (beheaded 1649), calling for increased parliamentary input in matters of Church reform and the choice of the King's ministers.
5. In the *Odyssey*, Mentor is the elderly friend and Ithaca neighbor to whom Ulysses, off to the Trojan War in Book II, confides the charge of his household and the education of his son, Telemachus. Disguised as Mentor, Pallas Athena persuades Telemachus to sail in search of his wayward father and to help him in deactivating his mother's suitors.
6. Verb[um] sap[ienti satis est]: a word to the wise (is sufficient). But Pumblechook's provincial readers are apt to mistake this for the columnist's pen name. "Blacksmith of Antwerp": Quentin (or Quintin) Matsys (also Massys, Metsys), Flemish painter (1465/66–1530), an early master of the northern Renaissance, started out as an apprentice blacksmith in his native Louvain; legend has it that he turned to painting because his bride, the daughter of a rich Antwerp artist, objected to the dirt and noise of the forge.

town—which was not Joe's side;[1] I could go there to-morrow—thinking about my patroness, and painting brilliant pictures of her plans for me.

She had adopted Estella, she had as good as adopted me, and it could not fail to be her intention to bring us together. She reserved it for me to restore the desolate house, admit the sunshine into the dark rooms, set the clocks a going and the cold hearths a blazing, tear down the cobwebs, destroy the vermin—in short, do all the shining deeds of the young Knight of romance, and marry the Princess. I had stopped to look at the house as I passed; and its seared red brick walls, blocked windows, and strong green ivy clasping even the stacks of chimneys with its twigs and tendons, as if with sinewy old arms, had made up a rich attractive mystery, of which I was the hero. Estella was the inspiration of it, and the heart of it, of course. But, though she had taken such strong possession of me, though my fancy and my hope were so set upon her, though her influence on my boyish life and character had been all-powerful, I did not, even that romantic morning, invest her with any attributes save those she possessed. I mention this in this place, of a fixed purpose, because it is the clue[2] by which I am to be followed into my poor labyrinth. According to my experience, the conventional notion of a lover cannot be always true. The unqualified truth is, that even when I loved Estella with the love of a man, I loved her simply because I found her irresistible. Once for all; I knew to my sorrow, often and often, if not always, that I loved her against reason, against promise, against peace, against hope, against happiness, against all discouragement that could be. Once for all; I loved her none the less because I knew it, and it had no more influence in restraining me, than if I had devoutly believed her to be human perfection.

I so shaped out my walk as to arrive at the gate at my old time. When I had rung at the bell with an unsteady hand, I turned my back upon the gate, while I tried to get my breath and keep the beating of my heart moderately quiet. I heard the side door open and steps come across the court-yard; but I pretended not to hear, even when the gate swung on its rusty hinges.

Being at last touched on the shoulder, I started and turned. I started much more naturally then, to find myself confronted by a man in a sober grey dress. The last man I should have expected to see in that place of porter at Miss Havisham's door.

"Orlick!"

"Ah, young master, there's more changes than yours. But come in, come in. It's opposed to my orders to hold the gate open."

I entered and he swung it, and locked it, and took the key out. "Yes!" said he, facing round, after doggedly preceding me a few steps towards the house. "Here I am!"

"How did you come here?"

"I come here," he retorted, "on my legs. I had my box brought alongside me in a barrow."

"Are you here for good?"

"I ain't here for harm, young master, I suppose."

I was not so sure of that. I had leisure to entertain the retort in my mind,

---

1. Miss Havisham lives at the eastern end of town; Pip's village lies four miles northwest.
2. Literally, thread. Perhaps an allusion to the legend of the Minotaur, a monster sporting a bull's head and a man's body (in some versions vice versa) who has been confined to a maze from which mortals can find their way out only by means of a thread they start to unwind from a ball on entering the monster's lair. The meaning is virtually spelled out in the waiter's "magic clue" in chapter 33.

while he slowly lifted his heavy glance from the pavement, up my legs and arms, to my face.

"Then you have left the forge?" I said.

"Do this look like a forge?" replied Orlick, sending his glance all round him with an air of injury. "Now, do it look like it?"

I asked him how long he had left Gargery's forge?

"One day is so like another here," he replied, "that I don't know without casting it up. How'sever, I come here some time since you left."

"I could have told you that, Orlick."

"Ah!" said he, drily. "But then you've got to be a scholar."   10

By this time we had come to the house, where I found his room to be one just within the side door, with a little window in it looking on the court-yard. In its small proportions, it was not unlike the kind of place usually assigned to a gate-porter in Paris.[3] Certain keys were hanging on the wall, to which he now added the gate key; and his patchwork-covered bed was in a little inner division or recess. The whole had a slovenly confined and sleepy look, like a cage for a human dormouse: while he, looming dark and heavy in the shadow of a corner by the window, looked like the human dormouse for whom it was fitted up—as indeed he was.

"I never saw this room before," I remarked; "but there used to be no Porter 20 here."

"No," said he; "not till it got about that there was no protection on the premises, and it come to be considered dangerous, with convicts and Tag and Rag and Bobtail[4] going up and down. And then I was recommended to the place as a man wot could give another man as good as he brought, and I took it. It's easier than bellowsing and hammering.—That's loaded, that is."

My eye had been caught by a gun with a brass-bound stock over the chimney-piece, and his eye had followed mine.

"Well," said I, not desirous of more conversation, "shall I go up to Miss Havisham?"   30

"Burn me, if I know!" he retorted, first stretching himself and then shaking himself; "my orders ends here, young master. I give this here bell a rap with this here hammer, and you go on along the passage till you meet somebody."

"I am expected, I believe?"

"Burn me twice over, if I can say!" said he.

Upon that, I turned down the long passage which I had first trodden in my thick boots, and he made his bell sound. At the end of the passage, while the bell was still reverberating, I found Sarah Pocket: who appeared to have now become constitutionally green and yellow by reason of me.

"Oh!" said she. "You, is it, Mr. Pip?"   40

"It is, Miss Pocket. I am glad to tell you that Mr. Pocket and family are all well."

"Are they any wiser?" said Miss Pocket, with a dismal shake of her head; "they had better be wiser, than well. Ah, Matthew, Matthew! You know your way, sir?"

Tolerably, for I had gone up the staircase in the dark, many a time. I ascended it now, in lighter boots than of yore, and tapped in my old way at

---

3. The "superintendent," or *concierge*, who lives in a small lodging near the front door of an apartment house, keeps the tenants' keys, collects their mail, etc.
4. "An assemblage of low people. . . . In dialect, tag-rag = a vagabond, hence a low rabble" (Grose).

the door of Miss Havisham's room. "Pip's rap," I heard her say, immediately; "come in, Pip."

She was in her chair near the old table, in the old dress, with her two hands crossed on her stick, her chin resting on them, and her eyes on the fire. Sitting near her, with the white shoe that had never been worn, in her hand, and her head bent as she looked at it, was an elegant lady whom I had never seen.

"Come in, Pip," Miss Havisham continued to mutter, without looking round or up; "come in, Pip, how do you do, Pip? so you kiss my hand as if I were a queen, eh?——Well?"   10

She looked up at me suddenly, only moving her eyes, and repeated in a grimly playful manner,

"Well?"

"I heard, Miss Havisham," said I, rather at a loss, "that you were so kind as to wish me to come and see you, and I came directly."

"Well?"

The lady whom I had never seen before, lifted up her eyes and looked archly at me, and then I saw that the eyes were Estella's eyes. But she was so much changed, was so much more beautiful, so much more womanly, in all things winning admiration had made such wonderful advance, that I seemed   20 to have made none. I fancied, as I looked at her, that I slipped hopelessly back into the coarse and common boy again. O the sense of distance and disparity that came upon me, and the inaccessibility that came about her!

She gave me her hand. I stammered something about the pleasure I felt in seeing her again, and about my having looked forward to it for a long, long time.

"Do you find her much changed, Pip?" asked Miss Havisham with her greedy look, and striking her stick upon a chair that stood between them, as a sign to me to sit down there.

"When I came in, Miss Havisham, I thought there was nothing of   30 Estella in the face or figure; but now it all settles down so curiously into the old——"

"What? You are not going to say, into the old Estella?" Miss Havisham interrupted. "She was proud and insulting and you wanted to go away from her. Don't you remember?"

I said confusedly that that was long ago, and that I knew no better then, and the like. Estella smiled with perfect composure, and said she had no doubt of my having been quite right, and of her having been very disagreeable.

"Is *he* changed?" Miss Havisham asked her.   40

"Very much," said Estella, looking at me.

"Less coarse and common?" said Miss Havisham, playing with Estella's hair.

Estella laughed, and looked at the shoe in her hand, and laughed again, and looked at me, and put the shoe down. She treated me as a boy still, but she lured me on.

We sat in the dreamy room among the old strange influences which had so wrought upon me, and I learnt that she had but just come home from France, and that she was going to London. Proud and wilful as of old, she had brought those qualities into such subjection to her beauty that it was   50 impossible and out of nature—or I thought so—to separate them from her beauty. Truly it was impossible to dissociate her presence from all those wretched hankerings after money and gentility that had disturbed my boyhood—from all those ill-regulated aspirations that had first made me ashamed of home and Joe—from all those visions that had raised her face in the glowing fire, struck it out of the iron on the anvil, extracted it from the darkness of night to look in at the wooden window of the forge and flit away. In a word, it was impossible for me to separate her, in the past or in the present, from the innermost life of my life.

It was settled that I should stay there all the rest of the day, and return to the hotel at night, and to London to-morrow. When we had conversed for a while, Miss Havisham sent us two out to walk in the neglected garden; on our coming in by-and-by, she said, I should wheel her about a little as in times of yore.

So, Estella and I went out into the garden by the gate through which I had strayed to my encounter with the pale young gentleman, now Herbert; I, trembling in spirit and worshipping the very hem of her dress; she, quite composed and most decidedly not worshipping the hem of mine. As we drew near to the place of encounter, she stopped and said:

"I must have been a singular little creature to hide and see that fight that day: but I did, and I enjoyed it very much."

"You rewarded me very much."

"Did I?" she replied, in an incidental and forgetful way. "I remember I entertained a great objection to your adversary, because I took it ill that he should be brought here to pester me with his company."

"He and I are great friends now," said I.

"Are you? I think I recollect though, that you read with his father?"

"Yes."

I made the admission with reluctance, for it seemed to have a boyish look, and she already treated me more than enough like a boy.

"Since your change of fortune and prospects, you have changed your companions," said Estella.

"Naturally," said I.

"And necessarily," she added, in a haughty tone, "what was fit company for you once, would be quite unfit company for you now."

In my conscience, I doubt very much whether I had any lingering intention left, of going to see Joe; but if I had, this observation put it to flight.

"You had no idea of your impending good fortune, in those times?" said Estella, with a slight wave of her hand, signifying in the fighting times.

"Not the least."

The air of completeness and superiority with which she walked at my side, and the air of youthfulness and submission with which I walked at hers, made a contrast that I strongly felt. It would have rankled in me more than it did, if I had not regarded myself as eliciting it by being so set apart for her and assigned to her.

The garden was too overgrown and rank for walking in with ease, and after we had made the round of it twice or thrice, we came out again into the brewery yard. I showed her to a nicety[5] where I had seen her walking on the

5. Precisely.

casks, that first old day, and she said, with a cold and careless look in that direction, "Did I?" I reminded her where she had come out of the house and given me my meat and drink, and she said, "I don't remember." "Not remember that you made me cry?" said I. "No," said she, and shook her head and looked about her. I verily believe that her not remembering and not minding in the least, made me cry again, inwardly—and that is the sharpest crying of all.

"You must know," said Estella, condescending to me as a brilliant and beautiful woman might, "that I have no heart—if that has anything to do with my memory."   10

I got through some jargon to the effect that I took the liberty of doubting that. That I knew better. That there could be no such beauty without it.

"Oh! I have a heart to be stabbed in or shot in, I have no doubt," said Estella, "and, of course, if it ceased to beat I should cease to be. But you know what I mean. I have no softness there, no—sympathy—sentiment—nonsense."

What *was* it that was borne in upon my mind when she stood still and looked attentively at me? Anything that I had seen in Miss Havisham? No. In some of her looks and gestures there was that tinge of resemblance to Miss Havisham which may often be noticed to have been acquired by children,   20 from grown persons with whom they have been much associated and secluded, and which, when childhood is past, will produce a remarkable occasional likeness of expression between faces that are otherwise quite different. And yet I could not trace this to Miss Havisham. I looked again, and though she was still looking at me, the suggestion was gone.

What *was* it?

"I am serious," said Estella, not so much with a frown (for her brow was smooth) as with a darkening of her face; "if we are to be thrown much together, you had better believe it at once. No!" imperiously stopping me as I opened my lips. "I have not bestowed my tenderness anywhere. I have never   30 had any such thing."

In another moment we were in the brewery so long disused, and she pointed to the high gallery where I had seen her going out on that same first day, and told me she remembered to have been up there, and to have seen me standing scared below. As my eyes followed her white hand, again the same dim suggestion that I could not possibly grasp, crossed me. My involuntary start occasioned her to lay her hand upon my arm. Instantly the ghost passed once more, and was gone.

What *was* it?

"What is the matter?" asked Estella. "Are you scared again?"   40

"I should be, if I believed what you said just now," I replied, to turn it off.

"Then you don't? Very well. It is said, at any rate. Miss Havisham will soon be expecting you at your old post, though I think that might be laid aside now, with other old belongings. Let us make one more round of the garden, and then go in. Come! You shall not shed tears for my cruelty to-day; you shall be my Page, and give me your shoulder."

Her handsome dress had trailed upon the ground. She held it in one hand now, and with the other lightly touched my shoulder as we walked. We walked round the ruined garden twice or thrice more, and it was all in bloom for me. If the green and yellow growth of weed in the chinks of the old wall,   50 had been the most precious flowers that ever blew, it could not have been more cherished in my remembrance.

There was no discrepancy of years between us, to remove her far from me; we were of nearly the same age, though of course the age told for more in her case than in mine; but the air of inaccessibility which her beauty and her manner gave her, tormented me in the midst of my delight, and at the height of the assurance I felt that our patroness had chosen us for one another. Wretched boy!

At last we went back into the house, and there I heard, with surprise, that my guardian had come down to see Miss Havisham on business and would 10 come back to dinner. The old wintry branches of chandeliers in the room where the mouldering table was spread, had been lighted while we were out, and Miss Havisham was in her chair and waiting for me.

It was like pushing the chair itself back into the past, when we began the old slow circuit round about the ashes of the bridal feast. But, in the funereal room, with that figure of the grave fallen back in the chair fixing its eyes upon her, Estella looked more bright and beautiful than before, and I was under stronger enchantment.

The time so melted away, that our early dinner-hour drew close at hand, and Estella left us to prepare herself. We had stopped near the centre of the 20 long table, and Miss Havisham, with one of her withered arms stretched out of the chair, rested that clenched hand upon the yellow cloth. As Estella looked back over her shoulder before going out at the door, Miss Havisham kissed that hand to her, with a ravenous intensity that was of its kind quite dreadful.

Then, Estella being gone and we two left alone, she turned to me, and said in a whisper:

"Is she beautiful, graceful, well-grown? Do you admire her?"

"Everybody must who sees her, Miss Havisham."

She drew an arm round my neck, and drew my head close down to hers 30 as she sat in the chair. "Love her, love her, love her! How does she use you?"

Before I could answer (if I could have answered so difficult a question at all), she repeated, "Love her, love her, love her! If she favours you, love her. If she wounds you, love her. If she tears your heart to pieces—and as it gets older and stronger, it will tear deeper—love her, love her, love her!"

Never had I seen such passionate eagerness as was joined to her utterance of these words. I could feel the muscles of the thin arm round my neck, swell with the vehemence that possessed her.

"Hear me, Pip! I adopted her to be loved. I bred her and educated her, to be loved. I developed her into what she is, that she might be loved. Love 40 her!"

She said the word often enough, and there could be no doubt that she meant to say it; but if the often repeated word had been hate instead of love— despair—revenge—dire death—it could not have sounded from her lips more like a curse.

"I'll tell you," said she, in the same hurried passionate whisper, "what real love is. It is blind devotion, unquestioning self-humiliation, utter submission, trust and belief against yourself and against the whole world, giving up your whole heart and soul to the smiter—as I did!"

When she came to that, and to a wild cry that followed that, I caught her 50 round the waist. For she rose up in the chair, in her shroud of a dress, and struck at the air as if she would as soon have struck herself against the wall and fallen dead.

All this passed in a few seconds. As I drew her down into her chair, I was conscious of a scent that I knew, and turning, saw my guardian in the room.

He always carried (I have not yet mentioned it, I think) a pocket-handkerchief of rich silk and of imposing proportions, which was of great value to him in his profession. I have seen him so terrify a client or a witness by ceremoniously unfolding this pocket-handkerchief as if he were immediately going to blow his nose, and then pausing, as if he knew he should not have time to do it before such client or witness committed himself, that the self-committal has followed directly, quite as a matter of course. When I saw him in the room, he had this expressive pocket-handkerchief in both hands, and was looking at us. On meeting my eye, he said plainly, by a momentary and silent pause in that attitude, "Indeed? Singular!" and then put the handkerchief to its right use with wonderful effect.

Miss Havisham had seen him as soon as I, and was (like everybody else) afraid of him. She made a strong attempt to compose herself, and stammered that he was as punctual as ever.

"As punctual as ever," he repeated, coming up to us. "(How do you do, Pip. Shall I give you a ride, Miss Havisham? Once round?) And so you are here, Pip?"

I told him when I had arrived, and how Miss Havisham had wished me to come and see Estella. To which he replied, "Ah! Very fine young lady!" Then he pushed Miss Havisham in her chair before him, with one of his large hands, and put the other in his trousers-pocket as if the pocket were full of secrets.

"Well, Pip! How often have you seen Miss Estella before?" said he, when he came to a stop.

"How often?"

"Ah! How many times. Ten thousand times?"

"Oh! Certainly not so many."

"Twice?"

"Jaggers," interposed Miss Havisham, much to my relief; "leave my Pip alone, and go with him to your dinner."

He complied, and we groped our way down the dark stairs together. While we were still on our way to those detached apartments across the paved yard at the back, he asked me how often I had seen Miss Havisham eat and drink; offering me a breadth of choice, as usual, between a hundred times and once.

I considered, and said, "Never."

"And never will, Pip," he retorted, with a frowning smile. "She has never allowed herself to be seen doing either, since she lived this present life of hers. She wanders about in the night, and then lays hands on such food as she takes."

"Pray, sir," said I, "may I ask you a question?"

"You may," said he, "and I may decline to answer it. Put your question."

"Estella's name. Is it Havisham or —— ?" I had nothing to add.

"Or what?" said he.

"Is it Havisham?"

"It is Havisham."

This brought us to the dinner-table, where she and Sarah Pocket awaited us. Mr. Jaggers presided, Estella sat opposite to him, I faced my green and yellow friend. We dined very well, and were waited on by a maid-servant whom I had never seen in all my comings and goings, but who, for anything I know, had been in that mysterious house the whole time. After dinner, a bottle of choice old port was placed before my guardian (he was evidently well acquainted with the vintage), and the two ladies left us.

Anything to equal the determined reticence of Mr. Jaggers under that roof, I never saw elsewhere, even in him. He kept his very looks to himself, and scarcely directed his eyes to Estella's face once during dinner. When she 10 spoke to him, he listened, and in due course answered, but never looked at her that I could see. On the other hand, she often looked at him, with interest and curiosity, if not distrust, but his face never showed the least consciousness. Throughout dinner he took a dry delight in making Sarah Pocket greener and yellower, by often referring in conversation with me to my expectations; but here, again, he showed no consciousness, and even made it appear that he extorted—and even did extort, though I don't know how—those references out of my innocent self.

And when he and I were left alone together, he sat with an air upon him of general lying by in consequence of information he possessed, that really 20 was too much for me. He cross-examined his very wine when he had nothing else in hand. He held it between himself and the candle, tasted the port, rolled it in his mouth, swallowed it, looked at the port again, smelt it, tried it, drank it, filled again, and cross-examined the glass again, until I was as nervous as if I had known the wine to be telling him something to my disadvantage. Three or four times I feebly thought I would start conversation; but whenever he saw me going to ask him anything, he looked at me with his glass in his hand, and rolling his wine about in his mouth, as if requesting me to take notice that it was of no use, for he couldn't answer.

I think Miss Pocket was conscious that the sight of me involved her in the 30 danger of being goaded to madness, and perhaps tearing off her cap—which was a very hideous one, in the nature of a muslin mop—and strewing the ground with her hair—which assuredly had never grown on *her* head.[6] She did not appear when we afterwards went up to Miss Havisham's room, and we four played at whist.[7] In the interval, Miss Havisham, in a fantastic way, had put some of the most beautiful jewels from her dressing-table into Estella's hair, and about her bosom and arms; and I saw even my guardian look at her from under his thick eyebrows, and raise them a little, when her loveliness was before him, with those rich flushes of glitter and colour in it.

Of the manner and extent to which he took our trumps into custody, and 40 came out with mean little cards at the ends of hands, before which the glory of our Kings and Queens was utterly abased, I say nothing; nor of the feeling that I had, respecting his looking upon us personally in the light of three very obvious and poor riddles that he had found out long ago. What I suffered from, was the incompatibility between his cold presence and my feelings towards Estella. It was not that I knew I could never bear to speak to him about her, that I knew I could never bear to hear him creak his boots at her,

6. Reminder that women habitually wore caps indoors, usually of linen, a custom that later devolved on domestics.
7. The forerunner of contract bridge. By Dickens's time easily the "King of Card Games."

that I knew I could never bear to see him wash his hands of her; it was, that my admiration should be within a foot or two of him—it was, that my feelings should be in the same place with him—*that*, was the agonising circumstance.

We played until nine o'clock, and then it was arranged that when Estella came to London I should be forewarned of her coming and should meet her at the coach; and then I took leave of her, and touched her and left her.

My guardian lay at the Boar in the next room to mine. Far into the night, Miss Havisham's words, "Love her, love her, love her!" sounded in my ears. I adapted them for my own repetition, and said to my pillow, "I love her, I love her, I love her!" hundreds of times. Then, a burst of gratitude came 10 upon me, that she should be destined for me, once the blacksmith's boy. Then, I thought if she were, as I feared, by no means rapturously grateful for that destiny yet, when would she begin to be interested in me? When should I awaken the heart within her, that was mute and sleeping now?

Ah me! I thought those were high and great emotions. But I never thought there was anything low and small in my keeping away from Joe, because I knew she would be contemptuous of him. It was but a day gone, and Joe had brought the tears into my eyes; they had soon dried, God forgive me! soon dried.

★

Chapter XXX.

AFTER well considering the matter while I was dressing at the Blue Boar 20 in the morning, I resolved to tell my guardian that I doubted Orlick's being the right sort of man to fill a post of trust at Miss Havisham's. "Why, of course he is not the right sort of man, Pip," said my guardian, comfortably satisfied beforehand on the general head, "because the man who fills the post of trust never is the right sort of man." It seemed quite to put him into spirits, to find that this particular post was not exceptionally held by the right sort of man, and he listened in a satisfied manner while I told him what knowledge I had of Orlick. "Very good, Pip," he observed, when I had concluded, "I'll go round presently, and pay our friend off." Rather alarmed by this summary action, I was for a little delay, and even hinted that our friend himself might 30 be difficult to deal with. "Oh no he won't," said my guardian, making his pocket-handkerchief-point with perfect confidence; "I should like to see him argue the question with *me*."

As we were going back together to London by the mid-day coach, and as I breakfasted under such terrors of Pumblechook that I could scarcely hold my cup, this gave me an opportunity of saying that I wanted a walk, and that I would go on along the London-road while Mr. Jaggers was occupied, if he would let the coachman know that I would get into my place when overtaken. I was thus enabled to fly from the Blue Boar immediately after breakfast. By then making a loop of about a couple of miles into the open country at the 40 back of Pumblechook's premises, I got round into the High-street again, a little beyond that pitfall, and felt myself in comparative security.

It was interesting to be in the quiet old town once more, and it was not disagreeable to be here and there suddenly recognised and stared after. One or two of the tradespeople even darted out of their shops and went a little way down the street before me, that they might turn, as if they had forgotten something, and pass me face to face—on which occasions I don't know whether they or I made the worse pretence; they of not doing it, or I of not seeing it. Still my position was a distinguished one, and I was not at all dissatisfied with it, until Fate threw me in the way of that unlimited miscreant, Trabb's boy.

Casting my eyes along the street at a certain point of my progress, I beheld Trabb's boy approaching, lashing himself with an empty blue bag.[1] Deeming that a serene and unconscious contemplation of him would best beseem me, 10 and would be most likely to quell his evil mind, I advanced with that expression of countenance, and was rather congratulating myself on my success, when suddenly the knees of Trabb's boy smote together, his hair uprose, his cap fell off, he trembled violently in every limb, staggered out into the road, and crying to the populace, "Hold me! I'm so frightened!" feigned to be in a paroxysm of terror and contrition, occasioned by the dignity of my appearance. As I passed him, his teeth loudly chattered in his head, and with every mark of extreme humiliation, he prostrated himself in the dust.

This was a hard thing to bear, but this was nothing. I had not advanced another two hundred yards, when, to my inexpressible terror, amazement, 20 and indignation, I again beheld Trabb's boy approaching. He was coming round a narrow corner. His blue bag was slung over his shoulder, honest industry beamed in his eyes, a determination to proceed to Trabb's with cheerful briskness was indicated in his gait. With a shock he became aware of me, and was severely visited as before; but this time his motion was rotatory, and he staggered round and round me with knees more afflicted, and with uplifted hands as if beseeching for mercy. His sufferings were hailed with the greatest joy by a knot of spectators, and I felt utterly confounded.

I had not got as much further down the street as the post-office, when I again beheld Trabb's boy shooting round by a back way. This time he was 30 entirely changed. He wore the blue bag in the manner of my great-coat, and was strutting along the pavement towards me on the opposite side of the street, attended by a company of delighted young friends to whom he from time to time exclaimed, with a wave of his hand, "Don't know yah!" Words cannot state the amount of aggravation and injury wreaked upon me by Trabb's boy, when, passing abreast of me, he pulled up his shirt-collar, twined his side-hair, stuck an arm akimbo, and smirked extravagantly by, wriggling his elbows and body, and drawling to his attendants, "Don't know yah, don't know yah, pon my soul don't know yah!" The disgrace attendant on his immediately afterwards taking to crowing and pursuing me across the bridge with crows 40 as from an exceedingly dejected fowl who had known me when I was a blacksmith, culminated the disgrace with which I left the town, and was, so to speak, ejected by it into the open country.

But unless I had taken the life of Trabb's boy on that occasion, I really do not even now see what I could have done save endure. To have struggled with him in the street, or to have exacted any lower recompense from him than his heart's best blood would have been futile and degrading. Moreover,

---

1. Very likely a laundry bag containing a ball of blue powder used in washing clothes.

he was a boy whom no man could hurt; an invulnerable and dodging serpent who, when chased into a corner, flew out again between his captor's legs, scornfully yelping. I wrote, however, to Mr. Trabb by next day's post, to say that Mr. Pip must decline to deal further with one who could so far forget what he owed to the best interests of society, as to employ a boy who excited Loathing in every respectable mind.

The coach, with Mr. Jaggers inside, came up in due time, and I took my box-seat again, and arrived in London safe—but not sound, for my heart was gone. As soon as I arrived, I sent a penitential codfish and barrel of oysters[2] to Joe (as reparation for not having gone myself), and then went on to Barnard's Inn.

I found Herbert dining on cold meat, and delighted to welcome me back. Having despatched The Avenger to the coffeehouse for an addition to the dinner, I felt that I must open my breast that very evening to my friend and chum. As confidence was out of the question with The Avenger in the hall, which could merely be regarded in the light of an ante-chamber to the key-hole, I sent him to the Play. A better proof of the severity of my bondage to that taskmaster could scarcely be afforded, than the degrading shifts to which I was constantly driven to find him employment. So mean is extremity, that I sometimes sent him to Hyde Park-corner[3] to see what o'clock it was.

Dinner done and we sitting with our feet upon the fender, I said to Herbert, "My dear Herbert, I have something very particular to tell you."

"My dear Handel," he returned, "I shall esteem and respect your confidence."

"It concerns myself, Herbert," said I, "and one other person."

Herbert crossed his feet, looked at the fire with his head on one side, and having looked at it in vain for some time, looked at me because I didn't go on.

"Herbert," said I, laying my hand upon his knee. "I love—I adore—Estella."

Instead of being transfixed, Herbert replied in an easy matter-of-course way, "Exactly. Well?"

"Well, Herbert? Is that all you say? Well?"

"What next, I mean?" said Herbert. "Of course I know *that*."

"How do you know it?" said I.

"How do I know it, Handel? Why, from you."

"I never told you."

"Told me! You have never told me when you have got your hair cut, but I have had senses to perceive it. You have always adored her, ever since I have known you. You brought your adoration and your portmanteau here, together. Told me! Why, you have always told me all day long. When you told me your own story, you told me plainly that you began adoring her the first time you saw her, when you were very young indeed."

"Very well, then," said I, to whom this was a new and not unwelcome

2. Nothing so expensive as they are today. Chaucer's "not worth an oyster" had lost none of its pertinence in Pip's day, when oysters could be had for eight pence a dozen. Thus Sam Weller in *Pickwick Papers*, chapter 22: "It's a wery remarkable circumstance . . . that poverty and oysters always seems to go together"; in *Oliver Twist*, chapter 27, Noah Claypole and Charlotte gorge themselves on oysters as a cheap aphrodisiac.
3. Pip is overdoing it: the Avenger has to walk more than two miles to consult the (authentic) clock at Hyde Park Corner.

light, "I have never left off adoring her. And she has come back a most beautiful and most elegant creature. And I saw her yesterday. And if I adored her before, I now doubly adore her."

"Lucky for you then, Handel," said Herbert, "that you are picked out for her and allotted to her. Without encroaching on forbidden ground, we may venture to say that there can be no doubt between ourselves of that fact. Have you any idea yet, of Estella's views on the adoration question?"

I shook my head gloomily. "Oh! She is thousands of miles away, from me," said I.

"Patience, my dear Handel: time enough, time enough. But you have   10 something more to say?"

"I am ashamed to say it," I returned, "and yet it's no worse to say it than to think it. You call me a lucky fellow. Of course, I am. I was a blacksmith's boy but yesterday; I am—what shall I say I am—to-day?"

"Say, a good fellow, if you want a phrase," returned Herbert, smiling, and clapping his hand on the back of mine, "a good fellow, with impetuosity and hesitation, boldness and diffidence, action and dreaming, curiously mixed in him."

I stopped for a moment to consider whether there really was this mixture in my character. On the whole, I by no means recognised the analysis, but   20 thought it not worth disputing.

"When I ask what I am to call myself to-day, Herbert," I went on, "I suggest what I have in my thoughts. You say I am lucky. I know I have done nothing to raise myself in life, and that Fortune alone has raised me; that is being very lucky. And yet, when I think of Estella—"

("And when don't you, you know?" Herbert threw in, with his eyes on the fire; which I thought kind and sympathetic of him.)

"—Then, my dear Herbert, I cannot tell you how dependent and uncertain I feel, and how exposed to hundreds of chances. Avoiding forbidden ground as you did just now, I may still say that on the constancy of one person   30 (naming no person) all my expectations depend. And at the best, how indefinite and unsatisfactory, only to know so vaguely what they are!" In saying this, I relieved my mind of what had always been there, more or less, though no doubt most since yesterday.

"Now, Handel," Herbert replied, in his gay hopeful way, "it seems to me that in the despondency of the tender passion, we are looking into our gift-horse's mouth with a magnifying glass.[4] Likewise, it seems to me that con-centrating our attention on that examination, we altogether overlook one of the best points of the animal. Didn't you tell me that your guardian, Mr. Jaggers, told you in the beginning, that you were not endowed with expec-   40 tations only? And even if he had not told you so—though that is a very large If, I grant—could you believe that of all men in London, Mr. Jaggers is the man to hold his present relations towards you unless he were sure of his ground?"

I said I could not deny that this was a strong point. I said it (people often do so, in such cases) like a rather reluctant concession to truth and justice; —as if I wanted to deny it!

4. The age of a horse can be estimated by looking at the wear of its teeth. Hence the expression "Never look a gift horse in the mouth" is an injunction never to question the worth of a gift. This excellent advice has been traced back to St. Jerome and the fourth century.

"I should think it *was* a strong point," said Herbert, "and I should think you would be puzzled to imagine a stronger; as to the rest, you must bide your guardian's time, and he must bide his client's time. You'll be one-and-twenty before you know where you are, and then perhaps you'll get some further enlightenment. At all events, you'll be nearer getting it, for it must come at last."

"What a hopeful disposition you have!" said I, gratefully admiring his cheery ways.

"I ought to have," said Herbert, "for I have not much else. I must acknowledge, by-the-by, that the good sense of what I have just said is not my own, 10 but my father's. The only remark I ever heard him make on your story, was the final one: 'The thing is settled and done, or Mr. Jaggers would not be in it.' And now before I say anything more about my father or my father's son, and repay confidence with confidence, I want to make myself seriously disagreeable to you for a moment—positively repulsive."

"You won't succeed," said I.

"Oh yes I shall!" said he. "One, two, three, and now I am in for it. Handel, my good fellow;" though he spoke in this light tone, he was very much in earnest: "I have been thinking since we have been talking with our feet on this fender, that Estella surely cannot be a condition of your inheritance, if 20 she was never referred to by your guardian. Am I right in so understanding what you have told me, as that he never referred to her, directly or indirectly, in any way? Never even hinted, for instance, that your patron might have views as to your marriage ultimately?"

"Never."

"Now, Handel, I am quite free from the flavour of sour grapes, upon my soul and honour! Not being bound to her, can you not detach yourself from her?—I told you I should be disagreeable."

I turned my head aside, for, with a rush and a sweep, like the old marsh winds coming up from the sea, a feeling like that which had subdued me on 30 the morning when I left the forge, when the mists were solemnly rising, and when I laid my hand upon the village finger-post, smote upon my heart again. There was silence between us for a little while.

"Yes; but my dear Handel," Herbert went on, as if we had been talking instead of silent, "its having been so strongly rooted in the breast of a boy whom nature and circumstances made so romantic, renders it very serious. Think of her bringing-up, and think of Miss Havisham. Think of what she is herself (now I am repulsive and you abominate me). This may lead to miserable things."

"I know it, Herbert," said I, with my head still turned away, "but I can't 40 help it."

"You can't detach yourself?"

"No. Impossible!"

"You can't try, Handel?"

"No. Impossible!"

"Well!" said Herbert, getting up with a lively shake as if he had been asleep, and stirring the fire; "now I'll endeavour to make myself agreeable again!"

So he went round the room and shook the curtains out, put the chairs in their places, tidied the books and so forth that were lying about, looked into 50

the hall, peeped into the letter-box, shut the door, and came back to his chair
by the fire: where he sat down, nursing his left leg in both arms.

"I was going to say a word or two, Handel, concerning my father and
my father's son. I am afraid it is scarcely necessary for my father's son to
remark that my father's establishment is not particularly brilliant in its housekeeping."

"There is always plenty, Herbert," said I: to say something encouraging.

"Oh yes! and so the dustman says, I believe, with the strongest approval,
and so does the marine-store-shop[5] in the back street. Gravely, Handel, for
the subject is grave enough, you know how it is, as well as I do. I suppose 10
there was a time once when my father had not given matters up; but if
ever there was, the time is gone. May I ask you if you have ever had an
opportunity of remarking, down in your part of the country, that the children
of not exactly suitable marriages, are always most particularly anxious to be
married?"[6]

This was such a singular question, that I asked him in return, "Is it so?"

"I don't know," said Herbert; "that's what I want to know. Because it is
decidedly the case with us. My poor sister Charlotte who was next me and
died before she was fourteen, was a striking example. Little Jane is the same.
In her desire to be matrimonially established, you might suppose her to have 20
passed her short existence in the perpetual contemplation of domestic bliss.
Little Alick in a frock has already made arrangements for his union with a
suitable young person at Kew. And indeed, I think we are all engaged, except
the baby."

"Then you are?" said I.

"I am," said Herbert; "but it's a secret."

I assured him of my keeping the secret, and begged to be favoured with
further particulars. He had spoken so sensibly and feelingly of my weakness
that I wanted to know something about his strength.

"May I ask the name?" I said.   30

"Name of Clara," said Herbert.

"Live in London?"

"Yes. Perhaps I ought to mention," said Herbert, who had become curiously crestfallen and meek, since we entered on the interesting theme, "that
she is rather below my mother's nonsensical family notions. Her father had
to do with the victualling of passenger-ships. I think he was a species of
purser."

"What is he now?" said I.

"He's an invalid now," replied Herbert.

"Living on ——?"   40

"On the first floor," said Herbert. Which was not at all what I meant, for
I had intended my question to apply to his means. "I have never seen him,
for he has always kept his room overhead, since I have known Clara. But I
have heard him constantly. He makes tremendous rows—roars, and pegs at

---

5. A dustman collects sewage and waste matter, which are sifted and sold for the manufacture of soap,
   fertilizers, glass, earthenware, etc.; a marine-store shop (originally suppliers of odds and ends to sailors
   in seaport towns) is a junk shop. The most famous exemplars of dustman and marine-store in English
   fiction are both found in Dickens: Old Harmon, the dust contractor in *Our Mutual Friend* 2.13, and
   Krook's Rag and Bottle Shop in *Bleak House*, chapter 5. Herbert is saying that between them the
   dustman and junk dealer divide the castoffs of the Pocket establishment.
6. For the autobiographical matrix of Herbert's axiom, see p. 571.

the floor with some frightful instrument." In looking at me and then laughing heartily, Herbert for the time recovered his usual lively manner.

"Don't you expect to see him?" said I.

"Oh yes, I constantly expect to see him," returned Herbert, "because I never hear him without expecting him to come tumbling through the ceiling. But I don't know how long the rafters may hold."

When he had once more laughed heartily, he became meek again, and told me that the moment he began to realise Capital, it was his intention to marry this young lady. He added as a self-evident proposition, engendering low spirits, "But you *can't* marry, you know, while you're looking about 10 you."

As we contemplated the fire, and as I thought what a difficult vision to realise this same Capital sometimes was, I put my hands in my pockets. A folded piece of paper in one of them attracting my attention, I opened it and found it to be the playbill I had received from Joe, relative to the celebrated provincial amateur of Roscian renown. "And bless my heart," I involuntarily added aloud, "it's to-night!"

This changed the subject in an instant, and made us hurriedly resolve to go to the play. So, when I had pledged myself to comfort and abet Herbert in the affair of his heart by all practicable and impracticable means, and when 20 Herbert had told me that his affianced already knew me by reputation and that I should shortly be presented to her, and when we had warmly shaken hands upon our mutual confidence, we blew out our candles, made up our fire, locked our door, and issued forth in quest of Mr. Wopsle and Denmark.[7]

Chapter XXXI.

ON our arrival in Denmark, we found the king and queen of that country elevated in two arm-chairs on a kitchen-table, holding a Court.[1] The whole of the Danish nobility were in attendance; consisting of a noble boy in the wash-leather boots of a gigantic ancestor, a venerable Peer with a dirty face who seemed to have risen from the people late in life, and the Danish chivalry 30 with a comb in its hair and a pair of white silk legs, and presenting on the whole a feminine appearance. My gifted townsman stood gloomily apart, with folded arms, and I could have wished that his curls and forehead had been more probable.

Several curious little circumstances transpired as the action proceeded. The late king of the country not only appeared to have been troubled with a cough at the time of his decease, but to have taken it with him to the tomb and to have brought it back. The royal phantom also carried a ghostly manuscript round its truncheon,[2] to which it had the appearance of occasionally referring,

7. On the evidence of its location in "the waterside neighbourhood of the Temple" and the architectooralooral ad, the theater historian V. C. Clinton-Baddeley argues (in *Dickensian* 57 [1961]: 150–59) that the playhouse in which Wopsle performs *Hamlet* corresponds to the Blacking Ware'us to which he dragged Joe in chapter 27—probably with an eye to engaging it for his production.

1. Either Pip and Herbert arrive late and come in at the start of scene 2, in which Claudius and his court (reduced to three actors) assemble in the state room at Elsinore and in which Hamlet first appears; or the production has been cut—an even more radical practice in Pip's day than in ours.

2. In this instance, a staff carried as a symbol of office. In 1.2.202–04, Horatio describes the ghost of Hamlet's father to Hamlet: "Thrice he walked . . . Within his truncheon's length."

and that, too, with an air of anxiety and a tendency to lose the place of reference which were suggestive of a state of mortality. It was this, I conceive, which led to the Shade's being advised by the gallery to "turn over!"[3]—a recommendation which it took extremely ill. It was likewise to be noted of this majestic spirit that whereas it always appeared with an air of having been out a long time and walked an immense distance, it perceptibly came from a closely contiguous wall. This occasioned its terrors to be received derisively. The Queen of Denmark, a very buxom lady, though no doubt historically brazen, was considered by the public to have too much brass about her; her chin being attached to her diadem by a broad band of that metal (as if she had a gorgeous toothache), her waist being encircled by another, and each of her arms by another, so that she was openly mentioned as "the kettle-drum."[4] The noble boy in the ancestral boots, was inconsistent; representing himself, as it were in one breath, as an able seaman, a strolling actor, a gravedigger, a clergyman, and a person of the utmost importance at a Court fencing-match, on the authority of whose practised eye and nice discrimination the finest strokes were judged.[5] This gradually led to a want of toleration for him, and even—on his being detected in holy orders, and declining to perform the funeral service—to the general indignation taking the form of nuts. Lastly, Ophelia was a prey to such slow musical madness, that when, in course of time, she had taken off her white muslin scarf, folded it up, and buried it, a sulky man who had been long cooling his impatient nose against an iron bar in the front row of the gallery, growled, "Now the baby's put to bed let's have supper!" Which, to say the least of it, was out of keeping.

Upon my unfortunate townsman all these incidents accumulated with playful effect. Whenever that undecided Prince had to ask a question or state a doubt, the public helped him out with it. As for example: on the question whether 'twas nobler in the mind to suffer, some roared yes, and some no, and some inclining to both opinions said "toss up for it;" and quite a Debating Society arose. When he asked what should such fellows as he do crawling between earth and heaven, he was encouraged with loud cries of "Hear, hear!" When he appeared with his stocking disordered (its disorder expressed, according to usage, by one very neat fold in the top, which I suppose to be always got up with a flat iron), a conversation took place in the gallery respecting the paleness of his leg, and whether it was occasioned by the turn the ghost had given him. On his taking the recorders—very like a little black flute that had just been played in the orchestra and handed out at the door

---

3. To turn the page and retrieve his lines. The royal phantom materializes on the Elsinore ramparts in 1.4 and 1.5.

4. Not the kettle-shaped timpani used in classical orchestras but the side drum suspended from the shoulders of street musicians and dangling in front of them. It's cylindrical, brazen, and—like the Danish Queen—encircled top and bottom by colored bands held together by rope-lashings.

5. Dickens, who knew *Hamlet* by heart, is very careful in parceling out the roles in this illustration of "doubling"—that is, using one and the same actor to assume different parts in the play when there aren't enough actors to go around. The able seaman appears in 4.6; the strolling actor in 2.2 and 3.2; and the authority on fencing—Osric, the only one of the five to be identifiable by name—in 5.2. Only the gravedigger and clergyman nearly overlap in 5.1, unless the gravedigger exits unceremoniously as soon as he finishes his lines and leaves Hamlet and Horatio alone to cope with Yorick's skull. Doubling—and Osric—come in for a lot of kidding by Dickens; in a *Hamlet* he watched in his youth, a "gentleman having been killed with much credit as Polonius, reappears in the part of Osric"—a resurrection that the awestruck spectators ascribed to the Ghost's supernatural interference ("Gaslight Fairies," *Household Words*, February 10, 1855).

—he was called upon unanimously for Rule Britannia.[6] When he recommended the player not to saw the air thus, the sulky man said, "And don't *you* do it, neither; you're a deal worse than *him!*" And I grieve to add that peals of laughter greeted Mr. Wopsle on every one of these occasions.

But his greatest trials were in the churchyard: which had the appearance of a primeval forest, with a kind of small ecclesiastical wash-house on one side, and a turnpike-gate on the other. Mr. Wopsle in a comprehensive black cloak being descried entering at the turnpike, the gravedigger was admonished in a friendly way, "Look out! Here's the undertaker a coming, to see how you're a getting on with your work!" I believe it is well known in a consti- 10 tutional country that Mr. Wopsle could not possibly have returned the skull, after moralising over it, without dusting his fingers on a white napkin taken from his breast;[7] but even that innocent and indispensable action did not pass without the comment "Wai-ter!" The arrival of the body for interment, in an empty black box with the lid tumbling open, was the signal for a general joy which was much enhanced by the discovery, among the bearers, of an individual obnoxious to identification. The joy attended Mr. Wopsle through his struggle with Laertes on the brink of the orchestra and the grave, and slackened no more until he had tumbled the king off the kitchen-table, and died by inches from the ankles upward.[8] 20

We had made some pale efforts in the beginning to applaud Mr. Wopsle; but they were too hopeless to be persisted in. Therefore we had sat, feeling keenly for him, but laughing, nevertheless, from ear to ear. I laughed in spite of myself all the time, the whole thing was so droll; and yet I had a latent impression that there was something decidedly fine in Mr. Wopsle's elocution—not for old associations' sake, I am afraid, but because it was very slow, very dreary, very up-hill and down-hill, and very unlike any way in which any man in any natural circumstances of life or death ever expressed himself about anything. When the tragedy was over, and he had been called for and hooted, I said to Herbert, "Let us go at once, or perhaps we shall meet him." 30

We made all the haste we could down stairs, but we were not quick enough either. Standing at the door was a Jewish man with an unnaturally heavy smear of eyebrow, who caught my eye as we advanced, and said, when we came up with him:

"Mr. Pip and friend?"

6. The nearest thing to a British national anthem after "God Save the Queen"—the *Dictionary of National Biography* calls it "perhaps the finest national song possessed by any nation." Words by James Thomson, music by Thomas Arne, from act 2 of *Alfred: A Masque* (1740) by Thomson and David Mallet. Thomson's refrain, "Rule Britannia, Britannia rule the waves; / Britons never will be slaves," furnished Dickens with countless occasions for civic irreverence, Dickens habitually multiplying *never* by a factor of four or five.

7. In 5.1, Hamlet moralizes over the court jester Yorick's skull. As Dickens notes, Hamlet's finicky gesture of wiping his fingers after fondling the skull was a standard gimmick in stage productions of the period (Guiliano/Collins).

8. A brief extract and chronicle of *Hamlet* happenings in the preceding paragraphs: Ophelia goes musically mad in 4.1 before drowning herself; the "churlish priest" who refuses to have a requiem sung for a suicide rouses her brother's wrath in 5.1; Hamlet pops both his existential question (in the most celebrated soliloquy in world literature) and his rhetorical question (to Ophelia) in 3.1; Ophelia has already complained to her father in 2.1 about the state of Hamlet's disordered ("fouled, ungartered, down-gyved" or tumble-down) stocking; Hamlet pilfers a recorder from one of the strolling actors in 3.2 and tries to teach the ornery Guildenstern how to play it, or pretends to try; his tips to the players open 3.2; the churchyard scene—comprising Hamlet's talk to the skull, the entrance of Ophelia's casket, and the fight with her brother—takes up 5.1; Hamlet begins to die in 5.2.244 and finishes dying in line 301, stabbing the King at about the half.

Identity of Mr. Pip and friend confessed.

"Mr. Waldengarver,"[9] said the man, "would be glad to have the honour."

"Waldengarver?" I repeated—when Herbert murmured in my ear, "Probably Wopsle."

"Oh!" said I. "Yes. Shall we follow you?"

"A few steps, please." When we were in a side alley, he turned and asked, "How do you think he looked?—I dressed him."[1]

I don't know what he had looked like, except a funeral;[2] with the addition of a large Danish sun or star hanging round his neck by a blue ribbon, that had given him the appearance of being insured in some extraordinary Fire   10
Office.[3] But I said he had looked very nice.

"When he come to the grave," said our conductor, "he showed his cloak beautiful. But, judging from the wing, it looked to me that when he see the ghost in the queen's apartment, he might have made more of his stockings."

I modestly assented, and we all fell through a little dirty swing-door, into a sort of hot packing-case immediately behind it. Here Mr. Wopsle was divesting himself of his Danish garments, and here there was just room for us to look at him over one another's shoulders, by keeping the packing-case door, or lid, wide open.   20

"Gentlemen," said Mr. Wopsle, "I am proud to see you. I hope, Mr. Pip, you will excuse my sending round. I had the happiness to know you in former times, and the Drama has ever had a claim which has ever been acknowledged, on the noble and the affluent."

Meanwhile, Mr. Waldengarver, in a frightful perspiration, was trying to get himself out of his princely sables.

"Skin the stockings off, Mr. Waldengarver," said the owner of that property, "or you'll bust 'em. Bust 'em, and you'll bust five-and-thirty shillings. Shakespeare never was complimented with a finer pair. Keep quiet in your chair now, and leave 'em to me."   30

With that, he went upon his knees, and began to flay his victim; who, on the first stocking coming off, would certainly have fallen over backward with his chair, but for their being no room to fall anyhow.

I had been afraid until then to say a word about the play. But then, Mr. Waldengarver looked up at us complacently, and said:

"Gentlemen, how did it seem to you, to go, in front?"

Herbert said from behind (at the same time poking me), "capitally." So I said "capitally."

9. Presumably a palpable hit at Samuel Waldegrave, bishop of Carlisle (1817–69), of whose Evangelical policies—notably his defense of the dreary Sunday Observances Law—Dickens took a dim view, and whose promotion to the episcopacy nearly coincided with Wopsle's debut as Waldengarver. Even without a specific attribution, it seems to be par "for these geniuses [to] assume fictitious names . . . with the double view of guarding against the discovery of friends or employers, and enhancing the interest of an assumed character" ("Private Theatres," *Sketches by Boz*, "Scenes," 13).
1. In the same essay Dickens talks about "Jews whose business, as lenders of fancy dresses, is a sure passport to the amateur stage" and here and elsewhere reminds us that dressers are themselves engaged in an almost exclusively Jewish profession.
2. Dressed in black.
3. Before the establishment of the London Fire Brigade in 1865, fire insurance companies (first formed after the Great Fire of London in 1666) placed metal plates on the buildings they insured, displaying simple emblems identifying their company: Star, Eagle, Phoenix, etc. That way rival brigades racing to a fire could tell at a glance which of them was entitled to put it out.

"How did you like my reading of the character, gentlemen?" said Mr. Waldengarver, almost, if not quite, with patronage.

Herbert said from behind (again poking me), "massive and concrete." So I said boldly, as if I had originated it, and must beg to insist upon it, "massive and concrete."

"I am glad to have your approbation, gentlemen," said Mr. Waldengarver, with an air of dignity, in spite of his being ground against the wall at the time, and holding on by the seat of the chair.

"But I'll tell you one thing, Mr. Waldengarver," said the man who was on his knees, "in which you're out in your reading. Now mind! I don't care 10 who says contrairy; I tell you so. You're out in your reading of Hamlet when you get your legs in profile. The last Hamlet as I dressed, made the same mistake in his reading at rehearsal, till I got him to put a large red wafer[4] on each of his shins, and then at that rehearsal (which was the last) I went in front, sir, to the back of the pit, and whenever his reading brought him into profile, I called out 'I don't see no wafers!' And at night his reading was lovely."

Mr. Waldengarver smiled at me, as much as to say "a faithful dependent —I overlook his folly;" and then said aloud, "My view is a little classic and thoughtful for them here; but they will improve, they will improve."   20

Herbert and I said together, Oh, no doubt they would improve.

"Did you observe, gentlemen," said Mr. Waldengarver, "that there was a man in the gallery who endeavoured to cast derision on the service—I mean, the representation?"

We basely replied that we rather thought we had noticed such a man. I added, "He was drunk, no doubt."

"Oh dear no, sir," said Mr. Wopsle, "not drunk. His employer would see to that, sir. His employer would not allow him to be drunk."

"You know his employer?" said I.

Mr. Wopsle shut his eyes, and opened them again; performing both cere- 30 monies very slowly. "You must have observed, gentlemen," said he, "an ig- norant and a blatant ass, with a rasping throat and a countenance expressive of low malignity, who went through—I will not say sustained—the rôle (if I may use a French expression) of Claudius King of Denmark. That is his employer, gentlemen. Such is the profession!"

Without distinctly knowing whether I should have been more sorry for Mr. Wopsle if he had been in despair, I was so sorry for him as it was, that I took the opportunity of his turning round to have his braces put on—which jostled us out at the doorway—to ask Herbert what he thought of having him home to supper? Herbert said he thought it would be kind to do so; therefore I 40 invited him, and he went to Barnard's with us, wrapped up to the eyes, and we did our best for him, and he sat until two o'clock in the morning, review- ing his success and developing his plans. I forget in detail what they were, but I have a general recollection that he was to begin with reviving the Drama, and to end with crushing it; inasmuch as his decease would leave it utterly bereft and without a chance or hope.

Miserably I went to bed after all, and miserably thought of Estella, and

4. A small disk of gum and flour used to seal letters before envelopes were introduced as part of the postal reforms in the 1840s. The color red identified the letter as business mail.

miserably dreamed that my expectations were all cancelled, and that I had to give my hand in marriage to Herbert's Clara, or play Hamlet to Miss Havisham's Ghost, before twenty thousand people, without knowing twenty words of it.

Chapter XXXII.

ONE day when I was busy with my books and Mr. Pocket, I received a note by the post, the mere outside of which threw me into a great flutter; for, though I had never seen the handwriting in which it was addressed, I divined whose hand it was. It had no set beginning, as Dear Mr. Pip, or Dear Pip, or Dear Sir, or Dear Anything, but ran thus:

"I am to come to London the day after to-morrow by the mid-day coach. I   10
believe it was settled you should meet me? At all events Miss Havisham has that impression, and I write in obedience to it. She sends you her regard. Yours,
ESTELLA."

If there had been time, I should probably have ordered several suits of clothes for this occasion; but as there was not, I was fain to be content with those I had. My appetite vanished instantly, and I knew no peace or rest until the day arrived. Not that its arrival brought me either; for, then I was worse than ever, and began haunting the coach-office in Wood-street, Cheapside, before the coach had left the Blue Boar in our town. For all that I knew this perfectly well, I still felt as if it were not safe to let the coach-office be out of   20
my sight longer than five minutes at a time; and in this condition of unreason I had performed the first half-hour of a watch of four or five hours, when Wemmick ran against me.

"Halloa, Mr. Pip," said he; "how do you do? I should hardly have thought this was *your* beat."

I explained that I was waiting to meet somebody who was coming up by coach, and I inquired after the Castle and the Aged.

"Both flourishing, thankye," said Wemmick, "and particularly the Aged. He's in wonderful feather. He'll be eighty-two next birthday. I have a notion of firing eighty-two times, if the neighbourhood shouldn't complain, and that   30
cannon of mine should prove equal to the pressure. However, this is not London talk. Where do you think I am going to?"

"To the office?" said I, for he was tending in that direction.

"Next thing to it," returned Wemmick, "I am going to Newgate. We are in a banker's-parcel case[1] just at present, and I have been down the road taking a squint at the scene of action, and thereupon must have a word or two with our client."

"Did your client commit the robbery?" I asked.

"Bless your soul and body, no," answered Wemmick, very drily. "But he

---

1. A case in which a bag of money was snatched from a bank messenger on the way to the bank or a fake bag substituted for the real thing.

is accused of it. So might you or I be. Either of us might be accused of it, you know."

"Only neither of us is," I remarked.

"Yah!" said Wemmick, touching me on the breast with his forefinger; "you're a deep one, Mr. Pip! Would you like to have a look at Newgate? Have you time to spare?"

I had so much time to spare, that the proposal came as a relief, notwithstanding its irreconcilability with my latent desire to keep my eye on the coach-office. Muttering that I would make the inquiry whether I had time to walk with him, I went into the office, and ascertained from the clerk with 10 the nicest precision and much to the trying of his temper, the earliest moment at which the coach could be expected—which I knew beforehand, quite as well as he. I then rejoined Mr. Wemmick, and affecting to consult my watch and to be surprised by the information I had received, accepted his offer.

We were at Newgate in a few minutes, and we passed through the lodge where some fetters[2] were hanging up on the bare walls among the prison rules, into the interior of the jail. At that time, jails were much neglected, and the period of exaggerated reaction consequent on all public wrongdoing—and which is always its heaviest and longest punishment—was still far off. So, felons were not lodged and fed better than soldiers (to say nothing of 20 paupers), and seldom set fire to their prisons with the excusable object of improving the flavour of their soup.[3] It was visiting time when Wemmick took me in; and a potman[4] was going his rounds with beer; and the prisoners behind bars in yards, were buying beer, and talking to friends; and a frowzy, ugly, disorderly, depressing scene it was.

It struck me that Wemmick walked among the prisoners, much as a gardener might walk among his plants. This was first put into my head by his seeing a shoot that had come up in the night, and saying, "What, Captain Tom? Are *you* there? Ah, indeed!" and also, "Is that Black Bill behind the cistern? Why, I didn't look for you these two months; how do you find your- 30 self?" Equally in his stopping at the bars and attending to anxious whisperers—always singly—Wemmick with his post-office in an immovable state, looked at them while in conference, as if he were taking particular notice of the advance they had made, since last observed, towards coming out in full blow at their trial.

He was highly popular, and I found that he took the familiar department of Mr. Jaggers's business: though something of the state of Mr. Jaggers hung about him too, forbidding approach beyond certain limits. His personal recognition of each successive client was comprised in a nod, and in his settling his hat a little easier on his head with both hands, and then tightening the 40

---

2. Leg irons.
3. Another one of the few topical references in the novel. In February 1861 the inmates of Chatham Convict Prison staged violent riots to protest the reduction in prison fare. Dickens, increasingly conservative in his views on penal reform—a view already elaborated scathingly ten years earlier in *David Copperfield*, chapter 61, "I Am Shown Two Interesting Penitents"—objects to the excessively lenient treatment of what he calls "Pet Prisoners" in a paper in *Household Words* for April 27, 1850, in which he attacks the "frightful disproportion" of prison diet "to the dietary of the free labourer," and for that matter the workhouse parishioners'. Chapter 32 of *Great Expectations* appeared in *All the Year Round* on April 23, 1861, and was presumably written within two or three weeks after the riots.
4. As the word implies, boy or man who delivers beer from a neighborhood tavern. Dickens's point is that prisoners were allowed all the beer they wanted, as long as they were able to pay the potman.

post-office, and putting his hands in his pockets. In one or two instances, there was a difficulty respecting the raising of fees, and then Mr. Wemmick, backing as far as possible from the insufficient money produced, said, "It's no use, my boy. I'm only a subordinate. I can't take it.[5] Don't go on in that way with a subordinate. If you are unable to make up your quantum, my boy, you had better address yourself to a principal; there are plenty of principals in the profession, you know, and what is not worth the while of one, may be worth the while of another; that's my recommendation to you, speaking as a subordinate. Don't try on useless measures. Why should you! Now, who's next?"

Thus, we walked through Wemmick's greenhouse, until he turned to me and said, "Notice the man I shall shake hands with." I should have done so, without the preparation, as he had shaken hands with no one yet.

Almost as soon as he had spoken, a portly upright man (whom I can see now, as I write) in a well-worn olive-coloured frock-coat, with a peculiar pallor overspreading the red in his complexion, and eyes that went wandering about when he tried to fix them, came up to a corner of the bars, and put his hand to his hat—which had a greasy spotty surface like cold broth—with a half-serious and half-jocose military salute.

"Colonel, to you!" said Wemmick; "how are you, Colonel?"

"All right, Mr. Wemmick."

"Everything was done that could be done, but the evidence was too strong for us, Colonel."

"Yes, it was too strong, sir—but *I* don't care."

"No, no," said Wemmick, coolly, "*you* don't care." Then, turning to me, "Served His Majesty this man. Was a soldier in the line and bought his discharge."

I said, "Indeed?" and the man's eyes looked at me, and then looked over my head, and then looked all round me, and then he drew his hand across his lips and laughed.

"I think I shall be out of this on Monday, sir," he said to Wemmick.

"Perhaps," returned my friend, "but there's no knowing."

"I am glad to have the chance of bidding you good-by, Mr. Wemmick," said the man, stretching out his hand between two bars.

"Thankye," said Wemmick, shaking hands with him. "Same to you, Colonel."

"If what I had upon me when taken, had been real, Mr. Wemmick," said the man, unwilling to let his hand go, "I should have asked the favour of your wearing another ring—in acknowledgment of your attentions."

"I'll accept the will for the deed," said Wemmick. "By-the-by; you were quite a pigeon-fancier." The man looked up at the sky. "I am told you had a remarkable breed of tumblers.[6] *Could* you commission any friend of yours to bring me a pair, if you've no further use for 'em?"

"It shall be done, sir."

"All right," said Wemmick, "they shall be taken care of. Good afternoon,

5. This penchant for shirking a dirty job by claiming to play second fiddle to an alleged or fictitious partner or boss or even employee is typical Dickens: prominently in the association of Dodson and Fogg in *Pickwick Papers*, Spenlow and Jorkins in *David Copperfield*, Pancks and Casby in *Little Dorrit*, and Riah and Fledgeby in *Our Mutual Friend* (Monod). See also Pumblechook's offer to be a "sleeping partner"—without bias—in chapter 19.
6. Species of domestic pigeon that tumbles head over heels in the air.

Colonel. Good-by!" They shook hands again, and as we walked away Wemmick said to me "A Coiner,[7] a very good workman. The Recorder's report is made to-day, and he is sure to be executed on Monday.[8] Still you see, as far as it goes, a pair of pigeons are portable property, all the same." With that, he looked back, and nodded at his dead plant, and then cast his eyes about him in walking out of the yard, as if he were considering what other pot would go best in its place.

As we came out of the prison through the lodge, I found that the great importance of my guardian was appreciated by the turnkeys, no less than by those whom they held in charge. "Well, Mr. Wemmick," said the turnkey, who kept us between the two studded and spiked lodge gates, and carefully locked one before he unlocked the other, "what's Mr. Jaggers going to do with that waterside murder? Is he going to make it manslaughter, or what's he going to make of it?"

"Why don't you ask him?" returned Wemmick.

"Oh yes, I dare say!" said the turnkey.

"Now, that's the way with them here, Mr. Pip," remarked Wemmick, turning to me with his post-office elongated. "They don't mind what they ask of me, the subordinate; but you'll never catch 'em asking any questions of my principal."

"Is this young gentleman one of the 'prentices or articled ones of your office?" asked the turnkey, with a grin at Mr. Wemmick's humour.

"There he goes again, you see!" cried Wemmick, "I told you so! Asks another question of the subordinate before his first is dry! Well, supposing Mr. Pip is one of them?"

"Why then," said the turnkey, grinning again, "he knows what Mr. Jaggers is."

"Yah!" cried Wemmick, suddenly hitting out at the turnkey in a facetious way, "you're as dumb as one of your own keys when you have to do with my principal, you know you are. Let us out, you old fox, or I'll get him to bring an action against you for false imprisonment."

The turnkey laughed, and gave us good day, and stood laughing at us over the spikes of the wicket[9] when we descended the steps into the street.

"Mind you, Mr. Pip," said Wemmick, gravely in my ear, as he took my arm to be more confidential; "I don't know that Mr. Jaggers does a better thing than the way in which he keeps himself so high. He's always so high. His constant height is of a piece with his immense abilities. That Colonel durst no more take leave of *him*, than that turnkey durst ask him his intentions respecting a case. Then, between his height and them, he slips in his subordinate—don't you see?—and so he has 'em, soul and body."

I was very much impressed, and not for the first time, by my guardian's subtlety. To confess the truth, I very heartily wished, and not for the first time, that I had had some other guardian of minor abilities.

7. Counterfeiter.
8. The Recorder of the City of London, an office dating back to the thirteenth century, acted as the Lord Mayor's juridical representative in order to stress the Mayor's authority within the City limits and his right "to try, hear, and determine" all offenses under his jurisdiction at the Old Bailey. As Senior Permanent Judge of the Central Criminal Court he is authorized to sentence the Colonel. The Recorder's general function is given in chapter 56.
9. A small gate or doorway, often located near or forming part of a larger one. Hence the "wicket-keeper" in chapter 27.

Mr. Wemmick and I parted at the office in Little Britain, where suppliants for Mr. Jaggers's notice were lingering about as usual, and I returned to my watch in the street of the coach-office, with some three hours on hand. I consumed the whole time in thinking how strange it was that I should be encompassed by all this taint of prison and crime; that in my childhood out on our lonely marshes on a winter evening I should have first encountered it; that it should have reappeared on two occasions, starting out like a stain that was faded but not gone; that it should in this new way pervade my fortune and advancement. While my mind was thus engaged, I thought of the beautiful young Estella, proud and refined, coming towards me, and I thought 10 with absolute abhorrence of the contrast between the jail and her. I wished that Wemmick had not met me, or that I had not yielded to him and gone with him, so that, of all days in the year on this day, I might not have had Newgate in my breath and on my clothes. I beat the prison dust off my feet as I sauntered to and fro, and I shook it out of my dress, and I exhaled its air from my lungs. So contaminated did I feel, remembering who was coming, that the coach came quickly after all, and I was not yet free from the soiling consciousness of Mr. Wemmick's conservatory, when I saw her face at the coach window and her hand waving to me.

What *was* the nameless shadow which again in that one instant had passed? 20

Chapter XXXIII.

IN her furred travelling-dress, Estella seemed more delicately beautiful than she had ever seemed yet, even in my eyes. Her manner was more winning than she had cared to let it be to me before, and I thought I saw Miss Havisham's influence in the change.

We stood in the Inn Yard while she pointed out her luggage to me, and when it was all collected I remembered—having forgotten everything but herself in the mean while—that I knew nothing of her destination.

"I am going to Richmond," she told me. "Our lesson is, that there are two Richmonds, one in Surrey and one in Yorkshire, and that mine is the Surrey Richmond.[1] The distance is ten miles. I am to have a carriage, and you are 30 to take me. This is my purse, and you are to pay my charges out of it. Oh, you must take the purse! We have no choice, you and I, but to obey our instructions. We are not free to follow our own devices, you and I."

As she looked at me in giving me the purse, I hoped there was an inner meaning in her words. She said them slightingly, but not with displeasure.

"A carriage will have to be sent for, Estella. Will you rest here a little?"

"Yes, I am to rest here a little, and I am to drink some tea, and you are to take care of me the while."

She drew her arm through mine, as if it must be done, and I requested a waiter who had been staring at the coach like a man who had never seen 40 such a thing in his life, to show us a private sitting-room.[2] Upon that, he

1. "Surrey Richmond," on the banks of the Thames southeast of London, one of the favorite excursion spots within easy reach of the city, has long endeared itself to painters, painterly poets, wealthy retirees, and tourists by its magnificent park, the view from Richmond Hill on the Thames Valley, and its picturesque Stuart and Hanoverian mansions and hunting lodges.
2. Inns at stage-coach stops provided small rooms in which passengers could take their refreshments in private. The charge was accordingly higher than the cost of public dining facilities.

pulled out a napkin, as if it were a magic clue without which he couldn't find the way up-stairs, and led us to the black hole of the establishment: fitted up with a diminishing mirror (quite a superfluous article considering the hole's proportions), an anchovy sauce-cruet,[3] and somebody's pattens. On my objecting to this retreat, he took us into another room with a dinner-table for thirty, and in the grate a scorched leaf of a copy-book under a bushel of coal-dust. Having looked at this extinct conflagration and shaken his head, he took my order: which, proving to be merely "Some tea for the lady," sent him out of the room in a very low state of mind.

I was, and I am, sensible that the air of this chamber, in its strong com-   10
bination of stable with soup-stock, might have led one to infer that the coaching department was not doing well, and that the enterprising proprietor was boiling down the horses for the refreshment department. Yet the room was all in all to me, Estella being in it. I thought that with her I could have been happy there for life. (I was not at all happy there at the time, observe, and I knew it well.)

"Where are you going to, at Richmond?" I asked Estella.

"I am going to live," said she, "at a great expense, with a lady there, who has the power—or says she has—of taking me about and introducing me, and showing people to me and showing me to people."   20

"I suppose you will be glad of variety and admiration?"

"Yes, I suppose so."

She answered so carelessly, that I said, "You speak of yourself as if you were some one else."

"Where did you learn how I speak of others? Come, come," said Estella, smiling delightfully, "you must not expect me to go to school to you; I must talk in my own way. How do you thrive with Mr. Pocket?"

"I live quite pleasantly there; at least——" It appeared to me that I was losing a chance.

"At least?" repeated Estella.   30

"As pleasantly as I could anywhere, away from you."

"You silly boy," said Estella, quite composedly, "how can you talk such nonsense? Your friend Mr. Matthew, I believe, is superior to the rest of his family?"

"Very superior indeed. He is nobody's enemy——"

"Don't add but his own,"[4] interposed Estella, "for I hate that class of man. But he really is disinterested, and above small jealousy and spite, I have heard?"

"I am sure I have every reason to say so."

"You have not every reason to say so of the rest of his people," said Estella,   40
nodding at me with an expression of face that was at once grave and rallying, "for they beset Miss Havisham with reports and insinuations to your disadvantage. They watch you, misrepresent you, write letters about you (anonymous sometimes), and you are the torment and the occupation of their lives. You can scarcely realise to yourself the hatred those people feel for you."

"They do me no harm, I hope?" said I.

Instead of answering, Estella burst out laughing. This was very singular to

---

3. Small glass bottle used to hold a condiment. "Diminishing mirror:" mirror that reduces the size of the object it reflects.
4. Pip is about to repeat the expression applied by Camilla Pocket to Matthew in chapter 11.

me, and I looked at her in considerable perplexity. When she left off—and she had not laughed languidly but with real enjoyment—I said, in my diffident way with her,

"I hope I may suppose that you would not be amused if they did me any harm."

"No, no, you may be sure of that," said Estella. "You may be certain that I laugh because they fail. Oh, those people with Miss Havisham, and the tortures they undergo!" She laughed again, and even now when she had told me why, her laughter was very singular to me, for I could not doubt its being genuine, and yet it seemed too much for the occasion. I thought there must really be something more here than I knew; she saw the thought in my mind, and answered it.

"It is not easy for even you," said Estella, "to know what satisfaction it gives me to see those people thwarted, or what an enjoyable sense of the ridiculous I have when they are made ridiculous. For you were not brought up in that strange house from a mere baby.—I was. You had not your little wits sharpened by their intriguing against you, suppressed and defenceless, under the mask of sympathy and pity and what not that is soft and soothing.—I had. You did not gradually open your round childish eyes wider and wider to the discovery of that impostor of a woman who calculates her stores of peace of mind for when she wakes up in the night.—I did."

It was no laughing matter with Estella now, nor was she summoning these remembrances from any shallow place. I would not have been the cause of that look of hers, for all my expectations in a heap.

"Two things I can tell you," said Estella. "First, notwithstanding the proverb that constant dropping will wear away a stone,[5] you may set your mind at rest that these people never will—never would, in a hundred years—impair your ground with Miss Havisham, in any particular, great or small. Second, I am beholden to you as the cause of their being so busy and so mean in vain, and there is my hand upon it."

As she gave it me playfully—for her darker mood had been but momentary—I held it and put it to my lips. "You ridiculous boy," said Estella, "will you never take warning? Or do you kiss my hand in the same spirit in which I once let you kiss my cheek?"

"What spirit was that?" said I.

"I must think a moment. A spirit of contempt for the fawners and plotters."

"If I say yes, may I kiss the cheek again?"

"You should have asked before you touched the hand. But, yes, if you like."

I leaned down, and her calm face was like a statue's. "Now," said Estella, gliding away the instant I touched her cheek, "you are to take care that I have some tea, and you are to take me to Richmond."

Her reverting to this tone as if our association were forced upon us and we were mere puppets, gave me pain; but everything in our intercourse did give me pain. Whatever her tone with me happened to be, I could put no trust in it, and build no hope on it; and yet I went on against trust and against hope. Why repeat it a thousand times? So it always was.

I rang for the tea, and the waiter, reappearing with his magic clue, brought

5. Job 14.19: "All the waters wear the stones." But the phrase appears repeatedly in the worldlier context of Ovid's *Art of Loving* (c. 1 B.C.) and his *Letters from Pontus* (c. A.D. 13).

in by degrees some fifty adjuncts to that refreshment, but of tea not a glimpse. A teaboard, cups and saucers, plates, knives and forks (including carvers), spoons (various), salt-cellars, a meek little muffin confined with the utmost precaution under a strong iron cover, Moses in the bulrushes typified by a soft bit of butter in a quantity of parsley, a pale loaf with a powdered head, two proof impressions of the bars of the kitchen fireplace on triangular bits of bread, and ultimately a fat family urn:[6] which the waiter staggered in with, expressing in his countenance burden and suffering. After a prolonged absence at this stage of the entertainment, he at length came back with a casket of precious appearance containing twigs.[7] These I steeped in hot water, and so from the whole of these appliances extracted one cup of I don't know what, for Estella.

The bill paid, and the waiter remembered, and the ostler[8] not forgotten, and the chambermaid taken into consideration—in a word, the whole house bribed into a state of contempt and animosity, and Estella's purse much lightened—we got into our post-coach[9] and drove away. Turning into Cheapside and rattling up Newgate-street, we were soon under the walls of which I was so ashamed.

"What place is that?" Estella asked me.

I made a foolish pretence of not at first recognising it, and then told her. As she looked at it, and drew in her head again, murmuring "Wretches!" I would not have confessed to my visit for any consideration.

"Mr. Jaggers," said I, by way of putting it neatly on somebody else, "has the reputation of being more in the secrets of that dismal place than any man in London."

"He is more in the secrets of every place, I think," said Estella, in a low voice.

"You have been accustomed to see him often, I suppose?"

"I have been accustomed to see him at uncertain intervals, ever since I can remember. But I know him no better now, than I did before I could speak plainly. What is your own experience of him? Do you advance with him?"

"Once habituated to his distrustful manner," said I, "I have done very well."

"Are you intimate?"

"I have dined with him at his private house."

"I fancy," said Estella, shrinking, "that must be a curious place."

"It is a curious place."

I should have been chary of discussing my guardian too freely even with her; but I should have gone on with the subject so far as to describe the dinner in Gerrard-street, if we had not then come into a sudden glare of gas.[1]

---

6. Vase-shaped hot-water container introduced about 1760 to replace the simpler tea kettle.
7. Pip is disparaging the tea he and Estella are served. A decent pot is brewed from dried tea leaves: the waiter has brought mere stalks.
8. Also hostler. Attendant on horses and carriages during their stop at an inn.
9. Fast-paced hired carriage seating two or four inside passengers.
1. Though gas lighting had been used experimentally in the West End as early as 1807, it wasn't generally introduced into London until twenty years later. Its glare may thus well have dazzled Pip, coming as he does from the dimly lit Newgate quarters. Pip recaptures this scene in chapter 48; earlier in the same chapter Dickens briefly describes the lamplighters' maneuvers: equipped with a short ladder to replace the long stick and torchlight of the pregaslight age, the nimble luminary was a familiar sight in Regency and Victorian England. (Dickens wrote a one-act farce—unproduced—called The Lamplighter for his friend Macready in 1838; under the same title he palmed this off as a story in Picnic Papers in 1841.)

It seemed, while it lasted, to be all alight and alive with that inexplicable feeling I had had before; and when we were out of it, I was as much dazed for a few moments as if I had been in Lightning.

So, we fell into other talk, and it was principally about the way by which we were travelling, and about what parts of London lay on this side of it, and what on that. The great city was almost new to her, she told me, for she had never left Miss Havisham's neighbourhood until she had gone to France, and she had merely passed through London then in going and returning. I asked her if my guardian had any charge of her while she remained here? To that she emphatically said "God forbid!" and no more.   10

It was impossible for me to avoid seeing that she cared to attract me; that she made herself winning; and would have won me even if the task had needed pains. Yet this made me none the happier, for, even if she had not taken that tone of our being disposed of by others, I should have felt that she held my heart in her hand because she wilfully chose to do it, and not because it would have wrung any tenderness in her, to crush it and throw it away.

When we passed through Hammersmith, I showed her where Mr. Matthew Pocket lived, and said it was no great way from Richmond, and that I hoped I should see her sometimes.

"Oh yes, you are to see me; you are to come when you think proper; you   20
are to be mentioned to the family; indeed you are already mentioned."

I inquired was it a large household she was going to be a member of?

"No; there are only two; mother and daughter. The mother is a lady of some station, I believe, though not averse to increasing her income."

"I wonder Miss Havisham could part with you again so soon."

"It is a part of Miss Havisham's plans for me, Pip," said Estella, with a sigh, as if she were tired; "I am to write to her constantly and see her regularly, and report how I go on—I and the jewels—for they are nearly all mine now."

It was the first time she had ever called me by my name. Of course she did so, purposely, and knew that I should treasure it up.   30

We came to Richmond all too soon, and our destination there, was a house by the Green:[2] a staid old house, where hoops and powder and patches,[3] embroidered coats, rolled stockings, ruffles, and swords, had had their court days many a time. Some ancient trees before the house were still cut into fashions as formal and unnatural as the hoops and wigs and stiff skirts they had cast their shadows on; but their own allotted places in the great procession of the dead were not far off, and they would soon drop into them and go the silent way of the rest.

A bell with an old voice—which I dare say in its time had often said to the house, Here is the green farthingale,[4] Here is the diamond-hilted sword, Here   40
are the shoes with red heels and the blue solitaire,[5]—sounded gravely in the

2. One of a series of row houses facing the Green, Maids-of-Honour Row, adjoining the palace of George II and named for Queen Caroline's ladies-in-waiting, for whom they were built (Hill).
3. Artificial beauty mark. In the seventeenth and eighteenth centuries ladies wore small, sometimes decoratively shaped pieces of black paper, plaster, or silk on their faces to emphasize their fair complexions or else hide blemishes, such as pockmarks. Thus Pope's description of Belinda's toilet in *Rape of the Lock* (1712; 1714) 1, line 138: "Puffs, powders, patches, Bibles, billet-doux."
4. Petticoat supported by wooden, wire, or whalebone hoops. Farthingales had been out of fashion for two hundred years.
5. Consistently annotated to describe a loose silk neckcloth worn by gents in the mid-1800s. But in context it surely refers to a jewel, usually a diamond, set singly in a ring or, as here, fastened to the top of a shoe.

moonlight, and two cherry-coloured maids came fluttering out to receive Estella. The doorway soon absorbed her boxes, and she gave me her hand and a smile, and said good night, and was absorbed likewise. And still I stood looking at the house, thinking how happy I should be if I lived there with her, and knowing that I never was happy with her, but always miserable.

I got into the carriage to be taken back to Hammersmith, and I got in with a bad heart-ache, and I got out with a worse heart-ache. At our own door, I found little Jane Pocket coming home from a little party escorted by her little lover; and I envied her little lover, in spite of his being subject to Flopson.

Mr. Pocket was out lecturing; for, he was a most delightful lecturer on domestic economy, and his treatises on the management of children and servants were considered the very best text-books on those themes. But Mrs. Pocket was at home, and was in a little difficulty, on account of the baby's having been accommodated with a needle-case to keep him quiet during the unaccountable absence (with a relative in the Foot Guards)[6] of Millers. And more needles were missing than it could be regarded as quite wholesome for a patient of such tender years either to apply externally or to take as a tonic.

Mr. Pocket being justly celebrated for giving most excellent practical advice, and for having a clear and sound perception of things and a highly judicious mind, I had some notion in my heart-ache of begging him to accept my confidence. But happening to look up at Mrs. Pocket as she sat reading her book of dignities after prescribing Bed as a sovereign remedy for baby, I thought—Well—No, I wouldn't.

★

Chapter XXXIV.

As I had grown accustomed to my expectations, I had insensibly begun to notice their effect upon myself and those around me. Their influence on my own character, I disguised from my recognition as much as possible, but I knew very well that it was not all good. I lived in a state of chronic uneasiness respecting my behaviour to Joe. My conscience was not by any means comfortable about Biddy. When I woke up in the night—like Camilla—I used to think, with a weariness on my spirits, that I should have been happier and better if I had never seen Miss Havisham's face, and had risen to manhood content to be partners with Joe in the honest old forge. Many a time of an evening, when I sat alone, looking at the fire, I thought, after all there was no fire like the forge fire and the kitchen fire at home.

Yet Estella was so inseparable from all my restlessness and disquiet of mind, that I really fell into confusion as to the limits of my own part in its production. That is to say, supposing I had had no expectations, and yet had had Estella to think of, I could not make out to my satisfaction that I should have done much better. Now, concerning the influence of my position on others, I was in no such difficulty, and so I perceived—though dimly enough, perhaps—that it was not beneficial to anybody, and, above all, that it was not

6. Transparent euphemism for boyfriend.

beneficial to Herbert. My lavish habits led his easy nature into expenses that he could not afford, corrupted the simplicity of his life, and disturbed his peace with anxieties and regrets. I was not at all remorseful for having un-wittingly set those other branches of the Pocket family to the poor arts they practised: because such littlenesses were their natural bent, and would have been evoked by anybody else, if I had left them slumbering. But Herbert's was a very different case, and it often caused me a twinge to think that I had done him evil service in crowding his sparely-furnished chambers with in-congruous upholstery work, and placing the canary-breasted Avenger at his disposal.   10

So now, as an infallible way of making little ease great ease, I began to contract a quantity of debt. I could hardly begin but Herbert must begin too, so he soon followed. At Startop's suggestion, we put ourselves down for elec-tion into a club called The Finches of the Grove:[1] the object of which insti-tution I have never divined, if it were not that the members should dine expensively once a fortnight, to quarrel among themselves as much as possible after dinner, and to cause six waiters to get drunk on the stairs. I know that these gratifying social ends were so invariably accomplished, that Herbert and I understood nothing else to be referred to in the first standing toast of the society: which ran "Gentlemen, may the present promotion of good feeling   20 ever reign predominant among the Finches of the Grove."

The Finches spent their money foolishly (the Hotel we dined at was in Covent-garden),[2] and the first Finch I saw, when I had the honour of joining the Grove, was Bentley Drummle: at that time floundering about town in a cab[3] of his own, and doing a great deal of damage to the posts at the street corners. Occasionally, he shot himself out of his equipage head-foremost over the apron;[4] and I saw him on one occasion deliver himself at the door of the Grove in this unintentional way—like coals. But here I anticipate a little, for I was not a Finch, and could not be, according to the sacred laws of the society, until I came of age.   30

In my confidence in my own resources, I would willingly have taken Her-bert's expenses on myself; but Herbert was proud, and I could make no such proposal to him. So, he got into difficulties in every direction, and continued

1. From Richard Brinsley Sheridan's *The Critic, or a Tragedy Rehearsed*, first performed in 1779 as an afterpiece for *Hamlet*. The "Tragedy" is *The Spanish Armada*, and in 2.2 of the play the crazed heroine, in a burlesque of Ophelia's ravings, hails "The lark! / The linnet! chaffinch! bullfinch! goldfinch! greenfinch! / But O, no joy can they afford! . . . nor marjoram, nor lark, / Linnet nor all the finches of the grove!"—the phrase "finches of the grove" providing her punch line and reminder to start howling.
2. A pretty raunchy location. By mid-eighteenth century, Covent Garden had turned into a hub of London coffeehouses, theaters, and brothels—for "Covent Garden abbess" read "procuress"; for "Cov-ent Garden ague," "syphilis"; for "Covent Garden nun," "whore" (Grose). The Finches' hotel has been variously identified as the Hummums (chapter 45) and the Tavistock Hotel, built on the site of the Great Piazza Coffee House, a favorite haunt of Dickens's, and before him patronized by the leading eighteenth-century actors and writers, including the author of the lines to which the Finches owe their name. Dickens never shook off his sense of "the fine secrecy and mystery about the Piazza— how you get up to these rooms above it, and what reckless deeds are done there" ("Where We Stopped Growing," *Household Words*, January 1, 1853).
3. Light open or hooded two-wheeled chaise, introduced into London about 1823. (But the contraction as Dickens uses it [from *cabriolet*, to describe the elastic motion of the carriage] is not found before 1830.) At the time Bentley bought his vehicle, cabs were still so much of a novelty that the citizenry gaped and wondered why anybody would risk his life to drive in one. See "The Streets—Morning," *Sketches by Boz*, "Scenes," 1.)
4. Wooden or leather covering to protect the cabdriver from getting his legs muddied by his horse's hooves.

to look about him. When we gradually fell into keeping late hours and late company, I noticed that he looked about him with a despondent eye at breakfast-time; that he began to look about him more hopefully about mid-day; that he drooped when he came in to dinner; that he seemed to descry Capital in the distance, rather clearly, after dinner; that he all but realised Capital towards midnight; and that at about two o'clock in the morning, he became so deeply despondent again as to talk of buying a rifle and going to America, with a general purpose of compelling buffaloes to make his fortune.

I was usually at Hammersmith about half the week, and when I was at Hammersmith I haunted Richmond: whereof separately by-and-by. Herbert would often come to Hammersmith when I was there, and I think at those seasons his father would occasionally have some passing perception that the opening he was looking for, had not appeared yet. But in the general tumbling up of the family, his tumbling out in life somewhere, was a thing to transact itself somehow. In the mean time Mr. Pocket grew greyer, and tried oftener to lift himself out of his perplexities by the hair. While Mrs. Pocket tripped up the family with her footstool, read her book of dignities, lost her pocket-handkerchief, told us about her grandpapa, and taught the young idea how to shoot,[5] by shooting it into bed whenever it attracted her notice.

As I am now generalising a period of my life with the object of clearing the way before me, I can scarcely do so better than by at once completing the description of our usual manners and customs at Barnard's Inn.

We spent as much money as we could, and got as little for it as people could make up their minds to give us. We were always more or less miserable, and most of our acquaintance were in the same condition. There was a gay fiction among us that we were constantly enjoying ourselves, and a skeleton truth that we never did. To the best of my belief, our case was in the last aspect a rather common one.

Every morning, with an air ever new, Herbert went into the City to look about him. I often paid him a visit in the dark back-room in which he consorted with an ink-jar, a hat-peg, a coal-box, a string-box, an almanack, a desk and stool, and a ruler; and I do not remember that I ever saw him do anything else but look about him. If we all did what we undertake to do, as faithfully as Herbert did, we might live in a Republic of the Virtues.[6] He had nothing else to do, poor fellow, except at a certain hour of every afternoon to "go to

5. To sprout; that is, to develop. The phrase, popularly quoted to describe the organic growth and development of a child, appears in part 1 of James Thomson's poem "The Seasons" (1726–30), lines 1151–55: "Delightful task! to rear the tender thought, / To teach the young idea how to shoot, / To pour the fresh instruction o'er the mind, / To breathe the enlivening spirit, and to fix / The generous purpose in the glowing breast." The association of childrearing with the rearing of plants is recognized in the term "kindergarten," the preschool institution founded by the German educator Friedrich Froebel in 1837. Note also Pip's reference to the Newgate inmates as Wemmick's "plants" and related botanical metaphors in chapter 32. By the end of the eighteenth century, Thomson's lines had turned into the kind of stock phrase that young ladies, like the heroine of Jane Austen's *Northanger Abbey* (begun 1798), were expected to know by heart, as one of six "serviceable and soothing" quotations to fit all occasions.

6. The concept of the Republic of Virtues, formulated by Jean-Jacques Rousseau (1712–1778), became the rallying cry of the radical Jacobins during the French Revolution, chiefly Maximilien Robespierre (b. 1758) and Antoine de St. Just (b. 1767; both guillotined 1794). Robespierre, who appointed a secular "Supreme Being" to rule over a society governed by Virtue, announced in his state of the union address on May 7, 1794 (or 18 Floréal II) that "Immorality is the basis for despotism, just as surely as Virtue is the very essence of the Republic." In *A Tale of Two Cities*, Dickens frequently used phrases like this with mock-seriousness: his way of inflating a trivial domestic transaction with ideological bombast.

Lloyd's"[7]—in observance of a ceremony of seeing his principal, I think. He never did anything else in connexion with Lloyd's that I could find out, except come back again. When he felt his case unusually serious, and that he positively must find an opening, he would go on 'Change at the busy time, and walk in and out, in a kind of gloomy country dance figure, among the assembled magnates. "For," says Herbert to me, coming home to dinner on one of these special occasions, "I find the truth to be, Handel, that an opening won't come to one, but one must go to it——so I have been."

If we had been less attached to one another, I think we must have hated one another regularly every morning. I detested the chambers beyond ex-   10
pression at that period of repentance, and could not endure the sight of the Avenger's livery: which had a more expensive and a less remunerative appearance then, than at any other time in the four-and-twenty hours. As we got more and more into debt, breakfast became a hollower and hollower form, and, being on one occasion at breakfast-time threatened (by letter) with legal proceedings, "not unwholly unconnected," as my local paper might put it, "with jewellery," I went so far as to seize the Avenger by his blue collar and shake him off his feet—so that he was actually in the air, like a booted Cupid[8]—for presuming to suppose that we wanted a roll.

At certain times—meaning at uncertain times, for they depended on our   20
humour—I would say to Herbert, as if it were a remarkable discovery:

"My dear Herbert, we are getting on badly."

"My dear Handel," Herbert would say to me, in all sincerity, "if you will believe me, those very words were on my lips, by a strange coincidence."

"Then, Herbert," I would respond, "let us look into our affairs."

We always derived profound satisfaction from making an appointment for this purpose. I always thought this was business, this was the way to confront the thing, this was the way to take the foe by the throat. And I know Herbert thought so too.

We ordered something rather special for dinner, with a bottle of something   30
similarly out of the common way, in order that our minds might be fortified for the occasion, and we might come well up to the mark. Dinner over, we produced a bundle of pens, a copious supply of ink, and a goodly show of writing and blotting paper. For, there was something very comfortable in having plenty of stationery.

I would then take a sheet of paper, and write across the top of it, in a neat hand, the heading, "Memorandum of Pip's debts;" with Barnard's Inn and the date very carefully added. Herbert would also take a sheet of paper, and write across it with similar formalities, "Memorandum of Herbert's debts."

Each of us would then refer to a confused heap of papers at his side, which   40
had been thrown into drawers, worn into holes in pockets, half-burnt in lighting candles, stuck for weeks into the looking-glass, and otherwise damaged. The sound of our pens going, refreshed us exceedingly, insomuch that I sometimes found it difficult to distinguish between this edifying business pro-

---

7. The company of shipowners, merchants, and insurers that originated in Edward Lloyd's coffeehouse in Lombard Street about 1680 before moving its headquarters to the Royal Exchange, where Herbert expects to be "hatched" in chapter 22. Known chiefly as pioneering marine insurers, Lloyd's initiated every sort of insurance: hurricane, earthquake—and the life of Napoleon. Herbert works for one of Lloyd's underwriters.
8. The Roman god of love is usually pictured as a lively winged barebottomed young imp; as he flies about, anybody pierced by his arrow is instantly smitten.

ceeding and actually paying the money. In point of meritorious character, the two things seemed about equal.

When we had written a little while, I would ask Herbert how he got on? Herbert probably would have been scratching his head in a most rueful manner at the sight of his accumulating figures.

"They are mounting up, Handel," Herbert would say; "upon my life, they are mounting up."

"Be firm, Herbert," I would retort, plying my own pen with great assiduity. "Look the thing in the face. Look into your affairs. Stare them out of countenance." 10

"So I would, Handel, only they are staring *me* out of countenance."

However, my determined manner would have its effect, and Herbert would fall to work again. After a time, he would give up once more, on the plea that he had not got Cobbs's bill, or Lobbs's, or Nobbs's, as the case might be.

"Then, Herbert, estimate it; estimate it in round numbers, and put it down."

"What a fellow of resource you are!" my friend would reply, with admiration. "Really your business powers are very remarkable."

I thought so too. I established with myself on these occasions, the reputa- 20 tion of a first-rate man of business—prompt, decisive, energetic, clear, cool-headed. When I had got all my responsibilities down upon my list, I compared each with the bill, and ticked it off. My self-approval when I ticked an entry was quite a luxurious sensation. When I had no more ticks to make, I folded all my bills up uniformly, docketed each on the back, and tied the whole into a symmetrical bundle. Then, I did the same for Herbert (who modestly said he had not my administrative genius), and felt that I had brought his affairs into a focus for him.

My business habits had one other bright feature, which I called, "leaving a Margin." For example; supposing Herbert's debts to be one hundred and 30 sixty-four pounds four-and-two pence, I would say, "Leave a margin, and put them down at two hundred." Or supposing my own to be four times as much, I would leave a margin, and put them down at seven hundred. I had the highest opinion of the wisdom of this same Margin, but I am bound to acknowledge that on looking back, I deem it to have been an expensive device. For, we always ran into new debt immediately, to the full extent of the margin, and sometimes, in the sense of freedom and solvency it imparted, got pretty far on into another margin.

But there was a calm, a rest, a virtuous hush, consequent on these examinations of our affairs that gave me, for the time, an admirable opinion of 40 myself. Soothed by my exertions, my method, and Herbert's compliments, I would sit with his symmetrical bundle and my own on the table before me among the stationery, and feel like a Bank of some sort, rather than a private individual.

We shut our outer door on these solemn occasions, in order that we might not be interrupted. I had fallen into my serene state one evening, when we heard a letter dropped through the slit in the said door, and fall on the ground. "It's for you, Handel," said Herbert, going out and coming back with it, "and I hope there is nothing the matter." This was in allusion to its heavy black seal and border. 50

The letter was signed TRABB & CO., and its contents were simply, that I was an honoured sir, and that they begged to inform me that Mrs. J. Gargery had departed this life on Monday last, at twenty minutes past six in the evening, and that my attendance was requested at the interment on Monday next at three o'clock in the afternoon.

Chapter XXXV.

IT was the first time that a grave had opened in my road of life, and the gap it made in the smooth ground was wonderful. The figure of my sister in her chair by the kitchen fire, haunted me night and day. That the place could possibly be, without her, was something my mind seemed unable to compass; and whereas she had seldom or never been in my thoughts of late, I had now   10 the strangest ideas that she was coming towards me in the street, or that she would presently knock at the door. In my rooms too, with which she had never been at all associated, there was at once the blankness of death and a perpetual suggestion of the sound of her voice or the turn of her face or figure, as if she were still alive and had been often there.

Whatever my fortunes might have been, I could scarcely have recalled my sister with much tenderness. But I suppose there is a shock of regret which may exist without much tenderness. Under its influence (and perhaps to make up for the want of the softer feeling) I was seized with a violent indignation against the assailant from whom she had suffered so much; and I felt that on   20 sufficient proof I could have revengefully pursued Orlick, or any one else, to the last extremity.

Having written to Joe, to offer him consolation, and to assure him that I would come to the funeral, I passed the intermediate days in the curious state of mind I have glanced at. I went down early in the morning, and alighted at the Blue Boar in good time to walk over to the forge.

It was fine summer weather again, and, as I walked along, the times when I was a little helpless creature, and my sister did not spare me, vividly returned. But they returned with a gentle tone upon them, that softened even the edge of Tickler. For, now, the very breath of the beans and clover whispered to   30 my heart that the day must come when it would be well for my memory that others walking in the sunshine should be softened as they thought of me.

At last I came within sight of the house, and saw that Trabb and Co. had put in a funereal execution[1] and taken possession. Two dismally absurd persons, each ostentatiously exhibiting a crutch done up in a black bandage—as if that instrument could possibly communicate any comfort to anybody—were posted at the front door; and in one of them I recognised a postboy[2] discharged from the Boar for turning a young couple into a sawpit on their bridal morning, in consequence of intoxication rendering it necessary for him to ride his horse clasped round the neck with both arms. All the children of   40 the village, and most of the women, were admiring these sable warders and the closed windows of the house and forge; and as I came up, one of the two

---

1. Trabb & Co. have taken over the place, like sheriff's officers executing a court order to seize the household goods of a debtor who can't pay up.
2. Boy put in charge of looking after horses or employed as postilion on a coach—riding or guiding the near horse of a pair that pulls a post chaise without a regulation coachman (Guiliano/Collins).

warders (the postboy) knocked at the door—implying that I was far too much exhausted by grief, to have strength remaining to knock for myself.

Another sable warder (a carpenter, who had once eaten two geese for a wager) opened the door, and showed me into the best parlour. Here, Mr. Trabb had taken unto himself the best table, and had got all the leaves up, and was holding a kind of black Bazaar, with the aid of a quantity of black pins. At the moment of my arrival, he had just finished putting somebody's hat into black long-clothes, like an African baby; so he held out his hand for mine. But I, misled by the action, and confused by the occasion, shook hands with him with every testimony of warm affection.   10

Poor dear Joe, entangled in a little black cloak tied in a large bow under his chin, was seated apart at the upper end of the room; where, as chief mourner, he had evidently been stationed by Trabb. When I bent down and said to him, "Dear Joe, how are you?" he said, "Pip, old chap, you knowed her when she were a fine figure of a —— " and clasped my hand and said no more.

Biddy, looking very neat and modest in her black dress, went quietly here and there, and was very helpful. When I had spoken to Biddy, as I thought it not a time for talking I went and sat down near Joe, and there began to wonder in what part of the house it—she—my sister—was. The air of the 20 parlour being faint with the smell of sweet cake, I looked about for the table of refreshments; it was scarcely visible until one had got accustomed to the gloom, but there was a cut-up plum cake upon it, and there were cut-up oranges, and sandwiches, and biscuits, and two decanters that I knew very well as ornaments, but had never seen used in all my life: one full of port, and one of sherry. Standing at this table, I became conscious of the servile Pumblechook in a black cloak and several yards of hatband, who was alternately stuffing himself, and making obsequious movements to catch my attention. The moment he succeeded, he came over to me (breathing sherry and crumbs), and said in a subdued voice, "May I, dear sir?" and did. I then 30 descried Mr. and Mrs. Hubble; the last-named in a decent speechless paroxysm in a corner. We were all going to "follow," and were all in course of being tied up separately (by Trabb) into ridiculous bundles.[3]

"Which I meantersay, Pip," Joe whispered me, as we were being what Mr. Trabb called "formed" in the parlour, two and two—and it was dreadfully like a preparation for some grim kind of dance; "which I meantersay, sir, as I would in preference have carried her to the church myself, along with three or four friendly ones wot come to it with willing harts and arms, but it were considered wot the neighbours would look down on such and would be of opinions as it were wanting in respect."   40

"Pocket-handkerchiefs out, all!" cried Mr. Trabb at this point, in a depressed business-like voice. "Pocket-handkerchiefs out! We are ready!"

So, we all put our pocket-handkerchiefs to our faces, as if our noses were bleeding, and filed out two and two; Joe and I; Biddy and Pumblechook; Mr. and Mrs. Hubble. The remains of my poor sister had been brought round by the kitchen door; and, it being a point of Undertaking ceremony that the six

---

3. Dickens's mirth in funeral pomp and his distaste for it form a staple of his writings, from the early chapters of *Oliver Twist* to his Last Will. He compared a funeral procession to "an army of beetles," and in his Testament, executed on May 12, 1869, he "emphatically directed . . . that those who attend my funeral wear no scarf, cloak, black bow, long hat-band, or any other such revolting absurdity." His wearing informal clothes at Macaulay's funeral in 1859 was the talk of the town.

bearers must be stifled and blinded under a horrible black velvet housing[4] with a white border, the whole looked like a blind monster with twelve human legs, shuffling and blundering along, under the guidance of two keepers—the postboy and his comrade.

The neighbourhood, however, highly approved of these arrangements, and we were much admired as we went through the village; the more youthful and vigorous part of the community making dashes now and then to cut us off, and lying in wait to intercept us at points of vantage. At such times the more exuberant among them called out in an excited manner on our emergence round some corner of expectancy, "Here they come!" "Here they are!" and we were all but cheered. In this progress I was much annoyed by the abject Pumblechook, who, being behind me, persisted all the way as a delicate attention in arranging my streaming hatband and smoothing my cloak. My thoughts were further distracted by the excessive pride of Mr. and Mrs. Hubble, who were surpassingly conceited and vainglorious in being members of so distinguished a procession.

And now, the range of marshes lay clear before us, with the sails of the ships on the river growing out of it; and we went into the churchyard, close to the graves of my unknown parents, Philip Pirrip, late of this parish, and Also Georgiana, Wife of the Above. And there, my sister was laid quietly in the earth while the larks sang high above it, and the light wind strewed it with beautiful shadows of clouds and trees.

Of the conduct of the worldly-minded Pumblechook while this was doing, I desire to say no more than that it was all addressed to me; and that even when those noble passages were read which remind humanity how it brought nothing into the world and can take nothing out, and how it fleeth like a shadow and never continueth long in one stay,[5] I heard him cough a reservation of the case of a young gentleman who came unexpectedly into large property. When we got back, he had the hardihood to tell me that he wished my sister could have known I had done her so much honour, and to hint that she would have considered it reasonably purchased, at the price of her death. After that, he drank all the rest of the sherry, and Mr. Hubble drank the port, and the two talked (which I have since observed to be customary in such cases), as if they were of quite another race from the deceased, and were notoriously immortal. Finally, he went away with Mr. and Mrs. Hubble—to make an evening of it, I felt sure, and to tell the Jolly Bargemen that he was the founder of my fortunes and my earliest benefactor.

When they were all gone, and when Trabb and his men—but not his boy: I looked for him—had crammed their mummery into bags, and were gone too, the house felt wholesomer. Soon afterwards, Biddy, Joe, and I, had a cold dinner together; but we dined in the best parlour, not in the old kitchen, and Joe was so exceedingly particular what he did with his knife and fork and the salt-cellar and what not, that there was great restraint upon us. But after dinner, when I made him take his pipe, and when I had loitered with him about the forge, and when we sat down together on the great block of stone

---

4. Ornamental cloth covering for the casket—the cloth frequently falling over the pallbearers' heads. But it could be used for other decorative purposes, such as covering the backs of horses in mourning.
5. From the "Burial Service" in *The Book of Common Prayer.* The first, from 1 Timothy 6.7, "For we brought nothing into this world, and it is certain that we can take nothing out," is spoken by the minister at the entrance to the cemetery; the second, from Job 14.2, "he fleeth also as a shadow, and continueth not," is recited at the graveside.

outside it, we got on better. I noticed that after the funeral Joe changed his clothes so far, as to make a compromise between his Sunday dress and working dress: in which the dear fellow looked natural and like the Man he was.

He was very much pleased by my asking if I might sleep in my own little room, and I was pleased too; for I felt that I had done rather a great thing in making the request.

When the shadows of evening were closing in, I took an opportunity of getting into the garden with Biddy for a little talk.

"Biddy," said I, "I think you might have written to me about these sad matters."

"Do you, Mr. Pip?" said Biddy. "I should have written if I had thought that."

"Don't suppose that I mean to be unkind, Biddy, when I say I consider that you ought to have thought that."

"Do you, Mr. Pip?"

She was so quiet, and had such an orderly, good, and pretty way with her, that I did not like the thought of making her cry again. After looking a little at her downcast eyes, as she walked beside me, I gave up that point.

"I suppose it will be difficult for you to remain here now, Biddy dear?"

"Oh! I can't do so, Mr. Pip," said Biddy, in a tone of regret, but still of quiet conviction. "I have been speaking to Mrs. Hubble, and I am going to her to-morrow. I hope we shall be able to take some care of Mr. Gargery, together, until he settles down."

"How are you going to live, Biddy? If you want any mo——"

"How am I going to live?" repeated Biddy, striking in, with a momentary flush upon her face. "I'll tell you, Mr. Pip. I am going to try to get the place of mistress in the new school nearly finished here. I can be well recommended by all the neighbours, and I hope I can be industrious and patient, and teach myself while I teach others. You know, Mr. Pip," pursued Biddy, with a smile, as she raised her eyes to my face, "the new schools are not like the old,[6] but I learnt a good deal from you after that time, and have had time since then to improve."

"I think you would always improve, Biddy, under any circumstances."

"Ah! Except in my bad side of human nature," murmured Biddy.

It was not so much a reproach, as an irresistible thinking aloud. Well! I thought I would give up that point too. So, I walked a little further with Biddy, looking silently at her downcast eyes.

"I have not heard the particulars of my sister's death, Biddy."

"They are very slight, poor thing. She had been in one of her bad states— though they had got better of late, rather than worse—for four days, when she came out of it in the evening, just at tea-time, and said quite plainly, 'Joe.' As she had never said any word for a long while, I ran and fetched in Mr. Gargery from the forge. She made signs to me that she wanted him to sit down close to her, and wanted me to put her arms round his neck. So I put them round his neck, and she laid her head down on his shoulder quite content and satisfied. And so she presently said 'Joe' again, and once 'Pardon,'

---

6. By the time Dickens was writing, the Dame Schools were being replaced by state-run National Schools—though Dickens, in novels like *Hard Times* and *Our Mutual Friend*, bitterly attacked the new breed of teachers for lacking in imaginative sympathy what Wopsle's great-aunt lacked in high seriousness.

and once 'Pip.' And so she never lifted her head up any more, and it was just an hour later when we laid it down on her own bed, because we found she was gone."

Biddy cried; the darkening garden, and the lane, and the stars that were coming out, were blurred in my own sight.

"Nothing was ever discovered, Biddy?"

"Nothing."

"Do you know what is become of Orlick?"

"I should think from the colour of his clothes that he is working in the quarries."

"Of course you have seen him then?—Why are you looking at that dark tree in the lane?"

"I saw him there, on the night she died."

"That was not the last time either, Biddy?"

"No; I have seen him there, since we have been walking here.—It is of no use," said Biddy, laying her hand upon my arm as I was for running out, "you know I would not deceive you; he was not there a minute, and he is gone."

It revived my utmost indignation to find that she was still pursued by this fellow, and I felt inveterate against him. I told her so, and told her that I would spend any money or take any pains to drive him out of that country. By degrees she led me into more temperate talk, and she told me how Joe loved me, and how Joe never complained of anything—she didn't say, of me; she had no need; I knew what she meant—but ever did his duty in his way of life, with a strong hand, a quiet tongue, and a gentle heart.

"Indeed, it would be hard to say too much for him," said I; "and Biddy, we must often speak of these things, for of course I shall be often down here now. I am not going to leave poor Joe alone."

Biddy said never a single word.

"Biddy, don't you hear me?"

"Yes, Mr. Pip."

"Not to mention your calling me Mr. Pip—which appears to me to be in bad taste, Biddy—what do you mean?"

"What do I mean?" asked Biddy, timidly.

"Biddy," said I, in a virtuously self-asserting manner, "I must request to know what you mean by this?"

"By this?" said Biddy.

"Now, don't echo," I retorted. "You used not to echo, Biddy."

"Used not!" said Biddy. "O Mr. Pip! Used!"

Well! I rather thought I would give up that point too. After another silent turn in the garden, I fell back on the main position.

"Biddy," said I, "I made a remark respecting my coming down here often, to see Joe, which you received with a marked silence. Have the goodness, Biddy, to tell me why."

"Are you quite sure, then, that you WILL come to see him often?" asked Biddy, stopping in the narrow garden walk, and looking at me under the stars with a clear and honest eye.

"Oh dear me!" said I, as if I found myself compelled to give up Biddy in despair. "This really is a very bad side of human nature! Don't say any more, if you please, Biddy. This shocks me very much."

For which cogent reason I kept Biddy at a distance during supper, and, when I went up to my own old little room, took as stately a leave of her as I could, in my murmuring soul, deem reconcilable with the churchyard and the event of the day. As often as I was restless in the night, and that was every quarter of an hour, I reflected what an unkindness, what an injury, what an injustice, Biddy had done me.

Early in the morning, I was to go. Early in the morning, I was out, and, looking in, unseen, at one of the wooden windows of the forge. There I stood, for minutes, looking at Joe, already at work with a glow of health and strength upon his face that made it show as if the bright sun of the life in store for him were shining on it.

"Good-by, dear Joe!—No, don't wipe it off—for God's sake, give me your blackened hand!—I shall be down soon, and often."

"Never too soon, sir," said Joe, "and never too often, Pip!"

Biddy was waiting for me at the kitchen door, with a mug of new milk and a crust of bread. "Biddy," said I, when I gave her my hand at parting, "I am not angry, but I am hurt."

"No, don't be hurt," she pleaded quite pathetically; "let only me be hurt, if I have been ungenerous."

Once more, the mists were rising as I walked away. If they disclosed to me, as I suspect they did, that I should not come back, and that Biddy was quite right, all I can say is—they were quite right too.

Chapter XXXVI.

HERBERT and I went on from bad to worse, in the way of increasing our debts, looking into our affairs, leaving Margins, and the like exemplary transactions; and Time went on, whether or no, as he has a way of doing; and I came of age—in fulfilment of Herbert's prediction, that I should do so, before I knew where I was.

Herbert himself had come of age, eight months before me. As he had nothing else than his majority to come into, the event did not make a profound sensation in Barnard's Inn. But we had looked forward to my one-and-twentieth birthday, with a crowd of speculations and anticipations, for we had both considered that my guardian could hardly help saying something definite on that occasion.

I had taken care to have it well understood in Little Britain, when my birthday was. On the day before it, I received an official note from Wemmick, informing me that Mr. Jaggers would be glad if I would call upon him at five in the afternoon of the auspicious day. This convinced us that something great was to happen, and threw me into an unusual flutter when I repaired to my guardian's office, a model of punctuality.

In the outer office Wemmick offered me his congratulations, and incidentally rubbed the side of his nose with a folded piece of tissue-paper that I liked the look of. But he said nothing respecting it, and motioned me with a nod into my guardian's room. It was November, and my guardian was standing before his fire leaning his back against the chimney-piece, with his hands under his coat-tails.

"Well, Pip," said he, "I must call you Mr. Pip to-day. Congratulations, Mr. Pip."

We shook hands—he was always a remarkably short shaker—and I thanked him.

"Take a chair, Mr. Pip," said my guardian.

As I sat down, and he preserved his attitude and bent his brows at his boots, I felt at a disadvantage, which reminded me of that old time when I had been put upon a tombstone. The two ghastly casts on the shelf were not far from him, and their expression was as if they were making a stupid apoplectic attempt to attend to the conversation.

"Now my young friend," my guardian began, as if I were a witness in the box, "I am going to have a word or two with you."

"If you please, sir."

"What do you suppose," said Mr. Jaggers, bending forward to look at the ground, and then throwing his head back to look at the ceiling, "what do you suppose you are living at the rate of?"

"At the rate of, sir?"

"At," repeated Mr. Jaggers, still looking at the ceiling, "the—rate—of?" And then looked all round the room, and paused with his pocket-handkerchief in his hand, half way to his nose.

I had looked into my affairs so often, that I had thoroughly destroyed any slight notion I might ever have had of their bearings. Reluctantly, I confessed myself quite unable to answer the question. This reply seemed agreeable to Mr. Jaggers, who said, "I thought so!" and blew his nose with an air of satisfaction.

"Now, I have asked *you* a question, my friend," said Mr. Jaggers. "Have you anything to ask *me*?"

"Of course it would be a great relief to me to ask you several questions, sir; but I remember your prohibition."

"Ask one," said Mr. Jaggers.

"Is my benefactor to be made known to me to-day?"

"No. Ask another."

"Is that confidence to be imparted to me soon?"

"Waive that, a moment," said Mr. Jaggers, "and ask another."

I looked about me, but there appeared to be now no possible escape from the inquiry, "Have—I—anything to receive, sir?" On that, Mr. Jaggers said, triumphantly, "I thought we should come to it!" and called to Wemmick to give him that piece of paper. Wemmick appeared, handed it in, and disappeared.

"Now, Mr. Pip," said Mr. Jaggers, "attend, if you please. You have been drawing pretty freely here; your name occurs pretty often in Wemmick's cashbook; but you are in debt, of course?"

"I am afraid I must say yes, sir."

"You know you must say yes; don't you?" said Mr. Jaggers.

"Yes, sir."

"I don't ask you what you owe, because you don't know; and if you did know, you wouldn't tell me; you would say less. Yes, yes, my friend," cried Mr. Jaggers, waving his forefinger to stop me, as I made a show of protesting:

"it's likely enough that you think you wouldn't, but you would. You'll excuse me, but I know better than you. Now, take this piece of paper in your hand. You have got it? Very good. Now, unfold it and tell me what it is."

"This is a bank-note," said I, "for five hundred pounds."

"That is a bank-note," repeated Mr. Jaggers, "for five hundred pounds. And a very handsome sum of money too, I think. You consider it so?"

"How could I do otherwise!"

"Ah! But answer the question," said Mr. Jaggers.

"Undoubtedly."

"You consider it, undoubtedly, a handsome sum of money. Now, that hand- 10 some sum of money, Pip, is your own. It is a present to you on this day, in earnest of your expectations. And at the rate of that handsome sum of money per annum, and at no higher rate, you are to live until the donor of the whole appears. That is to say, you will now take your money affairs entirely into your own hands, and you will draw from Wemmick one hundred and twenty-five pounds per quarter, until you are in communication with the fountain-head, and no longer with the mere agent. As I have told you before, I am the mere agent. I execute my instructions, and I am paid for doing so. I think them injudicious, but I am not paid for giving any opinion on their merits."

I was beginning to express my gratitude to my benefactor for the great 20 liberality with which I was treated, when Mr. Jaggers stopped me. "I am not paid, Pip," said he, coolly, "to carry your words to any one;" and then gathered up his coat-tails, as he had gathered up the subject, and stood frowning at his boots as if he suspected them of designs against him.

After a pause, I hinted:

"There was a question just now, Mr. Jaggers, which you desired me to waive for a moment. I hope I am doing nothing wrong in asking it again?"

"What is it?" said he.

I might have known that he would never help me out; but it took me aback to have to shape the question afresh, as if it were quite new. "Is it likely," I 30 said, after hesitating, "that my patron, the fountain-head you have spoken of, Mr. Jaggers, will soon —— " there I delicately stopped.

"Will soon what?" said Mr. Jaggers. "That's no question as it stands, you know."

"Will soon come to London," said I, after casting about for a precise form of words, "or summon me anywhere else?"

"Now here," replied Mr. Jaggers, fixing me for the first time with his dark deep-set eyes, "we must revert to the evening when we first encountered one another in your village. What did I tell you then, Pip?"

"You told me, Mr. Jaggers, that it might be years hence when that person 40 appeared."

"Just so," said Mr. Jaggers, "that's my answer."

As we looked full at one another, I felt my breath come quicker in my strong desire to get something out of him. And as I felt that it came quicker, and as I felt that he saw that it came quicker, I felt that I had less chance than ever of getting anything out of him.

"Do you suppose it will still be years hence, Mr. Jaggers?"

Mr. Jaggers shook his head—not in negativing the question, but in alto-gether negativing the notion that he could anyhow be got to answer it—and the two horrible casts of the twitched faces looked, when my eyes strayed up 50 to them, as if they had come to a crisis in their suspended attention, and were going to sneeze.

"Come!" said Mr. Jaggers, warming the backs of his legs with the backs of his warmed hands, "I'll be plain with you, my friend Pip. That's a question I must not be asked. You'll understand that, better, when I tell you it's a question that might compromise *me*. Come! I'll go a little further with you; I'll say something more."

He bent down so low to frown at his boots, that he was able to rub the calves of his legs in the pause he made.

"When that person discloses," said Mr. Jaggers, straightening himself, "you   10
and that person will settle your own affairs. When that person discloses, my part in this business will cease and determine.[1] When that person discloses, it will not be necessary for me to know anything about it. And that's all I have got to say."

We looked at one another until I withdrew my eyes, and looked thoughtfully at the floor. From this last speech I derived the notion that Miss Havisham, for some reason or no reason, had not taken him into her confidence as to her designing me for Estella; that he resented this, and felt a jealousy about it; or that he really did object to that scheme, and would have nothing to do with it. When I raised my eyes again, I found that he had been shrewdly   20
looking at me all the time, and was doing so still.

"If that is all you have to say, sir," I remarked, "there can be nothing left for me to say."

He nodded assent, and pulled out his thief-dreaded watch, and asked me where I was going to dine? I replied at my own chambers, with Herbert. As a necessary sequence, I asked him if he would favour us with his company, and he promptly accepted the invitation. But he insisted on walking home with me, in order that I might make no extra preparation for him, and first he had a letter or two to write, and (of course) had his hands to wash. So, I said I would go into the outer office and talk to Wemmick.   30

The fact was, that when the five hundred pounds had come into my pocket, a thought had come into my head which had been often there before; and it appeared to me that Wemmick was a good person to advise with, concerning such thought.

He had already locked up his safe, and made preparations for going home. He had left his desk, brought out his two greasy office candlesticks and stood them in line with the snuffers on a slab near the door, ready to be extinguished; he had raked his fire low, put his hat and great-coat ready, and was beating himself all over the chest with his safe-key, as an athletic exercise after business.   40

"Mr. Wemmick," said I, "I want to ask your opinion. I am very desirous to serve a friend."

Wemmick tightened his post-office and shook his head, as if his opinion were dead against any fatal weakness of that sort.

"This friend," I pursued, "is trying to get on in commercial life, but has no money and finds it difficult and disheartening to make a beginning. Now, I want somehow to help him to a beginning."

"With money down?" said Wemmick, in a tone drier than any sawdust.

1. Legalese for "terminate."

"With *some* money down," I replied, for an uneasy remembrance shot across me of that symmetrical bundle of papers at home; "with *some* money down, and perhaps some anticipation of my expectations."

"Mr. Pip," said Wemmick, "I should like just to run over with you on my fingers, if you please, the names of the various bridges up as high as Chelsea Reach.[2] Let's see: there's London, one; Southwark, two; Blackfriars, three; Waterloo, four; Westminster, five; Vauxhall, six." He had checked off each bridge in its turn, with the handle of his safe-key on the palm of his hand. "There's as many as six, you see, to choose from."[3]

"I don't understand you," said I.

"Choose your bridge, Mr. Pip," returned Wemmick, "and take a walk upon your bridge, and pitch your money into the Thames over the centre arch of your bridge, and you know the end of it. Serve a friend with it, and you may know the end of it too—but it's a less pleasant and profitable end."

I could have posted a newspaper in his mouth, he made it so wide after saying this.

"This is very discouraging," said I.

"Meant to be," said Wemmick.

"Then is it your opinion," I inquired, with some little indignation, "that a man should never——"

"—Invest portable property in a friend?" said Wemmick. "Certainly he should not. Unless he wants to get rid of the friend—and then it becomes a question how much portable property it may be worth to get rid of him."

"And that," said I, "is your deliberate opinion, Mr. Wemmick?"

"That," he returned, "is my deliberate opinion in this office."

"Ah!" said I, pressing him, for I thought I saw him near a loophole here; "but would that be your opinion at Walworth?"

"Mr. Pip," he replied, with gravity, "Walworth is one place, and this office is another. Much as the Aged is one person, and Mr. Jaggers is another. They must not be confounded together. My Walworth sentiments must be taken at Walworth; none but my official sentiments can be taken in this office."

"Very well," said I, much relieved, "then I shall look you up at Walworth, you may depend upon it."

"Mr. Pip," he returned, "you will be welcome there, in a private and personal capacity."

We had held this conversation in a low voice, well knowing my guardian's ears to be the sharpest of the sharp. As he now appeared in his doorway, towelling his hands, Wemmick got on his great-coat and stood by to snuff out the candles. We all three went into the street together, and from the doorstep Wemmick turned his way, and Mr. Jaggers and I turned ours.

I could not help wishing more than once that evening, that Mr. Jaggers had had an Aged in Gerrard-street, or a Stinger, or a Something, or a Somebody, to unbend his brows a little. It was an uncomfortable consideration on a twenty-first birthday, that coming of age at all seemed hardly worth while

---

2. Stretch of the Thames now flanked by Chelsea Bridge and Albert Bridge, west of the great London Docks. A reach is a stretch of water lying between two bends, or as much of the river as can be taken in at one glance.

3. Counting from east to west. Two of the six bridges in Wemmick's roll call help loosely to date the action: Southwark, the newest, went up in 1819, and Old London Bridge gave way to New London Bridge on August 1, 1831—though it had been a-building since 1823. Westminster Bridge dates from 1750, Blackfriars from 1769, Vauxhall from 1816, Waterloo from 1817.

in such a guarded and suspicious world as he made of it. He was a thousand times better informed and cleverer than Wemmick, and yet I would a thousand times rather have had Wemmick to dinner. And Mr. Jaggers made not me alone intensely melancholy, because, after he was gone, Herbert said of himself, with his eyes fixed on the fire, that he thought he must have committed a felony and forgotten the details of it, he felt so dejected and guilty.

Chapter XXXVII.

DEEMING Sunday the best day for taking Mr. Wemmick's Walworth sentiments, I devoted the next ensuing Sunday afternoon to a pilgrimage to the Castle. On arriving before the battlements, I found the Union Jack flying and the drawbridge up; but undeterred by this show of defiance and resistance, I   10 rang at the gate, and was admitted in a most pacific manner by the Aged.

"My son, sir," said the old man, after securing the drawbridge, "rather had it in his mind that you might happen to drop in, and he left word that he would soon be home from his arternoon walk. He is very regular in his walks, is my son. Very regular in everything, is my son."

I nodded at the old gentleman as Wemmick himself might have nodded, and we went in and sat down by the fireside.

"You made acquaintance with my son, sir," said the old man, in his chirping way, while he warmed his hands at the blaze, "at his office, I expect?" I nodded. "Hah! I have heerd that my son is a wonderful hand at his business,   20 sir?" I nodded hard. "Yes; so they tell me. His business is the Law?" I nodded harder. "Which makes it more surprising in my son," said the old man, "for he was not brought up to the Law, but to the Wine-Coopering."[1]

Curious to know how the old gentleman stood informed concerning the reputation of Mr. Jaggers, I roared that name at him. He threw me into the greatest confusion by laughing heartily and replying in a very sprightly manner, "No, to be sure; you're right." And to this hour I have not the faintest notion what he meant, or what joke he thought I had made.

As I could not sit there nodding at him perpetually, without making some other attempt to interest him, I shouted an inquiry whether his own calling   30 in life had been "the Wine-Coopering." By dint of straining that term out of myself several times and tapping the old gentleman on the chest to associate it with him, I at last succeeded in making my meaning understood.

"No," said the old gentleman; "the warehousing, the warehousing. First, over yonder;" he appeared to mean up the chimney, but I believe he intended to refer me to Liverpool; "and then in the City of London here. However, having an infirmity—for I am hard of hearing, sir — "

I expressed in pantomime the greatest astonishment.

"—Yes, hard of hearing; having that infirmity coming upon me, my son he went into the Law, and he took charge of me, and he by little and little made   40 out this elegant and beautiful property. But returning to what you said, you know," pursued the old man, again laughing heartily, "what I say is, No to be sure; you're right."

I was modestly wondering whether my utmost ingenuity would have en-

---

1. The retail wine trade; else, making and repairing wine barrels.

abled me to say anything that would have amused him half as much as this imaginary pleasantry, when I was startled by a sudden click in the wall on one side of the chimney, and the ghostly tumbling open of a little wooden flap with "JOHN" upon it. The old man, following my eyes, cried with great triumph "My son's come home!" and we both went out to the drawbridge.

It was worth any money to see Wemmick waving a salute to me from the other side of the moat, when we might have shaken hands across it with the greatest ease. The Aged was so delighted to work the drawbridge, that I made no offer to assist him, but stood quiet until Wemmick had come across, and had presented me to Miss Skiffins: a lady by whom he was accompanied.   10

Miss Skiffins was of a wooden appearance, and was, like her escort, in the post-office branch of the service. She might have been some two or three years younger than Wemmick, and I judged her to stand possessed of portable property. The cut of her dress from the waist upward, both before and behind, made her figure very like a boy's kite; and I might have pronounced her gown a little too decidedly orange, and her gloves a little too intensely green. But she seemed to be a good sort of fellow, and showed a high regard for the Aged. I was not long in discovering that she was a frequent visitor at the Castle; for, on our going in, and my complimenting Wemmick on his inge-nious contrivance for announcing himself to the Aged, he begged me to give   20 my attention for a moment to the other side of the chimney, and disappeared. Presently another click came, and another little door tumbled open with "Miss Skiffins" on it; then Miss Skiffins shut up, and John tumbled open; then Miss Skiffins and John both tumbled open together, and finally shut up together. On Wemmick's return from working these mechanical appliances, I expressed the great admiration with which I regarded them, and he said, "Well you know, they're both pleasant and useful to the Aged. And by George, sir, it's a thing worth mentioning, that of all the people who come to this gate, the secret of those pulls is only known to the Aged, Miss Skiffins, and me!"   30

"And Mr. Wemmick made them," added Miss Skiffins, "with his own hands out of his own head."

While Miss Skiffins was taking off her bonnet (she retained her green gloves during the evening as an outward and visible sign that there was company),[2] Wemmick invited me to take a walk with him round the property, and see how the island looked in winter-time. Thinking that he did this to give me an opportunity of taking his Walworth sentiments, I seized the opportunity as soon as we were out of the Castle.

Having thought of the matter with care, I approached my subject as if I had never hinted at it before. I informed Wemmick that I was anxious in   40 behalf of Herbert Pocket, and I told him how we had first met, and how we had fought. I glanced at Herbert's home, and at his character, and at his having no means but such as he was dependent on his father for: those, uncertain and unpunctual. I alluded to the advantages I had derived in my first rawness and ignorance from his society, and I confessed that I feared I had but ill repaid them, and that he might have done better without me and my expectations. Keeping Miss Havisham in the background at a great dis-

---

2. From the "Catechism," a set of questions and answers about religious doctrine, in *The Book of Com-mon Prayer*: "An outward and visible sign of an inward and spiritual grace." Women wore gloves indoors in company in an effort to look genteel.

tance, I still hinted at the possibility of my having competed with him in his prospects, and at the certainty of his possessing a generous soul, and being far above any mean distrusts, retaliations, or designs. For all these reasons (I told Wemmick), and because he was my young companion and friend, and I had a great affection for him, I wished my own good fortune to reflect some rays upon him, and therefore I sought advice from Wemmick's experience and knowledge of men and affairs, how I could best try with my resources to help Herbert to some present income—say of a hundred a year, to keep him in good hope and heart—and gradually to buy him on to some small partnership. I begged Wemmick, in conclusion, to understand that my help must 10 always be rendered without Herbert's knowledge or suspicion, and that there was no one else in the world with whom I could advise. I wound up by laying my hand upon his shoulder, and saying, "I can't help confiding in you, though I know it must be troublesome to you; but that is your fault, in having ever brought me here."

Wemmick was silent for a little while, and then said, with a kind of start, "Well you know, Mr. Pip, I must tell you one thing. This is devilish good of you."

"Say you'll help me to be good then," said I.

"Ecod," replied Wemmick, shaking his head, "that's not my trade." 20

"Nor is this your trading-place," said I.

"You are right," he returned. "You hit the nail on the head. Mr. Pip, I'll put on my considering-cap, and I think all you want to do, may be done by degrees. Skiffins (that's her brother) is an accountant and agent. I'll look him up and go to work for you."

"I thank you ten thousand times."

"On the contrary," said he, "I thank you, for though we are strictly in our private and personal capacity, still it may be mentioned that there *are* Newgate cobwebs about, and it brushes them away."

After a little further conversation to the same effect we returned into the 30 Castle, where we found Miss Skiffins preparing tea. The responsible duty of making the toast was delegated to the Aged, and that excellent old gentleman was so intent upon it that he seemed to me in some danger of melting his eyes. It was no nominal meal that we were going to make, but a vigorous reality. The Aged prepared such a haystack of buttered toast, that I could scarcely see him over it as it simmered on an iron stand hooked on to the top-bar;[3] while Miss Skiffins brewed such a jorum[4] of tea that the pig in the back premises became strongly excited, and repeatedly expressed his desire to participate in the entertainment.

The flag had been struck and the gun had been fired, at the right moment 40 of time, and I felt as snugly cut off from the rest of Walworth as if the moat were thirty feet wide by as many deep. Nothing disturbed the tranquillity of the Castle, but the occasional tumbling open of John and Miss Skiffins: which little doors were a prey to some spasmodic infirmity that made me sympathetically uncomfortable until I got used to it. I inferred from the methodical nature of Miss Skiffins's arrangements that she made tea there every Sunday night; and I rather suspected that a classic brooch she wore, representing the

---

3. Unlike oysters, buttered toast was much more of a luxury 150 years ago than it is today.
4. Large bowl, or its contents, generally used for punch rather than tea; or here simply "such a lot of tea."

profile of an undesirable female with a very straight nose and a very new moon, was a piece of portable property that had been given her by Wemmick.

We ate the whole of the toast and drank tea in proportion, and it was delightful to see how warm and greasy we all got after it. The Aged especially, might have passed for some clean old chief of a savage tribe, just oiled. After a short pause of repose, Miss Skiffins—in the absence of the little servant who, it seemed, retired to the bosom of her family on Sunday afternoons—washed up the tea-things in a trifling lady-like amateur manner that compromised none of us. Then she put on her gloves again, and we drew round the fire, and Wemmick said, "Now Aged Parent, tip us the paper." 10

Wemmick explained to me while the Aged got his spectacles out, that this was according to custom, and that it gave the old gentleman infinite satisfaction to read the news aloud. "I won't offer an apology," said Wemmick, "for he isn't capable of many pleasures—am you, Aged P.?"

"All right, John, all right," returned the old man, seeing himself spoken to.

"Only tip him a nod every now and then when he looks off his paper," said Wemmick, "and he'll be as happy as a king. We are all attention, Aged One."

"All right, John, all right!" returned the cheerful old man: so busy and so pleased, that it really was quite charming. 20

The Aged's reading reminded me of the classes at Mr. Wopsle's great-aunt's, with the pleasanter peculiarity that it seemed to come through a key-hole. As he wanted the candles close to him, and as he was always on the verge of putting either his head or the newspaper into them, he required as much watching as a powder-mill.[5] But Wemmick was equally untiring and gentle in his vigilance, and the Aged read on, quite unconscious of his many rescues. Whenever he looked at us, we all expressed the greatest interest and amazement, and nodded until he resumed again.

As Wemmick and Miss Skiffins sat side by side, and as I sat in a shadowy corner, I observed a slow and gradual elongation of Mr. Wemmick's mouth, 30 powerfully suggestive of his slowly and gradually stealing his arm round Miss Skiffins's waist. In course of time I saw his hand appear on the other side of Miss Skiffins; but at that moment Miss Skiffins neatly stopped him with the green glove, unwound his arm again as if it were an article of dress, and with the greatest deliberation laid it on the table before her. Miss Skiffins's composure while she did this was one of the most remarkable sights I have ever seen, and if I could have thought the act consistent with abstraction of mind, I should have deemed that Miss Skiffins performed it mechanically.

By-and-by, I noticed Wemmick's arm beginning to disappear again, and gradually fading out of view. Shortly afterwards, his mouth began to widen 40 again. After an interval of suspense on my part that was quite enthralling and almost painful, I saw his hand appear on the other side of Miss Skiffins. Instantly, Miss Skiffins stopped it with the neatness of a placid boxer, took off that girdle or cestus[6] as before, and laid it on the table. Taking the table to represent the path of virtue, I am justified in stating that during the whole

---

5. Mill for making gunpowder.
6. Latin for "belt." "A marriage-girdle that of old times the Bride used to wear, and the Bridegroom unloosed on the Wedding-night" (OED). Specifically, Aphrodite's magic girdle, which gave any woman who wore it the power to arouse male desires. In Skiffins's day an ad for crinolines advised its readers: "Come, Venus, you may give your maid your cestus / For Crinoline in future will invest us."

time of the Aged's reading, Wemmick's arm was straying from the path of virtue and being recalled to it by Miss Skiffins.

At last, the Aged read himself into a light slumber. This was the time for Wemmick to produce a little kettle, a tray of glasses, and a black bottle with a porcelain-topped cork, representing some clerical dignitary of a rubicund and social aspect. With the aid of these appliances we all had something warm to drink: including the Aged, who was soon awake again. Miss Skiffins mixed, and I observed that she and Wemmick drank out of one glass. Of course I knew better than to offer to see Miss Skiffins home, and under the circumstances I thought I had best go first: which I did, taking a cordial leave 10 of the Aged, and having passed a pleasant evening.

Before a week was out, I received a note from Wemmick, dated Walworth, stating that he hoped he had made some advance in that matter appertaining to our private and personal capacities, and that he would be glad if I could come and see him again upon it. So, I went out to Walworth again, and yet again, and yet again, and I saw him by appointment in the City several times, but never held any communication with him on the subject in or near Little Britain. The upshot was that we found a worthy young merchant or shipping-broker, not long established in business, who wanted intelligent help, and who wanted capital, and who in due course of time and receipt would want 20 a partner. Between him and me, secret articles were signed of which Herbert was the subject, and I paid him half of my five hundred pounds down, and engaged for sundry other payments: some, to fall due at certain dates out of my income: some, contingent on my coming into my property. Miss Skiffins's brother conducted the negotiation; Wemmick pervaded it throughout, but never appeared in it.

The whole business was so cleverly managed that Herbert had not the least suspicion of my hand being in it. I never shall forget the radiant face with which he came home one afternoon, and told me, as a mighty piece of news, of his having fallen in with one Clarriker (the young merchant's name), and 30 of Clarriker's having shown an extraordinary inclination towards him, and of his belief that the opening had come at last. Day by day as his hopes grew stronger and his face brighter, he must have thought me a more and more affectionate friend, for I had the greatest difficulty in restraining my tears of triumph when I saw him so happy.

At length, the thing being done, and he having that day entered Clarriker's House, and he having talked to me for a whole evening in a flush of pleasure and success, I did really cry in good earnest when I went to bed, to think that my expectations had done some good to somebody.[7]

A great event in my life, the turning-point of my life, now opens on my 40 view. But before I proceed to narrate it, and before I pass on to all the changes it involved, I must give one chapter to Estella. It is not much to give to the theme that so long filled my heart.

★

7. See "A Note on Dickens's Working Plans," p. 475.

Chapter XXXVIII.

IF that staid old house near the Green at Richmond should ever come to be haunted when I am dead, it will be haunted, surely, by my ghost. O the many, many nights and days through which the unquiet spirit within me haunted that house when Estella lived there! Let my body be where it would, my spirit was always wandering, wandering, wandering, about that house.

The lady with whom Estella was placed, Mrs. Brandley by name, was a widow, with one daughter several years older than Estella. The mother looked young, and the daughter looked old; the mother's complexion was pink, and the daughter's was yellow; the mother set up for frivolity, and the daughter for theology. They were in what is called a good position, and visited, and were visited by, numbers of people. Little if any community of feeling subsisted between them and Estella, but the understanding was established that they were necessary to her, and that she was necessary to them. Mrs. Brandley had been a friend of Miss Havisham's before the time of her seclusion.

In Mrs. Brandley's house and out of Mrs. Brandley's house, I suffered every kind and degree of torture that Estella could cause me. The nature of my relations with her, which placed me on terms of familiarity without placing me on terms of favour, conduced to my distraction. She made use of me to tease other admirers, and she turned the very familiarity between herself and me, to the account of putting a constant slight on my devotion to her. If I had been her secretary, steward, half-brother, poor relation—if I had been a younger brother of her appointed husband—I could not have seemed to myself, further from my hopes when I was nearest to her. The privilege of calling her by her name and hearing her call me by mine, became under the circumstances an aggravation of my trials; and while I think it likely that it almost maddened her other lovers, I know too certainly that it almost maddened me.

She had admirers without end. No doubt my jealousy made an admirer of every one who went near her; but there were more than enough of them without that.

I saw her often at Richmond, I heard of her often in town, and I used often to take her and the Brandleys on the water; there were pic-nics, fête days,[1] plays, operas, concerts, parties, all sorts of pleasures, through which I pursued her—and they were all miseries to me. I never had one hour's happiness in her society, and yet my mind all round the four-and-twenty hours was harping on the happiness of having her with me unto death.

Throughout this part of our intercourse—and it lasted, as will presently be seen, for what I then thought a long time—she habitually reverted to that tone which expressed that our association was forced upon us. There were other times when she would come to a sudden check in this tone and in all her many tones, and would seem to pity me.

"Pip, Pip," she said one evening, coming to such a check, when we sat apart at a darkening window of the house in Richmond; "will you never take warning?"

"Of what?"

"Of me."

---

1. Literally, "feast days" or festival days, often birthday celebrations; here probably outdoor entertainment. Richmond remains a favorite spot for boating excursions.

"Warning not to be attracted by you, do you mean, Estella?"

"Do I mean! If you don't know what I mean, you are blind."

I should have replied that Love was commonly reputed blind, but for the reason that I always was restrained—and this was not the least of my miseries—by a feeling that it was ungenerous to press myself upon her, when she knew that she could not choose but obey Miss Havisham. My dread always was, that this knowledge on her part laid me under a grave disadvantage with her pride, and made me the subject of a rebellious struggle in her bosom.

"At any rate," said I, "I have no warning given me just now, for you wrote 10
to me to come to you, this time."

"That's true," said Estella, with a cold careless smile that always chilled me.

After looking at the twilight without, for a little while, she went on to say:

"The time has come round when Miss Havisham wishes to have me for a day at Satis. You are to take me there, and bring me back, if you will. She would rather I did not travel alone, and objects to receiving my maid, for she has a sensitive horror of being talked of by such people. Can you take me?"

"Can I take you, Estella!"

"You can then? The day after to-morrow, if you please. You are to pay all 20
charges out of my purse. You hear the condition of your going?"

"And must obey," said I.

This was all the preparation I received for that visit, or for others like it: Miss Havisham never wrote to me, nor had I ever so much as seen her handwriting. We went down on the next day but one, and we found her in the room where I had first beheld her, and it is needless to add that there was no change in Satis House.

She was even more dreadfully fond of Estella than she had been when I last saw them together; I repeat the word advisedly, for there was something positively dreadful in the energy of her looks and embraces. She hung upon 30
Estella's beauty, hung upon her words, hung upon her gestures, and sat mumbling her own trembling fingers while she looked at her, as though she were devouring the beautiful creature she had reared.[2]

From Estella she looked at me, with a searching glance that seemed to pry into my heart and probe its wounds. "How does she use you, Pip; how does she use you?" she asked me again, with her witch-like eagerness, even in Estella's hearing. But when we sat by her flickering fire at night, she was most weird; for then, keeping Estella's hand drawn through her arm and clutched in her own hand, she extorted from her, by dint of referring back to what Estella had told her in her regular letters, the names and conditions of the 40
men whom she had fascinated; and as Miss Havisham dwelt upon this roll, with the intensity of a mind mortally hurt and diseased, she sat with her other hand on her crutched stick, and her chin on that, and her wan bright eyes glaring at me, a very spectre.

I saw in this, wretched though it made me, and bitter the sense of dependence and even of degradation that it awakened,—I saw in this, that Estella was set to wreak Miss Havisham's revenge on men, and that she was not

2. Gobbling up your relatives seems to run in the Pocket family: Camilla alludes to the same hobby in chapter 11. "Mumbling her . . . fingers": chewing or gnawing at her fingers, as if with toothless gums.

to be given to me until she had gratified it for a term. I saw in this, a reason for her being beforehand assigned to me. Sending her out to attract and torment and do mischief, Miss Havisham sent her with the malicious assurance that she was beyond the reach of all admirers, and that all who staked upon that cast were secured to lose. I saw in this, that I, too, was tormented by a perversion of ingenuity, even while the prize was reserved for me. I saw in this, the reason for my being staved off so long,[3] and the reason for my late guardian's declining to commit himself to the formal knowledge of such a scheme. In a word, I saw in this, Miss Havisham as I had her then and there before my eyes, and always had had her before my eyes; and I saw in this the distinct shadow of the darkened and unhealthy house in which her life was hidden from the sun.

The candles that lighted that room of hers were placed in sconces[4] on the wall. They were high from the ground, and they burnt with the steady dulness of artificial light in air that is seldom renewed. As I looked round at them, and at the pale gloom they made, and at the stopped clock, and at the withered articles of bridal dress upon the table and the ground, and at her own awful figure with its ghostly reflection thrown large by the fire upon the ceiling and the wall, I saw in everything the construction that my mind had come to, repeated and thrown back to me. My thoughts passed into the great room across the landing where the table was spread, and I saw it written, as it were, in the falls of the cobwebs from the centre-piece, in the crawlings of the spiders on the cloth, in the tracks of the mice as they betook their little quickened hearts behind the panels, and in the gropings and pausings of the beetles on the floor.

It happened on the occasion of this visit that some sharp words arose between Estella and Miss Havisham. It was the first time I had ever seen them opposed.

We were seated by the fire as just now described, and Miss Havisham still had Estella's arm drawn through her own, and still clutched Estella's hand in hers, when Estella gradually began to detach herself. She had shown a proud impatience more than once before, and had rather endured that fierce affection than accepted or returned it.

"What!" said Miss Havisham, flashing her eyes upon her, "are you tired of me?"

"Only a little tired of myself," replied Estella, disengaging her arm, and moving to the great chimney-piece, where she stood looking down at the fire.

"Speak the truth, you ingrate!" cried Miss Havisham, passionately striking her stick upon the floor; "you are tired of me."

Estella looked at her with perfect composure, and again looked down at the fire. Her graceful figure and her beautiful face expressed a self-possessed indifference to the wild heat of the other, that was almost cruel.

"You stock and stone!" exclaimed Miss Havisham. "You cold, cold heart!"

"What?" said Estella, preserving her attitude of indifference as she leaned against the great chimney-piece and only moving her eyes; "do you reproach me for being cold? You?"

"Are you not?" was the fierce retort.

3. Put off.
4. Wall brackets.

"You should know," said Estella. "I am what you have made me. Take all the praise, take all the blame; take all the success, take all the failure; in short, take me."

"O, look at her, look at her!" cried Miss Havisham, bitterly. "Look at her, so hard and thankless, on the hearth where she was reared! Where I took her into this wretched breast when it was first bleeding from its stabs, and where I have lavished years of tenderness upon her!"

"At least I was no party to the compact," said Estella, "for if I could walk and speak, when it was made, it was as much as I could do. But what would you have? You have been very good to me, and I owe everything to you. What would you have?" 10

"Love," replied the other.

"You have it."

"I have not," said Miss Havisham.

"Mother by adoption," retorted Estella, never departing from the easy grace of her attitude, never raising her voice as the other did, never yielding either to anger or tenderness, "Mother by adoption, I have said that I owe everything to you. All I possess is freely yours. All that you have given me, is at your command to have again. Beyond that, I have nothing. And if you ask me to give you what you never gave me, my gratitude and duty cannot do im- 20 possibilities."

"Did I never give her love!" cried Miss Havisham, turning wildly to me. "Did I never give her a burning love, inseparable from jealousy at all times, and from sharp pain, while she speaks thus to me! Let her call me mad, let her call me mad!"

"Why should I call you mad," returned Estella, "I, of all people? Does any one live, who knows what set purposes you have, half as well as I do? Does any one live, who knows what a steady memory you have, half as well as I do? I, who have sat on this same hearth on the little stool that is even now beside you there, learning your lessons and looking up into your face, when 30 your face was strange and frightened me!"

"Soon forgotten!" moaned Miss Havisham. "Times soon forgotten!"

"No, not forgotten," retorted Estella. "Not forgotten, but treasured up in my memory. When have you found me false to your teaching? When have you found me unmindful of your lessons? When have you found me giving admission here," she touched her bosom with her hand, "to anything that you excluded? Be just to me."

"So proud, so proud!" moaned Miss Havisham, pushing away her grey hair with both her hands.

"Who taught me to be proud?" returned Estella. "Who praised me when 40 I learnt my lesson?"

"So hard, so hard!" moaned Miss Havisham, with her former action.

"Who taught me to be hard?" returned Estella. "Who praised me when I learnt my lesson?"

"But to be proud and hard to *me!*" Miss Havisham quite shrieked, as she stretched out her arms. "Estella, Estella, Estella, to be proud and hard to *me!*"

Estella looked at her for a moment with a kind of calm wonder, but was not otherwise disturbed; when the moment was past she looked down at the fire again.

"I cannot think," said Estella, raising her eyes after a silence, "why you 50 should be so unreasonable when I come to see you after a separation. I have never forgotten your wrongs and their causes. I have never been unfaithful to you or your schooling. I have never shown any weakness that I can charge myself with."

"Would it be weakness to return my love?" exclaimed Miss Havisham. "But yes, yes, she would call it so!"

"I begin to think," said Estella, in a musing way, after another moment of calm wonder, "that I almost understand how this comes about. If you had brought up your adopted daughter wholly in the dark confinement of these rooms, and had never let her know that there was such a thing as the daylight 10 by which she has never once seen your face—if you had done that, and then, for a purpose had wanted her to understand the daylight and know all about it, you would have been disappointed and angry?"

Miss Havisham, with her head in her hands, sat making a low moaning, and swaying herself on her chair, but gave no answer.

"Or," said Estella, "—which is a nearer case—if you had taught her, from the dawn of her intelligence, with your utmost energy and might, that there was such a thing as daylight, but that it was made to be her enemy and destroyer, and she must always turn against it, for it had blighted you and would else blight her;—if you had done this, and then, for a purpose, had 20 wanted her to take naturally to the daylight and she could not do it, you would have been disappointed and angry?"

Miss Havisham sat listening (or it seemed so, for I could not see her face), but still made no answer.

"So," said Estella, "I must be taken as I have been made. The success is not mine, the failure is not mine, but the two together make me."

Miss Havisham had settled down, I hardly knew how, upon the floor, among the faded bridal relics with which it was strewn. I took advantage of the moment—I had sought one from the first—to leave the room, after be- seeching Estella's attention to her, with a movement of my hand. When I 30 left, Estella was yet standing by the great chimney-piece, just as she had stood throughout. Miss Havisham's grey hair was all adrift upon the ground, among the other bridal wrecks, and was a miserable sight to see.

It was with a depressed heart that I walked in the starlight for an hour and more, about the court-yard, and about the brewery, and about the ruined garden. When I at last took courage to return to the room, I found Estella sitting at Miss Havisham's knee, taking up some stitches in one of those old articles of dress that were dropping to pieces, and of which I have often been reminded since by the faded tatters of old banners that I have seen hanging up in cathedrals.[5] Afterwards, Estella and I played at cards, as of yore—only 40 we were skilful now, and played French games[6]—and so the evening wore away, and I went to bed.

I lay in that separate building across the court-yard. It was the first time I had ever lain down to rest in Satis House, and sleep refused to come near me. A thousand Miss Havishams haunted me. She was on this side of my pillow, on that, at the head of the bed, at the foot, behind the half-opened

5. Reference to the old custom of hanging up military banners in churches, either for safekeeping or as trophies of victory.
6. In Pip's day the English upper classes amused themselves by imitating French pastimes, including their card games. Pip and Estella have long since graduated from Beggar My Neighbour to imports like écarté, ombre, piquet, and vingt-et-un.

door of the dressing-room, in the dressing-room, in the room overhead, in the room beneath—everywhere. At last, when the night was slow to creep on towards two o'clock, I felt that I absolutely could no longer bear the place as a place to lie down in, and that I must get up. I therefore got up and put on my clothes, and went out across the yard into the long stone passage, design-ing to gain the outer court-yard and walk there for the relief of my mind. But I was no sooner in the passage than I extinguished my candle; for, I saw Miss Havisham going along it in a ghostly manner, making a low cry. I followed her at a distance, and saw her go up the staircase. She carried a bare candle in her hand, which she had probably taken from one of the sconces in her own room, and was a most unearthly object by its light. Standing at the bottom of the staircase, I felt the mildewed air of the feast-chamber, without seeing her open the door, and I heard her walking there, and so across into her own room, and so across again into that, never ceasing the low cry. After a time, I tried in the dark both to get out, and to go back, but I could do neither until some streaks of day strayed in and showed me where to lay my hands. During the whole interval, whenever I went to the bottom of the staircase, I heard her footstep, saw her candle pass above, and heard her ceaseless low cry.

Before we left next day, there was no revival of the difference between her and Estella, nor was it ever revived on any similar occasion; and there were four similar occasions, to the best of my remembrance. Nor, did Miss Hav-isham's manner towards Estella in anywise change, except that I believed it to have something like fear infused among its former characteristics.

It is impossible to turn this leaf of my life, without putting Bentley Drummle's name upon it; or I would, very gladly.

On a certain occasion when the Finches were assembled in force, and when good feeling was being promoted in the usual manner by nobody's agreeing with anybody else, the presiding Finch called the Grove to order, forasmuch as Mr. Drummle had not yet toasted a lady; which, according to the solemn constitution of the society, it was the brute's turn to do that day. I thought I saw him leer in an ugly way at me while the decanters were going round, but as there was no love lost between us, that might easily be. What was my indignant surprise when he called upon the company to pledge him to "Estella!"

"Estella who?" said I.

"Never you mind," retorted Drummle.

"Estella of where?" said I. "You are bound to say of where." Which he was, as a Finch.

"Of Richmond, gentlemen," said Drummle, putting me out of the ques-tion, "and a peerless beauty."

Much he knew about peerless beauties, a mean miserable idiot! I whispered Herbert.

"I know that lady," said Herbert, across the table, when the toast had been honoured.

"*Do* you?" said Drummle.

"And so do I," I added, with a scarlet face.

"*Do* you?" said Drummle. "*Oh*, Lord!"

This was the only retort—except glass or crockery—that the heavy creature was capable of making; but I became as highly incensed by it as if it had been barbed with wit,[7] and I immediately rose in my place and said that I could not but regard it as being like the honourable Finch's impudence to come down to that Grove—we always talked about coming down to that Grove, as a neat Parliamentary turn of expression[8]—down to that Grove, proposing a lady of whom he knew nothing. Mr. Drummle upon this, starting up, demanded what I meant by that? Whereupon, I made him the extreme reply that I believed he knew where I was to be found.[9]

Whether it was possible in a Christian country to get on without blood, after this, was a question on which the Finches were divided. The debate upon it grew so lively indeed, that at least six more honourable members told six more, during the discussion, that they believed *they* knew where *they* were to be found. However, it was decided at last (the Grove being a Court of Honour) that if Mr. Drummle would bring never so slight a certificate from the lady, importing that he had the honour of her acquaintance, Mr. Pip must express his regret, as a gentleman and a Finch, for "having been betrayed into a warmth which." Next day was appointed for the production (lest our honour should take cold from delay), and next day Drummle appeared with a polite little avowal in Estella's hand, that she had had the honour of dancing with him several times. This left me no course but to regret that I had been "betrayed into a warmth which," and on the whole to repudiate, as untenable, the idea that I was to be found anywhere. Drummle and I then sat snorting at one another for an hour, while the Grove engaged in indiscriminate contradiction, and finally the promotion of good feeling was declared to have gone ahead at an amazing rate.

I tell this lightly, but it was no light thing to me. For, I cannot adequately express what pain it gave me to think that Estella should show any favour to a contemptible, clumsy, sulky booby, so very far below the average. To the present moment, I believe it to have been referable to some pure fire of generosity and disinterestedness in my love for her, that I could not endure the thought of her stooping to that hound. No doubt I should have been miserable whomsoever she had favoured; but a worthier object would have caused me a different kind and degree of distress.

It was easy for me to find out, and I did soon find out, that Drummle had begun to follow her closely, and that she allowed him to do it. A little while, and he was always in pursuit of her, and he and I crossed one another every day. He held on, in a dull persistent way, and Estella held him on; now with encouragement, now with discouragement, now almost flattering him, now openly despising him, now knowing him very well, now scarcely remembering who he was.

The Spider, as Mr. Jaggers had called him, was used to lying in wait, however, and had the patience of his tribe. Added to that, he had a blockhead confidence in his money and in his family greatness, which sometimes did him good service—almost taking the place of concentration and determined

7. "And half mistrustful of her beauty's store, / She barbs with wit those darts too keen before." From "A Portrait," the dedicatory verses of Sheridan's comedy *The School for Scandal* (1777), some sixty rhymed couplets in which he totes up the graces of Frances Anne Lady Crewe, one of the famed beauties of the day and a collector of the political and artistic jet set.
8. Members of Parliament still speak of "coming down to this house"—the House of Commons. "Why," Dickens goes off, "must an honourable gentleman always '*come down*' to this house? Why can't he sometimes 'come up'—like a horse—or 'come in' like a man? ("A Few Conventionalities," *Household Words*, June 28, 1851).
9. Phrase used to challenge an opponent to a duel.

purpose. So, the Spider, doggedly watching Estella, outwatched many brighter insects, and would often uncoil himself and drop at the right nick of time.

At a certain Assembly Ball at Richmond (there used to be Assembly Balls[1] at most places then), where Estella had outshone all other beauties, this blundering Drummle so hung about her, and with so much toleration on her part, that I resolved to speak to her concerning him. I took the next opportunity: which was when she was waiting for Mrs. Brandley to take her home, and was sitting apart among some flowers, ready to go. I was with her, for I almost always accompanied them to and from such places.   10

"Are you tired, Estella?"

"Rather, Pip."

"You should be."

"Say rather, I should not be; for I have my letter to Satis House to write, before I go to sleep."

"Recounting to-night's triumph?" said I. "Surely a very poor one, Estella."

"What do you mean? I didn't know there had been any."

"Estella," said I, "do look at that fellow in the corner yonder, who is looking over here at us."

"Why should I look at him?" returned Estella, with her eyes on me instead.   20 "What is there in that fellow in the corner yonder—to use your words—that I need look at?"

"Indeed, that is the very question I want to ask you," said I. "For he has been hovering about you all night."

"Moths, and all sorts of ugly creatures," replied Estella, with a glance towards him, "hover about a lighted candle. Can the candle help it?"

"No," I returned; "but cannot the Estella help it?"

"Well!" said she, laughing, after a moment, "perhaps. Yes. Anything you like."

"But, Estella, do hear me speak. It makes me wretched that you should   30 encourage a man so generally despised as Drummle. You know he is despised."

"Well?" said she.

"You know he is as ungainly within, as without. A deficient, ill-tempered, lowering, stupid fellow."

"Well?" said she.

"You know he has nothing to recommend him but money, and a ridiculous roll of addle-headed predecessors; now, don't you?"

"Well?" said she again; and each time she said it, she opened her lovely eyes the wider.   40

To overcome the difficulty of getting past that monosyllable, I took it from her, and said, repeating it with emphasis, "Well! Then, that is why it makes me wretched."

Now, if I could have believed that she favoured Drummle with any idea of making me—me—wretched, I should have been in better heart about it; but in that habitual way of hers, she put me so entirely out of the question, that I could believe nothing of the kind.

1. Fashionable public balls frequented by the upper and upper-middle classes during the late eighteenth century and the Regency. Among academics, inevitably associated with Jane Austen.

"Pip," said Estella, casting her glance over the room, "don't be foolish about its effect on you. It may have its effect on others, and may be meant to have. It's not worth discussing."

"Yes it is," said I, "because I cannot bear that people should say, 'she throws away her graces and attractions on a mere boor, the lowest in the crowd.' "

"I can bear it," said Estella.

"Oh! don't be so proud, Estella, and so inflexible."

"Calls me proud and inflexible in this breath!" said Estella, opening her hands. "And in his last breath reproached me for stooping to a boor!"

"There is no doubt you do," said I, something hurriedly, "for I have seen 10 you give him looks and smiles this very night, such as you never give to— me."

"Do you want me then," said Estella, turning suddenly with a fixed and serious, if not angry, look, "to deceive and entrap you?"

"Do you deceive and entrap him, Estella?"

"Yes, and many others—all of them but you. Here is Mrs. Brandley. I'll say no more."

And now that I have given the one chapter to the theme that so filled my heart, and so often made it ache and ache again, I pass on, unhindered, to the event that had impended over me longer yet; the event that had begun 20 to be prepared for, before I knew that the world held Estella, and in the days when her baby intelligence was receiving its first distortions from Miss Havisham's wasting hands.

In the Eastern story, the heavy slab that was to fall on the bed of state in the flush of conquest was slowly wrought out of the quarry, the tunnel for the rope to hold it in its place was slowly carried through the leagues of rock, the slab was slowly raised and fitted in the roof, the rope was rove[2] to it and slowly taken through the miles of hollow to the great iron ring. All being made ready with much labour, and the hour come, the sultan was aroused in the dead of the night, and the sharpened axe that was to sever the rope 30 from the great iron ring was put into his hand, and he struck with it, and the rope parted and rushed away, and the ceiling fell. So, in my case; all the work, near and afar, that tended to the end, had been accomplished; and in an instant the blow was struck, and the roof of my stronghold dropped upon me.[3]

★

2. To reeve, or reef, is to pass a rope through or around a block or pulley. (But Guiliano/Collins, who cite it as the past participle of the verb "to rive"—to fix tightly around the object—find no sanction for Dickens's usage in the OED; one of Dickens's rare verbal lapses.)
3. Pip summarizes the story "The Enchanters, or, Misnar the Sultan of India," no. 6 in *The Tales of the Genii, or The Delightful Lessons of Horan, the Son of Asmar,* a collection of stories originally palmed off—in the heyday of the Oriental craze—as a translation from the Persian, but in fact written and published a year before his death by the Stepney-born Reverend James Ridley (born 1736). Two sorcerers have long hatched the Sultan's death. To trap them, a stone slab has been suspended over the royal coach; Misnar, defeated in battle by the Enchanters, is led to a cavern in a distant part of the sultanate and advised by his vizier, Horan, to sever a rope. This has been wired so to speak through miles of tunnel to the slab over the royal divan, on which the Enchanters are sleeping off their victorious battle fatigue, and the slab crushes *them.* The point is that Pip, like the Enchanters, is struck down when he least expects to be, at the height of his fortunes. Forty years earlier, the story inspired Dickens to compose, at age ten, his "lost tragedy," *Misnar, the Sultan of India.*

Chapter XXXIX.

I was three-and-twenty years of age. Not another word had I heard to enlighten me on the subject of my expectations, and my twenty-third birthday was a week gone. We had left Barnard's Inn more than a year, and lived in the Temple. Our chambers were in Garden-court, down by the river.[1]

Mr. Pocket and I had for some time parted company as to our original relations, though we continued on the best terms. Notwithstanding my inability to settle to anything—which I hope arose out of the restless and incomplete tenure on which I held my means—I had a taste for reading, and read regularly so many hours a day. That matter of Herbert's was still progressing, and everything with me was as I have brought it down to the close of the last chapter.

Business had taken Herbert on a journey to Marseilles. I was alone, and had a dull sense of being alone. Dispirited and anxious, long hoping that tomorrow or next week would clear my way, and long disappointed, I sadly missed the cheerful face and ready response of my friend.

It was wretched weather; stormy and wet, stormy and wet; and mud, mud, mud, deep in all the streets. Day after day, a vast heavy veil had been driving over London from the East, and it drove still, as if in the East there were an Eternity of cloud and wind. So furious had been the gusts, that high buildings in town had had the lead stripped off their roofs; and in the country, trees had been torn up, and sails of windmills carried away; and gloomy accounts had come in from the coast, of shipwreck and death. Violent blasts of rain had accompanied these rages of wind, and the day just closed as I sat down to read had been the worst of all.

Alterations have been made in that part of the Temple[2] since that time, and it has not now so lonely a character as it had then, nor is it so exposed to the river. We lived at the top of the last house, and the wind rushing up the river shook the house that night, like discharges of cannon, or breakings of a sea. When the rain came with it and dashed against the windows, I thought, raising my eyes to them as they rocked, that I might have fancied myself in a storm-beaten lighthouse. Occasionally, the smoke came rolling down the chimney as though it could not bear to go out into such a night; and when I set the doors open and looked down the staircase, the staircase lamps were blown out; and when I shaded my face with my hands and looked through the black windows (opening them ever so little, was out of the question in the teeth of such wind and rain) I saw that the lamps in the court were blown out, and that the lamps on the bridges and the shore were shud-

---

1. The Temple comprises two of the four Inns of Court, Middle Temple and Inner Temple, which are entitled to admit candidates to the bar once they have served their apprenticeship at the Inn of Chancery affiliated with it (see p. 134, n. 5). Named for the Knights Templar, who owned the property on which the Temple is built, the area (it extends from the Thames halfway toward Fleet Street) has been a domicile for lawyers and law students since the fourteenth century. The two Inns of Court date from 1501 and 1505, the Inner Temple occupying the eastern, the Middle Temple the western half of the grounds. Both lie sufficiently close to the river to serve essential narrative purposes later on.
2. The Victoria Embankment, the broad riverside road running along the north shore of the Thames from Westminster Bridge to Blackfriars Bridge, was not built until 1864–70; so the changes no doubt refer to alterations within Garden Court in 1830. The Embankment would have impeded virtually all direct access from Garden Court to the Thames.

dering, and that the coal fires in barges on the river were being carried away before the wind like red-hot splashes in the rain.

I read with my watch upon the table, purposing to close my book at eleven o'clock. As I shut it, Saint Paul's, and all the many church-clocks in the City—some leading, some accompanying, some following—struck that hour. The sound was curiously flawed by the wind; and I was listening, and thinking how the wind assailed it and tore it, when I heard a footstep on the stair.

What nervous folly made me start, and awfully connect it with the footstep of my dead sister, matters not. It was past in a moment, and I listened again, and heard the footstep stumble in coming on. Remembering then that the staircase-lights were blown out, I took up my reading-lamp and went out to the stair-head. Whoever was below had stopped on seeing my lamp, for all was quiet.

"There is some one down there, is there not?" I called out, looking down.

"Yes," said a voice from the darkness beneath.

"What floor do you want?"

"The top. Mr. Pip."

"That is my name.—There is nothing the matter?"

"Nothing the matter," returned the voice. And the man came on.

I stood with my lamp held out over the stair-rail, and he came slowly within its light. It was a shaded lamp, to shine upon a book, and its circle of light was very contracted; so that he was in it for a mere instant, and then out of it. In the instant, I had seen a face that was strange to me, looking up at me with an incomprehensible air of being touched and pleased by the sight of me.

Moving the lamp as the man moved, I made out that he was substantially dressed, but roughly: like a voyager by sea. That he had long iron grey hair. That his age was about sixty. That he was a muscular man, strong on his legs, and that he was browned and hardened by exposure to weather. As he ascended the last stair or two, and the light of my lamp included us both, I saw, with a stupid kind of amazement, that he was holding out both his hands to me.

"Pray what is your business?" I asked him.

"My business?" he repeated, pausing. "Ah! Yes. I will explain my business, by your leave."

"Do you wish to come in?"

"Yes," he replied; "I wish to come in, Master."

I had asked him the question inhospitably enough, for I resented the sort of bright and gratified recognition that still shone in his face. I resented it, because it seemed to imply that he expected me to respond to it. But I took him into the room I had just left, and, having set the lamp on the table, asked him as civilly as I could, to explain himself.

He looked about him with the strangest air—an air of wondering pleasure, as if he had some part in the things he admired—and he pulled off a rough outer coat, and his hat. Then I saw that his head was furrowed and bald, and that the long iron grey hair grew only on its sides. But I saw nothing that in the least explained him. On the contrary, I saw him next moment, once more holding out both his hands to me.

"What do you mean?" said I, half suspecting him to be mad.

He stopped in his looking at me, and slowly rubbed his right hand over his head. "It's disapinting to a man," he said, in a coarse broken voice, "arter having looked for'ard so distant, and come so fur; but you're not to blame for that—neither on us is to blame for that. I'll speak in half a minute. Give me half a minute, please."

He sat down in a chair that stood before the fire, and covered his forehead with his large brown veinous hands. I looked at him attentively then, and recoiled a little from him; but I did not know him.

"There's no one nigh," said he, looking over his shoulder; "is there?"

"Why do you, a stranger coming into my rooms at this time of the night, ask that question?" said I.

"You're a game one,"[3] he returned, shaking his head at me with a deliberate affection, at once most unintelligible and most exasperating; "I'm glad you've grow'd up, a game one! But don't catch hold of me. You'd be sorry arterwards to have done it."

I relinquished the intention he had detected, for I knew him! Even yet, I could not recall a single feature, but I knew him! If the wind and the rain had driven away the intervening years, had scattered all the intervening objects, had swept us to the churchyard where we first stood face to face on such different levels, I could not have known my convict more distinctly than I knew him now, as he sat in the chair before the fire. No need to take a file from his pocket and show it to me; no need to take the handkerchief from his neck and twist it round his head; no need to hug himself with both his arms, and take a shivering turn across the room, looking back at me for recognition. I knew him before he gave me one of those aids, though, a moment before, I had not been conscious of remotely suspecting his identity.

He came back to where I stood, and again held out both his hands. Not knowing what to do—for, in my astonishment I had lost my self-possession—I reluctantly gave him my hands. He grasped them heartily, raised them to his lips, kissed them, and still held them.

"You acted noble, my boy," said he. "Noble, Pip! And I have never forgot it!"

At a change in his manner as if he were even going to embrace me, I laid a hand upon his breast and put him away.

"Stay!" said I. "Keep off! If you are grateful to me for what I did when I was a little child, I hope you have shown your gratitude by mending your way of life. If you have come here to thank me, it was not necessary. Still, however you have found me out, there must be something good in the feeling that has brought you here, and I will not repulse you; but surely you must understand that—I——"

My attention was so attracted by the singularity of his fixed look at me, that the words died away on my tongue.

"You was a saying," he observed, when we had confronted one another in silence, "that surely I must understand. What, surely must I understand?"

"That I cannot wish to renew that chance intercourse with you of long

---

3. "You're a sharp one" (colloquial, especially in Australia [OED]).

ago, under these different circumstances. I am glad to believe you have repented and recovered yourself. I am glad to tell you so. I am glad that, thinking I deserve to be thanked, you have come to thank me. But our ways are different ways, none the less. You are wet, and you look weary. Will you drink something before you go?"

He had replaced his neckerchief loosely, and had stood, keenly observant of me, biting a long end of it. "I think," he answered, still with the end at his mouth and still observant of me, "that I *will* drink (I thank you) afore I go."

There was a tray ready on a side-table. I brought it to the table near the fire, and asked him what he would have? He touched one of the bottles without looking at it or speaking, and I made him some hot rum-and-water. I tried to keep my hand steady while I did so, but his look at me as he leaned back in his chair with the long draggled end of his neckerchief between his teeth—evidently forgotten—made my hand very difficult to master. When at last I put the glass to him, I saw with amazement that his eyes were full of tears.

Up to this time I had remained standing, not to disguise that I wished him gone. But I was softened by the softened aspect of the man, and felt a touch of reproach. "I hope," said I, hurriedly putting something into a glass for myself, and drawing a chair to the table, "that you will not think I spoke harshly to you just now. I had no intention of doing it, and I am sorry for it if I did. I wish you well, and happy!"

As I put my glass to my lips, he glanced with surprise at the end of his neckerchief, dropping from his mouth when he opened it, and stretched out his hand. I gave him mine, and then he drank, and drew his sleeve across his eyes and forehead.

"How are you living?" I asked him.

"I've been a sheep-farmer, stock-breeder, other trades besides, away in the new world," said he; "many a thousand miles of stormy water off from this."

"I hope you have done well?"

"I've done wonderful well. There's others went out alonger me as has done well too, but no man has done nigh as well as me. I'm famous for it."

"I am glad to hear it."

"I hope to hear you say so, my dear boy."

Without stopping to try to understand those words or the tone in which they were spoken, I turned off to a point that had just come into my mind.

"Have you ever seen a messenger you once sent to me," I inquired, "since he undertook that trust?"

"Never set eyes upon him. I warn't likely to it."[4]

"He came faithfully, and he brought me the two one-pound notes. I was a poor boy then, as you know, and to a poor boy they were a little fortune. But, like you, I have done well since, and you must let me pay them back. You can put them to some other poor boy's use." I took out my purse.

He watched me as I laid my purse upon the table and opened it, and he watched me as I separated two one-pound notes from its contents. They were

4. Magwitch here follows colloquial usage in omitting the verb.

clean and new, and I spread them out and handed them over to him. Still watching me, he laid them one upon the other, folded them long-wise, gave them a twist, set fire to them at the lamp, and dropped the ashes into the tray.

"May I make so bold," he said then, with a smile that was like a frown, and with a frown that was like a smile, "as ask you *how* you have done well, since you and me was out on them lone shivering marshes?"

"How?"

"Ah!"

He emptied his glass, got up, and stood at the side of the fire, with his heavy brown hand on the mantelshelf. He put a foot up to the bars, to dry and warm it, and the wet boot began to steam; but he neither looked at it, nor at the fire, but steadily looked at me. It was only now that I began to tremble.

When my lips had parted and had shaped some words that were without sound, I forced myself to tell him (though I could not do it distinctly), that I had been chosen to succeed to some property.

"Might a mere warmint ask what property?" said he.

I faltered, "I don't know."

"Might a mere warmint ask whose property?" said he.

I faltered again, "I don't know."

"Could I make a guess, I wonder," said the Convict, "at your income since you come of age! As to the first figure now. Five?"

With my heart beating like a heavy hammer of disordered action, I rose out of my chair, and stood with my hand upon the back of it, looking wildly at him.

"Concerning a guardian," he went on. "There ought to have been some guardian, or such-like, while you was a minor. Some lawyer, maybe. As to the first letter of that lawyer's name now. Would it be J?"

All the truth of my position came flashing on me; and its disappointments, dangers, disgraces, consequences of all kinds, rushed in in such a multitude that I was borne down by them and had to struggle for every breath I drew.

"Put it," he resumed, "as the employer of that lawyer whose name begun with a J, and might be Jaggers—put it as he had come over sea to Portsmouth, and had landed there, and had wanted to come on to you. 'However you have found me out,' you says just now. Well! However did I find you out? Why, I wrote from Portsmouth to a person in London, for particulars of your address. That person's name? Why, Wemmick."

I could not have spoken one word, though it had been to save my life. I stood, with a hand on the chair-back and a hand on my breast, where I seemed to be suffocating—I stood so, looking wildly at him, until I grasped at the chair, when the room began to surge and turn. He caught me, drew me to the sofa, put me up against the cushions, and bent on one knee before me: bringing the face that I now well remembered, and that I shuddered at, very near to mine.

"Yes, Pip, dear boy, I've made a gentleman on you! It's me wot has done it! I swore that time, sure as ever I earned a guinea, that guinea should go to you. I swore arterwards, sure as ever I spec'lated and got rich, you should get rich. I lived rough, that you should live smooth; I worked hard, that you should be above work. What odds,[5] dear boy? Do I tell it, fur you to feel a obligation? Not a bit. I tell it, fur you to know as that there hunted dunghill dog wot you kep life in, got his head so high that he could make a gentleman—and, Pip, you're him!"

The abhorrence in which I held the man, the dread I had of him, the repugnance with which I shrank from him, could not have been exceeded if he had been some terrible beast.

"Look'ee here, Pip. I'm your second father. You're my son—more to me nor any son. I've put away money, only for you to spend. When I was a hired-out shepherd in a solitary hut, not seeing no faces but faces of sheep till I half forgot wot men's and women's faces wos like, I see yourn. I drops my knife many a time in that hut when I was a eating my dinner or my supper, and I says, 'Here's the boy again, a looking at me whiles I eats and drinks!' I see you there, a many times, as plain as ever I see you on them misty marshes. 'Lord strike me dead!' I says each time—and I goes out in the air to say it under the open heavens—'but wot, if I gets liberty and money, I'll make that boy a gentleman!' And I done it. Why, look at you, dear boy! Look at these here lodgings o' yourn, fit for a lord! A lord? Ah! You shall show money with lords for wagers, and beat 'em!"

In his heat and triumph, and in his knowledge that I had been nearly fainting, he did not remark on my reception of all this. It was the one grain of relief I had.

"Look'ee here!" he went on, taking my watch out of my pocket, and turning towards him a ring on my finger, while I recoiled from his touch as if he had been a snake, "a gold 'un and a beauty; *that's* a gentleman's, I hope! A diamond, all set round with rubies; *that's* a gentleman's, I hope! Look at your linen; fine and beautiful! Look at your clothes; better ain't to be got! And your books too," turning his eyes round the room, "mounting up, on their shelves, by hundreds! And you read 'em; don't you? I see you'd been a reading of 'em when I come in. Ha, ha, ha! You shall read 'em to me, dear boy! And if they're in foreign languages wot I don't understand, I shall be just as proud as if I did."

Again he took both my hands and put them to his lips, while my blood ran cold within me.

"Don't you mind talking, Pip," said he, after again drawing his sleeve over his eyes and forehead, as the click came in his throat which I well remembered—and he was all the more horrible to me that he was so much in earnest; "you can't do better nor keep quiet, dear boy. You ain't looked slowly forward to this as I have; you wosn't prepared for this, as I wos. But didn't you never think it might be me?"

"O no, no, no," I returned. "Never, never!"

"Well, you see it *wos* me, and single-handed. Never a soul in it but my own self and Mr. Jaggers."

"Was there no one else?" I asked.

"No," said he, with a glance of surprise; "who else should there be? And, dear boy, how good-looking you have growed! There's bright eyes somewheres—eh? Isn't there bright eyes somewheres, wot you love the thoughts on?"

5. "What of it?" (Literally: "What's the difference?")

O Estella, Estella!

"They shall be yourn, dear boy, if money can buy 'em. Not that a gentleman like you, so well set up as you, can't win 'em off of his own game; but
money shall back you! Let me finish wot I was a telling you, dear boy. From
that there hut and that there hiring-out, I got money left me by my master
(which died, and had been the same as me), and got my liberty and went for
myself. In every single thing I went for, I went for you. 'Lord strike a blight
upon it,' I says, wotever it was I went for, 'if it ain't for him!' It all prospered
wonderful. As I giv' you to understand just now, I'm famous for it. It was the
money left me, and the gains of the first few year wot I sent home to Mr.   10
Jaggers—all for you—when he first come arter you, agreeable to my letter."

O, that he had never come! That he had left me at the forge—far from
contented, yet, by comparison, happy!

"And then, dear boy, it was a recompense to me, look'ee here, to know in
secret that I was making a gentleman. The blood horses of them colonists[6]
might fling up the dust over me as I was walking; what do I say? I says to
myself, 'I'm making a better gentleman nor ever you'll be!' When one of 'em
says to another, 'He was a convict, a few year ago, and is a ignorant common
fellow now, for all he's lucky,' what do I say? I says to myself, 'If I ain't a
gentleman, nor yet ain't got no learning, I'm the owner of such. All on you   20
owns stock and land; which on you owns a brought-up London gentleman?'
This way I kep myself a going. And this way I held steady afore my mind that
I would for certain come one day and see my boy, and make myself known
to him, on his own ground."

He laid his hand on my shoulder. I shuddered at the thought that for
anything I knew, his hand might be stained with blood.

"It warn't easy, Pip, for me to leave them parts, nor yet it warn't safe. But
I held to it, and the harder it was, the stronger I held, for I was determined,
and my mind firm made up. At last I done it. Dear boy, I done it!"

I tried to collect my thoughts, but I was stunned. Throughout, I had seemed   30
to myself to attend more to the wind and rain than to him; even now, I could
not separate his voice from those voices, though those were loud and his was
silent.

"Where will you put me?" he asked, presently. "I must be put somewheres,
dear boy."

"To sleep?" said I.

"Yes. And to sleep long and sound," he answered; "for I've been sea-tossed
and sea-washed, months and months."

"My friend and companion," said I, rising from the sofa, "is absent; you
must have his room."   40

"He won't come back to-morrow; will he?"

"No," said I, answering almost mechanically, in spite of my utmost efforts;
"not to-morrow."

"Because look'ee here, dear boy," he said, dropping his voice, and laying
a long finger on my breast in an impressive manner, "caution is necessary."

"How do you mean? Caution?"

"By G—, it's Death!"

"What's death?"

---

6. Emigrants to Australia by choice as distinguished from transported convicts.

"I was sent for life. It's death to come back. There's been overmuch coming back of late years, and I should of a certainty be hanged if took."[7]

Nothing was needed but this; the wretched man, after loading me with his wretched gold and silver chains for years, had risked his life to come to me, and I held it there in my keeping! If I had loved him instead of abhorring him; if I had been attracted to him by the strongest admiration and affection, instead of shrinking from him with the strongest repugnance; it could have been no worse. On the contrary, it would have been better, for his preservation would then have naturally and tenderly addressed my heart.

My first care was to close the shutters, so that no light might be seen from without, and then to close and make fast the doors. While I did so, he stood at the table drinking rum and eating biscuit; and when I saw him thus engaged, I saw my convict on the marshes at his meal again. It almost seemed to me as if he must stoop down presently, to file at his leg.

When I had gone into Herbert's room, and had shut off any other communication between it and the staircase than through the room in which our conversation had been held, I asked him if he would go to bed? He said yes, but asked me for some of my "gentleman's linen" to put on in the morning. I brought it out, and laid it ready for him, and my blood again ran cold when he again took me by both hands to give me good night.

I got away from him, without knowing how I did it, and mended the fire in the room where we had been together, and sat down by it, afraid to go to bed. For an hour or more, I remained too stunned to think, and it was not until I began to think, that I began fully to know how wrecked I was, and how the ship in which I had sailed was gone to pieces.

Miss Havisham's intentions towards me, all a mere dream; Estella not designed for me; I only suffered in Satis House as a convenience, a sting for the greedy relations, a model with a mechanical heart to practise on when no other practice was at hand; those were the first smarts I had. But, sharpest and deepest pain of all—it was for the convict, guilty of I knew not what crimes and liable to be taken out of those rooms where I sat thinking, and hanged at the Old Bailey door, that I had deserted Joe.

I would not have gone back to Joe now, I would not have gone back to Biddy now, for any consideration: simply, I suppose, because my sense of my own worthless conduct to them was greater than every consideration. No wisdom on earth could have given me the comfort that I should have derived from their simplicity and fidelity; but I could never, never, never, undo what I had done.

In every rage of wind and rush of rain, I heard pursuers. Twice, I could have sworn there was a knocking and whispering at the outer door. With these fears upon me, I began either to imagine or recall that I had had mysterious warnings of this man's approach. That for weeks gone by, I had passed faces in the streets which I had thought like his. That these likenesses

7. As Philip Collins points out, "Dickens conceals or ignores the fact that Magwitch's offence has notoriously ceased to be *de facto* capital by the time when the action of the novel takes place." A contemporary writer on penology (Edward Gibbon Wakefield, *Facts Relating to the Punishment of Death in the Metropolis*, 1831), notes that during the period from 1827 to 1830 out of eight convicted returned transports none was executed, and he spells out what has troubled some readers as an improbability later on in the novel: "The proof of this crime is more difficult than in many other cases; depending on identification, which the artful class of persons who commit the crime take great pains to prevent." Three years after Wakefield published his work, the death penalty for illegal reentry was officially taken off the statute books.

had grown more numerous, as he, coming over the sea, had drawn nearer. That his wicked spirit had somehow sent these messengers to mine, and that now on this stormy night he was as good as his word, and with me.

Crowding up with these reflections came the reflection that I had seen him with my childish eyes to be a desperately violent man; that I had heard that other convict reiterate that he had tried to murder him; that I had seen him down in the ditch tearing and fighting like a wild beast. Out of such remembrances I brought into the light of the fire, a half-formed terror that it might not be safe to be shut up there with him in the dead of the wild solitary night. This dilated until it filled the room, and impelled me to take a candle 10 and go in and look at my dreadful burden.

He had rolled a handkerchief round his head, and his face was set and lowering in his sleep. But he was asleep, and quietly too, though he had a pistol lying on the pillow. Assured of this, I softly removed the key to the outside of his door, and turned it on him before I again sat down by the fire. Gradually I slipped from the chair and lay on the floor. When I awoke, without having parted in my sleep with the perception of my wretchedness, the clocks of the Eastward churches were striking five, the candles were wasted out, the fire was dead, and the wind and rain intensified the thick black darkness. 20

THIS IS THE END OF THE SECOND STAGE OF PIP'S EXPECTATIONS.

Chapter XL.

It was fortunate for me that I had to take precautions to ensure (so far as I could) the safety of my dreaded visitor; for, this thought pressing on me when I awoke, held other thoughts in a confused concourse at a distance. The impossibility of keeping him concealed in the chambers was self-evident. It could not be done, and the attempt to do it would inevitably engender suspicion. True, I had no Avenger in my service now, but I was looked after by an inflammatory old female, assisted by an animated rag-bag[1] whom she called her niece, and to keep a room secret from them would be to invite curiosity and exaggeration. They both had weak eyes, which I had long attributed to their chronically looking in at keyholes, and they were 10 always at hand when not wanted; indeed that was their only reliable quality besides larceny. Not to get up a mystery with these people, I resolved to announce in the morning that my uncle had unexpectedly come from the country.

This course I decided on while I was yet groping about in the darkness for the means of getting a light. Not stumbling on the means after all, I was fain to go out to the adjacent Lodge[2] and get the watchman there to come with his lantern. Now, in groping my way down the black staircase I fell over something, and that something was a man crouching in a corner.

As the man made no answer when I asked him what he did there, but 20 eluded my touch in silence, I ran to the Lodge and urged the watchman to come quickly: telling him of the incident on the way back. The wind being as fierce as ever, we did not care to endanger the light in the lantern by rekindling the extinguished lamps on the staircase, but we examined the staircase from the bottom to the top and found no one there. It then occurred to me as possible that the man might have slipped into my rooms; so, lighting my candle at the watchman's, and leaving him standing at the door, I examined them carefully, including the room in which my dreaded guest lay asleep. All was quiet, and assuredly no other man was in those chambers.

It troubled me that there should have been a lurker on the stairs, on that 30 night of all nights in the year, and I asked the watchman as I handed him a dram at the door, on the chance of eliciting some hopeful explanation, whether he had admitted at his gate any gentlemen who had perceptibly been dining out? Yes, he said; at different times of the night, three. One lived in Fountain-court, and the other two lived in the Lane,[3] and he had seen them all go home. Again, the only other man who dwelt in the house of which my chambers formed a part, had been in the country for some weeks; and he certainly had not returned in the night, because we had seen his door with his seal on it as we came up-stairs.[4]

"The night being so bad, sir," said the watchman, as he gave me back my 40

---

1. Dickens consistently treats these menials with aversion as squalid fixtures of the Inns of Court.
2. Rooms occupied by a caretaker or watchman.
3. Middle Temple Lane, running from Fleet Street to the river, divides the Inner from the Middle Temple. Fountain Court, north of Middle Temple Gardens, gets its name from the single-jet fountain that has been spouting at least since Queen Elizabeth's days.
4. When going on a journey or absenting himself overnight, the tenant usually placed a wax seal on his door, so the watchman would know whether the chambers had been burglarized.

glass, "uncommon few have come in at my gate. Besides them three gentlemen that I have named, I don't call to mind another since about eleven
o'clock, when a stranger asked for you."

"My uncle," I muttered. "Yes."

"You saw him, sir?"

"Yes. Oh yes."

"Likewise the person with him?"

"Person with him!" I repeated, faltering.

"I judged the person to be with him," returned the watchman. "The person
stopped when he stopped to make inquiry of me, and the person took this   10
way when he took this way."

"What sort of person?"

The watchman had not particularly noticed; he should say, a working person; to the best of his belief, he had a dust-coloured kind of clothes on, under
a dark coat. The watchman made more light of the matter than I did, and
naturally; not having my reason for attaching weight to it.

When I had got rid of him, which I thought it well to do without
prolonging explanations, my mind was much troubled by these two circumstances taken together. Whereas they were easy of innocent solution apart—
as, for instance, some diner-out or diner-at-home, who had not gone near this   20
watchman's gate, might have strayed to my staircase and dropped asleep
there—and my nameless visitor might have brought some one with him to
show him the way—still, joined, they had an ugly look to one as prone to
distrust and fear as the changes of a few hours had made me.

I lighted my fire, which burnt with a raw pale flare at that time of the
morning, and fell into a doze before it. I seemed to have been dozing a whole
night when the clocks struck six. As there was full an hour and a half between
me and daylight, I dozed again; now, waking up uneasily, with prolix conversations about nothing, in my ears; now, making thunder of the wind in
the chimney; at length falling off into a profound sleep from which the day-   30
light woke me with a start.

All this time I had never been able to consider my own situation, nor could
I do so yet. I had not the power to attend to it. I was greatly dejected and
distressed, but in an incoherent wholesale sort of way. As to forming any plan
for the future, I could as soon have formed an elephant. When I opened the
shutters and looked out at the wet wild morning, all of a leaden hue; when
I walked from room to room; when I sat down again shivering, before the
fire, waiting for my laundress to appear; I thought how miserable I was, but
hardly knew why, or how long I had been so, or on what day of the week I
made the reflection, or even who I was that made it.   40

At length the old woman and the niece came in—the latter with a head
not easily distinguishable from her dusty broom[5]—and testified surprise at
sight of me and the fire. To whom I imparted how my uncle had come in
the night and was then asleep, and how the breakfast preparations were to be
modified accordingly. Then I washed and dressed while they knocked the
furniture about and made a dust, and so, in a sort of dream or sleep-waking,

5. Perhaps an echo of Swift's literary joke, "A Meditation upon a Broomstick" (1703): "SURELY MOR-
TAL MAN IS A BROOMSTICK . . . wearing his own Hair on his Head" (Monod). Grose gives
"Mopsqueeze" as slang for "a maid, servant, particularly a housemaid."

I found myself sitting by the fire again, waiting for—Him—to come to breakfast.

By-and-by, his door opened and he came out.[6] I could not bring myself to bear the sight of him, and I thought he had a worse look by daylight.

"I do not even know," said I, speaking low as he took his seat at the table, "by what name to call you. I have given out that you are my uncle."

"That's it, dear boy! Call me uncle."

"You assumed some name, I suppose, on board ship?"

"Yes, dear boy. I took the name of Provis."[7]

"Do you mean to keep that name?"   10

"Why, yes, dear boy, it's as good as another—unless you'd like another."

"What is your real name?" I asked him in a whisper.

"Magwitch," he answered, in the same tone; "chrisen'd Abel."

"What were you brought up to be?"

"A warmint, dear boy."

He answered quite seriously, and used the word as if it denoted some profession.

"When you came into the Temple last night——" said I, pausing to wonder whether that could really have been only last night, which seemed so long ago.   20

"Yes, dear boy?"

"When you came in at the gate and asked the watchman the way here, had you any one with you?"

"With me? No, dear boy."

"But there was some one there?"

"I didn't take particular notice," he said, dubiously, "not knowing the ways of the place. But I think there *was* a person, too, come in alonger me."

"Are you known in London?"

"I hope not!" said he, giving his neck a jerk with his forefinger that made me turn hot and sick.   30

"Were you known in London, once?"

"Not over and above,[8] dear boy. I was in the provinces mostly."

"Were you—tried—in London?"

"Which time?" said he, with a sharp look.

"The last time."

He nodded. "First knowed Mr. Jaggers that way. Jaggers was for me."

It was on my lips to ask him what he was tried for, but he took up a knife, gave it a flourish, and with the words, "And whatever I done is worked out and paid for!" fell to at his breakfast.

He ate in a ravenous way that was very disagreeable, and all his actions   40

---

6. Dickens's oversight: Magwitch has been locked in (unless the inadvertence is Pip's in leaving the door unlocked after checking up on Magwitch a page earlier).

7. The name may have been suggested by a petty criminal's, in whose case Dickens's detective friend Inspector Charles Frederick Field (1805?–1874) was involved. In 1853, after retiring from Scotland Yard, Field, having set up as a private sleuth, tracked down an impostor who claimed to be one Sir Richard Smyth but whose name was in fact Provis. Disguised as an invalid, Field wormed his way into the confidence of a Provis relation, a gabby valetudinarian responsive to Field's own imposture and large supplies of gin, and Field eventually bagged his man. On September 17, 1853, the *Times* published a report on Field's stunt and in the same article called attention to Dickens's appropriation of Field as Inspector Bucket in *Bleak House*.

8. Not especially.

were uncouth, noisy, and greedy. Some of his teeth had failed him since I saw him eat on the marshes, and as he turned his food in his mouth, and turned his head sideways to bring his strongest fangs to bear upon it, he looked terribly like a hungry old dog. If I had begun with any appetite, he would have taken it away, and I should have sat much as I did—repelled from him by an insurmountable aversion, and gloomily looking at the cloth.

"I'm a heavy grubber, dear boy," he said, as a polite kind of apology when he had made an end of his meal, "but I always was. If it had been in my constitution to be a lighter grubber, I might ha' got into lighter trouble. Sim'larly, I must have my smoke. When I was first hired out as shepherd 10 t'other side the world, it's my belief I should ha' turned into a molloncolly-mad sheep myself, if I hadn't a had my smoke."

As he said so, he got up from table, and putting his hand into the breast of the pea-coat[9] he wore, brought out a short black pipe, and a handful of loose tobacco of the kind that is called Negro-head.[1] Having filled his pipe, he put the surplus tobacco back again, as if his pocket were a drawer. Then he took a live coal from the fire with the tongs, and lighted his pipe at it, and then turned round on the hearthrug with his back to the fire, and went through his favourite action of holding out both his hands for mine.

"And this," said he, dandling my hands up and down in his, as he puffed 20 at his pipe; "and this is the gentleman what I made! The real genuine One! It does me good fur to look at you, Pip. All I stip'late, is, to stand by and look at you, dear boy!"

I released my hands as soon as I could, and found that I was beginning slowly to settle down to the contemplation of my condition. What I was chained to, and how heavily, became intelligible to me, as I heard his hoarse voice, and sat looking up at his furrowed bald head with its iron grey hair at the sides.

"I mustn't see my gentleman a footing it in the mire of the streets; there mustn't be no mud on *his* boots. My gentleman must have horses, Pip! Horses 30 to ride, and horses to drive, and horses for his servant to ride and drive as well. Shall colonists have their horses (and blood 'uns,[2] if you please, good Lord!) and not my London gentleman? No, no. We'll show 'em another pair of shoes than that, Pip; won't us?"

He took out of his pocket a great thick pocket-book, bursting with papers, and tossed it on the table.

"There's something worth spending in that there book, dear boy. It's yourn. All I've got ain't mine; it's yourn. Don't you be afeerd on it. There's more where that come from. I've come to the old country fur to see my gentleman spend his money *like* a gentleman. That'll be *my* pleasure. *My* pleasure 'ull 40 be fur to see him do it. And blast you all!" he wound up, looking round the room and snapping his fingers once with a loud snap, "blast you every one, from the judge in his wig, to the colonist a stirring up the dust, I'll show a better gentleman than the whole kit on you put together!"

"Stop!" said I, almost in a frenzy of fear and dislike, "I want to speak to you. I want to know what is to be done. I want to know how you are to be

---

9. Thick coat or jacket of coarse wool (Dutch *pij*), usually worn by seamen [OED].
1. Strong dark Cavendish tobacco, sweetened with molasses and pressed into square cakes; popular with sailors and workingmen [OED]. An inferior brand, to judge from the chewing contestant's gripe in *Huckleberry Finn* (1884), chapter 21: "You borry'd store tobacker and paid back nigger-head."
2. Pedigree.

kept out of danger, how long you are going to stay, what projects you have."

"Look'ee here, Pip," said he, laying his hand on my arm in a suddenly altered and subdued manner; "first of all, look'ee here. I forgot myself half a minute ago. What I said was low; that's what it was; low. Look'ee here, Pip. Look over it. I ain't a going to be low."

"First," I resumed, half groaning, "what precautions can be taken against your being recognised and seized?"

"No, dear boy," he said, in the same tone as before, "that don't go first. Lowness goes first. I ain't took so many year to make a gentleman, not without knowing what's due to him. Look'ee here, Pip. I was low; that's what I was; 10 low. Look over it, dear boy."

Some sense of the grimly-ludicrous moved me to a fretful laugh, as I replied, "I *have* looked over it. In Heaven's name, don't harp upon it!"

"Yes, but look'ee here," he persisted. "Dear boy, I ain't come so fur to be low. Now, go on, dear boy. You was a saying——"

"How are you to be guarded from the danger you have incurred?"

"Well, dear boy, the danger ain't so great. Without I was informed agen, the danger ain't so much to signify. There's Jaggers, and there's Wemmick, and there's you. Who else is there to inform?"

"Is there no chance person who might identify you in the street?" said I. 20

"Well," he returned, "there ain't many. Nor yet I don't intend to advertise myself in the papers by the name of A. M. come back from Botany Bay;[3] and years has rolled away, and who's to gain by it? Still, look'ee here, Pip. If the danger had been fifty times as great, I should ha' come to see you, mind you, just the same."

"And how long do you remain?"

"How long?" said he, taking his black pipe from his mouth, and dropping his jaw as he stared at me. "I'm not a going back. I've come for good."

"Where are you to live?" said I. "What is to be done with you? Where will you be safe?" 30

"Dear boy," he returned, "there's disguising wigs can be bought for money, and there's hair powder, and spectacles, and black clothes—shorts and what not.[4] Others has done it safe afore, and what others has done afore, others can do agen. As to the where and how of living, dear boy, give me your own opinions on it."

"You take it smoothly now," said I, "but you were very serious last night, when you swore it was Death."

"And so I swear it is Death," said he, putting his pipe back in his mouth, "and Death by the rope, in the open street not fur from this, and it's serious that you should fully understand it to be so. What then, when that's once 40 done? Here I am. To go back now, 'ud be as bad as to stand ground—worse. Besides, Pip, I'm here, because I've meant it by you, years and years. As to

3. An inlet five miles south of Sydney, Australia, discovered and seized as Crown territory by Captain James Cook (1728–1779) in 1770, and so named by the botanist on his expedition for the variety and opulence of its vegetation. On the government's use of Botany Bay as penal colony for transported convicts, see p. 17, n. 2. Although Botany Bay itself was declared unfit as a penal site, the place-name passed into the language as a generic term for all convict establishments in Australia.
4. Magwitch's sixteen-year absence from England is reflected in his obsolete taste in clothes and hair style. Wigs ceased to be worn after about 1810, except by members of the legal and ecclesiastical professions and by the smart set; hairpowder—taxable since 1795—persisted as an affectation among the very old-fashioned. Shorts—tight knee breeches—had been out of style for years, except as ceremonial dress among the clergy.

what I dare, I'm a old bird now, as has dared all manner of traps since first he was fledged, and I'm not afeerd to perch upon a scarecrow. If there's Death hid inside of it, there is, and let him come out, and I'll face him, and then I'll believe in him and not afore. And now let me have a look at my gentleman agen."

Once more he took me by both hands and surveyed me with an air of admiring proprietorship: smoking with great complacency all the while.

It appeared to me that I could do no better than secure him some quiet lodging hard by, of which he might take possession when Herbert returned: whom I expected in two or three days. That the secret must be confided to   10 Herbert as a matter of unavoidable necessity, even if I could have put the immense relief I should derive from sharing it with him out of the question, was plain to me. But it was by no means so plain to Mr. Provis (I resolved to call him by that name), who reserved his consent to Herbert's participation until he should have seen him and formed a favourable judgment of his physiognomy. "And even then, dear boy," said he, pulling a greasy little clasped black Testament out of his pocket, "we'll have him on his oath."

To state that my terrible patron carried this little black book about the world solely to swear people on in cases of emergency, would be to state what I never quite established—but this I can say, that I never knew him put it to   20 any other use. The book itself had the appearance of having been stolen from some court of justice, and perhaps his knowledge of its antecedents combined with his own experience in that wise, gave him a superstitious reliance on its powers as a sort of legal spell or charm. On this first occasion of his producing it, I recalled how he had made me swear fidelity in the churchyard long ago, and how he had described himself last night as always swearing to his resolutions in his solitude.

As he was at present dressed in a seafaring slop suit,[5] in which he looked as if he had some parrots and cigars to dispose of, I next discussed with him what dress he should wear. He cherished an extraordinary belief in the virtues   30 of "shorts" as a disguise, and had in his own mind sketched a dress for himself that would have made him something between a dean and a dentist.[6] It was with considerable difficulty that I won him over to the assumption of a dress more like a prosperous farmer's; and we arranged that he should cut his hair close and wear a little powder. Lastly, as he had not yet been seen by the laundress or her niece, he was to keep himself out of their view until his change of dress was made.

It would seem a simple matter to decide on these precautions; but in my dazed, not to say distracted, state, it took so long, that I did not get out to further them, until two or three in the afternoon. He was to remain shut up   40 in the chambers while I was gone, and was on no account to open the door.

There being to my knowledge a respectable lodging-house in Essex-street, the back of which looked into the Temple, and was almost within hail of my windows,[7] I first of all repaired to that house, and was so fortunate as to secure

---

5. Ready-made clothes issued to sailors from ship's stores, or sold by dealers in old clothes, whose slop-shops were clustered in the dockyard area [OED].

6. That is, between a high dignitary of the Church and a shabby professional man—dentists enjoyed notoriously little prestige in Dickens's day. "Certificates of fitness" were not issued to practicing dentists by the Royal College of Surgeons before 1859.

7. Essex Street, running from the Strand to what is now the Victoria Embankment, lies directly west of Garden Court: hence easily accessible to Pip's visits and surveillance.

the second floor for my uncle, Mr. Provis. I then went from shop to shop, making such purchases as were necessary to the change in his appearance. This business transacted, I turned my face, on my own account,[8] to Little Britain. Mr. Jaggers was at his desk, but, seeing me enter, got up immediately and stood before his fire.

"Now, Pip," said he, "be careful."

"I will, sir," I returned. For, coming along I had thought well of what I was going to say.

"Don't commit yourself," said Mr. Jaggers, "and don't commit any one. You understand—any one. Don't tell me anything: I don't want to know anything; I am not curious."

Of course I saw that he knew the man was come.

"I merely want, Mr. Jaggers," said I, "to assure myself that what I have been told is true. I have no hope of its being untrue, but at least I may verify it."

Mr. Jaggers nodded. "But did you say 'told,' or 'informed'?" he asked me, with his head on one side, and not looking at me, but looking in a listening way at the floor. "Told would seem to imply verbal communication. You can't have verbal communication with a man in New South Wales, you know."

"I will say, informed, Mr. Jaggers."

"Good."

"I have been informed by a person named Abel Magwitch, that he is the benefactor so long unknown to me."

"That is the man," said Mr. Jaggers, "—in New South Wales."

"And only he?" said I.

"And only he," said Mr. Jaggers.

"I am not so unreasonable, sir, as to think you at all responsible for my mistakes and wrong conclusions; but I always supposed it was Miss Havisham."

"As you say, Pip," returned Mr. Jaggers, turning his eyes upon me coolly, and taking a bite at his forefinger, "I am not at all responsible for that."

"And yet it looked so like it, sir," I pleaded with a downcast heart.

"Not a particle of evidence, Pip," said Mr. Jaggers, shaking his head and gathering up his skirts.[9] "Take nothing on its looks; take everything on evidence. There's no better rule."

"I have no more to say," said I, with a sigh, after standing silent for a little while. "I have verified my information, and there's an end."

"And Magwitch—in New South Wales—having at last disclosed himself," said Mr. Jaggers, "you will comprehend, Pip, how rigidly throughout my communication with you, I have always adhered to the strict line of fact. There has never been the least departure from the strict line of fact. You are quite aware of that?"

"Quite, sir."

"I communicated to Magwitch—in New South Wales—when he first wrote to me—from New South Wales—the caution that he must not expect me ever to deviate from the strict line of fact. I also communicated to him another caution. He appeared to me to have obscurely hinted in his letter at some

8. On my own behalf.
9. Coattails.

distant idea he had of seeing you in England here. I cautioned him that I
must hear no more of that; that he was not at all likely to obtain a pardon;
that he was expatriated for the term of his natural life; and that his presenting
himself in this country would be an act of felony, rendering him liable to the
extreme penalty of the law. I gave Magwitch that caution," said Mr. Jaggers,
looking hard at me; "I wrote it to New South Wales. He guided himself by
it, no doubt."

"No doubt," said I.

"I have been informed by Wemmick," pursued Mr. Jaggers, still looking
hard at me, "that he has received a letter, under date Portsmouth, from a   10
colonist of the name of Purvis, or ——"

"Or Provis," I suggested.

"Or Provis—thank you, Pip. Perhaps it *is* Provis? Perhaps you know it's
Provis?"

"Yes," said I.

"You know it's Provis. A letter, under date Portsmouth, from a colonist
of the name of Provis, asking for the particulars of your address, on behalf
of Magwitch. Wemmick sent him the particulars, I understand, by return of
post. Probably it is through Provis that you have received the explanation of
Magwitch—in New South Wales?"   20

"It came through Provis," I replied.

"Good day, Pip," said Mr. Jaggers, offering his hand; "glad to have seen
you. In writing by post to Magwitch—in New South Wales—or in communicating with him through Provis, have the goodness to mention that the
particulars and vouchers of our long account shall be sent to you, together
with the balance; for there is still a balance remaining. Good-day, Pip!"

We shook hands, and he looked hard at me as long as he could see me. I
turned at the door, and he was still looking hard at me, while the two vile
casts on the shelf seemed to be trying to get their eyelids open, and to force
out of their swollen throats, "O, what a man he is!"   30

Wemmick was out, and though he had been at his desk he could have
done nothing for me. I went straight back to the Temple, where I found the
terrible Provis drinking rum-and-water and smoking negro-head, in safety.

Next day the clothes I had ordered, all came home, and he put them on.
Whatever he put on became him less (it dismally seemed to me) than what
he had worn before. To my thinking, there was something in him that made
it hopeless to attempt to disguise him. The more I dressed him and the better
I dressed him, the more he looked like the slouching fugitive on the marshes.
This effect on my anxious fancy was partly referable, no doubt, to his old face
and manner growing more familiar to me; but I believe too that he dragged   40
one of his legs as if there were still a weight of iron on it, and that from head
to foot there was Convict in the very grain of the man.

The influences of his solitary hut-life were upon him besides, and gave
him a savage air that no dress could tame; added to these, were the influences
of his subsequent branded life among men, and crowning all, his consciousness that he was dodging and hiding now. In all his ways of sitting and
standing, and eating and drinking—of brooding about, in a high-shouldered
reluctant style—of taking out his great horn-handled jack-knife and wiping it
on his legs and cutting his food—of lifting light glasses and cups to his lips,

as if they were clumsy pannikins[1]—of chopping a wedge off his bread, and soaking up with it the last fragments of gravy round and round his plate, as if to make the most of an allowance, and then drying his finger-ends on it, and then swallowing it—in these ways and a thousand other small nameless instances arising every minute in the day, there was Prisoner, Felon, Bondsman,[2] plain as plain could be.

It had been his own idea to wear that touch of powder, and I had conceded the powder after overcoming the shorts. But I can compare the effect of it, when on, to nothing but the probable effect of rouge upon the dead; so awful was the manner in which everything in him that it was most desirable to repress, started through that thin layer of pretence, and seemed to come blazing out at the crown of his head. It was abandoned as soon as tried, and he wore his grizzled hair cut short.

Words cannot tell what a sense I had, at the same time, of the dreadful mystery that he was to me. When he fell asleep of an evening with his knotted hands clenching the sides of the easy-chair, and his bald head tattooed with deep wrinkles falling forward on his breast, I would sit and look at him, wondering what he had done, and loading him with all the crimes in the Calendar,[3] until the impulse was powerful on me to start up and fly from him. Every hour so increased my abhorrence of him, that I even think I might have yielded to this impulse in the first agonies of being so haunted, notwithstanding all he had done for me, and the risk he ran, but for the knowledge that Herbert must soon come back. Once, I actually did start out of bed in the night, and begin to dress myself in my worst clothes, hurriedly intending to leave him there with everything else I possessed, and enlist for India as a private soldier.

I doubt if a ghost could have been more terrible to me, up in those lonely rooms in the long evenings and long nights, with the wind and the rain always rushing by. A ghost could not have been taken and hanged on my account, and the consideration that he could be, and the dread that he would be, were no small addition to my horrors. When he was not asleep or playing a complicated kind of Patience[4] with a ragged pack of cards of his own—a game that I never saw before or since, and in which he recorded his winnings by sticking his jack-knife into the table—when he was not engaged in either of these pursuits, he would ask me to read to him—"Foreign language, dear boy!" While I complied, he, not comprehending a single word, would stand before the fire surveying me with the air of an Exhibitor,[5] and I would see him, between the fingers of the hand with which I shaded my face, appealing in dumb show to the furniture to take notice of my proficiency. The imaginary

---

1. Diminutive "pan"; small primitive metal drinking vessel; "a term exceedingly common in Australia."
2. Normally used to describe a person who is tied or bound by a covenant; here literally one who has worn bonds, an ex-convict.
3. *The Newgate Calendar, or Malefactors' Bloody Register*, a collection of brief biographies of eminent criminals tried or executed at Newgate; first compiled in 1771(?), though anticipated by similar collections throughout the eighteenth century. These mini-Lives pretended to be authentic autobiographies; their sources, in fact, were trial records, dying confessions, and the observations of the Newgate chaplains (or "ordinaries") who almost certainly wrote and published the *Calendar* anonymously as its "editors." The book enjoyed spectacular popularity with tabloid readers and was constantly reissued until at least 1826.
4. Solitaire [OED].
5. Donor of a scholarship or "exhibition," who would naturally interest himself in the stipendiary's performance; or simply a showman, exhibiting Pip as a spectacular curiosity to an empty room.

student pursued by the misshapen creature he had impiously made, was not more wretched than I, pursued by the creature who had made me, and recoiling from him with a stronger repulsion, the more he admired me and the fonder he was of me.[6]

This is written of, I am sensible, as if it had lasted a year. It lasted about five days. Expecting Herbert all the time, I dared not go out, except when I took Provis for an airing after dark. At length, one evening when dinner was over and I had dropped into a slumber quite worn out—for my nights had been agitated and my rest broken by fearful dreams—I was roused by the welcome footstep on the staircase. Provis, who had been asleep too, staggered 10 up at the noise I made, and in an instant I saw his jack-knife shining in his hand.

"Steady! It's Herbert!" I said; and Herbert came bursting in, with the airy freshness of six hundred miles of France upon him.

"Handel, my dear fellow, how are you, and again how are you, and again how are you? I seem to have been gone a twelvemonth! Why, so I must have been, for you have grown quite thin and pale! Handel, my——Halloa! I beg your pardon."

He was stopped in his running on and in his shaking hands with me, by seeing Provis. Provis, regarding him with a fixed attention, was slowly putting 20 up his jack-knife, and groping in another pocket for something else.

"Herbert, my dear friend," said I, shutting the double doors, while Herbert stood staring and wondering, "something very strange has happened. This is —a visitor of mine."

"It's all right, dear boy!" said Provis coming forward, with his little clasped black book, and then addressing himself to Herbert. "Take it in your right hand. Lord strike you dead on the spot if you ever split[7] in any way sumever! Kiss it!"

"Do so, as he wishes it," I said to Herbert. So Herbert, looking at me with a friendly uneasiness and amazement, complied, and Provis immediately 30 shaking hands with him, said, "Now you're on your oath, you know. And never believe me on mine, if Pip don't make a gentleman on you!"

Chapter XLI.

IN vain should I attempt to describe the astonishment and disquiet of Herbert, when he and I and Provis sat down before the fire, and I recounted the whole of the secret. Enough that I saw my own feelings reflected in Herbert's face, and, not least among them, my repugnance towards the man who had done so much for me.

What would alone have set a division between that man and us, if there

6. The titular hero of Mary Shelley's *Frankenstein* (see above, p. 169, n. 2) infuses life into the famous monster. Although the monster kills Frankenstein's small brother, his closest friend, and (during their wedding night) his wife, he only figuratively pursues the scientist by tormenting him for having given him life, then for his refusal to provide a mate; it is Frankenstein himself who eventually embarks on a pursuit of the creature and dies in the chase. Pip is saying that in his case the monster has made the man.
7. "If ever you turn informer."

had been no other dividing circumstance, was his triumph in my story. Saving his troublesome sense of having been "low" on one occasion since his return—on which point he began to hold forth to Herbert, the moment my revelation was finished—he had no perception of the possibility of my finding any fault with my good fortune. His boast that he had made me a gentleman, and that he had come to see me support the character on his ample resources, was made for me quite as much as for himself; and that it was a highly agreeable boast to both of us, and that we must both be very proud of it, was a conclusion quite established in his own mind.

"Though, look'ee here, Pip's comrade," he said to Herbert, after having 10 discoursed for some time, "I know very well that once since I come back— for half a minute—I've been low. I said to Pip, I knowed as I had been low. But don't you fret yourself on that score. I ain't made Pip a gentleman, and Pip ain't a going to make you a gentleman, not fur me not to know what's due to ye both. Dear boy, and Pip's comrade, you two may count upon me always having a gen-teel muzzle on. Muzzled I have been since that half a minute when I was betrayed into lowness, muzzled I am at the present time, and muzzled I ever will be."

Herbert said, "Certainly," but looked as if there were no specific consolation in this, and remained perplexed and dismayed. We were anxious for the 20 time when he would go to his lodging, and leave us together, but he was evidently jealous of leaving us together, and sat late. It was midnight before I took him round to Essex-street, and saw him safely in at his own dark door. When it closed upon him, I experienced the first moment of relief I had known since the night of his arrival.

Never quite free from an uneasy remembrance of the man on the stairs, I had always looked about me in taking my guest out after dark, and in bringing him back; and I looked about me now. Difficult as it is in a large city to avoid the suspicion of being watched, when the mind is conscious of danger in that regard, I could not persuade myself that any of the people within sight 30 cared about my movements. The few who were passing, passed on their several ways, and the street was empty when I turned back into the Temple. Nobody had come out at the gate with us, nobody went in at the gate with me. As I crossed by the fountain, I saw his lighted back windows looking bright and quiet, and when I stood for a few moments in the doorway of the building where I lived, before going up the stairs, Garden-court was as still and lifeless as the staircase was when I ascended it.

Herbert received me with open arms, and I had never felt before, so blessedly, what it is to have a friend. When he had spoken some sound words of sympathy and encouragement, we sat down to consider the question, What 40 was to be done?

The chair that Provis had occupied still remaining where it had stood—for he had a barrack way with him of hanging about one spot, in one unsettled manner, and going through one round of observances with his pipe and his Negro-head and his jack-knife and his pack of cards, and what not, as if it were all put down for him on a slate—I say, his chair remaining where it had stood, Herbert unconsciously took it, but next moment started out of it, pushed it away, and took another. He had no occasion to say, after that, that he had conceived an aversion for my patron, neither had I occasion

to confess my own. We interchanged that confidence without shaping a
syllable.

"What," said I to Herbert, when he was safe in another chair, "what is to
be done?"

"My poor dear Handel," he replied, holding his head, "I am too stunned
to think."

"So was I, Herbert, when the blow first fell. Still, something must be done.
He is intent upon various new expenses—horses, and carriages, and lavish
appearances of all kinds. He must be stopped, somehow."

"You mean that you can't accept——?"   10

"How can I?" I interposed, as Herbert paused. "Think of him! Look at
him!"

An involuntary shudder passed over both of us.

"Yet I am afraid the dreadful truth is, Herbert, that he is attached to me,
strongly attached to me. Was there ever such a fate!"

"My poor dear Handel," Herbert repeated.

"Then," said I, "after all, stopping short here, never taking another penny
from him, think what I owe him already! Then again: I am heavily in debt
—very heavily for me, who have now no expectations at all—and I have been
bred to no calling, and I am fit for nothing."   20

"Well, well, well!" Herbert remonstrated. "Don't say fit for nothing."

"What am I fit for? I know only one thing that I am fit for, and that is, to
go for a soldier. And I might have gone, my dear Herbert, but for the prospect
of taking counsel with your friendship and affection."

~~Of course I broke down there; and of course Herbert, beyond seizing a~~
warm grip of my hand, pretended not to know it.

"Anyhow, my dear Handel," said he presently, "soldiering won't do. If you
were to renounce this patronage and these favours, I suppose you would do
so with some faint hope of one day repaying what you have already had. Not
very strong, that hope, if you went soldiering! Besides, it's absurd. You would 30
be infinitely better in Clarriker's house, small as it is. I am working up towards
a partnership, you know."

Poor fellow! He little suspected with whose money.

"But there is another question," said Herbert. "This is an ignorant determined man, who has long had one fixed idea. More than that, he seems
to me (I may misjudge him) to be a man of a desperate and fierce character."

"I know he is," I returned. "Let me tell you what evidence I have seen of
it." And I told him what I had not mentioned in my narrative; of that encounter with the other convict.   40

"See, then!" said Herbert; "think of this! He comes here at the peril of his
life, for the realisation of his fixed idea. In the moment of realisation, after
all his toil and waiting, you cut the ground from under his feet, destroy his
idea, and make his gains worthless to him. Do you see nothing that he might
do, under the disappointment?"

"I have seen it, Herbert, and dreamed of it ever since the fatal night of his
arrival. Nothing has been in my thoughts so distinctly, as his putting himself
in the way of being taken."

"Then you may rely upon it," said Herbert, "that there would be great danger of his doing it. That is his power over you as long as he remains in England, and that would be his reckless course if you forsook him."

I was so struck by the horror of this idea, which had weighed upon me from the first, and the working out of which would make me regard myself, in some sort, as his murderer, that I could not rest in my chair but began pacing to and fro. I said to Herbert, meanwhile, that even if Provis were recognised and taken, in spite of himself, I should be wretched as the cause, however innocently. Yes; even though I was so wretched in having him at large and near me, and even though I would far far rather have worked at the forge all the days of my life, than I would ever have come to this! 10

But there was no raving off[1] the question, What was to be done?

"The first and the main thing to be done," said Herbert, "is to get him out of England. You will have to go with him, and then he may be induced to go."

"But get him where I will, could I prevent his coming back?"

"My good Handel, is it not obvious that with Newgate in the next street, there must be far greater hazard in your breaking your mind to him and making him reckless, here, than elsewhere. If a pretext to get him away could be made out of that other convict, or out of anything else in his life, now."

"There, again!" said I, stopping before Herbert, with my open hands held 20 out as if they contained the desperation of the case. "I know nothing of his life.[2] It has almost made me mad to sit here of a night and see him before me, so bound up with my fortunes and misfortunes, and yet so unknown to me, except as the miserable wretch who terrified me two days in my childhood!"

Herbert got up, and linked his arm in mine, and we slowly walked to and fro together, studying the carpet.

"Handel," said Herbert, stopping, "you feel convinced that you can take no further benefits from him; do you?"

"Fully. Surely you would, too, if you were in my place?" 30

"And you feel convinced that you must break with him?"

"Herbert, can you ask me?"

"And you have, and are bound to have, that tenderness for the life he has risked on your account, that you must save him, if possible, from throwing it away. Then you must get him out of England before you stir a finger to extricate yourself. That done, extricate yourself, in Heaven's name, and we'll see it out together, dear old boy."

It was a comfort to shake hands upon it, and walk up and down again, with only that done.

"Now, Herbert," said I, "with reference to gaining some knowledge of his 40 history. There is but one way that I know of. I must ask him point-blank."

"Yes. Ask him," said Herbert, "when we sit at breakfast in the morning."

---

1. In most editions, unsurprisingly corrected to "staving off." But "raving off" is unmistakably the MS reading and makes sense: the expression suggests Pip's pent-up tension and dread of Magwitch's and his own future. Thus in Emily Jolly's "A Wife's Story," which Dickens—recognizing the writer's potential greatness—ran as a brief serial in *Household Words* from September 1 to 15, 1855, the narrator, who is recovering from a fit of hysteria, writes: "When [the doctor] arrived, my passion had raved itself out." (But the rare usage of the term is reflected in its omission from the *OED*.)

2. In MS followed by the sentence "He is a mystery to me." Dickens may have struck as too closely echoing the preceding chapter: "Words cannot tell what a sense I had . . . of the dreadful mystery that he was to me."

For he had said, on taking leave of Herbert, that he would come to breakfast with us.

With this project formed, we went to bed. I had the wildest dreams concerning him, and woke unrefreshed; I woke, too, to recover the fear which I had lost in the night, of his being found out as a returned transport. Waking, I never lost that fear.

He came round at the appointed time, took out his jack-knife, and sat down to his meal. He was full of plans "for his gentleman's coming out strong, and like a gentleman," and urged me to begin speedily upon the pocket-book, which he had left in my possession. He considered the chambers and his 10 own lodging as temporary residences, and advised me to look out at once for a "fashionable crib" near Hyde Park, in which he could have "a shake-down."[3] When he had made an end of his breakfast, and was wiping his knife on his leg, I said to him, without a word of preface:

"After you were gone last night, I told my friend of the struggle that the soldiers found you engaged in on the marshes, when we came up. You remember?"

"Remember!" said he. "I think so!"

"We want to know something about that man—and about you. It is strange to know no more about either, and particularly you, than I was able to tell 20 last night. Is not this as good a time as another for our knowing more?"

"Well!" he said, after consideration. "You're on your oath, you know, Pip's comrade?"

"Assuredly," replied Herbert.

~~"As to anything I say, you know," he insisted. "The oath applies to all."~~

"I understand it to do so."

"And look'ee here! Whatever I done, is worked out and paid for," he insisted again.

"So be it."

He took out his black pipe and was going to fill it with negro-head, when, 30 looking at the tangle of tobacco in his hand, he seemed to think it might perplex the thread of his narrative.[4] He put it back again, stuck his pipe in a button-hole of his coat, spread a hand on each knee, and, after turning an angry eye on the fire for a few silent moments, looked round at us and said what follows.

Chapter XLII.

"DEAR boy and Pip's comrade. I am not a going fur to tell you my life, like a song or a story-book. But to give it you short and handy, I'll put it at once into a mouthful of English. In jail and out of jail, in jail and out of jail, in jail and out of jail. There, you've got it. That's *my* life pretty much, down to such times as I got shipped off, arter Pip stood my friend. 40

"I've been done everything to, pretty well—except hanged. I've been locked up, as much as a silver tea-kettle. I've been carted here and carted there, and

---

3. Improvised bed made up on the floor, usually of straw or hay. "Fashionable crib": thieves' cant for cheap lodging; also a disreputable public house or shop or any kind of shelter.
4. Magwitch fears that his story will become confused, muddled, or, metaphorically, tangled like his tobacco. In this sense (minus the tobacco) Othello's curtain-speech, 5.2.352–55: "Then must you speak . . . Of one not easily jealous but, being wrought, / Perplexed in the extreme."

put out of this town and put out of that town, and stuck in the stocks,[1] and whipped and worried and drove. I've no more notion where I was born than you have—if so much. I first become aware of myself, down in Essex, a thieving turnips for my living. Summun had run away from me—a man—a tinker—and he'd took the fire with him, and left me wery cold.

"I know'd my name to be Magwitch, chris'end Abel. How did I know it? Much as I know'd the birds' names in the hedges to be chaffinch, sparrer, thrush. I might have thought it was all lies together, only as the birds' names come out true, I supposed mine did.

"So fur as I could find, there warn't a soul that see young Abel Magwitch, with as little on him as in him, but wot caught fright at him, and either drove him off, or took him up.[2] I was took up, took up, took up, to that extent that I reg'larly grow'd up took up.

"This is the way it was, that when I was a ragged little creetur as much to be pitied as ever I see (not that I looked in the glass, for there warn't many insides of furnished houses known to me), I got the name of being hardened. 'This is a terrible hardened one,' they says to prison wisitors,[3] picking out me. 'May be said to live in jails, this boy.' Then they looked at me, and I looked at them, and they measured my head,[4] some on 'em—they had better a measured my stomach—and others on 'em giv me tracts what I couldn't read,[5] and made me speeches what I couldn't unnerstand. They always went on agen me about the Devil. But what the Devil was I to do? I must put something into my stomach, mustn't I?—Howsomever, I'm a getting low, and I know what's due. Dear boy and Pip's comrade, don't you be afeerd of me being low.

"Tramping, begging, thieving, working sometimes when I could—though that warn't as often as you may think, till you put the question whether you would ha' been over ready to give me work yourselves—a bit of a poacher, a bit of a labourer, a bit of a waggoner, a bit of a haymaker, a bit of a hawker,[6] a bit of most things that don't pay and lead to trouble, I got to be a man. A deserting soldier in a Travellers' Rest,[7] what lay hid up to the chin under a

---

1. The stocks, or pillory, one of the earliest torture instruments in England, officially adopted by the Statute of the Pillory and Tumbrel in 1266, had long outlived its usefulness by the time Magwitch was put on display. It was abolished in 1816 as distasteful and inhumane, its effectiveness as a deterrent chiefly dependent "on the whim of the multitude," that is, the fun-loving spectators.
2. Arrested him.
3. One of two dissimilar meanings: (1) "Moral missionaries" urging convicts to reform; (2) government-appointed inspectors who had to see to it that prison regulations were being carried out and that the prisoners were not being ill-treated.
4. Magwitch refers to the phrenologists, who studied the shape of the patient's (or criminal's) head to discover the contours of his personality and moral character. Dickens's friend and personal physician, Dr. John Elliotson (1791–1868), the founder of the Phrenological Society, lectured in 1823 on the phrenological symptoms of a famous murderer, who suffered from overdeveloped "bumps of amativeness, destructiveness, and acquisitiveness" (McMaster). The practice persisted throughout the century; in Conrad's *Heart of Darkness* (1899), Marlow has to have his head measured as part of his physical.
5. Dickens deplored the "utilitarian" practice of foisting edifying literature on the poor and the criminal classes, notably books issued by the Society for the Diffusion of Useful Knowledge, founded between 1825 and 1828 by liberals like the reformist politician Lord Brougham and the progressive criminologist M. D. Hill. In justice to the Society it should be said that most of its publications contained about as much moral uplift as a railway guide, consisting mostly of calendars, atlases, actuarial tables, and statistical rosters.
6. Huckster, or peddler. Hawkers were subject to fines for peddling their wares without a license—or peddling them, even with one, within two miles of a city or market town.
7. Roadside flophouse. "Traveler" could describe all sorts of derelicts: "thieves, swindlers, bullies, ruffians, beggars, &c.," and especially transported convicts, who, as Wemmick euphemistically says of Magwitch in chapter 45, travel to "a certain part of the world . . . not quite irrespective of the government's expense." Wemmick seems to be up on the latest slang: the expression dates from 1823.

lot of taturs,[8] learnt me to read; and a travelling Giant what signed his name at a penny a time learnt me to write.[9] I warn't locked up as often now as formerly, but I wore out my good share of key-metal still.

"At Epsom races,[1] a matter of over twenty year ago, I got acquainted wi' a man whose skull I'd crack wi' this poker, like the claw of a lobster, if I'd got it on this hob. His right name was Compeyson;[2] and that's the man, dear boy, what you see me pounding in the ditch, according to what you truly told your comrade arter I was gone last night.

"He set up fur a gentleman, this Compeyson, and he'd been to a public boarding-school and had learning. He was a smooth one to talk, and was a   10 dab[3] at the ways of gentlefolks. He was good-looking too. It was the night afore the great race, when I found him on the heath in a booth that I know'd on. Him and some more was a sitting among the tables when I went in, and the landlord (which had a knowledge of me, and was a sporting one) called him out, and said, 'I think this is a man that might suit you'—meaning I was.

"Compeyson, he looks at me very noticing, and I look at him. He has a watch and a chain and a ring and a breast-pin and a handsome suit of clothes.

" 'To judge from appearances, you're out of luck,' says Compeyson to   20 me.

" 'Yes, master, and I've never been in it much.' (I come out of Kingston Jail[4] last on a vagrancy committal.[5] Not but wot it might have been for something else; but it warn't).

" ~~'Luck changes,' says Compeyson; 'perhaps yours is going to change.'~~

"I says, 'I hope it may be so. There's room.'

" 'What can you do?' says Compeyson.

" 'Eat and drink,' I says; 'if you'll find the materials.'

"Compeyson laughed, looked at me again very noticing, giv me five shillings, and appointed me for next night. Same place.   30

"I went to Compeyson, next night, same place, and Compeyson took me on to be his man and pardner. And what was Compeyson's business in which we was to go pardners? Compeyson's business was the swindling, handwriting

8. Potatoes.
9. In Pip's day, giants, pygmies, and hunger artists did not have to earn their keep cooped up in a circus or as exhibits on fair days: itinerant physical freaks sold their autographs to pop-eyed passers-by. For the change in wording from MS "dwarf," see Cardwell, p. xiv.
1. Market town in Surrey, fifteen miles southwest of London—in Dickens's phrase, "the metropolis of English racing [since 1780], and fountain of Epsom salts." As a natural base for pickpockets, the Epsom racecourse provides a field day for Scotland Yard in "Three Detective Anecdotes—II," *Household Words*, September 14, 1850.
2. Grose (Suppl. 1839) gives "Compersome" as Derbyshire dialect for "frolicksome: generally applied to a horse." So Compeyson's name may be remotely allusive, given his debut at the derby.
3. Experienced hand. Presumably a corruption of "adept," originally in the sense of "sharpster," an "expert exquisite in Roguery" (Grose).
4. Prison for the temporary confinement of suspects. Kingston-on-Thames, the county town of Surrey, lies on the right bank of the Thames, kitty-corner from Hampton Court, some eleven miles southwest of London. From "King's Town," a reminder that most of the tenth-century West Saxon monarchs were crowned in Kingston before William the Conqueror moved the coronation to Westminster Abbey in 1066.
5. Vagrancy has generally been a misdemeanor, the earliest enactments prompted by the alarming increase of the migratory population in the Middle Ages and the arrival of the first gypsies in England in the early sixteenth century. The penalties fixed by the Vagrant Act of 1743 and the Rogues and Vagabonds Act of 1792, under which Magwitch would have been liable, ranged from one month's to two years' imprisonment. The leniency accorded to vagrants and the nature of Kingston Jail as a prison for short-timers suggest that Magwitch's detentions were brief; his own offhand phrase, "it might have been for something else," can be read as "it might have been worse."

forging, stolen bank-note passing, and such-like.[6] All sorts of traps as Compeyson could set with his head, and keep his own legs out of and get the profits from and let another man in for, was Compeyson's business. He'd no more heart than a iron file, he was as cold as death, and he had the head of the Devil afore mentioned.

"There was another in with Compeyson, as was called Arthur—not as being so chris'end, but as a surname. He was in a Decline, and was a shadow to look at. Him and Compeyson had been in a bad thing with a rich lady some years afore, and they'd made a pot of money by it; but Compeyson betted and gamed, and he'd have run through the king's taxes. So Arthur was a dying, and a dying poor and with the horrors[7] on him, and Compeyson's wife (which Compeyson kicked mostly) was a having pity on him when she could, and Compeyson was a having pity on nothing and nobody.

"I might a took warning by Arthur, but I didn't; and I won't pretend I wos partick'ler—for where 'ud be the good on it, dear boy and comrade? So I begun wi' Compeyson, and a poor tool I was in his hands. Arthur lived at the top of Compeyson's house (over nigh Brentford[8] it was), and Compeyson kept a careful account agen him for board and lodging, in case he should ever get better to work it out. But Arthur soon settled the account. The second or third time as ever I see him, he come a tearing down into Compeyson's parlour late at night, in only a flannel gown, with his hair all in a sweat, and he says to Compeyson's wife, 'Sally, she really is up-stairs alonger me now, and I can't get rid of her. She's all in white,' he says, 'wi' white flowers in her hair, and she's awful mad, and she's got a shroud hanging over her arm, and she says she'll put it on me at five in the morning.'

"Says Compeyson: 'Why, you fool, don't you know she's got a living body? And how should she be up there, without coming through the door, or in at the window, and up the stairs?'

" 'I don't know how she's there,' says Arthur, shivering dreadful with the horrors, 'but she's standing in the corner at the foot of the bed, awful mad. And over where her heart's broke—you broke it!—there's drops of blood.'

"Compeyson spoke hardy, but he was always a coward. 'Go up alonger this drivelling sick man,' he says to his wife, 'and Magwitch, lend her a hand, will you?' But he never come nigh himself.

"Compeyson's wife and me took him up to bed agen, and he raved most dreadful. 'Why look at her!' he cries out. 'She's a shaking the shroud at me! Don't you see her? Look at her eyes! Ain't it awful to see her so mad?' Next, he cries, 'She'll put it on me, and then I'm done for! Take it away from her, take it away!' And then he catched hold of us, and kep on a talking to her, and answering of her, till I half believed I see her myself.

"Compeyson's wife, being used to him, giv him some liquor to get the

---

6. These were all capital felonies. The Forgery Acts passed in the eighteenth and early nineteenth centuries emphasized the importance Parliament and the judiciary attached to property crimes. As the jurist John Holliday wrote in 1797, at about the time Magwitch and Compeyson were waging war on property, "Forgery is a stab to commerce, and only to be tolerated in a commercial nation when the foul crime of murder is pardoned." Forgery ceased to be a capital offense "in certain cases" in 1832, unconditionally five years later, replaced by sentences ranging from transportation for life to prison terms.

7. Delirium tremens.

8. County town in Middlesex, some eight miles west of London Bridge; one of the main thoroughfares in southern England before the railroad age. A popular resort in Shakespeare's day and after: legendary for its dirt, which so charmed George I as a reminder of his native Hanover that the royal carriage had to slow down whenever he passed through Brentford en route to and from Hampton.

horrors off, and by-and-by he quieted. 'Oh, she's gone! Has her keeper been for her?' he says. 'Yes,' says Compeyson's wife. 'Did you tell him to lock her and bar her in?' 'Yes.' 'And to take that ugly thing away from her?' 'Yes, yes, all right.' 'You're a good creetur,' he says, 'don't leave me, whatever you do, and thank you!'

"He rested pretty quiet till it might want a few minutes of five, and then he starts up with a scream, and screams out, 'Here she is! She's got the shroud again. She's unfolding it. She's coming out of the corner. She's coming to the bed. Hold me, both on you—one of each side—don't let her touch me with it. Hah! she missed me that time. Don't let her throw it over my shoul- 10 ders. Don't let her lift me up to get it round me. She's lifting me up. Keep me down!' Then he lifted himself up hard, and was dead.

"Compeyson took it easy as a good riddance for both sides. Him and me was soon busy, and first he swore me (being ever artful) on my own book— this here little black book, dear boy, what I swore your comrade on.

"Not to go into the things that Compeyson planned, and I done—which 'ud take a week—I'll simply say to you, dear boy, and Pip's comrade, that that man got me into such nets as made me his black slave. I was always in debt to him, always under his thumb, always a working, always a getting into danger. He was younger than me, but he'd got craft, and he'd got learning, 20 and he overmatched me five hundred times told and no mercy. My Missis as I had the hard time wi' —— Stop though! I ain't brought *her* in —— "

He looked about him in a confused way, as if he had lost his place in the book of his remembrance; and he turned his face to the fire, and spread his hands broader on his knees, and lifted them off and put them on again.

"There ain't no need to go into it," he said, looking round once more. "The time wi' Compeyson was a'most as hard a time as ever I had; that said, all's said. Did I tell you as I was tried, alone, for misdemeanour, while with Compeyson?"

I answered, No.   30

"Well!" he said, "I *was*, and got convicted. As to took up on suspicion, that was twice or three times in the four or five year that it lasted; but evidence was wanting. At last, me and Compeyson was both committed for felony— on a charge of putting stolen notes in circulation[9]—and there was other charges behind. Compeyson says to me, 'Separate defences, no communi- cation,' and that was all. And I was so miserable poor, that I sold all the clothes I had, except what hung on my back, afore I could get Jaggers.

"When we was put in the dock, I noticed first of all what a gentleman Compeyson looked, wi' his curly hair and his black clothes and his white pocket-handkercher, and what a common sort of a wretch I looked. When 40 the prosecution opened and the evidence was put short, aforehand, I noticed how heavy it all bore on me, and how light on him. When the evidence was giv in the box, I noticed how it was always me that had come for'ard, and could be swore to, how it was always me that the money had been paid to, how it was always me that had seemed to work the thing and get the profit. But, when the defence come on, then I see the plan plainer; for, says the counsellor for Compeyson, 'My lord and gentlemen, here you has afore you, side by side, two persons as your eyes can separate wide; one, the younger,

9. Again, a capital felony, although the sentences the Judge imposes more nearly reflect the actualities of contemporary penology.

well brought up, who will be spoke to as such; one, the elder, ill brought up, who will be spoke to as such; one, the younger, seldom if ever seen in these here transactions, and only suspected; t'other, the elder, always seen in 'em and always wi' his guilt brought home. Can you doubt, if there is but one in it, which is the one, and, if there is two in it, which is much the worst one?' And such-like. And when it come to character, warn't it Compeyson as had been to the school, and warn't it his schoolfellows as was in this position and in that, and warn't it him as had been know'd by witnesses in such clubs and societies, and nowt to his disadvantage? And warn't it me as had been tried afore, and as had been know'd up hill and down dale in Bridewells[1] and Lock-Ups?[2] And when it come to speech-making, warn't it Compeyson as could speak to 'em wi' his face dropping every now and then into his white pocket-handkercher—ah! and wi' verses in his speech, too—and warn't it me as could only say, 'Gentlemen, this man at my side is a most precious rascal'? And when the verdict come, warn't it Compeyson as was recommended to mercy on account of good character and bad company, and giving up all the information he could agen me, and warn't it me as got never a word but Guilty? And when I says to Compeyson, 'Once out of this court, I'll smash that face of yourn?' ain't it Compeyson as prays the Judge to be protected, and gets two turnkeys stood betwixt us? And when we're sentenced, ain't it him as gets seven year, and me fourteen, and ain't it him as the Judge is sorry for, because he might a done so well, and ain't it me as the Judge perceives to be a old offender of wiolent passion, likely to come to worse?"

He had worked himself into a state of great excitement, but he checked it, took two or three short breaths, swallowed as often, and stretching out his hand towards me said, in a reassuring manner, "I ain't going to be low, dear boy!"

He had so heated himself that he took out his handkerchief and wiped his face and head and neck and hands, before he could go on.

"I had said to Compeyson that I'd smash that face of his, and I swore Lord smash mine! to do it. We was in the same prison-ship, but I couldn't get at him for long, though I tried. At last I come behind him and hit him on the cheek to turn him round and get a smashing one at him, when I was seen and seized. The black-hole of that ship warn't a strong one, to a judge of black-holes that could swim and dive. I escaped to the shore, and I was a hiding among the graves there, envying them as was in 'em and all over, when first I see my boy!"

He regarded me with a look of affection that made him almost abhorrent to me again, though I had felt great pity for him.

"By my boy, I was giv to understand as Compeyson was out on them marshes too. Upon my soul, I half believe he escaped in his terror, to get

---

1. Originally a palace completed by Henry VIII in 1523 near St. Bridget's Well, south of Whitefriars, between the Temple and Carmelite (now New Bridge) Street. Under Edward VI "A House of Correction and House of Occupation" for vagrants, heretics, and whores. Notorious for its whipping post and appalling conditions generally, Bridewell persisted as a generic term for reformatories, in the sense in which Magwitch uses it.
2. "A spunging house; a public house kept by sheriff's officers, to which they convey the persons they have arrested, where they practice every species of imposition and extortion with impunity" (Grose). That is, a house of detention to which a debtor, against whom legal proceedings were pending, was confined at his own expense until he paid up or was bailed out or removed to a debtors' prison. Dickens's father spent three days in a lock-up before his removal to the Marshalsea in February 1824; on Pip's close call with sponging-house officers, see chapter 57.

quit of me, not knowing it was me as had got ashore. I hunted him down. I smashed his face. 'And now,' says I, 'as the worst thing I can do, caring nothing for myself, I'll drag you back.' And I'd have swum off, towing him by the hair, if it had come to that, and I'd a got him aboard without the soldiers.

"Of course he'd much the best of it to the last—his character was so good. He had escaped when he was made half wild by me and my murderous intentions; and his punishment was light. I was put in irons, brought to trial again, and sent for life. I didn't stop for life, dear boy and Pip's comrade, being here."   10

He wiped himself again, as he had done before, and then slowly took his tangle of tobacco from his pocket, and plucked his pipe from his button-hole, and slowly filled it, and began to smoke.

"Is he dead?" I asked, after a silence.

"Is who dead, dear boy?"

"Compeyson."

"He hopes I am, if he's alive, you may be sure," with a fierce look. "I never heerd no more of him."

Herbert had been writing with his pencil in the cover of a book. He softly pushed the book over to me, as Provis stood smoking with his eyes on the   20 fire, and I read in it:

"Young Havisham's name was Arthur. Compeyson is the man who professed to be Miss Havisham's lover."

I shut the book and nodded slightly to Herbert, and put the book by; but we neither of us said anything, and both looked at Provis as he stood smoking by the fire.

Chapter XLIII.

WHY should I pause to ask how much of my shrinking from Provis might be traced to Estella? Why should I loiter on my road, to compare the state of mind in which I had tried to rid myself of the stain of the prison before meeting her at the coach-office, with the state of mind in which I now re-   30 flected on the abyss between Estella in her pride and beauty, and the returned transport whom I harboured? The road would be none the smoother for it, the end would be none the better for it, he would not be helped, nor I extenuated.

A new fear had been engendered in my mind by his narrative; or rather, his narrative had given form and purpose to the fear that was already there. If Compeyson were alive and should discover his return, I could hardly doubt the consequence. That Compeyson stood in mortal fear of him, neither of the two could know much better than I; and that any such man as that man had been described to be, would hesitate to release himself for good from a   40 dreaded enemy by the safe means of becoming an informer, was scarcely to be imagined.

Never had I breathed, and never would I breathe—or so I resolved—a word of Estella to Provis. But, I said to Herbert that before I could go abroad, I must see both Estella and Miss Havisham. This was when we were left alone on the night of the day when Provis told us his story. I resolved to go out to Richmond next day, and I went.

On my presenting myself at Mrs. Brandley's, Estella's maid was called to tell me that Estella had gone into the country. Where? To Satis House, as usual. Not as usual, I said, for she had never yet gone there without me; when was she coming back? There was an air of reservation in the answer which increased my perplexity, and the answer was, that her maid believed she was only coming back at all for a little while. I could make nothing of this, except that it was meant that I should make nothing of it, and I went home again in complete discomfiture.

Another night-consultation with Herbert after Provis was gone home (I always took him home, and always looked well about me), led us to the conclusion that nothing should be said about going abroad until I came back from Miss Havisham's. In the mean time, Herbert and I were to consider separately what it would be best to say; whether we should devise any pretence of being afraid that he was under suspicious observation; or whether I, who had never yet been abroad, should propose an expedition. We both knew that I had but to propose anything, and he would consent. We agreed that his remaining many days in his present hazard was not to be thought of.

Next day, I had the meanness to feign that I was under a binding promise to go down to Joe; but I was capable of almost any meanness towards Joe or his name. Provis was to be strictly careful while I was gone, and Herbert was to take the charge of him that I had taken. I was to be absent only one night, and, on my return, the gratification of his impatience for my starting as a gentleman on a greater scale, was to be begun. It occurred to me then, and as I afterwards found to Herbert also, that he might be best got away across the water, on that pretence—as, to make purchases, or the like.

Having thus cleared the way for my expedition to Miss Havisham's, I set off by the early morning coach before it was yet light, and was out on the open country-road when the day came creeping on, halting and whimpering and shivering, and wrapped in patches of cloud and rags of mist, like a beggar. When we drove up to the Blue Boar after a drizzly ride, whom should I see come out under the gateway, toothpick in hand, to look at the coach, but Bentley Drummle!

As he pretended not to see me, I pretended not to see him. It was a very lame pretence on both sides; the lamer, because we both went into the coffee-room, where he had just finished his breakfast and where I ordered mine. It was poisonous to me to see him in the town, for I very well knew why he had come there.

Pretending to read a smeary newspaper long out of date, which had nothing half so legible in its local news, as the foreign matter of coffee, pickles, fish sauces, gravy, melted butter, and wine, with which it was sprinkled all over, as if it had taken the measles in a highly irregular form, I sat at my table while he stood before the fire. By degrees it became an enormous injury to me that he stood before the fire, and I got up, determined to have my share of it. I had to put my hand behind his legs for the poker when I went up to the fireplace to stir the fire, but still pretended not to know him.

"Is this a cut?"[1] said Mr. Drummle.

"Oh!" said I, poker in hand; "it's you, is it? How do you do? I was wondering who it was, who kept the fire off."

With that, I poked tremendously, and having done so, planted myself side
by side with Mr. Drummle, my shoulders squared and my back to the fire.

"You have just come down?" said Mr. Drummle, edging me a little away
with his shoulder.

"Yes," said I, edging *him* a little away with *my* shoulder.

"Beastly place," said Drummle.—"Your part of the country, I think?"

"Yes," I assented. "I am told it's very like your Shropshire."   10

"Not in the least like it," said Drummle.

Here Mr. Drummle looked at his boots, and I looked at mine, and then
Mr. Drummle looked at my boots, and I looked at his.

"Have you been here long?" I asked, determined not to yield an inch of
the fire.

"Long enough to be tired of it," returned Drummle, pretending to yawn,
but equally determined.

"Do you stay here long?"

"Can't say," answered Mr. Drummle. "Do you?"

"Can't say," said I.   20

I felt here, through a tingling in my blood, that if Mr. Drummle's shoulder had
claimed another hair's breadth of room, I should have jerked him into the window; equally, that if my own shoulder had urged a similar claim, Mr. Drummle
would have jerked me into the nearest box. He whistled a little. So did I.

"Large tract of marshes about here, I believe?" said Drummle.

"Yes. What of that?" said I.

Mr. Drummle looked at me, and then at my boots, and then said, "Oh!"
and laughed.

"Are you amused, Mr. Drummle?"

"No," said he, "not particularly. I am going out for a ride in the saddle. I   30
mean to explore those marshes for amusement. Out-of-the-way villages there,
they tell me. Curious little public-houses—and smithies—and that. Waiter!"

"Yes, sir."

"Is that horse of mine ready?"

"Brought round to the door, sir."

"I say. Look here, you sir. The lady won't ride to-day; the weather won't do."

"Very good, sir."

"And I don't dine, because I'm going to dine at the lady's."

"Very good, sir."

Then Drummle glanced at me, with an insolent triumph on his great-   40
jowled face that cut me to the heart, dull as he was, and so exasperated me,
that I felt inclined to take him in my arms as the robber in the story-book is
said to have taken the old lady, and seat him on the fire.[2]

---

1. "Are you snubbing me?"
2. Pip alludes to an incident in the life of Richard Turpin, the famous highwayman (1706–1739), as this
appears in *The Newgate Calendar*. Burglarizing the house of "an old woman at Loughton [in Essex]
who was in possession of seven or eight hundred pounds," Turpin threatened to "set her on the fire"
unless she produced the money. When she refused, Turpin and his gang "actually placed her on the
fire, where she sat till the tormenting pains compelled her to discover her hidden treasure." The story
enjoyed wide currency, often with sensational illustrations: Dickens may have found his source in one
of many chapbooks.

One thing was manifest to both of us, and that was, that until relief came, neither of us could relinquish the fire. There we stood, well squared up before it, shoulder to shoulder, and foot to foot, with our hands behind us, not budging an inch. The horse was visible outside in the drizzle at the door, my breakfast was put on table, Drummle's was cleared away, the waiter invited me to begin, I nodded, we both stood our ground.

"Have you been to the Grove since?" said Drummle.

"No," said I, "I had quite enough of the Finches the last time I was there."

"Was that when we had a difference of opinion?"

"Yes," I replied, very shortly.

"Come, come! They let you off easily enough," sneered Drummle. "You shouldn't have lost your temper."

"Mr. Drummle," said I, "you are not competent to give advice on that subject. When I lose my temper (not that I admit having done so on that occasion), I don't throw glasses."

"I do," said Drummle.

After glancing at him once or twice, in an increased state of smouldering ferocity, I said:

"Mr. Drummle, I did not seek this conversation, and I don't think it an agreeable one."

"I am sure it's not," said he, superciliously over his shoulder; "I don't think anything about it."

"And therefore," I went on, "with your leave, I will suggest that we hold no kind of communication in future."

"Quite my opinion," said Drummle, "and what I should have suggested myself, or done—more likely—without suggesting. But don't lose your temper. Haven't you lost enough without that?"

"What do you mean, sir?"

"Wa-iter!" said Drummle, by way of answering me.

The waiter reappeared.

"Look here, you sir. You quite understand that the young lady don't ride to-day, and that I dine at the young lady's?"

"Quite so, sir."

When the waiter had felt my fast-cooling teapot with the palm of his hand, and had looked imploringly at me, and had gone out, Drummle, careful not to move the shoulder next me, took a cigar from his pocket and bit the end off, but showed no sign of stirring. Choking and boiling as I was, I felt that we could not go a word further, without introducing Estella's name, which I could not endure to hear him utter; and therefore I looked stonily at the opposite wall, as if there were no one present, and forced myself to silence. How long we might have remained in this ridiculous position it is impossible to say, but for the incursion of three thriving farmers—laid on[3] by the waiter, I am inclined to think—who came into the coffee-room unbuttoning their great-coats and rubbing their hands, and before whom, as they charged at the fire, we were obliged to give way.

I saw him through the window, seizing his horse's mane, and mounting in his blundering brutal manner, and sidling and backing away. I thought he was gone, when he came back, calling for a light for the cigar in his mouth,

---

3. "Planted" or "put on the scent" [OED].

which he had forgotten. A man in a dust-coloured dress appeared with what was wanted—I could not have said from where: whether from the inn yard, or the street, or where not—and as Drummle leaned down from the saddle and lighted his cigar and laughed, with a jerk of his head towards the coffee-room windows, the slouching shoulders and ragged hair of this man, whose back was towards me, reminded me of Orlick.

Too heavily out of sorts to care much at the time whether it were he or no, or after all to touch the breakfast, I washed the weather and the journey from my face and hands, and went out to the memorable old house that it would have been so much the better for me never to have entered, never to have seen.

Chapter XLIV.

IN the room where the dressing-table stood and where the wax candles burnt on the wall, I found Miss Havisham and Estella; Miss Havisham seated on a settee near the fire, and Estella on a cushion at her feet. Estella was knitting, and Miss Havisham was looking on. They both raised their eyes as I went in, and both saw an alteration in me. I derived that, from the look they interchanged.

"And what wind," said Miss Havisham, "blows you here, Pip?"

Though she looked steadily at me, I saw that she was rather confused. Estella, pausing for a moment in her knitting with her eyes upon me, and then going on, I fancied that I read in the action of her fingers, as plainly as if she had told me in the dumb alphabet, that she perceived I had discovered my real benefactor.

"Miss Havisham," said I, "I went to Richmond yesterday to speak to Estella; and finding that some wind had blown *her* here, I followed."

Miss Havisham motioning to me for the third or fourth time to sit down, I took the chair by the dressing-table which I had often seen her occupy. With all that ruin at my feet and about me, it seemed a natural place for me, that day.

"What I had to say to Estella, Miss Havisham, I will say before you, presently—in a few moments. It will not surprise you, it will not displease you. I am as unhappy as you can ever have meant me to be."

Miss Havisham continued to look steadily at me. I could see in the action of Estella's fingers as they worked, that she attended to what I said; but she did not look up.

"I have found out who my patron is. It is not a fortunate discovery, and is not likely ever to enrich me in reputation, station, fortune, anything. There are reasons why I must say no more of that. It is not my secret, but another's."

As I was silent for a while, looking at Estella and considering how to go on, Miss Havisham repeated, "It is not your secret, but another's. Well?"

"When you first caused me to be brought here, Miss Havisham; when I belonged to the village over yonder that I wish I had never left; I suppose I did really come here, as any other chance boy might have come—as a kind of servant, to gratify a want or a whim, and to be paid for it?"

"Ay, Pip," replied Miss Havisham, steadily nodding her head; "you did."

"And that Mr. Jaggers——"

"Mr. Jaggers," said Miss Havisham, taking me up in a firm tone, "had nothing to do with it, and knew nothing of it. His being my lawyer, and his being the lawyer of your patron, is a coincidence. He holds the same relation towards numbers of people, and it might easily arise. Be that as it may, it did arise, and was not brought about by any one."

Any one might have seen in her haggard face that there was no suppression or evasion so far.

"But when I fell into the mistake I have so long remained in, at least you led me on?" said I.

"Yes," she returned, again nodding steadily, "I let you go on."

"Was that kind?"

"Who am I," cried Miss Havisham, striking her stick upon the floor and flashing into wrath so suddenly that Estella glanced up at her in surprise, "who am I, for God's sake, that I should be kind!"

It was a weak complaint to have made, and I had not meant to make it. I told her so, as she sat brooding after this outburst.

"Well, well, well!" she said. "What else?"

"I was liberally paid for my old attendance here," said I, to soothe her, "in being apprenticed, and I have asked these questions only for my own information. What follows has another (and I hope more disinterested) purpose. In humouring my mistake, Miss Havisham, you punished—practised on— perhaps you will supply whatever term expresses your intention, without offence—your self-seeking relations?"

"I did," said she. "Why, they would have it so! So would you. What has been my history, that I should be at the pains of entreating either them, or you, not to have it so! You made your own snares. *I* never made them."

Waiting until she was quiet again—for this, too, flashed out of her in a wild and sudden way—I went on.

"I have been thrown among one family of your relations, Miss Havisham, and have been constantly among them since I went to London. I know them to have been as honestly under my delusion as I myself. And I should be false and base if I did not tell you, whether it is acceptable to you or no, and whether you are inclined to give credence to it or no, that you deeply wrong both Mr. Matthew Pocket and his son Herbert, if you suppose them to be otherwise than generous, upright, open, and incapable of anything designing or mean."

"They are your friends," said Miss Havisham.

"They made themselves my friends," said I, "when they supposed me to have superseded them; and when Sarah Pocket, Miss Georgiana, and Mistress Camilla were not my friends, I think."

This contrasting of them with the rest seemed, I was glad to see, to do them good with her. She looked at me keenly for a little while, and then said quietly:

"What do you want for them?"

"Only," said I, "that you would not confound them with the others. They may be of the same blood, but, believe me, they are not of the same nature."

Still looking at me keenly, Miss Havisham repeated:

"What do you want for them?"

"I am not so cunning, you see," I said, in answer, conscious that I reddened a little, "as that I could hide from you, even if I desired, that I do want something. Miss Havisham, if you would spare the money to do my friend Herbert a lasting service in life, but which from the nature of the case must be done without his knowledge, I could show you how."

"Why must it be done without his knowledge?" she asked, settling her hands upon her stick, that she might regard me the more attentively.

"Because," said I, "I began the service myself more than two years ago, without his knowledge, and I don't want to be betrayed. Why I fail in my ability to finish it, I cannot explain. It is a part of the secret which is another person's and not mine."

She gradually withdrew her eyes from me, and turned them on the fire. After watching it for what appeared in the silence and by the light of the slowly wasting candles to be a long time, she was roused by the collapse of some of the red coals, and looked towards me again—at first vacantly—then with a gradually concentrating attention. All this time, Estella knitted on. When Miss Havisham had fixed her attention on me, she said, speaking as if there had been no lapse in our dialogue:

"What else?"

"Estella," said I, turning to her now, and trying to command my trembling voice, "you know I love you. You know that I have loved you long and dearly."

She raised her eyes to my face, on being thus addressed, and her fingers plied their work, and she looked at me with an unmoved countenance. I saw that Miss Havisham glanced from me to her, and from her to me.

"I should have said this sooner, but for my long mistake. It induced me to hope that Miss Havisham meant us for one another. While I thought you could not help yourself, as it were, I refrained from saying it. But I must say it now."

Preserving her unmoved countenance, and with her fingers still going, Estella shook her head.

"I know," said I, in answer to that action; "I know. I have no hope that I shall ever call you mine, Estella. I am ignorant what may become of me very soon, how poor I may be, or where I may go. Still, I love you. I have loved you ever since I first saw you in this house."

Looking at me perfectly unmoved and with her fingers busy, she shook her head again.

"It would have been cruel in Miss Havisham, horribly cruel, to practise on the susceptibility of a poor boy, and to torture me through all these years with a vain hope and an idle pursuit, if she had reflected on the gravity of what she did. But I think she did not. I think that in the endurance of her own suffering, she forgot mine, Estella."

I saw Miss Havisham put her hand to her heart and hold it there, as she sat looking by turns at Estella and at me.

"It seems," said Estella, very calmly, "that there are sentiments, fancies—I don't know how to call them—which I am not able to comprehend. When you say you love me, I know what you mean, as a form of words; but nothing more. You address nothing in my breast, you touch nothing there. I don't care for what you say at all. I have tried to warn you of this; now, have I not?"

I said in a miserable manner, "Yes."

"Yes. But you would not be warned, for you thought I didn't mean it. Now, did you not?"

"I thought and hoped you could not mean it. You, so young, untried, and beautiful, Estella! Surely it is not in Nature."

"It is in *my* nature," she returned. And then she added, with a stress upon the words, "It is in the nature formed within me. I make a great difference between you and all other people when I say so much. I can do no more."

"Is it not true," said I, "that Bentley Drummle is in town here, and pursuing you?"

"It is quite true," she replied, referring to him with the indifference of utter contempt.

"That you encourage him, and ride out with him, and that he dines with you this very day?"

She seemed a little surprised that I should know it, but again replied, "Quite true."

"You cannot love him, Estella!"

Her fingers stopped for the first time, as she retorted rather angrily, "What have I told you? Do you still think, in spite of it, that I do not mean what I say?"

"You would never marry him, Estella?"

She looked towards Miss Havisham, and considered for a moment with her work in her hands. Then she said, "Why not tell you the truth? I am going to be married to him."

I dropped my face into my hands, but was able to control myself better than I could have expected, considering what agony it gave me to hear her say those words. When I raised my face again, there was such a ghastly look upon Miss Havisham's, that it impressed me, even in my passionate hurry and grief.

"Estella, dearest dearest Estella, do not let Miss Havisham lead you into this fatal step. Put me aside for ever—you have done so, I well know—but bestow yourself on some worthier person than Drummle. Miss Havisham gives you to him, as the greatest slight and injury that could be done to the many far better men who admire you, and to the few who truly love you. Among those few, there may be one who loves you even as dearly, though he has not loved you as long, as I. Take him, and I can bear it better, for your sake!"

My earnestness awoke a wonder in her that seemed as if it would have been touched with compassion, if she could have rendered me at all intelligible to her own mind.

"I am going," she said again, in a gentler voice, "to be married to him. The preparations for my marriage are making, and I shall be married soon. Why do you injuriously introduce the name of my mother by adoption? It is my own act."

"Your own act, Estella, to fling yourself away upon a brute?"

"On whom should I fling myself away?" she retorted, with a smile. "Should I fling myself away upon the man who would the soonest feel (if people do feel such things) that I took nothing to him? There! It is done. I shall do well enough, and so will my husband. As to leading me into what you call this fatal step, Miss Havisham would have had me wait, and not marry yet; but I am tired of the life I have led, which has very few charms for me, and I am willing enough to change it. Say no more. We shall never understand each other."

"Such a mean brute, such a stupid brute!" I urged in despair.

"Don't be afraid of my being a blessing to him," said Estella; "I shall not be that. Come! Here is my hand. Do we part on this, you visionary boy— or man?"

"O Estella!" I answered, as my bitter tears fell fast on her hand, do what I would to restrain them; "even if I remained in England and could hold my head up with the rest, how could I see you Drummle's wife!" 10

"Nonsense," she returned, "nonsense. This will pass in no time."

"Never, Estella!"

"You will get me out of your thoughts in a week."

"Out of my thoughts! You are part of my existence, part of myself. You have been in every line I have ever read since I first came here, the rough common boy whose poor heart you wounded even then. You have been in every prospect I have ever seen since—on the river, on the sails of the ships, on the marshes, in the clouds, in the light, in the darkness, in the wind, in the woods, in the sea, in the streets. You have been the embodiment of every 20 graceful fancy that my mind has ever become acquainted with. The stones of which the strongest London buildings are made, are not more real, or more impossible to be displaced by your hands, than your presence and in- fluence have been to me, there and everywhere, and will be. Estella, to the last hour of my life, you cannot choose but remain part of my character, part of the little good in me, part of the evil. But, in this separation I associate you only with the good, and I will faithfully hold you to that always, for you must have done me far more good than harm, let me feel now what sharp distress I may. O God bless you, God forgive you!"

In what ecstasy of unhappiness I got these broken words out of myself, I 30 don't know. The rhapsody welled up within me, like blood from an inward wound, and gushed out. I held her hand to my lips some lingering moments, and so I left her. But ever afterwards, I remembered—and soon afterwards with stronger reason—that while Estella looked at me merely with incredulous wonder, the spectral figure of Miss Havisham, her hand still covering her heart, seemed all resolved into a ghastly stare of pity and remorse.

All done, all gone! So much was done and gone, that when I went out at the gate, the light of the day seemed of a darker colour than when I went in. For a while, I hid myself among some lanes and by-paths, and then struck off to walk all the way to London.[1] For, I had by that time come to myself 40 so far, as to consider that I could not go back to the inn and see Drummle there; that I could not bear to sit upon the coach and be spoken to; that I could do nothing half so good for myself as tire myself out.

It was past midnight when I crossed London Bridge. Pursuing the narrow intricacies of the streets which at that time tended westward near the Mid- dlesex shore of the river,[2] my readiest access to the Temple was close by the

1. A walk of twenty-six miles. Nothing extraordinary for a fantastic walker like Dickens, who once, in a fit of pique against his wife and in-laws, covered the same distance as Pip, from his London town house to Gad's Hill; and after his neuritic foot inhibited his gymnastics, he cheered himself up by arranging walking matches for his friends.
2. The north shore, as against the "Surrey side" of the Thames.

river-side, through Whitefriars.[3] I was not expected till to-morrow, but I had my keys, and, if Herbert were gone to bed, could get to bed myself without disturbing him.

As it seldom happened that I came in at that Whitefriars gate after the Temple was closed, and as I was very muddy and weary, I did not take it ill that the night-porter examined me with much attention as he held the gate a little way open for me to pass in. To help his memory, I mentioned my name.

"I was not quite sure, sir, but I thought so. Here's a note, sir. The messenger that brought it, said would you be so good as read it by my lantern."   10

Much surprised by the request, I took the note. It was directed to Philip Pip, Esquire, and on the top of the superscription were the words, "PLEASE READ THIS, HERE." I opened it, the watchman holding up his light, and read inside, in Wemmick's writing:

"DON'T GO HOME."

Chapter XLV.

TURNING from the Temple gate as soon as I had read the warning, I made the best of my way to Fleet-street, and there got a late hackney chariot and drove to the Hummums[1] in Covent Garden. In those times a bed was always to be got there at any hour of the night, and the chamberlain, letting me in at his ready wicket, lighted the candle next in order on his shelf, and showed   20 me straight into the bedroom next in order on his list. It was a sort of vault on the ground floor at the back, with a despotic monster of a four-post bedstead in it, straddling over the whole place, putting one of his arbitrary legs into the fireplace, and another into the doorway, and squeezing the wretched little washing-stand in quite a Divinely Righteous manner.[2]

As I had asked for a night-light, the chamberlain[3] had brought me in, before he left me, the good old constitutional rushlight[4] of those virtuous days—an object like the ghost of a walking-cane, which instantly broke its back if it were touched, which nothing could ever be lighted at, and which was placed in solitary confinement at the bottom of a high tin tower, perforated with   30 round holes that made a staringly wide-awake pattern on the walls. When I had got into bed, and lay there footsore, weary, and wretched, I found that I could no more close my own eyes than I could close the eyes of this foolish

3. Pip enters the Temple at the eastern gate leading to Whitefriars (named for the white mantles the friars wore over their brown habits), the site of the Carmelite monastery founded about 1241 and dissolved by Henry VIII in 1538. By Dickens's day, little more than a network of slums.
1. From *hammam*, Arabic for "bath": named for its location on the site of one of England's earliest Turkish baths (est. 1631), at the southeast corner of Covent Garden. Like most such "bagnios," a combination of steambath, eatery, health center, and brothel during the eighteenth century. The original Hummums was destroyed by fire in 1821 and rebuilt as a hotel; it may have been here that the Finches of the Grove convened: see chapter 34.
2. Facetious reference to the divine right of kings by which rulers like the Stuarts professed to govern.
3. Male chambermaid. Here probably with an ironic suggestion of an attendant on the nobility.
4. Candle made by stripping a rush plant and dipping the pith of the stems in tallow, the candle shaded by a perforated tin cylinder. Joe's bedside tattle in chapter 57—that Havisham has left Camilla "five pound fur to buy rushlights to put her in spirits when she wake up in the night"—reminds us that rushlights generally served as all-night fixtures; and they often formed an essential part of one's travel equipment.

Argus.[5] And thus, in the gloom and death of the night, we stared at one another.[6] What a doleful night! How anxious, how dismal, how long! There was an inhospitable smell in the room, of cold soot and hot dust; and, as I looked up into the corners of the tester[7] over my head, I thought what a number of blue-bottle flies from the butcher's, and earwigs from the market, and grubs[8] from the country, must be holding on up there, lying by for next summer. This led me to speculate whether any of them ever tumbled down, and then I fancied that I felt light falls on my face—a disagreeable turn of thought, suggesting other and more objectionable approaches up my back. When I had lain awake a little while, those extraordinary voices with which silence teems, began to make themselves audible. The closet whispered, the fireplace sighed, the little washing-stand ticked, and one guitar-string played occasionally in the chest of drawers. At about the same time the eyes on the wall acquired a new expression, and in every one of those staring rounds I saw written, DON'T GO HOME.

Whatever night-fancies and night-noises crowded on me, they never warded off this DON'T GO HOME. It plaited itself into whatever I thought of, as a bodily pain would have done. Not long before, I had read in the newspapers how a gentleman unknown had come to the Hummums in the night, and had gone to bed, and had destroyed himself, and had been found in the morning weltering in blood. It came into my head that he must have occupied this very vault of mine, and I got out of bed to assure myself that there were no red marks about; then opened the door to look out into the passages, and cheer myself with the companionship of a distant light, near which I knew the chamberlain to be dozing. But all this time, why I was not to go home, and what had happened at home, and when I should go home, and whether Provis was safe at home, were questions occupying my mind so busily, that one might have supposed there could be no room in it for any other theme. Even when I thought of Estella, and how we had parted that day for ever, and when I recalled all the circumstances of our parting, and all her looks and tones, and the action of her fingers while she knitted—even then I was pursuing, here and there and everywhere, the caution Don't go home. When at last I dozed, in sheer exhaustion of mind and body, it became a vast shadowy verb which I had to conjugate. Imperative mood, present tense: Do not thou go home, let him not go home, let us not go home, do not ye or you go home, let not them go home.[9] Then, potentially: I may not and I

---

5. In Greek mythology, Argus Panoptes, the All-Seeing, shut only two of his hundred eyes in his sleep. Under orders from Zeus to liberate Zeus's mistress Io, Hermes charmed Argus to sleep with his flute and lopped off his head; as a gesture of spite and restitution, Zeus's wife, Hera, transplanted Argus's eyes into the tail of her sacred bird, the peacock. One of Dickens's very rare uses of mythology without ironic edge (Monod); similarly, the reference to Argus in chapter 48 of *Bleak House*.
6. Pip's sensations recall *Oliver Twist*, chapter 12: "Oliver lay awake some time, counting the little circles of light, which the reflection of the rushlight-shade threw upon the ceiling."
7. Literally, headpiece: a flat canopy over a bedstead (or pulpit or altar), supported by four posts or suspended from the ceiling.
8. Beetles, moths. "Blue-bottle flies": large blowflies with hairy bodies and steel-blue abdomens. "Earwigs": insects so called from the popular error that they creep into one's ear.
9. Spoof on manuals of grammar, probably Lindley Murray's, from which Dickens almost certainly learned his conjugations. ("Potential Mood, Present Tense. I may or can love. Preterperfect Tense. I may or can have loved. Preterimperfect Tense. I might, could, would, or should love," etc.) Murray (1745–1826), the Pennsylvania-born "father of English grammar," published his *Grammar* in 1795; by about 1880, it had gone into nearly fifty editions, and he was enough of a household word to be given a place in Mrs. Jarley's waxworks in chapter 29 of *The Old Curiosity Shop*.

cannot go home; and I might not, could not, would not, and should not go home; until I felt that I was going distracted, and rolled over on the pillow, and looked at the staring rounds upon the wall again.

I had left directions that I was to be called at seven; for it was plain that I must see Wemmick before seeing any one else, and equally plain that this was a case in which his Walworth sentiments, only, could be taken. It was a relief to get out of the room where the night had been so miserable, and I needed no second knocking at the door to startle me from my uneasy bed.

The Castle battlements arose upon my view at eight o'clock. The little servant happening to be entering the fortress with two hot rolls, I passed through the postern and crossed the drawbridge, in her company, and so came without announcement into the presence of Wemmick as he was making tea for himself and the Aged. An open door afforded a perspective view[1] of the Aged in bed.

"Halloa, Mr. Pip!" said Wemmick. "You did come home, then?"

"Yes," I returned; "but I didn't go home."

"That's all right," said he, rubbing his hands. "I left a note for you at each of the Temple gates, on the chance. Which gate did you come to?"

I told him.

"I'll go round to the others in the course of the day and destroy the notes," said Wemmick; "it's a good rule never to leave documentary evidence if you can help it, because you don't know when it may be put in.[2] I'm going to take a liberty with you.—*Would* you mind toasting this sausage for the Aged P.?"

I said I should be delighted to do it.

"Then you can go about your work, Mary Anne," said Wemmick to the little servant; "which leaves us to ourselves, don't you see, Mr. Pip?" he added, winking, as she disappeared.

I thanked him for his friendship and caution, and our discourse proceeded in a low tone, while I toasted the Aged's sausage and he buttered the crumb of the Aged's roll.

"Now, Mr. Pip, you know," said Wemmick, "you and I understand one another. We are in our private and personal capacities, and we have been engaged in a confidential transaction before to-day. Official sentiments are one thing. We are extra official."

I cordially assented. I was so very nervous, that I had already lighted the Aged's sausage like a torch, and been obliged to blow it out.

"I accidentally heard, yesterday morning," said Wemmick, "being in a certain place where I once took you—even between you and me, it's as well not to mention names when avoidable — "

"Much better not," said I. "I understand you."

"I heard there, by chance, yesterday morning," said Wemmick, "that a certain person not altogether of uncolonial pursuits, and not unpossessed of portable property—I don't know who it may really be—we won't name this person — "

"Not necessary," said I.

"—had made some little stir in a certain part of the world where a good

1. Distant view.
2. Used as evidence.

many people go, not always in gratification of their own inclinations, and not quite irrespective of the government expense —— "

In watching his face, I made quite a firework of the Aged's sausage, and greatly discomposed both my own attention and Wemmick's; for which I apologised.

"—by disappearing from such place, and being no more heard of thereabouts. From which," said Wemmick, "conjectures had been raised and theories formed. I also heard that you at your chambers in Garden-court, Temple, had been watched, and might be watched again."

"By whom?" said I.   10

"I wouldn't go into that," said Wemmick, evasively, "it might clash with official responsibilities. I heard it, as I have in my time heard other curious things in the same place. I don't tell it you on information received. I heard it."

He took the toasting-fork and sausage from me as he spoke, and set forth the Aged's breakfast neatly on a little tray. Previous to placing it before him, he went into the Aged's room with a clean white cloth, and tied the same under the old gentleman's chin, and propped him up, and put his nightcap on one side, and gave him quite a rakish air. Then he placed his breakfast before him with great care, and said, "All right, ain't you, Aged P.?" To which   20 the cheerful Aged replied, "All right, John, my boy, all right!" As there seemed to be a tacit understanding that the Aged was not in a presentable state, and was therefore to be considered invisible, I made a pretence of being in complete ignorance of these proceedings.

"This watching of me at my chambers (which I have once had reason to suspect)," I said to Wemmick when he came back, "is inseparable from the person to whom you have adverted; is it?"

Wemmick looked very serious. "I couldn't undertake to say that, of my own knowledge. I mean, I couldn't undertake to say it was at first. But it either is, or it will be, or it's in great danger of being."   30

As I saw that he was restrained by fealty to Little Britain from saying as much as he could, and as I knew with thankfulness to him how far out of his way he went to say what he did, I could not press him. But I told him, after a little meditation over the fire, that I would like to ask him a question, subject to his answering or not answering, as he deemed right, and sure that his course would be right. He paused in his breakfast, and crossing his arms, and pinching his shirt-sleeves (his notion of in-door comfort was to sit without any coat), he nodded to me once, to put my question.

"You have heard of a man of bad character, whose true name is Compeyson?"   40

He answered with one other nod.

"Is he living?"

One other nod.

"Is he in London?"

He gave me one other nod, compressed the post-office exceedingly, gave me one last nod, and went on with his breakfast.

"Now," said Wemmick, "questioning being over;" which he emphasised and repeated for my guidance; "I come to what I did after hearing what I heard. I went to Garden-court to find you; not finding you, I went to Clarrikers to find Mr. Herbert."   50

"And him you found?" said I, with great anxiety.

"And him I found. Without mentioning any names or going into any details, I gave him to understand that if he was aware of anybody—Tom, Jack, or Richard—being about the chambers, or about the immediate neighbourhood, he had better get Tom, Jack, or Richard, out of the way while you were out of the way."

"He would be greatly puzzled what to do?"

"He *was* puzzled what to do; not the less, because I gave him my opinion that it was not safe to try to get Tom, Jack, or Richard, too far out of the way at present. Mr. Pip, I'll tell you something. Under existing circumstances there 10 is no place like a great city when you are once in it.[3] Don't break cover too soon. Lie close. Wait till things slacken, before you try the open, even for foreign air."

I thanked him for his valuable advice, and asked him what Herbert had done.

"Mr. Herbert," said Wemmick, "after being all of a heap for half an hour, struck out a plan. He mentioned to me as a secret, that he is courting a young lady who has, as no doubt you are aware, a bedridden Pa. Which Pa, having been in the Purser line of life, lies a-bed in a bow-window where he can see the ships sail up and down the river. You are acquainted with the young lady, 20 most probably?"

"Not personally," said I.

The truth was, that she had objected to me as an expensive companion who did Herbert no good, and that when Herbert had first proposed to present me to her she had received the proposal with such very moderate warmth, that Herbert had felt himself obliged to confide the state of the case to me, with a view to the passage of a little time before I made her acquaintance. When I had begun to advance Herbert's prospects by stealth, I had been able to bear this with cheerful philosophy; he and his affianced, for their part, had naturally not been very anxious to introduce a third person into their inter- 30 views; and thus, although I was assured that I had risen in Clara's esteem, and although the young lady and I had long regularly interchanged messages and remembrances by Herbert, I had never seen her. However, I did not trouble Wemmick with these particulars.

"The house with the bow-window," said Wemmick, "being by the riverside, down the Pool there between Limehouse and Greenwich,[4] and being kept, it seems, by a very respectable widow who has a furnished upper floor to let, Mr. Herbert put it to me, what did I think of that as a temporary tenement for Tom, Jack, or Richard? Now, I thought very well of it, for three reasons I'll give you. That is to say. Firstly. It's altogether out of all your beats, 40 and is well away from the usual heap of streets great and small. Secondly. Without going near it yourself, you could always hear of the safety of Tom, Jack, or Richard, through Mr. Herbert. Thirdly. After a while and when it

---

3. Dickens consistently describes London as a place of concealment. Thus, a novel like *Oliver Twist* is virtually framed by the hero's decision to head for London because "not even Mr. Bumble [the despotic parish beadle] could find him there" and the decision by the murderer Sikes to return from the countryside to London to escape capture.

4. Southeast of London; in Pip's day still the site of the Greenwich Observatory, established by Charles II in 1675 to advance the art of navigation. "Pool": stretch of the Thames between Tower Bridge and Limehouse Reach to the east. "Limehouse": east of London in Stepney, on the Thames, in the dockyard district.

might be prudent, if you should want to slip Tom, Jack, or Richard, on board a foreign packet-boat, there he is—ready."

Much comforted by these considerations, I thanked Wemmick again and again, and begged him to proceed.

"Well, sir! Mr. Herbert threw himself into the business with a will, and by nine o'clock last night he housed Tom, Jack, or Richard—whichever it may be—you and I don't want to know—quite successfully. At the old lodgings it was understood that he was summoned to Dover, and in fact he was taken down the Dover road[5] and cornered out of it. Now, another great advantage of all this, is, that it was done without you, and when, if any one was con- 10 cerning himself about your movements, you must be known to be ever so many miles off and quite otherwise engaged. This diverts suspicion and confuses it; and for the same reason I recommended that even if you came back last night, you should not go home. It brings in more confusion, and you want confusion."

Wemmick, having finished his breakfast, here looked at his watch, and began to get his coat on.

"And now, Mr. Pip," said he, with his hands still in the sleeves, "I have probably done the most I can do; but if I can ever do more—from a Walworth point of view, and in a strictly private and personal capacity—I shall be glad 20 to do it. Here's the address. There can be no harm in your going here to-night and seeing for yourself that all is well with Tom, Jack, or Richard, before you go home—which is another reason for your not going home last night. But after you have gone home, don't go back here. You are very welcome, I am sure, Mr. Pip;" his hands were now out of his sleeves, and I was shaking them; "and let me finally impress one important point upon you." He laid his hands upon my shoulders, and added in a solemn whisper: "Avail yourself of this evening to lay hold of his portable property. You don't know what may happen to him. Don't let anything happen to the portable property."

Quite despairing of making my mind clear to Wemmick on this point, I 30 forbore to try.

"Time's up," said Wemmick, "and I must be off. If you had nothing more pressing to do than to keep here till dark, that's what I should advise. You look very much worried, and it would do you good to have a perfectly quiet day with the Aged—he'll be up presently—and a little bit of —— you remember the pig?"

"Of course," said I.

"Well; and a little bit of *him*. That sausage you toasted was his, and he was in all respects a first-rater. Do try him, if it is only for old acquaintance' sake. Good-by, Aged Parent!" in a cheery shout.   40

"All right, John; all right, my boy!" piped the old man from within.

I soon fell asleep before Wemmick's fire, and the Aged and I enjoyed one another's society by falling asleep before it more or less all day. We had loin of pork for dinner, and greens grown on the estate, and I nodded at the Aged with a good intention whenever I failed to do it drowsily. When it was quite dark, I left the Aged preparing the fire for toast; and I inferred from the

5. The ancient Roman highway stretching from Westminster to Dover; until the nineteenth century the main artery in southern England. In Dickens, most familiarly associated with David Copperfield's trek (chapters 12–13) and the opening night-scene in *A Tale of Two Cities*. Gad's Hill Place, the red-brick mansion four miles northwest of Rochester that Dickens purchased in 1856, overlooked the Dover Road—and much of the marshy country Dickens describes in *Great Expectations*. See p. 47, n. 2.

number of teacups, as well as from his glances at the two little doors in the wall, that Miss Skiffins was expected.

Chapter XLVI.

EIGHT o'clock had struck before I got into the air that was scented, not disagreeably, by the chips and shavings of the long-shore boat-builders, and mast oar and block makers. All that water-side region of the upper and lower Pool below Bridge,[1] was unknown ground to me, and when I struck down by the river, I found that the spot I wanted was not where I had supposed it to be, and was anything but easy to find.[2] It was called Mill Pond Bank, Chinks's Basin;[3] and I had no other guide to Chinks's Basin than the Old Green Copper Rope-Walk.[4]

It matters not what stranded ships repairing in dry docks I lost myself among, what old hulls of ships in course of being knocked to pieces, what ooze and slime and other dregs of tide, what yards of ship-builders and ship-breakers, what rusty anchors blindly biting into the ground though for years off duty, what mountainous country of accumulated casks and timber, and how many rope-walks that were not the Old Green Copper. After several times falling short of my destination and as often over-shooting it, I came unexpectedly round a corner, upon Mill Pond Bank. It was a fresh kind of place, all circumstances considered, where the wind from the river had room to turn itself round; and there were two or three trees in it, and there was the stump of a ruined windmill, and there was the Old Green Copper Rope-Walk—whose long and narrow vista I could trace in the moonlight, along a series of wooden frames set in the ground, that looked like superannuated haymaking-rakes which had grown old and lost most of their teeth.

Selecting from the few queer houses upon Mill Pond Bank, a house with a wooden front and three stories of bow-window (not bay-window, which is another thing),[5] I looked at the plate upon the door, and read there, Mrs. Whimple. That being the name I wanted, I knocked, and an elderly woman of a pleasant and thriving appearance responded. She was immediately deposed, however, by Herbert, who silently led me into the parlour and shut the door. It was an odd sensation to see his very familiar face established quite at home in that very unfamiliar room and region; and I found myself looking

1. That is, downriver from (or east of) London Bridge; "below bridge" is virtually synonymous with the Pool of London. The "Upper Pool" extends from London Bridge past the Tower of London to Wapping, the "Lower Pool" from Wapping to Limehouse Reach. Dickens is slightly out of bounds in placing Magwitch's new lodgings, which are downriver from Limehouse Reach, within the Pool area in chapter 45; but see following notes.
2. Magwitch's retreat may have been one of seven row houses at the lower end of Rotherhithe (then Trinity) Street, east of the Surrey Commercial Docks in the London east end.
3. Presumably fictitious place-name, perhaps the part of the shipyard set aside for chinking (i.e., water-proofing) ships; or the name may have been suggested by the Chinese ships that anchored in the river before the construction of the West India and East India Docks. But the racial slur dates from the 1890s. "Mill Pond": a sheet of water seven hundred yards west of Magwitch's hideout, though the location is uncertain (Hill; see also *Dickensian* 34 [1934]: 117).
4. Long narrow shed or roofed-over alley in which rope makers twisted strands of jute or hemp into rope. But the modifiers "Old Green Copper" are obscure: the introduction of copper as an ingredient of rope and the manufacture of copper wire came later. The wooden frames that enclosed the rope-walk were protected from the weather by copper sheathing, much as ship's bottoms were, and had turned green from exposure.
5. Both describe windows that form a recess by projecting from the wall of the house: Dickens distinguishes the curved bow from the rectangular bay window.

at him, much as I looked at the corner-cupboard with the glass and china,
the shells upon the chimney-piece, and the coloured engravings on the wall,
representing the death of Captain Cook,[6] a ship-launch, and his Majesty King
George the Third in a state-coachman's wig, leather-breeches, and top-boots,
on the terrace at Windsor.[7]

"All is well, Handel," said Herbert, "and he is quite satisfied, though eager
to see you. My dear girl is with her father; and if you'll wait till she comes
down, I'll make you known to her, and then we'll go up-stairs. —— *That's* her
father!"

I had become aware of an alarming growling overhead, and had probably   10
expressed the fact in my countenance.

"I am afraid he is a sad old rascal," said Herbert, smiling, "but I have never
seen him. Don't you smell rum? He is always at it."

"At rum?" said I.

"Yes," returned Herbert, "and you may suppose how mild it makes his
gout. He persists, too, in keeping all the provisions up-stairs in his room, and
serving them out. He keeps them on shelves over his head, and *will* weigh
them all. His room must be like a chandler's shop."[8]

While he thus spoke, the growling noise became a prolonged roar, and
then died away.   20

"What else can be the consequence," said Herbert, in explanation, "if he
will cut the cheese? A man with the gout in his right hand—and everywhere
else—can't expect to get through a Double Gloucester[9] without hurting himself."

He seemed to have hurt himself very much, for he gave another furious
roar.

"To have Provis for an upper lodger is quite a godsend to Mrs. Whimple,"
said Herbert, "for of course people in general won't stand that noise. A curious
place, Handel; isn't it?"

It was a curious place, indeed; but remarkably well kept and clean.   30

"Mrs. Whimple," said Herbert, when I told him so, "is the best of house-
wives, and I really do not know what my Clara would do without her motherly
help. For, Clara has no mother of her own, Handel, and no relation in the
world but old Gruffandgrim."[1]

"Surely that's not his name, Herbert?"

"No, no," said Herbert, "that's my name for him. His name is Mr. Barley.
But what a blessing it is for the son of my father and mother to love a girl

6. Captain Cook was stabbed and bludgeoned to death in February 1779 in a scuffle with natives of the
   Sandwich Islands. Dickens probably alludes to the most authentic of several well-known pictures:
   the *Representation of the Murder of Captain Cooke at O-Wye-ee* (1785), a sketch by John Webber,
   the official draughtsman on the voyage.
7. An 1812 aquatint, after the portrait by Charles, or Carl, or Christian, Rosenberg (1745–1844), silhou-
   ette artist from Hanover (Hill).
8. A grocery or general food store. Here perhaps specifically a shop trading in ship's provisions. "Chandler": originally a candle merchant; generalized to mean grocer, who would normally stock candles
   among his supplies. In the early nineteenth century, the term often implied scorn.
9. A thick creamy cheese weighed in at from twelve to fifteen pounds. A Double Gloucester is twice as
   large and twice as old as a regular Gloucester. Herbert fears not that Barley would gorge himself by
   "getting through" the cheese but that he would slash his hand with the thin wire used to cut the
   cheese.
1. A familiar Dickensian formation: thus, the wooden-legged Greenwich pensioner Gruff and Glum,
   who presides at the runaway wedding match in *Our Mutual Friend* 4.4 and the sleeping (in this case,
   deceased) partner of Gruff and Tackleton, the baby-hating toy merchant in *Cricket on the Hearth*.
   "Old Mr. Grim" often appears as euphemism for death (Grose).

who has no relations, and who can never bother herself, or anybody else, about her family!"

Herbert had told me on former occasions, and now reminded me, that he first knew Miss Clara Barley when she was completing her education at an establishment at Hammersmith, and that on her being recalled home to nurse her father, he and she had confided their affection to the motherly Mrs. Whimple, by whom it had been fostered and regulated with equal kindness and discretion, ever since. It was understood that nothing of a tender nature could possibly be confided to Old Barley, by reason of his being totally unequal to the consideration of any subject more psychological than Gout, Rum, and Purser's stores.

As we were thus conversing in a low tone while Old Barley's sustained growl vibrated in the beam that crossed the ceiling, the room door opened, and a very pretty slight dark-eyed girl of twenty or so, came in with a basket in her hand: whom Herbert tenderly relieved of the basket, and presented blushing, as "Clara." She really was a most charming girl, and might have passed for a captive fairy whom that truculent Ogre, Old Barley, had pressed into his service.

"Look here," said Herbert, showing me the basket with a compassionate and tender smile after we had talked a little; "here's poor Clara's supper, served out every night. Here's her allowance of bread, and here's her slice of cheese, and here's her rum—which I drink. This is Mr. Barley's breakfast for to-morrow, served out to be cooked. Two mutton chops, three potatoes, some split peas, a little flour, two ounces of butter, a pinch of salt, and all this black pepper. It's stewed up together and taken hot, and it's a nice thing for the gout, I should think!"

There was something so natural and winning in Clara's resigned way of looking at these stores in detail, as Herbert pointed them out,—and something so confiding, loving, and innocent, in her modest manner of yielding herself to Herbert's embracing arm—and something so gentle in her, so much needing protection on Mill Pond Bank, by Chinks's Basin, and the Old Green Copper Rope-Walk, with Old Barley growling in the beam—that I would not have undone the engagement between her and Herbert, for all the money in the pocket-book I had never opened.

I was looking at her with pleasure and admiration, when suddenly the growl swelled into a roar again, and a frightful bumping noise was heard above, as if a giant with a wooden leg were trying to bore it through the ceiling to come at us. Upon this Clara said to Herbert, "Papa wants me, darling!" and ran away.

"There's an unconscionable old shark for you!" said Herbert. "What do you suppose he wants now, Handel?"

"I don't know," said I. "Something to drink?"

"That's it!" cried Herbert, as if I had made a guess of extraordinary merit. "He keeps his grog ready-mixed in a little tub on the table. Wait a moment, and you'll hear Clara lift him up to take some.—There he goes!" Another roar, with a prolonged shake at the end. "Now," said Herbert, as it was succeeded by silence, "he's drinking. Now," said Herbert, as the growl resounded in the beam once more, "he's down again on his back!"

Clara returning soon afterwards, Herbert accompanied me up-stairs to see our charge. As we passed Mr. Barley's door, he was heard hoarsely muttering

within, in a strain that rose and fell like wind, the following Refrain; in which
I substitute good wishes for something quite the reverse.

"Ahoy! Bless your eyes, here's old Bill Barley. Here's old Bill Barley, bless
your eyes. Here's old Bill Barley on the flat of his back, by the Lord. Lying
on the flat of his back, like a drifting old dead flounder, here's your old Bill
Barley, bless your eyes. Ahoy! Bless you."

In this strain of consolation, Herbert informed me the invisible Barley
would commune with himself by the day and night together; often, while it
was light, having, at the same time, one eye at a telescope which was fitted
on his bed for the convenience of sweeping the river.[2]   10

In his two cabin rooms at the top of the house, which were fresh and airy,
and in which Mr. Barley was less audible than below, I found Provis comfortably settled. He expressed no alarm, and seemed to feel none that was
worth mentioning; but it struck me that he was softened—indefinably, for I
could not have said how, and could never afterwards recall how when I tried;
but certainly.

The opportunity that the day's rest had given me for reflection, had resulted
in my fully determining to say nothing to him respecting Compeyson. For
anything I knew, his animosity towards the man might otherwise lead to his
seeking him out and rushing on his own destruction. Therefore, when Her-   20
bert and I sat down with him by his fire, I asked him first of all whether he
relied on Wemmick's judgment and sources of information?

"Ay, ay, dear boy!" he answered, with a grave nod, "Jaggers knows."

"Then I have talked with Wemmick," said I, "and have come to tell you
what caution he gave me, and what advice."

This I did accurately, with the reservation just mentioned; and I told him
how Wemmick had heard, in Newgate prison (whether from officers or prisoners I could not say), that he was under some suspicion, and that my chambers had been watched; how Wemmick had recommended his keeping close
for a time, and my keeping away from him; and what Wemmick had said   30
about getting him abroad. I added, that of course, when the time came, I
should go with him, or should follow close upon him, as might be safest in
Wemmick's judgment. What was to follow that, I did not touch upon; neither
indeed was I at all clear or comfortable about it in my own mind, now that
I saw him in that softer condition, and in declared peril for my sake. As to
altering my way of living, by enlarging my expenses, I put it to him whether
in our present unsettled and difficult circumstances, it would not be simply
ridiculous, if it were no worse?

He could not deny this, and indeed was very reasonable throughout. His
coming back was a venture, he said, and he had always known it to be a   40
venture. He would do nothing to make it a desperate venture, and he had
very little fear of his safety with such good help.

Herbert, who had been looking at the fire and pondering, here said that
something had come into his thoughts arising out of Wemmick's suggestion,
which it might be worth while to pursue. "We are both good watermen,
Handel, and could take him down the river ourselves when the right time
comes. No boat would then be hired for the purpose, and no boatmen; that

---

2. In describing Barley's room, Dickens may have gone to his source for Wemmick's Castle, Commodore
   Trunnion's house in Smollett's *Peregrine Pickle*. Barley himself recalls Trunnion's storage of provisions,
   the mounted telescope, and choleric swearing; cf. especially chapter 14.

would save at least a chance of suspicion, and any chance is worth saving. Never mind the season; don't you think it might be a good thing if you began at once to keep a boat at the Temple stairs,[3] and were in the habit of rowing up and down the river? You fall into that habit, and then who notices or minds? Do it twenty times or fifty times, and there is nothing special in your doing it the twenty-first or fifty-first."

I liked this scheme, and Provis was quite elated by it. We agreed that it should be carried into execution, and that Provis should never recognise us if we came below Bridge and rowed past Mill Pond Bank. But we further agreed that he should pull down the blind in that part of his window which gave upon the east, whenever he saw us and all was right.

Our conference being now ended, and everything arranged, I rose to go; remarking to Herbert that he and I had better not go home together, and that I would take half an hour's start of him. "I don't like to leave you here," I said to Provis, "though I cannot doubt your being safer here than near me. Good-by!"

"Dear boy," he answered, clasping my hands, "I don't know when we may meet again, and I don't like Good-by. Say Good Night!"

"Good Night! Herbert will go regularly between us, and when the time comes you may be certain I shall be ready. Good Night, Good Night!"

We thought it best that he should stay in his own rooms, and we left him on the landing outside his door, holding a light over the stair-rail to light us down stairs. Looking back at him, I thought of that first night of his return when our positions were reversed, and when I little supposed my heart could ever be as heavy and anxious at parting from him as it was now.

Old Barley was growling and swearing when we repassed his door, with no appearance of having ceased, or of meaning to cease. When we got to the foot of the stairs, I asked Herbert whether he had preserved the name of Provis? He replied, certainly not, and that the lodger was Mr. Campbell. He also explained that the utmost known of Mr. Campbell there, was, that he (Herbert) had Mr. Campbell consigned to him, and felt a strong personal interest in his being well cared for, and living a secluded life. So, when we went into the parlour where Mrs. Whimple and Clara were seated at work, I said nothing of my own interest in Mr. Campbell, but kept it to myself.

When I had taken leave of the pretty gentle dark-eyed girl, and the motherly woman who had not outlived her honest sympathy with a little affair of true love, I felt as if the Old Green Copper Rope-Walk had grown quite a different place. Old Barley might be as old as the hills, and might swear like a whole field of troopers, but there were redeeming youth and trust and hope enough in Chinks's Basin to fill it to overflowing. And then I thought of Estella, and of our parting, and went home very sadly.

All things were as quiet in the Temple as ever I had seen them. The windows of the rooms on that side, lately occupied by Provis, were dark and still, and there was no lounger in Garden-court. I walked past the fountain twice or thrice before I descended the steps that were between me and my rooms, but I was quite alone. Herbert coming to my bedside when he came in—for I went straight to bed, dispirited and fatigued—made the same report. Opening one of the windows after that, he looked out into the moonlight,

---

3. Temple Stairs used to be located directly below Middle Temple Lane, the walk separating the Inner from the Middle Temple.

and told me that the pavement was as solemnly empty as the pavement of any Cathedral at that same hour.

Next day, I set myself to get the boat. It was soon done, and the boat was brought round to the Temple-stairs, and lay where I could reach her within a minute or two. Then, I began to go out, as for training and practice: sometimes alone, sometimes with Herbert. I was often out in cold, rain, and sleet, but nobody took much note of me after I had been out a few times. At first, I kept above Blackfriars Bridge;[4] but, as the hours of the tide changed, I took towards London Bridge. It was Old London Bridge in those days,[5] and at certain states of the tide there was a race and a fall of water there which gave   10 it a bad reputation. But I knew well enough how to "shoot" the bridge[6] after seeing it done, and so began to row about among the shipping in the Pool, and down to Erith.[7] The first time I passed Mill Pond Bank, Herbert and I were pulling a pair of oars; and, both in going and returning, we saw the blind towards the east come down. Herbert was rarely there less frequently than three times in a week, and he never brought me a single word of intelligence that was at all alarming. Still, I knew that there was cause for alarm, and I could not get rid of the notion of being watched. Once received, it is a haunting idea; how many undesigning persons I suspected of watching me it would be hard to calculate.   20

In short, I was always full of fears for the rash man who was in hiding. Herbert had sometimes said to me that he found it pleasant to stand at one of our windows after dark, when the tide was running down, and to think that it was flowing, with everything it bore, towards Clara. But I thought with dread that it was flowing towards Magwitch, and that any black mark on its surface might be his pursuers, going swiftly, silently, and surely, to take him.

Chapter XLVII.

SOME weeks passed without bringing any change. We waited for a hint from Wemmick,[1] and he made no sign. If I had never known him out of Little Britain, and had never enjoyed the privilege of being on a familiar

---

4. Upriver from (or west of) Blackfriars Bridge.
5. By far the oldest bridge to span the Thames. The first recorded bridge, of timber, was built in the tenth century; in 1176, Peter the Bridge-Master, chaplain of St. Mary Colechurch, began to rebuild it as the first stone bridge in London. London Bridge was a miniature city and bastion, with drawbridges and fortified gates at either end, the roadway down the center flanked by shops and (above the shops) houses from three to seven stories high. For upwards of six hundred years it carried the London traffic across the Thames; and this is the Old Bridge that still stood in Pip's time. By the early nineteenth century it showed signs of collapse; and in 1824–25 John Rennie, the architect of Waterloo Bridge (1811), began to build New London Bridge 180 feet west of the old, completing it in 1831.
6. The piers, or pillars, of the Old London Bridge were so close to each other (the "starlings," or bases, supporting the piers taking up so much of the river bed), and the narrow arches of the bridge were so low, that at high water they obstructed the flow, which rushed through with tremendous force as the tide rose or fell. To "shoot the Bridge" was to seize the precise moment when the current would sweep the craft through one of the arches.
7. Small manufacturing town in Kent facing the Essex marshes, halfway between London Bridge and Gravesend.
1. Thus in MS only. All printed versions read "We waited for Wemmick." But the repetition of the phrase in the last paragraph of the chapter—the reminder to Wemmick "that we waited for his hint"—suggests a deliberate reprise: perhaps a typesetter's error that persisted in all editions.

ence) that it took half the evening to set things right, and then it was only brought about through an honest little grocer with a white hat, black gaiters, and red nose, getting into a clock, with a gridiron, and listening, and coming out, and knocking everybody down from behind with the gridiron whom he couldn't confute with what he had overheard. This led to Mr. Wopsle's (who had never been heard of before) coming in with a star and garter on, as a plenipotentiary[2] of great power direct from the Admiralty, to say that the Swabs were all to go to prison on the spot, and that he had brought the boatswain down the Union Jack,[3] as a slight acknowledgment of his public services. The boatswain, unmanned for the first time, respectfully dried his 10 eyes on the Jack, and then cheering up and addressing Mr. Wopsle as Your Honour, solicited permission to take him by the fin. Mr. Wopsle conceding his fin with a gracious dignity, was immediately shoved into a dusty corner while everybody danced a hornpipe;[4] and, from that corner, surveying the public with a discontented eye, became aware of me.

The second piece was the last new grand comic Christmas pantomime;[5] in the first scene of which, it pained me to suspect that I detected Mr. Wopsle with red worsted legs under a highly magnified phosphoric countenance and a shock of red curtain-fringe for his hair, engaged in the manufacture of thunderbolts in a mine, and displaying great cowardice when his gigantic 20 master came home (very hoarse) to dinner. But he presently presented himself under worthier circumstances; for, the Genius of Youthful Love being in want of assistance—on account of the parental brutality of an ignorant farmer who opposed the choice of his daughter's heart, by purposely falling upon the object, in a flour sack, out of the first-floor window—summoned a sententious Enchanter; and he, coming up from the antipodes[6] rather unsteadily, after an apparently violent journey, proved to be Mr. Wopsle in a high-crowned hat, with a necromantic work in one volume under his arm. The business of this enchanter on earth, being principally to be talked at, sung at, butted at, danced at, and flashed at with fires of various colours, he had a good deal of 30 time on his hands. And I observed with great surprise, that he devoted it to staring in my direction as if he were lost in amazement.

There was something so remarkable in the increasing glare of Mr. Wopsle's eye, and he seemed to be turning so many things over in his mind and to grow so confused, that I could not make it out. I sat thinking of it, long after he had ascended to the clouds in a large watch-case, and still I could not make it out. I was still thinking of it when I came out of the theatre an hour afterwards, and found him waiting for me near the door.

2. A person invested with someone else's power, such as the deputy or envoy of a sovereign. "Star and garter": badge of the Order of the Garter, the highest order of British knighthood.
3. Dickens kids the convention of bringing in the Union Jack at the end of the nautical drama and waving it over the hero's head to the tune of "Rule Britannia." Wopsle's dismissal to "a dusty corner" is equally hackneyed: at the end of the drama the deck is cleared for the hero while the "great power direct from the Admiralty" retreats to the side of the stage and meditates atop a barrel.
4. Lively dance to the tune of the instrument from which the term has been generalized, associated especially with sailors. Dickens hornpiped his way through his young manhood.
5. English pantomime is the invention of John Rich (1682?–1761), theatrical manager at Lincoln's Inn Fields Theatre, who between 1717 and 1760 produced elaborate spectacles in which the Italian harlequin figures were grafted onto classical myths or legendary stories like that of Dr. Faustus. The annual Christmas pantomime, a tradition from the 1720s on, involved extravagant scenery, dazzling special effects, and supernatural interferences; by the turn of the century, classical mythology had given way to fairy and nursery tales like "Cinderella," "Red Riding Hood," and "Mother Goose."
6. Through a trapdoor.

"How do you do?" said I, shaking hands with him as we turned down the street together. "I saw that you saw me."

"Saw you, Mr. Pip!" he returned. "Yes, of course I saw you. But who else was there!"

"Who else?"

"It is the strangest thing," said Mr. Wopsle, drifting into his lost look again; "and yet I could swear to him."

Becoming alarmed, I entreated Mr. Wopsle to explain his meaning.

"Whether I should have noticed him at first but for your being there," said Mr. Wopsle, going on in the same lost way, "I can't be positive; yet I think   10 I should."

Involuntarily I looked round me, as I was accustomed to look round me when I went home; for these mysterious words gave me a chill.

"Oh! He can't be in sight," said Mr. Wopsle. "He went out, before I went off. I saw him go."

Having the reason that I had, for being suspicious, I even suspected this poor actor. I mistrusted a design to entrap me into some admission. Therefore, I glanced at him as we walked on together, but said nothing.

"I had a ridiculous fancy that he must be with you, Mr. Pip, till I saw that you were quite unconscious of him, sitting behind you there, like a ghost."   20

My former chill crept over me again, but I was resolved not to speak yet, for it was quite consistent with his words that he might be set on to induce me to connect these references with Provis. Of course I was perfectly sure and safe that Provis had not been there.

"I dare say you wonder at me, Mr. Pip; indeed I see you do. But it is so very strange! You'll hardly believe what I am going to tell you. I could hardly believe it myself, if you told me."

"Indeed?" said I.

"No, indeed. Mr. Pip, you remember in old times a certain Christmas Day, when you were quite a child, and I dined at Gargery's, and some soldiers   30 came to the door to get a pair of handcuffs mended?"

"I remember it very well."

"And you remember that there was a chase after two convicts, and that we joined in it, and that Gargery took you on his back, and that I took the lead and you kept up with me as well as you could?"

"I remember it all very well." Better than he thought—except the last clause.

"And you remember that we came up with the two in a ditch, and that there was a scuffle between them, and that one of them had been severely handled and much mauled about the face, by the other?"   40

"I see it all before me."

"And that the soldiers lighted torches, and put the two in the centre, and that we went on to see the last of them, over the black marshes, with the torchlight shining on their faces—I am particular about that; with the torchlight shining on their faces, when there was an outer ring of dark night all about us?"

"Yes," said I. "I remember all that."

"Then, Mr. Pip, one of those two prisoners sat behind you to-night. I saw him over your shoulder."

"Steady!" I thought. I asked him then, "Which of the two do you suppose you saw?"

"The one who had been mauled," he answered readily, "and I'll swear I saw him! The more I think of him, the more certain I am of him."

"This is very curious!" said I, with the best assumption I could put on, of its being nothing more to me. "Very curious indeed!"

I cannot exaggerate the enhanced disquiet into which this conversation threw me, or the special and peculiar terror I felt at Compeyson's having been behind me "like a ghost." For, if he had ever been out of my thoughts for a few moments together since the hiding had begun, it was in those very moments when he was closest to me; and to think that I should be so unconscious and off my guard after all my care, was as if I had shut an avenue of a hundred doors to keep him out, and then had found him at my elbow. I could not doubt either that he was there, because I was there, and that however slight an appearance of danger there might be about us, danger was always near and active.

I put such questions to Mr. Wopsle as, When did the man come in? He could not tell me that; he saw me, and over my shoulder he saw the man. It was not until he had seen him for some time that he began to identify him; but he had from the first vaguely associated him with me, and known him as somehow belonging to me in the old village time. How was he dressed? Prosperously, but not noticeably otherwise; he thought, in black. Was his face at all disfigured? No, he believed not. I believed not, too, for, although in my brooding state I had taken no especial notice of the people behind me, I thought it likely that a face at all disfigured would have attracted my attention.

When Mr. Wopsle had imparted to me all that he could recall or I extract, and when I had treated him to a little appropriate refreshment after the fatigues of the evening, we parted. It was between twelve and one o'clock when I reached the Temple, and the gates were shut. No one was near me when I went in and went home.

Herbert had come in, and we held a very serious council by the fire. But there was nothing to be done, saving to communicate to Wemmick what I had that night found out, and to remind him that we waited for his hint. As I thought that I might compromise him if I went too often to the Castle, I made this communication by letter. I wrote it before I went to bed, and went out and posted it; and again no one was near me. Herbert and I agreed that we could do nothing else but be very cautious. And we were very cautious indeed—more cautious than before, if that were possible—and I for my part never went near Chinks's Basin, except when I rowed by, and then I only looked at Mill Pond Bank as I looked at anything else.

Chapter XLVIII.

THE second of the two meetings referred to in the last chapter, occurred about a week after the first. I had again left my boat at the wharf below Bridge; the time was an hour earlier in the afternoon; and, undecided where to dine, I had strolled up into Cheapside, and was strolling along it, surely the most unsettled person in all the busy concourse, when a large hand was laid upon

my shoulder, by some one overtaking me. It was Mr. Jaggers's hand, and he
passed it through my arm.

"As we are going in the same direction, Pip, we may walk together. Where
are you bound for?"

"For the Temple, I think," said I.

"Don't you know?" said Mr. Jaggers.

"Well," I returned, glad for once to get the better of him in cross-
examination, "I do *not* know, for I have not made up my mind."

"You are going to dine?" said Mr. Jaggers. "You don't mind admitting that,
I suppose?"   10

"No," I returned, "I don't mind admitting that."

"And are not engaged?"

"I don't mind admitting also, that I am not engaged."

"Then," said Mr. Jaggers, "come and dine with me."

I was going to excuse myself, when he added, "Wemmick's coming." So I
changed my excuse into an acceptance—the few words I had uttered serving
for the beginning of either—and we went along Cheapside and slanted off
to Little Britain, while the lights were springing up brilliantly in the shop-
windows, and the street lamp-lighters, scarcely finding ground enough to plant
their ladders on in the midst of the afternoon's bustle, were skipping up and   20
down and running in and out, opening more red eyes in the gathering fog
than my rushlight tower at the Hummums had opened white eyes in the
ghostly wall.

At the office in Little Britain there was the usual letter-writing, hand-
washing, candle-snuffing, and safe-locking, that closed the business of the day.
As I stood idle by Mr. Jaggers's fire, its rising and falling flame made the two
casts on the shelf look as if they were playing a diabolical game at bo-peep[1]
with me; while the pair of coarse fat office candles that dimly lighted Mr.
Jaggers as he wrote in a corner, were decorated with dirty winding-sheets,[2] as
if in remembrance of a host of hanged clients.   30

We went to Gerrard-street, all three together, in a hackney-coach: and as
soon as we got there, dinner was served. Although I should not have thought
of making, in that place, the most distant reference by so much as a look to
Wemmick's Walworth sentiments, yet I should have had no objection to
catching his eye now and then in a friendly way. But it was not to be done.
He turned his eyes on Mr. Jaggers whenever he raised them from the table,
and was as dry and distant to me as if there were twin Wemmicks and this
was the wrong one.

"Did you send that note of Miss Havisham's to Mr. Pip, Wemmick?" Mr.
Jaggers asked, soon after we began dinner.   40

"No, sir," returned Wemmick; "it was going by post, when you brought
Mr. Pip into the office. Here it is." He handed it to his principal, instead of
to me.

---

1. Peekaboo.
2. Solidified candle-drippings, dimly resembling a creased sheet and hence a shroud: superstitiously
   believed to be omens of death or disaster. A recurrent image used more effectively elsewhere in
   Dickens: in *A Tale of Two Cities* 2.4 Dickens takes stock of the drunken Sydney Carton, who has
   fallen "asleep in his arms, with his hair straggling over the table, and a long winding-sheet in the
   candle dripping down upon him"; and in *Our Mutual Friend* 2.16 the hollow men at a wedding
   anniversary "flutter like moths around that yellow wax candle, guttering down, and with some hint of
   a winding sheet in it."

"It's a note of two lines, Pip," said Mr. Jaggers, handing it on, "sent up to me by Miss Havisham, on account of her not being sure of your address. She tells me that she wants to see you on a little matter of business you mentioned to her. You'll go down?"

"Yes," said I, casting my eyes over the note, which was exactly in those terms.

"When do you think of going down?"

"I have an impending engagement," said I, glancing at Wemmick, who was putting fish into the post-office, "that renders me rather uncertain of my time. At once, I think."   10

"If Mr. Pip has the intention of going at once," said Wemmick to Mr. Jaggers, "he needn't write an answer, you know."

Receiving this as an intimation that it was best not to delay, I settled that I would go to-morrow, and said so. Wemmick drank a glass of wine and looked with a grimly satisfied air at Mr. Jaggers, but not at me.

"So, Pip! Our friend the Spider," said Mr. Jaggers, "has played his cards. He has won the pool."

It was as much as I could do to assent.

"Hah! He is a promising fellow—in his way—but he may not have it all his own way. The stronger will win in the end, but the stronger has to be 20 found out first. If he should turn to, and beat her——"

"Surely," I interrupted, with a burning face and heart, "you do not seriously think that he is scoundrel enough for that, Mr. Jaggers?"

"I didn't say so, Pip. I am putting a case. If he should turn to and beat her, he may possibly get the strength on his side; if it should be a question of intellect, he certainly will not.[3] It would be chance work to give an opinion how a fellow of that sort will turn out in such circumstances, because it's a toss-up between two results."

"May I ask what they are?"

"A fellow like our friend the Spider," answered Mr. Jaggers, "either beats, 30 or cringes. He may cringe and growl, or cringe and not growl; but he either beats or cringes. Ask Wemmick *his* opinion."

"Either beats or cringes," said Wemmick, not at all addressing himself to me.

"So here's to Mrs. Bentley Drummle," said Mr. Jaggers, taking a decanter of choicer wine from his dumb-waiter, and filling for each of us and for himself, "and may the question of supremacy be settled to the lady's satisfaction! To the satisfaction of the lady *and* the gentleman, it never will be. Now, Molly, Molly, Molly, Molly, how slow you are to-day!"

She was at his elbow when he addressed her, putting a dish upon the table. 40 As she withdrew her hands from it, she fell back a step or two, nervously muttering some excuse, and a certain action of her fingers as she spoke arrested my attention.

"What's the matter?" said Mr. Jaggers.

"Nothing. Only the subject we were speaking of," said I, "was rather painful to me."

The action of her fingers was like the action of knitting. She stood looking at her master, not understanding whether she was free to go, or whether he

---

3. In the MS, followed by the insertion "You saw him here," canceled in proof. Jaggers speaks as if interrogating a witness: he asks Pip to recall the dinner party in chapter 26.

had more to say to her and would call her back if she did go. Her look was
very intent. Surely, I had seen exactly such eyes and such hands, on a memorable occasion very lately!

He dismissed her, and she glided out of the room. But she remained before
me, as plainly as if she were still there. I looked at those hands, I looked at
those eyes, I looked at that flowing hair; and I compared them with other
hands, other eyes, other hair, that I knew of, and with what those might be
after twenty years of a brutal husband and a stormy life. I looked again at
those hands and eyes of the housekeeper, and thought of the inexplicable
feeling that had come over me when I last walked—not alone—in the ruined   10
garden, and through the deserted brewery. I thought how the same feeling
had come back when I saw a face looking at me, and a hand waving to me,
from a stage-coach window; and how it had come back again and had flashed
about me like Lightning, when I had passed in a carriage—not alone—
through a sudden glare of light in a dark street. I thought how one link of
association had helped that identification in the theatre, and how such a link,
wanting before, had been riveted for me now, when I had passed by a chance
swift from Estella's name to the fingers with their knitting action, and the
attentive eyes. And I felt absolutely certain that this woman was Estella's
mother.   20

Mr. Jaggers had seen me with Estella, and was not likely to have missed
the sentiments I had been at no pains to conceal. He nodded when I said
the subject was painful to me, clapped me on the back, put round the wine
again, and went on with his dinner.

Only twice more, did the housekeeper reappear, and then her stay in the
room was very short, and Mr. Jaggers was sharp with her. But her hands were
Estella's hands, and her eyes were Estella's eyes, and if she had reappeared a
hundred times I could have been neither more sure nor less sure that my
conviction was the truth.

It was a dull evening, for Wemmick drew his wine when it came round,   30
quite as a matter of business—just as he might have drawn his salary when
that came round—and with his eyes on his chief, sat in a state of perpetual
readiness for cross-examination. As to the quantity of wine, his post-office was
as indifferent and ready as any other post-office for its quantity of letters. From
my point of view, he was the wrong twin all the time, and only externally
like the Wemmick of Walworth.

We took our leave early, and left together. Even when we were groping
among Mr. Jaggers's stock of boots for our hats, I felt that the right twin was
on his way back; and we had not gone half a dozen yards down Gerrard-street
in the Walworth direction before I found that I was walking arm-in-arm with   40
the right twin, and that the wrong twin had evaporated into the evening air.

"Well!" said Wemmick, "that's over. He's a wonderful man, without his
living likeness; but I feel that I have to screw myself up when I dine with
him—and I dine more comfortably unscrewed."

I felt that this was a good statement of the case, and told him so.

"Wouldn't say it to anybody but yourself," he answered. "I know that what
is said between you and me, goes no further."

I asked him if he had ever seen Miss Havisham's adopted daughter, Mrs.
Bentley Drummle? He said no. To avoid being too abrupt, I then spoke of
the Aged, and of Miss Skiffins. He looked rather sly when I mentioned Miss   50

Skiffins, and stopped in the street to blow his nose with a roll of the head and a flourish, not quite free from latent boastfulness.

"Wemmick," said I, "do you remember telling me before I first went to Mr. Jaggers's private house, to notice that housekeeper?"

"Did I?" he replied. "Ah, I dare say I did. Deuce take me,"[4] he added, suddenly, "I know I did. I find I am not quite unscrewed yet."

"A wild beast tamed, you called her," said I.

"And what do *you* call her?" said he.

"The same. How did Mr. Jaggers tame her, Wemmick?"

"That's his secret. She has been with him many a long year."   10

"I wish you would tell me her story. I feel a particular interest in being acquainted with it. You know that what is said between you and me goes no further."

"Well!" Wemmick replied, "I don't know her story—that is, I don't know all of it. But what I do know, I'll tell you. We are in our private and personal capacities, of course."

"Of course."

"A score or so of years ago, that woman was tried at the Old Bailey for murder, and was acquitted. She was a very handsome young woman, and I believe had some gipsy blood in her.[5] Anyhow, it was hot enough when it   20 was up, as you may suppose."

"But she was acquitted."

"Mr. Jaggers was for her," pursued Wemmick, with a look full of meaning, "and worked the case in a way quite astonishing. It was a desperate case, and it was comparatively early days with him then, and he worked it to general admiration; in fact, it may almost be said to have made him. He worked it himself at the police-office, day after day for many days, contending against even a committal; and at the trial where he couldn't work it himself, sat under Counsel, and—every one knew—put in all the salt and pepper.[6] The mur-   30 dered person was a woman; a woman, a good ten years older, very much larger, and very much stronger. It was a case of jealousy. They both led tramping lives, and this woman in Gerrard-street here had been married very young, over the broomstick (as we say),[7] to a tramping man, and was a perfect fury in point of jealousy. The murdered woman—more a match for the man, certainly, in point of years—was found dead in a barn near Hounslow Heath.[8] There had been a violent struggle, perhaps a fight. She was bruised and scratched and torn, and had been held by the throat at last and choked. Now, there was no reasonable evidence to implicate any person but this woman, and, on the improbabilities of her having been able to do it, Mr. Jaggers

---

4. "I'll be damned." But also associated with the dice player's oath on making the lowest throw—a deuce, of course, meaning two.
5. Gypsies were routinely grouped with "vagabonds" and "rogues" in English law from the first Act in 1530 banning the immigration of "Egipcions" and ordering their deportation. The Poor Law Act of 1596 confirmed Gypsies to be rogues and vagabonds; under Acts of the 1820s and 1830s "any one pretending to tell fortunes by palmistry . . . [or] wandering abroad and lodging under any tent or cart" was liable to imprisonment. On vagrancy laws, see p. 260, n. 5.
6. Barred from addressing the jury himself, Jaggers supplies the barrister or "counsel" with spicy arguments on Molly's behalf. On his function as solicitor, see p. 133, n. 2.
7. That is, through a mock-marriage ceremony in which the partners "solemnize" the match by jumping over a broomstick and thereafter live as man and wife.
8. The heath stretching westward for five miles from Hounslow, Middlesex, some nine miles from London. Throughout the seventeenth and eighteenth centuries, synonymous with highway robbery and murder. Now more likely to be the site of hijacking: the precincts of Heathrow Airport.

principally rested his case. You may be sure," said Wemmick, touching me on the sleeve, "that he never dwelt upon the strength of her hands then, though he sometimes does now."

I had told Wemmick of his showing us her wrists, that day of the dinner party.

"Well, sir!" Wemmick went on; "it happened—happened, don't you see? —that this woman was so very artfully dressed from the time of her apprehension, that she looked much slighter than she really was; in particular, her sleeves are always remembered to have been so skilfully contrived, that her arms had quite a delicate look. She had only a bruise or two about her 10 —nothing for a tramp—but the backs of her hands were lacerated, and the question was, was it with finger-nails? Now, Mr. Jaggers showed that she had struggled through a great lot of brambles which were not as high as her face; but which she could not have got through and kept her hands out of; and bits of those brambles were actually found in her skin and put in evidence, as well as the fact that the brambles in question were found on examination to have been broken through, and to have little shreds of her dress and little spots of blood upon them here and there. But the boldest point he made, was this. It was attempted to be set up in proof of her jealousy, that she was under strong suspicion of having, at about the time of the murder, frantically 20 destroyed her child by this man—some three years old—to revenge herself upon him. Mr. Jaggers worked that, in this way. 'We say these are not marks of finger-nails, but marks of brambles, and we show you the brambles. You say they are marks of finger-nails, and you set up the hypothesis that she destroyed her child. You must accept all consequences of that hypothesis. For anything we know, she may have destroyed her child, and the child in clinging to her may have scratched her hands. What then? You are not trying her for the murder of her child; why don't you? As to this case, if you *will* have scratches, we say that, for anything we know, you may have accounted for them, assuming for the sake of argument that you have not invented them?' 30 To sum up, sir," said Wemmick, "Mr. Jaggers was altogether too many for the Jury, and they gave in."

"Has she been in his service ever since?"

"Yes; but not only that," said Wemmick. "She went into his service immediately after her acquittal, tamed as she is now. She has since been taught one thing and another in the way of her duties, but she was tamed from the beginning."

"Do you remember the sex of the child?"

"Said to have been a girl."

"You have nothing more to say to me to-night?"   40

"Nothing. I got your letter and destroyed it. Nothing."

We exchanged a cordial Good Night, and I went home, with new matter for my thoughts, though with no relief from the old.

★

Chapter XLIX.

PUTTING Miss Havisham's note in my pocket, that it might serve as my credentials for so soon reappearing at Satis House, in case her waywardness should lead her to express any surprise at seeing me, I went down again by the coach next day. But I alighted at the Halfway House, and breakfasted there, and walked the rest of the distance; for I sought to get into the town quietly, by the unfrequented ways, and to leave it in the same manner.

The best light of the day was gone when I passed along the quiet echoing courts behind the High-street. The nooks of ruin where the old monks had once had their refectories and gardens, and where the strong walls were now pressed into the service of humble sheds and stables, were almost as silent as the old monks in their graves. The cathedral chimes had at once a sadder and a more remote sound to me, as I hurried on avoiding observation, than they had ever had before; so, the swell of the old organ was borne to my ears like funeral music; and the rooks, as they hovered about the grey tower and swung in the bare high trees of the priory-garden, seemed to call to me that the place was changed, and that Estella was gone out of it for ever.[1]

An elderly woman whom I had seen before as one of the servants who lived in the supplementary house across the back court-yard, opened the gate. The lighted candle stood in the dark passage within, as of old, and I took it up and ascended the staircase alone. Miss Havisham was not in her own room, but was in the larger room across the landing. Looking in at the door, after knocking in vain, I saw her sitting on the hearth in a ragged chair, close before, and lost in the contemplation of, the ashy fire.

Doing as I had often done, I went in, and stood, touching the old chimney-piece, where she could see me when she raised her eyes. There was an air of utter loneliness upon her that would have moved me to pity though she had wilfully done me a deeper injury than I could charge her with. As I stood compassionating her, and thinking how in the progress of time I too had come to be a part of the wrecked fortunes of that house, her eyes rested on me. She stared, and said in a low voice, "Is it real!"

"It is I, Pip. Mr. Jaggers gave me your note yesterday, and I have lost no time."

"Thank you. Thank you."

As I brought another of the ragged chairs to the hearth and sat down, I remarked a new expression on her face, as if she were afraid of me.

"I want," she said, "to pursue that subject you mentioned to me when you were last here, and to show you that I am not all stone. But perhaps you can never believe, now, that there is anything human in my heart?"

When I said some reassuring words, she stretched out her tremulous right hand, as though she were going to touch me; but she recalled it again before I understood the action, or knew how to receive it.

"You said, speaking for your friend, that you could tell me how to do something useful and good. Something that you would like done, is it not?"

"Something that I would like done, very very much."

---

1. The single specific reference to Rochester and its Cathedral in the book. The Priory Gardens, or "Vines," which extend east of the cathedral, used to be what Dickens calls them in *Edwin Drood*, the "Monks' Vineyard."

"What is it?"

I began explaining to her that secret history of the partnership. I had not got far into it, when I judged from her look that she was thinking in a discursive way of me, rather than of what I said. It seemed to be so, for when I stopped speaking, many moments passed before she showed that she was conscious of the fact.

"Do you break off," she asked then, with her former air of being afraid of me, "because you hate me too much to bear to speak to me?"

"No, no," I answered, "how can you think so, Miss Havisham! I stopped because I thought you were not following what I said."   10

"Perhaps I was not," she answered, putting a hand to her head. "Begin again, and let me look at something else. Stay! Now tell me."

She set her hand upon her stick in the resolute way that sometimes was habitual to her, and looked at the fire with a strong expression of forcing herself to attend. I went on with my explanation, and told her how I had hoped to complete the transaction out of my means, but how in this I was disappointed. That part of the subject (I reminded her) involved matters which could form no part of my explanation, for they were the weighty secrets of another.

"So!" said she, assenting with her head, but not looking at me. "And how   20 much money is wanting to complete the purchase?"

I was rather afraid of stating it, for it sounded a large sum. "Nine hundred pounds."

"If I give you the money for this purpose, will you keep my secret as you have kept your own?"

"Quite as faithfully."

"And your mind will be more at rest?"

"Much more at rest."

"Are you very unhappy now?"

She asked this question, still without looking at me, but in an unwonted   30 tone of sympathy. I could not reply at the moment, for my voice failed me. She put her left arm across the crutched head of her stick, and softly laid her forehead on it.

"I am far from happy, Miss Havisham; but I have other causes of disquiet than any you know of. They are the secrets I have mentioned."

After a little while, she raised her head and looked at the fire again.

"It is noble in you to tell me that you have other causes of unhappiness. Is it true?"

"Too true."

"Can I only serve you, Pip, by serving your friend? Regarding that as done,   40 is there nothing I can do for you yourself?"

"Nothing. I thank you for the question. I thank you even more for the tone of the question. But, there is nothing."

She presently rose from her seat, and looked about the blighted room for the means of writing. There were none there, and she took from her pocket a yellow set of ivory tablets,[2] mounted in tarnished gold, and wrote upon them with a pencil in a case of tarnished gold that hung from her neck.

"You are still on friendly terms with Mr. Jaggers?"

---

2. A small notebook with covers made of two oblong pieces of ivory.

"Quite. I dined with him yesterday."

"This is an authority to him to pay you that money, to lay out at your irresponsible[3] discretion for your friend. I keep no money here, but if you would rather Mr. Jaggers knew nothing of the matter, I will send it to you."

"Thank you, Miss Havisham; I have not the least objection to receiving it from him."

She read me what she had written, and it was direct and clear, and evidently intended to absolve me from any suspicion of profiting by the receipt of the money. I took the tablets from her hand, and it trembled again, and it trembled more as she took off the chain to which the pencil was attached, and put it in mine. All this she did without looking at me.

"My name is on the first leaf. If you can ever write under my name, 'I forgive her,' though ever so long after my broken heart is dust—pray do it!"

"O Miss Havisham," said I, "I can do it now. There have been sore mistakes, and my life has been a blind and thankless one, and I want forgiveness and direction far too much to be bitter with you."

She turned her face to me for the first time since she had averted it, and, to my amazement, I may even add to my terror, dropped on her knees at my feet; with her folded hands raised to me in the manner in which, when her poor heart was young and fresh and whole, they must often have been raised to Heaven from her mother's side.

To see her with her white hair and her worn face, kneeling at my feet, gave me a shock through all my frame. I entreated her to rise, and got my arms about her to help her up; but she only pressed that hand of mine which was nearest to her grasp, and hung her head over it and wept. I had never seen her shed a tear before, and, in the hope that the relief might do her good, I bent over her without speaking. She was not kneeling now, but was down upon the ground.

"O!" she cried, despairingly. "What have I done! What have I done!"

"If you mean, Miss Havisham, what have you done to injure me, let me answer. Very little. I should have loved her under any circumstances.—Is she married?"

"Yes."

It was a needless question, for a new desolation in the desolate house had told me so.

"What have I done! What have I done!" She wrung her hands, and crushed her white hair, and returned to this cry, over and over again. "What have I done!"

I knew not how to answer, or how to comfort her. That she had done a grievous thing in taking an impressionable child to mould into the form that her wild resentment, spurned affection, and wounded pride, found vengeance in, I knew full well. But that, in shutting out the light of day, she had shut out infinitely more; that, in seclusion, she had secluded herself from a thousand natural and healing influences; that, her mind, brooding solitary, had grown diseased, as all minds do and must and will that reverse the appointed order of their Maker; I knew equally well. And could I look upon her without compassion, seeing her punishment in the ruin she was, in her profound unfitness for this earth on which she was placed, in the vanity of sorrow which

---

3. In the sense of "independent"; "responsible" to no one but oneself.

had become a master mania, like the vanity of penitence, the vanity of remorse, the vanity of unworthiness, and other monstrous vanities that have
been curses in this world?

"Until you spoke to her the other day, and until I saw in you a looking-
glass that showed me what I once felt myself, I did not know what I had
done. What have I done! What have I done!" And so again, twenty, fifty times
over, What had she done!

"Miss Havisham," I said, when her cry had died away, "you may dismiss
me from your mind and conscience. But Estella is a different case, and if
you can ever undo any scrap of what you have done amiss in keeping a part   10
of her right nature away from her, it will be better to do that, than to bemoan
the past through a hundred years."

"Yes, yes, I know it. But, Pip—my Dear!" There was an earnest womanly
compassion for me in her new affection. "My Dear! Believe this: when she
first came to me, I meant to save her from misery like my own. At first I
meant no more."

"Well, well!" said I. "I hope so."

"But as she grew, and promised to be very beautiful, I gradually did worse,
and with my praises, and with my jewels, and with my teachings, and with
this figure of myself always before her, a warning to back and point my lessons,   20
I stole her heart away and put ice in its place."

"Better," I could not help saying, "to have left her a natural heart, even to
be bruised or broken."

With that, Miss Havisham looked distractedly at me for a while, and then
burst out again, What had she done!

"If you knew all my story," she pleaded, "you would have some compassion
for me and a better understanding of me."

"Miss Havisham," I answered, as delicately as I could, "I believe I may say
that I do know your story, and have known it ever since I first left this neighbourhood. It has inspired me with great commiseration, and I hope I under-   30
stand it and its influences. Does what has passed between us give me any
excuse for asking you a question relative to Estella? Not as she is, but as she
was when she first came here?"

She was seated on the ground, with her arms on the ragged chair, and her
head leaning on them. She looked full at me when I said this, and replied,
"Go on."

"Whose child was Estella?"

She shook her head.

"You don't know?"

She shook her head again.   40

"But Mr. Jaggers brought her here, or sent her here?"

"Brought her here."

"Will you tell me how that came about?"

She answered in a low whisper and with great caution: "I had been shut
up in these rooms a long time (I don't know how long; you know what time
the clocks keep here), when I told him that I wanted a little girl to rear and
love, and save from my fate. I had first seen him when I sent for him to lay
this place waste for me; having read of him in the newspapers, before I and
the world parted. He told me that he would look about him for such an
orphan child. One night he brought her here asleep, and I called her Estella."   50

"Might I ask her age then?"

"Two or three. She herself knows nothing, but that she was left an orphan and I adopted her."

So convinced I was of that woman's being her mother, that I wanted no evidence to establish the fact in my own mind. But to any mind, I thought, the connexion here was clear and straight.

What more could I hope to do by prolonging the interview? I had succeeded on behalf of Herbert, Miss Havisham had told me all she knew of Estella, I had said and done what I could to ease her mind. No matter with what other words we parted; we parted.

Twilight was closing in when I went down stairs into the natural air. I called to the woman who had opened the gate when I entered, that I would not trouble her just yet, but would walk round the place before leaving. For I had a presentiment that I should never be there again, and I felt that the dying light was suited to my last view of it.

By the wilderness of casks that I had walked on long ago, and on which the rain of years had fallen since, rotting them in many places, and leaving miniature swamps and pools of water upon those that stood on end, I made my way to the ruined garden. I went all round it; round by the corner where Herbert and I had fought our battle; round by the paths where Estella and I had walked. So cold, so lonely, so dreary all!

Taking the brewery on my way back, I raised the rusty latch of a little door at the garden end of it, and walked through. I was going out at the opposite door—not easy to open now, for the damp wood had started[4] and swelled, and the hinges were yielding, and the threshold was encumbered with a growth of fungus—when I turned my head to look back. A childish association revived with wonderful force in the moment of the slight action, and I fancied that I saw Miss Havisham hanging to the beam. So strong was the impression, that I stood under the beam shuddering from head to foot before I knew it was a fancy—though to be sure I was there in an instant.

The mournfulness of the place and time, and the great terror of this illusion, though it was but momentary, caused me to feel an indescribable awe as I came out between the open wooden gates where I had once wrung my hair after Estella had wrung my heart. Passing on into the front court-yard, I hesitated whether to call the woman to let me out at the locked gate of which she had the key, or first to go upstairs and assure myself that Miss Havisham was as safe and well as I had left her. I took the latter course and went up.

I looked into the room where I had left her, and I saw her seated in the ragged chair upon the hearth close to the fire, with her back towards me. In the moment when I was withdrawing my head to go quietly away, I saw a great flaming light spring up. In the same moment I saw her running at me, shrieking, with a whirl of fire blazing all about her, and soaring at least as many feet above her head as she was high.

I had a double-caped great-coat on, and over my arm another thick coat. That I got them off, closed with her, threw her down, and got them over her; that I dragged the great cloth from the table for the same purpose, and with it dragged down the heap of rottenness in the midst, and all the ugly things that sheltered there; that we were on the ground struggling like desperate

---

4. Gotten loose; broken away from its fastenings.

enemies, and that the closer I covered her, the more wildly she shrieked and tried to free herself; that this occurred I knew through the result, but not through anything I felt, or thought, or knew I did. I knew nothing until I knew that we were on the floor by the great table, and that patches of tinder yet alight were floating in the smoky air, which, a moment ago, had been her faded bridal dress.

Then I looked round and saw the disturbed beetles and spiders running away over the floor, and the servants coming in with breathless cries at the door. I still held her forcibly down with all my strength, like a prisoner who might escape; and I doubt if I even knew who she was, or why we had struggled, or that she had been in flames, or that the flames were out, until I saw the patches of tinder that had been her garments, no longer alight but falling in a black shower around us.

She was insensible, and I was afraid to have her moved, or even touched. Assistance was sent for and I held her until it came, as if I unreasonably fancied (I think I did) that if I let her go, the fire would break out again and consume her. When I got up, on the surgeon's coming to her with other aid, I was astonished to see that both my hands were burnt; for I had no knowledge of it through the sense of feeling.

On examination it was pronounced that she had received serious hurts, but that they of themselves were far from hopeless; the danger lay, however, mainly in the nervous shock. By the surgeon's directions, her bed was carried into that room and laid upon the great table: which happened to be well suited to the dressing of her injuries. When I saw her again an hour afterwards, she lay indeed where I had seen her strike her stick, and had heard her say that she would lie one day.

Though every vestige of her dress was burnt, as they told me, she still had something of her old ghastly bridal appearance; for, they had covered her to the throat with white cotton-wool, and as she lay with a white sheet loosely overlying that, the phantom air of something that had been and was changed, was still upon her.

I found, on questioning the servants, that Estella was in Paris, and I got a promise from the surgeon that he would write to her by the next post. Miss Havisham's family I took upon myself; intending to communicate with Matthew Pocket only, and leave him to do as he liked about informing the rest. This I did next day, through Herbert, as soon as I returned to town.

There was a stage that evening when she spoke collectedly of what had happened, though with a certain terrible vivacity. Towards midnight she began to wander in her speech, and after that it gradually set in that she said innumerable times in a low solemn voice, "What have I done!" And then, "When she first came, I meant to save her from misery like mine." And then, "Take the pencil and write under my name, 'I forgive her!'" She never changed the order of these three sentences, but she sometimes left out a word in one or other of them; never putting in another word, but always leaving a blank and going on to the next word.

As I could do no service there, and as I had, nearer home, that pressing reason for anxiety and fear which even her wanderings could not drive out of my mind, I decided in the course of the night that I would return by the early morning coach: walking on a mile or so, and being taken up clear of the town. At about six o'clock of the morning, therefore, I leaned over her and touched her lips with mine, just as they said, not stopping for being touched, "Take the pencil and write under my name, 'I forgive her.'"

Chapter L.

MY hands had been dressed twice or thrice in the night, and again in the morning. My left arm was a good deal burned to the elbow, and, less severely, as high as the shoulder; it was very painful, but the flames had set in that direction, and I felt thankful it was no worse. My right hand was not so badly burnt but that I could move the fingers. It was bandaged, of course, but much less inconveniently than my left hand and arm; those I carried in a sling; and I could only wear my coat like a cloak, loose over my shoulders and fastened at the neck. My hair had been caught by the fire, but not my head or face.

When Herbert had been down to Hammersmith and seen his father, he came back to me at our chambers, and devoted the day to attending on me. He was the kindest of nurses, and at stated times took off the bandages, and steeped them in the cooling liquid that was kept ready, and put them on again, with a patient tenderness that I was deeply grateful for.

At first, as I lay quiet on the sofa, I found it painfully difficult, I might say impossible, to get rid of the impression of the glare of the flames, their hurry and noise, and the fierce burning smell. If I dozed for a minute, I was awakened by Miss Havisham's cries, and by her running at me with all that height of fire above her head. This pain of the mind was much harder to strive against than any bodily pain I suffered; and Herbert, seeing that, did his utmost to hold my attention engaged.

Neither of us spoke of the boat, but we both thought of it. That was made apparent by our avoidance of the subject, and by our agreeing—without agreement—to make my recovery of the use of my hands, a question of so many hours, not of so many weeks.

My first question when I saw Herbert had been, of course, whether all was well down the river? As he replied in the affirmative, with perfect confidence and cheerfulness, we did not resume the subject until the day was wearing away. But then, as Herbert changed the bandages, more by the light of the fire than by the outer light, he went back to it spontaneously.

"I sat with Provis last night, Handel, two good hours."

"Where was Clara?"

"Dear little thing!" said Herbert. "She was up and down with Gruffandgrim all the evening. He was perpetually pegging at the floor the moment she left his sight. I doubt if he can hold out long, though. What with rum and pepper—and pepper and rum—I should think his pegging must be nearly over."

"And then you will be married, Herbert?"

"How can I take care of the dear child otherwise?—Lay your arm out upon the back of the sofa, my dear boy, and I'll sit down here, and get the bandage off so gradually that you shall not know when it comes. I was speaking of Provis. Do you know, Handel, he improves?"

"I said to you I thought he was softened, when I last saw him."

"So you did. And so he is. He was very communicative last night, and told me more of his life. You remember his breaking off here about some woman that he had had great trouble with.—Did I hurt you?"

I had started, but not under his touch. His words had given me a start.

"I had forgotten that, Herbert, but I remember it now you speak of it."

"Well! He went into that part of his life, and a dark wild part it is. Shall I tell you? Or would it worry you just now?"

"Tell me by all means. Every word!"

Herbert bent forward to look at me more nearly, as if my reply had been rather more hurried or more eager than he could quite account for. "Your   10
head is cool?" he said, touching it.

"Quite," said I. "Tell me what Provis said, my dear Herbert."

"It seems," said Herbert, "—there's a bandage off most charmingly, and now comes the cool one—makes you shrink at first, my poor dear fellow, don't it? but it will be comfortable presently—it seems that the woman was a young woman, and a jealous woman, and a revengeful woman; revengeful, Handel, to the last degree."

"To what last degree?"

"Murder.—Does it strike too cold on that sensitive place?"

"I don't feel it. How did she murder? Whom did she murder?"   20

"Why, the deed may not have merited quite so terrible a name," said Herbert, "but she was tried for it, and Mr. Jaggers defended her, and the reputation of that defence first made his name known to Provis. It was another and a stronger woman who was the victim, and there had been a struggle—in a barn. Who began it, or how fair it was, or how unfair, may be doubtful; but how it ended, is certainly not doubtful, for the victim was found throttled."

"Was the woman brought in guilty?"

"No; she was acquitted.—My poor Handel, I hurt you!"

"It is impossible to be gentler, Herbert. Yes? What else?"   30

"This acquitted young woman and Provis," said Herbert, "had a little child: a little child of whom Provis was exceedingly fond. On the evening of the very night when the object of her jealousy was strangled, as I tell you, the young woman presented herself before Provis for one moment, and swore that she would destroy the child (which was in her possession), and he should never see it again; then she vanished.—There's the worst arm comfortably in the sling once more, and now there remains but the right hand, which is a far easier job. I can do it better by this light than by a stronger, for my hand is steadiest when I don't see the poor blistered patches too distinctly.—You don't think your breathing is affected, my dear boy? You seem to breathe quickly."   40

"Perhaps I do, Herbert. Did the woman keep her oath?"

"There comes the darkest part of Provis's life. She did."

"That is, he says she did."

"Why, of course, my dear boy," returned Herbert, in a tone of surprise, and again bending forward to get a nearer look at me. "He says it all. I have no other information."

"No, to be sure."

"Now, whether," pursued Herbert, "he had used the child's mother ill, or whether he had used the child's mother well, Provis doesn't say; but she had shared some four or five years of the wretched life he described to us at this   50 fireside, and he seems to have felt pity for her, and forbearance towards her. Therefore, fearing he should be called upon to depose about this destroyed child, and so be the cause of her death, he hid himself (much as he grieved for the child), kept himself dark, as he says, out of the way and out of the trial, and was only vaguely talked of as a certain man called Abel, out of whom the jealousy arose. After the acquittal she disappeared, and thus he lost the child and the child's mother."

"I want to ask——"

"A moment, my dear boy," said Herbert, "and I have done. That evil genius, Compeyson, the worst of scoundrels among many scoundrels, know- 10 ing of his keeping out of the way at that time, and of his reasons for doing so, of course afterwards held the knowledge over his head as a means of keeping him poorer, and working him harder. It was clear last night that this barbed the point of Provis's hatred."

"I want to know," said I, "and particularly, Herbert, whether he told you when this happened?"

"Particularly? Let me remember, then, what he said as to that. His expression was, 'a round score[1] o' year ago, and a'most directly after I took up wi' Compeyson.' How old were you when you came upon him in the little churchyard?" 20

"I think in my seventh year."[2]

"Ay. It had happened some three or four years then, he said, and you brought into his mind the little girl so tragically lost, who would have been about your age."

"Herbert," said I after a short silence, in a hurried way, "can you see me best by the light of the window, or the light of the fire?"

"By the firelight," answered Herbert, coming close again.

"Look at me."

"I do look at you, my dear boy."

"Touch me." 30

"I do touch you, my dear boy."

"You are not afraid that I am in any fever, or that my head is much disordered by the accident of last night?"

"N-no, my dear boy," said Herbert, after taking time to examine me. "You are rather excited, but you are quite yourself."

"I know I am quite myself. And the man we have in hiding down the river, is Estella's Father."

Chapter LI.

WHAT purpose I had in view when I was hot on tracing out and proving Estella's parentage, I cannot say. It will presently be seen that the question was not before me in any distinct shape, until it was put before me by a wiser 40 head than my own.

1. Fully twenty years.
2. Not entirely clear whether Pip was six or had just turned seven. The phrase "in my seventh year" literally suggests him to be six; in support of his being seven, see p. 115, n. 1 and below, p. 537.

But when Herbert and I had held our momentous conversation, I was seized with a feverish conviction that I ought to hunt the matter down—that I ought not to let it rest, but that I ought to see Mr. Jaggers, and come at the bare truth. I really do not know whether I felt that I did this for Estella's sake, or whether I was glad to transfer to the man in whose preservation I was so much concerned, some rays of the romantic interest that had so long surrounded her. Perhaps the latter possibility may be the nearer to the truth.

Any way, I could scarcely be withheld from going out to Gerrard-street that night. Herbert's representations that if I did, I should probably be laid up and stricken useless, when our fugitive's safety would depend upon me, alone   10 restrained my impatience. On the understanding, again and again reiterated, that come what would, I was to go to Mr. Jaggers to-morrow, I at length submitted to keep quiet, and to have my hurts looked after, and to stay at home. Early next morning we went out together, and at the corner of Giltspur-street[1] by Smithfield, I left Herbert to go his way into the City, and took my way to Little Britain.

There were periodical occasions when Mr. Jaggers and Wemmick went over the office accounts, and checked off the vouchers, and put all things straight. On those occasions Wemmick took his books and papers into Mr. Jaggers's room, and one of the up-stairs clerks came down into the outer   20 office. Finding such clerk on Wemmick's post that morning, I knew what was going on; but I was not sorry to have Mr. Jaggers and Wemmick together, as Wemmick would then hear for himself that I said nothing to compromise him. My appearance with my arm bandaged and my coat loose over my shoulders, favoured my object. Although I had sent Mr. Jaggers a brief account of the accident as soon as I had arrived in town, yet I had to give him all the details now; and the specialty of the occasion caused our talk to be less dry and hard, and less strictly regulated by the rules of evidence, than it had been before. While I described the disaster, Mr. Jaggers stood, according to his   30 wont, before the fire. Wemmick leaned back in his chair, staring at me, with his hands in the pockets of his trousers, and his pen put horizontally into the post. The two brutal casts, always inseparable in my mind from the official proceedings, seemed to be congestively[2] considering whether they didn't smell fire at the present moment.

My narrative finished, and their questions exhausted, I then produced Miss Havisham's authority to receive the nine hundred pounds for Herbert. Mr. Jaggers's eyes retired a little deeper into his head when I handed him the tablets, but he presently handed them over to Wemmick, with instructions to draw the cheque for his signature. While that was in course of being done,   40 I looked on at Wemmick as he wrote, and Mr. Jaggers, poising and swaying himself on his well-polished boots, looked on at me. "I am sorry, Pip," said he, as I put the cheque in my pocket, when he had signed it, "that we do nothing for *you*."

---

1. Giltspur Street runs from Newgate Street to West Smithfield; until mid-sixteenth century known as Knightrider's Street. The street names recall the period from the twelfth century when knights in gilt spurs rode to the jousting grounds at the "Smoothfield"; but the name may derive from the location of spurriers near Smithfield.
2. Indicating congestion or blockage by an accumulation of fluid such as blood. The two plaster casts made from the heads of hanged criminals are described in chapter 20 as being "peculiarly swollen, and twitchy about the nose" and again as "swollen faces": a classic case of congestion.

"Miss Havisham was good enough to ask me," I returned, "whether she could do nothing for me, and I told her No."

"Everybody should know his own business," said Mr. Jaggers. And I saw Wemmick's lips form the words "portable property."

"I should *not* have told her No, if I had been you," said Mr. Jaggers; "but every man ought to know his own business best."

"Every man's business," said Wemmick, rather reproachfully towards me, "is portable property."

As I thought the time was now come for pursuing the theme I had at heart, I said, turning on Mr. Jaggers: 10

"I did ask something of Miss Havisham, however, sir. I asked her to give me some information relative to her adopted daughter, and she gave me all she possessed."

"Did she?" said Mr. Jaggers, bending forward to look at his boots and then straightening himself. "Hah! I don't think I should have done so, if I had been Miss Havisham. But *she* ought to know her own business best."

"I know more of the history of Miss Havisham's adopted child, than Miss Havisham herself does, sir. I know her mother."

Mr. Jaggers looked at me inquiringly, and repeated "Mother?"

"I have seen her mother within these three days."   20

"Yes?" said Mr. Jaggers.

"And so have you, sir. And you have seen her still more recently."

"Yes?" said Mr. Jaggers.

"Perhaps I know more of Estella's history than even you do," said I. "I know her father too."

A certain stop that Mr. Jaggers came to in his manner—he was too self-possessed to change his manner, but he could not help its being brought to an indefinably attentive stop—assured me that he did not know who her father was. This I had strongly suspected from Provis's account (as Herbert had repeated it) of his having kept himself dark; which I pieced on to the fact   30 that he himself was not Mr. Jaggers's client until some four years later, and when he could have no reason for claiming his identity. But I could not be sure of this unconsciousness on Mr. Jaggers's part before, though I was quite sure of it now.

"So! You know the young lady's father, Pip?" said Mr. Jaggers.

"Yes," I replied. "And his name is Provis—from New South Wales."

Even Mr. Jaggers started when I said those words. It was the slightest start that could escape a man, the most carefully repressed and the soonest checked, but he did start, though he made it a part of the action of taking out his pocket-handkerchief. How Wemmick received the announcement I   40 am unable to say, for I was afraid to look at him just then, lest Mr. Jaggers's sharpness should detect that there had been some communication unknown to him between us.

"And on what evidence, Pip," asked Mr. Jaggers, very coolly, as he paused with his handkerchief half way to his nose, "does Provis make this claim?"

"He does not make it," said I, "and has never made it, and has no knowledge or belief that his daughter is in existence."

For once, the powerful pocket-handkerchief failed. My reply was so unexpected that Mr. Jaggers put the handkerchief back into his pocket without   50

completing the usual performance, folded his arms, and looked with stern
attention at me, though with an immovable face.

Then I told him all I knew, and how I knew it, with the one reservation
that I left him to infer that I knew from Miss Havisham what I in fact knew
from Wemmick. I was very careful indeed as to that. Nor did I look towards
Wemmick until I had finished all I had to tell, and had been for some time
silently meeting Mr. Jaggers's look. When I did at last turn my eyes in Wemmick's direction, I found that he had unposted his pen, and was intent upon
the table before him.

"Hah!" said Mr. Jaggers at last, as he moved towards the papers on the
table. "—What item was it you were at, Wemmick, when Mr. Pip came in?"

But I could not submit to be thrown off in that way, and I made a passionate, almost an indignant, appeal to him to be more frank and manly with
me. I reminded him of the false hopes into which I had lapsed, the length
of time they had lasted, and the discovery I had made; and I hinted at the
danger that weighed upon my spirits. I represented myself as being surely
worthy of some little confidence from him, in return for the confidence I had
just now imparted. I said that I did not blame him, or suspect him, or mistrust
him, but I wanted assurance of the truth from him. And if he asked me why
I wanted it and why I thought I had any right to it, I would tell him, little as
he cared for such poor dreams, that I had loved Estella dearly and long, and
that, although I had lost her and must live a bereaved life, whatever concerned
her was still nearer and dearer to me than anything else in the world. And
seeing that Mr. Jaggers stood quite still and silent, and apparently quite ob-
durate, under this appeal, I turned at last to Wemmick, and said, "Wemmick,
I know you to be a man with a gentle heart. I have seen your pleasant home,
and your old father, and all the innocent cheerful playful ways with which
you refresh your business life. And I entreat you to say a word for me to Mr.
Jaggers, and to represent to him that, all circumstances considered, he ought
to be more open with me!"

I have never seen two men look more oddly at one another than Mr. Jaggers
and Wemmick did after this apostrophe. At first, a misgiving crossed me that
Wemmick would be instantly dismissed from his employment; but it melted
as I saw Mr. Jaggers relax into something like a smile, and Wemmick become
bolder.

"What's all this?" said Mr. Jaggers. "You with an old father, and you with
pleasant and playful ways?"

"Well!" returned Wemmick. "If I don't bring 'em here, what does it
matter?"

"Pip," said Mr. Jaggers, laying his hand upon my arm, and smiling openly,
"this man must be the most cunning impostor in all London."

"Not a bit of it," returned Wemmick, growing bolder and bolder. "I think
you're another."

Again they exchanged their former odd looks, each apparently still distrustful that the other was taking him in.

"You with a pleasant home?" said Mr. Jaggers.

"Since it don't interfere with business," returned Wemmick, "let it be so.
Now, I look at you, sir, I shouldn't wonder if you might be planning and
contriving to have a pleasant home of your own, one of these days, when
you're tired of all this work."

Mr. Jaggers nodded his head retrospectively two or three times, and actually drew a sigh. "Pip," said he, "we won't talk about 'poor dreams;' you know more about such things than I, having much fresher experience of that kind. But now, about this other matter. I'll put a case to you. Mind! I admit nothing."

He waited for me to declare that I quite understood that he expressly said that he admitted nothing.

"Now, Pip," said Mr. Jaggers, "put this case. Put the case that a woman, under such circumstances as you have mentioned, held her child concealed, and was obliged to communicate the fact to her legal adviser, on his repre- 10 senting to her that he must know, with an eye to the latitude of his defence, how the fact stood about that child. Put the case that at the same time he held a trust to find a child for an eccentric rich lady to adopt and bring up."

"I follow you, sir."

"Put the case that he lived in an atmosphere of evil, and that all he saw of children, was, their being generated in great numbers for certain destruction. Put the case that he often saw children solemnly tried at a criminal bar, where they were held up to be seen; put the case that he habitually knew of their being imprisoned, whipped, transported, neglected, cast out, qualified in all ways for the hangman, and growing up to be hanged. Put the case that 20 pretty nigh all the children he saw in his daily business life, he had reason to look upon as so much spawn, to develop into the fish that were to come to his net—to be prosecuted, defended, forsworn, made orphans, be-devilled somehow."[3]

"I follow you, sir."

"Put the case, Pip, that here was one pretty little child out of the heap, who could be saved; whom the father believed dead, and dared make no stir about; as to whom, over the mother, the legal adviser had this power: 'I know what you did, and how you did it. You came so and so, this was your manner of attack and this the manner of resistance, you went so and so, you did such 30 and such things to divert suspicion. I have tracked you through it all, and I tell it you all. Part with the child, unless it should be necessary to produce it to clear you, and then it shall be produced. Give the child into my hands, and I will do my best to bring you off. If you are saved, your child is saved too; if you are lost, your child is still saved.' Put the case that this was done, and that the woman was cleared."

"I understand you perfectly."

"But that I make no admissions?"

"That you make no admissions." And Wemmick repeated, "No admissions."   40

"Put the case, Pip, that passion and the terror of death had a little shaken the woman's intellects, and that when she was set at liberty, she was scared out of the ways of the world and went to him to be sheltered. Put the case that he took her in, and that he kept down the old wild violent nature whenever he saw an inkling of its breaking out, by asserting his power over her in the old way. Do you comprehend the imaginary case?"

---

3. As Jaggers suggests, contemporary law did not distinguish between adult and juvenile offenders: young-sters like Oliver Twist and the Artful Dodger were tried in ordinary, not juvenile, courts. As late as 1816, when Pip would have been ten or so, one lexicographer of law defined "infant" as "any person under 21 years of age," whose infancy might, in exceptional cases, serve as a mitigating factor.

"Quite."

"Put the case that the child grew up, and was married for money. That the mother was still living. That the father was still living. That the mother and father unknown to one another, were dwelling within so many miles, furlongs,[4] yards if you like, of one another. That the secret was still a secret, except that you had got wind of it. Put that last case to yourself very carefully."

"I do."

"I ask Wemmick to put it to *himself* very carefully."

And Wemmick said, "I do."

"For whose sake would you reveal the secret? For the father's? I think he 10 would not be much the better for the mother. For the mother's? I think if she had done such a deed she would be safer where she was. For the daughter's? I think it would hardly serve her, to establish her parentage for the information of her husband, and to drag her back to disgrace after an escape of twenty years, pretty secure to last for life. But add the case that you had loved her, Pip, and had made her the subject of those 'poor dreams' which have, at one time or another, been in the heads of more men than you think likely, then I tell you that you had better—and would much sooner when you had thought well of it—chop off that bandaged left hand of yours with your bandaged right hand, and then pass the chopper on to Wemmick there, 20 to cut *that* off, too."

I looked at Wemmick, whose face was very grave. He gravely touched his lips with his forefinger. I did the same. Mr. Jaggers did the same. "Now, Wemmick," said the latter then, resuming his usual manner, "what item was it you were at, when Mr. Pip came in?"

Standing by for a little, while they were at work, I observed that the odd looks they had cast at one another were repeated several times: with this difference now, that each of them seemed suspicious, not to say conscious, of having shown himself in a weak and unprofessional light to the other. For this reason, I suppose, they were now inflexible with one another; Mr. Jaggers 30 being highly dictatorial, and Wemmick obstinately justifying himself whenever there was the smallest point in abeyance for a moment. I had never seen them on such ill terms; for generally they got on very well indeed together.

But they were both happily relieved by the opportune appearance of Mike, the client with the fur cap and the habit of wiping his nose on his sleeve, whom I had seen on the very first day of my appearance within those walls. This individual, who, either in his own person or in that of some member of his family, seemed to be always in trouble (which in that place meant Newgate), called to announce that his eldest daughter was taken up on suspicion of shoplifting.[5] As he imparted this melancholy circumstance to Wemmick, 40 Mr. Jaggers standing magisterially before the fire and taking no share in the proceedings, Mike's eye happened to twinkle with a tear.

"What are you about?" demanded Wemmick, with the utmost indignation. "What do you come snivelling here for?"

"I didn't go to do it,[6] Mr. Wemmick."

4. Eighth of an English mile, or 220 yards.
5. Like all forms of theft, shoplifting (above five shillings) remained technically a capital felony until the turn of the century.
6. "I didn't mean to do it."

"You did," said Wemmick. "How dare you? You're not in a fit state to come here, if you can't come here without spluttering like a bad pen. What do you mean by it?"

"A man can't help his feelings, Mr. Wemmick," pleaded Mike.

"His what?" demanded Wemmick, quite savagely. "Say that again!"

"Now, look here, my man," said Mr. Jaggers, advancing a step, and pointing to the door. "Get out of this office. I'll have no feelings here. Get out."

"It serves you right," said Wemmick. "Get out."

So the unfortunate Mike very humbly withdrew, and Mr. Jaggers and Wemmick appeared to have re-established their good understanding, and went to 10 work again with an air of refreshment upon them as if they had just had lunch.

Chapter LII.

FROM Little Britain I went, with my cheque in my pocket, to Miss Skiffins's brother, the accountant; and Miss Skiffins's brother, the accountant, going straight to Clarriker's and bringing Clarriker to me, I had the great satisfaction of completing that arrangement. It was the only good thing I had done, and the only completed thing I had done, since I was first apprised of my great expectations.

Clarriker informing me on that occasion that the affairs of the House were steadily progressing, that he would now be able to establish a small branch- 20 house in the East which was much wanted for the extension of the business, and that Herbert in his new partnership capacity would go out and take charge of it, I found that I must have prepared for a separation from my friend, even though my own affairs had been more settled. And now indeed I felt as if my last anchor were loosening its hold, and I should soon be driving with the winds and waves.

But there was recompense in the joy with which Herbert came home of a night and told me of these changes, little imagining that he told me no news, and sketched airy pictures of himself conducting Clara Barley to the land of the Arabian Nights, and of me going out to join them (with a caravan of 30 camels, I believe), and of our all going up the Nile[1] and seeing wonders. Without being sanguine as to my own part in these bright plans, I felt that Herbert's way was clearing fast, and that old Bill Barley had but to stick to his pepper and rum, and his daughter would soon be happily provided for.

We had now got into the month of March. My left arm, though it presented no bad symptoms, took in the natural course so long to heal that I was still unable to get a coat on. My right arm was tolerably restored;—disfigured, but fairly serviceable.

On a Monday morning, when Herbert and I were at breakfast, I received the following letter from Wemmick by the post. 40

1. The exotic attractions of Egypt must have been doubly vivid to the readers of *Great Expectations*. In 1858 the explorer John Hanning Speke (1827–1864) had discovered Lake Victoria and claimed it as the chief source of the Nile. By Pip's day, Egypt had long become a center of British trade with the Middle East, its importance consolidated by the establishment of an overland route from Alexandria to Suez in 1829. So Egypt had both romantic and commercial associations for Herbert.

"Walworth. Burn this as soon as read. Early in the week, or say Wednesday if the tide should suit, you might do what you know of if you felt disposed to try it. Now burn."

When I had shown this to Herbert and had put it in the fire—but not before we had both got it by heart—we considered what to do. For, of course my being disabled could now be no longer kept out of view.

"I have thought it over, again and again," said Herbert, "and I think I know a better course than taking a Thames waterman. Take Startop. A good fellow, a skilled hand, fond of us, and enthusiastic and honourable."

I had thought of him, more than once.   10

"But how much would you tell him, Herbert?"

"It is necessary to tell him very little. Let him suppose it a mere freak, but a secret one, until the morning comes: then let him know that there is urgent reason for your getting Provis aboard and away. You go with him?"

"No doubt."

"Where?"

It had seemed to me, in the many anxious considerations I had given the point, almost indifferent what port we made for—Hamburg, Rotterdam, Antwerp—the place signified little, so that he was got out of England. Any foreign steamer that fell in our way and would take us up, would do. I had 20
always proposed to myself to get him well down the river in the boat: certainly well beyond Gravesend,[2] which was a critical place for search or inquiry if suspicion were afoot. As foreign steamers would leave London at about the time of high-water, our plan would be to get down the river by a previous ebb-tide, and lie by in some quiet spot until we could pull off to one. The time when one would be due where we lay, wherever that might be, could be calculated pretty nearly, if we made inquiries beforehand.

Herbert assented to all this, and we went out immediately after breakfast to pursue our investigations. We found that a steamer for Hamburg was likely to suit our purpose best, and we directed our thoughts chiefly to that vessel. 30
But we noted down what other foreign steamers would leave London with the same tide, and we satisfied ourselves that we knew the build and colour of each. We then separated for a few hours; I, to get at once such passports as were necessary; Herbert, to see Startop at his lodgings. We both did what we had to do without any hindrance, and when we met again at one o'clock reported it done. I, for my part, was prepared with passports; Herbert had seen Startop, and he was more than ready to join.

Those two would pull a pair of oars, we settled, and I would steer; our charge would be sitter,[3] and keep quiet; as speed was not our object, we should make way enough. We arranged that Herbert should not come home 40
to dinner before going to Mill Pond Bank that evening; that he should not go there at all, to-morrow evening, Tuesday; that he should prepare Provis to come down to some Stairs hard by the house, on Wednesday, when he saw us approach, and not sooner; that all the arrangements with him should be concluded that Monday night; and that he should be communicated with no more in any way, until we took him on board.

2. A resort town some twenty-six miles downriver that serves the Port of London as pilot station, quarantine center, and customs station. Burial site of Pocahontas (d. 1617).
3. Passenger, as distinct from steersman or rowers.

These precautions well understood by both of us, I went home.

On opening the outer door of our chambers with my key, I found a letter in the box, directed to me; a very dirty letter, though not ill-written. It had been delivered by hand (of course since I left home), and its contents were these:

"If you are not afraid to come to the old marshes to-night or to-morrow night at Nine, and to come to the little sluice-house by the limekiln,[4] you had better come. If you want information regarding *your uncle Provis*, you had much better come and tell no one and lose no time. *You must come alone.* Bring this with you." 10

I had had load enough upon my mind before the receipt of this strange letter. What to do now, I could not tell. And the worst was, that I must decide quickly, or I should miss the afternoon coach, which would take me down in time for to-night. To-morrow night I could not think of going, for it would be too close upon the time of the flight. And again, for anything I knew, the proffered information might have some important bearing on the flight itself.

If I had had ample time for consideration, I believe I should still have gone. Having hardly any time for consideration—my watch showing me that the coach started within half an hour—I resolved to go. I should certainly not have gone, but for the reference to my Uncle Provis; that, coming on Wem- 20 mick's letter and the morning's busy preparation, turned the scale.

It is so difficult to become clearly possessed of the contents of almost any letter, in a violent hurry, that I had to read this mysterious epistle again, twice, before its injunction to me to be secret got mechanically into my mind. Yielding to it in the same mechanical kind of way, I left a note in pencil for Herbert, telling him that as I should be so soon going away, I knew not for how long, I had decided to hurry down and back, to ascertain for myself how Miss Havisham was faring. I had then barely time to get my great-coat, lock up the chambers, and make for the coach-office by the short by-ways. If I had taken a hackney-chariot and gone by the streets, I should have missed my 30 aim; going as I did, I caught the coach just as it came out of the yard. I was the only inside passenger, jolting away knee-deep in straw, when I came to myself.

For, I really had not been myself since the receipt of the letter; it had so bewildered me ensuing on the hurry of the morning. The morning hurry and flutter had been great, for, long and anxiously as I had waited for Wemmick, his hint had come like a surprise at last. And now I began to wonder at myself for being in the coach, and to doubt whether I had sufficient reason for being there, and to consider whether I should get out presently and go back, and to argue against ever heeding an anonymous communication, and, in short, 40 to pass through all those phases of contradiction and indecision to which I suppose very few hurried people are strangers. Still, the reference to Provis by name, mastered everything. I reasoned as I had reasoned already without knowing it—if that be reasoning—in case any harm should befall him through my not going, how could I ever forgive myself!

4. A furnace, or kiln, used to turn limestone or shells into lime. The limekiln would have had to be more distant—that is, farther inland—from the sluice-house than Dickens suggests; lime could hardly have burned in so watery an area. A number of limekilns at Cliffe were still burning chalk into lime at the time Dickens wrote the novel.

It was dark before we got down, and the journey seemed long and dreary to me who could see little of it inside, and who could not go outside in my disabled state. Avoiding the Blue Boar, I put up at an inn of minor reputation down the town,[5] and ordered some dinner. While it was preparing, I went to Satis House and inquired for Miss Havisham; she was still very ill, though considered something better.

My inn had once been a part of an ancient ecclesiastical house, and I dined in a little octagonal common-room, like a font. As I was not able to cut my dinner, the old landlord with a shining bald head did it for me. This bringing us into conversation, he was so good as to entertain me with my own story—of course with the popular feature that Pumblechook was my earliest benefactor and the founder of my fortunes.

"Do you know the young man?" said I.

"Know him!" repeated the landlord. "Ever since he was no height at all."

"Does he ever come back to this neighbourhood?"

"Ay, he comes back," said the landlord, "to his great friends now and again, and gives the cold shoulder to the man that made him."

"What man is that?"

"Him that I speak of," said the landlord. "Mr. Pumblechook."

"Is he ungrateful to no one else?"

"No doubt he would be, if he could," returned the landlord, "but he can't. And why? Because Pumblechook done everything for him."

"Does Pumblechook say so?"

"Say so!" replied the landlord. "He han't no call to say so."

"But does he say so?"

"It would turn a man's blood to white wine winegar to hear him tell of it, sir," said the landlord.

I thought, "Yet Joe, dear Joe, *you* never tell of it. Long-suffering and loving Joe, *you* never complain. Nor you, sweet-tempered Biddy!"

"Your appetite's been touched like, by your accident," said the landlord, glancing at the bandaged arm under my coat. "Try a tenderer bit."

"No, thank you," I replied, turning from the table to brood over the fire. "I can eat no more. Please take it away."

I had never been struck at so keenly, for my thanklessness to Joe, as through the brazen impostor Pumblechook. The falser he, the truer Joe; the meaner he, the nobler Joe.

My heart was deeply and most deservedly humbled as I mused over the fire for an hour or more. The striking of the clock aroused me, but not from my dejection or remorse, and I got up and had my coat fastened round my neck, and went out. I had previously sought in my pockets for the letter, that I might refer to it again, but could not find it, and was uneasy to think that it must have been dropped in the straw of the coach. I knew very well, however, that the appointed place was the little sluice-house by the limekiln on the marshes, and the hour nine. Towards the marshes I now went straight, having no time to spare.

★

---

5. Almost certainly The Mitre and Clarence (so named because William IV, as Duke of Clarence, once stopped off there), near the junction of Chatham and Rochester.

Marcus Stone, "On the Marshes, by the Lime-Kiln"

Chapter LIII.

IT was a dark night, though the full moon rose as I left the enclosed lands, and passed out upon the marshes. Beyond their dark line there was a ribbon of clear sky, hardly broad enough to hold the red large moon. In a few minutes she had ascended out of that clear field, in among the piled mountains of cloud.

There was a melancholy wind, and the marshes were very dismal. A stranger would have found them insupportable, and even to me they were so oppressive that I hesitated, half inclined to go back. But I knew them well, and could have found my way on a far darker night, and had no excuse for returning, being there. So, having come there against my inclination, I went 10 on against it.

The direction that I took, was not that in which my old home lay, nor that in which we had pursued the convicts. My back was turned towards the distant Hulks as I walked on, and, though I could see the old lights away on the spits of sand, I saw them over my shoulder. I knew the limekiln as well as I knew the old Battery, but they were miles apart; so that if a light had been burning at each point that night, there would have been a long strip of the blank horizon between the two bright specks.

At first, I had to shut some gates after me, and now and then to stand still while the cattle that were lying in the banked-up pathway, arose and blun- 20 dered down among the grass and reeds. But after a little while, I seemed to have the whole flats to myself.

It was another half-hour before I drew near to the kiln. The lime was burning with a sluggish stifling smell, but the fires were made up and left, and no workmen were visible. Hard by, was a small stone-quarry. It lay directly in my way, and had been worked that day, as I saw by the tools and barrows that were lying about.

Coming up again to the marsh level out of this excavation—for the rude path lay through it—I saw a light in the old sluice-house. I quickened my pace, and knocked at the door with my hand. Waiting for some reply, I looked 30 about me, noticing how the sluice was abandoned and broken, and how the house—of wood with a tiled roof—would not be proof against the weather much longer, if it were so even now, and how the mud and ooze were coated with lime, and how the choking vapour of the kiln crept in a ghostly way towards me. Still there was no answer, and I knocked again. No answer still, and I tried the latch.

It rose under my hand, and the door yielded. Looking in, I saw a lighted candle on a table, a bench, and a mattress on a truckle bedstead.[1] As there was a loft above, I called, "Is there any one here?" but no voice answered. Then I looked at my watch, and, finding that it was past nine, called again, 40 "Is there any one here?" There being still no answer, I went out at the door, irresolute what to do.

It was beginning to rain fast. Seeing nothing save what I had seen already, I turned back into the house, and stood just within the shelter of the doorway,

---

1. Or trundle bed: low bedstead, or cot, on wheels, that could be concealed beneath a larger standing bed during the day.

looking out into the night. While I was considering that some one must have been there lately and must soon be coming back, or the candle would not be burning, it came into my head to look if the wick were long. I turned round to do so, and had taken up the candle in my hand, when it was extinguished by some violent shock, and the next thing I comprehended, was, that I had been caught in a strong running noose, thrown over my head from behind.

"Now," said a suppressed voice with an oath, "I've got you!"

"What is this?" I cried, struggling. "Who is it? Help, help, help!"

Not only were my arms pulled close to my sides, but the pressure on my   10
bad arm caused me exquisite pain. Sometimes a strong man's hand, some-times a strong man's breast, was set against my mouth to deaden my cries, and with a hot breath always close to me, I struggled ineffectually in the dark, while I was fastened tight to the wall. "And now," said the suppressed voice with another oath, "call out again, and I'll make short work of you!"

Faint and sick with the pain of my injured arm, bewildered by the surprise, and yet conscious how easily this threat could be put in execution, I desisted, and tried to ease my arm were it ever so little. But it was bound too tight for that. I felt as if, having been burnt before, it were now being boiled.

The sudden exclusion of the night and the substitution of black darkness   20
in its place, warned me that the man had closed a shutter. After groping about for a little, he found the flint and steel he wanted, and began to strike a light.[2] I strained my sight upon the sparks that fell among the tinder, and upon which he breathed and breathed, match in hand, but I could only see his lips, and the blue point of the match; even those, but fitfully. The tinder was damp—no wonder there—and one after another the sparks died out.

The man was in no hurry, and struck again with the flint and steel. As the sparks fell thick and bright about him, I could see his hands, and touches of his face, and could make out that he was seated and bending over the table; but nothing more. Presently I saw his blue lips again breathing on the tinder,   30
and then a flare of light flashed up, and showed me Orlick.

Whom I had looked for, I don't know. I had not looked for him.[3] Seeing him, I felt that I was in a dangerous strait indeed, and I kept my eyes upon him.

He lighted the candle from the flaring match with great deliberation, and dropped the match and trod it out. Then he put the candle away from him on the table, so that he could see me, and sat with his arms folded on the table and looked at me. I made out that I was fastened to a stout perpendicular ladder a few inches from the wall—a fixture there—the means of ascent to the loft above.   40

"Now," said he, when we had surveyed one another for some time, "I've got you."

"Unbind me. Let me go!"

"Ah!" he returned, "I'll let you go. I'll let you go to the moon, I'll let you go to the stars. All in good time."

---

2. Before the use of friction matches, the customary way of getting a light: that is, by igniting tinder with the sparks struck off with flint and steel. Tinder generally consisted of charred linen, dry rags, or dried rotten wood.

3. Monod finds it surprising that Pip "should not have thought of Orlick from the moment he receives his mysterious message"; almost the first thing Pip tells us about him (chapter 15) is that "he lodged at a sluice-keeper's out on the marshes."

"Why have you lured me here?"

"Don't you know?" said he, with a deadly look.

"Why have you set upon me in the dark?"

"Because I mean to do it all myself. One keeps a secret better than two. Oh you enemy, you enemy!"

His enjoyment of the spectacle I furnished, as he sat with his arms folded on the table, shaking his head at me and hugging himself, had a malignity in it that made me tremble. As I watched him in silence, he put his hand into the corner at his side, and took up a gun with a brass-bound stock.

"Do you know this?" said he, making as if he would take aim at me. "Do   10
you know where you saw it afore? Speak, wolf!"

"Yes," I answered.

"You cost me that place. You did. Speak!"

"What else could I do?"

"You did that, and that would be enough, without more. How dared you to come betwixt me and a young woman I liked?"

"When did I?"

"When didn't you? It was you as always give Old Orlick a bad name to her."

"You gave it to yourself; you gained it for yourself. I could have done you   20
no harm, if you had done yourself none."

"You're a liar. And you'll take any pains, and spend any money, to drive me out of this country, will you?" said he, repeating my words to Biddy in the last interview I had with her. "Now, I'll tell you a piece of information. It was never so well worth your while to get me out of this country as it is to-night. Ah! If it was all your money twenty times told, to the last brass farden!" As he shook his heavy hand at me, with his mouth snarling like a tiger's, I felt that it was true.

"What are you going to do to me?"

"I'm a going," said he, bringing his fist down upon the table with a heavy   30
blow, and rising as the blow fell, to give it greater force, "I'm a going to have your life!"

He leaned forward staring at me, slowly unclenched his hand and drew it across his mouth as if his mouth watered for me, and sat down again.

"You was always in Old Orlick's way since ever you was a child. You goes out of his way, this present night. He'll have no more on you. You're dead."

I felt that I had come to the brink of my grave. For a moment I looked wildly round my trap for any chance of escape; but there was none.

"More than that," said he, folding his arms on the table again, "I won't have a rag of you, I won't have a bone of you, left on earth. I'll put your body   40
in the kiln[4]—I'd carry two such to it, on my shoulders—and, let people suppose what they may of you, they shall never know nothing."

My mind, with inconceivable rapidity, followed out all the consequences of such a death. Estella's father would believe I had deserted him, would be taken, would die accusing me; even Herbert would doubt me, when he compared the letter I had left for him, with the fact that I had called at Miss Havisham's gate for only a moment; Joe and Biddy would never know how

---

4. Like Pip's vision of Miss Havisham suspended from "the great wooden beam," this threat to Pip also recalls the Mannings, who threw their victim's body into a pit of quicklime (chapters 8 and 49); and the whole subject of death-by-limekiln looks forward to *Edwin Drood*.

sorry I had been that night; none would ever know what I had suffered, how true I had meant to be, what an agony I had passed through. The death close before me was terrible, but far more terrible than death was the dread of being misremembered after death. And so quick were my thoughts, that I saw myself despised by unborn generations—Estella's children, and their children—while the wretch's words were yet on his lips.

"Now, wolf," said he, "afore I kill you like any other beast—which is wot I mean to do and wot I have tied you up for—I'll have a good look at you and a good goad at you. Oh, you enemy!"

It had passed through my thoughts to cry out for help again; though few could know better than I, the solitary nature of the spot, and the hopelessness of aid. But as he sat gloating over me, I was supported by a scornful detestation of him that sealed my lips. Above all things, I resolved that I would not entreat him, and that I would die making some last poor resistance to him. Softened as my thoughts of all the rest of men were in that dire extremity; humbly beseeching pardon, as I did, of Heaven; melted at heart, as I was, by the thought that I had taken no farewell, and never never now could take farewell of those who were dear to me, or could explain myself to them, or ask for their compassion on my miserable errors; still, if I could have killed him, even in dying, I would have done it.

He had been drinking, and his eyes were red and bloodshot. Around his neck was slung a tin bottle, as I had often seen his meat and drink slung about him in other days. He brought the bottle to his lips, and took a fiery drink from it; and I smelt the strong spirits that I saw flare into his face.

"Wolf!" said he, folding his arms again, "Old Orlick's a going to tell you somethink. It was you as did for your shrew sister."

Again my mind, with its former inconceivable rapidity, had exhausted the whole subject of the attack upon my sister, her illness, and her death, before his slow and hesitating speech had formed these words.

"It was you, villain!" said I.

"I tell you it was your doing—I tell you it was done through you," he retorted, catching up the gun, and making a blow with the stock at the vacant air between us. "I come upon her from behind, as I come upon you to-night. I giv' it her! I left her for dead, and if there had been a limekiln as nigh her as there is now nigh you, she shouldn't have come to life again. But it warn't Old Orlick as did it; it was you. You was favoured, and he was bullied and beat. Old Orlick bullied and beat, eh? Now you pays for it. You done it; now you pays for it."

He drank again, and become more ferocious. I saw by his tilting of the bottle that there was no great quantity left in it. I distinctly understood that he was working himself up with its contents to make an end of me. I knew that every drop it held, was a drop of my life. I knew that when I was changed into a part of the vapour that had crept towards me but a little while before, like my own warning ghost, he would do as he had done in my sister's case —make all haste to the town, and be seen slouching about there, drinking at the ale-houses. My rapid mind pursued him to the town, made a picture of the street with him in it, and contrasted its lights and life with the lonely marsh and the white vapour creeping over it, into which I should have dissolved.

It was not only that I could have summed up years and years and years while he said a dozen words, but that what he did say presented pictures to me, and not mere words. In the excited and exalted state of my brain, I could not think of a place without seeing it, or of persons without seeing them. It is impossible to over-state the vividness of these images, and yet I was so intent, all the time, upon him himself—who would not be intent on the tiger crouching to spring!—that I knew of the slightest action of his fingers.

When he had drunk this second time, he rose from the bench on which he sat, and pushed the table aside. Then he took up the candle, and shading it with his murderous hand so as to throw its light on me, stood before me, looking at me and enjoying the sight.

"Wolf, I'll tell you something more. It was Old Orlick as you tumbled over on your stairs that night."

I saw the staircase with its extinguished lamps. I saw the shadows of the heavy stair-rails, thrown by the watchman's lantern on the wall. I saw the rooms that I was never to see again; here, a door half open; there, a door closed; all the articles of furniture around.

"And why was Old Orlick there? I'll tell you something more, wolf. You and her *have* pretty well hunted me out of this country, so far as getting a easy living in it goes, and I've took up with new companions, and new masters. Some of 'em writes my letters when I wants 'em wrote—do you mind?[5]—writes my letters, wolf! They writes fifty hands; they're not like sneaking you, as writes but one. I've had a firm mind and a firm will to have your life, since you was down here at your sister's burying. I han't seen a way to get you safe, and I've looked arter you to know your ins and outs. For, says Old Orlick to himself, 'Somehow or another I'll have him!' What! When I looks for you, I finds your uncle Provis, eh?"

Mill Pond Bank, and Chinks's Basin, and the Old Green Copper Rope Walk, all so clear and plain! Provis in his rooms, and the signal whose use was over, pretty Clara, the good motherly woman, old Bill Barley on his back, all drifting by, as on the swift stream of my life fast running out to sea!

"*You* with a uncle too! Why, I know'd you at Gargery's when you was so small a wolf that I could have took your weazen[6] betwixt this finger and thumb and chucked you away dead (as I'd thoughts o' doing, odd times, when I see you loitering amongst the pollards on a Sunday), and you hadn't found no uncles then. No, not you! But when Old Orlick come for to hear that your uncle Provis had mostlike wore the leg-iron wot Old Orlick had picked up, filed asunder, on these meshes ever so many year ago, and wot he kep by him till he dropped your sister with it, like a bullock,[7] as he means to drop you—hey?—when he come for to hear that—hey?" ——

In his savage taunting, he flared the candle so close at me, that I turned my face aside, to save it from the flame.

"Ah!" he cried, laughing, after doing it again, "the burnt child dreads the fire![8] Old Orlick knowed you was burnt, Old Orlick knowed you was a smuggling your uncle Provis away, Old Orlick's a match for you and knowed you'd come to-night! Now I'll tell you something more, wolf, and this ends it.

5. "Are you listening?"
6. Obsolete for "wesand"—windpipe; here, throat.
7. A castrated bull, which would be killed by being struck on the head with a heavy ax.
8. The sort of proverb that cuts across all periods and cultures: Aesop (c. 570 B.C.) points to a similar moral in his fable of "The Lion, the Ass, and the Fox," and since Aesop it has appeared in Sophocles, Cicero, Seneca, and, by way of geographical spread, in China, Germany, the Arabian countries, etc.

There's them that's as good a match for your uncle Provis as Old Orlick has been for you. Let him 'ware them, when he's lost his nevvy! Let him 'ware them, when no man can't find a rag of his dear relation's clothes, nor yet a bone of his body? There's them that can't and that won't have Magwitch— yes, I know the name!—alive in the same land with them, and that's had such sure information of him when he was alive in another land, as that he couldn't and shouldn't leave it unbeknown and put them in danger. P'raps it's them that writes fifty hands, and that's not like sneaking you as writes but one. 'Ware Compeyson, Magwitch, and the gallows!"

He flared the candle at me again, smoking my face and hair, and for an 10 instant blinding me, and turned his powerful back as he replaced the light on the table. I had thought a prayer, and had been with Joe and Biddy and Herbert, before he turned towards me again.

There was a clear space of a few feet between the table and the opposite wall. Within this space he now slouched backwards and forwards. His great strength seemed to sit stronger upon him than ever before, as he did this with his hands hanging loose and heavy at his sides, and with his eyes scowling at me. I had no grain of hope left. Wild as my inward hurry was, and wonderful the force of the pictures that rushed by me instead of thoughts, I could yet clearly understand that unless he had resolved that I was within a few mo- 20 ments of surely perishing out of all human knowledge, he would never have told me what he had told.

Of a sudden, he stopped, took the cork out of his bottle, and tossed it away. Light as it was, I heard it fall like a plummet. He swallowed slowly, tilting up the bottle by little and little, and now he looked at me no more. The last few drops of liquor he poured into the palm of his hand, and licked up. Then with a sud- den hurry of violence and swearing horribly, he threw the bottle from him, and stooped; and I saw in his hand a stone-hammer with a long heavy handle.

The resolution I had made did not desert me, for, without uttering one vain word of appeal to him, I shouted out with all my might, and struggled 30 with all my might. It was only my head and my legs that I could move, but to that extent I struggled with all the force, until then unknown, that was within me. In the same instant I heard responsive shouts, saw figures and a gleam of light dash in at the door, heard voices and tumult, and saw Orlick emerge from a struggle of men as if it were tumbling water, clear the table at a leap, and fly out into the night.[9]

After a blank, I found that I was lying unbound, on the floor, in the same place, with my head on some one's knee. My eyes were fixed on the ladder against the wall, when I came to myself—had opened on it before my mind saw it—and thus as I recovered consciousness, I knew that I was in the place 40 where I had lost it.

Too indifferent at first, even to look round and ascertain who supported me, I was lying looking at the ladder, when there came between me and it, a face. The face of Trabb's boy!

9. On Dickens's instructions to the printer here and the importance he attached to the spacing, see my "A Preface to *Great Expectations*: The Pale Usher Dusts His Lexicons," *DSA* 2 (1971): 304–06. (Hereafter, "A Preface to *GE*.")

"I think he's all right!" said Trabb's boy, in a sober voice; "but ain't he just pale though!"

At these words, the face of him who supported me, looked over into mine, and I saw my supporter to be —

"Herbert! Great Heaven!"

"Softly," said Herbert. "Gently, Handel. Don't be too eager."

"And our old comrade, Startop," I cried, as he too bent over me.

"Remember what he is going to assist us in," said Herbert, "and be calm."

The allusion made me spring up; though I dropped again from the pain in my arm. "The time has not gone by, Herbert, has it? What night is to- 10 night? How long have I been here?" For, I had a strange and strong misgiving that I had been lying there a long time—a day and night—two days and nights—more.

"The time has not gone by. It is still Monday night."

"Thank God!"

"And you have all to-morrow, Tuesday, to rest in," said Herbert. "But you can't help groaning, my dear Handel. What hurt have you got? Can you stand?"

"Yes, yes," said I, "I can walk. I have no hurt but in this throbbing arm."

They laid it bare, and did what they could. It was violently swollen and 20 inflamed, and I could scarcely endure to have it touched. But they tore up their handkerchiefs to make fresh bandages, and carefully replaced it in the sling, until we could get to the town and obtain some cooling lotion to put upon it. In a little while we had shut the door of the dark and empty sluice-house, and were passing through the quarry on our way back. Trabb's boy— Trabb's overgrown young man now—went before us with a lantern, which was the light I had seen come in at the door. But the moon was a good two hours higher than when I had last seen the sky, and the night though rainy was much lighter. The white vapour of the kiln was passing from us as we went by, and as I had thought a prayer before, I thought a thanksgiving now. 30

Entreating Herbert to tell me how he had come to my rescue—which at first he had flatly refused to do, but had insisted on my remaining quiet—I learnt that I had in my hurry dropped the letter, open, in our chambers, where he, coming home to bring with him Startop, whom he had met in the street on his way to me, found it, very soon after I was gone. Its tone made him uneasy, and the more so because of the inconsistency between it and the hasty letter I had left for him. His uneasiness increasing instead of subsiding after a quarter of an hour's consideration, he set off for the coach-office, with Startop, who volunteered his company, to make inquiry when the next coach went down. Finding that the afternoon coach was gone, and find- 40 ing that his uneasiness grew into positive alarm, as obstacles came in his way, he resolved to follow in a post-chaise.[1] So, he and Startop arrived at the Blue Boar, fully expecting there to find me, or tidings of me; but, finding neither, went on to Miss Havisham's, where they lost me. Hereupon they went back to the hotel (doubtless at about the time when I was hearing the popular local version of my own story) to refresh themselves, and to get some one to

1. As used here, a post-chaise did not necessarily convey mail: in the absence of letters, it operated as a passenger vehicle. Clearly Herbert engages it here, as do his rescuers later on, without its following a prescribed schedule.

guide them out upon the marshes. Among the loungers under the Boar's archway, happened to be Trabb's boy—true to his ancient habit of happening to be everywhere where he had no business—and Trabb's boy had seen me passing from Miss Havisham's in the direction of my dining-place. Thus, Trabb's boy became their guide, and with him they went out to the sluice-house: though by the town way to the marshes, which I had avoided. Now, as they went along, Herbert reflected that I might, after all, have been brought there on some genuine and serviceable errand tending to Provis's safety, and bethinking himself that in that case interruption might be mischievous, left his guide and Startop on the edge of the quarry, and went on by himself, and 10 stole round the house two or three times, endeavouring to ascertain whether all was right within. As he could hear nothing but indistinct sounds of one deep rough voice (this was while my mind was so busy), he even at last began to doubt whether I was there, when suddenly I cried out loudly, and he answered the cries, and rushed in, closely followed by the other two.

When I told Herbert what had passed within the house, he was for our immediately going before a magistrate[2] in the town, late at night as it was, and getting out a warrant. But I had already considered that such a course, by detaining us there or binding us to come back, might be fatal to Provis. There was no gainsaying this difficulty, and we relinquished all thoughts of 20 pursuing Orlick at that time. For the present, under the circumstances, we deemed it prudent to make rather light of the matter to Trabb's boy; who I am convinced would have been much affected by disappointment, if he had known that his intervention saved me from the limekiln. Not that Trabb's boy was of a malignant nature, but that he had too much vivacity to spare, and that it was in his constitution to want variety and excitement at anybody's expense. When we parted, I presented him with two guineas (which seemed to meet his views), and told him that I was sorry ever to have had an ill opinion of him (which made no impression on him at all).

Wednesday being so close upon us, we determined to go back to London 30 that night, three in the post-chaise; the rather as we should then be clear away, before the night's adventure began to be talked of. Herbert got a large bottle of stuff[3] for my arm, and by dint of having this stuff dropped over it all the night through, I was just able to bear its pain on the journey. It was daylight when we reached the Temple, and I went at once to bed, and lay in bed all day.

My terror, as I lay there, of falling ill and being unfitted for to-morrow, was so besetting, that I wonder it did not disable me of itself. It would have done so, pretty surely, in conjunction with the mental wear and tear I had suffered, but for the unnatural strain upon me that to-morrow was. So anxiously looked 40 forward to, charged with such consequences, its results so impenetrably hidden though so near!

No precaution could have been more obvious than our refraining from communication with him that day; yet this again increased my restlessness. I started at every footstep and every sound, believing that he was discovered and taken, and this was the messenger to tell me so. I persuaded myself that I knew he was taken; that there was something more upon my mind than a

2. Another term for a Justice of the Peace.
3. Medicine or potion.

fear or a presentiment; that the fact had occurred, and I had a mysterious knowledge of it. As the day wore on and no ill news came, as the day closed in and darkness fell, my overshadowing dread of being disabled by illness before to-morrow morning, altogether mastered me. My burning arm throbbed, and my burning head throbbed, and I fancied I was beginning to wander. I counted up to high numbers, to make sure of myself, and repeated passages that I knew, in prose and verse. It happened sometimes, that in the mere escape of a fatigued mind, I dozed for some moments, or forgot; then I would say to myself with a start, "Now it has come, and I am turning delirious!"

They kept me very quiet all day, and kept my arm constantly dressed, and gave me cooling drinks. Whenever I fell asleep, I awoke with the notion I had had in the sluice-house, that a long time had elapsed and the opportunity to save him was gone. About midnight I got out of bed and went to Herbert with the conviction that I had been asleep for four-and-twenty hours, and that Wednesday was past. It was the last self-exhausting effort of my fretfulness, for, after that, I slept soundly.

Wednesday morning was dawning when I looked out of window. The winking lights upon the bridges were already pale, the coming sun was like a marsh of fire on the horizon. The river, still dark and mysterious, was spanned by bridges that were turning coldly grey, with here and there at top a warm touch from the burning in the sky. As I looked along the clustered roofs, with Church towers and spires shooting into the unusually clear air, the sun rose up, and a veil seemed to be drawn from the river, and millions of sparkles burst out upon its waters. From me too, a veil seemed to be drawn, and I felt strong and well.

Herbert lay asleep in his bed, and our old fellow-student lay asleep on the sofa. I could not dress myself without help, but I made up the fire, which was still burning, and got some coffee ready for them. In good time they too started up strong and well, and we admitted the sharp morning air at the windows, and looked at the tide that was still flowing towards us.

"When it turns at nine o'clock," said Herbert, cheerfully, "look out for us, and stand ready, you over there at Mill Pond Bank!"

Chapter LIV.

IT was one of those March days when the sun shines hot and the wind blows cold: when it is summer in the light, and winter in the shade. We had our pea-coats with us, and I took a bag. Of all my worldly possessions I took no more than the few necessaries that filled the bag. Where I might go, what I might do, or when I might return, were questions utterly unknown to me; nor did I vex my mind with them, for it was wholly set on Provis's safety. I only wondered for the passing moment, as I stopped at the door and looked back, under what altered circumstances I should next see those rooms, if ever.

We loitered down to the Temple stairs, and stood loitering there, as if we were not quite decided to go upon the water at all. Of course I had taken care that the boat should be ready and everything in order. After a little show of indecision, which there were none to see but the two or three amphibious creatures belonging to our Temple stairs, we went on board and cast off; Herbert in the bow, I steering. It was then about high-water—half-past eight. Our plan was this. The tide, beginning to run down at nine, and being with us until three, we intended still to creep on after it had turned, and row against it until dark. We should then be well in those long reaches below Gravesend, between Kent and Essex, where the river is broad and solitary, where the water-side inhabitants are very few, and where lone public-houses are scattered here and there, of which we could choose one for a resting- 10 place. There, we meant to lie by, all night. The steamer for Hamburg and the steamer for Rotterdam would start from London at about nine on Thursday morning. We should know at what time to expect them, according to where we were, and would hail the first; so that if by any accident we were not taken aboard, we should have another chance. We knew the distinguishing marks of each vessel.

The relief of being at last engaged in the execution of the purpose, was so great to me that I felt it difficult to realise the condition in which I had been a few hours before. The crisp air, the sunlight, the movement on the river, and the moving river itself—the road that ran with us, seeming to sympathise 20 with us, animate us, and encourage us on—freshened me with new hope. I felt mortified to be of so little use in the boat; but, there were few better oarsmen than my two friends, and they rowed with a steady stroke that was to last all day.

At that time, the steam-traffic on the Thames was far below its present extent, and watermen's boats were far more numerous. Of barges, sailing colliers, and coasting-traders, there were perhaps as many as now;[1] but, of steam-ships, great and small, not a tithe or a twentieth part so many.[2] Early as it was, there were plenty of scullers[3] going here and there that morning, and plenty of barges dropping down with the tide; the navigation of the river 30 between bridges, in an open boat, was a much easier and commoner matter in those days than it is in these; and we went ahead among many skiffs and wherries,[4] briskly.

Old London Bridge was soon passed, and old Billingsgate market[5] with its

1. Throughout the chapter Dickens alludes to some dozen types of sailing craft common on the Thames at the time of action. "Barge: a flat-bottomed vessel of burden, for loading and unloading ships; and has various names, such as . . . a sand barge, a row barge, &c." "Sailing colliers: vessels employed to carry coals from one port to another, chiefly from the northern parts of England to the capital, and more southern parts, as well as to foreign markets" (Falconer). "Coasting traders": merchant ships confined mainly to domestic trade.
2. The first steam-driven vessel, or paddle wheeler, was used on the Thames in 1814. Within a decade, steamships were regularly crossing the Channel to France. By 1861, nearly one thousand steamers operated in and out of Britain. In the 1830s, steamers were still so unpopular that the most eminent steamship and railway pioneer of his day, Isambard Kingdom Brunel (1805–1859), was allegedly denied a hotel room on his arrival in Margate (McMaster).
3. "Sculler: a term used to denote a boat rowed on the river Thames by one man with two sculls, which is used in contradistinction to oars." "Scull: a kind of short oar, the loom of which is only each equal in length to half the breadth of the boat, whereby two may be managed by one man, one [scull] on each side" (Falconer).
4. Small light craft mainly intended for inland or estuary navigation.
5. London's oldest and largest fish market, just below London Bridge and next to the Customs House built in Pip's day. A wharf has been in use at Billingsgate from Saxon times; established as "a free and open market for fish" by Act of Parliament in 1698. As a synonym for foul language, "billingsgate" almost certainly antedates the establishment of the market; by 1700 it figures as a byword for "stupendous obscenity, nitrous verbosity, and malicious scurrility." Billingsgate was closed in 1982.

oyster-boats and Dutchmen,[6] and the White Tower and Traitors' Gate,[7] and we were in among the tiers of shipping. Here, were the Leith, Aberdeen, and Glasgow[8] steamers, loading and unloading goods, and looking immensely high out of the water as we passed alongside; here, were colliers by the score and score, with the coal-whippers[9] plunging off stages on deck, as counterweights to measures of coal swinging up, which were then rattled over the side into barges; here, at her moorings was to-morrow's steamer for Rotterdam, of which we took good notice; and here to-morrow's for Hamburg, under whose bowsprit we crossed. And now I, sitting in the stern, could see with a faster beating heart, Mill Pond Bank and Mill Pond stairs.   10

"Is he there?" said Herbert.

"Not yet."

"Right! He was not to come down till he saw us. Can you see his signal?"

"Not well from here; but I think I see it.—Now, I see him! Pull both. Easy, Herbert. Oars!"

We touched the stairs lightly for a single moment, and he was on board and we were off again. He had a boat-cloak with him, and a black canvas bag, and he looked as like a river-pilot as my heart could have wished.

"Dear boy!" he said, putting his arm on my shoulder as he took his seat. "Faithful dear boy, well done. Thankye, thankye!"   20

Again among the tiers of shipping, in and out, avoiding rusty chain-cables, frayed hempen hawsers[1] and bobbing buoys, sinking for the moment floating broken baskets, scattering floating chips of wood and shaving, cleaving floating scum of coal, in and out, under the figure-head of the John of Sunderland[2] making a speech to the winds (as is done by many Johns),[3] and the Betsy of Yarmouth[4] with a firm formality of bosom and her knobby eyes starting two inches out of her head, in and out, hammers going in ship-builders' yards, saws going at timber, clashing engines going at things unknown, pumps going in leaky ships, capstans going, ships going out to sea, and unintelligible sea-creatures roaring curses over the bulwarks at respondent lightermen,[5] in and   30 out—out at last upon the clearer river, where the ships' boys might take their fenders[6] in, no longer fishing in troubled waters with them over the side, and where the festooned sails might fly out to the wind.

6. Dutch fishing boats.
7. "White Tower": the central keep and earliest of a dozen strongholds comprising the Tower of London, England's most famous fortress, repository of the Crown Jewels, and one of London's chief tourist attractions; built in 1078 by William the Conquerer. "Traitors' Gate": the riverside entrance at the foot of Tower Hill through which prisoners-of-state convicted of treason were conveyed after being brought down the Thames from their trials at Westminster Hall. Its more charismatic passengers included Thomas More, Anne Boleyn, Jane Grey, and the Earl of Essex.
8. The chief Scottish seaports. Leith services Edinburgh.
9. Sailors who raised coal from ships and barges by means of pulleys, or "whips."
1. Rope cables.
2. Major seaport in Durham in northeast England near Newcastle-on-Tyne, known for its old shipbuilding yards and coal deposits.
3. Matthew 3.3: "In those days came John the Baptist, preaching in the wilderness of Judea, 'Repent, for the kingdom of heaven is at hand!'" Dickens may also have been thinking of Lord John Russell (1792–1878), dubbed "Johnny" by his colleagues and fans (McMaster). Russell, twice Prime Minister, was one of the few statesmen whom Dickens, who dedicated A Tale of Two Cities to him, admired unreservedly. As foreign secretary, Russell had unsuccessfully introduced a Reform Bill in 1860 to liberalize the franchise and he steadily opposed Napoleon III's annexation of Savoy.
4. Properly, Great Yarmouth, one of the world's largest herring-fishing ports and popular seaside resort on the east coast of Norfolk. Home of the Peggottys in David Copperfield.
5. Bargemen.
6. "Bumpers." "Certain pieces of old cable, timber, or other materials [mostly coiled rope] hung over the side of a vessel to prevent it from striking or rubbing against a wharf or quay; as also to preserve a smaller vessel from being damaged by a larger one" (Falconer).

At the Stairs where we had taken him aboard, and ever since, I had looked warily for any token of our being suspected. I had seen none. We certainly had not been, and at that time as certainly we were not, either attended or followed by any boat. If we had been waited on by any boat, I should have run in to shore, and have obliged her to go on, or to make her purpose evident. But, we held our own, without any appearance of molestation.

He had his boat-cloak on him, and looked, as I have said, a natural part of the scene. It was remarkable (but perhaps the wretched life he had led, accounted for it), that he was the least anxious of any of us. He was not 10 indifferent, for he told me that he hoped to live to see his gentleman one of the best of gentlemen in a foreign country; he was not disposed to be passive or resigned, as I understood it; but he had no notion of meeting danger half way. When it came upon him, he confronted it, but it must come, before he troubled himself.

"If you knowed, dear boy," he said to me, "what it is to sit here alonger my dear boy and have my smoke, arter having been day by day betwixt four walls, you'd envy me. But you don't know what it is."

"I think I know the delights of freedom," I answered.

"Ah," said he, shaking his head gravely. "But you don't know it equal to 20 me. You must have been under lock and key, dear boy, to know it equal to me—but I ain't a going to be low."

It occurred to me as inconsistent, that for any mastering idea, he should have endangered his freedom and even his life. But I reflected that perhaps freedom without danger was too much apart from all the habit of his existence to be to him what it would be to another man. I was not far out, since he said, after smoking a little:

"You see, dear boy, when I was over yonder, t'other side the world, I was always a looking to this side; and it come flat to be there, for all I was a growing rich. Everybody knowed Magwitch, and Magwitch could come, and 30 Magwitch could go, and nobody's head would be troubled about him. They ain't so easy concerning me here, dear boy—wouldn't be, leastwise, if they knowed where I was."

"If all goes well," said I, "you will be perfectly free and safe again, within a few hours."

"Well," he returned, drawing a long breath, "I hope so."

"And think so?"

He dipped his hand in the water over the boat's gunwale,[7] and said, smiling with that softened air upon him which was not new to me:

"Ay, I s'pose I think so, dear boy. We'd be puzzled to be more quiet and 40 easy-going than we are at present. But—it's a flowing so soft and pleasant through the water, p'raps, as makes me think it—I was a thinking through my smoke just then, that we can no more see to the bottom of the next few hours, than we can see to the bottom of this river what I catches hold of. Nor yet we can't no more hold their tide than I can hold this. And it's run through my fingers and gone, you see!" holding up his dripping hand.

"But for your face, I should think you were a little despondent," said I.

"Not a bit on it, dear boy! It comes of flowing on so quiet, and of that

---

7. Pronounced "gunnel." "'That piece of timber which reaches on either side of the ship, from the half-deck to the forecastle, being the uppermost bend'" (Falconer).

there rippling at the boat's head making a sort of a Sunday tune. Maybe I'm a growing a trifle old besides."

He put his pipe back in his mouth with an undisturbed expression of face, and sat as composed and contented as if we were already out of England. Yet he was as submissive to a word of advice as if he had been in constant terror, for, when we ran ashore to get some bottles of beer into the boat,[8] and he was stepping out, I hinted that I thought he would be safest where he was, and he said, "Do you, dear boy?" and quietly sat down again.

The air felt cold upon the river, but it was a bright day, and the sunshine was very cheering. The tide ran strong, I took care to lose none of it, and our steady stroke carried us on thoroughly well. By imperceptible degrees, as the tide ran out, we lost more and more of the nearer woods and hills, and dropped lower and lower between the muddy banks, but the tide was yet with us when we were off Gravesend. As our charge was wrapped in his cloak, I purposely passed within a boat or two's length of the floating Custom House,[9] and so out to catch the stream, alongside of two emigrant ships, and under the bows of a large transport with troops on the forecastle looking down at us. And soon the tide began to slacken, and the craft lying at anchor to swing, and presently they had all swung round, and the ships that were taking advantage of the new tide to get up to the Pool, began to crowd upon us in a fleet, and we kept under the shore,[1] as much out of the strength of the tide now as we could, standing carefully off from low shallows and mud-banks.

Our oarsmen were so fresh, by dint of having occasionally let her drive with the tide for a minute or two, that a quarter of an hour's rest proved full as much as they wanted. We got ashore among some slippery stones while we ate and drank what we had with us, and looked about. It was like my own marsh country, flat and monotonous, and with a dim horizon; while the winding river turned and turned, and the great floating buoys upon it turned and turned, and everything else seemed stranded and still.[2] For, now, the last of the fleet of ships was round the last low point we had headed, and the last green barge, straw-laden, with a brown sail, had followed, and some ballast-lighters,[3] shaped like a child's first rude imitation of a boat, lay low in the mud, and a little squat shoal-lighthouse on open piles, stood crippled in the mud on stilts and crutches,[4] and slimy stakes stuck out of the mud, and slimy stones stuck out of the mud, and red landmarks and tidemarks stuck out of the mud, and an old landing-stage and an old roofless building slipped into the mud, and all about us was stagnation and mud.

8. Probably from The White Hart Inn at Greenhithe, a small riverside village four miles west of Gravesend.
9. One of the customs launches from which officials would board the vessels at Gravesend. Pip draws near the launch either to disarm suspicion or to catch the stream by following the course the launch charted. "Floating custom houses" were familiar to Dickens from his Chatham boyhood.
1. Close to the shore.
2. Pip's party are creeping along the Essex shore as the more navigable and more sheltered from observation. Pip's "likening" the landscape to his "own marsh country" suggests the Essex rather than his "own" Kent marshes to the south. Pip's picnic spot may be a stony spit running inland from Mucking Flats (see note 4, below). Pip and his crew are now heading toward the open sea.
3. "A vessel fitted up to heave ballast from the bottom of a harbour or river, and to carry it to and from ships" (Falconer).
4. Lighthouse to mark a shoal, either a sandy elevation or a patch of shallow water, to alert navigators to sunken rocks. The Mucking Flats Lighthouse, to which Pip refers, is a small iron structure on open piles rising directly across the Cliffe marshes of Pip's childhood. But the detail belongs to the writer's day, not Pip's: the lighthouse Dickens describes was built in 1851. Observing it ten years later, in May 1861, while engaged in his research for the river journey, Dickens used this curious structure for an episode that took place some thirty years earlier (Hill).

We pushed off again, and made what way we could. It was much harder work now, but Herbert and Startop persevered, and rowed, and rowed, and rowed, until the sun went down. By that time the river had lifted us a little, so that we could see above the bank. There was the red sun, on the low level of the shore, in a purple haze, fast deepening into black, and there was the solitary flat marsh; and far away there were the rising grounds between which and us there seemed to be no life, save here and there in the foreground a melancholy gull.

As the night was fast falling, and as the moon, being past the full, would not rise early, we held a little council: a short one, for clearly our course was to lie by at the first lonely tavern we could find. So, they plied their oars once more, and I looked out for anything like a house. Thus we held on, speaking little, for four or five dull miles. It was very cold, and a collier coming by us, with her galley-fire smoking and flaring, looked quite a comfortable home. The night was as dark by this time as it would be until morning; and what light we had, seemed to come more from the river than the sky, as the oars in their dipping struck at a few reflected stars.

At this dismal time we were evidently all possessed by the idea that we were followed. As the tide made,[5] it flapped heavily at irregular intervals against the shore; and whenever such a sound came, one or other of us was sure to start and look in that direction. Here and there, the set of the current had worn down the bank into a little creek, and we were all suspicious of such places, and eyed them narrowly. Sometimes, "What was that ripple!" one of us would say in a low voice. Or another, "Is that a boat yonder?" And afterwards, we would fall into a dead silence, and I would sit impatiently thinking with what an unusual amount of noise the oars worked in the thowels.[6]

At length we descried a light and a roof, and presently afterwards ran alongside a little causeway made of stones that had been picked up hard-by. Leaving the rest in the boat, I stepped ashore, and found the light to be in the window of a public-house.[7] It was a dirty place enough, and I dare say not unknown to smuggling adventurers; but there was a good fire in the kitchen, and there were eggs and bacon to eat, and various liquors to drink. Also, there were two double-bedded rooms—"such as they were," the landlord said. No other company was in the house than the landlord, his wife, and a grizzled male creature, the "Jack"[8] of the little causeway, who was as slimy and smeary as if he had been low-water mark too.

With this assistant, I went down to the boat again, and we all came ashore, and brought out the oars, and rudder, and boat-hook, and all else, and hauled her up for the night. We made a very good meal by the kitchen fire, and then apportioned the bedrooms; Herbert and Startop were to occupy one; I and our charge the other. We found the air as carefully excluded from both, as if air were fatal to life; and there were more dirty clothes and bandboxes under the beds than I should have thought the family possessed. But we

---

5. Flowed more strongly.
6. Oarlocks.
7. Identified as The Lobster Smack, a tavern hidden away in an isolated inlet on the southeastern point of Canvey Island—itself a small and (then) sparsely populated island on the Essex coast near Southend. Magwitch directly faces the bay—Egypt Bay—where the prison hulk of the early chapters was moored. Despite Pip's injuries, the rowers had by now covered almost forty miles.
8. Jack-of-all-trades; general handyman [OED]. For its auxiliary uses, see chapter 2.

considered ourselves well off, notwithstanding, for a more solitary place we
could not have found.

While we were comforting ourselves by the fire after our meal, the Jack—
who was sitting in a corner, and who had a bloated pair of shoes on, which
he had exhibited while we were eating our eggs and bacon, as interesting
relics that he had taken a few days ago from the feet of a drowned seaman
washed ashore—asked me if we had seen a four-oared galley⁹ going up with
the tide? When I told him No, he said she must have gone down then, and
yet she "took up too,"¹ when she left there.

"They must ha' thought better on't for some reason or another," said the   10
Jack, "and gone down."

"A four-oared galley, did you say?" said I.

"A four," said the Jack, "and two sitters."²

"Did they come ashore here?"

"They put in with a stone two-gallon jar, for some beer. I'd ha' been glad
to pison the beer· myself," said the Jack, "or put some rattling physic in it."

"Why?"

"I know why," said the Jack. He spoke in a slushy voice, as if much mud
had washed into his throat.

"He thinks," said the landlord: a weakly meditative man with a pale eye,   20
who seemed to rely greatly on his Jack: "he thinks they was, what they·wasn't."

"I knows what I thinks," observed the Jack.

"You thinks Custum 'Us, Jack?" said the landlord.

"I do," said the Jack.

"Then you're wrong, Jack."

"Am I!"

In the infinite meaning of his reply, and his boundless confidence in his
views, the Jack took one of his bloated shoes off, looked into it, knocked a
few stones out of it on the kitchen floor, and put it on again. He did this,
with the air of a Jack who was so right that he could afford to do anything.   30

"Why, what do you make out that they done with their buttons then, Jack?"
asked the landlord, vacillating weakly.

"Done with their buttons?" returned the Jack. "Chucked 'em overboard.
Swallered 'em. Sowed 'em, to come up small salad.³ Done with their
buttons!"

"Don't be cheeky, Jack," remonstrated the landlord, in a melancholy and
pathetic way.

"A Custum 'Us officer knows what to do with his Buttons," said the Jack,
repeating the obnoxious word with the greatest contempt, "when they comes
betwixt him and his own light. A Four and two sitters don't go hanging and   40
hovering, up with one tide and down with another, and both with and against

---

9. "Row-Galley: an open boat, rowing six or eight oars, and used on the river Thames by custom-house
officers, press-gangs, and also for pleasure; hence the appellation of custom-house-galley, press-galley,
&c." (Falconer). The "floating custom-house" to which Pip refers earlier. Dickens consistently praises
the professional competence of the Thames River Police: see "Down with the Tide," Household Words,
February 5, 1853.
1. "Headed up river," that is, toward Gravesend, before doubling back. The Jack argues that only a
prowling customs galley would move up and down river within a short span of time, hence with and
against the same tide.
2. The boat seated four oarsmen and two "passengers," or police officers.
3. "Planted them and expected them to come up as 'small salad' "—the seedlings of mustard and cress.
The Jack's scornful proposition that the customs officers, to keep from being spotted, would conceal
their shining buttons.

another, without there being Custum 'Us at the bottom of it." Saying which, he went out in disdain; and the landlord, having no one to rely upon, found it impracticable to pursue the subject.

This dialogue made us all uneasy, and me very uneasy. The dismal wind was muttering round the house, the tide was flapping at the shore, and I had a feeling that we were caged and threatened. A four-oared galley hovering about in so unusual a way as to attract this notice, was an ugly circumstance that I could not get rid of. When I had induced Provis to go up to bed, I went outside with my two companions (Startop by this time knew the state of the case), and held another council. Whether we should remain at the house until near the steamer's time, which would be about one in the afternoon; or whether we should put off early in the morning; was the question we discussed. On the whole we deemed it the better course to lie where we were, until within an hour or so of the steamer's time, and then to get out in her track, and drift easily with the tide. Having settled to do this, we returned into the house and went to bed.

I lay down with the greater part of my clothes on, and slept well for a few hours. When I awoke, the wind had risen, and the sign of the house (the Ship) was creaking and banging about, with noises that startled me. Rising softly, for my charge lay fast asleep, I looked out of the window. It commanded the causeway where we had hauled up our boat, and, as my eyes adapted themselves to the light of the clouded moon, I saw two men looking into her. They passed by under the window, looking at nothing else, and they did not go down to the landing-place which I could discern to be empty, but struck across the marsh in the direction of the Nore.[4]

My first impulse was to call up Herbert, and show him the two men going away. But, reflecting before I got into his room, which was at the back of the house and adjoined mine, that he and Startop had had a harder day than I, and were fatigued, I forebore. Going back to my window, I could still see the two men moving over the marsh. In that light, however, I soon lost them, and, feeling very cold, lay down to think of the matter, and fell asleep again.

We were up early. As we walked to and fro, all four together, before breakfast, I deemed it right to recount what I had seen. Again, our charge was the least anxious of the party. It was very likely that the men belonged to the Custom House, he said quietly, and that they had no thought of us. I tried to persuade myself that it was so—as, indeed, it might easily be. However, I proposed that he and I should walk away together to a distant point we could see, and that the boat should take us aboard there, or as near there as might prove feasible, at about noon. This being considered a good precaution, soon after breakfast he and I set forth, without saying anything at the tavern.

He smoked his pipe as we went along, and sometimes stopped to clap me on the shoulder. One would have supposed that it was I who was in danger, not he, and that he was reassuring me. We spoke very little. As we approached the point, I begged him to remain in a sheltered place, while I went on to reconnoitre; for, it was towards it that the men had passed in the night. He complied, and I went on alone. There was no boat off the point, nor any boat drawn up anywhere near it, nor were there any signs of the men having

---

4. A sandbank in the Thames estuary, midway between the Essex and Kent coasts, three miles northeast of Sheerness near the confluence of the Thames and the Medway. The Nore is marked by a floating light that would be visible from Pip's hideout.

embarked there. But, to be sure, the tide was high, and there might have been some footprints under water.

When he looked out from his shelter in the distance, and saw that I waved my hat to him to come up, he rejoined me, and there we waited: sometimes lying on the bank wrapped in our coats, and sometimes moving about to warm ourselves: until we saw our boat coming round. We got aboard easily, and rowed out into the track of the steamer. By that time it wanted but ten minutes of one o'clock, and we began to look out for her smoke.

But, it was half-past one before we saw her smoke, and soon afterwards we saw behind it the smoke of another steamer. As they were coming on at full 10
speed, we got the two bags ready, and took that opportunity of saying good-by to Herbert and Startop. We had all shaken hands cordially, and neither Herbert's eyes nor mine were quite dry, when I saw a four-oared galley shoot out from under the bank but a little way ahead of us, and row out into the same track.

A stretch of shore had been as yet between us and the steamer's smoke, by reason of the bend and wind of the river; but now she was visible, coming head on. I called to Herbert and Startop to keep before the tide, that she might see us lying by for her, and I adjured Provis to sit quite still, wrapped in his cloak. He answered cheerily, "Trust to me, dear boy," and sat like a 20
statue. Meantime the galley, which was very skilfully handled, had crossed us, let us come up with her, and fallen alongside. Leaving just room enough for the play of the oars, she kept alongside, drifting when we drifted, and pulling a stroke or two when we pulled. Of the two sitters, one held the rudder lines, and looked at us attentively—as did all the rowers; the other sitter was wrapped up, much as Provis was, and seemed to shrink, and whisper some instruction to the steerer as he looked at us. Not a word was spoken in either boat.

Startop could make out, after a few minutes, which steamer was first, and gave me the word "Hamburg," in a low voice as we sat face to face. She was 30
nearing us very fast, and the beating of her paddles grew louder and louder.[5] I felt as if her shadow were absolutely upon us, when the galley hailed us. I answered.

"You have a returned Transport there," said the man who held the lines. "That's the man, wrapped in the cloak. His name is Abel Magwitch, otherwise Provis. I apprehend that man, and call upon him to surrender, and you to assist."

At the same moment, without giving any audible direction to his crew, he ran the galley aboard of us. They had pulled one sudden stroke ahead, had got their oars in, had run athwart us, and were holding on to our gunwale, 40
before we knew what they were doing. This caused great confusion on board of the steamer, and I heard them calling to us, and heard the order given to stop the paddles, and heard them stop, but felt her driving down upon us irresistibly. In the same moment, I saw the steersman of the galley lay his hand on his prisoner's shoulder, and saw that both boats were swinging round with the force of the tide, and saw that all hands on board the steamer were

5. On the introduction of steam-driven vessels, see p. 323, n. 2. Steamships are propelled by paddle wheels placed amidships on each side. Screw propellers were first used in 1843, the year after Dickens's first American voyage; by the time Dickens crossed the Atlantic in 1867, screw propulsion had entirely superseded paddle wheels, and the voyage had been shortened from eighteen to ten days.

running forward quite frantically. Still in the same moment, I saw the prisoner start up, lean across his captor, and pull the cloak from the neck of the shrinking sitter in the galley. Still in the same moment, I saw that the face disclosed, was the face of the other convict of long ago. Still in the same moment, I saw the face tilt backward with a white terror on it that I shall never forget, and heard a great cry on board the steamer and a loud splash in the water, and felt the boat sink from under me.

It was but for an instant that I seemed to struggle with a thousand mill-weirs[6] and a thousand flashes of light; that instant past, I was taken on board the galley. Herbert was there, and Startop was there; but our boat was gone, 10 and the two convicts were gone.

What with the cries aboard the steamer, and the furious blowing-off of her steam, and her driving on, and our driving on, I could not at first distinguish sky from water or shore from shore; but, the crew of the galley righted her with great speed, and, pulling certain swift strong strokes ahead, lay upon their oars, every man looking silently and eagerly at the water astern. Presently a dark object was seen in it, bearing towards us on the tide. No man spoke, but the steersman held up his hand, and all softly backed water, and kept the boat straight and true before it. As it came nearer, I saw it to be Magwitch, swimming, but not swimming freely. He was taken on board, and instantly 20 manacled at the wrists and ankles.

The galley was kept steady, and the silent eager look-out at the water was resumed. But, the Rotterdam steamer now came up, and apparently not understanding what had happened, came on at speed. By the time she had been hailed and stopped, both steamers were drifting away from us and we were rising and falling in a troubled wake of water. The look-out was kept, long after all was still again and the two steamers were gone; but, everybody knew that it was hopeless now.

At length we gave it up, and pulled under the shore towards the tavern we had lately left, where we were received with no little surprise. Here, I was 30 able to get some comforts for Magwitch—Provis no longer—who had received some very severe injury in the chest and a deep cut in the head.

He told me that he believed himself to have gone under the keel of the steamer, and to have been struck on the head in rising. The injury to his chest (which rendered his breathing extremely painful) he thought he had received against the side of the galley. He added that he did not pretend to say what he might or might not have done to Compeyson, but, that in the moment of his laying his hand on his cloak to identify him, that villain had staggered up and staggered back, and they had both gone overboard together; when the sudden wrenching of him (Magwitch) out of our boat, and the 40 endeavour of his captor to keep him in it, had capsized us. He told me in a whisper that they had gone down, fiercely locked in each other's arms, and that there had been a struggle under water, and that he had disengaged himself, struck out, and swum away.

I never had any reason to doubt the exact truth of what he had told me. The officer who steered the galley gave the same account of their going overboard.

When I asked this officer's permission to change the prisoner's wet clothes

6. Dam constructed across a stream to obstruct the water's flow and raise its level for use in turning a mill wheel.

by purchasing any spare garments I could get at the public-house, he gave it readily: merely observing that he must take charge of everything his prisoner had about him. So the pocket-book which had once been in my hands, passed into the officer's. He further gave me leave to accompany the prisoner to London; but, declined to accord that grace to my two friends.[7]

The Jack at the Ship was instructed where the drowned man had gone down, and undertook to search for the body in the places where it was likeliest to come ashore. His interest in its recovery seemed to me to be much heightened when he heard that it had stockings on. Probably, it took about a dozen drowned men to fit him out completely; and that may have been the reason 10 why the different articles of his dress were in various stages of decay.

We remained at the public-house until the tide turned, and then Magwitch was carried down to the galley and put on board. Herbert and Startop were to get to London by land, as soon as they could. We had a doleful parting, and when I took my place by Magwitch's side, I felt that that was my place henceforth while he lived.

For, now, my repugnance to him had all melted away, and in the hunted wounded shackled creature who held my hand in his, I only saw a man who had meant to be my benefactor, and who had felt affectionately, gratefully, and generously, towards me with great constancy through a series of years. I 20 only saw in him a much better man than I had been to Joe.

His breathing became more difficult and painful as the night drew on, and often he could not repress a groan. I tried to rest him on the arm I could use, in any easy position; but it was dreadful to think that I could not be sorry at heart for his being badly hurt, since it was unquestionably best that he should die. That there were, still living, people enough who were able and willing to identify him, I could not doubt. That he would be leniently treated, I could not hope. He who had been presented in the worst light at his trial, who had since broken prison and been tried again, who had returned from transportation under a life sentence, and who had occasioned the death of 30 the man who was the cause of his arrest.

As we returned towards the setting sun we had yesterday left behind us, and as the stream of our hopes seemed all running back, I told him how grieved I was to think that he had come home for my sake.

"Dear boy," he answered, "I'm quite content to take my chance. I've seen my boy, and he can be a gentleman without me."

No. I had thought about that, while we had been there side by side. No. Apart from any inclinations of my own, I understood Wemmick's hint now. I foresaw that, being convicted, his possessions would be forfeited to the Crown. 40

"Look'ee here, dear boy," said he. "It's best as a gentleman should not be knowed to belong to me now. Only come to see me as if you come by chance alonger Wemmick. Sit where I can see you when I am swore to, for the last o' many times, and I don't ask no more."

"I will never stir from your side," said I, "when I am suffered to be near you. Please God, I will be as true to you, as you have been to me!"

I felt his hand tremble as it held mine, and he turned his face away as he

---

7. On the complicity of Pip, Herbert, and Startop in Magwitch's attempt to escape, see pp. 461–62.

lay in the bottom of the boat, and I heard that old sound in his throat—softened now, like all the rest of him. It was a good thing that he had touched this point, for it put into my mind what I might not otherwise have thought of until too late: That he need never know how his hopes of enriching me had perished.

★

Chapter LV.

HE was taken to the Police Court next day, and would have been immediately committed for trial, but that it was necessary to send down for an old officer of the prison-ship from which he had once escaped, to speak to his identity. Nobody doubted it; but, Compeyson, who had meant to depose to it, was tumbling on the tides, dead, and it happened that there was not at that time any prison officer in London who could give the required evidence. I had gone direct to Mr. Jaggers at his private house, on my arrival over-night, to retain his assistance, and Mr. Jaggers on the prisoner's behalf would admit nothing. It was the sole resource, for he told me that the case must be over in five minutes when the witness was there, and that no power on earth could prevent its going against us.

I imparted to Mr. Jaggers my design of keeping him in ignorance of the fate of his wealth. Mr. Jaggers was querulous and angry with me for having "let it slip through my fingers," and said we must memorialise[1] by-and-by, and try at all events for some of it. But, he did not conceal from me that although there might be many cases in which the forfeiture would not be exacted, there were no circumstances in this case to make it one of them. I understood that, very well. I was not related to the outlaw, or connected with him by any recognisable tie; he had put his hand to no writing or settlement in my favour before his apprehension, and to do so now would be idle. I had no claim, and I finally resolved, and ever afterwards abided by the resolution, that my heart should never be sickened with the hopeless task of attempting to establish one.

There appeared to be reason for supposing that the drowned informer had hoped for a reward out of this forfeiture, and had obtained some accurate knowledge of Magwitch's affairs. When his body was found, many miles from the scene of his death, and so horribly disfigured that he was only recognisable by the contents of his pockets, notes were still legible, folded in a case he carried. Among these, were the name of a banking-house in New South Wales where a sum of money was, and the designation of certain lands of considerable value. Both these heads of information were in a list that Magwitch, while in prison, gave to Mr. Jaggers, of the possessions he supposed I should inherit. His ignorance, poor fellow, at last served him; he never mistrusted but that my inheritance was quite safe, with Mr. Jaggers's aid.

After three days' delay, during which the crown prosecution stood over[2] for the production of the witness from the prison-ship, the witness came, and

1. To draw up a memo setting out the particulars of a case; to petition.
2. Deferred the trial.

completed the easy case. He was committed to take his trial at the next Sessions,[3] which would come on in a month.

It was at this dark time of my life that Herbert returned home one evening, a good deal cast down, and said:

"My dear Handel, I fear I shall soon have to leave you."

His partner having prepared me for that, I was less surprised than he thought.

"We shall lose a fine opportunity if I put off going to Cairo, and I am very much afraid I must go, Handel, when you most need me."

"Herbert, I shall always need you, because I shall always love you; but my need is no greater now, than at another time." 10

"You will be so lonely."

"I have not leisure to think of that," said I. "You know that I am always with him to the full extent of the time allowed, and that I should be with him all day long, if I could. And when I come away from him, you know that my thoughts are with him."

The dreadful condition to which he was brought, was so appalling to both of us, that we could not refer to it in plainer words.

"My dear fellow," said Herbert, "let the near prospect of our separation— for, it is very near—be my justification for troubling you about yourself. Have 20 you thought of your future?"

"No, for I have been afraid to think of any future."

"But, yours cannot be dismissed; indeed, my dear dear Handel, it must not be dismissed. I wish you would enter on it now, as far as a few friendly words go, with me."

"I will," said I.

"In this branch house of ours, Handel, we must have a——"

I saw that his delicacy was avoiding the right word, so I said, "A clerk."

"A clerk. And I hope it is not at all unlikely that he may expand (as a clerk of your acquaintance has expanded) into a partner. Now, Handel——in short, 30 my dear boy, will you come to me?"

There was something charmingly cordial and engaging in the manner in which after saying "Now, Handel," as if it were the grave beginning of a portentous business exordium, he had suddenly given up that tone, stretched out his honest hand, and spoken like a schoolboy.

"Clara and I have talked about it again and again," Herbert pursued, "and the dear little thing begged me only this evening, with tears in her eyes, to say to you that if you will live with us when we come together, she will do her best to make you happy, and to convince her husband's friend that he is her friend too. We should get on so well, Handel!" 40

I thanked her heartily, and I thanked him heartily, but said I could not yet make sure of joining him as he so kindly offered. Firstly, my mind was too preoccupied to be able to take in the subject clearly. Secondly——Yes! Sec-

3. Any one of the four Terms (after 1873 changed to "Sittings") set aside for the transaction of judicial business. "Quarter sessions" originated in the custom, statutory since 1414, of convening a fixed number of Justices of the Peace four times a year, chiefly to deal with the growing problems of vagrants and fugitive laborers, many of whom found work elsewhere to escape the laws governing their shires. The quarterly sessions, each lasting some three to four weeks, took their names from festival days in the English calendar, the dates closely following those set down by Henry V in 1414: Hilary (second to last week in January); Easter (mid-April to May 8); Trinity (late May to mid-June); and Michaelmas (November 2 to 25). Magwitch's trial is scheduled to come on at Easter.

ondly, there was a vague something lingering in my thoughts that will come out very near the end of this slight narrative.

"But if you thought, Herbert, that you could, without doing any injury to your business, leave the question open for a little while——"

"For any while," cried Herbert. "Six months, a year!"

"Not so long as that," said I. "Two or three months at most."

Herbert was highly delighted when we shook hands on this arrangement, and said he could now take courage to tell me that he believed he must go away at the end of the week.

"And Clara?" said I.   10

"The dear little thing," returned Herbert, "holds dutifully to her father as long as he lasts; but he won't last long. Mrs. Whimple confides to me that he is certainly going."

"Not to say an unfeeling thing," said I, "he can hardly do better than go."

"I am afraid that must be admitted," said Herbert: "and then I shall come back for the dear little thing, and the dear little thing and I will walk quietly into the nearest church. Remember! The blessed darling comes of no family, my dear Handel, and never looked into the red book,⁴ and hasn't a notion about her grandpapa. What a fortune for the son of my mother!"

On the Saturday in that same week, I took my leave of Herbert—full of 20 bright hope, but sad and sorry to leave me—as he sat on one of the seaport mail coaches. I went into a coffee-house to write a little note to Clara, telling her he had gone off sending his love to her over and over again, and then went to my lonely home—if it deserved the name, for it was now no home to me, and I had no home anywhere.

On the stairs I encountered Wemmick, who was coming down, after an unsuccessful application of his knuckles to my door. I had not seen him alone, since the disastrous issue of the attempted flight; and he had come, in his private and personal capacity, to say a few words of explanation in reference to that failure.   30

"The late Compeyson," said Wemmick, "had by little and little got at the bottom of half of the regular business now transacted, and it was from the talk of some of his people in trouble (some of his people being always in trouble) that I heard what I did. I kept my ears open, seeming to have them shut, until I heard that he was absent, and I thought that would be the best time for making the attempt. I can only suppose now, that it was a part of his policy, as a very clever man, habitually to deceive his own instruments. You don't blame me, I hope, Mr. Pip? I am sure I tried to serve you, with all my heart."

"I am as sure of that, Wemmick, as you can be, and I thank you most 40 earnestly for all your interest and friendship."

"Thank you, thank you very much. It's a bad job," said Wemmick, scratching his head, "and I assure you I haven't been so cut up for a long time. What I look at, is the sacrifice of so much portable property. Dear me!"

"What *I* think of, Wemmick, is the poor owner of the property."

"Yes, to be sure," said Wemmick. "Of course there can be no objection to your being sorry for him, and I'd put down a five-pound note myself to get him out of it. But what I look at, is this. The late Compeyson having been

4. The *Peerage* Mrs. Pocket has been reading in chapter 23.

beforehand with him in intelligence of his return, and being so determined to bring him to book, I don't think he could have been saved. Whereas, the portable property certainly could have been saved. That's the difference between the property and the owner, don't you see?"

I invited Wemmick to come up-stairs, and refresh himself with a glass of grog before walking to Walworth. He accepted the invitation. While he was drinking his moderate allowance, he said, with nothing to lead up to it, and after having appeared rather fidgety:

"What do you think of my meaning to take a holiday on Monday, Mr. Pip?"   10

"Why, I suppose you have not done such a thing these twelve months."

"These twelve years, more likely," said Wemmick. "Yes. I'm going to take a holiday. More than that; I'm going to take a walk. More than that; I'm going to ask you to take a walk with me."

I was about to excuse myself, as being but a bad companion just then, when Wemmick anticipated me.

"I know your engagements," said he, "and I know you are out of sorts, Mr. Pip. But if you *could* oblige me, I should take it as a kindness. It ain't a long walk, and it's an early one. Say it might occupy you (including breakfast on the walk) from eight to twelve. Couldn't you stretch a point and manage it?"   20

He had done so much for me at various times, that this was very little to do for him. I said I could manage it—would manage it—and he was so very much pleased by my acquiescence, that I was pleased too. At his particular request, I appointed to call for him at the Castle at half-past eight on Monday morning, and so we parted for the time.

Punctual to my appointment, I rang at the Castle gate on the Monday morning, and was received by Wemmick himself: who immediately struck me as looking tighter than usual, and having a sleeker hat on. Within, there were two glasses of rum-and-milk prepared, and two biscuits. The Aged must have been stirring with the lark, for, glancing into the perspective of his   30 bedroom, I observed that his bed was empty.

When we had fortified ourselves with the rum-and-milk and biscuits, and were going out for the walk with that training preparation on us, I was considerably surprised to see Wemmick take up a fishing-rod, and put it over his shoulder. "Why, we are not going fishing!" said I. "No," returned Wemmick, "but I like to walk with one."

I thought this odd; however, I said nothing, and we set off. We went towards Camberwell Green,⁵ and when we were thereabouts, Wemmick said suddenly:

"Halloa! Here's a church!"⁶   40

There was nothing very surprising in that; but again, I was rather surprised, when he said, as if he were animated by a brilliant idea:

"Let's go in!"

We went in, Wemmick leaving his fishing-rod in the porch, and looked all

5. Camberwell, scene of the Barnwell murder in chapter 15, is a borough in Southwark, some two and a half miles south of the Thames. The stroll to Camberwell Green, a small park at the bottom of Camberwell Road, is less than a mile's walk from Wemmick's cottage in Walworth.
6. Probably St. George's Church, built in 1824, a few blocks south of the Walworth thickets, half a mile east of Camberwell Road. Its location near the Surrey Canal, a favorite spot for anglers, would give point to Wemmick's camouflage. Else St. Giles's, a few blocks east, the site of the Camberwell parish church since the seventh century (Hill).

round. In the mean time, Wemmick was diving into his coat-pockets, and getting something out of paper there.

"Halloa!" said he. "Here's a couple of pair of gloves! Let's put 'em on!"

As the gloves were white kid gloves, and as the post-office was widened to its utmost extent, I now began to have my strong suspicions. They were strengthened into certainty when I beheld the Aged enter at a side door, escorting a lady.

"Halloa!" said Wemmick. "Here's Miss Skiffins! Let's have a wedding."

That discreet damsel was attired as usual,[7] except that she was now engaged in substituting for her green kid gloves, a pair of white. The Aged was likewise 10 occupied in preparing a similar sacrifice for the altar of Hymen.[8] The old gentleman, however, experienced so much difficulty in getting his gloves on, that Wemmick found it necessary to put him with his back against a pillar, and then to get behind the pillar himself and pull away at them, while I for my part held the old gentleman round the waist, that he might present an equal and safe resistance. By dint of this ingenious scheme, his gloves were got on to perfection.

The clerk and clergyman then appearing, we were ranged in order at those fatal rails.[9] True to his notion of seeming to do it all without preparation, I heard Wemmick say to himself as he took something out of his waistcoat- 20 pocket before the service began, "Halloa! Here's a ring!"

I acted in the capacity of backer, or best-man, to the bridegroom; while a little limp pew opener[1] in a soft bonnet like a baby's, made a feint of being the bosom friend of Miss Skiffins. The responsibility of giving the lady away, devolved upon the Aged, which led to the clergyman's being unintentionally scandalised, and it happened thus. When he said, "Who giveth this woman to be married to this man?" the old gentleman, not in the least knowing what point of the ceremony we had arrived at, stood most amiably beaming at the ten commandments. Upon which, the clergyman said again, "WHO giveth this woman to be married to this man?" The old gentleman being still in a 30 state of most estimable unconsciousness, the bridegroom cried out in his accustomed voice, "Now, Aged P., you know; who giveth?" To which the Aged replied with great briskness, before saying that *he* gave, "All right, John, all right, my boy!" And the clergyman came to so gloomy a pause upon it, that I had doubts for the moment whether we should get completely married that day.

It was completely done, however, and when we were going out of church, Wemmick took the cover off the font, and put his white gloves in it, and put the cover on again. Mrs. Wemmick, more heedful of the future, put her white gloves in her pocket and assumed her green. "Now, Mr. Pip," said Wemmick, 40 triumphantly shouldering the fishing-rod as we came out, "let me ask you whether anybody would suppose this to be a wedding party!"

Breakfast had been ordered at a pleasant little tavern,[2] a mile or so away

---

7. As opposed to wearing the customary white bridal dress, which would give the show away. White gloves are worn on ceremonial occasions.
8. In Greek and Roman mythology, the marriage god.
9. In the sense of "fateful rails."
1. A functionary, long since replaced by a verger or usher, dating from the days of box pews. The job was usually given to an old woman, who expected to be tipped for opening the pew. Dickens cast a cold eye on pew openers as obsequious, moneygrubbing anomalies.
2. Presumably The Fox under the Hill, an old wayside inn half a mile beyond the Green. The "rising ground" is Denmark Hill, the continuation of Camberwell Road (Hill).

upon the rising ground beyond the Green; and there was a bagatelle board[3] in the room, in case we should desire to unbend our minds after the solemnity. It was pleasant to observe that Mrs. Wemmick no longer unwound Wemmick's arm when it adapted itself to her figure, but sat in a high-backed chair against the wall, like a violoncello in its case, and submitted to be embraced as that melodious instrument might have done.

We had an excellent breakfast, and when any one declined anything on table, Wemmick said, "Provided by contract,[4] you know; don't be afraid of it!" I drank to the new couple, drank to the Aged, drank to the Castle, saluted the bride at parting, and made myself as agreeable as I could.   10

Wemmick came down to the door with me, and I again shook hands with him, and wished him joy.

"Thank'ee!" said Wemmick, rubbing his hands. "She's such a manager of fowls, you have no idea. You shall have some eggs, and judge for yourself. I say, Mr. Pip!" calling me back, and speaking low. "This is altogether a Walworth sentiment, please."

"I understand. Not to be mentioned in Little Britain," said I.

Wemmick nodded. "After what you let out the other day, Mr. Jaggers may as well not know of it. He might think my brain was softening, or something of the kind."   20

Chapter LVI.

H̶E̶ ̶l̶a̶y̶ ̶i̶n̶ ̶p̶r̶i̶s̶o̶n̶ ̶v̶e̶r̶y̶ ill, during the whole interval between his committal for trial, and the coming round of the Sessions. He had broken two ribs, they had wounded one of his lungs, and he breathed with great pain and difficulty, which increased daily. It was a consequence of his hurt, that he spoke so low as to be scarcely audible; therefore, he spoke very little. But, he was ever ready to listen to me, and it became the first duty of my life to say to him, and read to him, what I knew he ought to hear.

Being far too ill to remain in the common prison, he was removed, after the first day or so, into the Infirmary. This gave me opportunities of being with him that I could not otherwise have had. And but for his illness he   30 would have been put in irons, for he was regarded as a determined prison-breaker, and I know not what else.

Although I saw him every day, it was for only a short time; hence, the regularly recurring spaces of our separation were long enough to record on his face any slight changes that occurred in his physical state. I do not recollect that I once saw any change in it for the better; he wasted, and became slowly weaker and worse, day by day, from the day when the prison door closed upon him.

The kind of submission or resignation that he showed, was that of a man who was tired out. I sometimes derived an impression, from his manner or   40 from a whispered word or two which escaped him, that he pondered over the question whether he might have been a better man under better circum-

---

3. A slanted oblong table, raised at one end; at the bottom a ball is released by means of a wooden cue or a plunger, and the aim is to drop the ball into one of nine numbered holes. In a more advanced version, the ball has to run an obstacle course of nails, pins, wire arches, etc.; functionally a forerunner of pinball. In Victorian England a standard fixture of taverns, much as darts are today.
4. Wemmick has paid a prearranged price, so his guests had better ingest all there is.

stances. But he never justified himself by a hint tending that way, or tried to bend the past out of its eternal shape.

It happened on two or three occasions in my presence, that his desperate reputation was alluded to by one or other of the people in attendance on him. A smile crossed his face then, and he turned his eyes on me with a trustful look, as if he were confident that I had seen some small redeeming touch in him, even so long ago as when I was a little child. As to all the rest, he was humble and contrite, and I never knew him complain.

When the Sessions came round, Mr. Jaggers caused an application to be made for the postponement of his trial until the following Sessions.[1] It was obviously made with the assurance that he could not live so long, and was refused. The trial came on at once, and, when he was put to the bar, he was seated in a chair. No objection was made to my getting close to the dock, on the outside of it, and holding the hand that he stretched forth to me.

The trial was very short and very clear. Such things as could be said for him, were said—how he had taken to industrious habits, and had thriven lawfully and reputably. But, nothing could unsay the fact that he had returned, and was there in presence of the Judge and Jury. It was impossible to try him for that, and do otherwise than find him Guilty.

At that time, it was the custom (as I learnt from my terrible experience of that Sessions) to devote a concluding day to the passing of Sentences, and to make a finishing effect with the Sentence of Death. But for the indelible picture that my remembrance now holds before me, I could scarcely believe, even as I write these words, that I saw two-and-thirty men and women put before the Judge to receive that sentence together.[2] Foremost among the two-and-thirty, was he; seated, that he might get breath enough to keep life in him.

The whole scene starts out again in the vivid colours of the moment, down to the drops of April rain on the windows of the court, glittering in the rays of April sun. Penned in the dock, as I again stood outside it at the corner with his hand in mine, were the two-and-thirty men and women; some defiant, some stricken with terror, some sobbing and weeping, some covering their faces, some staring gloomily about. There had been shrieks from among the women convicts, but they had been stilled, and a hush had succeeded. The sheriffs with their great chains and nosegays, other civic gewgaws and monsters,[3] criers, ushers, a great gallery full of people—a large theatrical audience—looked on, as the two-and-thirty and the Judge were solemnly confronted. Then, the Judge addressed them. Among the wretched creatures before him whom he must single out for special address, was one who almost

1. Jaggers wants the trial postponed to Trinity Term, May 22 to June 12.
2. Before the establishment of the Central Criminal Court in 1834, all prisoners found guilty of capital charges were sentenced collectively at the end of the Session, though, given the date of action, Dickens probably inflates the size of the group. The custom of hauling the prisoners to the dock in manacles and leg irons—a practice that all but condemned them in the eyes of the jury before the trial got underway—had been abandoned half a century earlier.
3. The nosegays and flowers the Judge and other high-court officials carry on them, as well as the herbs strewn about the court in the paragraph following, are vivid reminders of the noxious stench emanating from the Newgate prison cells next door and the constant threat of contagion—a virulent form of typhus—to the Old Bailey. The prophylactic was generally adopted after an epidemic of jail fever in 1750 killed the Lord Mayor of London, his aldermen, the jury, and spectators. In *A Tale of Two Cities* 2.2, Dickens reminds us how often "the Judge in the black cap pronounced his own doom as certainly as the prisoner's, and even died before him." "Civic gewgaws": useless ornaments [OED]; here perhaps in the sense of ornamental but useless officials.

from his infancy had been an offender against the laws; who, after repeated imprisonments and punishments, had been at length sentenced to exile for a term of years; and who, under circumstances of great violence and daring, had made his escape and been re-sentenced to exile for life. That miserable man would seem for a time to have become convinced of his errors, when far removed from the scenes of his old offences, and to have lived a peaceable and honest life. But, in a fatal moment, yielding to those propensities and passions, the indulgence of which had so long rendered him a scourge to society, he had quitted his haven of rest and repentance, and had come back to the country where he was proscribed. Being here presently denounced, he had for a time succeeded in evading the officers of Justice, but being at length seized while in the act of flight, he had resisted them, and had—he best knew whether by express design, or in the blindness of his hardihood—caused the death of his denouncer, to whom his whole career was known. The appointed punishment for his return to the land that had cast him out, being Death, and his case being this aggravated case, he must prepare himself to Die.

The sun was striking in at the great windows of the court, through the glittering drops of rain upon the glass, and it made a broad shaft of light between the two-and-thirty and the Judge, linking both together, and perhaps reminding some among the audience, how both were passing on, with ab- solute equality, to the greater Judgment that knoweth all things and cannot err. Rising for a moment, a distinct speck of face in this way of light, the prisoner said, "My Lord, I have received my sentence of Death from the Almighty,[4] but I bow to yours," and sat down again. There was some hushing, and the Judge went on with what he had to say to the rest. Then, they were all formally doomed,[5] and some of them were supported out, and some of them sauntered out with a haggard look of bravery, and a few nodded to the gallery, and two or three shook hands, and others went out chewing the fragments of herb they had taken from the sweet herbs lying about. He went last of all, because of having to be helped from his chair and to go very slowly; and he held my hand while all the others were removed, and while the audience got up (putting their dresses right, as they might at church or else-where) and pointed down at this criminal or at that, and most of all at him and me.

I earnestly hoped and prayed that he might die before the Recorder's Re-port[6] was made, but, in the dread of his lingering on, I began that night to write out a petition to the Home Secretary of State,[7] setting forth my knowl-edge of him, and how it was that he had come back for my sake. I wrote it as fervently and pathetically as I could, and when I had finished it and sent it in, I wrote out other petitions to such men in authority as I hoped were the most merciful, and drew up one to the Crown itself. For several days and nights after he was sentenced, I took no rest except when I fell asleep in my

4. Romans 2.2: "But we are sure that the judgment of God is according to truth against them which commit such things."
5. In pronouncing the death sentence, the Judge placed a small black piece of cloth on his head.
6. Though the Recorder (p. 201, n. 8) necessarily took his cue from the Judge and followed his notes, it was he, not the Judge, who reported all convictions for murder to the King and acted as final instance to instruct the Court whether the sentence should be carried out. Hence Jaggers's need to wait for the Recorder's official Report.
7. The minister in charge of the Home Office, responsible for law and order generally, including such areas as the police, prison, and security services. In one of his functions he advises the sovereign on the exercise of the prerogative of mercy: hence Pip's address to him—as well as to the Crown directly.

chair, but was wholly absorbed in these appeals. And after I had sent them in, I could not keep away from the places where they were, but felt as if they were more hopeful and less desperate when I was near them. In this unreasonable restlessness and pain of mind, I would roam the streets of an evening, wandering by those offices and houses where I had left the petitions. To the present hour, the weary western streets[8] of London on a cold dusty spring night, with their ranges of stern shut-up mansions and their long rows of lamps, are melancholy to me from this association.

The daily visits I could make him were shortened now, and he was more strictly kept. Seeing, or fancying, that I was suspected of an intention of carrying poison to him, I asked to be searched before I sat down at his bedside, and told the officer who was always there, that I was willing to do anything that would assure him of the singleness of my designs. Nobody was hard with him, or with me. There was duty to be done, and it was done, but not harshly. The officer always gave me the assurance that he was worse, and some other sick prisoners in the room, and some other prisoners who attended on them as sick nurses (malefactors, but not incapable of kindness, GOD be thanked!), always joined in the same report.

As the days went on, I noticed more and more that he would lie placidly looking at the white ceiling, with an absence of light in his face, until some word of mine brightened it for an instant, and then it would subside again. Sometimes he was almost, or quite, unable to speak; then, he would answer me with slight pressures on my hand, and I grew to understand his meaning very well.

The number of the days had risen to ten, when I saw a greater change in him than I had seen yet. His eyes were turned towards the door, and lighted up as I entered.

"Dear boy," he said, as I sat down by his bed: "I thought you was late. But I knowed you couldn't be that."

"It is just the time," said I. "I waited for it at the gate."

"You always waits at the gate; don't you, dear boy?"

"Yes. Not to lose a moment of the time."

"Thank'ee dear boy, thank'ee. God bless you! You've never deserted me, dear boy."

I pressed his hand in silence, for I could not forget that I had once meant to desert him.

"And what's best of all," he said, "you've been more comfortable alonger me, since I was under a dark cloud, than when the sun shone. That's best of all."

He lay on his back, breathing with great difficulty. Do what he would, and love me though he did, the light left his face ever and again, and a film came over the placid look at the white ceiling.

"Are you in much pain to-day?"

"I don't complain of none, dear boy."

"You never do complain."

He had spoken his last words. He smiled, and I understood his touch to mean that he wished to lift my hand, and lay it on his breast. I laid it there, and he smiled again, and put both his hands upon it.

8. "Western streets": the power elite whose influence Pip is seeking were residing chiefly in the wealthy West End of London: Piccadilly, Pall Mall, St. James's Street, Grosvenor Place.

The allotted time ran out while we were thus; but, looking round, I found
the governor of the prison standing near me, and he whispered, "You needn't
go yet." I thanked him gratefully, and asked, "Might I speak to him, if he
can hear me?"

The governor stepped aside, and beckoned the officer away. The change,
though it was made without noise, drew back the film from the placid look
at the white ceiling, and he looked most affectionately at me.

"Dear Magwitch, I must tell you, now at last. You understand what I say?"

A gentle pressure on my hand.

"You had a child once, whom you loved and lost."   10

A stronger pressure on my hand.

"She lived and found powerful friends. She is living now. She is a lady
and very beautiful. And I love her!"

With a last faint effort, which would have been powerless but for my yielding to it and assisting it, he raised my hand to his lips. Then, he gently let it
sink upon his breast again, with his own hands lying on it. The placid look
at the white ceiling came back, and passed away, and his head dropped quietly
on his breast.

Mindful, then, of what we had read together, I thought of the two men
who went up into the Temple to pray, and I knew there were no better words   20
that I could say beside his bed, than "O Lord, be merciful to him, a sinner!"[9]

Chapter LVII.

Now that I was left wholly to myself, I gave notice of my intention to quit
the chambers in the Temple as soon as my tenancy could legally determine,[1]
and in the meanwhile to underlet them. At once I put bills up in the windows;
for, I was in debt, and had scarcely any money, and began to be seriously
alarmed by the state of my affairs. I ought rather to write that I should have
been alarmed if I had had energy and concentration enough to help me to
the clear perception of any truth beyond the fact that I was falling very ill.
The late stress upon me had enabled me to put off illness, but not to put it
away; I knew that it was coming on me now, and I knew very little else, and   30
was even careless as to that.

For a day or two, I lay on the sofa, or on the floor—anywhere, according
as I happened to sink down—with a heavy head and aching limbs, and no
purpose, and no power. Then there came one night, which appeared of great
duration, and which teemed with anxiety and horror; and when, in the morning, I tried to sit up in my bed and think of it, I found I could not do so.

Whether I really had been down in Garden-court in the dead of the night,
groping about for the boat that I supposed to be there; whether I had two or
three times come to myself on the staircase with great terror, not knowing
how I had got out of bed; whether I had found myself lighting the lamp,   40
possessed by the idea that he was coming up the stairs, and that the lights
were blown out; whether I had been inexpressibly harassed by the distracted

9. On this embattled misquotation, see pp. 452–53 and 555.
1. Could be legally terminated.

talking, laughing, and groaning, of some one, and had half suspected those sounds to be of my own making; whether there had been a closed iron furnace in a dark corner of the room, and a voice had called out over and over again that Miss Havisham was consuming within it; these were things that I tried to settle with myself and get into some order, as I lay that morning on my bed. But, the vapour of a lime-kiln would come between me and them, disordering them all, and it was through this vapour at last that I saw two men looking at me.

"What do you want?" I asked, starting; "I don't know you."

"Well, sir," returned one of them, bending down and touching me on the 10 shoulder, "this is a matter that you'll soon arrange, I dare say, but you're arrested."

"What is the debt?"

"Hundred and twenty-three pound, fifteen, six. Jeweller's account, I think."

"What is to be done?"

"You had better come to my house," said the man. "I keep a very nice house."[2]

I made some attempt to get up and dress myself. When I next attended to them, they were standing a little off from the bed, looking at me. I still lay there.   20

"You see my state," said I. "I would come with you if I could; but indeed I am quite unable. If you take me from here, I think I shall die by the way."

Perhaps they replied, or argued the point, or tried to encourage me to believe that I was better than I thought. Forasmuch as they hang in my memory by only this one slender thread, I don't know what they did, except that they forebore to remove me.

That I had a fever and was avoided, that I suffered greatly, that I often lost my reason, that the time seemed interminable, that I confounded impossible existences with my own identity; that I was a brick in the house-wall, and yet entreating to be released from the giddy place where the builders had set me; 30 that I was a steel beam of a vast engine, clashing and whirling over a gulf, and yet that I implored in my own person to have the engine stopped, and my part in it hammered off; that I passed through these phases of disease, I know of my own remembrance, and did in some sort know at the time. That I sometimes struggled with real people, in the belief that they were murderers, and that I would all at once comprehend that they meant to do me good, and would then sink exhausted in their arms, and suffer them to lay me down, I also knew at the time. But, above all, I knew that there was a consistent tendency in all these people—who, when I was very ill, would present all kinds of extraordinary transformations of the human face, and would be much 40 dilated in size—above all, I say, I knew that there was an extraordinary tendency in all these people, sooner or later to settle down into the likeness of Joe.

After I had turned the worst point of my illness, I began to notice that while all its other features changed, this one consistent feature did not change. Whosoever came about me, still settled down into Joe. I opened my eyes in the night, and I saw in the great chair at the bedside, Joe. I opened my eyes in the day, and, sitting on the window-seat, smoking his pipe in the shaded

2. Sponging house. The "Lock-Up" Magwitch mentions in chapter 42. See p. 263, n. 2.

open window, still I saw Joe. I asked for cooling drink, and the dear hand that gave it me was Joe's. I sank back on my pillow after drinking, and the face that looked so hopefully and tenderly upon me was the face of Joe.

At last, one day, I took courage, and said, "Is it Joe?"

And the dear old home-voice answered, "Which it air, old chap."

"O Joe, you break my heart! Look angry at me, Joe. Strike me, Joe. Tell me of my ingratitude. Don't be so good to me!"

For, Joe had actually laid his head down on the pillow at my side and put his arm round my neck, in his joy that I knew him.

"Which dear old Pip, old chap," said Joe, "you and me was ever friends. And when you're well enough to go out for a ride—what larks!"

After which, Joe withdrew to the window, and stood with his back towards me, wiping his eyes. And as my extreme weakness prevented me from getting up and going to him, I lay there, penitently whispering, "O God bless him! O God bless this gentle Christian man!"

Joe's eyes were red when I next found him beside me; but, I was holding his hand, and we both felt happy.

"How long, dear Joe?"

"Which you meantersay, Pip, how long have your illness lasted, dear old chap?"

"Yes, Joe."

"It's the end of May, Pip. To-morrow is the first of June."

"And have you been here all the time, dear Joe?"

"Pretty nigh, old chap. For, as I says to Biddy when the news of your being ill were brought by letter, which it were brought by the post and being formerly single he is now married though underpaid for a deal of walking and shoe-leather, but wealth were not a object on his part, and marriage were the great wish of his hart——"

"It is so delightful to hear you, Joe! But I interrupt you in what you said to Biddy."

"Which it were," said Joe, "that how you might be among strangers, and that how you and me having been ever friends, a wisit at such a moment might not prove unacceptabobble. And Biddy, her word were, 'Go to him, without loss of time.' That," said Joe, summing up with his judicial air, "were the word of Biddy. 'Go to him,' Biddy say, 'without loss of time.' In short, I shouldn't greatly deceive you," Joe added, after a little grave reflection, "if I represented to you that the word of that young woman were, 'without a minute's loss of time.'"

There Joe cut himself short, and informed me that I was to be talked to in great moderation, and that I was to take a little nourishment at stated frequent times, whether I felt inclined for it or not, and that I was to submit myself to all his orders. So, I kissed his hand, and lay quiet, while he proceeded to indite a note to Biddy, with my love in it.

Evidently, Biddy had taught Joe to write. As I lay in bed looking at him, it made me, in my weak state, cry again with pleasure to see the pride with which he set about his letter. My bedstead, divested of its curtains, had been removed, with me upon it, into the sitting-room, as the airiest and largest, and the carpet had been taken away, and the room kept always fresh and wholesome night and day. At my own writing-table, pushed into a corner and cumbered[3] with little bottles, Joe now sat down to his great work: first choosing a pen from the pen-tray as if it were a chest of large tools, and tucking up his sleeves as if he were going to wield a crowbar or sledge-hammer. It was necessary for Joe to hold on heavily to the table with his left elbow, and to get his right leg well out behind him, before he could begin, and when he did begin, he made every down-stroke so slowly that it might have been six feet long, while at every up-stroke I could hear his pen spluttering extensively. He had a curious idea that the inkstand was on the side of him where it was not, and constantly dipped his pen into space, and seemed quite satisfied with the result. Occasionally, he was tripped up by some orthographical 10 stumbling-block, but on the whole he got on very well indeed, and when he had signed his name, and had removed a finishing blot from the paper to the crown of his head with his two forefingers, he got up and hovered about the table, trying the effect of his performance from various points of view as it lay there, with unbounded satisfaction.

Not to make Joe uneasy by talking too much, even if I had been able to talk much, I deferred asking him about Miss Havisham until next day. He shook his head when I then asked him if she had recovered.

"Is she dead, Joe?"

"Why you see, old chap," said Joe, in a tone of remonstrance, and by way 20 of getting at it by degrees, "I wouldn't go so far as to say that, for that's a deal to say; but she ain't——"

"Living, Joe?"

"That's nigher where it is," said Joe; "she ain't living."

"Did she linger long, Joe?"

"Arter you was took ill, pretty much about what you might call (if you was put to it) a week," said Joe; still determined, on my account, to come at everything by degrees.

"Dear Joe, have you heard what becomes of her property?"

"Well, old chap," said Joe, "it do appear that she had settled the most of 30 it, which I meantersay tied it up, on Miss Estella. But she had wrote out a little coddleshell[4] in her own hand a day or two afore the accident, leaving a cool four thousand to Mr. Matthew Pocket. And why, do you suppose, above all things, Pip, she left that cool four thousand unto him? 'Because of Pip's account of him the said Matthew.' I am told by Biddy, that air the writing," said Joe, repeating the legal turn as if it did him infinite good, "'account of him the said Matthew.' And a cool four thousand, Pip!"

I never discovered from whom Joe derived the conventional temperature of the four thousand pounds, but it appeared to make the sum of money more to him, and he had a manifest relish in insisting on its being cool. 40

This account gave me great joy, as it perfected the only good thing I had done. I asked Joe whether he had heard if any of the other relations had any legacies?

"Miss Sarah," said Joe, "she have twenty-five pound perannium fur to buy pills, on account of being bilious. Miss Georgiana, she have twenty pound down. Mrs——what's the name of them wild beasts with humps, old chap?"

"Camels?" said I, wondering why he could possibly want to know.

3. Cluttered.
4. Codicil.

Joe nodded. "Mrs. Camels," by which I presently understood he meant Camilla, "she have five pound fur to buy rushlights to put her in spirits when she wake up in the night."

The accuracy of these recitals was sufficiently obvious to me, to give me great confidence in Joe's information. "And now," said Joe, "you ain't that strong yet, old chap, that you can take in more nor one additional shovel-full to-day. Old Orlick he's been a bustin' open a dwelling-ouse."

"Whose?" said I.

"Not, I grant you, but what his manners is given to blusterous," said Joe, apologetically; "still, a Englishman's ouse is his Castle, and castles must not 10 be busted 'cept when done in war time. And wotsume'er the failings on his part, he were a corn and seedsman in his hart."

"Is it Pumblechook's house that has been broken into, then?"

"That's it, Pip," said Joe; "and they took his till, and they took his cash-box, and they drinked his wine, and they partook of his wittles, and they slapped his face, and they pulled his nose, and they tied him up to his bed-pust, and they giv' him a dozen, and they stuffed his mouth full of flowering annuals to prewent his crying out. But he knowed Orlick, and Orlick's in the county jail."

By these approaches, we arrived at unrestricted conversation. I was slow to 20 gain strength, but I did slowly and surely become less weak, and Joe stayed with me, and I fancied I was little Pip again.

For, the tenderness of Joe was so beautifully proportioned to my need, that I was like a child in his hands. He would sit and talk to me in the old confidence, and with the old simplicity, and in the old unassertive protecting way, so that I would half believe that all my life since the days of the old kitchen was one of the mental troubles of the fever that was gone. He did everything for me except the household work, for which he had engaged a very decent woman, after paying off the laundress on his first arrival. "Which I do assure you, Pip," he would often say, in explanation of that liberty; "I 30 found her a tapping the spare bed, like a cask of beer, and drawing off the feathers in a bucket, for sale. Which she would have tapped yourn next and draw'd it off with you a laying on it, and was then a carrying away the coals gradiwally in the soup-tureen and wegetable-dishes, and the wine and spirits in your Wellington boots."[5]

We looked forward to the day when I should go out for a ride, as we had once looked forward to the day of my apprenticeship. And when the day came, and an open carriage was got into the Lane, Joe wrapped me up, took me in his arms, carried me down to it, and put me in, as if I were still the small helpless creature to whom he had so abundantly given of the wealth of 40 his great nature.

And Joe got in beside me, and we drove away together into the country, where the rich summer growth was already on the trees and on the grass, and sweet summer scents filled all the air. The day happened to be Sunday, and, when I looked on the loveliness around me, and thought how it had grown and changed, and how the little wild flowers had been forming, and the voices of the birds had been strengthening, by day and by night, under the sun and

5. Long military boots of heavy black leather with chamois lining, covering the knee and cut away at the rear, allegedly devised (some time before Waterloo, 1815) by Wellington himself to be easily pulled on and off in soggy terrain. Napoleon wore them on St. Helena.

under the stars, while poor I lay burning and tossing on my bed, the mere remembrance of having burned and tossed there, came like a check upon my peace. But, when I heard the Sunday bells, and looked around a little more upon the outspread beauty, I felt that I was not nearly thankful enough—that I was too weak yet, to be even that—and I laid my head on Joe's shoulder, as I had laid it long ago when he had taken me to the Fair or where not, and it was too much for my young senses.

More composure came to me after a while, and we talked as we used to talk, lying on the grass at the old Battery. There was no change whatever in Joe. Exactly what he had been in my eyes then, he was in my eyes still; just 10 as simply faithful, and as simply right.

When we got back again and he lifted me out, and carried me—so easily —across the court and up the stairs, I thought of that eventful Christmas Day when he had carried me over the marshes. We had not yet made any allusion to my change of fortune, nor did I know how much of my late history he was acquainted with. I was so doubtful of myself now, and put so much trust in him, that I could not satisfy myself whether I ought to refer to it when he did not.

"Have you heard, Joe," I asked him that evening, upon further consideration, as he smoked his pipe at the window, "who my patron was?"   20

"I heerd," returned Joe, "as it were not Miss Havisham, old chap."

"Did you hear who it was, Joe?"

"Well! I heerd as it were a person what sent the person what giv' you the bank-notes at the Jolly Bargemen, Pip."

"So it was."

"Astonishing!" said Joe, in the placidest way.

"Did you hear that he was dead, Joe?" I presently asked, with increasing diffidence.

"Which? Him as sent the bank-notes, Pip?"

"Yes."   30

"I think," said Joe, after meditating a long time, and looking rather evasively at the window-seat, "as I did hear tell that how he were something or another in a general way in that direction."

"Did you hear anything of his circumstances, Joe?"

"Not partickler, Pip."

"If you would like to hear, Joe —— " I was beginning, when Joe got up and came to my sofa.

"Lookee here, old chap," said Joe, bending over me. "Ever the best of friends; ain't us, Pip?"

I was ashamed to answer him.   40

"Wery good, then," said Joe, as if I had answered; "that's all right; that's agreed upon. Then why go into subjects, old chap, which as betwixt two sech must be for ever onnecessary? There's subjects enough as betwixt two sech, without onnecessary ones. Lord! To think of your poor sister and her Rampages! And don't you remember Tickler?"

"I do indeed, Joe."

"Lookee here, old chap," said Joe. "I done what I could to keep you and Tickler in sunders, but my power were not always fully equal to my inclinations. For when your poor sister had a mind to drop into you, it were not so much," said Joe, in his favourite argumentative way, "that she dropped 50 into me too, if I put myself in opposition to her, but that she dropped into you always heavier for it. I noticed that. It ain't a grab at a man's whisker, nor yet a shake or two of a man (to which your sister was quite welcome), that 'ud put a man off from getting a little child out of punishment. But when that little child is dropped into, heavier, for that grab of whisker or shaking, then that man naterally up and says to himself, 'Where is the good as you are a doing? I grant you I see the 'arm,' says the man, 'but I don't see the good. I call upon you, sir, theerfore, to pint out the good.' "

"The man says?" I observed, as Joe waited for me to speak.

"The man says," Joe assented. "Is he right, that man?"   10

"Dear Joe, he is always right."

"Well, old chap," said Joe, "then abide by your words. If he's always right (which in general he's more likely wrong), he's right when he says this:— Supposing ever you kep any little matter to yourself when you was a little child, you kep it mostly because you know'd as J. Gargery's power to part you and Tickler in sunders, were not fully equal to his inclinations. Theerfore, think no more of it as betwixt two sech, and do not let us pass remarks upon onnecessary subjects. Biddy giv' herself a deal o' trouble with me afore I left (for I am most awful dull), as I should view it in this light, and, viewing it in this light, as I shouldser put it. Both of which," said Joe, quite charmed with   20 his logical arrangement, "being done, now this to you a true friend, say. Namely. You mustn't go a over-doing on it, but you must have your supper and your wine-and-water, and you must be put betwixt the sheets."

The delicacy with which Joe dismissed this theme, and the sweet tact and kindness with which Biddy—who with her woman's wit had found me out so soon—had prepared him for it, made a deep impression on my mind. But whether Joe knew how poor I was, and how my great expectations had all dissolved, like our own marsh mists before the sun, I could not understand.

Another thing in Joe that I could not understand when it first began to develop itself, but which I soon arrived at a sorrowful comprehension of, was   30 this: As I became stronger and better, Joe became a little less easy with me. In my weakness and entire dependence on him, the dear fellow had fallen into the old tone, and called me by the old names, the dear "old Pip, old chap," that now were music in my ears. I too had fallen into the old ways, only happy and thankful that he let me. But, imperceptibly, though I held by them fast, Joe's hold upon them began to slacken; and whereas I wondered at this, at first, I soon began to understand that the cause of it was in me, and that the fault of it was all mine.

Ah! Had I given Joe no reason to doubt my constancy, and to think that in prosperity I should grow cold to him and cast him off? Had I given Joe's   40 innocent heart no cause to feel instinctively that as I got stronger, his hold upon me would be weaker, and that he had better loosen it in time and let me go, before I plucked myself away?

It was on the third or fourth occasion of my going out walking in the Temple Gardens leaning on Joe's arm, that I saw this change in him very plainly. We had been sitting in the bright warm sunlight, looking at the river, and I chanced to say as we got up:

"See, Joe! I can walk quite strongly. Now, you shall see me walk back by myself."

"Which do not over-do it, Pip," said Joe; "but I shall be happy for to see you able, sir."

The last word grated on me; but how could I remonstrate! I walked no further than the gate of the gardens, and then pretended to be weaker than I was, and asked Joe for his arm. Joe gave it me, but was thoughtful.

I, for my part, was thoughtful too; for, how best to check this growing change in Joe, was a great perplexity to my remorseful thoughts. That I was ashamed to tell him exactly how I was placed, and what I had come down to, I do not seek to conceal; but, I hope my reluctance was not quite an unworthy one. He would want to help me out of his little savings, I knew, 10 and I knew that he ought not to help me, and that I must not suffer him to do it.

It was a thoughtful evening with both of us. But, before we went to bed, I had resolved that I would wait over to-morrow, to-morrow being Sunday, and would begin my new course with the new week. On Monday morning I would speak to Joe about this change, I would lay aside this last vestige of reserve, I would tell him what I had in my thoughts (that Secondly, not yet arrived at), and why I had not decided to go out to Herbert, and then the change would be conquered for ever. As I cleared, Joe cleared, and it seemed as though he had sympathetically arrived at a resolution too. 20

We had a quiet day on the Sunday, and we rode out into the country, and then walked in the fields.

"I feel thankful that I have been ill, Joe," I said.

"Dear old Pip, old chap, you're a'most come round, sir."

"It has been a memorable time for me, Joe."

"Likeways for myself, sir," Joe returned.

"We have had a time together, Joe, that I can never forget. There were days once, I know, that I did for a while forget; but I never shall forget these."

"Pip," said Joe, appearing a little hurried and troubled, "there has been larks. And, dear sir, what have been betwixt us—have been." 30

At night, when I had gone to bed, Joe came into my room, as he had done all through my recovery. He asked me if I felt sure that I was as well as in the morning?

"Yes, dear Joe, quite."

"And are always a getting stronger, old chap?"

"Yes, dear Joe, steadily."

Joe patted the coverlet on my shoulder with his great good hand, and said, in what I thought a husky voice, "Good night!"

When I got up in the morning, refreshed and stronger yet, I was full of my resolution to tell Joe all, without delay. I would tell him before breakfast. 40 I would dress at once and go to his room and surprise him; for, it was the first day I had been up early. I went to his room, and he was not there. Not only was he not there, but his box was gone.

I hurried then to the breakfast-table, and on it found a letter. These were its brief contents.

"Not wishful to intrude I have departed fur you are well again dear Pip and will do better without   "Jo.
"P.S. Ever the best of friends."

Enclosed in the letter, was a receipt for the debt and costs on which I had been arrested. Down to that moment I had vainly supposed that my creditor had withdrawn or suspended proceedings until I should be quite recovered. I had never dreamed of Joe's having paid the money; but, Joe had paid it, and the receipt was in his name.

What remained for me now, but to follow him to the dear old forge, and there to have out my disclosure to him, and my penitent remonstrance with him, and there to relieve my mind and heart of that reserved Secondly, which had begun as a vague something lingering in my thoughts, and had formed into a settled purpose? 10

The purpose was, that I would go to Biddy, that I would show her how humbled and repentant I came back, that I would tell her how I had lost all I once hoped for, that I would remind her of our old confidences in my first unhappy time. Then, I would say to her, "Biddy, I think you once liked me very well, when my errant heart, even while it strayed away from you, was quieter and better with you than it ever has been since. If you can like me only half as well once more, if you can take me with all my faults and disappointments on my head, if you can receive me like a forgiven child (and indeed I am as sorry, Biddy, and have as much need of a hushing voice and a soothing hand), I hope I am a little worthier of you than I was—not 20 much, but a little. And, Biddy, it shall rest with you to say whether I shall work at the forge with Joe, or whether I shall try for any different occupation down in this country, or whether we shall go away to a distant place where an opportunity awaits me, which I set aside when it was offered, until I knew your answer. And now, dear Biddy, if you can tell me that you will go through the world with me, you will surely make it a better world for me, and me a better man for it, and I will try hard to make it a better world for you."

Such was my purpose. After three days more of recovery, I went down to the old place, to put it in execution; and how I sped in it, is all I have left to tell. 30

Chapter LVIII.

THE tidings of my high fortunes having had a heavy fall, had got down to my native place and its neighbourhood, before I got there. I found the Blue Boar in possession of the intelligence, and I found that it made a great change in the Boar's demeanour. Whereas the Boar had cultivated my good opinion with warm assiduity when I was coming into property, the Boar was exceedingly cool on the subject now that I was going out of property.

It was evening when I arrived, much fatigued by the journey I had so often made so easily. The Boar could not put me into my usual bedroom, which was engaged (probably by some one who had expectations), and could only assign me a very indifferent chamber among the pigeons and post-chaises up 40 the yard. But, I had as sound a sleep in that lodging as in the most superior accommodation the Boar could have given me, and the quality of my dreams was about the same as in the best bedroom.

Early in the morning while my breakfast was getting ready, I strolled round by Satis House. There were printed bills on the gate, and on bits of carpet hanging out of the windows, announcing a sale by auction of the Household Furniture and Effects,[1] next week. The House itself was to be sold as old building materials and pulled down. LOT 1 was scrawled in white-washed knock-kneed letters on the brew house; LOT 2 on that part of the main building which had been so long shut up. Other lots were marked off on other parts of the structure, and the ivy had been torn down to make room for the inscriptions, and much of it trailed low in the dust and was withered already. Stepping in for a moment at the open gate and looking around me with the uncomfortable air of a stranger who had no business there, I saw the auc- 10 tioneer's clerk walking on the casks and telling them off for the information of a catalogue-compiler, pen in hand, who made a temporary desk of the wheeled chair I had so often pushed along to the tune of Old Clem.

When I got back to my breakfast in the Boar's coffee-room, I found Mr. Pumblechook conversing with the landlord. Mr. Pumblechook (not improved in appearance by his late nocturnal adventure) was waiting for me, and addressed me in the following terms.

"Young man, I am sorry to see you brought low. But what else could be expected! What else could be expected!"

As he extended his hand with a magnificently forgiving air, and as I was 20 broken by illness and unfit to quarrel, I took it.

"William," said Mr. Pumblechook to the waiter, "put a muffin on table. And has it come to this! Has it come to this!"

I frowningly sat down to my breakfast. Mr. Pumblechook stood over me, and poured out my tea—before I could touch the teapot—with the air of a benefactor who was resolved to be true to the last.

"William," said Mr. Pumblechook, mournfully, "put the salt on. In happier times," addressing me, "I think you took sugar? And did you take milk? You did. Sugar and milk. William, bring a watercress."

"Thank you," said I, shortly, "but I don't eat watercresses."   30

"You don't eat 'em," returned Mr. Pumblechook, sighing and nodding his head several times, as if he might have expected that, and as if abstinence from watercresses were consistent with my downfall. "True. The simple fruits of the earth. No. You needn't bring any, William."

I went on with my breakfast, and Mr. Pumblechook continued to stand over me, staring fishily and breathing noisily, as he always did.

"Little more than skin and bone!" mused Mr. Pumblechook, aloud. "And yet when he went away from here (I may say with my blessing), and I spread afore him my humble store, like the Bee,[2] he was as plump as a Peach!"

This reminded me of the wonderful difference between the servile manner 40 in which he had offered his hand in my new prosperity, saying, "May I?" and the ostentatious clemency with which he had just now exhibited the same fat five fingers.

"Hah!" he went on, handing me the bread-and-butter. "And air you a going to Joseph?"

---

1. "Furniture and Effects": auctioneer's phrase. The effects comprise all the movable property other than furniture.
2. Pumblechook is thinking of the busy little bee that collects its humble store (and improves each shining hour) by gathering honey all the day, from every opening flower—in song 20, "Against Idleness and Mischief," in Isaac Watts's *Divine Songs* (1715), the first hymnology for children. Famously parodied in *Alice in Wonderland* 150 years later.

"In Heaven's name," said I, firing in spite of myself, "what does it matter to you where I am going? Leave that teapot alone."

It was the worst course I could have taken, because it gave Pumblechook the opportunity he wanted.

"Yes, young man," said he, releasing the handle of the article in question, retiring a step or two from my table, and speaking for the behoof of the landlord and waiter at the door, "I *will* leave that teapot alone. You are right, young man. For once, you are right. I forgit myself when I take such an interest in your breakfast, as to wish your frame, exhausted by the debilitating effects of prodigygality, to be stimilated by the 'olesome nourishment of your forefathers. And yet," said Pumblechook, turning to the landlord and waiter, and pointing me out at arm's length, "this is him as I ever sported with in his days of happy infancy. Tell me not it cannot be; I tell you this is him!"

A low murmur from the two replied. The waiter appeared to be particularly affected.

"This is him," said Pumblechook, "as I have rode in my shay-cart. This is him as I have seen brought up by hand. This is him untoe the sister of which I was uncle by marriage, as her name was Georgiana M'ria from her own mother, let him deny it if he can!"

The waiter seemed convinced that I could not deny it, and that it gave the case a black look.

"Young man," said Pumblechook, screwing his head at me in the old fashion, "you air a going to Joseph. What does it matter to me, you ask me, where you air a going? I say to you, sir, you air a going to Joseph."

The waiter coughed, as if he modestly invited me to get over that.

"Now," said Pumblechook, and all this with a most exasperating air of saying in the cause of virtue what was perfectly convincing and conclusive, "I will tell you what to say to Joseph. Here is Squires of the Boar present, known and respected in this town, and here is William, which his father's name was Potkins if I do not deceive myself."

"You do not, sir," said William.

"In their presence," pursued Pumblechook, "I will tell you, young man, what to say to Joseph. Says you, 'Joseph, I have this day seen my earliest benefactor and the founder of my fortun's. I will name no names, Joseph, but so they are pleased to call him up-town, and I have seen that man.' "

"I swear I don't see him here," said I.

"Say that likewise," retorted Pumblechook. "Say you said that, and even Joseph will probably betray surprise."

"There you quite mistake him," said I. "I know better."

"Says you," Pumblechook went on, " 'Joseph, I have seen that man, and that man bears you no malice and bears me no malice. He knows your character, Joseph, and is well acquainted with your pig-headedness and ignorance; and he knows my character, Joseph, and he knows my want of gratitoode. Yes, Joseph,' says you," here Pumblechook shook his head and hand at me, " 'he knows my total deficiency of common human gratitoode. *He* knows it, Joseph, as none can. *You* do not know it, Joseph, having no call to know it, but that man do.' "

Windy donkey as he was, it really amazed me that he could have the face to talk thus to mine.

"Says you, 'Joseph, he gave me a little message, which I will now repeat.

It was, that in my being brought low, he saw the finger of Providence. He knowed that finger when he saw it, Joseph, and he saw it plain. It pinted out this writing, Joseph. *Reward of ingratitoode to earliest benefactor, and founder of fortun's.* But that man said that he did not repent of what he had done, Joseph. Not at all. It was right to do it, it was kind to do it, it was benevolent to do it, and he would do it again.' "

"It's a pity," said I, scornfully, as I finished my interrupted breakfast, "that the man did not say what he had done and would do again."

"Squires of the Boar!" Pumblechook was now addressing the landlord, "and William! I have no objections to your mentioning, either up-town or down-town, if such should be your wishes, that it was right to do it, kind to do it, benevolent to do it, and that I would do it again."

With those words the Impostor shook them both by the hand, with an air, and left the house; leaving me much more astonished than delighted by the virtues of that same indefinite "it." I was not long after him in leaving the house too, and when I went down the High-street I saw him holding forth (no doubt to the same effect) at his shop door, to a select group, who honoured me with very unfavourable glances as I passed on the opposite side of the way.

But, it was only the pleasanter to turn to Biddy and to Joe, whose great forbearance shone more brightly than before, if that could be, contrasted with this brazen pretender. I went towards them slowly, for my limbs were weak, but with a sense of increasing relief as I drew nearer to them, and a sense of leaving arrogance and untruthfulness further and further behind.

The June weather was delicious. The sky was blue, the larks were soaring high over the green corn, I thought all that country-side more beautiful and peaceful by far than I had ever known it to be yet. Many pleasant pictures of the life that I would lead there, and of the change for the better that would come over my character when I had a guiding spirit at my side whose simple faith and clear home-wisdom I had proved, beguiled my way. They awakened a tender emotion in me; for, my heart was softened by my return, and such a change had come to pass, that I felt like one who was toiling home barefoot from distant travel and whose wanderings had lasted many years.

The schoolhouse where Biddy was mistress, I had never seen; but, the little roundabout lane by which I entered the village for quietness' sake, took me past it. I was disappointed to find that the day was a holiday; no children were there, and Biddy's house was closed. Some hopeful notion of seeing her busily engaged in her daily duties, before she saw me, had been in my mind and was defeated.

But, the forge was a very short distance off, and I went towards it under the sweet green limes, listening for the clink of Joe's hammer. Long after I ought to have heard it, and long after I had fancied I heard it and found it but a fancy, all was still. The limes were there, and the white thorns were there, and the chestnut-trees were there, and their leaves rustled harmoniously when I stopped to listen; but, the clink of Joe's hammer was not in the midsummer wind.

Almost fearing, without knowing why, to come in view of the forge, I saw it at last, and saw that it was closed. No gleam of fire, no glittering shower of sparks, no roar of bellows; all shut up, and still.

But, the house was not deserted, and the best parlour seemed to be in use, for there were white curtains fluttering in its window, and the window was open and gay with flowers. I went softly towards it, meaning to peep over the flowers, when Joe and Biddy stood before me, arm in arm.

At first Biddy gave a cry, as if she thought it was my apparition, but in another moment she was in my embrace. I wept to see her, and she wept to see me; I, because she looked so fresh and pleasant; she, because I looked so worn and white.

"But, dear Biddy, how smart you are!"

"Yes, dear Pip."

"And Joe, how smart *you* are!"   10

"Yes, dear old Pip, old chap."

I looked at both of them, from one to the other, and then ——

"It's my wedding-day," cried Biddy, in a burst of happiness, "and I am married to Joe!"

     *   *   *   *   *

They had taken me into the kitchen, and I had laid my head down on the old deal table. Biddy held one of my hands to her lips, and Joe's restoring touch was on my shoulder. "Which he warn't strong enough, my dear, fur to be surprised," said Joe. And Biddy said, "I ought to have thought of it, dear Joe, but I was too happy." They were both so overjoyed to see me, so proud to see me, so touched by my coming to them, so delighted that I should have   20 come by accident to make their day complete!

My first thought was one of great thankfulness that I had never breathed this last baffled hope to Joe. How often, while he was with me in my illness, had it risen to my lips. How irrevocable would have been his knowledge of it, if he had remained with me but another hour!

"Dear Biddy," said I, "you have the best husband in the whole world, and if you could have seen him by my bed you would have —— But no, you couldn't love him better than you do."

"No, I couldn't indeed," said Biddy.

"And, dear Joe, you have the best wife in the whole world, and she will   30 make you as happy as even you deserve to be,[3] you dear, good, noble Joe!"

Joe looked at me with a quivering lip, and fairly put his sleeve before his eyes.

"And Joe and Biddy both, as you have been to church to-day, and are in charity and love with all mankind,[4] receive my humble thanks for all you have done for me, and all I have so ill repaid! And when I say that I am going away within the hour, for I am soon going abroad, and that I shall never rest until I have worked for the money with which you have kept me out of prison, and have sent it to you, don't think, dear Joe and Biddy, that if I could repay it a thousand times over, I suppose I could cancel a farthing   40 of the debt I owe you, or that I would do so if I could!"

They were both melted by these words, and both entreated me to say no more.

"But I must say more. Dear Joe, I hope you will have children to love, and

3. Not prejudicially, "as even *you* deserve to be," but judicially, "as in all fairness you deserve to be."
4. From the Holy Communion service of the Anglican Church: "You that do truly and earnestly repent you of your sins, and be in love and charity with your neighbours, and intend to lead a new life, following the commandments of God, and walking from henceforth in his holy ways: Draw near, and take this holy Sacrament to your comfort."

that some little fellow will sit in this chimney corner of a winter night, who may remind you of another little fellow gone out of it for ever. Don't tell him, Joe, that I was thankless; don't tell him, Biddy, that I was ungenerous and unjust; only tell him that I honoured you both, because you were both so good and true, and that, as your child, I said it would be natural to him to grow up a much better man than I did."

"I ain't a going," said Joe, from behind his sleeve, "to tell him nothink o' that natur, Pip. Nor Biddy ain't. Nor yet no one ain't."

"And now, though I know you have already done it in your own kind hearts, pray tell me, both, that you forgive me! Pray let me hear you say the words, 10 that I may carry the sound of them away with me, and then I shall be able to believe that you can trust me, and think better of me, in the time to come!"

"O dear old Pip, old chap," said Joe. "God knows as I forgive you, if I have anythink to forgive!"

"Amen! And God knows I do!" echoed Biddy.

"Now let me go up and look at my old little room, and rest there a few minutes by myself, and then when I have eaten and drunk with you, go with me as far as the finger-post, dear Joe and Biddy, before we say good-by!"

I sold all I had, and I put aside as much as I could, for a composition with my creditors—who gave me ample time to pay them in full—and I went out 20 and joined Herbert. Within a month, I had quitted England, and within two months I was clerk to Clarriker and Co., and within four months I assumed my first undivided responsibility. For, the beam across the parlour ceiling at Mill Pond Bank, had then ceased to tremble under old Bill Barley's growls and was at peace, and Herbert had gone away to marry Clara, and I was left in sole charge of the Eastern Branch until he brought her back.

Many a year went round, before I was a partner in the House; but, I lived happily with Herbert and his wife, and lived frugally, and paid my debts, and maintained a constant correspondence with Biddy and Joe. It was not until I became third in the Firm, that Clarriker betrayed me to Herbert; but, he then 30 declared that the secret of Herbert's partnership had been long enough upon his conscience, and he must tell it. So, he told it, and Herbert was as much moved as amazed, and the dear fellow and I were not the worse friends for the long concealment. I must not leave it to be supposed that we were ever a great House, or that we made mints of money. We were not in a grand way of business, but we had a good name, and worked for our profits, and did very well. We owed so much to Herbert's ever cheerful industry and readiness, that I often wondered how I had conceived that old idea of his inaptitude, until I was one day enlightened by the reflection, that perhaps the inaptitude had never been in him at all, but had been in me. 40

Chapter LIX.[1]

FOR eleven years,[2] I had not seen Joe nor Biddy with my bodily eyes— though they had both been often before my fancy in the East—when, upon an evening in December, an hour or two after dark, I laid my hand softly on

1. In MS chapters 58 and 59 run as one chapter, without a break in the text.
2. On the change from MS "eight years," see p. 506.

the latch of the old kitchen door. I touched it so softly that I was not heard, and looked in unseen. There, smoking his pipe in the old place by the kitchen firelight, as hale and as strong as ever though a little grey, sat Joe; and there, fenced into the corner with Joe's leg, and sitting on my own little stool looking at the fire, was——I again!

"We giv' him the name of Pip for your sake, dear old chap," said Joe, delighted when I took another stool by the child's side (but I did *not* rumple his hair), "and we hoped he might grow a little bit like you, and we think he do."

I thought so too, and I took him out for a walk next morning, and we 　10 talked immensely, understanding one another to perfection. And I took him down to the churchyard, and set him on a certain tombstone there, and he showed me from that elevation which stone was sacred to the memory of Philip Pirrip, late of this Parish, and Also Georgiana, Wife of the Above.

"Biddy," said I, when I talked with her after dinner, as her little girl lay sleeping in her lap, "you must give Pip to me, one of these days; or lend him, at all events."

"No, no," said Biddy, gently. "You must marry."

"So Herbert and Clara say, but I don't think I shall, Biddy. I have so settled down in their home, that it's not at all likely. I am already quite an old 　20 bachelor."

Biddy looked down at her child, and put its little hand to her lips, and then put the good matronly hand with which she had touched it, into mine. There was something in the action and in the light pressure of Biddy's wedding-ring, that had a very pretty eloquence in it.

"Dear Pip," said Biddy, "you are sure you don't fret for her?"

"O no—I think not, Biddy."

"Tell me as an old, old friend. Have you quite forgotten her?"

"My dear Biddy, I have forgotten nothing in my life that ever had a fore-most place there, and little that ever had any place there. But that poor dream, 　30 as I once used to call it, has all gone by, Biddy, all gone by!"[3]

Nevertheless, I knew while I said those words that I secretly intended to revisit the site of the old house that evening alone, for her sake. Yes, even so. For Estella's sake.

I had heard of her as leading a most unhappy life, and as being separated from her husband, who had used her with great cruelty, and who had become quite renowned as a compound of pride, avarice, brutality, and meanness. And I had heard of the death of her husband, from an accident consequent on his ill-treatment of a horse. This release had befallen her some two years before; for anything I knew, she was married again. 　　　　　　　　　40

The early dinner hour at Joe's, left me abundance of time, without hurrying my talk with Biddy, to walk over to the old spot before dark. But, what with loitering on the way, to look at old objects and to think of old times, the day had quite declined when I came to the place.

There was no house now, no brewery, no building whatever left, but the wall of the old garden. The cleared space had been enclosed with a rough fence, and, looking over it, I saw that some of the old ivy had struck root

3. The novel's original ending began at this point.

anew, and was growing green on low quiet mounds of ruin. A gate in the fence standing ajar, I pushed it open, and went in.

A cold silvery mist had veiled the afternoon, and the moon was not yet up to scatter it. But, the stars were shining beyond the mist, and the moon was coming, and the evening was not dark. I could trace out where every part of the old house had been, and where the brewery had been, and where the gates, and where the casks. I had done so, and was looking along the desolate garden-walk, when I beheld a solitary figure in it.

The figure showed itself aware of me, as I advanced. It had been moving towards me, but it stood still. As I drew nearer, I saw it to be the figure of a 10 woman. As I drew nearer yet, it was about to turn away, when it stopped, and let me come up with it. Then, it faltered as if much surprised, and uttered my name, and I cried out:

"Estella!"

"I am greatly changed. I wonder you know me."

The freshness of her beauty was indeed gone, but its indescribable majesty and its indescribable charm remained. Those attractions in it, I had seen before; what I had never seen before, was the saddened softened light of the once proud eyes; what I had never felt before, was the friendly touch of the once insensible hand. 20

We sat down on a bench that was near, and I said, "After so many years, it is strange that we should thus meet again, Estella, here where our first meeting was! Do you often come back?"

"I have never been here since."

"Nor I."

The moon began to rise, and I thought of the placid look at the white ceiling, which had passed away. The moon began to rise, and I thought of the pressure on my hand when I had spoken the last words he had heard on earth.

Estella was the next to break the silence that ensued between us. 30

"I have very often hoped and intended to come back, but have been pre-vented by many circumstances. Poor, poor old place!"

The silvery mist was touched with the first rays of the moonlight, and the same rays touched the tears that dropped from her eyes. Not knowing that I saw them, and setting herself to get the better of them, she said quietly:

"Were you wondering, as you walked along, how it came to be left in this condition?"

"Yes, Estella."

"The ground belongs to me. It is the only possession I have not relin-quished. Everything else has gone from me, little by little, but I have kept 40 this. It was the subject of the only determined resistance I made in all the wretched years."

"Is it to be built on?"

"At last it is. I came here to take leave of it before its change. And you," she said, in a voice of touching interest to a wanderer, "you live abroad still?"

"Still."

"And do well, I am sure?"

"I work pretty hard for a sufficient living, and therefore—Yes, I do well."

"I have often thought of you," said Estella.

"Have you?"

"Of late, very often. There was a long hard time when I kept far from me, the remembrance of what I had thrown away when I was quite ignorant of its worth. But, since my duty has not been incompatible with the admission of that remembrance, I have given it a place in my heart."

"You have always held your place in my heart," I answered. And we were silent again, until she spoke.

"I little thought," said Estella, "that I should take leave of you in taking leave of this spot. I am very glad to do so."

"Glad to part again, Estella? To me, parting is a painful thing. To me, the 10 remembrance of our last parting has been ever mournful and painful."

"But you said to me," returned Estella, very earnestly, " 'God bless you, God forgive you!' And if you could say that to me then, you will not hesitate to say that to me now—now, when suffering has been stronger than all other teaching, and has taught me to understand what your heart used to be. I have been bent and broken, but—I hope—into a better shape. Be as considerate and good to me as you were, and tell me we are friends."

"We are friends," said I, rising and bending over her, as she rose from the bench.

"And will continue friends apart," said Estella. 20

I took her hand in mine, and we went out of the ruined place; and, as the morning mists had risen long ago when I first left the forge, so the evening mists were rising now, and in all the broad expanse of tranquil light they showed to me, I saw the shadow of no parting from her.

The End of Great Expectations.

The Original Ending

It was two years more, before I saw herself. I had heard of her as leading a most unhappy life, and as being separated from her husband who had used her with great cruelty, and who had become quite renowned as a compound of pride, brutality, and meanness. I had heard of the death of her husband (from an accident consequent on ill-treating a horse), and of her being married again to a Shropshire doctor, who, against his interest, had once very manfully interposed, on an occasion when he was in professional attendance on Mr. Drummle, and had witnessed some outrageous treatment of her. I had heard that the Shropshire doctor was not rich, and that they lived on her own personal fortune.

I was in England again—in London, and walking along Piccadilly with little Pip—when a servant came running after me to ask would I step back to a lady in a carriage who wished to speak to me. It was a little pony carriage, which the lady was driving; and the lady and I looked sadly enough on one another.

"I am greatly changed, I know; but I thought you would like to shake hands with Estella too, Pip. Lift up that pretty child and let me kiss it!" (She supposed the child, I think, to be my child.)

I was very glad afterwards to have had the interview; for, in her face and in her voice, and in her touch, she gave me the assurance, that suffering had been stronger than Miss Havisham's teaching, and had given her a heart to understand what my heart used to be.

Adopted Readings

I have followed all substantive readings in *All the Year Round* with the following exceptions: (1) some twenty MS readings where the reading in AYR (and almost consistently in proof) clearly rests on a printer's error; (2) roughly sixty MS readings that are superior to all printed texts—frequently readings whose MS appearance encourages the MS adoption; (3) some fifty readings, based on the first (three-volume) edition of 1861, that may be plausibly attributed to Dickens, often changes in emphasis; (4) readings that first appeared in the one-volume Library Edition of 1862, nearly all of which persist through the Charles Dickens Edition of 1868 except for the very few 1868 readings that have been indicated separately. Readers who wish to consult the 1861 text have their choice of the Clarendon, Penguin, and St. Martin's editions; the 1868 text, with errors corrected, has been adopted by Robin Gilmour in the new Everyman. Some of the blemishes of the 1861 text have been spelled out by G. Thomas Tanselle in his "Problems and Accomplishments in the Editing of a Novel," *Studies in the Novel* 7 (1975): 323–60 (rept. in *Textual Criticism and Scholarly Editing* [Charlottesville: Virginia University Press, 1990] 179–270); most recently, with specific reference to *Great Expectations*, Joel J. Brattin's review article of the Clarendon edition in *DQ* 11 (1994): 138–47. The first reading below is the reading adopted; the second, the reading in *All the Year Round*.

MS Readings Adopted

10.26   MS **licking his lips at me**   AYR *omits* at me
18.24–25   MS **to think even now of what**   AYR to think of what
24.10   MS **orders to construct them**   AYR orders to make them
25.12   MS **had that very moment come to**   AYR *omits* very
26.37   MS **"Why," added Mr. Pumblechook, after**   AYR Mr. Pumblechook added, after
33.30   MS **half a dozen more men**   AYR some more men
34.11   MS **the means as I found out**   AYR *omits* as
35.44   MS **another pint, a separate pint**   AYR another pint, a separate matter
39.16–17   MS **must be received, however**   AYR *omits* however
41.4–5   MS **to be obleeged to have**   AYR to be obligated to have
44.19, 44.34   MS **Which some indiwidual**   AYR Which some individual
48.17   **no brewing was going on in it, however,**   AYR *omits* however
49.6–7   MS **As to strong beer, there's enough of that**   AYR As to strong beer, there's enough of it
58.29–30   MS **what results would ensue**   AYR what results would come
60.12   MS **continuing fur to keep**   AYR continuing for to keep
63.19   MS **he had all to himself**   AYR *omits* all
63.25   MS **Most meshes is solitary**   AYR Most marshes is solitary
67.24   MS **"Good Lord," said he**   AYR "Good Lord," says he

68.42   MS "And how do *you* come here?"   AYR "How do you come here?"

69.3–4   MS from her dressing-table   AYR from the dressing table

70.26   MS felt sufficiently disconcerted   AYR felt sufficiently discontented

71.23–24   MS it was otherwise. Still I wouldn't   AYR it was otherwise, still I wouldn't

76.18–19   MS knock me about until I was no more   AYR cuff me . . . more

79.4   MS Well! We went on in this way   AYR *omits* Well!

83.44   MS my own belief," assented Joe   AYR my own belief," answered Joe.

92.24   MS I'd hold you   AYR I'd hold you

94.25–26   MS I was happily hanged in my public character   AYR *omits* in my public character

111.24   MS tap an egg-shell   AYR pat an egg-shell

111.24–25   MS that harty welcome   AYR that hearty welcome

113.31   MS I felt in a manner offended   AYR I felt offended

118.18   MS Now, Mr. Trabb's boy   AYR *omits* Now,

121.26–27   MS I gave it as my opinion, "Wait a bit!"   AYR I gave it as my opinion. "Wait a bit!"

122.8   MS in the maintenance of a fiction that there was not a moment   AYR *omits* the maintenance of

122.41–42   MS to-morrow," I explained, exceedingly careful   AYR to-morrow," I was exceedingly careful

123.6   MS Not named, eh?   AYR Not named?

128.26   MS coachman glanced at Mr. Jaggers's name and answered   AYR *omits* glanced . . . name and

129.27   MS unless you wished   AYR unless you wish

130.38–39   MS the same disparaging mastery   AYR to same detrimental mastery

136.33–34   MS kept by one Barnard   AYR kept by Mr. Barnard

141.13   MS This of course I would not hear of   AYR This I would not hear of

149.21   MS holding his head with both hands   AYR *omits* with both hands

156.25   MS You took a particular fancy to me, didn't you   AYR You had a particular fancy to me, hadn't you

160.18   MS his defiance of 'em   AYR his defiance of them

166.25   MS seamed and scarred   AYR scarred and scarred

166.33   MS leisurely critical way   AYR leisurely critical style

167.50   MS to say a word of apology to my guardian   AYR *omits* of apology

170.11   MS a wery good inn   AYR a werry good inn

172.5–6   MS made the most extraordinary play   AYR *omits* the most

172.28   MS a sort of dignity in the look too   AYR *omits* too

172.42   MS as it were him   AYR as it wore him

172.43   MS looked upon as a playfeller   AYR looked upon as a playfellow

179.19   MS that even when I loved Estella   AYR *omits* even

180.8   MS How'sever, I come here   AYR However, I come here

180.25   MS a man wot could give   AYR a man who could give

180.43   MS any wiser?" said Miss Pocket   AYR any wiser?" said Sarah

180.43   MS dismal shake of her head   AYR dismal shake of the head

191.35 MS its having been so strongly AYR it's having been so strongly
193.22 MS that I should shortly be presented AYR *omits* shortly
197.12–13 MS made the same mistake AYR made the same mistakes
200.18 MS a greasy spotty surface AYR a greasy and fatty surface
206.35–36 MS hoops and wigs and stiff skirts they had cast their shadows
on AYR *omits* they . . . on
214.24 MS than that it was all addressed AYR *omits* than
215.45 MS laid her head down AYR laid her hand down
222.14 MS his afternoon walk AYR his afternoon's walk
223.6 MS waving a salute AYR waving a remote salute
225.14 MS am you, Aged P.? AYR are you, Aged P.?
228.7–8 MS under a grave disadvantage AYR under a heavy disadvantage
237.23 MS looking up at me AYR *omits* at me
240.36–37 MS However you have found me out AYR However, you . . .
out
245.31–32 MS as I handed him a dram at the door, on the chance of
eliciting some hopeful explanation AYR on the chance of eliciting some
hopeful explanation as I handed him a dram at the door
246.8 MS I repeated, faltering AYR *omits* faltering
249.22–23 MS and years has rolled away AYR and years have rolled away
250.23–24 MS gave him a superstitious reliance AYR gave him a
reliance
254.13 MS "Steady! It's Herbert!" AYR "Quiet! It's Herbert!'
254.32 MS if Pip don't make a gentleman AYR if Pip shan't make a
gentleman
267.42–43 MS laid on by the waiter, I am inclined to think AYR *omits*
am inclined to
279.26 MS not bay-window AYR not bay-windows
281.8–9 MS nothing . . . could possibly be confided to Old Barley AYR
omits possibly
284.27–28 MS We waited for a hint from Wemmick AYR *omits* a hint
from
303.41 MS in any distinct shape AYR in a distinct shape
306.25 MS I turned at last to Wemmick AYR *omits* at last
310.1–2 MS say Wednesday if the tide should suit AYR or say Wednesday *omits* if . . . suit
310.38 MS Those two would pull AYR Those two should pull
320.40 MS the afternoon coach AYR the afternoon's coach
321.25 MS [Trabb's boy] had too much vivacity to spare AYR [Trabb's
boy] had too much spare vivacity
327.23 MS [we] eyed them narrowly AYR [we] eyed them nervously
335.14 MS he can hardly do better AYR he cannot do better
336.2 MS I don't think he could have AYR I do not think . . . have
336.27–28 MS Wemmick himself: who immediately struck me AYR
omits immediately
340.19 MS linking both together AYR banding both together
343.7 MS it was through this vapour AYR it was through the vapour
343.38–39 MS there was a consistent tendency AYR there was a constant
tendency

344.31 MS you might be among strangers AYR you might be amongst strangers

349.3 MS but how could I remonstrate! AYR yet how could I remonstrate!

351.4 MS LOT 1 was scrawled AYR LOT 1 was marked

354.8 MS But, dear Biddy, how smart you are! AYR omits But,

1861 Readings Adopted

16.39–40 61 with a copper-stick AYR with the copper-stick

20.27–28 61 I handed him the file, and he laid it down in the grass AYR omits and he laid it down in the grass

23.6 61 Not a doubt of that AYR Not a doubt of it

31.30 61 in lively anticipation AYR in lively expectation

58.42 61 before the fire goes out AYR before the fire goes quite out

60.21 61 you'll never get to do it AYR omits get to

64.25–26 61 a most extraordinary shot AYR a most extraordinary one

67.12, 14, 26 ff. 61 Cousin Raymond AYR Cousin John

71.28–29 61 now, brushing . . . now, giving AYR now, brushing . . . and now giving

73.9 61 if it is done on this day AYR omits done

77.15 61 enjoy it greedily AYR enjoy it greedily in secret

79.1 61 you've given trouble enough AYR you've given trouble enough

91.26 61 he's a going uptown AYR he's going uptown

~~**96.13** 61 Joe Gargery was out AYR Joe was out~~

106.46–47 61 I don't ask you what you read just now AYR omits just now

109.25 61 When or where that intention AYR omits or where

136.11 61 They'll do it, if there's anything to be got by it AYR omits They'll do it begins If there

140.9 61 Miss Havisham's cousin AYR Miss Havisham's nephew [corrected in fn. in AYR two weeks later in number for March 16, 1861]

165.8 61 younger than she was AYR older than she was, as it is the manner of youth to do

175.20–21 61 the smaller suit of clothes AYR the smallest suit of clothes

179.20 61 I loved her simply AYR omits simply

197.4 61 must beg to insist upon it AYR omits beg to

198.23 61 Wemmick ran against me AYR Mr. Wemmick ran against me

201.30–31 61 to bring an action against you for false imprisonment AYR to bring an action of false imprisonment against you

222.6 61 forgotten the details of it AYR omits the details of

239.16 61 I saw with amazement AYR I saw with new amazement

245.21–22 61 the watchman to come AYR the watchman to come back

254.19 61 his running on AYR his rattling on

257.10 61 than I would ever have come to this AYR than I would have ever come to this

258.11–13 61 at once for a "fashionable crib" near Hyde Park, in which he could have "a shake-down." AYR at once for "a fashionable crib" in which he could have "a shake-down" near Hyde Park.

278.45   61 whenever I failed to do it drowsily   AYR whenever I failed to do it accidentally

284.8   61 as the hours of the tide   AYR as the hours of the tides

284.10   61 there was a race and a fall   AYR there was a race and fall

286.11   61 within the Lord Mayor's dominions   AYR in the Lord Mayor's dominions

293.18   61 A score or so of years   AYR omits or so

298.9   61 her cry had died away   AYR her cry died away

305.29–30   61 as Herbert had repeated it   AYR as Herbert had delivered it

306.50   61 tired of all this work   AYR omits all

307.4   61 But now, about this other matter.   AYR omits now,

308.37   61 My right arm   AYR my right hand

309.37   61 My right arm was tolerably restored   AYR My right hand was tolerably restored

315.15   61 I'll make short work of you   AYR I'll make short work of finishing you

320.5   61 Herbert! Great Heaven!   AYR Herbert! Good Heaven!

329.23–24   61 and they did not go down   AYR omits they

329.46–47   61 nor any boat drawn up   AYR omits any boat

330.22   61 Leaving just room enough   AYR Leaving just enough room

335.36–37   61 it was a part of his policy   AYR it was part of his policy

1862 Readings Adopted

25.3–4   62 our friend overhead   AYR my friend overhead

52.19   62 Her contempt for me was so strong   AYR omits for me

59.11   62 black welwet co — ch   AYR black welwet co-eh

61.10–11   62 put straws down   AYR put straws up

143.3–4   62 all the susceptibility she possessed   AYR omits the susceptibility

167.23   62 into your pocket   AYR in your pocket

169.16–17   62 I had made this monster   AYR I had made the monster

171.10   62 as you gets your elths   AYR as you get your elths

204.33   62 in the same spirit   AYR omits same

204.35   62 "What spirit was that?"   AYR "What was it?"

212.23   62 to offer him consolation   AYR omits him

212.23–24   62 assure him that I would   AYR assure him that I should

232.18   62 saw her candle   AYR saw her light

243.3–4   62 The wretched man after loading me with his wretched gold   AYR The wretched man after loading wretched me with his gold

251.7–8   62 coming along I had thought well of what I was going to say   AYR I had thought well of what I was going to say coming along

297.22   62 To see her with her white hair and her worn face, kneeling at my feet   AYR To see her with her white hair and her worn face kneeling at my feet

330.41–42   62 on board of the steamer   AYR omits of

1868 *Readings Adopted*

67.2   *68* **suppress a yawn**   *AYR* repress a yawn

73.15   *68* **play at cards**   *AYR omits* at

74.34   *68* **breaking out on his mouth**   *AYR* breaking out at his mouth

152.23   *68* **irrespective of the servants**   *AYR omits* the

226.35–36   *68* **so happy. [New Paragraph.] At length**   *AYR* so happy. At length

300.34–35   *68* **communicate with Matthew Pocket**   *AYR* communicate with Mr. Matthew Pocket

331.45   *68* **what he had told me**   *AYR* what he thus told me

Textual Notes

The abbreviations used in the textual notes are as follows:

MS = Manuscript, Wisbech and Fenland Museum
H = *Harper's Weekly*, New York
VA₁ = (?) First Corrected Proof, Victoria and Albert Museum
VA₂ = Later Corrected Proof, Victoria and Albert Museum
M = Corrected Proof, Pierpont Morgan Library
AYR = *All the Year Round*
61 = First Book Edition
62 = One-volume Edition
68 = Charles Dickens Edition
corr. = corrects
canc. = cancels

The table of variant readings that follows is meant to be selective, not exhaustive. Its aim is to suggest, somewhat more systematically than my commentary on Dickens's manuscript can convey, the revisions Dickens undertook from the time he began to write *Great Expectations* until he saw the Charles Dickens Edition through the press eight years later. At that, more than a dozen of these entries are being commented on discursively in the essay on the manuscript, if only to place them in context. The variants are not by and large of the eye-popping sort: I have salvaged those that tell us something about Dickens's workmanship and so lend themselves to discussion. Still, the people who worry why Henry James's Madame Merle, when we hear her tinker on the piano in *The Portrait of a Lady*, dropped Beethoven in favor of Schubert twenty-five years after her first performance won't find Dickens's second and third performances impenetrable conundrums.

I have made liberal use of "selectivity" by recording minor adjustments in the use of vulgarisms of the *he was, he were* sort and a few changes in punctuation and emphasis. Drummle's hyphenated "Wai-ter!" sounds more suggestively whiny and peremptory than the unhyphenated mating call to the "Waiter!" Then again, on a slightly lower level of textual altitude, we may wonder what Dickens gains by doubling and tripling the exclamation marks following Pumblechook's compassionate adjuration to *Joseph!! Joseph!!!* I have impounded half a dozen variants of suspect legitimacy: transparent misprints with which the pages of *Harper's Weekly* are riddled. But as a rule the entries are paradigmatic: where I cite one instance of the *whatsomnever/whatsoever* variety it's safe to assume that Dickens paraded a dozen.

The format of the individual entries differs slightly from the more austere shorthand hallowed by editorial usage (MS *Epimenides* to c.p. [F2] *Hammurabi* to [p.t.] Solon). As a working method, I have placed the earliest reading of a given variant into a slightly roomier context and indicated the later variant(s) in similarly discursive form. MS: *He handed me a slice of mince-meat* just as **Mrs. Joe collided with** Wopsle / AYR: *Joe administered my viaticum* just as *my sister ran into* Wopsle / 61 to 68 omit *just as . . . Wopsle.* Beyond that, a very few guidelines. (1) In every instance, the variant recorded last persists in all later texts: for example, where the last variant is assigned to *Harper's,* no changes were introduced subsequently. (2) Unless I explicitly specify cancellations and other corrections as these appear at proof stage, all readings in proof that are given silently suggest that Dickens made the change on a supposititious set of galleys that is no longer retrievable. As I have indicated, almost certainly two such sets have perished or disappeared. I have not bothered to assign a presumptive change in wording to a fugitive set of proofs by placing an identifying icon in brackets: the method, though of course indispensable to precisionists, seems to me needlessly cumbersome in the framework of this edition. (3) Textual scholars will notice that, except in one or two instances, I have ignored two editions: the 1863 Cheap Edition and the 1864 Library Edition. I have examined both line by line and found the variants so trifling that their inclusion would have pointlessly cluttered and inflated the tables.

FIRST STAGE

9.20–21
MS, H, VA$_1$: *My first* **distinct** *impression of the identity of things* AYR: *My first* **most vivid and broad** *impression of the identity of things*
9.23–24
MS, H: *that* **Tobias Pirrip,** *late of this parish* VA$_1$ corr. *to* **Philip Pirrip,** *late of this parish*
9.25–26
MS, H: *and that* **Abraham, George, and Robert,** *infant children of the aforesaid* VA$_1$ corr. *to and that* **Abraham, Tobias, and Roger,** *infant children of the aforesaid*
10.15
MS, H: *"Once more," said the man* VA$_1$ corr. *to "Once more," said the man,* **staring at me**
10.23
MS to AYR: *I saw the steeple under my* **legs** 61: *I saw the steeple under my* **feet**
10.30
MS, H: **Damned** *if I couldn't eat 'em* VA$_1$ corr. *to* **Darn Me** *if I couldn't eat 'em*
11.30
MS, H: *I am* **a Angel** *o'light* VA$_1$ corr. *to I am* **a Angel**
13.26–28
MS: *said Joe, slowly clearing the fire between the lower bars with the poker, "she* **rampaged out** H, VA$_1$: *said Joe, . . . with the poker, "she* **ram-paged out** AYR: *said Joe, . . . with the poker,* **and** *looking at it, "she Ram-paged out*
14.30–31
MS, H: *he sat feeling his right-side flaxen curls and whisker* VA$_1$ corr. *to he sat feeling . . . whisker* **with the palm of his hand** AYR: as in MS
14.34
MS, H: *she* **held** *the loaf* VA$_1$ corr. *to she* **jammed** *the loaf*
15.4
MS, H: *my larcenous researches* **in the dead of night** VA$_1$ canc. **in the dead of night**
16.3
MS, H: **such a honcommon Bolt** VA$_1$: *such a most* **honcommon Bolt** AYR, 61: *such a most* **uncommon Bolt** 62: *such a most uncommon bolt*
16.16–17
MS to 68: *a pint . . . was poured down my throat for my* **greater comfort** VA$_1$ only corr. *to a pint . . . for my* **better restoration**
16.41–17.1
MS, H: *the man with the* **iron** *on his leg* VA$_1$ corr. *to the man with the* **load** *on his leg*
17.1–2
MS: *[I] found the tendency . . .* **quite unconquerable** H: *[I] found the tendency . . .* **quite unmanageable and unconquerable** V$_1$ canc. **and unconquerable**
17.19
MS, H: **Drat** *that* **child** VA$_1$ corr. *to* **Drat** *that* **boy**

17.20
MS, H: *Ask no questions, and you'll be told no lies* VA₁ corr. to *Ask no questions, **child**, and . . . lies* AYR as in MS
18.9
MS, H: *because they murder, and . . . rob* VA₁ corr. to *because they murder, and . . . rob, **and forge***
18.31–32
MS, H: *There was no getting a light by easy friction **then*** VA₁ corr. to *There was **no venturing on the crime by night**, for there was no getting a light by easy friction **at that age of the world*** AYR: *There was **no doing it in the night**, for there was no getting a light by easy friction **then***
19.31
MS, H: *I couldn't help it!* VA₁ corr. to *I couldn't help it, **Sir!***
19.40
MS, H: *we would have such Larks there **as should recompense us for our constraint at home*** VA₁ canc. *as . . . home*
20.23–25
MS, H: *there was **the** man . . . waiting for me* VA₁ corr. to *there was **the right** man waiting for me*
20.27–28
MS to AYR: *I handed him the file* 61: *I handed him the file, **and he laid it down in the grass***
20.37–39
MS, H: *It was quite as much as he could do to keep the neck of the bottle between his teeth* VA₁ corr. to *It was . . . between his teeth, **without biting it off***
21.10–11
[*as this poor wretched warmint is* 1st installment in Harper's breaks off here; 2nd installment begins with paragraph following: **Something clicked in his throat**]
21.28
MS, H: *You won't leave any for him* VA₁ corr. to *I **am afraid** you won't leave any for him*
22.19–20
MS, H: *striking his . . . cheek with . . . of his hand* VA₁ corr. to *striking his . . . cheek **mercilessly** with . . . his hand*
24.10–11
MS: *the tailor had orders **to construct them** like a kind of Reformatory.* H: *the tailor had orders **to make them** . . . Reformatory*
24.35–36
MS, H, VA₁: *Mr. Wopsle, united to a Roman nose and a **large bald** forehead, had a **deep sonorous** voice* AYR: *Mr. Wopsle, united to . . . a **large shining bald** forehead, had a **deep voice***
26.19
MS, H, VA₁: **this** *mystery seemed too much for the company* AYR: **this moral** *mystery seemed too much for the company*
26.24–27
MS: [Paragraph beginning "*Joe's station . . . **half a pint**"* written separately on verso leaf, the insertion marked with an asterisk and the Spartan notation "**back**" (to the appropriate place in the text)]
26.24–25
MS, H: *[Joe] always aided and **abetted** me* VA₁ corr. to *[Joe] always aided and **comforted** me*
28.2
MS, H: *I held tight to the leg of the table* VA₁ corr. to *I held . . . the table, **under the cloth***
28.14–16
MS, H, VA₁: *he then became visible . . . violently **stamping** and expectorating* AYR: *he . . . visible . . . violently **plunging** and expectorating*
28.25–26
MS, H, VA₁: *how ever **could** it come there!* AYR: *how ever **could Tar** come there!*
29.6
M, H: *having deserved well of his fellow-creatures, **and having distinguished himself by his gift**, said **vivaciously*** VA₁ canc. *and . . . by his gift*; corr. to **quite** *vivaciously*
29.19
[**look sharp, come on!**" VA₁ ends here]
30.38–39
MS, H: *If you're ready, **the King** is* M: *If you're ready, **His Majesty the King** is*
32.1–2
MS, H: *when something **to drink** was going* M: *when something **moist** was going*
32.27
MS, H: *charging at the ditches **in the nimblest manner*** M: *charging . . . **like a hunter***
32.43–44
MS, H: *the shudder of **the whole dying day*** M: *the shudder of **the dying day in every blade of grass***

32.44
MS, H: *there was no break in the uniform stillness of the marshes* M: *there . . . break in the bleak stillness of the marshes*
33.9
MS to 62, 64: *we slanted to the right* 63, 68: *we started to the right*
33.11–12
MS, H: *It was . . . what Joe called "a buster"* M: *It was . . . "a Winder"*
33.12–13
MS, H: *over gates, and splashing into dykes:* M: *over gates, splashing into dykes, and breaking among coarse rushes:*
33.30
MS, H: *half a dozen more men went down into the ditch* M: *some more men went down into the ditch*
33.40
MS, H: *said my convict, with a terrible laugh* M: *said my convict with a greedy laugh*
34.7–8
MS, H: *I got clear of the prison-ship* M: *Single-handed I got clear of the prison-ship*
34.15
MS, H: *[he] was evidently in extreme fear of his companion* M: *[he] was evidently in extreme horror of his companion*
34.41–42
MS, H: *I looked at him . . . and moved my hands and shook my head* M: *I looked at him . . . and slightly moved my hands and shook my head*
35.18–19
MS, H: *the two wretched men . . . limped along* M: *the two prisoners . . . limped along*
35.26
MS, H: *an immense mangle* M: *an overgrown mangle*
35.27–29
MS, H: *Three or four soldiers who lay upon it . . . took a stare* M: *Three or four soldiers who lay upon it in their great-coats . . . took a sleepy stare,*
35.34–36
MS, H: *he stood before the fire looking at it, or putting up his miserable feet by turns upon the hob and looking at them as if he pitied them.* M: *he stood before the fire looking thoughtfully at it, or putting . . . upon the hob, and looking thoughtfully at them as if he pitied them for their recent adventures*
35.40–41
MS, H: *the sergeant, standing looking at him* M: *the sergeant, standing coolly looking at him*
36.11
MS, H: *"Oh!" said my convict to Joe in a moody manner* M: *"So," said my convict, turning his eyes on Joe in a moody manner*
36.16–17
MS, H: *We wouldn't have you starved to death for it, miserable fellow creetur, whatever it was* M to 68 omit *whatever it was*
36.22–24
MS, H: *No one seemed* [H: *appeared*] *glad to see him, or sorry to see him, or spoke a word, except that somebody called as if to dogs* M: *No one seemed surprised to see him, or interested in seeing him, or glad to see him, or sorry to see him, or spoke a word, except that somebody in the boat growled as if to dogs*
36.27–28
MS, H: *the prison-ship was ironed like the prisoners.* M: *the prison-ship seemed in my young eyes to be ironed like the prisoners.*
37.14–16
MS: *I had had no intercourse with people at that time, and I imitated none of the unaccountable host of people who act in this manner* H, M as in MS but canc. *unaccountable* AYR: *I had had no intercourse with the world . . . and I imitated none of its many inhabitants who act in this manner*
37.45
MS, H, M: *I seemed to have twenty boots on* AYR: *I seemed to have fifty boots on*
38.16–17
MS, H, M: *I was not to be what Mrs. Joe called "Pompeyed," or pampered* AYR: *I was not to be "Pompeyed," or (as I render it) pampered*
38.27–28
MS, H, M: *Mr. Wopsle's great-aunt . . . was an ancient woman* AYR: *Mr. Wopsle's great-aunt . . . was a ridiculous old woman*
38.30
MS, H, M: *who paid threepence per week each* AYR: *who paid twopence per week each*
38.36–39.2
MS, H: *I particularly venerated Mr. Wopsle as Fear, whistling to keep his courage up.* M corr. to *I particularly venerated Mr. Wopsle as Revenge, throwing his blood-stain'd sword*

in thunder down, and taking the War-denouncing trumpet with a withering look. [Corrections on Morgan proof begin with this entry]
39.39–40
MS, H: *old chap!" cried Joe, "what a scholar you are!"* M: *old chap!" cried Joe, opening his blue eyes wide, "what a scholar you are!"*
40.32–33
MS: *he was given to drink, and when he was overtook* H: *he were given to drink, and when he were overtook*
41.22–23
MS: *Whatsoe'er the failings on his part* H: *Whatsume'er the failings on his part*
42.30–31
MS: *Joe had obtained a divorce and settled her on* the Lords of the Admiralty H: *Joe had divorced her in favour of* the Lords of the Admiralty
43.11–13
MS: *Joe . . . stopped me by answering with a fixed look* H: *Joe . . . stopped me by arguing circularly, and answering with a fixed look*
43.42
MS: *and see no help or pity in the whole host* H: *and . . . pity in the whole glittering multitude* M: *and . . . pity in all the glittering multitude*
44.17–18
M, H: *"Well," said my sister in her short way. "Is the house a-fire?"* H: *"Well," said my sister in her snappish way. "Is the house a-fire?"* M: *"Well," . . . in her snappish way. "What are you staring at? Is the house a-fire?"*
44.20–21 [MS I–29]
unless you call Miss <Havish> Havisham a he [thus to 45.3; from 45.5 unhesitatingly *Havisham*]
45.10–11
MS: *my face was put into wooden bowls* H, M: *my face was forced into wooden bowls* AYR: *my face was squeezed into wooden bowls*
45.18–19
MS: *[I] was trussed up in my tightest suit* H: *[I] was trussed up in my tightest and fearfullest suit*
45.24
MS: *"God bless you, Joe!"* H: *"Good-bye, Joe!"*
45.28–30
MS: *why I was to play at Miss Havisham's, and what I was to play at* H: *why on earth . . . Miss Havisham's, and what on earth . . . play at*
49.6–7
MS: *As to strong beer, there's enough of that* H: *As . . . there's enough of it*
49.18
MS: *she was of about my own age—very little older.* H, M, AYR: *she was about my own age, or very little older* 61: *she was of about my own age*
49.18–19
MS: *She seemed older, of course* H: *She seemed much older than I, of course*
51.25
MS: *flashing a look of command at me* H: *flashing a look at me*
51.36
MS: *Why, he is a labouring boy!* H: *Why, he is a common labouring-boy!*
52.10–11
MS, M: *the frillings . . . on her bridal dress looking like earthy paper, and as if they would crumble under a touch* H omits *and* AYR to 68 omit *and . . . touch*
52.22–23
MS: *she denounced me for a stupid clumsy boy* H: *she denounced me for a stupid, clumsy labouring-boy*
53.12
MS, H, M: *Come again after three days* AYR: *Come again after six days*
53.30–32
MS, H, M: *She . . . gave me the bread and meat . . . as insolently as if I were a dog* AYR: *She . . . as insolently as if I were a dog in disgrace*
53.45–46
MS: *I am convinced there is nothing so finely perceived or so strongly felt* H: *I am convinced there is nothing so finely perceived or so finely felt* M canc. *I am convinced*
54.44–55.1
MS: *at this moment . . . a strange thing happened to my fancy.* H, M: *at this moment . . . my fancy. I thought it a strange thing then, and I thought it stranger long afterwards* AYR: *at this moment . . . my fancy. I thought it a strange thing then, and I thought it a stranger thing long afterwards.*
55.1
MS: *I turned my eyes—no doubt a little dazed* H: *I turned my eyes—little dimmed*
55.5–7
MS, H, M: *the face was Miss Havisham's, with the eyes open and with a movement . . . as if she were trying to call me* AYR to 68 omit *with the eyes open*

55.20–21
MS: *she touched me*—not **with a coarse hand**, *O no no!* H: *she touched me* **with a taunting hand**

55.24–25
MS, H, M: *You have been crying, and you are near crying again* AYR: *You have been crying till you are half blind, and you are near crying again*

55.26
MS: *She* **laughed** *. . . and locked the gate* H: *She* **laughed contemptuously** *. . . and locked the gate*

55.33
MS, H: *by that means* **got the better of it** M corr. to *by that means* **vanquished it**

56.13–15
MS, H, M: *there would be something coarse . . . in my dragging her . . . before the contemplation of Mrs. Joe* AYR: *there would be something coarse in my dragging her* **as she really was before** *. . . Mrs. Joe*

56.30–31
MS, H: *I . . . answered, "I mean pretty well."* M corr. to *I . . . answered,* **as if I had discovered a new idea,** *"I mean pretty well."*

56.35–36
MS, H, M: *Pumblechook then turned me towards him, as if he were going to cut my hair, or* **take out one of my teeth,** *or perform some such operation* AYR to 68 omit *or* **take** *. . . operation*

60.40
MS, H: *That was a memorable day . . . for it made great changes in me* **and in my fortunes** M canc. **and in my fortunes**

61.2–3
MS, H: *the best step . . . was to get out of Biddy everything she knew,* **and to pay the strictest attention to Mr. Wopsle when he read aloud** M canc. **and to pay** *. . .* **read aloud**

61.29–30
MS, H: *none of us having the least notion what we were reading about* M: corr. to *none of us having the least notion of,* **or reverence for,** *what we were reading about*

62.6–7
MS, H: *lending me, to copy at home,* **a German text or old English** D M corr. to *lending . . . home,* **a large old English** D

63.26–27
MS, H, M: *Do you find any gipsies . . . out there* **on those low lands** AYR to 68 omit **on those low lands**

67.34–35
MS: *I instantly went out . . . and bought* **the mourning** H: *I . . . bought* **the things**

68.45–46
MS: *Now mind," said he,* **threatening me with his great forefinger** H: *"Now" . . . said he,* **biting the side of his great forefinger as he frowned at me**

69.24–26
MS: *the high chimney-piece . . . disturbed and troubled its darkness* H: *the high chimney-piece . . .* **faintly disturbed and troubled** *its darkness* M canc. **and troubled**

70.25–26
MS: *I should have felt sufficiently* **disconcerted** H to 68: *I should have felt sufficiently* **discontented**

71.21–22
MS: *Camilla,* **whose upper lip and eyelids were now in a state of constant vibration,** *while her* [H: **whose**]*fermenting feelings appeared to rise from her legs* H to 68 omit **upper lip** *. . .* **vibration**

70.36–37
MS: *we were close to Camilla then* **and she had her hand out** H to 68 omit **and she had her hand out**

71.27
MS: *Miss Havisham and I had never once stopped* H to 68 omit **once**

71.38
MS: *Sarah Pocket (a blandly* **vicious** *old personage)* H to 68 omit **old**

72.16–17
MS, H, M: *to feast on one's relations* AYR: *to feast on one's relations*—**as if one was a Giant**

73.32–33
MS, H: *a spontaneous growth* **of feeble attempts** M corr. to *a spontaneous growth* **of weak attempts**

74.11
MS, H: *and* **ran it** *into my stomach* M corr. to *and* **butted it** *into my stomach*

74.12–14
MS, H: *it was . . .* **particularly disagreeable just after lunch** H: *it was . . .* **just after bread and meat**

74.35–36
MS, H: *he had a way . . . that was* **full of appearance and highly impressive** M canc. **and highly impressive**

75.1–2
MS: *I . . . saw him . . . with his face exceedingly fore-shortened* H: *I . . . saw him . . . with a bloody nose and his face exceedingly fore-shortened*
75.7
MS: *His spirit was extraordinary* H: *His spirit inspired me with great respect*
75.19
MS: *He seemed so brave and simple* H: *He seemed so brave and innocent*
75.21
MS: *I regarded myself . . . as a species of young wolf* H: *I regarded myself . . . as a species of savage young wolf*
75.22
MS: *I got dressed . . . wiping my face and nose* H: omits *and nose* M corr. to *I got dressed . . . wiping my sanguinary face*
76.27–29
MS, H, M: *I explored the garden . . . and all was lifeless and deserted* AYR to 68 omit *and deserted*
76.40–44
MS: *three hours at a stretch, or even more. I . . . fall into a general mention of the journeys as many . . . because I am now going to sum up a period of at least six or eight months.* H: *at a stretch. I . . . fall into a general mention of these journeys as numerous . . . because . . . eight or ten months.*
76.43–44
MS: *I am now going to sum up a period of at least six or eight months* H: *I . . . sum up . . . eight or ten months*
77.39–40
MS: *How could my temperament fail to be influenced* H: *How could my character . . . influenced*
77.6
M, H: *she seemed to like my being ignorant* M. corr. to *she seemed to prefer my being ignorant*
77.14–15
MS to AYR: *when I said yes . . . [she] seemed to enjoy it greedily in secret* 61–68 omit *in secret*
78.5–7
MS, H: *why Biddy had a deep concern in everything I told her, I did not know then, though I think I know now. Shade of poor Biddy, forgive me!* M corr. to *Shade . . . forgive me!*
78.26
MS: *what [Miss Havisham] would do with me* H: *what [Miss Havisham] would do with me and for me*
78.28–29
MS to AYR: *my sister spoke of me as if she were morally wrenching . . . my teeth* 61: *my sister spoke to me as if . . . my teeth*
78.41–42
MS, H: *my sister would . . . swoop upon me* M. corr. to *my sister would . . . yawn, and, catching hold of me as it were incidentally, would swoop upon me*
79.37–38
MS: *why he hadn't married a Negro slave* H: *why he hadn't married a Negress slave*
80.11
MS: *a Rampageous way of putting the case* H to 68 omit *Rampageous*
80.17–18
MS, H: *carrying . . . a pair of pattens, and an umbrella* M. corr. to *carrying a pair of pattens, a spare shawl, and an umbrella*
83.22
MS, H, M: *he was insanely proceeding up-stairs* AYR: *he was steadily proceeding up-stairs*
83.44–45
MS: *"Which that were my own belief," assented Joe—"her compliments to Mrs. Gargery"* H: *"Which . . . belief," answered Joe, her compliments to Mrs. J. Gargery"*
87.19
MS: *I never uttered a murmur* H: *I never breathed a murmur*
87.35–36
MS: *I was constantly haunted by the fear that [Estella] would . . . find me out* H to 68 omit *constantly*
88.36–38
MS: *the sails . . . looking as if they belonged to sunken ships* H: *the sails . . . belonged to sunken ships that were still sailing on at the bottom of the water*
90.15
MS: *"Yes, Joe, but look here. What I wanted to say* H: *"Yes, Joe; but what I wanted to say*
91.38
MS: *"Don't lose your temper, old man," said Joe* H to 68 omit *old man*
92.44–45
MS: *my sister, who had dropped at the window* H: *my sister, who had dropped insensible at the window*
93.26
MS: *Everything I saw was unchanged* H: *Everything was unchanged*

94.16
MS, H, M: *leaf after leaf, ever since he was taken up* AYR: *leaf . . . ever since his course began*

94.22–23
MS: *it became sheer monomania in Maria to care a button* H: *it became . . . in my master's daughter to care a button*

94.25–26
MS: *even after I was happily hanged in my public character* H to 68 omit *in my public character*

94.32–95.1
MS: *we found a heavy mist out, and it fell wet and thick without expending itself* H to 68 omit *without expending itself*

95.34–35
MS: *Mr. Wopsle died amiably at Camberwell, and exceedingly game on Bosworth Field* H: *Mr. Wopsle died . . . on Bosworth Field, and in the greatest agonies at Glastonbury*

95.36
MS: *Orlick sometimes growled, "Beat it out, Clem!" and took his right hand out of his pocket to make a blow at the air with* H to 68 omit *and took . . . the air with*

96.23
M to 62: *while she was wife of Joe* 68: *while she was the wife of Joe*

98.1–2
MS, H: *They took up several wrong people* M corr. to *They took up several obviously wrong people*

99.13–14
MS, H, M: *I bethought me of a crutch . . . and I borrowed one of a cripple in the village* AYR to 68 omit *of a cripple*

99.36–37
MS, H, M: *such as I have seen pervade the bearing of a frightened child* AYR to 68 omit *frightened*

101.1
MS: *"Biddy," I exclaimed* H: *"Biddy," I exclaimed in amazement*

101.35–36
MS: *the admission of Biddy into my most secret confidence:* H: *the admission of Biddy into my inner confidence*

102.1
MS: *shaking her head with a sorrowful and compassionate air* H to 68 omit *and compassionate*

104.44
MS: *I . . . tried perseveringly to have him dismissed* H to 68 omit *perseveringly*

104.6
MS: *When we came near the churchyard, by which our road home lay* H to 68 omit *by which . . . lay*

105.5–6
MS: *the plain honest working life . . . had nothing in it to be shirked or to be ashamed of* H to 68 omit *shirked or to be*

107.28
MS: *and had better stop in his reckless and shuffling career* H to 68 omit *and shuffling*

107.44–45
MS to AYR: Following *my second visit to Miss Havisham. His appearance was too remarkable for me to have forgotten* 61 to 68 omit sentence

108.16–17
MS: *the state-parlour . . . was feebly lighted by one candle and was very cold.* H to 68 omit *and was very cold*

109.9–10
MS to 61: *as a young fellow of great expectations* 62 to 68: *as a young fellow of Great Expectations*

109.25
MS to AYR: *When that intention may be carried out* 61: *When or where that intention may be carried out*

109.26
MS, H: *It may be years hence; even many years* M canc. *even many years*

109.31
MS: *the reasons of this condition* H: *the reasons of this prohibition*

109.35–36
MS: *the person from whom I take my instructions* H to 68: *person . . . my instructions, and for whom I am not otherwise responsible*

113.31
MS, H: *I felt in a manner offended* M: *I felt offended*

114.3
MS, H: *Mr. and Mrs. Hubble might like to see you in your new figure* M corr. to *Mr. and Mrs. Hubble . . . in your new gen-teel figure*

114.10
MS: "Ah, that indeed, Pip!" said Joe. "If you couldn't abear yourself, it wouldn't answer."
H: "Ah . . . ," said Joe. "If you couldn't abear yourself—"
114.20–21
MS: I soon exchanged a very affectionate good-night with [Biddy] and Joe H to 68 omit very
114.36
MS: I heard my name mentioned in a gentle loving tone H omits gentle M corr. to I heard . . . endearing tone
114.42–43
MS: a blessing from Joe—not obtruded on me H: a blessing from Joe—not obtruded on me or paraded before me
118.30
MS: with dreadful severity, evidently appreciating the danger H, M: with dreadful severity, foreseeing the danger AYR: with a dreadfully severe stare, foreseeing the danger
120.2
MS, H: Joseph! Joseph! M corr. to Joseph!! Joseph!!!
120.22–23
MS: "Ah poultry, poultry . . . !" said Mr. Pumblechook, shaking his head at the fowl H: "Ah . . . !" said Mr. Pumblechook, apostrophising the fowl
123.14–15
MS: you will always keep the name of Pip? H: you will always keep the name of Pip! M corr. to you will always keep the name of Pip, you know
123.46
MS: it might be so, or might seem to be so H to 68 omit or might seem to be so
124.1
MS: I wanted the heart to go downstairs H: I wanted the resolution to go downstairs
124.13–14
MS, H, M: I remained up there, trying to cheat myself by repeatedly unlocking . . . my small portmanteau AYR to 68 omit trying to cheat myself by
124.16
MS: It was a hurried breakfast with no taste in it, and it was a most unsatisfactory time. At last I got up from the meal H to 68 omit and it . . . At last
124.34
MS, H: we need never be ashamed of shedding tears M corr. to we need . . . of our tears
124, 38
MS, H: So subdued was I by those tears and by their breaking out more than once M canc. more than once
125.3–4
MS: it was now too late and too far to go back, and I went on heavily H to 68 omit heavily
125.4–5
MS, H: and the world was before me M corr. to and the world lay spread before me

SECOND STAGE

129.8
MS: whether it was not rather frowning, ugly, crooked, narrow, and smoky H: whether it was not rather ugly, crooked, narrow, and smoky M corr. to whether it was not rather ugly, crooked, narrow, and dirty
129.26
MS: The coachman glanced at Mr. Jaggers's name, and answered, "A shilling . . ." H to 68 omit glanced at Mr. Jaggers's name, and
130.24–25
MS: such as an old rusty pistol, a sword in a scabbard, an old horseman's great coat, several strange-looking boxes H to 68 omit an old . . . great coat
130.34–35
MS: I . . . became fascinated by the dismal spell H: I . . . became fascinated by the dismal atmosphere
131.29–30
MS: I thought myself well rid of him for a shilling, and fairly ran away H to 68 omit and fairly ran away
132.3–4
MS: a knot of three men and two women standing on the look-out at a corner H to 68 omit standing on the look-out
132.46
MS: "Then why the Devil," said Mr. Jaggers, "do you come here?" H to 68 omit the Devil
133.3–4
MS: I'll . . . let him slip through my fingers. I swear I will! H to 68 omit I swear I will!
134.9
MS: you blundering villain H: you blundering booby

135.15–16
MS: *We found a new set of* **suspicious-looking** *people lingering outside* H to 68 omit **suspicious-looking**
135.25–27
M: *The chisel . . . had given them up without an effort to smooth them off,* **and in the same absence of finish had left the deep lower lines of his face without a curve** H to 68 omit **and . . . curve**
135.27–28
MS: *I judged him to be a bachelor from* **the frayed and buttonless** *condition of his linen* H to 68 omit **and buttonless**
136.6
MS: **That depends on what you call very wicked.** *You may get cheated, robbed, and murdered, in London* H to 68 omit **That depends . . . wicked.**
136.22–23
MS, H: **At Hornsey, north of London** M corr. to **At Hammersmith, west of London**
136.35
MS, H: *I now found Barnard to be* **a ghost,** *or fiction* M corr. to *I now found Barnard to be* **a disembodied spirit,** *or fiction*
137.3–4
MS: *as if . . . the soul of Barnard were being slowly* **glutted** *by the gradual suicide* H: *as if . . . slowly* **appeased** *by the gradual suicide*
137.6–7
MS, H: *it had strewn ashes on its head* **and on all its members** M canc. **and on all its members**
140.9
MS to AYR: *My father is Miss* **Havisham's nephew** 61: *My father is Miss* **Havisham's cousin** [see Errata note at 168.21 below]
142.13–14
MS: *He married his second wife privately because he was proud* **and his daughter was proud** H to 68 omit **and his daughter was proud**
143.3–4
MS to 61: **all she possessed,** *certainly came out then* 62 to 68: **all the susceptibility she possessed,** *certainly came out then*
143.31–32
MS: *What was in [the letter], further than that it most heartlessly broke the marriage off, nobody knows* H: *What was in [the letter] . . .* **I can't tell you, because I don't know**
144.25
MS: *He replied,* **"a merchant"** H: *He replied,* **"A capitalist—an Insurer of Ships"**
144.25–27
MS: *he saw me glancing about the room in search of* **merchandise** H: *he saw me . . . in search of some tokens of* **Shipping, or capital**
144.28–30
MS: *I had grand ideas . . . of* **merchants** *in the City, and I began to think with awe of having laid a young* **merchant** *on his back . . . and cut his* **commercial** *head open* H: *I had grand ideas . . . of* **Insurers of Ships** *in the City, and I . . . laid a young* **Insurer** *on his back . . . and cut his* **responsible** *head open*
144.33–37
MS omits **I shall not rest satisfied with merely employing my capital in insuring ships. I shall buy up some good Life Assurance shares, and cut into the Direction. I shall do a little in the mining way. None of these things will interfere with my chartering a few thousand tons on my own account, I think**
145.3–4
MS: *I think I shall trade, also . . . for sugar, tobacco, and rum.* **Also to China.** *Also to Ceylon* H to 68 omit **Also to China.**
145.8–9
MS: *I asked him where* **he mostly traded to** H: *I asked him where* **the ships he insured mostly traded to**
145.11
MS: *that pursuit seemed more in keeping with Barnard's Inn,* **than either the East India trade or the Elephants' tusk trade** H to 68 omit **than either . . . tusk trade**
145.21–22
MS: *it would be difficult to lay by . . . capital from such a source of income,* **after defraying all current expences.** H to 68 omit **after . . . expences**
145.30–31
MS omits **When you have once made your capital, you have nothing to do but employ it.**
146.14–16
MS: *the eggs from which young* **merchants** *were hatched were incubated in dust and heat* H: *the eggs from which young* **Insurers** *were hatched . . . and heat*
146.35–36
MS: *I saw at once, quite as plainly as I ever saw afterwards, that Mr. and Mrs. Pocket's*

children H: omits *and* **Mrs.** M: canc. *at once* AYR: *I saw that Mr. and Mrs. Pocket's children*
146.38–39
MS: *two nursemaids* **who had a general air of being Mrs. Pocket's proprietors,** *were looking about them* H to 68 omit *who had* . . . *proprietors*

[*For substantive changes involving Mrs. Pocket in this and the following chapter, see pp. 455–61. The emendations are not separately recorded.*]

148.11–12
MS: *He was* **quite** *a young-looking man, in spite of his perplexities, and his manner seemed* **quite unstudied and natural** H: *He was a young-looking man,* . . . *perplexities, and his manner seemed* **natural** M corr. to *He was a young-looking man,* . . . *perplexities* **and his very grey hair,** *and his manner seemed* **quite natural**
148.12–15
MS omits *I* **use the word natural, in the sense of its being unaffected; there was something comic in his distraught way, as if it had been downright ludicrous but for his own perception that it was very near being so**
148.16–18
MS, H: *he said to Mrs. Pocket, "Belinda, I hope you have welcomed Mr. Pip?"* H: *he said to Mrs. Pocket,* **rather anxiously,** *"Belinda* . . . *Pip?"* M corr. to *he said to Mrs. Pocket,* **with a rather anxious contraction of his eyebrows, which were black and handsome,** *"Belinda* . . . *Pip?"*
149.15–19
MS: *Mr. Pocket* . . . *introduced me to* . . . **Jumble** *and Startop* H: *Mr. Pocket* . . . **Drummle** *and Startop* [MS **Jumble** through ch. 23; from ch. 25 (194.1) **Drummle**]
149.20–21
MS: *Startop,* **holding his head with both hands** H: omits **holding** . . . **hands**
149.41–42
MS: *dull blades* **whose fathers, when influential** H: *dull blades—of whom it was remarkable that their fathers—when influential*
150.3–6
MS: *he* . . . *had turned his acquirements* **to literary accounts** H: *he* . . . *had turned his acquirements* **to the account of literary compilation and correction**
150.7
MS concludes paragraph **Whether he was ever sensible in my day of anything like a waste of his life or of anything in it, will be deducible perhaps from my occasional record of him**
152.20
MS: *We all looked* . . . *at the table-cloth while this was going on* **and nothing extraneous was heard save an inarticulate moaning from Mrs. Coiler** H to 68 omit **and nothing** . . . **from Mrs. Coiler**
152.39
MS: **in a solemn, parental way** *he asked* H: **in a distant, Missionary way** *he asked*
153.10
MS: *Mr. Pocket was quite in good spirits* **(Mrs. Coiler having gone away)** H to 68 omit **(Mrs. Coiler** . . . **away)**
153.34–35
MS: *Mrs. Pocket.* **"Is it Mary Anne's position, or mine, to find out misconduct in the cook? Besides** H to 68 omit **Is it Mary Anne's** . . . **the cook?**
154.33
MS: *Mr. Jaggers, with a short laugh,* **and biting the side of his forefinger** H to 68 omit **and** . . . **forefinger**
155.6–7
MS: *Mr. Jaggers, with a knowing* **toss** H: *Mr. Jaggers, with a knowing* **and contradictory toss**
157.1
MS, H: *if he didn't* . . . *put the* . . . *testators to sleep,* **and it looked precious like it** M corr. to **and it looked precious like it**
157.43–158.1
MS: *my guardian* . . . *was striking* . . . *everybody present with* **deadly** *awe* H omits **deadly**
159.10–11
MS: *[Her disappointments] shed a* **pale** *reflected light* H: *shed a* **full** *reflected light* M: *shed a* **feeble** *reflected light*
159.34
MS, H: *Pick us out a good one, old* **fellow** M corr. to *Pick us out a good one, old* **Briton**
160.6–7
MS: *as if the remark* **followed on the housekeeper understood** H: *as if the remark* **bestowed on the housekeeper was understood** M: as in MS
160.33
MS: **five hundred** *thieves in this town* H: **seven hundred** *thieves in this town*
162.33–34
MS, H: *repair to the* **outworks** M corr. to *repair to the* **battery**

165.7–8
MS to AYR: *I may have thought her older than she was, as it is the manner of youth to do* 61: *I may have thought her younger than she was*
165.9
MS, H: *with large blue eyes, and a quantity of streaming light hair* M corr. to *with large faded-blue eyes, and . . . streaming hair* 61: *with large faded eyes, and . . . streaming hair*
165.14
MS, H: *like the faces I had seen rise out of the caldron* M: *the faces . . . out of the Witches' caldron*
165.27–28
MS, H: *a face that . . . derived from flowing light hair* M canc. *light* 68: *a face that . . . derived from flowing air*
166.2
MS, H: *my guardian (it could have been no one else) wound him up* M to 68 omit *(it . . . else)*
166.16–17
MS, H: *with her eyes attentively and timidly fixed* M: *with her eyes attentively and entreatingly fixed*
166.21–22
MS, H, M: *Jaggers . . . obstinately compressing his lips and looking at the other side of the room* AYR to 68 omit *compressing his lips and*
166.25
MS: *The last wrist was . . . deeply seamed and scarred* H: *The last wrist was . . . deeply scarred and scarred*
166.28–29
MS, H: *Jaggers, tracing out the sinews with his forefinger without touching them* M: *Jaggers, coolly tracing out . . . without touching them* AYR to 68 omit *without touching them*
167.10
MS, H: *"You do me justice," said Drummle* M: *"You are right," said Drummle*
167.23–24
MS, H: *as you put it in your pocket, you seemed to be immensely amused at his being such an ass as to lend it* M corr. to *as you . . . your pocket, very glad to have it, you seemed immensely amused at his being so weak as to lend you* AYR: *as . . . pocket, very glad to get it, you . . . as to lend it.*
167.34–36
MS, H: *Drummle . . . swore an oath, took up a large glass, and would infallibly have flung it* M: *Drummle . . . swore . . . and would have flung it*
167.49–50
MS, H: *I thought I would . . . say a word of apology to my guardian* M to 68 omit *of apology*
168.12–13
MS, H: *he is one of the true sort; I have not been disappointed in him* M canc. *I have not been disappointed in him*
168.21
MS, H add, following *family hole: He called me Blacksmith, when he went away, qualified to be an indifferent hostler or a bad gamekeeper* No. 220 AYR for 16 March 1861 carries this note beneath chapter XXVII: ERRATUM. In No. 97, Chapter XXII, of Great Expectations, page 481, second column, line 15 from the bottom, the word "nephew" is printed instead of "cousin." The line should read, "My father is Miss Havisham's cousin."
168.24
MS to 61: *in company of Mr. Wopsle* 62 to 68: *in company with Mr. Wopsle*
168.24–25
MS to 61: *Tuesday morning 9 o'clock* 62 to 68: *Tuesday morning at nine o'clock*
168.30–32
MS to 61: *Your affectionate / Servant / Biddy* 62 to 68: *Your affectionate servant Biddy*
169.3–4
MS: *My greatest comfort was, that he was coming to Barnard's Inn* H: *My greatest reassurance was . . . Inn*
169.16–17
MS, H: *I had made my monster* M corr. to *this monster*
169.40–41
MS, H: *the name of the avenging boy* M corr. to *the compromising name of the avenging boy*
170.3
MS, H: *I am delighted to see you, Joe* M corr. to *I am glad to see you, Joe*
171.27–28
MS, H: *since you are so kind as put that name to it* M corr. to *since you are so kind as make chice of coffee*
171.41–42
MS, H: *we didn't find that it come up to . . . the red picters at the shop-doors* M corr. to *we didn't . . . the red bills at the shop-doors*

173.11–13
MS: following *Miss A*, Dickens inserts **(see back)**; on verso leaf has "*Miss A., Joe! Miss Havisham?*" / "*Which I say, Sir,*" replied Joe, "*Miss A, or Havisham*" **(Printer Then run on)**
173.12–13
MS, H: *which I say, Sir,*" replied Joe M corr. to *which . . . Joe, **with an air of legal formality, as if he were making his will***
173.25–26
MS: *I wish you . . . prospering **more and more*** H: *I wish you . . . **to a greater and greater heighth***
173.44–46
MS, H: *you come . . . **and look at** [H: **see**] Joe . . . at the old work, **as he used to be when he first carried you about*** M corr. to *you come . . . **and see** Joe . . . **sticking to the old work***
174.5
MS: *I looked for him in the **streets*** H: *I looked . . . in the **neighbouring** streets*
176.24–25
MS, H: *The sensation was like being **touched with** some pungent acid . . .* M corr. to *The sensation was like being **touched in the marrow with** some pungent acid*
176.33–34
MS: *I ought to restore a couple of **guineas*** H: *I ought to restore a couple of **pounds*** M corr. to *I ought to restore a couple of **pounds sterling***
177.9–10
MS: ***Two guineas.*** H: ***Two one pound notes. I'd sell all the friends I ever had for one.*** M corr. to ***Two one pound notes. I'd sell all the friends I ever had for one, and think it a blessed good bargain***
177.19–20
MS, H: *He . . . got made a Lifer. **That's what he took by** his motion, and **that's all I know of him.*** M canc. *That's what . . . I know of him*
179.20
MS to AYR: *I loved her because I found her irresistible* 61: *I loved her **simply** because I found her irresistible*
179.21–23
MS: *I loved her against reason, against promise, against peace, against happiness* H: *I loved her against . . . peace, **against hope,** against happiness*
179.25
MS, H: *if I had devoutly **and conventionally** believed her to be human perfection* M canc. *and conventionally*
180.41–42
MS: ***your brother** and family are all well* H: ***Mr. Pocket** and family are all well*
181.47
MS: *She lured me on. **I was** every moment fascinated **more and more.*** H to 68 omit **I was . . . more and more.**
183.30
MS: *No! . . . I **have never given it away.*** H: *No! . . . I **have not bestowed my tenderness anywhere***
183.37–38
MS, H: *Instantly* [MS **And** *instantly*] *the ghost passed once more, **for the last time,** and was gone.* M canc. **for the last time**
183.43–44
MS: *that might be laid aside now with other old **incumbrances*** H: *that . . . old **belongings***
184.50
MS, H: *she came to . . . a **desperate** cry* M corr. to *she came to . . . a **wild** cry*
185.18–19
MS: *She . . . **said** he was as punctual as ever* H: *She . . . **stammered that** he was as . . . ever*
186.10–11
MS: *When she spoke to him, he **looked at the table-cloth and** listened* H to 68 omit **looked at the table-cloth and**
186.13
MS: *his face never showed the least consciousness **of being observed*** H to 68 omit **of being observed**
186.35–37
MS, H: *Miss Havisham, in a **wild** way, had put some of the most beautiful jewels . . . **into Estella's hair, and about her bosom and waist*** M corr. to *Miss Havisham, in a **fantastic** way, had put . . . jewels . . . **into Estella's hair, and about her bosom and arms***
187.7
MS: *in the room **next to me, and before he went to bed I could hear him dipping Miss Havisham's into the washing basin and blowing it out of himself like a whale. It would have been far better for me if I could have done the same.*** H: *in the room **next to mine.***
187.13–14
MS: *When should I awaken the heart within her, **if it were really mute and sleeping** now?* M corr. to *When . . . within her, **that was mute and sleeping** now?*

190.8
MS: *She is thousands of miles away,* **as yet** H: She is thousands of miles away, **from me**
190.45–46
MS: *I said it rather like a reluctant concession to truth* H: I said it rather **(people often do** **so, in such cases)** like a reluctant concession to truth
194.8–9
MS: *The Queen of Denmark, a very* **fine woman,** *though no doubt* **in conduct brazen** H: The Queen of Denmark, a very **buxom lady,** though . . . **historically brazen**
194.18
MS: *on his being detected* **in clerical disguise** H: on his being detected **in holy orders**
195.5–6
MS: *the churchyard . . . had the appearance of a* **wood** H: the churchyard . . . of a **primeval forest**
195.32–33
MS: **a man** *with an unnaturally heavy smear of eyebrow* H: **a Jewish man** with . . . *eyebrow*
196.9
MS, H: *with* **a large Danish order** *hanging round his neck* M corr. to with **a large Danish sun or star** hanging round his neck
197.3
MS, H: *Herbert said from behind . . .* **"massive and excellent"** M corr. to Herbert said . . . **"massive and concrete"**
200.31
MS, H: *I think I* **shall be off** *on Monday* M corr. to I think **I shall be out of this** on Monday
201.3
MS, H: *he is sure* **to be hanged** *on Monday* M corr. to he is sure **to be executed** on Monday
203.12–13
MS: *the . . . proprietor was boiling down the horses* H: the . . . proprietor was boiling down the horses **for the refreshment department**
204.2
MS: *she had not laughed languidly but with real* **mirth and** *enjoyment* H to 68 omit **mirth and**
204.40–41
MS: *Estella,* **shrinking away** *the instant I touched her cheek* H: Estella, **gliding away** the instant I touched her cheek
205.5
MS: *a pale* **unhealthy** *loaf* H: a pale loaf **with a powdered head**
207.21–22
MS: *I had some notion . . . of begging him to accept my confidence* **and telling him about Estella** H to 68 omit **and telling him about Estella**
209.3–4
MS: *he began to look about him* **more hopefully** *about mid-day* H: he began to look about him **more hopelessly** about mid-day M corr. to MS
209.30–31
MS: *in which he consorted with an ink-jar,* **an iron safe,** *a hat-peg* M to 68 omit **an iron safe**
211.33–34
MS, H: *I had the highest opinion of the wisdom* **and prudence** *of this same Margin* M canc. **and prudence**
212.6–7
MS: *and* **the gap** *it made in the smooth ground was wonderful* H: and **the depth of the gap . . .** was wonderful M corr. to MS
213.8
MS: *into black long-clothes, like* **a baby** H: into . . . clothes, like **an African baby**
213.11
MS, H: *Poor dear Joe,* **in a little black cloak** *tied in a large bow* M corr. to Poor dear Joe, **entangled in a little black cloak . . .** bow
214.20–21
MS: **And there, Joe and I standing side by side against the very grave stone on which the fugitive had put me that dismal evening long ago,** *my sister was laid quietly in the earth* H: And there, my sister was laid quietly in the earth
215.17
MS: *I did not like the thought of* **bringing tears into her eyes** H to 68: I . . . thought of **making her cry again**
215.45–46
MS, H: *she laid her* **hand** *down on his shoulder quite content* M corr. to she laid her **head** down . . . content
217.20
MS: *The mists were rising* **again** *as I walked away* H to 68: **Once more,** the mists were rising as I walked away
219.17–18
MS: *I am the mere agent* H: **As I have told you before,** I am the mere agent

220.11–12
MS: *When that person **appears**, my part in this business will cease* H: *When that person **discloses**, my part . . . will cease*
222.5–6
MS to AYR: *Herbert . . . thought . . . he must have committed a felony **and forgotten it*** 61: *Herbert . . . committed a felony **and forgotten the details of it***
223.12–13
MS: *[Miss Skiffins] might have been **some few years younger*** H: *[Miss Skiffins] might have been **some two or three years younger***
224.28–29
MS, H: *still, **there** are Newgate cobwebs about* M corr. to *still, **it may be mentioned that there** are Newgate cobwebs about*
226.38–39
MS: *I did really cry in good earnest when I went to bed.* H: *I . . . to bed, **to think that my expectations had done some good to somebody***
226.41–42
MS: *before I pass on to all the changes **and chances** [my life] involved, I must give **one chapter** to Estella* H to 68 omit ***and chances*** [MS, H: *I must give **a chapter**;* MS corr. to ***one chapter***]
226.42–43
MS omits final sentence: *It is not much to give to the theme that so long filled my heart*
228.3
MS: *I should have **retorted** that Love was . . . blind* H: *I should have **reported** that Love was . . . blind* M corr. to *I should have **replied** that Love was . . . blind*
229.9–10
MS: *Miss Havisham, as I had her . . . **before me**, and always had had her **before me*** H: *Miss Havisham, as I had her . . . **before my eyes**, and always had had her **before my eyes***
230.38
MS: *"So proud . . . !" moaned Miss Havisham . . . **as she contemplated Estella*** H to 68 omit ***as she contemplated Estella***
231.25–26
MS, H: *The success is not mine, the failure is not mine, but **the two together are me*** M corr. to *The success is not mine . . . **the two together make me***
231.45
MS, H, M: ***a million** of Miss Havishams haunted me* AYR: ***a thousand** . . . haunted me*
233.27
MS: *a contemptible, clumsy, **sulky fellow*** H: *a contemptible, clumsy, **sulky booby***
235.2–3
MS: *It may have its effect on others, **and I may mean it to have*** H: *It may . . . on others, **and may be meant to have***
235.24
MS: *the **crushing** slab that was to fall* H: *the **heavy** slab that . . . fall*
235.30–31
MS: *the rope was put into his hand* H: *the rope **from the great iron ring** was put into his hand*
235.32–33
MS: *all the work . . . that tended to the end, had **gradually** been accomplished* H to 68 omit ***gradually***
238.2
MS to 61: *"It's **disapinting** to a man," he said in a coarse broken voice* 62 to 68: *"It's **disappointing** to a man," he said in a coarse broken voice*
238.32
MS to 62: *"You acted **noble**, my boy," said he. "**Noble, Pip**."* 68: *"You acted **nobly**, my boy," said he. "**Noble Pip!**"*
239.16–17
MS to AYR: *I saw **with new amazement** that his eyes were full of tears* 61 to 68 omit ***new***
241.25–26
MS, H: *a beauty; that's a gentleman's . . . with rubies; that's a gentleman's* M corr. to *a beauty; that's a gentleman's, **I hope** . . . with rubies; that's a gentleman's, **I hope***
242.4–6
MS, H: *From that there hut and that there hiring out, **I got my liberty*** M corr. to *From . . . hiring out, **I got money left me by my master (which died, and had been the same as me), and got my liberty***
243.3–4
MS to 61: *the wretched man, after **loading wretched me with his gold*** 62: *the wretched man, after **loading me with his wretched gold***
243.24
MS: *I began fully to know how **cast adrift now** I was* H: *I began fully to know how **wrecked** I was*

243.41–42
MS: *I had had mysterious warnings of this man's **arrival*** H: *I had had mysterious warnings of this man's **approach***
244.12
MS, H: **There was still much of the old marsh character upon him, for** *he had rolled a handkerchief round his head* M canc. **There was still . . . upon him, for**

THIRD STAGE

246.25–26
MS, H: *my fire . . . burnt with a raw pale **look** at that **dead** time of the morning* M corr. *to my fire . . . burnt with a raw pale **flare** at . . . morning* AYR to 68 omit **dead**
247.4
MS: *he had **a more villainous look** by daylight* H, M: *he had **a villainous look** by daylight* AYR: *he had **a worse look** by daylight*
247.12
MS, H: *"What is **your own name?**" I asked him* M corr. to *"What is **your real name?**" I asked him*
247.38
MS, M: **wotever I done** *is worked out and paid for* H: **whatever I done** *is . . . for* 61: **what I done** *is . . . for*
248.3–4
MS: *he looked terribly **like an old dog*** H, M: *he looked terribly **like a hungry old dog***
248.38
MS, H, M: *Don't you be **afraid** on it* AYR: *Don't you be **afeerd** on it*
250.23–24
MS: *his experience . . . gave him **a superstitious reliance** on its powers* H to 68 omit **superstitious**
250.44–251.1
MS, H, M: *I . . . was so fortunate as to secure the second floor **for Mr. Provis*** AYR: *I . . . **for my uncle, Mr. Provis***
251.33
MS, H, M: *I pleaded with a **miserable** heart* AYR: *I pleaded with **a downcast** heart*
251.37–38
MS, H, M: *"I have no more to say," said I . . . after **standing downcast** for a little while* AYR: *"I . . . after **standing silent** for a little while*
250.16
MS, H: **Just so.** *A letter, under date Portsmouth* M corr. to **You know it's Provis.** *A letter, under date Portsmouth*
253.35–36
MS, H: *he would ask me to read to him—"**Some French**, dear boy!"* M corr. to *he would ask me to read to him—"**Foreign language**, dear boy!"*
254.11–12
MS: *I saw his jack-knife* H: *I saw his jack-knife **shining in his hand***
254.12
MS, H, M: *"**Steady!** It's Herbert!" I said* AYR: *"**Quiet!** It's Herbert!" I said*
254.29–30
MS, H: *Herbert, looking with a friendly **uneasiness** at me, complied* M corr. to *Herbert, looking at me with a friendly **uneasiness and amazement**, complied*
254.36
MS: *my insurmountable repugnance towards the man* H to 68 omit **insurmountable**
256.18–19
MS to AYR: *I . . . who have now no expectations **at all*** 61 to 68 omit **at all**
257.2
MS: *that would be **his revenge** if you forsook him* H: *that would be **his reckless course** if you forsook him*
257.9–10
MS: *I would far rather have worked **at journey-work** in the forge* H to 68 omit **at journey-work**
257.11
MS, M, AYR, 61, 62, 68: *there was no **raving** off the question, What was to be done?* H: *there was no **staving** off . . . done?*
257.21–22
MS: *I know nothing of his life. **He is a mystery to me.*** H to 68 omit **He is a mystery to me**
258.11–13
MS to AYR: *for a "fashionable crib" in which he could have a "shake-down" near Hyde Park* 61: *for a "fashionable crib" near Hyde Park, in which he could have a "shake-down"*
259.15–16
MS, H: *there warn't **many insides of houses** known to me* M corr. to *there warn't **many insides of furnished houses** known to me*

260.1–2
MS, H: *a travelling Dwarf . . . learnt me to write* M corr. to *a travelling Giant . . . learnt me to write*

260.4
MS, H: *At Epsom races, a matter of twenty year ago* M corr. to *At Epsom races a matter of over twenty year ago*

260.6
MS, H: *His right name was Compey* [thus until ch. 45] M corr. to *Compeyson* throughout

261.7
MS: *He was in a decline of his own bringing on* H to 68 omit *of his own bringing on*

262.3
MS: *take that ugly shroud away* H: *take that ugly thing away*

262.23–25
MS: *He looked about him in a confused way, as if he had lost his place in the book of his remembrance; and I thought that as he turned his face to the fire, and spread his hands broader on his knees, and lifted them off and put them on again, I saw something like the old click come into his throat* H to 68 omit *I thought that as* and *I saw something . . . into his throat*

262.47
MS, H: *My lord and gentlemen, here you have afore you* M corr. to *My lord . . . here you has afore you*

263.1–2
MS, H: *the elder . . . who will be spoke to as a hardened offender* M corr. to *the elder . . . spoke to as such*

263.11–13
MS: *and warn't it Compey as could speak to 'em . . . ah! and wi' verses in his speech, and, to the best of my belief, Latin too* H to 68 omit *and . . . Latin too*

263.21–22
MS: *and ain't it him as the Judge's woice trembles over* H: *and ain't it him as the Judge is sorry for because he might have done so well*

263.22–23
MS, H: *ain't it me as the Judge perceives to be a man of wiolent passion* M corr. to *ain't it me as the Judge perceives to be a old offender of wiolent passion*

263.38–39
MS: *he regarded me with a look of affection that made him abhorrent to me again, though I had been inclined to pity him* H: *he regarded me . . . almost abhorrent to me again, though I had felt great pity for him*

264.37–38
MS: *If Compey . . . should discover his return, I could hardly doubt that he would put the rope round his neck* H: *If Compeyson . . . should discover his return, I could hardly doubt the consequence*

265.24
MS: *I confess with remorse that I was capable of almost any meanness towards Joe* H to 68 omit *I confess with remorse that*

266.10
MS, H: *I am told it's very like Shropshire* M corr. to *I am told it's very like your Shropshire*

266.32
MS: *Curious little public-houses—and smithies—and convicts* H: *Curious little public-houses—and smithies—and that*

267.15–16
MS: *"I don't throw glasses." / "I do," said Drummle, and laughed* H to 68 omit *and laughed*

267.29
MS to 61: *"Wai-ter!" said Drummle* 62: *"Waiter!" said Drummle*

268.15
MS: *Miss Havisham was looking on with her hands on the head of her crutch-stick* H to 68 omit *with . . . stick*

270.37–38
MS, H: *It would have been cruel to practise on the affections of a poor boy* M corr. to *It . . . practise on the susceptibility of a poor boy*

270.40–41
MS to AYR: *in the endurance of her own suffering, she forgot mine* 61 to 68: *in . . . of her own trial, she forgot mine*

271.7
MS: *It is in the nature formed for me* H: *It is in the nature formed within me*

272.7
MS: *Do we part on this, you silly boy?* H: *Do we . . . this, you visionary boy?*

272.28–29
MS: *let me feel now what pain I may* H: *let . . . what distress I may* M corr. to *let . . . what sharp distress I may*

272.32
MS: *I held her hand to my cheek some lingering moments* H: *I held her hand to my lips some lingering moments*

272.39–40
MS: *I . . . then struck off to walk* **to London** H: *I . . . to walk* **all the way to London**
272.44
MS: *It was past midnight when I crossed* **old London Bridge** H: *It . . . when I crossed* **London Bridge**
273.12–15
MS: **Please read this, here.** *. . . * **Don't go home** H: PLEASE READ THIS HERE. . . . DON'T GO HOME
273.26–27
MS: *the chamberlain had brought me . . . the good old constitutional rushlight* **of those palmy days** H: *the chamberlain . . . constitutional rushlight* **of those virtuous days**
274.12–13
MS: *the fireplace sighed, the little washing-stand* **complained of pain** H: *the fireplace sighed, the little washing-stand* **ticked**
276.39–40
MS: *You have heard of a man of bad character, whose true name is* **Compeyson** [first appearance of Compeyson's name, -*son* added separately]
279.23–24
MS, H: *wooden frames . . . that looked like* **infirm** *hay-making rakes* M corr. to *wooden frames . . . that looked like* **superannuated** *hay-making frames*
281.19–20
MS, H: *"Look here," said Herbert, showing the basket* **with a smile** M corr. to *"Look here," said Herbert, showing the basket* **with a compassionate and tender smile**
281.20
MS: *here's Clara's supper* H: *here's* **poor** *Clara's supper*
282.18
MS to 68: *my* **fully** *determining to say nothing to him respecting* **Compeyson** [thus in MS hereafter]
283.39–40
MS: **thank God,** *there was redeeming youth and trust . . . in Chinks's Basin* H to 68 omit **thank God**
284.27–28
MS: **We waited for a hint from Wemmick,** *and he made no sign* H to 68 omit **a hint from**
286.8–13
MS: *I . . . wore out the time in . . . baking in a hot blast of dinners,* **like the meat in an unwholesome pie** H to 68 omit **like the meat . . . pie**
288.7
MS: *I could* **almost swear** *to him* H to 68 omit **almost**
290.22–23
MS: *my rushlight tower . . . had opened white eyes in the* **ghostly** *wall* H: *my rushlight . . . in the* **ghostly** *wall* M corr. to MS
291.25–26
MS: *if it should be a question of intellect* [Drummle] *certainly will not* [get the better of Estella]. **You saw him here** H to 68 omit **You saw him here**
292.30–31
MS: *It was a* **heavy** *evening, for Wemmick drew his wine . . .* **strictly** *as a matter of . . . business* H: *It was a* **dull** *evening, for Wemmick drew his wine . . .* **quite** *as a matter of business*
293.5
MS: **"D—it!"** *he added* H: **"Deuce take me,"** *he added*
293.10
MS: *She has been with him many a long year.* **A score of years.** H to AYR omit **A score of years**
293.18–19
MS: **A score of years ago,** *that woman was tried at the Old Bailey for murder* H: **A score or so of years ago,** *that woman was tried . . . for murder*
293.34–35
MS: *The murdered woman was found dead in a barn* H: *The murdered woman—***more a match for the man, certainly, in point of years***—was found dead in a barn*
294.12–13
MS: *she had* (?) **straggled** *through a great lot of brambles* H to 68: *she had* **struggled** *. . . brambles*
294.17–18
MS: *little shreds of her dress and little* (?) **spirts of blood . . .** **which were also put in evidence** H to 68 omit **which were also put in evidence** [H: **spirts** emended to **spots**]
294.18
MS: *But* **one of the boldest points he made** H: *But* **the boldest point he made**
296.30–31
MS: *She asked this question in a*[n] *. . . tone of sympathy* **that choked me** H to 68 omit **that choked me**
296.37
MS: *It is* **nobly forgiving** *in you to tell me that you have other causes of unhappiness* H: *It is* **noble** *in you to tell me . . . unhappiness*

298.21
MS: *I took her heart* away and put ice in its place H: *I stole her heart* away and put ice in its place
298.46–47
MS, H: *I told him that I wanted a little girl* **to rear and save** *from my fate* M corr. to *I . . . wanted a little girl* **to rear and love, and save** *from my fate*
299.48–300.1
MS, H: *we were on the ground, struggling* **madly** *like desperate enemies* M canc. **madly**
301 [3–4]
MS to AYR following "*I forgive her*" have in separate paragraph: **It was the first and the last time that I ever touched her in that way. And I never saw her more.**
301.19–20
MS: *I was awakened by Miss Havisham's cries, and by her* **running to the door** H: *I was awakened . . . by her* **running at me**
303.22
MS, H: *It had happened* **about four years,** *then* M corr. to *It had happened* **some four years,** *then* AYR: *It had happened* **some three or four years,** *then*
303.23–24
MS, H: *the little girl so tragically lost would have been* **your age** M corr. to *the little girl . . .* **about your age**
303.38 [Ch. LI]
[Corrected proof VA₂ begins here]
304.9
MS: *I should probably be laid up* **with a fever** H to 68 omit **with a fever**
305.29–30
MS to AYR: *Provis's account (as Herbert* **had delivered it)** 61: *Provis's account (as Herbert* **had repeated it)**
305.41
MS: *I was afraid to look at [Wemmick]* **at that juncture** H: *I . . . [Wemmick]* **just then**
306.34–35
MS *Wemmick became* **gradually** *bolder* H to 68 omit **gradually**
306.38–39
M: *Well! . . . If I don't bring 'em here,* **Sir,** *what does it matter?* H to 68 omit **Sir**
306.46
MS: **You** *with a pleasant home?* H: **You** *with a pleasant home?*
307.22–23
MS: *so much spawn . . . to be prosecuted, defended,* **examined** H: *spawn . . . to be prosecuted, defended,* **forsaken** M: *spawn . . . to be prosecuted, defended,* **forsworn**
307.32
MS: *Part with the child* **for ever,** *unless it should be necessary to produce it* H to 68 omit **for ever**
308.11–12
MS: *if she had done* **a murder,** *she would be safer* where *she was* H: *if she had done* **such a deed, she . . .** was
309.9–11
MS, H: *Jaggers and Wemmick . . . with* **a visible refreshment** *upon them* VA₂, M corr. to *Jaggers and Wemmick . . . with* **an air of refreshment** *upon them*
309.37
MS to AYR: *My right* **hand** *was tolerably restored* 61: *My right* **arm** *was tolerably restored*
310.1
MS: *Early in the week, or say Wednesday,* **if the tide should suit** H to 68 omit **if the tide should suit**
310.5–6
MS: *we considered what to do.* **Down to that time we had never interchanged a word on the subject of my being disabled, but of course it could be kept out of view no longer** H: *we considered what to do.* **For, of course my being disabled, could now be no longer kept out of view**
314.30–32
MS: *I looked about me, noticing how the house—***a mere cabin** *of wood with a tiled roof—would not be proof against the weather* H to 68 omit **a mere cabin**
314.42
MS: *irresolute what to do,* **and looked about me.** H to 68 omit **and looked about me**
315.15
MS to AYR: *I'll make short work of* **finishing you!** 61: *I'll make short work of* **you!**
316.2
MS to AYR: "*Don't you know?*" *said he, with a* **deadly look** 61: "*Don't you know?*" *said he, with a* **deadly leer**
316.36
MS: *He'll have no more on you.* **You're dead** H: *He'll . . . on you.* **You're as good as dead** MS, H, VA₂: **You're as good as dead!** M: **You're dead!**

317.24
MS to AYR: *I smelt the strong spirits that I saw **flash** into his face* 61: *I smelt the strong spirits that I saw **flare** into his face*
317.30
MS: *It **was** you!" said I* H: *It **was** you, villain!" said I*
317.46–48
MS: *My rapid mind . . . made a picture of the street, and contrasted its lights and life with the lonely marshes* H: *My rapid mind . . . made a picture of the street **with him in it,** and . . . marshes*
318.19
MS, H, VA$_2$: *I've took up with **new companions*** M corr. to *I've took up with **new companions and new masters***
318.30
MS: *all drifting by as on **the swift tide** of my life* H: *all drifting by, as on **the swift stream** of my life*
319.17–18
MS: *his **unrelenting** eyes scowling at me* H to 68 omit **unrelenting**
319.34–35
MS: *[I] saw Orlick emerge from a **struggle*** H: *[I] saw Orlick emerge from a **struggle of men***
319.34–36
MS to 61: *[I] saw Orlick . . . clear the table at a leap and fly out into the **night.*** 62–68: *[I] saw Orlick . . . fly out into the **night!***
[Dickens has: **Printer, two white lines here** (i.e., double space)]
321.25
MS, H, VA$_2$: *[Trabb's boy] had too much **vivacity to spare*** M corr. to *[Trabb's boy] . . . **spare vivacity***
321.28–29
MS: *[I] told him that I was sorry ever to have had an ill opinion of him **(which he was quite indifferent about)*** H: *[I] told . . . of him **(which made no impression on him at all)***
322.6
MS, H, VA$_2$: *I counted . . . **to make sure I was steady*** M corr. to *I counted . . . **to make sure of myself***
322.22–23
MS, H: *As I looked at **the clustered confusion of roofs** . . . the sun rose* M, VA$_2$ canc. **confusion of**
323.11–13
MS, H: *The steamer for Hamburg and the steamer for Rotterdam would start from London at about nine on Thursday morning, **and would be in our part of the river at about noon.*** M, VA$_2$ canc. **and would . . . about noon**
323.15–16
MS, H, M: *We **had a pocket-glass with us,** and knew the distinguishing marks of each vessel* VA$_2$: canc. **had a pocket-glass with us, and**
324.29–30
MS, H: *unintelligible **sea-monsters** roaring curses* M, VA$_2$ corr. to *unintelligible **sea-creatures** roaring curses*
325.34
MS: ***"Please God,"** said I, "you will be perfectly free"* H: ***"If all goes well,"** said I, "you . . . free."*
326.31–32
MS: *some ballast lighters, shaped like a child's first rude **drawing** of a boat* H: *some ballast lighters, shaped like a child's first rude **imitation** of a boat*
327.13–14
MS, H, VA$_2$: *a collier coming by us, with her galley-fire smoking and **flaring*** M corr. to *a collier . . . smoking and **blazing***
327.18–19
MS: *we were . . . all possessed by the idea that we were **chased*** H: *we were . . . **followed***
327.22–23
MS: *we . . . eyed them **narrowly*** H: *we eyed them **nervously***
329.2
MS, H: *he went out **disgusted*** M, VA$_2$ corr. to *he went out **in disdain***
329.23–25
MS to VA$_2$: *They . . . struck out in the direction **of the sea*** AYR: *They . . . struck out in the direction **of the Nore***
329.41–42
MS, H: *He . . . sometimes stopped to clap me on the shoulder, **or take me by the hand*** M, VA$_2$ canc. **or take me by the hand**
330.21–22
MS, W, M, VA$_2$: *Meantime the galley . . . had **borne down** upon us, crossed us and come alongside* AYR: *Meantime the galley . . . had **crossed us, let us come up with her, and fallen alongside***
330.36–37
MS: *I . . . call upon him to surrender, and you **gentlemen** to assist* H to 68 omit **gentlemen**

331.19–20
MS, H: *I saw it to be Magwitch, swimming* M, VA₂ corr. to *I saw it to be Magwitch, swimming, but not swimming freely*
331.31–32
MS: *Magwitch—Provis no more—had received a very severe contusion in the chest* H: *Magwitch—Provis no longer—had received some very severe injury in the chest*
332.17–18
MS, H, VA₂: *the hunted, wounded, ironed creature* M corr. to *the hunted, wounded, shackled creature*
332.27–28
MS, H, VA₂: *That he would be mercifully treated, I could not hope* M corr. to *That he would be leniently treated, I could not hope*
333.17
MS: *I imparted to Mr. Jaggers on the first day of the proceedings, my design* H to 68 omit *on the first day of the proceedings*
333.33–34
MS, H: *notes were still legible, folded in the case of the watch he wore* M, VA₂ corr. to *notes . . . folded in a case he wore* AYR: *notes folded . . . in a case he carried*
334.26
MS: *"Well! I will." I will," said I.* H to 68: *"I will."*
335.3–4
MS: *if you . . . could . . . leave the post open* H: *if you . . . could . . . leave the question open*
335.15–17
MS: *and then the dear little thing and I will walk into the nearest church* H: *and then I shall come back for the dear little thing, and the dear little thing . . . nearest church*
335.17–19
MS: *The blessed darling comes of no family . . . What a fortune for her husband!* H: *The blessed darling comes of no family. What a fortune for the son of my mother!*
340.17–19
MS, H, 61–68: *The sun . . . made a broad shaft of light between the two-and-thirty [condemned] and the Judge, linking both together* M, VA₂, AYR: *The sun . . . Judge, banding both together*
340.21–22
MS, H, M: *the greater Judgment that knoweth all things and never errs* VA₂ corr. to *the greater Judgment that . . . cannot err*
341.4–5
MS: *I would roam the streets . . . wandering by those offices and houses where I had left the petitions, and thence to the prison where he was confined, and thence back again* H to 68 omit *and thence to the prison . . . back again*
341.5–8
MS: *To the present hour, the weary streets of London . . . with their ranges of stern shut-up houses are . . . melancholy to me* H: *To the present hour, the weary western streets of London . . . of stern shut-up mansions are . . . melancholy to me*
341.25
MS: *The number of days had mounted up to eight when I saw a greater change in him* H, M, VA₂: *The number . . . had mounted up to ten* AYR: *The number . . . had risen to ten*
341.45
MS, H: *You never do complain, dear Magwitch* M, VA₂ canc. *dear Magwitch*
342.2–3
MS: *the governor of the prison standing by me . . . said, "You needn't go."* H: *the governor standing by me . . . whispered . . . go yet. "* M, VA₂ corr. to *the governor standing near me whispered . . . go yet."*
342.12
MS: *She lived and found rich friends* H: *She lived and found powerful friends*
342.15–16
MS: *he raised my hand . . . then he gently let it sink upon his heart again* H: *he raised my hand . . . then he gently let it sink upon his breast again*
342.20–21
MS: *There were no better words that I could say by his bed, through my rush of tears, than "O Lord, be merciful* H to 68 omit *through my rush of tears*
343.4
MS: *Miss Havisham was burning within it* H: *Miss Havisham was consuming within it*
345.32–33
MS: *leaving a cool three thousand to Mr. Matthew Pocket* H: *leaving a cool four thousand to Mr. Matthew Pocket*
345.41–42
MS, H, M, VA₂: *This account gave me great joy, as it perfected the only good thing I had done since I left the forge* AYR to 68 omit *since I left the forge*
346.5–7
MS: *you ain't that strong . . . that you can take in more nor one additional bit to-day* H: *you ain't . . . one additional shovel-full to-day*

346.29
MS: *after **paying off and dismissing** the laundress* H to 68 omit **and dismissing**
348.24
MS: *The delicacy with which Joe dismissed this **painful** theme* H to 68 omit **painful**
352.3
MS: *It was **the worst tone** I could have taken* H: *It was **the worst course** I could have taken*
353.1
MS: *in my being brought low, he saw **(not to deceive you, Joseph)** the finger of Providence* H to 68 omit **(not . . . Joseph)**
353.44–45
MS: *and their leaves **rustled** when I stopped to listen* H: *and their leaves **rustled harmoniously** when I stopped to listen*
355.3–4
MS: *Don't tell them, Biddy, that I was **ungenerous and petulant*** H: *Don't tell them, Biddy, that I was **ungenerous and unjust***
355.19
[Corrected proof VA$_2$ ends on the fragment *I **sold all I had, and put aside as much as***]
355.41
MS: *For **eight years**, I had not seen Joe nor Biddy* H, M corr. to *For **eleven years**, I . . . nor Biddy*
356.27
MS, M: *I am sure and certain, Biddy* H: *Oh no—I think not, Biddy*
356.29–30
MS: *I have forgotten nothing in my life **that ever had a foremost place there*** H to 68: *I have forgotten nothing in my life **that ever had a foremost place there, and little that ever had any place there***
356.31
[Following the phrase *"Biddy, all gone by!"* the revised ending printed in all texts begins without break except a paragraph break. The fragment of the original ending which has been preserved in MS takes up the bottom four lines of the slip (MS 9–26). Presumably, the slip on which the bulk of the ending appeared was destroyed. With a few minor corrections in Dickens's hand, the ending has been preserved *in toto* in the Morgan proofs; see below at 470.6–7 and my long note on "The Two Endings."]
356.36–37
MS: ~~who had become quite renowned as a compound of **pride, brutality, and** meanness~~
M: *who had . . . compound of **pride, avarice, brutality, and meanness***
357.3
MS: *A cold silvery mist **had come on in the afternoon*** H, M corr. to *A . . . mist **had veiled the afternoon***
357.16–18
MS, M: *The freshness of her beauty was indeed gone, **but its majesty** remained. **That,** I had seen before* H: *The freshness of her beauty was indeed gone, **but its indescribable majesty and its indescribable charm** remained. **Those attractions in it,** I had seen before*
357.30
MS: *Estella was the next **to break the silence*** M corr. to *Estella was the next **to break the silence that had ensued between us***
357.44
MS, M: *At last it is [to be built on]. **I have leased it for that purpose, and** came here to take leave of it before its change* H: *At last it is. **I** came here to take leave of it before its change*
357.49–358.7
Following **Yes, I do well** MS omits four paragraphs beginning *"**I have often thought of you**"* and ending **silent again, until she spoke.**
358.24
MS: *I saw **the shadow of no parting from her, but one*** M canc. **but one** M to 61: *I saw **the shadow of no parting from her** 62–68: *I saw **no shadow of another parting from her***
359.1
MS: ***It was four years more***
359.4
MS: ***Then I had heard***
359.5–6
[MS fragment ends **and of her being married again to a**]

Launching *Great Expectations*

In May 1858, Charles Dickens, the British icon and high priest of hearth and home, separated from his wife, Catherine, who had borne him ten children in the twenty-two years of their marriage. Despite the literature on the women in Dickens's life, his wife, at least until recently, has remained something of a shadowy figure. From the early accounts we have of her, she emerges as a slightly silly, easily flustered, awkward, rather obese woman, with an annoying habit of dropping things, whom Dickens, certainly in the waning years of their marriage, neglected, occasionally humiliated, and often left at home when he dined out. An American guest at Tavistock House describes her as "a plump, rosy, English, handsome woman, with a certain air of absent-mindedness"; one of Dickens's office boys remembers that "she was very stout and could hardly get her crinoline through the door."[1] At the time of the separation, Dickens rationalized the debacle as being rooted in their innate incompatibility; but the evidence that has come to light in the past few decades reveals a thoroughly affectionate relationship—which gradually soured on Dickens. The year before their formal rupture, Dickens had met a young woman, probably at a stage performance in which she played a minor role, Ellen Ternan, with whom he became infatuated and who almost certainly became his mistress, though not just yet; and his preoccupation with Ellen precipitated the marital breakup.[2]

At the time of his separation, Dickens was forty-six, but the wear and tear of work had taken their toll, and he looked ten years older. By 1858 he was also the most lionized writer in Europe, the author of a dozen enormously popular novels and five acclaimed Christmas Books, a gifted amateur actor in dramas that he produced to benefit impoverished brother-artists, a roving reader of his own works, and a tireless speaker on behalf of social betterment.

1. Grace Greenwood, "Charles Dickens: Recollections of the Great Novelist," *New York Daily Tribune*, July 5, 1870, in Collins, *Dickens: Interviews and Recollections* 2, 233; Catherine Van Dyke, "A Talk with Charles Dickens's Office Boy, William Edrupt of London," *Bookman* (New York), March 1921: 49–52, in *Interviews and Recollections* 2, 196.
2. Catherine Dickens's first outspoken champion was Bernard Shaw, who persuaded Dickens's younger daughter, Kate Perugini, to donate Dickens's letters to the British Museum in 1903 and, years later, justified his advice on the grounds "that posterity might sympathize much more with the woman who was sacrificed to the genius's uxoriousness to the appalling extent of having had to bear eleven children in sixteen years than with a grievance which, after all, amounted only to the fact that she was not a female Charles Dickens." See " 'This Ever-Diverse Pair,' To the Editor of *Time and Tide*," July 27, 1935, rept. in *Shaw on Dickens*, ed. Dan H. Laurence and Martin Quinn (New York: Frederick Ungar, 1985), 79–82; for the letter to Kate Perugini of June 2, 1903, see *Shaw on Dickens*, 62–64. (If Shaw is slightly off on the number of Dickens's children, so was their father.) Michael Slater's *Dickens and Women* (Stanford, Calif.: Stanford University Press, 1983), the best-informed and most balanced account of the subject, has brought us a good deal closer to Catherine than my comments suggest. See also the lively chapter in Phyllis Rose, *Parallel Lives: Five Victorian Marriages* (New York: Alfred A. Knopf, 1983), 145–91.

Since 1850 he had invested much of his time as editor and part-owner of a weekly journal, *Household Words*, a highly successful mixture of informal essays, verse, and pieces on topical matters, many of them written by Dickens himself, as well as short fiction, a very few novels—prominently Dickens's own *Hard Times*—and book-length nonfiction works, among them his *Child's History of England*. The weekly sold roughly thirty-five thousand copies at twopence the copy and attracted a flock of writers who, apart from durable people like Mrs. Gaskell, Harriet Martineau, and Wilkie Collins, have long been consigned to the dustbin of literary history but in their own day enjoyed considerable vogue: Mrs. Mulock, Richard Hengist Horne, James Hannay, the ladies Thomasina Ross and Louisa Anne Twamley, and Dickens's father-in-law. This is not the place to elaborate on Dickens's editorial methods or policies (though something about these will have to be said apropos of the failures of the novels that flanked *Great Expectations*); as the compiler of the *Household Words* contents notes, "Such principles as it had were the opinions Dickens held," and "as Dickens' mouthpiece, *Household Words* was a periodical in which opinions and ideas were advanced, not one in which opposing points of view were debated."[3] But by the late 1850s, the days of *Household Words* were numbered.

Apparently, Dickens held the opinion that there could be no better way to publicize his separation—and torpedo any rumors that linked him to Ellen —than to broadcast it to the world on the front page of his weekly. Accordingly, the readers of *Household Words* for June 12, 1858, were amazed to learn under the headline "Personal" that "some domestic trouble" of Dickens's, "of long-standing," on which he "would make no further remark than that it claims to be respected, as being of a sacredly private nature," had recently been settled to the satisfaction of all parties, but that "by some means, arising out of wickedness, or out of folly, or out of inconceivable wild chance, or out of all three, this trouble has been made the occasion of misrepresentation, most grossly false, most monstrous, and most cruel," and having discharged himself of this Hamletic blast of icy rhetoric, Dickens concluded with the malediction that he "most solemnly declare[d] * * * that all the lately whispered rumours * * * are abominably false. And that whoever repeats one of them after this denial, will lie as wilfully and as foully as it is possible for any witness to lie, before heaven and earth."[4] What confounded the readers of *Household Words* or provoked their mirth was both the message Dickens sent them and the medium. Who cared what went on under the rooftops of Tavistock Square? Dickens has been almost universally pilloried for washing his linen in public, especially when he himself in his Address had described the separation "as being of a sacredly private nature." Percy Fitzgerald, one of Dickens's "young men," recalls "the general wonder and confusion when the author's famous 'Personal' came out—a proclamation, *urbi et orbi*, which it required no request from the writer to insert in every journal with such alacrity"; exercising less restraint, the editor of *Reynolds' Weekly Newspaper*, which printed the Address in full, thought the affair either

3. Anne Lohrli, comp., "Introduction," *Household Words: A Weekly Journal, 1850–1859* (Toronto: Toronto University Press, 1973), 3–50; quoted matter pp. 4 and 12.
4. *Household Words* 17, 1; rept. in *PL* 8, 744.

"the daring emanation of a desperate criminality, or the deadly mistake of a slandered and frenzied innocence."[5]

The most concussive result of the Statement in *Household Words* was the cessation of *Household Words*—not because the Statement scared off the readers but because the publishers of the journal, Bradbury & Evans, who were also the owners of *Punch*, had declined to announce Dickens's matrimonial difficulties in their funny paper. Dickens had not, in fact, bothered to ask them; he took it for granted that the people who had profited by his pen for the past fifteen years and enriched themselves by his books from *The Chimes* to *Little Dorrit* would follow the precedent he had set in *Household Words* and anticipate his will and pleasure. *Household Words* was then and there to be "broken up, smashed, pulverized, and utterly destroyed";[6] and moreover, Dickens stopped talking to the editor of *Punch*, his good friend Mark Lemon, the darling of the Dickens children. In mid-June Bradbury & Evans learned of Dickens's decision, and they subsequently issued the sensible rejoinder that it wasn't their business to run "statements on a domestic and painful subject in the inappropriate columns of a comic miscellany" and that "the grievance of Mr. Dickens substantially amounted to this, that Bradbury & Evans did not take upon themselves, unsolicited, to gratify an eccentric wish by a preposterous action."[7] On November 15, John Forster, acting for Dickens (who refused to attend the talks), informed B & E that the partnership in *Household Words*—in which Dickens and his subeditor, William Henry Wills, owned three-quarters of the shares—would be dissolved; and after a series of complex negotiations, in which the enemy suffered a nearly total rout, the weekly was auctioned off, with very handsome results to Dickens, and ceased publication with the number for May 28, 1859. Dickens collected thirty-five hundred pounds, "a really enormous sum for an unproductive and now valueless object," and retained the copyright of the name "Household Words," which he incorporated in the title of its supercessor.[8]

The first number of the successor journal, *All the Year Round*, appeared on April 30, 1859, and as the initial (and accidental) repository of *Great Expectations* it merits a brief description. If Dickens had had his way, he would have called the new journal *Household Harmony*, apparently too obtuse, until it was pointed out to him, to notice the dissonance of the title and the event that had launched the periodical, and, once it was pointed out, too truculent to buy the objection. "I am afraid we must not be too particular about the possibility of personal references and applications: otherwise it is manifest that I never can write another book. I could not invent a story of any sort * * * incapable of being twisted into some such nonsensical shape." Having written himself into his heat, he cooled off, thought of calling the journal *Charles Dickens's Own* or *The Forge* or *Home-Music* or plain *Home* or *Twopence* or *The Rocket*, before he settled on what Percy Fitzgerald

5. Percy Fitzgerald, "Boz and His Publishers," *Dickensian* 3 (1907): 158; Reynolds is quoted in K. J. Fielding, "Dickens and the Hogarth Scandal," *Nineteenth-Century Fiction* 10 (1955): 64–74. The responses to the "Statement" are funny enough to be worth collecting in a Casebook.
6. Percy Fitzgerald, *Memories of Charles Dickens* (Bristol: J. W. Arrowsmith, 1913), 192.
7. "Mr. Charles Dickens and His Late Publishers," *Once a Week* 1 (May 31, 1859): 3; *PL* 9, 565–66.
8. Fitzgerald, *Memories*, 194; more fully, Robert L. Patten, *Dickens and His Publishers* (Oxford: Clarendon Press, 1978), 260–78.

thought the perfectly awful title he finally gave it—though the title may have been suggested to him by Wilkie Collins.[9]

Apart from its format and price (twenty-four pages at twopence), *All the Year Round* differed from *Household Words* in a number of ways. The first number alone sold one hundred thousand copies—in its palmiest days the sales of *Household Words* never exceeded forty thousand—and within a few months it outsold *The Times*. As early as May 28, the day the old *Household Words* expired, the new periodical could boast on its front page that "[The] fifth number [of *All the Year Round*] is published to-day, and its circulation, moderately stated, trebles that now relinquished in *Household Words*."[1] The success of *All the Year Round* is doubly impressive when you consider that in 1859 some 115 new periodicals were published in London alone, most of which barely outlasted the year. Even by mid-century so much cheap journalism still flourished throughout the country that in the very first number of *Household Words* Dickens had lit into these tabloids as "panders to the basest passions of the lowest natures—whose existence is a national reproach."[2] The very popularity of Dickens's earlier journal thus acted as a wholesome corrective.

The fact that *All the Year Round* upstaged its predecessor as much as it did may be largely explained by the changes the Chief introduced. Essays of topical sociopolitical interest were almost entirely tossed out—it is worth noting that at the time *Great Expectations* was being serialized, Dickens instructed his contributors to steer clear of the American Civil War (unless they checked out their essays with him first) as a subject totally unsuited to the aims of *All the Year Round*.[3] America herself could hardly be kept off limits; the journal was littered with essays about us. Leafing through the two-penny pages, you keep coming across pieces with titles like "American Snake Stories," "American Sleeping Cars," "American Street Railroads," "American Volunteer Firemen," "American Cotton," "Two Friends from Texas," "Scenery in South Carolina," "Love in Kentucky" (none of these implying a distinct bias in favor of the Rebels), "American Cemeteries," and for Britons who take their pleasures sadly, even a piece on "American Humour." Dickens seems to have been one of the earliest editors to appoint foreign correspondents—or correspondents who contributed native stuff but were given occasional foreign assignments. Thus Percy Fitzgerald all but blinded his readers with his pictures from Italy: "The Noble Roman," "The Common Roman," "A Roman Burgher," "A Roman Sunday," "A Roman Soldier," to say nothing of "Vatican Ornithology"—all this in consecutive numbers of the weekly—after all, Dickens couldn't subsidize Percy's Roman holiday forever (most of

9. Forster, book 8, chapter 5; Hoppé 2, 228. To Forster, [?January 25, 1859] (*PL* 9, 15–16 and 19, n. 2).
1. Ella Ann Oppenlander, ed., *Dickens's All the Year Round: Descriptive Index and Contributor List* (Troy, N.Y.: The Whitston Publishing Company, 1984), 49.
2. "A Preliminary Word," *Household Words* 1, 1, March 30, 1850; Oppenlander, 21; on the glut of weeklies, Walter J. Graham, *English Literary Periodicals* (New York: Octagon Books, 1966), 30. The use of the publisher's name as title of the journal was nothing unusual at a time when readers might subscribe to *Bentley's Miscellany* or buy *Douglas Jerrold's Shilling Magazine*, and the practice persists in the twentieth century in publications like *I. F. Stone's Weekly* or *Austen Kiplinger's Newsletter*.
3. Oppenlander, 38–39. But the letter she cites (correctly) to W. H. Wills, *NL* 3, 563, is dated October 1867, years after the Surrender. On Dickens's policy of soft-pedalling controversial events in *All the Year Round*, see P. A. W. Collins, "The Significance of Dickens's Periodicals," *Review of English Literature* 2 (1961): 55–64.

the contributors were reimbursed for their travel expenses); and after taking a last lingering look at "Our Roman Inn" and listening to "A Roman Cook's Oracle," Percy had to come home to the office. Then also a sprinkling of verse, from "The Unfinished Poem" to "Railway Reverie," "To His Love: Who Has Justly Rebuked Him," "Rabbi Ben Ephraim's Treasure," and "Fair Urience with the Yellow Hair." It wouldn't do to look for these titles in Palgrave's *Golden Treasury* or *The Norton Anthology*. They more nearly resemble the syndicated doggerel that appears in our dailies, the sort of thing in which the late James J. Metcalfe appealed to our uplift with titles like "Sweden Day," "The Usherette," and "House Painting." The number in which the first chapters of *Great Expectations* appeared provides a fair sample of what the readers of *All the Year Round* got for their twopence. First off, the opening of Dickens's novel. Next, the "Roman Cook's Oracle," followed by an essay of roughly the same length, "The Wolf at the Church Door." Next a rhymed item, "The World of Love," collapsed, despite its global promise, into a single column. Then an installment of Lever's novel *A Day's Ride*, which had been rezoned from the front pages to privilege *Great Expectations*. Two more essays: on "Dress and Food Five Hundred Years Ago" and on the "Inconveniences of Being a Cornish Man." The two serial novels and the Cornish Man accounted for thirty of the forty-eight columns. Dickens paid his authors at least a guinea a page for prose; the enfeement of poetry "varie[d] according to the nature of the lines."[4] Very likely it also varied according to the popularity of the poet. Dickens himself contributed barely one third of the essays he had contributed to *Household Words*, largely because he spent more and more time on the road and his public readings brought him into much closer contact—so essential to him—with his public than his columns did. Even so, if *All the Year Round* fell short of pieces by the Conductor, it did bring us *Great Expectations*.

The chief innovation of *All the Year Round* and a salient reason for its popularity in fact lay in Dickens's policy of giving prime space to serial fiction. In *Household Words* Dickens had skimped on novels and short fiction: *Hard Times*, like *Great Expectations* six years later, was spooned out as a weekly to boost the sagging sales of the journal; apart from this, Dickens's shortest novel, only Wilkie Collins's *Hide and Seek* and two novels by Mrs. Gaskell, whose *Mary Barton* Dickens admired no end. As has been pointed out elsewhere, in adopting full-length serials as a staple feature of the new weekly, Dickens took a considerable risk. He had, after all, little experience as a publisher of novels and would now have to compete with the commercial kings of the fiction market. At that, he could count on at least one predecessor in the aforementioned *Reynolds' Weekly*, whose editor used the journal to run his own novels in weekly serials for nearly a quarter century, from 1846 to 1869. But since Reynolds catered to the very panders Dickens had anathematized in *Household Words*, the resemblance between the two journals ends with the format.[5] And the success of *Hard Times*, which had nearly doubled the circulation of *Household Words*, persuaded Dickens that the innovation was worth the risk.

4. Oppenlander, 53; to Samuel Lover, June 5, 1862 (*PL* 10, 91).
5. Oppenlander, 20. On the competitive fiction market, J. A. Sutherland, *Victorian Novelists and Publishers* (Chicago: Chicago University Press, 1976), 166–87, and Oppenlander, 22–23.

The first number of *All the Year Round* led off with *A Tale of Two Cities*, which ran in thirty-one weekly installments, with the result that the circulation skyrocketed from the start. Elated by its success, Dickens could confidently spell out his policy in the number in which *A Tale* concluded: "We propose always reserving the first place in these pages for a continuous original work of fiction occupying about the same amount of time in its serial publication, as that which is just completed. * * * And it is our hope and aim, while we work hard at every other department of our journal, to produce, in this one, some sustained works of imagination that may become a part of English Literature."[6] How far he succeeded in this depends on what you call English Literature. Of the twenty-seven novels to appear in *All the Year Round* in the eleven years Dickens lived to edit it, six have so far escaped being bitten to death by the tooth of time: the two novels by Dickens, the three Wilkie Collins contributed—*The Woman in White, No Name*, and *The Moonstone*—and (arguably) Charles Reade's *Hard Cash*. A few more are apt to sneak their way into Companions to English Literature because the authors are still known to a handful of specialists or amateur buffs, even where the books have been long out of print: Charles Lever's *A Day's Ride*, Bulwer-Lytton's *A Strange Story*, and an interesting minor work of Mrs. Gaskell's, *A Dark Night's Work*. (Mrs. Gaskell would have been glad to call the novel *A Night's Work*, but Dickens persuaded her that the insertion of the modifier would act as a potent aphrodisiac.) Nobody nowadays would dispute that *Great Expectations* is the pick of the lot. What is worth noting about this list of survivors is their place in the ranks of the twenty-seven. Of the nine worthies, all but one appear among the first nine entries, and the loner, *The Moonstone*, lags years behind. Thus between *Hard Cash*, which ran from March to December 1863, and *The Moonstone*, which ran from January to August 1868, the field is littered with the corpses of forgotten writers whose names are about as familiar as those of our Vice Presidents and who, as Henry James said of his fictionalized Ouida, Greville Fane, "wrote from their elbows down" and "displayed an unequalled gift of squeezing large mistakes into small opportunities": Henry Spicer, Rosa Mulholland, Amelia Edwards, and Dickens's young protégés. But the obscurity of these people ought not to diminish Dickens's achievement as an enormously successful journalist—as well as a painstaking editor, who took hours off from *Little Dorrit* to rewrite other people's sentences, cut their paragraphs, sharpen their vocabularies, and accentuate the positive if their endings struck him as apt to lower his readers' pulse beats. At the same time, one may argue with Philip Collins that the unmistakable falling off in "quality" novels reflects Dickens's growing indifference to the merits of these books and perhaps his growing impatience with having to waste his time on an ill-written sentence by a second-rater.[7] Good or bad, the novels and stories became the essential features of the journal, sometimes to the near-exclusion of all others. The number for January 19, 1861, provides a good example. Along with the eighth installment of *Great Expectations* it offered its readers Portion the Third of Mrs. Gaskell's novella *The Grey Woman* and petered out with chapter 33 of *A Day's Ride*. Taken together, the stories took up more than two-thirds of the number.

6. *All the Year Round* 2, 95 (November 26, 1859). See also G. H. Lewes, November 14, 1859 (*PL* 9, 160).
7. Collins, "The Significance of Dickens's Periodicals," esp. 61.

Unlike the contributors to the shorter sallies, the novelists were paid not by the page but on the basis of their popularity and Dickens's personal estimate of or esteem for them, presumably along with the consideration of how much he could get away with. He certainly paid as well as any publisher of serials. Even so, one may find it objectionable to read that when in 1860 he solicited an eight-month serial from Mrs. Gaskell and an eight-month serial from Bulwer, he bought Mrs. Gaskell for four hundred pounds and bribed Bulwer by offering him fifteen hundred. As a prophet of success, Dickens was not always on target: Collins, who had already scored with *Woman in White* and *No Name*, collected seven hundred fifty pounds for the best-selling *Moonstone* (which Dickens disliked as "wearisome beyond endurance"), and Lever collected the same amount for the single most notorious failure among the novels.[8]

So much for the journal in which Pip first saw the light of day and for some of the oddments that surrounded Pip and Herbert and Magwitch and Uncle Pumblechook.

First Impressions

In following the progress of the novel's composition and the internal dating, the letters that have been reprinted below, scant as they are, are occasionally helpful in providing an overview of *Great Expectations*; they help, too, in establishing roughly the chronology of composition and sometimes suggest how far in advance of publication Dickens wrote a given segment. The earliest portents of a new work appear in a letter to the Earl of Carlisle of August 8, 1860: "I am prowling about, meditating a new book"; words to the same effect recur a few days later in a note to Alfred Wigan, the manager of the Olympic Theatre, and again in a letter of September 14 to Mrs. Richard Watson: "I * * * am on the restless eve of beginning a new book."[9] But we cannot be sure that these obiter dicta refer to *Great Expectations*, if we are to credit the note to John Forster, undated but almost certainly written end of September, that is generally accepted as the first mention of the book, Dickens presumably referring to it as an essay to be included in his ongoing series of papers *The Uncommercial Traveller*: "For a little piece I have been writing—or am writing; for I hope to finish it to-day—such a very fine, new, and grotesque idea has opened upon me that I begin to doubt whether I had not better cancel the little paper and reserve the notion for a new book. * * * I can see the whole of a new serial revolving around it, in a most singular and comic manner"—in a slightly later letter to Forster, Dickens describes the project as "exceedingly droll," "very funny," without "want of humour."[1] Readers may find this an odd prospectus for a book that starts out by serving up starving criminals, terrified little boys, and cannibalism (on Christmas Eve); but in assuring Forster that he would "not have to complain of the want of humor," Dickens may have been engaged in a species of damage control, the preceding novel, *A Tale of Two Cities*, having been trounced by the reviewers for its unremitting

---

8. Oppenlander, 54.
9. *PL* 9, 284, 285, 309.
1. *PL* 9, 310, 325 and below, pp. 531, 533. Hereafter letters that are excerpted or given in full below, pp. 531–36, are not separately identified here.

humorlessness—unfairly, for in fact the novel contains a good deal of humor, some of it unintended.[2] Forster's biography of Dickens, written within four years after Dickens's death by somebody who had known him intimately for more than thirty years, is rightly regarded as one of the handful of great nineteenth-century biographies. At the same time, Forster, partly from the prissiness inflicted on him by the age, partly from the desire to protect Dickens, and not least from personal vanity, tinkered with Dickens's correspondence unconscionably and amputated letters right and left, even from time to time quoting letters Dickens had written to somebody else as if they had been written to him. There seems to be no reason to look for self-serving motives in Forster's transcription of Dickens's note: we may assume that this was indeed "the germ of Pip and Magwitch," even if the scrap Forster cites is not 100 percent reliable. (At the time of writing the above-quoted memo, Dickens not only expected to have the paper finished the same day but, as Forster claims, proposed to send it to him as soon as it had come back from the printer, a procedure that suggests Forster's getting a finished sketch for *All the Year Round*, not the first chapters of a new novel.)[3] As early as October 2 Dickens decided to abandon the projected publication of the book in monthly number parts and to publish it instead in *All the Year Round*, beginning with the number for December 1. We have next the letters quoted by Forster as of October 4 and 6 and a third written a few days later. The letter of the 6th chiefly retails the financial grounds for "dashing in now" with the new novel, which are spelled out at greater length in the "business report" to Charles Lever, the culprit and catalyst of the change from monthly to weekly—a report of immaculate tact and sympathy: Dickens obviously knew his man and anticipated Lever's self-flagellations. The earlier note of October 4 confirms that Dickens had settled on the approximate length of the story and the title ("I think a good name?"). "A few more days," Forster writes, referring to a slightly later undated letter, "brought the first instalment of the tale and explanatory mention of it." The dating may be roughly established by the coincidence of a verbal detail: in chapter 2 Joe is introduced as "a mild, good-natured, sweet-tempered, easy-going, foolish, dear fellow"; in the letter: "I have put a child and a good-natured foolish man, in relations that seem to me very funny."

Whatever difficulties Forster's slipshod bookkeeping may have put in our path, it seems reasonably clear that by mid-October Dickens had the first four chapters or so in manuscript and had gotten through the Christmas dinner. By October 24 he informed Collins that "four weekly numbers have been ground off the wheel, and at least another must be turned before we meet."

2. In the *Life* (book 9, chapter 2; Hoppé 2, 283) Forster complains that "there was probably never a book by a great humorist, and an artist with so little humour and so few rememberable figures." Reviews of *A Tale* are collected in Philip Collins, *Dickens: The Critical Heritage* (London: Routledge & Kegan Paul, 1971); also Michael Wolff, "Victorian Reviewers and Cultural Responsibilities," 1859: *Entering an Age of Crisis*, ed. Philip Appleman, et al. (2nd ed., Bloomington: Indiana University Press, 1961), 269–89.

3. *Life*, book 9, chapter 3; Hoppé 2, 284. We had better give Forster the benefit of the doubt in all this; his account is substantially supported by Dickens's notation in early October that "the pivot on which the story will turn . . . was the tragi-comic conception that first encouraged me"; but in view of the muddled dating of the letters—did Forster in fact receive three separate ones or resort to one of his paste-and-scissors jobs? did he add phrases of his own invention?—the generally received account that *Great Expectations* originated in a short paper to be included in *The Uncommercial Traveller* can't be accepted unconditionally, and the conception of the novel may have differed somewhat from what everybody has thought it to be.

That is, by the last week of October Dickens had finished the first seven chapters—or the first monthly portion—and by the end of the month the chapter following, which introduces Pip to Satis House. On the whole, then, Dickens managed to keep very roughly six weeks ahead of publication in *All the Year Round*, but it has to be borne in mind that all these chapters appeared, though with far fewer proof corrections, in *Harper's* a week earlier and Dickens was correspondingly more squeezed for time. (Thus, his letter to Bulwer of June 7, 1861, about the timing of Bulwer's submissions of his forthcoming novel: "The No. in which it [the ad for Bulwer's novel] is, is stereotyped and gone to America. We are always obliged to be a fortnight in advance.") Most of November seems to have been shot by work on the Christmas Story, *A Message from the Sea*, to judge from Dickens's note to Austen Henry Layard, the archeologist turned politician, of December 4—"I have been taken off [the novel] for a month by other Christmas work"; a letter to Edmund Yates in late February suggests that Dickens worked on both during November: "Before Christmas, my story and what I had to do for Christmas kept me in actual bondage for weeks together"—"my story" here clearly refers to the novel.[4]

The letters that cover the succeeding months provide little more than intermittent flashes about Dickens's progress. December and January bring repeated complaints of ill health, from which Dickens seems not wholly recovered by the end of the month. On February 4 he temporarily vacated Gad's Hill and until mid-June he and Mamie moved into a furnished flat at Hanover Terrace. The novel suffered more interruptions by the series of six public readings ("a very great result") that Dickens delivered at St. James's Hall between March 14 and April 18—it is pleasant to think that at the opening reading the thirty-two-year-old Tolstoy, in town to investigate schooling methods to be exported to Yasnaya Polyana, his estate near Moscow, may have been among the listeners.[5] By April Dickens had gotten well into the third stage of the book. The covering letter to Forster containing the chapters "which open the third division of the tale" can be approximately dated (roughly mid-April) by two bits of circumstantial evidence: Forster, in commenting on these chapters, professes particular delight in Old Barley, who appears in the final chapter (44) of the seventh monthly portion, which came out on June 8; moreover, Dickens's confident assertion in the same letter, "Two more months will see me through, I trust," argues the kind of realistic prognosis typical of him—characteristically, he could write to Collins on May 24 from his retreat at Dover: "I hope—I begin to hope—that somewhere about the 12th of June will see me out of the book." The correspondence with Bulwer in mid-May indicates what my comments on the two endings bear out, that Dickens took time out to go painstakingly over the manuscript portion of Bulwer's *A Strange Story*, which was to follow *Great Expectations* as star attraction on August 10.

We next hear Forster's engaging narrative of the steamer journey from Blackwall to Southend that Dickens undertook the third week of May by way of field research for chapter 54. Forster's account is well known:

4. To Collins, *PL* 9, 329; to Bulwer, 423; to Layard, 345; to Yates, 387.
5. Dickens had been under medical treatment in late December and early January: see his complaints and progress reports (*PL* 9, 354 ff). On Tolstoy's uncertain presence, see my long footnote in *DSA* 2: 375, n. 11.

To make himself sure of the actual course of a boat in such circumstances, and what possible incidents the adventure might have, Dickens hired a steamer for the day from Blackwall to Southend. Eight or nine friends and three or four members of his family were on board, and he seemed to have no care, the whole of that summer day (22 May 1861), except to enjoy their enjoyment and entertain them with his own shape of a thousand whims and fancies; but his sleepless observation was at work all the time, and nothing had escaped his keen vision on either side of the river. The fifteenth chapter of the third volume is a masterpiece.[6]

For the all-but-final assault on the novel and "to get rid of my neuralgic face," Dickens indulged himself in a brief working holiday in Dover the last week of May; on the 24th, as we saw, he informed Collins that he expected to wind up the book "about the 12th of June"; and on June 11 he announced to his old friend Macready: "I have just finished my book of Great Expectations, and am the worse for wear." Meanwhile Dickens had arranged (on June 7) to stay with Bulwer from the 15th to the 18th, to submit proofs of the concluding chapters and discuss Bulwer's new serial. Within four days of his return, the last thread of the tale had been unwound and the story rethreaded; on June 23 he informed Collins of the revision, and the following day he dispatched the finished version to Bulwer. On Saturday, July 6—with some four weeks left to run in the journal, without loss of revenue and without loss of suspense to people who couldn't cough up the thirty-one shillings sixpence at which the book sold—*Great Expectations* appeared in all the glory of three plum-colored volumes. The same day Dickens instructed his binder, Eeles, "to bind Dedication copy of Great Expectations in Russia Leather and Gold, and do it as good as you can."[7]

To judge not only from Dickens's euphoric notes to his friends but also from the available sales figures, *Great Expectations* turned out to be an enormous success—the note of euphoria, nothing unusual for Dickens, had already been sounded while the novel was being serialized. The readership of the serial alone has been estimated at one hundred thousand. Chapman published five editions between July and November, of which roughly one-fourth were absorbed by the lending library established by Henry Mudie in 1838—a fact that alone would account for the scarcity of genuine "firsts."[8] At that, the issuance of separate "editions" may have been something of a promotional stunt: a collation of the first five issues reveals that these were all printed at a single impression and published by Chapman & Hall in the succeeding months with slightly misleading title pages, announcing them as new editions in order to imply (and encourage) a rapid sale. There was nothing dishonest in the procedure at a time when the word "edition" was fairly flexible and could be stretched to mean nothing more than "reprint" from the stereotypes, and what we think of as first editions were nothing more than first impressions. Both Dickens's correspondence and the account books in-

6. *Life*, book 9, chapter 3; Hoppé 2, 287.
7. To T. R. Eeles (*PL* 9, 434). The price of a triple-decker had been established by Walter Scott's *Kenilworth* in 1821. On Bulwer, see p. 491 ff.
8. Editions appeared on July 6, August 3 and 17, September 21, and November 2. Mudie's "Select Lending Library for Ladies and Gentlemen, Subscription One Guinea a Year" enormously broadened the readership of books that the buying public couldn't afford—some thirty readers left their fingerprints on a novel circulated by Mudie's.

dicate that the "editions" went out of print so quickly that Dickens himself had to go begging for a copy. An uncommonly expensive book that had already been read as a serial by an estimated one hundred thousand people from Carlyle to the cook warrants Robert Patten's recognition that "the enormous popularity of *Great Expectations* * * * can be measured by the fact that it sustained a large readership in *All the Year Round* * * * , then circulated (as few others of Dickens's works seem to have done) through the lending libraries, and still was in demand for an exceptionally high price as Dickens's serials go."[9] In the early 1990s, a rare bookdealer in Los Angeles who specializes in Dickens's firsts offered (as nearly as we can judge in comparable mint condition) *Oliver Twist* at $5,000; *A Tale of Two Cities* at $8,500; and *Great Expectations* at $45,000. But even at $45,000, *Great Expectations* turned out not to be a genuine first and had to be returned to Sotheby's. So Magwitch did handsomely by his dear boy.

Despite the copyright laws, which forbade prior publication in foreign countries, the serial began with a week's headstart in *Harper's Weekly*: "Splendidly Illustrated by John McLenan. Printed from the Manuscript and early Proof-sheets purchased from the Author by the Proprietors of 'Harper's Weekly'." The tight schedule to which Dickens was thus forced to work no doubt accounts for the many textual changes he introduced after sending advance proof to New York. *Harper's* would no doubt have maintained its timetable and beaten *All the Year Round* to the finishing line if it hadn't been for the omission of the number for January 26 (Installment 10), in which readers found the following "Shipping Intelligence":

> Owing to the long passage which the ocean steamers are making at this season, we did not receive our advance proof-sheets of the next part of Mr. DICKENS'S new Novel, GREAT EXPECTATIONS, in time to have it illustrated. We therefore omit it this week. It will appear in our next Number, with the usual graphic Illustrations by JOHN McLENAN, Esq.

McLenan appeared to be as indispensable as Dickens was; to a modern reader the ad may sound rather like the ad for *The Magic Flute*—by Emanuel Schikaneder, with music by W. A. Mozart. But the importance of the illustrator can perhaps be appreciated when we remember that the names of Boz and Phiz were as inseparable as those of the Siamese twins, or Gilbert and Sullivan's. By the week following, at all events, thanks to the truancy of the ocean steamers, *All the Year Round* had caught up with *Harper's*, and from hereon in the same installments ran concurrently in both weeklies. The journals ended in a dead heat on August 3, 1861, when, as somebody pointed out, "readers of *Harper's Weekly* had other things to worry about than what happened to Pip and Estella."[1]

9. Patten, *Dickens and His Publishers*, 292. As Patten notes, the use of the word "edition" had been given legal sanction three years earlier, the courts defining "a new 'edition' " as an edition "published whenever, having in his storehouse a certain number of copies, the publisher issues a fresh batch of them to the public."
1. John T. Winterich, *Great Expectations* (New York: Heritage Press, 1939), 8. The nearly complete set of corrected proof preserved in the Pierpont Morgan Library indicates that *Harper's* served Dickens as text on which he indicated his corrections before sending the corrected copy to the printers of *All the Year Round*. A reader of *Harper's* thus found himself stuck with a text that Dickens himself, operating under extreme pressure of time, thought far from satisfactory.

Table 1: Serial Installments in Harper's Weekly *and* All the Year Round

	Harper's Weekly			All the Year Round			
DATE	INSTALL-MENT	VOL. & NO.	CHAPTERS	INSTALL-MENT	VOL. & NO.	CHAPTERS	COLUMNS IN *AYR*
			First Stage				
Nov. 24	1	IV. 204	1, 2, first half of 3				
Dec. 1	2	205	rest of 3, 4	1	IV. 84	1, 2	10½
Dec. 8	3	206	5	2	85	3, 4	10½
Dec. 15	4	207	6, 7	3	86	5	8¼
Dec. 22	5	208	8	4	87	6, 7	9½
Dec. 29	6	209	9, 10	5	88	8	9½
Jan. 5	7	V. 210	10[1]	6	89	9, 10	10½
Jan. 12	8	211	11, 12	7	90	11	10¾
Jan. 19	9	212	13, 14	8	91	12, 13	10+
Jan. 26	[*omitted in* Harper's]			9	92	14, 15	10⅓
Feb. 2	10	214	15, 16	10	93	16, 17	10½
Feb. 9	11	215	17	11	94	18	10½
Feb. 16	12	216	18	12	95	19	11½
			Second Stage				
Feb. 23	13	217	19, 20	13	96	20, 21	10+
March 2	14	218	21	14	97	22	10⅓
March 9	15	219	22, 23	15	98	23, 24	11+
March 16	16	220	24, 25	16	99	25, 26	11½
March 23	17	221	26, 27	17	100	27, 28	11
March 30	18	222	28	18	V. 101	29	10
April 6	19	223	29, 30	19	102	30, 31	11
April 13	20	224	31, 32	20	103	32, 33	10+
April 20	21	225	33, 34	21	104	34, 35	10¾
April 27	22	226	35, 36	22	105	36, 37	11+
May 4	23	227	37	23	106	38	10+
May 11	24	228	38	24	107	39	9½

The plus symbol (+) indicates a slight overspill to the next column or page; the minus sign (−) denotes a corresponding shortage before the end of the column.

1. The chapter numbering for 10 obviously appeared twice. The printers almost certainly followed uncorrected Morgan proof, in which the faulty numbering is corrected by hand from chapter 11 on, evidently after *Harper's* had gone to press.

Table 1: *Serial Installments in* Harper's Weekly *and* All the Year Round *(cont.)*

	Harper's Weekly				All the Year Round		
DATE	INSTALL-MENT	VOL. & NO.	CHAPTERS	INSTALL-MENT	VOL. & NO.	CHAPTERS	COLUMNS IN *AYR*
			Third Stage				
May 18	25	229	39	25	108	40	10⅓
May 25	26	230	40, 41	26	109	41, 42	10
June 1	27	231	42, 43	27	110	43, 44	10–
June 8	28	232	44, 45	28	111	45, 46	11¾
June 15	29	233	46, 47	29	112	47, 48	10½
June 22	30	234	48, 49	30	113	49, 50	10¼
June 29	31	235	50, 51	31	114	51, 52	10⅓
July 6	32	236	52	32	115	53	10+
July 13	33	237	53	33	116	54	11+
July 20	34	238	54, 55	34	117	55, 56	10+
July 27	35	239	56	35	118	57	9½
August 3	36	240	57, 58[2]	36	119	58, 59	9+

2. The discrepancy in the numbering of chapters 58/59 logically follows the careless numbering beginning with the installment in *Harper's* for February 2 and thus has manuscript sanction (Worth, *Bibliography*, 17). But pace Cardwell (*Great Expectations*, xix, n. 24) the manuscript error had been rectified earlier: the numbers differ because in manuscript chapter 58 extends to the end of the book.

Table 2: *Monthly, Weekly, and 1861 Chapter Division*

Manuscript	All the Year Round	First Book Edition
	First Stage	
1st Monthly Chs. 1 to 7	Chs. 1, 2 Chs. 3, 4 Ch. 5 Chs. 6, 7	Vol. I Chapters I to XIX (numbering as in AYR)
2nd Monthly Chs. 8 to 13	Ch. 8 Chs. 9, 10 Ch. 11 Chs. 12, 13	
3rd Monthly Chs. 14 to 19	Chs. 14, 15 Chs. 16, 17 Ch. 18 Ch. 19	

Table 2: Monthly, Weekly, and 1861 Chapter Division (cont.)

Manuscript	*All the Year Round*	First Book Edition

Second Stage

4th Monthly Chs. 20 to 26		Vol.II
	Chs. 20, 21	Chapters XX to XXXIX
	Ch. 22	(correspond to chs. 20 to 39)
	Chs. 23, 24	
	Chs. 25, 26	
5th Monthly Chs. 27 to 33		
	Chs. 27, 28	
	Ch. 29	
	Chs. 30, 31	
	Chs. 32, 33	
6th Monthly Chs. 34 to 39		
	Chs. 34, 35	
	Chs. 36, 37	
	Ch. 38	
	Ch. 39	

Third Stage

7th Monthly Chs. 40 to 46		Vol. III
	Ch. 40	Chapters I to XX
	Chs. 41, 42	(correspond to chs. 40 to 59)
	Chs. 43, 44	
	Chs. 45, 46	
8th Monthly Chs. 47 to 53		
	Chs. 47, 48	
	Chs. 49, 50	
	Chs. 51, 52	
	Ch. 53	
9th Monthly Chs. 54 to 59		
	Ch. 54	
	Chs. 55, 56	
	Ch. 57	
	Chs. 58, 59	

Weekly Disbursements

In expressing the hope "to produce some sustained works of imagination that may become a part of English Literature," Dickens voices a sentiment that was perhaps more clearly formulated with an eye on *Great Expectations* by the reviewer in *The Athenaeum*, the literary and music critic H. F. Chorley:

that a good serial is one that "stands the test of collection * * * as few tales published in its fragmentary form can" and that "on reading through the romance as a whole [we sense] that we have to do with a Work of Art with power, progress, and a minuteness consistent with the widest apparent freedom." This matter has been discussed thoroughly by Jerome Meckier. "No self-respecting serialist with an eye on posterity," Meckier writes, "privileged the serial state at the expense of the completed work. The serial was often the money, the attention-getter, but the volume edition, as Dickens and Browning both knew, held the key to immortality."[2] In a famous postscript to *Our Mutual Friend*—and in a dozen letters—Dickens makes clear that nobody was more keenly aware of the difference between the two modes of publication than he himself, and his defense of the installment plan sounds like an apologetic afterthought:

> [The] difficulty [of revealing the design of the whole] was much enhanced by the mode of publication; for it would be very unreasonable to expect that many readers, pursuing a story in portions from month to month through nineteen months, will, until they have it before them complete, perceive the relations of its finer threads to the whole pattern which is always before the eyes of the story-weaver at his loom.

Perhaps in answer to the unspoken question "Then why do you do it?" he concludes with a less than brash Nevertheless: "Yet, that I hold the advantages of the mode of publication to outweigh its disadvantages, may be easily believed of one who revived it in the Pickwick Papers after long disuse, and has pursued it ever since."[3] Quite apart from his special discomfort in writing weekly as against monthly numbers (and *Our Mutual Friend*, unlike *Great Expectations*, is a monthly and thus the lesser of two evils), he insists again and again on how much his readers lose by not being privy to the full view, the organic whole, the hidden demon-traps. To his friend Mrs. William Howitt: "I hope that you will be confirmed [in your good opinion of *A Tale of Two Cities*] when you can better perceive my design in seeing it all together, instead of reading it in what Carlyle (writing to me of it, with great enthusiasm) calls 'Teaspoons.' " (It would have been unlike Dickens to suppress the parenthetical Mrs. Harrisism.) To Wilkie Collins, in answer to his objection that Dickens should have presented Dr. Manette's role at the outset: "I think the business of Art is to lay all that ground carefully, but with the care that conceals itself—to shew, by a backward light, what everything has been working to. . . . These are the ways of Providence—of which ways all Art is but a little imitation." To Forster, in sending him the first numbers of the third stage of *Great Expectations*: "It is a pity that the third portion cannot be read all at once, because its purpose would be much more apparent; and the pity is the greater, because the general turn and tone of the working out and winding up, will be away from all such things as they conventionally go."[4] All the subtle allusions and half-hidden clues, that whole unbroken stretch in which Dickens makes us feel what sociologists would call Pip's pervasive low-key unpleasure, is much more likely to get to us in a single

2. Review-essay of Linda K. Hughes and Michael Lund, *The Victorian Serial* (Charlottesville: University Press of Virginia, 1991), *DQ* 9 (1992): 82–89, 87. Chorley's notice appeared on July 13, 1861.
3. Dated September 2, 1865. There is evidence, though, that unlike his readers Dickens increasingly distanced himself from *Pickwick*.
4. August 28, 1959 (*PL* 9, 119), October 6, 1859 (127–28), [?Mid-April 1861] (403).

reading than to people brought up on brief six-page hebdomadal encounters, who have to look back over their shoulders to find out what's what.

Suppose we take another look at three of the people I spotlighted a few pages back: Magwitch, Herbert, and Uncle Pumblechook. Who the devil are they?

You and I find out within a week or two who they are, depending on our reading habits, interest threshold, deadline for a *Great Expectations* paper, etc. Whoever picked up the first number of the novel Dickens launched on December 1, 1860, didn't have to wait *too* long to meet Pumblechook: one week—but by then we speed-readers have already seen the last of him as he licks his chops over Pip's reward for his total deficiency in the human gratitude department. On the other hand, the readers who paid their twopence had to wait six weeks before they laid eyes on Herbert Pocket and then another six to find out who he is. Magwitch they met as soon as you and I did; but his name wasn't sprung on them for five months, and they had to wait nearly that long to get their second glimpse of him. In other words, one of the three pivotal characters is kept in storage from mid-winter to the following spring. But having introduced him with so much éclat, Dickens, though keeping him in storage, can't afford the risk of entirely hiding him all that time only to find his investors grumbling, "Oh 'im! I forgot all about 'im. I wonder wotever 'appened to his shopmite." You and I can hold our breaths pending Magwitch's reentry, but even if we're no smarter than the readers of *All the Year Round*, Dickens needs to prod *them* every so often to keep their memory of Magwitch green.

~~Magwitch gets lost, then, on December 15, at the end of chapter 5, after~~ unshackling himself with Joe's file. In chapter 10—that would bring us to January 5—Magwitch's squint-eyed emissary turns up at the Three Jolly Bargemen, stirring his rum *with a file*—the italics are Pip's, Dickens craftily both signaling to the reader and recording Pip's state of mind—and handing him his first down payment, the two fat sweltering pound notes. Three weeks later, on the 26th, Orlick fells Mrs. Joe. Pip naturally connects the assailant and the incriminating instrument of the assault. On February 23 Wemmick takes Pip on his first tour of Newgate—nothing directly to do with Magwitch, yet even the journal reader won't fail to relate the convicts' space to the person whom Pip refers to as "my convict"—a very weird double entendre. On March 23 (chapter 28) Pip is fated to share the coach to Rochester with two exceedingly smelly prisoners, one of whom Pip recognizes to be the man with the file, and he is forced to listen to him as he broadcasts the story of the transaction at the Bargemen in all its particulars to *his* mate. (The serial readers are bound to miss a joke here: the point of chapter 28, of course, is to alert us to the originator of the two pounds, Pip's benefactor; the chapter ends with the local intelligence Pip picks up in the dirty newspaper at the Blue Boar, in which a highly respected individual not entirely unconnected with the corn-and-seed trade introduces himself to his readers for the hundredth time as Pip's earliest patron and founder of his fortunes.) Finally, on May 11 Magwitch returns, though it takes Pip another week to shake off his blues long enough to ask him his name or names. To defray Magwitch for the two fat sweltering pound notes he sent Pip in early January, and to get rid of this horrible person, Pip hands him two "clean and new" notes (which Magwitch to his credit tosses into the fire)—a touch that (again) may be lost on the readers who don't remember the look and feel of the notes Mrs. Joe buried in the family urn back in January; and by the time they get to chapter 53, come July, they aren't likely to waste much thought on the complacency with which Pip presents Trabb's boy with *his* two guineas for saving his life.

Go back for a minute to the Pip–Magwitch "pivot." Our certainty that this isn't the last we've seen of Magwitch is fortified by the silent understanding at which they arrive at the end of chapter 5. It's December 15th, and we're reading the third installment. In chapter 8 Pip first visits Satis House. Dickens hands the readers another conundrum that will presumably keep them going: why has Miss Havisham subpoenaed Pip in the first place? The idea that she summoned him merely to play Beggar My Neighbour obviously won't wash. We ask ourselves in effect the same question Pip asked himself the week before: "[the stars] twinkled out, one by one, without throwing any light on the question why on earth I was going to play at Miss Havisham's, and what on earth I was expected to play at." Dickens provides enough false and true leads long enough—from late December to early June—to keep us hopping from one foot to the other, as if we had been brought up by hand on Tar-Water. The two crucial events themselves are separated by a decent interval of three months. On February 9 Jaggers springs the news of his Great Expectations on Pip; on May 11 Magwitch reveals their source. (Jaggers has really planted two questions in chapter 18: Who and When.) If you guessed incorrectly, you become a party to Pip's false expectations; and if you guessed correctly, you still have to figure out what to do about Magwitch Redux. After all, the novel has another twelve weeks to run. And in the long chapters 53 and 54, which deal with Orlick's brawl and Magwitch's capture, Dickens builds up so much tension that only after the capture can Dickens begin to wind things down. The Pip–Orlick fight has very complex implications, but, coming where it does, it provides first and foremost a canny delay tactic, since it raises the question whether Pip will be in a position to rescue Magwitch. (Indeed, where Orlick has probably gotten under more people's skin than anyone else in *Great Expectations*, the author of a study on Dickens as serial novelist regards Orlick as no more than another one of Dickens's loose ends.)[5] The very solution to a riddle, then, may invite, or inevitate, more riddles: Magwitch's return, for one; for another, the information on which Wemmick's recital about Molly's crime and trial concludes, that she gave birth to a girl. We know which girl; but then what? One of the revealing things here, especially for readers who regard Pip's snobbishness as the alpha and omega of *Great Expectations*, is his immunity to the disclosure of Estella's origins— apparently his snobbishness is selective or circumstantial. For somebody as socially conscious as Pip, he is markedly indifferent to Estella's—genetic— decline from riches to rags; and this kind of perception, coming as late as it does, may have pretty much the same impact on readers of the serial and of the finished text.

In any event, to rely all too much on the readers' memories can be a tricky affair. Every so often Dickens grabs his clients by concluding a weekly on a fairly obvious note of suspense. One of the most effective examples of a dramatic close appears at the end of the second installment, in which Pip, terrified because he thinks Mrs. Joe is about to discover the theft of the pork

---

5. Archibald C. Coolidge, Jr., *Charles Dickens as Serial Novelist* (Ames: The Iowa State University Press, 1967), 94.

pie, runs "head foremost into a party of soldiers with their muskets," one of whom holds out "a pair of handcuffs to [Pip], saying, 'Here you are, look sharp, come on!' " Pip naturally takes it for granted that the soldiers have come to arrest him for the robbery. The ominous end of installment 27—" 'Don't Go Home!' "—could as easily be the handiwork of an inferior mystery writer. Chapter 52, the second of the chapters that make up No. 31, is framed by two messages: the brief alert from Wemmick suggesting the day of the planned escape, and the summons by Orlick that threatens to frustrate the plan. It's a rare reader who can resist picking up No. 32. Elsewhere Dickens prepares you for an explosive event by telling you that something is about to explode. Of the two big discoveries—of the great expectations and of Magwitch's return—the first is anticipated by Pip's serving abrupt notice that his apprenticeship is about to be terminated; the second, by the famous parable from *The Tales of the Genii*, the chapter ending with the words "all the work, near and afar, that tended to the end, had been accomplished; and in an instant the blow was struck, and the roof of my stronghold dropped upon me."

Other discoveries or other narrative devices—I am drifting from the mechanics of the weekly to more general formal elements—may be about equally accessible to the "naive" reader of *All the Year Round* and the "advanced" reader of the volume. This is true especially of compositional elements that are found in close proximity to each other. The simplest kind of integrity can be found in Pip's movements in the opening number: chapter 1 ends with his racing home from the marshes in holy terror; chapter 2, in nearly identical language, with his racing back to the marshes. The second weekly (chapters 3 and 4) appeals to a more refined sense of discrimination. As Edwin Eigner notes,[6] both zero in on Christmas dinners—and both subvert our conventional notions of the comfy old-fashioned "Dickensian" feasts in which people like Tiny Tim ingest their turkeys audibly, chunk by chunk. In chapter 3 Magwitch gobbles down his Christmas viaticum like the hunted dog he is; in chapter 4 Pip is fed his gravy while he is being tormented and processed into pork by the domestic authorities round the dinner table. In both chapters the terror is intensified by the interposition of the Church: the black ox who has "to my awakened conscience something of a clerical air" and all but accuses Pip of his theft (chapter 3); "Under the weight of my wicked secret, I pondered whether the Church would be powerful enough to shield me from the vengeance of the terrible young man, if I divulged to that establishment" (chapter 4). (One—shallow—distinction between Pip's two patrons is that one plumes himself on being "a heavy grubber"; the other derives a kind of sadistic gratification from making an exhibition of starving herself—Jaggers later tells Pip that the old lady really cheats by nibbling on her asparagus when nobody is around to see her do it.)

Often within a single chapter Dickens will play funny tricks that can be shared alike by the readers of the weekly and of the novel. In the concluding chapter of the first stage Dickens makes his point by first having Pip humiliate Joe and Biddy and then getting Pip taken down any number of pegs by Trabb's boy, the born tormentor of class-casuists. The same contrapuntal effect appears in chapter 27, in which Joe visits Pip in London. It's difficult

6. Edwin M. Eigner, "A Modified Parts Approach to the Teaching of *Great Expectations*," *Reading Great Expectations*, ed. Murray Baumgarten (Santa Cruz: University of California, [1987]), 101–102.

to say who more acutely embarrasses Pip and more radically shames him: Joe or Trabb's Boy's awful double, who is known simply as The Avenger. What, or whom, is it he avenges? Joe, for one. But as Nicola Bradbury points out, he exists primarily to remind Pip of the misery his riches have brought him.[7] (Initially Pip calls him the Avenging Phantom, and though I think too much has been made of the *Hamlet* parallel, I'm willing to see The Avenger as a sort of debased Revenge Ghost, who haunts Pip's existence and recalls him to his responsibilities—just as the Stranger at the Play who first appears to that fallen Shakespearean, Wopsle, in chapter 47, "sitting behind [Pip] like a ghost," has some of the trappings of the vengeful *revenant*. But this sort of thing can be overdone.) In chapter 51, when all the relationships have been sorted out, Pip for once stuns the unflappable Jaggers by exploding the news that Magwitch is Estella's father. The information provokes not only undisguised shock in Jaggers for the first and last time but—for the first and last time—also a passionate outburst in which he reveals his deeply felt sympathy not perhaps so much for Molly and her kind as for their children and for all children whose lives have been poisoned by the atmosphere of crime in which they are reared. (His compassion is hardly compromised by his presenting his plaidoyer in the form of a hypothesis.) Brief though it is, the chapter accommodates something like a comic "subplot" in Jaggers's amazement that Wemmick is a family man: you (too) with a father! All these motifs—Jaggers's display of emotion, the aura of crime, the presence of the father and his offspring—give way to a grotesque coda: "the opportune appearance" of the sniveling thief Mike (virtually one of Pip's first London tourist attractions), announcing that his daughter has been arrested for shoplifting; and at the thought of his child he starts sniveling again. Wemmick won't have any of his disgusting noises; well, Mike blubbers, "A man can't help his feelings." "His what?" Wemmick savagely turns on him; and Jaggers throws him out of the office with a biting "I'll have no feelings here." A lot of chapters in *Great Expectations* work like this. I'm not prepared to say whether Dickens knew what he was about in bringing on Mike or whether, like Emerson's Michelango, he builded better than he knew; but you don't look inspiration in the mouth.

The organic structure of *Great Expectations*, except for the change from monthly to weekly, is not germane to a discussion of its textual history. But (going back to chapter 51, in which Pip reveals Estella's paternity) we may just notice that in swearing his listeners to silence Jaggers reenacts the confrontation in chapter 18, in which Pip is forbidden to ask any questions about the identity of his benefactor—of whom, by chapter 51, Pip knows more than Jaggers ever dreamed of. Let's stay with Jaggers. In chapter 29, Havisham, Jaggers, Pip, and Estella sit down to play whist. "Of the manner and extent to which he took our trumps into custody, and came out with mean little cards at the end of hands, before which the glory of our Kings and Queens was utterly abased; I say nothing." What is Jaggers doing but beggaring his neighbors? In other words, the control vested in Estella during Pip's first visits has now shifted to Jaggers: to Pip, whom she used to beggar, Estella appeared as an impenetrable enchantress; Jaggers knows her to be the child of the gypsy murderess. Molly's own first appearance is another rum affair. Jaggers

---

7. Nicola Bradbury, *Great Expectations* (New York: St. Martin's Press, 1990), 66.

shows her off to the boys at his dinner party in chapter 26. The only other character he singles out for his own amusement is Drummle. Not even the wiliest haruspex can guess at the significance of the relationship between Molly and Drummle until Dickens makes the connection about four months later. Both Bradbury and Meckier glance (from different perspectives) at the three fights in the first stage: Magwitch versus the liver-chewing young man, Pip versus the pale young gentleman, Joe versus Orlick.[8] All three antagonists seem to spring out of nowhere. Compeyson all but starts up from his grave; Pip "finds himself, to his great surprise," staring at a red-lidded anemic kid who (just like so) invites him to "Come and fight!"; Orlick hasn't been mentioned before Pip's request for a half holiday provokes his outburst and ends in his lying among the coal dust "as if he had been of no more account than the pale young gentleman." Estella, observing but unobserved during the combat with Herbert (Thomas Hardy virtually took out a patent on these concealed listening posts) appears unto Pip "with a bright flush upon her face, as though something had happened to delight her"; Mrs. Joe, "a most unscrupulous spy and listener," who looks *in* at one of the windows, gets a livelier sexual charge from seeing Orlick imbrued in blood. A final point (Bradbury again, independently). Pip's first encounters with his real and assumed benefactors could serve as studies in the manipulation of narrative tempi. Pip's meeting with Magwitch (" 'Hold your noise!' cried a terrible voice") comes with a shocking immediacy that doesn't give Pip (or us) a minute to think of what's happening. His first visit to Havisham occurs almost in slow motion. Pip first notices one thing, then another; he blinks at the light and gropes in the dark; Dickens allows him all the time in the world to get his bearings. "It was not in the first few moments that I saw all these things, though I saw more of them in the first moments than might be supposed." The sentence almost requires to be read slowly, reflectively, as if Pip were revisiting the experience. (Cf. "Hold your noise!") As happens so often in fiction, the very expansiveness of the narrative deepens the intensity of the experience. And this is, of course, the way we experience time: we recall a first happening more clearly and deliberately than the third and fifth, which have been dimmed by the eye of habit and routine. "As we began to become more used to one another . . ." When he does get used to Havisham he ratifies their familiarity by singing "Old Clem" to her: "Blow the fire, blow the fire—Old Clem! Roaring dryer, soaring higher—Old Clem." Perhaps Dickens remembered this when Miss Havisham perishes by fire five months later.[9] Chances are that the reader of the thirtieth weekly on June 22 was far too absorbed in Havisham's curtains or her burnt wedding dress to mind Old Clem. After all, before he can expect them to turn to the next number, Dickens has to make sure his readers are going to turn the page.

As a matter of record, Dickens himself, past master of the weekly serial, thoroughly disliked the format, and he complained about its constraints every time he sat down to write one. He looked on the monthly numbers as his proper métier, the format that allowed him the room and the time frame in which he felt most at home. Weeklies were almost always a function of ex-

---

8. Bradbury, 44, 46; Meckier, "*Great Expectations*: Symmetry in (Com)motion," *DQ* 15 (1998): 47, n. 8.
9. Bradbury, 32. The tempo of the Havisham scene is discussed in Gervais's essay below, p. 692.

ternal pressures: to fill up the pages of *Master Humphrey's Clock*; to give *Household Words* a booster shot; to get *All the Year Round* off to a handsome start. Thus of *Master Humphrey's Clock*, the weekly that accommodated *The Old Curiosity Shop* and *Barnaby Rudge*: "I cannot bear these jerking confidences which are no sooner begun than ended, and no sooner ended than begun again." Of *Hard Times*: "the difficulty of the space * * * is CRUSH-ING." Of *A Tale of Two Cities*: "the small portions thereof drive me frantic"; and again, "it has occasioned me the greatest misery by being presented in the 'tea-spoon-ful' form." Of *Great Expectations*: "as to planning out from week to week, nobody can imagine what the difficulty is, without trying."[1]

Even so, Dickens enjoyed at least *some* freedom in broaching his jerky confidences. In computing his weekly portions for a miscellany, Dickens was not, of course, so narrowly bound by considerations of space as he was in making up his monthly numbers, which required strict uniformity of length. The numbers for *Great Expectations* could vary by as many as nearly four columns, ranging from just over eight to just under twelve. But on the whole, he liked to keep things tidy. He advised his contributors that the ideal installment would be about eight columns, and he usually practiced what he preached. Beyond this, Dickens adopted the tripartite division he had already adopted in *A Tale of Two Cities* and, before this, in the book edition of *Hard Times*, and it may be worth noting that in coping with the larger units of Pip's three stages, Dickens gets back in uniformity of length what he gave away in the weekly serial: roughly 123 columns each. Jejune as all this sounds, in practice even so mechanical a business as the difference between the tripartite division of *Great Expectations* and *A Tale of Two Cities* (in which the short first book serves primarily as a prelude in which all motifs are introduced) leads the reader into basic questions of narratology or musicology.

In *A Tale of Two Cities*, the serial that had launched *All the Year Round*, Dickens had "struck out [the] rather bold and original idea" of publishing in both weekly and monthly installments, the novel running in weekly numbers from April to November 1859 and, with a decent handicap, issued in seven monthly parts from June to December. But the ho-hum sales in monthly wrappers failed to confirm Dickens in his speculation that a double blessing is a double grace. Accordingly, in serializing *Great Expectations* he dispensed with monthly publication—though both the manuscript pagination and internal evidence reflect Dickens's by now ingrained habit, in process of composition, of thinking in terms of monthly numbers, the format in which nearly all his loose baggy monsters had been marketed for the past quarter century. That he clearly had the monthly in mind is indicated by the breaks in the manuscript, in which this is spelled out at the head of the page: "Second Monthly Portion," "Fourth Monthly No.," etc. Two months into the book (and even after the first weekly number had gone on sale) he still spoke of

1. "To the Readers of 'Master Humphrey's Clock' " in *Master Humphrey's Clock* No. 79 (*Barnaby Rudge*, chapter 65), October 1841; to Forster, [?February] 1854 (*PL* 7, 282) and July 9, 1859 (*PL* 9, 92); to Thomas Carlyle, October 30, 1859 (145); to Forster, [April] 1861 (403). See R. C. Churchill, "The Monthly Dickens and the Weekly Dickens," *Contemporary Review* 234 (1979): 97–101; Ellen Casey, "That Specially Trying Mode of Publication: Dickens as Editor of the Weekly Serial," *Victorian Periodicals Review* 14 (1981): 97; Robert L. Patten, "Dickens and Serial Publication," in Baumgarten, *Reading Great Expectations*, 104–107.

the novel as nine months long.[2] Indeed, what needs to be remembered in all this is that when Dickens sat down to write *Great Expectations* at the end of September 1860 he fully planned to publish the book in monthly parts and that its issuance in weekly numbers was an accident of the trade, ultimately irrelevant to the conception and scaffolding of the book—a fiat by the editor-publisher of *All the Year Round*, not the biographer of Pip's fortunes.

Lever's Long Day's Journey into Night

As early as January 2, 1860, Dickens had invited the Anglo-American novelist Charles Lever to contribute a serial, either to follow directly on the heels of Collins's smashing *Woman in White*, scheduled to conclude in July 1860, or else to follow an intermediate serial by an author who had been approached in November but had so far refused to commit herself one way or the other—on January 13, Dickens identified the waffly subject as George Eliot. By February 21 Dickens informed Lever that Eliot had begged off— "Adam (or Eve) Bede is terrified by the novel difficulties of serial writing"— and that Lever was to succeed Collins in July.[3] Collins's serial took up more space than had been anticipated, and Lever's *A Day's Ride: A Life's Romance* was held over until the number for August 18, which carried the next-to-last installment of Collins's thriller; starting with the number for September 1, Lever's novel took pride of place on the front pages of *All the Year Round*.

But pride goeth before the fall; and if Collins's detective novel had been a publisher's dream, Lever's romance turned out to be a nightmare, or *Alpentraum*—Lever likes to sprinkle his prose with a little German. Though Dickens initially professed to be delighted with both the title and the drollness of the opening episodes, it soon became clear that the readers failed to appreciate whatever humor Dickens thought he had glimpsed; the *Ride* rambled on and on; within three installments, sales of *All the Year Round* were falling off drastically, and there was "nothing for it" but to arrest the slippage with a novel by the Conductor himself.

Not one of Lever's thirty-four novels is still in print; the last full-length study on him appeared almost sixty years ago, and its author, the distinguished Victorian scholar Lionel Stevenson, goes Forster one better by keeping the very dates of Lever's letters (and most other dates) a professional secret.[4] Within seven years of his death, a reviewer in *The Nation* could write that Lever "belongs to a completely bygone period, and * * * his reputation, whatever may become of it in the future, is almost as completely dead for the time being as if he had never written a line."[5] Very likely *A Day's Ride*, which even Lever's apologists have written off as minor Lever, would have disappeared from sight but for two circumstances: its contribution to the re-

2. To Bernhard Tauchnitz, [?Mid-November 1860] and November 21, 1860 (*PL* 9, 340, 341); to Austen Henry Layard (345). A basic fact of the calendar—that four weeks are not a month—explains why the novel ran for eight months, not, as Dickens keeps saying, for nine. In my section on "Monthly Numbers," *DSA* 2: 321–26, I have tried to make a case on internal stylistic evidence for Dickens's thinking in monthlies.
3. To Lever, January 2, 1860 (*PL* 9, 190–91); January 13 (197–98); February 21 (215–16); also Gordon S. Haight, *George Eliot: A Biography* (New York: Oxford University Press, 1968), 311, citing George Eliot's journal for November 18, 1859.
4. *Dr. Quicksilver: The Life of Charles Lever* (London: Chapman & Hall, 1939; rept. New York, Russell & Russell, 1969).
5. *The Nation* (New York) 29 (1879): 368.

cession of *All the Year Round* and the praise heaped on it by Bernard Shaw, its one genuine damned-if-I-won't champion.

Even though Yeats gave an early novel of Lever's a place (eleventh in his roster of thirteen) among Irish novels worth reading, Yeats spoke for most of his compatriots who thought of Lever as a renegade, a lost soul to the Irish cause—and anyway, what kind of ranking is eleven out of thirteen?[6] Lever's first two books, *The Confessions of Harry Lorrequer* (a name that became his sobriquet in the sense in which "Boz" became Dickens's) and *Charles O'Malley, the Irish Dragoon* (the one that made No. 11 on Yeats's list), both appeared in monthly installments in *The Dublin University Magazine*, the first intermittently over a period of three years between 1837 and 1840, the second from March 1840 to December 1841. The novels put Lever on the map and remain virtually the only two that have kept him there. *Lorrequer* and *O'Malley* brought something passingly innovative into English fiction in being the first books to deal with the whole subject of the English military in the Napoleonic Wars. That novel readers should have had to wait twenty-two years after Waterloo before they found their mini-Hemingways or mini-Mailers is remarkable enough: very likely, Englishmen suffered from a dearth of veteran-writers and war correspondents (for this was long before the days of photographs), and the despatches by the Duke of Wellington didn't make for more exciting reading than Lever—even though Dickens for one ranked them (to *"Great applause"*) among the topnotch publications (along with Macaulay's *History*, Tennyson's *Poems*, Layard's Nineveh *Researches*, and "the minutest truths * * * discovered by the genius of a Herschel or a Faraday").[7] It may be useful to remember that Lever's naval counterpart, the more seasoned and better-known Captain Marryat, had to wait twenty years after Trafalgar before coming out with his first (semi-autobiographical) novel, *Frank Mildmay*—his best-known novel, *Mr. Midshipman Easy*, preceded the first installment of *Lorrequer* by roughly a year—and *Captain* Marryat wrote from experience.[8] (Of the two big novels covering Waterloo from the enemy's side, the first, Stendhal's *Charterhouse of Parma*, appeared in 1839, and the hero of the second, Hugo's *Les Misérables*, waited so long to steal his loaf of bread that Pip had already stolen his sister's the year before.)

The adjectives always used to describe Lever, with the built-in reductiveness of these epithets, are things like "rollicking," "roisterous," "boisterous," "slap-dash," and "jolly," and everybody who knew him described him as a mercurial conversationalist. One of the subjects on which Lever tirelessly expatiated was his sloppiness as a writer; the haste with which he got rid of Character X; the languor, the fatigue, the apathy he experienced in writing about Y; the impossibility of his maintaining any interest in his plots once he had gotten them going; and not to get him started on the deadly boredom inflicted by the need to find an end to a novel—any end. From time to time, he offered his publishers a choice of endings: "You may have O'Donoghue warm with love or cold without, as may seem best to befit the temper and taste of our readers. I can wind up with Demosthenic abruptness in eleven

6. Letter to *The Daily Express* (Dublin), February 27, 1895, and "Irish National Literature: A List of the Best Irish Books," *Bookman* 9 (1895): 21–22; quoted in A. Norman Jeffares, "Reading Lever," in *Charles Lever: New Evaluations*, ed. Tony Bareham ("Ulster Editions and Monographs, 3"; Savage, Md.: Barnes and Noble Books, 1991), 26.
7. Banquet of Literature and Art, January 6, 1853; *Speeches*, 157.
8. Stevenson, 76.

numbers, the curtain falling amid the blue lightning and thunder that scattered the French fleet; or I can go on to a more Colburn and Bentley ending,
with love and marriage licenses, in thirteen numbers." Apparently, even this
was not enough for the publishers, and Lever obligingly volunteered to "give
it another turn * * *—anything in the world, even to marrying Sir Marma-
duke to Mrs. McKelly, and Lanty Lawlor to Miss Travers."[9] One recent critic
quotes him as admitting that " 'I was never sure when I started for Norway
that I might not end in Naples'; and that endings were always his weak point."[1]
    For somebody as prolific as Lever, he certainly groused immensely about
the miseries of composition. As Stevenson notes, he forever tried to bring
Lorrequer, which had begun as a disjointed group of sketches and midway
turned into a monthly serial, to an abrupt finish, wrote the final installments
under loud protest, and once he discovered that the public loved this labor
of discontent, noted that "if this sort of thing amuses them, thought I, I can
go on for ever." And apparently practice makes prodigal: from about 1850
on, his practice was to write two novels simultaneously ("I have * * * been
doing with my thoughts what they say has deteriorated Spanish nobility—
ruining them by frequent intermarriage"),[2] one written under his own name,
the other anonymously—and usually the one he published anonymously got
much better reviews—without, however, our being able to factor any personal
bias against him into the equation. One would have thought that, of all
people, Lever, who had rescued *The Dublin University Magazine*, in which
his own novels had been successfully serialized, from going under by assuming its editorship in 1842, should have known the demands of serial publication. But the assumption is really a specious one, and when one of Lever's
commentators points out that "[Lever] is absolutely the product of the
nineteenth-century vogue for serial publication" what he means is that this
mode of publication doesn't necessarily encourage constant self-monitoring
but can make for the happy-go-lucky slovenliness that nobody had to teach
Lever. Lever gave up the editorship after three years; for a couple of years the
Levers and their kids rambled around Germany and Italy; in 1847 they settled
in Florence, and in 1867 Lord Derby appointed him consul at Trieste, with
the observation, "Here is six hundred a year for doing nothing, and you are
just the man to do it."[3] All this explains a good deal about the handicap *A
Day's Ride* was bound to suffer: the predictable failure of a slapdash novel
(which might have done very well in his Irish journal) in *All the Year Round*;
the abrupt ending of the book, which is the more reprehensible, really, in
view of Lever's getting almost two months' notice to wind it up; and a reversal

9. Stevenson, 150; Roger J. McHugh, "Charles Lever," *Studies: An Irish Quarterly* 27 (1938): 259. The
    practice of providing optional endings persisted throughout Lever's life. Of *Sir Jasper Carew* (1852–
    54): "I am sorely distressed about the choice of two dénouements for the tale; like one of Peel's
    measures, it can be treated in various ways, with divers objections against each." Of *Sir Brook Fossbroke*
    (1865–66): "I can never put the people to bed with the propriety that I wish. Some won't come for
    their night-caps; some won't lie down; and some will run about in their shirts when I want to extinguish
    the candle" (Stevenson, 200, 272).
1. Tony Bareham, "Introduction: The Famous Irish Lever," *Charles Lever: New Evaluations*, 3.
2. Stevenson, 163. The composition of two books at the same time was not wholly foreign to Dickens,
    who published the last eight monthly installments of *Pickwick Papers* concurrently with the first nine
    installments of *Oliver Twist*, but this balancing act never became habitual to him: it was taken up,
    without detriment to either production, when he interrupted a novel to cough up his portions of the
    annual Christmas numbers.
3. W. J. Fitzpatrick, *The Life of Charles Lever* (2 vols., London: Chapman & Hall, 1879) 2, 341.

of the hero's five-hundred-page misadventures so sudden, in the antepenultimate paragraph, that the ending seems artificially grafted on to a much more morose conclusion.

The relations of Dickens and Lever got off to a very rocky start in the early forties, and Lever's comments about Dickens continued to reveal a good deal of malice, envy, and paranoia even after the two novelists had sheathed their swords. But Dickens obviously wouldn't have solicited a serial from him if he hadn't been convinced of its commercial potential. Fitzgerald notes that "it had been thought something of a *coup* to secure the vivacious Lever * * * whose mercurial style was certain to carry the readers with him. I recall the joyous starting, the very original opening, the anticipated enjoyment of the editors"; and his optimism was clearly shared by Dickens's staff.[4] What happened?

The easiest answer would be to say that Lever wasn't "with it." As usual, he was working on two books: *A Day's Ride* appeared in *All the Year Round* from August 18, 1860 to March 23, 1861; *One of Them*, in which Lever drew on his experiences as dispensary doctor at Portstewart, a spa in County Derry, in the thirties, and on his Florentine sojourn ten years later, was published in monthly parts from December 1859 to January 1861, and Lever clearly set greater store by the autobiographical book. "I am doing my best at *One of Them*," he told his friend Alexander Spencer. "*The Ride* I write as carelessly as a common letter, but I'd not be the least astonished to find the success in the inverse ratio of the trouble." Within a few weeks, as we know, the composition and the reception couldn't have been in more nearly direct ratio. What specially annoyed Lever was that "as ill luck would have it, it is just the moment the F[oreign] O[ffice] should call upon me for details about Italy"—in other words, should ask him to relapse just then into the work he was being paid to do. Elsewhere he confided to his friends that two months before he was to begin sending proof to Dickens, he had rummaged through some serialized stories he had published fifteen years earlier, *Tales of the Trains*, "to see if I could steal any of the incidents into my new tale for Dickens."[5] Greater minds than he were known to get multiple uses out of one composition, and Lever was too far behind the times to palm off his autoplagiarisms as "self-quotation," intertextuality, or montage. Dickens himself, counting on "the vivacious Lever's" gift for gab, had been much too cavalier in his instructions to Lever back in October 1859, at a time when he had a shorter serial in mind than the full-length serial he was to broach the following January.

4. Fitzgerald, *Memories*, 204. Dickens to Lever, January 2, 1860 (*PL* 9, 190); March 9, 1860 (219); June 21, 1860 (267–68). For a sampling of Lever's more acrimonious comments on Dickens, see the letters given in Franklin P. Rolfe, "Letters of Charles Lever to His Wife and Daughter," *Huntington Library Bulletin* 10 (1936): 149–88. But the later exchanges are very affectionate (Lever dedicated his next novel, *Barrington* [1863], to Dickens); and the view that the two got along famously is put forward by Hyder Rollins in *Charles Dickens's Letters to Charles Lever*, ed. Flora V. Livingston (Cambridge, Mass.: Harvard University Press, 1933), xvii.
5. To Alexander Spencer, September 17, 1860, in Edmund Downey, *Charles Lever: His Life in His Letters* (2 vols., Edinburgh: William Blackwood and Sons, 1906) 1, 362. For all his *je-m'en-fichisme*, Lever apparently got cold feet in getting started on the book and kept asking for delays: see his letters of February 27, 1860 (*PL* 9, 215, n. 9) and May 18, 1860 (255, n. 1); and while proof was already en route to America, on July 25, "Let me start * * * on a New Yr. with more hopeful mind & better courage" (275, n. 1). It would be difficult to think of two writers temperamentally further apart than Lever and Bulwer, but some of the parallels in their professional conduct are striking; see below, p. 496 ff.

The chronic malady that is to succeed mine, being already under medical treatment,[6] I reply—a paroxysm—in one, two, three, or four parts—anything in the way of fiction—anything in the way of actual observation and the reflection suggested by it—anything about Italy—anything grave or gay about anything in the wide world, that has filtered through the mind of a man who sees the world with bright and keen eyes such as yours. "Say what will suit you," say you. "*That* is what will suit me," say I.[7]

For a man like Lever this was an invitation to ignore the basic rules that guided serial novels in *All the Year Round*. What Dickens ought to have known was that the qualities of his own serial and Wilkie Collins's—the two that preceded *A Day's Ride*—as well as the one that followed it and for nearly four months kept it company just weren't within Lever's grasp. Whatever one may think of The Woman in White, Dickens thought her appearance on the Finchley Road at 1 A.M. ten pages into the novel one of the two most dramatic scenes in all literature; *A Tale of Two Cities*, which had gotten *All the Year Round* off to its start, makes readers jump out of their seats the moment (call it page eight) a passenger on the Dover Road unfolds a piece of paper that says "RECALLED TO LIFE"; and in the novel Lever inadvertently called to life, a terrible voice shouts "Hold your noise!" after the family introductions and the mise-en-scène have been disposed of in three paragraphs. Hence Dickens's memo to Lever on June 21, 1860, after seeing proof of the opening chapters: "The only suggestion I have to make (and that arises solely out of the *manner* of publication) is, that we ought to get at the action of the story, in the first No."; and, after the fall, on October 15, his explanation that "if you do not fix the people in the beginning, it is almost impossible to fix them afterwards."[8]

The central figure and narrator of Lever's novel, Algernon Sydney Potts, is the twenty-two-year-old scion of a long line of Dublin apothecaries, whose head has been turned by German romances and who labors under the triple misfortune of living a fantasy life, telling pathological lies, and being condemned to eavesdrop on conversations about himself from which he emerges as a ludicrous ass.[9] Potts suffers a brief stint at Trinity College, Dublin; decides to emulate German day-trippers by riding around Ireland; loses his horse in a drunken wager to a good-humored priest; falls into a brain fever; spends a couple of weeks in a summer cottage as guest of a friendly sport and his sister; finds that the cottage belongs to the worldly priest who talked him out of his horse (a plot!) and decamps when he thinks he has been found out as a fraud; sails for England; barely escapes being flogged by an irate old husband, whose jealousy Potts has provoked by confusing his wife with a mysterious young woman in mourning; is mistaken by the mysterious young woman's companion for a prince traveling incog. (an heir apparent to an obscure branch of the Bourbons); takes up with a liberty-loving clown and a grasping gypsy; and,

6. In plain and homely writ: The Woman in White, which is to succeed A Tale of Two Cities, being readied for publication.
7. October 16 (*PL* 9, 134).
8. *PL* 9, 267, 328.
9. Charles Lever's *A Day's Ride: A Life's Romance* [1860–61] (2 vols., Leipzig: Bernhard Tauchnitz, "Collection of British Authors," 1864), chapter 7. All quotations follow this, the "Copyright Edition," but since the edition begins chapter numeration afresh with volume 2, I follow, in giving chapters, *The Novels of Charles Lever* (2 vols., Boston: Little, Brown and Company, 1895). *A Day's Ride* appears in 2, 101–522.

in another case of mistaken identity, spends nine months in an Austrian dungeon; is rescued by the father of the young woman in mourning, with whom the Austrian gendarmerie got him mixed up; embarks for Constantinople and Russia; and turns up as a slightly seedy boulevardier in Paris. It *sounds* like a lot of happenings, but most of them are stifled in Potts's endless interior monologues, which lack all contours, as much as to prove that "There is nothing either good or bad but thinking makes it worse."[1]

One way to lie your way out of your frustrations is to indulge in fantasies, the psychedelic fantasies of the bodily meek, cowardly, and tacky. Occasionally, reading *A Day's Ride* is like reading six hundred pages of "The Secret Life of Walter Mitty"—which its author was smart enough to exhaust in six pages (and which self-destructed as a full-length movie); and as fantasts go, Münchhausen, with his ballistics, is not only incomparably more imaginative but a prototechnocratic visionary, the Jules Verne of liars. "Am I destined to drive the Zouaves into the sea by a bayonet charge of the North Cork Rifles?" (26). "With a tear to the memory of the poor French colonel that I killed at Sedan, I turned the conversation" (3). "In an episode about bear-shooting, I mentioned the Emperor of Russia, poor dear Nicholas, and told how we had exchanged horses" (3). "I remember one night—it was the fourth sitting of the Congress at Paris—that Sardinian fellow, you know his name, came to me and said, 'There's that confounded question of the Danubian Provinces coming on to-morrow, and Gortschakoff is the only one who knows about it. Where are we to get at anything like information?' 'When do you want it, count?' said I" (21), etc., etc. Whatever Potts may have known about the Danubian Provinces, Lever himself could certainly have bettered his instruction. At least one reviewer of *A Day's Ride* complained, with a certain justice tempered by insularity, that Lever's "repetition of scenes representative of a kind of society which is neither familiar nor pleasing to a large class of English readers" had long outlasted its usefulness, and that the British were tired of reading about "the frivolity of Continental society, [and] the vulgarity and mistakes of English travellers abroad."[2] Yet to readers unfamiliar with Lever, the way to read *A Day's Ride* is to catch him out in those parts of the book to which the reviewer in *Blackwood's* objects: the passages of social satire that are in large part based on the experienced actuality, sometimes, in fact, are little more than transcriptions from his correspondence, and especially those that ideologically connect up with some of Dickens's discontents. Lever had a very sharp and jaundiced view of the English in Europe, and though he couldn't have rendered a mindless tourist like Meagles in *Little Dorrit*, he would have recognized him on sight. But this would have bypassed or bored his readers.

---

1. The charge always leveled against Lever's novel is that of its being picaresque and for that reason alone obsolete. But the last thing to which Potts can lay any claims is to be mistaken for a picaro, i.e., a rogue, an unscrupulous scamp, a foil to his gullible master. Besides, the picaro keeps himself and the reader going by the profusion and variety of his whirlwind adventures; his character is the least interesting thing about him. But Potts would be unintelligible without his internal life, even if his mea culpas and smart would-be quid pro quos take up exactly those pages that tempt us to skip the rest. What qualifies *A Day's Ride* as picaresque are Potts's rambling all over Europe and the sloppiness of its construction—Potts going everywhere, the book going nowhere—which are secondary functions of the genre. The hero of *A Day's Ride* is no more a picaro than Arthur Dimmesdale or Mrs. Dalloway: characterologically he is the nearest thing to an antipicaro, a gull, Peter Schlemihl on horseback.

2. Unsigned review in *Blackwood's Magazine* 91 (1862): 452–72.

Then also Lever suffered the misfortune of having been booked by Dickens to follow an act nobody could have followed.

Had he consulted a horoscope, Dickens might have picked a different date on which to launch Lever on his foggy ride. When Potts mounted his horse on August 18, 1860, Wilkie Collins's breathtaking *Woman in White*, which turned out to be four numbers longer than anticipated, still had two weeks to run, and you couldn't very well assign Collins to the back pages just as he was winding up his thriller. (One can't talk about Collins's ever winding anything down.) Collins's readers were still reeling under the shock brought on by the discoveries that Sir Percival Glyde, the husband (or alleged widower) to the (allegedly dead) heroine, while burning the evidence that he hadn't the least claim to call himself Sir Percival anything, burned down the vestry of the church in which he had hidden the evidence and burned himself to death while he was about it; and that the odious Mrs. Catherick, with whom the late fake Sir Percival was thought to have had a scandalous liaison, had carried on no such affair with Sir Percival but with the heroine's late father, a charmer who had sired the heroine's half-sister, the half-sister having been on the point of revealing a "secret" for the past two hundred pages until she took her secret with her to the grave, a grave that Sir Percival and his co-conspirators had palmed off as the heroine's, or legitimate half-sister's, that of Sir Percival's captive wife. In the final two numbers, the two that rode twenty pages ahead of Lever's nag, the heroine had yet to establish her claims to the family fortune, and, with Sir Percival in cinders and her nearest relation indisposed to recognize her as anybody but the dead half-sister, the demystification devolved on the villain and power behind the conspiracy, Count Fosco, the darling of Collinsians, an oddly hollow man despite his three or four hundred pounds of flesh and his perchant for the small beasties whom T. S. Eliot talked about as if he were talking about Donne or the Duchess of Malfi ("who can forget the canaries and the white mice?"). Just before Lever's number came up, on August 11, the narrator discovers from an Italian connection, the silly Papa Pesca, that years ago Fosco betrayed a Secret Brotherhood and is a marked man. In the number in which Collins first went halves with Lever, Collins's hero confronts Fosco with his crimes against the Secret Mafia; in Collins's final installment and Lever's second, Hartwright (the hero) forces the Count into writing a forty-page confession, in which all the mysteries are explained; in the last pages of his novel Collins achieves a genuinely horrible scene, in which Hartwright, vacationing in Paris, stops off at the Morgue and finds Fosco's immense carcass lying on one of the slabs, the nosy Parisians gawking at such a handsome man. Then the wrap-up. All this while Potts gets drunk and barters away his horse.[3]

Even without Collins to stimulate odious comparisons, Lever didn't have

3. Wilkie Collins, *The Woman in White* [1859–60], ed. Harvey Peter Sucksmith (London: Oxford University Press, 1975), 538–84 (numbers 39 and 40). For three weeks in January, Lever shared the pages of the weekly not only with Dickens but also with Mrs. Gaskell, whose gruesome novella *The Grey Woman* bore the reassuring subtitle "In Three Portions," when the end of Lever wasn't in sight. Mrs. Gaskell spun out a first-person historical story, set in the late eighteenth-century French-German border provinces at a time when marauders on both sides of the border terrified the countryside. The timing of the novella, incidentally, suggests how far Dickens was occasionally willing to go in violating his editorial principles: though his subeditor, W. H. Wills, had instructions not to run two first-person articles or serials in one and the same number, Dickens had already ignored his injunction in publishing the Collins and Lever, both first-person narratives, in overlapping numbers; Lever and Dickens were coupled for seventeen numbers; and from January 5 to January 19, 1861, Dickens suffered the presence of three recitalists: Pip, Potts, and Mrs. Gaskell's.

a chance. As Dickens reminded him, Collins had "strung [his story] on the needful strong thread of interest, and made it a great success,"[4] but Lever's book, as I said, remained purely episodic—with a few links that Lever might have hammered into place if he hadn't been so lazy. For example in number 7 and 8, en route to London and Dover, Potts (a) overhears some funny talk about the malfeasances of an ancestral relation of the cottagers he'd been staying with, (b) meets the aforementioned young lady in mourning, and (c) divides his attention between the young lady in black and the brash young diplomat who accidentally leaves his attaché case with Potts. But by then, when things begin to look as if they might go somewhere, and the ancestor, the young woman in mourning, and the attaché case might be strung on the "needful strong thread of interest," the calendar in the Wellington Street offices pointed to October 6, and Dickens had already sent in his "business report" to Lever. On October 27 Dickens informed the public what Lever and the war cabinet had known for at least three weeks, that a new novel by Mr. Dickens was to begin publication "on Saturday, December the first, to be continued until completed in about eight months," an ad repeated in the numbers for November 3, 10, and 17, capped, lest anybody forget, on November 24 with the reminder that *Great Expectations* "will be commenced [next week] to be continued from week to week and completed in August." Accordingly, Dickens took over the front page on December 1, just before Potts had reached the halfway mark, and *A Day's Ride* took a backseat twelve pages into the journal. One may be tempted to blame Dickens for first announcing his advent so indecently soon and then forcing Lever from the front page (which Lever needed a lot more than Dickens did), but the survival of the journal obviously required some such draconian measures. On January 23, 1861, Wills told Lever to wrap up his story by March 23—Dickens liked to leave these peremptory notices to his subalterns.[5] On February 9, the day Dickens sprung the news of Pip's Great Expectations, readers were informed that in six weeks they would have seen the last of Potts. By February 9 *A Day's Ride* had long been relegated from page twelve to the final pages of the journal, taking a backseat to pieces like "More about Silkworms" and "Flaws in China"—the country, not the porcelain, I think, and (in the number following) to the "Scenery of South Carolina" and "A German Pedlar's Congress at the Foot of the Rauhe Alp in Würtemberg"—which really is the limit. The reminder of the March 23 deadline was repeated in the numbers for February 16 and 23, and March 2, in which the *Ride* is squeezed into three pages, a pale afterthought to "A New Chamber of Horrors." The number for February 16 had been devoted to Pip's leave-taking from the forge and completed the first stage; and there is perhaps a certain pathos in the reflection that in the same number Potts's darling gypsy lass leaves him. By March 23 Potts dismounted for good; but then Lever—and from what we know about his hopeful finales nobody will be shocked at the news—still had a surprise in store.

A Day's Ride, in fact, is an excellent demonstration of a book that doesn't work as a weekly but may just be worth salvaging in volume form. Though

---

4. October 6, 1860 (*PL* 9, 321).
5. *Charles Dickens's Letters to Charles Lever*, 30.

Shaw himself dipped into the book in *All the Year Round* (whether he finished it is a toss-up: Shaw didn't have to read books from cover to cover to praise or to bury them), as a serial Lever's novel, as we saw, defied every rule of the trade. Even as a novel it remains a very shaky affair, but the book has almost certainly been judged, and undervalued, by the odium attached to its serial history. For sympathetic souls, Shaw's brief—it appeared in his preface to *Major Barbara* in 1906—may begin to provide a key to the book's strengths. Shaw read Potts's interminable lies and soliloquies not as blarney but as the essential symptoms of an identifiable clinical case and Potts himself as a corrective to the stereotype of the romantic fantast who from time out of mind, from Aristophanes to R. L. S., has been drawn as a harmless lunatic. Lever substituted for these affable Don Quixotes a "piece of really scientific natural history," whose dislocation can be diagnosed and called "Potts's disease"—or Potts's Complaint, insofar as Potts dabbles in a kind of emotional autoeroticism. Writers like the creators of Alnaschar, Don Quixote, and Pickwick all lacked Lever's intransigence: in "relent[ing] over [their characters] they simply changed sides, and became friends and apologists where they had formerly been mockers."

In Lever's story there is a real change of attitude. There is no relenting towards Potts: he never gains our affection like Don Quixote and Pickwick. * * * But we dare not laugh at him, because, somehow, we recognize ourselves in Potts. We may, some of us, have enough nerve, enough muscle, enough luck, enough tact or skill or address or knowledge to carry things off better than he did * * * ; but for all that we know that Potts plays an enormous part in ourselves and in the world, and that the social problem is not a problem of story-book heroes of the older patterns, but a problem of Pottses, and of how to make men of them. To fall back on my old phrase, we have the feeling * * * that Potts is a piece of really scientific natural history as distinguished from funny story telling.[6]

Potts is in fact often his own best analyst. Occasionally, when he pauses for breath, he isn't above delivering an epigram straight out of Balzac: "like all awkward men, I grew garrulous where I ought to have been silent" (2). He ticks off his options in impressing some tourists: should he pretend to be a peer of the realm? a great writer? a heartbroken victim of infidelity? a dreadful criminal? He chooses the role of criminal, for "there is, to men who are not constitutionally courageous, a strong pleasure in being able to excite terror in others" (40). The romantic innocents whom Shaw parades could scarcely diagnose their delusional disorders the way Potts diagnoses his:

Most men who build "castles in Spain" * * * do so purely to astonish their friends. *I* indulged in these architectural extravagances in a very

---

6. "First Aid to Critics," *Major Barbara* [1906], *The Complete Bodley Head Plays of Bernard Shaw*, ed. Dan H. Laurence (7 vols., London: Bodley Head, 1970–74) 3 [1971], 15–18. Shaw had already taken notice of Lever's novel more than ten years earlier, in his review of *All's Well that Ends Well*, "Poor Shakespeare," *Saturday Review*, February 2, 1895, in which he describes the part of Parolles as "a capital study of the yarn-spinning society-struck coward, who also crops up again in modern fiction as the hero of Charles Lever's underrated novel, *A Day's Ride: A Life's Romance.*" See Stanley Weintraub, "Bernard Shaw, Charles Lever, and *Immaturity*," *The Shaw Bulletin* 2 (1957): 11–15. Weintraub proposes Potts as a model for the hero of Shaw's first novel (1879), "an amalgam of the immature Shaw and the immature hero of [his] novel." Shaw's hero, apparently as much of a dawdler as Potts, had to wait half a century before he appeared in print.

different spirit. I built my castle to live in it; from foundation to roof-tree, I planned every detail of it to suit my own taste, and all my study was to make it as habitable and comfortable as I could (20).

The complications and fun surface when he isn't merely deluded himself but is the cause of delusion in other people—in the old lady, say, who has convinced herself that he is pretender to the French throne—or, as he himself puts it: "from the moment I entered one of *their* castles, I felt myself in a strange house" (20). In fact, it is sometimes difficult to draw the line between Lever's clinical accuracy (Shaw) and his authorial lumpishness (everybody else). As has been suggested, Potts is apt to answer a perfectly commonplace question in two or three pages of the most stilted language: the impression isn't so much of a pompous puppy as it is of somebody who is clinically autistic. Before he approaches somebody he tries to impress, Potts—again sometimes for pages on end—rehearses what he is going to say: a sure symptom of the petrified personality.

Potts is also a great snob, and his snobbishness has furnished another (doubtful) reason for the failure of *A Day's Ride*: Lever's use of the same theme Dickens uses in *Great Expectations*, the theme of a snob's progress. A recent commentator who addresses himself to just this issue writes:

> [D]iscernible [too], particularly in Lever's later novels, is a fascination with rank or station. * * * He derives great pleasure from the depiction of characters who aspire beyond their station, and who cannot with ease or certainty be classified as authentically genteel or irredeemably vulgar. These characters exist in a transitional zone, perpetually threatened with exposure and humiliation if they fail to enunciate the shibboleths and passwords of gentility.[7]

And he quotes an axiom Lever articulates in *The Martins of Cro'Martin* (1856), that "no peasant in Europe puts so high a value on the intercourse with a rank above his own as does the Irish. The most pleasant flattery to his nature is the notice of 'the gentleman.' "[8] But the very character of snobbishness in Pip and Potts is so different as to make the comparison itself all but meaningless. The final sentence of the above quote, applied to Potts, should really read that characters like him are "perpetually threatened with exposure and humiliation the minute they enunciate the shibboleths and passwords of gentility." Potts's snobbishness is little more than another provocation for ridicule; as a social fact it exists (Shaw in despite) in vacuo, especially as Potts doesn't hurt a fly with his pretentions, which merely redound on himself. At worst, he manages to insult a few people, especially those to whom he happens to be attracted, but the insults leave no impression. There are no Joes and Biddys in Potts's universe. As we saw, one of Pip's most shaming experiences is his response to Joe's visit in chapter 27. This chapter was published in the same number as the final installment of Potts's story, and it shows up the difference between somebody who exercises his snobbishness because he exists in a society that provides him with foils and opportunities, and somebody who merely talks big.

Still, Lever's book contains at least one scene in which Potts's genuine, unconscious social snobbishness surfaces. About midway through the novel,

---

7. Richard Haslam, "Transitional States in Lever," in *Charles Lever: New Evaluations*, 75–85, 79.
8. Ibid., 82.

Potts joins up with a two-person circus: a gypsy and fortune-teller named Catinka and her adoptive father, a clown who (though he isn't Russian) is simply called Little Father, or Väterchen. There was a good deal of the Bohemian in Lever himself (when the Levers and their three children entered Florence on horseback, with manes as long as their horses', they were mistaken for the vanguard of a circus or hippodrome); he was also, like Väterchen—and Dickens—a sworn foe of the Austrian rule over Italy, of which Väterchen has been a victim. (We discover that he has been imprisoned for his refusal to feed and billet Austrian soldiers, and his clownish convulsions before he was led away to be flogged turned him into a professional clown.) Gypsy-complexioned as she is, Catinka goes by the nickname of "Tintenfleck," or "Inkspot." Early on in their acquaintance, Potts, in an effort to lower himself to her level, calls her by her nickname, only to find that she deeply resents this familiarity, which is natural to her equals, "where we all have similar nicknames, but that you, a great personage, high, and rich, and titled, should do so" wounds her deeply (27). Of course, Potts is none of these things, but this is irrelevant to her response, which is sensitive and dignified—and which we shall have reason to remember when these two last lay eyes on each other. At one point, in a long inset narrative (chapter 30), Väterchen tells Potts something about Catinka's past and ruminates: "Would that some rich person—it should be a lady—kind and gentle, and compassionate, could see her and take her away, from such associates, and this life of shame, ere it be too late." Chapter 30 coincided in *All the Year Round* with chapter 8 of *Great Expectations*, in which we have our first glimpse of Estella; and the parallel of Catinka's shady past and her adoption and Estella's (whose mother is in effect a gypsy) is at least an interestingly crooked one. At the same time, Potts's intermittent affection, unlike Pip's torments, yields some of the most simply touching passages of the *Ride*: "and we went along, side by side, very amicably, very happily" (32). There are no such sentences nor sentiments in *Great Expectations*.

These two enjoy one last encounter—the one part of the novel that a couple of commentators on *A Day's Ride* have had a swing at. Three pages before the end of the book, Lever recalls Catinka, who has vanished from sight three or four installments ago, for a final meeting with Potts. Potts has had a serious physical breakdown and has just returned not from Egypt but from the Crimea.

> It was about two years after this—my father had died in the interval, leaving me a small but sufficient fortune to live on, and I had just arrived in Paris * * *—I was standing one morning early in one of the small alleys of the Champs Elysées, watching with half-listless curiosity the various grooms as they passed to exercise their horses in the Bois de Boulogne.
>
> *   *   *
>
> I crossed the road, and had but reached the opposite pathway, when a carriage stopped, and the old horse drew up beside it. After a word or two, the groom took off the hood, and there was Blondel [the horse Potts bartered away at the start of the book]! But my amazement was lost in the greater shock, that the Princess, whose jewelled hand held out the sugar to him, was no other than Catinka!
>
> I cannot say with what motive I was impelled—perhaps the action was

too quick for either—but I drew nigh to the carriage, and, raising my hat respectfully, asked if her highness would deign to remember an old acquaintance. "I am unfortunate enough, sir, not to be able to recall you," said she, in most perfect Parisian French.

"My name you may have forgotten, madame, but scarcely so either our first meeting at Schaffhausen, or our last at Bregenz."

"These are all riddles to me, sir; and I am sure you are too well bred to persist in an error after you have recognised it to be such." With a cold smile and a haughty bow, she motioned the coachman to drive on, and I saw her no more. (48)

As far as I know, it was Shaw again who first drew attention to the resemblance between Dickens's original ending and the ending Lever had published. "[T]he passing carriage was unconsciously borrowed from A Day's Ride," Shaw noted, adding that "Dickens must have felt that there was something wrong with this ending, and Bulwer's objection confirmed his doubt. Accordingly, he wrote a new ending, in which he got rid of Piccadilly."[9] The problem of the two endings is more fully discussed elsewhere, but without reference to the Lever connection, which has since been strengthened by Sadrin.[1] The resemblance certainly can't be dismissed out of hand, and even if Dickens's borrowing was an unconscious one, clever readers might well have noticed it. Two lovers long separated, the man just having come back from the East and realized "modest profits," the couple thrown together by chance in the posh heart of Paris and the posh London West End respectively, he on foot, the lady unbending from a passing carriage, desultory conversation; finis. Pip and Estella need to part on a friendly note because these are the definitively final paragraphs of the novel and it won't do to take leave of an unrepentant Estella; Potts and Catinka can leave on a sour note because their relationship isn't, like Pip and Estella's, germane to the book (nothing is); besides, Lever has a few more paragraphs at his disposal and Catinka isn't the world's only Alien. Whether Dickens himself, reading over the final manuscript pages of *Great Expectations*, or Bulwer, reading the ending in proof the following week, discovered the resemblance ere Shaw came along remains moot. Sadrin inclines to the probability that Bulwer, whose serial was to follow Dickens's come August and who would have been specially sensitive to the two novels still current in *All the Year Round*, alerted Dickens to these embarrassing affinities and told him to "get rid of Piccadilly" and get that woman down from her carriage.[2] The possibility is intriguing and, in the nature of things, undemonstrable.

Lever could afford to get rid of Catinka because, in the paragraph following, Potts finds a letter that had been languishing for more than a year at the police, from the young lady in mourning, whose family had been trying to track down Potts, who, in a Western Union–sized last sentence, is about to

9. *Great Expectations*, "The Novel Library" (London: Hamish Hamilton, 1947), xvi.
1. Sadrin, *Great Expectations*, 171–75. But Sadrin prefaces her commentary with the polite reminder that her hypothesis, which jibes with Shaw's, "is just as tentative—and, no doubt, just as disputable" as any others. Cardwell (482) dismisses the whole Lever thing in a couple of lines as superficial and irrelevant, but as an orthodox Dickens editor she can't be absolved of being parti pris.
2. Sadrin, 174. The joke is that Lever himself, paranoid as he was, wouldn't have been aware of Dickens's theft: two years before it first came to light in Forster's biography, Lever had joined Dickens in Elysium. The other joke, of course, if Shaw is correct, is that Dickens should have gotten his ending from the very novel he had scuttled in order to salvage his own property. But Dickensians aren't likely to buy that option.

join them in Wales and live happily ever after. So, to stretch a point, even Lever at least came close to providing an unhappy ending and then, with two paragraphs to spare, reversed himself. But the two cases are admittedly very dissimilar. In fact, Lever's breathtakingly swift moodswing much more closely resembles Bulwer's equally breathtaking change of heart, which remains to be looked at.

A final tangential, probably meaningless scoring point before we let go of Lever. In number 7 (chapter 9) of his book, Potts spins out some bogus reason for his abrupt flight from his hosts and along the line writes: "I vaguely hinted at great expectations, and so on." The phrase is so common, especially in implying financial gains, that I shouldn't even bring it up if it weren't for the dating of the number: September 29th, 1860—within a couple of days, if not on the very day, Dickens began to write *Great Expectations* ("I think a good name?"). Naturally he had seen the number in proof a week or two earlier, about the time he must have started to wonder what to do about Lever. But even forgettable phrases resist being forgotten. So we are left with a worst-case scenario, which is probably accurate, and a best-case scenario, which we can take or leave, but may take under advisement. The worst-case scenario is the one everybody knows: that Lever delivered a serial that kept losing momentum by the week and cost Dickens a lot of money. The best-case scenario (for Lever) is that Dickens stood in his sloppy gambling friend's debt for supplying him with the alpha and omega of *Great Expectations*, from the title to the last paragraph—and, less incidentally, the format of a brilliantly built novel that might have failed to achieve such formal perfection had Dickens spun it out over twelve monthly numbers.

A Note on Early Editions

Even before Chapman printed a genuine second edition in one volume, the "Library Edition," priced at 7s. 6d., with frontispiece and illustrated title page by Marcus Stone, a number of editions appeared abroad bearing the 1861 date. In January, Dickens completed the agreement with Bernhard Tauchnitz, the prestigious Leipzig publisher, to bring out the novel in the "Collection of British Authors" that Tauchnitz had inaugurated in 1841 with Bulwer's *Pelham, Pickwick Papers*, and *Oliver Twist*. (Germany had entered into a copyright agreement with England as early as 1846, forty-five years before the United States followed suit.) Even before Dickens began composition of *Great Expectations* he informed Tauchnitz, whose liberality and integrity he greatly admired and who was to become a family friend, of the forthcoming book and handsomely asked him to set his own price—by then a customary practice between the two. For a hard-nosed writer like Dickens, who would have been the first to agree with Forster's comment that "publishers are bitter bad judges of an author" and who was notorious for driving hard bargains, the relations with Tauchnitz were uniquely cordial.[3] The two-volume *Great Expectations* in Tauchnitz's "Copyright Edition" followed *All the Year Round*, as do all 1861 editions known to me: the two-volume "House-

---

3. Curt Otto, *Der Verlag Bernhard Tauchnitz: 1837–1912* (Leipzig: Tauchnitz, 1912). The Baron's integrity did not keep him from committing interesting petty malpractices, such as giving fake dates to his publications: for example, he issued his three-volume *David Copperfield* under the date of 1849, before Dickens had finished writing the book. See esp. Simon Nowell-Smith, "Firma Tauchnitz: 1837–1900," *The Book Collector* 15 (1966): 423–36.

hold Edition" published by James Gregory, New York, and two editions published by the reprint house of T. B. Peterson & Brothers, Philadelphia, who had bought the rights from Harper: a one-volume edition based on *Harper's Weekly* and issued in wrappers, which sold for a staggering twenty-five cents —the first paperback of *Great Expectations*—and a slightly later hardcover, priced at $1.50, featuring McLenan's illustrations from *Harper's*.[4]

In England four more editions appeared during Dickens's lifetime: in 1863, Chapman published the "Cheap Edition," a near-likeness of the "Library Edition," reduced by four shillings threepence and richer by some thirty-five garbled readings. Dickens had inaugurated the "Cheap" back in 1847 as a series of reissues for readers who couldn't afford earlier book editions, assuring the owners of the more expensive texts that the "Cheap" would in no way undermine the value of their superior editions.[5] Lastly, two editions were both known as "Library Editions," one dated 1864, the other (which seems to have been universally overlooked) dated 1866, again virtual reprints of the 1862, marketed at the same price and containing all of Stone's eight woodcuts. The "Charles Dickens Edition" of 1868, too, contained the whole of Stone; it was priced at three shillings and bore descriptive headlines Dickens composed for each volume. The headlines are reprinted below, pp. 489–90.

4. Peter S. Bracher, "Harper & Brothers: Publishers of Dickens," *Bulletin of the New York Public Library* 79 (1976): 317–35, traces Dickens's long connection with Harper and charts the course of his worth in dollars and cents for the first book editions: 360 pounds for *Bleak House* (1853); 250 for *Little Dorrit* (1857); 1,000 each for *A Tale of Two Cities* (1859) and *Our Mutual Friend* (1865); and 1,250 for *Great Expectations* (1861).
5. Inserted in parts vi and vii (November and December 1846) of *Dombey and Son*. Simon Nowell-Smith, "The 'Cheap Edition' of Dickens's Works [First Series]: 1847–1852," *The Library*, 5th series (1967): 245–50.

CHARLES DICKENS, ESQ.—[FROM A LATE PHOTOGRAPH.]

fected to speak lightly of Doctor Manette. It is not uncommon to hear people say that he has written himself out. It may be remarked, however, that while the contemporaries of the Pickwick Papers deny that he has ever surpassed that work, there are numerous critics who consider "Oliver Twist" his master-piece, others who prefer "Nickleby," some who pronounce in favor of the "Old Curiosity Shop," and others in favor of "Dombey & Son;" while, judging from the sales of the published volumes, "Little Dorrit" has the best claim to preeminence; and from the actual number of readers, the "Tale of Two Cities" would probably hold the first rank. In a word, there is not the least reason for supposing that in any of the qualities which have raised Mr. Dickens to his present fame —humor, descriptive power, analytical perception of character, charm of style, fancy, pathos, or dramatic ability — there has been any decay since Boz first came before the public. We have no doubt that "Great Expectations" will have as many admirers as any of its predecessors, and that a new generation of readers will decide, when it is ended, that the Great Novelist has at last written his great work— leaving it to their children, or, at all events, to their successors in the reading world, to discover that, after all, the real master-piece was yet to come, and that a genius like that of Dickens is inexhaustible.

[Entered according to Act of Congress, in the Year 1860, by Harper & Brothers, in the Clerk's Office of the District Court for the Southern District of New York.]

CHARLES DICKENS.

WE accompany the first part of Mr. Dickens's new novel, "GREAT EXPECTATIONS," with a Portrait of the author, taken from a very recent photograph. Those who remember him during his visit to this country will notice the change which has taken place since then in his outward man.

Mr. Dickens was born at Portsmouth, England, on 7th February, 1812. His father was for many years a Paymaster in the British Navy; on his retirement he became a reporter on the London press,

first and sweetest of his Christmas stories—"A Christmas Carol," and "Martin Chuzzlewit"—a work of infinite power, and full of his peculiar humor, but marred by the faults which were so conspicuous in his previous work on America.

In 1846 Mr. Dickens appeared before the public as the editor of a daily newspaper—the Daily News —which was intended to inaugurate a new era in London journalism. He had previously filled, for a few months, the office of editor of Bentley's Miscellany; but this was his first experiment in political journalism. It is no discredit to him that it

GREAT EXPECTATIONS.

A NOVEL.

BY CHARLES DICKENS.

Splendidly Illustrated by John McLenan.

☞ Printed from the Manuscript and early Proof-sheets purchased from the Author by the Proprietors of "Harper's Weekly."

From first weekly number in *Harper's Weekly*, November 24, 1860
(detail reduced)

"THE STORY OF OUR LIVES FROM YEAR TO YEAR."—SHAKESPEARE.

ALL THE YEAR ROUND.

A WEEKLY JOURNAL.

CONDUCTED BY CHARLES DICKENS.

WITH WHICH IS INCORPORATED HOUSEHOLD WORDS.

Nº· 84.]   SATURDAY, DECEMBER 1, 1860.   [PRICE 2d.

GREAT EXPECTATIONS.

BY CHARLES DICKENS.

CHAPTER I.

My father's family name being Pirrip, and my christian name Philip, my infant tongue could make of both names nothing longer or more explicit than Pip. So, I called myself Pip, and came to be called Pip.

I give Pirrip as my father's family name, on the authority of his tombstone and my sister—Mrs. Joe Gargery, who married the blacksmith. As I never saw my father or my mother, and never saw any likeness of either of them (for their days were long before the days of photographs), my first fancies regarding what they were like, were unreasonably derived from their tombstones. The shape of the letters on my father's, gave me an odd idea that he was a square, stout, dark man with curly black hair. From the character and turn of the inscription, "Also Georgiana Wife of the Above," I drew a childish conclusion that my mother was freckled and sickly. To five little stone lozenges, each about a foot and a half long, which were arranged in a neat row beside their grave, and were sacred to the memory of five little brothers of mine—who gave up trying to get a living, exceedingly early in that universal struggle—I am indebted for a belief I religiously entertained that they had all been born on their backs with their hands in their trousers-pockets, and had never taken them out in this state of existence.

Ours was the marsh country, down by the river, within, as the river wound, twenty miles of the sea. My first most vivid and broad impression of the identity of things, seems to me to have been gained on a memorable raw afternoon towards evening. At such a time I found out for certain, that this bleak place overgrown with nettles was the churchyard; and that Philip Pirrip, late of this parish, and also Georgiana wife of the above, were dead and buried; and that Alexander, Bartholomew, Abraham, Tobias, and Roger, infant children of the aforesaid, were also dead and buried; and that the dark flat wilderness beyond the churchyard, intersected with dykes and mounds and gates, with scattered cattle feeding on it, was the marshes; and that the low leaden line beyond, was the river;

and that the distant savage lair from which the wind was rushing, was the sea; and that the small bundle of shivers growing afraid of it all and beginning to cry, was Pip.

"Hold your noise!" cried a terrible voice, as a man started up from among the graves at the side of the church porch. "Keep still, you little devil, or I'll cut your throat!"

A fearful man, all in coarse grey, with a great iron on his leg. A man with no hat, and with broken shoes, and with an old rag tied round his head. A man who had been soaked in water, and smothered in mud, and lamed by stones, and cut by flints, and stung by nettles, and torn by briars; who limped, and shivered, and glared and growled; and whose teeth chattered in his head as he seized me by the chin.

"O! Don't cut my throat, sir," I pleaded in terror. "Pray don't do it, sir."

"Tell us your name!" said the man. "Quick!"

"Pip, sir."

"Once more," said the man, staring at me. "Give it mouth!"

"Pip. Pip, sir."

"Show us where you live," said the man. "Pint out the place!"

I pointed to where our village lay, on the flat in-shore among the alder-trees and pollards, a mile or more from the church.

The man, after looking at me for a moment, turned me upside-down, and emptied my pockets. There was nothing in them but a piece of bread. When the church came to itself—for he was so sudden and strong that he made it go head over heels before me, and I saw the steeple under my legs—when the church came to itself, I say, I was seated on a high tombstone, trembling, while he ate the bread ravenously.

"You young dog," said the man, licking his lips, "what fat cheeks you ha' got."

I believe they were fat, though I was at that time undersized for my years, and not strong.

"Darn Me if I couldn't eat 'em," said the man, with a threatening shake of his head, "and if I han't half a mind to't!"

I earnestly expressed my hope that he wouldn't, and held tighter to the tombstone on which he had put me; partly, to keep myself upon it; partly, to keep myself from crying.

"Now then, lookee here!" said the man. "Where's your mother?"

Opening page of serial in *All the Year Round*, December 1, 1860 (reduced)

The Wisbech Manuscript (fragment of opening page, slightly reduced)

Writing *Great Expectations*†

Chapter 10 of *Great Expectations* begins with Dickens's self-delighted description of the Educational Scheme or Course established by Mr. Wopsle's great-aunt—one of the funniest scenes in the novel, and one that, but for the grace of Dickens's muse, would have been lost to posterity. I don't know how many readers have noticed the discontinuity of episodes within a given Dickens chapter; it's a tribute to Dickens's craft that, if we notice the discontinuity at all, it doesn't bother us. No sooner has Dickens done his duty by Wopsle's great-aunt than he transports us, without transition, to the scene at the Three Jolly Bargemen in which Pip gets his down payment of two fat sweltering one-pound notes from the itinerant convict. Of course, it's always possible to finesse the two halves into a coherent whole by talking about the kinds of corruption or contamination Pip suffers at Wopsle's great-aunt's and in being brought face to face with Magwitch's roving ambassador, or in suggesting how a lower-class pre-Victorian country lad is condemned to spend his weekday evenings (the great-aunt's of course is an evening school) and his weekend nights. The more immediate explanation is also the more prosaic. In the received text, the scene at the great-aunt's—it takes up roughly a third of the chapter—ends with Biddy's loan of the large old English D that Pip is to copy and "which I supposed, until she told me what it was, to be a design for a buckle," period; and this is directly followed by paragraph four, which begins: "Of course there was a public-house in the village, and of course Joe liked sometimes to smoke his pipe there." Now, the fact is that these are almost precisely the words with which the chapter itself originally started: "Of course, there was a public house in our village": the chapter began exactly where paragraph four of the chapter now begins, at the Jolly Bargemen. But Dickens then scratched his head, scratched the sentence, and began all over again: "The felicitous idea occurred to me a morning or two later . . . to get out of Biddy everything she knew," and he was launched. Had he not scratched the sentence, we should have been left without one of the most inspired lunacies in the book and a godsend to Dickens recitalists. Of course, Dickens might have introduced the Dame School elsewhere, but one may doubt whether he could have recaptured these first fine raptures even remotely. On her first appearance in chapter 7, by the way, Dickens brought on Biddy's mistress as Wopsle's aunt, got rid of the aunt in manuscript, and promoted her to the status by which we know her, either because an adult's great-aunt is even less qualified to run a Dame School than a mere aunt is, or because you had to be nearly senile to qualify as a Dame School teacher to start with.

As I said, the episodic incoherence in any one chapter is almost a given in Dickens, and very often the funny half and the sensational half may, like

† A longer version of section IX of this essay appeared as "Small Talk in Hammersmith: Chapter 23 of *Great Expectations*" in *Dickensian* 69 (1973): 90–101, and is reprinted with permission of the editors.

Dickens's famous layers of red and white in a side of streaky bacon, fry side by side.[1] Chapter 15, for example, offers a fairly clear division between the scene in which Pip talks Joe into letting him visit Miss Havisham and the one in which Orlick gets into a brawl with Mrs. Joe, and though the two are logically related by Orlick's claim that if Pip gets a half holiday, so should he, Dickens himself here is clearly conscious of the dividing line. The section begins with the words "Now, Joe kept a journeyman at weekly wages whose name was Orlick." Dickens originally dispensed with the introductory adverb and started the paragraph simply "Joe kept a journeyman," and then must have noticed that since this is the first time Orlick has been mentioned, some such adverbial clearing-of-the-throat may act as a sanitary alert. (Dickens follows the same procedure in introducing Trabb's boy in chapter 19: "Now, Mr. Trabb's boy was the most audacious boy in all that country-side"—in this instance, the preparatory cough failed to outlast *Harper's* and second proof, though in our text I have restored the manuscript reading to Trabb's boy.) As a matter of fact, the Orlick section began with a quite different sentence from the one we have. The original is so heavily ballooned out that it can be only imperfectly recovered to life; but what can be detected behind the balloons is Pip's reference to a journeyman "whom I have purposefully withheld from mentioning until now," or words very nearly like these, the conjunction "therefore" that ushers in the clause presumably telling us why Pip hasn't clued us in on Orlick before. Apparently this struck Dickens as too gawky and self-conscious by half, and so he replaced it with the brief three-letter chord with which he opens the sentence. Dickens is not always so vigilant: for example, in chapter 29, at a point when Pip has had plenty of opportunities to observe Jaggers, it suddenly occurs to him to inform us in what is one of the clumsier parentheses in the novel, "He always carried (I have not yet mentioned it, I think) a pocket-handkerchief." And thereafter (now that Pip has mentioned it), Jaggers obligingly hauls out that pocket-handkerchief as a bonus to readers who have a sharp eye for detail.[2]

The impulsive insertion of the Dame School passage is not the only afterthought of its kind, though its kind is rare. Early on, in chapter 8, a window is raised and a girl's voice asks the visitors who have come to call to identify themselves. This is, of course, the first encounter of Pip and Estella. But it's just possible that Dickens meant to keep Estella, however briefly, in ambush, for directly preceding the passage beginning "A window was raised" Dickens struck three exasperatingly puzzling words: "An elderly woman." What elderly woman! Hardly Miss Havisham, who isn't the sort to wheel herself to the window and scream, "Who's there?" A premature infiltration of the resident Satis House spy, Sarah Pocket? Could be, but improbable. Merely one of those charwomen for whom Dickens reserves his choicest anathemas and who must have done him an ill turn in Furnival's Inn? As we have no more than these three hurried words, struck no sooner than they appeared in the manu-

---

1. *Oliver Twist*, chapter 17: "It is the custom on the stage, in all good murderous melodramas, to present the tragic and the comic scenes, in as regular alternation, as the layers of red and white in a side of streaky bacon."
2. Just before we first meet Orlick, Pip, after debating the issue with Joe for two pages, stutters that he fully means to call on "Miss Est—avisham." Joe naturally reminds him, "Which her name * * * ain't Estavisham, Pip, unless she have been rechris'ened." What interests the Clarendon editor about this sentence is the change from manuscript "an't" to printed "ain't." What mostly interests me is the substitution of the phrase "unless she have been rechris'ened" for the canceled "unless she have took another [name]":—surely the emendation is a shade more graphic and more nearly in character.

script, Dickens almost certainly decided to change directions at once and push Estella into Pip's presence without more ado. Still, for a tantalizing few seconds, he must have had some lesser figure up his sleeve, and up his sleeve he kept her. Or did he? Yes and no. Well, yes, for some forty-one chapters. And then he brought her out briefly after all. Skip from Pip's first visit to Miss Havisham to his last.

There she comes, in the paragraph following the famous passage in which Dickens evokes the whole mournful atmosphere of Pip's town, the very rooks as they hover over the old Cathedral tower calling to him that the place was changed and that Estella was gone out of it forever. Chapter 49, paragraph 3, in full:

> An elderly woman whom I had seen before as one of the servants who lived in the supplementary house across the back court-yard, opened the gate. The lighted candle stood in the dark passage within, as of old, and I took it up and ascended the staircase alone. Miss Havisham was not in her own room, but was in the larger room across the landing. Looking in at the door, after knocking in vain, I saw her sitting on the hearth in a ragged chair, close before, and lost in the contemplation of, the ashy fire.

Pip may have seen her before, but we haven't—excepting the few of us (surely half a dozen is a generous estimate) who retrieved her from behind Dickens's fatty inkspots 175 manuscript leaves earlier. What a very strange deferment! What unaccountable tricks memory, or forgetfulness, won't play on your creative writers! Had the elderly woman, I wonder, somehow been stowed away in the attic or cellarage of Dickens's mind and made herself at home there for the six months that elapsed between her overhasty appearance and her appropriate one, between her being struck from the record and then, all quite wonderfully, been recalled to life, from late December 1860 to the third week of June 1861? There she is, still another person to be accounted for among Dickens's sixteen thousand characters—or among the 180 identifiable figures, give or take a few, who float in and out of *Great Expectations*.

Why did Dickens bother to introduce this born supernumerary anyhow? The answer probably depends on whether you are a novelist or a critic. The novelist will very likely tell you that he introduced her because somebody had to open the gate for Pip. The critic will tell you that he introduced her, of course, to remind the reader of the poignant difference between this visit and Pip's first, when Estella herself opened the door, a lifetime ago, before the rooks' appeals to his desolate loneliness. A couple of critics might even go on to make the point that the last gatekeeper at Satis House, Orlick (who had been sent packing at Pip's own instigation), brute though he is, supplies a more consolingly familiar figure—we're so *used* to him—than a nonentity of "an elderly woman," whose very anonymity points up the contrast between Pip's first interview and his last. Provided the critics notice her.

So far I have been squinting at a couple of cancellations, picked more or less at random, that Dickens made in mid-composition. In her memoir of her father, Mamie, Dickens's older daughter, mentions what any editor discovers soon enough: that his manuscripts were littered with "so many erasures, and such frequent interlineations, that a special staff of compositors was used for his work."[3] Compared with the changes he made on the manuscript itself (by my guess no fewer than 90 percent) the corrections he made in proof were slight, and the corrections he undertook between final proof and printed version even slighter—these last are mostly confined to changes in punctuation. One might have thought that Dickens would have tried to minimize printers' errors by copying manuscript pages, or at least chunks of writing that were specially hard to decode. But he consistently fought shy of this practice from his early days as a novelist. On the evidence of the manuscript, certainly, Dickens was one of those writers who simply wanted to get on with it and whose patience would have been severely tried by rewriting and thus covering ground he had already covered. As early as 1840 he wrote to one of his protégés, the cabinetmaker John Overs, "I never copy, correct but very little, and that invariably as I write," and to the same effect a few months later to the New York historian Charles Edwards Lester that the "scrap" from *Oliver* he is sending Lester is the original article—"I never copy."[4] Perhaps still more conclusive is a comment of his to Bulwer-Lytton written in August 1848. Bulwer had been heaping praise on what is nowadays considered the most maudlin of Dickens's *Christmas Books*, *The Battle of Life*, a story with which Dickens seems to have been especially dissatisfied because he felt that its material really demanded novelistic scope when it had to be compressed into the confines of the usual format of the Christmas novella. "I was wretched," he tells Bulwer, "to feel the great capacity there was in the idea, and the waste of it that the limits of the story hopelessly involved." And he continues (italics mine): *"But for an insuperable aversion I have to trying back in such a case, I should certainly forge that bit of metal again, as you suggest. One of these days perhaps—."*[5] As far as I know, no one among the commentators on the revised ending of *Great Expectations* has made an issue of Bulwer's having urged revision on Dickens at least once before—by the time Bulwer told him to recharge the last pages of *Great Expectations*, Dickens entertained an at least superable aversion to trying back.[6] In any event, we may be grateful that Dickens didn't inflate *The Battle of Life* into a three-hundred-page siege.

The memos to Overs and Lester are those of an author in his late twenties, and the comment "I correct but little" is clearly borne out by the manuscript leaves of *Oliver Twist* and the later *A Christmas Carol*, which are almost entirely legible even to nonspecialists. Not only are the corrections negligible but the number of words on a given page are roughly half the number he crams onto the pages of the later books; and Dickens's hand is especially poor in the *Great Expectations* manuscript. His young illustrator Marcus Stone records a comment of Dickens's that I am unable to date but that is clearly of a very late vintage (Stone was barely thirty when Dickens died). The comment suggests that Dickens went out of his way to complicate the lives of his

---

3. Mamie Dickens, *My Father As I Recall Him* [1897] (Westminster: Roxborough Press, 1912), 63.
4. To Overs, February 7?, 1840 (*PL* 2, 19 n.4); to Lester, July 19, 1840 (*PL* 2, 102). But cf. 102–03, n. 5: "there is evidence of his making fair copies of a few pages and various short passages of *Oliver.*"
5. August 4, 1848 (*PL* 5, 383). Dickens had already raised the same complaint in his letter to Bulwer of April 10, 1848 (*PL* 5, 274), and to John Forster, [October 26–29, 1846] (*PL* 4, 648): "What an affecting story I could have made of it in one octavo volume."
6. This information can, of course, be used to defend the position taken by the partisans of either the happy or the unhappy ending: since Dickens had rejected Bulwer's suggestion the first time around, his caving in to the second can suggest only his conviction that Bulwer's objections were unobjectionable; or else it can be argued that the difference is meaningless since Dickens himself didn't like *The Battle of Life*, whereas he praised *Great Expectations* almost nauseatingly before Bulwer entered the picture.

printers (never mind his editors, who started to cannibalize him much later), and that he knew to a T why he liked to make things difficult. "Never," he advised Stone, "make a fair copy of a much corrected manuscript. An MS with few or no corrections is always given to the boy beginner to set up, and you will get a proof full of errors. The MS which is difficult to decipher is put into the hands of a first rate compositor whose proof will give very little trouble."[7] The compositors who took *Great Expectations* in hand must have been absolutely first rate.

II

It should be clear from the foregoing remarks that our unchallenged (because unexamined and self-perpetuating) view of Dickens as one of our great spontaneous comic novelists needs to be taken with a grain of salt. To be sure, Dickens had to write against deadlines, much as he loathed them, and the prevailing truism may up to a point hold for his very early productions. But Dickens was hardly the sort of writer who could dash off a novel in the four days it took Voltaire to dash off *Candide*, nor the one week it took Dr. Johnson to dash off *Rasselas*, nor the seven weeks it took Stendhal to dash off *The Charterhouse of Parma*; and even if we lacked the many testimonials of his friends and family members who have described his working habits at Gad's Hill, one look at the manuscript pages of *Great Expectations*, as I have suggested, should be enough to convince anybody of the enormous pains Dickens took with his chapters, his paragraphs, his sentences.

The testimonials of Dickens's working habits by insiders have been handily assembled in Philip Collins's volumes of *Interviews and Recollections*,[8] and as this aspect of Dickens's craftsmanship has been relatively neglected, a few words ought to be said about it here, if only as a corrective to the prevailing pseudodoxies. Of course Dickens, like any good writer, couldn't have written a word without the pressure, or godsend, of inspiration, or an accumulation of inspirations; and, like any good writer, he would have shared Aldous Huxley's contempt for Edison's famous recipe for genius—1 percent inspiration and 99 percent perspiration—as the asinine edict of a Gradgrind or Bounderby, the gross Benthamites in *Hard Times*. His oldest son, Charley, for some years his employee and after Dickens's death his successor as editor of *All the Year Round*, is certainly less on target in his comment that Dickens "had no faith in the waiting-for-inspiration theory" (which is contradicted by the observed actuality Charley conveys elsewhere) than the obverse half of the sentence, "nor did he fall into the opposite error of forcing himself willy nilly to turn out so much manuscript every day."[9] The two aspects of Dickens's working habits that emerge most clearly from the accounts of his family appear at first glance to cancel each other out, but in practice of course don't: his compulsive regularity and, even away from his desk, his total immersion in his work-in-progress. According to Georgina Hogarth, his sister-in-law and the chatelaine of Gad's Hill, "Everything with him went as by clockwork; his movements, his absences from home, and the times of his return were all

---

7. From Autograph Notes, MS Dickens House; quoted in Collins 2, 189. Collins dates this 1912 on internal evidence.
8. Collins 1, passim.
9. Charles Dickens Jr., "Reminiscences of My Father," *Windsor Magazine*, Christmas Supplement 1934, 24–25; in Collins 1, 120.

fixed beforehand."[1] More recently, Malcolm Andrews has pointed out how frequently Dickens's characters reflect his own rage for order, from the constipated young gents who appear in his early *Sketches by Boz* to someone like Esther Summerson, the household spirit of *Bleak House*, who would be lost without her rattling door keys[2]—the type Chekhov was to consolidate in his great story "The Man in the Case." After his years of apprenticeship as a novelist, when he was a good deal more flexible in his schedule, Dickens generally wrote from ten to noon, and from two to four, unless he happened to be in the heat of creation and needed another hour or so to cool off. "I have made it a rule that the inimitable [his almost lifelong joshing reference to himself] is invisible, until two every day. I shall have half the number done, please God, to-morrow."[3] But the picture of Dickens chained to his desk four hours a day is very misleading. Despite Georgina's conceit, Dickens would hardly have understood an Anthony Trollope, writing so many hours a day facing a clock, stopping the minute the bell tolled for him, and continuing where he left off the next day. Nearly everyone in his family circle has commented on his extraordinary absorption in his work, even while he found himself surrounded by company. His capacity for totally disregarding people around him, his silences and his absent-mindedness over lunch or during his strolls with Charley, with Henry, with Boxer (his dog), suggest that Dickens's working hours could in fact be extended ad lib, and that the compulsion outweighed the clockwork regularity. During his walks ("striding along with his regular four-miles-an-hour-swing" and knitting his brow) he might forget all about his companion, leave him paces behind, talk to himself as he "worked," and, the knitting done, join his silent partner on their walk to Rochester and resume the conversation as though it had never been interrupted. Mamie records similar patterns indoors: her father would come in for luncheon, altogether preoccupied, "take something to eat in a mechanical way," and return to his study without once having opened his mouth except to ingest his frugal diet, unconscious of the table talk all about him.[4] (A funny and almost certainly trumped-up story about Joseph Conrad comes to mind: it took Conrad two years to finish one of his novels; all this time he took his meals regularly with his family and thus saw his children once or twice every day; the day he finished the book, walking into the dining room, he took a look at his young hopefuls and burst out, "Good Lord, they've grown!") On the other hand, another diner at Gad's Hill reports that Dickens got into a mild fit, pushed back his chair, and raced off whenever somebody talked to him during his lapses into creation.

Then, too, we are so used to picturing Dickens as scribbling away a mile a minute that it comes as a surprise to learn from Charley how often his father might sit at his desk for an entire morning without writing a word, without even one visit by his daimon. "To-day and yesterday I have done nothing. Though I know what I want to do, I am lumbering on like a stage-

1. Adolphus William Ward, *Dickens* (1882); in Collins 1, 119.
2. Malcolm Andrews, *Dickens on England and the English* (New York: Harper & Row, 1979), 186 and passim. I probably owe Dr. Andrews an apology for drawing on a book that I happened to scorch in a review-essay shortly after the book appeared. But as it greatly improves with time, very likely mea culpa.
3. To Forster, [Early August 1849] (*PL* 5, 590).
4. Charles Dickens Jr., "Reminiscences," in Collins 1, 121; Mamie Dickens, *My Father As I Recall Him*, 64.

waggon." Or again: "I have entered on the first stage of * * * composition this morning, which is, sitting frowning horribly at a quire of paper, and falling into a state of inaccessibility and irascibility which utterly confounds and scares the House. The young family peep at me through the banisters as I go along the hall; and Kate and Georgina quail (almost) when I stalk by them."[5] But the point was to stick it out at the desk all the same and hope that the words, which had kept him waiting, would arrive—by luck, by brooding, by inspiration—next day; and they always did.

One more incident deserves to be docketed, which displays him in a more volatile way and throws a curious light on his methods of writing and his relations to his characters. During the Dickenses' sojourn at Tavistock House in the 1850s, Mamie, then in her mid-teens, became seriously ill, and during her convalescence Dickens had her moved into his study. Mamie writes: "On one of these mornings, I was lying on the sofa endeavouring to keep perfectly quiet, while my father wrote busily and rapidly at his desk, when he suddenly jumped from his chair and rushed to a mirror which hung near, and in which I could see the reflection of some extraordinary facial contortions which he was making. He returned rapidly to his desk, wrote furiously for a few moments, and then went again to the mirror. The facial pantomime was resumed, and then turning toward, but evidently not seeing me, he began talking rapidly in a low voice. Ceasing this soon, however, he returned once more to his desk, where he remained silently writing until luncheon time."[6] Dickens was working on *Hard Times* just then and it would be nice to know which character he was trying out. The lithping circus owner, Slearly? Slackbridge, the trade union agitator? Mrs. Sparsit, relict to the spendthrift who died aged twenty-four ("the scene of his decease, Calais, and the cause, brandy")? All of the above? But very likely not even Mamie could have identified the creatures he mimicked once they had been translated into language.

The people who describe him at the time he wrote *Great Expectations* describe Dickens as rather florid, stylishly dressed or over-dressed, laughing uproariously when something struck him as funny (I have never read a description of Dickens smiling), abstemious rather than otherwise (though he apparently chain-smoked in his editorial offices), somebody who found an outlet for his restlessness on his walks and in the company he craved, when it was convenient for him to crave them, and someone who enjoyed the role of squirearch and liked to arrange cricket matches with his neighbors. And for four hours a day (or more) he wrote, mostly novels, on manuscript pages that go some way toward helping us unravel the way he wrote.

III

The first obstacle, then, that the editor of *Great Expectations* faces is Dickens's hand. Dickens's handwriting in all his later novels is exasperatingly small as well as unsteady—one has to remember here that while working on *Great Expectations* between September 1860 and June 1861 Dickens suffered prolonged bouts of illness and much of the time was under medical treatment for neuralgia. (On January 29, 1861, he serves notice on his physician Beard:

5. To Forster, [April 19?, 1849] (*PL* 5, 526); to the Hon. Mr. Watson, October 5, 1848 (*PL* 5, 419); on the dinner anedote, Collins 1, 126, n. 6, quoting Thomas Wright, *Life of Charles Dickens* (1935), 311.
6. Mamie Dickens, *My Father As I Recall Him*, 47–49.

"I should like to be inspected—though I hope I can offer no new attractions.")[7] The entire manuscript takes up some 271 leaves—again, half the number of pages to which most editions run. And these leaves teem with interlineations, cancellations, canceled interlineations, ink so faded and dimmed by time that whole lines have nearly vanished from sight. Moreover, Dickens frequently adopts a kind of personal shorthand that, to be sure, can be decoded by the trained eye but nonetheless ruffles or arrests any sort of continuous target practice. For example, Dickens habitually treats the adverbial ending **ly** as a spidery downward squiggle, often petering out into illegibility; his **e**'s and **l**'s, **g**'s and **q**'s, **n**'s and **z**'s often look so interchangeable that even his best printers can't be blamed for printing "**a quiet mind**" where Dickens had written "**a guilty mind**." A great many of these errors unsurprisingly crept into *Harper's Weekly*, which lacked the skilled workers who had learned to cope with Dickens's **g**'s and **q**'s, **e**'s and **l**'s, and some of these errors (which almost certainly went past the earliest readers, especially within the open-ended format of a weekly installment) sound zany enough to those of us in the know. For example, it appears to Pip's guilty (or quiet) mind that he catches the dead hare hanging by the heels in the Gargery kitchen **waking** instead of **winking** at him; the sergeant who finally catches up with Magwitch and Compeyson during the chase in chapter 4 and who means to announce the discovery by panting "**Here are both men!**" instead pants "**Here are lots more!**"—a happy catch for the sergeant and his men, a trial to the captain of the hulk who has barely room to accommodate the two. In one of his slightly moralizing asides to the reader, which is meant to start off with the question "**Why did you, who read this**," Dickens (improbably, given his truculent self-assurance) asks the readers of *Harper's* "**Why did you read this**," and so on. Some of the misreadings are not only pardonable but would certainly go unnoticed by readers of the authorized versions. Pip's information that "Joe **fenced** me up the chimney" is no doubt the more graphic wording, but it wouldn't occur to anybody who read that Pip was **forced** up the chimney to raise an eyebrow; and, still more forgivably, the idea, in the description of Wopsle's duties, that "he **finished** the Amens tremendously" may be all the more acceptable than Pip's comment that "he **punished** the Amens tremendously" to people who're not sure what Pip is talking about and who wonder why anybody would want to "**punish**" an Amen.

If Dickens gave his compositors a run for their money, he also allowed their tempi to vary considerably. Mark Van Doren said somewhere of Shakespeare's plays that "these plays had to be written quickly to be written at all," and—again—our habit of looking on Dickens as our great inspired comic writer makes it come as something of a surprise when we find that the passages he took the greatest pains with are most often just those that sound as though he had poured them out on the page: the funny descriptions of Wopsle's performance of *Barnwell* or of the Dame School Dickens all but forgot to open or the famous spoof on Wopsle's *Hamlet*. These are the scenes that roused Dickens to the most finicky and fastidious exertions and that he blotted a thousandfold in an effort to get them quite right; and the very spontaneity that so impresses us reflects the success with which he covered his tracks. The "easy" manuscript pages by contrast are by and large those that most

7. *PL* 9, 377.

people dismiss as inferior Dickens: much of the sensational hocus-pocus in Satis House, the often maudlin tra-la-la between Pip and Estella; almost every scene in which our local demon waves her crutched stick (or magic wand): these things, one feels, Dickens could do in his sleep; the banal talk proceeds without effort and presents no obstacle to printer or editor. It is difficult, in other words, to come away from the manuscript without concluding at least provisionally that the manifest expenditure of labor is in almost direct proportion to the success of the product: a comforting conclusion in a meritocracy and one that Dickens himself would have respected. This needs perhaps to be qualified by the more general notation that Dickens seems to be nearly always most at his ease in dialogue—or simply in reproducing spoken language. After all, *Great Expectations* contains a number of long monologues: Magwitch himself is a born storyteller; so are Herbert and Joe. In these passages, then, whether they are the genuine comic article or melodramatic panache, Dickens could let himself go, though the sensational chunks of conversation probably outnumber the funny ones. A good example of "easy" writing in the noisy mode appears in chapter 38, in which Miss Havisham and Estella exchange radioactive reproaches and frigid reproaches; another, a couple of decibels lower, in chapter 49, in which Miss Havisham cries her mea culpa just before the old lady catches fire. In both episodes Dickens exploits a familiar gimmick that Sylvère Monod has described as it operates in *A Tale of Two Cities*, the use of melodramatic repetition—though nothing in *Great Expectations* can quite live up to Lucie Manette's soap-operatic jeremiads before her long-lost father, that impossible row of conditionals, "If you hear [a voice that once was sweet music] weep for it, weep for it! If you touch [a head once beloved], weep for it, weep for it! If I bring back [the remembrance of your Home], weep for it, weep for it!"[8] and the echo murmurs, "Too much of water hast thou, poor Ophelia, and therefore I forbid these tears." The comparable scenes in *Great Expectations*—with their liturgical "**Soon forgotten! Soon forgotten!**" "**So proud! So proud!**" "**What have I done! What have I done!**"—whatever they may do to sensitive stomachs, are a positive boon to typesetters and editors. The passage in chapter 38 (too long to quote) beginning "**Soon forgotten!** * * * **Times soon forgotten!**" and going on for two hundred words contains some ten cancellations, all but two of them retrievable, half of them substitutions of the **retorted** for **returned** and **contemplated** for **looked at** variety, and a very few slightly more material ones, each of them characteristic of Dickens at Work. In one of her fits, Miss Havisham is described as **raising herself in her chair**; this sounds a little too bland to suit the occasion, and so Dickens spruces her up and presents her a shade more excitably as **pushing away her grey hair with both her hands**. Elsewhere Dickens may cancel a word or phrase and aim at a kind of lyrical embellishment. In reply to Havisham's accusation of forgetfulness and ingratitude, Estella corrects her: "Not forgotten, **but recalled**"—this followed by an adamantly resistant word; the phrasing altered to read "Not forgotten, **but treasured up in my memory**." Miss Havisham's passion spent—or momentarily in suspension—we are told that "Estella looked at her **in amazement**"; interlineation, cancellation, and substitution rephrase this to read that "Estella

8. "Some Stylistic Devices in *A Tale of Two Cities*," in Robert Partlow, ed., *Dickens the Craftsman: Strategies of Presentation* (Carbondale: Southern Illinois University Press, 1970), 265–86. But Monod spares us this particular passage (from *A Tale of Two Cities*, 1.6).

looked at her **for a moment with a kind of calm wonder**." Earlier in the course of their altercation, Estella "touched **her heart** with her hand"; Dickens removes **her heart** and in its place puts **her bosom**, if only because the presence of the **heart** would make a liar out of Estella, who has been insisting all along on her heartlessness, or, as our sponsor would say, "vehemently repudiated the possession of that indispensable organ which, if we are not mistaken, has been universally regarded as the very organ the absence of which would involve our vociferous young woman in the greatest perplexity were she to persevere in publicly insisting upon its absence."

Dickens never entirely conquered these mouthfuls even in his latest and leanest novels—though this, as a general problem of style, goes beyond the immediate topic. "I think," says Pip after Havisham has told him to play, "it will be conceded by my most disputatious reader, that she could hardly have directed an unfortunate boy to do anything in the wide world more difficult to be done under the circumstances"—though Dickens seems to have started the sentence with a much simpler construction. A few lines before this, in answer to Miss Havisham's question whether she scares him, "I regret to state that I was not afraid of telling the enormous lie comprehended in the answer 'No.'" The fight with Joe leaves no "other traces of discomposure than a slit in one of Orlick's nostrils, which was neither expressive nor ornamental"—a replay, this, of *Nicholas Nickleby*, in which the schoolmaster Wackford Squeers is introduced as "possessed of but one eye, when the popular prejudice runs in favor of two," this information mitigated by the consoling reminder that "the eye he had was decidedly useful but not ornamental," etc., etc. There are moments when we find ourselves in the world of Henry Fielding and his contemporaries: "At first with such discourse, and afterwards with conversation of a more general nature, did Mr. Wemmick and I beguile the time and the road, until he gave me to understand that we had arrived in the district of Walworth." In repaying the visit, Wemmick fails to find Pip at home, not after knocking on Pip's door but "after an unsuccessful application of his knuckles" thereonto.

Before I look at a few of the more conspicuous manuscript changes, I may indicate a few minor substantive changes that Dickens introduced for one of a number of reasons: to substitute sense for downright nonsense, or plausibility for implausibility, or to supply incidental explanations to matters the reader might not be clued in on, or else to cleanse his narrative of the ludicrously obvious. Dickens rarely indicated these changes within the manuscript but more often in proof, occasionally at a still later stage, when these peccadilloes first struck him. For example, when we first meet Pip and Joe in the Gargery kitchen, gulping down their hunks of bread as it were responsively, we are told that Joe "took a **semicircular bite** out of his slice, which he didn't seem to enjoy." Whether he enjoyed it or not, since semicircularity is one of the properties of the bite among dentally healthy mammals, the adjective is canceled in proof, and Joe treats himself to a merely **generous** bite instead. To stick with bodily details for a minute: a great deal has been written about the importance of hands in *Great Expectations*. In chapter 8, Miss Havisham, "with an impatient movement of **all** the fingers of her right hand," orders Pip to play. I think it will be conceded by Dickens's most disputatious reader that she could hardly have directed an unfortunate boy to do anything in the world "with an impatient movement of **two or three fingers** of her right hand"; so **all** is canceled—this time Dickens already caught the hands in the manuscript. (What difference, by the way, does it make whether Miss Havisham orders Pip about with her right or her left hand?) Skipping ahead to chapter 56, following the mass-sentencing of Magwitch and his fellow convicts, Dickens briefly describes the conduct of the condemned men thus: "**one or two shook hands.**" ("What is the sound of one hand clapping?") Dickens was too good an editor not to see through the difficulty of such a maneuver (I like to think that he himself burst out laughing), and on their next appearance the handshakers were increased to the minimum number of players, two or **three**. Following Mistress Quickly in moving our own hands up (or down) so-and-so's body, we hear Pip telling us that after his struggle with Miss Havisham he made his way to Jaggers "with [his] arms bandaged." As this would virtually immobilize Pip and suggest a not very apropos picture of the Monumental Crusader kind, Dickens decides that one bandaged arm will do fine, and with one arm bandaged (and his coat loose over his shoulders) Pip gets into print. A few pages later, Pip informs us that "**down to that time we had never interchanged a word on the subject of my being disabled, but of course it could be kept out of view no longer.**" Not, I think, very likely. That so conspicuous a detail as Pip's bodily disability should go unmentioned among Pip, Herbert, Startop, and Magwitch strains belief, especially among people who communicate as freely as Pip and Herbert communicate. Accordingly, Dickens lops off the first half of the sentence and retains the second: "**For, of course my being disabled could now no longer be kept out of view**"—the phrase **out of view** of course to mean "out of account" or "out of consideration"; it would be almost as difficult to keep Pip's disability literally out of view as it would be to have Joe take a fully circular bite. It doesn't perhaps matter much whether Pip is asked to return to Satis House and his compulsory gambling after three days (manuscript) or six days (proof stage); but as he has to negotiate a round-trip of eight miles and hasn't yet turned into the restless flaneur he (like his author) will become as an adult, the six days make more sense—and speak well for Miss Havisham's solicitude, which goes into remission for the next three hundred pages. By the time Pip's visits to Satis House become routine, Miss Havisham gets Pip to confess that, yes, Estella grows prettier and prettier each time, and he notes that Miss H. seemed "to enjoy [his romantic agony] greedily **in secret**." Strictly speaking, the secrecy involves a self-contradiction since Pip is there to observe it; so out it goes—very late: it persists in *All the Year Round*. (A line or two later Pip talks about Havisham's "**greedy relish** of Estella's moods"; evidently Dickens noticed the repetition and in manuscript allows Havisham her diet of "**miserly relish**"—a leaner and in some ways still meaner affect.)

Lastly, a couple of—unrelated—matters of pedagogy. The teaching aids with which the great-aunt implements her Educational Scheme and that Biddy commends to Pip as useful models to copy at home include "**a German text** or large old English D." Though the presence of the German text underlines the idiocy and futility of the great-aunt's curriculum, as well as her granddaughter's intellectual purity—and would nicely extend the linguistic boundaries of a novel that includes Latin (Compeyson), Greek (Wemmick's plant, the Yah Bounceable in chapter 23—the felons in *Great Expectations* seem to enjoy a monopoly on the languages of Pindar and Horace), French (the Pip of the manuscript before his Exhibitor Magwitch invites his dear boy to explain himself in any "foreign language"), Latin (again) and Hebrew (two of Estella's etymologies to explain the meaning of Satis House)—the likelihood of scaring up a German book in a remote early-nineteenth-century village on the Hoo Peninsula defies the most elementary probabilities and is scorched accordingly. Two other amendments involve the great-aunt's great-nephew. In his funny description of Wopsle's recital of *The London Merchant* in chapter 15 Dickens changes manuscript **Maria** ("it became sheer monomania in Maria to care a button for me") to read "**my master's daughter.**" Presumably he took it for granted that not every reader of *Great Expectations* had read Lillo's play and that the manuscript reading invited the question "Who's Maria?" To the objection that he didn't do as much for Millwood, the likeliest answer is that Millwood, Barnwell's nemesis, had entered the public domain as a byword for harlotry and a snare to apprentices almost as soon as she appeared a century earlier. (Even readers who have no trouble in identifying Lady Macbeth without having read *Macbeth* would be hard put to give you the number let alone the names of Lady Macbeth's children.) And at the beginning of chapter 10, Pip makes up his mind that "the best step [he] could take towards making [himself] uncommon was to get out of Biddy everything she knew, **and to pay the strictest attention to Mr. Wopsle when he read aloud.**" Even at eleven Pip must have recognized that he had precious little to gain by rattling off chunks of *Barnwell* and *King John* in front of Estella, who as likely as not would tell Miss Havisham, "Listen to the coarse and common way that common labouring boy speaks." Though Wopsle may be a man of many parts, his playing Mentor to Pip's Telemachus is not one of them.

IV

How are those of us who haven't been trained on the job to make sense of this recalcitrant script? The editor of *Great Expectations*, like the editor of any book, has to cope with three sorts of changes: cancellations, interlineated matter, which presumably reflects the writer's second thoughts, and the variants between manuscript and later readings. The cancellations themselves are, of course, the stuff of which eyestrain and migraines are made; and besides, the attempt to decode these hopelessly blotted phrases can become as hideously addictive as solving crossword puzzles, with no better than a 1 percent chance of decoding as many as half of them. I can think of four (time-consuming, frustrating, and generally unavailing) methods of breaking the code. One is to turn myself into that literate specimen Joe Gargery and puzzle out a word by studying the formation of single letters: "why, here's a **a** and here's a **w** and here's a **s** equal to anythink. A **a** and a **w** and a **s**: why, if it ain't a '**orse**, Pip! *Astonishing!*" Fallible as the method is, it is often by some such procedure (sometimes in combination with others) that we can resurrect buried jewels, or custom jewels. Thus (to stick to the first paragraphs) we discover that the stone lozenges that are sacred to the memory of Pip's five little brothers used to be sacred to the memory of five little brothers **and a sister** of his—whoever thought of Pip's having had a little sister? The little sister is decidedly out of place in the monosexual community of the deceased infant brothers, and besides, what sisterling could rival the one sister who survives, with a more than twenty-year headstart on Pip—"more than twenty years," by the way, substituted for the canceled "at least twenty years"—a subtly malicious change. The five brothers as we know them appear as Alexander, Bartholomew, Abraham, Tobias, and Roger. Tobias and Roger clearly usurped the places of George and Robert in first proof; but it takes Joe Gargery and my research assistant to piece together the Esau and Isaac who folded their tents to make room for George and Robert, who begat Tobias and Roger. Perhaps Dickens thought Abraham, Esau, and Isaac too heavily Old Testamental to launch a novel about a child and a mild good-natured sweet-tempered easy-going foolish dear man, or he may have found something unnatural in sticking the hairy Esau between his grandfather and his father. The name changes in proof defy explanation, though the well-known change of the father's name from Tobias to Philip is a handy one to readers who make much of Pip's sonship.

A second method of decoding Dickens's hand, and a simpler one, is to be on the lookout for canceled words that are plainly written out elsewhere in the same sentence or a contiguous one. Like most writers, Dickens frequently restructures his word order, and perhaps more than most, he can't leave well enough alone but tends to trick out what he wrote to begin with. This kind of change is difficult to reproduce; one example will do. In talking about Mrs. Joe's fit after Orlick's injury to her reputation in chapter 15, Dickens originally wrote that "Each of [her] explanations was a shriek; and I must say of my sister as of all the violent women I have ever seen that passion was no excuse for her because she deliberately took pains to work herself into a state" (the last three words are conjectural). The cancellations here can be reconstructed from the slightly embroidered text: "Each of [her] explanations was a shriek; and I must remark of my sister, what is equally true of all the violent women I have ever seen, that passion was no excuse for her, because it is undeniable that instead of lapsing into passion, she consciously and deliberately took extraordinary pains to force herself into it." A third and much the least satisfactory way available to the lay cryptographer is to hunt up likely synonyms or approximations. The method is obviously fraught with risks: for one thing, Dickens may not have replaced the original with anything like a synonym; for another, our usage has changed too much from his to make the method really workable. Even so, once in a while the thesaurus can provide a clue or, more reliably, a convenient check. For example, in the passage preceding the maledictions on Mrs. Joe, Pip expatiates on Orlick's improbable first name and notes that in view of his obstinacy he thinks him to have been "the prey of no delusion in this particular" but to have foisted the name on the village "as an affront to its understanding." The detective eye discovers that the delusion used to be a misapprehension and the affront an outrage. The word misapprehension almost certainly needs no thesaurus for its apprehension, though it's nice to have it confirmed; affront supplied me with perhaps a dozen options, and there is no doubt that it originated in outrage.

There is yet another way to get at these concealed squiggles and pollywogs; and this is once more to crawl into Joe's hide—not Joe the painstaking abecedarian but Joe the inspired poet of tombstone inscriptions, who without knowing how or why but as if he were striking out a horseshoe complete in a single blow, got a couplet out of the rhyming words part and hart, was never so much surprised in his life that he did—couldn't credit his own ed,

hardly believed it *were* his own ed. In other words, much the best way to make sense of the manuscript is to wait for the words to come leaping out from the page, complete in a single blow. This kind of coup almost invariably brings to light not a single word but a phrase, a clause, an entire sentence: I was never so much surprised in my life! Incidentally, apropos of Joe's tribute to his father, whatsumever the failings on his part, Sylvère Monod, for one, fails to see why Dickens should go out of his way to misspell the Gargery Senior's **hart**, omitting the **e**, when after all the word sounds the same, **e** or no **e**.[9] But the point is that it doesn't *look* the same, certainly not to its analphabetic author; and anyhow Dickens gets a mildly infantile kick out of these kinky misconstructions. Thus, in *Martin Chuzzlewit* our great Prairie State is forever referred to as **Illi-noy**, presumably to keep Monod's compatriots from pronouncing it **Illinoa** and Germans from pronouncing it **Illinoise**. And in *Nicholas Nickleby*, Lillyvick, who as a collector of water rates naturally has a vested interest in this, casts a very cold eye on a fishy language like French, in which the word for **water** is spelled **lo**, as in **lo and behold** or **Lo-li-ta**: " 'Lo, eh? I don't think anything of that language—nothing at ball.' "
On the subject of graphics, and by a natural association with Lillyvick's two-letter **lo**, I subjoin that in manuscript Dickens almost consistently distinguished between capital **O** (without **h**) and capital **O-h**: the vocative **O** ("O that Shakespeherian Rag") is generally used to indicate high drama: "**O**, don't cut my throat, sir!", "**O** Joe, you break my heart!", Pip's valediction on Magwitch: "**O** Lord, be merciful to him," Pip's valediction on Estella, "**O** God bless you," Mrs. Joe's theatrical "**O! O! O!**" Against this, Wemmick's conversational "**Oh**, I don't know about bad blood!", Biddy's "**Oh**, I wouldn't [try to be a gentleman], if I was you!" and so on—a practice editors haven't always followed with the desirable piety. Thus where Dickens had written " '**O! O!**' [Miss Havisham] cried, despairingly. 'What have I done!' " a lot of modern texts based on the 1868 edition retain the chatty **Oh**, as if to say, "**Oh** dear me, what in the world have I done now, I wonder."

V

Whatever detective method we find most helpful (or whichever catches us by surprise), would-be resurrectionists will find that the opening paragraphs of *Great Expectations* alone contain dozens of changes, any number of which entail the painful letter-by-letter game. In the very first sentence, along with much inked-out matter, Dickens diluted the information that Pip's "infant tongue could make out nothing longer or more explicit than Pip" by (uncertainly) adding the clumsy phrase "my infant tongue, **as it began to speak**"; in the sentence following, Dickens nearly spoiled the neat "so I called myself Pip, and came to be called Pip" by interpolating the word **originally**. Again, the readers who worry about the importance of Pip's paternity will have their anxieties allayed by the textual evidence of the opening words of the second paragraph, in which Dickens strikes the word **family** on its first appearance and substitutes **father's family**; the simpler explanation, of course, suggests that most people take their father's surnames. The parents' **likeness**, which Pip never got to see, replaces the parents' **portrait**—perhaps Dickens thought

9. Sylvère Monod, *Dickens the Novelist* (Norman, Okla., University of Oklahoma Press, 1968), 479.

C. D. 1

My father's family name being Pirrip, and my christian name Philip, my infant tongue could make of both names nothing longer or more explicit than Pip. So I called myself Pip, and came to be called Pip.

I give Pirrip as my father's family name, on the authority of his tombstone and my sister— Mrs. Joe Gargery, who married the blacksmith. As I never saw my father or my mother, and never saw any likeness of either of them (for their days were long before the days of photographs), my first fancies regarding what they were like were unreasonably derived from their tombstones. The shape of the letters on my father's, gave me an odd idea that he was a square, stout, dark man with curly black hair. From the character and turn of the inscription, "*also Georgiana wife of the above*," I drew a childish conclusion that my mother was freckled and sickly. To five little stone lozenges, each about a foot and a half long, which were arranged in a neat row beside their grave, and were sacred to the memory of five little brothers of mine—who gave up trying to get a living exceedingly early in that universal struggle—I am indebted for a belief I religiously entertained that they had all been born on their backs with their hands in their trousers-pockets, and had never taken them out in this state of existence.

Ours was the marsh country, down by the river, within, as the river wound, twenty miles of the sea. My first distinct impression of the identity of things seems to me to have been gained on a memorable raw, damp afternoon towards evening. At such a time I found out for certain, that this bleak place overgrown with nettles was the churchyard; and that Tobias Pirrip, late of this parish, and also Georgiana wife of the above, were dead and buried; and that Alexander, Bartholomew, Abraham, George, and Robert, infant children of the aforesaid, were also dead and buried; and that the dark, flat wilderness beyond the churchyard, intersected with dykes and mounds and gates, with scattered cattle feeding on it, was the marshes; and that the low leaden line beyond was the river; and that the distant savage lair from which the wind was rushing, was the sea; and that the small bundle of shivers growing afraid of it all and beginning to cry, was Pip.

"Hold your noise!" cried a terrible voice, as a man started up from among the graves at the side of the church porch. "Hold your noise, you little devil, or I'll cut your throat!"

A fearful man, all in grey, with a great iron on his leg. A man with no hat, and broken shoes, and with an old rag tied round his head. A man who had been soaked in water and smothered in mud, and lamed by stones, and cut by flints, and stung by nettles, and torn by

Philip/
Tobias/
Roger/
coarse/

Corrected proof (detail, enlarged)

441

the word too graphic for once (as a rule, a given object gains in concreteness in revision), or he may have felt that the Pirrips couldn't afford the price of a print, let alone an oil. It's just as well that Pip finds out that Philip Pirrip Late of This Parish and Also Georgiana Wife of the Above are effectively **dead and buried** instead of discovering that in their earliest appearance, before Dickens thought better of it, Philip Pirrip and Also Georgiana used to be **tombstones**, and so were the little brothers. Again, critics who argue that Pip is as it were born into existence by his meeting with Magwitch, and that before the encounter in the churchyard—that is, before the book starts— Dickens kept him afloat in a sort of prenatal gill-slit, will derive comfort from the manuscript change by which Pip's "first distinct impression of the **world**[1] **of things**" (**distinct** altered in proof to read **most vivid and broad**) is emended to read **identity of things**." The argument that Pip didn't to all intents "exist" before Magwitch kicked him into life has been used to justify Pip's innocent question "what's hulks?": surely, these critics argue, no manchild who has spent six years within shooting distance of sunset guns would ask a question like that unless he has been pent up all this time in a soundproof womb. I wonder. Very likely Dickens sets up the question "what's hulks?" not because Pip but because the reader doesn't know "what's hulks" and therefore depends on Mrs. Joe for an answer—admittedly, a clumsy way of dishing out information. In support of the far-out interpreters, it's only fair to add that the emended wording anticipates, however remotely, the opening words of Magwitch's *récit* some three hundred pages later, "I first became aware of myself down in Essex, a thieving turnips"—the **turnips** again planted in the manuscript only after it occurred to Dickens that his readers might like to know just what it was Magwitch stole.

In describing Pip's dismal surroundings in the paragraphs following, Dickens consistently sharpens the object and deepens the gloom: the low **white** line in the distance that Pip makes out to be the Medway is assimilated into the general grayness of things by being retouched as a low **leaden** line in the distance; "**the dark place beyond the churchyard** [but here an intermediate phrase eludes me] **intersected with ditches and mounds**" turns into "**the dark flat wilderness intersected with dykes and mounds**." In the first dramatic frame of the book, Magwitch's emergence from his *Urschleim*, Dickens, as the text stands, startles the reader almost as much as he terrifies Pip with that out-of-nowhere " **'Hold your noise!' cried a terrible voice**"; beneath that terrible voice, the more terrifying for remaining impersonal and unidentified, we detect the bland " **'Hold your noise!' said a man**"; and (we are still on manuscript page 1, with dozens of cancellations kept in reserve for the next session), Dickens divests his varmint of the old **handkerchief** he wore as a headgear and, much more in keeping with the old golem's appearance, ties an old **rag** round his head. In blackmailing Pip—as though his own presence weren't blackmail enough—with the threat of producing the young man in comparison with which young man he himself is **a Angel** (or **a Angel o'light** until the 1861 text extinguished the halo), it's perhaps a toss-up which prospect is more frightening: that the young man is going to **tear** [Pip] **to pieces** (canceled) or **tear** [him] **open** (our reading).

A touching reminder that Pip's terror—though the terror is surely the op-

---

1. The word is almost certainly **worldly**; so Dickens may not have had a different noun in mind.

erative motive for the robbery—is tinged with a child's compassion may be just barely felt in the change in wording as he watches Magwitch limp back to his hideout: "As I saw him go, * * * **I fancied that**" changed to read "As I saw him go, * * * **he looked in my young eyes as if** he were eluding the hands of the dead people." Another wonderful touch, in which a single (four-letter) word conveys a world of childish innocence, childish routine, childish dependence. In chapter 10, the shaven-headed stranger who pops up in the Three Jolly Bargemen invites Pip to sit next to him. Pip nicely declines the invitation: " 'No, thank you, sir,' and **took** [no, strike that] **crept** [good try] **fell** into the space Joe made for me on the opposite settle." This even before the convict frightens the wits out of Pip by producing his nightmarish file: he's simply a strange person, and Pip isn't used to sitting anywhere except next to Joe. The file is nightmarish, all right, at least by association: near the close of the chapter, after Mrs. Joe has safe-deposited the two one-pound notes ("that seemed to have been on terms of the warmest intimacy with all the cattle markets in the county") in her ornamental teapot, Pip tells us: "There, they remained, a nightmare to me, many and many a <**long**> night and day."[2] The commas are perfectly in place here: one of those instances in which editors would do well to follow the manuscript punctuation.

Magwitch's apparition among the nettles and his agent's hot money under the dried rose leaves aren't the only things that scare Pip. Two chapters after the roving convict leaves his legacy, Pip suffers another bout of anxiety at the idea of having "the pale young gentleman's blood" on his head and his conviction that "pitching into the studious youth of England" is no way for village boys to behave; and he all but locks himself into the forge, making sure that the coast is clear before he goes on an errand, "**apprehensive** that the officers **of peace** would be **lying in wait for me**." Dickens apparently felt that this is much too long-winded to convey Pip's fright; and so he has Pip peek out the door "**lest** the officers **of the County Jail** should **pounce upon me**." Pip's first and actual confrontation with the constabulary on Christmas Eve gains in tension by similar incidental compressions. A-Version: "**I half expected** to find a Constable in the kitchen, waiting **to take me straight to one of the Hulks**." After the smoke has cleared: "**I fully expected** to find a Constable in the kitchen, **waiting to take me up**." One of Dickens's office boys has been quoted as saying that "I think Mr. Dickens was a man who lived a lot by his nose. He seemed to be always smelling things."[3] Clearly he was also a man who lived by his eyes and ears; Forster was hardly alone in making much of Dickens's "keen vision." The keen vision and its reflection on paper are probably what Katherine Mansfield meant when she marveled at "those pencil sharpeners" of Charley's.[4]

2. Throughout this essay, where this is not spelled out in the text, cancellations in manuscript appear boldface in angle brackets; emendations and obvious "second thoughts" appear boldface in square brackets.

3. In Collins 2, 194–95, quoting Catherine Van Dyke, "A Talk with Charles Dickens's Office Boy, William Edrupt of London," *Bookman* (New York), March 1921, 49 ff.

4. *The Letters of Katherine Mansfield*, ed. John Middleton Murry (London: Constable & Co., 1928), as quoted in George Ford, *Dickens and His Readers: Aspects of Novel-Criticism Since 1836* (Princeton: Princeton University Press, 1955; rpt. New York: W. W. Norton, 1965), 226. Forster's phrase appears in his description of the steamer journey in May 1861; see p. 398.

VI

Of the thousands of cancellations with which the manuscript is littered (and the hundreds that can be confidently recovered), it will be convenient to pick another dozen or so ad hoc. Often Dickens will strike a phrase or a clause because it introduces a discordant note. In chapter 2, in answer to Mrs. Joe's question, Pip informs her that he has been to the churchyard, and Mrs. Joe, in her sisterly way, allows that if it weren't for her, Pip would "have been in the churchyard long ago and stayed there." But the way she originally hectored Pip read: "If it weren't for me, you'd have been in the churchyard long ago, **with your five brothers** and stayed there." Dickens must have felt that any allusion to the five brothers beyond the opening, on which Pip's whole history is predicated, somehow violates their status, as if their being so much as mentioned were a species of grave-robbery; and Pip never alludes to them again. Miss Havisham is first mentioned in chapter 7; and Pip comments, "I had heard of Miss Havisham up town," then adds that "**everybody in our neighbourhood had heard of Miss Havisham up town.**" The manuscript change from "**everybody in our neighbourhood**" to "**everybody for miles round, had heard of Miss Havisham**" wonderfully reflects not merely an enlargement of Miss Havisham's fame but, more suggestively, the sense of some isolated windswept stretch of land that the very word **neighbourhood**, with its implied sense of domestic coziness, quite negates. By the same token, we may regret the loss (though not by deletion in manuscript but presumably in proof) of a mere four words. In chapter 18, just before Pip learns of his great expectations, Joe, Pip, and Jaggers walk home from the Jolly Bargemen. "Our conference," Pip tells us, "was held in the state parlour, which was feebly lighted by one candle **and was very cold.**" That final phrase, preserved in the manuscript only, provides the perfect atmospheric touch, a detail straight out of Chekhov: Pip ought to shiver physically, in every bone of his body, when Jaggers explodes his bombshell. We have squinted at Pip's putative benefactor. In chapter 11 Miss Havisham stands "looking at the table as if she **saw her own figure lying there**"; after canceling, she stands "looking at the table **as if she stood looking at her own figure lying there.**" The substitution serves to combine Havisham's permanent paralysis with the momentary activity implicit in the phrase **looking at**, which—momentarily— turns her into a debased Cassandra, who is willfully staring doom in the face.

A change of a rather different sort. During Wopsle's *Hamlet*, the wretched actor who has to double and more than double as a strolling actor, a grave-digger, and Osric finally loses his audience once they detect him in **clerical disguise**—or ought it to be **in holy orders**? The earlier reading—**clerical disguise**—is all wrong: it draws all the attention to the artifice itself in a context in which, as a recent critic puts it, Dickens pointedly abolishes theatrical space and invests Wopsle's Denmark with the reality of a place in an atlas (after all, the chapter introduces us to the theater with the phrase "on our arrival in Denmark"), and to that kind of reality the conceit **holy orders** is plainly adequate.[5]

Often the simplest change in wording captures the characters more naturally than the original does. Magwitch is much less likely, in asking Pip where

5. Rodney Stenning Edgecombe, "Dickens, Hunt and the 'Dramatic Criticism' in *Great Expectations*: A Note," *Dickensian* 88 (1992): 82–90.

he lives, to tell him to "pint out the **area!**" than to "pint out the **place!**"—with the substitution before us, the word *area*, coming from Magwitch, sounds much too hoity-toity. In chapter 42, the delirious Arthur Havisham, who keeps hallucinating his half-sister's reappearance clad in a shroud, after railing at Compeyson's wife "to take **that ugly shroud** away from her" (manuscript), charges her (in print) with "taking **that ugly thing** away from her"—the shroud having already figured in Arthur's ravings a dozen times. (Who, by the way, ever remembers the obliging Sally Compeyson—and whatever happened to her?) Even Trabb's "do me the favour **to be seated, sir**" is just that much more obsequious than the invitation "**to take a seat, sir**." In chapter 5, no more than a couple of modifiers separate **the sergeant** of the manuscript, who refers to Pip as "**this young shaver**" and expresses the honor of making Joe's "**wife's acquaintance**," from the **gallant sergeant** in first proof, who butters up Pip as "**this smart young shaver**" and Joe (or Mrs. Joe) by making "**his fine wife's acquaintance**." Some manuscript cancellations reveal a wonderful sense of tact and discrimination. Again, one small example may stand for dozens. In chapter 22 Herbert barges breathlessly into Barnard's from his shopping spree at Covent Garden, apologizing to Pip for getting his timetables mixed up, explaining that he has been out shopping on Pip's account, and parenthetically qualifying this, "**if that is any excuse**." Herbert himself being the soul of tact, he at once recalls himself—in manuscript—by correcting his "**if that is any excuse**" to the finely shaded "**not that that is any excuse**." As for Herbert's opinion of Estella, "**She** [no: **That girl**] . . . has been brought up to wreak vengeance on all **our** [no: **the male**] sex."

Estella, of course—though she has been mentioned in passing—deserves a couple of sentences to herself. It is not much to give to the theme that so long filled Pip's heart. (This last, by the way, the coda to chapter 37, is one of the few chapter endings that does not appear in manuscript; as a very loose rule, Dickens added these slightly moralizing *sententia* in proof.) Dickens appears to have had almost as much trouble with her as Pip does. For example: in chapter 8, once Dickens has gotten rid of the elderly woman, a window is "**<lifted> raised** . . . and then a **<pretty> <young>** [**young**] **<girl>** [**lady**]" comes tripping across the courtyard. Pumblechook—whose lease on Satis House is no stronger than the elderly woman's and who is about to be ~~sent packing back to the High-street in his shay cart~~—introduces our hero: "**<Oh> This is Pip, is it?**" returns "the **<young woman> <girl>** [**young lady**] who was very pretty"—and who seems to be very proud. A little later on, again in a heavily canceled passage, Estella is promoted from **Princess** to **Queen**. Once the two have grown up, Dickens finds it heartrendingly difficult to decide what's proper to the rejected Prince Consort and what isn't. In chapter 44, just before he parts from Estella, ought Pip to hold her hand to his **lips** or his **cheek**? As I make out the sequence in which he tortures the options, he first tries out **lips**, decides against **lips**, tries out **cheek**, doesn't like **cheek**, gives the **lips** one more chance, conclusively nixes **lips**, settles on **cheek**; but in print the **lips** have it.

Though the final manuscript leaves, in which Pip and Estella are reunited in the Ruined Garden, present special difficulties (in the number of cancellations, the constant hesitations, the recuperations of canceled words, and not least the extraordinarily poor condition in which these leaves, and hence the aging lovers, are preserved), two things can be said with some confidence. For one, Dickens rather thickens the sentimental touches and enhances Estella's credentials—for reasons that need to be spelled out in their place. In describing Estella, Pip first tries to invest her with **dignity**, then tries out **magic**, and he finally delivers himself in manuscript of the simple and decorous observation: "The freshness of her beauty was indeed gone, but **its majesty** remained. **That** I had seen before." What the readers of *All the Year Round* get is this: "The freshness of her beauty was indeed gone, but **its indescribable majesty and its indescribable charm** remained. **Those attractions in it,** I had seen before." The simplicity of the manuscript phrasing here is as patent as the self-indulgence of the printed text. Nobody is likely to take issue with Estella's majestic, or queenly, endowments; but when in the last twenty-eight years has Pip ever been "caught by her charms"—as if Dickens were (literally) talking about Scarlett's catch of the Tarleton Twins?[6] The second quality Dickens's cancellations reveal in this final passage is more difficult to get at; and one has to look for it—really and figuratively—between the lines. By canceling three words and substituting, Dickens achieves a remarkable change in two brief sentences: **seemed to come** changed to read **soon showed itself; approached** to **advanced, coming** to **moving.** As we have it, the sentence reads: "**The figure showed itself aware of me, as I advanced. It had been moving towards me, but it stood still.**" The rest of the brief paragraph should be cited; I note that just before Pip utters Estella's name the phrase **I exclaimed** is changed to read **I cried out.** "**As I drew nearer yet, it was about to turn away, when it stopped, and let me come up with it.** ~~Then, it faltered as if much surprised, and uttered my name, and I cried~~ out: 'Estella!' " As I read these lines, I feel as if I were reading about two sleepwalkers, people who are not moving by an act of volition but are drawn along by invisible strings—an effect enhanced, I suppose, by the use of the passive in the first sentence and, perhaps still more strikingly, by the use of the impersonal pronoun—Estella is as yet an *it*. (In the normative novel, the third-person pronoun is used to define a character at the start, not the end, of the text, almost always a child who is barely recognizable, unformed, and often reified by adults: Oliver is an *it*; Heathcliff, when Earnshaw picks him out of the Liverpool gutters, is an *it*—but Estella?) So that when Pip cries out the name, the impression is, all uncannily, that of someone who has just been waking from a dream, or a very deep sleep. And the still more modest change in verbs, from Pip's observation that "Estella was the next **to speak**" to "Estella was the next **to break the silence**" has the effect of capturing the awkwardness of this unexpected dreamlike encounter between two people who have yet to connect. It has, after all, been a very long time since she slapped his face and gave him permission to kiss her.

As long as I have mentioned Dickens's treatment of colloquial speech as this is reflected in manuscript changes, it may be well to jump ahead for a moment and glance at the changes in idiom he introduced at later stages of revision.[7] Not only the manuscript itself but more often a comparison of the manuscript with the corrected galleys and the early printed versions show

---

6. *Gone with the Wind*, 1.1: "Scarlett O'Hara was not beautiful, but men seldom realized it when caught by her charms as the Tarleton Twins were."

7. Cardwell, esp. xxxv f.

how enormously (and often how unavailingly) Dickens fussed over the idiom of his lower-class characters—a procedure already evident in his treatment of the Lancashire factory workers in *Hard Times*.[8] The speech habits of the entirely debased characters in *Great Expectations* (Compeyson, Orlick) did not much interest Dickens; on the other hand, he spent, or wasted, a good deal of time in cleaning up Joe's and more thoroughly Magwitch's idiom, without ever quite achieving consistency. Dickens, whose ear registered all vibrations of speech, knew that there is no status symbol like verbal usage; and if people like Joe and Magwitch display no significant refinement in their table manners in their passage from manuscript to print, their speech habits become at times conspicuously more genteel. In writing up Magwitch's talk with Pip after his return from Botany Bay, for example, and in transcribing Magwitch's recital in chapter 42, Dickens refined all his **wots**—**wot** I have, **wot** a gentleman, and **wot** not—to the regulation **what** at proof stage. If vulgarity is a function of sincerity, one may well feel that these people talked rather more like themselves before Dickens decided to civilize them. But, to repeat, the practice is often arbitrary. Joe frequently lapses from standard usage into preposterous Gargerisms; elsewhere a word like manuscript **afraid** turns up as **afeerd** in print: perhaps Dickens's way of discriminating the coarse from the picturesque. A similar prissiness operates every so often in changes not only in spelling but in vocabulary. In chapter 32, Wemmick conducts Pip on a tour of the Newgate "greenhouse," and after exacting from one of his "plants," the serenely moribund "Colonel," the promise of leaving him a pair of pigeons, informs Pip that the pigeon-fancier ("A Coiner, a very good workman") "is sure to be **hanged** on Monday." Like hundreds of the original readings that Dickens had no time to spoil before *All the Year Round* went to press, the "Colonel" lasted long enough to be **hanged** in *Harper's*; but thereafter the friendly counterfeiter was "sure to be **executed** on Monday." And in chapter 43, Pip himself fears realistically enough that "if Compeyson . . . should discover [Magwitch's] return, I could hardly doubt **that he would put the rope round his neck**." This time not even the readers of *Harper's* were given the benefit of the rope but, like everybody else, found out that Pip "could hardly doubt **the consequence**."

VII

So far I have been sampling the cancellations Dickens made in mid-composition, along with a very few later changes. The other important changes, the interlineated matter and the variants between manuscript and later readings, are obviously easy to get at since they survive the passage from manuscript to print, though interlineations, as obviously, aren't identified in the apparatus—a practical impossibility but a pity all the same, since they can tell us every bit as much about the way Dickens's mind worked as cancellations tell us. Thus, at the risk of my covering some of the chapters of *Great Expectations* already looked at, they need to be glanced at, too, in the light of Dickens's interpolations. Very often, Dickens inserts or marginally adds words or phrases that act as catchy modifiers. In the opening paragraphs, in which Pip rounds up his family, his father remains the comparatively pallid

8. *Hard Times*, eds. George Ford and Sylvère Monod (New York: W. W. Norton, 2nd ed., 1990), 236. More fully: Monod, "Dickens at Work on the Text of *Hard Times*," *Dickensian* 64 (1968): 86–99.

ghost of "a stout dark man" until Dickens invests him with **curly black hair**; the little brothers who are "all born with their hands in their pockets," now that Dickens looks at them again, are "born **on their backs** with their hands in their **trousers**-pockets"; the little things gave up their attempts to survive not in the struggle against their presumably innate infirmities but in that **universal** struggle that Darwin had predicated as a condition of life less than a year before we find out that Pip's brothers had succumbed to it. Magwitch's embarrassments in the churchyard are compounded by such incidental impediments as the **broken shoes** that Dickens puts him into and in his being not merely smothered in mud and lamed by stones but **stung by nettles** to complete his discomfort. The first encounter with Magwitch teems with these improvised verbal fortifications. "After looking at his leg," Pip tells us, " * * * [he] tilted me back as far as he could hold me; so that his eyes looked down into mine, and mine looked up into his." Changed to read: "After **darkly** looking at his leg * * * [he] tilted me back as far as he could hold me; so that his eyes looked **most powerfully** down into mine, and mine looked **most helplessly** up into his." Skipping from Pip's earliest adventure back home to his earliest adventures in the big city, we find that practically the first Londoners he sets eyes on are "a red-eyed Jew * * * in company with a second Jew." Something is obviously missing here, and so Dickens adds the obligatory "red-eyed **little** Jew * * * in company with a second **little** Jew," as though statuesque red-eyed Jews were a thing of nought. Back on the farm, all that Pip remembers of that virtual supernumerary, Mrs. Hubble, the wheelwright's wife, is "a person in blue," as though she had sat for Gainsborough in a former incarnation or Picasso in a later one. As "a **little curly sharp-edged** person in **sky**-blue," Mrs. H. not only assumes the minimal characteristics necessary if the reader is to visualize her, but seven chapters later strips Herbert Pocket of his **sky-blue** suit and stuffs him into a **grey** one, as no two persons in all of *Great Expectations* could look less alike than the wheelwright's wife and the accidental deceased knight's grandson. (Before he became a wheelwright, Hubble apparently followed a different profession, which I've been unable to coax into legibility, after racking my brains for hours to ponder every conceivable trade—after all, a pretty limited quantity—available to these Lower Highamites. At that, I've no assurance that the word Dickens struck gave Hubble's profession, but it makes sense that it would; in the sentence preceding, the introduction of "Mr. Wopsle" is followed by the appositive "our clerk at church.")

Plainly a lot of these fillers are not merely descriptive; often they define or explain an event, a response, a character. On his first visit to Satis House, for example, Pip is sufficiently nonplussed by Havisham's perfectly weird directive to Estella—"I thought I overheard Miss Havisham answer, 'Well? You can break his heart'"—to comment parenthetically: "I thought I overheard Miss Havisham answer—**only it seemed so unlikely**—'Well? You can break his heart.'" In the first of two very brief recapitulatory chapters—the kind that in *David Copperfield* bear the titles "A Retrospect" and "Another Retrospect"— Pip, though he is ashamed of being ashamed of his home as a coarse and common affair, vows that he "would not have had **Estella** see it on any account." But then he adds **Miss Havisham** to the people for whom the forge is off limits—Pip's shame, you see, is not purely a function of his dream girl's contempt but defines the whole class barrier that separates Miss Havisham's bridal chamber from Mrs. Joe's front parlor. Not that Estella, as we've had plenty of chance to see, isn't bad enough in her own right. Pip is promoted from **Pip** to **a boy**, from **a boy** to **a labouring boy**, from **a labouring boy** to **a common labouring boy**, from **a common labouring boy** to **a common coarse labouring boy**, and from **a common coarse labouring boy** to **a little monster**, somebody, or something, at all events, to whom at one moment she brings his food "as if [he] were **a dog**," the next "as if he were **a dog in disgrace**"—these last invectives, which turn Pip into a sort of infant Magwitch, taken not from manuscript changes, however, but from changes added in proof. And (reverting to the MS), Pip draws the inescapable conclusion from Estella's invitation to kiss her after he's raised her blood pressure by drawing blood from the boy in the gray flannel suit. "I kissed her cheek as she turned it to me." Then three incremental admissions: "**I think I would have gone through a great deal to kiss her cheek.**" Then: "But, I felt that she"—this followed by a canceled construction to the effect that she regarded the kiss as a reward, the active construction replaced by the throwaway phrase "**the kiss was given** to the coarse common boy," given, Pip concludes, "**as a piece of money might have been**, and that it was worth nothing."

We are left with one nifty detail—again Dickens kept it under wraps until 1861, when it must have struck him as an essential clue to the narrative, a dramatic foreshadowing that he should have thought of before. During his second encounter with Magwitch, Pip observes that "[Magwitch's] eyes looked so awfully hungry, too, that when I handed him the file, it occurred to me he would have tried to eat it, if he had not seen my bundle." In 1861 Dickens introduced eight low words: "when I handed him the file, **and he laid it down in the grass**, it occurred to me he would have tried to eat it"— that is, it occurred to Dickens (but not until after the serial had run its run) that it would be expedient to plant the file where it can be picked by anybody who chose to lay his hands on it. When we next see the file (or its cousin), one of Magwitch's connections dumbfounders Pip by using it as a swizzle stick, stirring his rum and rubbing his leg, in a very odd way.

A number of interlineations draw special attention to themselves because Dickens very obviously squeezed them between two lines in noticeably small letters. For example, it will be remembered that during the Christmas dinner, while everybody else is turning Pip into pork, Joe comforts him by serving him gravy. "[Joe] **always aided and comforted me** * * * **by giving me gravy**, if there were any. There being plenty of gravy to-day, Joe spooned into my plate, at this point, about half a pint." Some ten manuscript lines later Dickens squeezes in tiny letters between the lines as a separate paragraph: "**Joe gave me some more gravy.**" Eight manuscript lines later, same thing, same squeeze: "**Joe gave me some more gravy.**" Some thirteen lines later: "**Joe offered me more gravy**, which I was afraid to take." Here Dickens is just trying to be funny. Elsewhere this giveaway format has more substantial implications. Dr. Cardwell has pointed out that in Pip's farewell visit to Miss Havisham before he sets out for London, "the addition on proof of two words seems designed to emphasize [Havisham's] collusion."[9] The sentence all but concludes the scene. "Good-by, Pip!—you will always keep the name of Pip,

---

9. Cardwell, xxv, n. 40.

you know." The addition not only seems calculated to mislead us into reading a spurious connection into the transaction, but, by the same token, fortifies Sarah Pocket in her venal viridescence. Still more telling than Cardwell's reminder seems to me evidence once more buried within the manuscript and hence hidden from variorum readings. A few lines before the final farewell, Pip and the fairy godmother exchange some snatches of conversation: of the seven lines two have been crowded in tiny script between the lines, in the manner of Joe's gravy. In answer to Havisham's "so you go to-morrow?":

> "Yes, Miss Havisham."
> "And you are adopted by a rich person?"
> "Yes, Miss Havisham."
> **"Not named, eh?"**[1]
> **"No, Miss Havisham."**
> "And Mr. Jaggers is made your guardian?"
> "Yes, Miss Havisham."

In this catechism in which Experience leads Innocence by the nose, the inserted question surely represents the strongest and most transparent tease of all. Pip would have to be a thoroughgoing skeptic at this point to resist Havisham's come-on and abandon his poor dreams—at the very moment when he has every reason to think that they are about to be translated into the experienced actuality. And of course if Pip is gullible, so is everybody else back at the forge and on the Rochester High-street.

VIII

Even before the *Great Expectations* manuscript had gone to the printer, Dickens still had ample room for revision. As I mentioned earlier, nearly all remaining corrections were made at proof stage after the sheets had been shipped to New York, so that to all intents *All the Year Round* represents Dickens's finished text. Additional emendations were introduced—not always correctly—in the three-volume book edition of 1861. The changes that remain to be recorded here, then, are those Dickens undertook after he had "just finished [his] book of Great Expectations, and [felt] the worse for wear."[2]

A study of the variant readings urges the conclusion that the printed text is all the better for the revisions Dickens undertook in proof. To cite a few obvious small improvements from the first couple of chapters. In describing Mrs. Joe's "trenchant way of cutting bread-and-butter" in the manuscript, Pip makes a mental note of the way "Mrs. Joe **held** the loaf * * * against her bib," but Mrs. Joe's sad and sour ferocity is more sharply conveyed in the substitution of **jammed** for **held**. Joe's amiable hebetude, which is reflected in the manuscript by his "slowly **biting** and meditating before the fire," is a little more graphically suggested in his "slowly **munching** and meditating." The **overgrown mangle**, a stand-in for the bedstead in the guardhouse in chapter 5, more nearly conveys the sense of confinement than the manuscript **immense** mangle; it displays, too, Dickens's famous trick of "paralytically animating" the inanimate, a suggestion quite absent from the neutral **immense**. But here again Dickens's method is by no means consistent. Forging

1. "Eh?" in manuscript only.
2. To W. C. Macready (see p. 535).

ahead to chapter 46, we discover that the "series of wooden frames" in the rundown dockyard area near Chinks's Basin resemble "**infirm** haymaking-rakes which had grown old and lost most of their teeth" before Dickens alters their appearance, with the same liabilities, to resemble "**superannuated** haymaking-rakes." In chapter 45, in which Pip miserably tosses and turns in his nocturnal hideaway at the Hummums, Dickens reverses the pathetic fallacy altogether. In manuscript Pip is forced to listen as "the closet whispered, the fireplace sighed, the little washing-stand **complained of pain**"; in *All the Year Round* he is forced to hear how "the closet whispered, the fireplace sighed, the little washing-stand **ticked**." Here Dickens perhaps wanted to keep the verbal parallelism more nearly intact; besides, that everlasting ticking is bound to exacerbate Pip's nerve-racking wake. Why would the chamberlain at the hotel want to bring Pip "the good old constitutional rushlight of those **virtuous** days" instead of the "**palmy** days" that prevailed in the manuscript? Probably because in the preceding paragraph the four-post bedstead has been described as a "despotic monster" that has been lording it over the room in "quite a Divinely Righteous manner," and the despotism associated with the wicked Stuarts calls for the ironic contrast with a kinder, gentler constitutionally governed generation, not with an age of affluence.

Dickens's refinements can perhaps best be gauged if we look at two brief parallel passages, in which the modification of fewer than half a dozen verbs displays Dickens's art in cameo. At the beginning of chapter 3, Pip braves the rimy and damp morning air to bring Magwitch his file and his wittles. Here is the second paragraph, first as it appears in manuscript, then after Dickens corrects it in proof.

> The gates and dykes and banks came bursting at me through the mist, as if they cried as plainly as could be, "A boy **with a pork pie!** Stop him!" **The black cattle** came upon me with like suddenness, staring out of their eyes, and **smoking** out of their nostrils, "Halloa, young thief!" One black ox, with a white cravat on—who even had to my awakened conscience something of a clerical air—fixed me so **steadily** with his eyes, and moved his blunt head round in such an accusatory manner as I moved round, that I **called out** to him, "**I couldn't help it!** It wasn't for myself I took it!"

> The gates and dykes and banks came bursting at me through the mist, as if they cried as plainly as could be, "A boy with **Somebody-else's pork pie!** Stop him!" **The cattle** came upon me with like suddenness, staring out of their eyes, and **steaming** out of their nostrils, "Halloa, young thief!" One black ox, with a white cravat on—who even had to my awakened conscience something of a clerical air—fixed me so **obstinately** with his eyes, and moved his blunt head round in such an accusatory manner as I moved round, that I **blubbered out** to him, "**I couldn't help it, sir!** It wasn't for myself I took it!"

The "**sir!**" provides the crowning touch in conveying Pip's terror no less than the littleness of a boy who (in moments of terror) clings to his belief in animism. There are many oddities not unlike this: for example, in asking "**Why, how ever could Tar come there?**" where Dickens had first written "**Why, how ever could it come there!**" Pip talks as if Tar had the power to move on its own, unless someone or other propelled it by steam. Just before Magwitch is marched off to the prison ship, he and Pip exchange glances. "I looked at him * * * and moved my hands and shook my head" altered to read "I looked at him * * * and **slightly** moved my hands and shook my head"—there is nothing slight about the force of the modification. Very often—as in the manuscript cancellations and substitutions—the changes serve the purpose of character definition. In the same chapter, just as the convicts are caught, Compeyson's "extreme **fear** of his companion" (manuscript) sounds lame compared with his "extreme **horror** of his companion" (in print): coming upon the passage on a second reading, we recall Arthur Havisham's delirium tremens and the horror *he* entertains towards *his* companion. Of Arthur, we are told (chapter 42) that "he was in a Decline, **of his own bringing on,** and was a shadow to look at"; by deleting in proof the phrase **of his own bringing on,** Dickens underlines Compeyson's role as Arthur's "evil genius."

Dickens's (or Pip's) attitude toward Magwitch is extremely complicated and the change not perhaps always wholly believable. Herbert is almost the first to insinuate the barest softening by warning Pip that since Magwitch owes his power over Pip to his certainty of Pip's affection, he might choose to forfeit his life if Pip were to disabuse him of his illusion, "and that would be his **revenge** if you forsook him." But revenge suggests malicious intent, and as Magwitch is much too buoyed up by his illusion, Herbert is more nearly on target by commuting the charge of **revenge** to the less felonious one of pursuing a **reckless course.** Pip himself is so circumspect in his mood swings that his comment after Magwitch's capture, "For, now, my repugnance to him had all melted away," sounds a little specious. In manuscript: "He regarded me with a look of affection that made him **abhorrent** to me again, though **I had been inclined to pity him.**" The modifier **abhorrent** is shaded to **almost abhorrent,** and the **inclination to pity** to **I had felt great pity for him:** not perhaps an earthshaking metamorphosis. A little earlier, toward the end of Magwitch's narrative, Pip watches him "as he spread his hands broader on his knees, and lifted them off and put them on again," and in manuscript he goes on to observe, "**I saw something like the old click come into his throat.**" By silencing the old click in proof, Dickens may want to distance the reader from the criminal bogeyman back in the meshes and divest him of these unpleasant canine noises of old.

At least one of the changes resolves a crux that has exercised critics for years. As everyone knows, Pip, in his last words to Magwitch, perverts Luke 18.13 by pharisaically substituting the third for the first person: "O Lord, be merciful to him, a sinner!" Is the misreading, or misremembering, a deliberate slap in Pip's face, a final exposure of his dying obtuseness? I doubt it. In the printed text, Pip leads up to the prayer with the phrase "I knew there were no better words that I could say beside his bed." But in the manuscript this reads: "[I] knew there were no better words that I could say beside his bed **through my rush of tears.**" Surely Dickens blotted the tears not because they obscured any intended irony but because he saw them as blemishes on Pip's dignity: the weeping fit is all out of place. The hydraulics in the manuscript reflect Pip's unquestionable sincerity, and Dickens would hardly have changed his mind so thoroughly about Pip's attitude while correcting proof. So, if there is any unconscious hocus-pocus, the lapse is Dickens's, not Pip's.

Besides, as Jean Callahan notes in her piece on the reading version of *Great Expectations*, the reading ends precisely at this point, with Magwitch's death and Pip's prayer, exactly as it stands in the novel.[3] Dickens would hardly have terminated the story with a calculated gesture of denigration, on an abrupt note of ironic reproach, as much as to say: the boy is really impossible. By the end of the chapter Dickens had probably written himself into the condition of mournful complacency in which people easily and a little drowsily lapse into error—and so we may be merciful to him.

Of the comparatively few sentences Dickens struck in manuscript or deleted in proof or *All the Year Round* or (more rarely) added in proof, half a dozen or so may be worth glancing at. In chapter 12, Pip confesses that while he shrinks from sullying Miss Havisham's and Estella's names by dragging them over the threshold of the forge, he feels no such constraints toward "poor Biddy," and he winds up the passage in which he picks his emotional scabs with the invocation "**Shade of poor Biddy, forgive me!**" Dickens no doubt struck the sentence to preclude any misreading the word "Shade" might invite, dispel any suggestion that poor Biddy may have perished from this Earth, and defuse any great expectations of a Dickensian death scene. Dickens is fond of engaging in these sentimentally pious apostrophes elsewhere, without harboring any intimations of mortality. Thus, during the critical three-way conference with Jaggers in chapter 18: "**O dear good Joe, * * * I see you again, with your muscular blacksmith's arm before your eyes * * * and your voice dying away**"—right on, Pyramus: "I see a voice. . . ." A number of sentences involve closure. Chapter 26 ends with Drummle's departure and the comment that "to the great relief of all the house, but Mrs. Pocket, he went home to the family hole." Dickens struck the sentence that follows in the manuscript: "**He called me Blacksmith, when he went away, qualified to be an indifferent hostler or a bad gamekeeper.**" He may have canceled simply because he felt the reference to the young nobleman's "family hole" to be the supreme insult, a good terse, nasty way to pack him off, from which any addition would be tantamount to subtraction. The closing sentence of chapter 49—our final farewell from Miss Havisham—is familiar, if only because she keeps repeating it. "**Take the pencil and write under my name, 'I forgive her.'**" ~~But originally Dickens had taken his leave of her in~~ a separate paragraph: "**It was the first and last time that I ever touched her in that way. And I never saw her more.**" Again Dickens may have struck for a number of reasons: because he wanted to foreground the act of forgiveness, not the farewell, or perhaps because he wanted to keep the options open— that Pip might see her again—or because he thought it important to stress the liturgical repetition, the identical sentence having appeared some lines before. Occasionally Dickens remembers to add a sentence within the manuscript as a slightly transparent sop to the reader. For example, meeting Jaggers again at The Jolly Bargemen just before he springs his surprise, Pip needlessly reminds you that "**his appearance was too remarkable for me to have forgotten.**" One cancellation should have been resurrected, I think, and I've no idea what Dickens disliked about it. During the obsequies in chapter 27, a masterpiece of pathos and comedy, or bacon-streaking, Pip remembers:

3. See below, p. 555.

"And there, Joe and I standing side by side against the very grave stone on which the fugitive had put me that dismal evening long ago, my sister was laid quietly in the earth while the larks sang high above it." (Dickens had written **convict** before he settled on **fugitive**, perhaps already looking ahead to Magwitch's rehabilitation.) The recollection seems to me all the more movingly appropriate since Dickens had laid the groundwork for it in Pip's remembrance at the start of the chapter, in the famous passage that Graham Greene has singled out as an instance of Dickens's "secret prose, that sense of a mind speaking to itself with no one there to listen"[4] and to which I alluded earlier:

> It was fine summer weather again, and, as I walked along, the times when I was a little helpless creature, and my sister did not spare me, vividly returned. But they returned with a gentle tone upon them that softened even the edge of Tickler. For, now, the very breath of the beans and clover whispered to my heart that the day must come when it would be well for my memory that others walking in the sunshine should be softened as they thought of me.

Not all of Dickens's ornamentations are guaranteed to please, and he is likeliest to lose himself in gushing rhetoric whenever he heaps Ossa on Pelion. I have already mentioned his "improving" touches on the Estella of the ruined garden. These sentimental obtrusions are, of course, noticeable elsewhere. An instructive instance can be observed in Clara Barley's debut in chapter 46. In the manuscript, we have: " 'Look here,' said Herbert, showing me the basket, 'here's Clara's supper.' " But this won't do. Dickens proceeds to interlineate: " 'Look here,' said Herbert, showing me the basket, **with a smile after we had talked a little**, 'here's Clara's supper.' " (The interpolation, though it seems to cheer Dickens up, does nothing for the sentence, as we don't know what to do with Herbert's smile. But Dickens is about to come to our rescue, adjectivally.) " 'Look here,' said Herbert, **showing me the basket with a compassionate and tender smile after we had talked a little;** 'here's **poor** Clara's supper.' " The one excuse that I can find for Pip's confession to his being "**in an agony of apprehension**" at the discovery of his theft after he had been "**in mortal terror**" of it is also a sufficient one, that Pip has found himself in mortal terror just a little earlier: "I was **in mortal terror** of the young man who wanted my heart and liver; I was **in mortal terror** of my interlocutor with the ironed leg; I was **in mortal terror** of myself, from whom an awful promise had been extracted."

Despite his lapses, most of the time Dickens is his own best editor, and where he spots what he himself regards as a blemish he makes the necessary adjustments. When, for example, Pip talks about Orlick's "**unrelenting** eyes scowling at me" Dickens strikes the modifier as smacking not only of redundancy but of fine writing. Every so often Dickens fudges and compromises. Before fetching Magwitch his midnight viaticum, Pip explains in manuscript chapter 2, again simply enough, that "there was **no getting a light** by easy friction then." In *Harper's* and first proof this reads: "There was **no venturing**

---

4. "The Young Dickens," *The Lost Childhood and Other Essays* (London: Eyre & Spottiswoode, 1951), 53.

on the crime by night, for there was no getting a light by easy friction at that age of the world." After correction at proof stage, Dickens preserved the substance of the elaborated version but dropped the cosmic talk: "There was no doing it in the night, for there was no getting a light by easy friction then." The sentence that concludes the first stage of Pip's expectations and launches him from his meshes into the New Babylon is well known and touching in the form in which we know it: "And the mists had all solemnly risen now, and **the world lay spread before me**." Yet even here an editor might be justified in feeling that the barest difference in the manuscript wording preserves the Miltonic echo simply and movingly: "And the mists had all solemnly risen now, and **the world was before me**." I confess that this is one of the few occasions on which my knowledge of the manuscript interferes with and taints my respect for the improved text: as though Dickens, poetically compromising, had withdrawn from me something perfectly shaped and in its place served up a somewhat cheaply purchased stereotype.

IX

One measure of Dickens's craftsmanship and his almost consistent success in revision may be found in the one significant departure from the manuscript. Chapter 23 of the *Great Expectations* manuscript contains a fairly sustained passage that Dickens partly canceled in proof. Elsewhere in the same chapter Dickens introduced at proof stage a rather longer passage than the rejected manuscript paragraphs, which differs materially from the manuscript text and is nowhere anticipated in the manuscript. Its suppression, taken together with a number of changes scattered throughout chapters 22 and 23, reveals a thoroughgoing reorientation of Mrs. Pocket's character and of her role within the social ambience of the novel generally. Its suppression may also be of autobiographical relevance. For starters I may mention that in the Ur-text, the Pockets' toady neighbor, a minor character named Mrs. Coiler, appears as Mrs. Pocket's mother, and that accordingly poor Mr. Pocket, before he emerged in *Harper's* and *All the Year Round*, found himself shackled not to the daughter of some accidental deceased Knight but to the Miss Coiler that was.

First the printed passage. Pip pays his first visit to Hammersmith toward the end of chapter 22 to meet his prospective tutor and settle in; enter the small Pockets and the domestics; Mrs. Pocket discovered reading; to them, at the close of the chapter, Mr. Pocket. The opening snatches of chapter 23 (epitome of Matthew Pocket's looks) are crudely similar in both manuscript and print, but so crudely by even the most relaxed standards of textual homework that only the more marked differences need be spelled out, in a footnote.[5] Then follow two longish paragraphs that are in the nature of an expository brief (ancestry and matrimonial history of Mr. and Mrs Pocket); and these are the paragraphs that are nowhere to be found in the manuscript.

5. "He was quite a young-looking man, in spite of his perplexities, and his manner seemed unstudied and natural." Revised to read: "He was a young-looking man, in spite of his perplexities and his very grey hair, and his manner seemed quite natural. I use the word natural, in the sense of its being unaffected; there was something comic in his distraught way, as though it would have been downright ludicrous but for his own perception that it was very near being so." Thus already in *Harper's* except for the phrase "**and his very grey hair**," which Dickens added in proof.

The passage begins with Pip's observation "I found out within a few hours
* * * that Mrs. Pocket was the only daughter of a certain quite accidental
deceased Knight"; it concludes: "Mrs. Pocket was in general the object of a
queer sort of respectful pity, because she had not married a title; while Mr.
Pocket was the object of a queer sort of forgiving reproach because he had
never got one." For the purpose of making up the installment of *All the Year
Round* Dickens did not really need the paragraphs (the installment that contains chapter 23 exceeds the preceding one by fully a column), and we may
assume that he introduced them to satisfy a conscious artistic impulse, not
an editorial mandate.

None of this, then, appears in the manuscript. The three paragraphs that
follow are again substantially alike in both manuscript and print: Pip's introduction to Drummle and Startop, the Pockets' god-awful servant problems,
and Mr. Pocket's professional enfeeblement. In course of revision, Dickens
tossed out the sentence with which he rounds off the expository matter in the
manuscript, one of those garrulous editorials, or asides, that the wisdom of
second thoughts moved him to suppress as a tactless intrusion here and elsewhere in the novel: "Whether [Matthew] was ever sensible in my day of
anything like a waste of his life or of anything in it, will be deducible perhaps
from my occasional record of him." (It won't.) Mrs. Coiler's appearance in
the seventh paragraph introduces the "lost passage" of *Great Expectations*.
Not entirely lost: some two-fifths survive in print. Dickens obviously thought
it a waste of time to mutilate a perfectly good piece of prose where the
manuscript wording merely required to be touched up to bring it into line
with his altered intention. The sentences that are preserved verbatim appear
in square brackets. Mrs. Pocket has a mother.

Mrs. Pocket had a mother; a widow lady of that highly sympathetic
nature that she agreed with everybody (except Mr. Pocket), blessed everybody (with the same exception) and shed smiles and tears for everybody (with the same exception). When visiting at the house, she usually
maintained one gentle uniform continual watery assertion of Mrs.
Pocket. If her feelings towards Mr. Pocket ever had assumed that hydraulic form of demonstration, I might have been better able to account
for it now and then. [This lady's name was Mrs. Coiler, and I had the
honour of taking her down to dinner on the day of my installation. She
gave me to understand on the stairs, that it was a blow to dear Mrs.
Pocket that dear Mr. Pocket should be under the necessity of receiving
gentlemen to read with him. That did not extend to Me, she told me,
in a gush of love and confidence (at that time, I had known her something less than five minutes); if they were all like Me, it would be quite
another thing.]
     "But my dear Belinda has so large a family," said Mrs. Coiler, "and
requires so much affection —— "
     ["Yes ma'am," said I, to stop her, for I was afraid she was going to
cry.]
     "And she is of so sweet a disposition, and ever was as a child; for if
she had plenty to eat and drink and was never interfered with, she was
always so amiable —— "
     ["Yes ma'am," I said again, with the same object as before.]

"——that it *is* hard," said Mrs. Coiler, with red eyelids, "to have Mr. Pocket's time and attention diverted from Belinda."

[I could not help thinking that it might be harder if the butcher's time and attention were diverted from dear Mrs. Pocket; but I said nothing, and indeed had enough to do in keeping a bashful watch upon my company-manners.]

"How do you think her looking, Mr. Pip?" asked Mrs. Coiler with an air of extreme solicitude.

"Mrs. Pocket, Ma'am?" I said: considering it an odd question to put to me, who had never seen its fair subject before.

"Yes. My dear dear Belinda."

Bluff was the only word I could have used with honesty; but not being honest under the moistened eye of Mrs. Coiler, I said "delicate." She highly approved of the reply, and was resuming "With Belinda's large family——" when Mr. Pocket, whom I had observed to be out of sorts at the bottom of the table, struck into our conversation.

"Pray Mrs. Coiler," said Mr. Pocket, "is anything the matter?"

"Matter? No," returned Mrs. Coiler, with a kind of jocund resignation.

"You seemed to be low, Ma'am, I thought," said Mr. Pocket.

"Why should I be low?" answered Mrs. Coiler with a sprightly tear, "at dear Belinda's table?"

So much for the stifled table talk. I need to retrieve two more paragraphs, which have also dropped from sight. The first occurs toward the end of chapter 22, shortly after Pip is first presented to the "fair subject" by Herbert (typical of Herbert, incidentally, that he should introduce him in the phrase "Mamma * * * this is young Mr. Pip"). In the printed text, the eighth paragraph from the end of the chapter concludes simply: "Mrs. Pocket read all the time, and I was curious to know what the book could be." In the manuscript, the paragraph, though silent on Pip's curiosity, is much elaborated. Lost passage, chapter 22:

> Mrs. Pocket read all the time. At last she looked at me again and asked me if I was "fond of travelling?" I was so very much surprised by the abstract character of the question that I answered "No"—which, without any intention or meaning whatever on my part, seemed agreeable to Mrs. Pocket. "No," she said; "so much hurry and trouble, isn't there?" and Flopson then struck in with the observation, "It ain't the thing for you, Mum;" upon which Mrs. Pocket said, "No, Flopson," and laughed and went on reading.

We have next a succinct paragraph—again canceled in its entirety—lifted from the dinner scene in chapter 23; this trails the passage cited earlier (both the suppressed conversation and the printed version) by three paragraphs. Interpolated between Pip's description of the seating arrangement and the introduction of the Young Nobles:

> We had all sorts of things for dinner and Mrs. Pocket sweetly consumed them at the head of the board. Startop afterwards disrespectfully informed me when I said how sweet she was, that I had better say how sticky. I was rather disposed to say it, too, before I had done with the family.

What changes, then, have been wrought in Mrs. Pocket's complexion in her passage from manuscript to print, and why? As Dickens originally conceived her, to judge from the manuscript amputations, Mrs. Pocket emerges as an adequately anserine, debile, vapid, spoiled, absent-minded, idiotically helpless, and lethargic female. She is also sweet and affectionate, but the sweetness and affection are cheaply bought, a function of her silliness and a positive disservice in her total inadequacy as a mother and in her surrender—of the children, of the household, of self—to the domestic staff.[6] Certainly a "character"—but to the integrity of the novel no more serviceable than her hydraulic mother. To say that by the time *Great Expectations* appeared, a person like Mrs. Pocket (the manuscript Mrs. Pocket, without the published increments) had gone stale is perhaps to beg the question; and to suggest that the Mrs. Pocket of the manuscript is a figure out of situation farce and the Mrs. Pocket of the printed text is a figure out of social satire is not to downgrade one form of mimicry and elevate the other, merely a way of discriminating the two. But the change confirms Barbara Hardy's conclusion that Dickens "is weak in farce," and that his "comedy needs the stiffening either of satire or of the macabre, and where his comedy is neither satiric nor dark, it is always least successful."[7]

The "reformed" Mrs. Pocket of the printed text, without relinquishing the follies Dickens foists on her in the manuscript, has more serious things to offer. The whole point of the expository paragraphs Dickens subsequently introduced is to show up in the most glaring light Mrs. Pocket's incurable snobbishness, her inherited pretensions to class values that are based on trumped-up claims, her allegiance to a social status in which class consciousness has declined into the silliest exhibition of class casuistry: a perversion of the noblesse oblige principle, by which the noblesse, the obligation, and the principle persist merely as empty husks. The manuscript passage makes no issue whatever of Mrs. Pocket's class bearings, any more than it tells us what kind of book Mrs. Pocket ogles. How deliberately Dickens strove to make his point—in gratuitously inflating the copy for *All the Year Round*—has been mentioned. The stress is all on Mrs. Pocket's ancestry and nurture—on the fact that the accidental deceased Knight, her father, himself invents a baronetcy of which the grandfather has been mysteriously defrauded, that Mrs. Pocket has been "brought up from her cradle as one who in the nature of things must marry a title," and so on. And this is important, not least because it explains Herbert's matrimonial choice of Clara Barley, with its explicit repudiation of heraldic and genealogical humbug—"the blessed darling" who "comes of no family * * * and hasn't a notion about her grandpapa. What a fortune for the son of my mother!" The failure of the Pockets' own marriage, of course, is in part rooted in social "inequality," in Belinda's approval of the consensus that she has married hopelessly beneath her station. No wonder that she pounces on Bentley Drummle as the only genuine grandee within earshot—this in a passage on which the manuscript is again silent and that

---

6. A nosecount of the Pocket children reveals that Mrs. Pocket has, in Plato's phrase, experienced "birth in beauty" nine times, and is in process of experiencing it for the tenth. Dickens encyclopedists and census-takers may record their names. First, Herbert; next, a sister, Charlotte, who "died before she was 14" (chapter 30); two little boys: Master Alick and little Joe; four little girls: Miss Jane, little Fanny, and two unidentified items of mortality; "besides the baby who might have been either [boy or girl]" (but whose sex is established by Jane's reference to "hith eyeth"), "and the baby's next successor who was as yet neither" (chapters 22, 23).
7. *The Moral Art of Dickens* (New York: Oxford University Press, 1970), 84–85.

Dickens must have introduced at that stage of revision when the satiric muse
told him how to pump life into his bloodless subject; and this almost certainly
is the passage Dickens substituted directly for Mrs. Coiler's meanderings. In
the manuscript, her muffled parting shot, "Why should I be low?" leads directly to Matthew's (rather tiresome) gesture of lifting himself up by his hair
to keep from going quite daft. What is missing from the manuscript is the
following (to revert to the text):

> It came to my knowledge, through what passed between Mrs. Pocket
> and Drummle * * * that Drummle * * * was actually the next heir but
> one to a baronetcy. It further appeared that the book I had seen Mrs.
> Pocket reading in the garden was all about titles, and that she knew the
> exact date at which her grandpapa would have come into the book, if
> he ever had come at all. Drummle didn't say much, but in his limited
> way (he struck me as a sulky kind of fellow) he spoke as one of the elect,
> and recognised Mrs. Pocket as a woman and a sister. No one but them-
> selves and Mrs. Coiler the toady neighbour showed any interest in this
> part of the conversation, and it appeared to me that it was painful to
> Herbert; but it promised to last a long time.

To the earlier conception of Mrs. Pocket this is all quite extraneous. With
the business of Matthew's spastic rise and subsidence, manuscript and text
coincide again. But whenever Dickens gets near Mrs. Pocket the two versions
never quite coincide in phrasing and hence never in presentation. Once Dickens found out Mrs. Pocket—found, that is, a place for her in the scheme of
the book—certain changes in wording forced themselves on him in process
of transforming a goose into a peacock and a sweet ninny into a fainéant
snob. Startop's description—"how sticky"—is everywhere confirmed in the
manuscript. In the manuscript, Pip allows that Mrs. Pocket received him with
an **appearance of amiable enthusiasm, and I thought her the sweetest
woman I had ever seen;** in the revised text, she received him with an **appearance of amiable dignity**, and the sweetness quietly evaporates. She fixes
her eyes upon him **in the sweetest manner** in manuscript; she fixes her eyes
upon him, full stop, in *All the Year Round*; she smiles upon him **with great
sweetness** in the vaults of the Wisbech and Fenland Museum; she smiles
upon him **in an absent state of mind** in the offices at Wellington Street or
at Gad's Hill. The **sweet disposition** Mother Coiler professes to discover in
her yields to the discovery of her **aristocratic disposition** by Mrs. Coiler the
toady neighbor; her **conversational hospitality** lapses into **conversational condescension.** In Mother Coiler's vocabulary, she requires **so much affection;**
in Neighbor Coiler's, she requires **so much luxury and elegance.** The infants
are hauled onstage: initially Mrs. Pocket gazes merely at **them,** but by the
time she looks at them again she gazes at **the young Nobles that might have
been.** She alarms Pip by falling into **a state of serene contemplation** in
her maiden appearance; she alarms him by falling into **a discussion with
Drummle respecting two baronetcies** in her maturity. Little Jane impudently
tries to keep Baby from killing himself with a nutcracker, and Mrs. Pocket—
at all times mistress of the non sequitur—rouses herself: "I hope **I know my
position**"; on second thought, she remembers to "hope **I know my poor
grandpapa's position.**" Last scene of all: the snooping housemaid squeals on
the drunken cook; Mrs. Pocket bridles—not at the cook, for boozing and

stealing, but at the housemaid for peddling unpleasant truths. Manuscript: "Am I to be nothing in the house? . . . Besides, the cook has always been **a very nice woman, and went on very quietly.**" Tailored to read: "Am I, **grandpapa's granddaughter,** to be nothing in the house? . . . Besides, the cook has always been **a very nice respectful woman, and said in the most natural manner when she came to look after the situation, that she felt I was born to be a Duchess.**" Shackled to the born Duchess, ringed round by seven Nobles, Matthew rises to the occasion by dying like the Gladiator.

So we begin with a Mrs. Pocket who lounges in a social and artistic vacuum, a goose of a woman cast adrift in a book called *Great Expectations*. We end with a Mrs. Pocket who is drawn into the whole ambience of misplaced snobbishness, failed ambition, frustrated hopes, that endows the book with its essential substance. One of the least original comments about *Great Expectations*, the acknowledged truism, insists on the total propriety of the title, which in one way or another defines the fortunes of Pip and Estella, Magwitch and Miss Havisham, Wopsle and Orlick, Matthew Pocket and Mrs. Joe, and all the lickspittles and hangers-on who play Raven and Vulture to Miss Havisham's Volpone. In this class-conscious fantasy, this national gallery of snobs, Dickens has found a small niche—not for Mrs. Coiler's daughter but for her listlessly disillusioned, listlessly disinherited hostess.

A word on what I started to talk about: the change in relationship between Mesdames Coiler and Pocket. In the manuscript, of course, Mrs. Coiler augments Matthew's grievances in her position of mother-in-law, and he can't wait for her to get out of the house. There was not much life left in that joke by 1861: the gag of the sweetly shrewish mum-in-law had gone stale long before Mrs. Coiler arrived to exclude Matthew from her smiles and benedictions. For that matter, Dickens had achieved much funnier and more weirdly novel results far earlier in his treatment of the monstrous Quilp and Mrs. Jiniwin in *The Old Curiosity Shop*, in which the stereotyped relationship is neatly twisted: as these configurations go, the son-in-law who lords it over the wife's intimidated mother is perhaps a more intriguing specimen than the henpecked Matthew. Aside from the shabbiness of the joke, Dickens may have had his own reasons for hesitating to grin too emphatically at the spectacle of strenuous in-laws. Naturally one speculates at one's peril here; but it is surely very likely that in 1860–61 Dickens had good reasons to shun even the dimmest echo of his wife's family as distasteful. At the time he began to write *Great Expectations*, as we saw, Dickens had been separated for some two and a half years—not a very long time measured by the seismic intensity of the shocks that the event generated. Enough documentation has come to light to identify the "wicked persons" whom, in that whole sad story, Dickens singled out as the objects of his special venom and whom he forced to retract in writing any rumors about his sex life they might have set in motion and any aspersions they might have cast on his unchivalrous conduct. I raise the point diffidently, only to drop it again. Dr. Cardwell has adduced plenty of evidence to support the autobiographical matrix; but perhaps the last word on the subject ought to be K. J. Fielding's recognition that "no understanding can be reached without appreciating what those who took part in the affair were like, and with the exception of the overshadowing figure of Dickens they all remain obscure."[8]

Herbert will be the last to regret Mrs. Coiler's dismissal from the family. The boy has quite enough to put up with as it is. A chlorotic mother; an enfeebled sire; unspeakable cousins; so many little siblings that Clarriker & Co. may well have to provide for them one day; the fiancée's raving father, whose death is awaited with bated breath: Herbert may thank his stars for his narrow escape from being ambushed by an incense-breathing grandmama.

• • •

As I make out the matter, Herbert has had a narrow escape of quite another stripe. So has Pip. The thing requires a brief departure from the discussion of textual niceties.

Earlier on I looked at some of Dickens's slightly risible peccadilloes, nearly all of which he caught in proof. A very few errors or inconsistencies survive in print—they, too, for the most part of the kind any writer is likely to introduce in the heat of creation. Dickens's one serious miscalculation is almost certainly an unconscious one, and it has escaped general notice, I think, because Dickens scholars have fallen into the habit of stressing the growing leniency of the courts after about 1815, to the exclusion of the punishable offenses still on the books—and very much on Pip's mind. (Why should Pip keep worrying about the deadly consequences of firing a rick, if firing a rick has been reduced from a capital crime to a misdemeanor?) The legal histories I have combed suggest that in the 1820s, whatever ameliorations had been introduced, the myrmidons of justice were still busily at it. In helping Magwitch escape, Pip, Herbert, and Startop are technically "accessories after the fact"—after the fact since Magwitch's initial crime is not his illegal attempt to escape but his return from Botany Bay. With minor variations in wording, all texts define an accessory after the fact as "one who, knowing a felony to have been committed by another, receives, relieves, comforts, or assists the felon." One might have expected Dickens to be especially alert to this particular transgression since the passage of the Accessories and Abettors Act coincided roughly with the publication of *Great Expectations* and had been debated before and while Dickens wrote the novel. Other things being equal, Magwitch's three accomplices would have gotten off with a comparatively mild sentence—two years in jail or "any term not exceeding two years." Yet even this embarrassment is never talked about. For that matter, Pip and his pals might have been given a much stiffer sentence by an impartial jury. For in fact they have been indirectly implicated in and responsible for Compeyson's murder: the judge who sentences Magwitch, after ticking off Magwitch's lifelong offenses, leads up to the ultimate charge that Magwitch "whether by express design, or in the blindness of his hardihood—caused the death of his denouncer, to whom his whole career was known." Technically, an accessory after the fact to murder could be transported or imprisoned for life, though this, too, could be commuted to transportation or imprisonment for no more

8. Cardwell, xxix–xxx; Fielding, "Dickens and the Hogarth Scandal," *Nineteenth-Century Fiction* 10 (1955): 74. Also Fielding's "Charles Dickens and His Wife: Fact or Forgery?" *Etudes Anglaises* 8 (1955): 212–22; Ada Nisbet, *Dickens and Ellen Ternan* (Berkeley and Los Angeles, 1952: University of California Press), 65 ff.; and the useful summary of the facts as assembled in A. J. Hoppé's long note in his edition of Forster's *Life* 2, 448–59.

than four years. What almost certainly saved Pip and Herbert from being sent to the very spot from which Magwitch returned was not the increased leniency of the courts but Dickens's absentmindedness. Else the issue might at least have been raised; the silence speaks for itself. Very likely it never occurs to —or if it does, fails to bother—the reader, who thinks in broadly ethical not legalistic terms; and in trying to smuggle Magwitch out of England the young men are performing a service of love and courage. To imagine Pip and Herbert in jail for as long as two days defies the imagination, especially now that we know them to be snugly ensconced in Egypt. Besides, it's quite enough to give your reader a choice between a happy and an unhappy ending without increasing the dosage by adding a very unhappy ending. Dickens forgets to tell us what happened to Startop.

X

I conclude with two or three very general comments. A good deal has been made of Dickens's names and the nominal changes he introduced in *Great Expectations*. Most of them are reasonably familiar, and most (though not quite all) have been recorded by the Clarendon editor. Throughout chapters 23 and 24, **Drummle** appears as **Jumble**, which sounds as inoffensive as Jingle and Sweedlepipe and may have been discarded by Dickens precisely because of its harmless comicality as unsuited to horse-whippers and wife-beaters, or he may have found the name uncomfortably near-homologous to **Bumble** or **Pumblechook**. The virtual supernumerary **Mary Anne** initially appears as a fixture in the Pocket ménage, but Mary Anne is not nearly a fine enough name to suit the likes of Mrs. Pocket, who is on easier terms with an **odious Sophia** than with the **odious Mary Anne** of the manuscript; and so Dickens finds a place for **Mary Anne** in the leveling milieu of the Castle. **Startop's** original name has been canceled beyond recognition; he enters as **Startop** together with the refurbished **Drummle**, though, unlike Drummle's, Startop's name appears as corrective to the canceled original from the first. Then we have **Orlick**: the first half dozen times Dickens refers to him by name, he calls him **Horlick**, exactly as he appears in the notebook Dickens kept as a storehouse for incidents, names, ideas, from 1855 on, Dickens canceling the initial in manuscript, as if the likes of **Orlick** were too coarse altogether to deserve the dignity of being aspirated any more than a horse deserves to be, or perhaps because this is how Joe would pronounce his name. (Mr. George Newlin has pointed out to me the curious fact that among the thousands of Dickens's characters, Orlick is one of the two important ones whose surname begins with a vowel, the other being the née Akersham in *Our Mutual Friend*—and *she* drops her maiden name first off.)

Much—too much, I think—has been made of **Magwitch's** Christian name, if that is the right word. Whatever Dickens may have thought of the dead young **Abraham** and the aborted **Esau** and **Isaac**, he appears to have hesitated at least for a second in naming Pip's godfather **Abel**. Dickens had already struck **George** (almost certainly twice) and (uncertainly) still another name before he introduced Magwitch as **Abe**; he then, pace Dr. Cardwell, transformed **Abe** into **Abel** by adding the l, again clearly on second thought. I doubt, though, that in this and a myriad other instances, "thought" had anything to do with the change. I doubt, that is, that in adding the l to his **Abe**,

Dickens all consciously had his mind on the symbolic propriety of Magwitch's being hounded to death by a criminal British fraternity, his pastoral pursuits down under, etc. And though Dickens certainly wouldn't have called him Cain Magwitch, he probably pinned the name Abel on him because it felt right. It looked right; it sounded right: let it be Abel. This flies in the face of dozens of exegetes, but that is not my fault. It would be asinine to suggest that Dickens was deaf to scriptural nomenclature; but to entitle a chapter in *Our Mutual Friend* "**Better to Be Abel than Cain**" or to have young David Copperfield refer to himself as a **little Cain** or to keep referring to hulks as **wicked Noah's arks** or, for that matter, to talk unmistakably about **Stephen Blackpool's martyrdom** in *Hard Times* is obviously something else altogether. Of course, one could always argue that Dickens called Pecksniff **Seth**, Adam's youngest, because it's a great convenience to be an architect and land surveyor if you have to start building from scratch east of Eden, and that our intro- duction to **Noah** Claypole as the son of a washerwoman and a drunken soldier points unambiguously to the ubiquitous presence of water and tipsi- ness in Genesis 6 to 8, but I doubt that anyone would. **Abel** Garland in *The Old Curiosity Shop*, a shy young city merchant, whom Dickens decks out with a clubfoot because the bloke is so dull that he has to do *something* for him, and who marries "the bashfullest girl that ever was," has about as much in common with **Abel Magwitch** as either has with the **Abel** of Genesis 4, especially to interpreters who have read Robert Hughes's history of the Aus- tralian settlement, *The Fatal Shore*, and find in Magwitch traces not of the self-made agrarian merchant-prince but of the cannibal—I recognize that in some economic circles the two are not mutually exclusive. It seems only right that—again pace Cardwell—the thoughtless formation **Abe** persisted in the first American book edition (in *Harper's* he appears as Abel): at the time Magwitch first springs his names on Pip, on May 18, 1861, Americans were more likely to keep their eyes on the new president than on the Old Testa- ment, the gentleman from Illi-noy having been nominated on May 18, 1860, and assumed office just a couple of weeks before Pip first meets his warmint on manuscript page 1.

I suspect that the same reservations apply to Miss Havisham. (We're never told her first name—which saves critics a lot of time.) In the manuscript, she appears as Havish the first six times she is named (the name in German suggests both a bird of prey and the soul of avarice) before Dickens adds the final syllable. Dickens makes no bones about her being Pip's "fairy god- mother" or (in what is really the same mode) "the witch of the place," any more than he blinds the reader to Magwitch's acting out the role of the scapegoat; but I've a hunch that he added the last syllable to Havish for no better reason than he added the last syllable to Compey—the name Compey itself having pejorative implications in Kentish dialect. Jaggers's name is struck and/or blotted some six times before the name appears unhesitatingly; Dick- ens then cancels the name again paragraphs later before reinstating Jaggers as Jaggers; cancels again; finally comes up with nothing better. The procedure suggests little or no forethought, despite all the lists of names Dickens had drawn up by then. I find a good deal of sense in the meaning of **Estella** to signify **Star**; but this gets me into no end of trouble with the innocent **Startop**. In the bawdy language of Honest Iago, who here tops whom? Does **Startop** top **Star** or does **Star** top **Startop**? In the history of onomastics, Estella occupies a unique place: to all intents Dickens introduced her name into the language. Though there are plenty of cognate Esthers, you can no more find an Estella before 1861 than (by an obverse relation of life to literature) the educated American reading public could, a century later, baptize a child Lolita and get away with it.[9]

One final point, which, in the most modest sense, may shed a ray of light on Dickens's view of his novel. Clearly the tripartite division was very important to him and almost certainly suggested itself to him from the start. In ending the first stage, Dickens, in the first of his three valedictions, canceled "This is the End of the First Stage of **Pip's** Expectations," rephrased it to read "This is the End of the First Stage of **Great Expectations**," struck "**Great Expectations**," and gave the last word to Pip. Dickens's indecisiveness at this point and his decision (on third thought) in favor of Pip obviously could not affect the book's title, on which Dickens had settled from the very outset and under which the serial had run for nearly three months. The likeliest guess is that at the end of a clear break in Pip's life, Dickens wanted to stress the biographical aspect of his bildungsroman. This is supported by the wording at the end of stage two, which reads unhesitatingly "**This is the End of the Second Stage of Pip's Expectations**." That at the very end, on manuscript page 29 of his ninth monthly portion, Dickens should want to revert to the title "**This is the End of Great Expectations**"—that, too, is wonderfully appropriate: Pip may go on and on, but the artificer has closed his account.

A Note on Accidentals

SPELLING AND HYPHENATION

I have briefly anticipated the subject of accidentals in my tangential remarks on Dickens's distinction between the hieratic **O** and chatty **Oh**. I should introduce one other change by first noting that Dickens is very circumspect in his treatment of God, and in three cases out of four secularizes phrases like **Please God** to read **If all goes well**. This reticence breaks down completely in the late chapters, especially in the scenes dealing with Magwitch's last hours, and this is relevant to this business of accidentals only because in these final scenes, apart from invoking the Almighty by name a dozen times, Dickens gets caught up in an unprecedented riot of capitalization. "It was impossible [not to] find [Magwitch] **Guilty**"; the concluding day is given over to "the passing of **Sentences**, and to make a finishing effect with the **Sentence of Death**"; "the appointed punishment * * * being **Death** * * * he must prepare himself to **Die**"; Magwitch, in bowing to earthly **Justice** at the same time acknowledges that he has received his "sentence of **Death** from **God**," etc. It is difficult to imagine the rest of the moribundi in *Great Expectations*—Compeyson, Arthur Havisham, Arthur's half-sister, even Mrs. Joe—enjoying the dignity of **Dying**, in caps. Similarly, in chapter 57 Pip asks His blessings on Joe, "this gentle **Christian** man!" where, in the more wordly context of the Higham churchyard in the opening sentence of the novel, Pip

---

9. Anyone interested in the uses of Dickensian nomenclature ought to read the wonderfully suggestive essay by C. A. Bodelsen, "The Physiognomy of the Name," *Review of English Literature* 3 (1961): 39–48, rept. in C. A. Bodelsen, *Essays and Papers* (Copenhagen: The Nature Method Centre, 1964), 75–83. René Belletto goes to fantastic lengths to deconstruct Pip's name in his *Les grandes espérances* (Paris: P.O.L., 1994), passim.

refers to his **christian** name; and it goes without saying that Orlick alleges his **christian** name to be Dolge, not his **Christian** one. It may be objected that Dickens is here at the mercy of Victorian conventions of feeling and spelling; but a glance at novels where this kind of scrappy orthography might be expected (in Charlotte Brontë's, for instance) reveals that the heavens are much more likely to fall on M. Emanuel than Heaven. Elsewhere, Dickens may use caps for emphasis, or ironically, where we would place these words in quotation marks: in the notation in chapter 28, say, apropos of the convicts en route from London whose guard treats them as if they "were an interesting **Exhibition** not formally open at the moment, and he the **Curator**"; similarly, Magwitch, warming himself by the fire and surveying his protégé "with the air of an **Exhibitor**"; but elsewhere still (Heaven knows why) Dickens may go on the **Rampage** by capitalizing anything from **Coiners** to **Sulks** and from **Bed** to **Eternity**. Indeed, his respect for capitals appears to be so small that he is apt to use one and the other in one and the same line: Miss Havisham may wail "O **Dear**, what have I done!" and then, perhaps on the presumption that capitals *should* be treated with diffidence, follows this up with the wail "O **dear**, what have I done!"

For the rest, Dickens's spelling calls for little comment. He usually favors the American **z** over the homegrown **s**, and the terminal **-or** over the native **-our**. But, again, he distributes his favors and honors promiscuously. On his trip to London in chapter 27, Joe talks feelingfully about a pig's "meller **flavor**," and in trying to disengage Pip from Estella three chapters later, Herbert assures him that he is "quite free from the **flavour** of sour grapes." Here all editors have adopted the standard British usage. I have similarly followed the less uniform practice of modernizing the terminal **l** in words like **befal** and **downfal** by doubling ("I do not **recal** that I felt any tenderness of conscience in reference to Mrs. Joe"). To a modern reader these spellings (precisely because they look like misspellings) have a way of interfering with our reading habits, jumping out from the page and attracting a degree of attention the writer never intended them to attract: we read these constructions not as "I **recal** her" or "it **befel** him" but as "I **RECAL** her" and "it **BEFEL** him." Until about fifty years ago, four-letter obscenities used to affect our reading habits in much the same way. I have already talked about the phonetic spelling in which Joe or the zany Yanks in *Martin Chuzzlewit* find refuge.

John Butt, the pioneering Dickens textualist, has already pointed out that Dickens is equally cavalier in his hyphenation. His tendency is to omit the hyphen where we would normally place one, but here again it would be idle to look for any consistent usage. As far as I know, editors have not bothered to normalize but rather have followed whatever copy-text they pick, even where the result can be mildly ludicrous. Thus Jaggers recommends—I beg pardon, he *mentions*—the vehicle Pip may wish to take to his office: accordingly, Pip has his choice of taking "a **hackney coach** at the **stage coach office**" (manuscript), "a **hackney-coach** at the **stage-coach office**" (*AYR*), or "a **hackney-coach** at the **stage coach-office**" (1861 to 1868). As a very loose rule, I have adopted two procedures: in view of his pervasively lazy omissions, wherever Dickens takes the trouble of hyphenating, the hyphen should be paid double and be retained; and certain words seem to need the hyphen (which Dickens usually introduces here anyway) if we are to feel their full force. A **heart-ache** suggests a deeper pain than a **heartache**, and where Pip finds himself **spell-bound**, so do I. These words simply read differently from their unhyphenated step-brothers; the eye glides over Pip's heartaches and his being spellbound as it doesn't over the (intentionally?) separated halves. *Webster's* and house-styling apart, bookshelves, armchairs, and stage coach offices can do as they please.

PUNCTUATION

If Dickens hyphenates sparingly or indifferently, he overcompensates in his punctuation: a far more important element of style in proportion as it affects our reading as spelling and syllabification don't. English teachers are familiar with the weird penchant of students for placing a comma just as they list, and the more commas the better, as if the commission of a comma were in itself a demonstration of stylistic proficiency. (At that, these people haven't even the excuse of Dickens's friend Bulwer, a pragmatic eccentric who on one occasion ended a sentence with 101 exclamation marks because he was being paid by the letter, and no publisher would risk the loss of so high-prized a commodity as Bulwer by fooling with his punctuation.) Dickens, without the least mercenary motives but by a habit that he acquired early in his career, adopted a system of internal punctuation in which he introduced colons where other writers would place commas or semicolons or omit punctuation altogether. Moreover, especially at the beginning of sentences, his conjunctions frequently take commas: And, But, For, Nor—pretty much as we ourselves, in the 1990s, use commas following adverbs: Moreover, However, Nevertheless. In his wonderful essay *"Great Expectations"* (reprinted below) Christopher Ricks singles out one such punctuation mark—in Pip's answer to Havisham's question in chapter 49 whether there is anything she can do for Pip himself beyond subsidizing Herbert's partnership: "I thank you * * * for the tone of the question. But, there is nothing." Ricks comments that "that comma after 'But' must be the least careless comma in Dickens—the decent mystery of leaving the rest unsaid."[1] Very likely Ricks, by pouncing on this as Dickens's most deeply meditated punctuation mark, is not fully aware of Dickens's practice; on the other hand, if we were to read Dickens with the same attention to pauses and stresses as Ricks reads him, we might be all the better for it. (For the record, our copy-text, *All the Year Round*, most perversely forgets all about the comma, but I didn't have it in my heart to cross Professor Ricks and, with the freedom of the eclectic, restored it, for his sake, and the readers'.)

Dickens's punctuation is bound to draw attention to itself, and editors have been surprisingly faithful in following manuscript precedent. Taking at random a middling-long paragraph from chapter 22 that is thirteen lines long in print, I find that of nineteen manuscript punctuation marks, nearly all texts retain at least the same seventeen, which isn't a bad score. The opening sentence of the paragraph happens to be an object lesson in Dickens's usage. Its seventeen words read: **"On a moderate computation, it was many months, that Sunday, since I had left Joe and Biddy."** Presumably, we would either omit all commas or retain the one that sets off "computation" —but there is no reason why we can't follow Dickens. A lot of students would.

1. See below, p. 672.

In fact, a number of editors, as if they thought Dickens a little stingy, add a few commas of their own, and some of them make for curious reading. While Magwitch is teasing Pip toward the horrible truth, Pip allows that Magwitch's thank-you call at least proves that he can't be all bad. "**Still, however you have found me out**, there must be something good in the feeling that brought you." Sure enough, the 1868 text and the texts it spawned read "**Still, however, you have found me out**," etc., in this emulating the famous misreading in Shakespeare, "**Wherefore are thou, Romeo?**" Elsewhere, as in the opening paragraph of chapter 56, the paragraph beginning "He lay in prison very ill," Dickens's heavy punctuation virtually imitates Magwitch's laborious breathing, a triumph of composition for which Flaubert scores a lot of points in rendering Félicité's last breaths in the concluding sentences of *A Simple Heart*. On the other hand, Dickens (though infrequently) piles modifiers on modifiers without the expected breaks: for example, on first seeing Herbert's Intended, what Pip sees is "**a very pretty slight dark-eyed girl of twenty or so**," as if to suggest that he takes her in in one sweeping glance.

One final paragraph. It appears in chapter 54 and describes Magwitch and the young parties to his escape taking a break on shore. The passage runs to a little over two hundred words and, aside from the full stops, has twenty-four punctuation marks. Here I follow the manuscript, which (with one exception) gives commas throughout—to convey a sense both of the tempo and of the hypnotic effect induced by identical punctuation, where all printed texts commute between commas and semicolons without particular rhythmic or grammatical laws of discrimination.

> Our oarsmen were so fresh, by dint of having occasionally let her drive with the tide for a minute or two, that a quarter of an hour's rest proved full as much as they wanted. We got ashore among some slippery stones while we ate and drank what we had with us, and looked about. It was like my own marsh country, flat and monotonous, and with a dim horizon; while the winding river turned and turned, and the great floating buoys upon it turned and turned, and everything else seemed stranded and still. For, now, the last of the fleet of ships was round the last low point we had headed, and the last green barge, straw-laden, with a brown sail, had followed, and some ballast-lighters, shaped like a child's first rude drawing of a boat, lay low in the mud, and a little squat shoal-lighthouse on open piles, stood crippled in the mud on stilts and crutches, and slimy stakes stuck out of the mud, and slimy stones stuck out of the mud, and red landmarks and tidemarks stuck out of the mud, and an old landing-stage and an old roofless building slipped into the mud, and all about us was stagnation and mud.

The attention Dickens himself paid to these pauses is reflected in the number of changes he introduced at proof stage. He might substitute a semicolon for a comma or a full stop, or a full stop or question mark for an exclamation mark. His tendency was to tone down his sentences; thus: " '**Is she married?**' / '**Yes!**' " (manuscript to *AYR*); " '**Is she married?**' / '**Yes.**' " (1861 ff); " '**Tell me by all means! Every word!**' " (manuscript to *AYR*); " '**Tell me by all means. Every word.**' " (1861 ff). As a rule, where the change from the declamatory to the resigned mood seems to me the more effective and characterologically sound alternative and has sanction in proof, I follow 1861; on the other hand, more than half the time the *All the Year Round* text is demonstrably more dependable. Often readers have their choice. Where, Magwitch wants to know in the churchyard, did Pip see t'other one? " 'Yes! There!' " *(AYR)* " 'Yes, there!' " (1861). I should give this, along with a good many substantive changes, to *All the Year Round*; but others may prefer the later reading.

A Note on Dickens's
Working Plans

From the time he composed *Dombey and Son* (1846–48), Dickens made it a practice to draw on loose sheets of paper a series of working memoranda to guide him in the progress of the narrative. These *Mems.*, as he called them—briefly worded notations and reminders of names, snatches of phrasing, bits and pieces of plot machinery—were especially serviceable to him in the composition of his longer and more complex novels, which were issued in monthly numbers and required him to anticipate, recollect, and keep a check on his work-in-progress.[1] Nearly all the *Mems.* are written in light blue ink on facing half sheets, each half sheet approximately 7½ inches by 4½ inches. Generally Dickens used the left-hand sheet to scribble names and phrases he wanted to keep in reserve and the right-hand side to jot down a fairly accurate outline of the action, usually adding chapter titles and numbers. (But the *Mems.* could serve ancillary functions: for example, Dickens uses up fully ten half sheets on working titles for *Bleak House*, from *The East Wind* to *The Solitary House where the grass grew*, and seventeen for *David Copperfield*, from *Copperfield Complete* to *The Copperfield Survey of the world as it rolls*.)

The working plans for *Great Expectations* are conspicuously briefer and more fragmentary than those for any other novel—of the later books, *A Tale of Two Cities* alone lacks *Mems.* altogether. Dickens seems to have had the main action of *Great Expectations* fairly well mapped out from the early stages of composition and could dispense with most of the working plans as he went along, nor did he bother with the incidental reminders and queries—names, sequence of action, problems of "tone"—that we find in the other *Mems.* What we are left with are a scant five half sheets, written like all the *Mems.* in blue ink on pale blue laid paper; these are bound in with the Wisbech manuscript and evidently guided Dickens in composing the final chapters of the novel. First we have two half sheets entitled "Dates"; next, two half sheets headed "General Mems."; and, on a separate page, a brief memo headed "Tide." The memos on "Dates" and "General Mems." are reproduced in photographic facsimile below; all three memoranda are given in typographic transcription.

---

1. The memoranda have been superbly reproduced in Harry Stone's volume *Dickens' Working Notes for His Novels* (Chicago: Chicago University Press, 1987). Stone's introduction provides the most detailed discussion of the *Mems.* we are likely to see, and he furnishes helpful headnotes for each of the novels. On *Great Expectations* see [314]–19.

Dates

The half sheets headed "Dates" were almost certainly written earlier than either "General Mems." or "Tide," which they precede at the back of the manuscript. "Dates" reconstructs the chronology of the Havisham-Compeyson affair and Magwitch's association with Compeyson, citing the approximate ages of the major characters "in the last stage of Pip's Expectations," each entry preceded by the qualifying "about": "Pip about 23 / Estella about 23," and so on. Compeyson here bears the original name "Compey," the name he bears in the manuscript through chapter 42; in manuscript chapter 45 the last three letters are added separately; it is only in chapter 47 that the name first appears unhesitatingly as "Compeyson," the form in which it appears in the "General Mems." John Butt, who was the first to conduct a thorough study of the Wisbech Plans, reasonably infers that these memoranda were written at some point after Magwitch's narrative in chapter 42 and before chapter 45, when Compey is invested with his full name.[2] Perhaps more safely before chapter 47, since we have no way of knowing just when Dickens went back to the manuscript to add the final syllable to Compey's name; and even this later dating is open to challenge insofar as the original name may well have lingered in Dickens's mind after he made the formal change in the manuscript.

In jotting down "Dates," as Butt suggests, Dickens intended to guard against major gaffes by reviewing his earlier detective work—even though, as Butt also points out, "the novel was too far gone in print for material alterations"; if Dickens "had discovered some discrepancy at this point, there was not much he could have done about it."[3] The memorandum confirms, too, Dickens's tendency to blur the ages of his characters in the main part of the narrative and so disinfect the danger of local inaccuracies. After all, it doesn't matter very much whether Miss Havisham is 56 or "about 56" and Wemmick is 50 or "near 50"; but he clearly felt that to approximate was safer than to specify. The discursive matter in the memorandum consistently reflects this in the phrasing: "Say Pip was about 7 at the opening of the story"; "say that the matter was a year or so in hand"; "At that time, Pip is say 18 or 19," and so forth. The care with which Dickens went about this (and perhaps the strongest evidence for dating these sheets) is apparent in a number of minor textual revisions he undertook in chapters 48, 49, and 50. In manuscript chapter 48, for example, in answer to Pip's question how Jaggers managed to tame Molly, Wemmick replies: "That's his secret. She has been with him many a long year. A score of years." In the printed text the final sentence disappears. Dickens in this instance may have deleted it simply because in reading proof he discovered the sentence to be nearly redundant, for a few paragraphs later Wemmick launches into his story of Molly's crime with the words "a score of years ago, that woman was tried at the Old Bailey for murder and was acquitted." But even here the wording "a score of years ago," as it stands in the manuscript, is toned down to read "a score or so of years ago." Similar refractions, or hedges, can be detected in Pip's questions about Estella's infancy in the Satis House conversation in chapter 49 and again in his

2. "Dickens's Plan for the Conclusion of *Great Expectations*," *Dickensian* 45 (1949): 78–80, the piece in which "Dates" first appeared in print.
3. Ibid., 80.

conference with Herbert toward the end of chapter 50, just as Pip is about
to spring on Herbert the disclosure of Magwitch's paternity.[4] All these changes
are trifling enough, but an altered phrase betrays an altered intention, especially where the changes become systemic. Clearly Dickens didn't want to
commit himself overmuch: hence the cautious insertion of all these *abouts*
and *would have beens*. I think it fair to assume that Dickens jotted down
"Dates" at the time he began chapter 48, or a trifle earlier, a conjecture
supported not only by the evidence of the manuscript revisions in this part
of the novel but also by the equally probative circumstance that the entire
reconstruction of Molly's history and the attendant Magwitch-Compey-Estella
complications are begun in chapter 48 and run through chapter 51. So chapter 48 would have been a natural place for Dickens to pause for a general
review of the chronology.

"Dates" reveals something else, which bears on the whole reach of retrospect in *Great Expectations*. The biographies of Miss Havisham, Magwitch,
Estella, and Molly can be revealed only in long inset narratives and flashbacks: Herbert's in chapter 22, Magwitch's in chapter 42, the more compressed information Wemmick serves up in chapter 49, and Jaggers two
chapters later. Despite Magwitch's genius and Herbert's gift as storytellers, the
very device of the flashback often has a way of lowering the narrative pressure.
But in a little more than a page of the *Mems.* (always granted that they were
intended as an aide-mémoire to himself and not to his readers), Dickens jolts
us back into the past and by reminding himself reminds us of the catastrophic
events thirty years ago that engendered the fortunes and misfortunes of Pip
and Estella. From a purely actuarial interest, as Anny Sadrin reminds us,
"Dickens [in the section on 'Dates'] tells himself more about the ages of his
characters than he ever tells us in his novel, where only Pip's and Herbert's
ages are specified"[5]—we may safely, within a year (or two), add Estella's. It
may come as something of a surprise to find that Jaggers is only a year younger
than Miss Havisham: to most readers they are more likely to mark the difference between old age and middle age. Again, it is only fitting that Biddy,
Pip's mentor, should be at least a year or two "the elder in [her] love time"
with Pip; that she should marry a man who is nearly twice her age, given the
other determinants, is perfectly plausible. As it's difficult to imagine Wemmick mooning over a woman in her twenties or thirties, it makes sense that
he and Skiffins should be of roughly the same vintage—when Pip first meets
her in chapter 37, he judges her to be "some two or three years younger than
Wemmick," whose own age is given in the Memoranda of Dates as "near
fifty."

The cases of Pip's patrons—the imaginary and the real one—are rather
more striking. Miss Havisham is a mere thirty-three years older than Pip, when
most of us would have thought her somewhere been Mrs. Coiler and Wopsle's
great-aunt in age. When Pip first meets her, Havisham is no older than thirty-
nine or forty and thus in the prime of life. At the time of her self-immolation,

---

4. In puzzling out the time of Molly's disappearance and Estella's arrival in Satis House, Herbert asks
    Pip at what age he first met Magwitch, and, in the manuscript wording, concludes: "It had happened
    about four years then, [Magwitch] said, and you brought into his mind the little girl so tragically lost,
    who would have been your age." This is straightforward enough—too much so, for Dickens subse-
    quently altered the phrase "about four years" to read "some three or four years," and in the final
    clause he blurred the downright "your age" to read, a shade less definitely, "about your age."
5. Sadrin, 21.

Dickens informs us, she is fifty-six (or about fifty-six). The odd thing is that she has nothing to show for the passage of sixteen years. In chapter 8, Pip asks her when he should come back to play, only to be cut short—"I know nothing of the days of the week; I know nothing of the weeks of the year." We should like to, though, and we would expect her to have more to show for that dismal sixteen-year interval than a sense of existence in vacuo. In a way, Dickens here falls victim to the very objections he voiced against *Robinson Crusoe*, a book he scorched as "perfectly contemptible, in the glaring defect that it exhibits the man who was 30 years on that desert island with no visible effect made on his character by that experience."[6] Admittedly, the defect is more glaring in a person who has been shipwrecked, spent weeks in salvaging biscuits, nails, and survival kits from the wreck, built himself a summer pavilion, suffered from tropical fever, experienced a religious conversion, turned a childish factotum into a byword for a day in the week, married, took to the sea again, lived forever and died rich in *moidores* and pieces of eight than it is in a woman who appears as though she had been preserved in formaldehyde, who spends her undifferentiated days and nights immured in one or two airless candlelit rooms and likes to be pushed about in a species of pram for senior citizens. But this is really a specious difference; ask any student to guess Havisham's age at the time Pumblechook first escorts Pip to Satis House, and the answer is likely to be anywhere upwards of fifty-five—that is, the age at which she catches fire some sixteen years later. As if bent on getting even with Dickens and making the most of the gap, the first illustrator of *Great Expectations*, Marcus Stone, working without the customary instructions by Dickens, seized on the difference in age so glaringly that the two Miss Havishams, the woman of forty and the woman of fifty-six, no longer bear the faintest resemblance to each other: the first (whom Pip meets in chapter 8) a ripe, ravishing, raven-haired, bosomy specimen whom anybody would mistake for Estella (or Edith Dombey) if it weren't for young Pip's dancing attendance on her; the second (playing a rubber with Pip, Estella, and Jaggers in chapter 29) a pinched, vinegary, suspicious old thing, a near relation, in temperament if not social status, to old Mrs. Gummidge, the crabby professional widow, the "lone lorn creetur," in *David Copperfield*.

The passage of years that separates Magwitch's first from his last appearance works rather the other way: there is no mistaking the metamorphosis from varmint to parvenu and rags to riches. On the other hand, a number of commentators, with some justice, have lectured Dickens on the improbability of Magwitch's being identified after his sixteen-year absence on the nether side of the globe. As the *Mems.* inform us, Magwitch is forty-four when he jumps Pip in the churchyard and sixty when the appearance of the witness in chapter 55 seals his doom. Well, a person of sixty very often retains an unmistakable resemblance to his younger double—often a photographic likeness. The changelessness of a Robinson Crusoe or Miss Havisham isn't, of course, merely or primarily cosmetic but involves something like a total stasis. Magwitch, on the other hand, has experienced a marked change, has lived a violent and volatile history in his sixteen years down under—Dickens making sure all the while that the old grubber retains enough of his old characteristics

6. Forster, *Life*, book 7, chapter 5 n; Hoppé, 2, 431–32.

to sustain our faith in certain immutabilities in behavior.[7] Moreover, we are told that the deponent had been "an old officer of the prison-ship from which [Magwitch] had once escaped," and the escape may well have generated enough commotion to stick in the officer's mind. Even so, the number of such escape artists in the heyday of transportation, the brevity of the confrontation between convict and officer sixteen years back, and the confusion of the arrest perhaps suffice to vindicate the skeptics. The ideal eyewitness would have been a much closer and more recent acquaintance of Magwitch's from the penal settlement, and *he* would be the last to come forward—in the certainty of sharing the gallows with Magwitch and doubling the Recorder's already grinding workload. But it is too late to do anything about that now.

General Mems.

"General Mems." were almost certainly written about the time Dickens dispatched to Forster the letter in which he expressed his chagrin "that the third portion cannot be read all at once, because its purpose would be much more apparent; and the pity is all the greater, because the general turn and tone of the working out and winding up, will be away from all such things as they conventionally go." The letter can be pretty confidently dated April 1861, when Dickens would have been working on the installments for June, perhaps early July.[8]

The memoranda may be at least nearly dated by a few chunks of internal evidence. Apart from the first three entries the "General Mems." provide only for chapters 54 through 58—that is, for the ninth (and last) monthly portion of the novel, if we except the brief allusion to Orlick that is worked out in chapter 53. The first twelve chapters of the third stage go almost entirely unnoticed in the *Mems*. By any reasonable explanation, therefore, these chapters had already been written by the time the *Mems*. were drawn up (Professor Butt's view) or (if we wish to give Dickens a little leeway) sufficiently imprinted in Dickens's mind to obviate their inclusion in the *Mems*. "Compeyson" here appears, without fuss, as "Compeyson," the name, as we saw, he had borne since chapter 47.

Clearly, Dickens diverged very little from the "General Mems." in working out the final chapters of the novel. The plan is not 100 percent prescient: for example, Magwitch is not rescued by Pip, as the *Mems*. indicate, and Herbert leaves for Egypt before, not after, Magwitch's trial. Lesser incidents, like Wemmick's wedding in chapter 57 and Orlick's last hurrah in 58—incidents that plainly moved in an aura of Dickens's creative leisure—"could be be left . . . for the improvisation of the moment."[9]

From among the very few "signs" Dickens has left us about this most

---

7. Forster's description of Magwitch as convict and repatriate in book 9, chapter 3 of the *Life* (Hoppé, vol. 2, p. 287)—"Magwitch's convict habits strangely blend themselves with his wild pride in . . . Pip"—remains as apt as ever, as do his remarks on the parallel structure of the book, which begins with one chase and ends with its sequel. On Dickens's efforts in course of revision to mitigate Magwitch's aboriginal ways (and Pip's corresponding revulsion), see my comments on the manuscript, especially p. 452.
8. See pp. 397–98.
9. John Butt and Kathleen Tillotson, *Dickens at Work* (London: Methuen, 1957), 33. Unlikely as this appears, the daunting chance that Dickens drew up a full set of *Mems*. for the novel (and a full set for *A Tale of Two Cities*), which disappeared, can't be rejected out of hand.

autonomous of his novels,[1] the "General Mems." reveal two matters of some importance, one of these by negative reference.

(1) The purely narrative part of the Wisbech notes concludes with the penultimate (or antepenultimate) entry, which informs us that Pip's plan to marry Biddy has been foiled by her marriage to Joe and that Pip joins Herbert abroad. Full stop. In other words, the *Mems.* stop short of the vexed conclusion. Any reunion with Estella (at this stage it could only have been the brief encounter in Piccadilly, not the "dignified and commodious sacrament" to which the revised ending points) may not have been part of Dickens's master plan—unless, again, we assume, reasonably enough, that he took the Piccadilly ending too much for granted to make an issue of it in the *Mems.* Still, Dickens may just have regarded the novel as finished with Pip's departure for Cairo—the point at which an increasing number of critics wish he *had* finished it—without his necessarily having felt so strongly about the issue as his commentators have felt. Humphry House's uncomplicated reading of Estella's absence from the "General Mems." has the merit of just that—its level-headedness:

> The plan [plainly says] that Pip's main reason for going down to the marsh Village again after recovering from his illness was "to propose to Biddy." After "Finds Biddy married to Joe" there is no mention of Pip's love affairs. All this fits the rounded careful plot that Pip was to lose both the fortune and the girl, and that both were to derive from Magwitch. I find it hard to believe that this firm symmetry was only achieved in the last stage of writing; and it seems unlikely that proof can now be given that it was so.[2]

The *Mems.* provide an oddly skewed way of getting at House's reading elsewhere. One of the earliest entries—the last of the three that precede the plan for the five or six final chapters (that is, for the substance of the "General Mems.")—reads "Estella. Magwitch's daughter." This, pace Sadrin, was probably jotted down some time before the composition of chapter 50. The chapter is almost entirely taken up by the conversation between Pip and Herbert and in its final sentence springs on the reader the information their talk has been leading up to: "And the man we have in hiding down the river is Estella's Father." One may well ask oneself (Sadrin does) why Dickens felt any need to memorialize the Magwitch-Estella relationship, on which so much of the plot has been hinging throughout: "the expression, 'Estella, as Magwitch's child' which he uses in 'Dates' shows that the relationship between the two characters was for him a matter of course." The point here lies less in Dickens's (ultimately irretrievable) motives for scribbling a wholly

1. See below, p. 476.
2. "G.B.S. on *Great Expectations*," *Dickensian* 54 (1948): 184, House locking horns with John Butt. Butt first published the "General Mems." in his pilot study "Dickens at Work," *Durham University Journal*, N.S. 9 (1948): 76, Butt speculating that their composition coincided with the end of the second stage. That is, Butt read the "General Mems." as a record of Dickens's indecisiveness about where to go after he reached the end of the second stage. Butt's view was challenged by House in his piece on "G.B.S." (in a section that I omitted from House's essay in the "Criticism" section below as impairing its continuity). House, who had predicated the first installment of his essay on the "importance . . . of the fact that Estella is . . . shown to be Magwitch's daughter," rejected the idea that her parentage should have occurred to Dickens so late in the novel—why, in that case, Molly's buildup as early as chapter 26? Butt concurred in House's dating and he published his recantation in "Dickens's Plan," in which House's conclusion is supported by internal evidence that House had kept out of court.

superfluous note to himself than in its very superfluity, its alluding to "a matter of course."[3]

(2) The "General Mems." conclude on a suitably resolute note: "The one good thing he did in his prosperity, the only thing that endures and bears good fruit." Shortly before the passage just quoted, House writes of the final entry:

> The very emphasis that Dickens gives this note, by placing it as his last comment on the whole plan, gives it almost the status of a leading "moral." . . . It is entirely consistent with Dickens's mainly sentimental and individualistic ethic that Pip's one good deed should have its reward, even for himself.[4]

House (as Butt reminds him) might have strengthened his argument by pointing out that the leading "moral" had been anticipated, in nearly identical words, as early as chapter 37, long before Dickens began the Mems. At the end of chapter 37, Pip tells us: "At length, the thing being done, and [Herbert] having that day entered Clarriker's House, and he having talked to me for a whole evening in a flush of pleasure and success, I did really cry in good earnest when I went to bed, to think that my expectations had done some good to somebody." For the record (though Butt overlooks this), the final words of the plan had not merely been anticipated in chapter 37 but also recur in the opening passage of chapter 52, in language that resembles the final entry in the Mems. still more closely than the earlier observation. Pip, having just concluded the arrangements with Clarriker, reflects: "It was the only good thing I had done, and the only completed thing I had done, since I was first apprised of my great expectations." The near identity in phrasing supports, I think, the presumption that the two formulations—in the Mems. and in the novel—must have been written in very close conjunction to each other. We needn't conclude that the sentence as it stands in the Mems. was written first, but the inference is at least a reasonable one, and it would favor the view that Dickens composed the Mems. about the time he tackled chapter 52. The importance Dickens attached to this is plainly reflected, too, in the reading version of Great Expectations, in which the leading moral is given similar prominence by concluding the second stage, "Pip's Minority": "Wemmick was as good as his word, and I made a secret treaty, by virtue of which I did buy Herbert into a partnership at last, and was proud and happy to think that my expectations had at last done good to somebody."[5]

The formulaic "one good thing," "only good thing" recurs still elsewhere, though its application differs slightly from its earlier occurrences. Very near the end, Joe, having finally brought himself to inform Pip—not exactly of Miss Havisham's death ("that's nigher where it is; she ain't living")—basks in the "cool four thousand" she has left to Herbert's father; and Pip writes: "This account gave me great joy, as it perfected the only good thing I had done."

3. Sadrin, Great Expectations, 22–23. The Russians stole a fifty-year march on all these people in giving primacy to Estella and Magwitch; the Russian title for Great Expectations translates to read The Criminal's Daughter: or From Rags to Riches (Moscow, 1895)—just as the Brazilians got at the real meaning of A Tale of Two Cities (and beat Dickens at his own game) by issuing it as Love and the Guillotine (São Paulo, 1957).
4. "G.B.S. on Great Expectations," 184.
5. Great Expectations. A Reading ([London]. Privately Printed [by William Clowes and Sons], circa 1866), 116; more accessibly, Philip Collins, ed., Charles Dickens: The Public Readings (London: Clarendon Press, 1975), 347–48 and below, p. 555.

Parenthetically, we might note that in manuscript and early proof, Dickens had written: "the only good thing I had done since I left the forge." After all, he had done a very good thing in ministering to Magwitch before the mists began to rise and show him the world. By the time the sentence appeared in *All the Year Round*, the forge had been banished from the text, perhaps as an intrusive distraction from Pip's immersion in the present and future; or perhaps it had simply become irrelevant. Although Pip here clearly is not thinking about his dealings with Clarriker but his friendly claims on Miss Havisham, I think that the recurrence of the phrase toward the end of the book, now that Pip has completed his education in the school of hard knocks and been taught to recognize the genuine meaning of "profit," reinforces the view that Pip's intercession in behalf of his friends constitutes "a leading 'moral' of the book." We need merely to readjust a little, or broaden a little, the area of Pip's legitimate gratifications; and there is no need for us to take a narrow view of morality.

Tide

Dickens's tables of tides, first printed by T. W. Hill in 1960 in his "Notes to *Great Expectations*"[6] no doubt coincided very nearly with the composition of the "General Mems." For it is early in chapter 52, also, that this subject occupies Pip for the first time.

> As foreign steamers would leave London at about the time of high-water, our plan would be to get down the river by a previous ebb-tide, and lie by in some quiet spot until we could pull off to one. The time when one would be due where we lay, wherever that might be, could be calculated pretty nearly; if we made inquiries beforehand.

A few paragraphs earlier, Pip receives Wemmick's curt message that establishes the day when to go ahead with the projected flight: "Early in the week, or say Wednesday, you might do what you know of if you felt disposed to try it," and this detail finds its way (or has found its way) into the second and somewhat more nearly specific of the two tables. The manuscript here reads: "or Wednesday, if the tide should suit." Very likely Dickens had figured out by the time he drew up the second of the two tables that the tide suited all right and altered the phrase accordingly. I assume that some time (probably no more than a few days) elapsed between the composition of the two tables. How "pretty nearly" Dickens had calculated is borne out by the record of these *Mems*.

6. *Dickensian* 56 (1960): 122–23.

A Note on Antecedents

K. J. Fielding's essay "The Critical Autonomy of *Great Expectations*" — the crux of his argument is reprinted below[7] — remains one of the very best pieces on the novel, both as a stimulus to editorial activity and as a deterrent to extravagance. As his title suggests, Fielding predicates his piece on the nearly total absence of "clues" to the novel that Dickens has left in the way of autocriticism, memoranda, correspondence, etc.: "was there ever," Fielding asks, "a more ludicrous contrast between what critics have written about a great work, and what Dickens had to say when he started it." *Great Expectations*, like *Hard Times*, was issued without a preface; like *Hard Times*, too, its first edition appeared without illustrations (which can tell us a good deal about Dickens's thoughts); and the bulk of the foregoing note has dealt with Dickens's uniquely fragmentary Working Plans to *Great Expectations*. It would be mulish to take issue with Fielding's argument: my own research has left the critical autonomy of *Great Expectations* as nearly intact as Fielding found it, and I subjoin my own commentaries as a collection of miniature exhibits demonstrating the measure of my own "desperation in looking for signs." We have a very few documents sounding the note of preparation, which may be briefly summarized — and which, in their very paucity, confirm Fielding's point.

(a) One is the *Book of Memoranda* Dickens kept in the last fifteen years of his life, in which he jotted down ideas for his novel and stories: some 115 entries ranging from a phrase or snatch of dialogue to the outline of a scene or even an entire work, as well as a few long rosters of names.[8] Between 1855 and 1870, Dickens finished four novels and wrote half of another one, initiated and collaborated on four long Christmas Stories, and wrote more than a dozen papers for *All the Year Round* and a dozen miscellaneous fictions; and though a good many of the entries have not been traced to a particular work, most of them can be at least tentatively attributed. Half of the entries relate to *Little Dorrit* and *Our Mutual Friend*; of the 115, at most three can be confidently assigned to *Great Expectations*, another three or four conjecturally. At least one of the entries foreshadows the introduction of the Toadies and Humbugs in chapter 11; one or two others deal with Drummle; one is almost certainly a passing reference to that nearly forgotten specimen, Miss Havisham's father, and yet more forgotten shadow, her mother. Not a very impressive haul, even if we add a dozen names or so that found their way into the novel, not always in quite the form in which they appear in the notebook.

(b) A second place to look for brief previews of *Great Expectations* is the novellas — three of them Christmas Stories — that Dickens wrote in collaboration, the first two with Wilkie Collins. Again only brief summaries can be given here. *The Perils of English Prisoners* (1857),[9] a story inspired by the Indian Mutiny and a dismal reflection (itself a reflection of the national mood) of Dickens's distasteful view of The Races Not so Blessed as We,

---

7. *Review of English Literature* 2 (1961): 75–88 and below, p. 663.
8. *Charles Dickens' Book of Memoranda*, ed. Fred Kaplan (New York: The New York Public Library, 1981).
9. Charles Dickens, *The Christmas Stories*, ed. Ruth Clancy (London: J. M. Dent, 1996), 171–256. Glancy's edition is by far the best now available. The full title of *Perils* reveals the priorities: *The Perils of Certain English Prisoners, and Their Treasure in Women, Children, Silver, and Jewels.*

anticipates Pip's infatuation with a woman whose social status (in this instance less spurious than Estella's) precludes any intimacy: the principals are a common soldier and a thoroughbred regimental daughter.[1] Apart from his jaundiced view of minorities, especially blacks, Dickens maintained a large dose of bigotry against certain fringe types; and it's revealing that two of the stories in one way or another deal with the Havisham syndrome: recluses, hermits, and their ilk. The pertinent incident in the story *The Lazy Tour of Two Idle Apprentices* (October 1858), the story of "The Bride's Chamber," has been discussed intensively by Harry Stone.[2] The narrator—by the time Dickens and Collins meet him, a ghost—revenges himself on a woman who has spurned his courtship by forging her will and gaining control of her daughter, whom he keeps locked up in a deserted mansion, marries, and wills to die. Given Dickens's marital blight at the time, it's hardly surprising that the story should combine the destruction of an unwanted wife with the motif of an unattainable love.[3] Dickens's initial idea for *A House to Let* (1858), spelled out in a letter to Collins, again unmistakably foreshadows Miss Havisham: "Some disappointed person, man or woman, prematurely disgusted with the world for some reason or no reason . . . retired to an old lonely house . . . : resolved to shut out the world and hold no communion with it."[4] Dickens held this over until 1861, when the idea materialized in *Tom Tiddler's Ground*—written, in fact, after Dickens had finished the novel. But Dickens was no doubt familiar with the principal's prototype, the Hertfordshire hermit Mad Lucas, whose story he must have heard from Bulwer, and whom he had peeked in on, as one peeks in on an eohippus or creodont, on his visit to Bulwer in June 1861.[5] Nowhere is Dickens's distaste for fringe types more unpleasantly on exhibit and nowhere is Miss Havisham's "lifestyle" taken to nastier extremes than in his description of this "slothful unsavoury nasty reversal of the laws of human nature." The parallel is no less striking for Pip's turning Havisham into a kindlier Lucas in his final judgment on her that "in shutting out the light of day . . . her mind, brooding solitary, had grown diseased, as all minds do and must and will that reverse the appointed order of their Maker."[6]

The resemblances between the novel and Dickens's contribution to the actualized *A House to Let*, the comic interlude "Going into Society," are slighter. The story stars a performing dwarf, Chops, who experiences a sudden rise in station after winning a lottery and then, with the help of some scoundrels who worm their way into his confidence, loses every penny. Perhaps

---

1. The very name of Pip's alter ego, Gill Davis, betrays him: the opening lines, in which Gill talks about the truncation of the name Gilbert to Gill, clearly echo (or anticipate) the same procedure that turns Philip into Pip in the opening paragraph of the novel—down to the assonance of the names: "the name given to me in the baptism * * * was Gilbert * * * but I always understood my christian name to be Gill." Rephrase the opening of *Great Expectations* to read: "The name given to me being Pirrip, and my christian name Philip, I always understood my name to be Pip."
2. *Dickens and the Invisible World* (Bloomington: Indiana University Press, 1979), 288–94 and below, p. 556–61; more fully, *The Night Side of Dickens: Cannibalism, Passion, Necessity* (Columbus: Ohio State University Press, 1994), 286–345.
3. Stone, as anyone might, gets mileage out of the fact that the Bride whom Dickens places on his Catherine wheel should bear the name Ellen. He might have strengthened his case by adding that the Ellen of "The Bride's Chamber" appears to be the only Ellen among all of Dickens's sixty-five hundred named characters. His Kates are a dime a dozen.
4. August 29, 1857; *PL* 8, 423 and n. 1.
5. *The Christmas Stories*, 417–48. See esp. Susan Shatto, "Miss Havisham and Mr. Mopes the Hermit: Dickens and the Mentally Ill," part 1, *DQ* 2 (1985): 79–83 and Richard Whitmore, *Mad Lucas: The Strange Story of England's Most Famous Hermit* (Hitchin: North Hertfordshire District Council, 1983).
6. Chapter 49; *Christmas Stories*, 419.

Chops's conviction that he is entitled to property may be seen as a form of great expectations and in its fatuity recalls Magwitch's "low" gloating over *his* gentleman. Chops points out his own moral: "The secret of this matter is, that it ain't so much that a person goes into Society as that Society goes into a person."[7] The interest that attaches to the sketch lies as much in its origins as in these rather perfunctory details: Dickens had thought of withdrawing the piece from the printer in order to use the idea, "which appears to me so humorous, and so available at greater length," for a novel, and Dr. Cardwell has argued persuasively that the letter in which he broaches this to his sub-editor, Wills, in its verbal resemblance to Dickens's earliest specific mention of *Great Expectations*, may be our first intimation of the novel to come.[8]

(c) By the time Dickens had inspected Mad Lucas, he had published the series of sixteen essays that appeared under the title *The Uncommercial Traveller* between January 29 and October 13, 1860.[9] The essays have been combed for more clues to *Great Expectations*, unsurprisingly: nearly all of them appeared just before Dickens began to write the novel; moreover, Forster identified the series as the projected repository of the "little piece" that has been widely accepted as the germ of *Great Expectations*; and as first-person narratives the essays anticipate the autobiographical form Dickens chose for the novel. Two, which bear on *Great Expectations* and which Dickens himself published together as *Associations of Childhood*, "Dullborough Town" and "Nurse's Stories" (the last excerpted here), have been taken, perhaps too literally, as unvarnished autobiographical reminiscences;[1] both, in their grotesque introduction of cannibalistic motifs, the terror experienced by children, and, in "Dullborough Town," the nostalgic and futile attempts to retrieve the past, suggest interesting affinities.[2] The essay "Chambers" has occasionally been cited for verbal parallels; though set in Gray's Inn, the milieu could easily double as Jaggers's office. Other essays—"City of London Churches," "Shy Neighbourhoods," "Night Walks," "Arcadian London"— present incidental analogues, in topographical definitions, identity of detail, and even similarity in language.[3]

So much for the preliminaries. They sound a lot more promising than they are. Compared with the ample documentation we have for Dickens's other works, the pickings are as slim as Fielding and I infer from the evidence, insofar as we can find any.

---

7. *Christmas Stories*, 280. "Going into Society," 271–84.
8. *PL* 8, 709–10; Cardwell, xiii.
9. Charles Dickens, *The Uncommercial Traveller and Reprinted Pieces*, ed. Leslie C. Staples (London: Oxford University Press, 1958). Eleven more papers were added for the Cheap Edition of 1865 and eight more were added posthumously for the Illustrated Library Edition of 1875.
1. But see Michael Slater's caution against the autobiographical fallacy, "How Many Nurses Had Charles Dickens? *The Uncommercial Traveller* and Dickensian Biography," *Prose Studies* 10 (1987): 250–58.
2. For the fullest account of "Dullborough Town" and one of the finest papers on *The Uncommercial Traveller*, see Malcolm Andrews, "Dullborough—The Birthplace of His Fancy," *Dickensian* 87 (1991): 37–49.
3. E.g., F. S. Schwarzbach, *Dickens and the City* (London: University of London Press, 1979), 178–84; Scott Foll, "Great Expectations and the 'Uncommercial Sketch Book,'" *Dickensian* 81 (1985): 109–16; George Worth, "*The Uncommercial Traveller* and *Great Expectations*: A Further Note," *Dickensian* 83 (1987): 19–21.

Dates

Habert Pocket speaks of mrs Havisham's
matter having happened "five and twenty years
ago." at that time Pip is say 18 or 19.
consequently it happened 6 or 7 years before
Pip, & and Estella — who is about his age —
were born.

But say that the matter was a year or so in
hand — which it used to — that used reduces
it to ~~to a decapssso~~ 5 or 6 years before
they were born.

Magwitch tells his story in the Temple, where
Pip is 23. Magwitch is then about 60.
Say Pip was about 7 at the opening of the story. Magwitch's
escape saved him 16 years ago. If Magwitch
says he first knew Compey about 20 years ago, that
used leave or is it 4 years for his knowledge of
Compey and whole association with him at the
time of the escape. That used also make him
about 40 when he knew Compey, and Compey was
younger than his.

---

when Magwitch ~~became~~ became known to Compey,
the end of mrs Havisham's matter used has just
taken place about 7 or 8 years before him.

Estella, as Magwitch's child, must have been born

Dickens's Working Notes, "Dates"

about 3 years before he knew Compey.

The ages in the last stage of Great Expectations stand thus:

Pip about 23
Estella .. 23
Herbert . 23
Magwitch . 60
Compey . 52 or 53
Miss Havisham . 56 (Query, her to have seen the older in the Continent)
Biddy . 24 or 25
Joe . 45

Jaggers 55, Wemmick near 50, and so for the rest.

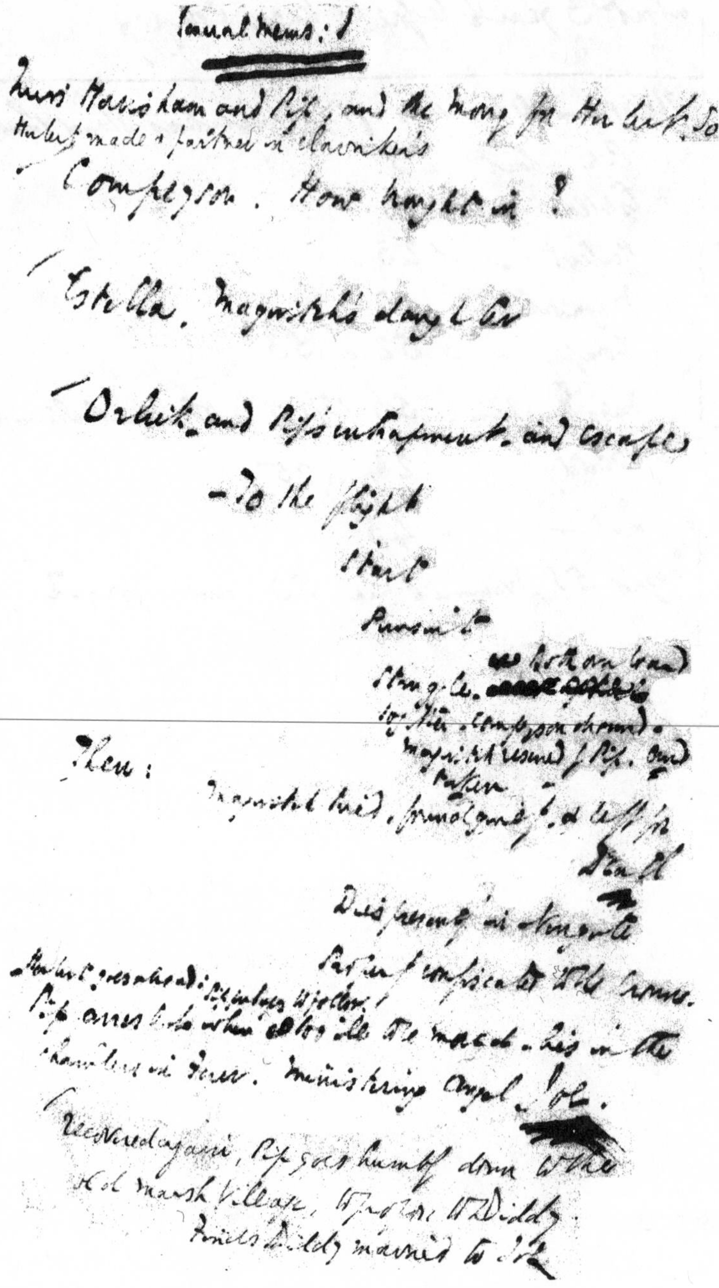

Dickens's Working Notes, "Mems."

So goes abroad to Herbert (happily married to Clara Barly), and becomes his clerk.

The one good thing he did in his prosperity, the only thing that endures and bears good fruit

<u>Dates</u>

Herbert Pocket speaks of Miss Havisham's
matter having happened "five and twenty years
ago." At that time, Pip is say—18 or 19.
Consequently it happened 6 or 7 years before
Pip,—and Estella——who is about his age——
were born.

But say that the matter was a year or so in
hand—which it would be—that would reduce
it to ~~4 or 5 years~~ 5 or 6 years before
they were born.

Magwitch tells his story in the Temple, when
Pip is 23. Magwitch is then about 60.
Say Pip was about 7 at the opening of the story. Magwitch's
escape would then be ∧^about 16 years ago. If Magwitch
says he first knew Compey about 20 years ago, that
would leave about 4 years for his knowledge of
Compey and whole association with him up to the
time of the escape. That would also make him
about 40 when he knew Compey, and Compey was
younger than he.

When Magwitch ~~knew Comp~~ became known to Compey
the end of Miss Havisham's matter would thus have
taken place about 7 or 8 years before.

Estella, as Magwitch's child, must have been born

[Page 1—Right-hand side]

(Dates) 2

about 3 years before he knew Compey.

The ages in the last stage of Pip's Expectations, stand thus:

Pip	about	23
Estella	"	23
Herbert	"	23
Magwitch	"	60
Compey	"	52 or 53
Miss Havisham	"	56 (I judge her to have been the elder in the love time)
Biddy	"	24 or 25
Joe	"	45

Jaggers 55, Wemmick near 50, and so forth.

General Mems: 1

Miss Havisham and Pip, and the Money for Herbert. So
Herbert made a partner in Clarriker's[1]
Compeyson. How brought in?
Estella. Magwitch's daughter
Orlick—and Pip's entrapment—and escape
—To the flight
start
Pursuit

Both overboard
Struggle— <   >
together—Compeyson drowned—

Magwitch rescued by Pip. And

taken
Then:
Magwitch tried, found guilty, & left for

Death
Dies presently in Newgate
Property confiscated to the Crown.
Herbert goes abroad:
Pip perhaps to follow.
Pip arrested when too ill to be moved—lies in the
chambers in Fever. Ministering Angel Joe.

recovered again, Pip goes humbly down to the
old marsh Village, to propose to Biddy.
Finds Biddy married to Joe.

---

1. This appears as "clarriker's" in all transcriptions. On Dickens's erratic use of capitals, see pp. 464–65,
though this would hardly apply to personal names or place-names.

General Mems: 2

So goes abroad to Herbert (happily married to Clara Barley), and becomes his clerk.

The one good thing he did in his prosperity, the only thing that endures and bears good fruit

Tide

Down at	up
9 AM	3 PM
till	till
3 PM	9 PM
Down 9 PM	
till 3 morning	

Down at 9 A.M till 3 P.M. Wednesday
Up at 3 PM—till 9. P.M. Wednesday
Down at 9 PM.—till 3 AM Thursday morning
Up at 3 AM.—till 9. AM Thursday morning
when the boat starts

The Descriptive Headlines†

† Where these headlines are not self-explanatory, I have provided a brief bracketed gloss.

House]. Chapter XXVIII. Convicts outside the Coach. Pumblechook, the founder of my fortunes! Chapter XXIX. Estella grown a Woman. Of whom does Estella remind me? Arrival of Mr. Jaggers [at Satis House]. Chapter XXX. In the old town again. Herbert knows that I love Estella! Herbert's Sweetheart. Chapter XXXI. Mr. Wopsle as Hamlet. Chapter XXXII. A note from Estella [announcing her impending arrival in London]. Wemmick at home in Newgate. Chapter XXXIII. Estella tells me where she is going. I take Estella to her destination [in Richmond]. Chapter XXXIV. The Finches of the Grove. Herbert and I look our affairs in the face. Chapter XXXV. My Sister's Funeral. I take Biddy to task [for her failure to inform Pip personally of Mrs. Joe's death]. Chapter XXXVI. I have a word or two with my Guardian [about the identity of Pip's benefactor]. My question remains unanswered. Chapter XXXVII. Another Pilgrimage to the Castle. I take Wemmick into confidence [on the subject of financing Herbert's mercantile ventures]. I befriend Herbert without his knowing it. Chapter XXXVIII. Estella with Miss Havisham again. True to the lesson, or false? [of Estella's training in Satis House]. Drummle claims to know Estella. Chapter XXXIX. A stormy night in the Temple. I recognise my Visitor. He explains my great mistake. And I wake from my dream.

The Third Stage of Pip's Expectations. Chapter XL. Provis. Death, if identified. I try in vain to hide him. Much virtue in an Affidavit. Chapter XLI. Necessary to know his History. Chapter XLII. He relates his Life and Adventures. He continues his Narrative. The end of the Narrative. Chapter XLIII. I encounter Drummle [at the Blue Boar]. Chapter XLIV. I speak to Miss Havisham and Estella [on their allowing him to persist in his illusions]. My love is unintelligible to Estella. I receive a warning [not to go home]. Chapter XLV. I toast a sausage for the Aged P. Wemmick's advice and management [to lodge Magwitch with Old Barley and lay hands on Magwitch's "portable property"]. Chapter XLVI. Old Barley. I begin to get a boat ready. Chapter XLVII. The Nautical Drama. Mr. Wopsle alarms me. Chapter XLVIII. I know now of whom Estella reminded me. Information from Wemmick [about Molly's criminal past]. Chapter XLIX. A Loan from Miss Havisham. Miss Havisham tells me all she knows [of Estella's past]. Chapter L. Herbert becomes my Nurse. A conversation with my Nurse [revealing Estella's parentage]. Chapter LI. I appeal to Mr. Jaggers [to be "more frank and manly" in his disclosures]. A pair of Impostors [Jaggers and Wemmick]. Chapter LII. A Letter from Wemmick [suggesting the timing of Magwitch's escape]. Chapter LIII. Out on the Marshes. I am entrapped. I stand face to face with Death. My Life is preserved. Chapter LIV. The time draws near for his escape. We take him on Board. A Four-oared Galley about. The Galley boards us. I accompany the Prisoner. Chapter LV. Herbert leaves me for the last. Wemmick married. Chapter LVI. He is tried and sentenced. Chapter LVII. Joe tends me in my sickness. Joe and I talk things over [Miss Havisham and her legatees]. Things necessary and unnecessary [necessary that Pip regain his strength; unnecessary that he dwell on the subject of Magwitch]. Joe delicately leaves me. Chapter LVIII. The Founder of my Fortunes holds forth. I am too late, and become penitent. Chapter LIX: The Figure in the Ruin.

Putting an End to
Great Expectations†

Nothing in *Great Expectations* has generated more heat than Dickens's decision to rewrite the conclusion of the novel, with the result that he left critics with two endings to fight over. As an editorial crux and a problem in "sincerity," the two endings of *Great Expectations* are crudely comparable with things like the moral rehabilitation of Walter Gay, the slick, time-serving young fellow in *Dombey and Son*, who was intended to perish at sea but was then kept in reserve to marry the young Miss Dombey; or the insertion of the American episodes in *Martin Chuzzlewit*, a quick fix to boost the flagging monthly sales of the novel; or Dickens's decision to kill Little Nell, the adolescent heroine of *The Old Curiosity Shop*, who, in Ruskin's famous phrase, "was simply killed for the market, as a butcher kills a lamb."[1] The question whether Pip and Estella were in effect mated for the market has exercised Dickens scholars in the 125 years since the original ending first came to light in the third volume of Forster's biography. Blasphemous as the suggestion may sound, just maybe those of us who have written on the subject have rather inflated its importance: had Dickens written one ending only—either one—it wouldn't have occurred to us to take issue with it. Had he stuck to the unhappy ending, we should all have bought the unhappy ending and thought no more about it; and had he all along gone for the happy ending, we might have been equally happy. But now that this double monster has affronted a hundred operatives, clairvoyants after the fact, prophets of hindsight, it would be cowardice to run from it.

The chronology leading up to the composition of the second ending may be briefly summarized here. To judge from his note to his old friend, the actor Charles Macready, Dickens finished the novel on Wednesday, June 11, 1861—possibly the day before. He arranged to spend part of the following week with his fellow artist Bulwer-Lytton on Bulwer's estate Knebworth, in Hertfordshire, to submit the proofs of the final chapters of *Great Expectations* to Bulwer, whose opinion he greatly valued, and to discuss Bulwer's serial *A Strange Story*, which had been scheduled to succeed *Great Expectations* on the front pages of *All the Year Round* on August 10. Dickens had written to solicit a full-length contribution from Bulwer as early as August 1860; throughout autumn and winter the format of the story and the business details were settled, and by January 1861 Dickens was able to express his delight "in

† A more frugal version of this piece appeared as "Last Words on *Great Expectations*: A Textual Brief on the Six Endings," *Dickens Studies Annual* 9 (1981): 87–115. Grateful acknowledgment is made to AMS Press, Inc.
1. "Fiction, Fair and Foul" [1880]; in E. T. Cook and A. Wedderburn, eds., *The Works of John Ruskin*, 37 vols. (London: George Allen, 1908) 34, 275 n. But the change in Walter Gay had been preceded by serious second thoughts; see letter to Forster, [July 5, 1846] (*PL* 4, 593).

pride, brutality, and meanness. I had heard of the death of her husband (from an accident consequent on ill-treating a horse), and of her being married again to a Shropshire doctor, who, against his interest, had once very manfully interposed, on an occasion when he was in professional attendance on Mr. Drummle, and had witnessed some outrageous treatment of her. I had heard that the Shropshire doctor was not rich, and that they lived on her own personal fortune.

I was in England again—in London, and walking along Piccadilly with little Pip—when a servant came running after me to ask would I step back to a lady in a carriage who wished to speak to me. It was a little pony carriage, which the lady was driving; and the lady and I looked sadly enough on one another.

"I am greatly changed, I know; but I thought you would like to shake hands with Estella too, Pip. Lift up that pretty child and let me kiss it!" (She supposed the child, I think, to be my child.)

I was very glad afterwards to have had the interview; for, in her face and in her voice, and in her touch, she gave me the assurance, that suffering had been stronger than Miss Havisham's teaching, and had given her a heart to understand what my heart used to be.

THE END OF GREAT EXPECTATIONS.

The unhappy and happy endings at proof stage

I had heard of her as leading a most unhappy life, and as being separated from her husband who had used her with great cruelty, and who had become quite renowned as a compound of pride, avarice, brutality, and meanness. And I had heard of the death of her husband, from an accident consequent on his ill-treatment of a horse. This release had befallen her some two years before; for anything I knew, she was married again.

The early dinner hour at Joe's, left me abundance of time without hurrying my talk with Biddy, to walk over to the old spot before dark. But what with loitering on the way, to look at old objects and to think of old times, the day had quite declined when I came to the place.

There was no house now, no brewery, building whatever left but the wall of the old garden. The cleared space had been enclosed with a rough fence, and, looking over it, I saw that some of the old ivy had struck root anew, and was growing green on low quiet mounds of ruin. A gate in that fence standing ajar, I pushed it open, and went in.

A cold silvery mist had come on in the afternoon, and the moon was not yet up to scatter it. But the stars were shining beyond the mist, and the moon was coming, and the evening was not dark. I could trace out where every part of the old house had been, and where the brewery had been, and where the gates, and where the casks. I had done so, and was looking along the desolate garden-walk, when I saw a solitary figure in it.

The figure soon showed itself aware of me, as I advanced. It had been moving towards me, but it stood still. As I drew nearer, I saw it to be the figure of a woman. As I drew nearer yet, it was about to turn away, when it stopped, and let me come up with it. Then it faltered as if much surprised, and uttered my name, and I cried out:

"Estella!"

"I am greatly changed. I wonder you know me."

The freshness of her beauty was indeed gone, but its majesty remained. That, I had seen before; what I had never seen before, was the saddened softened light of the once proud eyes; what I had never felt before, was the friendly touch of the once insensible hand.

We sat down on a bench that was near, and I said, "After so many years, it is strange that we should thus meet again, Estella, here where our first meeting was! Do you often come back?"

"I have never been here since," she said.

"Nor I."

The moon began to rise, and I thought of the placid look at the white ceiling, which had passed away. The moon began to rise, and I thought of the pressure on my hand when I had spoken the last words he had heard on earth.

Estella was the next to break silence.

"I have very often hoped and intended to come back, but have been prevented by many circumstances. Poor, poor old place!"

The silvery mist was touched with the first rays of the moonlight, and the same rays touched the tears that dropped from her eyes. Not knowing that I saw them, and setting herself to get the better of them, she said quietly:

"Were you wondering, as you walked along, how it came to be left in this condition?"

"Yes, Estella."

"The ground belongs to me. It is the only possession I have not relinquished. Everything else has gone from me, little by little, but I have kept this. It was the subject of the only determined resistance I made in all the wretched years."

"Is it to be built on?"

"At last it is. I have leased it for that purpose, and came here to take leave of it before its change. And you," she said, in a voice of touching interest to a wanderer, "you live abroad still?"

"Still."

"And do well, I am sure?"

"I work pretty hard for a sufficient living, and therefore—Yes, I do well."

"I little thought," said Estella, "that I should take leave of you in taking leave of this spot. I am very glad to do so."

"Glad to part again, Estella? To me, parting is a painful thing. To me, the remembrance of our last parting has been ever mournful and painful."

"But you said to me," returned Estella, very earnestly, "' God bless you, God forgive you!' And if you could say that to me then, you will not hesitate to say that to me now—now, when suffering has been stronger than all other teaching, and has taught me to understand what your heart used to be. I have been bent and broken, but—I hope—into a better shape. Be as considerate and good to me as you were, and tell me we are friends."

"We are friends," said I, bending over her, as she rose from the bench.

"And will continue friends apart," said Estella.

I took her hand in mine, and we went out of the ruined place; and, as the morning mists had risen long ago when I first left the forge, so the evening mists were rising now, and in all the broad expanse of tranquil light they showed to me, I saw the shadow of no parting from her but one.

THE END OF GREAT EXPECTATIONS.

.d thought of standing side by side with you before this great audi-
From Saturday the 15th to Tuesday the 18th, then, Dickens and the
ladies of Gad's Hill, Georgina and Mamie, spent a long weekend on
lwer's estate—a fantastic piece of Tudor architecture, with its battlements,
urrets, domes, gargoyles, catacombs, and "heraldic monstrosities" set in the
middle of the peaceful Hertfordshire pastures, the sort of place in which
Wemmick might have felt at home if he had owned as much portable property as the Earl of Lytton.

Even if by 1860 Dickens had long hobnobbed with all the best people,
including the prime minister and the richest woman in England, the "thought
of standing side by side" with Bulwer may well have gratified Dickens's never
wholly subdued sense of his own *arrivisme*. Though Bulwer was not knighted
until 1838 and raised to the peerage until 1866, the Bulwers traced their
lineage to the eleventh century; Dickens's lineage more nearly approximated
Noah Claypole's in *Oliver Twist*, of whom he notes with the unconscious
snobbishness of those who are one step ahead in the game that he "could
trace his genealogy all the way back to his parents."[3] Dickens and Bulwer
first met in the late thirties; their friendship dated from 1850, Bulwer playing
host to Dickens and his amateur theatrical troupe at Knebworth and collab-
orating with Dickens in establishing a Guild of Literature and Art designed
to help impoverished writers and artists. Bulwer had burst on the literary scene
in 1828 with a sardonic novel about a Regency dandy, *Pelham*; though the
book was written largely as a dig at its hero's foppishness and the whole
frippery associated with George IV, the physical—notably the sartorial—presentation far overshadowed the intended critique; the French, who might have
been expected to plume themselves on their own chic, hailed it as *"le manuel
du dandysme le plus pur et le plus parfait,"* a guidebook, as the *Revue des
Deux Mondes* described it, "to English society in all the salons, cafés, and
clubs of Paris"; Pushkin started a novel with the working title *Pelymov* or
Russkiy Pelam in which the denizens of Piccadilly and the Faubourg Saint-
Germain act out their boredom on the shores of the Neva; and 170 years
after Pelham's appearance the Western world remains the plaything of Bulwer's playboy, who, after centuries of plum-colored clothes, was the first to
introduce black evening wear, and black it has been ever since.[4] Today, *Pelham* is scarcely readable, and hence no longer read.

By the time the two writers met, Bulwer had published seventeen novels,
including among his earliest books after *Pelham* two—*Paul Clifford* (1830)
and *Eugene Aram* (1832)—in which Bulwer to all intents invented the short-
lived genre of the "Newgate Novel" and set the vogue for presenting roman-

2. August 3, 1860 (*PL* 9, 280); November 30, (?misdated Nov 29; *PL* 9, 343); December 4, 1860 (*PL*
9, 345–46); January 23, 1861 (*PL* 9, 374).

3. Chapter 5. Bulwer's full name after his appearance on Queen Victoria's first birthday list in 1837 read
Sir Edward George Earle Lytton, Bulwer, Bart., a mouthful that gave his archenemy Thackeray the
desired opening in signing his parody of Bulwer in his *Punch's Prize Novelists* (1847) as "Sir
E.L.B.L.B.B.L.L.B.B.BLLL,Bart." On this, see Robert Lee Wolff, *Strange Stories and Other Explora-
tions in Victorian Fiction* (Boston: Gambit, 1971), 334 n.

4. Ellen Moers, *The Dandy: Brummel and Beerbohm* (New York: Viking Press, 1960), 68–83; James
Campbell, Sr., *Edward Bulwer Lytton* (Boston: Twayne Publishers, 1986), 27–28; on Pushkin, Tur-
genev, and Dostoevsky, Régis Messac, "Bulwer-Lytton et Dostoievski: de Paul Clifford à Raskolnikoff,"
Revue de litterature comparée 6 (October–December 1926), 638–53; Patrick Waddington, "Two Au-
thors of Strange Stories: Bulwer-Lytton and Turgenev," *New Zealand Slavonic Journal* (1992), 32 ff.;
also Robert Lytton, First Earl of Lytton, *Life, Letters, and Literary Remains of Edward Bulwer, Lord
Lytton, by His Son*, 2 vols. (New York: Harper and Brothers, 1884) 1, 488, and Michael Sadleir,
Bulwer: A Panorama (Boston: Little, Brown and Co., 1931), 204 ff.

ticized criminals as vehicles for attacks on judiciary and penal conditions.[5] In *Paul Clifford*, Bulwer explicitly set himself the job of exposing a "vicious Prison-discipline and a sanguinary Criminal Code"; its hero anticipates Oliver Twist in being caught on a pickpocket charge of which he is innocent and the hero of Robert Louis Stevenson's *Weir of Hermiston* (1896) in being sentenced to death by his own father. The novel concludes with John Wilkes's famous axiom that "THE VERY WORST USE TO WHICH YOU CAN PUT A MAN IS TO HANG HIM." Nowadays, the impact of the final sentence of *Paul Clifford* is lost in its legendary opening words, which are syndicated in thousands of American and European dailies—though its (canine) author rather cheats by giving you only the first seven words of a sentence that goes on for another packed fifty-two.[6] Since the (aborted) beginning has inspired at least one American college to sponsor a Bulwer-Lytton contest, in which the creator of the worst opening sentence collects an award for his pains, it needs no Mark Twain to document the literary offenses of Bulwer-Lytton; and it is only fair to note that *Paul Clifford* has been singled out for its awful prose: Bulwer's grandson (and official biographer) himself laughs at Grandfather's idiocies in calling a bedroom a "somnambular accommodation" and beer a "nectarean beverage," in describing the acts of lighting a pipe as "applying the Promethean spark to his tube," and of amusing somebody as "exciting his risible muscles."[7] Incidentally, *Paul Clifford* did not have to wait for Snoopy to give it class: its first edition, the largest printing of any modern novel until then, sold out the first day.

Bulwer's genius for cutting his clothes to the latest literary fashion has been conceded by his most sympathetic commentators, and once the flush days of the Newgate Novel were starting to fade, Bulwer (to get his most widely read books down and out) turned his attention to the uses of ancient and medieval history and to the one novel whose title alone still rings a just-audible bell among people who have otherwise never heard of him—and that still enjoys a fugitive and cloistered favor among specialists—*The Last Days of Pompeii* (1834), a meticulously researched romance, which, as one Bulwer scholar submits, "offered Bulwer the chance to comment on the decadence of the late Regency Englishmen while seeming to portray only that of early imperial Romans."[8] One hundred and twenty years later the novel might have been written to order for Hollywood, and it was in fact made into a feature film precisely a hundred years ago and into at least eight more movies in the hundred years since. Today its filmic qualities, apart from the spectacular stuff, are transparent in the sort of gimmick by which the audience is alerted to the foreignness of the product by the wackiest and showiest lingo. If the opening sentence of *Paul Clifford* makes for good newspaper copy, the opening lines of *The Last Days of Pompeii* can be purloined verbatim by Warner Bros. "Ho, Diomed, well met. Art off to sup with Glaucus tonight? . . . By Jove, a scurvy trick," etc. The same attention to linguistic propriety may be

---

5. See Keith Hollingsworth, *The Newgate Novel: 1830–1847* (Detroit: Wayne State University Press, 1963); on Bulwer, 65–98.
6. *Paul Clifford*, preface to the 1840 edition. Bulwer liked to settle his readers into the weather from his earliest to his latest novels. For "It was a dark and stormy night," read "It was the evening of a soft warm day in the May of 17—" (*The Disowned*, 1829); "It was a bright day in the early spring of 1869" (*The Parisians*, 1873), etc.
7. Earl of Lytton, *Bulwer-Lytton*, 46. On the Bulwer-Lytton Prize awarded by San Jose State University see *The Wall Street Journal*, May 5, 1983, 1 and 5.
8. Wolff, *Strange Stories*, 151.

observed in his next, at the time still more popular, romance, *Rienzi* (1835), which inspired Wagner's opera. (Not the least remarkable thing about Bulwer is his penchant for eschatological alerts: *The Last Days of Pompeii*; *Harold*, *The Last of the Saxons*; *The Last of the Barons*; *Rienzi* is subtitled *The Last of the Tribunes*.)

Nowadays, as the above suggests, Bulwer's enormous prestige in his own day and his usefulness to Dickens are apt to strike us as one of the curiosities of literature. For Percy Fitzgerald, writing in 1913, "the great quartet of story-tellers which distinguished the Victorian Era [consisted of] Bulwer-Lytton, Dickens, Thackeray, and Charles Reade"; more than one contemporary reviewer narrowed the quadrumvirate to a triumvirate by tossing out Reade, and it was not uncommon to find Bulwer and Dickens mentioned in one and the same breath. Bulwer's grandson, citing the testimonials of Bulwer's contemporaries, talks of Dickens as "his [single] greatest rival in literature"—it's instructive that the word "rival" should automatically leap to his mind at a time when Dickens appears to have had nothing but rivals. But as he enjoyed an eight-year headstart on Dickens, Bulwer, at least for a while, could claim the full fair field for himself; and one recent commentator notes that after *Eugene Aram* appeared, "as a result of his six published novels, Bulwer was recognized as the most popular novelist of his time."[9] And it is difficult to shrug off a novelist who "influenced" artists as far apart as Pushkin, Villiers de l'Isle-Adam, Carlyle, Dostoevsky, Shaw, Disraeli, Turgenev, Barbey d'Aurevilly, Robert Louis Stevenson, Richard Wagner, and Snoopy the Dog—artists who had nothing remotely in common except the sponsorship of Bulwer-Lytton. In a famous passage in *The Nigger of the "Narcissus"* (1897), Joseph Conrad marvels at

> the popularity of Bulwer Lytton in the forecastles of Southern-going ships [as] a wonderful and bizarre phenomenon. What ideas do his polished and so curiously insincere sentences awaken in the simple minds of the big children who people those dark and wandering places of the earth? What meaning can their rough, inexperienced souls find in the elegant verbiage of his pages? What excitement?—what forgetfulness?—what appeasement? Mystery! Is it the fascination of the incomprehensible? is it the charm of the impossible? . . . Mystery!

—as if the author of *Pelham*, instead of dining at Lady Blessington's in black jacket and tails, had just emerged from the bowels of the Earth after impaling the heads of a dozen Congolese tribesmen.[1]

But if Bulwer has pretty well written himself into obscurity, in 1860 a writer of his credentials could hardly have failed to pay off more handsomely than did Lever's *A Day's Ride*, whose prolix and bustling immobility, as we saw,

9. Campbell, *Edward Bulwer Lytton*, 47; Percy Fitzgerald, *Memories of Charles Dickens* (Bristol: J. W. Arrowsmith, 1913), 210; Victor Lytton, *The Life of Sir Edward Bulwer, First Lord Lytton, By His Grandson* [hereafter given as *Life*], 2 vols. (London: Macmillan & Co., 1913) 2, 495. Cf. Joseph I. Fradin, " 'The Absorbing Tyranny of Every-day Life': Bulwer-Lytton's *A Strange Story*," *Nineteenth-Century Fiction* 16 (1961): 1: "In 1855, an anonymous critic for *Blackwood's Magazine*, writing a series of articles on Dickens, Thackeray, and Bulwer-Lytton, concluded that, of the three, Bulwer-Lytton seemed most sure of a lasting reputation. One man, he wrote, 'the greatest novelist of his time,' has a broader grasp, a fuller life, than any one of his contemporaries."
1. Joseph Conrad, *The Nigger of the "Narcissus,"* ed. Robert Kimbrough (New York: W. W. Norton, 1979), 3.

had so bored the readers of *All the Year Round* that its soggy reception forced Dickens to change the whole packaging and marketing of *Great Expectations*. Unlike the sloppy, slapdash Lever, Bulwer was a highly fastidious, nervous, fidgety artist, as well as a serious theorist of fiction; and instead of fretting, like Lever, about keeping deadlines, he worried about substantive issues like the theme and intelligibility of his book. The new serial—Bulwer's first flight into the occult in the nearly twenty years since he published his own favorite, "Rosicrucian" novel *Zanoni*—evidently gave him much trouble; throughout May and June 1861, at about the time he and Dickens arranged to meet, he kept urging on Dickens his anxieties about the suitability of the story to the demands of the journal, whose readers might easily be scared off by the occult scaffolding of the tale; and for months after the story began to appear in print he kept unfreighting his worries on Dickens, their mutual friend Forster, his own family, and anyone else who would listen. "My doubts are not as to the force of the writing, but the nature of the subject. . . . The whole may go too much against the grain of the reader. It is my object to give you as good a thing for your paper as I can write, and my fear is that it may not exactly suit so wide an audience." And to Forster: "[The story] is original and a psychological curiosity. But I am by no means sure of its effect either with the few or the many." Then the usual fuss about a fetching title. *The Steel Casket. The Lost MS. Maggie. Life and Death. Margrave and the Criminous Shadow. Is and Is Not.* After much soul-searching, Bulwer settled on *A Strange Story*: "[It] is modest and quiet; suggests much and reveals nothing."[2]

Though the letter closest in time to the June conference is imprecisely dated (in another hand than his), Bulwer refers to his being "deep in the back numbers" of *Great Expectations* in a letter to Dickens on April 27, 1861, some six weeks before the meeting; and it is reasonable to assume that the progress of *A Strange Story*, not the ending of *Great Expectations*, headed the agenda.[3] It is entirely in character that from the time Bulwer began to submit proof, Dickens, immersed in winding up his own novel, immersed himself deeply in Bulwer's, assuring Bulwer of his—quite genuine—enthusiasm for the book. The enthusiasm was plainly mutual: if Bulwer found himself "literally" bewitched by Miss Havisham, Dickens found himself entranced, or jinxed, by the early proofs of Bulwer's romance: "I COULD NOT lay them aside, but was obliged to go on with them in my bedroom until I had got into a very ghostly state indeed." Dickens was not the only reader "obliged to go on": in a note that might serve as a blueprint for publishers, he reassured Bulwer that Wills, his managing editor, "who is no genius, [and] is in literary matters, sufficiently commonplace to represent a very large proportion of our readers" was "enchained" too "and thinks [the story] will certainly make a sensation." Besides, Dickens must have read Bulwer's MS with special attention to its suitability to the demands of a weekly serial; especially after the heartaches and the thousand shocks he had experienced on just this score with writers like Mrs. Gaskell and Lever, Bulwer's story appeared to come as a very godsend. As late as September 17, 1861 (admittedly only two numbers into *All the Year Round*, but of course Dickens had

2. Fitzgerald, *Memories*, no date given; April 2, 1861, as quoted in Fitzgerald, *Memories*, 215; July 29, 1861, *Life* 2, 341–51.
3. *PL* 9, 571.

been reading ahead): "the exquisite art with which you have . . . overcome the difficulties of the mode of publication, has fairly staggered me. I know pretty well what the difficulties are; and there is no other man who could have done it, I swear." As to Bulwer's "misgiving" that the story might be too arcane to take a hold on the readers, Dickens had already assured him that "most decidedly there is NOT sufficient foundation for it" and that he for one did "not share [Bulwer's fears] in the least," and that "on more imaginative readers, the tale will fall (or I am greatly mistaken) like a spell."[4] If Dickens's parenthetical comment turned out to be more prophetic than anything else he told Bulwer, nobody could have faulted him on his enthusiasm for the exciting events that got him into his ghostly state to begin with. Some time, then, between June 15th and 18th, while Dickens and Bulwer were trading compliments about each other's scary bedtime reading, Bulwer lodged his earthshaking objection to the ending of *Great Expectations* and persuaded Dickens to have another go at it: as a result, between the 18th and 24th, back at Gad's Hill, Dickens proceeded to "unwind the thread" and stitch it up again; on the 24th he returned the expanded final portion to Bulwer, commending him, in impeccably diplomatic language, on "the alteration that is entirely due to you."[5]

I will look at Bulwer's grounds for urging the change on Dickens in the teacherly note at the end of this discussion. But something about Bulwer's *Strange Story* ought to be briefly anticipated here as bearing directly on Dickens's (rare) lapses in editorial judgment and Bulwer's almost infallible nose for the market. In the first of his Barsetshire novels, *The Warden* (1855), in which he lampoons Dickens as "Mr. Popular Sentiment" and pitches into his serial installments as particular sops to popular sentiment, Anthony Trollope had written rather maliciously that "his first numbers always are well done"—leaving it to the reader to supply the initial "Only."[6] The put-down, though Trollope is hardly being fair to Dickens, was to apply pretty much to Bulwer's meanderings. Though Dickens pretended (as he hardly pretended with lesser contributors) to keep the faith, he couldn't blink the fact that as Bulwer's novel trailed its slow length along, the sales of *All the Year Round* dropped badly enough to suggest that Bulwer had pulled another Lever—not quite, but alarmingly enough. If Lever had bored his readers by the absence of any dramatic momentum, any narrative contours, Bulwer's readers were obviously confused and bored silly by Bulwer's ectoplasmic hocus-pocus, metaphysical abracadabra, and misapplied erudition. The narrative, with its physical transformations, its fountains of youth and puddles of death, its clumsy flashbacks and long interpolated remembrances of times past (and Bulwer's remembrancers are neither Marcels nor Magwitches), defeats any attempt at recapitulation; and whenever readers stumble on an elixir, a clairvoyant, a sleepwalker, a vital spirit, an Oriental powder, a magic wand, a Damascus steel casket, a Ghost of Aleppo, the antique science of Rhabdomancy, and the Luminous Shadow, they are advised to duck. But since the Luminous Shadow illuminates or overshadows every page, it's hard to keep out of his way.

---

4. September 17, 1861 (*PL* 9, 459); May 12, 1861 (*PL* 9, 412); May 15, 1861 (*PL* 9, 415); to Wilkie Collins, July 12, 1861 (*PL* 9, 439).
5. June 24, 1861 (*PL* 9, 428–29).
6. Chapter 15.

When it comes to footnotes, some of Bulwer's are twice as long as any to be found in the Norton Critical Edition of *Great Expectations*. Some go on for more than seventy lines, and occasionally a footnote contains more verbiage than the chapter it annotates. Bulwer likes to begin a note with some such come-on as "See Liebig, 'Organic Chemistry,' Playfair translation, p. 363" and in the next thirty-two lines he may cite a couple of other authorities to support or refute Liebig, in the Playfair translation.[7] In this, Bulwer's strategy nowhere departs from academic protocol—location of source, citation of supporting or clashing authorities. But in a novel? The question, so put, isn't merely philistine but vulgar. "Vulgar critics," Bulwer tells his son, "say I dismiss [the character who typifies the Social World] too soon. So I do if the novel is only a novel. But if you look into the deeper meaning" you'll find no mere novelistic hodgepodge but such "symbolical truths" as Bulwer is really after.[8] That the two are not incompatible may not have occurred to him; but at least the authors of books like *Lord Jim*, *Shamela*, and *The Metamorphosis* leave the annotation to Professors Moser, Battestin, and Corngold. The conversation isn't conversation in the ordinary sense (Smith yelling at Jones and Jones telling Smith to keep quiet), but takes the form of long scientific debates. As the chief character somewhere remarks with unconscious irony, "If some chance passer-by . . . overheard any part of our strange talk, the listener must have been mightily perplexed" (chapter 34). Since these debates—on magic, on the rational basis of the irrational, on the relation between belief and skepticism, on the constitution of the soul—go on for as many as twenty or thirty pages, readers forget that they are reading a novel, if only because the voices of the disputants are indistinguishable both from one another's and from Bulwer's. Ford Madox Ford says somewhere of Conrad's narrator that "Marlow recites written Conrad"; still more jarringly (because she lacks Marlow's introspectiveness), Esther Summerson, the heroine of *Bleak House*, slides into written Dickens, as has been said, whenever Dickens drops the pretense that she sounds like herself. But Bulwer goes Conrad and Dickens one better. As long as he has to serve up arcane textbook materials and wants his characters to do all the talking, Bulwer takes the line of least resistance by getting X and Y to *quote* their authorities, as if they had memorized long learned passages by rote and now reeled them off like clockwork. Why bother the reader with a clumsy construction like "See the observation on La Place and La Marck in the introduction to Kirby's 'Bridgewater Treatise' " when the characters can swap all those observations literally, having memorized Bacon, Reichenbach, and the unforgettable Chalmers? "How nobly and how truly has Chalmers said," the old doctor pipes up before launching into Chalmers and proceeding to quote twenty-one lines that he dutifully annotates: "Chalmers, 'Bridgewater Treatise,' vol. II, pp. 28, 30" (between Kirby and Chalmers it's a marvel how many learned volumes Bridgewater has on its conscience); and this is followed by Bulwer's philosophy of composition: "Perhaps I should observe, that here and elsewhere in the dialogue between Faber and Fenwick, it has generally been thought better to substitute the words of the author quoted for the mere outline or purport of the quotation which memory affords to the interlocutor" (ch. 73, 412, n. 1).

---

7. Ch. 24. All references to *A Strange Story* are to the Editions de Luxe (Boston: Estes & Lauriat, 1892). [The preferred Knebworth Edition has been unavailable to me.]
8. April 15, 1862, *Life* 2, 349.

The procedure at least saves Bulwer the trouble of writing his own sentences.

But the blame for this and related maneuvers falls in fact on Bulwer's editor, who could not have known what he was in for. "Where you can avoid notes . . . and get their substance into the text," Dickens had advised him, "it is highly desirable in the case of so large an audience, simply because, as so large an audience necessarily reads the story in small portions, it is of the greatest importance that they should retain as much of its argument as possible. Whereas the difficulty of getting numbers of people to read notes . . . is wonderful." Dickens obviously failed to anticipate that in avoiding footnotes, Bulwer, instead of translating their substance into the text, got the notes themselves into it by lifting them from the foot of the page. Similar advice backfired when Dickens urged Bulwer to scotch the idea of spelling out the meaning of his hero's metaphysical disputes with old Dr. Faber in so many words in a hefty explanatory aside: "I urge you most strongly . . . NOT to enter upon any explanation beyond the title-page and the motto. . . . Let the book explain itself." And (whether he meant it or not): "It speaks for itself with a noble eloquence."[9] But if Bulwer is temperamentally prosy, few writers excel him in brevity where brevity is the object. "At length—at length—life was rescued, was assured! Life came back, but Mind was gone."

By chapter 62 readers who couldn't wait to find out when Mind would return were sadly outnumbered by those who had long ceased to care about such trifles. Bulwer had shown a much keener sense of the "suitability of the story" to *All the Year Round* than the Chief had shown. As early as October 12, a mere two months after the hero's arrival on page 1 and the start of the intrigues he set in motion, the installment carried the ominous *Mene, Mene* ("numbered, numbered"), "To be completed next March." This in the tenth installment, with twenty to go. In February, readers were repeatedly assured of the story's liquidation, with Wilkie Collins about to come to the rescue with his new shocker, *No Name.* Bulwer, the old wizard, who had been right all along, was very bitter. The entire debacle ended in his virtually blaming Dickens for accepting and running a self-defeating romance when he should have known better. "Even with my long authorship," he wrote to his son, "if I had my time over again, I would not have published *A Strange Story*, nor do I think if I had shown it, on the whole, to an anxious friend, that he would have counselled me to publish it."[1] Evidently Dickens's anxiety threshold, though high, had been lower than Bulwer's.

Textual Brief: The Happy Ending

In briefly retracing and updating the history of the two endings that the textual record reveals, it is convenient to reverse the chronology—beginning, that is, with the received text of the second ending and working back to the earliest available record of the original. Some of the admittedly minor verbal changes that crept into the later version, especially those that affect the final sentence of the novel, have occasionally been noted before, but without reference to the manuscript. The textualist has, in fact, to consider not two endings but six.

(1) In all modern texts, the final clause of the novel reads

9. December 18, 1861 (*PL* 9, 543); November 20, 1861 (*PL* 9, 510).
1. *Life* 2, 351.

> I saw no shadow of another parting from her.

The reading dates from the Library Edition of 1862; it is fair to assume that Dickens introduced it deliberately; it was allowed to stand in the Charles Dickens Edition six years later, and it has been the familiar exit line ever since. (2) The sentence as we know it reflects a slight modification of the phrase as it appears in all texts earlier than 1862 (the serial versions, first edition, and early American editions based on *All the Year Round*), in which the book concludes

> I saw the shadow of no parting from her.

As far as I know, the first to point this out was Charles Dickens Jr., who noted it, without comment, in his introduction to the novel in the Macmillan Edition of 1904.[2] The discrepancy has been briefly vented in print a number of times, the commentators assigning a greater degree of clarity or else ambiguity to one sentence or the other, though the critical brouhaha merely leads to the further question whether Dickens really intended to end on a note of ambiguity or simply wrote himself into one. More than one reader (who finds the original phrasing hopelessly muddled) argues that Dickens rephrased the sentence precisely in order to preclude any misreading and to leave no shadow of another doubt about his intentions to marry off the principals; others read the sentences in the opposite light. Thus Angus Calder submits that "in revision, Dickens deliberately made the last phrase less definite, and even ambiguous. For the later version carries the buried meaning: '. . . at this happy moment, I did not see the shadow of our subsequent parting looming over us.' Perhaps Pip did not marry Estella; the reader may believe what he likes." A more sophisticated if slightly strained argument has been advanced by an interpreter (Albert A. Dunn) who speculates that Dickens may have wanted to balance out Pip's failure to foresee the "shadow of another parting" from Estella with his failure to anticipate the shadow "of another meeting" with her; and he goes on to suggest (more plausibly) that Dickens may have been animated by the canny desire to propitiate Bulwer without quite caving in to him and so engaged in the sort of double-talk that didn't entirely rule out the original ending. That is, where Calder parades Dickens as merely lukewarm, Dunn at least dignifies him with the capacity for sabotage, or subterfuge, or trimming. The most persuasive as well as concise interpretation is also one of the most recent: looking at the three options (all other commentators, by ignoring the MS reading—on which see below—confined themselves to the two printed versions) Robin Gilmour notes that "each [of the three] envisages the future in negative rather than positive terms—as a parting not seen rather than a union looked forward to. A 'shadow' is invoked even in the act of denying it."[3]

2. Charles Dickens Jr., "Introduction, Biographical and Bibliographical," *Great Expectations* (London: Macmillan & Co., 1904), xii. Charley died in 1896, eight years before the volume containing both *Great Expectations* and *Hard Times* (vol. 16) appeared, so that I have been unable to date the composition of his introductory essay. But since the first eleven volumes of the twenty-one-volume Macmillan Edition were published as early as 1892, we may plausibly assign the composition to the early 1890s.
3. *Great Expectations*, ed. Robin Gilmour (London: Everyman, 1994), 447; see a.o. "The End of *Great Expectations*," *Dickensian* 34 (1938): 82; *Great Expectations*, ed. Angus Calder (Harmondsworth: Penguin, 1965), 496 (but Calder errs in dating the change from 1868); A. A. Dunn, "The Altered Endings of *Great Expectations*: A Note on Bibliography and First-Person Narrative," *DSN* 9 (June 1978): 40–42.

(3) The Ur-ending of the altered version, in the MS reading, first appeared in print in my own essay some fifteen years ago. It reveals a small and exquisite difference by the addition of two words. Last words on *Great Expectations*:

> I saw the shadow of no parting from her, but one.

This, certainly, is explicit enough to disinfect any possibility of misreading. Why, then, did Dickens strike the last phrase? (The cancellation is clearly indicated in proof.) On the face of it, the cancellation of the two operative words strengthens Calder's argument—that Dickens entertained second thoughts about too definitely committing Pip to Estella and therefore decided to introduce the shadow of a doubt after all, a shadow that had sufficiently deepened by 1862 to urge his final revision. One might even take the position taken by Dunn, that if Dickens at bottom disliked the ending foisted on him by Bulwer, he found the deepening shadow as good a way to scuttle Bulwer's friendly advice as any. Against this, it can be argued that of the two published readings, the reading introduced in '62 is in effect much the less equivocal and more nearly resolves the ambiguity than the earlier one. Besides (though this begs the question), the whole notion that Dickens went out of his way to skirt the issue in the final sentence of his novel ignores, I think, his creative procedures.

Though one can only guess at his intention here, it seems very unlikely that in blotting the last phrase Dickens endeavored to obscure a plain text. He may simply have disliked the phrase on artistic grounds: in playing these shapely sentences by ear, he may well have discovered that last chord to be a needless, needlessly distracting obtrusion on an already long and moving sentence, which reaches its appropriate climax in the parting words to which the cadences lead up. Possibly, too, he objected to the mawkishness of the phrase or, more emphatically, refused to end the novel on a quasi-religious note as being out of harmony with the scene—the note, precisely, that the phrase "but one" conveys. Death may have its dominion over Pip and Estella, but it has no place in a novel that ends on a note of muted recognition and self-recognition. Some such possibility can't be discounted, and it gains piquancy by a curious echo: for if Dickens had stuck to the original coda, "til death do us part," the ending of Pip's story and Estella's would have carried a resonance uncomfortably redolent of the pious flourish on which *David Copperfield* ends, with its vocative "O Agnes, O my soul," and concluding with the words "when I close my life indeed, so may I . . . still find thee near me, pointing upward!" But what was all right for Agnes would hardly do for Estella: in whatever light Pip may see her, she hardly presents herself to his mind's eye as a figure fit to be glazed into a stained-glass window or to qualify as the Angel in the House. Leaving aside the biblical "thees" and "thous" with which David cheers himself up (and which, one is made to feel, Dickens escaped narrowly in the closing paragraphs of *Hard Times*), simply imagine what the final sentence of *Great Expectations* would sound like had Dickens banged it out, as David bangs out his story, with an exclamation mark: "I saw the shadow of no parting from her, but one!"

Having struck the phrase, Dickens was left with the vexed sentence that appears in the early texts and in '62 reshaped it once more—very likely to minimize, or obviate, confusion, perhaps also again on "musical" grounds: certainly, as we have it, the sentence beckons to us more rhythmically than the gaunt string of monosyllables it supplanted, the nine low words that creep in one dull line. But surely any explanation by which Dickens is made to invite the reader, all cavalierly, to "believe what he likes," smacks of a desperate pococurantism. After all, we lose sight of the lovers holding hands as they leave the ruined garden; and after all, Marcus Stone's last plate for the novel bears the caption "With Estella, After all." Some readers, in fact, in resolving the marriage question, use identical arguments to arrive at opposite conclusions. A. L. French, for example, is sure that Pip must have remained an aging celibate, or he would have told us in so many words that he married Estella, French assuming that Pip wrote his autobiography about the time Dickens fictionalized it. And in 1861 Pip, with about a six-year headstart on Dickens, would have been at least in his mid-fifties. More recently Jerome Meckier, who shares French's dating of Pip's manuscript as the work of a seasoned elder, concludes by pretty much the same reasoning that Pip must have been married, or he would have told us in so many words that he wasn't. At the same time, precisely because the composition of Pip's story coincides with Dickens's, Meckier would have you believe that Estella must have been dead by 1861 or she would have collapsed of shock at reading her shaming story in the pages of *All the Year Round*. I can't be the only biped in creation who finds the very notion of Estella's reading any issue of *All the Year Round* deeply distressing—there is nothing in Meckier's plaidoyer against her living just long enough to enjoy *A Tale of Two Cities* in the same journal or dip into the opening number of Lever's serial, which might have killed her by acting as a literary overdose of laudanum.[4] Meckier, a militant votary of the happy ending, bases his death sentence on Pip's promise to Jaggers in chapter 51 that he would never, never reveal Estella's origins—a promise Pip makes weeks before Dickens dreamt of keeping the lovers together. Naturally it would have been easy for Pip to deliver a gentlemanly promise of secrecy about a woman he'll never lay eyes on again, but that he should have kept his mouth shut during twenty years of married intimacy opens out startling possibilities in the construction of relationships. Very likely, like Lohengrin's Elsa, he would have talked out of turn during their honeymoon. If nothing else, he'd probably talk in his sleep.

Aside from the reconstruction of the final sentence, the manuscript and proof of the altered ending elsewhere shed oblique light (by negative reference) on Dickens's intentions and thus on any scrupulous reading of the conclusion. For neither MS nor proof contains a brief passage of dialogue that Dickens evidently introduced at a very late stage in proofing, presumably just before he dispatched the last chapters to *Harper's*. The interpolation— almost certainly the very last touches Dickens added to the novel—follows Estella's question about Pip's professional success and his answer, "Yes, I do well." MS and proof omit:

---

4. Jerome Meckier, "Charles Dickens's *Great Expectations*: A Defense of the Second Ending," *Studies in the Novel* 25 (1993): 28–58; A. L. French, "Old Pip: The Ending of *Great Expectations*," *Essays in Criticism* 209 (1979): 357–60. Meckier's argument, of course, has precedent in Cervantes, postmodernists, and lesser writers who like to get their people to talk about the book by virtue of which they exist; but that is another story. Dickens himself, in fact, has one such self-referential joke in *Somebody's Luggage*, the Christmas bonus for 1862, in which the MS on which the story turns is revealed in the final segment to be a submission to *All the Year Round*.

"I have often thought of you," said Estella.

"Have you?"

"Of late, very often. There was a long hard time when I kept far from me, the remembrance of what I had thrown away when I was quite ignorant of its worth. But, since my duty has not been incompatible with the admission of that remembrance, I have given it a place in my heart."

"You have always held your place in my heart," I answered. And we were silent again, until she spoke.

MS and proof then pick up again with Estella's line "I little thought," etc. Within the general scheme of the second ending, the four brief paragraphs are certainly defensible and artistically appropriate: Estella's confession, in its insistence on *remembrance*, on *heart*, on the changes wrought in her during the long intermittence, foreshadows the paragraphs that follow and reinforces them by anticipation. Dickens, in other words, wants to establish as unmistakably as possible the genuine efficacy of Estella's reformation and is at pains to remind the reader of this. "At pains"—for it must be admitted that taken by itself the passage sounds oddly bromidic, the quality of afterthought (now that we know it to be one, without Bulwer's spectral dictation at issue) too strained: "since my duty has not been incompatible with the admission of that remembrance" is fagged out Emma Woodhouse, not ripened Estella, as if, really, Dickens himself, having finished the novel twice over, found himself hamstrung by the performance of a boring duty incompatible with his art.[5] On the other hand, Dickens may really have felt that he owed Estella the extra booster shot to make her quite safe for Pip, even if his needle had been rather blunted by the end of June.

That Dickens may have felt some such debt to Estella and sensed that he may have short-changed her role in the final chapters is apparent elsewhere in the MS corrections. Necessarily, a good deal has been made of the implication, for Pip and Estella, of their meeting in the Satis House garden and, related to this, the propriety of extending Pip's humbling and rehabilitation to Estella. Where few people question the legitimacy of Pip's conversion (even where they question the legitimacy of the reward), can the same allowances be made for Estella, whose change of heart takes place offstage and is supported merely by her own say-so (the old song about "showing" versus "telling")? As I have noted earlier in discussing the textual changes, Dickens, in working over the altered ending, clearly decided to make the most of Estella's legitimate claims on Pip's susceptibility and, within the decent limits set by their middle-aged reunion, to apply his varnish more lavishly in revision.

In this matter of puffing Estella as well as accounting for the compressed character of even the altered ending, something else should be noted here. In the revised ending Estella does practically all the talking and Pip is oddly reticent—again, as if either Pip or Dickens or both were less than enthusiastic about reactivating the conversation. Pip is all gab in Joe's and Biddy's com-

5. One may even take the uncharitable view that Dickens, in discharging this, his final debt to Pip, wasn't thinking of art at all but of word count. A good many critics, as we shall see, have faulted both endings, the "unhappy" and less emphatically the "happy" one, as unconvincingly abrupt—after all, the second ending is only two pages longer than the first. The brevity even of the second, somewhat elaborated conclusion can't be argued out of the world, and on the evidence of suppressions and additions in proof throughout Dickens's writings, we know that he liked to keep his installments tidy —the monthly numbers, of course, required uniform length. Since the interpolated four paragraphs add very little to the story, their insertion at the last moment may suggest more of editorial expediency than artistic intention.

pany in the pages preceding, before the two endings go their separate ways. Pip, in a passage in which the word *old* appears a dozen times, makes his way to the ruined garden; Estella rises out of the mist, and Pip, having conquered his surprise at her appearance and his amazement at the coincidence of their meeting, falls into the silent mood—a silence that reminds us a little of the shyness he displayed in the days when he used to be a coarse and common laboring boy nearly thirty years ago. Now they confront each other for the last time. *She*: had he been wondering why the poor old place had been left such a dreary wreck? *He*: "Yes, Estella." *She*: that this would be her final visit before the place was to be restored, and by the way did he still live abroad? *He*: "Still." She expects that he is doing well in his job. *He*: "I work pretty hard for a sufficient living, and therefore—Yes, I do well." She allows that she has often thought of him. *He*: "Have you?" Then her four-line speech quoted earlier, that after having tried to put him out of her mind, she found that she couldn't after all. *He*: "You have always held your place in my heart." *She* (in the longest speech in the scene): that since he forgave her long ago and she has learned her lesson in the school of hard knocks she hopes that they can be friends again. *He*: "We are friends." Not only does Estella get in about four times as many lines as he does—the only two sustained questions or repartees are hers—but it is she who picks up the thread whenever it slips from them in what must be both an awkward and an overpowering encounter. So Dickens spares no pains in giving Estella her due.

Taken together, the textual changes of the "happy" ending and the care —or labor—Dickens bestowed on them really leave very little room for the view that the final sentence of the book "may presage anything" and that the ending is therefore an impatient cop-out. That the ending represents, as the same critic goes on to say, "a final lack of conviction [by Dickens] in his own scheme, a reluctance to face, close-up, the implications of his hero's behavior," is really a separate charge, which doesn't necessarily follow from the first.[6]

Textual Brief: The Unhappy Ending

(4) The original ending of the novel was first published in the last volume of Forster's *Life*, Forster printing the conclusion as a footnote to his commentary on the novel. Forster prefaced the footnote with the comment that

> There was no Chapter XX as now [Forster refers to the three-volume edition of 1861, in which the chapters were separately numbered for each volume]; ("For eleven years" in the original, altered to "eight years") followed the paragraph about his business partnership with Herbert, and led to Biddy's question whether he is sure he does not fret for Estella ("I am sure and certain, Biddy" as originally written, altered to "O no—I think not, Biddy"): from which point here was the close.[7]

Volume 3 of the *Life* appeared in 1874, thirteen years after Dickens composed the ending, and Forster's footnote has been the sole authority for all subsequent transmissions and necessarily the source of all critical comment. Until 1937, when Bernard Shaw famously claimed to be the first to restore

6. Milton Millhauser, "*Great Expectations*: The Three Endings," DSA 2 (1972): 267–77; quoted matter, 270.
7. Forster, book 9, chapter 3; Hoppé 2, 441.

the original ending to the text for the Limited Editions Club, editors habitually ignored the first ending, at most acknowledging the fact of the two endings in the prefatory matter; since the late 1940s it has been customary to print both endings, editors unexceptionally concluding the text with the revised ending and running the original as a trailer.[8] The comment with which Forster ushers in the original ending contains one obvious blunder; and the footnote that comprises the ending, as we shall see, has been imperfectly transcribed. As Forster has it, in the earlier version Pip remains abroad for eleven years; in rewriting the ending, Dickens reduced his absence to eight. But this, on the face of it, makes no sense. For whereas the first ending proper begins with Pip's comment that "it was two years [after his return], before I saw herself," the second ending unites the lovers the day he returns. Assuming that Dickens intended Pip and Estella to be roughly the same age in both endings (an assumption borne out by the memoranda of "Dates" [see p. 484] in which both Pip and Estella are said to be "about 23" "in the last stage of Pip's Expectations"), elementary arithmetic suggests that in rewriting the ending, Dickens extended Pip's sojourn abroad to bring it temporally into line with the garden scene. Presumably Dickens thought thirty-three—thirty-four in the original ending—to be more suited to their mellowed condition than thirty-one, and once he advanced the meeting with Estella he had to adjust the length of Pip's Egyptian phase accordingly. Evidently, Forster's figures need to be read upside down: For "eight years" in the original, altered to "eleven years" in revision.

(5) We are left with the question whether a source for the unhappy ending earlier than Forster's note can be discovered; and here I make free to jumble the inverted chronology by introducing MS evidence before concluding with the evidence of the corrected proof. We know that Shaw, in trying to track down his prey to the MS, affirmed that the MS contained the altered ending only, without a trace of the original.[9] But the scout who had been commissioned to copy the whole of the Wisbech MS at a time when Limited Editions intended to publish the entire text verbatim from the MS, pardonably overlooked Dickens's cancellations. For, in fact, roughly one fourth of the Ur-ending is preserved in the MS. Following the words "Biddy, all gone by!" the MS continues after a paragraph break for seventy-three words to the bottom of the slip—a mere four lines in Dickens's cramped hand—the text beginning where Forster begins and going as far as "of her being married to a." The omission of anything more than a simple paragraph break—two lines of space or the insertion of a rule—suggests that the ending was to follow quite organically. Dickens canceled the passage not by ballooning out the words but by drawing broad diagonal strokes across it—the practice he generally followed in canceling entire passages in his manuscripts—so that the canceled matter

---

8. "Preface," *Great Expectations* (Edinburgh: Limited Editions, 1937), xiii. Minor corruptions of Forster's note have been introduced into nearly all editions that print the first ending—in accidentals of punctuation and in introducing a paragraph break preceding Estella's "I am greatly changed," where Forster prints the entire ending as a single paragraph. Where these corruptions occur, the editors almost certainly based their text on Shaw's 1937 edition rather than on Forster's note, Shaw himself apparently following not Forster but a flawed transcription of Forster by Hugh Mann, which appeared in Robert Blatchford's column "In the Library" in *The Clarion* for May 16, 1902. On Shaw's editorial mystifications, see my "Last Words on *Great Expectations*," 111–12.

9. *The Mystery of the Unhappy Ending* (New York: n.p., 1937), which gives the correspondence (August 28, 1935, to December 24, 1936) among Shaw's secretary Blanche Patch, the Edinburgh editor William Maxwell, and the publisher of Limited Editions, George Macy.

is entirely legible. It ends where it does only because the slip ends there, and we may regret that this, our only preserve of the original in Dickens's hand, did not begin farther up the slip and uncover correspondingly more attractions. The altered ending, "Nevertheless, I knew while I said those words," begins at the top of the slip following; its position leaves uncertain whether Dickens meant to indicate a break here.

The MS tallies with Forster's note except in two small points. Whereas Forster begins "It was two years more, before I saw herself," the MS has "It was four years more," and where Forster starts the second sentence "I had heard of her as leading a most unhappy life," the MS leads off "Then I had heard of her. . . ." Again, Dickens struck "four" and substituted "two" in proof, and the adverbial "Then"—that is, "at that time"—disappears: perhaps because Dickens, beyond his general unwillingness to tie himself down to too specific a calendar, felt that since Estella had "at that time" already been separated from Drummle, as the clause following makes clear, and as nothing could be worse than Bentley's beastly conduct, she had weathered the worst of her unhappiness at the point at which Pip learns about this. And we may reasonably assume that Dickens decided to reduce the interval of Pip's return from Egypt and the Piccadilly meeting by two years in order to bring the events of Estella's separation, Drummle's death, and her remarriage closer to the time of action. In the second paragraph of the revised ending (the paragraph taken over almost verbatim from the original except for the Shropshire doctor), Dickens spells this out: "This release [Bentley's death] had befallen her some two years before."[1]

(6) As an editorial guideline the corrected proof necessarily supersedes the authority of the manuscript where the corrections are demonstrably intentional, and our only check on Forster remains the proof. Two things about Forster's transcription need to be kept in mind here: that it appeared thirteen years after composition, and that Forster ran it as a footnote. The proofs of the original ending are preserved with the bound proofs in the Pierpont Morgan Library, where, following a lead by Professor K. J. Fielding, I unearthed them sometime in the seventies. They incorporate Dickens's final corrections and reveal precisely how Dickens intended the first ending to be printed.[2]

1. Dickens introduces at least two more minor emendations to which Robert Greenberg has drawn attention. In the first ending, Drummle is described "as a compound of pride, brutality, and meanness"; in the second, his offenses are compounded by the vice of "avarice." Greenberg sensibly concludes that "by the addition of 'avarice' Dickens is able to eliminate reference to [Estella's] impoverished second husband . . . and, more important, to retain from his original version the fact of her reduced circumstances." (Against this, Q. D. Leavis: "We don't, I think, ask how it is that Estella is now poor . . . and since Drummle himself was by definition rich, avaricious, and mean, why should he lose his fortune?") Where the two endings very nearly correspond in their wording, Greenberg records another variant: the first ending concludes with the narrator's comment on Estella that "suffering had been stronger than Miss Havisham's teaching"; the second ending, with Estella's confession that "suffering has been stronger than all other teaching." Evidently Bentley has contributed his mite. Robert A. Greenberg, "On Ending *Great Expectations*," *Papers on Language and Literature* 6 (1970): 159; Q. D. Leavis, "How We Must Read *Great Expectations*," in F. R. and Q. D. Leavis, *Dickens the Novelist* (London: Chatto and Windus, 1970), 425.
2. The credit for this goes entirely to Fielding, who, as long ago as 1968 or '69, conveyed to me his hunch that the original ending was preserved in the Morgan proof book, which he had himself examined briefly some years earlier. The Morgan proof, too, at first sight seemed to have only the altered ending; but in going over the (suspiciously bulky) proofs for the final chapter, I found, as anyone might have, that these were pasted over other galleys; moreover, since some of the marginal corrections could refer only to the concealed, not the overlaid, sheets, it was clear that Professor Fielding's hunch was within inches of being verified. Mr. Douglas C. Ewing, Curator of Manuscripts and Modern Books, agreed that the unhappy ending in its most nearly impeccable text deserved to be uncovered and proceeded to have the overlaid galleys steamed open—a half-hour operation of astounding interest and suspense.

The set of corrected proof at the Victoria and Albert Museum is quite un-availing here: it abruptly ends midway through the first sentence of the pen-ultimate paragraph of chapter 58, "I sold all I had, and I put aside as much as I." The possibility that the V & A proofs gave the original ending and that this was either destroyed or found its way into a collection to which I have been unable to track it down cannot, of course, be dismissed; but this would in any case have been superseded by the corrected Morgan proof.

The Morgan text is close enough to Forster to defeat any great expectations of a brand-new discovery and just distinct enough to yield "a sufficient living" and modest profits. Materially it differs in nothing from Forster's note and corroborates the accuracy of his transcription: in substance *Great Expectations* ends as he ends it. The difference lies not in what Dickens reveals but in quite how he reveals it. Anybody who has studied Dickens's galleys is struck by the pains he takes in altering paragraph breaks at proof stage, either string-ing separate paragraphs together or breaking a single paragraph into two or three or more. One is struck, in other words, by the importance he attaches to the nuances and modulations, as well as the appearance—the purely optical effect—of his text. The importance of the Morgan proof lies in nothing more than this: in conveying a quite different sense of tempo, of rhythm, to the first ending, and hence a different sense of poetic closure to the novel. Where Forster, restricting himself to a footnote, jams the ending into a single para-graph, Dickens lays out the conclusion in four paragraphs; and this necessarily affects the way in which we ultimately read the ending. Factually, to repeat, this alters nothing. At most it confutes (and, at that, perhaps by a narrow literalism) those commentators who object that "the original ending, amount-ing to but a long paragraph, could hardly have been more concise."[3] Yet exactly this objection, as I have indicated, has been lodged against the endings (both endings, but more damnably against the first) too often and too righ-teously to be quite passed over; and it is but to do justice to Dickens to assuage—or bribe—the opposition by presenting it with four quietly modu-lated paragraphs instead of a single hurried one.

Options

So much for the textual-housekeeping details. To soak up the immense amount of ink that has been spilled on the two endings does not, in the occupational jargon, lie within the scope of this commentary. Each of the critics may be said to fit roughly into one of three slots: (1) the supporters of the first ending; (2) the supporters of the second ending; and (3) the neither/nors, who argue that Dickens botched both endings about equally and whose views boil down to the argument that Dickens should have discharged Pip on his return to Lower Higham and kept Estella out of it entirely. As for (1) and (2), the spectrum of opinion ranges from those who put down the altered ending as "preposterous," "outrageous," "pointless," "a falsification of all that

3. Greenberg, "On Ending *Great Expectations*," 155. Though the abruptness of the ending has often been noted, critics respond to this in different ways. Thus, of three commentators picked at random, all of whom agree that the ending betrays signs of haste, Humphry House prefers the first ending (*The Dickens World* [London: Oxford University Press, 1941], 28, 156–57); R. George Thomas prefers the second (*Charles Dickens*: Great Expectations [London: Arnold, 1964], 55–56); and Martin Meisel finds both equally irrelevant ("The Ending of *Great Expectations*," *Essays in Criticism* 15 (1965): 326; on the increasing acceptance of Meisel's position, see below.

has taken place," to those who, like Mrs. Leavis, find the preference for the original ending "incomprehensible." Caught in this crossfire of critical grape-shot, the editor is confronted by the raw question which of two veteran con-testants more nearly deserves to be rescued. The argument raised by the neither/nors is of course textually irrelevant: an editor can't very well rip out the last four or five pages and keep Estella married to Drummle or separated from him to gratify clever narratologists. As I have said, editors have habitually printed the second ending, variously alleging their genuine preference for it or arguing that "it was, after all, the one Dickens published," and the practice has by now turned into a self-perpetuating tic. And there is no blinking the fact that the weight of critical comment has not only been increasingly in favor of the ruined garden, but that its sponsors have argued their case on the whole more eloquently and more convincingly than the sponsors of Piccadilly.

In following the precedent set by earlier editors and printing the second ending, I myself am guided not so much by protocol and usage, nor by the steadily mounting critical bias (which may count for very little in the long run). From any strictly textual point of view, the argument that it was "the one Dickens published" remains, I suppose, the single overriding argument in favor of its maintenance. Editors who set aside the author's published product always do so at their peril. In this, too, the example of Shaw remains an instructive if unavailing one: Shaw, while trying to dig up the first ending, cast a rather cold eye on the publisher's plan to print the novel from manu-script. In keeping his errand boys from intruding on Dickens's privacy, Shaw speaks for a great many writers who feel that their final printed words are the only ones that matter, and who thus look on textualists as a breed of Peeping Toms or resurrectionists. In editing anything, one has, naturally, to keep the author's knowable, or guessable, wishes steadily in mind by establishing the text that most nearly tallies with the book the author wrote—that is, by mi-croscopic attention to the alternatives. The double ending, to be sure, presents a special problem—divorced as it is from Dickens's known intention both by the intervention of time and by the interference of a well-meaning confrère. And, indeed, there seem to me cogent reasons for printing the ending Dickens wrote before Bulwer talked him out of it and assigning the second ending a backseat in the appendix; and future editors may well restore it in its course. This commentary therefore cannot be complete without my playing devil's advocate for those who may wish to flout both editorial practice and the critical consensus, and, on grounds of editorial propriety alone, restore priority to Piccadilly.

(1) What of Dickens's own preference? Though critics can afford to moot anything smacking of the intentional fallacy, editors have no such license; and if Dickens's own response to the altered ending can be at all gauged, it deserves a hearing. To say that the second ending was, after all, the one Dickens published is one thing; to say that it was the one Dickens preferred is another; and I am not really impressed with the argument that if Dickens had not liked Bulwer's suggestion he would have lumped it. Certainly the language of what little correspondence there is sounds guarded enough on this point, singularly guarded for a novelist who, in speaking of his compo-

sitions, assaults his friends with a steady drumfire of self-applause, and whose autocritical reports hardly ever record anything less than an A+. In his pithy essay on the novel, Martin Meisel notes that in justifying the revised ending to Forster "Dickens seems to have done his best to hang himself" by the "coy and philistine smugness with which he promotes the new conclusion ('I have put in as pretty a little piece of writing as I could and I have no doubt the story will be more acceptable for the alteration')."[4] It may be cold comfort to Professor Meisel to be reminded that this is strictly par for the course and that the other comments on the novel are hardly more modest: "such a very fine, new, and grotesque idea has opened upon me"; "I have made the opening, I hope, in its general effect exceedingly droll"—and the rest are little more than the self-satisfied noises of the buoyant merchandiser: "Pray read Great Expectations. . . . It is a very great success and seems universally liked"; "I am glad to find you so faithfully following Great Expectations, which story is an immense success"; "the journal is doing gloriously, and Great Expectations is a great success." Apart from these rather tiresome Odes to a Balance Sheet, Dickens's hosannas to the merits of his productions seemed to be habitual to him and persisted throughout his career. Pick up any volume of the *Pilgrim Letters* and you will find that the comments on *Great Expectations* differ barely from the self-approving notices twenty years earlier: "Behold No. XII which I think a good 'un. No. XIII will finish the part at rather a good point, I expect"; "Number 15, which I began to-day, I anticipate great things from. There is a description . . . with which, if I had read it as anybody else's writing, I think I should have been very much struck"—if Dickens hangs himself once with his pretty complacencies, he hangs as often as Pangloss; and, like Pangloss, he escapes with his skin intact. This needs to be stressed on two counts: that the purely monetary rewards and the elation they occasioned reflect the success of the novel not primarily after its publication but during its serial run; and that if Dickens pulls all the stops elsewhere, he rather pulls his punches in talking of the second ending. *"Upon the whole,* I think it is for the better" suggests acquiescence, not enthusiasm; "I think the story more *acceptable* for the alteration"—the operative term skirts merit in favor of market; the note to Bulwer—"I hope you will like the alteration that is entirely due to you"—is at best a worldly compliment and at worst (to those who care to stretch the issue further than I should) a nice invitation to supply the unwritten "certainly not to me" and to turn an overt compliment into an implied reproof, a gesture of abdication, as if Dickens really wanted to wash his hands of the whole business. Perhaps even more revealing is Dickens's comment expressed in his covering note to Forster of April—at the time he dispatched the first installments of stage three—in which he registers his regret that "the third portion cannot be read all at once": regrettable "because the general turn and tone of the working out or winding up will be away from all such things as they conventionally go." Evidently Dickens took a certain pride and pleasure in the "unconventionality" of the original ending as he himself perceived it.[5]

    Can we infer anything about Dickens's preference from the earliest appearance of these final pages? In my comments on the manuscript I tried to

4. Meisel, "The Ending of *Great Expectations*," 326–31, quoting from letter of July 1, 1861 (*PL* 9, 433).
5. *PL* 9, 403.

show that Dickens's "difficult" passages are often his most successful, and I mentioned that the final MS leaves—those that contain the revised ending— are in especially poor condition. Moreover, they teem with cancellations that are more difficult to unriddle than almost any others in the manuscript. The very plethora of revision would suggest that Dickens went over them with the same painstaking care he lavished on what were to be some of the most wonderful things in the book. I think not. Though this is manifestly beyond all proof, I can't escape the impression that the revisions are less a product of the conscientious craftsman happy in his sense that all his labor will pay off than they are a product of *fatigue*. I have implied as much in my comments on the uncharacteristically stilted language in which Estella beckons to Pip in the brewery yard. In no other parts of the MS has Dickens so consistently canceled words or phrases, substituted, and gone back to the original—a procedure, as has also been noted, evident throughout the manuscript, conspicuously in the heavily marked opening paragraph. But unless I willfully misread, the procedure here reflects less of sanguine effort, the writer at his happiest, than of futility; less of the snappy thought "hullo: my first instinct paid off!" than the resigned "let's face it: this is the best that I can do." As I say, this can be no more than speculation—an affair compounded of inference, sympathy, and impure guesswork. But here and there, between this cancellation and the next, I keep detecting the (quite un-Dickensian) sound of the scrivener, who would prefer not to.

(2) Then Forster came. Allowing for the usual amount of twaddle by contemporary reviewers, whose judgments often strike us as deplorably vulgar and astigmatic (and who could not have known about the first ending anyway), we may refrain from belittling the tributes of the well-informed and sensible readers of a generation closer to Dickens than our own. J. Hillis Miller and Peter Brooks are certainly better critics than Charles Dickens Jr. and, as novel-critics, quite as good as Shaw; but the perspective that distance confers is often more warped than the shorter view, and one may even argue that the testimony of the immediate post-Dickensians is the more reliable for their being closer to the Spirit in Which the Author Writ. Certainly their unanimity in favor of the first ending, once it was brought to their attention, is difficult to shrug off, and it would be asinine to assume that these people were actuated by nothing more ennobling than professional spite against Bulwer. Forster's preference for the pre-Bulwer ending—the only recorded verdict by a strict contemporary—is all the more telling in view of Forster's lifelong esteem for Bulwer, unless we uncharitably impute his judgment to his private pique at not having been consulted.[6] After Forster came Charley Jr., who, pilfering the words out of his father's mouth, allowed the story to be "more acceptable" for the alteration, but went on to docket his own opinion "that the only really natural as well as artistic conclusion to the story was that which was originally intended"; and by the time Charley wrote this, his disdain for the second ending already reflected, in his words, "the soundness of the general judgment."[7] In the thirty years or so following Dickens's death, critics as

6. No reason to, considering the amicable correspondence between the two at this time about Bulwer's *A Strange Story*. See Wolff, *Strange Stories*, 291, and *Life* 2, 341 ff. But Bulwer and Forster had been friends for years.
7. "Introduction," *Great Expectations*, xi–xii.

far apart as Gissing and Chesterton, though they agreed on nothing else about
Dickens, concurred in their preference for the Piccadilly ending; ditto William Dean Howells and Shaw's early socialist friends on *The Clarion*. If much
of the early criticism errs on the side of the shrill and peremptory, it has the
merit of being cleanly forthright and assured and is entirely untainted by the
sort of special pleading that spoils so much of the later academic criticism
that has rallied round the reunited lovers in the moonlight.

(3) Gissing, Shaw, Chesterton, and Howells, of course, were themselves
novelists as well as critics; so were Orwell, Robert Liddell, Edmund Wilson,
and Angus Wilson. Good (or middling) novelists may be notoriously unreliable as critics, if only because they have their own axes to grind or
because their literary tastes are more crotchety than those of the
average-educated critic. A writer's estimate of another writer always invites a
certain wariness. But in judging the local problem of the two endings, these
novelists may, I think, be absolved of ulterior motives: indeed, I should like
to think that they respond to this with the special sensitivity and imaginative
sympathy and an intuitive sense for the real right thing that their craft confers.
And if all these people, in varying degrees of heat and voltage, are united in
favoring the earlier ending, perhaps the significance of their vote ought to be
taken at its proper valuation. This is not merely a question of name-dropping
(in that case, one should have to add, among the academic critics, nearly
all the leading Dickens scholars of the past decades) but a matter of recognizing, for what it may be worth, the substantial size of the creative-writing
lobby.

(4) The raw question of artistic merit is more complex than any of the
foregoing and forces us to ponder the character of the criticism. Forster's
opinion of the first ending as "more consistent with the drift, as well as the
natural working out, of the tale" has to all intents been echoed by all subsequent partisans of the first ending, who, whatever they may think of Dickens's motives, object to the altered ending as (minimally) out of line with the
rest of the book or (at worst) an artistically indefensible as well as morally
shoddy about-face, Dickens torpedoing in the last three pages of the novel
everything he has set adrift in the four hundred pages leading up to the end.
In this view, Pip ultimately gets more than his deserts and Dickens not only
muddles the narrative integrity of the book and explodes the reader's just
expectations but also muddles the socio-moral lesson he has all along been
preaching and so nullifies the very theme of *Great Expectations*. I deliberately
overstate the case here, but some such line has been taken by nearly all the
apostles of the first ending. Estella's conversion has unsurprisingly occasioned
much talk among them and been viewed as a decisive issue in all this. The
First Endians generally object to her change of heart as colliding with the
very logic of the narrative and the whole of Estella's education: "the logical
consequence of such an upbringing . . . [would] unfit her for any sort of
marriage"; "everything that we know of Miss Havisham and her bringing up
of Estella is made hollow by this softening of Estella, since we find, not that
we must forgive the tragic Miss Havisham, but that there was not really anything to forgive"; "the shaping of a lifetime in Estella [is] miraculously undone." As a result, Pip "is as much prepared to live on unearned income in
his emotional life as in his life as a gentleman"; the modest profits he earns,
and deserves to earn, are morally of no use to him; and Pip's own education

into disillusionment is made hollow, "miraculously undone" by the discovery that the disillusionment has itself been illusory.[8]

Against this view, we have a crowd of writers who defend the altered ending as ratifying much more harmoniously than the first the recurrent patterns and images of the novel, the interwoven motifs of union and separation and reconciliation, who stress the deep linkage of the past and present and make much of the "atmospheric" propriety that informs the garden scene—it's a rare writer who forgets to quote Milton at this point. Moreover, at least a few of the Second Endians claim as much coherence for the second ending as the First Endians claim for the first, arguing that the lovers have been sufficiently humanized by their griefs to deserve whatever morsel of happiness Dickens hands them. The Happy Endgamers by and large condone Estella's redemption as an artistically fitting function of Pip's own amendment and a moving result of her personal harrowing. Their case rests on the conviction that Pip's growth suggests the possibility of a similar process in Estella, that Estella's change of heart is supported by Pip's conduct and Bentley Drummle's and that anyhow, as Harvey Sucksmith argues, as long as "the regeneration of Estella is improbable in the new ending, then it is improbable in the rejected ending too." In anticipating "the valid objection [that] the themes of regeneration and reconciliation violate the tone of pessimistic irony which pervades and helps to unify the novel," Sucksmith remarks that "this objection may be levelled equally against both endings; perhaps critics do not object to the rejected ending because the break in tone is much weaker and therefore overlooked." In any event, "it is a satisfying conclusion that, as Magwitch's daughter, [Estella] should find happiness with Pip."[9] To oversimplify a complex issue: whereas the First Endians argue their case on the grounds of plot-logic and moral authority, the Second Endians argue theirs on the grounds of symbolic recurrence and the redemptive relativism of experience; and insofar as these are the points at issue, the scales seem to me to tip in favor of the First Endians. If the first ending supports the logic of the book and the second doesn't, no amount of atmospheric pressure will relieve the garden scene; and Justice, nervously poised between Forster and Lytton, lifts her blindfold just long enough to tip a nod toward Forster.

(5) The argument raised by the neither/nors, the people who veto both a brief encounter with Estella and a lifelong one, assumes that Dickens rushed the novel to its conclusion with indecent haste and that both endings reflect hardly more "than a cursory gesture of compliance with the fictional proprieties." The phrase appears in what has become one of the staple works on the subject, Milton Millhauser's "*Great Expectations*: The Three Endings," in which Millhauser browbeats Dickens for racing to the finish line, or rather for overshooting his mark when he should have known where to stop. The

8. T. A. Jackson, *Charles Dickens: Progress of a Radical* (London: Lawrence & Wishart, 1937), 194; Christopher Ricks, "*Great Expectations*," below, p. 668; Edgar Johnson, *Charles Dickens: His Tragedy and Triumph*, 2 vols. (New York: Simon & Schuster, 1952) 2, 992–93; H. M. Daleski, *Dickens and the Art of Analogy* (London: Faber & Faber, 1970), 254.
9. Sucksmith, *The Narrative Art of Charles Dickens*, 112. Of the numerous pieces along similar lines, see esp. Barbara Hardy, "The Change of Heart in Dickens' Novels," *Victorian Studies* 5 (1961): 49–67, esp. 61–63, and Hardy's *The Moral Art of Dickens* (New York: Oxford Univ. Press, 1970), 73–75; James Reed, "The Fulfilment of Pip's Expectations," *Dickensian* 55 (1959): 16; Kurt Tetzeli von Rosador, "*Great Expectations*: Das Ende eines Ich-Romans," *Neuere Sprachen* NF 18 (1969): esp. 407–08; John Kucich, "Action in the Dickens Endings: *Bleak House* and *Great Expectations*," *Nineteenth-Century Fiction* 33 (1978): 102–07; Douglas Brooks-Davies, *Great Expectations* (Harmondsworth: Penguin, 1989); and the "Closure" section of the bibliography, below, p. 742.

three endings Millhauser presents as alternatives are (1) Pip's return to the forge and reunion with Joe, (2) his second visit, after he "has found his métier and carried forward his moral education," and (3) what Millhauser regards as no more than a postscript to either one of the actualized endings—it doesn't finally matter which. Either way, "one is left with the impression that the book is hurried to a conclusion, through scenes about which the author does not greatly care."[1] Millhauser was probably one of the earliest advocates of this amputation theory, one that has found a respectable number of accessories, not least among Freudians and deconstructionists. In defending their objections to what they regard as an artificially inflated conclusion, a number of commentators point out that, after all, the working memoranda, in which Dickens charted the course of the later chapters, stop short of the meeting with Estella in Piccadilly—though, as has also been suggested, the omission of the final scenes of the *Mems.* in itself is less likely to suggest the last-minute improvisation of a writer in search of an ending than the opposite: a conclusion too firmly planted in Dickens's mind to require a written reminder.[2]

The problem whether Estella's reappearance (either ending) is really as dysfunctional as these champions of retrenchment (or body snatchers) accuse it of being really straddles aesthetic and affective grounds. In dumping Estella (never mind that Dickens, for better or for worse, enlarged her role) one is at least entitled, it seems to me, to anticipate and empathize with the readers' expectations, not just those of Dickens's contemporaries but also our own. We have had our last glimpse of Estella all of fourteen chapters earlier, some one hundred pages before the terminal reconciliation. We last saw her, that is, in the scene in which Pip confronts Miss Havisham with her duplicity and Estella informs him that she is going to marry Drummle; and our last direct news of her comes five chapters later, some seventy pages before the end, when, in answer to Pip's "needless question," Havisham confirms that Estella has indeed married the brute. One can surely forgive readers who feel they are being not overpaid by being brought up to date at the last minute but a little short-changed at being so thoroughly left in the dark about the future of the person who has been all in all to Pip. Ought Dickens really to ditch her so cavalierly some three-fourths through the novel? Naturally, the very last thing we should want is the kind of last-chapter summary, "A Last Retrospect"—as often as not "A Final Prospect"—in which the reader is told what happened, or what will happen, to everybody, the sort of Copperfield-Biedermaier tableau — or "pantomime" — in which each character takes a half-minute curtain call—Aunt Betsey; Rosa Dartle; old Mrs. Steerforth; Tommy Traddles; the good, feeble Dr. Strong; Jack Maldon; Agnes—to be applauded or whistled at. Besides, in *Great Expectations* we know what happened to everybody—except, unless Dickens revives her, Estella.[3] The idea of her being permanently trapped by the Spider is a little distasteful, though Dickens is certainly spunky enough to face up to this; I am not sure—given her flashes

1. Millhauser, "*Great Expectations*: The Three Endings," 268, 270.
2. See Peter Brooks, "Repetition, Repression and Return," below, p. 679; D. A. Miller, "Afterword," *Narrative and its Discontents* (Princeton: Princeton UP, 1970), 222–23; Meisel, "The Ending of *Great Expectations*," 326; Moshe Ron, "Autobiographical Narration and Formal Closure in *Great Expectations*," *Hebrew University Studies in Literature* 5 (1977): 37–66; Greenberg, "On Ending *Great Expectations*," 156; Millhauser, "The Three Endings," 274; Thomas M. Leitch, "Closure and Teleology in Dickens," *Studies in the Novel* 18 (1986): 143–56.
3. Ditto Startop and Orlick; see "Writing *Great Expectations*," above, p. 462.

of fury and contempt along with her frigidity—that she would choose to stick it out with him, a contingency anyhow obviated by what we are told about Drummle's death and Estella's modest transfiguration in the first ending. But in the absence of more recent information—and with all the deference in the world to her vanishing advocated by literary Houdinis like Brooks, Miller, Meisel, Sadrin, Robin Gilmour[4]—I shouldn't blame the reader for feeling a little cheated at being left to wonder. A diplomatic acquiescence in the "fictional proprieties"—if that is what we are talking about—seems to me preferable to an obtrusive iconoclasm. Dickens showed a good deal of acumen, I think, in (for example) reminding us of Edith Dombey's emotional mutilatedness long after she has played any active part in the novel, or leaving no doubt of Louisa Gradgrind's solitary destiny in *Hard Times*, and in neither case does he recoil from the desolate future these people face. Even if Pip's story is (arguably) complete by the time he returns to the forge, either before he joins Clarriker's or eleven years later, when he is home on holiday, isn't the closure as we know it not only more gratifying but narratologically appropriate, whether the lovers fade out—just the two of them—in the romantic moonshine of the ruined garden or the sexless daylight of Piccadilly, with little Pip gazing up at the strange lady in the pony carriage, suffering her to lift him up to kiss her (a wonderfully droll replay of her earliest humiliating invitation to the young Pip, "You may kiss me, if you like"), and probably tugging at the sleeves of his middle-aged would-have-been godfather?

(6) One final argument in favor of the unhappy ending ought to be taken under advisement. It all has to do with what Sucksmith, in the passage I cited, calls the "the break in tone" that is so much more noticeable in the second than the first ending. Sucksmith's intuitive insight apart, I have never heard the point raised except by undergraduates and graduate students, and they respond to this with refreshing vigor. What jars on them has to do with the language of the penultimate paragraph of the revised ending, the radical "break in tone." The difference between reported and direct speech could scarcely be more sharply felt than it is at this point, and it is in this that (for my students) the difference between the two endings is so revealing and Dickens's weakness so much "exposed." I cite two paragraphs everyone knows by heart.

> (1) I was very glad afterwards to have had the interview; for, in her face and in her voice, and in her touch, she gave me the assurance, that suffering had been stronger than Miss Havisham's teaching, and had given her a heart to understand what my heart used to be.

> (2) "But you said to me," returned Estella, very earnestly, " 'God bless you, God forgive you!' And if you could say that to me then, you will not hesitate to say that to me now—now, when suffering has been stronger than all other teaching, and has taught me to understand what your heart used to be. I have been bent and broken, but—I hope—into a better shape. Be as considerate and good to me as you were, and tell me we are friends."

Why should the students object to this sort of talk when they have weathered the most melodramatic, declamatory ballyhoo at Miss Havisham's? What

4. *Great Expectations*, ed. Robin Gilmour, 447; Sadrin, ch. 12; Richard J. Dunn, "Far Far Better Things: Dickens' Later Endings," *DSA* 7 (1978): 21–36; and n. 2 above.

is happening—and this again may reflect the novelist's weariness—is that Dickens simply deputizes Estella to speak for the narrator; what would sound at least inoffensive in the mouth of the observer sounds (to my students) unpleasantly intrusive in the speaker's. In back of this stylized lingo we have, I think, rather different conceptions of Estella, which have also gone begging for attention. In the original ending she remains very much the lady, the *grande dame*, who seems to be more at home in Piccadilly than in Shropshire, who maintains a certain agreeably lofty distance and acts even a trifle condescending. However much she has aged, however much her suffering excels Miss Havisham's teaching, the resemblance is close enough so that we recognize the Estella whom we loved to hate—and who hasn't, for all her griefs, gotten Richmond quite out of her system. The altered ending involves (for my students) a face-lift—but then the sight of the face-lift in turn is obscured by the sight of Estella's picking her moral scabs. As a result, instead of feeling at least a little sorry for her, the students, when they aren't up in arms, laugh at Estella's penitential prattle.

(7) The meeting in Piccadilly is always called an "accident."[5] On empirical grounds alone (to be a pigsticker about this) the Piccadilly meeting is, of course, no such thing: if anything, the meeting in Satis House is an accident. You are much more likely, after an eight-year absence, to run into an old chum at a time and in a place entirely disconnected from local associations in the past than to collide with him or her, as Pip collides with Estella—of all places and of all nights—in the very spot from which, after years of childhood togetherness, they both have been separated for years, in the very nick of time, on the eve of Estella's last visit. Naturally, the novel can absorb such coincidences, which are perhaps hardly felt to be coincidences by the reader. Still, one ought not to miscall the thing in the name of artistic seemliness and to foist on the West End the sins of the brewery garden.[6]

Without our torturing the vocabulary, insofar as "coincidence" plays a role in the final passage at all, we have to admit that the meeting in Piccadilly is far more nearly in line with Dickens's very notion of chance—and in back of this his fascination with the whole weirdly chancy way in which people happen to meet. The passage in which Forster describes Dickens's view of coincidence has often been cited; it is worth quoting again:

> On the coincidences, resemblances, and surprises of life, Dickens liked especially to dwell, and few things moved his fancy so pleasantly. The world, he would say, was so much smaller than we thought; we were all so connected by fate without knowing it; people supposed to be far apart were so constantly elbowing each other; and to-morrow bore so close a resemblance to nothing half so much as to yesterday.[7]

5. By R. George Thomas, *Charles Dickens*: Great Expectations, 54; Greenberg, "On Ending *Great Expectations*," 156; Millhauser, "*Great Expectations*: The Three Endings," 274; Leavis, "How We Must Read *Great Expectations*," 425; Meckier, "A Defense of the Second Ending," 36–37.
6. An advocate of the ruined garden seems to me to hit the nail on the head in a wonderful parenthetical qualifier—italics mine: "Accepting without question the appropriateness of the meeting—*the convincing atmosphere and medium of the narrative cleverly discourage our calculating the probability of their coming across each other that particular evening in December*—we are moved in our hearts by Pip's obvious happiness and by the inference we draw from his final words." See David Paroissien, ed., *Selected Letters of Charles Dickens* (Boston: Twayne Publishers, 1985), 290–91.
7. Forster, book 1, chapter 5; Hoppé 2, 59. On Dickens's defense of the use of "the interposition of accident * * * where it is strictly consistent with the whole design," see his very important letter to Bulwer of June 5, 1860 (PL 9, 259–60).

The last clause might well invite you to interpret the final scene in the garden as a conscious echo of earlier meetings—the tomorrow (or today) that recalls yesterday. But the whole drift of the passage, when taken together with strikingly similar passages throughout Dickens's novels, favors the notion that in the Dickens universe the "coincidence" of Piccadilly is so much the rule that to all intents it cancels out its coincidentality—or that this kind of coincidentality turns into its epistemological opposite, that is, the norm. "What connection can there be," Dickens asks in a well-known passage in chapter 15 of *Bleak House*, "between many people in the innumerable histories of this world, who, from opposite sides of great gulfs, have nevertheless been very curiously brought together!" Dickens uses very nearly the same language in chapter 2 of *Little Dorrit*, when in answer to one of her fellow passengers' parting "Good-bye! We may never meet again," the one unsociable, independent soul on board ("a handsome young Englishwoman who had . . . either withdrawn herself from the rest or been avoided by the rest") tells him: "In our course through life we shall meet the people who are coming to meet us, from many strange places and by many strange roads . . . and what it is set to us to do to them, and what it is set to them to do to us, will all be done"; and she goes on to compound the well-meaning gent's discomfiture by informing his daughter that "you may be sure that there are men and women already on their road, who have their business to do with you. . . . They may be coming hundreds, thousands, of miles over the sea there; they may be close at hand now; they may be coming, for anything you know, or anything you can do to prevent them." To be sure, Miss Wade's words suggest that coincidence is finally tantamount or akin to something like fate, and thus predestined. But they are as much Dickens's as Miss Wade's, and similar passages can be found in *A Tale of Two Cities*. And what is common to all of them is the unpredictability and ineluctability of the event (*che sarà sarà*) as well as the underlying notion of spatial remoteness. These characters are going to meet somewhere, but who is to say where? Probably anywhere: this is the nature of Dickensian coincidence. Estella happens to be in town from Shropshire, Pip from Cairo: "people who are supposed to be far apart"; Pip and Estella are brought together "from opposite sides of great gulfs"; "people . . . are coming to meet us, from many strange places and by many strange roads." If my reading of this is correct, then the chance meeting in Piccadilly is the genuine Dickens article, and the carefully staged encounter in the ruined garden isn't. Part of the trouble with the garden scene is just that—its pure *staginess*—which may be one reason why Shaw, pioneering champion of the first ending, or *Why She Would Not* (whose stage directions are almost as much fun to read as the smart talk they prepare you for is), turned tails and made common cause with the Second Endians by notarizing the garden scene as "atmospherically perfect."

(8) All this raises a more fundamental question. In resting their claims so emphatically on the seamless interdependence of the machinery in the second ending and the devices and themes that punctuate the novel earlier on —in relating, that is, the emblematic and thematic components of the second ending to analogical materials throughout the novel and thus investing the second ending with a retrospective weight that the original ending allegedly lacks—even the very best of these critics leave the disturbing impression that Dickens did not really know what he was doing before he talked to Bulwer

and that the real meaning of *Great Expectations*, which is essentially comprehended in the revised final pages, flashed on him only during or after the Knebworth conference. It is of course possible, though undemonstrated and even unlikely, that Dickens reread the novel after his chat with Bulwer or that Bulwer alerted him to specific clues and motifs that had been anticipated earlier in the book and could be usefully reapplied.[8] But the larger implications in back of this assume a greater degree of ignorance or sloppiness in Dickens than one may care to contemplate. Indeed, the best evidence against this is the memo to Forster already alluded to: "It is a pity that the third portion cannot be read all at once, because its purpose would be much more apparent"—more apparent, it would seem, than a good many of the Second Endians are willing to credit. And perhaps, when all is said and done, Bulwer's remains a hauntingly intrusive and embarrassing presence. If, therefore, the traditional second ending concludes my own edition of *Great Expectations* (with the first duly annexed in its finally rehabilitated form) as the only ending that Dickens authorized and allowed to appear in print, its priority is being recognized grudgingly, with a certain bad conscience and bad grace, and a sneaky desire to revert to the status quo that prevailed on June 11, 1861. That at least the proverbial one editor unconditionally prefers the original ending should by now be obvious. It is also beside the point.

A Note on Bulwer's Meddling

A word needs to be said here about Bulwer's role in persuading Dickens to alter the ending of *Great Expectations*. Precisely what grounds he alleged for tampering with the original can only be guessed at. All we know is that he "stated his reasons so well" and "supported his views with such good reasons" that Dickens chose to take his advice. Nor do we know just how far he instructed Dickens in guiding him toward the ruined garden: did he merely suggest the bare-bones fact of a permanent union between Pip and Estella; did he volunteer details? One needs to raise these questions in fairness to Bulwer; for whereas the result of his persuasiveness has in turn persuaded a lot of sophisticated readers, the instrument of persuasion has until recently been steadily damned as a money-minded cosmetician, the Max Factor of fiction, whose "imbecile suggestion" (in Gissing's phrase) Dickens should have ignored. The reader has a choice of epithets: for "Lytton's imbecile suggestion" read "the vulgar opinion of a tawdry novelist," "the opinion of a facile writer . . . devoid of genius," that of a "romantic humbug" and writer of "adventurous schoolboy romances"—"Lytton's most wrong headed intervention" is about the mildest you get.[9] Else, if you happen to like the revised end but object to Bulwer's interference and wish Dickens had thought of it all by himself, without Bulwer in the prompter's box, you take the line sug-

8. Greenberg, "On Ending *Great Expectations*," 152–53.
9. G. C. Rosser, ed., *Great Expectations* (London: University of London Press, 1964), 45. George Gissing, *Charles Dickens: A Critical Study* (London: Blackie and Son, 1897), 179, and below, p. 629; Hesketh Pearson, *Dickens: His Character, Comedy and Career* (London: Methuen & Co., 1949), 296; Sylvère Monod, *Dickens the Novelist* (Norman: University of Oklahoma Press, 1968), 476; Bernard Shaw, "From Dickens to Ibsen," British Museum Additional MS 506 90 [1897] as quoted in B. G. Knepper, "Shaw's Debt to *The Coming Race*," *Journal of Modern Literature* 1 (1971), 341, the entire essay reprinted in Dan H. Laurence and Martin Quinn, eds., *Shaw in Dickens* (New York: Frederick Ungar, 1985), 5–21, in which the essay is dated as begun in 1889 and Bulwer is teamed up with Disraeli as "a pair of romantic humbugs" (p. 10).

gested by critics like Dunn, that Dickens, while ostensibly buying Bulwer's advice, craftily sabotaged it by supplying a conclusion just murky enough to defuse Bulwer's fog-bomb. Of two leading Dickens scholars, one asks rhetorically whether Dickens "would . . . really have acceded to Mrs. Grundy in the mask of Bulwer Lytton"; another urges us to "forget that Lytton originated the change and remember that Dickens wholeheartedly accepted it."[1] The fact that nobody could have taped the Knebworth conversation and that we have no record of it has hardly prevented a nearly unanimous jury from imputing Bulwer's advice to his fair-weather commercialism or his glib preference for a conventionally comfy ending or both. Bernard Shaw's "Lytton moidered him [i.e., scared the devil out of him] for fear of the sales" sums up the view of those who see the whole deal in terms of the cash nexus; but most commentators relate the profit motive to the prevailing literary trendiness: one talks about Bulwer's "deference to Victorian sentimentality," another boos Dickens's "evident willingness to accommodate an importunate friend and a weak-minded public."[2]

Of the hundred-odd commentators (hyphen optional) who have dealt with the double ending, an increasing number have come to Bulwer's rescue in the past twenty-five years or so, but only three readers, to my knowledge, have offered anything like a reasonable and sustained defense of his motives. Of the three (their pieces all appeared as early as 1970), one, Robert Greenberg, is in fact less interested in Bulwer's reasons for selling the second ending on Dickens than in Dickens's reasons for buying it; the others, Edwin M. Eigner and Harvey Sucksmith, speculate sympathetically and plausibly on Bulwer's motives in the light of his known literary theories.[3] Greenberg predicates his case largely on Dickens's genuine belief in the soundness of Bulwer's judgment, as this is reflected not only in his reports to Forster and Wilkie Collins but in his going out of the way to take Bulwer's advice—unique in a writer who, in Greenberg's arguable reading, "never seems to have had second thoughts." In support of Bulwer's own integrity, Greenberg cites a frequently quoted memo by Dickens, written in answer to one of Bulwer's own tortured queries about the propriety of killing the heroine of *A Strange Story*, Dickens giving Bulwer the green light to go ahead and kill her by all means "so long as that, beyond question, whatever the meaning of the story tends to, is the proper end." Surely Bulwer, "having won this ready concession from his editor for his own work," wouldn't then urge Dickens a month later to "violate the 'meaning . . . the story tends to' by altering 'its proper end.' " (Whatever

---

1. Monod, *Dickens the Novelist*, 477; J. Hillis Miller, *Charles Dickens: The World of His Novels* (Cambridge, Mass.: Harvard University Press, 1958), 278. Both cited in this context by Edwin Eigner; see n. 5 below. It has even been suggested that the second ending had been Dickens's idea all along, that the thing had been written before the meeting with Bulwer, of whom Dickens wanted no more than a friendly go-ahead. But why should Dickens have lied so brazenly to Forster and so sanctimoniously flattered Bulwer? Are we to read his acknowledgment of Bulwer's godfatherly role to mean that Bulwer merely rubber-stamped a fait accompli? Thus Meckier, "A Defense of the Second Ending," 39–40.
2. Meisel, "The Ending of *Great Expectations*," 326; G. C. Rosser, *Great Expectations*, 45. In both *Dickens Romancier* (Paris: Hachette, 1953), 446, and its translation, *Dickens the Novelist*, 476, Monod submits that Dickens's and Forster's suggestibility can be explained only by their sense of class inferiority toward someone of Bulwer's credentials. With respect to Forster, this ignores three obtrusive details: that he preferred the original ending, that he wasn't consulted about the change, and that he and Bulwer were on the best of terms; see n. 6, p. 511, above.
3. Greenberg, "On Ending *Great Expectations*"; Edwin M. Eigner, "Bulwer-Lytton and the Changed Ending of *Great Expectations*," *Nineteenth-Century Fiction* 25 (1970), 104–08; Sucksmith, *The Narrative Art of Charles Dickens*, 110–65.

his intentions and Dickens's assurances may have been, Bulwer in fact experienced a change of heart about the character of the "proper end"—a twist I shall need to revert to.)[4]

In alleging as part of his argument Bulwer's initial plan to round off *A Strange Story* with the spectacle of a moribund heroine and a mournfully aging hero, Greenberg collides sideways with Eigner and Sucksmith, who defend Bulwer on similar grounds and by consulting much the same sources. Eigner accepts Bulwer's preference for happy endings as a donnée—not on the grounds always urged against Bulwer, as a sop to the public, but as a stubbornly cherished aesthetic canon. Bulwer saw nothing trendy in a happy ending at a time when the reading public was turning increasingly toward conventionally dismal and disastrous endings—Eigner cites among recent novels *Uncle Tom's Cabin* (1852), Thackeray's *The Newcomes* (1855), Meredith's *Richard Feverel* (1859), George Eliot's *The Mill on the Floss* (1860), as well as *A Tale of Two Cities*. Pace Eigner, Bulwer, who based his theories on the "durable popularity" of the time-honored masterpieces by Cervantes, Goethe, Fénelon, and the seventeenth- and eighteenth-century picaresque novelists, distrusted the fair-weather vogue for conventionally happy endings, which were being turned loose by writers of the 1850s. "I hold it a principle of true art," he wrote to his publisher John Blackwood, "because a vital element in durable popularity, which true art must always study, that the soul of a very long fiction should be pleasing"; and the same formulation is to be found in Bulwer's essays on the aesthetics of the novel. "Thus as regards *Great Expectations*, Dickens was probably urged to forego what his friend considered a fashionably unhappy ending, designed to gain immediate popularity, and encouraged to substitute for it a conclusion more in keeping with what looked in 1861 like the time-tested rules of English narrative romance."[5]

Unlike Eigner, Sucksmith is as much interested in Dickens's creative processes—the alterations he undertook in manuscript, proof, and printed text—as he is in Dickens's artistic creeds; like Eigner, he explores in some detail Bulwer's essays on literary aesthetics and their influence on Dickens. Sucksmith notes that both "in his scattered comments on narrative art and more especially in his practice, Dickens shares a great many concepts with Bulwer": he instances Dickens's uses of the multiple catastrophe, "the severe demands made by verisimilitude in the novel"; the uses of subplots to convey a sense of the society from which the main plot derives its validity; and not least the portrayal of the criminal mentality;[6] and while a dozen other Victorian writers share rather the same concerns, the link between Bulwer and

---

4. Greenberg, 153 and 154, citing Dickens's letter of May 20, 1861 (*PL* 9, 417), 156. Greenberg disposes of the "moneybags" charge by pointing out that the altered ending obviously could not have affected the sales of *All the Year Round*, in which *Great Expectations* was about to finish in either version; and the idea that Bulwer should have projected ahead to sales in hardcovers strains belief. Greenberg assumes the omission of either ending from Dickens's working plans to mean that Dickens, in what Greenberg a little fuzzily calls "an ironical, though not totally unaffirmative" ending, intended Pip to live out his life in Egypt and then, in process of composition, "at some time, perhaps in the act of concluding the novel," may have changed *his* mind.
5. Eigner, "Bulwer-Lytton and the Changed Ending," 107–08; letter to Blackwood, January 25, 1858, cited p. 106. Eigner develops and elaborates on his thesis on Bulwer as theorist and craftsman in his pioneering study *The Metaphysical Novel in England and America* (Berkeley: U of California P, 1978).
6. Sucksmith, *The Narrative Art of Charles Dickens*, 118; also Allan Conrad Christensen, *Edward Bulwer-Lytton: The Fiction of New Regions* (Athens: The University of Georgia Press, 1976), 233 ff. On "double plot," Barry V. Qualls, *The Secular Pilgrims of Victorian Fiction: The Novel as Book of Life* (Cambridge: Cambridge University Press, 1982), ix.

Dickens seems to be uniquely strong. Perhaps more nearly than either Greenberg or Eigner, Sucksmith connects the altered ending to Bulwer's theoretical writings, notably Bulwer's early (1838) essay "On Art in Fiction," in which Bulwer insists on the need for the reader's sympathetic involvement in the lives of the characters. Taking this and later essays, most of them dating from the 1860s but formulated much earlier, for his text, Sucksmith speculates that "in the matter of *Great Expectations*, Bulwer may well have pointed out that the harsh ironic fate of the hero needs to be balanced by a more compassionate ending, that too severe a judgment on Pip would leave the reader with a cynical vision of life, alienate his sympathy, and spoil the final effect of the book."[7]

This is all very fine; but one may still wonder whether Bulwer's defendants are in the last resort entirely free from a certain clammy special pleading. First we face the problem of the importance one ought to attach to the influence of aesthetic theories on Dickens's practice. The argument, convincing as it sounds in theory, that Bulwer's rules of narrative rubbed off on Dickens strikes me as highly questionable on the face of it and on the empirical evidence of Dickens's stylistic habits and plot constructions. Dickens may have been familiar with a number of Bulwer's essays and may even have expressed his praise of Bulwer's aesthetics conversationally or in correspondence with him. My own sense is that Dickens didn't care twopence for Bulwer's theories and cared a great deal about Bulwer's fiction, in which he had a vested interest. Nowhere is this more clearly shown than in the very exhibits Sucksmith brings forward in support of his argument, five letters— four to contributors, one to his subeditor—that unmistakably demonstrate the degree of Dickens's interest in narrative theory. They are about as theoretical as Hamlet's advice to the players. In other words, they are models of practical criticism, more suited to a course in writing than in literary theory, as we might expect from our brief inspection of Dickens's correspondence with Bulwer. The latest of the five, to Mrs. Brookfield (February 20, 1866), is also the best known and is always cited as an instance of Dickens's editorial imperatives. Dickens begins by pointing out the unfitness of her story to the demands of a weekly serial—a very old story by now; he goes on to specify four essential elements of a successful weekly, none of which she knows how to handle ("the scheme of the chapters, the manner of introducing the people, the progress of the interest, the places in which the principal places fall"), and he submits a brief list of suggested (or required) readings for aspirants to the craft by ticking off the titles of the novels that had appeared in *All the Year Round*: his own, Bulwer's, Wilkie Collins's, and Charles Allston Collins's *At the Bar*, which had appeared shortly before Dickens returned Mrs. B's story. The letter to Emily Jolly (May 30, 1857) expresses his conviction that the writer is biting off more than she can chew, can't possibly do justice to her characters within the confines of the story, and as a result produces people in whom no reader believes. One of the figures, as he nicely puts it, "carries a train of anti-climax after her"; another is "for ever exploding like a great firework without any background, . . . glares and wheels and hisses, and goes

---

7. Sucksmith, 117. See "On Art in Fiction," *Pamphlets and Sketches*, Knebworth Edition, 34 (1874), 344 ff.; on Sucksmith's comments on the essay, 113–19. My quibbles in despite, Sucksmith's work remains after thirty years one of the essential texts on Dickens.

out, and has lighted nothing." The letter to Mrs. Gaskell (May 3, 1853) mostly reflects his concern for her using the proper words in the proper places and ends on a characteristic note of friendly pedagogy: that the heroine of Gaskell's *Ruth* would never address her seducer as "Sir"—"a girl pretending to be what she really was, would have done it, but she—never!" The brief letter to Miss [Louisa Lucy Juliana] King (February 24, 1855) informs the lady that her story, as is, should be cut in half; that it has the makings of a novel, though he would be the last to send her on that treacherous journey; and that she obviously knows nothing about the way Italians talk. (An earlier and longer letter to King [February 9, 1855], which Sucksmith omits from his roster, is more substantial and voices one of Dickens's persistent complaints: that the writer, instead of letting her characters talk and act for themselves, talks and acts for them—and that only brats who speak substandard English require the author's help to civilize them.) His objection to the submission of an unidentified MS by his subeditor (April 13, 1855) couldn't be expressed more tersely: "It is all working machinery, and the people are not alive." This followed by examples of the way Wills should have handled his episodes.[8] A great many of Dickens's strictures are the kinds of things that students in Elementary Composition might find at the end of their papers: "The word 'both' is [mistakenly] used as applied to several things. The word 'all,' with a slight alteration in the pointing, will express what he means." "The Italics (of which, take care not one is left), and the marks of elision . . . are as irritating and vulgar as the offenses complained of." "I wish [the novelist James] Hannay would not imitate Carlyle. Pray take some of the innumerable dashes out of his article."[9] Elsewhere he goes to absurd lengths to explain the difference between *lie* and *lay*—not to one of his children but to Wilkie Collins. In effect, Dickens is telling his hirelings to "speak the speech . . . trippingly on the tongue . . . nor do not saw the air too much with your hands, thus . . . be not too tame, neither; but let your own discretion be your tutor. Suit the action to the word, the word to the action. . . . Go make you ready." In none of this do I detect the metaphysical strains the commentators praise in him in their efforts to stress his discipleship to Bulwer.

Then, too, I find it hard to believe that Bulwer was quite the disinterested arbiter elegantiarum he is made out to be and to ignore the consensus of writers, alluded to earlier, who make an issue of Bulwer's "uncanny sense of the literary market"; his "almost uncanny knack for perceiving what the reading public wanted and providing it"; his genius as an "infallible reflector of changes in taste," somebody who hoodwinked the public by "habitually us[ing] his literary dexterity to pass off mere smattering of scholarship"; and so on. Even Eigner, in the essay from which I have quoted, gives Mammon his due: whether or not Bulwer really grasped the implications of the fad for tear-jerking endings, he couldn't have missed its commercial implications, "for he must have remembered that years before, when his literary theories were unformed, both he and Dickens had achieved great popular success with unhappy conclusions. Bulwer's all-time best-seller, *Rienzi*, had ended tragically, and the great heartthrob of English fiction before Little Nell had been provided by the death of Nydia in *The Last Days of Pompeii*. Clearly

8. To Mrs. Brookfield, NL 3, 461–62; to Emily Jolly, PL 8, 335–36; to Mrs. Gaskell, PL 7, 76; to Miss King, PL 7, 546–47, 529–30; to W. H. Wills, PL 7, 590–91.
9. January 2, 1862 (PL 10, 2); November 15, 1855 (PL 7, 745); July 11, 1851 (PL 6, 430).

there was money to be made through tears."[1] And the top-notch writer on the Newgate Novel, in his comments on *Eugene Aram*, damns Bulwer for ruining an "original and important theme" by "subject[ing] it to indignity and triviality . . . [and] cheapening the whole with a plaster covering of sentiment according to current fashions."

Hollingsworth is referring to what is probably Bulwer's most notorious change in one of his own novels, the change he undertook in overhauling *Eugene Aram* in an effort to silence his readers. What fascinates Bulwer in *Aram* are the mental operations and the behavior of the criminal, a subject that was to mesmerize Dickens in nearly every novel from *Oliver Twist* to *Edwin Drood*. *Aram* is based on historical incidents, a murder committed in 1744 by Aram and one Richard Houseman and Aram's execution in 1759. The case made considerable noise in its own day and it had just gotten a new lease on life by the publication of a hugely successful recital piece, Thomas Hood's "The Dream of Eugene Aram"—the "Invictus" or "If" of the 1820s. The story of Aram's crime had all the trappings of a great novel, and it's a shame that it had to be wasted on Bulwer. The murder was the more remarkable for having been committed not by some career criminal like Dick Turpin but by a modest village schoolmaster and, as nearly as this can be established, a self-taught scholar of arcane languages—Chaldee, Celtic, Arabic, Hebrew. Like any historical novelist, Bulwer tinkers with the historical Aram by turning the schoolmaster into a brooding, overwrought intellectual, and he Bulwerizes a sordid murder into the desperate act of a middle-aged mini-Raskolnikov, goaded by poverty, illness, and hubris into an act of violence almost in spite of himself. The romantic element is provided by a wealthy young infatuée who is determined to marry Aram, just as her spurned lover, while traveling to forget his lost Lenore, unearths instead evidence that Aram had been his father's killer. "Bulwer," as Hollingsworth notes, "tidied Aram up for romantic presentation, making him attractive in everything except the central fact of being a murderer."[2]

The fact of the murder obviously couldn't be undone, anymore than the executions of John the Baptist or Marie Antoinette.[3] Bulwer undid it anyway, though not just then. *Aram* became an instantaneous best-seller, and what is bound to strike us as fustian now, both in Aram's deadly monologues and Bulwer's psychobabble, appeared in its own day to be profound and innovative. (Wopsle would have had a field day with Aram's morose communings—Bulwer's penchant for italicizing his sentences providing him with a clue how to read his lines.) But in the years after its appearance the public turned against the glorification of these first-degree homicides, especially a fright like

1. Eigner, "Bulwer-Lytton and the Changed Ending," 107; Kathleen Tillotson, *Novels of the Eighteen-Forties* (London: Oxford University Press [1954], 2nd impression, 1961), 85 n. 2, quoting Matthew Whiting Rosa, *The Silver Fork School: Novels of Fashion Preceding "Vanity Fair"* (New York: Columbia University Press, 1936), 86; John Cloy, "Two Altered Endings," 170; Tillotson, *Novels of the Eighteen-Forties*, 141; Shaw, "From Dickens to Ibsen," as quoted in Knepper, "Shaw's Debt to *The Coming Race*," 341; Sadleir, *Bulwer: A Panorama*, 251; Wolff, *Strange Stories*, 151; Hollingsworth, *The Newgate Novel*, 91–92.
2. Hollingsworth, *The Newgate Novel*, 86–87.
3. It could, but preferably with characters who (insofar as they aren't anyhow fictitious and therefore free to be parodied) have at least passed into the realm of the legendary. Thus, Joan of Arc, who was burned at the stake in 1431, can be transformed into a soldier who dies on the battlefield (Schiller), a Protestant (Shaw), an American factory worker (Brecht), a Nazi victim in occupied France headed for a euthanasia hospital disguised as a nunnery (Brecht/Feuchtwanger), a Joan of Arc who enjoys a happy ending (Anouilh), etc. This, however, exonerates neither Bulwer nor Eugene Aram.

Aram, who, in addition to everything else, had deserted his wife and seven children. In a preface to *Aram* written in 1840 for a new edition of his collected novels—some twenty by then—Bulwer defended his treatment of Aram by setting him apart from your normal everyday thug as someone whose views are completely at variance with "those with which profligate knavery and brutal cruelty revolt and displease us in the literature of Newgate and the Hulks." As Byron might have said, "He was the mildest mannered man / that ever scuttled ship or cut a throat." Evidently, by the (unwritten) laws of historical fiction, Bulwer was entitled to introduce characterological changes he felt would make Aram more palatable to the public than the real one. But by 1849, ninety years after Aram had been hanged for murder and seventeen years after Bulwer had stuck to the verdict the judge had handed him, Bulwer trespassed across the threshold of the credible by giving the novel as happy an ending as you could wish, short of reviving Aram: he announced that he had changed his mind about Aram's guilt and that (never mind the conclusive evidence) someone of Aram's mettle couldn't have killed a fly. From 1849 on, then, the Eugene Aram you read about is guilty of nothing more than being accessory to the robbery that led to a murder wholly at odds with his nature.

Is Bulwer being serious or hoodwinking the lot of us? Had any other writer played any trick like that, we should all cry foul. But with Bulwer you're never quite safe. In him, an uncanny sense of the market seems to have coexisted with a superstitious view of the world, the flesh, and the spirit that mocked all rational ordinances and found refuge in "the fascination of the incomprehensible"—to steal Conrad's jesuitical rhetoric out of his own mouth. Even Dickens, who for all his distrust of eccentrics, liked Bulwer dearly, thought him a rather weird client, though a canny, useful, and pretty expensive one. Sadleir, who is particularly down on *Aram*, simply caves in by commenting on the futility of judging the book by "standards purely literary," and he faults the critics who fault Bulwer as a trendy hack, for missing the point: "They ignore one element in his novel-writing—the opportunist element of giving the public what it wanted. . . . Logic in characterisation, accuracy in legal procedure, retention of historical fact—all these were unimportant beside the imperative need to conciliate the taste . . . of the day." But Sadleir's anathema leads him into the more intriguing problem of Bulwer's private epistemological perplexities and the broad road that leads from success to imposture and self-deception: "Unfortunately . . . opportunism grew with success into a second nature. Not only, while he was actually writing *Eugene Aram*, did Bulwer begin to believe in his own rendering of the murderer's character—indeed, later on, he became so convinced that the man had been in fact innocent of the crime that he altered the novel's ending."[4] In his *Treatise on Human Nature* (part 3, section 5) Hume had written that "an idea of the imagination may acquire such a force and vivacity, as to pass for an idea of the memory, and counterfeits its effects on the belief and judgment." In the case of *Aram*, though, external pressure may have acted more forcibly than wishful thinking, and it is at least reasonable to take under advisement the conclusion that "taking the line of least resistance himself,

---

4. Sadleir, *Bulwer: A Panorama*, 251–52.

Bulwer was ready to impose it on his friend."[5] Admittedly, the changed ending of *Aram* is separated from the changed ending of *Great Expectations* by fully twelve years—nor is the magnitude of the change the same. More pertinent and instructive—because so much closer in time to the composition of *Great Expectations* and the occasion, as we saw, of a good deal of correspondence between Knebworth and Gad's Hill—is the conclusion of *A Strange Story*, the serial that was to succeed Dickens's novel in *All the Year Round*; and here I need to revert to the text I took for an airing early on in this essay.

Not the least of the worries Bulwer kept foisting on Dickens had to do with the ending of *A Strange Story*. Should the heroine die? or should the heroine live? In line with the logic of the narrative and his professed aesthetic on the superior merits of unhappy endings, Bulwer tried to persuade Dickens, though nervously, that he thought the girl had better die and her lover decline into old age; what did Dickens think about that? Absolutely, said Dickens: "As to Isabel's dying [the heroine's working name] and Fenwick's growing old, I would say, that, beyond question, whatever the meaning of the story tends to, is the proper end."[6] The Pilgrim editors wittily annotate this, "In fact, Lilian recovers."[7] But somewhere along the line, Bulwer discovered a different, still more logical meaning, which entailed an equally logical and appropriate ending, and having just persuaded his mentor, guide, and publisher to bring his ever-diverse pair to the fateful rails, could he himself do any less for *his* principals?

Bulwer, as I said, looked on his people as so many little building blocks, on each of whom he pinned some scientific or pseudoscientific label. First we have the narrator and hero, young Dr. Fenwick (Dickens didn't think the name Fenwick "startling enough") who breezes into the town of L— (Dickens, who thought these dashes puerile, asked Bulwer to invent a fictitious place-name instead, but Bulwer liked his L— and stuck to it); and to Fenwick, who has written a book disproving the reality of a higher power, Bulwer parcels out the "Image of Intellect, Obstinately Separating All Its Inquiries from the Belief in the Spiritual Essence and Destiny of Man" (capitals mine). Fenwick himself introduces himself as "espous[ing] a school of medical philosophy severely rigid in its inductive logic," as contemptuous of people "who accepted with credulity what they could not explain by reason," and as somebody whose "favorite phrase was 'common sense.'"[8] (To anybody familiar with Bulwer the phrase "common sense" carries roughly the same deadly charge that, say, the information that "Ivan Ilyich was totally happy" carries in Tolstoy.) Fenwick's mettle is put to the test almost at once, when he is picked to supplant his chief rival doctor, whom society dismisses as a crackpot once he takes up "somnambular clairvoyance"; and, as Bulwer writes, "while cracked poets may be all the better for being cracked, doctors are not." The doctor's humiliation brings on a stroke (we are only at the end of chapter 2) and his dying malediction on Fenwick: "Verily, retribution shall await you! Hist! I see them already! The gibbering phantoms are gathering round you!"[9]

5. John Cloy, "Two Altered Endings: Dickens and Bulwer Lytton," *University of Mississippi Studies in English* NS 10 (1992): 172.
6. *PL* 9, 17.
7. Ibid., n. 2.
8. Preface, ix and *A Strange Story*, p. 8.
9. *A Strange Story*, p. 15.

Little wonder these early horrors kept Dickens and Georgina awake and justified Dickens's most sanguine prognostics.

Then things begin to slow down. About one fourth into the book, L— (and
the novel) are startled out of their slumbers by the arrival of a dazzling young
stranger, a species of *enfant sauvage*, who lacks any conscience, warbles
strange Eastern chants at the sun, is deadly scared of growing old, and tries
to horn in on Fenwick's experiments. This gate-crasher has been assigned to
personate "the image of sensuous, soulless Nature, such as the Materialists
had conceived it."[1] Fenwick has meanwhile fallen in love with an eighteen-
year-old, a beautiful, impressionable, ailing young heiress, "one of the elfin
people," whose tag reads: "erring but pure-thoughted visionary, seeking overmuch on this earth to separate soul from mind, till innocence itself is led
astray * * * and reason is lost in the space between earth and the stars." We
may define these three people as Mind, Animal Energy, and Soul. The Ap-
pollonian Stranger, or Luminous Shadow, gains control over young Lilian,
whose soulfulness he hopes to exploit as a way of prolonging his life; literally
entranced by the Shadow, she vanishes from L—. Eventually, she and Fenwick attempt to start a new life in Australia (which Bulwer, who had been
secretary of state for the colonies in 1859, romanticizes in the by then fashionable way); the final pages are taken up by an exorcism designed to exorcise
all competing exorcisms; the Shadow is scalded to death (I think); and Lilian,
who has been sickly or slumbering through most of the book, intermittently
close to death, enjoys a lovely, unexpected recovery.

Marionettes can be moved about pretty much at will; and Bulwer had his
puppets all ready for Dickens to look at. The point of his romance, as he
rationalized it, was to bring about Fenwick's conversion by curing him of his
godless intellectualism, and, redressing the balance, to bring about Lilian's
metamorphosis by curing her of her lymphatic and narcoleptic intervals and
restoring her Mind. But we had better take a leaf out of Bulwer and quote
him directly, if only on paper: "Fenwick is the type of the intellect that
divorces itself from the spiritual * * * ; Lilian is the type of the spiritual
divorcing itself from the intellectual, and indulging in mystic ecstasies which
end in the loss of reason. Each has need of the other, * * *—Fenwick recognising soul and God thro' love and sorrow * * * ; Lillian struggling back
to reason and life."[2] By the time Bulwer despatched this, he seems to have
discarded an earlier and in many ways more natural outcome, which Dickens
had approved from the start. In other words, Bulwer had at least two objects
in mind, both of which he discarded. Since Lilian had been pining away to
the point where she has got to perish from this Earth, it seemed reasonable
to conclude the book with her death—not, of course, a death that would be
made meaningless by her persistent imbecility but one that presumed a reconciliation with Fenwick. And since Fenwick himself has been converted to
a belief in the immortality of the soul and hence a reunion more permanent
than their earthly one, it made sense to grant him his allotted life span and
anticipate their togetherness in the Kingdom Everlasting. What we should
have expected and what Bulwer had had in mind, would have been a slow
fade-out. Instead—whatever his good intentions and Dickens's assurance that

---

1. Preface, ix.
2. Victor Lytton, *Life* 2, 346. For a fuller explanation, see Bulwer's letter to Dickens of late December
1860 (*PL* 9, 571–73).

his good intentions were also the most nearly logical ones—Bulwer not only refrained from killing his heroine but rescued her in the last pages of the novel in a breathless photo-finish that makes the "hurriedly telescoped" ending of *Great Expectations* sound slower than Wagner's *Ring* or Bruckner's Ninth Symphony in comparison; and he discharged his hero, who was to fade into pious old age, at the pinnacle of his manhood.

Literary history has provided us with a simultaneously happy and unhappy ending: an unexpectedly happy ending to the narrative (presuming our preference for happily married couples in L— to partners in heaven); an unexpectedly dismal balance on the account books of *All the Year Round*. Technically, of course, we are not dealing with two different endings, since the unhappy one never materialized; but de facto there probably are two, the one Bulwer meant to write and the one he decided to write. Anybody who has read this far may feel that he has heard all this before. With all their differences—in ancestry, income, professional success, degree of intimacy with their sponsor—the similarities of Bulwer and Lever, in the context in which I discussed them, are uncomfortably out in the open. Contributors who got off to a slam-bang start; whose powers as storytellers dwindled within a few weeks, the initial excitement giving way to blank tedium; who, as a result, within weeks lost their audiences (one because his hero soliloquized himself to death, the other because his lost himself in gothic metaphysics); whose stories had to be sped to a premature end by the Conductor; and who, at the very last moment and as if to make up for all that dawdling, propitiated the readers by giving them two endings apiece. Had there been two authentic alternatives, we have at least the assurance that they would have spawned less discussion than the two endings of *Great Expectations*. Or so one would hope.

BACKGROUNDS

DICKENS'S LETTERS ON *GREAT EXPECTATIONS*†

As one of England's great letter writers, Dickens has often been coupled with Keats. At their best, his letters display the same vitality and delight in language his novels display so abundantly. The example of Keats calls to mind an important reservation, however, one that is perhaps best expressed in Bernard Shaw's testy dismissal of them (in conversation with Dickens's biographer) as " 'roast beef and Yorkshire pudding letters,' explaining that what he meant * * * was that they were all concerned with things done, places visited, what people looked like and how they acted, limited to the concrete, sensuous, and immediate, that Dickens had nothing to say about art, philosophy, sociology, religion—in short, no interest in what Shaw has elsewhere called 'the great synthetic ideals.' "[1] Shaw's judgment is patently biased and ignores the many letters in which Dickens talks openly, even eagerly, about his craft and writing habits. Still, his letters can be disappointing to anybody who looks for subtle aesthetic formulations and confessions of the artist. Even for a novelist habitually reticent about these things, Dickens is exceptionally reserved in his comments on *Great Expectations*. By and large, he tends to be most revealing about his work when writing from abroad, eager to keep John Forster and Wilkie Collins abreast of his intentions and progress; when in town he could broach such matters conversationally. But no student of the novel can ignore the available correspondence: the dozen brief letters we have form a sort of running commentary on the novel-in-the-making, especially those, to Forster and Charles Lever, that deal with the origin of the book, and the bundle to Bulwer, Collins, and Forster, in which Dickens vindicates the altered ending. In printing titles, I have followed Dickens's inconsistent use of italics.

To John Forster

[?Mid-September 1860]

For a little piece I have been writing—or am writing; for I hope to finish it to-day—such a very fine, new, and grotesque idea has opened upon me, that I begin to doubt whether I had not better cancel the little paper, and reserve the notion for a new book. You shall judge as soon as I get it printed. But it so opens out before *me* that I can see the whole of a serial revolving on it, in a most singular and comic manner.

To John Forster

4 October 1860, from Gad's Hill Place

Last week I got to work on the new story. I had previously very carefully considered the state and prospects of *All the Year Round*, and, the more I

---

† From *The Letters of Charles Dickens*, ed. Kathleen Tillotson, Graham Storey, et al., 10 vols. (1965–   ). Reprinted by permission of The Clarendon Press, Oxford and The British Academy. All citations are taken from vol. 9 (1997), ed. Graham Storey. Page references as follows: to John Forster, 310, 319–20, 320, 325, 403, and 432–33; to Charles Lever, 321–22 and 323–28; to William de Cerjat, 383; to W. C. Macready, 424; to Wilkie Collins, 428; to Edward Bulwer Lytton, 428–29.

1. Edgar Johnson, ed., *The Heart of Charles Dickens, as Revealed in His Letters to Angela Burdett-Coutts* (Boston: Little Brown, 1952), 22.

considered them, the less hope I saw of being able to get back, *now*, to the profit of a separate publication in the old 20 numbers. However I worked on, knowing that what I was doing would run into another groove; and I called a council of war at the office on Tuesday. It was perfectly clear that the one thing to be done was, for me to strike in. I have therefore decided to begin the story as of the length of the *Tale of Two Cities* on the First of December—begin publishing, that is. I must make the most I can out of the book. You shall have first two or three weekly parts to-morrow. The name is GREAT EXPECTATIONS. I think a good name?

Now the preparations to get ahead, combined with the absolute necessity of my giving a good deal of time to the Christmas number, will tie me to the grindstone pretty tightly.[2] It will be just as much as I can hope to do.

To John Forster

[6 October 1860]

The sacrifice of *Great Expectations* is really and truly made for myself. The property of *All the Year Round* is far too valuable, in every way, to be much endangered. Our fall is not large, but we have a considerable advance in hand of the story we are now publishing, and there is no vitality in it, and no chance whatever of stopping the fall; which on the contrary would be certain to increase. Now, if I went into a twenty-number serial, I should cut off my power of doing anything serial here for two good years—and that would be a most perilous thing. On the other hand, by dashing in now, I come in when most wanted; and if Reade and Wilkie follow me, our course will be shaped out handsomely and hopefully for between two and three years. A thousand pounds are to be paid for early proofs of the story to America.[3]

To Charles Lever

[6 October 1860, from the Office of *All the Year Round*]

My Dear Lever,

I have a business report to make, that I fear I can hardly render agreeable to you. The best thing I can say in the beginning, is, that it is not otherwise

2. The Christmas bonus for 1860, *A Message from the Sea*, appeared in *All the Year Round* on December 13. The message, stuffed into a green bottle washed ashore on a North Devon village, contains allegations of theft against the hero's deceased father, a paragon of North Devon thrift, who is cleared by the evidence of a shipwreck, a piece of paper used as hat lining, the forced coexistence on a remote island of the hero's lost brother (the bottle thrower), and the story's villain, a sallow man with the suspicious name Clissold. The presiding genius is a Yankee seadog whom Dickens modeled on an acquaintance and who engages in the unmistakably national habits of slapping his knees in spasms of mirth and starting every third sentence with a sanguine "wa'al now." Dickens and Collins had gone to Devon in early September to collect scenic material for the story, to which they contributed all but one very long chapter. *A Message* sold some 250,000 copies.
3. On the American serialization of the novel, see pp. 396–97. Charles Reade (1814–1884), with Dickens and Collins one of the triumvirs of "sensation fiction," spiked his sensationalism with topical social protest. His *Very Hard Cash*, an attack on the conditions of insane asylums (and thus an unlikely subject for *All the Year Round*) appeared between March and December 1863. Collins's *No Name* takes *its* name from the stigma of illegitimacy that is pinned on two sisters whose father, in neglecting to update his will, has deprived of their heritage. Dickens thought *No Name* "as far and beyond *The Woman in White* as *that* was beyond the wretched common law of fiction-writing" (*PL*, vol. 10, 128).

disagreeable to *me* than as it imposes this note upon me. It causes me no other uneasiness or regret.

We drop, rapidly and continuously, with the Day's Ride. Whether it is too detached and discursive in its interest for the audience and the form of publication, I can not say positively; but it does not *take hold*. The consequence is, that the circulation becomes affected, and that the subscribers complain. I have waited week after week, for these three or four weeks, watching for any sign of encouragement. The least sign would have been enough. But all the tokens that appear, are in the other direction; and therefore I have been driven upon the necessity of considering how to act, and of writing to you.

There is but one thing to be done. I had begun a book which I intended for one of my long twenty-number Serials. I must abandon that design and forego its profit (a very serious consideration, you may believe), and shape the story for these pages. I must get into these pages, as soon as possible, and must consequently begin my story in the No. for the 1st. of December. For as long a time as you continue afterwards, we must go on together.

This is the whole case. If the publication were to go steadily down, too long, it would be very, very, very difficult to raise again. I do not fear the difficulty at all, by taking this early and vigorous action. But without it there is not a doubt that the position would be serious.

Now do, pray, I entreat you, lay it well to heart that this might have happened with any writer. It was a toss-up with Wilkie Collins, when he began his story,[4] on my leaving off. But he strung it on the needful strong thread of interest, and made a great success. The difficulties and discouragements of such an undertaking are enormous, and the man who surmounts them today may be beaten by them tomorrow.

To John Forster

[Early October 1860]

The book will be written in the first person throughout, and during these first three weekly numbers you will find the hero to be a boy-child, like David. Then he will be an apprentice. You will not have to complain of the want of humour as in *The Tale of Two Cities*. I have made the opening, I hope, in its general effect exceedingly droll. I have put a child and a good-natured foolish man, in relations that seem to me very funny. Of course I have got in the pivot on which the story will turn too—and which indeed, as you will remember, was the grotesque tragi-comic conception that first encouraged me. To be quite sure I had fallen into no unconscious repetitions, I read *David Copperfield* again the other day, and was affected by it to a degree you would hardly believe.

---

4. On Collins's *Woman in White* see pp. 410, 415–16 and Mrs. Oliphant's comment below, p. 627, as well as her extended remarks on Collins in the same review (in a long section not printed here).

To Charles Lever

15 October 1860, from the Office of *All the Year Round*

My Dear Lever,

I cannot tell you how exceedingly distressed I am by your letter received this morning, or with what reluctance I wrote the note to which it is a reply, or with what care and pains I have applied myself to the whole subject.

But I do entreat you most earnestly, to understand that my original opinion of your Serial remains quite unchanged—that I believe it to be the best you ever wrote—that I think it full of character and humour—that I have not in my mind the slightest atom of reservation respecting it—that I am proud and glad to have it—that I value it exactly as I valued it when we first corresponded about it. I implore you to understand that, and not to let any feeling interpose to obscure this truth. *For such a purpose*, it does not do what you and I would have it do. I suppose the cause to be, that it does not lay some one strong ground of suspended interest; I know the fact; I have the effect before me; but I cannot be sure of the cause.

I beg and pray you not to do yourself and me so great a wrong as to think of our connexion as having been a "misfortune" to me. * * * Some of the best books ever written would not bear the mode of publication; and one of its most remarkable and aggravating features is, that if you do not fix the people in the beginning, it is almost impossible to fix them afterwards. Surely my dear Lever, not quite to succeed in such a strange knack, or lottery, is a very different thing from having cause to be struck in one's self-respect and just courage. It was but the other day that Bulwer and Adam Bede[5] were both speaking to me with a kind of scared wavering between temptation and repulsion—and each with a direct personal reference—on this very head.

As to winding up—you are to consider your own reputation, your own knowledge of the book as a whole, your own desire what it shall be, and your own opinion what it ought to be. In considering all these things you best consider me. Our connexion never can be a "misfortune" to me, so long as you will think of me in it as if I were your other self, and will recognize no possibility of any interest on my part arising out of it, which is capable of being placed in any kind of opposition to your own.

Now, do take heart of Grace and cheer up. * * *

To William de Cerjat[6]

1 February 1861, from the Office of *All the Year Round*

This journal is doing gloriously, and Great Expectations is a great success. Lever's story has been a dead-weight, and obliged me to rush in to the rescue.

---

5. George Eliot.
6. Dickens struck up a neighborly friendship with William Woodley Frederick de Cerjat, scion of an old-established Swiss family, during his sojourn in Lausanne, where Dickens rented a villa from June to November 1846 and began to write *Dombey and Son*. Until de Cerjat's death in 1869, Dickens kept up a nearly unbroken correspondence with him, which is revealing as a running commentary on Dickens's views on foreign affairs and as a chronicle of family gossip.

But it will soon be finished now, and we shall be all the better yet for that desirable consummation. * * *

Dear me, when I have to shew you about London, and we dine en garçon at odd places, I shall scarcely know where to begin! Only yesterday, I walked out from here in the afternoon, and thought I would go down· by the Houses of Parliament. When I got there, the day was so beautifully bright and warm, that I thought I would walk on by Mill Bank,[7] to see the river. I walked straight on *for three miles* on a splendid broad esplanade overhanging the Thames, with immense factories, railway work, and what not, erected on it, and with the strangest beginnings and ends of wealthy streets pushing themselves into the very Thames. When I was a rower on that river, it was all broken ground and ditch, with here and there a public house or two, an old mill, and a tall chimney. I had never seen it in any state of transition, though I suppose myself to know this rather large city as well as any one in it.

To John Forster

[?Mid-April 1861]

* * * It is a pity that the third portion cannot be read all at once, because its purpose would be much more apparent; and the pity is the greater, because the general turn and tone of the working out and winding up, will be away from all such things as they conventionally go. But what must be, must be. As to the planning out from week to week, nobody can imagine what the difficulty is, without trying. But, as in all such cases, when it is overcome the pleasure is proportionate. Two months more will see me through it, I trust. All the iron is in the fire, and I have "only" to beat it out. * * *

To William Charles Macready[8]

11 June 1861, from the *All the Year Round* Office

* * * I have just finished my book of Great Expectations, and am the worse for wear. Neuralgic pains in the face have troubled me a good deal, and the work has been pretty close. But I hope that the book is a good book, and I have no doubt of our very soon throwing off the little damage it has done me.

7. The "broad esplanade" extending along the Thames from Parliament to Vauxhall Bridge. The offices of *All the Year Round* were located at 26 Wellington Street, Strand, north of Waterloo Bridge. "En garçon": bachelor-fashion.
8. The greatest Shakespearean actor-manager of his generation, Macready (1793–1873) first achieved eminence as Richard III in 1819; his Lear, Hamlet, and Macbeth consolidated his position as rival and successor to Edmund Kean. As manager of both Covent Garden and Drury Lane, Macready played a major role in rescuing English drama from its trashy repertoire and in restoring Shakespeare's texts from their eighteenth-century corruptions. Macready had been friendly with Dickens since Forster introduced them in 1837; two years later Dickens ratified their friendship by dedicating *Nicholas Nickleby* to and naming his second daughter for him. A man of ungovernable temper, Macready took to Dickens's reading performances with unbridled enthusiasm.

To Wilkie Collins

23 June 1861, from Gad's Hill Place

As yet, I have hardly got into the enjoyment of thorough laziness. Bulwer was so very anxious that I should alter the end of Great Expectations—the extreme end, I mean, after Biddy and Joe are done with—and stated his reasons so well, that I have resumed the wheel and taken another turn at it. Upon the whole I think it is for the better. You shall see the change when we meet.

To Sir Edward Bulwer Lytton

24 June 1861, from Gad's Hill Place

My Dear Bulwer Lytton. I send you enclosed, the whole of the concluding weekly No. of Great Expectations, in order that you may the more readily understand where I have made the change.

My difficulty was, to avoid doing too much. My tendency—when I began to unwind the thread that I thought I had wound for ever—was to labour it, and get out of proportion.

So I have done it in as few words as possible; and I hope you will like the alteration that is entirely due to you.

To John Forster

1 July 1861, from Gad's Hill

* * * You will be surprised to hear that I have changed the end of *Great Expectations* from and after Pip's return to Joe's, and finding his little likeness there. Bulwer, who has been, as I think you know, extraordinarily taken by the book, so strongly urged it upon me, after reading the proofs, and supported his views with such good reasons, that I resolved to make the change. You shall have it when you come back to town. I have put in as pretty a little piece of writing as I could, and I have no doubt the story will be more acceptable through the alteration. * * *

I will add no more to this, or I know I shall not send it; for I am in the first desperate laziness of having done my book, and think of offering myself to the village school as a live example of that vice for the edification of youth.

ANNY SADRIN

A Chronology of *Great Expectations*†

An Inner Chronology

In a late chapter of the novel, acting the detectives, Herbert and Pip investigate into the past of 'Uncle Provis' at the time when he lost his little child and they try to work out an exact chronology of some early events which are seminal to the plot:

> 'I want to know,' said I, 'and particularly, Herbert, whether he told you when this happened?'
> 'Particularly? Let me remember, then, what he said as to that. His expression was, "a round score o' year ago, and a'most directly after I took up wi' Compeyson." How old were you when you came upon him in the little churchyard?'
> 'I think in my seventh year.'
> 'Ay. It had happened some three or four years then, he said, and you brought into his mind the little girl so tragically lost, who would have been about your age.' (chapter 50)

Suddenly alerted to the imperfection of our own information, we may feel at this stage desirous to establish a more consistent time-scheme and to retrace our steps right back to the beginning, looking for signposts we might have missed in the course of our reading. Dickens himself, at about this period, had felt it necessary to take his bearings, check upon what he had written so far, write the plan for the last episodes of the novel and sort out the ages of the different characters.[1]

His sorting out, however, is not perfectly congruent with the text, at least as regards Pip's age at the beginning of the book. 'Pip', Dickens writes in his memoranda, 'was about 7 at the opening of the story' and, even though his 'about' (repeated throughout when he lists the ages of the various characters) shows that he does not wish to commit himself too much, we take him to have meant that Pip was 'about' half-way between 6 and 8. Whereas, if Pip means what he says, 'I think in my seventh year', he is informing us that he was not yet 7 during the churchyard scene; and, considering that the scene takes place on Christmas Eve and that, as we shall learn later, his birthday is in November (chapter 36), we may even deduce that he has just celebrated his sixth anniversary of his birth and is therefore closer to six than to seven, which would make him a year younger than he is usually considered to have been. 'At the beginning he is a child of seven',[2] writes Mary Edminson, the authority on chronology, not 'about' 7 or 'in his seventh year', just 'seven'.

---

† From Anny Sadrin, *Great Expectations* (London, 1988), 30–43. Reprinted, slightly modified and updated, by permission of the author.
1. See "A Note on Dickens's Working Plans," above, pp. 469–79.
2. Mary Edminson, "The Date of the Action in *Great Expectations*," *Nineteenth-Century Fiction* 13 (1958): 26. Since the appearance of my book, the honorific "authority on chronology" may be shared by Jerome Meckier, whose piece "Dating the Action in *Great Expectations*," *Dickens Studies Annual* 21 (1992): 157–94, remains the most exhaustive treatment of the subject. Meckier's piece, a result of his and Edgar Rosenberg's research on the novel, takes into account all previous chronologers, and though I dissent from some of his conclusions—notably the narrowing of the date of action on the basis of a single passing reference in chapter 19—Meckier has examined all options.

This is assuredly a minor point, but it raises the question whether, on such matters, we ought to trust Dickens the novelist or Dickens editing Dickens or critics editing Dickens's own edition of his text.

[Sadrin here examines in detail the options I briefly cite on p. 78, n. 4 (chap. 12), giving as her chief sources two complementary essays: T. W. Hill, "Notes on *Great Expectations*," *Dickensian* 53 (1957): 185, and Daniel P. Deneau, "Pip's Age and Other Notes on *Great Expectations*," *Dickensian* 60 (1964): 28.]

Dickens, in his memoranda, leaves no doubt as to what he wanted us to believe, which confirms the thesis put forward by Hill: 'at that time', he writes, 'Pip is—say 18 or 19'. This also tallies more nearly with what we learn in chapter 22 of Miss Havisham's story. According to Herbert, 'this happened five-and-twenty years ago (before you and I were, Handel)'. Judging by Dickens's reckoning in the notes appended to his manuscript, Miss Havisham is thirty-three years older than Pip (she is 'about' 56 when Pip is 'about' 23 and 'Compey' 'about' 52 or 53); if Pip is 18 when Herbert relates to him the Compeyson/Havisham story, it means that Miss Havisham, who is now 51, was jilted by her lover when she was 26 and he 22 or 23, which is plausible enough; if Pip is five or six years younger, we have to accept the idea of a young lady of 20 being forsaken on her wedding-day by a bridegroom of no more than 17 or 18, which is far less likely. * * * We might actually reconsider the teller's words and take them less literally: 'Within a single year, all this was changed' might have meant simply that Pip's first year at Satis House was enough to make a new boy of him and that the following years merely confirmed the change. Yet, we cannot help regretting that Dickens should have been so indefinite about just these years and that a number of odd years of Pip's life during the Satis House period should have been lost on his way from childhood to adolescence!

Things get worked out more neatly in the later episodes. Pip comes of age in chapter 36, eight months after his friend Herbert. At the beginning of chapter 39, when Magwitch reappears, he is 23: 'I was three-and-twenty years of age . . . and my twenty-third birthday was a week gone' he writes, from which we may infer that Magwitch returns in late November or early December. He pays his last visit to the old village in the following June and leaves England 'within a month', an indication that he is still in his twenty-fourth year. He returns in December eleven years later, presumably shortly after his thirty-fifth birthday.

In its final version, therefore, the novel covers a time-span of about twenty-seven years: the sixteen years or so which constitute the main bulk of the story, followed by another batch of eleven years that Pip spends in the East between the penultimate chapter and the epilogue. (In the original version, the last meeting of hero and heroine in Piccadilly was postponed for another two years: 'It was two years more, before I saw herself'.)

Dating Pip's Manuscript

How long it took from that point for the hero to make up his mind to write his memoirs the text never says. His keen awareness as a narrator of the gap in years between 'then', when it all happened, and 'now, as I write' (chapter

32) does not prevent him from being obstinately vague as to what 'then' and 'now' exactly correspond to. He refers throughout, almost provocatively, to 'those days', 'that time': 'Since that time, which is far enough away now', as he writes in the second chapter, is typical of his phrasing.

Comparisons between the vaguely distant past and the 'unspecified present'[3] are very numerous but of a general nature, and merely serve to enhance the idea of change: Joe's house, for instance, is described as 'a wooden house, as many of the dwellings in our country were—most of them, at that time' (chapter 2); the road between Hammersmith and London is 'not so pleasant a road as it was then' (chapter 25); London is no longer the same as it used to be: 'Alterations have been made in that part of the Temple since that time' (chapter 39). The stress is clearly, as Edminson remarks, on the 'changing scene'.[4]

In spite of such vagueness, it must have been assumed by Dickens's first readers that the time of writing was more or less simultaneous with the serialization of the story. Nowhere is there any suggestion that it might be otherwise; no reason is ever put forward why the manuscript should have been shelved for any length of time and publication delayed.[5] On the contrary, one or two details point to an exact coincidence between the 'now' of the writer and the 'now' of his first readers. As early as page one, the passing remark about 'that universal struggle' must have been taken by many as an allusion to Darwin's recently published *The Origin of Species*, and the ideological debate of the book on true gentlemanliness must have been redolent of that other best-seller, Samuel Smiles's *Self-Help*, also published in 1859.

> [In the rest of the section, Sadrin discusses a number of topical allusions that are explained in the notes to the text: the references to "the Mediums of the present Day" (chap. 4, p. 28, n. 9); to "Rantipole" (chap. 13, p. 84, n. 7); to the Chatham Prison Riots (chap. 32, p. 198, n. 3); and to Lord John Russell (chap. 54, p. 324, n. 3).]

By creating the illusion of contemporaneity, topical allusions were clearly a means of strengthening the relationship between reader and narrator and of providing the right perspective (especially . . . on matters of penal and social reform). As the story was set back in time, it was important that the standpoint should be that of a man who shared his readers' preoccupations and, it is hoped, their convictions and ideals. The message would be easier to perceive, coming from someone who might be a friend or a next-door neighbour than from some remote source of writing.

Dating the Story

Dating the story proper is certainly more delicate than dating the moment of writing: 'verification', says Edminson, 'demands close consideration of appar-

---

3. Edminson, "The Date of the Action," 26.
4. Ibid.
5. The case is succinctly argued in A. L. French, "Old Pip: The Ending of *Great Expectations*," *Essays in Criticism* 39 (1979): 358–59: "it seems only natural to assume that this Present [from which Pip is looking back] is the present of the date of publication. . . . It is true that *Great Expectations* [unlike *David Copperfield* and *Bleak House*] ends in the past tense, but a past implies a present and this present, in the absence of any reasons for thinking otherwise, can only be taken as the first readers' present, viz. 1861."

ently trifling remarks scattered throughout the novel', especially as Dickens
was so very careful to make the date as vague as possible. Rosenberg even
draws our attention to the fact that many slight changes in the manuscript
obviously tended to make the text approximative and imprecise: 'a score of
years ago' is changed to 'a score *or so* of years ago'; and he goes on to note
how frequently Dickens bandied about his *abouts* and *might have beens*.[6]
Obviously, Dickens the serialist wanted to avoid inconsistencies, knowing that,
should they occur, it would be too late for him to correct discrepancies, given
his method of publication. But those critics who have annotated the text and
placed it under cross-examination—T. W. Hill, M. Edminson, A. Calder, E.
Rosenberg, to whom this chapter is heavily indebted—are all agreed that
Dickens was exceptionally consistent in this novel and has succeeded, thanks
to slight hints and period touches, in placing his story within a very precise
time-frame ('1807–10 to 1823–26' in Edminson's estimation).[7]

   The first time-indication in the novel occurs very early, when Pip refers to
his parents' looks: 'I never saw my father or my mother,' he writes, 'and never
saw any likeness of either of them (for their days were long before the days
of photographs' (chapter 1). This is vague enough, but it is a way of letting
us know that Pip was born 'long before' 1839, when the first photographic
print was made on paper by Fox Talbot, a year after Daguerre discovered the
process.

   It soon appears very clearly that the whole novel is set in pre-Victorian days.
The presence of the Hulks and the gibbet in the opening chapters is not in
itself sufficient proof of an early date, for gibbets and hulks remained a familiar feature in the British landscape long after they were in disuse. But the
last gibbeting occurred in 1832[8] and Pip's fear of meeting the fate of the
pirate would have been less justified had the events related taken place long
after that date (although we must make allowances for the fact that, even to
this day, hanging and pirates belong to the lore of children). More significantly, the general acceptance by the Gargerys and the villagers of the convict-
ship, and the gusto with which they join the hunt, seem to indicate that the
novel begins before the system was condemned by a Parliamentary Committee in 1837, and very probably before it became objectionable.

   As early as chapter 5, we get confirmation of our guesses: the soldiers who
interrupt the Christmas festivities at the Gargerys explain to the company that
they are 'on a chase in the name of the king'. There is no telling so far who
that King is and it merely implies a date earlier than 1837, the year Queen
Victoria acceded to the throne. Only later, after the cross-checking of other
details, will the King appear to have been George III and the date prior to
1820.

                                *   *   *

   But there are two indices (or series of indices) which do enable us to narrow
the margin. The first is to be found in chapter 10 when, at the Three Jolly
Bargemen, Pip is offered 'two fat sweltering one-pound notes' by a stranger.
The time-indication given by this remark has either passed unnoticed or
been the source of inaccurate approximations. Hill takes it as a sign that

---

6. Edminson, "Dating the Action," 23; Rosenberg, "A Preface," 332.
7. Edminson, "Dating the Action," 34.
8. See Collins, *Dickens on Crime*, 5 and below, p. 593.

'The period of the story is therefore placed before 1826': 'Notes for £1 and 10/- are since 1914 current', he writes, 'but before that date and ever since 1826 no note of less value than £5 was used in England'. And Calder reproduces the inaccuracy: 'One-pound notes were not current between 1826 and 1914'.[9] But Dickens was better informed: in a two-part article on 'Bank note forgeries' published in *Household Words* for 7 and 21 September 1850, he explains that forgeries had been so numerous after 1797, when one-pound notes were first put into circulation, that in 1819 a committee was appointed by the government to inquire into the best means of prevention and that 'the true expedient for at least lessening the crime was adopted in 1821' when the issue of small notes 'was wholly discontinued, and sovereigns were brought into circulation'.[1]

Confirmation of Dickens's dates is to be found in the Bank of England's publication, *The Bank of England Note: A Short History*:

> . . . in 1797 a shortage of specie developed and the Bank obtained an Order of the Privy Council authorising them to stop paying notes in gold and silver; consequently notes for £1 and £2 were issued in payment . . . In 1821 the Bank resumed the payment of their notes in gold and silver . . . At the same time the Bank ceased to issue notes for less than £5 and this continued to be the rule until 1928, apart from an isolated issue of £1 notes in 1825–26—an emergency measure at a time of financial crisis.[2]

Forgery was so widespread and so severely punished in the early years of the century that the measure adopted in 1821 could almost be described as a social reform: 'Social concern', writes Joe Cribb, 'centred on poor and uneducated people who could not distinguish genuine from forged notes, and who thus fell foul of the law themselves'.[3] In 1819 George Cruikshank, the cartoonist who was later to collaborate with Dickens, after seeing a woman hanged outside Newgate Prison 'for passing a forged note', sketched his famous 'Bank Restriction Note':

> His design is a horrific parody of a banknote, festooned with skulls and gibbets and ships for transportation. A ghastly Britannia gobbles infants, the pound sign is a noose and the note is signed by 'J. Ketch', the common nickname for a hangman. Along the left-hand edge of the note, Cruikshank printed sardonically 'Specimen of a Bank Note—not to be imitated.'[4]

Dickens was only nine when the restriction began, but it is quite probable that he heard of it even at the time: both the government motives in taking these measures and their consequences on practical life must have been discussed in his home and the connection with the world of criminals and counterfeiters cannot but have appealed to his childish imagination. Forty years later, it still appealed to his imagination as a novelist when he wrote *Great Expectations*, as the presence of Compeyson shows. And if Compeyson

9. Hill, "Notes," 184; Calder, *Great Expectations*, 501–02.
1. "Two Chapters on Bank Note Forgeries," *Household Words*, vol. 1, 618.
2. Reprinted from the *Bank of England Quarterly Bulletin* (June 1969), 212–23.
3. Joe Cribb (ed.), *Money from Cowrie Shells to Credit Cards* (London: British Museum Publications, 1986), 151.
4. Ibid.

was to be transported for forgery and Magwitch for passing forged notes, the story of their conviction and transportation had to take place during the pre-restriction days. Knowing from his *Household Words* article on forgeries how conversant Dickens was with the facts concerning bank note circulation, we can also assert unhesitatingly that Pip was offered his 'two fat sweltering one-pound notes' before 1821: had the scene occurred later, Mrs Joe would never have hoarded them in the 'ornamental tea-pot on the top of a press in the state parlour' (chapter 10).

Later in the novel, we find another reference to one-pound notes, which enables us to date the events with increased preciseness: travelling down from London to the marsh country by stage-coach, Pip overhears the conversation of convicts who are being carried to the dockyards; among them is the stranger who had, some years before, given him the money and whom he has just recognized:

> The very first words I heard them interchange as I became conscious were the words of my own thought, 'Two One Pound notes.'
> 'How did he get 'em?' said the convict I had never seen.
> 'How should I know?' returned the other. 'He had 'em stowed away somehows. Giv him by friends, I expect.'
> 'I wish,' said the other, with a bitter curse upon the cold, 'that I had 'em here.'
> 'Two one pound notes, or friends?'
> 'Two one pound notes. I'd sell all the friends I ever had, for one, and think it a blessed good bargain . . .' (chapter 28)

It is clear that when this conversation takes place one-pound notes are still in circulation; otherwise, the convict would have no reason to express such lust for useless pieces of paper money. And since the scene takes place when Pip is eighteen, we infer that his eighteenth birthday cannot have occurred later than 1820, which pushes back the beginning of the novel to a period prior to 1809.

A third occurrence compels us to push the events even further back in time. When Magwitch returns, Pip alludes to the messenger who brought him the notes:

> 'He came faithfully, and he brought me the two one-pound notes. I was a poor boy then, as you know, and to a poor boy they were a little fortune. But, like you, I have done well since, and you must let me pay them back. You can put them to some other poor boy's use.' I took out my purse.
> He watched me as I laid my purse upon the table and opened it, and he watched me as I separated two one-pound notes from its contents. They were clean and new, and I spread them out and handed them over to him. Still watching me, he laid them one upon the other, folded them long-wise, gave them a twist, set fire to them at the lamp, and dropped the ashes into the tray. (chapter 39)

The scene takes place a week after Pip's twenty-third birthday and, since the notes are said to be 'clean and new' and liable to be of some use to some poor boy, we must deduce that the date cannot be later than December 1820.

But then the margin has narrowed to the point of overlapping. For it has appeared from a previous conversation that Pip cannot have been twenty-one before 1819 at the very earliest.

[Sadrin cites the roster of bridges Wemmick ticks off in chapter 36 and the dates of construction (p. 220, n. 3); the most recent, Southwark Bridge, went up in 1819.]

We are therefore told indirectly that the scene takes place after 1819. Later in the novel, Pip, referring to London Bridge, will remark 'It was Old London Bridge in those days, and . . . I knew well enough how to "shoot" the bridge' (chapter 46). 'Shooting the bridge', Calder explains, 'involved choosing the exact moment when the current would sweep a small boat through one of the many narrow arches that were a feature of the Old London Bridge, which was pulled down in 1831'. This enables us of course to realize that the action of this particular section is 'definitely not later than 1831', but also 'indeed possibly not later than 1824', the year when the first pile of New London Bridge was driven, since, as Edminson notes, 'Dickens nowhere mentions the building of a new bridge in his descriptions of the river scene.'[5]

The time-frame, therefore, is narrower than one would like it to be and Dickens's inconsistency (the almost inevitable consequence of his mode of publication) compels us, like him, to use some 'abouts' and 'might have beens'. All that can be asserted is that Pip must have been born with the century or slightly earlier and that he was Dickens's senior by 'about' ten years.

JEAN CALLAHAN

The (Unread) Reading Version of *Great Expectations*†

Beginning with his first paid reading—of A *Christmas Carol*, on April 29, 1858, at St. Martin's Hall, London—Dickens entertained what was virtually a second career as a brilliant performer of his own work, as what one enthusiast called "the greatest reader of the greatest writer of the age."[1] Dickens crowded some 445 paid public readings into the last twelve years of his life,[2] but even before a combination of monetary, personal, and professional pressures propelled him onto the stage in 1858, he had been toying with the idea of paid readings for years. As early as 1846, after auditioning a private reading in Lausanne of a section of *Dombey and Son*, he wrote to Forster: "I was thinking the other day that in these days of lecturings and readings, a great deal of money might possibly be made (if it were not *infra dig*) by one's having Readings of one's own books. It would be an *odd* thing. I think it would take immensely. What do you say?"[3] In 1846, Forster said no, and he continued to say no on the grounds that, as Dickens himself had acknowl-

---

5. Calder, *Great Expectations*, 502; Edminson, "Dating the Action," 29–30.
† This previously unpublished essay appears here by permission of the author.
1. Jack Shaw, "Dickens in Ireland," *Dickensian* 5 (1909): 89–90.
2. *Charles Dickens: The Public Readings*, ed. Philip Collins (Oxford: Clarendon Press, 1975), xxiii–iv.
3. John Forster, *The Life of Charles Dickens*, ed. J. W. T. Ley (New York: Doubleday, 1928), 424–25.

edged, public readings of one's own books would be beneath his dignity as artist. Indeed, then and now, purists have been uncomfortable with the way Dickens abandoned himself and his artistic integrity to a cluster of baser motives. It is scarcely a coincidence that George Dolby, the most intimate and best-known of Dickens's agents, consulted P. T. Barnum in planning Dickens's tours.[4]

From the very beginning Dickens gained a sense of euphoria from watching the effects he could work on his friends by reading to them. Charles Macready's reaction after Dickens read *The Chimes* (an eighty-page Christmas Book) to a group of friends is well known. As Britain's leading tragedian, Macready might have been expected to be hardened to Dickens's effects, but no: next day, Dickens wrote to his wife: "If you had seen Macready last night—undisguisedly sobbing, and crying on the sofa, as I read—you would have felt, (as I did) what a thing it is to have Power."[5] Over the years the audience turned out to be Dickens's "fix," but to say so is not necessarily to belittle Dickens's motives for going onstage. His enthusiasm seems to have been inseparable from a genuine sense of mission: to respond to a public need that he alone could satisfy: the need to leave behind the everyday cares of "the most hard worked people on earth" and enter into a collective imaginative experience that exercised the affections and replenished the stocks of moral sympathy.

The reviews, along with Dickens's many letters in which he describes the audiences' overwhelming response to his performances, suggest that Dickens was spectacularly successful at giving them just what they craved. Philip Collins, the authority on Dickens as reader, has proposed, persuasively, that Dickens's reading repertoire consisted of "the essential[6] 'popular' Dickens," the Dickens of the Christmas Books and stories and of the early novels that had made Dickens a household word in the 1830s and '40s: *Pickwick, Oliver Twist, Nicholas Nickleby, Chuzzlewit*. Apart from the late addition of *Sikes and Nancy*, with its horrifying centerpiece of the murder of Nancy, the two dominant modes of the readings were humor and pathos; in other words, the audience wanted to laugh, cry, and indulge their emotions.

The reviews suggest, too, Dickens's enormous talent as a reader—and actor. For his readings were in fact less readings than dramatic performances that entailed careful rehearsal (Dickens claimed to have rehearsed *Dr. Marigold* two hundred times)[7] and ongoing revisions and refinements of his "scripts"; marginal notes in the reading book for *The Cricket on the Hearth*, for example, give instructions for delivery such as "domestic pathos," "surprise coming, mystery," "quick," "earnest," "very pathetic," "very strong to the end."[8] In the famous scene of the storm in *David Copperfield*, in which David's friend Steerforth drowns (the scene that Tolstoy thought one of the peaks of literature along with the Gospels and Rousseau's *Confessions*), Dickens's sub-

4. Paul Schlicke, *Dickens and Popular Entertainment* (London: Allen & Unwin, 1985), 243; George Dolby, *Charles Dickens as I Knew Him* (Philadelphia: J. B. Lippincott, 1885), 125. Another, later client of Dolby's, Mark Twain, described him somewhere as "a gladsome ape." Dolby's biography of Dickens remains one of the best of the early crop; see Jerome Meckier, *Innocent Abroad: Dickens's American Engagements* (Lexington: University Press of Kentucky, 1990).
5. *Pilgrim Letters*, vol. 4, p. 235.
6. *Charles Dickens: The Public Readings*, lxvi.
7. *Charles Dickens: The Public Readings*, xxxii.
8. L. A. Kennethe [Walter Dexter?], "The Unique Reading Books," *Dickensian* 39 (1943): 75.

stitution of gesture for language at the moment David asks Peggotty, "Has a body come ashore?" provoked a characteristically pious observation:

> Here Mr. Dickens displayed his dramatic power in a very remarkable manner. The tone in which David, knowing what the answer will be, and yet dreading to hear it, asks, "Has a body come ashore?"—strikes to the heart of every person within reach of his voice. And the answer! In the book it is simply "yes" but Mr. Dickens, in the person of the old fisherman, does not speak,—he only bows his head; and in that simple action conveys the whole story which the lips cannot speak. Acting more impressive than this we have never witnessed.[9]

Dickens's fiction, of course, is inherently dramatic in its emphasis on often oddly distinctive characters who reveal themselves through dialogue and monologue rather than through narrative exposition and analysis. The "live" Dickens used the ability he himself described as "a strong perception of character and oddity, and a natural power of reproducing in my own person what I observe in others"[1] to embody vividly for the senses the well-loved characters from his fiction. In the extremely popular "Pickwick and Bardell" reading Dickens played all eight characters in what must have been virtuoso performances.

In our own time, Emlyn Williams, who himself took to the podium as the century's most acclaimed imitator of Dickens as Reader, noted that "Dickens the actor did not do full justice to Dickens the author, in the material he chose to perform."[2] This judgment may equally be applied to the way he translated his original materials into reading texts. Philip Collins ultimately dismisses the idea that "Dickens's choice and arrangement of scripts also reflect his critical judgment of his writings."[3] But while we cannot pretend that a reading version represents what Dickens thought the heart of a work's value or meaning, what Dickens did, as a practical matter or with a view to pleasing the audience, still has interpretive and aesthetic *effects*. And any version of an original has the effect (even if unintended) of showing the work in a new light, making visible certain veins, or making us freshly aware of the importance of what is not there.[4]

II

Dickens almost certainly devised the reading version of *Great Expectations* in the summer of 1861, in preparation for a tour spanning the years 1861 to 1863. *Great Expectations* was one of five reading texts Dickens prepared but never performed; only one other, *The Bastille Prisoner*, was taken from a novel. Unlike the reading copy of *The Bastille Prisoner*, which bears the marks

9. *New York Times*, December 11, 1867. Cited in Philip Collins, *Sikes and Nancy* (London: Dickens House, 1982), 166, n. 4.
1. Forster, *Life*, 59 as cited in Philip Collins, "How Many Men Was Dickens the Novelist?" *Studies in the Later Dickens*, Jean-Claude Amalric, ed. (Montpellier: Université Paul Valéry, 1973), 153.
2. Emlyn Williams, "Dickens and the Theatre," in E. W. F. Tomlin, ed., *Charles Dickens: 1812–1870* (London, 1969), 192. Cited in Schlicke, 242.
3. *Charles Dickens: The Public Readings*, xlii.
4. For an extremely interesting study of the narratological effects of Dickens's changes for the reading version, see W. J. M. Bronzwaer, "Implied Author, Extradiegetic Narrator and Public Reader: Gérard Genette's Narratological Model and the Reading Version of *Great Expectations*," *Neophilologus* 62 (Jan 1978): 1–18; unfortunately, I discovered this too late to take it into account in the present essay.

of extensive preparation for performance, the printed reading text of *Great Expectations*, to repeat, is untouched, as if Dickens had ceased to consider it as a possible part of his repertoire as soon as it was printed. We cannot be certain of Dickens's reasons, but the likeliest one would have been the sheer length of the reading version. A typical program consisted of two selections: a long piece of seventy or eighty minutes, followed by a shorter, usually comic "afterpiece" of thirty or forty minutes. *Great Expectations* amounted to over one hundred and sixty pages—about thirty thousand words; a reading of the unabridged text would have taken more than three hours, almost an hour more than the reading text of *David Copperfield* in its initial form. Still, Dickens had successfully reduced other long readings. For example, he cut over ten thousand words from the *Copperfield* prompt-copy, so that by January 1862 he could read it along with a shorter item within two hours. Similarly, the *Carol*, which took three hours to read at its first performance in 1853, could be read in half that time by 1858. Length alone, then, does not account for Dickens's decision to omit *Great Expectations* from his repertory.

One reason *Great Expectations* was so long, and perhaps also a reason why Dickens did not attempt to condense it, was that it was far more comprehensive in scope than the other readings taken from the novels. Before *David Copperfield*, Dickens's adaptations had focused on dramatizing either one character (e.g., Mrs. Gamp from *Martin Chuzzlewit*), a single episode (the trial from *Pickwick*), or a limited area of the story (the first quarter of *Dombey and Son*). In *Great Expectations* Dickens attempts to tell in condensed form the main plot of the novel from beginning to end.[5] The main plot, for Dickens, meant the Pip-Magwitch plot. The reading version opens, as does the novel, with Pip's first, terrifying encounter with Magwitch, and it closes with Magwitch's redemption and death. Such simplicity of structure could not be achieved without victims, first and foremost Estella, whose absence, along with Biddy's, works to foreground the sentimental relations between Pip and two (unequally) benevolent older male figures, Joe Gargery and Abel Magwitch. Scenes with Miss Havisham, Mrs. Joe, and Herbert form a less extensive, but still relatively substantial, part of the text, although Miss Havisham, Joe, and Mrs. Joe vanish from the story once Pip goes to London. Their disappearance is disconcerting if the adaptation is read, but in performance the dramatic immediacy would absorb the attention, so that the continuities and connections generated by a literal or mental flipping back through the pages would not be missed. What is perhaps most immediately striking about this scenario is its so completely recapturing and dramatizing Dickens's "new and grotesque idea," the putting "a child and a good-natured foolish man in relations that seem to me very funny," and his having "got in the pivot on which the story will turn." In the beginning, that is, Dickens created Pip, Joe, and Magwitch, and these are the central characters on which the reading version will turn.

Like the novel, the reading version is divided into three "stages" of Pip's development, but the two works are sliced up differently. The first stage of the reading version, "Pip's Childhood," covers the first seven chapters of the

5. *Charles Dickens: The Public Readings*, 374.

novel and closes, after Pip's invitation to Miss Havisham's, with the last sentence of chapter 7: "But [the stars] twinkled out one by one, without throwing any light on the questions why on earth I was going to play at Miss Havisham's, and what on earth I was expected to play at." The second stage, "Pip's Minority," corresponds to chapters 8 through 37 in the novel, and takes us from Pip's first visit to Miss Havisham to Pip's visit to Walworth and his negotiation of a partnership for Herbert Pocket. The third stage, "Pip's Majority," corresponding to chapters 39 to 56, begins with Magwitch's visit to the twenty-three-year-old Pip at the Temple and ends with Magwitch's death. We can compare this organization to the novel's, whose first stage ends with Pip's departure from the forge for London, and whose second stage begins with Pip's journey to London and ends with Magwitch's visit to Pip's lodgings at the Temple. In addition to chapters 57 to 59, which form the conclusion of the novel, the reading text omits entirely chapters 6, 9, 10, 15–17, 20, 23–24, 26, 28–33, 35, 38, and 44–53. Other reading texts drawn from novels are based on a comparatively small number of chapters: *Nicholas Nickleby*, for example, has four chapters, derived from five proximate chapters in the novel; *David Copperfield* consists of six chapters, based primarily on nine chapters in the novel, though it includes parts of thirteen others. But the three stages of *Great Expectations* draw on twenty-eight chapters from most parts of the novel.

Among the episodes and characters discarded, in no particular order: everything to do with Estella (including Molly and Drummle), Biddy, Herbert's Clara, the scenes with Trabb and Trabb's boy, Mrs. Wopsle's great-aunt's school, Orlick and the assault on and death of Mrs. Joe, Joe's visit to London, the stranger at The Three Jolly Bargemen and the convicts on whom Pip eavesdrops in the carriage from London, Pip's first visit to Jaggers in Little Britain and his dinner on Gerrard Street, his strolls through Smithfield, Newgate, and his visit to the police court, the scenes at the Pockets' home and with the Finches of the Grove, and Wopsle's performances. Dickens retained two of the most charming scenes in the novel: Pip's Walworth visit with Wemmick, the Aged, and even (an abbreviated) Miss Skiffins; and Pip's and Herbert Pocket's complacent ritual of confronting their debts and "leaving a margin." These episodes are fairly self-contained and are included for their own sake, but as we shall see, they also serve the particular slant Dickens chose to present in the reading text. Despite the necessity of eliminating many of the minor characters and scenes and details, Dickens preserves his early characterizations of Mr. and Mrs. Hubble, Wopsle, and, more extensively, Pumblechook, although none of them outlives the Christmas dinner. Dickens most nearly preserved the feel of the original in his disproportionately generous use of the novel's opening chapters; what makes up one-tenth of the novel occupies one-fourth of the reading text.

Dickens, then, reduced the novel to a length suitable for performance by omitting chapters, cutting or condensing passages, eliminating sentences and even words. He went about this in certain characteristic ways. For example, in the *Great Expectations* as in other reading texts, Dickens generally eliminated from dialogue indications of who is speaking and how, that is, aspects of the text that could be performed through gesture, facial expression, and voice. Compare these snatches of dialogue:

"Whatever family opinions, or whatever the world's opinions, on the subject may be, Pip, your sister is," Joe tapped the top bar with the poker after every word following, "a-fine-figure-of-a-woman!"

I could think of nothing better to say than "I am glad you think so, Joe."[6]

"Whatever family opinions, or whatever the world's opinions on that subject may be, Pip, your sister is a fine figure of a woman."

"I am glad you think so, Joe!"[7]

The removal of even such small details of gesture and pacing is felt by the silent reader of the performing version as a decrease in the vividness and expressiveness of the moment, but Dickens could have evoked something of Joe's percussive accompaniment to his pronouncement on Mrs. Joe through the rhythm and emphasis of his voice.

Another technique Dickens used to reduce his texts, which particularly served his larger intention in *Great Expectations* of telling the entire main plot, was to conflate two, three, or more parallel scenes from the novel into a single episode. Pip's first visit to Miss Havisham in the reading version includes parts of the second visit (the description of the mouldering wedding cake and the walks round the room with Miss Havisham) and the third visit (when Pip begins to propel Miss Havisham round the room in a wheelchair). As a result, almost immediately after the first visit Miss Havisham remarks how tall Pip has grown and pays for his apprenticeship. Similarly, the two visits to Wemmick's Walworth are conflated into one in the reading version. More materially, the crucial dialogue between Pip and Magwitch that occurs on four different days in the novel (and is spread over an even longer period) is condensed into one long conversation the night Magwitch first arrives at Pip's lodgings, Herbert returning just in time to hear Magwitch's monologue.

By giving us only one each of these scenes that in the novel are recurrent events in Pip's life, the novel's natural depiction of time—the dailiness, the sense of a gradual accumulation of experience—is sacrificed to pure straight-forward plot. The reading version is structured simply around one return, that of Magwitch, who opens and closes the story. Apart from this one return, the narrative conveys a linear feel, and the pattern of returning in the novel fades away—the shuttling between London and the marsh country, between Satis House and the forge, and the final return to Satis House at the end, that plays so vital a structural and thematic role.

To be sure, the conflation of scenes not only helps condense the novel but arguably allows Dickens to preserve some of the best parts of the original, just as in process of devising other reading texts he incorporates "gems" res-cued from parts of the novel he discards. Even so, Dickens can be surprisingly cavalier (or is it savvy?) in the way he manipulates the language of the original. Here are the first two paragraphs of the reading text:

My father's family name being Pirrip, and my christian name Philip, my infant tongue could make of both names nothing longer than Pip. So I called myself Pip, and I came to be called Pip.

I give my family name on the authority of the family tombstones and of my sister—Mrs. Joe Gargery, who married the blacksmith. The tomb-

6. *Great Expectations*, chapter 7.
7. *Charles Dickens: The Public Readings*, 322.

stones recorded that Philip Pirrip, late of this parrish, was dead and buried, and also Georgiana, wife of the above. But my childish construction even of their simple meaning was not very correct, for I read 'Wife of the Above' as a complimentary reference to my father's exaltation to a better world: and if any of my deceased relatives had been referred to as 'Below,' I have no doubt I should have formed the worst opinions of that member of the family.[8]

It *sounds* like *Great Expectations* but could only be mistaken for it by inattentive—or tone-deaf—readers. In the first, two-sentence paragraph, Dickens makes a few small changes: for example, where the novel has "nothing longer or more explicit than Pip," the altered text has "nothing longer than Pip." The effect of the first change is perhaps negligible; the words "or more explicit" lengthen the approach to and hence set off the brevity of the word "Pip"; we lose the subtle humor of placing a Latinate "adult" word next to the product of an infant tongue. We can only guess at what he would have done in performance (and he was known to extemporize), but it seems likely that he would have compensated for the omission of "or more explicit" by playing up the short, plosive sound of the name "Pip." Similarly, when Dickens adds some words to a sentence later on in chapter 1—after Magwitch's threatening request, Pip replies, in the novel, "I said I would get him the file" and in the reading version, "I said under those circumstances I would certainly get him the file"[9]—it seems fairly clear that Dickens would have emphasized these orotund mouthfuls in performance to comic effect.

An eye on humoring the audience as well as on economizing may also account for the changes Dickens made to the second paragraph of the chapter, notably the omission of the long, wonderful sentence that introduces the graves of the five little brothers. The prose sounds more flat and generic, while the sort of plodding clarity gained by the insertion of "of" ("on the authority of the family tombstones and *of* my sister") dissipates the startling, Popean equivalence suggested by the compression of "his tombstone and my sister." Dickens excises the remaining sentences of the second paragraph, and in their place inserts bits and pieces of text from other parts of the novel. Thus, the third and fourth sentences should sound familiar: they are in fact lifted from the beginning of chapter 7, where the narrator glances back at the opening scene of the novel. Why did Dickens make such a substitution? Length again is certainly a consideration, and Dickens preferred transferring shorter sentences intact from the novel to deforming the longer sentences. The joke at the beginning of chapter 7, it could be argued, is simpler, the humor broader and more likely to get out-loud laughs. By contrast, the last, mind-taxing sentence of the novel's first paragraph, with its deferred main clause, comprises eighty-five words, contains an allusion to Darwin, and is urbanely witty:

> To five little stone lozenges, each about a foot and a half long, which were arranged in a neat row beside their grave, and were sacred to the memory of five little brothers of mine—who gave up trying to get a living exceedingly early in that universal struggle—I am indebted for a belief I religiously entertained that they had all been born on their backs with

---

8. *Charles Dickens: The Public Readings*, 307; *Great Expectations*, chapter 1.
9. *Great Expectations*, chapter 1; *Charles Dickens: The Public Readings*, 308.

their hands in their trousers-pockets, and had never taken them out in this state of existence.

By the time he was done, Dickens had reduced the paragraph to about half its original length.

Among the cuts in chapter 1, one in particular sets a pattern for cuts in the rest of the first stage, a pattern that fundamentally alters the character of Pip and indeed of the novel itself, and that is the omission of the fictitious "young man" Magwitch conjures up to terrorize Pip into obedience. In this opening chapter, Dickens blots descriptive and (relatively) minor narrative passages—much of the turning-upside-down business or again the paragraph describing Magwitch as he walks away hugging himself. But in dispensing with Magwitch's companion, Dickens suppresses a substantial, dramatically effective portion of dialogue. The monstrous young man represents Pip's animus, linking Pip intimately to Magwitch, and Magwitch's evocation of him in chapter 1 foreshadows the devouring, appetitive social climber—the "robber" of Mrs. Joe and potentially of Miss Havisham, whose house is fortified against robbers—which threatens to gain ascendancy in Pip's character. Naturally, if he is to be consistent, Dickens must erase all subsequent allusions to the omitted passage. In Pip's psyche, the young man, even more than Magwitch, signifies the guilt-intensified terror engendered in him by his encounter with the convict, and to remove all references to the young man is to remove the deepest, most unconscious part of Pip's response.

Dickens, in fact, is consistent in silencing the darker aspects of Pip's psyche even when the young man is not involved. Thus, he omits a paragraph in chapter 2 in which Pip speaks of his "mortal terror of [him]self," and a passage in Chapter 4 in which Pip describes feeling the weight of his "wicked secret" while in church with Joe. Dickens also tends to omit suggestions of Pip's identification (conscious or unconscious) with the convict—Pip's twinge of empathy with the experience of wearing a leg iron, for example, and the conversation about the Hulks. The absence in the reading version of the attack on Mrs. Joe and of Pip's encounters with Orlick ensures that the connection between Pip's fear and guilt and his own unconscious violent desires is not repressed in the reading version, but simply nonexistent.

Indeed, a comparison of the novel and the reading text reveals that Dickens almost systematically dropped passages in the novel that concern themselves at all with Pip's state of mind. We find a typical example of this in the way Dickens altered chapter 39. In the novel, Pip's conversation with Magwitch on the night he shows up at the Temple is followed by nine paragraphs, most of which are devoted to the psychological impact of the revelation, and to the thoughts and memories that crowd in on him—of his loss of Estella, his shameful behavior toward Joe and Biddy, his childhood memories of Magwitch. In the reading version, all but one of the paragraphs evoking Pip's interior life are omitted. Admittedly, such passages constitute static moments that do not advance the plot. And certainly, self-dramatization through dialogue and action rather than self-observation were likely to be effective in performance. These alterations bear out Paul Schlicke's point that in his readings, Dickens's emphasis was on a theatrical "intensity of expression rather than on complexity of psychology."[1] Still, the effect is to make the story

1. Schlicke, 230.

less rich, Pip's character flatter, his motives simpler and less ambivalent, and to throw the emphasis on an external chain of events. The reading version has, at times, much more the feel of an adventure story for boys than a bildungsroman.

Other examples of the ways in which Dickens, in devising the reading text, used "cut and paste" techniques to telescope a scene or a passage of dialogue suggest that Dickens simply ignored the degree to which his alterations violated the original logic of his text. Take, for instance, the issue of Mr. Wopsle's Roman nose, a feature on which Pip mentally vents his moral indignation at being the sitting target of endless insinuations and nasty sermons during the Christmas dinner. In both novel and reading text, the paragraph in which Mrs. Joe treats the guests to her "fearful catalogue of all the illnesses I had been guilty of . . . and all the times she had wished me in my grave, and I had contumaciously refused to go there" is followed by a paragraph that begins like this:

> I think the Romans must have aggravated one another very much, with their noses. Perhaps they became the restless people they were, in consequence. Anyhow, Mr. Wopsle's Roman nose so aggravated me, during the recital of my misdemeanours, that I should have liked to pull it until he howled.

In the novel, the paragraph continues:

> But, all I had endured up to this time, was nothing in comparison with the awful feelings that took possession of me when the pause was broken which ensued upon my sister's recital, and in which pause everybody had looked at me (as I felt painfully conscious) with indignation and abhorrence.[2]

Then two events in which Pip's robbery threatens to be found out—Uncle Pumblechook's gulping down the god-awful tar water and Mrs. Joe's announcement that the pork pie is about to be served. The last two paragraphs of chapter 4 and the first of chapter 5 run as follows:

> My sister went out to get it. I heard her steps proceed to the pantry. I saw Mr. Pumblechook balance his knife. I saw re-awakening appetite in the Roman nostrils of Mr. Wopsle. I heard Mr. Hubble remark that "a bit of savoury pork pie would lay atop anything you could mention, and do no harm," and I heard Joe say, "You shall have some Pip." I never have been absolutely certain whether I uttered a shrill yell of terror, merely in spirit, or in the bodily hearing of the company. I felt that I could bear no more, and that I must run away. I released the leg of the table and ran for my life.
>
> But I ran no further than the house door, for there I ran head foremost into a party of soldiers with their muskets: one of whom held out a pair of handcuffs to me, saying, "Here you are, look sharp, come on!"
>
> [Chapter V]
> The apparition of a file of soldiers ringing down the butt-ends of their loaded muskets on our door-step caused the dinner party to rise from

2. *Great Expectations*, chapter 4.

the table in confusion and caused Mrs. Joe, re-entering the kitchen empty-handed, to stop short and stare.

In the reading version the paragraph about Mr. Wopsle's nose goes like this:

> I think the Romans must have aggravated one another very much, with their noses. Perhaps they became the restless people they were, in consequence. Anyhow, Mr. Wopsle's Roman nose so aggravated me, during the recital of my misdemeanours, that I should have liked to pull it until he howled. But the apparition of a file of soldiers ringing down the butt-ends of their loaded muskets on our door-step changed the current of my thoughts, and caused us all to rise from the table in confusion.[3]

Gone is the impeccably timed choreography of Pip's dash to the door straight into the arms of the law. Gone, too, is the dramatic sense that, for a moment, Pip's guilty fantasy world has taken solid shape in the external world. In the novel, Pip's fear of discovery has been mounting with the tar-water and pork-pie business, and he has reached a pitch of "terror" (again, the word associated with the monstrous "young man") when he makes a run for it. If the police have come for him in the reading version, they are apparently taking him up because he has had naughty thoughts about a guest's nose. And, in fact, their entrance only, in Dickens's rather dull, neutral words, "changed the current of [Pip's] thoughts": what is going on in Pip's head has nothing to do with the arrival of the police.

Something similar happens in a passage of dialogue between Pip and Magwitch that takes place the day after Magwitch arrives at Pip's lodgings. In the reading version we have this:

> He ate of my supper in a ravenous way that was very disagreeable. Some of his teeth had failed him since I saw him eat on the marshes, and as he turned his food in his mouth, and turned his head sideways to bring his strongest fangs to bear upon it, he looked terrible, like a hungry old dog.
> "I'm a heavy grubber, dear boy," he said, as a polite kind of apology when he had made an end of his meal; "but I always was. If it had been in my constitution to be a lighter grubber, I might ha' got into lighter trouble. Similarly, I must have my smoke. When I was first hired out as shepherd t'other side the world, it's my belief I should ha' turned into a molloncolly-mad sheep myself, if I hadn't a had my smoke. But this is low talk. Look'ee here, Pip. Look over it. I ain't a going to be low. Look'ee here, Pip. I was low; that's what I was; low. Look over it, dear boy."[4]

In the novel, a short paragraph separates the first and second paragraphs quoted here, in which Pip records the aversion Magwitch's "grubbing" inspires in him. The second paragraph is taken verbatim from the novel, except that in the novel the passage stops with the words "if I hadn't a had my smoke." Magwitch doesn't chastise himself for being "low" until after about another page of dialogue, and by then "low" means something very different from its meaning in the reading version, where it is difficult to pinpoint whether Magwitch feels himself low for being a heavy grubber, or for being

3. *Charles Dickens: The Public Readings*, 317.
4. Ibid, 352.

like a mad sheep without his smoke, or for referring to his transportation. "Low" has an ambiguous referent in the novel, too, but for other, more complex reasons. After lighting his pipe in the novel, Magwitch begins to gloat, to salivate, over "his" gentleman. He uses the word "gentleman" half a dozen times: " 'I've come to the old country fur to see my gentleman spend his money *like* a gentleman. That'll be *my* pleasure. *My* pleasure.' " And cursing " 'every one from the judge in his wig, to the colonist,' " he ends by vowing that " 'I'll show a better gentleman than the whole kit on you put together.' " Pip stops Magwitch "in a frenzy of fear and dislike," and Magwitch begins to apologize: " 'I forgot myself half a minute ago. What I said was low' "[5] "Low," at this point, seems to signify the sort of resentment and crass lust for (vicarious) social prestige that could be felt only by someone of the lower class—or, at least, only exhibited so shamelessly. In fact, Magwitch makes remarks about "gentlemen" at least six more times in the last part of the novel, and none of these gets into the reading version. In Magwitch's account of his standing trial with Compeyson, Dickens significantly censors everything Magwitch says about Compeyson's defense being based on his social advantages and Magwitch's commonness.

III

Philip Collins has noted that Dickens avoided all passages of social commentary in his reading texts, citing as an example Dickens's omission of the visions of Ignorance and Want in *A Christmas Carol*. In the *Great Expectations* reading text we find similar suppressions throughout. To cite one small example: in describing Magwitch's trial, the narrator deletes all references to the thirty-two condemned men present in court. Evocations of political realities are avoided too in the reading versions. In *The Bastille Prisoner*, as Michael Slater has remarked, "we hardly hear the rumblings (so insistent in the novel) of the approaching storm of the Revolution . . . the historical novel being transformed into a domestic drama."[6] Clearly, Dickens's (successful) conception of the "essential 'popular' Dickens" excluded serious references to the political and social conditions in which his audience lived.

What is striking about *Great Expectations* is the degree to which Dickens pursued this criterion for "popularity." Collins writes of Dickens's "deletions" of "passages of social criticism."[7] A close inspection of the reading version of *Great Expectations* reveals that a more gruesome operation took place that might be described as gutting. *Great Expectations* may not tell us anything new about Dickens's methods in devising his reading texts, but it shows us how resolutely Dickens sweetened away the less-than-universal truths of class, and any suggestion that these truths might shape and be hidden in the deepest parts of the psyche. Of course, not every cut is determined by the desire to avoid all sociopolitical commentary; still, what remains of *Great Expectations* in the reading version is pretty much emptied of such critiques, from Pumblechook's and Mrs. Joe's gloating contemplation of Pip's expectations, to Mrs. Pocket's lament over having married a man who is "under the necessity of receiving gentlemen to read with him" instead of a peer of the

5. *Great Expectations*, chapter 40.
6. Michael Slater, "The Bastille Prisoner: A Reading Dickens Never Gave," *Études Anglaises* 23 (1970): 190–96.
7. *Charles Dickens: The Public Readings*, xxxvi.

realm, to Joe's visit to London and (perhaps most immediately revealing) Trabb's Boy's showing up of Pip. Indeed, one is hard pressed to find any part of the reading version, except for what is inherent in the Havisham/Magwitch plots themselves, and one or two remarks on Pip's patronizing treatment of Joe, that raises the issues of class consciousness.

To be sure, structurally what Dickens carved out of his original work does have its own coherence. A look at what emerges after Dickens has whittled down the middle portion of the novel—from Pip's arrival in London to the visit of Magwitch—provides a good example of his craftsmanship, along with his soft-pedaling "unpleasant" topics and vistas. Frequently, when Dickens eliminates a long stretch of text, as he does after Pip leaves the forge, he reestablishes continuity by writing a concise and helpful summarizing bridge paragraph. After Pip "broke into tears after all" after leaving the forge, Dickens spares Pip his introduction to London in its more ugly, depressing aspects (the scenes in and around Jaggers's office), skips his introduction to Herbert and necessarily his recognition of him as the "pale young gentleman," since this doesn't appear in the reading version, and by means of a bridging paragraph moves to Pip's and Herbert's first bachelor dinner at Barnard's Inn. Pip breaks into tears, dries his tears, and proceeds:

> I found Mr. Matthew Pocket an excellent tutor, and (as he said of himself) not at all an alarming personage; and I arranged to live with his son Herbert, in Barnard's Inn, Holborn. I liked Herbert Pocket much better than Barnard's Inn, which appeared to me to be a very forlorn creation on the part of Barnard, and in fact the dingiest collection of shabby buildings ever squeezed into a rank corner as a club for Tom cats. Herbert was about my own age, very amiable and cheerful, very frank and easy, not rich, but carried off his rather old clothes much better than I carried off my very new suit.[8]

What Dickens's omissions set into high relief is a thread of plot Samuel Smiles, the Victorian high priest of self-help, might have endorsed: the friendship and the disposition of money on the part of two young men. We follow Pip's foolish youthful excesses as they lead to his corruption of Herbert (who has no expectations); we watch Pip's moral character bud once he ceases to encourage Herbert's lavishness and instead uses his own expectations to secure Herbert a position that will help him become financially self-sufficient. The relationship of Pip's giddy materialism to class issues of social ambition and social shame is strongly muted in this part of the story, which, of course, lacks the tension created in Pip's psyche by the lingering presence of Joe and Biddy in the corresponding section of the novel. There is none of the novel's painful ambivalence implicit in our recognition that Pip's disloyalty to the simple, pure-hearted working-class Joe is on one level immoral and on another necessary.

The principles dictating the division into stages of the reading version are in many ways self-explanatory, but two effects are worth stressing here. First, the division emphasizes one of the main themes of the novel, the theme of false versus true expectations and true and false benefactors, by establishing clear parallels between Pip's visit to Miss Havisham's Satis House and Mag-

8. *Charles Dickens: The Public Readings*, 335.

witch's visit to Pip's lodgings. Second, new prominence is given to Pip's good deed and the use of his "expectations" to increase the happiness and wealth of someone other than himself. The shift in Pip's character entails his acceptance of Magwitch's benevolence—an acceptance, as we have seen, that is purified in the reading version of its class casuistry once Dickens cuts from the scene substantial swatches of the "warmint's" distasteful gloating over having made Pip a "gentleman." The second stage of the reading version ends with the words, "I * * * was proud and happy to think that my expectations had at last done good to somebody"—substantially the very words, as we know, on which Dickens's Working *Mems:* end: "The one good thing that endures and bears good fruit." The critical placement of the sentence in the performing version surely corroborates John Butt's and Edgar Rosenberg's reading of the sentence as at least one of the leading morals of *Great Expectations*.[9] So put, the reading version turns the novel into little more than a heartwarming morality tale, Victorian in its emphasis on the value of hard work and selflessness and on the crossing of social boundaries through sympathy, but largely independent of a specific social and economic milieu. That the reading version ends with Pip's misquotation of the parable ought to resolve once and for all the crux it presents in the novel: it would jar no end with the purely sentimental tendencies that pervade the reading version to wind up on the ironic note some critics have perceived in this (inadvertent) transformation of the original "Lord, forgive me, a sinner."[1]

A final note, that I may have anticipated. One function of Dickens's changes is the purging of all feminine influence in Pip's story—a striking change, perhaps, but one that ought not to surprise us when we remember the novel's disenchantment with the redemptive possibilities of the feminine or, for that matter, the shrinking back into the omphalos of masculine sentimental relations from which the novel seems to have sprung. Estella and Biddy are absences; Miss Havisham and Mrs. Joe, having played their roles in the first part of the story, simply vanish. It could be argued, moreover, that in the reading version Miss Havisham and Mrs. Joe serve more or less as foils—Mrs. Joe to set off Joe's simple, loyal (if foolish) heart, specifically in the scene in which Joe informs Pip that Mrs. Joe is a "fine-figure-of-a-woman!" and Miss Havisham, who is neither rescued from fire nor forgiven, to set off the true benefactor, Magwitch. They serve this function in the novel as well, of course, but in a less reductive way. The relationship between Miss Havisham and Magwitch is certainly simplified by the absence of Estella, who embodies the connection between the two plots in the novel. Dickens may well have tossed out Estella and Biddy because they are too closely bound up with Pip's class consciousness and some of the unresolvable conflicts between moral values and social ambition that Dickens avoids in the reading version. From what we have seen of Dickens's systematic erasure of references to the "gentlemanly ideal" in the reading version, the absence of Estella surprises us less than it might, since one of Estella's foremost functions is to make Pip feel acutely and explicitly his "coarse" and "common" social inferiority, and to inspire him to move up in the world; and it would have been difficult for Dickens to avoid such troubling themes with Estella on board.

9. See comments by Butt and Rosenberg, above, p. 475.
1. See p. 453 and n. 3 and the commentaries by Moynahan and Fielding, pp. 655 and 666.

And Biddy more actively and articulately than Joe rankles Pip's conscience about his social aspirations and the values they imply and exclude.

Given Dickens's choice not so much as to mention the word "gentleman" in a self-conscious or socially conscious way in the reading version of *Great Expectations*, it is interesting that Forster complained of Dickens's reading career: "it had so much the character of a public exhibition for money as to raise, in the question of respect for his calling as a writer, a question also of respect for himself as a gentleman."[2] Perhaps we should take Dickens's omissions and elisions of serious social content as a form of class unconsciousness that, like the one Forster disapproves of, he adopted not only to make a fortune but in the spirit of a generous good will. If I have sounded (perhaps unwarrantably) captious in my comments on the reading version, it should be remembered that this, after all, has been another silent, solitary reading of *Great Expectations*, and Dickens's public performances of his works were, it should be clear by now, an entirely different—and in the end irretrievable—story.

HARRY STONE

The Genesis of a Novel: *Great Expectations*†

Pause you who read this, and think for a moment of the long chain of iron or gold, of thorns or flowers, that would never have bound you, but for the formation of the first link on one memorable day.

Great Expectations

* * *

* * * Some of the crucial themes which became *Great Expectations*, and some of the everyday experiences which became Miss Havisham and ordained her fiery destruction, can be traced to the most casual happenstance of Dickens's early and late years. In the case of Miss Havisham this is surely a paradox, for she is often pointed to as a character who is totally unreal. She is too bizarre, runs the arraignment, too Dickensian; she is unbelievable. Whatever the validity of this judgment, one thing is certain: Miss Havisham is constructed out of everyday events. But there is another, still greater irony, and it is this: Dickens consciously suppressed the wilder, the more 'Dickensian' aspects of the everyday reality he drew upon.

That reality—'the formation of the first link', to use Dickens's phrase—commenced with childhood. As a boy, Dickens had seen a strange lady wandering through the streets of London. The sight of this grotesque creature, and the romantic and tragic speculations he attached to her, sank into his memory and became an evocative part of his consciousness. Many years later, in 1853, in his magazine, *Household Words*, he wrote an essay about the

---

2. Forster, *Life*, 641 as cited in Schlicke, 242.
† From Harry Stone, "The Genesis of a Novel: *Great Expectations*," in E. W. F. Tomlin, ed., *Charles Dickens, 1812–1870: A Centennial Volume* (New York, 1970), 110–31. Originally printed by Weidenfeld & Nicolson. Reprinted by permission of Simon and Schuster and the Orion Publishing Group, Ltd.

indelible impressions of his boyhood. He called the essay 'Where We Stopped Growing', and in it he described the strange lady of his youth:

> Another very different person who stopped our growth, we associate with Berners Street, Oxford Street; whether she was constantly on parade in that street only, or was ever to be seen elsewhere, we are unable to say. The White Woman is her name. She is dressed entirely in white, with a ghastly white plaiting round her head and face, inside her white bonnet. She even carries (we hope) a white umbrella. With white boots, we know she picks her way through the winter dirt. She is a conceited old creature, cold and formal in manner, and evidently went simpering mad on personal grounds alone—no doubt because a wealthy Quaker wouldn't marry her. This is her bridal dress. She is always walking up here, on her way to church to marry the false Quaker. We observe in her mincing step and fishy eye that she intends to lead him a sharp life. We stopped growing when we got at the conclusion that the Quaker had had a happy escape of the White Woman.

Here already are most of Miss Havisham's attributes: her externals—bridal dress, all-white accoutrements, and ever-present staff (represented for the moment by an umbrella); her personality—cold, formal, conceited, eccentric, and man-hating; and her history—jilted and thereby frozen forever (she too has stopped growing!) in the ghastly garments of her dead love. But this White Woman—the White Woman of 'Where We Stopped Growing'—is not the simple figure of Dickens's boyhood. He had long since begun to surround the original image with fantasies of his own creation. * * *

His imagination may have embroidered or intertwined some of these motifs shortly after he turned nineteen, that is, several years after he had first seen the Berners Street White Woman. On the evening of 18 April 1831, at the Adelphi Theatre in London, Charles Mathews the elder, a great favourite of the youthful Dickens, opened in the twelfth of his annual 'At Homes'. One segment of the 1831 'At Home', a sketch entitled ' "No. 26 and No. 27" or Next Door Neighbours', featured a 'Miss Mildew', a character based upon the Berners Street White Woman. Miss Mildew, played by Mathews, was an eccentric old lady in white who had been jilted by her first love forty years earlier. On the day originally set for her marriage, Miss Mildew had donned her wedding garments, and every day since, in those yellowing weeds, she had made her way through London streets to a place bearing a startling name: the 'Expectation Office'. At the Expectation Office she inquires fruitlessly after her lost love. Her next door neighbour * * * dresses all in black and constantly calls at the Expectation Office to collect a vast fortune that never arrives: another theme central to *Great Expectations*.

* * *

Many years later * * * another, more fantastic cluster of associations merged with Dickens's boyhood White Woman and helped shape Miss Havisham and the basic structure of *Great Expectations*. The second cluster of associations apparently entered Dickens's mind in 1850, that is nineteen years after Miss Mildew's brief life and three years before he wrote 'Where We Stopped Growing'. In 1850 Dickens launched a monthly supplement to the weekly *Household Words*. He called this supplement the *Household Narrative* *of Current Events*, gave it a departmentalized format, and sold it for twopence. In the first issue, that is, in the January 1850 *Household Narrative*, in the section entitled 'Narrative of Law and Crime', appeared the following paragraph:

> An inquest was held on the 29th, on Martha Joachim, a *Wealthy and Eccentric Lady*, late of 27, York-buildings, Marylebone, aged 62. The jury proceeded to view the body, but had to beat a sudden retreat, until a bull-dog, belonging to deceased, and which savagely attacked them, was secured. It was shown in evidence that on the 1st of June, 1808, her father, an officer in the Life Guards, was murdered and robbed in Regent's Park. A reward of 300*l.* was offered for the murderer, who was apprehended with the property upon him, and executed. In 1825, a suitor of the deceased, whom her mother rejected, shot himself while sitting on the sofa with her, and she was covered with his brains. From that instant she lost her reason. Since her mother's death, eighteen years ago, she had led the life of a recluse, dressed in white, and never going out. A charwoman occasionally brought her what supplied her wants. Her only companions were the bull-dog, which she nursed like a child, and two cats. Her house was filled with images of soldiers in lead, which she called her 'body-guards.' When the collectors called for their taxes, they had to cross the garden-wall to gain admission. One morning she was found dead in her bed; and a surgeon who was called in, said she had died of bronchitis, and might have recovered with proper medical aid. The jury returned a verdict to that effect.

Reading about this eccentric white woman, Dickens must have recalled his own boyhood White Woman, and perhaps, if the association existed, Miss Mildew as well, for when he came to write about his Berners Street White Woman three years later in *Household Words*, he seems to have overlaid his early memories with details and associations from the history of Martha Joachim—that is, he projected upon his Berners Street White Woman the Martha Joachim–Miss Mildew syndrome of rejection and ensuing madness. Miss Havisham herself, who was not conceived until 1860—that is, not until almost ten years after the *Household Narrative* paragraph, and eight years after 'Where We Stopped Growing'—is indebted in yet other ways to the *Household Narrative* account of Martha Joachim. Miss Havisham, like Martha Joachim (but unlike the boyhood or the *Household Words* White Woman, and unlike Miss Mildew) is wealthy, is associated with crime and murder, undergoes an instantaneous breakdown caused by her suitor, becomes a recluse, surrounds herself with toylike mementoes of her past, and lives in a house with a walled garden. But Dickens—softening, as he so often did, life's own outrageous brand of 'Dickensian' exaggerations—left out such proto-Dickensian touches as the pampered bulldog, the lead-soldier bodyguards, and the splattering brains.

Selection and suppression, then, there surely is; and yet there is also a seemingly indiscriminate absorptiveness. Can scraps and bits such as these, we wonder, help shape, perhaps even help inaugurate, a great novel? And is it not curious that these trivially encountered and swiftly scanned details should become crucial parts of an artist's consciousness, or that years later they should be reproduced so faithfully, yet so wonderfully transformed?

* * * [But] Dickens was always a snapper up of unconsidered trifles; his genius made those trifles meaningful, and when an image or association held a special emotional charge for him—as the image of the White Woman had since boyhood—he unconsciously sifted out every scrap of consonant material scattered through his life, even as a magnet sifts out every scrap of iron scattered through a heap of dust.

*   *   *

But perhaps the most extraordinary example of how happenstance and association can help shape art occurs in yet another paragraph in the January 1850 issue of the *Household Narrative*. Under the section entitled 'Narrative of Accident and Disaster', just a leaf removed from the Martha Joachim history, appears the following paragraph:

> An accident, fortunately not serious in its results, occurred on the evening of the 7th at the residence of W. O. Bigg, Esq., of Abbot's Leigh. There was a large party at the house, and during the night a '*German Tree*,' about five feet high, with its branches covered with bon-bons and other Christmas presents, and lit with a number of small wax tapers, was introduced into the drawing-room for the younger members of the party. While leaning forward to take some toy from the tree, the light gauze overdress of one young lady, Miss Gordon, took fire, and blazed up in a most alarming manner. One of the lads present, whose quickness and presence of mind were far superior to his years, with much thought and decision threw down the young lady, and folding her in a rug that was luckily close by, put out the flame before it had done any serious damage beyond scorching her arms severely.

Here, in brief, close enough to become forever entangled in Dickens's mind with those other *Household Narrative* themes destined for *Great Expectations*—with made gentlemen, transported convicts, hiding one's past, jilted white-robed recluses, and his own boyhood White Woman—occurs the accident, the rescue, and the wound that he will later attach to *his* burning white woman and her rescuer when he comes to write *Great Expectations*. For in *Great Expectations* Miss Havisham's gauzy white dress blazes up when she approaches too close to a fire, Pip puts out the flames by throwing her down and folding her in coats and a tablecloth that are luckily nearby, and Pip's hands and arm are severely scorched.

[The *Household Narrative* associations took on especially strong meaning for Dickens because they resonate with "vital configurations in Dickens's life." The fact that Martha Joachim died in York Buildings must have struck a uniquely resonant chord: not only had Dickens lived a hundred yards from York Buildings for the past eleven years, but York Buildings itself was also the name of one of the streets surrounding the Blacking Factory in which Dickens had worked as a young boy. The name must have stirred up in Dickens all the humiliating memories of a time when his family was imprisoned and he himself mingled with convicts and other social pariahs.]

But the 'long chain' was only partly formed. In the late 1850s other links of 'iron or gold' were hammered into place. During the 1850s Dickens's imagination was increasingly haunted by the figure of a blighted woman in white, and during the same period he increasingly associated that figure with themes that were to dominate *Great Expectations*. His most striking antici- pation of those tangled themes appeared in *The Lazy Tour of Two Idle Ap- prentices*, a series of five travel articles that he and Wilkie Collins wrote for the October 1857 issues of *Household Words*. Most of *The Lazy Tour* is by Dickens, and most of it is autobiographical; the series was designed to give a fanciful, highly personalized account of a trip he and Collins made to Car- lisle, Wigton, Allonby, Lancaster, and Doncaster a few weeks earlier. In a section of *The Lazy Tour* by Dickens, a section set at the King's Arms Inn, Lancaster, Dickens interrupted his travel account to introduce a wild ghost story—I shall call the story 'The Bride's Chamber'—and this story, and the circumstances that produced it, shed additional light on the origins of *Great Expectations*.

The trip itself grew out of Dickens's need to escape into activity, an escape made necessary by one of the great emotional crises of his life. * * * The causes of his restlessness seemed beyond remedy. He was miserable in his twenty-year marriage with Catherine Hogarth, and he was in love with one of the actresses in *The Frozen Deep*, teen-aged Ellen Ternan. Yet a remedy of sorts was close at hand, for his restlessness was the onset of a storm of emotions which would cause him, a few weeks later, to separate from his wife. On 27 August 1857, with the storm mounting, he wrote to Collins in 'grim despair'. 'I want,' he said, 'to . . . go anywhere—take any tour—see anything. . . . We want something for Household Words, and I want to escape from myself.' At the same time he was confessing to Forster: 'Poor Catherine and I are not made for each other, and there is no help for it. . . . She is . . . amiable and complying; but we are strangely ill-assorted for the bond there is between us. God knows she would have been a thousand times hap- pier if she had married another kind of man . . . I am often cut to the heart by thinking what a pity it is, for her own sake, that I ever fell in her way.' To Mrs Watson[1] he later wrote additional confessions:

> * * * I wish I had been born in the days of Ogres and Dragon-guarded Castles. I wish an Ogre with seven heads (and no particular evidence of brains in the whole of them) had taken the Princess whom I adore—you have no idea how intensely I love her!—to his stronghold on top of a high series of mountains, and there tied her up by the hair. Nothing would suit me half so well this day, as climbing after her, sword in hand, and either winning her or being killed.—*There's* a frame of mind for you, in 1857.

* * *

'The Bride's Chamber' * * * is soon told. A scheming, mercenary man, put aside by a tormenting woman for a moneyed suitor, and then, when the lady becomes a rich widow, again tormented by her and again denied her, this time owing to her sudden death, determines that since he allowed himself to be tormented for money, and since he was put aside for money, he will

---

1. Widow of wealthy liberal MP at whose ancestral home in Northamptonshire, Rockingham Castle (the model for Bleak House) Dickens often staged his amateur theatricals. [*Editor.*]

compensate himself with money. His plan is to rear and eventually marry the widow's daughter, Ellen, now ten, and his ward, and then to do away with her. The method of destruction he chooses is slow and terrible, but within the law—through long years of isolation, indoctrination, and psychological imposition, he destroys her ego and makes her a supine instrument of his will. She soon becomes compliant and fearful, and she performs a useless litany of propitiation; she constantly begs his pardon, pledges to do anything he wishes, pleads to be forgiven. At last, on her twenty-first birthday, he marries her, causes her to sign over her property to him, and then, while she begs to be forgiven, commands her to die. The isolated girl, deprived of any will or ego, constantly pleading to be forgiven, and constantly exhorted to die, proceeds in the course of time to do just that—the mercenary man has committed a murder which is no murder.

But for years he has been observed by a young man who has climbed a tree in the garden of the house and peered through a window into the Bride's Chamber. The young man has fallen hopelessly in love with Ellen, has received a tress of hair from her, but has felt incapable of rescuing her. Now, with Ellen dead, the young man confronts the husband and accuses him of murder. The husband, seized by a spasm of uncontrollable hate, dashes a billhook through the young man's skull, and buries the body under the garden tree. Years go by and the mercenary man, fearful of discovery, remains in his dark mansion, compounding and multiplying his purloined riches. But one night a bolt of lightning cleaves the garden tree even as the young man's skull was cleft, and scientists who later come to examine the strangely split tree and to dig around its roots discover the young man's body and the billhook in his skull. The husband is apprehended, accused, ironically, of murdering his wife as well as the young man, and hanged. But even in death the husband has no peace. Every night his unshriven ghost is haunted by his innocent victims; and periodically, in doomed attempts to disburden himself, he must tell his guilty tale to spellbound listeners—Dickens at the moment is one such listener—who sojourn in the precincts of the Bride's Chamber.

* * *

The white-clad bride is treated in two very different ways, both of which reflect Dickens's state. As a wife, the bride is destroyed by her husband; as the object of a forbidden love, she is secretly adored by her admirer. The husband's chief crime, the destruction of his wife's identity through the imposition of his dominating will, is a version of Dickens's current treatment of his wife, Catherine (Catherine also is a weak, self-effacing woman, soon to be put away); at the same time, the husband's crime is a version of Dickens's treatment of his 'Princess', Ellen (Ellen, like the Ellen of the story, is an inexperienced, teen-aged girl overwhelmed by a masterful, middle-aged man). In the story this destructive domination of another's personality is accompanied by massive externalized guilt. Dickens not only makes his protagonist a murderer, but requires that the villain's ghost be haunted through all eternity by the innocent creatures he has so grievously subdued. * * * On the other hand, two other aspects of Dickens's emotional predicament are bodied forth in the two male adversaries of the story: Dickens the restless husband, in the middle-aged, unloving, wife-tormenting villain; Dickens the illicit adorer, in the young, passionate, disqualified lover. And fittingly, if one looks upon these adversaries as conflicting aspects of Dickens's emotional state, it is Dickens the husband who makes impossible or 'murders' Dickens the lover.

These emotional tensions underlie 'The Bride's Chamber'. But the emotions are wedded to images and themes that have been accumulating for years. The bride is more than a bride, more even than an autobiographical Dickensian bride; she is a version of the blighted spectre in white who had seized Dickens's youthful imagination. Here is how that white spectre appears in her new, ghost-story role:

> When he came into the Bride's Chamber . . . he found her withdrawn to the furthest corner, and there standing pressed against the paneling as if she would have shrunk through it: her flaxen hair all wild about her face, and her large eyes staring at him in vague terror.
> . . . .
> There were spots of ink upon the bosom of her white dress, and they made her face look whiter and her eyes look larger as she nodded her head. There were spots of ink upon the hand with which she stood before him, nervously plaiting and folding her white skirts.

And here is the way his blighted, white-clad bride appears at the moment of her death: 'Paler in the pale light, more colourless than ever in the leaden dawn, he saw her coming, trailing herself along the floor towards him—a white wreck of hair, and dress, and wild eyes.'

The blighted bride lives in a blighted house—a gloomy version of the isolated house in which white-clad Martha Joachim had imprisoned herself; a remarkable premonition of the ruined mansion and ruined bride's chamber in which white-clad Miss Havisham would soon be immured. Here is a glimpse of this desolate precursor of Satis House: 'Eleven years she lived in the dark house and its gloomy garden. He was jealous of the very light and air getting to her, and they kept her close. He stopped the wide chimneys, shaded the little windows, left the strong-stemmed ivy to wander where it would over the house-front, the moss to accumulate on the untrimmed fruit-trees in the red-walled garden, the weeds to over-run its green and yellow walks. He surrounded her with images of sorrow and desolation.'

Added to this atmosphere of decay, imprisonment, and manipulation, and superimposed upon the figure of the blighted white-clad bride, is the corrupting influence of money. As in *Great Expectations*, the sin of valuing money more than men pervades and integrates the story. But the pecuniary similarities go further. In both works the destructive forces are set in motion when a projected marriage is broken off for monetary considerations. And again in both works the injured party destroys himself and all those around him in attempts to assuage his injury by monetary means. In 'The Bride's Chamber' the money nexus works with fable-like simplicity. The villain, who has been denied marriage owing to lack of money, seeks recompense through a marriage that will bring him money. Dickens underlines this mercenary equation by means of a refrain which recurs throughout the story: 'He wanted compensation in Money.' The refrain, in turn, is elaborated and counterpointed by dozens of images and episodes. The villain's awareness that the white-clad bride is dead is conveyed, for example, as follows: 'He was not at first so sure it was done, but that the morning sun was hanging jewels in her hair—he saw the diamond, emerald, and ruby, glittering among it in little points, as he stood looking down at her.' The implication, in terms of the fable, is clear. The villain now has his longed-for 'compensation in money', but his treasure, as this scene hints and as we finally see, is as illusory as the insubstantial jewels which glitter momentarily in his dead victim's hair. One is reminded of the glittering jewels which Miss Havisham hangs in Estella's hair. They too preach a message of false values and deluded longing. * * *

The relationship between 'The Bride's Chamber' and *Great Expectations* is profound, but it is also limited. * * * The brief ghost story with its pervasive supernaturalism and its folklore elements is no miniature *Great Expectations*. What is of special interest here is the way Dickens enlarged and refashioned old images and motifs. The Berners Street White Woman and Martha Joachim are now associated with larger considerations: with the manipulation of other human beings and with the corrosive effects of money. Places have been similarly transformed. The walled mansion of the *Household Narrative* is now more than a walled mansion: it has become the physical correlative of isolation, repression, and imprisonment. There is rearrangement as well as elaboration. Old themes have been joined in fresh configurations: commercial ethics, hopeless passion, and murderous aggression, brought together in naked conjunction, whisper of darker connections. A great centripetal force is silently working. The Berners Street eccentric, the *Household Narrative* news columns, the break-up of Dickens's marriage, and the other forces which shaped *Great Expectations* are being pulled into orbit; Pip and Magwitch, Miss Havisham and Satis House are waiting to be born.

* * *

CONTEXTS

Dickens and the World of Pip

JAMES T. FIELDS

[Dickens among the Tombstones] †

Leaving the hurry and bustle of the Post-Office behind us, we strolled out into the streets of London. It was past eight o'clock, but the beauty of the soft June sunset was only then overspreading the misty heavens. * * * We came through White Friars to the Temple, and thence into the Temple Garden, where our very voices echoed. Dickens pointed up to Talfourd's room,[1] and recalled with tenderness the merry hours they had passed together in the old place. Of course we hunted out Goldsmith's abode, and Dr. Johnson's, saw the site of the Earl of Essex's palace,[2] and the steps by which he was wont to descend to the river, now so far removed. But most interesting of all to us there was "Pip's" room, to which Dickens led us, and the staircase where the convict stumbled up in the dark, and the chimney nearest the river where, although less exposed than in "Pip's" days, we could well understand how "the wind shook the house that night like discharges of cannon, or breakings of a sea." We looked in at the dark old staircase, so dark on that night when "the lamps were blown out, and the lamps on the bridges and the shore were shuddering," and then went on to take a peep, half shuddering ourselves, at the narrow street where "Pip" by and by found a lodging for the convict. Nothing dark could long survive in our minds on that June night, when the whole scene was so like the airy work of imagination. Past the Temple, past the garden to the river, mistily fair, with a few boats moving upon its surface, the convict's story was forgotten, and we only knew this was Dickens's home, where he had lived and written, lying in the calm light of its fairest mood.

---

† From James T. Fields, "Dickens," *Yesterdays with Authors* (Boston: James R. Osgood, 1872), 207–8; 224–26; 234–35. All footnotes are by the editor of this Norton Critical Edition.
    Fields (1817–1881), head of Ticknor & Fields, Dickens's American publisher, met Dickens during his first American visit in February 1842. Himself a familiar literary figure (he and his second wife, Annie Adams, conducted what has been called the first American salon), Fields introduced American readers to most of the leading British authors, with many of whom he was friends. The passages printed here record Fields's impression on his last visit to Gad's Hill and London in May and June 1869. The essay from which they are taken first appeared in a shorter version as an obituary tribute in the *Atlantic Monthly* (August 1870), which Fields edited from 1861 to 1870.
1. Friendly with Dickens from his days as a law reporter, Sir Thomas Noon Talfourd (1795–1854) divided his time between law and literature, rising to become Sergeant-at-Law, one of the highest ranking judicial officers, and writing successful historical tragedies. Talfourd maintained quarters in the Middle Temple, and these presumably are the rooms to which Fields alludes.
2. From 1764 until his death Oliver Goldsmith (1728–1774) rented chambers in the Temple, where he wrote his most enduringly popular works. Dr. Samuel Johnson (1709–1784) completed his edition of Shakespeare and wrote his *Prefaces* to the plays while leading a life of "poverty, total idleness, and the pride of literature" inhabiting "three very dirty rooms" in Inner Temple Lane from 1760 to 1765. Robert Devereux, second Earl of Essex (1566–1601), inherited the mansion named for him, located just west of Inner Temple, on the death of his stepfather, the Earl of Leicester, in 1588.

* * *

One of the weirdest neighborhoods to Gad's Hill, and one of those most closely associated with Dickens, is the village of Cooling. A cloudy day proved well enough for Cooling; indeed, was undoubtedly chosen by the adroit master of hospitalities as being a fitting sky to show the dark landscape of "Great Expectations." The pony-carriage went thither to accompany the walking party and carry the baskets; the whole way, as we remember, leading on among narrow lanes, where heavy carriages were seldom seen. We are told in the novel, "On every rail and gate, wet lay clammy, and the marsh mist was so thick that the wooden finger on the post directing people to our village—a direction which they never accepted, for they never came there—was invisible to me until I was close under it." The lanes certainly wore that aspect of never being accepted as a way of travel; but this was a delightful recommendation to our walk, for summer kept her own way there, and grass and wild-flowers were abundant. It was already noon, and low clouds and mists were lying about the earth and sky as we approached a forlorn little village on the edge of the wide marshes described in the opening of the novel. This was Cooling, and passing by the few cottages, the decayed rectory, and straggling buildings, we came at length to the churchyard. It took but a short time to make us feel at home there, with the marshes on one hand, the low wall over which Pip saw the convict climb before he dared to run away; "the five little stone lozenges, each about a foot and a half long, . . . sacred to the memory of five little brothers, . . . to which I had been indebted for a belief that they all had been born on their backs, with their hands in their trousers pockets, and had never taken them out in this state of existence";—all these points, combined with the general dreariness of the landscape, the far-stretching marshes, and the distant sea-line, soon revealed to us that this was Pip's country, and we might momently expect to see the convict's head, or to hear the clank of his chain, over that low wall.

We were in the churchyard now, having left the pony within eye-shot, and taken the baskets along with us, and were standing on one of those very lozenges, somewhat grass-grown by this time, and deciphering the inscriptions. On tiptoe we could get a wide view of the marsh, with the wind sweeping in a lonely limitless way through the tall grasses. Presently hearing Dickens's cheery call, we turned to see what he was doing. He had chosen a good flat gravestone in one corner (the corner farthest from the marsh and Pip's little brothers and the expected convict), had spread a wide napkin thereupon after the fashion of a domestic dinner-table, and was rapidly transferring the contents of the hampers to that point. The horrible whimsicality of trying to eat and make merry under these deplorable circumstances, the tragic-comic character of the scene, appeared to take him by surprise. He at once threw himself into it (as he says in "Copperfield" he was wont to do with anything to which he had laid his hand)[3] with fantastic eagerness. Having spread the table after the most approved style, he suddenly disappeared behind

3. David Copperfield, chapter 42, on his practicing "that tremendous shorthand": "whatever I have tried to do in life I have tried with all my heart to do well. . . . Never to put my hand to anything, on which I could throw my whole self; and never to affect depreciation of my work, whatever it was; I find, now, to have been my golden rules."

the wall for a moment, transformed himself by the aid of a towel and napkin into a first-class head-waiter, reappeared, laid a row of plates along the top of the wall, as at a bar-room or eating-house, again retreated to the other side with some provisions, and, making the gentlemen of the party stand up to the wall, went through the whole play with most entire gravity. When we had wound up with a good laugh, and were again seated together on the grass around the table, we espied two wretched figures, not the convicts this time, although we might have easily persuaded ourselves so, but only tramps gazing at us over the wall from the marsh side as they approached, and finally sitting down just outside the churchyard gate. They looked wretchedly hungry and miserable, and Dickens said at once, starting up, "Come, let us offer them a glass of wine and something good for lunch." He was about to carry them himself, when what he considered a happy thought seemed to strike him. "*You* shall carry it to them," he cried, turning to one of the ladies; "it will be less like a charity and more like a kindness if one of you should speak to the poor souls!" * * * We feasted on the satisfaction the tramps took in their lunch, long after our own was concluded; and, seeing them well off on their road again, took up our own way to Gad's Hill Place.

* * *

* * * In answer one day to a question, prompted by psychological curiosity, if he ever dreamed of any of his characters, his reply was, "Never; and I am convinced that no writer (judging from my own experience, which cannot be altogether singular, but must be a type of the experience of others) has ever dreamed of the creatures of his own imagination. It would," he went on to say, "be like a man's dreaming of meeting himself, which is clearly an impossibility. Things exterior to one's self must always be the basis of dreams." The growing up of characters in his mind never lost for him a sense of the marvellous. "What an unfathomable mystery there is in it all!" he said one day. Taking up a wineglass, he continued: "Suppose I choose to call this a *character*, fancy it a man, endue it with certain qualities; and soon the fine filmy webs of thought, almost impalpable, coming from every direction, we know not whence, spin and weave about it, until it assumes form and beauty, and becomes instinct with life."

EDGAR ROSENBERG

Dickens in 1861†

I suppose that everybody who has written or thought about *Great Expectations* has seen it as one of Dickens' most deeply personal books, as much so, in its way, as *Copperfield* is in its more expansive fashion. Readers and commentators have inescapably linked Dickens' early chagrins to Pip's; but the novel bears traces, too, of Dickens' more immediately pressing concerns and anxieties. One may indeed wonder whether he didn't have his family

† Adapted from my "A Preface to GE," pp. 318–20. Reprinted with permission of the AMS Press.

very much in mind while he wrote *Great Expectations,* and in a very direct sense. He had good reason to worry, not just about Ellen (who wasn't Family) but about his near-relations, his in-laws, and especially his older sons. Two months before Dickens started work on the novel, on 27 July, his brother Alfred died of pleurisy; on 3 August Dickens wrote to Miss Coutts: "My poor brother's death is a sad calamity, to which there are five little witnesses"; is it really very fanciful to imagine that Dickens would have quite failed to recall this when he composed his opening epitaph about the "five little stone lozenges . . . sacred to the memory of five little brothers of mine"? Alfred's death meant more claims on Dickens' pocket, more sponging and toadying: "I declare to you," he wrote to Wills on 11 March 1861, "that with my mother—and Alfred's family—and my wife—and a Saunders or so—I seem to stop sometimes like a steamer in a storm, and deliberate whether I shall go on whirling, or go down."

Above all Dickens viewed with weary moroseness the prospects of his older sons, who were reaching that stage in their expectations when fathers ask themselves certain hard-nosed questions about their offspring's future. Charley was twenty-three when Dickens started the novel (the same age as Pip when the bubble burst) and, though born on Epiphany, turned out to be something less than a gift to the god; even Forster, writing to Carlyle, could merely growl about him as "representing his father alas! in no one particular but his name." Walter was twenty, running up debts in India; Frank and Alfred, aet. sixteen and fifteen, were lumbering through adolescence in Hamburg and Wimbledon. (Henry, the one son who vindicated Dickens' hopes by his success in college and provoked the one moment when Dickens "broke down completely" with fatherly pride, was still in knee pants.) Dickens, in writing up Pip's and Herbert's domestic mismanagement, did not have to look very far beyond his own table. In *Copperfield,* after all, it had been chiefly the father's orotund alter ego who stood for insolvency, the "waiter on Providence" in his most literal embodiment; in *Great Expectations,* the economic bungling and the keeping up with the Finches is all the young men's doing, specifically Pip's, who takes the blame for dragging Herbert into debt.

I think that Charley in particular left his traces on these parts of the novel. In May 1860 Charley had gone out to Hongkong, "strongly backed up by Baring's, to buy tea on his own account, as a means of forming a connection and seeing more of the practical part of a merchant's calling, before starting in London for himself." By February '61 he was back in England, before *Great Expectations* was being finalized. It is difficult to believe that Dickens could have helped thinking of Charley's prospects in describing Herbert's ambitions as an overseas trader in chapter xxii and the commercial voyages for Clarriker & Co. toward the end of the book; and in fact some of the MS readings in chapter xxii tend to support this. In the printed text, Herbert, in answer to Pip's question "what he was," roundly declares himself to be "A capitalist—an Insurer of Ships"; in the MS, the answer is "a merchant"; the talk is all about trading in the Orient; all references to insurance and insurer originally read "merchandise" and "merchant"; virtually the entire paragraph beginning "I shall not rest satisfied with merely employing my capital in insuring ships" is absent from the MS; and where Herbert in the published text proposes to trade "Also to Ceylon, especially for elephants' tusk," Dickens originally had him trade "Also to China for teas"—no doubt *that* detail struck too close to home.[1]

It is even possible to detect uncomfortably loud echoes of Dickens' matrimonial muddle in certain parts of the book, and of its effects on the children. Toward the end of chapter xxx Herbert broaches to Pip his engagement to Clara; he leads up to this by asking: "May I ask if you have ever had an opportunity of remarking, down in your part of the country, that the children of not exactly suitable marriages, are always most particularly anxious to be married?" and he goes on to describe in a paragraph charged with sardonic whimsy the marriage-itch that epidemically afflicts the small Pockets.

Dickens was in a brown study about this. Katie had married Charles Alston Collins in July 1860, and Dickens' hysterical *mea culpa* after the couple drove off is well known.[2] In November 1861 Charley compounded his filial delinquencies by marrying the daughter of Dickens' old enemy Frederick Evans, and Dickens cast a cold eye on the match in a letter of 3 November: "I wish I could hope that Charley's marriage may not be a disastrous one. There is no help for it, and the dear fellow does what is unavoidable—his foolish mother would have effectually committed him if nothing else had; chiefly I suppose because her hatred of the bride and all belonging to her, used to know no bounds, and was quite inappeasable. But I have a strong belief founded on careful observation of him, that he cares nothing for the girl." Thus Dickens (later he talked about Charley's "preposterous child") in a letter to the companion of Miss Coutts, that luckless would-be mediator between the parties to a "not exactly suitable marriage:"[3]

In an excellent discussion of Dickens' relations with his children, Philip Collins argues in the opposite direction, that Dickens' "imagination was not seized by his offspring, either in their relation to himself or to one another" and that "Dickens the parent seems to have little direct relevance to Dickens the novelist." As a general proposition about the earlier novels, this is perhaps true; with respect to *Great Expectations*, I am not sure: I tend to think, with K. J. Fielding, that Dickens "may have learnt something about Pip from his own family"—Fielding means his sons.[4] Imagination being what it is, the two views may not be mutually exclusive.

1. On Alfred's death, *PL* 9, 280; to Willis, 391; Forster to Carlyle, September 8, 1870, quoted in Adrian, *Georgina Hogarth and the Dickens Circle*, 158; on Dickens's breakdown, Henry Fielding Dickens, *Memoirs of My Father*, 19–20; on Charley's travels, to William de Cerjat, May 3, 1860, *PL* 9, 246–47. Saunders has not been identified (by me), but for a reluctant guess see *PL* 9, 391, n. 5.

2. Kate, or "Tinderbox," Dickens's second daughter, married Collins (1828–1873), Wilkie's younger brother, a Pre-Raphaelite painter turned writer, on July 19, chiefly to get away from a household that had become increasingly unstable since Dickens's separation. After the couple drove off on their pro forma honeymoon, Kate's older sister Mamie found Dickens sobbing in Kate's bedroom: "But for me, Katey would not have left home." The marriage fell apart during Collins's lingering illness; Kate survived him by fifty-five years.

3. Angela Georgina Burdett-Coutts (1814–1906), the youngest daughter of the radical politician Sir Francis Burdett, inherited, at twenty-three, her stepgrandmother's fortune and became the second richest woman in England after the Queen—by some accounts the richest. A fervent Evangelist, she devoted her life to social betterment, pouring millions into schemes for urban development and school reform. In the 1840s she joined forces with Dickens in a dozen projects, most famously in establishing a reformatory asylum for prostitutes in Shepherd's Bush (the prostitutes were graded on their behavior) and in improving the conditions of Ragged charity schools for pauper children. The Dickenses tirelessly obtruded their marital ennuis on her and her companion, Hannah Meredith Brown (d. 1878). See letter to Mrs. Brown, November 3, 1861, *PL* 9, 494; to Thomas Beard, November 15, 1862, *PL* 10, 161.

4. Philip Collins, *Dickens and Education* (London, 1963), 28–29; K. J. Fielding, *Charles Dickens: A Critical Introduction* (rev. ed., Boston, 1965), 219.

HUMPHRY HOUSE

[Pip's Upward Mobility]†

A great deal has been written and said about Dickens as a writer for 'the people'. Yet his chief public was among the middle and lower-middle classes, rather than among the proletarian mass. His mood and idiom were those of the class from which he came, and his morality throve upon class distinctions even when it claimed to supersede them. He belonged to the generation which first used the phrase 'the great unwashed' and provided a Chadwick[1] to scrub the people clean. His 'class' character was well described by *Blackwood's* in June 1855:

> We cannot but express our conviction that it is to the fact that he represents a class that he owes his speedy elevation to the top of the wave of popular favour. He is a man of very liberal sentiments—an assailer of constituted wrongs and authorities—one of the advocates in the plea of Poor *versus* Rich, to the progress of which he has lent no small aid in his day. But he is, notwithstanding, perhaps more distinctly than any other author of the time, a *class* writer, the historian and representative of one circle in the many ranks of our social scale. Despite their descents into the lowest class, and their occasional flights into the less familiar ground of fashion, it is the air and breath of middle-class respectability which fills the books of Mr. Dickens.

It should hardly be necessary to stress the substantial truth of this judgement; but Dickens has so often been claimed as popular in other senses—by Chesterton as if he were the leader of a kind of peasants' revolt in Bloomsbury; by Mr. Jackson as if his heart were really devoted to the uniting of the workers of the world[2]—that some insistence on it here * * * must be forgiven.

* * *

Many misunderstandings have been caused by the fact that Dickens himself so often and in so many voices proclaimed the gospel that class distinctions do not matter so much as common humanity, nor rank so much as virtue. In his speeches he loved to quote

> The rank is but the guinea stamp,
> The man's the gowd for a' that.[3]

† From Humphry House, *The Dickens World* (London, 1941), 152–60. Reprinted by permission of Oxford University Press. Unless otherwise indicated, all footnotes are by the editor of this Norton Critical Edition.

1. A leading social activist, Edwin Chadwick (1800–1890) is best known for his pioneering work in the fields of slum clearance and sanitary reform, and his authorship of the Poor Law Report of 1834. Chadwick's Sanitary Report (1842), an instant best-seller and textbook on the subject, led to the passage of the Public Health Act of 1848 and helped to wipe out the cholera epidemics that periodically afflicted England. As House suggests, sanitation was all the rage in the 1830s and 1840s: Victoria's consort, Prince Albert, ranked hygiene a few notches below religion and found it in a dead heat with literature. Chadwick's chief work was issued in 1889 under the lucrative title *The Health of Nations*.
2. T. A. Jackson, *Charles Dickens: The Progress of a Radical* (New York: International Publishers, 1938), one of the first Marxist studies of Dickens. Chesterton's coupling of a peasants' revolt with Bloomsbury, the metonym for the intellectual set of the 1920s and 1930s, is meant to suggest, of course, the wooliness of his position.
3. Robert Burns (1759–1796), "For A' That and A' That" (1794), lines 7–8. That is, For all that an honest man, however poor, surpasses all the tinseled dukes and princes. "Gowd" here means "gold." Dickens, never much of a punster, introduced the lines with a reference to "the burning works of your Northern poet" at a banquet in his honor at Edinburgh in June 1841 (*Speeches*, 10).

In one speech (1844) he quoted 'the words of a great living poet, who is one of us, and who uses his great gifts, as he holds them in trust, for the general welfare—

> Howe'er it be, it seems to me,
>   'Tis only noble to be good.
> True hearts are more than coronets,
>   And simple faith than Norman blood.'[4]

But that he *could* make such quotations, as he did, to audiences of working men, without the slightest trace of self-consciousness or condescension, only shows the confidence he had in his own class position. In the same speech in which he made the Tennyson quotation he also said: 'Differences of wealth, of rank, of intellect, we know there must be, and we respect them.'[5] Sentiments like that of Tennyson, so frequent in Victorian literature, have their origin more in the assertion by the bourgeois of his essential similarity to the aristocrat than in any levelling denial of all differences everywhere. The English aristocracy, for centuries recruited from the middle classes, was forced into still closer cultural and social contact with them in the generation after 1832: only then began those interminable controversies about what a gentleman is, and the countless jokes about snobs. Compared with Thackeray and most of the *Punch* circle, for instance, Dickens steered through these dangers handsomely.[6]

* * *

The general vagueness about class distinctions in these books has sometimes been attributed to a supposed deficiency in young Dickens's knowledge of the world; but Dickens's 18 was most men's 25, and in his work in Doctors' Commons and Parliament and in miscellaneous reporting all over the country he must have had unusually good opportunities of observing all the details of social difference; and *David Copperfield* is reason enough for supposing that he did observe them. But why were they not used till 1849–50? The answer seems to be that the social atmosphere of the 'forties led him to revise his pattern of interpretation; and that as the shifting and mingling of classes became more *apparent* in the habits of London society he was better able to understand the implications of what he had observed in earlier years.

Dombey himself is the first full-length Dickens business-man to be sol-

---

4. Alfred Lord Tennyson, "Lady Clara Vere de Vere" (1842; written c. 1835), lines 53–56. The title figure is a blue-blooded femme fatale whose frustrated suitors slit their throats. The speaker, her next would-be quarry, who much prefers his country lass to Lady Clara, suggests that she seek a cure from her boredom in the pursuit of charitable works.

5. Mechanics' Institution, Liverpool, February 26, 1844 (*Speeches*, 55). Elsewhere Dickens is fond of quoting from the same poem "the gardener Adam's and his wife's" disparagement of the pedigrees of the Vere de Veres: this appropriately in his talks to the Gardeners' Benevolent Institution, June 9, 1851, and June 14, 1852 (*Speeches*, 133, 146). The term "Mechanics' Institution" refers to an early form of adult education for working men established in 1823 by Dr. George Birkbeck (1776–1841), stressing the need for public lectures, libraries, and reading rooms "appropriate to the avocation of the industrial classes."

6. Thackeray's *The Snobs of England, by One of Themselves* appeared in *Punch* from 1846–47 (*The Women of England, The Daughters of England, The Mothers of England* having glutted the market) before he collected the sketches under the mock-biblical title *The Book of Snobs*. The word *snob* gained currency at Cambridge, Thackeray's alma mater, as a cant term of abuse against local townies; but Thackeray redefined the term by substituting for its class moorings a morally charged meaning, which could be applied to any flunkey—anybody who "meanly admires mean things." Dickens for one loathed the book.

emnly self-conscious about his 'station and its duties', and a good deal of his pride is class-pride. * * * He differs from business-men like Pickwick, Brownlow, the Cheerybles, and the Chuzzlewits not only in living far more expensively, but in the importance he attaches to doing so.[7] * * * Historically, he represents the process of taming the aristocrats till they are fit for bourgeois society: he is successful only through his daughter, which is as it should be. Dickens originally set himself in Dombey a problem in personal psychology: he did not make it very interesting; but in proportion as he failed to make convincing the workings of Dombey's mind he gave more attention to the money-class context in which they were expressed. The effectiveness of his later portraits of middle-class snobs—Merdles, Podsnaps, Veneerings,[8] and the rest—is that this is artistically wrong, as the final marriage to Estella is wrong: for the book is the sincere, uncritical expression of a time when the whole class-drift was upwards and there was no reason to suppose that it would ever stop being so. The social ideals of Pip and Magwitch differ only in taste. Though Pip has shuddered at the convict for being coarse and low, he consoles him on his death-bed with the very thought that first fired and then kept alive his own love for Estella: 'You had a child. . . . She is a lady and very beautiful.'

Here is the story allegorized by Mr. Jackson, writing as a Marxist:

> Self-satisfied, mid-Victorian, British society buoyed itself up with as great 'expectations' of future wealth and glory as did poor, deluded Pip. If it had but known, its means of ostentation came from a source (the labour of the depressed and exploited masses) to which it would have been as shocked to acknowledge indebtedness as Pip was to find he owed all his acquired gentility to the patronage of a transported felon. Magwitch differed little from the uncouth monster which respectable society envisaged to itself as the typical 'labouring man'. And in literal truth, good, respectable society owed as much to these working men, and was as little aware of it, as was Pip of the source of his advantages. And respectable society is as little grateful as Pip, whenever the truth is revealed.[9]

This would be very plausible if only the rest of the class distinctions in the novel were what Mr. Jackson makes them out to be:

> Such class-antagonism as there is in Great Expectations is not that between aristocrats (as such) and common people, but that between, on the one side, the 'gentlemen' (who are for one reason or another either crazily vengeful or callously cold-hearted and corrupt) and with them

7. Mr. Pickwick is the elderly bachelor whose travels and embarrassments made Dickens famous. Brownlow: the kindly suburbanite who provides Oliver Twist with a home and tracks down his parentage. The Cheerybles are benevolent old gents who employ Nicholas Nickleby in their counting house. Chuzzlewits: old-fashioned misers.
8. Merdle (Little Dorrit) is one of the great capitalist-swindlers in nineteenth-century literature. Podsnaps (Our Mutual Friend): an officious ass who prides himself on his xenophobia, solves the world's ills by sweeping them from him, and bristles at anything low enough to "bring a blush to the cheek of the young person." The Veneerings, "bran-new people in a bran-new house in a bran-new quarter of London," reflect Dickens's distaste for the London parvenues. Chesterton is sure they're Jews (Appreciations and Criticisms, "Introduction," x–xii).
9. Jackson, Charles Dickens, 197.

their sycophants and attendant slum-hooligans and on the other, the honest, working section of the population.[1]

Applied in detail this means Bentley Drummle, Compeyson, and Pumble-chook on one side, with Joe, Biddy, Matthew and Herbert Pocket, Jaggers, and Wemmick all lumped together on the other. This is virtually to say that in the end class distinctions are identical with moral distinctions, without even being particularly nice about morals; it is to ignore all the facts of class difference that Dickens was so subtly analysing. It is in things like Estella's early treatment of Pip, Pip's first weeks with Herbert, Jaggers's treatment of Estella's mother, and the behaviour of Trabb's boy, that these real differences are to be found.

Chesterton professed to find in Trabb's boy the last word upon the tri-umphant revolutionary sarcasm of the English democracy;[2] you might almost as well find the ultimate English democrat in old Orlick, the soured 'hand' turning to crime because of his inferior status, whom Mr. Jackson just leaves as a 'blackguard'—a man who in another novel might well have been the leader of a no-Popery mob[3] or of physical-force Chartists.[4] The assault of Trabb's boy, which brings Pip's class-consciousness to a head, is more per-sonal than political: Dickens doesn't mean that good clothes are worse than bad or that they are intrinsically funny and that the class that wears them is doomed to die of jeers. * * * As things were he was a good pin to prick Pip's conceit; but if he himself had come into a fortune, he would have been just as nasty about it as Pip in his own way; and his way might have been worse.

Great Expectations is the perfect expression of a phase of English society: it is a statement, to be taken as it stands, of what money can do, good and bad; of how it can change and make distinctions of class; how it can pervert virtue, sweeten manners, open up new fields of enjoyment and suspicion. The mood of the book belongs not to the imaginary date of its plot, but to the time in which it was written; for the unquestioned assumptions that Pip can be transformed by money and the minor graces it can buy, and that the loss of one fortune can be repaired on the strength of incidental gains in voice and friends, were only possible in a country secure in its internal economy, with expanding markets abroad: this could hardly be said of England in the 'twenties and 'thirties.

Pip's acquired 'culture' was an entirely bourgeois thing: it came to little more than accent, table manners, and clothes. In these respects a country gentleman with an estate in a remoter part of England would probably have been, even at Queen Victoria's accession, more like the neighbouring farmers than like Mr. Dombey. The process of diffusing standard 'educated', London and Home Counties, speech as the norm expected of a gentleman was by no

1. Jackson, 195.
2. Introduction to *Great Expectations* (London: J. M. Dent, 1907), xi–xii.
3. The no-Popery Riots of 1780, in which a crowd of hooligans, convicts, and crazies acting in the name of the fanatically anti-Catholic and mildly insane Lord Gordon, looted, sacked, and burnt down dozens of Catholic homes and churches (but also the interdenominational Newgate Prison), take up a long section in Dickens's first historical novel, *Barnaby Rudge*.
4. The Chartists, so called for their support of a "People's Charter" drawn up in 1838, advocated political reform, specifically universal male suffrage, equal electoral districts, vote by ballot, and the abolition of property qualifications for members of Parliament. The dissension within their ranks—between the anti-industrialists of Northern England and the London and Midland factions—led to deadly riots in Birmingham and Newport in November 1839.

means complete: its rapid continuance through the Dickens period was an essential part of the increasing social uniformity between the middle and upper classes, helped on by the development of the 'public' schools.[5]

We are told that Pip 'read' a great deal, and that he enjoyed it; but we do not know what he read, or how it affected his mind, or what kind of pleasures he got from it. He knew enough about Shakespeare and acting to realize that Mr. Wopsle turned Waldengarver was ridiculous; but what other delights he found in theatre-going in his prosperous days we are left to judge for ourselves; painting and music certainly had no large part in his life. People like Pip, Herbert Pocket, and Traddles have no culture but domestic comfort and moral decency. They are sensitive, lovable, and intelligent, but their normal activities are entirely limited to a profession and a fireside. When one of their kind extends his activities beyond this range it is in the direction of 'social work', and even that is likely to be governed by his profession, as Allan Woodcourt is a good doctor, and Mr. Milvey a good parson.[6] David Copperfield's other activity is to write novels like *Great Expectations* and *David Copperfield*: so we come full circle.

ROBIN GILMOUR

[The Pursuit of Gentility]†

It used to be said of Dickens that he could not describe a gentleman. Behind this charge often lurked the snobbish assumption that he could not describe gentlemen because he was not a gentleman himself. Thus when Forster's *Life* appeared in 1871 with its revelations of his father's imprisonment for debt and his own childhood employment in the blacking factory, the worst suspicions of the *Times* reviewer were confirmed: Dickens the man, he observed, was 'often vulgar in manners and dress . . . ill at ease in his intercourse with gentlemen . . . something of a Bohemian in his best moments'.[1] It was G. K. Chesterton who put the matter in its proper perspective:

> When people say that Dickens could not describe a gentleman, what they mean is . . . that Dickens could not describe a gentleman as gentlemen feel a gentleman. They mean that he could not take that atmosphere easily, accept it as the normal atmosphere, or describe that world from the inside . . . Dickens did not describe gentlemen in the way that gentlemen describe gentlemen . . . He described them . . . from the outside, as he described any other oddity or special trade.[2]

5. It is interesting that there is no description of such a school anywhere in Dickens, though he described so many different kinds of private school, and sent his own sons to Eton. The extension of the term 'public school' to an increasing number of boarding schools was a process of the 'forties. (See, for instance, McCulloch's *Account of the British Empire*, 3rd. ed., 1847, Vol. II, p. 329.) It was, of course, the most influential expression of the 'gentleman' idea. [*Author.*]
6. Alan Woodcourt is the romantic lead in *Bleak House*, who *would* court the heroine, Esther Summerson, and in his role of physician, attends the deathbed of an opium addict, ministers to a young typhoid-stricken slum dweller, and while on naval duty, looks after the survivors of a shipwreck. The Reverend Frank Milvey (*Our Mutual Friend*) acts as consultant to an elderly childless couple in adopting a child (who dies before the adoption).
† From Robin Gilmour, *The Idea of the Gentleman in the Victorian Novel* (London: Allen & Unwin, 1981), 105–48. Used by permission of Routledge.
1. Quoted in G. H. Ford, *Dickens and His Readers*, 2nd ed. (New York: Norton, 1956), 162.
2. G. K. Chesterton, *Criticisms and Appreciations*, 125.

In this, as in so much else, Dickens contrasts with his great rival Thackeray. Thackeray took to the gentlemanly atmosphere naturally; it forms a shared basis of assumption between author and reader and is one source of the distinctive authorial tone in his novels. * * *

Both Thackeray and Dickens, we can now see, were novelists of the middle-class emergence, but at opposite ends of the scale. Thackeray's province is that 'debateable land between the aristocracy and the middle classes', as W. C. Roscoe called it.[3] * * * Dickens is concerned with the lower reaches of the middle class in its most anxious phase of self-definition, struggling out of trade and domestic service and clerical work into the sunshine of respectability. * * * Thackeray once wrote that 'an English gentleman knows as much about the people of Lapland or California as he does of the aborigines of the Seven Dials or the natives of Wapping.' Dickens's unique qualification was that he could not share the gentleman's conventional ignorance. * * * Dickens knew what the natives of Wapping were like, and how they saw the gentleman; he discovered for himself how thin and precarious was the partition that separated a lower-middle-class family from the abyss of urban poverty in the early nineteenth century; and he knew from his own experience how intensely that partition might be valued by those threatened with the drop into the abyss, how desperately an aspiring young gentleman would struggle to escape working 'from morning to night, with common men and boys, a shabby child'.[4] For most of his life Dickens did not 'know' these things objectively, as a man more detached from middle-class aspirations might have done; he experienced them subjectively, in all their complexity and ambivalence. But in one marvellous novel, *Great Expectations* (1860–1), he found a fictional form capable of expressing the social ironies underlying both his own and his generation's preoccupation with the idea of the gentleman, and in doing so delivered what is in many ways his most profound commentary on Victorian civilisation and its values.

Dickens could write *Great Expectations* because he was so deeply involved in the process of social evolution which * * * lies at the heart of the novel. 'He typifies and represents, in our literary history', one contemporary critic said of him, 'the middle class ascendancy prepared for by the Reform Bill.'[5] Dickens came of age in the year after the 1832 Reform Bill, and he has all that parvenu generation's fascination with the idea of the gentleman. Not surprisingly we find him pulled this way and that by the conflicting images of gentlemanliness abroad in the early Victorian period. Ellen Moers has suggested that the young clerks and medical students in the early novels belong (as perhaps the young Dickens did himself) to the species known in the 1830s as 'The Gent'. The 'Gent' was 'a second-hand shop-worn imitation of the dandy'[6]—young men at the very bottom of the respectable class who

---

3. G. Tillotson and D. Hawes (eds.), *Thackeray: The Critical Heritage* (London: Routledge & Kegan Paul, 1968), 272.
4. Forster, book 1, chapter 2; Hoppé, vol. 1, 25. This is how David Copperfield describes his sensations in slaving for Murdstone & Quinby in chapter 11. [*Editor.*]
5. Quoted in P. A. W. Collins (ed.), *Dickens: The Critical Heritage* (London: Routledge & Kegan Paul, 1971), 476. Review by James Hannay (1827–1873) in his *Course of English Literature* (1866), 321. [*Author.*] The Reform Bill of 1832 represented a long-delayed effort to keep up with the radical demographic changes in Britain in the early part of the century, especially the massive migrations from rural to industrialized areas. The First Reform Act abolished "Rotten Boroughs" and redistributed electoral seats [*Editor.*]
6. Ellen Moers, *The Dandy: From Brummel to Beerbohm*, 215.

wore flashy clothes and cheap jewellery and worshipped fashionable life at a distance. * * * And although she distorts some of the later novels to make her case, she shows how Dickens's growing revulsion from the stuffy, Podsnap side of Victorian middle-class life in the 1850s and 1860s inclined him to a more sympathetic portrayal of the dandy-type, in characters like Sydney Carton in A *Tale of Two Cities* (1859) and Eugene Wrayburn in *Our Mutual Friend* (1864–5).[7]

More conventionally, Dickens shared to the full in the Victorian ambivalence about the relative claims of inherited and acquired status: like the fictional John Halifax[8] * * * Dickens was capable of asserting his qualities as a self-made man as well as his claims as a gentleman's son. The latter tend to dominate in his treatment of the heroes in early novels like *Oliver Twist* (1837–9) and *Nicholas Nickleby* (1838–9), who struggle to recover and reassert a lost birthright of gentility, and can still be discerned in a letter written a year before he died, where he spoke of his father's coat-of-arms: 'I beg to inform you that I have never used any other armorial bearings than my father's crest; a lion couchant, bearing in his dexter paw a Maltese cross. I have never adopted any motto, being quite indifferent to such ceremonies.'[9] (The movement of thought here, from the modest assertion of inherited gentility—'my father's crest'—to the protested indifference to 'such ceremonies', is of course characteristically ambivalent, simultaneously claiming the status and dissociating himself from those who take it too seriously.) On the other side Dickens could, and frequently did, align himself with the self-help virtues, particularly in his middle period—the years from *Dombey and Son* (1846–8) to *Bleak House* (1852–3)—when he was most in sympathy with the progressive momentum of what he called in *Bleak House* 'the moving age', against the 'perpetual stoppage' (ch. 12) of the moribund, tradition-ridden elements in mid-Victorian life. * * * This was the Dickens who was as successful an example of self-help as any in Smiles's book, and who throughout his career used his fame to champion the rights and dignity of his profession, an important campaign which helped to destroy the old patronage system and the snobbish assumption (to which Thackeray was prone) that a professional writer could not be a gentleman. It was the progressive, self-made Dickens who spoke of the rewards of self-help to those institutions of Victorian self-help, the Mechanics' Institutes and Athenaeums,[1] and who identified with

---

7. Both are lawyers—aimless, languid, cynical. Carton shuttles between bouts of drinking and gallantry before he sacrifices his life for the heroine by taking her husband's place on the guillotine; Wrayburn, who yawns his way through the London upper crust, falls in love with the daughter of a riverside ruffian. [*Editor.*]

8. In *John Halifax, Gentleman* (1856), Mrs. Craik (Dinah Mulock, 1820–1887) presents a young tanner who personifies the virtues and benefits of "self-help," the Victorian *ideé fixe* and a subject anticipated twenty-five years earlier by her husband's *Pursuit of Knowledge under Difficulties*, a biographical dictionary of famous Self-Helpers. Ambitious, persevering, a practitioner of the Christian virtues, Halifax marries into money and thrives as factory owner; by the end of the novel he is revealed to have been a gentleman (by birth) all along and so has the best of both worlds: those of inherited and achieved gentility. Samuel Smiles's canonical text *Self-Help* (1859) not only told Britons how to get on in life but created a market for latter-day blockbusters like Dale Carnegie's *How to Win Friends and Influence People* (1936), Norman Vincent Peale's *The Power of Positive Thinking* (1952), and via Carnegie and Peale, for all the "How-To" therapeutants that litter our supermarkets. See (or hear) also Stanley Fish, "How to Stop Worrying by Stopping Reading" (cassette, 1976). [*Editor.*]

9. *NL* 3, 717. [*Editor.*]

1. Athenaeum: from the temple of Athens, in which orators and poets read their compositions; since the nineteenth century a literary club room, reading room, library. In England the establishment dates from the founding of the Athenaeum Club in London in 1824 as a sanctuary for intellectual Brahmins. [*Editor.*]

the 'manly' character of the reformed English gentleman which Dr Arnold and others had struggled to bring into being.[2] * * *

The total picture is complex, as one would expect: the gent, the dandy, the traditional gentleman by birth, the self-made man, the manly Victorian gentleman—Dickens's imaginative response to these competing images of social style fluctuates with changes in his attitude to his own experience and to the life of a changing society. * * * The bohemian streak which many contemporaries discerned in his showy dress was the outward sign of a defiant non-respectability deep inside Dickens; the famous coloured waistcoats were in deliberate rebellion against the cautious sobriety of mid-Victorian gentlemanly fashion. Seeing gentlemen from the outside he came to appreciate both the centrality of the gentlemanly idea in Victorian culture and its underlying irony, that however earnestly it might be moralised the concept depended for its existence upon exclusion, on separating gentlemen from non-gentlemen. *Great Expectations* is the fruit of that recognition. Dickens was in a unique position to write it because, looking back and coming to understand the ironies of the great expectations which had inspired his own social rise, he could see how central these expectations had been for the class and generation to which he belonged. * * *

* * *

As we have seen, Dickens the man was divided between the claims of inherited and acquired status, between the part of himself which wanted to believe that he was a gentleman's son and the part which took pride in having overcome Bulwer Lytton's 'twin jailers of the daring heart—Low birth and iron fortune'.[3] Both attitudes are a perfectly natural response to the insecurities of his early years in London and the never-forgotten brief exposure, in the blacking factory and the debtors' prison, to the prospect of total social disinheritance. In *Oliver Twist*, his first fictional treatment of the orphan's story, this experience and his reaction to it can be discerned in two conflicting impulses at the heart of the novel: a horror of the criminal underworld when seen through the terrified eyes of the child Oliver, and a sympathetic understanding of the same underworld from a different, more realistic and socially compassionate perspective. * * * The shrinking Oliver becomes the respectable reader's point of entry into the social underworld: he is made to feel the menace of that world, its power to suck in the innocent and the vulnerable, and in this way Dickens is able to bring across his message more effectively than by overt denunciation—the message that it is the accident of birth which condemns a child to the workhouse, and the fault of society that the road from the workhouse should lead so naturally to the life of crime. * * *

2. Thomas Arnold (1775–1842), the father of the poet—and of the modern public (i.e., private) school —was headmaster of Rugby from 1828 until his death. His credo has been summed up in one of his letters: "A thorough English gentleman—Christian, manly, and enlightened—is * * * a finer specimen of human nature than any other country, I believe, could furnish" (quoted in Gilmour, 88; A. P. Stanley, *The Life and Correspondence of Thomas Arnold, D.D.*, 12th ed., 2 vols. [London: John Murray, 1881] vol. 2, 339). [*Editor.*]

3. *The Lady of Lyons; or Love and Pride* (1838) 3.2: "Then did I seek to rise / Out of the prison of my mean estate; / And, with such jewels as the exploring Mind / Brings from the caves of Knowledge, buy my ransom / From those twin gaolers of the daring heart— / Low Birth and iron Fortune." Bulwer's play, a potpourri of farce and melodrama written for Charles Macready, takes place during the France of Napoleon's Directory and deals with the attempt to break down class barriers and the rise of a humble gardener's son to wealth and fortune. Gilmour has earlier quoted the passage on which the lines end: Dickens obviously knew the passage by heart. [*Editor.*]

* * * [Oliver's] improbable immunity from the environment which corrupts all the other underworld characters is justified by the discovery that he is after all the son of a gentleman. From Oliver's point of view the novel insists on the utter incompatibility between the underworld and the life of respectable society, as opposed as heaven and hell, and yet from another point of view suggests that if Fagin's den seems more human than the workhouse, the life of crime preferable to the official charity institutions of society, then the responsibility for this lies at the door of that same respectable society.

*   *   *

David Copperfield is of course different from *Oliver Twist*: the underworld with which it deals is merely disreputable and not criminal, and David's rise in the world is accompanied by a convincing affirmation of the self-help values of hard work and earnestness congenial to Dickens at this stage of his career. But David is really not much more of a self-made man than Oliver: both are gentlemen by birth whose tenacious hold on an inner conviction of gentility throughout their sufferings is rewarded by fairy godparents. In *Great Expectations* this genteel underpinning to the orphan's story is knocked away and the fantasy exposed. Pip is always and only the blacksmith's boy, his struggle is to acquire rather than to recover gentility, and he is not allowed to forget or ever truly escape from his rude beginnings. The fairy godparents of the earlier novels reappear, but in an ironic reversal of the inheritance theme. Miss Havisham is a grotesque version of [David's] Aunt Betsey,[4] an eccentric single lady who in taking Pip up seems to have recognised his innate fitness to become a gentleman, but as her name suggests she is a sham, a witch, while the money that makes Pip's pursuit of gentility possible comes from another 'witch', Magwitch, and thus from the underworld—literally the underworld of Australia where he has made his money, and symbolically from the social underworld of violent crime with which he is associated in Pip's mind for most of the novel.

And Dickens gives a further twist to the orphan myth in *Great Expectations*. The story of David Copperfield's threatened disinheritance still has power to move us partly because of the tension in the hero's mind between the world of the social outsider to which he feels condemned, and the comforts and decency of the middle-class family life for which he longs. This tension is interesting because it is not a simple question of black and white: the outsider's world undoubtedly has its seamy side, but qualities of sympathy and fellow-feeling also flourish there. Moreover it exhibits, at times, certain kinds of human attractiveness lacking in the more respectable society of the novel —one thinks of Micawber's gaiety and his liberating extravagance, and there is the strange paradox that in a novel so preoccupied with marital relations the disreputable Micawbers should provide almost the only example of a marriage that triumphantly works.[5] * * *

In *Great Expectations*, however, there is no such resistance on Dickens's part to the human claims of the underworld. Far from endorsing the sense

---

4. Betsey Trootwood, David's crusty and kindly great-aunt, who presides at his birth and, as his sole blood-relation after his mother's death, shelters him in her madcap ménage in Dover.
5. Emma Micawber's spousal "I shall never desert Mr. Micawber" remains one of the venerable Dickensian tags. And she never does. [*Editor.*]

of class division in Pip's mind, Dickens constantly undermines it; he is not concerned to justify Pip's rise in station but rather to suggest and analyse the guilt, the inhibition, the personal betrayals which this involves. While David succeeds through a combination of hard work and good fortune, Pip is given the economic basis of the genteel life only to discover in the end that he owes it to a man whose whole history and way of life seem a denial of the refinement to which Pip aspires. In this way the social contrasts which threatened the equilibrium of David's progress are made the very agents of meaning in the later work, and what had been implicit in David's sense of shame—that his middle-class status had somehow been compromised by his association with the likes of Micawber and the boys in the warehouse—these fears are brought into the open and given objective expression in the plot, in the secret bond of complicity between Pip and the convict Magwitch.

* * *

The greatness of Great Expectations, as Lionel Trilling observed, begins in its title: 'modern society bases itself on great expectations which, if they are ever realized, are found to exist by reason of a sordid, hidden reality.' * * *6 Much modern criticism of the novel has been rightly preoccupied with the relationship between cellarage and drawing-room, between the gentility of Pip's life and the criminal outcast who makes it possible; and discussion has tended to focus on the hero's seemingly excessive sense of guilt and the encompassing 'taint of prison and crime' (ch. 32) which pervades his upward rise. 'Snobbery is not a crime', Julian Moynahan points out in an influential article and asks 'Why should Pip feel like a criminal?'7

It is an important question, because Pip's guilty conscience is the link between cellarage and drawing-room in the novel, but the terms in which Moynahan and others have phrased and answered it are questionable on both instrinsic interpretive and extrinsic historical grounds. How true is it, for instance, to say that Pip is a snob? * * * The real snobs in Great Expectations, the characters blinded to human considerations by the worship of wealth and social position, are Pumblechook and Mrs Pocket, and Pip sees through them both from the start. What the view of the novel as a 'snob's progress' ignores, as Q. D. Leavis has convincingly demonstrated, is the sympathy and complexity with which Dickens treats Pip's predicament: to call him a snob is to suggest that he was wrong to feel discontented with life on the marshes and could have chosen to act otherwise than he did, whereas much of the energy of Dickens's imagination in the early part of the novel goes in showing how mean and limiting that life is, and how helpless Pip himself is in face of the contradictory forces at work on him. * * * Similarly with Pip's great expectations, the burden of most modern criticism has been to stress that these are only illusory, that the 'real thing' (as Trilling says) is not Pip's gentility but what goes on in the cellarage of the novel, that his expectations are indeed even dangerous and anti-social, as Moynahan argues. But such arguments are in varying degrees unhistorical, ignoring the fact that Pip's desire to become a gentleman is 'real' too and has a representatively positive element, in the sense that it is bound up with that widespread impulse to improvement, both

6. L. Trilling, "Manners, Morals and the Novel," in The Liberal Imagination (London: Secker & Warburg, 1951), 211.
7. J. Moynahan, "The Hero's Guilt: the Case of Great Expectations," Essays in Criticism 10 (1960), 60.

personal and social, which is a crucial factor in the genesis of Victorian Britain. * * *

* * *

The basic *donnée*[8] of the book, the pivot on which Dickens's 'grotesque tragi-comic conception' turns, is the fact that Magwitch is Pip's benefactor and the father of Estella. But so firm is Dickens's control of his theme * * * that long before the convict's return he has been able to suggest this inherent contradiction in his hero's expectations. * * * For example, when Pip visits Satis House for the second time the smoke from the dining-room fire reminds him of 'our own marsh mist' (ch. 11), just as the cobwebs on Miss Havisham's bridal cake recall the damp on the hedges, like 'a coarser sort of spiders' webs' (ch. 3), on the morning when he sneaks out of the forge to carry the food to Magwitch. Such delicate tracery of interrelationship serves to unify the atmosphere of the novel, undermining the opposition Pip is setting up between the savagery of the marshes and the refinement of Satis House, and thereby preparing the way for the revelations to come.

The separation of the two worlds is also undermined in the case of Bentley Drummle. * * * Drummle is heavy, brutish, cruel and violent; he is an upper-class equivalent of the journeyman Orlick, with whom he is associated at the end of chapter 43. The function of this character in the scheme of the novel is to remind us that violence and brutality are not confined to life on the marshes, that they also exist in the supposedly refined society of London. And Estella's marriage to Drummle provides another dimension to our understanding of her character. This 'proud and refined' girl who is the very incarnation of the civilised life to which Pip aspires can prefer a coarse brute like Drummle because there exists, deep within her, a violent animal nature which Pip ignores. Dickens suggests this fact in chapter 11, where Pip fights and beats Herbert. Unknown to him, Estella has been watching the fight and when she comes down to let him out 'there was a bright flush upon her face, as though something had happened to delight her'. She offers to let Pip kiss her, and he does so, without realising the significance of her sudden response; he feels that 'the kiss was given to the coarse common boy as a piece of money might have been, and that it was worth nothing'. The brief scene enacts the supreme paradox of Pip's life: Estella can only respond to him when he exhibits those qualities of physical force and animal aggression which, in order to win her, he is at pains to civilise out of himself. It is her one spontaneous gesture to Pip and he misreads it, feeling only guilt and remorse at this exercise of his blacksmith's arm.

* * *

8. A "given": the basic assumption in back of the thing. [*Editor.*]

Childhood Lessons

CHARLES DICKENS

[Captain Murderer] †

* * * [W]hen I was at Dullborough one day, revisiting the associations of my childhood as recorded in previous pages of these notes,[1] my experience in this wise was made quite inconsiderable and of no account, by the quantity of places and people—utterly impossible places and people, but none the less alarmingly real—that I found I had been introduced to by my nurse before I was six years old, and used to be forced to go back to at night without at all wanting to go. If we all knew our own minds (in a more enlarged sense than the popular acceptation of that phrase), I suspect we should find our nurses responsible for most of the dark corners we are forced to go back to, against our wills.

The first diabolical character who intruded himself on my peaceful youth (as I called to mind that day at Dullborough), was a certain Captain Murderer. This wretch must have been an offshoot of the Blue Beard family, but I had no suspicion of the consanguinity in those times. His warning name would seem to have awakened no general prejudice against him, for he was admitted into the best society and possessed immense wealth. Captain Murderer's mission was matrimony, and the gratification of a cannibal appetite with tender brides. On his marriage morning, he always caused both sides of the way to church to be planted with curious flowers; and when his bride said, "Dear Captain Murderer, I never saw flowers like these before: what are they called?" he answered, "They are called Garnish for house-lamb," and laughed at his ferocious practical joke in a horrid manner, disquieting the minds of the noble bridal company, with a very sharp show of teeth, then displayed for the first time. He made love in a coach and six, and married in a coach and twelve, and all his horses were milk-white horses with one red spot on the back which he caused to be hidden by the harness. For, the spot *would* come there, though every horse was milk-white when Captain Murderer bought him. And the spot was young bride's blood. (To this terrific point I am indebted for my first personal experience of a shudder and cold beads on the forehead.) When Captain Murderer had made an end of feasting and revelry, and had dismissed the noble guests, and was alone with his wife on the day month after their marriage, it was his whimsical custom to produce

---

† From "The Uncommercial Traveller," *All the Year Round*, September 8, 1860; as "Nurse's Stories," *The Uncommercial Traveller*, First Series (1861), chapter 15.

1. "Dullborough Town," a sketch in which Dickens describes his return to Chatham and Rochester, and which is often regarded as one of his most nostalgic autobiographical pieces, had appeared in *All the Year Round* on June 30. The entertaining nurse has been identified as Mary Weller, an adolescent inmate of the Chatham Workhouse, in the employ of the Dickenses. [*Editor.*]

a golden rolling-pin and a silver pie-board. Now, there was this special feature in the Captain's courtships, that he always asked if the young lady could make pie-crust; and if she couldn't by nature or education, she was taught. Well. When the bride saw Captain Murderer produce the golden rolling-pin and silver pie-board, she remembered this, and turned up her laced-silk sleeves to make a pie. The Captain brought out a silver pie-dish of immense capacity, and the Captain brought out flour and butter and eggs and all things needful, except the inside of the pie; of materials for the staple of the pie itself, the Captain brought out none. Then said the lovely bride, "Dear Captain Murderer, what pie is this to be?" He replied, "A meat pie." Then said the lovely bride, "Dear Captain Murderer, I see no meat." The Captain humorously retorted, "Look in the glass." She looked in the glass, but still she saw no meat, and then the Captain roared with laughter, and suddenly frowning and drawing his sword, bade her roll out the crust. So she rolled out the crust, dropping large tears upon it all the time because he was so cross, and when she had lined the dish with crust and had cut the crust all ready to fit the top, the Captain called out, "I see the meat in the glass!" And the bride looked up at the glass, just in time to see the Captain cutting her head off; and he chopped her in pieces, and peppered her, and salted her, and put her in the pie, and sent it to the baker's, and ate it all, and picked the bones.

Captain Murderer went on in this way, prospering exceedingly, until he came to choose a bride from two twin sisters, and at first didn't know which to choose. For, though one was fair and the other dark, they were both equally beautiful. But the fair twin loved him, and the dark twin hated him, so he chose the fair one. The dark twin would have prevented the marriage if she could, but she couldn't; however, on the night before it, much suspecting Captain Murderer, she stole out and climbed his garden wall, and looked in at his window through a chink in the shutter, and saw him having his teeth filed sharp. Next day she listened all day, and heard him make his joke about the house-lamb. And that day month, he had the paste rolled out, and cut the fair twin's head off, and chopped her in pieces, and peppered her, and salted her, and put her in the pie, and sent it to the baker's, and ate it all, and picked the bones.

Now, the dark twin had had her suspicions much increased by the filing of the Captain's teeth, and again by the house-lamb joke. Putting all things together when he gave out that her sister was dead, she divined the truth, and determined to be revenged. So, she went up to Captain Murderer's house, and knocked at the knocker and pulled at the bell, and when the Captain came to the door, said: "Dear Captain Murderer, marry me next, for I always loved you and was jealous of my sister." The Captain took it as a compliment, and made a polite answer, and the marriage was quickly arranged. On the night before it, the bride again climbed to his window, and again saw him having his teeth filed sharp. At this sight she laughed such a terrible laugh at the chink in the shutter, that the Captain's blood curdled, and he said: "I hope nothing has disagreed with me!" At that, she laughed again, a still more terrible laugh, and the shutter was opened and search made, but she was nimbly gone, and there was no one. Next day they went to church in a coach and twelve, and were married. And that day month, she rolled the pie-crust out, and Captain Murderer cut her head off, and chopped her in pieces, and peppered her, and salted her, and put her in the pie, and sent it to the baker's, and ate it all, and picked the bones.

But before she began to roll out the paste she had taken a deadly poison of a most awful character, distilled from toads' eyes and spiders' knees; and Captain Murderer had hardly picked her last bone, when he began to swell, and to turn blue, and to be all over spots, and to scream. And he went on swelling and turning bluer, and being more all over spots and screaming, until he reached from floor to ceiling and from wall to wall; and then, at one o'clock in the morning, he blew up with a loud explosion. At the sound of it, all the milk-white horses in the stables broke their halters and went mad, and then they galloped over everybody in Captain Murderer's house (beginning with the family blacksmith who had filed his teeth) until the whole were dead, and then they galloped away.[2]

Hundreds of times did I hear this legend of Captain Murderer, in my early youth, and added hundreds of times was there a mental compulsion upon me in bed, to peep in at his window as the dark twin peeped, and to revisit his horrible house, and look at him in his blue and spotty and screaming stage, as he reached from floor to ceiling and from wall to wall. The young woman who brought me acquainted with Captain Murderer had a fiendish enjoyment of my terrors, and used to begin, I remember—as a sort of introductory overture—by clawing the air with both hands, and uttering a long low hollow groan. So acutely did I suffer from this ceremony in combination with this infernal Captain, that I sometimes used to plead I thought I was hardly strong enough and old enough to hear the story again just yet. But, she never spared me one word of it, and indeed commended the awful chalice to my lips as the only preservative known to science against "The Black Cat"—a weird and glaring-eyed supernatural Tom, who was reputed to prowl about the world by night, sucking the breath of infancy, and who was endowed with a special thirst (as I was given to understand) for mine. * * *

MRS. SHERWOOD

["Naterally Wicious: Many a Moral for the Young"]†

One morning, as Mr. Fairchild was coming down stairs, he heard the little ones quarreling in the parlour; and he stood still to hearken to what they said.

2. For a less graphic analogue to "Captain Murderer," see the Grimms' fairy tale "The Robber Bridegroom."

† From Mrs. [Mary Martha Butt] Sherwood, *The History of the Fairchild Family; or, the Child's Manual: Being a Collection of Stories Calculated to Shew the Importance and Effects of a Religious Education* (London: J. Hatchard, 1818), 53–60.

A clergyman's daughter, Mary Martha Butt Sherwood (1775–1851) wrote the earliest of her four-hundred-some stories and tracts as an infantry captain's wife in India, largely to keep the children of British colonials immunized against the heathen native instructors. The immense success of her first published stories, *The History of Little Henry and His Bearer* (1814) has been compared to the popularity of *Uncle Tom's Cabin*; four years later came *The Fairchild Family*, the book for which she is best known and which formed a staple of every middle-class child's education during the first half of the nineteenth century. A deeply religious woman, steeped in the Evangelical doctrine in which she was raised, Mrs. Sherwood shared the Puritan belief in the innate depravity of children, whose first duty it is to obey their parents as God's deputies and who are therefore best served by being terrified into piety and flogged into godliness.

"You are very ill-natured, Lucy," said Henry: "why won't you let me play with the doll?"

"What have boys to do with dolls?" said Lucy: "you shan't have it."

"But he shall," said Emily.

And Mr. Fairchild saw her, through the parlour door, snatch the doll from her sister, and give it to Henry, who ran with it behind the sofa. Lucy tried to get the doll away from her brother; but Emily ran in between them, and the two sisters began to fight. Lucy bit Emily's arm, and Emily scratched her sister's face; and, if Mr. Fairchild had not run in and seized hold of them, I do not know what they would have done to each other; for, when Emily felt the bite, she cried out,

"I hate you! I hate you with all my heart, you ill-natured girl!"

And Lucy answered,

"And I hate you too; that I do!"

And they looked as if what they said was true too; for their faces were as red as fire, and their eyes full of anger. Mr. Fairchild took the doll away from Henry; and, taking a rod out of the cupboard, he whipped the hands of all the three children till they smarted again, saying:

> "Let dogs delight to bark and bite,
> For God has made them so;
> Let bears and lions growl and fight,
> For 'tis their nature too:
>
> But children, you should never let
> Such angry passions rise:
> Your little hands were never made
> To tear each other's eyes."[1]

After which he made them stand in a corner of the room, without their breakfasts; neither did they get any thing to eat all the morning; and what was worse, their papa and mamma looked very gravely at them. * * *

* * *

Then Mr. Fairchild kissed his children, and forgave them; and they kissed each other; and Mr. Fairchild gave them leave to dine with him as usual. After dinner, Mr. Fairchild said to his wife:

"I will take the children this evening to Blackwood, and shew them something there which, I think, they will remember as long as they live: and I hope they will take warning from it, and pray more earnestly for new hearts, that they may love each other with perfect and heavenly love."

* * *

"What is there at Blackwood, Papa?" cried the children.

"Something very shocking," said Mr. Fairchild. "There is one there," said Mr. Fairchild, looking very grave, "who hated his brother."

"Will he hurt us, Papa?" said Henry.

"No," said Mr. Fairchild; "he cannot hurt you now."

---

1. From Isaac Watts's "Against Quarrelling and Fighting," *Divine Songs*, 16. As a dyed-in-the-wool dissenter, who shared the gloomy Fairchild religion, Watts and his sermons and threats would be grist to the Fairchilds' mill. [*Editor.*]

When the children and John were ready, Mr. Fairchild set out. They went down the lane nearly as far as the village; and then, crossing over a long field, they came to the side of a very thick wood. * * * At last they saw, by the light through the trees, that they were come near to the end of the wood; and, as they went further on, they saw an old garden wall[.] * * * Just between [the wall] and the wood stood a gibbet, on which the body of a man hung in chains: it had not yet fallen to pieces, although it had hung there some years. The body had on a blue coat, a silk handkerchief round the neck, with shoes and stockings, and every other part of the dress still entire: but the face of the corpse was so shocking, that the children could not look at it.

"Oh! Papa, Papa! what is that?" cried the children.

"That is a gibbet," said Mr. Fairchild; "and the man who hangs upon it is a murderer—one who first hated, and afterwards killed his brother! When people are found guilty of stealing, they are hanged upon a gallows, and taken down as soon as they are dead; but when a man commits a murder, he is hanged in iron chains upon a gibbet, till his body falls to pieces, that all who pass by may take warning by the example."

Whilst Mr. Fairchild was speaking, the wind blew strong and shook the body upon the gibbet, rattling the chains by which it hung.

"Oh! let us go, Papa!" said the children, pulling Mr. Fairchild's coat.

"Not yet," said Mr. Fairchild: "I must tell you the history of that wretched man before we go from this place."

So saying, he sat down on the stump of an old tree, and the children gathered close round him.

"When I first came into this country, before any of you, my children, were born," said Mr. Fairchild, "there lived, in that old house which you see before you, a widow lady, who had two sons. * * * The old lady kept an excellent table, and was glad to see any of her neighbours who called in upon her. Your mamma and I used often to go; and should have gone oftener, only we could not bear to see the manner in which she brought up her sons. She never sent them to school, lest the master should correct them, but hired a person to teach them reading and writing at home; but this man was forbidden to punish them. They were allowed to be with the servants in the stable and kitchen, but the servants were ordered not to deny them any thing: so they used to call them names, swear at them, and even strike them. * * *

"From quarreling with the servants, these angry boys went on to quarrel with each other. James, the eldest, despised his brother Roger, because he, as eldest, was to have the house and land; and Roger, in his turn, hated his brother James. As they grew bigger, they became more and more wicked, proud and stubborn, sullen and undutiful. * * * One evening in autumn, after one of [their] quarrels, James met his brother Roger returning from shooting, just in the place where the gibbet now stands: they were alone, and it was nearly dark. Nobody knows what words passed between them; but the wicked Roger stabbed his brother with a case-knife, and hid the body in a ditch under the garden, well covering it with dry leaves. A year or more passed before it was discovered by whom this dreadful murder was committed. Roger was condemned, and hung upon that gibbet; and the poor old lady, being thus deprived of both her sons, went quite mad, and is shut up in a place where such people are confined. Since that time no one has lived in the house, and, indeed, nobody likes to come this way."

"O what a shocking story!" said the children: "and that poor wretch who hangs there is Roger, who murdered his brother? Pray let us go, Papa."

"We will go immediately," said Mr. Fairchild; "but I wish first to point out to you, my dear children, that these brothers, when they first began to quarrel in their play, as you did this morning, did not think that death and hell would be the end of their quarrels. Our hearts by nature, my dear children," continued Mr. Fairchild, "are full of hatred. People who have not got new hearts do not love any body but themselves; and they hate those who have offended them, or those whom they think any way better than themselves. * * * [W]hen, through faith in my dying Redeemer, I receive a new heart * * * then I shall 'love my enemies, bless them that curse me, do good to them that hate me, and pray for them that despitefully use me and persecute me,' (Matt. v. 44); like my beloved Redeemer, who prayed upon the cross for his enemies, saying, 'Father, forgive them, for they know not what they do.' (Luke xxiii. 34.)"

"Papa," said Lucy, "let us kneel down in this place, and pray for new hearts."

"Willingly, my child," said Mr. Fairchild. So he knelt upon the grass, and his children round him; and afterwards they all went home.[2]

THE NEWCASTLE COMMISSION

[Dame Schools and Bible Studies][†]

Infant schools fall into two well-marked classes. The private or dames' schools, and the public infant schools, which frequently form a department of an ordinary school. Dames' schools are very common both to the country and in towns. They are frequently little more than nurseries, in which the nurse collects the children of many families into her own house instead of attending upon the children of some one family. The general character of these schools is the same in every part of the country. Women are always the teachers. They are generally advanced in life, and their school is usually their kitchen, sitting and bed-room, and the scene of all their domestic occupations. In remote villages, where there are not children enough to support an infant school, or in towns where the distance of such schools from the residence of the parents makes it dangerous for the children to resort to them, such establishments are useful; but there can be no doubt that, in many cases, the

2. Gibbeting was abolished in 1834. Assuming the narrative of *The Fairchild Family* to be roughly contemporaneous with its composition, Emily, Lucy, and Henry thus had to take their own children somewhere other than Blackwood for their religious education—unless Roger remained on display as a skeleton. [*Editor.*]

† Report of the Commissioners appointed to Inquire into the State of Popular Education in England [Newcastle Commission]. Parliamentary Papers, 21, 6 vols., pts. 1–6. (London: Eyre & Spottiswoode, 1861). All footnotes are by the editor of this Norton Critical Edition.

In 1858 the government appointed a "Commission to Inquire into the Present State of Popular Education in England, and to Consider and Report What Measures, if any, are Required for the Extension of Sound and Cheap Elementary Instruction to all Classes of People." The commission, headed by Henry Pelham, Duke of Newcastle (1811–1864), surveyed all branches of elementary schooling from training colleges to "the education of vagrant and criminal children." The spadework was farmed out to ten assistant commissioners who were assigned "specimen districts" in five fields: agricultural, manufacturing, mining, maritime, and metropolitan districts. In their report the commissioners blamed the chief defects of the system on the high—and rising—tuition, unqualified teachers, a reluctance to extend government funding to the poorer schools, and the unwieldy bureaucracy of the Office of Education.

continued existence of such schools indicates great deficiency in the supply
of a very important branch of popular education. The dames' schools are apt
to be close, crowded, and dirty. "The usual scene of these schools," says
[Assistant Commissioner] Mr. Winder * * * "is a cottage kitchen, in which
the mistress divides her time between her pupils and her domestic duties.
The children sit round the room, often so thickly stowed as to occupy every
available corner, and spend the greater part of their time in knitting and
sewing. At intervals the mistress calls them up, one or two at a time, and
teaches the alphabet and easy words, the highest proficiency attained being
the power of reading a little in the New Testament." * * * The teachers of
these schools are of course of characters as various as the schools which they
teach, but they have rarely been in any way trained to their profession, and
they have almost always selected it, either because they have failed in other
pursuits, or because, as in the case of widows, they have been unexpectedly
left in a state of destitution. * * * [Assistant Commissioner] Mr. Wilkinson
says that the profession, as such, hardly exists, and that it is a mere refuge for
the destitute, and enumerates grocers, tobacconists, linen drapers, tailors, attorneys, painters, German, Polish, and Italian refugees, bakers, widows or
daughters of clergymen, barristers, and surgeons, housekeepers, ladies' maids,
and dressmakers, as being found amongst the teachers of private schools. Mr.
Winder says that hardly any one is brought up to the business unless he suffers
from some bodily infirmity. He called, without design, on five masters successively, all of whom were more or less deformed; one, who taught in a
cellar, being paralytic and horribly distorted. * * * [Assistant Commissioner]
Dr. Hodgson's Report shows [that] "When other occupations fail, even for a
time, a private school can be opened, with no capital beyond the cost of a
ticket in the widow. Any room, however small and close, serves for the purpose; the children sit on the floor, and bring what books they please: whilst
the closeness of the room renders fuel superfluous, and even keeps the children quiet by its narcotic effects. If the fees do not pay the rent, the school
is dispersed or taken by the next tenant."

*   *   *

[From the Report by Assistant Commissioner A. F. Forster]

I met with very few day schools indeed in which it seemed that the words
read or repeated from a book, even with apparent ease, conveyed any idea to
the mind of the pupil. For instance, a smart little boy read the first verse of
the ninth chapter of St. Matthew's Gospel, "And he entered into a ship, and
passed over, and came into his own city." I asked, "What did he enter into?"
"Don't know, thank you, Sir," replied the boy politely. "Read it again. Now
what did he come into?" "Don't know, thank you, Sir." In another school, a
girl of about 13 years of age was directed to "say her geography" to me, and
after she had repeated the boundaries of several countries, I asked, "What is
a boundary?" "It's a year's wages." My question had suggested to her mind
the terms on which the pitmen are in some collieries *bound* for a year to
their employment. Doubtless she did not dream of its connexion with the
lesson she had just repeated. These are fair specimens of the usual results of
any effort to elicit the children's apprehension of what they were learning—
either total silence or an answer perfectly irrelevant. The truth which has

been forced upon me in a way it never was before is, that the language of books is an unknown tongue to the children of the illiterate, especially in remote situations. It is utterly unlike their vernacular dialect, both in its vocabulary and construction, and, perhaps, not less unintelligible than Latin generally was to the vulgar in the middle ages. * * *

* * *

[From the Report by Assistant Commissioner Dr. W. B. Hodgson]

* * * [N]one [of the Dame School teachers] are too old, too poor, too ignorant, too feeble, too sickly, too unqualified in any or every way to regard themselves, and to be regarded by others, as unfit for school-keeping. Nay, there are few, if any, occupations regarded as incompatible with school-keeping, if not as simultaneous, or at least as preparatory employment. Domestic servants out of place; discharged barmaids; venders of toys or lollipops; keepers of small eating-houses, of mangles, or of small lodging-houses; needle-women, who take in plain or slop work; milliners, consumptive patients in an advanced stage; cripples almost bedridden; persons of at least doubtful temperance; outdoor paupers; men and women of 70 and even 80 years of age; persons who spell badly (mostly women, I grieve to say), who can scarcely write, and who cannot cipher at all; such are some of the teachers, not in remote rural districts, but in the heart of London, the capital of the world, as it is said to be, whose schools go to make up two-thirds of English schools, and whose pupils swell the muster roll that some statistical philanthropists rejoice to contemplate, and to inscribe with the cheering figure, 1 in 8. * * *

The following letter [by the keeper of a Dame-School], addressed to me, is copied *literatim:*—

"Sir, I regret that I am not able to attend to all the rules lade down in thee in closed, as my school is of to numbel a cast to meat eyes (of thee publick gaze) at thee same time Sir, I shal be moust appay to refur you to my Children's Parents, as kindly favord me with thir children for some Years any further information that you require Sir, I shall bee moust appey to give Pardone defects I remain

Your most Numbel Servant,
Elen D."

* * *

The instruction in all Sunday schools [Hodgson continues], whether of the established or of dissenting churches, or even non-demonination, is certainly not secular, but as purely as possible religious, that is theological; in no one instance have I found writing to be taught, and reading is taught only incidentally, and by means of Bible lessons. In one school I found a class of infants being taught their letters, but even here every letter was made a peg on which to hang a Scripture narrative, A standing for *Abraham* or *Abel* (instead of the *Archer* or *Apple-pie* of ancient primers). I was used to introduce Isaac, and the teacher recounted Abraham's attempted sacrifice of his son at such length as to endanger the effect of the lesson in its literary bearing. The Bible reading was usually drowsy and sing-song; the questions, if any, were of the leading sort, to which the answer was almost inevitable, *e.g.*, God,

Christ, Heaven, Hell, Sin &c. One (certificated) teacher, from whom I had expected better things, unable to extract from his class what it was that man had committed against God to deserve his anger, told them that the word began with S, whereupon arose a general shout of "Sin;" and so the word "Mediator" was suggested by the announcement that it began with M. * * * One thing is very striking, that what is called "THE WAY OF LIFE," including all human duties, the subject which, may fairly be regarded as the pith and marrow of true religious teaching, is not precisely left to chance, but assigned to the fifth Sunday in the month, when there happens to be one (in 1859 there are four such Sundays), a thirteenth of the year's available time; and the subjects chosen for those four days are Repentance, Faith, Prayer, and Holiness. Among the subjects selected for other Sundays I observe "Absalom's Rebellion and Death," "Jehoshaphat's Reign," "Elijah's Last Days," "Elijah's Last Miracles," "The Reign of Joash," &c.[1] Am I wrong in my conviction that such teaching can have little influence in fitting for the struggle with the dangers, the trials, the temptations of actual daily, English, nineteenth-century life? * * *

Again, it may fairly be questioned whether the repetition of Scripture texts, with the full reference of chapter and verse, be an efficient mode of awakening the moral sentiment, and applying moral principle to the complicated relations of daily modern life. * * * It is distressing to hear how texts are rattled over in schools, and to observe how seldom an explanation is given or thought to be required. "What passage in Scripture commands 'duty to parents?'" asks the master of a school that I visited. Twenty arms are extended: one pupil is fixed on, and he shouts out—"Exodus, 20th chapter and 12th verse, 'Honour thy father and mother, that thy days may be long in the land that the Lord thy God giveth thee.'" But neither pupil nor teacher seemed to have ever inquired whether, or how this applies to them. Is Middlesex or Surrey the promised land here spoken of? * * * I venture to think that neither morality nor intelligence can be promoted by teaching children (as I was myself taught) that they must not lie because Ananias and Sapphira were struck dead,[2]—or that sleeping in church is a sin, because Eutychus "fell down from the third loft," and was "taken up (as one) dead," (though he afterwards recovered), "as Paul was long preaching," (Acts xx. 9).[3] * * *

*　　*　　*

1. Absalom's rebellion against King David and his murder by David's field-commander Joab forms the substance of 2 Samuel 12–18. Jehoshaphat, fourth king of Judah, reigned piously and prosperously from 870 to 845 B.C., introducing legal reforms, purging the kingdom of pagan idolaters, and concluding the feud with Israel by intermarriage (2 Chronicles 17–20; 1 Kings 22.41–50). Elijah the Tishbite, by means of a fire curse, destroyed two royal messengers and their contingents to penalize Ahaziah, ninth king of Israel, for seeking deathbed medical advice from Baal-ze-bub the god of Ekron instead of consulting the God of Israel: a miracle followed shortly afterwards by Elijah's translation to heaven in a chariot of fire (2 Kings 1–2). Joash I, ninth king of Judah, whose forty-year reign from 835 to 796 B.C. witnessed large-scale religious defections and military defeats and ended in his being murdered by his servants (2 Kings 11–12; 2 Chronicles 24), compares unfavorably with Joash II, twelfth king of Israel, who, between 793 and 782, defeated the Syrians and subdued Judah, capturing both Jerusalem and the king of Judah, Amaziah, son of Joash I (2 Kings 13.10–14; 2 Chronicles 25.17–24).
2. Ananias, a member of the primitive church of Jerusalem, in collusion with his wife Sapphira, defrauded the common fund by claiming a smaller profit on real estate than he had realized. Charged by Peter with deceit, husband and wife were struck dead (Acts 5.1–10).
3. During Paul's stop-over at the Aegean seaport of Troas, Eutychus, a young citizen, fell from a third-floor window-seat in the middle of Paul's evening lecture, narcotized either by the garish illumination or Paul's longwindedness. Though taken up as dead, he was apparently revived by Paul in time to join the farewell party for the Apostle next day (Acts 20.7–12).

[Dr. Hodgson's Report: Sources and Evidence]

* * *

I extract one or two answers from the report of the examiner on Holy Scripture. A question is asked about the first temptation and the evil that was entailed by disobedience upon mankind. Almost all the answers limit the cause to the necessity of human labour, and no wonder, as the examiner observes, that with such prevailing notions chaplains and country prisons are necessary. Here is one reply, "That evil is, if a wount work neither shall he heat." Another says, "They was turned out of the garden, had to work hard all day, and had skins of animals for clothes." Another, questioned about St. Paul's conversion, tells us "he was then taken to an inn where he stayed for a short time; here was afterwards converted, and his eyes were opened. From then he became a true disciple of Christ. He afterwards visited Itily, Malto, Jimica, and afterwards was sent to the Isle of White."[4]

"In scripture, I find nothing commoner than a knowledge of such facts as the weight of Goliath's spear, the length of Noah's ark, the dimensions of Solomon's temple, or what Samuel did to Agag,[5] by children who can neither explain the atonement, the sacraments, or the parables with moderate intelligence, or tell you the practical teaching of Christ's life: their spelling and English are often equally bad." (J. C. Symons, Esq., Essay read at Educational Conference, June 1857.)

---

4. Obviously a garbled version of Paul's complicated itinerary, which the scribe traces in Acts 9 to 28. Paul's "eyes are opened" in Acts 9.8 and 22.6–11. The student of Genesis 3 occasions confusion: our first parents are expelled not for their idleness but for their tasting of forbidden fruit. But they are clothed in coats of skin in Genesis 3.21 all right and forced to work the earth in 3.23.
5. The dimensions of Noah's Ark are given as three hundred cubits in length, fifty cubits in width, and thirty cubits in height (Genesis 6.15). If we translate the cubit (approximately) into a foot and a half, the Ark assumes the size, virtually, of the *Queen Elizabeth*. Goliath's spear weighed six hundred shekels of iron, or about 350 pounds avoirdupois; Goliath himself stood 9'6" (1 Samuel 17.5–7). Solomon's temple measured 90 ft. × 30 × 45 (1 Kings 6.3). Samuel, enraged by Saul's half-hearted compliance with God's command to destroy the Amalekites, especially by Saul's failure to kill the Amalekite King Agag, subpoenaed the captive king: "And Samuel hewed Agag into pieces before the Lord in Gilgal" (1 Samuel 15.33).

Reformatory: Down and Out in London and Botany Bay

WILLIAM SYKES

[On Gibbeting]†

I am sure you will overlook the intrusion of a letter from a private individual calling your notice to the longer continuance of the revolting spectacle exhibited on the bank of the Thames, and which excites feelings of disgust in the breasts of numerous voyagers to Ramsgate, Margate, France, the Netherlands, &c. &c. I allude to the scare-crow remains of the poor wretches who long since expiated by death their crimes, now hanging upon gibbets. It is said that "persecution ceases in the grave." Let these poor remains find a grave, and the remembrance of their offences pass away. I have heard many ladies anxiously inquire if the boats had passed the gibbets, and not until then would they come upon deck. I have heard seamen say "What honest man would like to have a halter held up to him in menace, and why should they (following their lawful and honest employ) have the hint thus ingeniously prolonged to them?"

* * * Tyburn, Kennington, Hounslow, Wimbledon are all freed from the sad practice: why should it be perpetuated to the disgrace and nuisance of the Port of London? * * * The remains of mortality is a sad sight under any circumstances; under *such* circumstances it is revolting, disgusting, pitiable, dishonourable to the law's omnipotence, and discreditable to the administration of the law.

---

† Letter to Robert Peel, September 15, 1824; Public Record Office, Home Office, 44/14, as quoted in A. Aspinall and E. Anthony Smith, *English Historical Documents* 11 (London, 1959), 401. Reprinted with permission of Eyre & Spottiswoode.
   Robert Peel (1788–1850), the son of a Lancashire cotton manufacturer and a ranking Tory statesman, headed the government from 1841 to 1846. As Home Secretary in Liverpool's ministry he introduced lasting penal reforms that drastically reduced the number of capital crimes and, in 1829, he achieved a breakthrough in public surveillance by founding the Metropolitan Police: see p. 98, n. 2. On the function of the Home Secretary, see p. 340, n. 7.

SIR HENRY HAWKINS

[Firing a Rick and Breaking the Sabbath][†]

* * *

Presently—and deeply is the event impressed on my mind after seventy years of a busy life, full of almost every conceivable event—I saw, emerging from a bystreet that led from Bedford Gaol, and coming along through the square and near the window where I was standing, a common farm cart, drawn by a horse which was led by a labouring man. As I was above the crowd on the first-floor, I could see there was a layer of straw in the cart at the bottom, and above it, tumbled into a rough heap as though carelessly thrown in, a quantity of the same; and I could see also from all the surrounding circumstances, especially the pallid faces of the crowd, that there was something sad about it all. The horse moved slowly along, at almost a snail's pace, while behind walked a poor sad couple with their heads bowed down, and each with a hand on the tail-board of the cart. They were evidently overwhelmed with grief.

Happily we have no such processions now; even Justice itself has been humanized to some extent, and the law's cruel severity mitigated. The cart contained the rude shell into which had been laid the body of this poor man and woman's only son, *a youth of seventeen, hanged that morning at Bedford Gaol for setting fire to a stack of corn!*

He was now being conveyed to the village of Willshampstead, six miles from Bedford, there to be laid in the little churchyard where in his childhood he had played. He was the son of very respectable labouring people of Willshampstead; had been misled into committing what was more a boyish freak than a crime, and was hanged. That was all the authorities could do for him, and they did it.

* * *

In all cases of unusual gravity three Judges sat together. Offences that would now be treated as not even deserving of a day's imprisonment in many cases were then invariably punished with death. It was not, therefore, so much the nature of the offence as the importance of it in the eyes of the Judges that caused three of them to sit together and try the criminals.

They sat till five o'clock right through, and then went to a sumptuous dinner provided by the Lord Mayor and Aldermen. They drank everybody's

---

† From *The Reminiscences of Sir Henry Hawkins, Baron Brampton*, ed. Richard Harris, K.C., 2 vols. (London: Edward Arnold, 1904); I, 3–4, 31–32, 33–34, 40–45, 112–13, 114–15, 165–66, 169–70; II, 200–04.

   Sir Henry Hawkins, Baron Brampton (1817–1907), was a highly successful and esteemed judge on the Queen's bench from 1876 to 1898, a period that saw the severity with which criminals were punished earlier in the century give way to greater leniency. Hawkins was admired for his masterful methods of cross-examination; his role in high-profile cases like Orsini's assassination attempt on Napoleon III helped make his reputation as a lawyer. Though known popularly as "Hanging Hawkins," he set an example in favoring light punishments for first-time offenders. Some doubt has been cast on the accuracy of his memoirs, which seem to have been freely transcribed. On the place of Hawkins's dossier in current critical controversy, see K. J. Fielding's essay below, which alerted me to the memoirs.

health but their own, thoroughly relieved their minds from the horrors of the court, and, having indulged in much festive wit, sometimes at an alderman's expense, and often at their own, returned into court in solemn procession, their gravity undisturbed by anything that had previously taken place, and looking the picture of contentment and virtue.

Another dinner was provided by the Sheriffs; this was for the Recorder, Common Serjeant,[1] and others who took their seats when their lordships had arisen.

I ought to mention one important dignitary—namely, the chaplain of Newgate—whose fortunate position gave him the advantage over most persons, for he *dined at both these dinners*, and assisted in the circulation of the wit from one party to another; so that what my Lord Chief Justice had made the table roar with at five o'clock, the Recorder and the Common Serjeant roared with at six, and were able to retail at their family tables at a later period of the evening. It was in that way so many good things have come down to the present day.

*   *   *

Let me illustrate it [the rapidity with which after-dinner trials were conducted] by a trial which I heard. Jones was the name of the prisoner. His offence was that of picking pockets, entailing, of course, a punishment corresponding in severity with the barbarity of the times. It was not a plea of 'Guilty,' when, perhaps, a little more inquiry might have been necessary: it was a case in which the prisoner solemnly declared he was 'Not guilty,' and therefore had a right to be tried.

The accused having 'held up his hand,' and the jury having solemnly sworn to hearken to the evidence, and 'to well and truly try, and true deliverance make,' etc., the witness for the prosecution climbs into the box, which was like a pulpit, and before he has time to look round and see where the voice comes from, he is examined as follows by the prosecuting counsel:

'I think you were walking up Ludgate Hill on Thursday 25th, about half-past two in the afternoon and suddenly felt a tug at your pocket and missed your handkerchief which the constable now produces. Is that it?'

'Yes, sir.'

'I suppose you have nothing to ask him?' says the Judge. 'Next witness.'

Constable stands up.

'Were you following the prosecutor on the occasion when he was robbed on Ludgate Hill, and did you see the prisoner put his hand into the prosecutor's pocket and take this handkerchief out of it?'

'Yes, sir.'

Judge to prisoner: 'Nothing to say, I suppose?' Then to the jury: 'Gentlemen, I suppose you have no doubt? I have none.'

Jury: 'Guilty, my lord,' as though to oblige his lordship.

Judge to prisoner: 'Jones, we have met before—we shall not meet again for some time—seven years' transportation—next case.'

Time: two minutes, fifty-three seconds.

---

1. A judicial officer of the Corporation of the City of London, the Common Serjeant acted as assistant to the Recorder and a judge of the Central Criminal Court; in the nineteenth century sometimes used interchangeably with "Sergeant-at-Law" (see p. 567, n. 1). The functions of the Recorder are explained in chapters 32 (p. 201, n. 8) and 56 (p. 340, n. 6).

Perhaps this case was a high example of expedition, because it was not always that a learned counsel could put his questions so neatly; but it may be taken that these after-dinner trials did not occupy on the average more than *four minutes* each.

*   *   *

On one occasion, before Maule,[2] I had to defend a man for murder. It was a terribly difficult case, because there was no defence except the usual one of insanity. * * *

We * * * called the clergyman of the village where the prisoner lived. He said he had been Vicar for thirty-four years, and that up to very recently, a few days before the murder, the prisoner had been a regular attendant at his church. He was a married man with a wife and two little children, one seven and the other nine.'

'Did the wife attend your ministrations, too?' asked Maule.

'Not so regularly. Suddenly,' continued the Vicar, after suppressing his emotion, 'without any apparent cause, the man became *a Sabbath-breaker*, and absented himself from church.'

[Judge Maule then examines the Vicar to establish the assiduity of his preaching during the years the defendant attended his service.]

His lordship then turned and addressed his observations on the result to me.

'This gentleman, Mr. Hawkins, has written with his own pen and preached or read with his own voice to this unhappy prisoner about *one hundred and four Sunday sermons or discourses, with an occasional homily, every year.'*

There was an irresistible sense of the ludicrous as Maule uttered, or rather growled, these words in a slow enunciation, and an asthmatical tone. He paused as if wondering at the magnitude of his calculations, and then commenced again more slowly and solemnly than before.

'These,' said he, 'added to the week-day services—make—exactly *one hundred and fifty-six sermons, discourses, and homilies for the year.'* (Then he stared at me, asking with his eyes what I thought of it.) 'These, again, being continued over a space of time, comprising, as the reverend gentleman tells us, no less than *thirty-four years*, give us a grand total of *five thousand three hundred and four sermons, discourses, or homilies* during this unhappy man's life.'

Maule's eyes were now riveted on the clergyman as though he were an accessory to the murder. * * *

'I was going to ask you, sir [Maule asked the Vicar], did the idea ever strike you when you talked of this unhappy being suddenly leaving your ministrations and turning Sabbath-breaker, that after thirty-four years * * * the man might think he had had enough of it?'

'It might, my lord.'

---

2. Called to the bar in 1814, Sir William Henry Maule (1788–1858) became King's Counsel at age twenty-three, and after a brief stint as liberal MP, served for sixteen years on the Court of Common Pleas. Maule's memory on the bench was almost legendary, but his caustic wit merely confused jury members.

'And would not that in your judgment, instead of showing that he was insane, prove that he was *a very sensible man?*' * * *

'And,' continued Maule, 'that he was perfectly sane, although he murdered his wife?'

All this was very clever, not to say facetious, on the part of the learned Judge, but as I had yet to address the jury, I was resolved to take the other view of the effect of the Vicar's sermons, and I did so. I worked Maule's quarry, I think, with some little effect; for after all his most strenuous exertions to secure a conviction, the jury believed, probably, that no man's mind could stand the ordeal; and, further, that any doubt they might have, after seeing the two children of the prisoner in court dressed in little black frocks, and sobbing bitterly while I was addressing them, would be given in the prisoner's favour, which it was. * * * On the same evening I was dining at the country house of a Mr. Hardcastle, and near me sat an old inhabitant of the village where the tragedy had been committed.

'You made a touching speech, Mr. Hawkins,' said the old inhabitant.

'Well,' I answered, 'it was the best I could do under the circumstances.'

'Yes,' he said; 'but I don't think you would have painted the little home in such glowing colours if you had seen what I saw last week when I was driving past the cottage. No, no; I think you'd have toned down a bit.'

'What was it?' I asked.

'Why,' said the old inhabitant, 'the little children who sobbed so violently in court this morning, and to whom you made such pathetic reference, were playing on an ash-heap near their cottage; and they had a poor cat with a string round its neck, swinging backwards and forwards, and as they did so they sang:

> ' "This is the way poor daddy will go!
> This is the way poor daddy will go!"

Such, Mr. Hawkins, was their excessive grief!'

Yes, but it got the verdict.

*   *   *

I was born in times when the law sent crowds of people to the gallows after every assize and at every sitting of the Old Bailey, and the calendar which is before me is a record of that portion of English history which is the least creditable to its sense of justice. Its punishments had been too brutal for words to express. Most of those which involved torture had been abolished before my day, but the punishment of death was inflicted for almost every offence of stealing which would now be thought sufficiently dealt with by a sentence of a week's imprisonment. The struggle to turn King's evidence was great, and it was almost a competitive examination to ascertain who knew most about the crime, and he being generally the worst of the gang, was accepted accordingly. * * *

It was in such times that Mr. Justice Graham[3] was called upon to administer the law, and on one occasion particularly he vindicated his character for courtesy to all who appeared before him. He was a man unconscious of

---

3. Appointed to the bench of the exchequer in 1799, a position he filled for twenty-seven years, Sir Robert Graham (1744–1836) was an urbane, inefficient judge, known chiefly for his unfailing politeness.

humour and yet humorous, and was even unconscious of the extreme civility which he exhibited to everybody and upon all occasions, especially to the prisoner.

People went away with a sense of gratitude for his kindness, and when he sentenced a batch of prisoners to death he did it in a manner that might make anyone suppose, if he did not know the facts, that they had been awarded prizes for good conduct. * * *

The learned Mr. Justice Graham asked [a prisoner indicted for murder] if he had any objection to the case being postponed until the next assizes, on the ground, as the prosecution had alleged, that their most material witness could not be produced. His lordship put the case as somewhat of a misfortune for the prisoner, and made it appear that it would be postponed, if he desired it, as a favour to *him*.

Notwithstanding the Judge's courteous manner of putting it, the prisoner most strenuously objected to any postponement. It was not for him to oblige the Crown at the expense of a broken neck, and he desired above all things to be tried in accordance with law. He stood there on his 'gaol delivery.'

Graham was firm, but polite, and determined to grant the postponement asked for. In this he was doubtless right, for the interests of justice demanded it. But to soften down the prisoner's disappointment and excuse the necessity of his further imprisonment, his lordship addressed him in the following terms, and in quite a sympathetic manner:

'Prisoner, I am extremely sorry to have to detain you in prison, but *common humanity* requires that I should not let you be tried in the absence of an important witness for the prosecution, although at the same time I can quite appreciate your desire to have your case speedily disposed of; one does not like a thing of this sort hanging over one's head. But now, for the sake of argument, prisoner, suppose I were to try you to-day in the absence of that material witness, and yet, contrary to your expectations, they were to find you guilty. What then? Why, in the absence of that material witness, I should have to sentence you to be hanged on Monday next. That would be a painful ordeal for both of us.

'But now let us take the other alternative, and let us suppose that if your trial had been put off, and the material witness, when called, could prove something in your favour—this sometimes happens—and that that something induced the jury to acquit you, what a sad thing that would be! It would not signify to you, because you would have been hanged, and would be dead!'

Here his lordship paused for a considerable time, unable to suppress his emotion, but, having recovered himself, continued:

'But you must consider what my feelings would be when I thought I had hanged an innocent man!'

At the next assizes the man was brought up, the material witness appeared; the prisoner was found guilty, and hanged.

* * *

If a man about to be tried for his life could look on [a specially hideous cell in Newgate] and its horrors unmoved, he would certainly be a fit subject for the attentions of the hangman, and deserving of no human sympathy. It was enough to shake the nerves of the hangman himself.

We were in an apartment on the north-east side of the quadrangular building, where the sunshine never entered. Even daylight never came, but only a feeble, sickening twilight, precursor of the grave itself. It was not merely the gloom that intensified the horrors of the situation, or the ghastly traditions of the place, or the impending fate of our callous client; but there was a tier of shelves occupying the side of the apartment, on which were placed in dismal prominence the plaster of Paris busts of all the malefactors who had been hanged in Newgate for some hundred years.[4]

No man can look attractive after having been hanged, and the indentation of the hangman's rope on every one of their necks, with the mark of the knot under the ear, gave such an impression of all that can be conceived of devilish horror as would baffle the conceptions of the most morbid genius.

Whether these things were preserved for phrenological purposes or for the gratification of the most sanguinary taste I never knew, but they impressed me with a disgust of the brutal tendency of the age.

*   *   *

THE CROWN CALENDAR

FOR THE LINCOLNSHIRE LENT ASSIZES[5]

Holden at the Castle of Lincoln on Saturday the 7th of March, 1818, before the Right Honorable Sir Vicary Gibbs and the Honorable Sir William Garrow

JOHN CHARLES LUCAS CALCRAFT, Esq., Sheriff

1. William Bewley, aged 49, late of Kingston upon Hull, pensioner from the 5th Regt. of foot, committed July 29, 1817, charged on suspicion of having feloniously broken into the dwelling house of James Crowder at Barton, no person being therein, and stealing 1 bottle green coat, 1 velveteen jacket, 3 waistcoats, &c. Guilty—Death.

2. John Giddy, aged 22, late of Horncastle, tailor, com. Aug. 5, 1817, charged with stealing a silver watch with a gold seal and key, from the shop of James Genistan of Horncastle. Six Months Imprisonment.

*   *   *

5. George Crow, aged 15, late of Frith Ville, com. Sept. 23, 1817, charged on suspicion of having entered the dwelling house of S. Holmes of Frith Ville, about 7 o'ck in the morning, breaking open a desk, and stealing three £1 notes, 3s. 6d. in silver, and a purse. Guilty—Death.

6. Thomas Young, aged 17, late of Firsby, laborer, com. Sept. 23, 1817, charged with having, about 11 o'ck at night, entered the dwelling house of John Ashlin of Firsby, with intent to commit a robbery. Guilty—Death.

4. The busts are evidently next of kin to Jaggers's "ill-looking relations" in chapter 20.
5. Name given to the court, time, or place where, by special commission from the Crown, judges were sent on circuits throughout the kingdom to take indictments, and with the help of a jury from the county in which the trial took place, to try disputed cases issuing out of the courts at Westminster.

*   *   *

9. John Marriott, aged 19, late of Osgodby, laborer, com. Oct. 18, 1817, charged with maliciously and feloniously setting fire to an oat stack, the property of Thomas Marshall of Osgodby. Guilty—Death.

*   *   *

11. Elizabeth Firth, aged 14, late of Burgh cum Girsby, spinster, com. Nov. 22, 1817, charged with twice administering a quantity of vitriol or verdigrease powder, or other deadly poison, with intent to murder Susanna, the infant daughter of George Barnes of Burgh cum Girsby. No true Bill.[6]

12. John Moody, aged 28, late of Stallingborough, laborer, com. Dec. 24, 1817, charged with having committed the odious and detestable crime and felony called sodomy. Indicted for misdemeanor. Two years imprisonment.

*   *   *

14. Richard Randall, aged 27,⎫
15. John Tubbs, aged 29, ⎬ both late of Lutton, laborers,
com. Dec. 29, 1817, charged with feloniously assaulting Wm. Rowbottom of Holbeach Marsh, between 11 and 12 o'ck in the night, in a field near the king's highway, and stealing from his person 3 promissory £10 notes, 8 or 10 shillings in silver, one silver stop and seconds watch, and various other goods and chattels. Both Guilty—Death.

16. William Hayes, aged 20, late of Braceby, weaver, com. Jan. 6, 1818, charged with feloniously stealing a mare, together with a saddle and bridle, the property of Ed. Briggs of Hanby. Guilty—Death.

*   *   *

21. William Bell, alias John Brown, aged 30, late of Alvingham, laborer, com. Feb. 19, 1818, charged with burglariously breaking into the shop of Wm. Goy of Alvingham, and stealing 1 pair of new shoes, 1 half boot, and 1 half boot top. Guilty—Death.

22. John Hoyes, aged 48, late of Heckington, com. Feb. 24, 1818, charged with feloniously stealing 2 pigs of the value of £3 the property of John Fairchild of Wellingore. Acquitted.

*   *   *

---

6. Bill of indictment endorsed by a grand jury once the evidence convinces them of the probable truth of the accusation.

IN HIS MAJESTY'S GAOL IN THE CITY OF LINCOLN

1. Daniel Elston, aged 34, late of Waddington, cordwainer, com. Sep. 22, 1817, charged with feloniously stealing from the dwelling-house of Rd. Blackbourn of Waddington, one silver watch, and a pair of new quarter boots.— Guilty of stealing only—7 years transportation.

2. William Kehos, aged 22, a private soldier in the 95th Regt. of foot, com. Nov. 17, 1817, charged with feloniously slaughtering and stealing from the close of Mathew White of Lincoln one wether hog.—Guilty—Death.

JEREMY BENTHAM

Of Transportation†

I. The main object or end of penal justice is *example*—prevention of similar offences, on the part of individuals at large, by the influence exerted by the punishment on the minds of bystanders, from the apprehension of similar suffering in case of similar delinquency. Of this property, transportation is almost destitute: this is its radical and incurable defect. * * * Punishments which are inflicted at the antipodes—in a country of which so little is known, and with which communication was so rare, could make only a transient impression upon the minds of people in this country. "The people," says an author who had deeply considered the effects of imagination, "the mass of the people make no distinction between an interval of a thousand years and of a thousand miles."[1] It has been already said, but cannot be too often repeated and enforced, that the utility and effect of example is not determined by the amount of suffering the delinquent is made to endure, but by the amount of apparent suffering he undergoes. It is that part of his suffering which strikes the eyes of beholders, and which fastens on their imagination, which leaves an impression strong enough to counteract the temptation to offend. However deficient they may be in respect of exemplarity, the sufferings inflicted on persons condemned to this mode of punishment are not the less substantial and severe: confinement for an unlimited time in prisons or in the hulks—a voyage of from six to eight months, itself a state of constant

† From *Principles of Penal Laws* (1802), part 2, book 5, chapter 2; *Works* 1: 490–97.
  Jeremy Bentham (1748–1832), seminal political economist, is the father (with James Mill) of Utilitarianism, a philosophy rooted in the belief that happiness and utility are best served by self-interest. For Bentham, the end of social and private well-being lay in "the greatest happiness of the greatest number"—the catchphrase to which Bentham's twenty volumes of prose are frequently melted down. (Bentham almost certainly didn't originate it, but he did invent a "felicific calculus," or happiness gauge, which apparently failed to be operational.) A pioneer of prison reform, Bentham crusaded against the futility and viciousness of transportation. In his longest essay on the subject, *Panopticon vs. New South Wales*, cast in the form of two letters to the Home Secretary, Lord Pelham (November and December 1802), he played off the evils of transportation against his hobbyhorse, the construction of a government-sponsored penitentiary, a circular fortress with a central watchtower from which a thousand eyes kept continuous watch over the inmates—a scary forerunner of Big Brother's televised omnipresence in George Orwell's *1984* (1947), and a subject that continues to fascinate sociocultural historians, most recently Gertrude Himmelfarb, "The Haunted House of Jeremy Bentham," *Victorian Minds* (New York: Knopf, 1968), 32–81, and Michel Foucault in his study on the origins of prisons *Surveiller et punir* (*Discipline and Punish*, 1975).
1. Not traced. But throughout this excerpt and his other essays that deal with Australian penal settlements, Bentham acknowledges his debt to the eyewitness account by David Collins, *Account of the English Colony in New South Wales from Its First Settlement in January 1788 to August 1801* (London: T. Cadell Jun. and W. Davies, 1798–1802; rept. Adelaide: Libraries Board of South Australia, 1971). [*Editor.*]

sufferance from the crowded state of the ships and the necessary restraint to which convicts are subjected—the dangers of the sea—exposure to contagious diseases, which are often attended with the most fatal consequences.

* * *

* * * Here, then, is punishment, partly intentional, partly accidental, dealt out with the most lavish profuseness; but compared with its effects in the way of example, it may be considered as so much gratuitous suffering, inflicted without end or object. A sea of oblivion flows between that country and this. It is not the hundredth, nor even the thousandth part of this mass of punishment, that makes any impression on the people of the mother country—upon that class of people who are most likely to commit offences, who neither read nor reflect, and whose feelings are capable of being excited, not by the description, but by the exhibition of sufferings. The system of transportation has, moreover, this additional disadvantage, which not merely neutralizes its effects in the discouragement of offences, but renders it, in many cases, an instrument of positive encouragement to the commission of offences: A variety of pleasing illusions will, in the minds of many persons, be connected with the idea of transportation, which will not merely supplant all painful reflections, but will be replaced by the most agreeable anticipations.[2] It requires but a very superficial knowledge of mankind in general, and more especially of the youth of this country, not to perceive that a distant voyage, a new country, numerous associates, hope of future independence, and agreeable adventures, will be sufficiently captivating to withdraw the mind from the contemplation of the painful part of the picture, and to give uncontrouled sway to ideas of licentious fascinating enjoyment.

* * *

The punishment of transportation, which, according to the intention of the legislator, is designed as a comparatively lenient punishment, and is rarely directed to exceed a term of from seven to fourteen years, under the system in question is, in point of fact, frequently converted into capital punishment. What is the more to be lamented is, that this monstrous aggravation will, in general, be found to fall almost exclusively upon the least robust and least noxious class of offenders—those who, by their sensibility, former habits of life, sex and age, are least able to contend against the terrible visitation to which they are exposed during the course of a long and perilous voyage. Upon this subject the facts are as authentic as they are lamentable.

* * *

Whatever may be the precautions employed, by any single accident or act of negligence, death, under its most terrific forms, is at all times liable to be introduced into these floating prisons, which have to traverse half the surface of the globe, with daily accumulating causes of destruction within them, before the diseased and dying can be separated from those who, having es-

---

2. Not many years ago, two young men, the one about 14, the other about 16 years of age, were condemned, for a petty theft, to be transported. Upon hearing this unlooked for sentence, the youngest began to cry. "Coward," said his companion, with an air of triumph, "who ever cried because he had to set out upon the grand tour?" This fact was mentioned to me by a gentleman who was witness to this scene, and was much struck with it. [Author.]

caped infection, will have to drag out a debilitated existence in a state of bondage and exile.

Can the intention of the legislator be recognised in these accumulated aggravations to the punishment denounced? Can he be said to be aware of what he is doing, when he denounces a punishment, the infliction of which is withdrawn altogether from his controul—which is subjected to a multiplicity of accidents—the nature of which is different from what it is pronounced to be—and in its execution bears scarce any resemblance to what he had the intention of inflicting? Justice, of which the most sacred attributes are certainty and precision—which ought to weigh with the most scrupulous nicety the evils which it distributes—becomes, under the system in question, a sort of lottery, the pains of which fall into the hands of those that are least deserving of them. Translate this complication of chances, and see what the result will be: "I sentence you," says the judge, "but to what I know not—perhaps to storm and shipwreck—perhaps to infectious disorders—perhaps to famine—perhaps to be massacred by savages—perhaps to be devoured by wild beasts. Away—take your chance—perish or prosper—suffer or enjoy: I rid myself of the sight of you: the ship that bears you away saves me from witnessing your sufferings—I shall give myself no more trouble about you."

A CONVICT'S RECOLLECTIONS OF NEW SOUTH WALES†

Written by Himself

[The following very curious, and in some points of view, very instructive account, is the genuine composition of one Mellish who had returned from transportation; and, being again committed to the gaol of one of the midland counties, set himself about describing what he had seen for the amusement of the gaoler's wife. The manuscript has been faithfully adhered to in all respects. On the back is inscribed MELLISH'S BOOK OF BOTANY BAY. The manuscript terminates abruptly. It is written in a copy-book, which is filled to the very covers; but the story breaks off in the middle of a sentence. The following title is Mellish's own.—Ed.]

An Account of the Treatment of Convicts, and How They Are Dispos'd of in New South Wales

When they first leave the hulks, every man pulls of his hulk dress, and has given him a fresh dress, jacket and trowsers; then goes on board the Bay ship, there every man is examined by the doctor; if he thinks any of them is not fit for the voyage, they are sent back to the hulks and others sent in lieu of them; then all their names is call'd over and every man sent down between decks, every man in dubble iron's, but very light ones; then the doctor and one of the mates comes down, and puts 6 men in a birth, each birth about three I may say 4 yards wide; * * * then there is an hospital in the same

---

† *The London Magazine* 2 (May 1825): 49–67. The bracketed note above is the magazine editors'. Unless otherwise noted, footnotes are by the editor of this Norton Critical Edition.

deck, a small place petishioned of, and if any of the men is sick, or in a dangerous state, they are put there, and every attention paid to them. I understand the doctor as[1] a guinea for every one he lands in New South Wales alive[2][.] * * * As to provishions there is not much reason to find fault; on Sunday's, plumb pudding with suet in it, about a pound to each man, likewise a pound of beef; Monday, pork a pound and peas with it; Tuesday, beef and rice; Wednesday, same as on Sunday; Thursday, same as Monday; Friday, beef and rice and pudding; Saturday, pork only, for breakfast oatmeal boil'd, with about 2 ozs. of sugar to each man. * * * The only place they stop at is Riodiginaro,[3] some time a week and some times not so long, as the captain thinks proper; a very pretty view of the town; plenty of bum boates[4] comes along side with fruit and tobacco. * * * Captain and mates in general purchase tobacco and rum and sugar; tobacco 1¼d. a pound; rum and sugar very cheap. Convicts are allowd to purchase any thing but spirits; coffee 1½d. pound; sugar 2½d. lb.; tea very good at about 3s. 6d. lb.[5] Convicts as serv'd to them, while they are in the harbor, fresh beef and broth, with a deal of garden stuff with it; beef very thin, no fat on it, very bad indeed.

Then when we saile from there, the captain begins to nock of the iron's, about 6 a day, according to the behavior of the men, till they are all off. The next land we see is the Bay; and as soon as a ship is in sight, a flag is histed at a place calld South Head, the mouth of the harbor, which gives the inteliganc to Sydney;[6] * * * then in less than 10 minutes there is no less than 30 or 40 boates full of people round the ship; all hands on deck, but none of the boat people is allow'd to come on board, but close along side; then all the cry is, who is come? is there any body from such a place? and how is such a one? and so on[.] * * * [T]he reason the governor wont allow any one to go on board is, that they should not tell or give them any information respecting the rules and ways of the colony:—for instance, if a man is a good macanick, they will tell them not to say what trade they are, then when they come on shore they are not thought so much of by government; in consequence of that, he is very easy to be got of the stores by his friend; when that is done, he can go to work at his own trade for himself. Then again others will tell their friends on board, to say they are some trade or other, with the view of keeping them from being sent up the country. After they have been in the harbor 4 days, every man gets a fresh supply of cloathing given him, 2 blue jackets, 2 pair of trowsers, 2 pair of shoes, 2 handkerchiefs, 2 waste-

1. Has. Similarly, *is* for *his*, *are* for *hair*, *youse*, *tommy auck*, etc. But Mellish spells no worse than most people of his time and his class. At that, two thirds of the convicts were no more able to sign their names than Joe was.
2. During the run of the Second Fleet in 1790, more than 30 percent of the convicts perished at sea or after debarkation. Once the machinery of transportation was in gear, the death rate dropped noticeably—by the time Mellish sailed in 1810, he had a better than 95 percent chance of arriving intact. Even so, physicians continued to collect tips for delivering their live cargo in one piece.
3. To stock up on provisions, the early convict ships cast anchor at Tenerife, Rio, and Cape Town before clearing the decks for the final haul of sixty-five hundred miles to Botany Bay—for a total distance of nearly sixteen thousand miles. The First Fleet took 258 days (from May 13, 1787, to January 20, 1788) to complete the trip; Mellish, some twenty-two years later, managed the journey in 165 days.
4. "A small boat used to sell vegetables, etc. to ships lying at a distance from the shore" (Falconer).
5. In 1817 sugar at eight pence a pound fetched more than three times as much as in England; and for every pound of coffee he bought in England (eight shillings), Mellish could buy sixty-four pounds in Brazil.
6. Once the First Fleet sailed into Botany Bay, the region revealed itself to be so uninhabitable that Captain Arthur Philipp's convoy sailed to Port Jackson—about to be christened Port Sydney—some fifteen miles to the north. Philipp (1738–1814) became the first governor of the colony and Sydney the unofficial capital, around which the earliest penal settlements were built.

coats, 2 pair stockings, a hat, 3 cotton stripe shirts, a fresh bed and 2 very good blankets, all new; not a single thing of what has been in youse on board to be allowd to go on shore. Then when that is done, every man clean shaved, wash'd, and his are cut in a moderate way; then Superintender of Government Works, and the Commersary General[7] with is Cleark, comes on board, then the men's names are all call'd over, and as they answer their names they pass by one by one; the Superintender ask what trade are you? so and so; have you any complaints to make in respect to your treatment on the voyage? if they have any they relate it; and so on with every one; and if there is a general complaint, the Captain or Doctor gets a very severe reprimand by the Governor; I have known one or two captains to have been try'd for it; but I think its only a matter of form, for they in jeneral win. When all hands has answered there names, they all get into boates and goes on shore; then the town is all of an uproar; a deal of shaking hands and so on: then when all there boxes and bags and bundles are all got on shore togather, a few soldiers is left to guard them, or else they would not remain there long; then all hands walk two by two into a large square, there they stand as they do in this yard[8] only two deep; then the Governor, Superintender, and Doctor, &c. comes; the Governor addresses them, by saying what a fine fruiteful country they are come to, and what he will do for them if there conduct merits it; likewise tells them if they find themselves anyways dessatesfied with there imployer, to go (immediately) to the madjestrate of the district, and he will see him righted.[9]

When that part of the ceremony is perform'd, the Governor, &c. &c. leaves, after complimenting the Doctor a little; then they are all left to the Superintender to dispose of as he thinks proper, he begins first to pick out so many to go to Parramatta, some fit for farmers, and some for difrant trades; then so many to be sent to Windsor; some to Georges River; and the remainder he will dispose of in the town (Sydney),[1] some for grooms, some coachmen, some to one trade and some to an other; those that are made application for by there friends, they are allow'd to take them with them; but if the Superintender knows he his a good trade, he will keep him for Government[.] * * *

It is very seldom that any thieves is sent up the country, as most of the

---

7. Official in charge of food supplies, stores, and transport.
8. Meaning the yard of the prison in which he was at the time of writing confined. [Editors, London Magazine.]
9. Mellish's arrival nearly coincided with the installation of Lachlan Macquarie (1762–1824), the most durable of the colony's twelve governors. Macquarie was sworn in on New Year's Day 1810 and for the next twelve years hardly ever failed to meet the prison ships in the harbor and treat the new recruits to a fatherly pep talk. Macquarie is credited with sweeping innovations in both the appearance and policy of the colony: by recruiting convicts for government service instead of farming them out on private assignments, he carried out massive urban-renewal projects, transforming Sydney and its precincts from a hodgepodge of decaying shanties into respectable Georgian towns, equipped with hospitals, churches, and liveable convict barracks. In depriving the established settlers of their monopoly on convict labor, he antagonized the whole network of Old Boys, with their strong ties to England. This cost him his job, but not before he had insured his survival by dotting the map of eastern Australia with dozens of Macquaries: the index to his own Journals of His Tours in New South Wales and Van Dieman's Land 1818–22 (Sydney: Library of Australian History, 1979), which cover his years as proconsul, lists Macquarie District, Macquarie Fields, Macquarie Grove, Macquarie Pier, Macquarie Plains, Macquarie Points, Macquarie Reach, Macquarie River, Macquarie Springs, a couple of Macquarie Streets, and Port Macquarie.
1. Windsor lies thirty-six miles northwest of Sydney; the source of George's River, which feeds into Botany Bay, lies twenty miles south. Parramatta, sixteen miles west of Sydney, one of the few places to retain the name given it by the blacks (most of the others were named for the empire builders and power brokers in Downing Street and the Colonial Office), had, by 1792, become the most prosperous real estate in the colony.

gentlemen resides in Sydney, and would sooner take for his servant a man that he knows has been a regular thief at home, than one of those barn dore gentlemen;[2] why is it, he knows he can depend on them, for they wont see no tricks play'd with his master's property, nor play none himself; you never hear tell of a thief geting into any trouble; but there is very few goes, when I went, out of 200 men, there was but 5 regular thieves in the whole.[3] If a man commits any crime, he his delt with exactly the same as in England, if found guilty of any thing which wont take their lives, they get a sentence according to the crime; those for short sentance, any thing under 7 year, are sent into the *goal gang*;[4] their cloathing is very dark brown jackets and trowsers, with one side of them white, double iron'd very light, work for Goverment from sun rise to nearly sun down, and then sleep in the goal at night[.] * * * Then on Sunday, every man that is at work for Goverment comes to church in the morning, * * * and if [the Superintendent] sees any man not clean shaved, or with a dirty shirt on, he calls a constable and sends him to goal while Monday morning; and a second time sends him to goal every day after he has done his work for a week; and if any man is absent from church without lief, he is treated in a simular way; and if that wont do, they sometimes get what we call a civel check,[5] 25 lashes, which cures them in jeneral the first dressing.

Now we will return again to say what sentence men are liable to.[6] If they get more than 2 year for a crime [committed on the colony's grounds], they are sent to a place call'd the Coal River, about 400 miles by water, some for 7 year, 14 year, and life. There they work at geting coales up to there middle in water. Then if they transgress again, they are sent by the madjestrate up to the lime burners.[7] They make lime out of oyster shells; they can't stand that work long, for it is very unholesome and gets into there eyes and blinds them; gets the same provishions as usual. If they commit any murder, which is very frequently the case, they are sent to Sydney and try'd for it, and if found guilty, they are taken back, and as neer to the spot as possable executed. A great many murders committed, and in jeneral by the Irish people.[8]

A man after he has served his master 3 years, and no complaint, is entitled

2. A peasant convict who, unlike his slick double from the city, lacks the brains of the professional thief and so can't be trusted to protect his master's house.
3. Four-fifths of the transportees from the U.K. (and more than nine-tenths from England) had been convicted of some form of theft. Presumably Mellish is talking not about pedestrian offenses against property like shoplifting or stealing a cow but commutable capital crimes like stealing an heiress or assaulting a Privy Councillor.
4. Chain gang.
5. A reprimand: Mellish's caustic understatement for flogging.
6. If it is a Judge's sentence, his former sentence stands still till his collonian one is done, then it begins again; but if a madjestrate's sentence his old sentence goes on. [*Mellish's note.*] Magistrates, who generally lack legal training, are regarded as inferior judicial officers.
7. As Mellish implies, the two extreme punishments. But they were almost certainly inflicted not four hundred miles from Sydney but seventy—at Coal Harbor, a swamp near Newcastle, the first of the penal outposts, which was activated north of Sydney in 1801. Newcastle itself, a shanty town teeming with sandflies, mosquitoes, and poisonous snakes, was rife with dysentery and cholera.
8. One-fourth of the convicts, many of them political offenders, were Irish—at a time when the population of Ireland made up one-third of the population of the entire U.K. The Irish formed the largest and most cohesive minority in the colonies, the most despised, repressed, brutalized—and the most feared, as likely insurrectionists both at sea and on land. As victims of political cleansing, they were given the deadliest jobs in the most infamous places of the colony. Even the humane Mellish speaks of them with bland disdain. The last convicts to be dumped on Australia—by then to the West Coast—were a boatload of Fenian rebels, members of the short-lived Irish revolutionary movement, which had spread from America to Ireland proper in 1865, three years before they became the last transportees.

to a ticket of leave,[9] that is to go any ware and work for himself, but receives nothing out of the stores. The regular way of obtaining a ticket of leave, is in first place to get a petition signed by your master, the parson of the town you belong to, and by the madjestrates of the same place; the Governor receives petitions the first Monday in the month, then you take or send your petition to Goverment House; then next 1st Monday you must go yourself, and the Governor if he thinks proper will signe it; and if the man conducts himself for a few years longar, 4 or 5, the Governor will give him an emansipation, by petitioning him in same way as before; and that will make him quite free in the country.

* * *

---

9. A good-conduct certificate that granted convicts limited freedom of movement and permission to work before their sentence expired: a seven-year transportee could be paroled after four years (but Mellish speaks of three), a fourteen-year convict after six, and a Lifer after eight. In practice the ticket had to be renewed every year and could be revoked at any time or withheld by the convict's master.

Theatrical

SAMUEL RICHARDSON

The Apprentice's Vade Mecum*
[A Gloss on George Barnwell]†

The Word *Apprentice* is derived * * * from the French *Apprentisse,* from the Latin *Apprehendere,* which signifies to *apprehend* or to *learn,* which is the Duty of a young Man entering into an Engagement to *learn* or *apprehend* the Art or Mystery to which he is bound *Apprentice.*

* * *

During which Term the said Apprentice his said Master faithfully shall serve, his Secrets keep, i.e., All those Secrets which relate to his Family-Affairs or Business, or to any Part of his Concerns, which being revealed, might be detrimental to his Master's Reputation or Interest. * * * There cannot be a more infamous Breach of the Rules of sound Morality, than for a Person to betray his Master's Secrets; which, but for the Confidence placed in his Integrity, and the just Expectations his Master had of his Fidelity and bounden Duty, had never come to his Knowledge; and which therefore is so vile a Breach of Trust, so high a Degree of Treachery, that it ought to make him odious to all Men.

* * *

The * * * Restriction, *viz.* "Not to haunt *Play-houses,*" is likewise of great Importance, and deserves to be consider'd very attentively. * * * We would not, like some narrow Minds, argue against the *Use* of any thing, because of the *Abuse* of it: And therefore shall frankly acknowledge it as our Opinion, that under proper Regulations, the *Stage* may be made subservient to excellent Purposes, and be an useful Second to the *Pulpit* itself: Even as it *is* conducted, which every sober Person I believe will allow is far from being done in an unexceptionable Manner, the Stage may be a tolerable Diversion to such as know not how to pass their Time, and who perhaps would spend it much worse, either in Drinking, Gaming, &c. if they did not go to the Play-house. But for a young *Tradesman* himself, much more an *Apprentice,* to make this a favourite Diversion, and to *haunt* or frequently go to a Play-house, who can bestow his Time much more to the Advantage of his Business,

---

* Lit., "Go with me." Richardson's subtitle, *Young Man's Pocket Companion,* defines the general meaning as "pocket guide" or "manual."
† From Samuel Richardson, *The Apprentice's Vade Mecum, 1734 and A Seasonable Examination of Playhouses* (London: J. Roberts, 1734 and 1735). Reprinted in *Richardsoniana I* (New York and London, 1974), 1–33, with permission of Garland Publishing, Inc.

which 'tis probable will suffer by it must be allowed to be of very pernicious Consequence. * * *

* * *

Most of our modern Plays, and especially those written in a late licentious Reign,[1] which are reckon'd the best, and are often acted, are so far from being so much as *intended* for Instruction to a Man of Business, that such Persons are generally made the Dupes and Fools of the Hero of it. To make a Cuckold of a rich Citizen, is a masterly Part of the Plot; and such Persons are always introduced under the meanest and most contemptible Characters. * * * And this in a Kingdom which owes its Support, and the Figure it makes abroad, intirely to Trade; the Followers of which are infinitely of more Consequence, and deserve more to be incourag'd, than any other Degree or Rank of People in it. Can it then be prudent, or even decent, for a Tradesman to encourage by his Presence, or support by the Effects of his Industry, Diversions so abusive of the Possession by which he lives, and by which not only these Catterpillars themselves, but the whole Nation, is supported? * * *

* * *

But to follow the arduous Subject a little closer: Let it be consider'd how little suited to the Circumstance of this Class of Youth, is the *Time* which the seeing of a Play requires. The Play generally begins about Six in the Evening, and the usual Time of an Apprentice's Business holds him * * * till Eight or Nine: About which last Hour, except prolong'd by some of the modern Farce, or wretched Pantomime, the Play generally ends. So here are three Hours in every Day that the young Man goes to the Play, (which is near a *Fourth* Part of it) stollen from the Master, and, as it may happen, turn'd to the worst Use that can possibly be made of it, both for Master and Servant. Then again it ought to be consider'd, that most Plays are * * * intirely unsuitable to People of Business and Trade, who, as we observ'd before, are always represented in the meanest and most sordid Lights in which the human Species can possible appear. I know but of one Instance, and that a very late one, where the Stage has condescended to make itself useful to the City-Youth, by a dreadful Example of the Artifices of a lewd Woman, and the Seduction of an unwary young Man; and it would savour too much of Partiality, not to mention it. I mean, the Play of *George Barnwell*, which has met with the Success that I think it well deserves; and I could be content to compound with the young City Gentry, that they should go to this Play once a Year, if they would condition, not to desire to go oftner, till another Play of an equally good Moral and Design were acted on the Stage. * * * Instead

---

1. The twenty-five-year reign of Charles II (1630–85; crowned 1660), the period known as the Restoration, which has been damned and celebrated as a second Sodom in works from John Milton's *Paradise Lost* (1667) to Kathleen Windsor's *Forever Amber* (first printing, 1944). Partly as a function of Charles's own profligacy and unconcealed whoring, partly as a reaction to the surly and acrimonious Puritans who had ruled the roost from 1649 to 1660, the Restoration stage (associated with the playwrights William Congreve, William Wycherly, Sir John Vanbrugh, and George Farquhar) throve on urbane, rakish, suggestive, often salacious plots. Though full five reigns separated Charles's misrule from the publication of Richardson's rule-book, the taste for farces rich in sexual innuendo and outright smut persisted into Richardson's day; one of its chief practitioners, Henry Fielding (1707–1754), titillated the public with titles like *The Debauchee, or The Jesuit Caught*; *The Intriguing Chambermaid*; *The Virgin Unmasked*; *The Coffee House Politician, or Rape upon Rape*—until he was driven from the theater by the Stage Licensing Act of 1737 and forced to abandon trashy plays for great novels. Thus, from 1737 on, apprentices could go to the playhouse without fear of contamination.

of inculcating among [our Youth] such wholesome Rules, to have planted among them an infamous Troop of wretched Strollers, who by our very Laws are deemed Vagabonds, and a collected String of abandon'd Harlots * * * impudently propagating, by heighten'd Action and Scenical Example, to an *underbred* and *unwary* Audience, Fornication, Adultery, Rapes and Murders, and at best teaching them to despise the Station of Life, to which, or worse, they are inevitably destin'd; this surely must have fatal Effects on the Morals both of Men and Women so circumstanced. * * *

* * *

HENRY FIELDING

[*Hamlet* Before Wopsle]†

* * *

Mr. Jones * * * he agreed to carry an appointment, which he had before made, into execution. This was, to attend Mrs. Miller and her younger daughter into the gallery at the playhouse, and to admit Mr. Partridge as one of the company.[1] For as Jones had really that taste for humour which many affect, he expected to enjoy much entertainment in the criticisms of Partridge, from whom he expected the simple dictates of nature, unimproved, indeed, but likewise unadulterated, by art.

In the first row, then, of the first gallery did Mr. Jones, Mrs. Miller, her youngest daughter, and Partridge take their places. Partridge immediately declared it was the finest place he had ever been in. When the first music was played, he said, 'It was a wonder how so many fiddlers could play at one time, without putting one another out.' While the fellow was lighting the upper candles, he cried out to Mrs. Miller, 'Look, look, madam, the very picture of the man in the end of the common-prayer book before the gunpowder-treason service.'[2] Nor could he help observing, with a sigh, when all the candles were lighted, 'That here were candles enough burnt in one night, to keep an honest poor family for a whole twelve-month.'

As soon as the play, which was Hamlet, Prince of Denmark, began, Partridge was all attention, nor did he break silence till the entrance of the ghost; upon which he asked Jones, 'What man that was in the strange dress;

† From Henry Fielding, *The History of Tom Jones: A Foundling* (1749), book 16, chapter 5.
1. Tom's treat and an instance of his goodness. Mrs. Miller is Tom's London landlady; Tom's intercession has kept Nancy Miller from being jilted by the fop who has gotten her pregnant; Partridge, the superstitious, henpecked schoolmaster and barber in the parish in which Tom grows up, has been hounded from his village for allegedly having fathered Tom; he meets up with his putative son en route to London, where the two keep company. At two shillings, the gallery was the second-cheapest seat in the house, a notch above the upper gallery at one shilling.
2. In what is known as the Gunpowder Plot, a number of Catholics, bitterly opposed to the severity of King James I's anti-Roman policies, tried to blow up the King during the opening of Parliament on November 5, 1605. The job of laying and firing the charge devolved on one Guy (or Guido) Fawkes, an obscure Yorkshireman and latecomer to the conspiracy. In 1606 Parliament instituted a thanksgiving service for the Church of England; in revised form this was incorporated into *The Book of Common Prayer* in 1622. On the accession of William III, who landed on English soil on November 5, 1688, eighty-three years to the day after the failed plot, the service was further updated to celebrate Britain's double anniversary. The service, preceded by an etching of Guy Fawkes with dark lantern in hand, became official in 1690; and this would have been the one Partridge knew.

something,' said he, 'like what I have seen in a picture. Sure it is not armour, is it?'—Jones answered, 'That is the ghost.'—To which Partridge replied with a smile, 'Persuade me to that, sir, if you can. Though I can't say I ever actually saw a ghost in my life, yet I am certain I should know one, if I saw him, better than that comes to. No, no, sir, ghosts don't appear in such dresses as that, neither.' In this mistake, which caused much laughter in the neighbourhood of Partridge, he was suffered to continue, till the scene between the ghost and Hamlet, when Partridge gave that credit to Mr. Garrick[3] which he had denied to Jones, and fell into so violent a trembling, that his knees knocked against each other. Jones asked him what was the matter, and whether he was afraid of the warrior upon the stage? 'O la! sir,' said he, 'I perceive now it is what you told me. I am not afraid of anything; for I know it is but a play. And if it was really a ghost, it could do one no harm at such a distance, and in so much company; and yet if I was frightened, I am not the only person.'—'Why, who,' cries Jones, 'dost thou take to be such a coward here besides thyself?'—'Nay, you may call me coward if you will; but if that little man there upon the stage is not frightened, I never saw any man frightened in my life. Ay, ay: go along with you: ay, to be sure! Who's fool then? Will you? Lud have mercy upon such fool-hardiness!—Whatever happens, it is good enough for you.——Follow you? I'd follow the devil as soon. Nay, perhaps it is the devil——for they say he can put on what likeness he pleases.—Oh! here he is again.——No farther! No, you have gone far enough already; farther than I'd have gone for all the king's dominions.' Jones offered to speak, but Partridge cried, 'Hush, hush! dear sir, don't you hear him?' And during the whole speech of the ghost, he sat with his eyes fixed partly on the ghost and partly on Hamlet, and with his mouth open; the same passions which succeeded each other in Hamlet succeeding likewise in him.

When the scene was over Jones said, 'Why, Partridge, you exceed my expectations. You enjoy the play more than I conceived possible.'—'Nay, sir,' answered Partridge, 'if you are not afraid of the devil, I can't help it; but, to be sure, it is natural to be surprised at such things, though I know there is nothing in them: not that it was the ghost that surprised me, neither; for I should have known that to have been only a man in a strange dress; but when I saw the little man so frightened himself, it was that which took hold of me.'—'And dost thou imagine, then, Partridge,' cries Jones, 'that he was really frightened?'—'Nay, sir,' said Partridge, 'did not you yourself observe afterwards, when he found it was his own father's spirit, and how he was murdered in the garden, how his fear forsook him by degrees, and he was struck dumb with sorrow, as it were, just as I should have been, had it been my own case?— But hush! O la! what noise is that? There he is again.——Well, to be certain, though I know there is nothing at all in it, I am glad I am not down yonder, where those men are.' Then turning his eyes again upon Hamlet, 'Ay, you may draw your sword; what signifies a sword against the power of the devil?'

During the second act, Partridge made very few remarks. He greatly admired the fineness of the dresses; nor could he help observing upon the king's countenance. 'Well,' said he, 'how people may be deceived by faces! *Nulla*

---

3. David Garrick (1717–1779), the greatest actor of his age and one of Fielding's closest friends, played Hamlet several times at Covent Garden in May 1746—though at the time of Tom's visit he happened to be performing in Ireland. Below medium height, he would naturally strike Partridge, who is tall as a beanpole, as "that little man."

fides fronti is, I find, a true saying.[4] Who would think, by looking in the king's face, that he had ever committed a murder?' He then inquired after the ghost; but Jones, who intended he should be surprised, gave him no other satisfaction than 'that he might possibly see him again soon, and in a flash of fire.'

Partridge sat in a fearful expectation of this; and now, when the ghost made his next appearance, Partridge cried out, 'There, sir, now; what say you now? is he frightened now or no? As much frightened as you think me, and, to be sure, nobody can help some fears. I would not be in so bad a condition as what's his name, squire Hamlet, is there, for all the world. Bless me! what's become of the spirit? As I am a living soul, I thought I saw him sink into the earth.'—'Indeed, you saw right,' answered Jones.—'Well, well,' cries Partridge, 'I know it is only a play; and besides, if there was anything in all this, Madam Miller would not laugh so; for, as to you, sir, you would not be afraid, I believe, if the devil was here in person.—There, there—Ay, no wonder you are in such a passion; shake the vile wicked wretch to pieces. If she was my own mother, I would serve her so. To be sure, all duty to a mother is forfeited by such wicked doings.——Ay, go about your business, I hate the sight of you.'

Our critic was now pretty silent till the play which Hamlet introduces before the king. This he did not at first understand, till Jones explained it to him; but he no sooner entered into the spirit of it than he began to bless himself that he had never committed murder. Then turning to Mrs. Miller, he asked her, 'If she did not imagine the king looked as if he was touched; though he is,' said he, 'a good actor, and doth all he can to hide it. Well, I would not have so much to answer for as that wicked man there hath, to sit upon a much higher chair than he sits upon. No wonder he run away; for your sake I'll never trust an innocent face again.'

The grave-digging scene next engaged the attention of Partridge, who expressed much surprise at the number of skulls thrown upon the stage. To which Jones answered, 'That it was one of the most famous burial-places about town.'—'No wonder, then,' cries Partridge, 'that the place is haunted. But I never saw in my life a worse grave-digger. I had a sexton, when I was clerk, that should have dug three graves while he is digging one. The fellow handles a spade as if it was the first time he had ever had one in his hand. Ay, ay, you may sing. You had rather sing than work, I believe.'—Upon Hamlet's taking up the skull, he cried out, 'Well! it is strange to see how fearless some men are: I never could bring myself to touch anything belonging to a dead man, on any account.—He seemed frightened enough too at the ghost, I thought. *Nemo omnibus horis sapit*.'[5]

Little more worth remembering occurred during the play, at the end of which Jones asked him, 'Which of the players he had liked best?' To this he answered, with some appearance of indignation at the question, 'The king, without doubt.'—'Indeed, Mr. Partridge,' says Mrs. Miller. 'You are not of the same opinion with the town; for they are all agreed that Hamlet is acted by the best player who ever was on the stage.'—'He the best player!' cries Par-

---

4. From Juvenal, *Satires* (c. A.D. 100–130) 2.6, slightly transposed: "Appearances are deceptive." But Partridge's quotation is not very apropos: Juvenal is lampooning Roman drag queens.
5. Slightly abridged from Pliny the Elder, *Naturalis Historia* (c. A.D. 77) 7.40.1: *"quid quod nemo mortalium omnibus horis sapit?"* ("What of the fact that none among mortal is wise at all times?") Fielding, who almost certainly picked this up from the "Syntaxis" of William Lily's sixteenth-century *Shorte Introduction of Grammar*, appears to have been partial to Pliny's adage, which he quotes three times in the course of *Tom Jones*.

tridge, with a contemptuous sneer; 'why, I could act as well as he myself. I am sure, if I had seen a ghost, I should have looked in the very same manner, and done just as he did. And then, to be sure, in that scene, as you called it, between him and his mother, where you told me he acted so fine, why, Lord help me, any man, that is, any good man, that had such a mother, would have done exactly the same. I know you are only joking with me; but indeed, madam, though I was never at a play in London, yet I have seen acting before in the country: and the king for my money; he speaks all his words distinctly, half as loud again as the other.—Anybody may see he is an actor.'

* * *

Thus ended the adventure at the playhouse; where Partridge had afforded great mirth, not only to Jones and Mrs. Miller, but to all who sat within hearing, who were more attentive to what he said than to anything that passed on the stage.

He durst not go to bed all that night, for fear of the ghost; and for many nights after sweated two or three hours before he went to sleep, with the same apprehensions, and waked several times in great horrors, crying out, 'Lord have mercy upon us! there it is.'

CRITICISM

Contemporary Reviews and Early Comments

FROM *THE SATURDAY REVIEW*†

[Dickens's Comeback]

Mr. Dickens may be reasonably proud of these volumes. After the long series of his varied works—after passing under the cloud of *Little Dorrit* and *Bleak House*—he has written a story that is new, original, powerful, and very entertaining. * * * It is in his best vein, and although unfortunately it is too slight, and bears many traces of hasty writing, it is quite worthy to stand beside *Martin Chuzzlewit* and *David Copperfield*. It has characters in it that will become part of common talk, and live even in the mouths of those who do not read novels. Wemmick strikes us as the great creation of the book, and his marriage as the funniest incident. How often will future jokers observe, "Halloa, here's a church; let's have a wedding." It is impossible not to regret that a book so good should not have been better. Probably the form in which it was first published may have had something to do with its faults. The plot ends before it ought to do. The heroine is married, reclaimed from harshness to gentleness, widowed, made love to, and remarried, in a page or two. This is too stiff a pace for the emotions of readers to live up to. We do not like to go beyond a canter through the moral restoration of a young lady. Characters, too, are entirely altered, in order to make the story end rapidly. Herbert, one of the most pleasing characters Mr. Dickens ever drew, starts as an amiable dreamy creature, incapable of business, and living on the vaguest hopes. But at the close of the tale it becomes necessary to provide for the hero. So Herbert comes out all at once as a shrewd, successful Levant merchant, and takes the hero into partnership. Villains, again, are sketched in and then smeared out again. Old Orlick, the gigantic lout of a blacksmith, commits every kind of atrocity, from breaking the skull of his mistress to purposing to burn the hero in a limekiln, and yet all we hear of him at the end is, that he is taken up for a burglary which forms no part of the story. * * * It is rather a story with excellent things in it than an excellent story.

* * *

† 12 (July 20, 1861): 69–70. All notes in "Contemporary Reviews and Early Comments" are by the editor of this Norton Critical Edition.

FROM *THE SPECTATOR*†

["The Most Successful of His Works Have Been His Most Incoherent"]

The reader of *Great Expectations*, unless he has profited by his experience of Mr. Dickens's recent tales, is placed in much the same position as its hero. He has great and well-founded hopes at the beginning which are bitterly disappointed before the novel is half completed. The disappointment, however, is of an opposite kind. The reader is led to hope, when he begins the tale, that its course is to run continuously through that low life which Mr. Dickens describes with such marvellous accuracy and such delightful humour, to wind quietly among convicts and attorneys' clerks, henpecked blacksmiths, and tailors' apprentices; here we find ourselves, and here we ardently trust we may remain, but the circumstances which raise Mr. Pip's hopes gradually depress ours; when his Ideal fairly enters the tale, we are discomforted, and when Mr. Dickens bursts into lyrics, melodrama, and recitative, we almost make up our mind finally to abandon the story, and are only tempted on by those indications of a flagging wing which suggest that the author must sink again before long into that vulgar life which his genius has thoroughly matured, out of that thin sentimental region where it is utterly paralyzed, or rather transformed into noxious rant.

The cause which renders Mr. Dickens's great genius so comparatively impotent in the more cultivated sphere of life and sentiment which he sometimes essays to paint, is not far to find. In the uneducated classes character is far more characteristically expressed, if we may use the expression, than in the higher. The effect of cultivation is to draw a certain thin semi-transparent medium over the whole surface of human nature, so that the effects of individual differences of character, though by no means hidden, are softened and disguised, and require, not so much a subtle discrimination to discern, as a subtler artistic faculty to delineate without falsification. The power of painting, by the turn of a phrase, by a transposition in a sentence, by a movement, by a mode of receiving or accosting another, the bias of a man's character, is a power apparently of a finer order, but really much less rare and remarkable than the intellectual instrument with which Mr. Dickens fascinates us. There are twenty or thirty writers, many of them ladies, who can use the former faculty to perfection. There is not one who can attempt to rival Mr. Dickens in his own field. The truth is, that to play upon an instrument that demands great delicacy, though it gives out little volume of sound, is far easier than to produce the highest effects from a coarser and rougher organ. * * *

And his special power lies in the manipulation of such well-defined habits of thought, whether professional or otherwise, as mark themselves sharply on the outward bearing of men, and their broadest forms of speech. To these he can give an almost endless and illimitable variety; he will immerse and steep himself in them till he is thoroughly saturated, and then bring them into the most humorous contrast with all things human. * * * But he requires a habit of mind with a definite body to it, and this is so essential to him that he often mistakes the one for the other, and pounces upon some eccentric feature which he has noticed as if a class character could be extorted out of it, when it is quite incapable of yielding anything of the sort. * * * It is one of the disappointing traits in his recent tales that these mere tricks—the accidents, not the essence of human character—have taken the place of that large assemblage of minute, coherent habits which go to make up such a figure as Mrs. Gamp or Mr. Weller[1][.] * * * In this tale, we are sorry to say, and even in the better parts of it, this weakness abounds. * * *

* * *

Mr. Dickens has made another mistake in the attempt which he has obviously made to construct a coherent tale, though it is obvious that his purpose has often wavered, and that many "undeveloped formations" have been finally abandoned before its close. His genius is not suited to a unity of plot. He needs the freedom to ramble when he will and where he will. The most successful of his works have uniformly been the most incoherent of tales. The truth is that he gets too much interested in his own plot, and forgets the characters in his interest in the story. What he does so powerfully cannot be undone under the strain of any exciting emotion. He is great when he accumulates details to illustrate such homely roundabout miscellaneous types of character as he loves most to sketch; but he is very small when he becomes lyrical, and he cannot deal with the destinies of his heroes and heroines without becoming lyrical.

* * *

If Mr. Dickens could only see how much he would gain if he could take a vow of total abstinence from the "Estella" element in all future tales, and limit himself religiously to vulgar life—we do not use the word in the depreciating sense—he might still increase the number of his permanent additions to English literature. This, *Great Expectations* certainly has not done.

HENRY CRABB ROBINSON

["I Would Rather Read a Good Review of It"][†]

July 22nd. . . . I was seduced to read a few chapters in Dickens's *Great Expectations* in consequence of the great praise of the *Saturday Review*, as if it were a revival of his early excellence. I am not sure that I shall go on with it. I do not feel impressed with its truth, though I feel the force of the description of the poverty of the family of the blacksmith and extreme ferocity of the escaped convicts of the prison ship. . . .

---

1. Sairey Gamp is the gin-soaked midwife and nurse in *Martin Chuzzlewit* (1843–44), who speaks a highly personal cockney idiom and keeps quoting a fictitious lady-friend to sing her praises; Sam Weller is Mr. Pickwick's manservant, who cheers himself up with pithy similes and macabre anecdotes.

† From *Diaries*, July to August 1861; in *Henry Crabb Robinson on Books and Their Writers*, ed. Edith J. Morley, 3 vols. (London: J. M. Dent, 1938), vol. 2, 802–3.
   A former reporter, barrister, and friend of Wordsworth and Coleridge, Robinson (1775–1867) is best known as an inveterate chronicler, author of thirty-two volumes of travel journals and thirty-five manuscript volumes of diaries, in which he registers his neural reactions to nearly all of Dickens's novels.

⁂

Aug. 20th. . . . I skimmed volume one of Dickens's last novel. ⁂ It is one of the least agreeable by him that I ever read. . . . Why it has been so praised I cannot conceive. Whether I go on with it or not will depend on circumstances. I would rather read a good review of it.

⁂

Aug. 26th. . . . I devoted the day to the concluding volume of *Great Expectations*. This third volume is far better than the other two, though at the best a disagreeable story. One feels an interest in volume three, but at the best there is an untruth and improbability in all the incidents and characters that destroys it entirely as a novel. One can't believe that a villain like the convict could feel so romantic a love to the boy, who partly from terror and for no other reasonable motive keeps his word to him. Miss Havisham has no truth about her character. And why Jaggers the lawyer and Wemmick the clerk should have so much good as well as bad? Were Jaggers a humorist one might reconcile much. The most important incidents are told short. The poetically conceived Estella consents to marry a wretch, and one cares nothing about her when at the very last her brute of a husband, after cruelly treating her, dies, and the hero by chance falls in with her and we are given to understand they never part. I cannot comprehend the praise given to this tale, which at least interested me; but I regret throwing three days away upon it. Herbert, the generous friend, [son] of the scholar by whom the hero is educated, but of which [whom?] we hear nothing, is a fine character, but he is not made out. The scenes are admirably painted in volume three; the endeavour to escape and capture of the convict, whose riches, by the bye, had they been, would have given him ample means of escape. . . .

[E. S. DALLAS]

[Dickens as Serial Writer]†

The method of publishing an important work of fiction in monthly instalments was considered a hazardous experiment, which could not fail to set its mark upon the novel as a whole. Mr. Dickens led the way in making the experiment, and his enterprise was crowned with such success that most of the good novels now find their way to the public in the form of a monthly dole. We cannot say that we have ever met with a man who would confess to having read a tale regularly month by month, and who, if asked how he liked Dickens's or Thackeray's last number, did not instantly insist upon the impossibility of his getting through a story piecemeal. Nevertheless, the monthly publication succeeds, and thousands of a novel are sold in minute doses, where only hundreds would have been disposed of in the lump.

† From *The Times* 6 (October 7, 1861): columns 3–4.
  In his chief critical work, *The Gay Science* (1860), and in his contributions to Britain's leading dailies and weeklies E(neas) S(weetland) Dallas (1828–1879) sought to explain the psychological sources of "reader response" to poetry, fiction, and rhetoric.

Charles Lamb somewhere speaks of books which are not books,[1] and there is a reading which men accustomed to study will not permit themselves to regard as reading. There are little half-hours and quarters throughout the day which we sometimes know not how to fill up, and in which our idle humour would not allow of our taking up any important work, unless it came before us in the fragments of a monthly issue. Rolling in the railway train or waiting for dinner at the club we get through a chapter or two. We are amused, but we cannot call it reading, and our chief pleasure in turning over the pages is to ascertain whether the novel will be worthy of perusal when it comes out complete. On the whole, perhaps, the periodical publication of the novel has been of use to it, and has forced English writers to develope a plot and work up the incidents. Lingering over the delineation of character and of manners, our novelists began to lose sight of the story and to avoid action. Periodical publication compelled them to a different course. They could not afford, like Scheherazade, to let the devourers of their tales go to sleep at the end of a chapter. * * * Hence a disposition to wind up every month with a melodramatic surprise that awakens curiosity in the succeeding number.

But what are we to say to the new experiment which is now being tried of publishing good novels week by week? Hitherto the weekly issue of fiction has been connected with publications of the lowest class—small penny and halfpenny serials that found in the multitude some compensation for the degradation of their readers. The sale of these journals extended to hundreds of thousands, and so largely did this circulation depend on the weekly tale, that on the conclusion of a good story it has been known to suffer a fall of 40,000 or 50,000. * * * Lust was the alpha and murder the omega of these tales. When the attempt was made to introduce the readers of the penny journals to better authors and to a more wholesome species of fiction, it was an ignominious failure. And the question was naturally raised—is this failure due to the taste of the readers or to the form of the publication? * * * Mr. Dickens has tried another experiment. The periodical which he conducts is addressed to a much higher class of readers than any which the penny journals would reach, and he has spread before them novel after novel specially adapted to their tastes. The first of these fictions which achieved a decided success was that of Mr. Wilkie Collins—*The Woman in White*.[2] * * * The novel was most successful, but if we are from it to form a judgment of the sort of story which succeeds in a weekly issue our estimate will not be very high. Everything is sacrificed to the plot—character, dialogue, passion, description; and the plot, when we come to examine it, is not merely improbable—it is impossible. We are fascinated with a first reading of the tale, but, having once had our curiosity appeased, we never wish to take it up again. * * * [*Great Expectations*] is quite equal to *The Woman in White* in the management of the plot, but, perhaps, this is not saying much when we have to add that the story, though not impossible like Mr. Wilkie Collins's,

---

1. Charles Lamb (1775–1834), "Detached Thoughts on Books and Reading" (*London Magazine*, July 1822; *The Last Essays of Elia*, 1834): "In this catalogue *of books which are not books—biblia-a-biblia—* I reckon Court Calendars, Directories, Pocket Books . . . and, generally, all those volumes which 'no gentleman's library should be without.' "
2. The comparison of Collins's *Woman in White* and Dickens's serials that flanked Collins's novel in *All the Year Round—A Tale of Two Cities* and *Great Expectations*—turned into a critical fad almost from the moment these novels appeared, a comparison encouraged by their success as weeklies. For a good discussion, see Jerome Meckier, *Hidden Rivalries in Victorian Fiction* (Lexington: University of Kentucky Press, 1988).

is very improbable. If Mr. Dickens, however, chose to keep the common herd of readers together by the marvels of an improbable story, he attracted the better class of readers by his fancy, his fun, and his sentiment. Altogether, his success was so great as to warrant the conclusion, which four goodly editions already justify, that the weekly form of publication is not incompatible with a very high order of fiction.

* * *

FROM *THE DUBLIN UNIVERSITY MAGAZINE*†

[Dickens's Tiresome Clowning]

Of those who may have had the boldness to expect great things, even in these latter days, from the growing weakness of a once mighty genius, there can be few who have not already chewed the cud of a disappointment bitter in proportion to the sweetness of their former hopes. * * * * * * After a careful reading of "Great Expectations," we must own to having found the book in most ways better than our very small expectations could have foreboded. But, in saying this much, we are very far from endorsing the notion that it comes in any way near those earlier works which made and which alone are likely hereafter to keep alive their author's fame. * * * [T]ime, flattery, and self-indulgence have robbed his phrases of half their whilom happiness; the old rich humour shines wan and watery through an ever-deepening film of fancies farfetched or utterly absurd; while all the old mannerisms and deformities that once seemed to impart a kind of picturesque quaintness to so many neighbour beauties, have been growing more and more irredeemably ungraceful and pitilessly obtrusive.

* * *

The extravagance of Mr. Dickens's nature often tempts him to harp too much on the same string, to spin too fine a thread out of even his happiest ideas. * * * Whatever grains of humour might have suggested the likening of anybody's mouth to a post-office, their effect is wholly lost in the tiresome frequency with which that likeness is pointed out, until poor Wemmick cannot eat his dinner without being said to post it. So, too, among other bits of illustrative humour touching the Convict's first appearance to little Pip, we are told that as he limped his way in fetters over the churchyard brambles and nettles, he looked, in Pip's young eyes, "as if he were eluding the hands of the dead people, stretching up cautiously out of their graves to get a twist upon his ankle and pull him in." Perhaps the most daring stretch of fancy in the whole book is the account of little Pip's frightened pleading to the face of a black ox, seen through the white marsh-mists, whom his guilty conscience mistook for some minister of punishment come to accuse him of his unwilling theft. In this merciless pumping-up of grotesque or ridiculous fancies Mr. Dickens recalls the similar weakness of an otherwise different writer, whose

† 58 (December 1861): 685–93.

sickly straining after sentimental subtleties marred the great literary merits of "Transformation."[1] But Mr. Hawthorne's whimsies could hardly go down with any but the sickliest of American schoolgirls, while those of Mr. Dickens will often evoke an irrepressible laugh from English boys and men who can sometimes allow themselves to feel like boys.

* * *

About Pip himself, * * * we hardly know what to say. * * * Under Joe's roof, even during the years of his apprenticeship, he seems to win for himself a little of the love so largely due from us to his companion. But * * * Pip's acquaintance with Estella seems gradually to turn him into as feeble a snob as ever was palmed off on the novel reader for a hero. Under the blighting influence of Satis House, his character grows as shadowy as the greatness of his own expectations proves at last to be. The growth of his mad love for a girl of mere moonshine, melts away his manlier qualities, and renders him weakly ungrateful alike to his first and his latest benefactor. Between his departure for London in the character of a new made gentleman and the reappearance of Abel Magwitch, the story of his life is a broad waste of sluggish unreality.

* * *

[J. M. CAPES AND J. E. E. D. ACTON]

["Dickens Knows Nothing of Sin When It Is Not Crime"]†

If we were asked to name the walk in which English literature has in late years most distinguished itself by the side of the literatures of other European countries, we should be disposed to give the palm to our novelists. Not that their works form the most important body of books in positive value; but, in comparison with what is done in other countries, they have carried their peculiar matter to a pitch of excellence unknown elsewhere. In this excellence we must give a very high place to the moral respectability that characterises all our great novelists since Bulwer's reformation,[1] with only so few

---

1. The title under which Nathaniel Hawthorne's last romance appeared in England shortly before its American debut as *The Marble Faun*, in which a mysterious young Italian is transformed from a prelapsarian innocence to a tragic sense of life after murdering his sweetheart's nemesis. The book served as the Michelin of its day—"read," Henry James notes, "by every English-speaking traveller who arrives [in Rome], who has been there, or who expects to go" (*Hawthorne*, 1879).

† From *Rambler* n.s. 6 (January 1862): 274–76.

John Emerich Edward Dalberg Acton, First Baron Acton (1834–1902), the great political essayist and historian of ideas, wrote voluminously on Dickens over more than twenty-five years. A major figure in the liberal Catholic movement and MP from 1859–65, Acton succeeded John Henry Newman as editor of the Catholic monthly the *Rambler*. Acton was among the first to recognize the importance of Karl Marx and the Danish philosopher Søren Kierkegaard.

John More Capes (1812–1889), founder of the *Rambler* and by 1861 its proprietor, author of theological tracts and musicological studies, seesawed between Anglicanism and Catholicism before "seceding to Rome" permanently. Capes drafted the bulk of the review; Acton contributed the first three paragraphs.

1. "Bulwer's reformation" dates from roughly 1850, when he abandoned historical fiction (*Devereux, Last Days of Pompeii, Rienzi*) and stopped glamorizing criminals (*Paul Clifford, Eugene Aram*) to spin domestic tales (*The Caxtons, My Novel*, etc.)

exceptions—perhaps Currer Bell, and perhaps Kingsley[2]—that they serve rather as a foil to the rest. But this respectability was not in fashion when "Boz" began to write; then, the corrupt Bulwer was in the ascendent, and the author of *Pickwick*, to his immense credit, resisted and overcame the evil influence, and won the foremost place in popularity, without pandering for a moment to the prevailing taste for indecency. The thorough youthfulness, fun, and animal spirits of *Pickwick* will always make it the characteristic work of the author; but it is not so decidedly his best book as to deserve to be always referred to as such. Nancy refusing to be delivered from Sikes, when her love for the child had brought her a chance of redemption, and Charley Bates turning against the murderer, are in a higher style than any thing in *Pickwick*.[3]

But both the fun of *Pickwick* and the genuine pathos of *Oliver Twist* soon degenerated into a tedious reiteration of some superficial absurdity that does duty for humour, and into the pathos of a melodrama at a minor theatre. We trace this fall partly to Mr. Dickens's views about religion; he reminds us of certain Germans of the last century, of whom we may take Herder[4] as the type: they saw no divine element in Christianity, but they made humanity their God, and so made their religion simply human, and taught that man was perfectible, but childhood perfect. So they used to die full of benevolence for all men, and of admiration for the sun, the moon, their children, their dog, and their home. * * * They professed a kind of natural religion, adorned with poetry and enthusiasm, quite superior to the narrowness and lowness of Christianity.

Mr. Dickens is very like these men. Nothing can be more indefinite or more human than his religion. He loves his neighbour for his neighbour's sake, and knows nothing of sin when it is not crime. Thus one whole lobe of the human soul is dark to him; he cannot see a whole character, or perhaps has disabled himself from seeing it by his persevering purpose to write up his own particular views. This partly explains his defects of humour—his giving us so few characters and so many caricatures. And these caricatures have been the winding-sheet and the leaden coffin of his humour. For what fun can any one person find in describing a man by an ever-recurring absurdity, by his ever sucking his thumb, by his having a mouth like a letter-box, or by his firing a gun at sundown? It is the mere poverty of an imagination self-restrained to one narrow field of human nature, that makes him search curiously for such follies, and ransack newspapers for incidents to put into his books. * * *

It is the determination to make every thing subservient to this fetishism of

2. Charlotte Brontë (1816–1855) wrote under the pseudonym Currer Bell. Charles Kingsley (1819–1875), writer, clergyman, and early feminist, is best known for his working-class novels *Yeast* (1848) and the autobiographical *Alton Locke, Tailor and Poet* (1849–50), in which he describes the hardships of the agricultural laborer and the London artisan. As Christian Socialist (in 1850 and later, read "anarchist") and promoter of "Muscular Christianity," Kingsley would hardly endear himself to Acton. His anti-Catholic sentiments sparked one of the century's great spiritual autobiographies, Newman's *Apologia Pro Sua Vita* (1864).
3. In *Oliver Twist* the thug Bill Sikes clubs his common-law wife, Nancy, to death for ratting on the gang in order to rescue Oliver and, while escaping from his pursuers, accidentally hangs himself. Charlie Bates, the sunniest of the teen gangsters, reforms under the shock of Nancy's murder.
4. A theologian and seminal thinker, Johann Gottfried von Herder (1744–1803) fell early on under the spell of the enlightened sentimental English and French philosophers. A pioneering student of primitive cultures and languages and John the Baptist of the "Storm and Stress" movement in German literature, Herder is best known for his groundbreaking works *On the Origin of Languages* (1772), *Of the Spirit of Hebrew Poetry* (1782–3), and his *Ideas on the Philosophy of History* (1784–91).

sentimental civilisation that spoils not only the humour of Mr. Dickens, but the temper of his intelligent readers. They do not choose to be insulted with the negative sermons of those pathetic death-beds which are made so much happier by the want of all spiritual assistance, and where the "babbling of green fields"[5] is the all-sufficient substitute for the sterner truths of which dying Christians naturally think.

Yet, with all his faults, we should be puzzled to name Mr. Dickens's equal in the perception of the purely farcical, ludicrous, and preposterously funny, though not so much now, perhaps, as in the days when he had not adopted the stage-trick of putting some queer saying into his characters' mouths, and making them utter it on every possible occasion. It is by a partial flickering up of this bright gift that *Great Expectations* has proved an agreeable surprise to so many of his readers. * * * Wemmick, the lawyer's clerk, who lives in a cockney castle at Walworth, and fires off his gun at sundown every night, is a conception, barring the last characteristic, worthy of Dickens's happiest days. The walk to the wedding is delicious. And, on the whole, then, we may rejoice that even in Mr. Dickens's ashes still live his wonted fires. Perhaps, if he would but lie fallow for a year or two, and let his thoughts range at will, and eschew every thing that is tragic, sentimental, or improving, especially in his particular line of improvement, we need not despair of seeing a still more lively reproduction of the delightful absurdities with which he charmed his readers a quarter of a century ago.

[MRS. OLIPHANT]

["Specimens of Oddity Run Mad"]†

So far as 'Great Expectations' is a sensation novel, it occupies itself with incidents all but impossible, and in themselves strange, dangerous, and exciting; but so far as it is one of the series of Mr Dickens's works, it is feeble, fatigued, and colourless. One feels that he must have got tired of it as the work went on, and that the creatures he had called into being, but who are no longer the lively men and women they used to be, must have bored him unspeakably before it was time to cut short their career, and throw a hasty and impatient hint of their future to stop the tiresome public appetite. * * *

* * * As the story progresses, we learn that [Miss Havisham], who is perfectly sane, much as appearances are against her, has lived in her miraculous condition for five-and-twenty years. Not very long ago we heard an eminent Scotch divine pause in the middle of his exposition to assure his hearers that it was not necessary to believe that the garments of the children of Israel were literally preserved from the wear and tear of the forty years in the wilderness,

5. Mistress Quickly, hostess of the Boar's Head Tavern in Eastcheap, describing the death of Falstaff in *Henry V* 2.3.15–16.
† "Sensation Novels," *Blackwood's Edinburgh Magazine* 91 (May 1862): 564–84.
"Mrs. Oliphant," wrote Virginia Woolf, "sold her brain, her very admirable brain, prostituted her culture and enslaved her intellectual liberty in order that she might earn her living and educate her children" (*Three Guineas*, 1938). Widowed at thirty-one, Margaret Oliphant née Wilson (1828–1897) furnished so many popular histories, travel guides, biographies, and novels set in her native Scotland that one encyclopedia entry docketing her productions peters out with the phrase "and 112 other books." An equally tireless critic, she contributed more than three hundred pieces to *Blackwood's* alone.

but simply that God provided them with clothing as well as food.[1] We should like to know what the reverend gentleman would say to that wedding-dress of Miss Havisham's, which, in five-and-twenty years, had only grown yellow and faded, but was still, it appears, extant in all its integrity, no tatters being so much as inferred, except on the shoeless foot, the silk stocking on which "had been trodden ragged."

* * *

* * * The narrative [recounting Magwitch's escape attempt] is close and rapid, and told without much unnecessary detail; but notwithstanding its undeniable effectiveness as a whole, it must be admitted that neither its successive incidents nor even its crisis strikes sharp upon the course of the story, or stands out with any distinctness from its general level. We watch the second boat stealing out upon the river without any sudden thrill of interest. We see the two convicts go down together into the water churned by the agitating passage of the great steamer which lowers over them like a castle in the water, but we draw our breath as calm as before. The means, in short, are superabundant, and full of all the natural elements of wonder, pity, and terror, but the effect is *not* produced. Perhaps most readers will make sure of what is going to happen to Abel Magwitch before they retire to their peaceful pillows, but once there, the returned convict will not haunt them. He will neither interfere with their sleep, nor startle their leisure with any uncomfortable consciousness of his own lurking, clandestine figure. At first, when he was out on the marsh, there seemed some likelihood that he might—but he has died, so far as his faculty of exciting a sensation goes, for long before he dies in prison. * * * The * * * deathbed sketch, however, is full of a subdued pathos and tenderness, without exaggeration or overdoing, dismissing in pity and charity, but without any attempt to make him a wonder either of remorse or reformation, the lawless soul who has been the overshadowing terror of the book[.]

The secondary persons of this book, however—almost entirely separated as they are from the main action, which is connected only in the very slightest way with the rest of the story—are, so far as they possess any individual character at all, specimens of oddity run mad. The incredible ghost, in the wedding-dress which has lasted for five-and-twenty years, is scarcely more *outré* than the ridiculous Mrs Pocket. * * * Of the same description is the ingenious Mr Wemmick, the lawyer's clerk, who lives in a little castle at Walworth, and calls his old father the Aged, and exclaims, "Hulloa! here's a church—let's go in!" when he is going to be married. Is this fun? Mr Dickens ought to be an authority in that respect, seeing he has made more honest laughter in his day than any man living, and called forth as many honest tears; but we confess it looks exceedingly dull pleasantry to us, and that we are slow to accept Mr Wemmick's carpentry as a substitute for all the homely wit and wisdom in which Mr Dickens's privileged humorists used to abound. * * * And again [in Orlick's entrapment of Pip] Mr Dickens misses fire—he rouses himself up, indeed, and bethinks himself of his old arts of word and composition, and does his best to galvanise his figures into momentary life. But it is plain to see all along that he means nothing by it; we are as sure

1. Deuteronomy 8.4: "Thy raiment waxed not old upon thee, neither did thy foot swell, these forty years."

that help will come at the right moment, as if we saw it approaching all the time; and the whole affair is the most arbitrary and causeless stoppage in the story—perhaps acceptable to weekly readers, as a prick of meretricious excitement on the languid road, perhaps a little stimulant to the mind of the writer, who was bored with his own production—but as a part of a narrative totally uncalled for, an interruption and encumbrance, interfering with the legitimate interest of the story, which is never so strong as to bear much trifling with[.] In every way, Mr Dickens's performance must yield precedence to the companion work of his disciple and assistant.[2] * * *

GEORGE GISSING

[Dickens's Shrews]†

Great Expectations (1861), would be nearly perfect in its mechanism but for the unhappy deference to Lord Lytton's judgment, which caused the end to be altered. * * * Observe how finely the narrative is kept in one key. It begins with a mournful impression—the foggy marshes spreading drearily by the seaward Thames—and throughout recurs this effect of cold and damp and dreariness; in that kind Dickens never did anything so good. Despite the subject, we have no stage fire—except around the person of Mr. Wopsle, a charming bit of satire, recalling and contrasting with the far-off days of *Nickleby*. * * * No story in the first person was ever better told.

* * *

It results from Dickens's weakness in the devising of incident, in the planning of story, that he seldom develops character through circumstance. There are conversions, but we do not much believe in them; they smack of the stage. * * * From this point of view Dickens's best bit of work is Pip, in *Great Expectations*; Pip, the narrator of his own story, who exhibits very well indeed the growth of a personality, the interaction of character and event. One is not permitted to lose sight of the actual author; though so much more living than Esther Summerson,[1] Pip is yet embarrassed, like her, with the gift of humour. We know very well whose voice comes from behind the scenes when Pip is describing Mr. Wopsle's dramatic venture. Save for this, we acknowledge a true self-revelation. What could be better than the lad's picture of his state of mind, when, after learning that he has "great expectations", he quits the

---

2. Wilkie Collins, whose *Woman in White* Mrs. Oliphant praised at length in the same review.

† From George Gissing, *Charles Dickens: A Critical Study* (London: Blackie & Sons, 1898), 60, 95, 129–30, 135, 141–43.
    Destitute and chronically unlucky, George Gissing (1857–1903) translated his vision of late-Victorian England into a series of powerful naturalistic novels, in which he examines the effects of poverty (*Workers in the Dawn*, 1880), the conditions of near-starvation (*Nether World*, 1889), and the ruin by indigence and overwork of a writer's creative impulse (*New Grub Street*, 1891). A lifelong Dickens disciple, he published a number of studies that went a long way toward vindicating Dickens's reputation. The prefaces Gissing wrote for the aborted Rochester Edition were collected under the title *The Immortal Dickens* in 1925.

1. Esther Summerson, the central figure of *Bleak House*, is the bastard daughter of a London drug addict and a low bourgeoise who has married into the landed gentry, and ward to a party in the longest law suit in English literature. Gissing's dim view of Esther reflects the general view held by early commentators who are repelled by her goody-goodyness—Mark Twain called her a "Joan of Arc in petticoats."

country home of his childhood and goes to London? "I formed a plan in outline for bestowing a dinner of roast beef and plum-pudding, a pint of ale, and a gallon of condescension upon everybody in the village" (chap. xix.). It is one of many touches which give high value to this book.

* * *

* * * [S]etting aside his would-be tragic figures, * * * it is obvious that Dickens wrote of women in his liveliest spirit of satire. Wonderful as fact, and admirable as art, are the numberless pictures of more or less detestable widows, wives, and spinsters which appear throughout his books. Beyond dispute, they must be held among his finest work; this portraiture alone would establish his claim to greatness. And I think it might be forcibly argued that, for incontestable proof of Dickens's fidelity in reproducing the life he knew, one should turn in the first place to his gallery of foolish, ridiculous, or offensive women. * * *

Through his early life, Dickens must have been in constant observation of these social pests. In every lodging-house he entered, such a voice would surely be sounding. His women use utterance such as no male genius could have invented; from the beginning he knew it perfectly, the vocabulary, the syntax, the figurative flights of this appalling language. "God's great gift of speech abused" was the commonplace of his world. Another man, obtaining his release from those depths, would have turned away in loathing; Dickens found therein matter for his mirth, material for his art. When one thinks of it, how strange it is that such an unutterable curse should become, in the artist hands, an incitement to joyous laughter! As a matter of fact, these women produced more misery than can be calculated. That he does not exhibit this side of the picture is the peculiarity of Dickens's method; a defect, of course, from one point of view, but inseparable from his humorous treatment of life. Women who might well have wrecked homes, are shown as laughable foils for the infinite goodness and patience of men about them. Justly, by the by, a matter of complaint to the female critic. * * *

It certainly is a troublesome fact for sensitive female readers that this, a great English novelist of the Victorian age, so abounds in women who are the curse of their husbands' lives. A complete list of them would, I imagine, occupy nearly a page of this book. * * * But there remains one full-length picture which we may by no means neglect, its name Mrs. Joe Gargery.

Mrs. Gargery belongs to Dickens's later manner. * * * The blacksmith's wife is a shrew of the most highly developed order. If ever she is good-tempered in the common sense of the word, she never lets it be suspected; without any assignable cause, she is invariably acrid, and ready at a moment's notice to break into fury of abuse. It gratifies her immensely to have married the softest-hearted man that ever lived, and also that he happens to be physically one of the strongest; the joy of trampling upon him, knowing that he who could kill her with a backhand blow will never even answer the bitterest insult with an unkind word! It delights her, too, that she has a little brother, a mere baby still, whom she can ill-use at her leisure, remembering always that every harshness to the child is felt still worse by the big good fellow, her husband. Do you urge that Dickens should give a cause for this evil temper? Cause there is none—save of that scientific kind which has no place in English novels. It is the peculiarity of these women that no one can conjecture why they behave so ill. * * *

Notice, now, that in Mrs. Gargery, though he still disguises the worst of the situation with his unfailing humour, Dickens gives us more of the harsh truth than in any previous book. That is a fine scene where the woman, by a malicious lie, causes a fight between Joe and Orlick; a true illustration of character, and well brought out. Again, Mrs. Joe's punishment. Here we are very far from the early novels. Mrs. Gargery shall be brought to quietness; but how? By a half-murderous blow on the back of her head, from which she will never recover. Dickens understood by this time that there is no other efficacious way with these ornaments of their sex. A felling and stunning and all but killing blow, followed by paralysis and slow death. A sharp remedy, but no whit sharper than the evil it cures. Mrs. Gargery, under such treatment, learns patience and the rights of other people. We are half sorry she cannot rise and put her learning into practice, but there is always a doubt. As likely as not she would take to drinking, and enter on a new phase of ferocity. * * *

* * *

* * * Dickens meant, and rightly meant, to end [*Great Expectations*] in the minor key. The old convict, Magwitch, if he cannot be called a tragical personality, has feeling enough to move the reader's deeper interest, and in the very end acquires through suffering a dignity which makes him very impressive. Rightly seen, is there not much pathos in the story of Pip's foolishness? It would be more manifest if we could forget Lytton's imbecile suggestion, and restore the original close of the story.

Essays

E. M. FORSTER

[Autumnal England]†

Great Expectations. Alliance between atmosphere and plot (the convicts) make it more solid and satisfactory than anything else of D. known to me. Very fine writing occasionally (*end of Pt. I.*).[1] Pip adequate, Joe Gargery not a stick. Occasional hints not developed—e.g. Mrs. G.'s and Jaggers's character *does* nothing, Herbert Pocket's has to be revised: But all the defects are trivial, and the course of events is both natural and exciting. Now and then (e.g. in the return of Magwitch) D. grasps at subtleties which would impede him if he grasped them always. Pip's cold disgust and fundamental decency.

Beating heart—instead of good digestion of Scott.

Chilly mist—chill without mist in D. Copperfield. Autumnal England.
And the river—cf. Our Mutual Friend.
Cannot express its merits properly. One of the few masterpieces in my copious catalogue.

⁂

BERNARD SHAW

Introduction to *Great Expectations*†

'Great Expectations' is the last of the three full-length stories written by Dickens in the form of an autobiography. Of the three, *Bleak House*, as the autobiography of Miss Esther Summerson, is naturally the least personal, as Esther is not only a woman but a maddening prig, though we are forced to

† 1926; from E. M. Forster, *Commonplace Book*, ed. Philip Gardner (Stanford, Calif., 1985), 18–19. Reprinted by permission of Stanford University Press and the Scolar Press.
  Forster's *Commonplace Book* covers the years 1925 to 1956. A good many of the early entries make their way into his seminal *Aspects of the Novel*, the series of lectures he delivered at Cambridge in 1927, in which his comments on Dickens are far more patronizing.
1. Beneath the entry Forster transcribed excerpts from the final paragraphs of Stage I of the novel, from "I walked away" to the end of the chapter, elliptical dots indicating the omission of the two intermediate paragraphs.
† From Bernard Shaw, "Introduction," *Great Expectations* (London: Hamish Hamilton, 1947), v–xx. Reprinted by permission of the Society of Authors. An earlier version appeared as preface to the Limited Editions Club of New York (1937), v–xxii. Neither text could have been written later than December 1936. All footnotes are by the editor of this Norton Critical Edition.

admit that such paragons exist and are perhaps worthy of the reverent admiration with which Dickens regarded them. Ruling her out, we have *David Copperfield* and *Great Expectations*. David was, for a time at least, Dickens's favourite child,[1] perhaps because he had used him to express the bitterness of that episode in his own experience which had wounded his boyish self-respect most deeply. For Dickens, in spite of his exuberance, was a deeply reserved man: the exuberance was imagination and acting (his imagination was ceaseless, and his outward life a feat of acting from beginning to end); and we shall never know whether in that immensely broadened outlook and knowledge of the world which began with *Hard Times* and *Little Dorrit*, and left all his earlier works behind, he may not have come to see that making his living by sticking labels on blacking bottles and rubbing shoulders with boys who were not gentlemen, was as little shameful as being the genteel apprentice in the office of Mr. Spenlow, or the shorthand writer recording the unending twaddle of the House of Commons and electioneering bunk on the hustings of all the Eatanswills in the country.[2]

That there was a tragic change in his valuations can be shown by contrasting Micawber with William Dorrit, in which light Micawber suddenly becomes a mere marionette pantaloon with a funny bag of tricks which he repeats until we can bear no more of him, and Dorrit a portrait of the deadliest and deepest truth to nature.[3] Now contrast David with Pip; and believe, if you can, that there was no revision of his estimate of the favorite child David as a work of art and even as a vehicle of experience. The adult David fades into what stage managers call a walking gentleman. The reappearance of Mr. Dickens in the character of a blacksmith's boy may be regarded as an apology to Mealy Potatoes.[4]

Dickens did in fact know that *Great Expectations* was his most compactly perfect book. In all the other books, there are episodes of wild extravagance, extraordinarily funny if they catch you at the right age, but recklessly grotesque as nature studies. Even in *Little Dorrit*, Dickens's masterpiece among many masterpieces, it is impossible to believe that the perfectly authentic Mr. Pancks really stopped the equally authentic Mr. Casby in a crowded street in London and cut his hair; and though Mr. F.'s aunt is a first-rate clinical study of senile deficiency in a shrewd old woman, her collisions with Arthur Clennam[5] are too funny to be taken seriously. * * *

* * *

1. So Dickens claimed in his preface to the 1869 edition of *David Copperfield*.
2. In *Pickwick Papers*, chapter 13, Dickens lampoons the brouhaha at the borough election contest of Eatanswill. (Hustings are the raised platforms from which the campaigners broadcast their electioneering bunk.) Spenlow is the hard-nosed attorney in Doctors' Commons to whom David Copperfield is articled and whose daughter he marries once death has removed any fatherly interferences.
3. Micawber and Dorrit, the veteran prisoner and self-appointed father of the Marshalsea, are both modeled on John Dickens though no clueless reader could trace them to one and the same original: Micawber unalterably sanguine, Dorrit growing morbidly attached to the prison world. Between them they virtually exemplify E. M. Forster's distinction between "flat" and "round" characters.
4. The only workmate of David Copperfield's at Murdstone & Grinby's (chapter 11) who questions David's privileged status as "the little gent."
5. The male lead in *Little Dorrit*, a middle-aged China merchant, whose will has been sapped by his Calvinistic childhood. Mr. F. (the name is Finching) is the late husband of Clennam's youthful sweetheart grown into a giddy magpie. Casby, her father, is an extortionist landlord who radiates a benevolent paternalism; Pancks, his agent, is also his most aggrieved victim; and the aunt is precisely what Shaw says she is, a senile fright who intermittently surfaces from her narcoma with vindictive non sequiturs.

In *Great Expectations* we have Wopsle and Trabb's boy; but they have their part and purpose in the story and do not overstep the immodesty of nature. It is hardly decent to compare Mr. F.'s aunt with Miss Havisham; but as contrasted studies of madwomen they make you shudder at the thought of what Dickens might have made of Miss Havisham if he had seen her as a comic personage. For life is no laughing matter in *Great Expectations*; the book is all of one piece and consistently truthful as none of the other books are, not even the compact *Tale of Two Cities*, which is pure sentimental melodrama from beginning to end, and shockingly wanting in any philosophy of history in its view of the French Revolution.

Dickens never regarded himself as a revolutionist, though he certainly was one. His implacable contempt for the House of Commons, founded on his experience as a parliamentary reporter, never wavered from the account of the Eatanswill election and of Nicholas Nickleby's interview with Pugstyles to the Veneering election in *Our Mutual Friend*.[6] * * * And this was not mere satire, of which there had been plenty. Dickens was the first writer to perceive and state definitely that the House of Commons, working on the Party system, is an extraordinarily efficient device for dissipating all our reforming energy and ability in Party debate and when anything urgently needs to be done, finding out 'how not to do it.'[7] It took very little time to get an ineffective Factory Act. It took fifty years to make it effective, though the labour conditions in the factories and mines were horrible.[8] After Dickens's death, it took thirty years to pass an Irish Home Rule Bill, which was promptly repudiated by the military plutocracy, leaving the question to be settled by a competition in slaughter and house burning, just as it would have been between two tribes of savages.[9] Liberty under the British parliamentary system means slavery for nine-tenths of the people, and slave exploitation or parasitic idolatry and snobbery for the rest. * * *

* * *

Marx and Dickens were contemporaries living in the same city and pursuing the same profession of literature;[1] yet they seem to us like creatures of a different species living in different worlds. Dickens, if he had ever become conscious of Karl Marx, would have been classed with him as a revolutionist. The difference between a revolutionist and what Marx called a bourgeois is that the bourgeois regards the existing social order as the permanent and natural order of human society, needing reforms now and then and here and there, but essentially good and sane and right and respectable and proper and everlasting. To the revolutionist it is transitory, mistaken, objectionable, and pathological: a social disease to be cured, not to be endured. We have

6. Pugstyles is a comic extra in *Nicholas Nickleby*, chapter 10, who presents a Westminster MP with a ludicrous list of grievances; the Veneerings, as varnished as their name suggests, head the list of nouveaux riches in *Our Mutual Friend*.
7. The phrase that describes the Circumlocution Office, Dickens's satire on the nightmarish bureaucratic muddle in *Little Dorrit*, chapter 10.
8. The Factory Act of 1833, to all intents the work of Lord Shaftesbury (1801–1885), sought to alleviate the conditions of child labor, chiefly by lowering working hours; an act of 1840 banned the employment of children as chimney sweeps, the high-risk labor so memorably rendered by writers like Blake and the Dickens of *Oliver Twist*. But employers found so many ways of dodging the legislation as to rob it of all effectiveness.
9. The defeat of the second Home Rule Bill in the House of Lords in 1893, after its passage in the Commons, led to the dissolution of William Gladstone's fourth ministry and thus the virtual demise of England's leading liberal prime minister of the past thirty years.
1. Marx fled to London in 1849 and lived there until his death in 1883.

only to compare Thackeray and Trollope with Dickens to perceive this contrast. Thackeray reviled the dominant classes with a savagery which would have been unchivalrous in Dickens: he denied to his governing class characters even the common good qualities and accomplishments of ladies and gentleman, making them mean, illiterate, dishonest, ignorant, sycophantic to an inhuman degree, whilst Dickens, even when making his aristocrats ridiculous and futile, at least made gentlemen of them. Trollope, who regarded Thackeray as his master and exemplar, had none of his venom, and has left us a far better balanced and more truthful picture of Victorian well-off society, never consciously whitewashing it, though allowing it its full complement of black sheep of both sexes.[2] But Trollope's politics were those of the country house and the hunting field just as were Thackeray's. * * * [Dickens] was told that he could not describe a gentleman and that *Little Dorrit* is twaddle. And the reason was that in his books the west-end heaven appears as a fool's paradise that must pass away instead of being an indispensable preparatory school for the New Jerusalem of Revelation. A leading encyclopedia tells us that Dickens had 'no knowledge of country gentlemen.'[3] It would have been nearer the mark to say that Dickens knew all that really mattered about Sir Leicester Dedlock[4] and that Trollope knew nothing that really mattered about him. Trollope and Thackeray could see Chesney Wold; but Dickens could see through it. * * *

The difference between Marx and Dickens was that Marx knew that he was a revolutionist whilst Dickens had not the faintest suspicion of that part of his calling. Compare the young Dickens looking for a job in a lawyer's office and teaching himself shorthand to escape from his office stool to the reporters' gallery, with the young Trotsky, the young Lenin, quite deliberately facing disreputable poverty and adopting revolution as their profession with every alternative of bourgeois security and respectability much more fully open to them than to Dickens.[5]

And this brings us to Dickens's position as a member of the educated and cultured classes who had neither education nor culture. This was fortunate for him and for the world in one way, as he escaped the school and university routine which complicates cultural Philistinism with the mentality of a Red Indian brave. Better no schooling at all than the schooling of Rudyard Kipling and Winston Churchill.[6] But there are homes in which a mentally acquisitive

---

2. Thackeray's distaste for the ruling classes is reflected in his portrayal of illiterates and debauchees like Sir Pitt Crawley and Lord Steyne in *Vanity Fair* (1848); Trollope's study of midcentury politics may be found in his series of parliamentary novels *Phineas Finn* (1869), *The Prime Minister* (1876), and others. The comparison of Dickens and Thackeray as the two leading rival novelists had already turned into a critical tic in the authors' lifetime.

3. *Encyclopaedia Britannica*, Ninth Edition, article by William Minto.

4. The conservative, class-complacent head of one of the great county families in *Bleak House* who entertains the vegetative nobility at his estate in Lincolnshire.

5. From 1827 to 1829 Dickens clerked for a couple of solicitors; in 1831–32 he was hired as general reporter by one newspaper, as parliamentary reporter by another. Lenin (1870–1927) matriculated at Kazan University in 1887 and passed his bar exam in 1891 before his arrest and deportation in 1897. Trotsky (1879–1940), the son of prosperous Jewish farmers, took first-class honors in secondary school; after a dramatic escape from Siberia in 1907, he supported himself in Vienna and Paris by working on newspapers and in a chemical factory during the prewar years. Shaw's point is that neither Lenin nor Trotsky lost sight of his revolutionary aims in exile or captivity.

6. Rudyard Kipling (1865–1936), after being sent home from India at age five to a narrowly pious Methodist kinswoman, who broke the boy's spirit by beating him and bullying him with her Bible and her pathological mistrust, was enrolled, at age twelve, in a cheap boarding school, the United Services College in Devon, a place notorious for its brutality. Winston Churchill (1874–1965), at seven, was enrolled in a rich boarding school in Ascot, where "flogging with the birch . . . was a great feature of the curriculum." Shaw damns these schools less for their "Dickensian" beastliness than for the military-imperialist complex they instilled in their recruits.

boy can make contact with the fine arts. I myself learnt nothing at school, but gained in my home an extensive and highly educational knowledge of music. I had access to illustrated books on painting which sent me to the National Gallery; so that I was able to support myself as a critic of music and painting as Dickens supported himself by shorthand. I devoured books on science and on the religious controversies of the day. It is in this way, and not in our public schools and universities that such culture as there is in England is kept alive.

Now the Dickenses seem to have been complete barbarians. Dickens mentions the delight with which he discovered in an attic a heap of eighteenth-century novels. But Smollett was a grosser barbarian than Dickens himself; and *Don Quixote* and *The Arabian Nights*, though they gave the cue to his eager imagination, left him quite in the dark as to the philosophy and art of his day. * * * To Dickens as to most Victorian Englishmen metaphysics were ridiculous, useless, unpractical, and the mark of a fool. He was musical enough to have a repertory of popular ballads which he sang all over the house to keep his voice in order; and he made Tom Pinch[7] play the organ in church as an amiable accomplishment; but I cannot remember hearing that he ever went to a classical concert, or even knew of the existence of such entertainments. The articles on the National Gallery in *All the Year Round*, though extremely funny in their descriptions of 'The Apotheosis' of 'William the Silent' (the title alone would make a cat laugh),[8] and on some profane points sensible enough, are those of a complete Philistine. * * * When Dickens introduced in his stories a character whom he intensely disliked he chose an artistic profession for him. Henry Gowan in *Little Dorrit* is a painter. Pecksniff is an architect. Harold Skimpole is a musician. There is real hatred in his treatment of them.[9]

* * * [A]ll the truth to life of Dickens's portraiture cannot extenuate the fact that the cultural side of art was as little known to Dickens as it is possible for a thing so public to remain to a man so apprehensive. You may read the stories of Dickens from beginning to end without ever learning that he lived through a period of fierce revivals and revolutionary movements in art, in philosophy, in sociology, in religion: in short, in culture. Dean Inge's remark that 'the number of great subjects in which Dickens took no interest whatever

---

7. The softheaded assistant to the architect Pecksniff in *Martin Chuzzlewit*.
8. "The Apotheosis of William the Taciturn . . . is a picture representing a gentleman going up to Heaven in a cuirass and jack-boots, assisted by numerous angels, who look heavy enough to require some aid themselves in getting off the ground, and one of whom has a helmet on. A disagreeable-looking man, who probably found the Silent William a congenial companion, is trying to hold him down to earth, while a strange, and hitherto unknown animal, compounded of a lioness, a mastiff, and a bull-calf, is kicking up his heels in evident joy at William's removal from a sphere where he contributed so little to the general satisfaction of society" ("Our Eye-Witness at the National Gallery," *All the Year Round*, June 16, 1860, article written anonymously by Dickens's son-in-law). The painting has been identified as the work of Peter Paul Rubens (1577–1640), the greatest of Flemish artists, and the subject of the apotheosis is not William the Silent, Prince of Orange (born 1533, assassinated 1584) but George Villiers, First Duke of Buckingham (born 1592, assassinated 1628), who almost certainly commissioned the painting some time before 1625. An allegorical commentary on Buckingham's aspirations, its genuine title reads "Minerva and Mercury conduct the Duke of Buckingham to the Temple of Virtus." About the turn of the century, when art experts had firmly disowned William but not yet decisively taken up George, the painting bore the cagey title "The Apotheosis of a Prince."
9. Henry Gowan is pictured as a shiftless dilettante who sexually torments his wife; Pecksniff (*Martin Chuzzlewit*) as a sycophant who uses his profession as a front to endear himself to his wealthy relatives; Harold Skimpole (*Bleak House*) as an engagingly shameless sponge, whose flute playing, like his improvised conversation, is a refuge from work.

is amazing' hits the nail exactly on the head.[1] As to finding such a person as Karl Marx among his characters, one would as soon look for a nautilus in a nursery.

* * *

And yet Dickens never saw himself as a revolutionist. It never occurred to him to found a Red International, as Marx did, not even to join one out of the dozens of political reform societies that were about him. He was an English gentleman of the professional class, who would not allow his daughter to go on the stage because it was not respectable. He knew so little about revolutionists that when Mazzini called on him and sent in his card, Dickens, much puzzled, concluded that the unknown foreign gentleman wanted money, and very kindly sent him down a sovereign to get rid of him.[2] He discovered for himself all the grievances he exposed, and had no sense of belonging to a movement, nor any desire to combine with others who shared his subversive views. To educate his children religiously and historically he wrote A Child's History of England which had not even the excuse of being childish, and a paraphrase of the gospel biography which is only a belittling of it for little children.[3] He had much better have left the history to Little Arthur and Mrs. Markham and Goldsmith,[4] and taken into account the extraordinary educational value of the Authorized Version as a work of literary art. He probably thought as seldom of himself as a literary artist as of himself as a revolutionist; and he had his share in the revolt against the supernatural pretensions of the Bible which was to end in the vogue of Agnosticism and the pontificate of Darwin.[5] It blinded that generation to the artistic importance of the fact that at a moment when all the literary energy in England was in full eruption, when Shakespear was just dead and Milton just born, a picked body of scholars undertook the task of translating into English what they believed to be the words of God himself. Under the strain of that conviction they surpassed all their normal powers, transfiguring the original texts into literary masterpieces of a splendor that no merely mortal writers can ever again hope to achieve. But the nineteenth century either did not dare think of the Bible in that way, it being fetish, or else it was in such furious reaction against the fetishism that it would not allow the so-called Holy Scriptures even an artistic merit. At all events Dickens thought his Little Nell style better

1. Untraced, though [William Ralph] Inge (1860–1954), the "Gloomy Dean" of St. Paul's from 1911 to 1934, one of the more politicized as well as highly educated British clergymen, might have said it. Like Shaw, Inge had no use for rule by parliament and (like Shaw) he enjoyed a brief honeymoon with Hitler.
2. Giuseppe Mazzini (1805–1872), the founder of "Young Italy" and leading figure in the struggle for Italian unification, spent much of his life as an exile in London, where Dickens first met him in 1848. Shaw's account is misleading: Dickens was introduced to Mazzini after handing money to an impostor who had used Mazzini's name as carte d'entrée—which rather blunts the edge of Shaw's putdown (Forster, book 6, chapter 6; Hoppé, vol. 2, 84).
3. Dickens's Child's History of England appeared in 1853; The Life of Our Lord, written for his children between 1846 and 1849 and based chiefly on the Gospel of Luke, was first published in 1934.
4. "Mrs. Markham," pseudonym for Elizabeth Penrose (1780–1837), published a History of England (1823) and a History of France (1828) from which all the "horrors" of history and snake pits of party politics were expunged as unsuitable for the young. Oliver Goldsmith turned out a number of sloppy abridgments and compilations of English, Roman, and Greek history for use in schools.
5. Agnostics: a group of Oxford intellectuals active in the 1870s, prominently including Thomas Henry Huxley (1825–1895), Leslie Stephen (1832–1904), and John Morley (1838–1923), who maintained that the entire realm of speculative thought was immune to scientific interpretation and who insisted on the importance of moral action independent of religious belief. Darwin's Origin of Species appeared in 1859.

for his children than the English of King James's inspired scribes.[6] He took them (for a time at least) to churches of the Unitarian persuasion, where they could be both sceptical and respectable; but it is hard to say what Dickens believed or did not believe metaphysically or metapolitically, though he left us in no doubt as to his opinion of the Lords, the Commons, and the ante-Crimean Civil Service.[7]

* * *

Meanwhile he overloaded himself and his unfortunate wife with such a host of children that he was forced to work himself to death prematurely to provide for them and for the well-to-do life he led. The reading public cannot bear to think of its pet authors as struggling with the economic pressures that often conflict so cruelly with the urge of genius. This pressure was harder on Dickens than on many poorer men. He had a solid bourgeois conscience which made it impossible for him to let wife and children starve whilst he followed the path of destiny. Marx let his wife go crazy with prolonged poverty whilst he wrote a book which changed the mind of the world. But then Marx had been comfortably brought up and thoroughly educated in the German manner. Dickens knew far too much of the horrors of impecuniosity to put his wife through what his mother had gone through, or have his children pasting labels on blacking bottles. He had to please his public or lapse into that sort of poverty. Under such circumstances the domestic conscience inevitably pushes the artistic conscience into the second place. We shall never know how much of Dickens's cheery optimism belied his real outlook on life. He went his own way far enough to make it clear that when he was not infectiously laughing he was a melancholy fellow * * * I will not go so far as to say that Dickens's novels are full of melancholy intentions which he dares not carry through to their unhappy conclusions; but he gave us no vitally happy heroes and heroines after Pickwick (begun, like Don Quixote, as a contemptible butt). Their happy endings are manufactured to make the books pleasant. Nobody who has endured the novels of our twentieth-century emancipated women, enormously cleverer and better informed than the novels of Dickens, and ruthlessly calculated to leave their readers hopelessly discouraged and miserable, will feel anything but gratitude to Dickens for his humanity in speeding his parting guests with happy faces by turning from the world of destiny to the world of accidental good luck; but as our minds grow stronger some of his consolations become unnecessary and even irritating. And it happens that it is with just such a consolation that *Great Expectations* ends.

It did not always end so. Dickens wrote two endings, and made a mess of both. In the first ending, which Bulwer Lytton persuaded him to discard, Pip takes little Pip for a walk in Piccadilly and is stopped by Estella, who is passing in her carriage. She is comfortably married to a Shropshire doctor, and just says how d'y'do to Pip and kisses the little boy before they both pass on out

6. The Authorized (King James) Version was first printed in 1611. "Little Nell style": the maudlin prose that pollutes large chunks of *The Old Curiosity Shop* and reaches its apogee in Little Nell's death.
7. The administrative chaos before and during the Crimean War (1854–56) is expressed not only in the Circumlocution Office but in a dozen essays in *Household Words*. The Crimean conflict, in which England, France, and (as always at the last moment) Italy teamed up against Russia, is mostly remembered for Florence Nightingale, the charge of the Light Brigade, and the fact that 150 years after they had disappeared from the face of man, beards started to sprout again—an act of homage to British soldiers who returned from the front unshaven.

of one another's lives. This, though it is marred by Pip's pious hope that her husband may have thrashed into her some understanding of how much she has made him suffer, is true to nature. But it is much too matter-of-fact to be the right ending to a tragedy. Piccadilly was impossible in such a context; and the passing carriage was unconsciously borrowed from *A Day's Ride: A Life's Romance*, the novel by Lever which was so unpopular that *Great Expectations* had to be written to replace it in *All The Year Round*. But in Lever's story it is the man who stops the carriage, only to be cut dead by the lady. Dickens must have felt that there was something wrong with this ending; and Bulwer's objection confirmed his doubt. Accordingly, he wrote a new ending, in which he got rid of Piccadilly and substituted a perfectly congruous and beautifully touching scene and hour and atmosphere for the meeting. He abolished the Shropshire doctor and left out the little boy. So far the new ending was in every way better than the first one.

Unfortunately, what Bulwer wanted was what is called a happy ending, presenting Pip and Estella as reunited lovers who were going to marry and live happily ever after; and Dickens, though he could not bring himself to be quite so explicit in sentimental falsehood, did, at the end of the very last line, allow himself to say that there was 'no shadow of parting' between them. If Pip had said 'Since that parting I have been able to think of her without the old unhappiness; but I have never tried to see her again, and I know I never shall' he would have been left with at least the prospect of a bearable life. But the notion that he could ever have been happy with Estella: indeed that anyone could ever have been happy with Estella, is positively unpleasant. I can remember when the Cowden Clarks[8] ventured to hint a doubt whether Benedick and Beatrice had a very delightful union to look forward to; but that did not greatly matter, as Benedick and Beatrice have none of the reality of Pip and Estella. Shakespear could afford to trifle with *Much Ado About Nothing*, which is avowedly a potboiler;[9] but *Great Expectations* is a different matter. Dickens put nearly all his thought into it. It is too serious a book to be a trivially happy one. Its beginning is unhappy; its middle is unhappy; and the conventional happy ending is an outrage on it.

Estella is a curious addition to the gallery of unamiable women painted by Dickens. In my youth it was commonly said that Dickens could not draw women. The people who said this were thinking of Agnes Wickfield and Esther Summerson, of Little Dorrit and Florence Dombey, and thinking of them as ridiculous idealizations of their sex.[1] Gissing put a stop to that by

8. Charles Cowden Clarke (1787–1877) lectured and wrote on Shakespeare. A number of his books were jointly written with his wife, Mary Victoria Novello (1809–1898), herself "the lady to whom the world owes incomparably the best *Concordance* to Shakespeare" (Forster, book 6, chapter 1; Hoppé, vol. 2, 17) and the Mistress Quickly in Dickens's production of Shakespeare's *Merry Wives* in 1848. Mrs. Cowden Clarke describes her engagements with Dickens in her *Recollections of Writers* (New York: Scribners, 1878).
9. Benedick and Beatrice are the sparring lovers in *Much Ado About Nothing* (1598–1600) whose persiflage is a staple of Shakespeare talk. Shaw, who thought the very title of the play an insult to the audience, found Benedick's badinage coarse enough to make a cabman blush and "Much-Adoodle-do" "a shocking bad play" (to Gordon Craig, June 3, 1903).
1. Dickens's sentimental heroines. Agnes Wickfield: daughter of the Canterbury solicitor with whom David Copperfield boards while at school, David's tutelary angel and second wife—Orwell calls her "the real legless angel of Victorian romance." Little Dorrit: the self-sacrificing heroine of the novel named for her, who is born and raised in debtors' prison and continues to hover as ministering angel over her family after their release. Florence Dombey: the humiliated daughter of the purse-proud Dombey clan, whose father, in prosperity, spurns her for not being a male and, in adversity, comes to depend on her samaritan surveillance.

asking whether shrews like Mrs. Raddle, Mrs. Macstinger, Mrs. Gargery, fools like Mrs. Nickleby and Flora Finching, warped spinsters like Rosa Dartle and Miss Wade, were not masterpieces of woman drawing.[2] And they are all unamiable.* * * Of course Dickens with his imagination could invent amiable women by the dozen; but somehow he could not or would not bring them to life as he brought the others. We doubt whether he ever knew a little Dorrit; but Fanny Dorrit[3] is from the life unmistakably. So is Estella. She is a much more elaborate study than Fanny, and, I should guess, a recent one.

Dickens, when he let himself go in *Great Expectations*, was separated from his wife and free to make more intimate acquaintances with women than a domesticated man can. * * * It is not necessary to suggest a love affair; for Dickens could get from a passing glance a hint which he could expand into a full-grown character. The point concerns us here only because it is the point on which the ending of *Great Expectations* turns: namely, that Estella is a born tormentor. She deliberately torments Pip all through for the fun of it; and in the little we hear of her intercourse with others there is no suggestion of a moment of kindness: in fact her tormenting of Pip is almost affectionate in contrast to the cold disdain of her attitude towards the people who were not worth tormenting. It is not surprising that the unfortunate Bentley Drummle, whom she marries in the stupidity of sheer perversity, is obliged to defend himself from her clever malice with his fists: a consolation to us for Pip's broken heart, but not altogether a credible one; for the real Estellas can usually intimidate the real Bentley Drummles. At all events the final sugary suggestion of Estella redeemed by Bentley's thrashings and waste of her money, and living happily with Pip for ever after, provoked even Dickens's eldest son to rebel against it, most justly.[4]

Apart from this the story is the most perfect of Dickens's works. In it he does not muddle himself with the ridiculous plots that appear like vestiges of the stone age in many of his books, from *Oliver Twist* to the end. The story is built round a single and simple catastrophe: the revelation to Pip of the source of his great expectations. There is, it is true, a trace of the old plot superstition in Estella turning out to be Magwitch's daughter; but it provides a touchingly happy ending for that heroic Warmint. Who could have the heart to grudge it to him?

As our social conscience expands and makes the intense class snobbery of the nineteenth century seem less natural to us, the tragedy of *Great Expectations* will lose some of its appeal. I have already wondered whether Dickens himself ever came to see that his agonizing sensitiveness about the blacking bottles and his resentment of his mother's opposition to his escape from them was not too snobbish to deserve all the sympathy he claimed for it. Compare the case of H. G. Wells, our nearest to a twentieth-century Dickens. Wells hated being a draper's assistant as much as Dickens hated being a warehouse boy; but he was not in the least ashamed of it, and did not blame his mother

2. Assorted shrews, termagants, and hysterics. Mrs. Raddle: vitriolic landlady in *Pickwick Papers*. Mrs. Macstinger: imperious widow in *Dombey and Son*, hell-bent on a second marriage. Mrs. Nickleby: the hero's mother, given to nonstop twaddle. Rosa Dartle: the repressed and masochistic housecompanion in *David Copperfield*, in love with the voluptuary son of the house. Miss Wade: a headstrong young woman in *Little Dorrit*, whose "History of a Self-Tormentor" (book 2, chapter 21) is often cited as evidence of Dickens's grasp of abnormal types.
3. Little Dorrit's go-getting older sister, who marries into the Merdle plutocracy.
4. In his introduction to the novel in the Macmillan Edition (1904). For his judgment on the conclusion of *Great Expectations*, see also the discussion above, p. 500.

for regarding it as the summit of her ambition for him.[5] Fate having imposed on that engaging cricketer Mr. Wells's father an incongruous means of livelihood in the shape of a small shop, shopkeeping did not present itself to the young Wells as beneath him, whereas to the genteel Dickens being a warehouse boy was an unbearable comedown. Still, I cannot help speculating on whether if Dickens had not killed himself prematurely to pile up money for that excessive family of his, he might not have reached a stage at which he could have got as much fun out of the blacking bottles as Mr. Wells got out of his abhorred draper's counter.

Dickens never reached that stage; and there is no prevision of it in *Great Expectations*; for in it he never raises the question why Pip should refuse Magwitch's endowment and shrink from him with such inhuman loathing. Magwitch no doubt was a Warmint from the point of view of the genteel Dickens family and even from his own; but Victor Hugo would have made him a magnificent hero, another Valjean.[6] Inspired by an altogether noble fixed idea, he had lifted himself out of his rut of crime and honestly made a fortune for the child who had fed him when he was starving. If Pip had no objection to be a parasite instead of an honest blacksmith, at least he had a better claim to be a parasite on Magwitch's earnings than, as he imagined, on Miss Havisham's property. It is curious that this should not have occurred to Dickens; for nothing could exceed the bitterness of his exposure of the futility of Pip's parasitism. If all that came of sponging on Miss Havisham (as he thought) was the privilege of being one of the Finches of the Grove, he need not have felt his dependence on Magwitch to be incompatible with his entirely baseless self-respect. But Pip—and I am afraid Pip must be to this extent identified with Dickens—could not see Magwitch as an animal of the same species as himself or Miss Havisham. His feeling is true to the nature of snobbery; but his creator says no word in criticism of that ephemeral limitation.

The basic truth of the situation is that Pip, like his creator, has no culture and no religion. Joe Gargery, when Pip tells a monstrous string of lies about Miss Havisham, advises him to say a repentant word about it in his prayers; but Pip never prays; and church means nothing to him but Mr. Wopsle's orotundity. In this he resembles David Copperfield, who has gentility but neither culture nor religion. Pip's world is therefore a very melancholy place, and his conduct, good or bad, always helpless. This is why Dickens worked against so black a background after he was roused from his ignorant middle-class cheery optimism by Carlyle. When he lost his belief in bourgeois society and with it his lightness of heart he had neither an economic Utopia nor a credible religion to hitch on to. * * * [B]ut at least he preserved his intellectual innocence sufficiently to escape the dismal pseudo-scientific fatalism that was descending on the world in his latter days, founded on the preposterous

---

5. H. G. Wells (1866–1946), the prolific author of science fiction, popular histories, and novels about lower-middle-class life (*Kipps, Tono Bungay, Mr. Polly*), began life as a draper's apprentice at thirteen, after his father, a shopkeeper and part-time professional cricketer, was crippled in an accident and his mother had to abandon the Wells's failing china shop to work as a housekeeper. As Shaw suggests, Mrs. Wells free-associated drapery with the tuxedos and tailcoats of the very rich who passed in front of the shop; per Wells himself, "Almost as unquestioning as her belief in Our Father and Our Saviour was her belief in drapers." As Shaw also suggests, Wells—no Trabb's boy—loathed his job and ran away at sixteen to become an usher—a teaching assistant.
6. Jean Valjean, the central figure in Victor Hugo's novel of social repression *Les Misérables* (1862).

error as to causation in which the future is determined by the present, which has been determined by the past. The true causation, of course, is always the incessant irresistible activity of the evolutionary appetite.

GEORGE ORWELL

Charles Dickens†

No one, at any rate no English writer, has written better about childhood than Dickens. In spite of all the knowledge that has accumulated since, in spite of the fact that children are now comparatively sanely treated, no novelist has shown the same power of entering into the child's point of view. I must have been about nine years old when I first read *David Copperfield*. The mental atmosphere of the opening chapters was so immediately intelligible to me that I vaguely imagined they had been written *by a child*. And yet when one re-reads the book as an adult and sees the Murdstones, for instance, dwindle from gigantic figures of doom into semi-comic monsters, these passages lose nothing. Dickens has been able to stand both inside and outside the child's mind, in such a way that the same scene can be wild burlesque or sinister reality, according to the age at which one reads it. Look, for instance, at the scene in which David Copperfield is unjustly suspected of eating the mutton chops;[1] or the scene in which Pip, in *Great Expectations*, coming back from Miss Havisham's house and finding himself completely unable to describe what he has seen, takes refuge in a series of outrageous lies—which, of course, are eagerly believed. All the isolation of childhood is there. And how accurately he has recorded the mechanisms of the child's mind, its visualising tendency, its sensitiveness to certain kinds of impression. Pip relates how in his childhood his ideas about his dead parents were derived from their tombstones:

> The shape of the letters on my father's, gave me an odd idea that he was a square, stout, dark man, with curly black hair. From the character and turn of the inscription, "ALSO GEORGIANA, WIFE OF THE ABOVE", I drew a childish conclusion that my mother was freckled and sickly. To five little stone lozenges, each about a foot and a half long, which were arranged in a neat row beside their grave, and were sacred to the memory of five little brothers of mine . . . I am indebted for a belief I religiously entertained that they had all been born on their backs with their hands in their trouser-pockets, and had never taken them out in this state of existence.

There is a similar passage in *David Copperfield*. After biting Mr Murdstone's hand, David is sent away to school and obliged to wear on his back

† From George Orwell, "Charles Dickens," *The Collected Essays, Journalism, and Letters*, ed. Sonia Orwell and Ian Angus, 4 vols. (London, 1968), vol. 1, 413–60. Reprinted by permission of Secker & Warburg.
1. In chapter 5, David, en route from his home to public school, stops off at an inn in which a foxy waiter talks him into surrendering his ale, chops, and pudding to him, the meal disappearing so fast that David's fellow passengers on the coach afterwards twit David on his insatiable appetite and he goes hungry for the rest of the trip. [*Editor.*]

a placard saying, "Take care of him. He bites". He looks at the door in the playground where the boys have carved their names, and from the appearance of each name he seems to know in just what tone of voice the boy will read out the placard:

> There was one boy—a certain J. Steerforth—who cut his name very deep and very often, who, I conceived, would read it in a rather strong voice, and afterwards pull my hair. There was another boy, one Tommy Traddles, who I dreaded would make game of it, and pretend to be dreadfully frightened of me. There was a third, George Demple, who I fancied would sing it.[2]

When I read this passage as a child, it seemed to me that those were exactly the pictures that those particular names would call up. The reason, of course, is the sound-associations of the words (Demple—"temple"; Traddles—probably "skedaddle"). But how many people, before Dickens, had ever noticed such things? * * *

*   *   *

* * * Dickens * * * shows less understanding of criminals than one would expect of him. * * * As soon as he comes up against crime or the worst depths of poverty, he shows traces of the "I've always kept myself respectable" habit of mind. The attitude of Pip (obviously the attitude of Dickens himself) towards Magwitch in *Great Expectations* is extremely interesting. Pip is conscious all along of his ingratitude towards Joe, but far less so of his ingratitude towards Magwitch. When he discovers that the person who has loaded him with benefits for years is actually a transported convict, he falls into frenzies of disgust. "The abhorrence in which I held the man, the dread I had of him, the repugnance with which I shrank from him, could not have been exceeded if he had been some terrible beast", etc etc. So far as one can discover from the text, this is not because when Pip was a child he had been terrorised by Magwitch in the churchyard; it is because Magwitch is a criminal and a convict. There is an even more "kept-myself-respectable" touch in the fact that Pip feels as a matter of course that he cannot take Magwitch's money. The money is not the product of a crime, it has been honestly acquired; but it is an ex-convict's money and therefore "tainted". There is nothing psychologically false in this, either. Psychologically the latter part of *Great Expectations* is about the best thing Dickens ever did; throughout this part of the book one feels "Yes, that is just how Pip would have behaved." But the point is that in the matter of Magwitch, Dickens identifies with Pip, and his attitude is at bottom snobbish. The result is that Magwitch belongs to the same queer class of characters as Falstaff and, probably, Don Quixote—characters who are more pathetic than the author intended.

*   *   *

Significantly, Dickens's most successful books (not his *best* books) are *The Pickwick Papers*, which is not a novel, and *Hard Times* and *A Tale of Two Cities*, which are not funny. As a novelist his natural fertility greatly hampers him, because the burlesque which he is never able to resist is constantly

---

2. Chapter 5. Murdstone is David's stepfather. [*Editor.*]

breaking into what ought to be serious situations. There is a good example of this in the opening chapter of *Great Expectations*. The escaped convict, Magwitch, has just captured the six-year-old Pip in the churchyard. The scene starts terrifyingly enough, from Pip's point of view. The convict, smothered in mud and with his chain trailing from his leg, suddenly starts up among the tombs, grabs the child, turns him upside down and robs his pockets. Then he begins terrorising him into bringing food and a file:

> He held me by the arms in an upright position on the top of the stone, and went on in these fearful terms:
>
> "You bring me, tomorrow morning early, that file and them wittles. You bring the lot to me, at that old Battery over yonder. You do it, and you never dare to say a word or dare to make a sign concerning your having seen such a person as me, or any person sumever, and you shall be let to live. You fail, or you go from my words in any partickler, no matter how small it is, and your heart and liver shall be tore out, roasted and ate. Now, I ain't alone, as you may think I am. There's a young man hid with me, in comparison with which young man I am a Angel. That young man hears the words I speak. That young man has a secret way pecooliar to himself, of getting at a boy, and at his heart, and at his liver. It is in wain for a boy to attempt to hide himself from that young man. A boy may lock his door, may be warm in bed, may tuck himself up, may draw the clothes over his head, may think himself comfortable and safe, but that young man will softly creep and creep his way to him and tear him open. I am keeping that young man from harming you at the present moment, but with great difficulty. I find it wery hard to hold that young man off of your inside. Now, what do you say?"

Here Dickens has simply yielded to temptation. To begin with, no starving and hunted man would speak in the least like that. Moreover, although the speech shows a remarkable knowledge of the way in which a child's mind works, its actual words are quite out of tune with what is to follow. It turns Magwitch into a sort of pantomime wicked uncle, or, if one sees him through the child's eyes, into an appalling monster. Later in the book he is to be represented as neither, and his exaggerated gratitude, on which the plot turns, is to be incredible because of just this speech. As usual, Dickens's imagination has overwhelmed him. The picturesque details were too good to be left out. Even with characters who are more of a piece than Magwitch he is liable to be tripped up by some seductive phrase. Mr. Murdstone, for instance, is in the habit of ending David Copperfield's lessons every morning with a dreadful sum in arithmetic. "If I go into a cheesemonger's shop, and buy five thousand double-Gloucester cheeses at fourpence halfpenny each, present payment," it always begins. Once again the typical Dickens detail, the double-Gloucester cheeses.[3] But it is far too human a touch for Murdstone; he would have made it five thousand cashboxes. Every time this note is struck, the unity of the novel suffers. Not that it matters very much, because Dickens is obviously a writer whose parts are greater than his wholes. He is all fragments, all details—rotten architecture, but wonderful gargoyles—and never better than

---

3. Chapter 4: the "appalling sums" Murdstone forces him to learn. [*Editor.*]

when he is building up some character who will later on be forced to act inconsistently.

* * *

HUMPHRY HOUSE

G. B. S. on *Great Expectations*†

The publication for the first time in England of an essay by Mr Shaw on Dickens is not an event to let slip with just a casual notice. * * *

* * *

Mr Shaw says that in *Great Expectations* Dickens "let himself go". The critical importance of these words varies with the emphasis: they are more important if the emphasis is on "himself" than if it is on "go". For in countless other parts of his work he "let go" his other self, the impersonator, the actor who grimaced and spoke the words of his characters aloud as he wrote about them, forgetting all the details of ordinary life. His great grotesques are all "lettings-go" in this sense. And his great criminal, distorted, evil characters are "lettings-go" of a secret inner strain of his. But in *Great Expectations* it was his more open, social, autobiographical self he let go; it is the pendant to the first part of *David Copperfield*, the more mature revision of the progress of a young man in the world.

* * *

It is, of course, a snob's progress; and the novel's greatest achievement is to make it sympathetic. When Pip plays Beggar-my-Neighbour and, later on, sophisticated French games of cards with Estella; when he has just heard of his fortune, and the cattle on the marshes seem "in their dull manner, to wear a more respectful air now"; when he first dines with Herbert Pocket; when he visits the town in the Havisham-Pocket context without calling on Joe at the forge, and then, on getting back to London, sends him some fish and a barrel of oysters to salve his conscience; above all, when Magwitch comes to his rooms in the Temple—on these and countless other such occasions Dickens is touching the very quick of that delicate, insinuating, pervasive class-consciousness which achieved in England a subtle variegation and force to which other countries, with fewer gradations between the feudal and the "low", have scarcely aspired. Many of our novels have played on class themes, but none with such lingering, succulent tenderness. Mr Shaw says that "as our social conscience expands and makes the intense class snobbery of the nineteenth century seem less natural to us, the tragedy of *Great Expectations* will lose some of its appeal". It may need a little more effort to understand—and the novel is indeed already a historical document of the first importance; but its permanent appeal derives from its adaptation of an age-old theme to a particular complex modern society.

† From Humphry House, *All in Due Time* (London, 1955), 201–18. Reprinted by permission of John House. Originally published as a review of Shaw's introduction in *Dickensian* 44 (1948): 63–70, 183–86. All footnotes are by the editor of this Norton Critical Edition.

Many critics have seen in it an allegory or at least a symbolism. The disappointment of Pip's expectations, following upon the discovery of their source, is taken to be an expression of disgust at the groundless optimism and "progressive" hope of mid-Victorian society. What Mr Shaw calls the bitterness of Dickens's "exposure of the futility of Pip's parasitism" is often taken to be a bitterness in the knowledge that all the material wealth and boasted progress of that age were parasitic on the drudgery of an exploited working-class, a hideous underworld of labour. * * *

All this is very important. It is plain that in the later novels—*Little Dorrit, Great Expectations*, and *Our Mutual Friend* above all—Dickens's attitude to money and to the power of money in life has undergone a drastic revision, and that this reflects the development of capitalism in mid-century: the joint-stock company and investment have taken the place of the old-fashioned honest "counting-house" businessmen of the Fezziwig-Cheeryble-Garland type,[1] who plainly worked for their living and often lived over the office. The new power of money is vaster, anonymous and secret; and those who make the big fortunes do not work for them, but juggle with paper. Merdle, Veneering, and Lammle are the new businessmen. The clearest expression of Dickens's opinion about the effect of this upon society is in the rhythmical satiric exhortation to "Have Shares" and be mighty, in *Our Mutual Friend*.[2] The plots of all these three novels turn on Big Money; and in each a main point is that the money bears no intelligible relation to the amount and quality of the work put into earning it. Pip's is an extreme case: he does not even know where the money comes from. When he learns he is appalled: his fortune turns to dust and ashes.

The special unity of the book, which Mr Shaw and all its admirers particularly stress, is brought out by the ingenuity of plot through which both the amorous and social expectations are ultimately seen to derive from the same source. When Pip has made that discovery he reveals to Magwitch on his deathbed a secret of his own heart. * * * That deathbed scene is the confession from Pip that ultimately he and Magwitch had been actuated by the same sort of motive. Mr Shaw does not quite give full weight to this scene:

> But Pip—and I am afraid Pip must be to this extent identified with Dickens—could not see Magwitch as an animal of the same species as himself or Miss Havisham. His feeling is true to the nature of snobbery; but his creator says no word in criticism of that ephemeral limitation.

Surely this last scene is criticism enough without any labouring of the point. "Dear Magwitch," says Pip; at the moment of death he can use the word of love, can recognise the kinship, can even admit community of ultimate thought. This is indeed too terribly true to the nature of snobbery; Pip could never have maintained such a mood with Magwitch alive, and if he had

---

1. Types of the sentimental private philanthropists who appear in Dickens's early novels. Fezziwig is the eupeptic merchant with whom the young Scrooge serves his apprenticeship in *A Christmas Carol*, Garland a sterling fatherly do-gooder in *The Old Curiosity Shop*.
2. Part 1, chapter 10: "Have no antecedents, no established character, no cultivation, no ideas, no manners: have Shares. . . . What are his tastes? Has he any principles? . . . What squeezes him into Parliament? Shares. . . . Sufficient answer to all: Shares." The enormous traffic in shares reflected the economic boom of the early 1860s, which was about to collapse at the time Dickens wrote *Our Mutual Friend*. Lammles: newcomers to the Veneering circle, who marry each other for money only to discover that both are penniless. On Merdle and Veneerings, see House's earlier comments on p. 574.

thought he would recover he would never have told him about Estella. It was a sort of viaticum. And surely Dickens knew what he was doing.

Mr Shaw rather complains that Dickens

> never raises the question why Pip should refuse Magwitch's endowment and shrink from him with such inhuman loathing. . . . Inspired by an altogether noble fixed idea, he had lifted himself out of his rut of crime and honestly made a fortune for the child who had fed him when he was starving. If Pip had no objection to be a parasite instead of an honest blacksmith, at least he had a better claim to be a parasite on Magwitch's earnings than, as he imagined, on Miss Havisham's property. It is curious that this should not have occurred to Dickens.

The novel is not an essay in ethics; this may have occurred to Dickens, but the important point is that it did not occur to Pip; and that is in general keeping with the truth to life which Mr Shaw praises. The horror of Magwitch which Pip had as a child in the churchyard and during the fight with Compeyson in the ditch on the marshes would have stayed with him for life; he had indelible memories of terror linked to Magwitch; the beginning of the book is so fine, so well in keeping with all that follows, because it gives the full weight and proportion to those childish fears; and those very fears are caught up again into the mood of apparently crude snobbery in the Temple. This is one of Dickens's greatest novels just because the moral problems are not seen too simply. Pip is not a young philosopher acting and feeling on argued moral principle. The childish fears hitched on to social snobbery by a complex, unconscious process in which the sexual love for Estella had the strongest play. It is just because Pip could not have rationally defended his loathing of the Warmint that it is so strong and awful. And indeed it does seem to be going a little far to say that Magwitch's fixed idea is "altogether noble"; for he was not concerned so much about Pip's true well-being as about his own capacity to make a "gentleman" of him; Pip was to be Magwitch's means of self-expression, just as Estella was to be Miss Havisham's; they each wanted to use a child to redress the balance of a world gone wrong, to do vicariously what they had failed to do direct. In the Temple Magwitch is not really concerned much about the grateful return for Pip's help on the marshes; he is concerned to view, assess, appraise the "dear boy" as his own creation. For Magwitch is a snob too. It is curious that this should not have occurred to Mr Shaw. A main theme of the book, running in two parallel strands of the plot, is that the attempt through money and power to exploit a child will lead to ingratitude and even more bitterness. Pip's presence both at the death of Magwitch and at the awful scene of Miss Havisham's repentance is meant to show him as the channel through which they purge themselves of their errors too.

Thus, emotionally as well as socially and financially, Pip appears as "helpless". He directs nothing; things happen to him; everybody except Joe and Biddy uses him for purposes of their own. They let him go his own way and help him out of scrapes. But there is never any question of his return to the village for good, with an effective, working reconciliation with them. His new class character—amounting to very little more than voice and table manners and range of friends—is firmly established and he is left to continue in it. Dickens was not going to say that all his gains were negligible. Of the two children used for experiment Estella suffers in the long run more than Pip; she is not of the receptive kind. * * *

* * *

Far too much that has been written and said about Dickens's politics has been written and said with the misguided expectation of finding something definite and almost systematic. * * * [He] was suspicious of both theoretical systems and practical systems because he thought of the individual human element as more important, and ultimately more powerful, than they. But this individualistic humanism was qualified in two respects. It was qualified first by experience; as time went on Dickens began to see its weakness. The more bitter and less sanguine mood of his later books can be missed only by a reader who has been befogged by the earlier. The old expansive Christmas ethic is almost dead. * * * Magwitch is no benevolent idealist whose goodness may regenerate society; he is a power-lover and a snob, whose specious generosity all but corrupts Pip and brings about his good almost by chance. The old Christmas ethic is represented by Joe, in whom it is humble, narrow and cautious. Joe's relations with Old Orlick could be quoted to illustrate the break-down of the kind of employer-employed relationship which Dickens had earlier loved to idealise. Orlick never seems to be intrinsically evil in himself as Compeyson is shown to be evil; he is jealous, revengeful, full of hate; but he seems all the time to have been thwarted by something outside himself, something it is beyond Joe's range to understand. He is indeed a baffling figure to a modern reader, and seems to me to represent an unresolved (perhaps only half-conscious) problem in Dickens's own mind.

Mr Shaw writes that Dickens never "called on the people themselves". This is not wholly true of his journalism; there was, for instance, his article *To Working Men* about Public Health in *Household Words* for 7th October 1854; there were other particular articles, such as *A Poor Man's Tale of a Patent*.[3] But in general I think it is true that he was suspicious of the people in the mass. The curious passage in *The Old Curiosity Shop* showing the dread of physical-force Chartism has its counterparts in the description of the popular riots in *A Tale of Two Cities* and in *Barnaby Rudge*.[4] Old Orlick seems in his own individual self to echo this dread of the mass in action. He is less a criminal than a turbulent, discontented underdog, and I think many readers of *Great Expectations*, if they look into their minds carefully about the matter, will find that they have been all along according him a sort of uneasy sympathy touched with fear. Orlick represents the element in English society with which Dickens never came to terms. He could assimilate the pitiable underdog; but the rash, independent, strong, turbulent, losing underdog, who became criminal more by accident than by choice, always disturbed him. Orlick is far more interesting than Compeyson or Magwitch, because his author did not put him flat and fair in the criminal department.

3. *Household Words*, October 19, 1850. The story details a workingman's frustrations in trying to patent an (unspecified) invention. His figure was to be fleshed out in the inventor Daniel Doyce in *Little Dorrit*.
4. *Old Curiosity Shop*, chapter 44; *Tale of Two Cities*, book 1, chapters 21–22 and *passim*; *Barnaby Rudge*, chapters 63–65. Dickens likens the Chartists to the violent proletarian elements of the French Revolution and Lord Gordon's street gang in the No-Popery Riots of 1780. *Old Curiosity Shop* appeared in 1840–41, when the Chartist agitation would be instant newspaper copy.

There was an underlying fear that "the people" in the mass might turn out to be Orlicks.

* * *

DOROTHY VAN GHENT

On *Great Expectations*†

"The distinguishing quality of Dickens's people," says V. S. Pritchett,

> is that they are solitaries. They are people caught living in a world of their own. They soliloquize in it. They do not talk to one another; they talk to themselves. The pressure of society has created fits of twitching in mind and speech, and fantasies in the soul . . . The solitariness of people is paralleled by the solitariness of things. Fog operates as a separate presence, houses quietly rot or boisterously prosper on their own . . . Cloisterham[1] believes itself more important than the world at large, the Law sports like some stale and dilapidated circus across human lives. Philanthropy attacks people like a humor or an observable germ. The people and the things of Dickens are all out of touch and out of hearing of each other, each conducting its own inner monologue, grandiloquent or dismaying. By this dissociation Dickens brings to us something of the fright of childhood . . .[2]

Some of the most wonderful scenes in *Great Expectations* are those in which people, presumably in the act of conversation, raptly soliloquize; and Dickens' technique, in these cases, is usually to give the soliloquizer a fantastic private language as unadapted to mutual understanding as a species of pig Latin. Witness Mr. Jaggers' interview with Joe Gargery, in which the dignified lawyer attempts to compensate Joe financially for his part in Pip's upbringing, and Joe swings on him with unintelligible pugilistic jargon.

> "Which I meantersay . . . that if you come into my place bull-baiting and badgering me, come out! Which I meantersay as sech if you're a man, come on! Which I meantersay that what I say, I meantersay and stand or fall by!"

Or Miss Havisham's interview with Joe over the question of Pip's wages; for each question she asks him, Joe persists in addressing his reply to Pip rather than herself, and his replies have not the remotest relation to the questions. Sometimes, by sheer repetition of a phrase, the words a character uses will assume the frenzied rotary unintelligibility of an idiot's obsession, as does Mrs. Joe's "Be grateful to them which brought you up by hand," or Pumblechook's mincing "May I?—May I?" The minimal uses of language as an instrument

---

† From Dorothy Van Ghent, "On *Great Expectations*," *The English Novel: Form and Function* (New York, 1953), 125–38. Reprinted by permission of Holt, Rinehart & Winston Co. All footnotes are by the editor of this Norton Critical Edition.

1. The cathedral town in which Dickens's last novel, *Edwin Drood*, is set: Pip's "market town" by another name.

2. V. S. Pritchett, *The Living Novel* (New York: Reynal & Hitchcock, 1947), 88.

of communication and intellectual development are symbolized by Pip's progress in the school kept by Mr. Wopsle's great-aunt, where the summit of his education consists in his copying a large Old-English "D," which he assumes to be the design for a belt buckle; and by Joe's pleasure in the art of reading, which enables him to find three "J's" and three "O's" and three "J-O, Joes" in a piece of script.

* * * Language as a means of communication is a provision for social and spiritual order. You cannot make "order" with an integer, one thing alone, for order is definitively a relationship among things. Absolute noncommunication is an unthinkable madness for it negates all relationship and therefore all order, and even an ordinary madman has to create a kind of order for himself by illusions of communication. Dickens' soliloquizing characters, for all their funniness (aloneness is inexorably funny, like the aloneness of the man who slips on a banana peel, seen from the point of view of togetherness), suggest a world of isolated integers, terrifyingly alone and unrelated.

The book opens with a child's first conscious experience of his aloneness. Immediately an abrupt encounter occurs—Magwitch suddenly comes from behind a gravestone, seizes Pip by the heels, and suspends him upside down.

> "Hold your noise!" cried a terrible voice, as a man started up from among the graves at the side of the church porch. "Keep still, you little devil, or I'll cut your throat!"

Perhaps, if one could fix on two of the most personal aspects of Dickens' technique, one would speak of the strange languages he concocts for the solitariness of the soul, and the abruptness of his tempo. His human fragments suddenly shock against one another in collisions like those of Democritus'[3] atoms or of the charged particles of modern physics. Soldiers, holding out handcuffs, burst into the blacksmith's house during Christmas dinner at the moment when Pip is clinging to a table leg in an agony of apprehension over his theft of the pork pie. A weird old woman clothed in decayed satin, jewels and spider webs, and with one shoe off, shoots out her finger at the bewildered child, with the command: "Play!" A pale young gentleman appears out of a wilderness of cucumber frames, and daintily kicking up his legs and slapping his hands together, dips his head and butts Pip in the stomach. These sudden confrontations between persons whose ways of life have no habitual or logical continuity with each other suggest the utmost incohesion in the stuff of experience.

* * *

Dickens lived in a time and an environment in which a full-scale demolition of traditional values was going on, correlatively with the uprooting and dehumanization of men, women, and children by the millions—a process brought about by industrialization, colonial imperialism, and the exploitation of the human being as a "thing" or an engine or a part of an engine capable of being used for profit. This was the "century of progress" which ornamented its steam engines with iron arabesques of foliage as elaborate as the anti-

---

3. The Greek atomist and moral philosopher (460?–370? B.C.) who maintained that reality is to be found in the infinitely swirling world of atoms and that thought and sensation were mere surface appearances. As the author of two lost essays, *On Laughter* and *On Cheerfulness*, he has been known as "The Laughing Philosopher."

macassars[4] and aspidistras and crystal or cut-glass chandeliers and bead-and-feather portieres of its drawing rooms, while the human engines of its welfare groveled and bred in the foxholes described by Marx in his *Capital*.[5] (Hauntingly we see this discordance in the scene in *Great Expectations* where Miss Havisham, sitting in her satin and floral decay in the house called Satis, points her finger at the child and outrageously tells him to "play." For though the scene is a potent symbol of childish experience of adult obtuseness and sadism, it has also another dimension as a social symbol of those economically determined situations in which the human soul is used as a means for satisfactions not its own, under the gross and transparent lie that its activity is its happiness, its welfare and fun and "play"—a publicity instrument that is the favorite of manufacturers and insurance agencies, as well as of totalitarian strategists, with their common formula, "We're just a happy family.") The heir of the "century of progress" is the twentieth-century concentration camp, which makes no bones about people being "things."

Dickens' intuition alarmingly saw this process in motion, a process which abrogated the primary demands of human feeling and rationality, and he sought an extraordinary explanation for it. People were becoming things, and things (the things that money can buy or that are the means for making money or for exalting prestige in the abstract) were becoming more important than people. People were being de-animated, robbed of their souls, and things were usurping the prerogatives of animate creatures—governing the lives of their owners in the most literal sense. This picture, in which the qualities of things and people were reversed, was a picture of a daemonically motivated world, a world in which "dark" or occult forces or energies operate not only in people (as modern psychoanalytic psychology observes) but also in things: for if people turn themselves or are turned into things, metaphysical order can be established only if we think of things as turning themselves into people, acting under a "dark" drive similar to that which motivates the human aberration.

There is an old belief that it takes a demon to recognize a demon, and the saying illustrates the malicious sensibility with which things, in Dickens, have felt out and imitated, in their relationship with each other and with people, the secret of the human arrangement. A four-poster bed in an inn, where Pip goes to spend the night, is a despotic monster that straddles over the whole room,

> putting one of his arbitrary legs into the fireplace, and another into the doorway, and squeezing the wretched little washing-stand in quite a Divinely Righteous manner.

Houses, looking down through the skylight of Jaggers' office in London, twist themselves in order to spy on Pip like police agents who presuppose guilt. Even a meek little muffin has to be "confined with the utmost precaution under a strong iron cover," and a hat, set on a mantelpiece, demands constant attention and the greatest quickness of eye and hand to catch it neatly as it tumbles off, but its ingenuity is such that it finally manages to fall into the

---

4. Coverlets draped over the backs of chairs and sofas to keep them from soilure, specifically a protection against hair oil (imported from the Indonesian seaport Makassar).
5. See esp. book 1, chapter 25, section 5, in which Marx, citing the *Public Health Reports* for 1865–66, attacks the appalling living conditions of English workingmen.

slop basin. The animation of inanimate objects suggests both the quaint gaiety of a forbidden life and an aggressiveness that has got out of control—an aggressiveness that they have borrowed from the human economy and an irresponsibility native to but glossed and disguised by that economy.

Dickens' fairly constant use of the pathetic fallacy[6] (the projection of human impulses and feelings upon the nonhuman, as upon beds and houses and muffins and hats) might be considered as incidental stylistic embellishment if his description of people did not show a reciprocal metaphor: people are described by nonhuman attributes, or by such an exaggeration of or emphasis on one part of their appearance that they seem to be reduced wholly to that part, with an effect of having become "thinged" into one of their own bodily members or into an article of their clothing or into some inanimate object of which they have made a fetish. Dickens' devices for producing this transposition of attributes are various. * * * Many of what we shall call the "signatures" of Dickens' people—that special exaggerated feature or gesture or mannerism which comes to stand for the whole person—are such dissociated parts of the body, like Jaggers' huge forefinger which he bites and then plunges menacingly at the accused, or Wemmick's post-office mouth, or the clockwork apparatus in Magwitch's throat that clicks as if it were going to strike. The device is not used arbitrarily or capriciously. In this book, whose subject is the etiology of guilt and of atonement, Jaggers is the representative not only of civil law but of universal Law, which is profoundly mysterious in a world of dissociated and apparently lawless fragments; and his huge forefinger, into which he is virtually transformed and which seems to act like an "it" in its own right rather than like a member of a man, is the Law's mystery in all its fearful impersonality. Wemmick's mouth is not a post-office when he is at home in his castle but only when he is at work in Jaggers' London office, where a mechanical appearance of smiling is required of him. And as Wemmick's job has mechanized him into a grinning slot, so oppression and fear have given the convict Magwitch a clockwork apparatus for vocal chords.

* * *

Through the changes that have come about in the human, as humanity has leaked out of it, the atoms of the physical universe have become subtly impregnated with daemonic aptitude. Pip, standing waiting for Estella in the neighborhood of Newgate, and beginning dimly to be aware of his implication in the guilt for which that establishment stands—for his "great expectations" have already begun to make him a collaborator in the generic crime of using people as means to personal ends—has the sensation of a deadly dust clinging to him, rubbed off on him from the environs, and he tries to beat it out of his clothes. Smithfield, that "shameful place," "all asmear with filth and fat and blood and foam," seems to "stick to him" when he enters it on his way to the prison. The nettles and brambles of the graveyard where Magwitch first appears "stretch up cautiously" out of the graves in an effort to get a twist on the branded man's ankles and pull him in. The river has a malignant potentiality that impregnates everything upon it—discolored copper, rot-

6. As a formal term in literary criticism, the phrase first appears in John Ruskin's *Modern Painters*, volume 3, part 4, chapter 12 (1856), in which he imputes the fallacy to writers who are "over-dazzled by emotion" without sufficient mental powers to control their feelings: "the state of mind which attributes the characters of a living creature to [non-human phenomena] is one in which the reason is unhinged by grief" or by any other sensation that ends by falsifying the object.

ten wood, honeycombed stone, green dank deposit. The river is perhaps the most constant and effective symbol in Dickens, because it establishes itself so readily to the imagination as a daemonic element, drowning people as if by intent, disgorging unforeseen evidence, chemically or physically changing all it touches, and because not only does it act as an occult "force" in itself but it is the common passage and actual flowing element that unites individuals and classes, public persons and private persons, deeds and the results of deeds, however fragmentized and separated. Upon the river, one cannot escape its action; it may throw the murderer and his victim in an embrace. At the end of *Great Expectations*, it swallows Compeyson, while, with its own obscure daemonic motivation, though it fatally injures Magwitch, it leaves him to fulfill the more subtle spiritual destiny upon which he has begun to enter. The river scene in this section, closely and apprehensively observed, is one of the most memorable in Dickens.

* * *

What brings the convict Magwitch to the child Pip, in the graveyard, is more than the convict's hunger; Pip (or let us say simply "the child," for Pip is an Everyman) carries the convict inside him, as the negative potential of his "great expectations"—Magwitch is the concretion of his potential guilt. What brings Magwitch across the "great gulfs" of the Atlantic to Pip again, at the moment of revelation in the story, is their profoundly implicit compact of guilt, as binding as the convict's leg iron which is its recurrent symbol. The multiplying likenesses in the street as Magwitch draws nearer, coming over the sea, the mysterious warnings of his approach on the night of his reappearance, are moral projections as "real" as the storm outside the windows and as the crouched form of the vicious Orlick on the dark stairs. The conception of what brings people together "coincidentally" in their seemingly uncaused encounters and collisions—the total change in the texture of experience that follows upon any act, public or private, external or in thought, the concreteness of the effect of the act not only upon the conceiving heart but upon the atoms of physical matter, so that blind nature collaborates daemonically in the drama of reprisal—is deep and valid in this book.

* * *

Pip first becomes aware of the "identity of things" as he is held suspended heels over head by the convict; that is, in a world literally turned upside down. Thenceforth Pip's interior landscape is inverted by his guilty knowledge of this man "who had been soaked in water, and smothered in mud, and lamed by stones, and cut by flints, and stung by nettles, and torn by briars." The apparition is that of all suffering that the earth can inflict, and that the apparition presents itself to a child is as much as to say that every child, whatever his innocence, inherits guilt (as the potential of his acts) for the condition of man. The inversion of natural order begins here with first self-consciousness: the child is heir to the sins of the "fathers." Thus the crime that is always pervasive in the Dickens universe is identified in a new way—not primarily as that of the "father," nor as that of some public institution, but as that of the child—the original individual who must necessarily take upon himself responsibility for not only what is to be done in the present and the future, but what has been done in the past, inasmuch as the past is part and parcel of the present and the future. The child is the criminal, and it is for this reason that he is able to redeem his world; for the world's guilt is his guilt, and he can expiate it in his own acts.

The guilt of the child is realized on several levels. Pip experiences the psychological *form* (or feeling) of guilt before he is capable of voluntary evil; he is treated by adults—Mrs. Joe and Pumblechook and Wopsle—as if he were a felon, a young George Barnwell (a character in the play which Wopsle reads on the night when Mrs. Joe is attacked) wanting only to murder his nearest relative, as George Barnwell murdered his uncle. This is the usual nightmare of the child in Dickens, a vision of imminent incarceration, fetters like sausages, lurid accusatory texts. He is treated, that is, as if he were a thing, manipulable by adults for the extraction of certain sensations: by making him feel guilty and diminished, they are able to feel virtuous and great. But the psychological *form* of guilt acquires spiritual *content* when Pip himself conceives the tainted wish—the wish to be like the most powerful adult and to treat others as things. At the literal level, Pip's guilt is that of snobbery toward Joe Gargery, and snobbery is a denial of the human value of others. Symbolically, however, Pip's guilt is that of murder; for he steals the file with which the convict rids himself of his leg iron, and it is this leg iron, picked up on the marshes, with which Orlick attacks Mrs. Joe; so that the child does inevitably overtake his destiny, which was, like George Barnwell, to murder his nearest relative. But the "relative" whom Pip, adopting the venerable criminality of society, is, in the widest symbolic scope of intention, destined to murder is not Mrs. Joe but his "father," Magwitch—to murder in the socially chronic fashion of the Dickens world, which consists in the dehumanization of the weak, or in moral acquiescence to such murder. Pip is, after all, the ordinary mixed human being, one more Everyman in the long succession of them that literature has represented, but we see this Everyman as he develops from a child; and his destiny is directed by the ideals of his world—toward "great expectations" which involve the making of Magwitches—which involve, that is, murder. These are the possibilities that are projected in the opening scene of the book, when the young child, left with a burden on his soul, watches the convict limping off under an angry red sky, toward the black marshes, the gibbet, and the savage lair of the sea, in a still rotating landscape.

*   *   *

As the child's original alienation from "natural" order is essentially mysterious, a guilty inheritance from the fathers which invades first awareness, so the redemptive act is also a mysterious one. The mysterious nature of the act is first indicated, in the manner of a motif, when Mrs. Joe, in imbecile pantomime, tries to propitiate her attacker, the bestial Orlick. In Orlick is concretized all the undefined evil of the Dickens world, that has nourished itself underground and crept along walls, like the ancient stains on the house of Atreus.[7] He is the lawlessness implied in the unnatural conversions of the

7. The sanguinary and accident-prone family in Greek mythology, whose titular head numbered among his crimes and miscalculations the murder of a half-brother, the accidental murder of a son who had been sent to kill him, and the murder of two nephews whose flesh he set before their father at a banquet and whose sister he married after she had become pregnant by the father. Students of Greek tragedy are apt to be more familiar with the second generation of Atreus, which involves the intrafamilial murders of Agamemnon, Clytemnestra, and Aegisthus.

human into the nonhuman, the retributive death that invades those who have grown lean in life and who have exercised the powers of death over others. He is the instinct of aggression and destruction, the daemonism of sheer external Matter as such; he is pure "thingness" emerging without warning from the ooze where he has been unconsciously cultivated. As Orlick is one form of spiritual excess—unmotivated hate—Joe Gargery is the opposed form—love without reservation. Given these terms of the spiritual framework, the redemptive act itself could scarcely be anything but grotesque—and it is by a grotesque gesture, one of the most profoundly intuitive symbols in Dickens, that Mrs. Joe is redeemed. What is implied by her humble propitiation of the beast Orlick is a recognition of personal guilt in the guilt of others, and of its dialectical relationship with love. The motif reappears in the moment of major illumination in the book. Pip "bows down," not to Joe Gargery, toward whom he has been privately and literally guilty, but to the wounded, hunted, shackled man, Magwitch, who has been guilty toward himself. It is in this way that the manifold organic relationships among men are revealed, and that the Dickens world—founded in fragmentariness and disintegration —is made whole.

JULIAN MOYNAHAN

The Hero's Guilt: The Case of *Great Expectations*†

Two recent essays on *Great Expectations* have stressed guilt as the dominant theme. They are Dorothy Van Ghent's 'On Great Expectations' (*The English Novel: Form and Function*, New York, 1953) and G. R. Stange's 'Dickens's Fable for his Time' (*College English*, XVI, October 1954). Mr. Stange remarks *inter alia* that 'profound and suggestive as is Dickens's treatment of guilt and expiation in this novel, to trace its remoter implications is to find something excessive and idiosyncratic'; and he has concluded that 'compared to most of the writers of his time the Dickens of the later novels seems to be obsessed with guilt'. He does not develop this criticism, if it is a criticism, but one might guess he is disturbed by a certain discrepancy appearing in the narrative between the hero's sense of guilt and the actual amount of wrong-doing for which he may be said to be responsible. Pip has certainly one of the guiltiest consciences in literature. He not only suffers *agenbite of inwit*[1] for his sin of snobbish ingratitude toward Joe and Biddy, but also suffers through much of the novel from what can only be called a conviction of criminal guilt. Whereas he expiates his sins of snobbery and ingratitude by ultimately accepting the convict Magwitch's unspoken claim for his protection and help, by willingly renouncing his great expectations, and by returning

---

† From Julian Moynahan, "The Hero's Guilt: The Case of *Great Expectations*," *Essays in Criticism* 10 (1960): 60–79. Reprinted by permission of the author. All footnotes are by the editor of this Norton Critical Edition.

1. "Remorse of conscience." Originally the title of a penitential manual written in French in the late thirteenth century by one Friar Lorenz, the phrase owes its vogue to James Joyce's repeated use of it in the early episodes of *Ulysses* (1922) to describe the guilt from which his autobiographical hero, Stephen Dedalus, suffers after his refusal to pray at his mother's deathbed and at his failure as a son generally.

in a chastened mood to Joe and Biddy, he cannot expiate—or exorcise—his conviction of criminality, because it does not seem to correspond with any real criminal acts or intentions.

Snobbery is not a crime. Why should Pip feel like a criminal? Perhaps the novel is saying that snobbery of the sort practiced by Pip in the second stage of his career is not very different from certain types of criminal behaviour. For instance, a severe moralist might point out that snobbery and murder are alike in that they are both offences against persons rather than property, and both involve the culpable wish to repudiate or deny the existence of other human beings. On this view, Pip reaches the height of moral insight at the start of the trip down the river, when he looks at Magwitch and sees in him only 'a much better man than I had been to Joe'. By changing places with the convict here, he apparently defines his neglectful behaviour toward Joe as criminal. Does this moment of vision objectify Pip's sense of criminality and prepare the way for expiation? Perhaps, but if so, then Pip's pharisaic rewording of the publican's speech, which occurs a few pages later while he is describing Magwitch's death in the prison, must somehow be explained away:

> Mindful, then, of what we had read together, I thought of the two men who went up into the Temple to pray, and I thought I knew there were no better words that I could say beside his bed, than 'O Lord, be merciful to him, a sinner!'

Even Homer nods, and Dickens is not, morally speaking, at his keenest in deathbed scenes, where his love of the swelling organ tone is apt to make him forget where he is going. Still, we ought not to explain anything away before the entire problem of Pip's guilt has been explored at further length.

Other answers to the question I have raised are possible. Consider the following passage, wherein Pip most fully expresses his sense of a criminal 'taint'. He has just strolled through Newgate prison with Wemmick and is waiting near a London coach office for the arrival of Estella from Miss Havisham's:

> I consumed the whole time in thinking how strange it was that I should be encompassed by all this taint of prison and crime; that, in my childhood out on our lonely marshes on a winter evening I should have first encountered it; that, it should have reappeared on two occasions, starting out like a stain that was faded but not gone; that, it should in this new way pervade my fortune and advancement. While my mind was thus engaged, I thought of the beautiful young Estella, proud and refined, coming toward me, and I thought with absolute abhorrence of the contrast between the jail and her. I wished that Wemmick had not met me, or that I had not yielded to him and gone with him, so that, of all days in the year, on this day I might not have had Newgate in my breath and on my clothes. I beat the prison dust off my clothes as I sauntered to and fro, and I shook it out of my dress, and I exhaled its air from my lungs. So contaminated did I feel, remembering who was coming, that the coach came quickly after all, and I was not yet free from the soiling consciousness of Mr. Wemmick's conservatory, when I saw her face at the coach window and her hand waving at me.

Without question, Pip here interprets the frequent manifestations in his experience of criminal elements—the runaway prisoner on the marshes, the man with the two pound notes, the reappearance of the same man in chains on the coach going down into the marsh country, the reappearance of Magwitch's leg iron as the weapon which fells Mrs. Joe, the accident making the criminal lawyer Jaggers, whose office is beside Newgate prison, the financial agent of his unknown patron—as signs that indicate some deep affinity between him and a world of criminal violence. But a question that the reader must face here and elsewhere in the novel is whether to accept Pip's interpretation. If we conclude that Pip is in fact tainted with criminality, we must rest our conclusion on a kind of symbolic reading of the coincidences of the plot. Through these coincidences and recurrences, which violate all ordinary notions of probability, Dickens, so this argument must go, weaves together a net in whose meshes his hero is entrapped. Regardless of the fact that Pip's association with crimes and criminals is purely adventitious and that he evidently bears no responsibility for any act or intention of criminal violence, he must be condemned on the principle of guilt by association.

Nevertheless, if the reader is himself not to appear a bit of a pharisee, he must be able to show good reason for accepting the principle of guilt by association in settling the question of the hero's criminality. Both Mr. Stange and Miss Van Ghent present readings of the guilt theme which are an attempt to validate this principle. Mr. Stange decides that 'the last stage of Pip's progression is reached when he learns to love the criminal and to accept his own implication in the common guilt'. He believes that one of Dickens's major points is that 'criminality is the condition of life'. Pip, therefore, feels criminal guilt because he is criminal as we are all criminal. Along similar lines, Miss Van Ghent remarks, 'Pip . . . carries the convict inside him, as the negative potential of his 'great expectations'—Magwitch is the concretion of his potential guilt.' The appearance of Magwitch at Pip's apartment in the Temple is 'from a metaphysical point of view . . . that of Pip's own unwrought deeds.' Finally, she maintains that Pip bows down before Magwitch, who has been guilty towards him, instead of bowing down before Joe, toward whom Pip has been guilty. In so doing Pip reveals by a symbolic act that he takes the guilt of the world on his shoulders—rather in the style of Father Zossima[2] in *The Brothers Karamazov*. This is shown particularly by the fact that Pip assumes culpability in a relationship where he is, in fact, the innocent party.

Objections to these metaphysical readings can be raised. If criminality is the condition of life, and if guilt is universal in the world of the novel, what world may Joe Gargery, Biddy, and Herbert Pocket be said to inhabit? Miss Van Ghent's theory of Pip's guilt as the negative potential of his great expectations is more promising, because it seems to exempt humble people from the guilt attaching itself to a society of wealth and power which thrives on the expropriation of the fruits of labour of its weaker members. But in her description of Pip's redemptory act, Miss Van Ghent insists upon the pervasiveness of guilt throughout the Dickens world. Less disturbing than this contradiction but still questionable is her assumption that Magwitch has been

2. The saintly father superior in Dostoyevski's *The Brothers Karamazov* (1880), who instructs the youngest of the sons, Alyosha, and prostrates himself before Alyosha's libertine half-brother Dmitri (part 1, book 2, chapter 6), presumably because he knows that Dmitri will be accused of a parricide he did not commit. Zossima's history is given in a long interpolated section in book 4.

guilty of great wrong-doing towards Pip. Metaphysics aside, how badly has he treated Pip? Does his wrong-doing stand comparison with the vicious practices of an Orlick or even a Miss Havisham? Who, in the light of the virtues of faithfulness and love, virtues which the novel surely holds up for admiration, is the better, Magwitch or his daughter Estella?

*   *   *

II

In my opinion, Pip's relation to the criminal milieu of *Great Expectations* is not that of an Everyman to a universal condition. It is rather a more concrete and particularised relation than the metaphysical approach would indicate, although the novel defines that relation obliquely and associatively, not through discursive analysis. Miss Van Ghent has suggested a metaphoric connection between Magwitch and Pip. Her proposal of such implicit relations between character and character, even though they do not become rationalised anywhere, is an illuminating insight into the artistic method of the mature Dickens. But her principle can be applied differently and yield rather different results.

I would suggest that Orlick rather than Magwitch is the figure from the criminal milieu of the novel whose relations to him come to define Pip's implicit participation in the acts of violence with which the novel abounds. Considered by himself, Orlick is a figure of melodrama. He is unmotivated, his origins are shrouded in mystery, his violence is unqualified by regret. In this last respect he is the exact opposite of Pip, who is, of course, filled with regret whenever he remembers how he has neglected his old friends at the forge.

On the other hand, if we consider Orlick in his connections with Pip, some rather different observations can be made. In the first place, there is a peculiar parallel between the careers of the two characters. We first encounter Orlick as he works side by side with Pip at the forge. Circumstances also cause them to be associated in the assault on Mrs. Joe. Orlick strikes the blow, but Pip feels, with some justification, that he supplied the assault weapon. Pip begins to develop his sense of alienation from the village after he has been employed by Miss Havisham to entertain her in her house. But Orlick too turns up later on working for Miss Havisham as gatekeeper. Finally, after Pip has become a partisan of the convict, it turns out that Orlick also has become a partisan of an ex-convict, Compeyson, who is Magwitch's bitter enemy.

Up to a point, Orlick seems not only to dog Pip's footsteps, but also to present a parody of Pip's upward progress through the novel, as though he were in competitive pursuit of some obscene great expectations of his own. Just as Pip centres his hopes successively on the forge, Satis House, and London, so Orlick moves his base of operations successively from the forge, to Satis House, and to London. From Pip's point of view, Orlick has no right to interest himself in any of the people with whom Pip has developed close ties. For instance, he is appalled when he discovers that his tender feeling for Biddy is given a distorted echo by Orlick's obviously lecherous interest in the same girl. And when he discovers that Orlick has the right of entry into Satis

House he warns Jaggers to advise Miss Havisham to get rid of him. But somehow he cannot keep Orlick out of his affairs. When Magwitch appears at Pip's London lodging half-way through the novel, Orlick is crouching in darkness on the landing below Pip's apartment. And when Pip is about to launch the escape attempt down the Thames, his plans are frustrated by the trick which brings him down to the marshes to face Orlick in the hut by the limekiln. * * * [T]he confrontation of Orlick and Pip on the marshes is crucial for an understanding of the problem I am discussing, because it is the scene in which Dickens comes closest to making explicit the analogy between the hero and the novel's principal villain and criminal.

Orlick inveigles Pip to the limepit not only to kill him but to overwhelm him with accusations. Addressing Pip over and over again as 'Wolf', an epithet he might more readily apply to himself, he complains that Pip has cost him his place, come between him and a young woman in whom he was interested, tried to drive him out of the country, and been a perpetual obstacle in the path of his own uncouth ambitions. But the charge he makes with the greatest force and conviction is that Pip bears the final responsibility for the assault on Mrs. Joe:

> 'I tell you it was your doing—I tell you it was done through you,' he retorted, catching up the gun and making a blow with the stock at the vacant air between us. 'I come upon her from behind, as I come upon you to-night. I giv' it to her! I left her for dead, and if there had been a limekiln as nigh her as there is now nigh you, she shouldn't have come to life again. But it warn't old Orlick as did it; it was you. You was favoured, and he was bullied and beat. Old Orlick bullied and beat, eh? Now you pays for it. You done it; now you pays for it.'

The entire scene has a nightmare quality. This is at least partly due to the weird reversal of rôles, by which the innocent figure is made the accused and the guilty one the accuser. As in a dream the situation is absurd, yet like a dream it may contain hidden truth. On the one hand Orlick, in interpreting Pip's character, seems only to succeed in describing himself—ambitious, treacherous, murderous, and without compunction. On the other hand, several of Orlick's charges are justified, and it is only in the assumption that Pip's motives are as black as his own that he goes wrong. We know, after all, that Pip is ambitious, and that he has repudiated his early associates as obstacles to the fulfilment of his genteel aspirations. Another interesting observation can be made about Orlick's charge that 'it was you as did for your shrew sister'. Here Orlick presents Pip as the responsible agent, himself merely as the weapon. But this is an exact reversal of Pip's former assumptions about the affair. All in all, Orlick confronts the hero in this scene, not merely as would-be murderer, but also as a distorted and darkened mirror-image. In fact, he presents himself as a monstrous caricature of the tender-minded hero, insisting that they are two of a kind with the same ends, pursued through similarly predatory and criminal means. This is what his wild accusations come down to.

III

* * *

In *Great Expectations*, as in its legendary prototypes, the theme of ambition is treated under the two aspects of desire and will, the search for a super-abundance of love and the drive for power. And it is in his presentation of the theme in the latter aspect that Dickens makes the more profound analysis of the immoral and criminal elements in his hero's (and the century's) favourite dream.

But Pip's ambition is passive. He only becomes active and aggressive after he has ceased to be ambitious. How then does *Great Expectations* treat the theme of ambition in terms that are relevant to the total action of which Pip is the centre? I have already begun to suggest an answer to the question. Ambition as the instinct of aggression, as the pitiless drive for power directed against what we have called authority-figures is both coalesced and disguised in the figure of Orlick. And Orlick is bound to the hero by ties of analogy as double, *alter ego* and dark mirror-image. We are dealing here with an art which simultaneously disguises and reveals its deepest implications of meaning, with a method which apparently dissociates its thematic materials and its subject matter into moral fable-*cum*-melodramatic accompaniment, yet simultaneously presents through patterns of analogy a dramatic perspective in which the apparent opposites are unified. In *Great Expectations* criminality is displaced from the hero on to a melodramatic villain. But on closer inspection that villain becomes part of a complex unity—we might call it Pip-Orlick—in which all aspects of the problem of guilt become interpenetrant and co-operative. The only clue to this unity which is given at the surface level of the narrative is Pip's obsession of criminal guilt. Pip tells us over and over again that he feels contaminated by crime. But we do not find the objective correlative of that conviction until we recognise in the insensate and compunctionless Orlick a shadow image of the tender-minded and yet monstrously ambitious young hero.

What is the rationale of this elusive method? In my opinion it enabled Dickens to project a radical moral insight which anticipated the more sophisticated probings of novelists like Dostoievsky and Gide without abandoning the old-fashioned traditions of melodrama and characterisation in which he had worked for more than a quarter of a century before *Great Expectations* was published. Pip, by comparison with Raskolnikov,[3] is a simple young man. But through the analogy Pip-Orlick, *Great Expectations* makes the same point about ambition as *Crime and Punishment*, and it is a very penetrating point indeed. In the *Brothers Karamazov* Ivan comes to recognise during the course of three tense interviews with his half-brother, Smerdyakov, how he shares with that brother a criminal responsibility for the murder of their father, although Smerdyakov alone wielded the weapon. The comparable scene in *Great Expectations* is the limekiln scene. Orlick even adopts the tone of a jealous sibling during the interview, as in the remark, 'You was favoured, and he was bullied and beat.' But Dickens is not a Dostoievsky. Pip does not recognise Orlick as a blood-relation, so to speak. The meaning remains sub-

---

3. Rodion Raskolnikov, the homicidal student in *Crime and Punishment* (1866), whose spiritual pride and atonement provide the novel with its essential content.

merged and is communicated to the reader through other channels than the agonised confessions of a first-person narrator. Indeed, the profoundest irony of the novel is not reached until the reader realises he must see Pip in a much harsher moral perspective than Pip ever saw himself.

IV

Recognition that Pip's ambition is definable under the aspect of aggression as well as in terms of the regressive desire for passive enjoyment of life's bounty depends upon the reader's willingness to work his way into the narrative from a different angle than the narrator's. The evidence for the hero's power-drive against the authority-figures, the evidence of his 'viciousness' if you will, is embodied in the story in a number of ways, but a clear pattern of meaning only emerges after the reader has correlated materials which are dispersed and nominally unrelated in the story *as told*. Orlick, thus far, has been the figure whose implicit relations to the hero have constituted the chief clue to the darker meaning of Pip's career. He continues to be important in any attempt to set forth the complete case, but there are also some significant correlations to be made in which he does not figure. * * *

We might begin with the apparently cynical remark that Pip, judged on the basis of what happens to many of the characters closely associated with him, is a very dangerous young man. He is not accident-prone, but a great number of people who move into his orbit decidedly are. Mrs. Joe is bludgeoned, Miss Havisham goes up in flames, Estella is exposed through her rash marriage to vaguely specified tortures at the hands of her brutal husband, Drummle. Pumblechook has his house looted and his mouth stuffed with flowering annuals by a gang of thieves led by Orlick. All of these characters, with the exception of Estella, stand at one time or another in the relation of patron, patroness, or authority-figure to Pip the boy or Pip the man.

* * * Furthermore, all of these characters, including Estella, have hurt, humiliated, or thwarted Pip in some important way. All in some way have stood between him and the attainment of the full measure of his desires. All are punished.

Let us group these individual instances. Mrs. Joe, the cruel foster-mother, and Pumblechook, her approving and hypocritical relation by marriage, receive their punishment from the hands of Orlick. Mrs. Joe hurts Pip and is hurt in turn by Orlick. Pip has the motive of revenge—a lifetime of brutal beatings and scrubbings inflicted by his sister—but Orlick, a journeyman who does not even lodge with the Gargerys, bludgeons Mrs. Joe after she has provoked a quarrel between him and his master. If we put together his relative lack of motive with his previously quoted remarks at the limekiln and add to these Pip's report of his own extraordinary reaction upon first hearing of the attack—

> With my head full of George Barnwell, I was at first disposed to believe that *I* must have had some hand in the attack upon my sister, or at all events that as her near relation, popularly known to be under obligations to her, I was a more legitimate object of suspicion than anyone else—

we arrive at an anomalous situation which can best be resolved on the assumption that Orlick acts merely as Pip's punitive instrument or weapon.

With regard to Pumblechook's chastisement, the most striking feature is not that Orlick should break into a house, but that he should break into Pumblechook's house. Why not Trabb's? One answer might be that Trabb has never stood in Pip's light. Pumblechook's punishment is nicely proportioned to his nuisance value for Pip. Since he has never succeeded in doing him any great harm with his petty slanders, he escapes with a relatively light wound. Although we are told near the end of the novel that Orlick was caught and jailed after the burglary, we are never told that Pip reported Orlick's murderous assault on him or his confessions of his assault on Mrs. Joe to the police. Despite the fact that there is enough accumulated evidence to hang him, Orlick's end is missing from the book. Actually, it seems that Orlick simply evaporates into thin air after his punitive rôle has been performed. His case needs no final disposition because he has only existed, essentially, as an aspect of the hero's own far more problematic case.

Estella receives her chastisement at the hands of Bentley Drummle. How does this fit into the pattern we have been exploring? In the first place, it can be shown that Drummle stands in precisely the same analogical relationship to Pip as Orlick does. Drummle is a reduplication of Orlick at a point higher on the social-economic scale up which Pip moves with such rapidity through the first three-quarters of the novel. Drummle, like Orlick, is a criminal psychopath. At Jaggers's dinner party the host, a connoisseur of criminal types, treats Drummle as 'one of the true sort', and Drummle demonstrates how deserving he is of this distinction when he tries to brain the harmless Startop with a heavy tumbler.

But the most impressive evidence that Orlick and Drummle are functional equivalents is supplied by the concrete particulars of their description. To an extraordinary degree, these two physically powerful, inarticulate, and dark-complexioned villains are presented to the reader in terms more often identical than similar. Orlick, again and again, is one who lurks and lounges, Drummle is one who lolls and lurks. When Pip, Startop, and Drummle go out rowing, the last 'would always creep in-shore like some uncomfortable amphibious creature, even when the tide would have sent him fast on his way; and I always think of him as coming after us in the dark or by the back-water, when our own two boats were breaking the sunset or the moonlight in mid-stream'. When Startop walks home after Jaggers's party, he is followed by Drummle but on the opposite side of the street, 'in the shadow of the houses, much as he was wont to follow in his boat'. The other creeper, follower and amphibian of *Great Expectations* is Orlick, whose natural habitat is the salt marsh, who creeps his way to the dark landing below Pip's apartment to witness the return of Magwitch from abroad, who creeps behind Biddy and Pip as they walk conversing on the marshes and overhears Pip say he will do anything to drive Orlick from the neighbourhood, who appears out of the darkness near the turnpike house on the night Pip returns from Pumblechook's to discover that his sister has been assaulted, and who, finally, creeps his way so far into Pip's private business that he ends by acting as agent for Compeyson, Magwitch's—and Pip's— shadowy antagonist.

Like Orlick, Drummle is removed from the action suddenly; Pip is given no opportunity to settle old and bitter scores with him. In the last chapter we hear that he is dead 'from an accident consequent on ill-treating a horse'.

This is the appropriate end for a sadist whose crimes obviously included wife-beating. But more important to the present argument is our recognition that Drummle has been employed to break a woman who had, in the trite phrase, broken Pip's heart. Once he has performed his function as Pip's vengeful surrogate he can be assigned to the fate he so richly deserves.

Mrs. Joe beats and scrubs Pip until she is struck down by heavy blows on the head and spine. Pumblechook speaks his lies about him until his mouth is stuffed with flowers. Estella treats his affections with cold contempt until her icy pride is broken by a brutal husband. In this series Orlick and Drummle behave far more like instruments of vengeance than like three-dimensional characters with understandable grudges of their own. In terms of my complete argument, they enact an aggressive potential that the novel defines, through patterns of analogy and linked resemblances, as belonging in the end to Pip and to his unconscionably ambitious hopes.

When Miss Havisham bursts into flames, there is no Orlick or Drummle in the vicinity to be accused of having set a match to her. In the long series of violence which runs through *Great Expectations* from the beginning to end, this is one climax of violence that can be construed as nothing more than accidental. And yet it is an accident which Pip, on two occasions, has foreseen. Before Miss Havisham burns under the eye of the horror-struck hero, she has already come to a violent end twice in his hallucinated fantasies—in Pip's visionary experiences in the abandoned brewery, where he sees Miss Havisham hanging by the neck from a beam. He has this vision once as a child, on the occasion of his first visit to Satis House, and once as an adult, on the occasion of his last visit, just a few minutes before Miss Havisham's accident occurs. What are we to make, if anything, of these peculiar hallucinatory presentiments and of the coincidence by which they come true? * * *

How do these hallucinations, the second followed immediately by Miss Havisham's fatal accident, add to the burden of the hero's guilt? The answer is obvious. Because Pip's destructive fantasy comes true in reality, he experiences the equivalent of a murderer's guilt. As though he had the evil eye, or as though there were more than a psychological truth in the old cliché, 'if looks could kill', Pip moves from the brewery, where he has seen Miss Havisham hanging, to the door of her room, where he gives her one long, last look—until she is consumed by fire. But here the psychological truth suffices to establish imaginative proof that Pip can no more escape untainted from his relationship to the former patroness than he can escape untainted from any of his relationships to characters who have held and used the power to destroy or hamper his ambitious struggles. In all these relationships the hero becomes implicated in violence. With Estella, Pumblechook, and Mrs. Joe, the aggressive drive is enacted by surrogates linked to the hero himself by ties of analogy. With Miss Havisham the surrogate is missing. Miss Havisham falls victim to the purely accidental. But the 'impurity' of Pip's motivation, as it is revealed through the device of the recurrent hallucination, suggests an analogy between that part of Pip which wants Miss Havisham at least punished, at most removed from this earth for which she is so profoundly unfit, and the destroying fire itself.

* * *

[Moynahan briefly discusses Pip's brainfever as a reflection of his destructive impulses and his helplessness.]

When Pip wakes up from his delirium he finds himself a child again, safe in the arms of the angelic Joe Gargery. But the guilt of great expectations remains inexpiable, and the cruelly beautiful original ending of the novel remains the only possible 'true' ending. Estella and Pip face each other across the insurmountable barrier of lost innocence. The novel dramatises the loss of innocence, and does not glibly present the hope of a redemptory second birth for either its guilty hero or the guilty society which shaped him. I have already said that Pip's fantasy of superabundant love brings him at last to a point of alienation from the real world. And similarly Pip's fantasy of power brings him finally to a point where withdrawal is the only positive moral response left to him.

The brick is taken down from its giddy place, a part of the engine is hammered off. Pip cannot redeem his world. In no conceivable sense a leader, he can only lead himself into a sort of exile from his society's power centres. Living abroad as the partner of a small, unambitious firm, he is to devote his remaining life to doing the least possible harm to the smallest number of people, so earning a visitor's privileges in the lost paradise where Biddy and Joe, the genuine innocents of the novel, flourish in thoughtless content.

K. J. FIELDING

The Critical Autonomy of *Great Expectations*†

Over the past twenty years there has been an astounding change in the critical value set on Charles Dickens. It may be said to have begun with the two long essays by George Orwell and Edmund Wilson,[1] and *The Dickens World* by Humphry House, about 1940–41. It took some while for it to sink in that Dickens was 'incomparably the greatest writer of his time'; it took even more to appreciate that he might show 'complexity and depth'.[2] Yet it fairly soon came to be generally understood that it had not been enough for someone such as Q. D. Leavis to explain away Dickens's 'best seller' success on the grounds that he was writing 'for a new, a naive public', and one for which he was well fitted as a novelist mainly because he was 'emotionally not only uneducated but also immature'.[3] * * *

*   *   *

The three studies of the novel that have given me the greatest insights are 'G.B.S. on *Great Expectations*' by Humphry House (1948; reprinted in *All in Due Time*, 1955), the chapter in *Charles Dickens, The World of His Novels* by J. Hillis Miller (1958), and 'The Hero's Guilt: the Case of *Great Expectations*' by Julian Moynahan (in *Essays in Criticism*, January 1960, Vol. X).

† From K. J. Fielding, "The Critical Autonomy of *Great Expectations*," *Review of English Literature* 2 (1961): 75–88. Reprinted by permission of the author.
1. In George Orwell, *Inside the Whale*, 1940, and Edmund Wilson, *The Wound and the Bow*, 1941.
2. *The Wound and the Bow*, rev. ed., London, 1952, 3.
3. Q. D. Leavis, *Fiction and the Reading Public*, 1932, 156–57.

Each offers a subtle interpretation; each is informed, thoughtful, persuasive, even brilliant; and they each explicitly recognise both the greatness and the complexity of the novel. Humphry House interpreted it as 'a snob's progress'; Miller regards it as showing a search for 'authentic selfhood'; and Moynahan presents it as an expression of the universal fantasy of 'great expectations', the outcome for the individual's unbounded demand for love and power which is inevitably linked with a sense of guilt. * * *

There is much in common between these three recent criticisms, and acceptance of one by no means involves a complete rejection of the others. Yet they are different enough to offer an elementary demonstration of how in creating *Great Expectations*, perhaps more than with any of his other novels, Dickens succeeded in creating a world of his own which he left to express itself, which is not bounded by his comments, nor limited by it being possible to identify too obviously the author's point of view. Whatever may be true of some of the other novels (of *Bleak House*, for example, as seen by E. M. Forster in *Aspects of the Novel*, iv) Dickens never depended less on 'bouncing' the reader into accepting what was happening, nor more successfully and deliberately detached himself from his work so that it stands almost completely on its own, offering the reader what he can make of it for himself.[4]

This is fairly well recognised. Certainly all three critics of *Great Expectations* are circumspect about straying away from the novel to search for evidence of Dickens's intentions. * * * All three, perhaps, while recognising the meagreness of our information, might have said a little more about how strange this was. It is true that, like Dickens's other novels, the book grew enormously in meaning beyond its first conception; but was there ever a more ludicrous contrast between what critics have written about a great work, and what Dickens had to say when he started it? * * *

* * *

There is, in fact, nothing to guide us. Though Forster, it may well be thought, talked over the novel with Dickens, and the critical comments in his biography of his friend *may* even have been written with the benefit of a knowledge of Dickens's intentions, there is nothing in them to show this one way or the other. * * * If Dickens had any other purpose than writing a 'tragicomic' story dealing in a fairly conventional way with the three stages in the development of Pip, he kept it more closely from his friends than the mystery of *Edwin Drood*. * * *

In general it is clear from Dickens's letters that when he discussed his novels it was usually in unsophisticated terms. There are occasional hints that it may have been possible to draw him out, and it is easy to believe that his understanding of creative processes and critical problems went much further than he reveals. Yet it is up-hill work trying to demonstrate this part from what is implied in the novels themselves. * * * Melville is sometimes held up to us as a writer who preserved a dignified reserve in comparison, say, with Mark Twain. Even so, he could write such a letter to Nathaniel Hawthorne as the one in which he says of himself, amid much else: 'It is but

---

4. In his discussion of fictional characters in *Aspects of the Novel*, Forster disparages the aesthetic that requires a rigidly consistent viewpoint from which the narrative is to be told, and he cites the success with which the dual viewpoint is assumed in *Bleak House*. "Logically, *Bleak House* is all to pieces, but Dickens bounces us [into submission], so that we do not mind the shiftings of the viewpoint" (79). [*Editor.*]

nature to be shy of a mortal who boldly declares that a thief in jail is as honourable a personage as Gen. George Washington.'[5] Whereas Dickens, though this might be thought to be the main implication of *Great Expectations*, hardly once looks out from under cover. Surely we do not get anywhere near 'the heart of Charles Dickens' in his letters?[6] * * *

The more one learns of his life, therefore, the more one is bound to agree that it is entirely justifiable (with the later novels at least) to seek the heart of what he had to say within the novels, even when it is apparently at variance with what we know of the outward incidents of his life. This is what most recent criticism tries to do: it is concerned to analyse the kind of personal experience that Dickens was trying to convey, while being rather detached and tentative in estimating the merits of his writing.

Yet this already poses other problems. For once we have assented to this, what is one to make of Dickens as a novelist when it seems that he may be writing a story which has not merely a variety of implications, but possibly a number of contradictory ones?[7] And what if we have to suppose that he was unaware of many of them? It may be wrong to assume that he was. Yet, as an assumption, it is no greater than Mr. Moynahan's, for example, when he says of a certain incident in the novel, that 'we need not deny Dickens the insight necessary to the imagining of so ambivalent a response' in Pip—a response, the ambivalence of which lies in his being able to express and even think that he feels forgiveness for Miss Havisham at one moment, and yet a moment or two afterwards to show (by his vision of her hanging from the beam in the old brewery) that he 'hates her in the depths of his being'.

We *need* not deny Dickens this insight, but what if we do? It may quite as well be that the insight we have here (and a valuable one) is Mr. Moynahan's, that it is true to the character of Pip, and yet that the imaginative power that created the character and the incident worked almost blindly. It makes it no easier to assent when Mr. Moynahan goes on to say that 'we should not commit the anachronism of demanding that this response be defined in the novel analytically and self-consciously—that the hero should tell us, "I forgave Miss Havisham as fully as I could, but continued to think how well it would have been for me if she had never set foot on this earth."'

It is hard to see that to have written like this would have been an anachronism: indeed, it is very like a good deal of *Great Expectations*, as when Pip graciously 'extends his clemency' to Biddy, or describes his feelings towards Joe on the hat-dropping visit to Barnard's Inn (chapters xix and xxvii). Dickens was quite capable of explicitly recognising that a character might behave in a contradictory way towards other characters.[8] On the other hand, it *is* perhaps rather difficult (and possibly anachronistic) to imagine that—at least any earlier in his career than this—he could intentionally have shown this kind of behaviour and have refrained from clearly underlining its implications for the reader. * * *

5. *Letters of Herman Melville*, ed. M. R. Davis and W. H. Gilman, New Haven, 1960, 127; letter of 1 June 1851.
6. Crack at the American edition of Dickens's letters to Angela Burdett-Coutts, which bears the title placed by Fielding in sarcastic quotation marks. [*Editor*.]
7. As an example of the first, I would instance *Great Expectations*, of the second, *Our Mutual Friend*.
8. The memorandum book suggests that the "germ" for a Dickens character often lay in his perception of a contradiction.

* * *

The whole question is illustrated again by a problem which Mr. Moynahan sets the reader at the beginning of his article. He points out that, at the end of Chapter lvi, as Pip describes how he took Magwitch's hand at the moment of the convict's death, he writes: 'Mindful, then, of what we had read together, I thought of the two men who went into the Temple to pray, and I knew that there were no better words that I could say beside his bed, than "O Lord, be merciful to him, a sinner!" ' Obviously * * * this is a ludicrous or pharisaic perversion of the publican's prayer, 'God be merciful to me a sinner' (St. Luke, xviii). But what are we to make of it? There are perhaps, three main alternatives: the first that Dickens simply mis-quoted, without a thought, as he was capable of doing, and that it has no especial significance; secondly, that he was, indeed, unaware of it, and it indicates how superficial his frequent by-play with biblical references in the novels can be; and thirdly that Pip, the former blacksmith's boy and respectable partner in Clarriker & Co., was still so unperceptive and snobbish enough neither to know what he was thinking at the moment of Magwitch's death, nor even to be aware of it twelve years or more later when he was telling the story.

Putting aside the first two alternatives, we are presented by the third with quite a complex character in Pip, for it seems that we can never accept at face-value anything he has to say. The whole novel is not merely 'a snob's progress', but one in which we can never be sure just what progress has been made. This was implicit in House's analysis of Pip's behaviour in the same death-bed scene. He maintained that Pip was still a snob. Unaware of the possible irony in the prayer, House nevertheless believed that in spite of 'the horror that he feels for Magwitch', Pip revealed to him the story of Estella, addresses him as 'dear Magwitch', recognised their common humanity and took his hand, actions that were 'indeed too terribly true to the nature of snobbery', for: 'Pip could never have maintained such a mood with Magwitch alive, and if he had thought he would recover he would never have told him about Estella. It was a sort of viaticum. And surely Dickens knew what he was doing'.[9]

Surely Dickens knew. But what is one to make of this interpretation on turning back several pages to the end of Chapter liv, in which Pip had said, 'I took my place by Magwitch's side', and 'I felt that that was my place henceforth while he lived'. Is this then also self-deception? Did Pip really still have to overcome 'horror' at his benefactor as Magwitch was dying, and are we really to disbelieve him when he says of himself directly after the arrest: 'For now my repugnance to him had all melted away, and in the hunted, wounded, shackled creature who held my hand in his, I only saw a man who had meant to be my benefactor, and who had felt affectionately, gratefully, and generously towards me with great constancy through a series of years. I only saw in him a much better man than I had been to Joe.' On one interpretation, therefore, these words would evidently mark the climax of Pip's self-deception; yet on another they are believed to mark the transformation after which 'Magwitch thinks only of Pip . . . and Pip thinks only of Magwitch'.[1]

9. House, 208–09; see also above, 645–46.
1. Miller, 276.

*　　*　　*

*　*　* We hear of critics who wish to treat the novels as 'autonomous works of art'.[2] But with *Great Expectations* one has little alternative: it is largely imposed by the author and form of the novel, rather than a self-limitation set by the reader.

One may wonder, even, whether this respect for the autonomy of the novels on the part of every critic is altogether a good thing. As adopted by Trilling and Miller, it would be asinine to complain. Yet it may be that some of our critical problems in discussing the novels are largely self-imposed. It may be that we make too much, for example, of the whole question of Pip's personal 'guilt'. Turning away from the world of the novels once more, and looking for a moment at the real world by which Dickens was so passionately disturbed, one can catch glimpses of a society the members of which did well to raise a feeling of guilt at its recent treatment of crime and punishment. *　*　*

Taking up, at random, a volume of memoirs rescued from the shilling-box in a second-hand bookshop, *The Reminiscences of Sir Henry Hawkins, Baron Brampton* (1817–1907) it seems to me that even in the pages of such a book we can begin to share the world of a reader of the time which is not altogether irrelevant to understanding the novel. These memoirs tell the story of a famous advocate whose most unforgettable childhood recollection was of the sight of the corpse of a young man, executed for rick-burning, being borne past his schoolroom window by the young man's parents. It was a world in which he found that the law 'at every assize, was like a tiger let loose upon the district', in which prisoners were sentenced to death in batches, as Magwitch was in the memorable scene at the Old Bailey. It was a time *　*　* when even the unsentimental Hawkins found that his 'greatest delight . . . was the obtaining an acquittal of someone whose guilt nobody could doubt'. Newgate itself, as he describes it, still had a room as late as 1852 in which counsel might interview prisoners, which was decorated in the style of Little Britain by countless death-masks showing the 'indentation of the hangman's rope under the ear'. These impressed even Hawkins 'with a disgust at the brutal tendency of the age' he had lived through; and he was a contemporary of Dickens, and one of his amateur players in the company at Knebworth.[3]

It all proves nothing, yet one never knows quite what to make of Dickens's own openly-expressed views on crime. Against certain passages in *Great Expectations* one might set the passionate outburst one finds in a letter to Forster at the Home Secretary's pardon for a poisoner convicted of murder. It was written about this time (25 August 1859) and followed by a furious article in *All the Year Round* ('Five Points of the Criminal Law', 24 September 1859). It seems to me that it may have a reference to the treatment of Orlick and Mrs. Joe; but that is not to be dealt with here. The same murderer, as it happens, was immediately passed on to Sir Henry Hawkins, who managed to inflict on him the penalty of twelve months for bigamy.

We do well to remember that Dickens was writing in a world in which an Attorney-General could address the young men of a Y.M.C.A. and assure

---

2. Miller, viii, referring to his "own approach" and Trilling's essay on *Little Dorrit*.
3. Thanks to Professor Fielding's alert, I have rescued seven pages from Hawkins's *Reminiscences*, above, pp. 594–601. [*Editor.*]

them: 'I am perfectly confident that the principle of mutual benevolence, of a universal desire to do good, derived from Christianity . . . is one of the best and most sure modes of securing even temporary success in life (Cheers).'[4] It may prove nothing once again, but it puts the novel back into a world ripe for irony; and it may be, as regards Hawkins, that Pip's feeling of the 'taint of prison or crime', immediately after his visit to Newgate, was shared by others who had lived through the first half of the century, and that Pip's own sense of guilt has been rather exaggerated.

* * *

CHRISTOPHER RICKS

Great Expectations†

The most important things about *Great Expectations* are also the most obvious—a fact that is fortunate for the book, but unfortunate for the critic. The greatly deplored deficiency of modern criticism is its inability to deal adequately with what is at the heart of most novels: 'scenes, actions, *stuff*, people' (Christopher Caudwell).[1] That is, in a way as specific as is usual in the discussion of poetry, relying more on cognition and less on ejaculation than did an earlier generation. Yet at the heart of *Great Expectations* are all those obvious sorts of greatness which embarrass the modern critic—convincing and often profound characterization, a moving and exciting story, and a world observed with both literal and moral fidelity. * * *

If the critic quiets his conscience, more or less ignores 'scenes, actions, *stuff*, people', and turns instead to symbols and themes, he does at any rate know where he is * * * [The] symbols [in *Great Expectations*] are striking, and strikingly used, but the novel could have managed without them; to ignore them would mar but not ruin the novel. Admittedly, this is partly because, at their best, Dickens's symbols do not make the fundamental mistake of appearing to owe their presence to their symbolic function. It is not difficult to design consciously or erupt obsessively a pattern of cross-connecting themes or symbols; and the virtue of cross-connection is felt only when the *raison d'être* of the separate moments is something other than that they will be connected. The important image or gesture or word should owe its existence to some non-symbolic necessity (as it almost always does in Shakespeare)—to plausible characterization, say, or likely incident. * * * 'Only connect'[2] will not really do, either for author or critic.

But at his best, Dickens can make the separate moments true in themselves,

---

4. Joseph Irving, *Annals of Our Time*, 1869, 402, entry for 4 October 1859.
† From Christopher Ricks, "*Great Expectations*," *Dickens and the Twentieth Century*, ed. John Gross and Gabriel Pearson (London, 1962), 187–211. Reprinted by permission of Routledge and Kegan Paul. Unless otherwise indicated, footnotes are by the editor of this Norton Critical Edition.
1. In *Illusion and Reality: A Study of the Sources of Poetry* (New York: International Publishers, 1937), 200: "The novel blots out external reality by substituting a more or less consistent mock reality which has sufficient 'stuff' to stand between reader and reality. . . . [R]hythm, 'preciousness,' and style are alien to the novel: . . . novels are not composed of words. They are composed of scenes, actions, *stuff*, people."
2. The epigraph to E. M. Forster's novel *Howards End* (1910), which dramatizes the division among the English social classes. But Forster's imperative may have its sources in Indian teaching.

so that the cross-connection is not only beautiful, but, what is even better, convincing. Magwitch's first act of gratitude to Pip for saving him from starvation is to send two pound notes to him *via* a discharged convict—'Nothing less than two fat sweltering one-pound notes that seemed to have been on terms of the warmest intimacy with all the cattle markets in the county.' Simply as description, it is vivid and plausible; but its subterranean energy comes out clearly when Pip, still thinking that Miss Havisham is his great benefactor, tries to pay back the returned Magwitch:

> 'Like you, I have done well since, and you must let me pay them back. You can put them to some other poor boy's use.' I took out my purse.
> He watched me as I laid my purse upon the table and opened it, and he watched me as I separated two one-pound notes from its contents. They were clean and new, and I spread them out and handed them over to him. Still watching me, he laid them one upon the other, folded them longwise, gave them a twist, set fire to them at the lamp, and dropped the ashes into the tray. (Ch. 39.)

Here too the account of the notes is apt to Pip and his station; and then the descriptions ignite, and we see in a flash the parable of Pip and his money. For him the money from the convict, fat and sweltering from the cattle markets, is a very different thing from that of Miss Havisham, 'clean and new'. But he is wrong about his benefactor, and he is wrong in thinking that some money is mysteriously cleaner than other money. When Magwitch burns the clean money, Dickens means more by it than Magwitch does. Magwitch means to shock and waken Pip, but he also burns Pip's dreams of a clean gentlemanly fortune. * * *

                    *   *   *

Yet cross-connections, symbols or themes do not really grapple with the book. Humphry House did, when he said that

> The final wonder of *Great Expectations* is that in spite of all Pip's neglect of Joe and coldness towards Biddy and all the remorse and self-recrimination that they caused him, he is made to appear at the end of it all a really better person than he was at the beginning. It is a remarkable achievement to have kept the reader's sympathy throughout a snob's progress.[3]

How then *does* Pip keep our sympathy? It is a crucial question, and some of the more general answers are obvious enough—indeed they throng in. That our first sight of him in the churchyard shows him not only defenceless but also compassionate and generous; that he is ill-treated by his sister Mrs. Joe and by all the visitors to the house, especially Pumblechook; that he early shows what is surely a praiseworthy wish to get on, and a willingness to spend his time and his pocket-money on learning to read and write—and all that before he has met Estella and caught her 'infectious' contempt for his commonness: all these dispose us well towards him. * * * Moreover, we are disinclined to pursue vengefully a sinner who gets so little pleasure out of his sin; remorse at his ingratitude to Joe, fear and insecurity about his great

---

3. *The Dickens World*, 156. [*Author.*]

expectations, and hopeless yearning for Estella, all combine to make him appropriately unhappy. 'We were always more or less miserable.' At the profoundest level, Pip's feelings of guilt (as Mr. Julian Moynahan has imaginatively and convincingly shown[4]) can be compared to Dostoievsky, with reservations but without absurdity. Yet in a more elementary way Pip's unhappiness is one of the strongest reasons why we keep our sympathy for him. And without that sympathy the novel could not begin to express its darker purpose.

Not that it is only Pip's behaviour and state of mind which control our feelings. If Pip thinks that it is Miss Havisham who is making his fortune, that is more because he has been deceived by others than self-deceived. The very first time Pip is to go to Satis House, his sister and Pumblechook insist 'that for anything we can tell, this boy's fortune may be made by his going to Miss Havisham's'. It is never forgotten that it is they who stuff Pip's head with 'nonsensical speculations about Miss Havisham, and about what she would do with me and for me'. Nor is this the limit of the mitigation; Pip is the victim not only of the chatter of his sister and Pumblechook, but also of the deliberate intrigue of Miss Havisham and Jaggers—and he 'deep as Australia', a man against whom no one has a chance. Pip's mistaken guess is precipitated by Jaggers's mention of Miss Havisham's relations the Pockets, and by Miss Havisham's own gloating knowledge of his new fortune and its conditions. She herself admits that she deliberately let Pip go on in his mistake, and we are not to believe her when she flashes out 'You made your own snares. I never made them.' At the very least, Pip's wishful thinking had been swollen by others, by ignorant speculations and by knowing deceptions. * * *

Yet not even these extenuations really explain why we feel so little malice towards Pip, who has behaved so badly. Perhaps only one thing can make us accept as likeable a boy so ungrateful and snobbish, and that is that he should admit it—which is of course just what Pip's first-person narrative does. The effect of using the first-person is completely to reverse the normal problem about keeping a reader's sympathy. We do not, in the ordinary way, have much difficulty in liking someone who tells us how bad he has been; we are perhaps less sympathetic to someone who talks about his good deeds. And, conversely, we are likely to feel sympathy with a man seen from the outside as acting well, but not otherwise. Goodness should not talk about itself, but badness may be absolved, or mitigated, by doing so. Not that there are no problems for the novelist who lets his bad character confess; but they are the opposite of what would ordinarily be suggested by Humphry House's remark. The real difficulties are two: can his confession always ring true, and not sound like disingenuous breast-beating?; and can he keep our sympathy even when he is telling us of his good actions?

Dickens's task here is made easier since Pip does very few good actions— and we are less suspicious about a good action when it comes after a frank admission of so many bad ones. * * *

Yet since, within limits, we tend to like people who admit faults, we must be convinced that they are not admitting the faults only as a way of getting us to like them, meanwhile securely complacent. Most of the time Dickens

---

4. "The Hero's Guilt," *Essays in Criticism* 10 (1960): 60–79. [*Author.*]

gets exactly the right tone for Pip—open but not abased, willing to admit faults but not positively enjoying it. At its best, such a confession has a brisk-ness, an unwillingness to luxuriate, which renders it immediately authentic: 'Whatever [learning] I acquired, I tried to impart to Joe. This statement sounds so well, that I cannot in my conscience let it pass unexplained. I wanted to make Joe less ignorant and common, that he might be worthier of my society and less open to Estella's reproach.' (Ch. 15.) Brief and simple, that is all that is said. Or, when Pip hears that Joe is coming to see him in London:

> Let me confess exactly, with what feelings I looked forward to Joe's coming.
> Not with pleasure, though I was bound to him by so many ties; no; with considerable disturbance, some mortification, and a keen sense of incongruity. If I could have kept him away by paying money, I certainly would have paid money. (Ch. 27.)

Again it is dry and terse, convincing and therefore likeable.

To discuss the less convincing confessions means first granting with plea-sure that there are few of them, and that they do throw into relief the innu-merable times when the poise is perfect. There is a spectrum of unsatisfying moments, ranging from the faintly uneasy to the hotly embarrassing. So Pip tells us that 'I know right well that any good that intermixed itself with my apprenticeship came of plain contented Joe, and not of restless aspiring dis-contented me'; where uneasiness might focus on the staunchness of 'I know right well', on the condescension in 'plain contented Joe', and on the height-ened self-reproach of 'restless aspiring discontented me' (three adjectives to the two that Joe gets). Brevity is the soul of confession, or we start to see the shadow of the impure motive. But the example is admittedly not a gross one; it is not, for example, Pip's final expiation: 'Don't tell him, Joe, that I was thankless; don't tell him, Biddy, that I was ungenerous and unjust; only tell him that I honoured you both, because you were both so good and true, and that, as your child, I said it would be natural to him to grow up a much better man than I did.' (Ch. 58.) * * *

                    *   *   *

But most of the time Dickens catches the right tone for Pip's admissions. His handling of the other difficulty, Pip's good actions, is just as skilful. The three important ones are his secret act of kindness in buying Herbert a part-nership, his final refusal to accept money from Miss Havisham or from Mag-witch, and his love for Magwitch. And the greatest of these three is love, which redeems him.

At first sight the incident of Herbert's partnership is not perhaps quite satisfactory. The early mentions of it are plausible enough, but verge on the mawkish: 'I did really cry in good earnest when I went to bed, to think that my expectations had done some good to somebody.' But what strengthens and elevates it is simply the fact that Pip is unable to complete the good act casually himself, since he no longer has any money. He has to go to Miss Havisham and ask a favour, one which runs the risk of being misunderstood both by her and by Jaggers. (Her instructions to him were 'evidently intended to absolve me from any suspicion of profiting by the receipt of the money'.)

The incident succeeds not merely because Pip does not go on about it, but also because it means that he must ignore his proud wish to be independent of the woman who tricked him. * * * Dickens's tact here is at its finest. In a way, this moment ought to be the long-awaited answer to Pip's dreams; all along he has thought of his 'great expectations' from Miss Havisham, and now at last they can be realized. Yet the power of this incident comes precisely from the fact that Dickens, who is so often over-explicit, does not need to mention how Pip's dreams are here finally destroyed. By leaving the rest unsaid, and by not at any point showing Pip meditating on such an offer or on his refusal of it, Dickens makes the incident all the more moving. And the simple dignity of Pip's refusal is a far truer evidence of his maturity than is the self-abasement before Joe:

> 'Can I only serve you, Pip, by serving your friend? Regarding that as done, is there nothing I can do for you yourself?'
> 'Nothing. I thank you for the question. I thank you even more for the tone of the question. But, there is nothing.' (Ch. 49.)

That comma after 'But' must be the least careless comma in Dickens—the decent mystery of leaving the rest unsaid.

Pip's refusal to take any more money from Magwitch is plainly right. One should not take money from someone whom one finds repugnant. And by the time that Pip loves Magwitch, the convict's fortune has been forfeited to the Crown. It was easy enough for Dickens to make convincing Pip's early shrinking from the money; the latter attitude needed to be more delicately handled. What happens is not a grand renunciation of the money, but a firm resignation to losing it; the firmness makes Pip admirable, the resignation instead of renunciation makes him plausible. Jaggers

> did not conceal from me that although there might be many cases in which forfeiture would not be exacted, there were no circumstances in this case to make it one of them. I understood that very well. I was not related to the outlaw, or connected with him by any recognisable tie; he had put his hand to no writing or settlement in my favour before his apprehension, and to do so now would be idle. I had no claim, and I finally resolved, and ever afterwards abided by the resolution, that my heart should never be sickened with the hopeless task of attempting to establish one. (Ch. 55.)

'I *finally* resolved . . .': those are the words not of a plaster saint, but of a decent man who manages not to repine.

But of all Pip's good deeds it is his loyal love for Magwitch which most matters. It more than counterbalances his ingratitude to Joe and Biddy, partly for the good reason that Pip's love for Magwitch is so strongly felt, partly for the bad reason that Joe and Biddy, despite all their occasional vividness, remain characters sadly insubstantial compared with Magwitch (or at any rate *become* so as soon as Pip grows up). The fact that, when Magwitch first returns, Pip feels nothing but repugnance for him, is not only the most powerful reason why his final love is so moving, but also the most powerful reason why it is so convincing. It is likely enough that Pip would shrink from Magwitch; the danger for Dickens here is that this may topple the reader over into disliking Pip. What retrieves the situation is the stroke of having Herbert

Pocket react at first in just the same way to Magwitch—Herbert, the simple, unsnobbish and good-natured:

> I saw my own feelings reflected in Herbert's face, and, not least among them, my repugnance towards the man who had done so much for me . . .
> [Magwitch's] chair remaining where it had stood, Herbert unconsciously took it, but next moment started out of it, pushed it away, and took another. He had no occasion to say, after that, that he had conceived an aversion for my patron, neither had I occasion to confess my own. We interchanged that confidence without shaping a syllable. (Ch. 41.)

* * *

Not that *Great Expectations* is flawless; rather, it is that compared with Dickens's other novels it has less flaws. * * * It is more than a pity that the coincidences on which the plot depends (Jaggers being the lawyer of both Miss Havisham and Magwitch, and Magwitch being Estella's father) should not be revealed until almost the end of the novel. *Données* are not usually looked in the mouth; but when they are offered as late as this it is easy to feel that they exist not, legitimately, as a means to writing the novel, but, illegitimately, as a means to rounding it off. And it is a matter for at least dismay that Dickens changed the original ending and allowed Pip to marry Estella; everything that we know of Miss Havisham and her bringing up of Estella is made hollow by this softening of Estella, since we find, not that we must forgive the tragic Miss Havisham, but that there was not really anything to forgive.

Such flaws are mainly technical, though some of them are serious. But there is one flaw of sympathy which is more grave. In the early scenes, the villain Compeyson is seen with the same compassionate realism as Magwitch:

> This man was dressed in coarse grey, too, and had a great iron on his leg, and was lame, and hoarse, and cold, and was everything that the other man was; except that he had not the same face, and had a flat, broad-brimmed, low-crowned felt hat on. (Ch. 3.)

But as soon as Compeyson disappears from our sight, he becomes merely a villain, and the villainy is rather hollowly denounced: 'that evil genius, Compeyson, the worst of scoundrels among many scoundrels'—'They fell into deeper shame and degradation—if there can be deeper—and ruin.' The denouncing words are too empty to weigh much in the scale against that 'flat, broad-brimmed, low-crowned felt hat'. * * *

It is not that some people are not wickeder than others; rather that the loose melodrama with which Compeyson is treated exerts an unwanted pressure on Magwitch. It puts the novel in danger of saying, not that Magwitch is a criminal whom we must love, but that he is not really a criminal. Real criminals we are left free to hate as before. Not that this is anything like the total impression which the book in fact makes. There *is* a failure of compassion in the treatment of Compeyson ('tumbling on the tides, dead'), but it is almost as nothing when set against the love of Pip and Magwitch. That love is made compellingly real; the whole novel is perhaps Dickens's most straightforwardly realistic; and even the fairy-tale elements look slightly different if one remembers that James Joyce received a letter from Slack Monro Saw & Co.:

> Dear Sir,
> We are instructed to write to you on behalf of an admirer of your writing, who desires to be anonymous, to say that we are to forward you a cheque for £50 on the 1st May, August, November, and February next, making a total of £200, which we hope you will accept without any enquiry as to the source of the gift.[5]

IAN WATT

Oral Dickens†

In *A Room of One's Own*, Virginia Woolf asserts that "it is part of the novelist's convention not to mention soup and salmon and ducklings" when he describes luncheon parties; the novelists "seldom spare a word for what was eaten."[1]

One knows what she means, but she's wrong. Actually, there are two kinds of novelists: those that do and those that don't. Among the moderns, Joyce, Hemingway, Thomas Wolfe, and Scott Fitzgerald, not to mention Philip Roth, typically activate our tastebuds, while Conrad and Lawrence[2] and Henry James[3] don't, although people occasionally pass the port, meet in the Café Royal, or pour cups of tea. Earlier, there's very little about food and drink in Melville, but lots in the English novelists of the nineteenth century—in Mrs. Gaskell and Meredith as well as in Surtees and Trollope. In the richness and variety of his treatment of food and drink Dickens is the indisputable master among the Victorian novelists; as, equally indisputably, he is both the heir of the tradition of Fielding and Smollett, and profoundly original.

✻   ✻   ✻

The first gastric phase in Dickens lasts for something like a decade. Accounts of eating and drinking diminish very little, but, although they are normally of a relatively straightforward kind, Dickens also begins to use them to show larger moral and social conflicts. Thus *Oliver Twist* (1838) and *Nicholas Nickleby* (1839) make much of the contrast between grownup overeating and youthful starvation. The two are memorably juxtaposed in such famous scenes as Oliver Twist in the workhouse asking for more, or Nicholas Nickleby hungering at Dotheboys Hall: in each case, Dickens, by insisting on the

---

5. London solicitors; letter dated February 22, 1917. The anonymous admirer was Harriet Shaw Weaver (1877–1961), a member of Ezra Pound's London circle and successor to Pound as editor of the journal *The New Freewoman* (after 1913 *The Egoist*). Weaver first touched base with Joyce in 1914 and the same year published the first (limited) edition of his *Portrait of the Artist*. Despite their often rocky relations, she continued to support Joyce for the rest of his life—and beyond: she paid for his funeral.
† From Ian Watt, "Oral Dickens," *Dickens Studies Annual*, ed. Robert B. Partlow, Jr., 3 (1974): 165–81. Reprinted by permission of AMS Press, Inc.
1. *A Room of One's Own* (London, 1935), p. 16.
2. Though food figures vitally and frequently in such travel books as Lawrence's *Sea and Sardinia* (New York, 1936), pp. 40–41, 65, 78–79, 98–107, 144–45.
3. Though a *cotelette de veau à l'oseille* [veal cutlet with purée of sorrel] at the *Cheval Blanc* is specified (in Henry James's *The Ambassadors* [1903], book 11, chapter 3).

choice fare on the tables of the elders, dramatizes the naked intergenerational power play.

* * *

Quite early, then, Dickens expanded the role of food and drink so that they played a vital part both in the plot structure and in the moral significance of his novels. In the second phase, in the novels which follow *The Christmas Carol*, those from *Martin Chuzzlewit* (1844) and *Dombey and Son* (1848) to *Hard Times* (1854) and *Little Dorrit* (1857), these characteristics continue; there is still a great deal of eating and drinking, but in keeping with Dickens' new fictional directions, there is less simple celebration of the pleasures of the table, while the appetites are presented in a much larger psychological and social perspective.

Martin Chuzzlewit anticipates much of the darker side of the later novels, and in so doing reveals an important advance in Dickens' presentation of the varied pathologies of oral appetite. There are, for instance, the boarders at Major Pawkins': "Dyspeptic individuals bolted their food in wedges; feeding, not themselves, but broods of nightmares"; and much the same could be said of Jonas Chuzzlewit's hectic and joyless drunkenness. At the same time the basic theme of the predatory relatives fighting among themselves for old Chuzzlewit's fortune is consistently presented in terms of vampirism, scavenging, and cannibalism. Dickens' comic aim, though, mitigates the consequences of these individual and social perversions of appetite.* * *

* * *

* * * *Great Expectations* (1861) offers perhaps the supreme example in Dickens of a comprehensive integration of eating and drinking into every aspect of the novel. Most obviously, food and drink are mentioned hundreds of times; and the attitude of almost every character toward the subject is presented, not only in itself, but as diagnostic of his moral essence and his social role. The rather few characters whom we can think of as good—notably Pip, Joe, Wemmick, Herbert Pocket, Abel Magwitch—are all fond of good food and drink; and in their various ways they express their love and consideration for others through the giving of food. * * *

The novel begins with Magwitch terrifying Pip: "You know what wittles is. . . . You get me wittles." Next morning Pip raids the Christmas larder and smuggles out his haul. When he sees Magwitch wolfing down mincemeat and pork pie and cheese with terrifying animality, Pip's sympathy finally gets the better of his terror and disgust: "Pitying his desolation . . . I made bold to say, 'I am glad you enjoy it.' " At first Magwitch doesn't hear him, but when Pip repeats his civility, Magwitch answers, "Thankee, my boy, I do." "The rudest meal in the novel," Barbara Hardy comments, is thereby turned "into an introductory model of ceremony."[4]

This early reciprocity of compassion and gratitude is immediately rewarded. Magwitch, soon captured, protects Pip by concealing his theft of the food; and Joe easily forgives the theft itself when, in answer to Magwitch's apology, he answers, "God knows you're welcome to it." Later, Magwitch, no longer threatening to eat Pip's "fat cheeks," determines to provide Pip with his great

---

4. "Food and Ceremony in *Great Expectations*," *Essays in Criticism*, XIII (1963), 354.

expectations; in his convict exile, he often imagined: "Here's the boy again, a looking at me whiles I eats and drinks!" But by the time Magwitch returns to England, snobbery has inhibited Pip's natural humanity; when Magwitch visits him in his Temple chambers, Pip at first intends to remain standing and let his guest drink his hot rum-and-water alone; he only changes his mind when, to his uncomprehending amazement, he notices that there are tears in Magwitch's eyes.

In this scene with Magwitch Pip is in a sense only repeating the way Mrs. Joe used to stand over Pip and Joe while she fed them, and the even more contemptuous rejection of Pip by Estella, when she first brought him beer and bread and meat at Satis House, "without looking at me, as insolently as if I were a dog in disgrace." The human importance of these reciprocities, or their damning absence, is expanded in two other episodes of the novel. First, the scene when Joe comes up to London and has breakfast with Pip and Herbert Pocket; Pip, ashamed of Joe's rough country manners, allows the reunion to become painfully embarrassing. He later blames himself: "I had neither the good sense nor the good feeling to know that this was all my fault." His own memory should really have afforded him a corrective parallel, for when, a country bumpkin himself and also just arrived in London, Pip had dinner with Herbert Pocket, his host so kindly corrected his table manners that "we both laughed and I scarcely blushed." "In London," says Pocket, "it is not the custom to put the knife in the mouth—for fear of accidents— and . . . while the fork is reserved for that use, it is not put further in than necessary."

Magwitch himself, of course, had originally become a criminal out of hunger; he first came to consciousness "down in Essex, a thieving turnips for my living." So Compeyson only had to tempt him: "What can you do?" he asked, and Magwitch replied, "Eat, drink . . . if you'll find the materials." Magwitch remains, in his own words, "a heavy grubber," and for the same psychological reasons, no doubt, a heavy smoker; but we are obviously meant to see him as a victim of a sick society, not as psychologically maimed himself, as so many of the other characters in *Great Expectations* are.

Outside this quartet of benevolent eaters, Pip, Joe, Magwitch, and Herbert Pocket (and perhaps some of their echoes, like Clara, Wemmick and his Aged Parent), attitudes to food in *Great Expectations* are diagnostic in quite a different way. Most obviously there is the petty egotistical tyranny of Pumblechook, bringing his Christmas offering of port and sherry to Mrs. Joe, but then dispensing hospitality with it to the sergeant of the search party and claiming all the credit; or Wopsle with his Christmas sermon on the gluttony of swine—the memory haunts Pip, and is only exorcised when he later toasts a sausage made from Wemmick's pig. Mr. Jaggers is tyrannical in a different way: he "cross-examined his very wine," and "seemed to bully his very sandwich as he ate it." Then there is the way that social pressure dictates the mode of eating: Wemmick is a vastly congenial table companion at his Walworth home; but in the official world of Little Britain, he merely "put[s] fish into the post-office" of his mouth. The implication of this gastric mutation is extended when Wemmick and Jaggers, united as proper unfeeling citizens of Little Britain, bully their poor client Mike for insulting them with his tears: "Get out of this office. I'll have no feelings here. Get out," says Jaggers; Mike does, and the two then go back "to work again with an air of refreshment upon them as if they had just had lunch."

As is usual in Dickens, it is the women characters who present the strongest examples of individual and social pathology, and almost without exception their symptoms are manifested through their attitudes to food. Mrs. Joe Gargery, who had married beneath her, even takes out her revenge on the bread and butter; she holds the bread against her "square impregnable bib . . . stuck full of pins and needles," and slaps the butter on "as if she were making a plaister." The vultures around Miss Havisham are all carrion-hungry, waiting until they can "come to feast upon her"; there is Camilla, who claims, "If I could be less affectionate and sensitive, I should have a better digestion and an iron set of nerves"; Georgiana, "an indigestive single woman, who called her rigidity religion and her liver love"; and Miss Sarah Pocket, who, Joe reports, on Miss Havisham's death is left "twenty-five pound per-annium fur to buy pills, on account of being bilious."

Satis House is itself an ironically named symbol of unsatisfied appetite. Once the home of a wealthy brewer who married his cook, it is now the mausoleum of love, betrayed twenty-five years ago and now turned into hatred of others and the self. Miss Havisham lives on, waiting to replace the decaying bride cake on the great table with her own dead body; pretending to herself that she can rise above the humanity that has wounded her, she not only stops the clocks and refuses to see the light of day, but "has never allowed herself to be seen doing either [eating or drinking], since she lived this present life of hers."

All the kinds of frustration and rejection, like all the kinds of satisfaction and acceptance, go together.

*   *   *

A good many biographical connections seem plausible, though also somewhat general and hypothetical. Not that Dickens was an infant starveling; it seems likelier that he had a difficult but not unhappy early childhood, if only because trust of others, success in work, and a great capacity for pleasure feature prominently not only in the novels but in his own character. The crucial biographical episode is more probably the five months or so at Warren's blacking warehouse. Dickens was then twelve; he would be nearing the end of the latency period when infantile sexual attitudes again come to the fore and are shaped into the basic sexual pattern of the future. But Dickens' mother had failed him on every count; he was expelled from home and family; he was hungry, and had to find his own food; all his hopes for the future were, it seemed, permanently doomed; and he seems to have laid the blame on his mother—the very mother who, in Dickens' case, had performed not only the usual maternal offices, but had taught him to read. On the other hand, it was his father—the Micawberish grandiloquent spendthrift—who eventually decided to take him out of Warren's warehouse and send him back to school. It was natural, therefore, that Dickens should have fallen back on the oral patterns of the distant past; that he should set out to achieve his early ambitions through prodigiously hard work; and that these ambitions should be connected with never going hungry, to be sure, but also with finding mother-substitutes rather than sexual experience.

As to the relationship between "oral regression" and Dickens' development as writer and oral performer, some connections seem fairly clear. We don't need Rabelais' Gargantua to teach us that what every baby would like to do at birth is shout: "*A boire! A boire! A boire!*"[5] For most children, though, in this unlike Gargantua, or even John Henry[6] for that matter, words normally come later, after weaning; but when words are finally mastered they provide new ways of obtaining nourishment, approval, and other modes of pleasure. * * *

The readings themselves were mainly taken from early works—the latest were from *David Copperfield* (1850); and they mainly feature feast scenes, comic scenes, or scenes where young children die—Nancy and Paul Dombey. In going back to an earlier stage of his development in literary subject matter, Dickens may have been enacting the same regressive impulse as in giving the readings themselves, which can be seen as reviving an earlier and more direct investment in oral satisfaction. He could burn many of the records of the past, cast off Catherine, and defy the world, but the strong oral components in his personality merely diverted their expression into an equally oral outlet in the readings: they would—and in fact did—at last persuade Dickens that he really could make the whole world hang, visibly and palpitatingly, upon his very lips.

* * *

For Dickens, and indeed for the Victorian child in general, all older people would tend to be seen in two main roles: as eaters, drinkers, and talkers themselves; and as powerful dispensers or withholders of his own oral pleasures. This itself comes close to supplying a perspective for understanding why so many of the basic conflicts in Dickens' novels can be reduced to the simple primitive choice between eating or being eaten. The sociological perspective would reinforce the psychological. We know that Victorian parents habitually used the giving or withholding of food as an instrument of religious, moral, and social discipline. Presumably, therefore, the child not only categorized adults as good or bad according to whether he was being well fed or not. Giving or consuming good food was deeply equated with goodness; and this equation was reinforced by economic and class factors, since there was a much greater difference then than now between the staple diets of different classes.[7]

As for the connection between the three senses of *oral*, a few concluding generalizations seem called for. First, as regards speech, it seems that there is still much to say about the way Dickens makes speaking itself both a directly

---

5. "As soon as he was born, he didn't cry, like other children, 'Wa! Wa!' Instead he shouted at the top of his voice, 'Drink! Drink! Drink!,' as if inviting the whole world to join him." In book 1, chapter 6 of François Rabelais's encyclopedic farrago *Gargantua and Pantagruel* (1534–54), the monster-baby Gargantua (the name translates "How Big You Are!") is squeezed from his mother's womb to her shoulders by way of her diaphragm and "taking a left-hand turn" comes out of her ear, dying of thirst and dying to talk after his long day's journey into light. [*Editor*.]

6. John Henry, the black folk hero who worked the railroad tracks in the mid-nineteenth-century South, has inspired innumerable ballads, "hammer songs," and blues, glorifying his prowess in fighting a steam drill whose uses jeopardized the need for human labor. In at least one version he weighs forty-four pounds at birth and bursts into a river song before he gulps down an enormous soul-food breakfast. [*Editor*.]

7. See John Burnett, *Plenty and Want: A Social History of Diet in England from 1815 to the Present Day* (London, 1866), especially the chapters on the food of the town workers and of the rich in the early Victorian period.

physical reality in his novels, and also an infinitely symbolic activity; more generally, that there is still much to learn about the physical, physiological and psychosexual functions of the act of speech.

Secondly, we should surely challenge the adverse judgment on all the oral functions which is implicit in our current terminology. The basic reason for this adverse judgment on oral satisfactions is presumably not so much the puritan objection to gluttony or the pleasures of the physical appetites in general, as it is Freud's biologically based evolutionary model for psychological development: oral satisfactions are "regressive" because they denote a deflection from, or a failure to achieve, "mature genitality," that "psychoanalytic Utopia," as Erik Erikson has called it.[8] Erikson's irony points to the reductive and pejorative connotations of such terms as *oral*, or, for that matter, *anal*. In any case, all surviving biological species have presumably achieved their genital Utopia; and though human civilization has done much with the genital component as a basis—romantic love and the family for instance—it is no more impressive than what man has done with the oral components, and it is certainly not so distinctive of man. All human societies have developed cooking, and no others have; man is indeed, as Boswell defined him, a "Cooking Animal."[9] Among the other oral components of culture which are unique to man one should at least list three that are particularly important for Dickens' novels. First, the invention of fermented beverages, which was no inconsiderable achievement; second, social laughter, which is basic to comedy; and third, of course, speech. *Homo loquens* is a reality, and were it not, we would not even have been able to christen him, however presumptuously, *homo sapiens*.[1]

PETER BROOKS

Repetition, Repression, and Return: The Plotting of *Great Expectations*†

Great Expectations is exemplary for a discourse on plot in many respects, not least of all for its beginning. For what the novel chooses to present at its outset is precisely the search for a beginning. As in so many nineteenth-century novels, the hero is an orphan, thus undetermined by any visible inheritance, apparently unauthored. * * * There may be sociological and sentimental reasons to account for the high incidence of orphans in the nineteenth-century novel, but clearly the parentless protagonist frees an author from struggle with preexisting authorities, allowing him to create afresh all

8. Erik Erikson, *Childhood and Society*, 2nd ed. (New York, 1963), 92, 76. One of the leading psychoanalysts of the second half of the century, Erik [Homburger] Erikson (1902–1994) applied the tools of Freudian analysis to cultural anthropology, developmental psychology, history, and biography in the text cited by Watt and in books like *Young Man Luther* (1958) and *Gandhi's Truth* (1969). Largely as a function of his biographical research, Erikson introduced the vogue for identity crises. [*Editor.*]
9. *Journal of a Tour to the Hebrides with Samuel Johnson, LL.D.*, ed. R. W. Chapman (London, 1961), pp. 179–80. Burke replied, "Your definition is good, and I now see the full force of the common proverb, 'There is *reason* in roasting of eggs.'"
1. Literally, "knowing man"; *homo loquens*: "speaking man." [*Editor.*]
† From Peter Brooks, "Repetition, Repression, and Return: The Plotting of *Great Expectations*," *Reading for the Plot: Design and Intention in Narrative* (New York, 1984), 113–42. Reprinted by permission of Alfred A. Knopf. A slightly shorter version of the chapter appeared in *New Literary History* 11 (1980): 503–26.

the determinants of plot within his text. He thus profits from what Gide called the "lawlessness" of the novel[1] by starting with an undefined, rule-free character and then bringing the law to bear upon him—creating the rules—as the text proceeds. With Pip, Dickens begins as it were with a life that is for the moment precedent to plot, and indeed necessarily in search of plot. Pip when we first see him is himself in search of the "authority"—the word stands in the second paragraph of the novel—that would define and justify— authorize—the plot of his ensuing life.

The "authority" to which Pip refers here is that of the tombstone which bears the names of his dead parents, the names that have already been displaced, condensed, and superseded in the first paragraph, where Pip describes how his "infant tongue" (literally, a speechless tongue: a catachresis that points to a moment of emergence, of entry into language) could only make of the name, Philip Pirrip, left to him by the dead parents, the monosyllabic Pip. "So, I called myself Pip, and came to be called Pip" (chapter 1). This originating moment of Pip's narration and his narrative is a self-naming that already subverts whatever authority could be found in the text of the tombstones. The process of reading that text is described by Pip the narrator as "unreasonable," in that it interprets the appearance of the lost father and mother from the shape of the letters of their names. The tracing of the name—which he has already distorted in its application to self—involves a misguided attempt to remotivate the graphic symbol, to make it directly mimetic, mimetic specifically of origin. Loss of origin, misreading, and the problematic of identity are bound up here in ways we will further explore later on. The question of reading and writing—of learning to compose and to decipher texts—is persistently thematized in the novel.[2]

The decipherment of the tombstone text as confirmation of loss of origin —as unauthorization—is here at the start of the novel the prelude to Pip's *cogito*,[3] the moment in which his consciousness seizes his existence as other, alien, forlorn:

> My first most vivid and broad impression of the identity of things seems to me to have been gained on a memorable raw afternoon towards evening. At such a time I found out for certain, that this bleak place overgrown with nettles was the churchyard; and that Philip Pirrip, late of this parish, and also Georgiana, wife of the above, were dead and buried; and that Alexander, Bartholomew, Abraham, Tobias, and Roger, infant children of the aforesaid, were also dead and buried; and that the dark flat wilderness beyond the churchyard, intersected with dykes and mounds and gates, with scattered cattle feeding on it, was the marshes; and that the low leaden line beyond was the river; and that the distant savage lair from which the wind was rushing, was the sea; and that the

1. André Gide (1869–1951) preached and practiced the subversion of conventional plot constructions and character definitions in nearly all of his later works, most famously in *The Counterfeiters* (1925). For Gide the behaviour and function of the characters reveal themselves by trial and error, often by chance or in answer to questions Gide himself puts to them—pretty much in the way scientists come by their information in conducting their research. In the central chapter of *The Counterfeiters* to which Brooks refers, "Edouard Explains His Theory of the Novel" (part 2, chapter 3), Gide's alter ego expresses his opinion—by now, thanks largely to Gide, a commonplace—that "of all literary genres, the novel remains the freest, the most *lawless*" (Gide uses the English word). [*Editor.*]

2. On the theme of reading in the novel, see Max Byrd, " 'Reading' in *Great Expectations*," PMLA 91, no. 2 (1976), 259–65.

3. "I think" (Latin). By hitching an English (or any other modern) noun, pronoun, or article to the verb, the writer arrives at some such meaning as "awareness" or the cognate "cogitation." [*Editor.*]

small bundle of shivers growing afraid of it all and beginning to cry, was Pip.

"Hold your noise!" cried a terrible voice. . . . (chapter 1)

The repeated verbs of existence—"was" and "were"—perform an elementary phenomenology of Pip's world, locating its irreducible objects and leading finally to the individual subject as other, as aware of his existence through the emotion of fear, fear that then appears as the origin of voice, or articulated sound, as Pip begins to cry: a cry that is immediately censored by the command of the convict Magwitch, the father-to-be, the fearful intrusive figure of future authorship who will demand of Pip: "Give us your name." * * * For purposes of my study of plot, it is important to note how this beginning establishes Pip as an existence without a plot, at the very moment of occurrence of that event which will prove to be decisive for the plotting of his existence, as he will discover only two-thirds of the way through the novel. Alien, unauthorized, self-named, at the point of entry into the language code and the social systems it implies, Pip will in the first part of the novel be in search of a plot, and the novel will recount the gradual precipitation of a sense of plot around him, the creation of portents of direction and intention.

Schematically, we can identify four lines of plot that begin to crystallize around the young Pip, the Pip of Part 1, before the arrival of his "Expectations":

1. Communion with the convict/criminal deviance.
2. Naterally wicious/bringing up by hand.
3. The dream of Satis House/the fairy tale.
4. The nightmare of Satis House/the witch tale.

These plots, we will see in a moment, are paired as follows: 2 / 1 = 3 / 4. That is, there is in each case an "official" and censoring plot standing over a "repressed" plot. In terms of Pip's own choices, we could rewrite the formula: 3 / 4 / 2 / 1, to show (in accordance with one of Freud's favorite models) the archaeological layering of strata of repressed material.[4] When the Expectations are announced by Jaggers at the end of part one, they will apparently coincide with Pip's choices ("My dream was out; my wild fancy was surpassed by sober reality" [chapter 18]), and will thus appear to take care of the question of plot. But this will be so only on the level of official plots; the Expectations will in fact only mask further the problem of the repressed plots.

I choose the term "communion" for the first plot because its characteristic symbolic gesture is Pip's pity for the convict as he swallows the food Pip has brought him, a moment of sympathetic identification which focuses a series of suggestive sympathies and identifications with the outlaw: the bread and butter that Pip puts down his leg, which makes him walk like the chained convict; Mrs. Joe's belief that he is on his way to the Hulks; Pip's flight from the Christmas dinner table into the arms of a soldier holding out handcuffs, to give a few examples. Pip is concerned to assure "his" convict that he is not responsible for his recapture, a point he conveys in a mute exchange of glances which the convict understands and which leads him to make a public

---

4. On the archeological model in Freud, see in particular the use he makes of Pompeii in "Delusions and Dreams in Jensen's *Gradiva*" [*Der Wahn und die Traeume in W. Jensens Gradiva*] (1907), in *The Standard Edition of the Complete Psychological Works of Sigmund Freud*, ed. James Strachey (London: Hogarth Press, 1953–74), vol. 9, pp. 3–95.

statement in exoneration of Pip, taking responsibility for stealing the food. This in turn provokes an overt statement of community with the outlaw, which comes from Joe: "We don't know what you have done, but we wouldn't have you starved to death for it, poor miserable fellow-creatur.—Would us, Pip?" (chapter 5)

The fellowship with the convict here stated by Joe will remain with Pip, but in a state of repression, as what he will later call "that spell of my child-hood" (chapter 16), an unavowable memory. It finds its official, adult, re-pressive version in the conviction—shared by all the adults in Pip's life, with the exception of the childlike Joe—that children are naturally depraved and need to be corrected, kept in line with the Tickler, brought up by hand lest their natural willfulness assert itself in plots that are deviant, transgressive. * * * The "nateral wiciousness" of children legitimates communion with the outlaw, but legitimates it as that which must be repressed, forced into other plots—including, as we shall see, "binding" Pip as an apprentice.

The dream of Satis House is properly a daydream, in which * * * Miss Havisham is made to play the role of Fairy Godmother, her crutch become a magic wand, explicitly evoked twice near the close of part 1 [chapter 19]. This plot has adult sanction; its first expression comes from Pumblechook and Mrs. Joe when they surmise that Miss Havisham intends to "do some-thing" for Pip, and Pip comes to believe in it, so that when the "Expectations" arrive he accepts them as the logical fulfillment of the daydream, of his "long-ings." Yet to identify Satis House with the daydream is to perform a repression of all else that Satis House suggests and represents—all that clusters around the central emblem of the rotting bride-cake and its crawling things. The craziness and morbidity of Satis House repose on desire fixated, become fet-ishistic and sadistic, on a deviated eroticism that has literally shut out the light, stopped the clocks, and made the forward movement of plot impos-sible. * * *

*   *   *

We have, then, a quadripartite scheme of plots, organized into two pairs, each with an "official" plot, or interpretation of plot, standing over a repressed plot. The scheme may lead us in the first instance to reflect on the place of repression as one of the large "orders" of the novel. Repression plays a dom-inant role in the theme of education which is so important to the novel, from Mrs. Joe's bringing up by hand, through [Mr. Wopsle's great-aunt's] school-room, to Mr. Pocket's career as a "grinder" of dull blades (while his own children meanwhile are "tumbling up"). Bringing up by hand in turn suggests Jaggers's hands, representation of accusation and the law, which in turn sug-gest all the instances of censorship in the name of high authorities evoked from the first scene of the novel onward: censorship is repression in the name of the Law.[5] Jaggers's sinister hand-washings point to the omnipresent taint of Newgate, which echoes the earlier presence of the Hulks, to which Mrs. Joe verbally assigns Pip. Then there is the moment when Pip is "bound" as apprentice blacksmith before the magistrates, in a scene of such repressive appearance that a well-meaning philanthropist is moved to hand Pip a pam-

---

5. On the role of the law as one of the formal orders of the novel, see Moshe Ron, "Autobiographical Narration and Formal Closure in *Great Expectations*," *Hebrew University Studies in Literature*, 5, no. 1 (1977), pp. 37–66.

phlet entitled *To Be Read in My Cell*. There is a constant association of education, repression, the threat of prison, criminality, the fear of deviance. * * *

* * *

Repetition is, of course, a complex phenomenon, and one that has its history of commentary in philosophical as well as psychoanalytic thought. * * * In *Great Expectations*, the repetitions associated with Satis House, particularly as played out by Miss Havisham herself, suggest the reproductive in that they aim to restore in all its detail the traumatic moment—recorded by the clocks stopped at twenty minutes to nine—when erotic wishes were abruptly foreclosed by Compeyson's rupture of faith. On the other hand, the repetitions of the convict material experienced by Pip all imply something to come—something to come that, as we shall see, will take him back, painfully, to the primal scene, yet take him back in the context of difference. Repetition in the text is a return, a calling back or a turning back. * * *

The novelistic middle * * * is in this case notably characterized by the return. Quite literally: it is Pip's repeated returns from London to his home town that constitute the organizing device of the whole of the London period, the time of the Expectations and their aftermath. Pip's returns are always ostensibly undertaken to make reparation to the neglected Joe, an intention never realized; and always implicitly an attempt to discover the intentions of the putative donor in Satis House, to bring her plot to completion. Yet the returns also always bring his regression, in Satis House, to the status of the "coarse and common boy" (chapter 29) whose social ascension is hallucinatorily denied, his return to the nightmare of unprogressive repetition; and, too, a revival of the repressed convict association, the return of the childhood spell. Each return suggests that Pip's official plots, which seem to speak of progress, ascent, and the satisfaction of desire, are in fact subject to a process of repetition of the yet unmastered past, the true determinant of his life's direction.

The pattern of the return is established in Pip's first journey back from London, in chapter 28. His decision to visit Joe is quickly thrown into the shade by the presence on the stagecoach of two convicts, one of whom Pip recognizes as the man of the file and the rum and water, Magwitch's emissary. There is a renewed juxtaposition of official, genteel judgment on the convicts, voiced by Herbert Pocket—"What a vile and degraded spectacle"—and Pip's inward avowal that he feels sympathy for their alienation. On the roof of the coach, seated in front of the convicts, Pip dozes off while pondering whether he ought to restore the two one-pound notes that the convict of the file had passed him so many years before. Upon regaining consciousness, the first two words he hears, continuing his dream thoughts, are: "Two one-pound notes." There follows the convict's account of his embassy from "Pip's convict" to the boy who had saved him. Although Pip is certain that the convict cannot recognize him, so changed in age, circumstance, and even name (since Herbert Pocket calls him "Handel"), the dreamlike experience forces a kind of recognition of a forgotten self, refound in fear and pain:

> I could not have said what I was afraid of, for my fear was altogether
> undefined and vague, but there was great fear upon me. As I walked on
> to the hotel, I felt that a dread, much exceeding the mere apprehension

of a painful or disagreeable recognition, made me tremble. I am confident that it took no distinctness of shape, and that it was the revival for
a few minutes of the terror of childhood. (chapter 28)

The return to origins has led to the return of the repressed, and vice versa.
Repetition as return becomes a reproduction and reenactment of infantile
experience: not simply a recall of the primal moment, but a reliving of its
pain and terror, suggesting the impossibility of escape from the originating
scenarios of childhood, the condemnation forever to replay them.

This first example may stand for the other returns of the novel's middle,
which all follow the same pattern, which all double return to with return of
and show Pip's ostensible progress in the world to be subverted by the irrad-
icable presence of the convict-communion and the Satis House nightmare.
It is notable that toward the end of the middle—as the novel's dénouement
approaches—there is an acceleration in the rhythm of these returns, as if to
affirm that all the clues to Pip's future, the forward movement of his plot, in
fact lie in the past. * * * In the moment of crisis before the climax of the
novel's action, Pip is summoned back to the marshes associated with his
infancy to face extinction at the hands of Orlick—who has throughout the
novel acted the role of Pip's "bad double," a hateful and sadistic version of
the hero—in a threatened short-circuit of the text, as Pip indicates when he
thinks how he will be misunderstood by others if he dies prematurely, without
explanation: "Misremembered after death . . . despised by unborn generations" (chapter 53). Released from this threat, Pip attempts to escape from
England, but even this voyage out to another land and another life leads him
back: the climax of Magwitch's discovery and recapture are played out in the
Thames estuary, where "it was like my own marsh country, flat and monotonous, and with a dim horizon" (chapter 54). We are back in the horizontal
perspectives and muddy tidal flats that are so much a part of our perception
of the childhood Pip.

                              *   *   *

Magwitch poses unanswerable questions, about the origins of Pip's property
and the means of his social ascent, which force home to Pip that he has
covered over a radical lack of original authority. Like Oedipus—who cannot
answer Tiresias's final challenge: who are your parents?—Pip does not know
where he stands. The result has been the intrusion of an aberrant, contingent
authorship—Magwitch's—in the story of the self. Education and training in
gentility turn out to be merely an agency in the repression of the determinative convict plot. Likewise, the daydream/fairy tale of Satis House stands
revealed as a repression, or perhaps a "secondary revision," of the nightmare.
* * * Pip has in fact misread the plot of his life.

The misreading of plots and the question of authority bring us back to the
question of reading with which the novel began. Pip's initial attempt to decipher his parents' appearance and character from the letters traced on their
tombstones has been characterized as "childish" and "unreasonable." Pip's
decipherment in fact appears as an attempt to motivate the arbitrary sign, to
interpret signs as if they were mimetic and thus naturally tied to the object
for which they stand. Deriving from the shape of the letters on the tombstones

that his father "was a square, stout, dark man, with curly hair," and that his mother was "freckled and sickly," for all its literal fidelity to the graphic trace, constitutes a dangerously figural reading, a metaphorical process unaware of itself, the making of a fiction unaware of its status as fiction making. Pip is here claiming natural authority for what is in fact conventional, arbitrary, dependent on interpretation.

The question of texts, reading, and interpretation is, as we earlier noted, consistently thematized in the novel: in Pip's learning to read (using that meager text, [Mr. Wopsle's great-aunt's] catalogue of prices), and his attempts to transmit the art of writing to Joe; the expressive dumb shows between Pip and Joe; messages written on the slate, by Pip to Joe, and then (in minimum symbolic form) by the aphasic Mrs. Joe; the uncanny text of Estella's visage, always reminding Pip of a repetition of something else which he cannot identify; Molly's wrists, cross-hatched with scratches, a text for the judge, and eventually for Pip as detective, to decipher; Mr. Wopsle's declamations of *George Barnwell* and *Richard III.* * * *

*   *   *

The novel constantly warns us that texts may have no unambiguous referent and no transcendent signified. Of the many examples one might choose in illustration of the status of texts and their interpretation in the novel, perhaps the most telling is the case of Mr. Wopsle. Mr. Wopsle, the church clerk, is a frustrated preacher, ever intimating that if the church were to be "thrown open," he would really "give it out." This hypothetical case never coming to realization, Mr. Wopsle is obliged to content himself with the declamation of a number of secular texts, from Shakespeare to Collins's ode. The church indeed remains resolutely closed (we never in fact hear the word of the preacher in the novel, only Mr. Wopsle's critique of it), and Mr. Wopsle "has a fall": into play-acting. He undertakes the repetition of fictional texts which lack the authority of that divine word he would like to "give out." We next see him playing *Hamlet,* which is of course the text par excellence about usurpation, parricide, lost regal authority, and wrong relations of transmission from generation to generation. Something of the problematic status of textual authority is suggested in Mr. Wopsle's rendition of the classic soliloquy:

> Whenever that undecided Prince had to ask a question or state a doubt, the public helped him out with it. As for example: on the question whether 'twas nobler in the mind to suffer, some roared yes, and some no, and some inclining to both opinions said "toss up for it"; and quite a Debating Society arose. (chapter 31)

From this uncertainty, Mr. Wopsle has a further fall, into playing what was known as "nautical melodrama," an anonymously authored theater played to a vulgar public in the Surreyside houses. When Pip attends this performance, there occurs a curious mirroring and reversal of the spectacle, where Mr. Wopsle himself becomes the spectator, fascinated by the vision, in the audience, of what he calls a "ghost" from the past—the face of the novel's hidden arch-plotter, Compeyson. The vision leads to a reconstruction of the chase and capture of the convicts, from the early chapters of the novel, a kind of analytic dialogue in the excavation of the past, where Mr. Wopsle repeatedly

questions: "You remember?" and Pip replies: "I remember it very well . . . I
see it all before me." * * *

* * *

Mr. Wopsle's career may stand as a figure for Pip's. Whereas the model of
the *Bildungsroman*[6] seems to imply progress, a leading forth, and developmental change, Pip's story—and this may be true of other nineteenth-century
educative plots as well—becomes more and more as it nears its end the
working through of past history, an attempted return to the origin as the
motivation of all the rest, the clue to what must else appear, as Pip puts it to
Miss Havisham, a "blind and thankless" life (chapter 49). The past needs to
be incorporated *as past* within the present, mastered through the play of
repetition in order for there to be an escape from repetition: in order for there
to be difference, change, progress. In the failure ever to recover his own
origin, Pip comes to concern himself with the question of Estella's origin,
searching for her patronymics where knowledge of his own is ever foreclosed.
Estella's story in fact eventually links all the plots of the novel: Satis House,
the aspiration to gentility, the convict identity, "naterally wicious" (the status
from which Jaggers rescued her), bringing up by hand, the law. Pip's investigation of her origins as substitute for knowledge of his own has a certain
validity in that, we discover, he appeared originally to Magwitch as a substitute
for the lost Estella, his great expectations a compensation for the impossibility
of hers: a chiasmus of the true situation. Yet when Pip has proved himself to
be the successful detective in this quest, when he has uncovered the convergence of lines of plot that previously appeared distinct and indeed proved
himself more penetrating even than Jaggers, he discovers the knowledge he
has gained to be radically unusable. When he has imparted his knowledge
to Jaggers and Wemmick, he reaches a kind of standoff between what he has
called his "poor dreams" and the deep plot he has now exposed. As Jaggers
puts it to him, there is no gain to be had from knowledge. We are in the
heart of darkness, and the articulation of its meaning must simply be repressed. In this novel full of mysteries and hidden connections, detective work
turns out to be both necessary and useless. It can offer no comfort and no
true illumination to the detective himself. Like deciphering the letters on the
tombstone, it produces no authority for the plot of life.

The novel in fact toward its end appears to record a generalized breakdown
of plots: none of the schemes machinated by the characters manages to ac-
complish its aims. The proof *a contrario*[7] may be the "oversuccessful" result
of Miss Havisham's plot, which has turned Estella into so heartless a creature
that she cannot even experience emotional recognition of her benefactress.
Miss Havisham's plotting has been a mechanical success but an intentional
failure, as her final words, during her delirium following the fire, may suggest:

6. "Novel of formation" or "novel of education" (German). The paradigmatic bildungsroman traces the
hero's formative years from childhood to maturity and from innocence to experience, a process often
attended by external struggles as well as spiritual crises and illuminations. As the term suggests, the
genre originates in the German novel, specifically Goethe's *Wilhelm Meister's Apprenticeship* (1795–
96); and it includes texts as diverse as *David Copperfield*, Thackeray's *Henry Esmond*, Balzac's *Père
Goriot*, Stendhal's *The Red and the Black*, Butler's *The Way of all Flesh*, and Joyce's *Portrait of the
Artist as a Young Man*. Generally the protagonist's education involves a move from rural simplicity
to urban sophistication and intrigue, though occasionally the move may be reversed (as in Thomas
Mann's *Magic Mountain*). [*Editor*.]
7. Lit. "by the opposite" (Latin). Proof, usually by means of an example, that what has been maintained
or demonstrated needs to be stood upside down.

Towards midnight she began to wander in her speech, and after that it gradually set in that she said innumerable times in a low solemn voice, "What have I done?" And then, "When she first came, I meant to save her from misery like mine." And then, "Take the pencil and write under my name, 'I forgive her!' " She never changed the order of these three sentences, but she sometimes left out a word in one or other of them; never putting in another word, but always leaving a blank and going on to the next word. (chapter 49)

The cycle of three statements suggests a metonymic movement in search of arrest, a plot that can never find satisfactory resolution, that unresolved must play over its insistent repetitions, until silenced by death. Miss Havisham's deathbed scene transmits a "wisdom" that is in the deconstructive mode, a warning against plot.

* * *

The ultimate situation of plot in the novel may suggest an approach to the vexed question of Dickens's two endings to the novel: the one he originally wrote and the revision (substituted at Bulwer Lytton's suggestion) that was in fact printed. I think it is entirely legitimate to prefer the original ending, with its flat tone and refusal of romantic expectation, and find that the revision, with its tentative promise of reunion between Pip and Estella, "unbinds" energies that we thought had been thoroughly bound and indeed discharged from the text. We may also feel that choice between the two endings is somewhat arbitrary and unimportant in that the decisive moment has already occurred before either of these finales begins. The real ending may take place with Pip's recognition and acceptance of Magwitch after his recapture—this is certainly the ethical dénouement—and his acceptance of a continuing existence without plot, as celibate clerk for Clarrikers. The pages that follow may simply be *obiter dicta*.[8]

If we acknowledge Pip's experience of and with Magwitch to be the central energy of the text, it is significant that the climax of this experience, the moment of crisis and reversal in the attempted escape from England, bears traces of a hallucinatory repetition of the childhood spell—indeed, of that first recapture of Magwitch already repeated in Mr. Wopsle's theatrical vision:

In the same moment, I saw the steersman of the galley lay his hand on the prisoner's shoulder, and saw that both boats were swinging round with the force of the tide, and saw that all hands on board the steamer were running forward quite frantically. Still in the same moment, I saw the prisoner start up, lean across his captor, and pull the cloak from the neck of the shrinking sitter in the galley. Still in the same moment, I saw that the face disclosed was the face of the other convict of long ago. Still in the same moment, I saw the face tilt backward with a white terror on it that I shall never forget, and heard a great cry on board the steamer and a loud splash in the water, and felt the boat sink from under me. (chapter 54)

If this scene marks the beginning of a resolution—which it does in that it brings the death of the arch-villain Compeyson and the death sentence for

8. Literally, "things said in passing." [*Editor.*]

Magwitch, hence the disappearance from the novel of its most energetic plotters—it is resolution in the register of repetition and working through, the final effort to master painful material from the insistent past. Pip emerges from this scene with an acceptance of the determinative past as both determinative and as *past*, which prepares us for the final escape *from* plot. It is interesting to note that where the "dream" plot of Estella is concerned, Pip's stated resolution has none of the compulsive energetic force of the passage just quoted, but is rather a conventional romantic fairy-tale ending, a conscious fiction designed, of course, to console the dying Magwitch, but possibly also a last effort at self-delusion: "You had a child once, whom you loved and lost. . . . She lived and found powerful friends. She is living now. She is a lady and very beautiful. And I love her!" (chapter 56). If taken as anything other than a conscious fiction—if taken as part of the "truth" discovered by Pip's detections—this version of Pip's experience leads straight to what is most troubling in Dickens's revised version of the ending: the suggestion of an unbinding of what has already been bound up and disposed of, an unbinding that is indeed perceptible in the rather embarrassed prose with which the revision begins: "Nevertheless, I knew while I said these words, that I secretly intended to revisit the site of the old house that evening alone, for her sake. Yes, even so. For Estella's sake" (chapter 59). Are we to understand that the experience of Satis House has never really been mastered? Is its nightmare energy still present in the text as well? The original end may have an advantage in denying to Pip's text the possibility of any reflux of energy, any new aspirations, the undoing of anything already done, the unbinding of energy that has been bound and led to discharge.

As at the start of the novel we had the impression of a life not yet subject to plot—a life in search of the sense of plot that would only gradually begin to precipitate around it—so at the end we have the impression of a life that has outlived plot, renounced plot, been cured of it: life that is left over. What follows the recognition of Magwitch is left over, and any renewal of expectation and plotting—such as a revived romance with Estella—would have to belong to another story. It is with the image of a life bereft of plot, of movement and desire, that the novel most appropriately leaves us. * * *

[Brooks elaborates on the notion that plot is inherently a kind of "deviance" or "error," arguing that *Great Expectations* is exemplary in showing that plot is at once necessary if life is to have a meaningful, "readable" order, and something always erroneous because always a subjective imposition on reality: thus, in continually searching for his origins Pip continually returns to a scene of "unauthorized self-naming."]

What, finally, do we make of the fact that Dickens, master-plotter in the history of the novel, in this most tightly and consistently plotted of his novels seems to expose plot as a kind of necessary error? Dickens's most telling comment on the question may come at the moment of Magwitch's sentencing. The judge gives a legalistic and moralistic version of Magwitch's life story, his violence, his crimes, the passions that made him a "scourge to society" and led him to escape from deportation, thus calling upon his head the death sentence. The passage continues:

The sun was striking in at the great windows of the court, through the glittering drops of rain upon the glass, and it made a broad shaft of light between the two-and-thirty [prisoners at the bar] and the Judge, linking both together, and perhaps reminding some among the audience, how both were passing on, with absolute equality, to the greater Judgment that knoweth all things and cannot err. Rising for a moment, a distinct speck of face in this way of light, the prisoner [Magwitch] said, "My Lord, I have received my sentence of Death from the Almighty, but I bow to yours," and sat down again. There was some hushing, and the Judge went on with what he had to say to the rest. (chapter 56)

The passage is sentimental but also, I think, effective. It juxtaposes human plots—including those of the law—to eternal orders that render human attempts to plot, and to interpret plot, not only futile but ethically unacceptable. The greater Judgment makes human plots mere shadows. There is another end that recuperates passing human time, and its petty chronologies, to the timeless. Yet despite the narrator's affirmations, this other end is not visible, the other orders are not available. As Mr. Wopsle's case suggested, the divine word is barred in the world of the novel (it is suggestive that Christmas dinner is interrupted by the command to repair handcuffs). If there is a divine masterplot for human existence, it is radically unknowable.

In the absence or silence of divine masterplots, the organization and interpretation of human plots remains as necessary as it is problematic. Reading the signs of intention in life's actions is the central act of existence, which in turn legitimizes the enterprise of reading for the reader of *Great Expectations*—or perhaps, vice versa, since the reading of plot within the text and as the text are perfectly analogous, mirrors of one another. If there is by the end of the narrative an abandonment of the attempt to read plot, this simply mirrors the fact that the process of narration has come to a close—or, again, vice versa. But that there should be a cure from the reading of plot within the text—before its very end—and the creation of a leftover, suggests a critique of reading itself, which is possibly like the judge's sentence: human interpretation in ignorance of the true vectors of the true text. * * * But if the mastertext is not available, we are condemned to the reading of erroneous plots, granted insight only insofar as we can gain disillusion from them. We are condemned to repetition, rereading, in the knowledge that what we discover will always be that there was nothing to be discovered. Yet the process remains necessary if we are not to be caught perpetually in the "blind and thankless" existence, in the illusory middle. Like Oedipus, like Pip, we are condemned to reinterpretation of our names. But it is rare that the name coincides so perfectly with a fullness and a negation of identity as in the case of Oedipus. In a post-tragic universe, our situation is more likely to be that of Pip, compelled to reinterpret the meaning of the name he assigned to himself with his infant tongue, the history of an infinitely repeatable palindrome.

DAVID GERVAIS

The Prose and Poetry of *Great Expectations*†

[*Great Expectations* is regarded by critics as Dickens's one "assured 'artistic success'," "poetic" in the sense of event and character being shaped into meaningfulness by an artistic consciousness. Following T. S. Eliot's definition of "poetic" as the immediacy with which a character is conveyed in language, Gervais will work from the idea that the early Dickens is poetic and determine what happens to that immediacy of emotional expression in *Great Expectations*.]

To read *Great Expectations* is, first of all, to listen to it. It is the gravely lyrical tone that Dickens sustains in the pondering rhythms of Pip's voice that makes us so intensely susceptible to his experience. In no other nineteenth-century novel I can think of, except for *L'Education Sentimentale*,[1] is narrative so musical. Yet if its cadences are essential to its power, they may also be inseparable from its limitations. Its incantatory rhythms, dying falls and beautifully turned sentences lodge in the mind. For example:

> I saw that the bride within the bridal dress had withered like the dress, and like the flowers, and had no brightness left but the brightness of her sunken eyes.

Such stately magic is not what we recall either from the early books or of the galvanic prose of *Bleak House* or *Our Mutual Friend*. None of them seeks to sustain for so long [or would if they could] the note of trancelike and meditative lassitude that informs what Graham Greene finely calls "Dickens' secret prose."[2] In them, energy would have made off with half the controlled beauty of a recollection like the following, which, for all its mounting drama, seems to spring from some central tranquillity in Pip:

> Ours was the marsh country, down by the river, within, as the river wound, twenty miles of the sea. My first most vivid and broad impression of the identity of things, seems to me to have been gained on a memorable raw afternoon towards evening. At such a time I found out for certain, that this bleak place overgrown with nettles was the churchyard; and that Philip Pirrip, late of this parish, and also Georgiana wife of the above, were dead and buried; and that Alexander, Bartholomew, Abraham, Tobias, and Roger, infant children of the aforesaid, were also dead and buried; and that the dark flat wilderness beyond the churchyard, intersected with dykes and mounds and gates, with scattered cattle feeding on it, was the marshes; and that the low leaden line beyond, was the river; and that the distant savage lair from which the wind was rushing,

---

† From David Gervais, "The Prose and Poetry of *Great Expectations*," *Dickens Studies Annual* 13 (1984): 85–114. Reprinted by Permission of AMS Press, Inc. Unless otherwise indicated, all footnotes are by the editor of this Norton Critical Edition; some of the author's notes have been omitted.
1. Like *Great Expectations*, Flaubert's *Education of the Feelings* (1869), his most nearly autobiographical novel, is steeped in retrospect and the hero's remembrance of things past.
2. "The Young Dickens," *The Lost Childhood and Other Essays* (Harmondsworth, England: Penguin, 1962), p. 59. [*Author.*]

was the sea; and that the small bundle of shivers growing afraid of it all and beginning to cry, was Pip.

Pip is then surprised by Magwitch ("Hold your noise!"); but even in the next paragraph, he is never jolted out of these delicately weighed rhythms which savor their own note of subdued drama ("and that . . . and that") and rich suggestiveness ("the low leaden line beyond," "the distant savage lair"). Within the drama of childhood grief that the narrator recalls, there is a less dramatic note, a solemn lingering pathos, almost a mournfulness, that, but for its greater actuality, would remind us of elegiac poems like "Tears, Idle Tears"[3] and "Dover Beach."[4] This plangency is as much part of the spell the passage casts as is the mounting emotion of its repetitions. If it makes the prose seem deliberately less elastic than other late Dickensian prose, a new firmness and authority accrues from its slowness. The movingly delayed image of Pip as a "small bundle of shivers," for instance, is the touch of a writer who knows how to bide his time. Each detail in the passage is left to fill the mind at its own appropriate pace. * * *

[Gervais sees as a central issue in Dickens's work the problem of channeling the energy characteristic of early Dickens: the overflow of exuberant humor, energy, and emotion, the tendency of his characters and stories to "enact and embody moral qualities" rather than to self-consciously and explicitly "pass judgment on them." But he will challenge the usual critical view that as Dickens matured as a writer he learned to discipline his genius, subordinating this exuberant emotion to a "conscious thematic structure." He argues that, in Dickens, emotions shape plot rather than vice versa, and replaces the model of art shaping emotions with that of self-mastery, adducing as evidence the many characters who seem barely able to contain their explosive feelings. Gervais asks, where does this energy go in *Great Expectations*?]

One fancies that Hamlet meant every bit as much to the Dickens of *Great Expectations* as he did to Mr. Wopsle. The voice with which Pip recounts his "first most vivid and broad impression of the identity of things" has the music of soliloquy, quite shorn of rhetoric. * * * * " Pip's tone invites barely conscious thoughts into his mind, thoughts that remain unsaid in his workaday world. Though his grave, meditative rhythm is strongly measured, it never suggests someone who is trying to rationalize his experience: its antitheses and pauses are not logical but a patient waiting for the truth to emerge.

It is the prose, then, which first tells us that *Great Expectations* has more to offer than the edifying acuities of the *bildungsroman*. The almost magically natural way Dickens sustains it throughout the novel is enough to tell us to expect more than just the moral progress of a "character," some subtler ver-

---

3. One of the half dozen intercalated lyrics and songs that anthologists have salvaged from Tennyson's verse romance *The Princess* (1847), an arch, half-hearted plug for women's education. Tennyson described "Tears, Idle Tears" as expressing "the passion of the past, the abiding in the transient," inspired "on the yellowing autumn-tide at Tintern Abbey," the locale (and title) of Wordsworth's great lyrical meditation on the poet's use of reminiscence (1798).
4. In what is perhaps Matthew Arnold's finest lyric (c. 1851; published 1867), the speaker, gazing out on the English Channel, finds in the moonlit scene a mournful echo of the slow withdrawal of the "Sea of Faith," and, beyond it, the denudation of all spiritual values. The famous closing image, in which the world has turned into "a darkling plain . . . Where ignorant armies clash by night," captures the confusion, aimlessness, and intellectual anarchy of modern life.

sion of Wopsle's much admired *Tragedy of George Barnwell*. Pip's voice-music embodies something too deep to be seen simply in ethical terms. We are listeners first and judges only later and only then because the mature Pip succumbs more and more to his need to judge himself. But to the end, we always feel in him a mystery which no amount of self-rebuke and resignation can ever wholly illumine. Without such resonance, Dickens' fable would not have been so elusive and rich as readers always find it. A proposition to begin from is, then, that the novel's central and explicit moral concerns are sustained and animated by a more imaginative soil than ethics alone could provide. Often, of course, the moral and the imaginative work organically together (in Magwitch's first appearances, for example) while, at other times, they conflict. What is very hard to determine, but quite crucial, is whether it is only Pip the narrator who is trying to impose a moral pattern on his life or whether the novelist himself connives at moralizing his own poetry. * * *

* * *

Nowhere do the beauty and mystery of the book come together more vividly than in the first spectral apparition of Miss Havisham, all "waxwork and skeleton." The early chapters have been brought to a point in this one strange image of a life that has been wasted away by its own passion. The liturgical movement of the prose seems to set her at a remove from real living:

> It was not in the first few moments that I saw all these things, though I saw more of them in the first moments than might be supposed. But, I saw that everything within my view which ought to be white, had been white long ago, and had lost its lustre, and was faded and yellow. I saw that the bride within the bridal dress was withered like the dress, and like the flowers, and had no brightness left but the brightness of her sunken eyes. I saw that the dress had been put upon the rounded figure of a young woman, and that the figure upon which it now hung loose, had shrunk to skin and bone.

The incantatory chiming of the repetitions in this makes us dwell on Miss Havisham as if we saw her in slow motion. Despite the highly melodramatic subject, there is none of Dickens' usual kinesis. The hush in Pip's voice is too considered for excitement. A phrase like "It was not in the first moments that I saw all these things" has rather the still, visionary mood of some Romantic poetry, where the simplest words are given an unusual poise and weight, the mood of things like:

> . . . it had past
> The lily and the snow; and beyond these
> I must not think now, though I saw that face—
> But for her eyes I should have fled away.[5]

For Miss Havisham is as much part of a spiritual vision as is Moneta. Only the later Dickens could have made her so haunting in so unflashy a way. Yet

---

5. Keats, *The Fall of Hyperion: A Dream*, canto 1, lines 260–64. The second of two related fragments written a few months apart in Keats's "great year," 1819. The major part of *The Fall* is cast in the form of a dream-vision in which the speaker dilates on the poet's identity, growth, and function, while the place of Mnemosyne is assigned to her Latin equivalent Moneta, Keats prioritizing her role as monitor and guide.

if the rhythm of his prose here is endlessly suggestive, it is also an index of his powerful conscious control over his material. * * *

* * *

In speaking of the sense of "psychological mystery"[6] in *Great Expectations*, I mean that its moral content, at its deepest, lies at a different level from that of Pip's own overt self-judgments. For instance, there is one telling difference between the child Pip and the Pip of Volume III, the Pip who will tell the story. As a child, he judges himself every bit as harshly as he does when he takes Magwitch down the river at the end; but in the early chapters, we know just how limited those judgments are, what crude instruments they make for understanding what is happening to him. We even laugh a little at his dis-proportionate anguish over something as comic as the pork pie. But by Volume III, it is less clear how far we are being asked to see round Pip's self-judgments. Sometimes it seems as if his sad, penitent self-rebukes are meant to represent a true self-knowledge. We hear him at the confessional and commend him for seeing the error of his ways: ". . . I lay there, penitently whispering, 'O God bless him [Joe]! O God bless this gentle Christian man!'" Pip sounds just a little bit like Tiny Tim here. It is, in short, the directly moral moments which import a little softening sentiment into this grave and unremitting novel. More profound, in the scene just quoted from, is the sense that Pip, beneath his gentlemanly carapace, is still the same child of the marshes that he was at the beginning. The perception may be in danger of being sentimentalized by the presence of "gentle Joe," but it belongs to a deeper moral level in the book: Pip is so real because, more than with almost any character in fiction, we feel in him the continued presence of the un-deciphered child on which his adult self has been built. His behavior to Joe and to Magwitch accounts for only a part, and that the easiest part, of what there is to judge and understand in him. When Pip sees in Magwitch a "much better man than I had been to Joe," it may well seem a moot point whether this is the final truth which resolves the book's psychological mystery or whether, instead, Dickens may not be conniving with the narrator to corroborate his hero's own indelible feelings of guilt.

Great Expectations owes some of its renown in our century to the fact that we have subscribed heavily to the notion that what we learn about life we learn—if at all—from experience, that self-doubt is the necessary prelude to self-knowledge. It is worth asking whether such an idea could provide Dickens with enough room for that celebration of natural energy which is usually such a spontaneous part of his characterization. To do this one needs to look at Pip's moments of self-chastisement. They include some of the rare occasions when his wise and even tone of voice falters. An early one, in chapter 6, has him reflecting on his failure to confess to Joe that he has stolen food from the pantry:

> In a word, I was too cowardly to do what I knew to be right, as I had been too cowardly to avoid doing what I knew to be wrong. I had had no intercourse with the world at that time, and I imitated none of its

6. In this, as in much else, Dickens anticipates Freud. Pip provides a perfect illustration of what the latter calls "projection" and "introjection." (It is a brilliant stroke that the one person whom he sees clearly, undistorted by either impulse, should be Joe—the one person whose love he can trust.) [*Author.*]

many inhabitants who act in this manner. Quite an untaught genius, I made the discovery of the line of action for myself.

The word "cowardly" is simply insensitive, as is Pip the narrator's ponderous sarcasm. Why call himself "untaught," given the strange and fierce duress under which he had acted? Instead of witnessing the mysterious birth of compassion out of terror, we get facetious copybook sermonizing. Pip's real anguish of mind is substituted by a picture of the moral man tut-tutting at the thoughtlessness of his youth. It is surely the child Pip who has the finest moral sense, who plays Maisie to his older self's Mrs. Wix.[7] The narrator only seems to want to disguise and dilute the traumas of his younger self. He is less interested than he should be in remembering the emotional intensity which prompted him to act as he did. So we wonder whether he really can still remember what it was that made him invent the dogs with the veal cutlets and also made him love Estella.

Pip's *ex post facto* earnestness, then, is not quite convincing as the main legacy from the "spell" of his childhood. It seems too orthodox an outcome to the very special events that shape his life. * * * But we need not feel as bound as Pip is to the moral truths that gnaw at his conscious mind. They are always symptoms of the particular individual he is too. And at another level of the prose, we can hear a voice less prone to praise or blame, a voice that is more merciful to others than it is to itself, and more honest about them. Here, for instance, from his description of his sister's funeral:

> It was the first time that a grave had opened in my road of life, and the gap it made in the smooth ground was wonderful. The figure of my sister in her chair by the kitchen fire, haunted me night and day. That the place could possibly be, without her, was something my mind seemed unable to compass. . . .
>
> Whatever my fortunes might have been, I could scarcely have recalled my sister with much tenderness. But I suppose there is a shock of regret which may exist without much tenderness.

This voice is larger and subtler than the self-expiatory one, though recognizably akin to it. The interplay of the two is not, however, any simple index of discrepancy and contradiction in the telling of the story. Both represent parts of the whole Pip. A problem only arises when the narrator unwittingly denigrates the inner life of his younger self, wishing to make his history exemplary, and one voice begins to drown out the other. This is more likely to happen toward the end of the novel, but the potential for it is there from the start. What is at stake is the fate of energy in the somber, twilit *Great Expectations* world. We already have a hint of this in the fate of Mrs. Joe. On the rampage with "tickler" and tar-water, she is a rebarbative but exciting figure, full of a coarse and spiteful life; but, after she has been attacked by Orlick and pacified, her image becomes more easy to assimilate into the tone of melancholy reminiscence. In this her fate resembles that of Magwitch, who,

7. In Henry James's comic masterpiece *What Maisie Knew* (1897), Maisie's governess, Miss Wix, a fatuous, languishing widow, by appealing to Maisie's "moral sense," implores her young ward to talk her stepparents into separating, thus "saving" the stepfather, Sir Claude—on whom Wix herself has designs—from his illicit relationship. (Maisie's blood parents are divorced and their second spouses, in a game of mixed doubles, have become lovers and Maisie's parent-substitutes). In the final scene of the novel, Maisie, torn between Wix and Sir Claude and unable to pry Sir Claude loose from his lover, throws in her lot with the governess.

by the end, is well on the way to gentle Joedom. Pip's own energy is most pointedly downgraded in his relations with Herbert Pocket. He first meets Herbert when a "prowling boy" in the ruined garden of Satis House where Herbert challenges him to a boxing bout. Pip draws blood. The "pale young gentleman" is weak, foolhardy and plucky; the forge child has real blood in his veins. For a long time this impression does not change much. Herbert is still innocent and ineffectual as Pip's roommate in London, needing Pip just as much as Pip needs him. He admires in Pip a complexity that is happily absent from his own open nature. Yet, by the end of the novel, Pip has come to look up to Herbert's as the finer character and one that reminds him of his own faults:

> We owed so much to Herbert's ever cheerful industry and readiness, that I often wondered how I had conceived that old idea of his inaptitude, until I was one day enlightened by the reflection, that perhaps the inaptitude had never been in him at all, but had been in me.

The betraying note of facetiousness reminds us that we know better than to believe him. Pip surely needs some finer reason for rapping himself so often over the knuckles than a desire to become a "pale young gentleman." He is a sort of Hamlet who aspires to play Horatio.[8] In the process, he tends to look down on his past self with something of the condescension to which he once treated Joe. It is as if he wanted to look back on a world that has been defused, a world in which Magwitch has become Provis, as if the very telling of his story is an attempt to make safe some unexploded bomb that lies in his memory. This is not, of course, the whole story—Pip's music would seep out of his voice if it were—but there is nonetheless something diluted in the novel's measured prose, some energy that has been too perfectly harnessed. Pip's moral maturity entails some thinning down of his blood. It is perhaps not unrelated to this that most of the novel's richest comedy comes in the opening chapters, before Pip learns to emulate the gentlemanly self-control of the Pockets.

*   *   *

In Miss Havisham, the libido that survives in the shape of a self-destructive will has an intensity that Estella's cool beauty and Pip's yearning for her both lack. A great deal of the fire in Pip's experience comes to him from other people—Mrs. Joe, Magwitch, Miss Havisham herself—but if Estella is desirable, she feels no desire herself. Her starlike coldness inspires in him a love that is warm enough to endure, to go on feeding itself over the years, but not hot enough to act to claim its object. It is the fact that she is out of reach that makes her so desirable:

> When I first went into it [the ruined brewery], and, rather oppressed by its gloom, stood near the door looking about me, I saw her pass among the extinguished fires, and ascend some light iron stairs, and go out by a gallery high overhead, as if she were going out into the sky.

---

8. Horatio, the exemplary Renaissance friend, is Hamlet's closest companion and confidant—Pip's Herbert—and the obligatory surviving witness to the hero's tragedy. Presumably Gervais suggests that Pip wants to exchange his introspective and doubting self for that of his uncomplicated, commonsensical friend.

Pip's abiding sense of Estella is given early: a lighted candle receding down the darkened passages of Satis House, beckoning as it recedes. The afterimage of her that lingers with him is cold and beautiful like diamonds. Whether she scorns or beguiles him, her spell arrests him in a dumb and unresolved longing. Not that the novel puts her on a pedestal, like Agnes: Pip cannot help seeing her as a very real, as well as very elegant, young lady too. There is a hint of the theatrical about her, but she is not ethereal. It is, indeed, precisely the discrepancy between what he wishes her to be morally and what he fears she really is that entices Pip. He loves her for what is unlovable in her, for her very indifference. It is inside this treacherous rift between desire and its object that Eros has delicately insinuated himself.

Pip's love enables him to go on inhabiting the same old territory of guilt and self-dispraise of his childhood. For all her beauty, Estella could never have made him want to call the Jacks Knaves but for what Mrs. Joe had done to him. It is as though some hidden complicity between his persecuting sister and Miss Havisham has fitted him to love Estella. She is shaped to despise him as he is shaped to feel despised. This lack of freedom in his desire makes his love seem romantically star-crossed so that, for all her spitefulness, Estella can still symbolize for him everything beyond the forge that his imagination craves for. She holds sway in his memory, the chief link between his life with and his life without expectations, a link with his pre-London world which, unlike Joe, he can still acknowledge to the Finches of the Grove. Estella occupies such an expanse of time in his mind, from before puberty to manhood, that she comes to seem like a symbol of sexuality itself, not just *one* beautiful woman. * * * That Pip's love is unrequited is not due simply to Estella herself (Bentley Drummle is rumored to have beaten her) but to his own delighted pain in contemplating her in a beautiful beyond outside him. His love, like Miss Havisham's, sets her aside from life. Because of it, he sets aside a part of himself as well. She never again kisses him so spontaneously as on the day when she watched him knock down Herbert Pocket.

The means which give us Pip's feeling for Estella are essentially poetic. She is not presented as a case for the psychologist or the moralist, any more than she is that to Pip. In this he is simply truthful, not deceived. A New Testament ethic, coupled with an acute consciousness of class, may provide the spur for a better understanding of Joe or Magwitch, but they would be too prosaic to fathom his love for Estella. She makes all his usual moral categories dizzy. This is not because she is simply an accomplished tease; it is Pip who teases himself. Part of her charm for him is an exquisite frigidity that allures and then rebuffs him. * * * Personally, she is rather bored by her beauty. This listlessness makes her a more malleable image for Pip's fantasy and, if she manipulates him, he also manipulates her in his mind. * * * In Estella, as the novel renders her, the flesh seems distilled without being quite spiritualized; she is poised gracefully between being a body and a dream. It is in Pip's nature to cling to such an image and consonant with much else in his history that he should be smitten by a woman the very thought of whom seems to quell his blood. Possibly, Dickens wished to hint that his devotion was a way of coping with his fear of Estella's real sexuality. Certainly, her marriage to the bearish and insensitive Drummle can be taken as a sort of riposte to Pip's own lack of aggression. But it would be wrong to proffer any too definite interpretation of a love whose description is so much more atmospheric than analytic. This is the part of the novel where Dickens leaves most to our imagination and most avoids glossing the mystery he evokes.

The treatment of death in *Great Expectations* has something in common with its faintly wistful treatment of love. In the presence of death, Pip best understands both himself and others. Deaths like his sister's, Magwitch's and Miss Havisham's are the stepping stones over which he treads through life. His tone of voice constantly modulates from reminiscence to the mood of an epitaph (in a sense the whole book *is* an epitaph). The deaths in *Great Expectations* feel more elegiac than those in earlier books: we are too attuned to them in advance for them to surprise us. Sensation would be discordant; we hear instead the beat of muffled drums. * * *

Within this muted atmosphere, Dickens maintains his old fascination with the last moments of consciousness. He is drawn to death by its disclosure of a vital spark in people, beneath the level of moral differences, that seems to hover most vividly on the brink of extinction. This spark is brightest in the starving Magwitch on the marshes, in the paralyzed Mrs. Joe beckoning to Biddy to bring the slate and in the terrified Pip about to be murdered by Orlick. It is there too in the returned Magwitch for a while, as we see from the wild weather that brings him back, yet little vestige of it remains in the touching prison scene when he looks for the last time at the white ceiling of his cell and all is swathed in a consoling sublimity. It is telling that at this moment Pip lies to him about Estella, while the truth-seeking narrator makes not the faintest demur. * * * When Pip prays, "O Lord, be merciful to him, a sinner!" we have half-forgotten what Magwitch needs to be forgiven for. To think back from this hallowed moment to the escaped felon shivering on a gravestone is, however moved we may be, to feel a regret that the poetic fable of volume I has become, by volume III, such a perfectly controlled moral fable. The fact that Magwitch's last scene is so perfectly written only makes one wonder whether the perfection of *Great Expectations* itself may not also be its greatest drawback.

* * *

It seems, then, that moral awareness not only liberates Pip by the end but that, with the connivance of Dickens' art, it also diminishes things in him which stood in need of liberation. Much has to remain absent from his voice for its music to be so unbroken. Perhaps as a result of his pressing wish to be a good man, he reneges on some of his bodily energy. As Trabb's Boy remarks after the limekiln ordeal, "Ain't he pale, though?" At times, indeed, he almost resembles the "pale young gentleman," quelled into making the best of life, with honesty if without enthusiasm:

> I must not leave it to be supposed that we were ever a great House, or that we made mints of money. We were not in a grand way of business, but we had a good name, and worked for our profits, and did very well.

This decent, undistinguished Pip, full of prosaic wisdom, so moving in his honesty, has somehow dwindled from the Everyman figure one looked to find in him in volume I. What is missing in him is not just the higher culture, as Bernard Shaw predictably felt, but something which, faced with the attenuated vitality of his lonely self, we can find in abundance in Dickens' less "artistic" books. To say so is not to wish that *Great Expectations* had ended more romantically than with the picture of an upright Victorian merchant; it is rather to surmise that when Dickens wrote it he was consciously and unerringly holding a part of his genius in check. Perhaps he could only describe sadness like Pip's by keeping it aesthetically in check.

* * *

We are still too near to the Victorians—nearer than we used to be—to say whether *Great Expectations* is enough of a classic to come free of the particular culture from which it grew. There is surely something in it which, recalling the sentiment of other writers of the time, will prompt the description "Victorian." But though Pip's voice often puts us in mind of the melodious gravity of a poet like Tennyson, it feels less bound to its age than Tennyson's and has a clearer ring. * * * It sounds most clearly in plain statements, for example in "I have forgotten nothing in my life that ever had a foremost place there, and little that ever had any place there." Great as a poem like *In Memoriam* is, it is more tied to its times; when it tries to rise above them (as in "Strong Son of God, immortal Love")[1] it feels, however eloquent, too dateably nineteenth-century. There is something in *Great Expectations* that, by facing Victorian England so squarely, transcends it, something subtler than its art and deeper than its morals, for which poetry is as good a name as any. Other Dickens novels are in some respects greater or more "Dickensian," but this is the one whose magic most eludes every attempt to define and pin it down. It is a Scarlet Pimpernel[2] among novels, unparaphraseable as good poems are, a mystery that grows more mysterious as it is explained.

MICHAL PELED GINSBURG

Dickens and the Uncanny: Repression and Displacement in *Great Expectations*†

In *Great Expectations*, Pip the narrator tells the story of how Pip the character gradually found out the truth about his great expectations. The story is that of an education, of the passage from a state of mystification (or misreading) to that of demystification (or correct interpretation). Having found out the truth, Pip can probably agree with Jaggers that there was "not a particle of evidence" to support his interpretation that his benefactor was Miss Hav-

---

1. The opening line of the prologue to *In Memoriam* (1833–1850), Tennyson's elegy on his friend, youthful mentor, and prospective brother-in-law Arthur Henry Hallam, who had died in September 1833, at age twenty-two. The topicality of the poem derives in large measure from Tennyson's—and his generation's—search for a solution to the deepening rift between religious and scientific truth, a rift symptomatized by the agitated debate on evolution. In the prologue, written after the bulk of the elegy was completed, Tennyson returned to the orthodox nineteenth-century position with its vestigial belief that "God is love" (John 4.8–9).
2. In effect, a vanishing act; another way of stressing the elusiveness of *Great Expectations*. In one of the perennially popular romances (1905) about the French Revolution, the Hungarian-born Baroness Orczy (1865–1947) lets loose a band of Englishmen whose mission it is to rescue the victims of the Reign of Terror, and whose titular hero succeeds not only in eluding the French but in concealing his identity from the Brits back home.
† Michal Peled Ginsburg, "Dickens and the Uncanny: Repression and Displacement in *Great Expectations*," *Dickens Studies Annual*, ed. Michael Timko, Fred Kaplan, and Edward Guiliano, 13 (1984): 115–24. Reprinted by permission of AMS Press, Inc. Figures in parentheses refer to chapter numbers of the novel. Some of the author's notes have been omitted.

isham. And yet, as he himself pleads in front of the lawyer, "it looked so like it" (40). The question which every interpretation of the novel has to answer is why "it looked so like it" or, more precisely: why was it *necessary* for Pip to misinterpret the signs which pointed toward Magwitch as pointing toward Miss Havisham.

The obvious answer to this question is that this necessity is a narrative one: if there were no misinterpretation there would have been no story. There can be no story of demystification if there is no error or mystification first.[1] But what this answer, in its present formulation, leaves unexplained is why the particular *misinterpretation* involved in the imaginary substitution of Miss Havisham for Magwitch is necessary. That is to say, how Dickens' particular way of plotting reveals something about the nature of narration in general. In order to answer this question, we should see first what the opposition between Miss Havisham and Magwitch involves.

On a first, most elementary level, the opposition between Miss Havisham and Magwitch is one which underlies the novels of Dickens in general. The world of Miss Havisham is for Pip the world of fairy tales and fantasy as opposed to reality. Enclosed within a wall, unknown to the world at large, with its clocks all stopped and its windows and doors locked, the world of Satis House appears to Pip as strange, and Miss Havisham, its mistress and emblem, is "the strangest lady I have ever seen, or shall ever see" (8). The fact that Miss Havisham is "perfectly incomprehensible" to Pip (9) means that he cannot interpret her actions according to the laws of reality which govern his own world. Since he cannot understand the motivation for her strange behavior, he sees this behavior as gratuitous and subject to no con- straint: the world of Satis House is a world where the impossible can happen. Hence Miss Havisham is the "fairy godmother" who, for no particular reason, will endow Pip with all that his heart desires. Or she is the witch who holds in her castle, in complete isolation, the imprisoned princess. Pip himself is the (arbitrarily) chosen fairy child, or the Prince, who would "restore the desolate house . . . tear down the cobwebs . . . in short, do all the shining deeds of the young Knight of romance, and marry the Princess" (29). The world of Magwitch, on the other hand, is the world of what in the nineteenth- century novel was regarded as "reality"—the world of squalor and need, of destructive passions and crime. Pip's misinterpretation can be seen as a rep- resentation of the heart's desire to escape from the world of reality (governed by strict, immutable laws) into the world of pure imagination and fantasy (arbitrary and gratuitous), a desire which is crushed by the inevitable discovery that such an escape is impossible. The plot which will reveal Miss Havisham's connection with Compeyson and Estella's relation to Magwitch will precisely serve as a demonstration of the fact that the world of Satis House is controlled by the same laws and powers as the world outside it. According to such an analysis, which sees the opposition between the world of Miss Havisham and that of Magwitch as an opposition between fantasy and reality, the necessity which informs Pip's misinterpretation is a necessity particular to Dickens' poetic world-view; it teaches us something about Dickens' art rather than about the nature of narration in general. It is, however, precisely this question of narration in general that I would like to discuss here and in order to do

---

1. For a detailed treatment of this point see Moshe Ron, "Autobiographical Narration and Formal Clo- sure in *Great Expectations*," *Hebrew University Studies in Literature*, 5 (1977), 37–66.

that we should look at the opposition between Magwitch and Miss Havisham from a slightly different angle.

The appearance of Magwitch predates that of Miss Havisham; it is represented as a primal event, contemporaneous with the formation of personal identity and its definition in relation to the world outside it: the moment in which Pip takes cognizance of the "identity of things" (1) around him, and of his own identity as "the small bundle of shivers growing afraid of it all," is the moment in which "a fearful man" (1), who eventually will define himself as a father ("I'm your second father," 39) appears. The reaction to that appearance is that of fear, and it immediately entangles Pip in a net of guilt: "the guilty knowledge that I was going to rob Mrs. Joe" (2), the guilty feeling towards Joe, for having not told him the truth (6), the need to assure the convict that he, Pip, is not guilty of his having been captured (5). It is this guilt Pip feels as a result of his encounter with the convict which causes him, in these early chapters, to see himself repeatedly as similar to the convict, as himself a criminal: for example, the explanation by Joe of the word "convict" is interpreted by Pip as a pronouncement of his own name, he sees the load of bread in his leg as similar to the iron on the convict's leg, etc.

It is clear, however, that the encounter with the convict does not simply *create*, or *originate* the feeling of guilt; rather, it *confirms* a feeling of guilt which predates it and which is equivalent to life itself. Thus Pip is both guilty because he associates with convicts and associates with convicts because he is guilty. This feeling of guilt which the encounter with the convict confirms is the basis of the relation between Pip and his sister, who only too willingly repeats "a fearful catalogue of all illnesses [he] had been guilty of, and all the acts of sleeplessness [he] had committed" (4). Mrs. Joe does not show much motherly feeling toward Pip; she is described throughout the novel as a violent and domineering figure who inspires only fear; both to Pip and to childlike Joe she appears as "all powerful" (2). When we add to this the fact that she is never called by her first name—a naming which would have defined her as a woman—but is always referred to by way of a masculine name—Mrs. Joe—we should see that an attempt was made to represent Pip's sister as occupying the place of the father rather than that of a mother. As two figures of the father Magwitch and Mrs. Joe inspire the same feelings—fear and guilt. It is this parallelism between them which explains the fact that Pip, against all reason, sees Magwitch's second appearance as a return of the dead Mrs. Joe. When he hears the steps of Magwitch on the stairs we read: "What nervous folly made me start, and awfully connect it with the footsteps of my dead sister, matters not" (39). Pip's negation[2]—"matters not"—is the sign that this association reveals a truth which has to be repressed.

In blaming Pip for being alive, Mrs. Joe also suggests that his life is going to be her death ("You'll drive *me* to the churchyard," 2, Dickens' emphasis). And indeed when she does die, Pip feels somehow guilty of her death. Moreover, it is his double, Orlick, who is the agent of Mrs. Joe's death, while at the same time, this same Orlick, in a passage of hallucinatory logic, accuses Pip of the deed. The guilt Pip feels in his relation to his sister who functions

---

2. Negation, or *Verneinung*, is one of the defense mechanisms described by Freud which functions, at the same time, as a revelation of the repressed. See his essay "Negation" in *The Standard Edition of the Complete Psychological Works of Sigmund Freud*, ed. James Strachey, 24 vols. (London: Hogarth Press, 1953–74), XIX (1955), 235–239.

as a father surrogate is hence a guilt toward a father, for having been alive while he, the father, is dead: it is a guilt for the death of the father, for having killed the father. The meeting with Magwitch is, as we have said, both the origin and the confirmation of this feeling of guilt: it is, in other words, an "original repetition" of this same structure of relations. The first encounter with Magwitch takes place in the churchyard, by the tomb of the father;[3] Magwitch, "start[ing] up from among the graves" (1) appears more dead than alive "as if he were eluding the hands of the dead people, stretching up cautiously out of their graves, to get a twist upon his ankle and pull him in" (1), while Pip is very much alive, as Magwitch himself makes clear when he comments on his "fat cheeks" (1).

Pip describes the death of his sister—this female father surrogate—as "a gap": "the gap it made in the smooth ground [of my road of life] was won- derful" (35). The guilty killing of the father is an event which has to be repressed, wiped out of memory, and becoming repressed it manifests itself precisely as a hole, a gap in the text of one's life. But having become repressed and unconscious, it is being repeated. Contrary to what Pip says, his sister's death is not "the first time that a grave had opened in [his] road of life," as the tombstones which open his story clearly indicate; it too is already a rep- etition. The death of the father is that which cannot stop being repeated, as the doubling of Mrs. Joe by Magwitch (or vice versa) already shows. And this repetition goes on: Pip "kills" Magwitch in his mind again and again when he thinks that "he [Magwitch] was dead to me, and might be veritably dead into the bargain" (19) and the return of Magwitch is the return of the dead father, who returns in order to die, once again. It is the return of the dead even in his *first* appearance: when Pip leaves Magwitch in the marshes he imagines him to be a "pirate come to life, and come down [off the gibbet], and going back to hook himself up again" (1).

It is because the death of the father is that which is constantly repeated that the appearance of Magwitch is both the origin and the confirmation of Pip's guilt, its cause, projection, and dramatization. The meeting with the convict is an event which, to use Freud's term, originates *nachträglich*[4] Pip's guilt. Miss Havisham's appearance, on the other hand, obeys a different logic: rather than being an external manifestation of internal feelings, it marks the birth of a totally new experience: "I had never thought of being ashamed of my hands before; but I began to consider them a very indifferent pair" (8). * * * While the encounter with Magwitch repeats a sense of guilt which is as old as life and consciousness itself, the meeting with Estella and Miss Havisham is the birth of a new concept of the self: it dates the first perception of the self as deficient, as defined by lack and hence as a subject to desire. The desire for Estella and Pip's feeling of insufficiency are two sides of the same coin: desire *is* the feeling of a lack. It is Estella's perfection and self- sufficiency (her pride) that show Pip that he is lacking, and it is the fact that she makes him feel lacking that transforms her in his eyes to a perfect and totally self-sufficient creature.

---

3. It is true, of course, that the scene takes place by the graves of the entire family. But the father's tombstone is given a special status as the site of the authority for the family's identity: "I give Pirrip as my father's name on the authority of his tombstone." The other members of the family are clearly inscribed as dependent on him (hence secondary), in life as in death, in as much as they are defined "Wife of the Above" and "children of the aforesaid."

4. Belatedly; after the event (German). [*Editor.*]

From the moment Pip visits Miss Havisham and sees Estella for the first time, he feels himself lacking and desiring; and the great expectations which eventually are revealed to him are the fulfillment of this desire; they are the transformation which eliminates or "fills up" the lack. It is because Pip first feels himself lacking and desiring at Miss Havisham's, because his desire for a change is born in Satis House (whose name is hence doubly ironic), that he associates his great expectations with Miss Havisham and Estella. The meeting with Magwitch was just another manifestation of an already known predicament, a powerful instance of an ever-existing feeling, a repetition of that which is constantly to be repressed and forgotten; the visit to Miss Havisham's is, on the contrary, "a *memorable* day" which "made great changes in me" (9, my emphasis).

The association with Miss Havisham is experienced by Pip as the revelation of something totally new which does not correspond to any internal reality that predates it and which could have produced it. While the association with the convict causes and confirms Pip's feeling of guilt, the appearance of Miss Havisham in Pip's life is a chance event which does not depend on him. Even the association of Miss Havisham with "great expectations" does not originate in Pip but rather in Mrs. Joe and Pumblechook who "had no doubt that Miss Havisham would 'do something' for me" (9). Yet this eruption of a new reality is repeatedly linked to the old feeling of guilt. The moment before Mrs. Joe and Pumblechook enter the house to reveal the fact that Miss Havisham would like Pip to come and play in her house, Pip was thinking: "A man would die to-night of lying out on the marshes" (7). Throughout the novel, every encounter with the world of Miss Havisham, Estella, and great expectations will be preceded by a return of the world of the convict, of crime, and of guilt. * * * Jaggers's announcement of the great expectations follows a discussion of murder at the Three Jolly Bargemen; going down to see Miss Havisham, Pip finds himself in a carriage with two convicts; before meeting Estella in London, Pip is taken by Wemmick to Newgate.

This constant association between the world of Miss Havisham and that of Magwitch, between the world of desire and that of guilt, is represented in the novel as the result of pure chance. It is not based on a similarity between the two worlds but rather on their contiguity. It is seen as an association imposed from the outside, rather than being created by the inherent qualities of the two worlds thus linked. But the compulsive repetition of this association which transforms it into a law that governs Pip's world indicates that even if the origin of this association is totally accidental, this accident is being embraced by Pip as revealing his own truth. The burden of the plot, like the burden of Pip's life, is precisely to transform this gratuitous, accidental association into a metaphorical, organic link: hence Miss Havisham's relation to Estella is revealed to be parallel to Magwitch's relation to Pip, hence Magwitch is discovered (through Pip's effort and obsession) to be Estella's father.

*   *   *

Throughout the novel Pip is engaged in two contradictory activities: on the one hand he insists on misinterpreting his destiny, on seeing his great expectations as linked to Miss Havisham and Estella rather than to Magwitch. On the other hand he insists on linking these two worlds, first only in his imagination, and finally "in reality," when he discovers the true parentage of Estella. It is clear that these two activities function as plot devices, the first one being a delay mechanism and the second a mechanism of anticipation. But our analysis permits us now to assign to these two activities the particular meaning they have in this novel. Pip's misinterpretation can now be phrased as the wish to see desire as totally independent of guilt, and the lesson Pip learns is that such a separation is impossible. But the process through which Pip gradually links the world of Miss Havisham with that of Magwitch gives a slightly different meaning to this relation between desire and guilt. It is not simply that there is no desire without guilt (a fact of oedipal psychology), but that, more importantly, repressed guilt manifests itself as desire (in the same way that, in Freud's studies on hysteria, for example, repressed desire manifests itself as guilt) *because the repressed cannot manifest itself in any other way but through something else.* This something else is always more or less arbitrary, more or less accidental and external—it is always something "strange" (as are Miss Havisham and Satis House). But once it becomes arbitrarily and accidentally linked to the repressed as its manifestation it reveals itself to be partaking of the familiarity of the repressed.

It is important to note here that the fact that Magwitch turns out to be Estella's real father does not mean that the link between repressed guilt and desire is a "given" of Pip's world, rather than an arbitrary association, revealed retrospectively to constitute truth. The "truth" of Estella's parentage has a very special status in the novel, different, for example, from the "truth" about Pip's real benefactor. While the latter is an objective fact, known to others (to Magwitch himself, to Jaggers) and gradually discovered by Pip, Estella's parentage is a construct of Pip's imaginative association and linking, it is a new "fact" which rather than being confirmed by the knowledge of others, is introduced to the story to the great surprise even of the all-knowing Jaggers.

I have described the manifestation of the repressed as the linking of that which is familiar to something which is external and accidental—hence strange—a linking through which the strange becomes familiar and the arbitrary acquires a certain kind of necessity. This convergence of the familiar and the strange reminds one of Freud's definition of the uncanny as the familiar (*heimlich*) becoming strange (*unheimlich*) through the act of repression.[5] These two formulations are only superficially different: repression and the manifestation of the repressed—hiding and revealing—are one and the same thing; the repressed does not exist anywhere in a "pure," undisplaced form. But their *seeming* difference, or inversion—the strange becoming familiar versus the familiar becoming strange—is still of great importance because it alerts us to the problematic status of the notion of origin in psychoanalytical theory and which we have already seen in our discussion of Pip's meeting with Magwitch.

In his analysis of Hoffmann's story "The Sandman" (in his essay on the uncanny) Freud claims that the fear of losing one's eyes produces an uncanny effect only to the extent that it is a substitute (*i.e.*, a displacement) for the fear of castration. But Freud does *not* see the fear of castration as an unambiguous *origin* of the fear of losing one's eyes because the fear of castration is not simply the "justifiable dread" of losing a precious organ.[6] The fear of castration *itself* refers to something other than itself, castration itself, rather

5. Freud, "The Uncanny," in the *Standard Edition*, XVIII (1955), 219–252.
6. "The Uncanny," 231.

than being first (*origin*) and last (*meaning*) is one element in a chain of substitutions. Thus the "strange" fear of losing one's eyes is not simply the result of a substitution of something "familiar" (the fear of castration) because the "familiar" itself is a result of a substitution: the "familiar" becomes "strange" and the "strange" becomes "familiar." This ever-regressing series of substitutions, this constant transformation of the strange into the familiar and the familiar into the strange, makes it impossible to posit a point of origin, that is to say, a moment in which the familiar was wholly familiar, a stage before repression, without an unconscious: the primal murder, the primal scene, like primary repression, are mythic moments which one cannot locate within experience.

The impossibility of locating a point of origin joins another impossibility already mentioned: that of "pure" repression without displacement, of pure repetition without difference. In *Beyond the Pleasure Principle*, written approximately at the same time as the essay on the uncanny, Freud treats precisely this impossibility: pure repetition cannot exist in the sense that it is equivalent to instantaneous death.[7] In other words, pure repetition cannot create life—or a story. In *Great Expectations* we see clearly how the repressed in itself, in as much as it *is* pure repetition, cannot generate a story. Magwitch who stands for the world of crime and guilt (which is being repressed) does not have a story: "In jail and out of jail, in jail and out of jail, in jail and out of jail. There, you've got it. That's *my* life pretty much" (42, Dickens' emphasis), says Magwitch. It is only when the repressed manifests itself as something other than itself—that is to say, when there is an act of substitution and displacement (a "detour," to use the phraseology of *Beyond the Pleasure Principle*) into something which is totally unrelated (hence arbitrary), new, and different, that a story becomes possible which is not simply a pure repetition * * *. When Pip comes back from his first meeting with Magwitch and when he comes back from his first visit to Miss Havisham, his reaction is the same: he does not tell the truth. But in the case of Magwitch, this withholding of truth takes the shape of *silence*: there is no other story possible but the repetition of guilt, the addition of another item to the catalogue of misdeeds. The visit to Miss Havisham's, on the other hand, produces lies: it generates a fiction, a story, and this creative act is the result of the new feeling of desire: "I told Joe . . . that there had been a beautiful young lady at Miss Havisham's who was dreadfully proud, and that she had said that I was common, and that I knew that I was common, and that I wished I was not common, and that the lies had come out of it somehow, though I didn't know how" (9). The act of displacement from guilt to desire is not only an act of repression; as an act of substitution and displacement, it opens up a space where a story can be told.

---

7. *Beyond the Pleasure Principle*, in the *Standard Edition*, XVIII (1955), especially the fifth section, pp. 34–43. On the relation between *Beyond the Pleasure Principle* and a theory of plot, see Peter Brooks, "Freud's Masterplot," in *Yale French Studies*, 55/56 (1977), 280–300; on this problem in its particular relation to *Great Expectations*, see his "Repetition, Repression, and Return: *Great Expectations* and the Study of Plot," *New Literary History*, XI (1980), 503–26 [see p. 679 in this Norton Critical Edition]. I am greatly indebted to both these studies.

LINDA RAPHAEL

A Re-Vision of Miss Havisham: Her Expectations and Our Responses†

* * *

Perhaps one of the most significant figures in *Great Expectations* in terms of affective power is Miss Havisham. Dickens's contemporary readers probably understood, either consciously or subconsciously, that Miss Havisham's ill-fated marriage and her consequent behavior made a peculiar sort of sense in their world. On the other hand, since stories like Miss Havisham's have been re-told, from Dickens's day to ours, in the continuing narrative of western experience and have been articulated in theoretical conceptions as well as in other fictional works, this frustrated spinster may seem very familiar to present-day readers. Like Dickens's contemporaries, we respond to the codes that inform *Great Expectations* almost intuitively: the difference is that our intu-itions are informed by a century of additional developments, both cultural and literary. The characterization of Miss Havisham provides a model of the power of repressive forces, especially in their dual roles as agents of society at large acting on the individual and as internalized matter directing one to govern the conduct of self and others according to unstated principles. For the late twentieth-century reader, the richness of this novel may be enhanced by an analysis that pays attention to the cultural dynamics at work during Dickens's time with an emphasis on what more recent psycho-analytic, social, and literary narratives offer us for understanding.

Embodying the mythic horrors of countless cruel mothers, stepmothers, and witch-like figures, Miss Havisham has often been described by critics as one more instance of an irrational and vindictive female figure. * * * [Thomas] Vargish's claim [that Miss Havisham is "the most clearly culpable"[1] compared to Magwitch], which depends on his assertion that Miss Havisham "was brought up as a lady, with a lady's advantages," raises the question of what it meant to be brought up as a lady, in general, or in Miss Havisham's case, in particular. Dickens probably counted on his readers' ability to answer the "in general," since he provides only a brief summary of her life, offered to Pip by Herbert Pocket. However, her significance in the novel may be positively linked to the brevity of details about her background rather than in spite of it. In other words, readers may have always responded to Miss Hav-isham with an almost automatic comprehension of her state of mind and her actions—and clearly this sort of reaction depends on the text's evocation of shared cultural, and often literary, concepts.

Miss Havisham—bedecked in her withered bridal gown and half-arranged veil, resembling grave-clothes and a shroud, one shoe on, one off—creates a vivid and lasting image for the reader, one which is made more grotesque

---

† From Linda Raphael, "A Re-Vision of Miss Havisham: Her Expectations and Our Responses," *Studies in the Novel* 21 (Winter 1989). Copyright 1989 by University of North Texas. Reprinted by permission of the publisher.
1. Thomas Vargish, *The Providential Aesthetic in Victorian Fiction* (Charlottesville: Univ. of Virginia Press, 1985), pp. 152–53.

because of its convolution of the symbolic import of a wedding scene. Since at least biblical times, depictions of betrothal and marriage scenes have functioned as literary devices.[2] However, rather than signifying the celebration of a joyous social and personal event in which private lives are endorsed by public ceremony, the remains of the aborted wedding—the table still laid for a feast and the jilted bride in her yellowed gown—visibly enact a gap between opportunity and desire which frequently occurred in the lives of Victorian women. The dismal scene mirrors Miss Havisham's failure to make her private dream a public reality and to create an identity outside her private sphere. In making the point that "there is nothing that is not social and historical—indeed, that everything is in the last analysis political," Frederic Jameson defines the "structural, experiential, and conceptual gap between the public and private [as] maim[ing] our existence as individual subjects and paralyz[ing] our thinking about time and change."[3] And surely Dickens depicts in Miss Havisham's experience a social, historical, and "in the last analysis political" event. Few authors, with the notable exception of Faulkner, particularly in "A Rose for Emily" and The Sound and the Fury, create characters so paralyzed in thinking about time and change as Dickens does in the case of Miss Havisham.[4]

Miss Havisham's choice—if we can call it a choice finally—to live reclusively in the inner space of Satis House, enduring in a fetid atmosphere which threatens also to engulf young Estella, repeats the fate of many Victorian women. As Elaine Showalter concludes in her analysis of "The Rise of the Victorian Madwoman":

> the rise of the Victorian madwoman was one of history's self-fulfilling prophecies. In a society that not only perceived women as childlike, irrational, and sexually unstable but also rendered them legally powerless and economically marginal, it is not surprising that they should have formed the greater part of the residual categories of deviance from which doctors drew a lucrative practice and the asylums much of their population.[5]

Because of the macabre nature of Miss Havisham's environment—one which has resisted all but the most negative effects of the passage of time—we may not immediately connect her existence to those of other nineteenth-century fictional females, such as Jane Eyre, whose confinement to closed spaces is a metaphor for entrapment in a society whose functioning depends in part on females' complicity with their own imprisonment. Herbert Pocket's report to Pip of Miss Havisham's past—that she was a motherless young girl whose father, anxious about his newly-achieved financial status, doted on her and

---

2. Robert Alter provides an illuminating narrative analysis of betrothal scenes in The Art of Biblical Narrative (New York: Basic Books, 1981).
3. Fredric Jameson, The Political Unconscious: Narrative as a Socially Symbolic Act (Ithaca: Cornell Univ. Press, 1981), p. 20.
4. In Faulkner's first major novel (1929), Quentin Compson, the oldest of four children of an effete Southern clan, has been paralyzed by the past: obsessed with his sister's loss of virginity, conditioned by his father's nihilism and his deadly drinking—resembling in Sartre's famous formulation "a man sitting in an open car and looking backwards"—Quentin drowns himself in the Charles River at the end of his freshman year at Harvard. But Quentin's idiot brother Benjy and their mother, a hypochondriac who spends most of the day in bed, indulging in self-recriminations and panegyrics on an illusory past, also qualify as characters for whom time has stopped. On "A Rose for Emily," see below, n. 6. [Editor.]
5. Sandra Gilbert and Susan Gubar, Madwoman in the Attic: The Woman Writer and the Nineteenth Century Literary Imagination (New Haven: Yale Univ. Press, 1979), p. 73.

neglected his son, who in turn resented the child so clearly favored over him—recounts, on one level, the history of a spoiled woman who, when her expectations are sorely disappointed by a jilting fiancé, will spend the rest of her life impotently raging at the forces that worked against her. Thus, readers have generally considered Miss Havisham's isolation as self-inflicted, but probing into the causes of her tortured manner of living reveals the workings of a complex system which has made her reclusiveness inevitable. While her financial independence has allowed her to escape confinement to an asylum, a fate we would imagine for a woman who behaved as she but did not have property or money, she lives as disconnected from the outside world as if she were institutionalized.

The "madwoman" who spends her life thus has many fictional counterparts, whose thrashings in a world deaf to their cries symbolize the same sort of unsatiated female passion and desire that smoulder in Miss Havisham. It is instructive, for example, to connect Faulkner's Emily with Miss Havisham because of their similar roles as daughters who held a special place in their fathers' imaginations.[6] The world of *Great Expectations*, like that of "A Rose for Emily," refracts complex and changing social values. Each work concerns itself particularly with those changes which challenge the privileged status of a family as a source of identity but simultaneously frustrate individual identity. Ironically, they seem to say, the same system which esteems individual enterprise limits the ability of those not powerful or lucky enough to find a secure niche within a competitive system that renders all things, including human relationships, subordinate to their profit and exchange value: Miss Havisham and Emily remain within the privacy of their homes, perhaps initially filling a role like the one Davidoff and Hall describe in their social history, *Family Fortunes*, as common to a young motherless woman: she might serve as an emotional focus for her father, protecting him from an "ill-considered" remarriage while gaining for herself "responsibility, respect and affection without a break from familiar surroundings and the necessity to cope with a new, sexual relationship."[7]

*   *   *

Although Miss Havisham has the privileges that Vargish associates with a "lady," the prerogatives she enjoys essentially limit her exchange value to the small marketplace she has created in Satis House. Again like Emily, who could not function in her post-Civil War American southern town which no longer apprized the social status of her family, Miss Havisham's worth to Compeyson and then to her relatives, and even to some extent to Pip (he imagines that she is a means to attaining the love of Estella as well as a source of material wealth), is measured by the monetary gains they believe they can realize from her. What a surprise for a woman who had no dealings with the public world in her years of growing up and who had received preferential

---

6. Emily is Miss Emily Grierson, a Mississippi spinster "with insanity in the family," whose domineering, class-conscious father has been largely responsible for her spinsterhood: all "eligible" young men are socially ineligible and need not apply. After the father's death, she is courted, then jilted, by the foreman of a Yankee construction company, whom she poisons and whose body she accommodates in her bedroom until her own decomposition thirty years later. Like Miss Havisham, Miss Emily lives out her life shut up in her barren home; unlike her, she avenges herself on the male sex by simpler means than the use of a surrogate. [*Editor.*]

7. Leonore Davidoff and Catherine Hall, *Family Fortunes: Men and Women of the English Middle Class, 1780–1850* (London: Hutchinson, 1987), p. 347.

treatment at the hands of her father, who himself had stature in his community.

* * *

In terms of Miss Havisham's marital plans, a brief history of traditional modes of arrangement helps to explain her special position vis-à-vis the male alliance between her step-brother and Compeyson. Until the eighteenth century, alliances between children of propertied families had been arranged by their families. Since the move toward arranging one's own courtship and marriage was in harmony with other social movements toward autonomy, Miss Havisham's choice to marry someone for whom she felt "all the passion of which she was susceptible" may be interpreted as a response to new social possibilities. However, the self-determined woman, often associated in popular culture with witch-like old maids, would have good cause to feel vulnerable to social criticism and to potential rejection from her object of desire. Herbert reports that when his father warned Miss Havisham that she was placing herself too much in Compeyson's power, she responded in an angry rage—a response that we might interpret as a sign of her fear that he was right as well as a sign that she behaved explosively as a young woman. Thus, Miss Havisham's half-brother, while hardly an upstanding member of the family, ostensibly protects her in two ways. He provides a socially acceptable context by introducing a friend to marry his sister, since the custom of a male family member arranging a marriage when parents were deceased follows the pattern which was still somewhat in place at the time; and his intermediary status deflects somewhat the passion with which Miss Havisham approaches this relationship. Thus, the homosocial alliance finds its strength in norms which reflect women's subordination in legal, social, and emotional affairs.

* * *

* * * [John] Kucich's claims about the ways in which repressed material forms identity help to explain how Miss Havisham has repressed her desire to punish Compeyson for his rejection of her and has used this energy to create her self-image.[8] Thus, she may see herself as powerful, the owner of Satis House and an authority over Estella. In each of these powerful roles, she represents the Victorian male figure rather than the female: she owns property and she possesses a female—and her own female addition to this is that she also gains power over a male, Pip. * * * For despite Estella's practical dependence on her adoptive mother, she is forced into an uncomfortably powerful position which places her in the role of master to the alternately vicious and pathetic woman who pleads for her approval and acceptance. The reversibility of the slave-master relationship reveals itself continually through the novel, so that in one of the turns of the screw, when Estella turns on Miss Havisham with controlled but significant anger, we enjoy a release of our hostile feelings toward this manipulative witch-like figure through the expression of repressed rage of the female, Estella. And even though ulti-

8. John Kucich, *Repression in Victorian Fiction* (Berkeley: University of California Press, 1987), 252 ff. For detailed theoretical studies of the way women function as objects of exchange between men within the institution of marriage, see Gayle Rubin, "The Traffic in Women: Notes on the 'Political Economy' of Sex," in Rayna Reiter, ed., *Toward an Anthropology of Women* (New York: Monthly Review Press, 1975), 157–210, and Luce Irigaray, *This Sex Which Is Not One*, trans. Catherine Porter (Ithaca: Cornell University Press, 1985). [*Editor.*]

mately Estella represents the "angel in the house" image for which Dickens is famous, the reversal of her character remains unconvincing in contrast to the representation of her as an abused and abusing female.

* * *

We have no reason to suspect that Miss Havisham understands her own misery as a consequence of more than having been jilted. The tragedy of her life is not that Compeyson failed to show up at the altar; it is not even that he and her step-brother had plotted against her—it is that she fails to understand the system that works against her. Rather than seeking whatever small, but personally significant, change she might effect, she seeks to revenge herself against society on its own terms. In other words, she acts on the belief that it is only through dehumanizing and often brutal deceit and abuse that desire can be satisfied. Miss Havisham thus fails to offer a hope for a different future for the next generation. This is Dickens at his most pessimistic—the Dickens who reveals the vicious circularity of individual and social misery. The illusion that Miss Havisham holds onto sustains the dream that the role she intended to assume was one that could offer satisfaction. Dickens unmasks this illusion in various ways throughout the novel, but the world he depicts offers no alternative.

* * *

SUSAN WALSH

Bodies of Capital: *Great Expectations* and the Climacteric Economy†

Taken together, Miss Havisham and her derelict brewery present stunning images of insolvency. Senescent, irascible, decaying like the barrels with their "sour remembrance of better days," Miss Havisham is characterized by how her garden grows: rankly. * * * As Herbert Pocket recounts her history, years ago Miss Havisham had been bilked, jilted, and humiliated by a false fiancé; in response, she had immolated her woman's body and the brewery's manufacturing economy in one furious sweep. In so doing, she effectually repudiated the role of women's economic and bodily capital within the family enterprise system, a business model still central to Victorian culture in general, and crucial in particular to this novel's conservationist nostalgia. When Pip casts Miss Havisham in the role of fairy godmother and himself as the "dummling" youngest son, he unwittingly invokes more than the popular *Märchen*[1] story of up-from-below success. He draws upon an established nineteenth-century pattern of advancement in which young men's economic agency is partially underwritten by female relatives expected to invest annuities, legacies, and independent funds in manufacturing and trade.

† From Susan Walsh, "Bodies of Capital: *Great Expectations* and the Climacteric Economy," *Victorian Studies* 37.1 (1993): 73–98. Reprinted by permission of the publisher.
1. Folk or fairy tale. The "dummling" is the legendary simpleton. [*Editor.*]

Miss Havisham, I want to argue, is an important index to the local economics beneath the more ahistorical fairy tale motifs that structure *Great
Expectations*; she is one of the means by which Dickens demarcates the
commercial parameters within which Victorian men operated. Her history as
a swindled investor enacts the rash speculation and reckless overtrading
which, to some observers, had led to the stock frauds, bankruptcies, and bank
crashes of the middle decades. Her history as an unmarried heiress conjures
up mid-century debates about women's changing roles and financial com-
mitments. For just when the rise of larger corporations seemed to augur the
breakdown of traditional forms of commercial organization and, in the wake
of the Limited Liability Act of 1855,[2] to encourage dangerously incautious
business practices, more middle-class women began to argue their right to
enter the work force. Additionally, reformers began to advocate that the married woman be granted the power to own and dispose of property as a "*feme
sole*."[3] Miss Havisham, as a moderately wealthy "*feme sole*," already enjoys
these prerogatives. Before the novel begins, she has acted independently of
male advice, squandered her money upon an imposter and, at least initially,
fallen delinquent in her duty to offer monetary support to real or surrogate
male relatives. From a conservative point of view, her errors as a single woman
would seem to reflect badly upon measures aimed at giving all women greater
freedom to modify or reject their customary economic roles.

However meticulously plotted in the 1820s, Dickens's "Copperfield of the
inner man" offers a ruminative response to the shifting socio-economic
grounds of the 1840s and 1850s.[4] * * *

I

The homologous relationship between the social body and the human body
has a long history, from Plato's *Republic*[5] to Hobbes' *Leviathan* to Herbert
Spencer's writings on political economy.[6] However, as Catherine Gallagher
has argued, in nineteenth-century England not everyone agreed about how
the homology was to be configured or about what it ultimately revealed. * * *

Mid-century proponents of laissez-faire drew upon Hume and Smith's * * *
traditional analogy in characterizing financial panics as free market "convulsions" in which circulation has been hampered by "constriction" or "obstruction."[7] Writing *Great Expectations* against the backdrop of mid-century
commercial crises, Dickens appears to modify this homology so that the sick
human body becomes aged and female. The reason isn't far to seek. Women's
bodies, as advertisements, medical handbooks, and health manuals made
clear, were the human bodies most agitated by cyclical "crises." W. Tyler

---

2. Legislation allowing the formation, without permission from Parliament, of companies in which individual shareholders could be held liable only for a limited percentage of losses incurred by the
   company as a whole. [*Editor.*]
3. Legal term for an unmarried woman. [*Editor.*]
4. Martin Meisel, "Miss Havisham Brought to Book," *PMLA* 81 (1966), 278.
5. Plato's seminal work, in which he explores the nature of the ideal state. [*Editor.*]
6. Herbert Spencer (1820–1903), one of the founders of sociology, endeavored to apply the doctrine of
   evolution to his utilitarian and economic free-market principles. In his magnum opus, *Leviathan*
   (1651), Thomas Hobbes (1588–1679) defends absolute government on the grounds that it meets the
   subject's need for protection. [*Editor.*]
7. In his *Treatise of Human Nature* (1739), the philosopher and historian David Hume (1711–1790)
   anticipated his disciple and friend Adam Smith (1723–1790) in defending the freedom of commerce
   and industry against state interference, a thesis elaborated by Smith in his revolutionary *Wealth of
   Nations* (1776). [*Editor.*]

Smith, for instance, argued that although older men and women both suffer from "climacteric disease," periodicity is nevertheless "more indelibly marked upon the female than upon the male constitution." In fact, the "climacteric" (menopausal) woman faced greater hazards as she struggled towards "the death of the reproductive faculty" than did women who contended with menarche or pregnancy.[8] The older female body, therefore, became available as a potent analogue for economic as well as reproductive "bankruptcy," the complete foreclosure of the machinery of material production. Dickens draws from the representational reservoirs of medicine and economics when the half-"waxwork," half-exhumed "skeleton" of Miss Havisham makes her gruesome debut.[9]

More specifically, Dickens introduces his infamous recluse into a cultural context within which it made sense to link the afflicted economic body with the disordered female body. Artists for *Punch*,[1] for example, waggishly depicted the financial crises of 1847 and 1857 as an ailing Old Lady of Threadneedle Street, her prominent, balloon-shaped bottom half sketched as a giant money bag partly covered by an apron of bank bills. In one 1847 cartoon (fig. 1), a groaning Old Lady grasps a bedpost while Prime Minister Peel,[2] his face flinty with determination, reins in her midriff in a preposterous gesture of husbandly help. For an actual older woman, this maneuver would constitute a painful and misguided attempt to recreate the supple elasticity of youth. In the Bank of England's case, the tight-lacing pantomimes the credit restrictions imposed by the Bank Charter Act of 1844, which drew shut the purse strings of the Issue Department's precious metal reserves whenever bullion could not cover all the notes it ostensibly backed. A zealous supporter of the Charter Act, Peel was utterly convinced that it would, in Colonel Torrens's words, finally prevent "the recurrence of those commercial revulsions—those cycles of commercial excitement and depression, which . . . result from the alternate expansion and contraction of an ill-regulated circulation."[3] Yet far from insuring tranquility, in October of 1847 the Charter Act incited panic when the Bank limited its extension of credit and in some instances suspended it altogether. Accordingly, *Punch*'s 1847 cartoon travesties the Act by illustrating its effects upon the body of Mrs. Threadneedle, whose vascular tract stands in for the Bank's own circulatory system. For as any medical student or political economist could have predicted, and as the Old Lady's billowing extremities attest, vital currents blocked in one direction will either find egress somewhere else or burst their vessels. As suggested by her pinched waist and her distended feet, the Old Lady of Threadneedle Street appears to have arrived at this apoplectic juncture. "Oh! Oh!," she moans, "I

---

8. W. Tyler Smith, "The Climacteric Disease in Women: A Paroxysmal Affection Occurring at the Decline of the Catamenia," *London Journal of Medicine* 7 (July 1849): 601.
9. *Great Expectations*, ed. Angus Calder (New York: Penguin, 1965), 87.
1. Weekly comic magazine founded in 1841. [*Editor.*]
2. As Prime Minister, Peel moved England toward a free-trade policy. See above, pp. 98, n. 2 and 593. [*Editor.*]
3. Colonel Torrens, one of the "currency" men and partisan advocates of the Act quoted by James Wilson in the House of Commons (*Hansard's* 95 [30 Nov. 1847]: 422). Members of Parliament used a variety of medical metaphors in their debates over the crises of 1847 and 1857. In 1847, the Chancellor of the Exchequer defended the 1844 Charter Act by likening it to an approved course of medical treatment which, in special cases, might be departed from without impugning the "ordinary" curative principle on which it was based (377). By contrast, Lord Portman argued that England's commercial malady "was not like a chronic disease which could await the careful and deliberate attention of the physician, but it was a case which required the active hand of a skilful surgeon" (*Hansard's* 148 [3 Dec. 1857]: 7).

THE EFFECTS OF TIGHT LACING ON THE OLD
LADY OF THREADNEEDLE STREET.

"The Effects of Tight Lacing on the Old Lady of Threadneedle
Street." *Punch* 13 (July–Dec. 1847): 115.

shall go. I'm sure I shall go if you don't loose me—." *Punch's* Threadneedle Street cartoon thus seems based on a familiar blood-currency analogy. * * *

In nineteenth-century parlance, however, the "obstruction," "constriction," or "depression" of an "ill-regulated circulation" in women meant more than digestive or circulatory arrest: these terms were code words for stopped menses, whether the result of delayed menarche, pregnancy, menopause, or a general ovario-uterine "derangement." Countless remedies offered to "purify," "restore," and "regulate" malfunctioning menstrual systems. Frampton's Pills of Health, advertised in the London *Times*, promised to relieve females of "all obstructions," in addition to "the distressing headaches so very prevalent with the sex, depression of spirits, dullness of sight, nervous affections, blotches, pimples, and sallowness of the skin"; other nostrums guaranteed the same. What exercised physicians most was the necessity of alleviating "constriction"—not so much the problem of menstruation itself but its suppression.[4] Doctors and quack advertisers agreed: even under relatively normal conditions, a woman's uterus could become "a disturbing radiator" in her reproductive "economy,"[5] behaving like a badly calibrated engine that periodically throws its entire assembly into "violent commotion."[6]

* * *

Considering the challenge that economic "convulsions" posed to bourgeois doctrines of success predicated upon diligence, self-help, and shrewd business acumen, the Old Lady of Threadneedle Street cartoons are more than humorous; they are ideologically useful. By representing women's economies as the circulatory systems periodically undermined by paroxysm, they work to alleviate apprehensions about corporate and individual bankruptcy, about anarchic market forces beyond anyone's power to predict or command. The problem is displaced, transported away from men and resituated within women's bodies. * * * What helps to make the *Punch* parodies and cartoons funny rather than alarming is their use of medical language itself, because it offers the promise of mastery through diagnosis and cure. * * *

* * *

II

Where *Punch's* Mrs. Threadneedle points to the increasing agedness of England's own "Motherbank," a short essay published in Dickens's *All the Year Round* (1859) focuses upon the individual investors whose monies constitute the Bank itself. Entitled "Great Meeting of Creditors," this sketch presents an array of typical fundholders which concludes in an arresting portrait of the British investor as a decrepit yet dangerous old woman. * * * Most dramatically, the sketch demonstrates the sheer numbers of women involved in sustaining the economy; on "creditor's day" at the Bank of England, they seem to emerge from every socio-economic nook and cranny.

4. Sally Shuttleworth, "Female Circulation: Medical Discourse and Popular Advertising in the Mid-Victorian Era," 64. In Jacobus, Keller, and Shuttleworth, eds., *Body/Politics: Women and the Discourses of Science* (New York: Routledge, 1990), 47–68.
5. Charles Meigs, *Females and Their Diseases: A Series of Letter to His Class* (Philadelphia: Lea and Blanchard, 1848), 49.
6. Colombat d'Isere (Marc Columbat), *A Treatise on the Diseases and Special Hygiene of Females*, trans. Charles Meigs (Philadelphia: Lea and Blanchard, 1845), 19.

However, "Great Meeting of Creditors" does not paint a reassuring picture of the hidden female investor. The AYR "reporter" begins by describing the vivid, cross-class panoply of shareholders and annuitants who underwrite the National Debt, "that numerical abstraction, that perilous jungle for currency doctors."[7] Like lepers to the healing founts of quarterly profits, he tells us, "the lame, the blind, the palsied, the jaundiced" flock to the Bank of England on dividend day. * * * Scores of women arrive to secure their profits; fully one-third of the descriptions involves widows, matrons, spinsters, young women, and girls. Indeed, the essay's culminating and most elaborate portrait of the female creditor is that of an ancient bundle of unwashed rags "borne in like a nodding Guy Fawkes in November . . . on an old, brown, creaking Windsor chair."[8] Her stare is vacant and glazed; her chin lies submerged in her chest. She has been transported to the Bank because rules stipulate that fundholders apply for their dividends in person. Her incapacity, however, requires special dispensation from a head clerk, with whose assistance she makes "the sacred sign which stands for new life in either state of existence." And yet it was not always so:

> When first she became a creditor of the state, she was young, and, per-
> haps, sightly. . . . Now, her helpless withered arm is lifted up, and clum-
> sily made to form a thick inky cross, with a juicy full-charged quill, as
> it might have been unresistingly lifted up and made to stab a Rotunda
> beadle. When her money is, at last, procured, it turns out to be some
> thirty shillings, which are passed before her listless eyes to give her com-
> fort, and then placed in her pocket under her cold, bloodless, listless
> touch.[9]

Cadaverous and awful, this old woman personifies the female investor's potential for committing violence against the economy and its male managers. * * * Yet this female shareholder, like all female shareholders, is willingly accommodated by the Bank even though she may damage, intentionally or not, the system it is her proper function to support. Like Miss Havisham, she is a grotesque old woman who wields phallic economic power—the "juicy full-charged quill"—in a manner almost as horribly powerful as it is pathetically impotent.

For some readers, Miss Havisham and the aged "Guy Fawkes" of "Great Meeting of Creditors" might well have suggested worrisome things about women's financial powers, especially within the context of general anxiety about the health, tractability, and essential fairness of a burgeoning industrial marketplace. In Great Expectations, women provide at least two sorts of relief. They act as angels in the house who conserve old-style domestic and economic arrangements, or alternatively, they become places where economic trouble can be displaced and thereby symbolically disposed of. Miss Havisham offers the second kind of solution, and she is eventually rehabilitated enough also to offer the first. Before we can see how she both represents and finally helps to compensate for a pitiless economy, however, we need to understand how Dickens proves the economic problems of his day upon the pulses of his male characters.

7. "Great Meeting of Creditors," All the Year Round (11 June 1859), 153.
8. "Great Meeting," 155.
9. "Great Meeting," 155–56.

By mid-century it had become increasingly evident, amidst calamitous tales of broken banks and broken men, that although the ethos of self-determining individualism was borne out in the prosperity of some, it was nothing but a tantalizing illusion in the careers of others. If laborers were "slaves to necessity," as Samuel Martin claimed in 1773, it required little stretch of the imagination to recognize that masters too could be the bondsmen of market forces beyond their control.[1] As Sally Shuttleworth has pointed out, while the proponents of laissez-faire commerce extolled economic man as a "rational, independent actor" with Smilesian[2] talents for upward mobility, critics of industrial capitalism characterized him as an exploited drudge, a shackled automaton or an insentient cog.[3] In *Great Expectations* these competing definitions become hallucinogenically real. In his delirium following Magwitch's death, Pip dreams that he has become soldered into an implacable industrial machine, fixed like "a steel beam of a vast engine, clashing and whirling over a gulf"; at the same time, he envisions himself standing outside the nightmare apparatus pleading "in my own person to have the engine stopped, and my part in it hammered off."[4] But he can no more entirely disengage himself from the mechanics of wage-earning and production than he can live out the fairy-tale plot of benevolent godmothers, beautiful princesses, and kingdoms distributed to worthy youngest sons.

For as Dickens well knew, in the 1850s economic conditions had been particularly unforgiving for young men like the chastened Pip and the irrepressible Herbert Pocket "looking about" them for the main chance.[5] By the time of *Great Expectations*, biographers report, Dickens had begun to view the undistinguished careers of his sons with exasperation and dismay. Seriously concerned about their inaptitude, and fearful that they had inherited their mother's laziness and their paternal grandfather's genius for debt, he steered his sons away from dim domestic prospects and towards foreign venues like Hong Kong and Australia.[6] * * * Dickens's own ineffectual sons also haunt the opening paragraphs of *Great Expectations* where, amidst echoes of Wordsworth and Blake, they seem to make cameo appearances as Pip's small deceased brothers. Close by the graves of Philip and Georgiana Pirrip * * * lie five stone lozenges "sacred to the memory of five little brothers of mine —who gave up trying to get a living, exceedingly early in that universal struggle." To the little lozenges Pip owes his "religiously entertained" belief that his brothers "had all been born on their backs with their hands in their trousers-pockets, and had never taken them out in this state of existence."[7]

In Pip's imagination, therefore, his brothers assume the posture of indolent little slackers, their premature deaths apparently the natural result of a congenital inability to get on in life. * * * With hands in empty pockets, they seem compliant casualties of that universal economic struggle where mastery,

1. Quoted in Catherine Gallagher, *Industrial Reformation of English Fiction, 1832–1867* (Chicago: U of Chicago P, 1985), 7.
2. Samuel Smiles (1812–1904), Scottish writer and social reformer, author of best-selling books promoting self-improvement, notably *Self Help* (1859). See also Robin Gilmour's discussion, p. 578 and n. 8. [*Editor.*]
3. Shuttleworth, 54.
4. GE, 471–72.
5. GE, 207.
6. Fred Kaplan, *Dickens: A Biography* (New York: Avon, 1988), 420–23.
7. GE, 35.

as Carlyle proclaimed in *The French Revolution*,[8] is conferred by the "least blessed fact" upon which "necessitous mortals have ever based themselves . . . . : That *I* can devour *Thee*."[9] *Great Expectations*, as Elliot Gilbert has remarked, is so rife with literal and metaphoric devouring that here, as in many Dickens novels, the ravenous boast from *The French Revolution* modulates into an even more distressing rule of public and private consumption: "Try as I will, I cannot *keep* from devouring thee."[1]

* * *

According to Sarah Ellis, John Ruskin,[2] and other writers of domestic economy, Wemmick's society of potentially felonious men was an almost inevitable result of cutthroat capitalism. Men struggling within a merciless public arena had to contend not only with their competitors' foul play but also with powerful daily inducements to behave treacherously themselves. Only the meliorative influence of gentle Christian women, whose spiritual teaching provides "a kind of second conscience," Ellis remarks, helps to preserve embattled husbands, sons, and brothers from "the snares of the world . . . and temptations from within and without."[3] But in *Great Expectations*, Ruskin and Ellis's deferential helpmate takes a perverse, exaggerated form in Miss Havisham. Miss Havisham is a voluptuary of pain, spokeswoman for the masochistic dark side of domestic ideology. "Real love," in her hissed definition, means "blind devotion, unquestioning self-humiliation, utter submission, trust and belief against yourself and against the whole world, giving up your whole heart and soul to the smiter."[4] She strikes back at the "smiter" by training an avenging angel, Estella, to "break [the] hearts" of aristocrats, masters, and men, to retaliate against the brotherhood of unscrupulous plotters who, in the persons of Compeyson and Arthur Havisham, first defrauded her adoptive mother. Set loose in the world like an enemy agent, Estella is no moral "guarantor," the role Mary Poovey suggests nineteenth-century domestic ideology imagined for women within laissez-faire capitalism.[5] Rather, she is a cold-blooded anti-monitoress who seems to atomize rather than harmonize the competing interests of covetous men.[6]

[Although Miss Havisham seems to subvert the role of domestic angel by heightening hostility between men, Walsh argues that hatred between men over the women whom they are competing to possess cements bonds between

<hr />

8. Thomas Carlyle (1795–1881), Scottish essayist, historian, and first of the Victorian social prophets, opposed the spread of democracy and harshly criticized laissez-faire economics. *The French Revolution* (1837) portrayed the revolution as an inevitable, renovating destruction of defunct values and a sham aristocracy. [*Editor.*]

9. Quoted in Elliot L. Gilbert, " 'In Primal Sympathy': *Great Expectations* and the Secret Life," *Dickens Studies Annual* 11 (1983), 92.

1. Gilbert, 98.

2. Art and social critic, who attacked the Victorian culture of materialism and self-interest, and in *Sesame and Lilies* (1865) idealized a private domestic sphere ruled by feminine values as a corrective. Sarah Stickney Ellis (1799–1882) wrote novels and conduct books that instructed women in self-denial, subordination to men, and domestic duty. [*Editor.*]

3. Quoted in Gallagher, *Industrial Reformation*, 118.

4. *GE*, 261.

5. Mary Poovey, "Speaking of the Body: Mid-Victorian Constructions of Female Desire," 36. In Jacobus, Keller, and Shuttleworth, 36.

6. See Gallagher, *Industrial Reformation*, and Nancy Armstrong, *Desire and Domestic Fiction: A Political History of the Novel* (New York: Oxford UP, 1987).

men as much as does cooperation. Miss Havisham and Estella cannot escape their economic role as "commodities." In *Great Expectations*, self-swindling characters like Pip, Estella, and Miss Havisham misconstrue the true economic nature of their romantic relationships.]

Judged according to the conventions of Victorian economic practice, Miss Havisham, like Mrs. Threadneedle and Maria Jolly Motherbank, illustrates a significant sort of female failure. Because she wrecks the brewery and refuses to sponsor her male relatives, she blocks her financial capital from circulating within the proper channels of investment and trade, thus rendering it economically barren. And because she dedicates herself to angry spinsterhood, she condemns her sexual body to infertile disuse and enters her forties as a textbook case of the tragically embittered climacteric woman. Under the best of circumstances, physicians reported, the climacteric sufferer often feels driven to "revenge supposed grievances by making miserable those under her control."[7] She chews "the cud of baleful introspection"[8] and "peoples the void with imaginary evils . . . [sitting] alone for weeks and months, in the darkened room of some gloomy dwelling, without any other enjoyment than solitude, or that of brooding over unbegotten evils."[9] Such women turn "sour, excitable, irascible; often falling into passion without provocation, they become unjust toward every body."[1] Some, experiencing a recrudescence of sexual desire, become "tyrannized by the memory of past love," which nearly always leads to "the most formidable results."[2] Health manuals and conduct books, likewise, urged the climacteric woman to cast aside perverse obsessions with youth and chastely eschew "every thing calculated to cause regret for charms that are lost, and enjoyments that are ended forever."[3] For notwithstanding these grim prognoses, writers assured her, the apocalypse of menopause would almost certainly give way to the millenium of peaceful old age. And while nothing can bring back the splendor in the grass, climacteric survivors may yet find strength in what remains behind—charitable works, newfound serenity, relief from the hazards of childbearing—once "their features are stamped with the imprint of age, and their genital organs are sealed with the signet of sterility."[4]

Contrary to advice, Miss Havisham keeps the idea of a sexual self always before her, gleefully watching the gap widen between bridal promise and atrophied reality. Her perambulations with Pip, as he wheels her about the decayed remains of the wedding feast, not only parody the breakdown of economic "circulation" (the defunct production-and-exchange life of her father's brewery) but also mimic the mental orbits of the older woman trapped in the circular grooves of memory. Incongruous images of youth characterize Miss Havisham to the end. When Estella reproves her for her harsh curriculum of heartbreaking, she falls prostrate with her long grey hair "all adrift upon the ground, among the other bridal wrecks," more like the adulterous

7. Tilt, *Change*, 158.
8. Tilt, *Change*, 101.
9. Tilt, *Change*, 159.
1. Columbat, 40.
2. Columbat, 40.
3. Columbat, 551.
4. Columbat, 549.

wife in Augustus Egg's *Past and Present*[5] than a castigated mother.[6] Later, when she kneels for Pip's forgiveness, she presses one of his hands as he clasps her supplicating body, and then, much to his horror, sinks further "down upon the ground," drawing him with her.[7] Finally, when she bursts into flames in the spectacular fire scene filled with sexual overtones of assault and rape, Pip works hard to extinguish not so much the return of the repressed but the last, furious eruption of the all-too-expressed.

As in the case of Mrs. Threadneedle and Mrs. Motherbank, the same paranoia, sleeplessness, and desolation that identify Miss Havisham as a climacteric woman also mark her as the quintessential swindled capitalist. At the urging of Compeyson, her husband-to-be, she had bought out her brother Arthur's brewery stock at an enormously inflated rate so that her husband might exercise absolute control over the business. When the "handwriting forging, stolen bank-note passing" lover betrayed her, she fell victim to a version of the uncontrolled speculation and fraud many thought had precipitated the 1840's railway crises and the Depression of 1858.[8] And like her predecessors Mrs. Threadneedle and Mrs. Motherbank, as an older woman Miss Havisham offers a displaced resolution to the macroeconomic problem of financial crisis, to the microeconomic threat of individual bankruptcy, and to the general predicament of toiling men whose powers of economic self-determination seemed cramped, thwarted, or nullified entirely. Pip succeeds in forging a modest competency within the humanizing offices of Clarriker and Company. But Miss Havisham, despite making contrite atonements, despite awaiting death wrapped in gauze bandages, essentially departs from the novel in a blaze, as if she were the self-consuming engine of old finally burned up by its own overheated works. Hers is the tyrannized body and shackled mind, the internal "clashing and whirling" within a terrible apparatus. Where Pip awakes from his fevered hallucinations into renewed life, she moves inexorably from nightmare into death.

*   *   *

III

Great Expectations makes the past usable for the present even as it acknowledges that "the old order changeth, yielding place to new."[9] The careful signposts by which Dickens recognizes the gap between England in the first quarter of the century and the moment in which the novel is read call attention to how difficult it is to row against the currents of time. But not impossible: we *can* go back again, the novel suggests, by clinging to those who move forward in slow, conservative ways. This is the message of Biddy and Joe's forge, complete with tiny replicas of Biddy and Pip ("and there, fenced into the corner with Joe's leg, and sitting on my own little stool looking at

5. Augustus Egg (1816–1863), English painter and close friend of Dickens's, whose tripartite painting *Past and Present* (1858) depicts the aftermath of a woman's adultery. [*Editor.*]

6. *GE*, 325.

7. *GE*, 410.

8. *GE*, 362. See J. R. T. Hughes, "The Commercial Crisis of 1857," *Oxford Economic Papers*, New Series 8 (June 1956), 194–222; S. G. Checkland, *The Rise of Industrial Society in England 1815–1885* (London: Longmans, 1964); E. A. J. Johnson, *An Economic History of England* (New York: Thomas Nelson, 1939); and Francois Crouzet, *The Victorian Economy* (New York: Columbia UP, 1982).

9. From Tennyson's "The Passing of Arthur" (1869), 1.408. [*Editor*].

the fire, was—I again!"[1]) Within the model family, Biddy performs the maternal and economic duties Miss Havisham had abdicated. She not only supplies an infant Pip for the cottage corner, but also replaces with the "light pressure" of the wedding ring on her "good matronly hand" the clenched fists and explosive passions of Mrs. Joe, Molly, and Miss Havisham. As Pip noticed as a boy, Biddy knew the smithing business so minutely that "theoretically, she was already as good a blacksmith as I, or better."[2] Proficiencies that might masculinize her, such as her "theoretical" forge skills or her scholarly learning, at which she also excelled as a girl, become her woman's contribution to the family enterprise. Good wives like Biddy guarantee historical continuity and economic equilibrium by perpetuating values and practices from one generation to the next; they become one of the means by which Dickens "figures history as home."[3] They do so as reproducers of people and cultures without themselves being the "subjects," Carlylean heroes and makers,[4] of the official historical record.

The plot line involving Pip, however, does not fully participate in the novel's recuperative ending, hindered not only by Pip and Estella's emotional exhaustion but also by the representational limits of Dickens's narrative. After all, like the *Punch* artists and parodists before him, Dickens cannot change the mechanizing and dehumanizing dynamics of laissez-faire commerce by locating them within an older woman's climacteric body. "Analogizing" the problem may offer symbolic resolutions yet must inevitably stop short of effecting "real" reforms of a recalcitrant material culture, the world "out there" filled with journeyman Pips. * * * But cyclical crises remained a problem for the Victorian economy, as was amply demonstrated in the "depressions" of 1862 and 1868.[5] * * *

* * *

Perhaps, this doubt is the final legacy of the "immensely rich and grim lady" of Satis House. For if Miss Havisham is a symbolic indicator of economic problems, she is also an actual, monied woman whose economic transgressions have lasting, discernible effects upon the commercial and marital destinies of the novel's young people. When the famous mists of the novel's last line rise to reveal a "broad expanse of tranquil light" in which Pip, in that ambiguous phrase, sees "no shadow of another parting from her," they also disclose a future not yet under construction. What Pip and Estella stand upon is the "desolate" ground of the family enterprise leveled by Miss Havisham, the dupe and perpetuator of a ruthless, "Beggar My Neighbor" economics. Even the triumphs of the more fortunate are subtly qualified. No married couple in the novel has successfully merged domestic felicity and commercial engagement without also being dissociated from contemporary England in some way. Joe and Biddy inhabit an idealized forge already rel-

1. GE, 490.
2. GE, 153.
3. Christina Crosby, *The Ends of History: Victorians and "The Woman Question"* (New York: Routledge, 1991), 70.
4. A reference to Thomas Carlyle's *On Heroes, Hero-Worship, and the Heroic in History*, a series of lectures delivered in 1840, published in 1841, in which Carlyle maintains that "Universal history * * * is at bottom the history of * * * Great Men" and in support of his view cites people like Odin as an example of The Hero as Divinity, Mohammed (The Hero as Prophet), Luther (The Hero as Priest), et al. [*Editor.*]
5. Crouzet, 57.

egated to the past; Herbert and Clara prosper in Cairo, a foreign annex of Britain's trading empire; Wemmick and Miss Skiffins live in a moated, miniature castle that epitomizes the *cordon sanitaire*[6] Victorians drew around "Walworth sentiments" to protect them from "Little Britain" heartlessness.

Pip and Herbert Pocket turn out to be tolerably good specimens of the modern economic man, but they can only do so abroad, a crucial limitation. It is as if, in *Great Expectations*, Dickens can see his way clear towards preserving the capitalist dream of the self-determining male economic agent, yet cannot tell a lie. Propertied godmothers do not always underwrite young men, or raise up dutiful daughters as future partners within the family enterprise. The climacteric body of Great Britain's Motherbank cannot really escape the periodic convulsions typical of older women in "catemenial decline." In this novel, when young men with empty pockets "look about" them in a world destabilized by shifting women's roles and a fickle, exclusionary marketplace, they cannot always wake from their economic dream to find it real.

---

6. Lit. "sanitary cordon" or "quarantine line"; barrier designed to keep contaminated areas (or undesirable contacts) from spreading to healthy neighborhoods (and safe contacts).

Charles Dickens: A Chronology

Life

1812–16 Friday Feb. 7: CD born at Mile End Terrace, Landport Portsmouth, second child and oldest son of John Dickens (1785/86–1851, m. 1809), clerk in the Navy Pay Office, and Elizabeth Barrow (1789–1863). Baptized (Mar. 4) Charles John Huffam Dickens. John Dickens is posted to the Admiralty Office in London (Jan. 1815–Dec. 1816).

1817–23 John Dickens transferred to Chatham, "the birthplace of [CD's] fancy." CD attends Dame School with his older sister Fanny (1810–1848), then (1821–22) the Rev. William Giles's School. Learns rudiments of Latin and grammar from his mother. John recalled to London (summer 1822). Dickenses (with six children by now) move from one lodging to another, chiefly in Camden Town, a largely rural area three miles north of London. Mrs. D opens a stillborn school for young ladies (Dec. 1823). Growing indigence of John D.

1824–27 Feb. 1824–June 1824: CD is sent to work at Warren's [Shoe] Blacking, Hungerford Stairs, the Strand ("No words can express the secret agony of my soul, as I sunk into this companionship"). Feb. 20–May 28, 1824: John imprisoned for debt at the Marshalsea, his wife and the younger children taking up residence with him at the jail some five weeks later. Released under the Insolvent Debtor's Act, retires from Naval Pay Office after nineteen years' service. CD attends Wellington House Academy, Hampstead Road (June 1824–Mar. 1827), where he takes the Latin prize and participates in school theatricals until John Dickens's financial embarrassments force him to withdraw from school.

Works

1822 Composes first tragedy, **Misnar, the Sultan of India**, modeled on *The Tales of the Genii*.

721

1827–33 Solicitor's clerk at Symond's Inn (Mar.–May 1827), at Gray's Inn (May 1827–Nov. 1828). Learns shorthand and becomes freelance reporter at Doctors' Commons, one of the ecclesiastical courts (1829?–1831?). Admitted as reader at the British Museum on his eighteenth birthday. Falls in love (May 1830) with Maria Beadnell, a banker's daughter (1810–1886); packed off to finishing school in Paris, she breaks off the romance (May? 1833).

1834–37 Late 1834?/early 1835: CD meets William Hogarth's oldest girl, Catherine (1815–1879), whom he marries Apr. 2, 1836, three days after he begins to write **Pickwick Papers**, and whom he installs in chambers in Furnivall's Inn, along with her younger sister Mary (b. 1819). Winter 1836–37: Introduced to John Forster (1812–1876), hereafter his closest friend and advisor, and his future hagiographer.

1837 Jan. 6: First child, Charles Culliford "Boz" (the pseudonym CD had adopted in 1834) born (d. 1896). Catherine bears nine more children: Mary (Mamie; 1838–1896), Kate Macready (1839–1929), Walter Landor (1841–1863, d. in India), Francis Jeffrey (1844–1886, d. in America), Alfred D'Orsay Tennyson (1845–1912, d. in America), Sidney Smith Haldimand (1847–1872, d. at sea), Henry Fielding (1849–1933), Dora Annie (Aug. 1850–Apr. 1851), Edward Bulwer Lytton (1852–1902, d. in Australia). Apr.: Family moves to Doughty St. (since 1924 the Dickens House). First of CD's public speeches (Literary Fund Anniversary, May 3). CD's much loved live-in sister-in-law Mary Hogarth dies

1831–33 Shorthand reporter for *The Mirror of Parliament* (transcripts of parliamentary debates). From May–July 1832 works concurrently as reporter for a new evening paper, the *True Sun*. Private theatricals at his parents' home (1833). First farce, **O'Thello** (unpublished). First story, "**A Dinner at Poplar Walk**" (later retitled "**Mr. Minns and His Cousin**") appears in all the glory of print" in the *Monthly Magazine* on Dec. 1, 1833.

1834–36 Jan. 1834–Feb. 1835: Eight more stories in *Monthly Magazine*. CD joins staff of the *Morning Chronicle* (Aug. 1834–Nov. 1836), which publishes his first "**Street Sketches**" and where he meets George Hogarth, Scottish music critic, editor of the *Evening Chronicle*, and his future father-in-law. Between Sept. 1834 and Jan. 1836 contributes more than forty sketches and tales ("**Street Sketches**," "**Sketches of London**," "**Scenes and Characters**") to *Monthly Magazine*, *Morning Chronicle*, *Evening Chronicle*, *Bell's Life in London*. Feb. 1836: CD's first volume, **Sketches by Boz, First Series**, published. **A Second Series** appears Dec. The publishers Chapman & Hall approach CD (Feb. 10) with a proposal that leads to the composition of **Pickwick Papers**, the novel that launches CD's popularity; published in nineteen monthly numbers (Mar. 1836–Oct. 1837). Apr.: Begins his long partnership with his illustrator Hablot Knight Browne ("Phiz"). Produces his first three farces, 1836–37: **The Strange Gentleman**, **The Village Coquettes**, **Is She His Wife?** Enters on a number of acrimonious relationships with his publishers (John Macrone, Richard Bentley).

1837–38 Jan. 1837: Begins editing *Bentley's Miscellany*. Jan. number contains the first of three **Mudfog Papers**; papers 2 and 3 in Oct. 1837. To gather material for **Nicholas Nickleby**, CD and Browne inspect the notorious Yorkshire boarding schools (Jan. 30–Feb. 6, 1837). **Oliver Twist** in twenty-four monthly installments (Jan. 1837–Apr. 1839) in *Bentley's*. (From Jan.–Oct. 1837 CD writes **Pickwick** and **Oliver** concurrently.) Feb. 1838: **Sketches of Young Gentlemen**. Edits **Memoirs of Grimaldi**, the great clown's autobiography; published Feb. 26. **Nicholas Nickleby** in monthly numbers (Mar. 1838–Oct. 1839). Nov.: A farce, **The Lamplighter** (first aired in 1879).

(May 7); CD suspends June publication of **Pickwick** and **Oliver** and composes an epitaph worthy of a grammarian's funeral: "Young, beautiful, and good, God numbered her among his angels at the early age of 17." July: First visit to the Continent (France and Belgium).

1839–41 CD's parents exiled to a cottage in Devon. Family moves to 1 Devonshire Terrace, Regent's Park (Dec. 1839). CD invited but declines to stand as Liberal MP for Reading (May 29, 1841). Tours Scotland: lionized at Edinburgh and given Freedom of the City, his first public honor (June 29).

1842 Jan. 4–22: CD and Kate sail from Liverpool to Boston. Speaks on international copyright in Boston, Hartford, New York; inspects prisons in NY, Philadelphia, Pittsburg (and meets Pres. John Tyler in Washington); tours Midwest by steamboat; Niagara, Canada. Meets Longfellow ("a frank, accomplished man"), William Cullen Bryant ("a sad one and very reserved"), Washington Irving ("a great fellow"). June 7–29: Voyage home. Kate's youngest sister, Georgina, joins the household. CD enters into informal philanthropic partnership (till about 1858) with the fantastically wealthy heiress Angela Burdett Coutts (1814–1906).

1844–45 The first of prolonged sojourns on the Continent: CD and the clan (Kate, Georgina, six children, servant, courier, and dog) settle in Genoa for nearly a year (July 1844–June 1845). Apr. 1845: CD detours to Paris and London, where he reads his Christmas Book **The Chimes** to a group of illustrious friends. Produces and acts in Ben Jonson's *Every Man in His Humour* in Soho (Sept. 20, 1845), the first of many amateur performances.

1839–41 Begins to write, then shelves, his first historical novel, **Barnaby Rudge** (Jan. 1839). Feb.: Informs Bentley that he will deliver completed **Barnaby** by Jan. 1, 1840. Dec.: Informs Bentley that he won't. **Sketches of Young Couples** (Feb. 1840). Contracts with Chapman & Hall to edit a weekly miscellany of tales and sketches, **Master Humphrey's Clock**, largely as an outlet for his own fiction (first number Apr. 1840). **The Old Curiosity Shop** in forty weekly installments in **Master Humphrey** Apr. 1840–Feb. 1841. **Barnaby Rudge** directly follows **Curiosity Shop** Feb.–Nov. 1841. Aug. 9: **Pic Nic Papers**, a three-vol. potpourri of stories, essays, poems, ed. by CD with contributions by lesser writers in aid of the family of CD's first publisher, John Macrone (1809–1837). Vol. 1 leads off with a narrative adaptation of CD's luckless farce **The Lamplighter**.

1842 **American Notes**, an often derisive account of CD's adventures among the Yankees in two vols. (Oct. 1842), riles the natives. **Martin Chuzzlewit** in monthly numbers Dec. 1842–June 1844. To boost its sagging sales, CD packs his hero off to America in no. 7: sales instantly rise and so do colonial tempers, bilious at CD's treatment of everything from NY journalism to Midwestern land speculation. (At a burlesque performance of *Macbeth* in Boston, **Chuzzlewit** is pitched into the witches' cauldron, along with worthless Pennsylvania bonds and Mexican rifles.)

1843–45 Dec. 19, 1843: **A Christmas Carol**, the first and best-known of CD's five Christmas Books (and the rest of his work). Succeeded in following years (late Dec.) by **The Chimes** (1844), **The Cricket on the Hearth** (1845), **The Battle of Life** (1846), **The Haunted Man** (1848). Livid at the proceeds from the sales of **Christmas Carol** CD leaves Chapman & Hall for Bradbury & Evans ("I opened the Carol account on Saturday Night . . . [and] I have slept as badly

Life

1846–48 More foreign travels. Lausanne and Geneva (June–Nov. 1846). Paris (Nov. 1846–Feb. 1847). CD meets his French confrères: Lamartine, Gautier, Dumas père, Victor Hugo ("who looks a Genius . . . from head to foot. His wife is a handsome woman with flashing black eyes, who looks as if she might poison his breakfast any morning"). With the help of Burdett Coutts, CD sets up a "Home for Homeless [i.e., 'Fallen'] Women" (Urania Cottage) in Shepherd's Bush (opens Nov. 1847). First amateur performances in the provinces ("Splendid Strolling") in Manchester and Liverpool to benefit indigent writers Leigh Hunt and John Poole (July 1847). More performances mid-May 1848 at the Haymarket, Victoria and Albert attending (May 7). CD's most talented sibling, Fanny, dies Sept. 2, 1848.

1850–51 Explores with Bulwer-Lytton the creation of a "Guild of Literature and Art" to assist needy writers and artists. Kate suffers nervous breakdown (Mar. 1851), John Dickens dies (Mar. 31), Dora Annie dies (Apr. 14), Bulwer's *Not So Bad As We Seem* premieres (May 16) before the royals. Purchases Tavistock House, Bloomsbury (July). Catherine Dickens publishes her maiden (and final) work, the cookbook *What Shall We Have For Dinner?* under the pseudonym Lady Maria Clutterbuck.

1852–55 On the verge of nervous collapse, CD escapes to Boulogne with his family (June–Oct. 1853). To Switzerland and Italy (Oct.–Dec. 1853) with his protégé Wilkie Collins (1824–1889) and the painter Augustus Egg (1816–1863). Increasingly cultivates the friendships of younger writers (G. A. Sala, 1829–1896; James Payn, 1830–1898; Edmund Yates, 1831–1894; Percy Fitzgerald, 1834–

Works

as Macbeth ever since.") Edits **Evenings of a Working Man** by John Overs (1808–1844), fatally ill cabinet maker and patient of CD's mesmerist friend, John Elliotson.

1846–49 Briefly edits *Daily News* (Jan. 21–Feb. 5, 1846). Continues to write for the paper, notably his letters on capital punishment (Feb.–Mar. 1846). **Pictures from Italy** (May 1846), an engaging travel book marred (often with unintended hilarity) by CD's anti-Catholic bigotry and insular view of the visual arts. **Dombey and Son** in monthly numbers Sept. 1846–Mar. 1848, much of it written in Lausanne and Paris. **An Appeal to Fallen Women** (Oct.? 1847) written to promote Urania Cottage. Hands Forster his "**Autobiographical Fragment**" on his shaming work in the blacking factory (Jan. 1849; probably written 1845/46). CD's presence at the hanging of George and Maria Manning at Horsemonger Gaol provokes his letters to the *Times*, in which he pillories public executions (Nov. 14 and 18, 1849). **David Copperfield** in monthly numbers (Apr. 1849–Oct. 1850).

1850–51 Mar. 27, 1850 (to May 28, 1859): edits, publishes, and owns half shares in the weekly *Household Words*, to which he contributes personal and polemical essays; the journal carries an annual Christmas Number, containing novellas written in collaboration with other writers—a practice to be continued in the successor journal *All the Year Round*. CD dictates (an exceptional practice) **A Child's History of England** to Georgina; this appears in *HW* from Jan. 1851 to Dec. 1853.

1852–55 **Bleak House** in monthly numbers Feb. 1852–Sept. 1853. In Preston, Lancashire (late Jan. 1854) to observe millworkers' strike and collect background for **Hard Times**; in twenty weekly installments in *Household Words*, Apr.–Aug. 1854. **Little Dorrit** in monthly numbers (Nov. 1855–June 1857). Christmas Numbers: **The Seven Poor Travellers** (1854), **The Holly Tree** (1855).

1925). Dec. 27–30, 1853: First public readings for charity (**Christmas Carol**) in aid of Birmingham and Midland Institute—readings for charity continue till 1858. Dines (and sermonizes) at Lord John Russell's, with Meyerbeer the composer as rapt audience (July).

1856–57 Purchases Gad's Hill Place, the red-brick mansion north of Rochester on the Dover Road, from his fellow writer Eliza Lynn Linton (Mar. 1856). Fall 1856: Rehearsals of Wilkie Collins's *The Frozen Deep*, one of the sources of **A Tale of Two Cities**; first performance Jan. 6, 1857. CD's future mistress, the eighteen-year-old Ellen Ternan (1839–1914); her mother; and her older sister join the cast in August. (CD's first meeting with Ellen uncertainly the previous Apr.) That "bony bore" (Mamie's and Katie's putdown) Hans Christian Andersen is invited to Gad's for two weeks and stays five (June–July 1857). His childishness and unintelligible prattle drive his hosts dotty. ("In French or Italian he [is] the Wild boy; in English, the Deaf and Dumb Asylum.").

1858 Apr. 29–July 22: First public readings for profit. These turn virtually into CD's second profession. More provincial readings; readings in Ireland and Scotland; occasional Christmas or Easter auditions. (Eighty-three readings alone Aug.–Nov. 1858.) CD and Kate separate (May 1858) after twenty-three years of marriage; they never meet again. Charley to stay with Kate (who is banished to Regent's Park); the other children plus Georgina with CD. CD publicizes his separation in the *Times* and *Household Words* (June 7 and 12) to defuse rumors of his having bedded Ellen (or Georgina).

1860–62 CD's daughter Kate marries Wilkie's brother, the pre-Raphaelite painter Charles Allston Collins (1828–1875) on July 17, 1860; the mother is not invited. CD destroys all correspondence in auto-da-fé at Gad's Hill (Sept. 3). Tavistock House sold (Sept. 4) to Jewish banker J. B. Davies ("Tavistock House is cleared today and possession delivered up to the house of Israel"). Settles into Gad's Hill as his permanent home but maintains quarters in the office of *All the Year Round*.

1857–58 Sept. 7–22: With Wilkie Collins in Cumberland to collect material for **A Lazy Tour of Two Idle Apprentices**, in *HW* Oct. 3–31. Devotes himself to work for Sick Children's Hospital (Nov.). Breach with Thackeray following a social flap (Nov.). Official breach with the publishers and editor of *Punch*, Bradbury & Evans and his friend Mark Lemon, for their refusal to publish CD's domestic trials (July 1858). Breach with "Phiz." Christmas Numbers: **The Perils of Certain English Prisoners** (1857), **Going into Society** (1858).

1859 Apr. until CD's death: *All the Year Round* supplants *Household Words*. (After CD's death the editorship devolves on Charley.) **A Tale of Two Cities** is launched in its opening number in thirty weekly installments (Apr.–Nov.), concurrently in monthly numbers (June–Dec.). By May 28, the circulation of *All the Year Round* has trebled that of *Household Words*; will reach a circulation of three hundred thousand within ten years. **Hunted Down**, story based on the career of artist/critic/family-poisoner (Aug. 20, 27, Sept. 3, 1859). Christmas Number: **The Haunted House.**

1860–61 Begins series of papers **The Uncommercial Traveller** in *All the Year Round* (Jan. 28, 1860); fifteen more papers appear between Feb. and Oct. containing pieces directly relevant to **Great Expectations** ("Dullborough Town," "Chambers," "Nurse's Stories," "Arcadian London"). Published as **The Uncommercial Traveller, First Series** (Dec. 1860). With Wilkie Collins in North Devon to collect material for their joint Christmas Story "A Message from the

Sea" (Nov.). First installment of **Great Expectations** (opening two and a half chapters) published from early proof in *Harper's Weekly*, New York (Nov. 24, 1860); in weekly installments in *All the Year Round* (Dec. 1860–Aug. 1861). Three-volume (first) edition July 5, 1861. Christmas Number for 1861: **Tom Tiddler's Ground**.

1862–66 **Our Mutual Friend** in monthly installments (May 1864–Nov. 1865). Christmas Numbers: **Somebody's Luggage** (1862); **Mrs. Lirriper's Lodgings** (1863); **Mrs. Lirriper's Legacy** (1864); **Doctor Marigold** (1865); **Mugby Junction** (1866).

1867–68 "**George Silverman's Explanation**" and "**A Holiday Romance**" written for American market: "**Silverman**" published in *Atlantic Monthly* (Jan.–Mar. 1867), "**Holiday Romance**" (four stories written as though told by children) in *Our Young Folks* (Jan.–May 1868). His final Christmas Story (with Wilkie Collins), **No Thoroughfare** (Oct./Nov. 1867; dramatized Dec. 1867). Chauncy Hare Townsend, dedicatee of **Great Expectations**, dies Feb. 25, 1868; CD edits Townsend's **Religious Opinions**; published 1869.

Engages 3 Hanover Terrace, Regent's Park (Jan. 1861) as a temporary London pied-à-terre. Charley marries Bessie Evans, daughter of CD's estranged publisher; CD declines to attend the wedding (Nov. 1861). Rents 16 Hyde Park Gate (Feb. 1862), partly "for [his] daughter's sake"—that is, to provide Mamie with the male company and close encounters she lacks at Gad's Hill. Reluctantly declines offer of ten thousand pounds for eight-month reading tour in Australia (June 1862).

1863–66 Depletions at home and abroad: CD's mother dies, hopelessly senile (Sept. 13, 1863); Thackeray dies (Dec. 1863), reconciled with CD, who writes his obit in the *Cornhill Magazine* (Feb. 1864); Walter dies in Calcutta (Dec. 31, 1863); Frank leaves for India (Jan. 1864); Alfred sails for Australia (May 29, 1865); youngest brother, Augustus, dies penniless in Chicago (Oct. 6, 1866). CD's own health worsens alarmingly; early symptoms of thrombosis. On return journey from Paris holiday, CD and Ellen are in spectacular railway accident at Staplehurst, Kent (June 9, 1865). CD administers aid and brandy to the wounded and dying (thus, pace Bernard Shaw, insuring their deaths) and recovers manuscript of **Our Mutual Friend** from the wreckage. Takes a house for Ellen in Slough (Jan.? 1866–July 1867).

1867–68 Secures Windsor Lodge, Peckham for Ellen (June? 1867–July 1870). Against all medical advice, undertakes reading tour in America Dec. 1867–Apr. 1868. Itinerary includes (Dec.–Jan.) Boston, New York (Henry Ward Beecher's chapel in Brooklyn), Philadelphia, Washington (Pres. Andrew Johnson having him in for a meal at the White House), Baltimore; (Mar.–Apr.) upstate New York ("Syracuse is a rather depressing feather in the [American] eagle's wing, when considered on a Sunday and in a thaw"), New England. Entertains American friends at Gad's Hill (summer 1868). CD's youngest and favorite son, Edward ("Plorn"), sails for Australia (Sept. 26); the one promising son, Henry, wins scholarship to Trinity College, Cambridge (Oct.). Fred Dickens dies Oct. 20. CD tries out the chilling "**Sikes and Nancy**" episode from **Oliver Twist** on his friends (Nov.).

1869–70 First public airing of **"Sikes and Nancy"** (Jan. 5), CD running up a pulse of 120. Reports to Mamie on Jan. 27 that the murder produced "a contagion of fainting," at Clifton: "I should think we had from a dozen to twenty ladies taken out stiff and rigid." Readings abandoned after CD's collapse at Preston (Apr. 22, 1870). Makes his will (May 1869). Final farewell reading at St. James Hall (Mar. 15): "From these garish lights I now vanish forevermore . . ." Audience at Buckingham Palace (May 9). June 8: After a full day's work on **Edwin Drood** CD suffers a stroke—not clear whether at home or at Ellen's. June 9: Dies of cerebral hemorrhage at Gad's Hill at 6:10 P.M. without having regained consciousness. June 14: CD's body conveyed by train from Gad's Hill to Charing Cross for private funeral. Burial in Poet's Corner, Westminster Abbey.

1869–70 Begins composition of **The Mystery of Edwin Drood** (Oct. 1869); monthly numbers Apr.–Sept. 1870. First bound publication of the unfinished **Drood** Aug. 12, 1870, two months after CD's death.

727

Selected Bibliography

Essays and books from which material has been excerpted for "Contexts," "Early Comments," and "Essays" in this edition are not included. I have, however, absorbed titles that are cited in my footnotes; without them, I should be left without a bibliography altogether.

I. Periodicals

The most widely read and historically much the most informative of the journals is *The Dickensian*, issued three times a year (originally quarterly) by the Dickens Fellowship, London, since 1905. Now in its ninety-third year, the journal reflects the shifting scholarly and critical attitudes of nearly a century, from the early fuzzy anecdotal pieces, Dickens quizzes, mock trials of *Edwin Drood*, and life-threatening feuds over topographical sources to current critical methods—though still comparatively conservative, the journal, under its most recent editors, has ventured an occasional poststructuralist piece. *The Dickensian* has attracted every major scholar in the field (and a great many first-rate nonacademic writers, from Shaw and G. K. Chesterton on down) and has been an invaluable source for researchers, if only because it publishes absolutely anything that might be of interest to Dickensians, from the awesome prospect that the GE manuscript might have to be sold to America to the embarrassing disclosure that at least three of Dickens's novels were avidly read by the Nuremberg war criminals (*Pickwick Papers, Oliver Twist, A Tale of Two Cities*). The American quarterly, *Dickens Studies* (Boston, Mass.), founded in 1965, died with its editor, Noel Peyrouton, in 1969. It was succeeded in 1970 by *The Dickens Studies Newsletter* (Louisville, Ky.), a deceptively diffident title discarded in favor of *Dickens Quarterly* in 1984. Under the editorships of Duane DeVries and David Paroissien, *The Quarterly* (the official organ of the American Dickens Society) publishes scholarly and critical articles, review-essays, and reviews of a very high caliber, and it regularly features what is now the most exhaustive bibliographical aid, a "Dickens Checklist," which has become the more nearly indispensable since the bibliography by George Worth (q.v.) stops in 1983. The bibliographical entries from *The Newsletter* have been collected in a volume by Alan Cohn and K. K. Collins, *The Cumulated Dickens Checklist: 1970–1979* (1982). *Dickens Studies Annual: Essays on Victorian Fiction*, founded and edited by Robert Partlow in 1970 (Carbondale: Southern Illinois Press), edited since 1980 by Michael Timko, Fred Kaplan, and Edward Guiliano (New York: AMS Press), is roomy enough—300 to 350 pages—to accommodate much longer articles than those that appear in the journals; a great many of the pieces that have appeared in its twenty-six volumes to date contain the best that has been thought and said of Dickens. A thorough but reasonably selective survey of

"Recent Dickens Studies," generally written by a seasoned Dickensian, usually comes with the *Annual*.

II. Bibliographies

The indispensable text remains George J. Worth, *GE: An Annotated Bibliography* (1986), in the excellent series of Garland bibliographies of Dickens.
It covers the years 1860 to 1983 and cites early editions, and though it runs
to more than 1,110 entries, Worth's arrangement is helpful in locating the
desired items, and a useful subject index is included. The most substantial
discursive bibliographies are to be found in the two volumes entitled *Victorian
Fiction: A Guide to Research*, the first, ed. Lionel Stevenson (1964), the Dickens chapter by Ada Nisbet, 44–113; the second, ed. George Ford (1978), the
Dickens chapter by Philip Collins, 34–113. Unlike Worth, both Nisbet and
Collins include the more important foreign imports. Useful by Philip Collins,
too, especially for its citation of primary sources, is the reprint of his bibliography from *The New Cambridge Bibliography of English Literature*, ed.
George Watson (Cambridge University Press and The Dickens Fellowship),
vol. 3, 779–850. The long essay "Dickens and Fame: 1870–1970," *The Dickensian Centenary Number 66* (May 1970): 73–182, with contributions by
K. J. Fielding, Sylvère Monod, Michael Slater, Philip Collins, and George
Ford, provides a fascinating overview of Dickens criticism by five leading
scholars. Timed to appear on the same anniversary, Joseph Gold, *The Stature
of Dickens: A Centenary Bibliography* (1971) remains a compact bibliography
with foreign entries assembled by Donald Fanger; on GE, 167–74. John J.
Fenstermaker, in *Charles Dickens: 1940–75—Analytical Subject Index to Periodical Criticism of the Novels and Christmas Books* (1979), opts for a handy
arrangement by topic; on GE, 199–217. The two compilations that address
Dickens's periodicals, both containing essential biographies of contributors,
are Anne Lohrli, *Household Words: A Weekly Journal 1850–1859* (1973), and
Ella Ann Oppenlander, *Dickens' All the Year Round: A Descriptive Index
and Contributor List* (1984). The best brief descriptive survey of modern
Dickens criticism is Anny Sadrin's commentary in her chapter "Prefaces to
the Next" in her *GE* (q.v.), 245–75, which not only has the advantage of its
brevity but is also as intelligent an arrangement by topic as these things allow
for.

III. Biographies of Dickens

If four of anything can be definitive, the definitive biographies are John
Forster's *Life of Charles Dickens* (1872–74), Edgar Johnson's *Charles Dickens:
His Tragedy and Triumph* (2 vols., 1952), Fred Kaplan's *Dickens: A Biography*
(1988), and Peter Ackroyd's *Dickens* (1990). As I have indicated earlier, Forster has been rapped over the knuckles for the liberties he took with his
materials—not least with Dickens's letters—to present both his subject and
himself in the best light; but despite these blemishes, the *Life* remains one
of the major texts of the period. And for all of Forster's prissiness, the book
has the unique merit that intimacy with the subject confers, and arguably
nobody since has rivaled him. J. W. T. Ley's one-volume edition (1928) has
long been used as a convenient text; this has been superseded by J. A. Hoppé

(2 vols., 1966 and 1969) with its richly amplified annotation, which makes full use of materials that would have made Forster's hair stand on end. For hurried readers who want the benefit of Forster but not the full benefit, the *Life* has been abridged to 350 pages by Dickens's first major critic, George Gissing (1903). Edgar Johnson's biographical update has had the singular twice-blessed fortune of being a monumentally academic, enormously researched work that has also sold nearly three hundred thousand copies, though it is doubtful whether the members of the Book of the Month Club soaked up all its footnotes and genealogical charts. Johnson's prose is not elegant, and almost from day one Johnson was criticized for mixing matter and impertinency by overstepping the biographer's job and lacing his text with long critical interchapters on each novel as his slow passage came to a stop at each. These were removed, and the book was reissued with great editorial tact at half its length twenty-five years later (1977). Once its irritating qualities are overlooked, the original Johnson, though not free from errors (in dating, attribution, etc.), remains, in Jamesian phrase, the most richly "done." A biographer of Dickens and James both, Fred Kaplan, coming almost forty years after Johnson, has written what is the all-round most polished and most readable of the lives, Kaplan again using materials unavailable to earlier biographers tactfully, with a refined will to selection. A decade after its publication, the book remains psychologically the most penetrating, and Kaplan steers clear from both the hero worship and the emotional self-indulgence of his more ambitious precursors. Far and away the tersest part of Ackroyd's recent twelve-hundred-page blockbuster is its seven-letter title. Unlike the others, Ackroyd is primarily a novelist and a poet, and one glance at his *Dickens* (to cite its full title) should persuade one that it has much more nearly the makings of a best-seller than Johnson's ponderous labor of love. Not unexpectedly, Ackroyd has a wonderful sense for the anecdotal and a gift for bouncing Dickens's friends into instant life. In many ways Ackroyd (like Julius Caesar and Matthew Pocket) is his own worst enemy: his garrulousness conceals the fund of reading and research that is buried in every sentence (Ackroyd dispenses with footnotes as if superscript numbers were ill-favored poppy seeds); and every so often he interrupts the narrative to make room for an improving chat between himself and an imaginary interviewer, or other self, on the way he wrote *Dickens*. If it were less compelling, the book would be better read in bits and pieces.

IV. Biographical Studies and Reminiscences

In addition to the four large *Lives*, a number of shorter studies deserve to be cited (Jerome Meckier noted that at the time it appeared Ackroyd's was the thirty-seventh Dickens biography—a very conservative estimate, I think): notably Christopher Hibbert, *The Making of Charles Dickens* (1967), perhaps the best and most pleasingly written account covering the years from Dickens's childhood to his early career as a journalist; spanning the same period, the engaging early biography by Robert Langton, *The Childhood and Youth of Dickens* [1891] (1912); most thoroughly (and, for specialists, indispensably), Michael Allen's detective work in dating Dickens's moves through the 1820s, *Charles Dickens's Childhood* (1988). Of the earlier full-length biographies, worth singling out are T. A. Jackson, *Charles Dickens: The Progress of a*

Radical (1937); Una Pope-Hennessy's *Charles Dickens: 1812–1870* (1946); Jack Lindsay, *Charles Dickens* (1950); and Angus Wilson, *The World of Charles Dickens* (1970), the most beautifully illustrated of the short Lives; and, most recently, Graham Smith, *Charles Dickens: A Literary Life* (1996), which usefully foregrounds CD's relation to his publishers, his journalism, readings, and showmanship. Thomas Wright of Olney stood the world on its ear with his disclosure of Dickens's twelve-year liaison with Ellen Ternan in his *The Life of Charles Dickens* (1935). Following Wright's volcanic exposé, the murky Ternan affair was given a fresh airing in Ada Nisbet, *Dickens and Ellen Ternan* (1952); since then, more fully (than necessary), Claire Tomalin, *The Invisible Woman: The Story of Nellie Ternan and Charles Dickens* (1991). Given his credentials, it is hardly a surprise that Dickens should have attracted more than the usual number of reminiscences by his contemporaries and members of his family. Philip Collins has assembled extracts from dozens of these, including oral histories, in his *Interviews and Recollections* (2 vols., 1981), from Dickens's nurse to his office boys. One of the most intimate portraits emerges from the manager of Dickens's readings, George Dolby: *Charles Dickens as I Knew Him: The Story of His Reading Tours in Great Britain and America* [1885] (1912)—pace Collins, Dickens's daughter Mamie thought this the single best book about her father. All of Dickens's "young men" have written about him, prominently George Augustus Sala in his *Charles Dickens* (1870) and *Life and Adventures of George Augustus Sala* (2 vols., 1896), and Percy Fitzgerald, *Memoirs of an Author* (1895), *Life of Charles Dickens* (2 vols., 1905), and *Memories of Charles Dickens* (1913), the last containing detailed accounts of Dickens's editorial activities. Though Philip Collins calls Fitzgerald a liar and deplores Dickens's trust in him, his lies are never less than engaging and some of them so pointless that they may well be half-truths. Though nearly all of Dickens's children have left recollections of life with Father, the two most tersely informative (despite the inevitably pious voice) are Mary [Mamie] Dickens, *My Father as I Recall Him* [1897] (1912), and Henry Fielding Dickens, *Memories of My Father* (1928). To these should be added the close-ups by Charles Kent, *Charles Dickens as a Reader* (1872), and by his closest American friend, James T. Fields, *Yesterdays with Authors* (1872). Finally, of the full-length accounts not by but of Dickens's family, arguably the two most important are Michael Slater, *Dickens and Women* (1983), notably part 1, and Arthur A. Adrian, *Georgina Hogarth and the Dickens Circle* (1957). Though one would not think that a book that ostensibly deals with one of Dickens's sisters-in-law can be more than an in-group exercise, Adrian's biography gives what remains perhaps the most detailed account of Dickens's later years.

V. Aids to Research

In my prefatory note to his correspondence about *GE*, I suggested that as a letter writer Dickens is nearly peerless, and he seems to have written incomparably more than anyone else. The ongoing edition of his complete letters, the Pilgrim Edition of *The Letters of Charles Dickens* (1965–), a project initiated by Humphry House before his death in 1955, which will run to some twelve or thirteen volumes (the volumes ranging from seven hundred to nearly one thousand pages), is generally regarded as the single most monumental work of Dickens scholarship now in the works. Under the editorship of the late Madeline House, Graham Storey, Kathleen Tillotson, K. J. Fielding, and others, ten volumes have appeared as of 1998, taking Dickens to 1864. The letters covering the period 1859–61 appear in vol. 9, ed. Graham Storey et al. (1996). For the years 1864–70, readers need to consult the *Nonesuch Letters*, ed. Walter Dexter (3 vols., 1938), the best edition until 1965. The annotation of the Pilgrim *Letters* itself is staggering enough to make Quintilian stare and gasp and has been invaluable to scholars. Naturally, a lot of the letters are scraps of the "Can you come for chops?" variety. Briefer volumes contain *The Letters of Charles Dickens 1833–1870 by His Sister-in-Law and Eldest Daughter* (1893), with good interstitial commentary by Georgina and Mamie; much more recently, F. W. Dupee, *Selected Letters of Charles Dickens* (1960), and, more copiously, David Paroissien, *Selected Letters* (1985). Other needful tools for research include *The Speeches of Charles Dickens*, ed. K. J. Fielding (1960); *Charles Dickens: The Public Readings*, ed. Philip Collins (1975), on GE, 305–63; also by Collins, his collection of contemporary reviews, *Dickens: The Critical Heritage* (1971), 427–42. The critical history of GE, with generous chunks of extracts and an excellent bibliography, is now available in Nicholas Tredell, *Charles Dickens: Great Expectations* (1998). David Paroissien's indispensable *The GE Companion* (1999) provides the fullest available annotation of the novel. Anybody interested in Dickens's habits of composition will want to consult the notebook Dickens kept from 1855 to his death as a brief storehouse of ideas, *Charles Dickens's Book of Memoranda: A Photographic and Typographic Facsimile*, ed. Fred Kaplan (1981), and the "number plans" Dickens jotted down while writing his books, *Dickens' Working Notes for His Novels*, ed. Harry Stone (1987), again with photographic and typographic reproductions on facing pages, the most scrupulously and beautifully reproduced holograph writing of Dickens to be had anywhere. To Stone, too, we are indebted for his rescuing Dickens's composite writings, *Charles Dickens' Uncollected Writings from Household Words: 1850–1859*, with a copious apparatus by the editor (2 vols., 1968). Among the most massive and concrete aids to reflection to appear in the past few years are the volumes of *Dickens's Journalism* from *Sketches by Boz* to *All the Year Round* (so much of which feeds into *Great Expectations*), impeccably edited by Michael Slater; of the four projected volumes, three have appeared so far (1994, 1996, 1999). Pending the publication of the last volume (and for people whom Slater's two thousand pages would put out of pocket), readers will find a handy shortcut to the later essays in *Charles Dickens: Selected Journalism 1850–1870* (1997), edited for Penguin by David Pascoe, who is both a discriminating optant and a model annotator.

VI. *Backgrounds*

Of the titles that follow, a number deal with problems that apply to the period generally; a number apply to GE specifically. (On these last, see also "VII. Special Studies," below.) Anyone pressed for time is advised to pick two complementary books: Humphry House's by now classic (and brief) *The Dickens World* (1942), one of the texts (along with George Orwell's and Edmund Wilson's, q.v.) that salvaged Dickens's reputation for modern readers and is being rediscovered by students with the unexampled zest of novelty; and

Robin Gilmour, *The Victorian Period: The Intellectual and Cultural Context* (1993). Social and cultural background: [John Wade], *History of the Middle and Working Classes* [1833] (rept. 1966); Samuel Smiles, *Self-Help: With Illustrations of Conduct and Perseverance* [1859], ed. Asa Briggs (1958); George C. T. Bartley, *The Schools for the People: Containing the History . . . of English School for the Industrial and Poorer Classes* (1871); W. Cunningham, *The Growth of English Industry and Commerce in Modern Times* (3 vols., 1903); Jerome Hamilton Buckley, *The Victorian Temper: A Study in Literary Culture* [1951] (1969); Asa Briggs, *Victorian People: A Reassessment of Persons and Themes: 1851–67* [1955] (1972); Walter E. Houghton, *The Victorian Frame of Mind: 1830–1870* (1957); and Richard D. Altick, *Victorian People and Ideas* (1973). On crime: Christopher Hibbert, *The Roots of Evil: A Social History of Crime and Punishment* (1963), esp. 51–181, and Douglas Hay, Peter Linebaugh, et al., *Albion's Fatal Tree* (1975). Australia and Penal Settlements: the finest, most comprehensive book on the subject (and simply one of the grand books of the past quarter-century, period) is Robert Hughes's magisterial *The Fatal Shore: The Epic of Australia's Founding* (1988); still very useful answers to "What's Hulks?" are Charles Bateson, *The Convict Ships* (1959); L. L. Robson, *The Convict Settlers of Australia* (1965); and A. G. L. Shaw, *Convicts and the Colonies* (1971). For the uses of Australia in Dickens and his contemporaries, see Coral Lansbury, *Arcady in Australia: The Evocation of Australia in Nineteenth-Century English Literature* (1970).

VII. *Special Studies*

The rubrics here necessarily overlap; most of the titles can be left to speak for themselves, and all bear immediate relevance to GE. First, a number of first-rate miscellaneous items: Philip Collins, *Dickens and Education* [1963] (1965); Philip Collins, *Dickens and Crime* [1961] (3rd ed., 1994); Fred Kaplan, *Dickens and Mesmerism: The Hidden Springs of Fiction* (1975). Robert L. Patten, *Charles Dickens and His Publishers* (1978), has been mined by nearly every Dickens scholar, despite (or because of) the daunting fiduciary tables. Two studies in reception aesthetics: George Ford, *Dickens and His Readers: Aspects of Novel Criticism since 1836* [1955] (1965), and, antedating Ford, Irma Rantavaara, *Dickens in the Light of English Criticism* [1944] (1971). On Dickens and the city: Donald Fanger, *Dostoevski and Romantic Realism* (1965), 75–91, which remains one of the very best comparative studies; Raymond Williams, *The Country and the City* (1973); F. S. Schwarzbach, *Dickens and the City* (1979), on GE, 171–74, 184–93; Gabriel Pearson, "Dickens and London," *London in Literature* (1979), 94–109; Alexander Welsh, *The City of Dickens* [1971] (1986). Illustrations: Frederic G. Kitton, *Dickens and His Illustrators* (1899), on Marcus Stone, 192–203; J. R. Harvey, *Victorian Novelists and Their Illustrators* (1971); Jane Rabb Cohen, *Dickens and His Original Illustrators* (1980), on Stone: 203–09. Both Kitton and Rabb Cohen are opulently illustrated. For a rationale for/against illustration, see the piece by Q. D. Leavis, "The Dickens Illustrations: Their Functions," in F. R. and Q. D. Leavis, *Dickens the Novelist* [1970] (1972), 429–79. For essential books on the literary background and the types of fiction that are relevant to GE: Peter Coveney, *Poor Monkey: The Child in Literature* (1957), 71–119 and passim; Edgar Rosenberg, *From Shylock to Svengali: Jewish Ste-*

reotypes in English Fiction (1960); Keith Hollingworth, The Newgate Novel, 1830–1847: Bulwer, Ainsworth, Dickens and Thackeray (1963), esp. 111–31; Edwin Eigner, The Metaphysical Novel in England and America: Dickens, Bulwer, Hawthorne, Melville (1978); Harry Stone, Dickens and the Invisible World: Fairy Tales, Fantasy, and Novel Making (1979), 279–339; Janice Carlisle, The Sense of an Audience: Dickens, Thackeray, and George Eliot at Mid-Century (1981); Michael Hollington, Dickens and the Grotesque (1984), 216–30; Robin Gilmour, The Novel in the Victorian Age: A Modern Introduction (1986); Jerome Meckier, Hidden Rivalries in Victorian Fiction: Dickens, Realism, and Revaluation (1987), 122–52. GE as Bildungsroman and the Uses of the Past: K. J. Fielding, "Dickens and the Past: The Novelist of Memory," in Roy Harvey Pearce, Experience in the Novel (1968), 107–31; Jerome Hamilton Buckley, Season of Youth: The Bildungsroman from Dickens to Golding (1974), 28–62; the same writer's brief discussion in The Turning Key: Autobiography and the Subjective Impulse Since 1800 (1984), 114–30; Barry Westburg, The Confessional Fictions of Charles Dickens (1977), esp. 33–71 and 115–87; Franco Moretti, The Way of the World: the Bildungsroman in European Culture, tr. Albert J. Sbragia (1987), 181–228. The autobiographical elements of the novel have been brilliantly explored by Philip M. Weinstein in The Semantics of Desire: Changing Models of Identity from Dickens to Joyce (1984). Literary marketplace: Q. D. Leavis, Fiction and the Reading Public [1932] (1990); Amy Cruse, The Victorians and Their Reading [1935] (1962); Kathleen Tillotson, Novels of the Eighteen-Forties (1954, 1956); Richard D. Altick, The English Common Reader: A Social History of the Mass Reading Public, 1800–1900 (1957); Guinevere L. Griest, Mudie's Circulating Library and the Victorian Novel (1970); James M. Brown, Dickens: Novelist in the Market-Place (1982); Norman N. Feltes, Modes of Production of Victorian Novels (1986); John O. Jordan and Robert L. Patten, Literature in the Marketplace: Nineteenth-Century British Publishing and the Circulation of Books (1995). Serialization (but this and the foregoing are generally found in one and the same compartment): Walter Phillips, Dickens, Reade, and Collins: Sensation Novelist [1919] (1962); William F. Axton, "Keystone Structure in Dickens' Serial Novels," University of Toronto Quarterly 37 (1967): 31–50; Archibald C. Coolidge, Jr., Dickens as Serial Novelist (1967); J. Don Vann, Victorian Novels in Serial (1985), 1–17 and 61–75; R. C. Churchill, "The Monthly Dickens and the Weekly Dickens," Contemporary Review 234 (1979): 97–101; Edwin Eigner, "A Modified Parts Approach to GE," in Baumgarten, Reading Great Expectations (q.v.), 101–03; Robert L. Patten, "Charles Dickens and Serial Publication," in Baumgarten, 104–08; Linda K. Hughes and Michael Lund, The Victorian Serial (1991); Jerome Meckier, "Great Expectations: Symmetry in (Com)motion," DQ 15 (1998): 28–49. Dickens and popular entertainment: one of the best studies remains Paul Schlicke, Dickens and Popular Entertainment (1985); of importance also William F. Axton, Circle of Fire: Dickens' Vision and Style and the Popular Victorian Theater (1966); George J. Worth, Dickensian Melodrama: A Reading of the Novels (1978); William Wilson, "The Magic Circle of Genius: Dickens' Translations of Shakespearean Drama in GE," NCF 40 (1985): 154–74; Carol Hansbury Mackay, Dramatic Dickens (1989). On film, Ana L. Zambrano, Dickens and Film (1977); Julian Moynahan, "Seeing the Book, Reading the Movie," in The English Novel and the Movies, ed. Michael Klein and Gillian Parkes (1981), 143–54; Barry Tharaud, "GE as Literature and Film," *Dickensian* 87 (1991): 102–10. The study of topography has fallen on lean and Lenten days, but an informed full-length study needs to be cited, Laurence W. Gadd, *The GE Country* (1929). Since Gadd locates Pip's village at Lower Higham, a few miles north of Gad's Hill, his book has provoked much ire among the people who opt for Cooling, a few more miles northwest of Lower Higham.

VIII. Reference Works

A writer as prolific as Dickens—one, moreover, whose life has attracted so much attention—has naturally energized the compilers of Dickens dictionaries, Dickens encyclopedias, Dickens companions, etc.; these were all the rage through about 1930. Among the very earliest, at least one, Gilbert A. Pierce and William A. Wheeler, *The Dickens Dictionary* (1872), which went through twelve editions, is still a valuable adjunct. See also Alex J. Philip and W. Laurence Gadd, *A Dickens Dictionary* (2nd ed., 1928); more recently, Michael and Mollie Hardwick's comprehensive *The Charles Dickens Encyclopaedia* (1973) and, handier than any of these, Norman Page, *A Dickens Companion* (1984). Donnish bibliographers may want to shut their eyes to a book entitled *What Jane Austen Ate and Charles Dickens Knew*, penned by Daniel Pool (1993), but the book happens to be extraordinarily helpful to Americans (and other non-Brits) who haven't a clue about English currency, whether a viscount precedes an archbishop to the table at the Lord Mayor's Banquet or an archbishop outmaneuvers a viscount, and by a natural association of ideas think of Boxing Day as a prelude to the Super Bowl. A little off to one side is Fred Levit, *A Dickens Glossary* (1990), which is of use to annotators who worry about things like cucumber frames. By far the best guides are nothing alike in tonnage, availability, and cost: Nicolas Bentley, Michael Slater, and Nina Burgis, *The Dickens Index* (1990), excels all the aforementioned guides in its compressed inclusiveness and choice of entries; second, a product of the computer age, George Newlin's behemoth three-volume *Everyone in Dickens* (1995), though it sounds tailor-made for quiz kids and crossword addicts, is an immensely serviceable and detailed affair— as much a study in onomastics as it is an awesome catalog. To these now needs to be added what is in some ways the most ambitious (and most nearly indispensable) reference work we are likely to have: the encyclopaedic *Oxford Reader's Companion to Dickens* (1999) under the general editorship of Paul Schlicke, with contributions by some sixty experts in their fields and hundreds of entries ranging from "À Beckett, Gilbert" to "Yates, Frederick" via "Drink and Temperance," "Russia," and "Waxworks."

IX. Critical Introductions

The best-known and in many ways still the most satisfactory is K. J. Fielding, *Charles Dickens: A Critical Introduction* (1958; 2nd enlarged ed., 1965); useful by Fielding, too, is the brief but packed "Charles Dickens" in the "Bibliographical Supplements to British Book News on Writers and Their Work" 37 (n.d.). The most recent concise text, a sort of summa by a well-known critic, is James Lucas, *Charles Dickens: The Major Novels* (1992), on

GE, 124–44. Two earlier introductions hold up extremely well: Julian Symons, *Charles Dickens* (1951), and E. D. H. Johnson, *Charles Dickens: An Introduction to His Novels* (1969). Perhaps more thorough than any of these is Philip Hobsbaum, *A Reader's Guide to Charles Dickens* (1973); on GE, 221–42.

X. Collections of Critical Studies

Of the general collections of critical essays on Dickens, by far the most opulent is the recent four-volume edition by Michael Hollington, *Charles Dickens: Critical Assessments* (1995), which runs to over three thousand pages and is unique not only for its inclusiveness but for Hollington's splendid selections, which range from the early reviews to the present. The first three volumes are ordered along broadly chronological lines by critic (and, within this ordering, canonically by Dickens's works); volume 4 is arranged by topos. For the section on GE, which includes pieces by Claude Lévi-Strauss, Edward Said, and Jeremy Tambling, see vol. 3, 517–86 and vol. 4 passim. It labors under the same liability as George Newlin's volumes in that its cost restricts its accessibility to libraries, wealthy collectors, and addicts. Less ambitious but more maneuverable are two first-rate anthologies: George Ford and Lauriat Lane, Jr., *The Dickens Critics* (1961), and especially Stephen Wall's *Charles Dickens* in the Penguin Critical Anthologies series (1970). Wall's knowledge of sources seems almost as encyclopedic as Hollington's, Wall crowding into his 540 pages everything from Emerson's journal to Kafka's diaries; moreover, the volume contains Dickens's most important commentaries on his craft. Excellent brief general collections that focus on contemporary criticism include editions by John Gross and Gabriel Pearson, *Dickens and the Twentieth Century* (1962), 199–211; Martin Price, *Dickens: A Collection of Critical Essays* (1967), 158–68; A. E. Dyson, *Dickens* (1968); and Robert Partlow, *Dickens the Craftsman: Strategies of Presentation* (1970). The pervasive critical trends of the past twenty-five years are on display in Steven Connor's first-rate collection *Charles Dickens* (1996), with contributions by contemporary icons on the order of D. A. Miller, Terry Eagleton, and Eve Kosofsky Sedgwick; on GE, the now obligatory pieces by Peter Brooks (q.v.), Jeremy Tambling (q.v.), and Christopher D. Morris (q.v.). Critical pieces on GE alone have been assembled in Richard Lettis and William Morris, *Assessing Great Expectations* (1960), and Michael Cotsell, *Critical Essays on GE* (1990), and though one might expect the two volumes to show up the passage of the thirty years that separate them, the Lettis and Morris has held up remarkably well. Roger D. Sell's *Great Expectations: Charles Dickens* (1994) hosts both postmodern and plain modern contributors. More difficult to track down and in short supply is an impressive collection (cited earlier) of original contributions as well as excerpts from published materials, *Reading Great Expectations* (n.d., 1987?), ed. Murray F. Baumgarten, a folio-sized volume of papers read at the University of California Dickens Institute at Santa Cruz. The institute, now known as the Dickens Project, has turned into the major annual Dickens conference; it attracts the leading Dickens scholars and combines a "general education course" for the public with a few days' worth of academic showmanship, each year devoted to a single Dickens novel. (By the whirligig of the years, GE, first taught in 1981, had its second turn in 1995.) Two volumes of *Dickens Studies Annual* contain half a dozen pieces—most of them first-rate—on GE: volumes 2 (1970) and 11 (1983).

(E.R.)

XI. Full-Length Critical Studies

The fecundity of the novel for critics is reflected in the book-length studies devoted entirely to GE that have appeared in the past twenty years. The most impressive by far are Anny Sadrin's compact and sophisticated GE (1988, rept. 1999) and René Belletto's 650-page *Les grandes espérances* (1994). Sadrin, the more generally accessible of the two, covers the historical context of Dickens's preoccupation with criminality and gentlemanliness, Pip's sonship, narrative techniques, and the two endings, and provides a most useful critical history and selective bibliography. Belletto offers an at times microscopic scrutiny of GE. His work is creatively informed by psychoanalytic and poststructuralist thought and committed to uncovering the repressed secrets of Pip's and Dickens's identity, primarily through extremely close attention to words and their materiality, teasing out puns, multiple meanings, etymologies, etc., in order to read against the grain. Jerome Meckier's book has not been available to us thus far; at least four substantial pieces by him on GE—two of these products of his brief collaboration with E. R.—have appeared since 1992. Three of the essays deal with the date of action, the double ending, and the symmetrical structure of the novel; a fourth offers the most exhaustive treatment we are likely to get of the spurious "Dartmouth Notes" (a dozen [mainly forged] words jotted into the flyleaf of Dickens's copy of Dr. Johnson's *Dictionary* that were thought to suggest the genesis of the book years before Dickens dreamt of writing it)—Meckier's meticulous detective work yields what must surely be one of the longest pieces of negative reference on record. Other full-length works on GE to appear in the past fifteen years or so are in the nature of monographs and hence more modest in scope than Sadrin's and Belletto's books, but all of them are worth looking at. One of the earliest, R. G. Thomas, *Charles Dickens: GE* (1964), is an elementary but useful survey. Graham Martin, in his GE (1985), has provided a most intelligently edited and intelligently illustrated booklet, published for and by Open University. A useful Casebook for neophytes, which focuses on Dickens criticism and in which the discussion of *Great Expectations* cohabits with discussions of *Hard Times* and *Our Mutual Friend*, is *Charles Dickens*, edited for the "Casebook Series" by Norman Page (1979). Rather more challenging is Douglas Brooks-Davies's GE (1989), in which Brooks-Davies undertakes a reading of the novel chapter by chapter, emphasizing biblical symbolism, doubling of characters, and Pip's search for a lost father. Among the shorter books, Nicola Bradbury's monograph *Charles Dickens' GE* (1990) is the pick of the lot: it provides an extremely cogent introduction to the text itself, and Bradbury is especially good at discovering thematic and verbal patterns and hidden linkages no one else seems to have unearthed. Bradbury, an elegant stylist, is partial to Steven Connor's commanding Lacanian poststructuralist study (q.v.) and Kate Flint's *Dickens* (1986)—both of which, however, engage the Dickens oeuvre generally. Earlier than Brooks-Davies and Bradbury, and straddling the twilit zone between book and monograph, Bert G. Hornback, in his *GE: A Novel of Friendship* (1987), is perhaps more user-friendly to novices than most other writers are: his text is very much that of a dedicated teacher who looks at the significant aspects of the book as he might in a classroom. (The volume contains a number of student responses.) Another instructor might prefer to assign the postmodern soft-porn feminist *GE* by the iconic Kathy Acker, author of *Blood and Guts in High School* and *Empire of the Senseless*, a pastiche of spoofs on *GE*, Proust's *Remembrance*, Woolf's *Orlando* et al. Allowing for a couple of totally hilarious "quotations" from the genuine *GE*, Acker's novel hasn't much more in common with Dickens's than a book with the windy title *GE: An Illustrated Guide to Your Pregnancy, Your Birth, Your Baby* (1993), and then also the Acker contains so many four-letter words per page that it isn't likely to be found on even the most chip-proof branch of the Dickens Fellowship. Still, it's great fun to read; and it commands a lot more attention on and off college reading lists than all of the other books cited in this paragraph lumped together. And lastly, Peter Carey's fictional adaptation *Jack Maggs* (1997), in which Carey turns the spotlight (or sunset-gun) on Magwitch's alter ego, offers a fascinating post-colonial reading—performing for *GE* somewhat the same service that *Wide Sargasso Sea* performs more famously for *Jane Eyre*.

(E. R. and J. C.)

XII. Criticism

Along with Humphry House's seminal study *The Dickens World* (q.v.), the publication of George Orwell's "Charles Dickens," *Inside the Whale* (1940), and Edmund Wilson's "Charles Dickens: The Two Scrooges," *The Wound and the Bow* (1941), inaugurated a new era of Dickens criticism, one that established Dickens as an author who ought, after all, to be taken seriously. The corpus of Dickens criticism is now so extensive and *GE* makes up so substantial an area of the Dickens industry that a representative, inevitably inadequate sampling of what has been said about the novel is all that is possible here. The critical history of *GE* to some extent follows the contours of the history of Anglo-American literary criticism, but certain themes, cruxes, and approaches persist, determined by the form of the novel itself.

To begin with what are arguably the most nearly essential works. At the time of its appearance in 1958, J. Hillis Miller's *Charles Dickens: The World of His Novels* was widely regarded as the single most seminal critical study since the pioneering essays by Orwell and Wilson; the comments on *GE*, 249–78, focus on Pip's difficult self-confrontations. Two studies that remain indispensable to students of Dickens's evolving craftsmanship are John Butt and Kathleen Tillotson, *Dickens at Work* (1957)—see especially their comments on "Dickens as Serial Novelist," 13–34—and what is perhaps the single most important work on a related topic, Harvey Peter Sucksmith's brilliant *The Narrative Art of Charles Dickens: The Rhetoric of Sympathy and Irony in His Novels* (1970). Nobody before Sucksmith had examined nearly all of Dickens's manuscripts with anything like his thoroughness. Q. D. Leavis's essay "How We Must Read *GE*," in F. R. and Q. D. Leavis, *Dickens the Novelist* (1970), 277–331, used to be one of the most hotly debated pieces about the novel, an instant candidate for Frederick Crews's *The Pooh Perplex*, largely because of the stridently apodictic voice reflected in the title and its parochial conviction that nobody outside the United Kingdom can begin to understand GE. But Mrs. Leavis's intemperance against Professors Dabney and Garis (q.v.) is tempered by her mercy toward Pip, and once you get over her splenetic asides, you remain to admire her gritty intelligence and persuasive sympathy. Of the chapters on GE included, like Miller's, in full-length studies of Dickens, H. M. Daleski's reading in his *Dickens and the Art* of *Analogy* (1970), 237–69, remains perhaps unsurpassed in its linking Pip to other characters in GE.

Other studies of Dickens useful to students of our novel include A. O. J. Cockshut, *The Imagination of Charles Dickens* (1961); Sylvère Monod, *Dickens Romancier* (1953; English translation, 1968); Robert Garis, *The Dickens Theatre: A Reassessment of the Novels* (1965), which considers Dickens's novels as performances rather than new-critical icons; Ross Dabney, *Love and Property in the Novels of Dickens* (1967), which examines the effect of social and economic factors on human relationships in the novel; Grahame Smith, *Dickens, Money and Society* (1968); and Geoffrey Thurley, *The Dickens Myth: Its Genesis and Structure* (1976). Barry Westburg devotes two major chapters to GE in his *The Confessional Fictions of Charles Dickens* (1977). An earlier short piece on GE that helped define the agenda of GE criticism is Robert G. Stange, "Expectations Well Lost: Dickens' Fable for His Time," *College English* 16 (1954): 9–17.

A number of the essays on GE unsurprisingly concentrate on a single character, and Wemmick, Jaggers, and Havisham in particular seem to have stimulated critical activity. On Wemmick: L. J. Dessner, "GE: The Tragic Comedy of John Wemmick," *Ariel* 6 (1975): 65–80; James Phelan, "Reading for the Character and Reading for the Progression: John Wemmick and GE," *Journal of Narrative Technique* 19 (1989): 70–84; Alexander Welsh, *The City of Dickens* [1971] (1986), 143–44; Garrett Stewart, *Dickens and the Trials of Imagination* (1974), 187–97; most recently, Jay Clayton, "Is Pip Postmodern? Or Dickens at the End of the Twentieth Century," in GE, ed. Janice Carlisle (1996), 606–24. On Jaggers: A. F. Dilnot, "The Case of Mr. Jaggers," *Essays in Criticism* 25 (1975): 437–43; A. L. French, "Mr. Jaggers," *Essays in Criticism* 26 (1976): 278–82; Stanley Tick, "Towards Jaggers," *DSA* 5 (1976): 133–49, 207. Miss Havisham has attracted more attention than any other single figure in the novel. Short pieces devoted to her character and origins prominently include Martin Meisel, "Miss Havisham Brought to Book," *PMLA* 81 (1966): 278–85; Harry Stone's important study of the genesis of her character in "Genesis of a Novel" (reprinted in this edition) and even more expansively in *The Night Side of Dickens: Cannibalism, Passion, Necessity*; Susan Shatto, "Miss Havisham and Mr. Mopes the Hermit: Dickens and the Mentally Ill," *DQ* 2 (1985): 43–50, 79–84; Evelyn M. Romig, "Twisted Tale, Silent Teller: Miss Havisham in GE," *DQ* 5 (1988): 18–22. Of the books dealing with character types, perhaps the best recent study (though GE takes a backseat to *Dombey* and *Copperfield*) remains Malcolm Andrews, *Dickens and the Grown-Up Child* (1994). Essays that focus primarily on Dickens's treatment of human and social relationships, often with special reference to ingestion, include Barbara Hardy's "Food and Ceremony in GE," *Essays in Criticism* 13 (1963): 351–63; Katherine Carolan, "Dickens's Last

Christmases," *Dalhousie Review* 52 (1972): 373–83; Anya Taylor, "Devoured Hearts in GE," *DSN* 13 (1982): 65–71; John Cunningham, "The Figure of the Wedding Feast in GE," *DQ* 10 (1993): 87–91; Carol Siegel, "Postmodern Women Novelists Review Victorian Male Masoschism," *Genders* 11 (1991): 1–16.

To all intents, the preoccupation with the novel's imagery and symbolism dates from mid-century: most intelligently, Taylor Stoehr, *Dickens: The Dreamer's Stance* (1965), 101–37; Robert Barnard, "Imagery and Theme in GE," *DSA* 1 (1970): 238–51; John P. McWilliams, Jr., "GE: the Beacon, the Gibbet, and the Ship," *DSA* 2 (1972): 255–66, 371–72; Paulette Michel-Michot, "The Fire Motif in GE," *Ariel* 8 (1977), 49–69; more recently, Naomi Lightman, "The 'Vulcanic Dialect' of GE," *Dickensian* 82 (1986): 33–38.

In serving notice to the readers of her most "Victorian" novel that she would let other pens than hers dwell on such odious subjects as guilt and misery, Jane Austen bequeathed a very rich harvest to her successors and their critics, who wouldn't quite know what to do without them. Guilt and shame have been a staple of Dickens commentary, from psychoanalytic, moral, and sociological points of view. Social shame and class consciousness are explored in Grahame Smith, *Dickens, Money and Society* (1968), 169–81; Barnard (above); Dudley Flamm, "The Prosecutor Within: Dickens's Final Explanation," *Dickensian* 66 (1970): 16–23; A. E. Dyson, "GE: The Immolations of Pip," in *The Inimitable Dickens* (1970), chapter 11. L. J. Dessner, "GE: 'The Ghost of a Man's Own Father,'" *PMLA* 91 (1976): 436–49, considers oedipal guilt; Robert Newsom's influential "The Hero's Shame," *DSA* 11 (1983): 1–24, builds on Moynahan's essay "The Hero's Guilt," and Brian Cheadle, "Sentiment and Resentment in GE," *DSA* 20 (1991): 147–72, illuminates the way class resentment tinctures relationships in GE. Albert Hutter, "Crime and Fantasy in GE," in *Psychoanalysis and the Literary Process*, ed. Frederick Crews (1970), is an illuminating Freudian analysis of Pip's ambivalent relationship to father figures and to two sides of nineteenth-century economic life.

For a writer who used to be thought *the* comic novelist in the language, Dickens the humorist has gotten rather short shrift in the past decades. There are exceptions, of course: again, a few examples will have to suffice. Douglas Bush's essay modestly entitled "A Note on Dickens's Humor" (but in fact one of the best things on the subject), in Robert C. Rathburn and Martin Steinman, Jr., eds., *From Jane Austen to Joseph Conrad* (1958), 82–91, traces the type of the comic self-dramatizer. In his spirited "Dickens and the Comedy of Humor," in Roy Harvey Pearce (q.v.), 49–81, Northrop Frye traces Dickens's humor to the New Comedy of Plautus, with its division between "congenial" and "obstructive" societies, in an essay that has retained all its sheen and allusiveness in the thirty years since its appearance. Henri Talon, "On Some Aspects of the Comic in GE," *Victorian Newsletter* 42 (1972): 6–11, tackles the subject with the brevity inseparable from wit. Sylvia Mannings's comments on GE in her *Dickens the Satirist* (1971) are disappointingly brief in an otherwise insightful if uneven book. Rodney Stenning Edgecombe, "Violence, Death and Euphemism in GE," *Victorian Institute Journal* 22 (1994): 85–92, looks at the way humor is generated by inflation and evasiveness. Patrice Hannon writes about "The Aesthetics of Humor in GE" in

Dickensian 92 (1996): 106–10. Although one of the very best books on the subject, James R. Kincaid's *Dickens and the Rhetoric of Laughter* (1971), rather slights *GE*, it glances in passing at the itself slight, slighted episode about Pumblechook's comeuppance. Edgecombe's essay really straddles the topic of humor with the more "in" topic of Pip's relationship to different kinds and uses of language: thus, for starters, Ian Ousby, "Language and Gesture in *GE*," *MLR* 72 (1977): 784–93, and Melanie Young,"Distorted Expectations: Pip and the Problems of Language," *DSA* 7 (1978): 203–20. In the 1970s the narratological aspects of *GE*—the complexity of the narrative's temporality and point of view—became a focal point for critics, although R. B. Partlow, Jr., broke ground much earlier in "The Moving I: A Study of the Point of View in *GE*," *College English* 23 (1961): 122–31. W. J. M. Bronzwaer explores the relationship between narrator and narrated in "Implied Author, Extradiegetic Narrator and Public Reader: Gérard Genette's Narratological Model and the Reading Version of *GE*," *Neophilologus* 62 (1978): 1–18; Mary Galbraith closely analyzes self-identifications and self-dissociations of the narrative consciousness in her more recent "Pip as 'Infant Tongue' and as Adult Narrator in Chapter One of *GE*," in *Infant Tongues: The Voice of the Child in Literature*, ed. Elizabeth Goodenough (1994).

From the 1970s on—but more particularly in the last two decades—analyses of the narrative have become increasingly and skeptically concerned with Pip's self-creation through storytelling or through acts of reading and writing, and thus with the self-reflexivity of the novel. Moshe Ron's excellent, deconstruction-inflected "Autobiographical Narration and Formal Closure in *GE*," *Hebrew U Studies in Lit.* 5 (1977): 37–66, discusses Pip's retrospective self-fashioning. Murray Baumgarten, "Calligraphy and Code: Writing in *GE*," *DSA* 11 (1983): 61–72, and other essays in *DSA* 11 treat *GE* as a novel about writing and the subject's relationship to the language that constitutes it; see esp. Robert Tracy, "Reading Dickens' Writing," 37–59, and John O. Jordan, "The Medium of *GE*," 73–88. Among influential deconstructive readings along with O'Connor's, see prominently Eiichi Hara, "Stories Present and Absent in *GE*," *ELH* (1986): 593–614; Christopher Morris, "The Bad Faith of Pip's Bad Faith: Deconstructing *GE*," *ELH* (1987), 941–55. A different kind of application of deconstruction is given in Edward Said's "Criticism Between Culture and System," in *The World, the Text, and the Critic* (1983), in which Said shows how Wopsle's performance of *Hamlet* enacts Derrida's theories of representation. Elsewhere, Nabokov's "Viennese witch-doctor" has left his fingerprints to splendid effect on Dianne Sadoff's wonderful *Monsters of Affection* (1982), 22–38; Ned Lukacher, "Dialectical Images: Benjamin/ Dickens/Freud" in his *Primal Scenes: Literature, Philosophy, Psychoanalysis* (1986), 275–333, and Roland R. Thomas, *Dreams of Authority: Freud and the Fictions of the Unconscious* (1990). Among psychocritical studies, Lawrence Frank's *Charles Dickens and the Romantic Self* (1984) remains arguably unsurpassed; see esp. 151–83, but the entire book is extremely astute and readable. So, in a related mode, is Anny Sadrin's *Parentage and Inheritance in the Novels of Charles Dickens* (1994), 95–120. For briefer studies, see the essays by the psychoanalyst Leonard F. Manheim, "The Dickens Hero as Child," *Studies in the Novel* 1 (1969): 189–95 and "Dickens' HEROES, heroes and heroids," *DSA* 5 (1976): 1–22. Recent treatments of more traditional questions include J. B. Reed, "Astrophel and Estella: A Defense of

Poesy," *SEL* 30 (1990): 655–79, which explores the way Dickens sets a view of the novel as instrument of social reform against the novel as "high culture," the latter encoded in allusions to Petrarchan love and style.

In the last decade or so, approaches to *GE* that foreground issues of gender and sexuality—from feminist and historical materialist perspectives—have begun to appear. Gail Turley Houston, "Pip and Property: (Re)production of the Self in *GE*," *Studies in the Novel* 24 (1992): 13–25, considers the failure of the feminine private sphere to save Pip from the market forces that produce people as consumers and consumed. On autoeroticism and the disciplining of sexual desire in *GE*, William A. Cohen's witty "Manual Conduct in *GE*," *ELH* 60 (1993): 217–59. One of the best (of few) feminist treatments of *GE* is Hilary Schor, " 'If He Should Turn to and Beat Her': Violence, Desire, and the Woman's Story in *GE*," in Janice Carlisle's *GE*, 541–57; earlier, Lucy Frost, "Taming to Improve: Dickens and the Women in *GE*," *Meridian* 1 (1982): 11–20. Of the full-length feminist studies, Catherine Waters's excellent *Dickens and the Politics of the Family* (1997), 150–74, should be consulted, as should Laurie Langbauer's *Women and Romance: The Consolations of Gender in the English Novel* (1990), 127–87. Daniel Cottom, "Paranomasia, Culture, and the Power of Meaning," *Text and Culture: The Politics of Interpretations* (1989), 103–53, looks at *GE* with an awareness that the construction of meaning is always contingent and politically "interested." Jeremy Tambling, "Prison-Bound: Dickens and Foucault," *Essays in Criticism* 37 (1996): 37–59, reads *GE* through the lens of Foucault's revisionary work on modern forms of social and political power.

It would be impossible to conclude this section without drawing attention to what remains one of the finest, most durable, and most balanced studies of Dickens in the past thirty-five years (though we have to wait for volume two for a discussion of *GE*): Steven Marcus, *Dickens: From Pickwick to Dombey* (1965).

XIII. Closure

Here, listed alphabetically by author, is a selection of the interventions that have been made since 1949 in the novel's two endings (for sortings-out see the essay in this volume on the two endings and Anny Sadrin's remarks in *GE* [1988]: 256–59): John Butt, "Dickens's Plan for the Conclusion of *GE*," *Dickensian* 45 (1949): 78–80; John Cloy, "Two Altered Endings—Dickens and Bulwer-Lytton," *U of Mississippi Studies in English* (1992): 170–72; David M. Craig, "Origins, Ends and Pip's Two Selves," *Research Studies* (Washington State U) 47 (1979): 16–26; Albert A. Dunn, "The Altered Endings of *GE*," *DSN* 9 (1978): 40–42; Richard J. Dunn, "Far, Far Better Things: Dickens' Later Endings," *DSA* 7 (1978): 221–36, 262; Edwin M. Eigner, "Bulwer-Lytton and the Changed Ending of *GE*," *NCF* 25 (1970): 104–08; A. L. French, "Old Pip: The Ending of *GE*," *Essays in Criticism* 29 (1979): 357–60; Robert A. Greenberg, "On Ending *GE*," *PLL* 6 (1970): 152–62; John C. Kucich, "Action in the Dickens Ending: *Bleak House* and *Great Expectations*," *NCF* 33 (June 1978): 88–109; Thomas M. Leitch, "Closure and Teleology in Dickens," *Studies in the Novel* 18 (1986): 143–56; David Lodge, "Ambiguously Ever After: Problematic Endings in English Fiction," in *Working with Structuralism* (1981), 143–55; Gregory W. Marshall, "Value and

Meaning in GE: The Two Endings Revisited," *Essays in Criticism* 19 (1969): 402–09; Jerome Meckier, "Charles Dickens' GE: A Defense of the Second Ending," *Studies in the Novel* 25 (1993): 28–58; Martin Meisel, "The Ending of GE," *Essays in Criticism* 15 (1965): 326–31; Milton Millhauser, "GE: The Three Endings," *DSA* 2 (1972): 265–77; Robert Polhemus, who supplies a sophisticated comparison of the two endings of GE and *Villette* in his *Erotic Faith: Being in Love from Jane Austen to D. H. Lawrence* (1990); Moshe Ron (preceding page); John T. Smith, "The Two Endings of GE: A Reevaluation," *Thoth* 12 (1971): 11–17; Robert Stein, "Repetitions During Pip's Closure," *DSA* 21 (1992): 143–56; Harvey Sucksmith, (q.v.), 110–19; Douglas H. Thomson, "The Passing of Another's Shadow: A Third Ending of GE," *DQ* 1 (1984): 94–96.

(J. C.)

XIV. Editions

The editions of the novel printed in Dickens's lifetime have been cited in the sketch on the novel's publication. A few later editions may be aired for what interest the introductory matter furnishes: very nearly all but the most recent ones have been briefly described in Worth's bibliography, 19–26. Edwin Whipple, one of Dickens's earliest and smartest reviewers, introduced the novel in the New Illustrated Library Edition (1877); Andrew Lang, like Jaggers and President Coolidge a man of few words and unlike Bulwer a perfect Scrooge in his annotation (nine footnotes), in the Gadshill Edition (1898); Charles Dickens the Younger, one of the very few early editors to glance at the problem of the two endings, in the volume in the Macmillan Edition (1904); G. K. Chesterton with a substantial if pontifical leadoff to the first Everyman Edition (1907); "John Oxenham" in the Waverley Edition (1914), the first, despite Shaw's claims at primacy, to print the unhappy ending—but as part of the prefatory matter; Bernard Shaw, in the "Introduction" to the Limited Editions Club (1937), credited with first printing the original ending, this followed by the revised version of his "Preface" for the Novel Library Edition (1947); Lauriat Lane, Jr., in the Harper's Modern Classics Edition (1961); John T. Winterich, in the Heritage Press Edition (1939); Monroe Engel, in the Riverside Edition (1962); Angus Wilson, in the Signet Edition (1963); Christopher Hibbert, in the London Folio Society Edition (1981). It should be added that the Household Edition (1870s) features illustrations by F. A. Fraser; the Gadshill, illustrations by Charles Green; the Heritage Press Edition, by Edward Ardizzone; Limited Editions, by Gordon Ross; and the Oxford Illustrated Edition (1953), for many years the most widely used of the modern hardcovers, the twenty-one plates furnished by F. W. Pailthorpe (1838–1914), after Marcus Stone the best-known of the early illustrators of GE and the provider of the Norton Critical cover. Pailthorpe's plates have been reproduced more recently in a handsome reprint of the 1907 Everyman (1992; not to be confused with Gilmour's paperback, below), featuring a compact introduction by Michael Slater as well as Chesterton's original salutatory. Ronald Searle has furnished the illustrations for the Norton GE (1962), edited by Doris Dickens.

Probably every Dickens illustrator known to humanity is featured in Edward Guiliano's and Philip Collins's sumptuous two-volume *The Annotated Dickens* (1985): Harry Furniss, Green, Fraser, Stone, Charles Keeping (Folio Society)—the lot. The edition, which also reproduces stills from every film adaptation, from Nordisk to eternity, is far and away the most amply annotated. Over and above the annotation proper, Guiliano/Collins offer a marvelous assortment of annotatable (and annotated) reproductions of almost every place mentioned in *GE*. But the book has been out of print for some years, weighs a ton, and so fails to qualify as portable property, and it costs a mint—though it's worth every penny. The next best merchandise in the way of illustrations is the very recent New York Public Library Collector's Edition, published by Doubleday (1997), in which, as the editors (or producers) inform you, "Four very different artists . . . vie for your attention"—Pailthorpe, "Kyd" (J. Clayton Clarke), Fraser, and Sol Eytinge, Jr. Priced as an ideal present for a person you like, but not too much.

Books in Print for 1997–98 dockets some forty-five editions of GE (exclusive of impertinent stuff like the *Guide to Pregnancy* or *Great Expectations: Preparing for Evangelism through Bible Study*); and the latest number of *DQ* for June 1998 lists four new ones, one introduced by the distinguished Shaw scholar-critic Stanley Weintraub. Of the editions in print, other than the Clarendon, though none contains quite as much freight as the Norton Critical, by far the best text for our times is Janice Carlisle's edition in the Case Studies in Contemporary Criticism (1996); this, apart from printing "Essays from Five Contemporary Perspectives" (psychoanalytic, deconstructive, feminist, cultural, and gender criticism), leads off with a splendidly compact history of Dickens criticism. By far the best all-around of the less expensive paperbacks is Robin Gilmour's in the new Everyman series (1994), which is the only paperback to contain (in addition to essays on the two endings and Dickens criticism) all of Stone's original illustrations. The recent edition by Tim Seward in the Cambridge Literature series (1995), though very much a student edition ("How does *Great Expectations* present its subject?") contains arguably the most useful maps in the business. Of the two "standard" paperbacks, the recent Penguin, edited by David Trotter and Charlotte Mitchell (1996), improves markedly on the earlier (1965) text; its chief drawback and that of the World's Classics (1994)—the paperback version of the Clarendon minus the textual apparatus—lies in its preserving the annoyingly outdated chapter numeration of the 1861 edition (Book II, chapter 11, when all you want to find is chapter 30 instead of fumbling back and forth to discover what II, 11 corresponds to). That the Penguin sells circles around the elsewhere competitive World's Classics (by a factor of roughly nine to one) may be assigned to one or both of two causes: the waywardness of the market and/or the inelegant, or inappropriate, cover illustration to the World's Classics of a fat red-cheeked youth, doing his best to look as if he were sitting for Sir Henry Raeburn. The World's Classics GE can also be had in a handsome one-volume trilogy, cheek by jowl with *Hard Times* and *A Tale of Two Cities*, but sans footnotes and even without the original ending. Alan Sillitoe has provided a brief preface to the 1999 edition of Oxford World's Classics. A *Portable Dickens* seems, God Bless Us, a thing of nought, but Angus Wilson has made the best of an unlikely job; unsurprisingly, *GE* takes up two-thirds of the *Portable*. The more inexpensively disposable texts (Signet, Avon, Bantam, Collier, Airmont, Panther, TOR Classics, Washington Square) can't begin to compete with the Gilmour, which is a steal. The *GE* just issued by Cyber Classics (1997) comes with software.

I started out this book with an *hommage* to the many French commissioned spirits who continue to take *Great Expectations* under their wings; so it is only fitting to all but conclude by saluting three distinguished French journals that regularly carry pieces on Dickens in both English and French: *Études Anglaises* (Paris, 1937–), *Revue de littérature comparée* (Paris, 1921– [inclusion of pieces in English from 1930 on]), and *Cahiers Victoriens et Édouardiens* (Université Paul Valéry, Montpellier (1978–); a fourth, the annual *Q/W/E/R/T/Y* (Université de Pau, 1991–) is running some six or eight pieces on *GE* in their October 1999 volume.

This roster cannot be logically complete without three distinctly modern productions, though the earliest of the three appeared fifty years ago: the editions of *Classics Comic Illustrated* published in 1947 (No. 43), 1990, and 1997. Pace Jay Clayton (q.v.), who has ventilated the first two, the first has the distinction of being the most valuable of all the *Classics Illustrated* since the publishers, proud of their highbrow merchandise, withdrew the issue in a great huff as a result of its being attacked for the brutality of its illustrations ("Am I correct in classifying this as a crime comic?") by Dr. Fredric Wertham in his *Seduction of the Innocents* (1954). The 1990 adaptation by Rick Geary is a good deal cozier, and its Pip does not compare unfavorably with whoever appears on the cover of the World's Classics. The latest comic (1997), a dwarfish rerun of the 1947, using the same text and illustrations, is sponsored by the Dickens Project, which is issuing the entire canon, farming out its editions to graduate students and faculty, who supply ten pages' worth of notes for discussion. As the 1997, like the '47, is told in the third person ("His family name was Pirrip, but all who knew the boy called him Pip for short"), the text is tailor-made to encourage an in-class discussion on the merits of the third-person viewpoint. All instructors ought to avail themselves of it.

(E.R.)

Norton Critical Editions

ANDERSON *Winesburg, Ohio* edited by Charles E. Modlin and Ray Lewis White
AQUINAS *St. Thomas Aquinas on Politics and Ethics* translated and edited by Paul E. Sigmund
AUSTEN *Emma* edited by Stephen M. Parrish *Third Edition*
AUSTEN *Mansfield Park* edited by Claudia L. Johnson
AUSTEN *Persuasion* edited by Patricia Meyer Spacks
AUSTEN *Pride and Prejudice* edited by Donald Gray *Second Edition*
BALZAC *Père Goriot* translated by Burton Raffel, edited by Peter Brooks
BEHN *Oroonoko* edited by Joanna Lipking
Beowulf (the Donaldson translation) edited by Joseph F. Tuso
BLAKE *Blake's Poetry and Designs* selected and edited by Mary Lynn Johnson and John E. Grant
BOCCACCIO *The Decameron* selected, translated, and edited by Mark Musa and Peter E. Bondanella
BRONTË, CHARLOTTE *Jane Eyre* edited by Richard J. Dunn *Second Edition*
BRONTË, EMILY *Wuthering Heights* edited by William M. Sale, Jr., and Richard Dunn *Third Edition*
BROWNING, ELIZABETH BARRETT *Aurora Leigh* edited by Margaret Reynolds
BROWNING, ROBERT *Browning's Poetry* selected and edited by James F. Loucks
BURNEY *Evelina* edited by Stewart J. Cooke
BYRON *Byron's Poetry* selected and edited by Frank D. McConnell
CARROLL *Alice in Wonderland* edited by Donald J. Gray *Second Edition*
CERVANTES *Don Quijote* translated by Burton Raffel edited by Diana de Armas Wilson
CHAUCER *The Canterbury Tales: Nine Tales and the General Prologue* edited by V. A. Kolve and Glending Olson
CHEKHOV *Anton Chekhov's Plays* translated and edited by Eugene K. Bristow
CHEKHOV *Anton Chekhov's Short Stories* selected and edited by Ralph E. Matlaw
CHOPIN *The Awakening* edited by Margo Culley *Second Edition*
The Classic Fairy Tales edited by Maria Tatar
CLEMENS *Adventures of Huckleberry Finn* edited by Sculley Bradley, Richmond Croom Beatty, E. Hudson Long, and Thomas Cooley *Second Edition*
CLEMENS *A Connecticut Yankee in King Arthur's Court* edited by Allison R. Ensor
CLEMENS *Pudd'nhead Wilson and Those Extraordinary Twins* edited by Sidney E. Berger
CONRAD *Heart of Darkness* edited by Robert Kimbrough *Third Edition*
CONRAD *Lord Jim* edited by Thomas C. Moser *Second Edition*
CONRAD *The Nigger of the "Narcissus"* edited by Robert Kimbrough
CRANE *Maggie: A Girl of the Streets* edited by Thomas A. Gullason
CRANE *The Red Badge of Courage* edited by Donald Pizer *Third Edition*
DARWIN *Darwin* selected and edited by Philip Appleman *Second Edition*
DEFOE *A Journal of the Plague Year* edited by Paula R. Backscheider
DEFOE *Moll Flanders* edited by Edward Kelly
DEFOE *Robinson Crusoe* edited by Michael Shinagel *Second Edition*
DE PIZAN *The Selected Writings of Christine de Pizan* translated by Renate Blumenfeld-Kosinski and Kevin Brownlee, edited by Renate Blumenfeld-Kosinsk
DICKENS *Bleak House* edited by George Ford and Sylvère Monod

DICKENS   *David Copperfield*   edited by Jerome H. Buckley

DICKENS   *Hard Times*   edited by George Ford and Sylvère Monod   *Second Edition*

DICKENS   *Oliver Twist*   edited by Fred Kaplan

DONNE   *John Donne's Poetry*   selected and edited by Arthur L. Clements   *Second Edition*

DOSTOEVSKY   *The Brothers Karamazov*   (the Garnett translation)   edited by Ralph E. Matlaw

DOSTOEVSKY   *Crime and Punishment*   (the Coulson translation)   edited by George Gibian   *Third Edition*

DOSTOEVSKY   *Notes from Underground*   translated and edited by Michael R. Katz

DOUGLASS   *Narrative of the Life of Frederick Douglass, an American Slave, Written by Himself*   edited by William L. Andrews and William S. McFeely

DREISER   *Sister Carrie*   edited by Donald Pizer   *Second Edition*

DU BOIS   *The Souls of Black Folk*   edited by Henry Louis Gates, Jr., and Terri Oliver

Eight Modern Plays   edited by Anthony Caputi

ELIOT   *Middlemarch*   edited by Bert G. Hornback

ELIOT   *The Mill on the Floss*   edited by Carol T. Christ

ERASMUS   *The Praise of Folly and Other Writings*   translated and edited by Robert M. Adams

FAULKNER   *The Sound and the Fury*   edited by David Minter   *Second Edition*

FIELDING   *Joseph Andrews with Shamela and Related Writings*   edited by Homer Goldberg

FIELDING   *Tom Jones*   edited by Sheridan Baker   *Second Edition*

FLAUBERT   *Madame Bovary*   edited with a substantially new translation by Paul de Man

FORD   *The Good Soldier*   edited by Martin Stannard

FORSTER   *Howards End*   edited by Paul B. Armstrong

FRANKLIN   *Benjamin Franklin's Autobiography*   edited by J. A. Leo Lemay and P. M. Zall

FULLER   *Woman in the Nineteenth Century*   edited by Larry J. Reynolds

GOETHE   *Faust*   translated by Walter Arndt   edited by Cyrus Hamlin

GOGOL   *Dead Souls*   (the Reavey translation)   edited by George Gibian

HARDY   *Far from the Madding Crowd*   edited by Robert C. Schweik

HARDY   *Jude the Obscure*   edited by Norman Page   *Second Edition*

HARDY   *The Mayor of Casterbridge*   edited by James K. Robinson

HARDY   *The Return of the Native*   edited by James Gindin

HARDY   *Tess of the d'Urbervilles*   edited by Scott Elledge   *Third Edition*

HAWTHORNE   *The Blithedale Romance*   edited by Seymour Gross and Rosalie Murphy

HAWTHORNE   *The House of the Seven Gables*   edited by Seymour Gross

HAWTHORNE   *Nathaniel Hawthorne's Tales*   edited by James McIntosh

HAWTHORNE   *The Scarlet Letter*   edited by Seymour Gross, Sculley Bradley, Richmond Croom Beatty, and E. Hudson Long   *Third Edition*

HERBERT   *George Herbert and the Seventeenth-Century Religious Poets*   selected and edited by Mario A. DiCesare

HERODOTUS   *The Histories*   translated and selected by Walter E. Blanco   edited by Walter E. Blanco and Jennifer Roberts

HOBBES   *Leviathan*   edited by Richard E. Flathman and David Johnston

HOMER   *The Odyssey*   translated and edited by Albert Cook   *Second Edition*

HOWELLS   *The Rise of Silas Lapham*   edited by Don L. Cook

IBSEN   *The Wild Duck*   translated and edited by Dounia B. Christiani

JAMES   *The Ambassadors*   edited by S. P. Rosenbaum   *Second Edition*

JAMES   *The American*   edited by James W. Tuttleton

JAMES   *The Portrait of a Lady*   edited by Robert D. Bamberg   *Second Edition*

JAMES   *Tales of Henry James*   edited by Christof Wegelin

JAMES   *The Turn of the Screw*   edited by Deborah Esch and Jonathan Warren   *Second Edition*

JAMES *The Wings of the Dove* edited by J. Donald Crowley and Richard A. Hocks

JONSON *Ben Jonson and the Cavalier Poets* selected and edited by Hugh Maclean

JONSON *Ben Jonson's Plays and Masques* selected and edited by Robert M. Adams

KAFKA *The Metamorphosis* translated and edited by Stanley Corngold

LAFAYETTE *The Princess of Clèves* edited and with a revised translation by John D. Lyons

MACHIAVELLI *The Prince* translated and edited by Robert M. Adams *Second Edition*

MALTHUS *An Essay on the Principle of Population* edited by Philip Appleman

MANN *Death in Venice* translated and edited by Clayton Koelb

MARX *The Communist Manifesto* edited by Frederic L. Bender

MELVILLE *The Confidence-Man* edited by Hershel Parker

MELVILLE *Moby-Dick* edited by Harrison Hayford and Hershel Parker

MEREDITH *The Egoist* edited by Robert M. Adams

Middle English Lyrics selected and edited by Maxwell S. Luria and Richard L. Hoffman

Middle English Romances selected and edited by Stephen H. A. Shepherd

MILL *Mill: The Spirit of the Age, On Liberty, The Subjection of Women* selected and edited by Alan Ryan

MILL *On Liberty* edited by David Spitz

MILTON *Paradise Lost* edited by Scott Elledge *Second Edition*

Modern Irish Drama edited by John P. Harrington

MORE *Utopia* translated and edited by Robert M. Adams *Second Edition*

NEWMAN *Apologia Pro Vita Sua* edited by David J. DeLaura

NEWTON *Newton* edited by I. Bernard Cohen and Richard S. Westfall

NORRIS *McTeague* edited by Donald Pizer *Second Edition*

Restoration and Eighteenth-Century Comedy edited by Scott McMillin *Second Edition*

RHYS *Wide Sargasso Sea* edited by Judith R. Raiskin

RICH *Adrienne Rich's Poetry and Prose* edited by Barbara Charlesworth Gelpi and Albert Gelpi

ROUSSEAU *Rousseau's Political Writings* edited by Alan Ritter translated by Julia Conaway Bondanella

ST. PAUL *The Writings of St. Paul* edited by Wayne A. Meeks

SHAKESPEARE *Hamlet* edited by Cyrus Hoy *Second Edition*

SHAKESPEARE *Henry IV, Part I* edited by James L. Sanderson *Second Edition*

SHAW *Bernard Shaw's Plays* edited by Warren Sylvester Smith

SHELLEY, MARY *Frankenstein* edited by J. Paul Hunter

SHELLEY, PERCY BYSSHE *Shelley's Poetry and Prose* selected and edited by Donald H. Reiman and Sharon B. Powers

SMOLLETT *Humphry Clinker* edited by James L. Thorson

SOPHOCLES *Oedipus Tyrannus* translated and edited by Luci Berkowitz and Theodore F. Brunner

SPENSER *Edmund Spenser's Poetry* selected and edited by Hugh Maclean and Anne Lake Prescott *Third Edition*

STENDHAL *Red and Black* translated and edited by Robert M. Adams

STERNE *Tristram Shandy* edited by Howard Anderson

STOKER *Dracula* edited by Nina Auerbach and David J. Skal

STOWE *Uncle Tom's Cabin* edited by Elizabeth Ammons

SWIFT *Gulliver's Travels* edited by Robert A. Greenberg *Second Edition*

SWIFT *The Writings of Jonathan Swift* edited by Robert A. Greenberg *Second Edition*

TENNYSON *In Memoriam* edited by Robert H. Ross

TENNYSON *Tennyson's Poetry* selected and edited by Robert W. Hill, Jr. *Second Edition*

THACKERAY *Vanity Fair* edited by Peter Shillingsburg

750